TOM'S CROSSING

Mark Z. Danielewski

TOM'S CROSSING

by

E.L.M.

Transcribed

by

A Western

Pantheon Books, New York

First Hardcover Edition Published by Pantheon Books

© 2025 by Mark Z. Danielewski

Published by Pantheon Books, a division of Penguin Random House LLC, 1745 Broadway, New York, NY 10019.

Pantheon Books and colophon are registered trademarks of Penguin Random House LLC.

Library of Congress Cataloging-in-Publication Data
Names: Danielewski, Mark. Z., author.
Title: Tom's crossing : a western / by ████████████.
Description: First edition. | New York : Pantheon Books, 2025.
Identifiers: LCCN 2025000564 | ISBN 9781524747718 (hardcover) |
ISBN 9781524747725 (ebook)
Subjects: LCGFT: Western fiction. | Novels.
Classification: LCC PS3554.A5596 T66 2025 | DDC 813/.54—dc23/eng/20250408
LC record available at https://lccn.loc.gov/2025000564

markzdanielewski.com
penguinrandomhouse.com | *pantheonbooks.com*

Jacket design by Atelier Z

FONTS:

Title: Dante MT
Description: Century Handtooled
©: Apollo | Dedication: ITC Legacy Serif
Main: Elysium Std Book & Italic
Folio: Revival565 BT
Amanuensis: Lapidary333BT

Printed in Canada

2 4 6 8 9 7 5 3 1

The authorized representative in the EU for product safety and compliance is Penguin Random House Ireland, Morrison Chambers, 32 Nassau Street, Dublin D02 YH68, Ireland, https://eu-contact.penguin.ie.

For her

Part One:

The Horses

Some
of What
Happened
Before

Hard to figure how so much awful horror could've started out with just them two horses and not a one yet named, both mindin their own business on that spring afternoon near the Tree Streets, nosin hay scraps at the back of Paddock A, with the new kid mindin his own business too, sittin hisself real quiet on a fence rail and, just like them horses, also nibblin on a blade of grass.

Peaceful as peaceful gets.

Rayleen Roundy, Orvop original, with braids and braces in her younger days, and still with braids in her elder years, would try once with paint to get at that moment, before she erased it with more pain, paint that is, *Clop-Clop-clip-Clop*, this time tryin for stacked logs of red elm, then asters, then attemptin to paint a cloud-encroached sky, and then the whole of it lost to the fires of Time. But if you'd've beheld her tableau and forgiven some of the lopsidedness of the horses, Rayleen bein no great artist, and surely not up for no Homeric echoes or the unaltered consequences of unbearable weapons or the dangerous enchantments of nine ordinary gates; if you'd've overlooked the mislaid perspectives of that fenced-in patch of dusty maltreated earth, well then you might've still seen how she caught with her lovin brushstrokes the lollin flow of the hour's cool breeziness, as well as in her shadowless composition found a kind of portentless calm that we would all count ourselves lucky to enjoy, when campfire stories, as good as those can be, don't dare interrupt the sun, and Journeys of the Dead don't cross no one's mind neither.

In the years that followed, good folks like Gil Stubbs and Anton Smiley; Amelia Beltran of course, the same Amelia who would become lifelong friends with Rayleen; along with Irene Wren, Courtney Resnick, Eldon McKennan, Craig Sandower, and fer sure Simon Bickette, would try their darndest through the materials of their practice to at least preserve the joy, and if joy is goin too far, then the pure idleness of livin, right before the heedless future, with no regard for Wile, Wrath, let alone Determination, or for that matter any thought of Love, Beauty, or Justice, chewed it all up: this one moment, and only this moment, of just a scrawny kid still sittin on a fence rail, still enjoyin the sight of that black mare and blood bay geldin, who were likewise also still enjoyin themselves.

What could be better?

And then Lindsey Holt charged up.

Hey! he hollered, but the new kid either didn't hear him or didn't care to hear him, because he just kept starin at the horses. *Hey, I'm talkin to you!* Lindsey shouted again, closin fast the gap between hisself and the object of his fury.

The new kid did at least turn around then.

Don't talk to me! Lindsey bellowed at once.

I didn't say nothin, the new kid finally answered.

There you done it again!

And Lindsey, satisfied with the logic of this, yanked the new kid right off the fence. And then, as if that weren't enuf, got to kickin him.

Lindsey probably would've kept on kickin too, and achieved some terrible damage upon that helpless and bewildered youth, if none other than Tom Gatestone hisself hadn't passed by right then. Not that Tom did much except stop in a riot of laughter, which is how Tom often found hisself, couldn't help hisself, could laugh about pretty much everythin, includin when the moment came for him to die.

Tom's big ears went bright red, and he howled hisself so hard, he got fast to coughin, gaggin some, enuf to get him diggin loose the leaf at his gum, because it was either that or cease breathin.

Of course, upon seein Tom Gatestone in such a state, Lindsey stopped his commotions at once, and only after the new kid had scrambled away did Lindsey reckon he had no idea what was so funny, whereupon this confused look overtook him, which only made Tom laugh harder, doublin him over again, because, see, Lindsey weren't the smartest of kids, and this confused look of his only helped make more evident that particular claim.

Now it should be noted it weren't no riskless endeavor to laugh at Lindsey Holt. Fer starters, havin what was thought of in those environs a girl's name, this bein Orvop, Utah County, in the year of our Lord 1982, why you'd either have to get strong quick or hightail it to California. On top of that, and makin matters a heckuva lot harder on poor Lindsey, in his younger years he even looked like a girl, a real pretty one too, before that first tickle of chin hair finally came to his rescue, and by then he was steer strong and about as ornery as one strung tight with a buckin strap in a Bascom rodeo chute.

When he was grown to near match the size of such a bovine, and maybe just to provoke some foolish soul to snicker at either his name or his tender features and hence justify the decidely untender beatdown that would follow, Lindsey kept his blond hair long, layered and feathered, parted in the middle too, in the way you'd see a cheerleader like Nadeen Garriman wear hers, she fer sure copyin the Dallas Cowboys Cheerleaders, or at least Cami Lark, or maybe a poster model in a red bathin suit. Lindsey spent near an hour every mornin gettin his hair blow-dried right. It helped that his sister, Lara, was a hairdresser.

Tom, though, paid Lindsey no mind, nor did he abate his chucklin when he offered his hand to the new kid, like Tom always done for the lost cause he had no business goin out of his way for, because lost means lost, as his daddy Dallin Gatestone always tried to tell all three of his noble-afflicted children, because no help any child has had to offer ever changed the outcome of this world, or so their dear daddy tried to make clear, even if his noble-afflicted children could see he was just sayin that for their sakes, not quite believin the words hisself.

You know him, Tom? Lindsey asked, more than a little surprised.

I do not.

Huh. What's so frickin funny then?

Funny?! Don't start me up again, Lindsey. You're funny! Kickin like you don't know how to use your own feet! I never seen no one kick like that! Gosh-darn, I can't even describe it. Worse than my little sister, and she's been perplexed her whole life, tryin to keep her legs movin in just the one direction.

Which was an unkind thing to say about his sister, especially with her not bein there to defend herself, though it was true, she did have in her gait a wanderin way some called lame but their Aunt Lissie called a signature of beauty, because beauty ain't beautiful if it ain't unique.

Lindsey darkened at Tom's directness, but to have a laugh like Tom's, Lord given his momma would swear, requires a sensitivity the likes of which most in Orvop could not summon let alone answer.

Now hold on, Lindsey! Tom hollered, hands up fast, as if a big dumb kid like Lindsey was the tin-star Law itself, which might then have even crossed Tom's mind, as his long, beautiful face started to redden again with that endless mirth. *Don't get all worked up twice! I can see you meant business, and far as I can tell by the wallopin you was givin this pup, you done already settled that business, and in your favor too. Unless, that is, he killt your whole family. Did he kill your whole family?*

No.

Then just your folks?

No.

Then your brothers? I don't care much for Dwayne.

No, Tom, he did not kill my brothers.

See now, and Tom's smile seemed to ignite deep in his eyes a dark glint. *You've won.*

Like a lizard to a hot rock, Lindsey took quick to the compliment and even laughed a bit, like he and Tom was laughin together, which they weren't, like he and Tom was friends, which they weren't, though you couldn't blame a kid like Lindsey for wishin Tom Gatestone was his friend.

What he done to you? Tom asked.

I come to see the horses is all, the new kid finally spoke up, his words comin out as certain as the spit on his lips was red, tryin then to slap the dust off his jeans, rubbin the back of an arm too, his right elbow tore up enuf to bleed through the long sleeve.

This weren't about no horses, Tom, Lindsey made clear. *I'm done sick of his shoes.*

His shoes? Tom's face again reddened.

Look at em! Every day! Same pair! I even warned him not to wear them no more. I don't care if he ain't from Orvop, but he can at least act like he's from Orvop. But did he listen? Nuh-uh. Have you ever seen such prissy things?!

Lindsey weren't wrong either. No kid, certainly not in Orvop, had ever seen such a pair, like a moccassin, only too worn for even the poorest Indian, and blue, though a blue faded to near gray, with leather laces and rubber soles. Called Top-Siders. They was made for a boat, though this kid sure didn't look like he'd ever set foot on a dock let alone a deck.

You got to kickin him because you didn't like his shoes?!

This time Tom doubled over so low, he had to drop to his knees, cryin so hard, he really couldn't breathe.

Fought like his shoes too! Like a girl! Lindsey further disclosed, as if that might solve it all.

That's true, the new kid even admitted. *I never could fight. Not that fightin crossed my mind when I seen this big yak runnin over like he wanted to marry me.*

Now on your knees is near low as you can get, but Tom got lower, rollin on his side in the hard dirt, which in the end was what arrested Lindsey's charge. See, not carin to be called a yak, Lindsey had at once lowered his head like he figured his skull bore horns fit to gouge the poor kid, all the while Tom kept makin this high-pitched wheezin sound, not a part of his face unred, his eyes squoze shut, a-leakin with tears. Tom was havin hisself one heckuva good time, and then his big black hat tumbled from his head and rolled right into Lindsey's path. Not that Tom depended solely on the errant way of his hat, such hats when they appear, especially black ones, or white ones, best just regarded as warnins.

And Lindsey did stumble before it, though truth be told, unbeknownst to that maraudin galoot, it was Tom's boot tip, faster than a cat's paw, that kissed Lindsey's heel just enuf to tangle him up, just enuf to force Lindsey to catch hisself, which he did, easily. He weren't the Orvop startin defensive tackle for nothin. But that moment of rebalancin was all that was needed, so instead of followin up on the kid's insult, Lindsey reached down for Tom's Stetson, and like it were the headgear or aegis of Achilles or Ares or even Athena herself, or any other one of them ancient or god-derived warriors Ms. Melson, Mr. Rudder, and Mrs. Annserdodder liked to teach about, he set to dustin off the wide brim and cattleman crown, surmisin maybe that this exchange would cement permanent their nascent friendship.

Lindsey never noticed that the new kid, through all these antics, had not moved one inch. Now even Tom, who was pretty nimble hisself, would never have thought to stand tall with Lindsey chargin him like a bull blind on rage. And maybe it was this boy's stolidity that quieted Tom's own cachinnations some, Tom noticin what Lindsey kept missin even as Lindsey handed Tom back his hat and gave him a hand up too, how the new kid showed no concern over the abuse he'd just taken and would likely have taken more of if Tom hadn't chosen on that Tuesday afternoon, April 13 to be exact, to walk home by way of Willow and Oak instead of takin Ninth straight to Briar. It was like he'd already plumb forgot about both Lindsey and Tom, returnin to the paddock to resume gazin upon them two horses.

And that sure got Tom's attention.

Tom's game was bulls, but his life was horses, which is hardly surprisin to anyone familiar with the Gatestones, given their familial and ancestral loyalty to equines of all shapes and sizes. Tom had already demonstrated a kind of skill and ease teachers and rodeo folks alike couldn't help but take note of. He was the elected FFA president for next year, with a closetful of ribbons and a dresser stacked with silver. He'd gained some regional fame when he'd sat eight seconds on Hightower, a bull that had pretty much terrorized the Springville Fairgrounds last summer. Snow College had already intimated he'd have any scholarship money he needed, though the Gatestones had no need for scholarship money. You don't have all their horses with land to match if you don't got a little cash.

You wanna ride them? Tom asked the new kid, winkin at Lindsey, mischief already layin claim to territories beyond the limits of the kindest heart.

Not that Lindsey was as quick to follow so wicked a plan. *Tom, these are Old Porch's ponies. He'd kill us if he found out.*

That is a certainty, Lindsey. Though I reckon if we play this right, them two horses might kill us first.

Heck, Tom, we don't even have a saddle.

You need a saddle? the new kid asked then, and thunder might as well have broke the dome of Heaven plus split the fence poles and leveled the barn, which really any puff of wind should've knocked down years ago, though to be sure the day was as bright as Mrs. Hallie Plummer's crystal is clear, with not even a wisp of cloud up there let alone one that might summon thunder.

Tom didn't laugh then, but his smile sure got bigger.

There's a halter right over there, the new kid even added.

Boy, how Tom started rubbin his hands together then. With absolute glee! And soon a little rodeo was arranged, Tom insistin on one dollar each, he bein the first to lay down a crisp bill, the new kid draggin out of his pockets just enuf change. Lindsey, however, didn't have on him even one dime. Tom said Lindsey could owe him, which almost made Lindsey quit the whole arrangement, because he didn't like owin nothin to no one. Nonetheless, Lindsey put aside his pecuniary preferences, as holdin to them might've suggested he was afraid to even have a try, not to mention concedin from the outset that Tom was the better rider, which Tom was by far, but this bein Orvop, no kid could ever admit to anythin but bein the best even in the face of the best, especially in a little contest like this.

Tom slipped between the fence rails easy as air and, easier still, haltered the dark mare. And if you know nil about our equine consorts, a halter ain't got no bit nor reins. It's just a soft harness for the head with a metal ring under the chin to attach a rope, called the lead, Tom bein capable enuf with knots to modify that lead so the end was retied again under the chin, hence makin a sorta set of reins, or really a loop, which you'd be a fool to think would offer you any help if the animal got to fumin.

Not that this horse here seemed anywhere close to fumin. Of course, underestimatin that mare was an easy thing to do. She weren't big by any means, and though Tom could guess she was a mustang, and he was right, in appearance she had a leanness that weren't so dissimilar from a thoroughbred. Plenty others would have devalued her on account of her size and even conformation, but Tom didn't care about none of that. He listened to her personality in the way she moved, though the mare didn't move much then nor cast much by way of a shadow so that who she was remained hid.

As Tom laid his hand on her back and patted her croup, the black mare's nostrils might've widened some, but only just. And when he laid his hand lightly on her withers, why then maybe an ear twitched, and fer sure the tail switched back and forth too, but just once. Otherwise, from muzzle to stifles, this great little mustang stood rock still. And of the slashes on her gaskins or other scars around her hind parts, a few even on her back, and on her belly too, who's to say what they was tellin Tom?

When at last Tom took hold of the rope, lacin too her long black mane between the fingers of his left hand, not a hint of objection stirred in her big brown eyes, but as soon as he swung up his right leg, and he did so easily, all easiness left the ring. That black mare at once threw down her head, pinned back both ears, and shot forward, kickin both her back legs skyward before rearin up just as fast and then doin everythin in her wily powers to scrape Tom off on the fence.

How Tom hooted with surprise and happiness, his long legs loose as a puppet with too much string, both flyin up in a jangle, slappin down in a jangle, his belt buckle the size of a hubcap tradin winks with the sun, while his right hand as light as nothin kept that big black cowboy hat pinned in place, magic it seemed pinnin his narrow buttocks just south of the withers, for all five seconds, and then even a sixth second accordin to Lindsey's watch, at which point the magic didn't actually abate but moved from Tom's steadiness on the horse to the manner by which Tom left the horse.

Tom sure was somethin to behold that afternoon. And if to the dumb-eyed he was just another brown-haired brown-eyed boy, albeit long and lanky, especially in the chaos of that ride, why on that day you'd still have to be extra clueless to miss how his dark features suddenly sparkled light as, say, the Orvop River bottom on a summer day, alive with moss-covered rocks, weightless trout, sand bright as gold dust, with his big teeth brighter than when them riverbanks are blanketed with first snow. That was Tom, one moment a river, the next a cat, why not a goat. Whether feathered, scaled, clawed, or a current on earth or above it, he was allways wild beyond us. Wild inhabited him, and endless laughter was the result, because he was forever. For a moment at least.

And even when Tom admitted defeat, none of his glories were subdued. Quite the contrary; he was easy in his goins. After all, what every one of us eventually finds out but Tom somehow already knew: the world will always leave you behind. Tom begrudged no endins, even when this mare denied him a subsequent second, much to his amusement, catchin him off guard with a sudden double reverse which lifted him, just enuf in the air to seal his fate. Tom weren't no fool; a quarter inch, a whole yard, they was the same. The horse was out from under him and Tom laughed, even as he was slidin off the off side, but far from fallin, more like lopin off, his right leg long enuf to make reachin the ground seem somehow possible, though lordy how he managed to swing that left leg out of the way too, without a hitch from that wild buckin animal, and follow it all through with what looked like an easy jog, not walkin on water, as far as miracles go, but near as good when it comes to walkin away from an ill-tempered horse, which is really the closest thing to a miracle these boys had ever seen, that mare still lashin skyward with her hooves and black tail not to mention givin that vault of unencumbered Vastness a good view of her nether places, all while Tom trotted back to the fence, hat in hand, not a hair outta place, with a smile larger than the Lord's and all of Heaven's vaults.

Ain't she made of surprises! Wanted nothin to do with me!

Or a seventh second, Lindsey added.

Lindsey seemed encouraged by this fact, at least at that moment. But he didn't last even three seconds. Tom generously gave him three too, considerin how long it took for Lindsey to get even sideways of the mare. It weren't pretty how the big football player had dug both his hands in her mane, grabbin up in his powerful hands some of the lead rope too, and then draggin hisself up onto her back. It was somewhat of a marvel that he'd managed to then get seated and hadn't just stayed draped across her, belly down. In all his maneuverins, his knees had got up so high, it looked for an instant like he was gonna stand up on the horse, sorta like the way he looked when he was doin a cannonball in the Jurgenvins' pool, which was pretty much what he did look like when he left that frenzied horse; fortunately for his sake and the Orvop High School football team, his trajectory flew away from the fence, though a mean hoof did nick him on the back of his left buttock as he sailed toward where the manure was deepest.

Lindsey emerged covered in it too, manure in his mouth, in his nose, even in one ear. This dressin-down, so to speak, beat a fractured skull, but he sure weren't grinnin when he got back to the fence. He'd lost a dollar he didn't have to Tom, and on top of that was just beginnin to realize how he'd gone from the satisfaction of beatin on a scrawny kid to now havin the crap kicked out of him. That was some of Tom's genius on display right there, how he'd gotten Lindsey to go from pickin on someone half his size to someone a good five times his size.

Lindsey had only one measure of pleasure left to take from this fast-sourin day, and that was to see this new kid in his prissy shoes not only get thrown but maybe kicked too, and this time kicked right, maybe even sent to the hospital, maybe even killt, a thought that actually seethed through young Lindsey's mind.

Now you can see what you're up against, Tom said to the new kid, nice like, but also aimin to rob Lindsey of the malice that big brute was incapable of concealin. *There ain't no shame in forfeitin that dollar to your elders. This here is Lindsey Holt, a junior like myself. He's an esteemed member of the FFA and already a star on the Orvop varsity football team. One day you might even see him on television with the professionals. You might even take pride in the fact that he even noticed you enuf to give you a welcomin kick in the rear.*

He'll get more than that if he don't get up on that horse fast, Lindsey growled. He really had it out for this kid, and maybe for the first time that day, a hint of irritation showed on Tom's face.

What's your name? the new kid asked Tom then, calm as flax.

Tom Gatestone.

The new kid extended his hand. *Kalin March. I don't think I've ever seen someone ride as good as you. That was a real honor to behold. I'm mighty grateful.*

And no lyin here, Tom went a little slackjawed because the last thing he expected from a small fry like this was a compliment like that, with the strangest part bein how such a young voice could utter it with such sincerity that it made Tom feel like it was comin from a teacher or a ward bishop or even from his own daddy, which panged him plenty.

Now there are a handful who swear that this was their true bindin moment. Llewellyn Bailey and Carter Roylance, to name just two, would get in quite the argument outside Farrer Junior High. Llewellyn mowed the Roylances' lawn, and Carter's sisters babysat for the Baileys as well as the Apples and the Trunnells. Llewellyn would swear it was the handshake, while Carter would hold tight to the exchangin of names. By contrast, Shamayne Apple would wind up arguin with her younger sister, them two squallin out in front of the Erville Family Mortuary of all places, swearin that the only moment that mattered was when Kalin declared his gratitude.

Whether these or any other moments can be satisfactorily proclaimed the bindin one, except the one that we all know, what will always resound through History, sworn to in that awful hospital room, Kalin hopped off the fence then and headed over to the mare, though not straight at her, but stickin to a long easy arc, and bidin his time as well, so that when he reached her, what she'd noticed comin her way at first she might near have forgotten about when he arrived. Once again she was still. And when Kalin slid up on her back, she didn't move then either. He lay against her neck for a while, strokin her and whisperin in her ear. She did lower her head some but didn't leap forward, and then when he sat up and slowly lifted her head with the lead rope, she didn't rear back. She even trotted ahead, though not for long, slowin quick enuf back to a walk, snortin a couple of times, her beautiful chest heavin in and out, and soon after takin a long walk around the paddock.

Tom and Lindsey was both hysterical, Tom with laughter, of course, and Lindsey with ire.

I ain't owin him a dollar for ridin a horse you and me tired out! Lindsey fumed.

Tom cocked his head to the side, findin that the hardest part of this utterance was how Lindsey had in fact made a fair point, even if Tom bein Tom sensed there was more at work here than just a tired pony.

Kalin eventually slipped off the mare, unbuckled the halter too, the whole time carryin on whatever conversation the two had enjoyed thus far. Fallin in love they was, as some still say.

He also ain't half our size, Tom, Lindsey groused. *That horse didn't even know there was but an ugly bug on its back.*

Not one to refuse any excuse to laugh, Tom chuckled some, though he remained puzzled. No question Lindsey plain loathed this kid and weren't gonna let up. But, also, this kid had somethin on them both that Tom hadn't begun to figure out yet.

You wanna give the other one a go? Tom asked Kalin, soft like and low, surpisin hisself with the deferential music in his own voice.

Kalin just handed Tom the halter and headed back out to greet the blood bay, Lindsey slumpin back some then on the fence, gettin smugger still with each step the new kid took through the deeper manure in the center, not that Kalin cared a whit, his gaze steady on the squat geldin, who quick enuf got wise to the approach. This weren't just a prey animal; he was a prey animal that had learned to survive worse than Kalin for millennia. But like the other, as if soft lit from all directions, little shadow betrayed who he was. The horse did flatten his ears, though, and exposed more and more teeth the closer Kalin got.

By the time Kalin reached the geldin's flank, he had to keep dancin outta the way of all them attempted bites. The horse refused completely his near side, but Kalin didn't defend no plan, headin instead around to the off side, or what those not familiar with equine polarities would call the right side when lookin the way a horse looks.

Since that horse's barrel of a belly might as well have rivaled a tank's girth, Kalin took the widest arc yet, which also helped to communicate no incursion and lesson calm, as well as avoid any wild kicks from this mostly quarter horse, Kalin's guess, correct too. Like the mare, the geldin's coat was shaggy and neglected due to a lack of brushin and attention. Unlike the mare, the geldin bore no scars, though Kalin sensed there was age here, maybe immense age, and no matter how well hidden, age always gathers its scars.

By the time Kalin eased up to the off side, the geldin had relaxed some, a might bit overconfident that Kalin's purpose was spent, though still snappin at the air to make sure of it. Not that Kalin was one bit diminished by where he stood and then no longer stood, movin so smooth, it should've seemed far too fast if it weren't also so natural. Kalin just needed two skips and a light post with two hands on the withers. Swifter than a tired man takin a seat, Kalin was swung up and settled before that horse could get a notion about what had just happened. In fact that big-bellied brawler even took a few trots forward before he understood he had a friend now. Not that the horse didn't react, rearin back faster than he could think, with that scrawny boy holdin on to nothin but the long tangled mane, though a better eye would've spotted quick that that mane was hardly gripped, with the real work happenin at the knees, the inside of each expertly fused with the motions of that protestin storm. Tom saw all this, of course, releasin that beautiful whistle of his high above, to circle the globe, out of reach of weather or any other disturbance, likely circlin there still.

When his rearin proved unsuccessful, that bellicose blood bay tried next to play the plough, throwin his head down, and so low a somersault might've seemed likely if he hadn't instead opted at the last second for a spin around, not once, not twice, but a full three times. Like a little tornado. That horse even gave it a shot the other way around. But Kalin was hardly disturbed, his dark brown hair hardly flutterin, even less than the mane, his dark brows lowerin far less than the horse's ears. Kalin weren't so much on that horse as he was the horse.

After that the blood bay just bolted straight at the fence where Tom and Lindsey sat. Lindsey was so startled, he near fell off backward. Tom, though, was quite the opposite, leanin forward, so thrilled just to see what would happen next: Would the new kid bail? Throw his weight to the lead? Instead Kalin, usin not just his knees but the insides of both his legs, like he already knew what was comin, rose up, leanin only slightly back as the horse pulled up hard, no doubt fully expectin to throw this burdensome trespasser right over his shoulders. But Kalin weren't goin nowhere, just as still as that pony was now in his dead halt, the two of them locked together in shared petrification, until the geldin with a big snort unpetrified them both, shakin his head side to side as if acceptin then that it weren't no use to try to shake loose your own back. Kalin, knowin that anythin more weren't meant for that day, accepted the draw and hopped off, pattin a shoulder before the blood bay offered a half-hearted snap of his teeth and trotted off.

Kalin had stayed atop that combative creature of scramblin discontent an easy dozen seconds, but his weren't a performance like Tom's, or even one Lindsey might assay, both of them too often tryin to equal those overly popular images of cowboys on buckin steeds. That was not for Kalin. Kalin would never participate in the deliberate act of troublin an animal. His gift had nothin to do with the acrobatics of domination but rather in the bestowin of calm, which in fact is how on that first day Kalin left the little tornado, gone of storm, as if once again returned to the grasp of a familiar and gentle memory assumed long gone, nuzzlin the mare first before next gettin after more alfalfa.

Not that the storm was ever far off. Lindsey never even got a hand on that geldin, and seein that big boy chase after that kickin pony made Tom this time laugh hisself off the fence.

Tom, fer his part, did manage to get a hand on the horse's withers, by which time that treacherous creature seemed asleep, not even twitchin an ear let alone tryin for a bite, Tom then swingin hisself up even quicker than the Kalin kid, though not fast enuf to outsmart that little tornado's schemes. No sooner had Tom's rear grazed but a hair than that horse's back was risin up, bouncin Tom up like he was an inflated stadium ball, except with long floppy arms and legs. Up he went and over, landin nimbly enuf, light as a gymnast dismountin from a pommel horse, if somewhat disbelievin too, but still extra amused, swattin that geldin's rump with his big black Stetson by way of conciliation. Though even with the swat, the horse only ever so slowly strolled away, well aware of his victory, liftin his tail then to drop steamy globs of satisfaction.

Tom's smile never wavered, oh heck it grew, but Lindsey was already yellin. *That don't count!* His eyes fillin with even more disbelief when Tom handed back over to the new kid his change plus the one crisp dollar bill.

Fair is fair, Lindsey. This boy just done whooped both our butts.

The heck I'm owin even one red cent to that— Lindsey couldn't even spit out one word more, stompin off, cursin everythin in sight, even the crows that had landed on the neighborin peach trees no doubt to laugh at them all.

So whatever you've heard, and no doubt you've heard plenty about what happens later, what none who know it will forget, and so long as stars keep sheddin light more than just a handful will never stop talkin about either; no matter how much the talk ices your veins, especially when it's late and the moon's missin and your campfire's no longer holdin even an ember; when you've still found the courage to turn from modern claims on your attention to listen there in your solitude to the great Breath that holds us all in its Grace, mullin over the sheer impossibility as well as inevitability of all that was about to transpire, those terrible odds, with the even more terrifyin consequences such odds decreed; what will make any heart glad for the bedsheets another night grants, what a new day of old routines helps deny; that which renders contemptible if not outright cowardly even the greatest acts of darin, the measure of which makes any man who thinks he's such a man know hisself as far lesser; what makes any woman gladder for knowin the world is made of lesser men; because if what is to come were the standard by which we are all measured, well then, as you likely also know, not even a few would find themselves still standin let alone with strength enuf to share the tale.

Clop-Clop-clip-Clop.

Or to put it another way: whatever you've heard, put that nonsense aside, especially gross mistellins by the lamentable likes of Abigail Fathwell and Darin Burdelong, who in their recountin in the River Bottoms, just outside the Lark residence in fact, and this in 1992, would never mention Tom but twice! That's right! Or Eugene Johnson, who at the same location but on a separate occasion mentioned Tom not even once, with Abigail and Darin there too and neither makin a point to object! And these three bein but just examples of the bad origins of even worse dialogues that would extend throughout the valley and over the years well beyond the state. Know this right now, here's how the friendship between Kalin March and Tom Gatestone truly began.

Though fer starters, so as also not to appear too disputatious toward other accounts, theirs was not a common friendship. To this day no one can recall the two sharin so much as a word in the halls of Orvop High School that spring. Not that such a 3A athlete-centric educational establishment demonstrated any of the intersectional socializin so lauded, say, in the twenty-first century. Football players stayed as much to themselves as the basketball players and wrestlers did to themselves. Baseball weren't worth much at Orvop. Sure, there were some who excelled at both football and wrestlin, Nigel Thorne doin just that, and baseball as well, and with a paper route, but he was the exception, and anyways still firmly situated among the jocks, just like the thespians stuck with the thespians, and the stoners with stoners, and the soccer club with the soccer club as well as the stoners because everyone knew anyone who played soccer was a stoner too.

The FFA folks had about the same presence as the football players, but they was their own thing. Like everyone else, except maybe the stoners, they was churchgoers but also carryin on traditions that were fer sure older than any high school athletic program and maybe even church. A few boys like Lindsey Holt could claim FFA membership and still locker with the football team on Main Hall. Curiously that very spring Lindsey appeared in the school's stagin of *Much Ado About Nothin*. That was so weird a thing that no one said a thing. Not even Tom's little sister, which, if you knew her, was plenty surprisin, though maybe she'd kept mum because she'd seen him in *Carousel* some years earlier and he weren't half bad, though he hardly sang; she loved the whole production and even sang *You'll Never Walk Alone* over and over for one whole interminable summer, interminable not because she had a bad voice, she had a great voice, it's just that, well, one song for a whole summer, that's a lot to ask of anyone, especially Tom.

Anyway, a boy like Kalin, havin just moved to town and startin up school midway through the year as a sophomore, had to make friends fast or keep to hisself, which is what he did, keepin to hisself, stayin out of anyone's way as best he could, which bein no tall poppy he mostly succeeded at doin, to the point of bein near a boy without a shadow, if now and then Lindsey would still slug Kalin in the shoulder or, even worse, frog him. Welcome to Orvop High. Froggin, see, was a mean practice of runnin up to some unsuspectin kid, usually while he was at his locker, and drivin a knee into the side of his thigh, which would cause any recipient to bounce first off the locker before collapsin on the floor in pain. Lindsey hit Kalin so hard one time he near got stuck in his locker. Lindsey barely slowed, grinnin at the cheerleaders or flag twirlers, sometimes at even the likes of Emily Larsen and Jennie Stall, who made to look appalled, though not a one of them said a thing, and a couple of their friends on the drill team even smiled back at Lindsey. Maybe it made some kinda queer sense to the folks around that if you was good at runnin into folks on a football field, why shouldn't you do the same thing in those halls? Lindsey's teammate, Mattock Jurgenvin, told Lindsey to knock it off, but anyone could see Mattock was equally amused.

When they noticed, folks sure liked to point out what Kalin was bad at, like dressin or not fittin in, but no one ever asked Kalin what he was good at. Tom, though, he knew. And Lindsey's attacks soon ceased when Tom, more frequently than any odds would've predicted, unless the dice were lead-loaded, would suddenly show up like some great white cat born of mists and spells with a shadow blacker than soot, and right behind that big blond-haired Holt boy too, spittin his tobacco in a Sprite can, his already long bowed legs goin more bowed for the fun of it, tellin one of his buddies, either Thurgood or Hogencamp, and loud enuf for Lindsey to hear and hear that plenty others were hearin it too: *I could never get with no girl Lindsey's been with! No Sir-*

ree, not with my teeny little pecker. Would be like tryin to screw a glass of water. Which admittedly was a coarse thing to say, but sometimes you need a little coarseness to rattle up the cage of bad behavior. *Throw some sand in their gears*, as Tom's momma, Sondra Gatestone, might say now and then, when she was feelin coarse, with *sand in their gears* bein as coarse as she got.

Tom's joshin with Lindsey sure put on display his indefatigable cunnin, what with how in the collective wave of laughter that followed Lindsey lost hold of his actions, sorta like how he lost sight of chargin after Kalin that afternoon by the paddocks when Tom's big black Stetson had rolled in front of him, him turnin his attention to Tom once again, with Kalin already disappearin down D-Wing, Lindsey even warmin to the compliment and only vaguely sensin somethin awry, especially comin from the likes of Tom Gatestone accused once of tapin a cucumber to his inner thigh until it was voluntarily and happily proven that there weren't no such produce section on his person.

So often Tom would appear right as Lindsey readied an attack on Kalin that eventually Lindsey, like a good dog, learned to look away from the boy whenever he saw the boy, lookin for Tom instead, which weren't wholly a good thing to do either, seein as how he still owed the Kalin kid a dollar and Tom knew it, though Tom never did bring up that matter again.

Kalin never did stop wearin those boat shoes either, all the way up to and through summer, wearin the same jeans too, rotatin but three shirts, all of which he kept clean and ironed. What spiteful fun students who'd knowd each other since before first grade had had at his expense. When two of Lindsey's teammates took a turn at him, as incensed by Kalin's dress as Lindsey was, Kalin didn't back down, but true to his word, he sure couldn't fight. Finally though, like any dog will tire of a bone, especially one that's used up and ground plenty with dirt, the teasin stopped. This was about when May drew up tall and ready as school started to wind down.

Tom had done his best to keep an eye out for the boy. He understood how little Kalin and his momma had, findin out over time how she worked durin the weekdays at the Rome mall, and weekends at the Cassidy Ski Shop, and often six nights a week at the movie theater, also at the Rome mall. Kalin was on his own most of the time, not that this arrangement seemed to trouble the kid much, bein obviously the way of it for quite some time now, no matter what town they was callin home. Maybe the fact that Tom's momma was single made Kalin's circumstances that much more relatable. Tom invited Kalin over for dinner but just once. It was a small gatherin at a big table, in the Gate-stone's big kitchen with them high ceilins, just Tom, his little sister, and his momma, but no matter how casual the gatherin, Kalin couldn't manage to say more than *Thank you* or *Yes, ma'am*. Tom and his sister thought it was pretty hysterical, them both sharin a similar sense of humor. Tom's momma sure didn't see no stormy petrel seated with them that night, though she would've at least sensed that a compar-ison to a bird, any bird, was wrong. Without explanation, she found herself absolutely fascinated by Kalin, maybe because she had no idea why Tom had invited him over in the first place. Since when did Tom hang around with a kid like this one? And you can be sure Tom never brought up nothin about stealin Old Porch's horses.

Who knows how Tom would find out, but somehow he'd get wind that Old Porch was away or his hands were otherwise occupied at Porch Meats or at some of the other Porch properties, and then Tom would get word to Kalin and they'd meet at Paddock A on Willow and Oak, Tom bringin two saddles, halter-bridles, reins, and bits. Early on he brought an extra pair of black boots, which he made Kalin keep. Tom's daddy once wore them, and as Tom had correctly guessed, they proved a perfect fit. Kalin accepted the gift, though he only wore them when he rode with Tom.

To this day, no one knows how long it took to get either horse accustomed to a saddle let alone the snaffle, though by early summer Tom and Kalin were disappearin for hours up into the foothills.

By then the horses had names. Navidad was the black mare with them awful scars and a white star on her forehead. Kalin chose her for their first stroll, and they was pretty much together from then on. That first time out the gate Navidad seemed at once to revive to some former self, with maybe even the damage done to her vanishin some as well, now that she was once again held by the arms of the great world surroundin that brutal corral. It was like she couldn't get enuf of the air, and not just the nearby scents that drew her down to graze on stalks of slender green beside many of the trails, but the breezes them-selves rollin down off the high mountains. She'd lift her nose up to inspect their news, sometimes snortin contentedly, a couple of times pinnin her ears fast, retreatin faster, which Kalin turned still faster into an easy lope back to the trail and more grass. Who could say what she sensed high above there, a mountain lion, a wolf, a leopard, why not get a little fantastical now and then?, and anyway what neither boy could fairly guess at, though even at their young ages they was still wise enuf to shudder before what she knew.

Tom in turn pretty much always rode Mouse, who they also called

Little Twister from time to time, and even Runaway, because twice, for reasons as invisible as Navidad's huffs and darts, that ornery blood bay with a white blaze would suddenly clamp down on the bit and lunge off ahead, runnin until Tom was dumped, what happened once to Kalin as well, lest this depiction thus far imply he was somehow invulnerable upon any horse.

Tom, though, swore he'd never seen no one handle a horse like Kalin. It was a gift the origins of which not even time would ever make clear. The tragedy, Tom would say, is that Kalin was born with but two gifts with neither one of them truly suited for this world. Kalin knew it too, and it troubled him plenty, for these talents were particular and did not apply to fightin or football or even serve as the barest social lubricant to let his place there in that dusty sun-beaten valley not seem so deservin of mockery and at times cruelty.

Except for Tom, no one else welcomed him into their fold. True, Kalin and his momma weren't churchgoers anymore, and Orvop was primarily of the Church, with wards on top of wards and even a temple to mark the ne plus ultra of civilization before the severe gap that marked the entrance to Isatch Canyon, toward where Tom would lead Kalin, ridin well above the temple as well as all the various homes, up to the higher foothill slopes still under construction, plenty of lots there so designated by the city, with a good bunch, yes, already sold, but without so much as a brick to mark progress or even a paved road to find a driveway. In other words, the perfect place to gallop those powerful horses.

Still higher up waited great vantage points where Tom liked to pause in order to make clear for Kalin the layout of that dovecote community called Orvop, pointin out where the pioneers first settled, where Fort Utah might've stood, how the settlement eventually spread all the way to Mud Lake, a shallow but expansive body of water, decades dulled by the now-closed lakeside Zurich Steel Mill in an area just above the city called Vineland, Tom indicatin then where, to the north, Orvop stopped bein Orvop and Rome became Rome; or indicatin where, to the south, Springville became Springville; with nothin east except the Isatch Range, now at their backs, them first set of peaks risin so high and wide they refused all notice, which might seem an odd way to describe such an enormous heave of earth and rock so heaven-bent, but ponder for just a moment the sky, how its immensity is so frequently denied, especially to the average onlooker fixed on a breakfast doughnut or an office tribulation or some saucy motel visit, none the wiser beneath such inhumane expanses so difficult to behold.

Not that Kalin lingered much on such sublimes either, carryin on more often than not his whispered conversations with Navidad while Tom carried on about frontier folk arrivin to establish Fort Orvop in 1849, *On April first too! If that don't say it all!,* followed by the Indian troubles, the Battle Crick Massacre, Church field cannons firin chain shot, then the beheadins that would follow and other such atrocities committed, which he and others swore still haunted Isatch Canyon if not the city of Orvop itself. Even worse, they was crimes committed in the name of the Lord, the same Lord to whom Tom and his family had prayed for generations and still prayed.

Tom then with a dark smile brought up Wild Bill Hickman as well as Garrison Porch and the Gatestones' consanguineous patriarch, Alfred Gatestone, before he drifted off to topics like copper, coal, and even topaz, which the state was rich with, eventually pointin out the more local centers of industry, fer sure the already mentioned steel mill, now a hulkin corpse of shadow and cinder, once required for the Second World War, about when, the late '40s, the land wars heated up between the state, the Church, and other interests, specifically the Gatestones and Porches. *We was all here pretty much from the start, some say even before the start, and the whole time fightin.*

As far as the more recent Porch vs. Gatestone affairs went, there was the Applebaum Snake Altercation, concernin a cherry orchard and a trespassin donkey, don't ask about the snake, settled in 1954; or the Gatliner Realty Dispute, settled in 1963; and then the relitigation of the Gatliner Realty Dispute, resettled in 1968; and then the Harvest-Meadow Development Suit, which included the Gatliner property, settled in 1973. The lawfare surroundin the Ridgeline Meadow Estates Claim was settled in 1980 after the death of Tom's daddy, with the lands fairly apportioned between the Porches and Gatestones, though the land weren't much by way of them estates or developments that Old Porch kept dreamin on, the Gatestones wantin the parcels just for pasture. *The lawyers got the most out of it anyways,* Tom laughed as he went on to describe how both Gatestones and Porches became settlors. *We had to give them the properties up at the Cassidy Ski Resort. Don't ask me how those lots got mixed up in the rowl. And the Porches did the same. From what I hear, them lawyers are neighbors now, and each got big cabins right on the slopes.* Tom admitted to bein marked by this endurin conflict, even if his obvious delight over every turn and twist of this near genea-logical enmity seemed to far outweigh what still held other hearts tight with vengeance. Tom had plenty of cousins who kept tellin the stories. The Porches were no different. Some say the universe bends toward Justice, but when it don't, stories mend the trajectory. As Tom's great-great-somethin-grandfather on Tom's daddy's side would put it:

Stories are a rebalancin of injustice, whether enacted within their narrative or purposed to enact certain reactions by the listeners. Stories are the lexical fashionins of vengeance. At least the good ones are. Tom didn't hesitate to convey with a grin that this great-great-somethin-grandfather, the very son of Alfred Gatestone, was a dark man whom most had failed to understand and who had hisself confessed to not understandin one bit many of the motives that afflicted him.

Mostly, though, Tom just pointed out to Kalin the various parts of town, like the Tree Streets right below where Lindsey Holt lived; the Roundy sisters; and the Wongs too, who had a lot with a proper house but pretty much lived in a trailer in the back because the house was in such disrepair; or, higher up, the Wittenbachs, the Hoveys, and the Riggs.

Now the Riggs, there was a story right there. They'd all gone away one summer and hired Tyler Stokes to water the lawn. *Now Tyler's a bit short on whatever smart sauce he puts on his burger,* Tom explained. *He figured he could get paid for the whole summer but only have to water the lawn once if he just left the hose runnin. And he did just that. And two months later, with all that water still goin, slowly underminin the foundation, half the house slid down the hill. It'd be tragic if it weren't so funny.* Kalin asked what had happened to Tyler Stokes. *What happens too often to idjits: nothin.*

Tom then pointed out Sherwood Hills, a richer neighborhood to the north, where Chloe Pew, Fenny Young, and Milly Lesson lived, Eva Thorn too, no relation to Nigel Thorne, Eva's name spellt without the *e*; these folks all goin to Timpview High. Some also lived down by the River Bottoms, like the Lark sisters and Carmen Shupe.

As for Orvop, downtown consisted of Main Street and Ninth Street, which were easily spotted from where they next stood; as was city hall, the police department, and a number of small local parks. Isatch University was near a city unto itself with all its white-and-orange brick buildins, the big stadium where Jim McMahon was the reignin quarterback, and the Milkinson Center near, well, the center of campus, loaded with arcade games, a miniature golf course, bowlin alley, an immense window depictin in stained glass the Church history, which included, hidden beneath the wings of seagulls and such, tiny figures from *Star Trek* and *The Lord of the Rings*; the campus even had its own toy cops to enforce hair standards, dress standards, and general appearances as mandated by the Church.

By them Tom had been detained for countless offenses, mostly havin to do with chewin tobacco or whistlin at a gal or tellin too loudly an impolite dumb-Polack joke, though Tom had never met a Polack in the real but always got a laugh. Every time the private IU security force demanded his name, Tom would answer as penitent as he could muster: *I am sorry. My name is Jeff Cannon.*

Tom also pointed out Grandview, where Jordan Heaton, Howie Dirker, and Carly Bunningham lived, the Whitneys, the Rowes, all the kids wantin to be doctors like their parents who saved many lives but couldn't save Evan's, nor Tom's when the time came, in fact couldn't save no Gatestone. The Thurgoods and Hogencamps, who got their money from cement and asphalt, were also up in Grandview.

After that, and a little farther west toward the lake, was where the Porches mostly lived.

But they's all over here like lice, Tom explained. *Egan Porch got a house and barn just down over there, near adjacent to Isatch Canyon. Just like us.* Tom pointed out his family's paddocks and barns, and then where his home stood, which Kalin by then already knew havin walked there hisself the one time for dinner.

One of the smaller and perhaps sadder mysteries forever resoundin through these events is why Tom had only invited Kalin over for just the one meal. Kalin hadn't been that bad a guest, and Tom's momma was always thrilled to have new folks at the big Gatestone table. No matter your shape, color, or size, she'd make sure you didn't leave hungry, servin up like she did for Kalin some of her peach pie with ice cream she'd made herself the day before. Not that there ain't speculations on even this point: Wade Clayson and Shaylan Chandler would one early July afternoon in 1983 at Boyer's Car Care Center manage to convince each other that Tom had a deep-seated disdain for Kalin and his supposed kindness, and all that friendly horsin around was just a piece of theater to lure young Kalin into a very bad situation.

Leavin such speculations aside for the moment, there's no question that the more Tom and Kalin rode together, the less attention they paid to the dusty valley below and more to what rose up above them, that first battalion of peaks presidin over Orvop: Agoneeya Mountain, pronounced like *Agony* with an *uh* at the end, also called *I*-Mountain for the I on its front; and Kaieneewa Mountain just to the north, like *Kye-a-knee-wah*; and between them none other than that darned Isatch Canyon.

They likely didn't enter the breach with any seriousness until late June. By then the undeveloped lots and dirt roads weren't nothin compared to Tom's favorite place, where even in the furnace of July you could still taste the cold poolin in the shadows. Tom loved that canyon, and he delighted in pointin out the obvious: how them dark sheer sides rose up near vertical, and how between Agoneeya and, on the Kaieneewa side, Squaw Peak, whose dolomite-and-limestone promontory they would've passed beneath every time they entered, weren't nothin compared to what rose up beyond, those higher ridges where, in the thinnin air, wide patches of snow would persist throughout summer, accountin for the little *crick*, as Tom called it, or *creek,* as Kalin called it, that *runs the whole length of Isatch Canyon,* Tom also describin the rapids of melt that fer sure would come with spring before falterin some by late August, but, no matter the flow, the thrillin cold always testifyin to the freezin summits where its waters were born.

Probably on one of those rides, just far enuf along to manage a first glimpse of Mount Katanogos and whisper then some about the not-yet-visible Upecksay Headwall, risin all the way up to the Katanogos Summit, an area known to many as the Four Summits, which really is mainly the Katanogos back side extendin southeast beyond the Stawberry Reservoir and northeast up to Wallsburg, its center includin the apex as well as those three lesser peaks along the summit ridge known as South Katanogos, Halo's Pike, and Bella's Horn, all with beautiful bowls of snow come winter and wildflowers come spring; why it would've been right around then, *Clop-Clop-clip-Clop,* that Tom told Kalin about the Crossin.

There's plenty of debate, especially by folks who were neither witnessess nor in possession of a firsthand account but nonetheless more than willin to connect some dots, embellishin what they'd heard and makin up what they hadn't heard, like whether or not Tom and Kalin would've really made a try that summer, though no question they'd already got to tacklin many parts of it, while speculatin about the rest of it, like for instance about how many days and nights they'd need, which Kalin never could nail down because Tom refused to divulge anythin beyond the initial stages of their journey. Tom also didn't divulge too much about Orwin Porch, or Old Porch as he was called, though he weren't but fifty-nine.

While Tom had fairly set out that the Gatestones and Porches were anythin but close, he also saw no need to keep fillin the new kid's ear with what poison had been simmerin and boilin over and refilled and simmered again for decades, Old Porch would say generations, and on that point alone he and Tom's momma would've agreed, knowin better than anyone alive the long ugly history between those two families.

Not that you needed a member from either family to attest to as much. Almost any local who has some years in their spine will do. Find yourself a hushed moment, a sincere one at least, and you'll get the idea pretty quick. Especially when it comes to the current Porch patriarch. As personable as he might seem in your average moment, when set flat before the light of social decency, Old Porch was a mean seed upon the land, a puttock, a violent thief, with the mild but too often stiff-necked Gatestones set there solely to either cut him back from his greedy designs or suffer his afflictions, which the Gatestones did suffer, regularly and terribly, Tom's older brother, Evan, when he was but seventeen, dyin racin trucks against Egan Porch, Egan havin walked away unscratched and the police declarin no fault, though it was hard to say it was just teenagers bein stupid when the two involved came from families with such a long history of endurin disdain.

Where Dallin, the Gatestone patriarch, had countless friends, Old Porch had countless collaborators. Old Porch managed to take advantage of folks dumb enuf to think they could use him all the while he was gettin around to usin them better. Plenty couldn't stand his guts, but it would be unfair to say he was hated by everyone, feared maybe, but not hated, and by quite a few admired. Few would dispute that he was a fierce survivor: raw, crude but definitely indomitable, and also successful, and whatever about him might rub you wrong, you couldn't say he weren't of the land and its troublin history. Plus, as Reed Beacham would say, *He had the stink of money on him, and that's pretty good cologne.* Reed Beacham, and more than likely that same local you found to discuss all this with, would also add that any troubles with the Porches might very well lie with the Gatestones for gettin high-minded or just stickin their noses where noses don't belong.

After all, just stealin Porch's two horses, and doin so over and over, is a fine example. True, Tom in his defense would've just claimed that he couldn't help hisself, and there'd been a truth in that too, the seriousness of it all then dissipatin because Tom would've gotten to laughin, which always seemed to lighten even the worst situations. Kalin, though, never rightly considered how the Porches were part of every one of those afternoon escapes, and that didn't just mean Old Porch but all of them, down to the last Porch boy. Not that Kalin would've paid much mind to the extra company. He just loved to ride, especially Navidad; he loved to abandon the city, goin higher and higher into the hills, gettin above it all but more so beyond it all, if such a feat is really ever possible, at least gettin a taste of a place where the bonds of birth and fortune have loosened their hold.

It's hard to argue with Orly Vanleuven, who, in the Orvop High parkin lot in the winter of 1989, would declare it was *nothin short of Providence that led them boys to Navidad and Mouse.* Orly Vanleuven was a character fer sure: he did indeed keep as a pet a genuine full-grown cougar, name of Killer Soul, who would spring from wherever he was hidin and land on Orly with them fierce big cat paws and bigger cat kisses; though just because Orly Vanleuven was *eccentric* didn't mean he didn't have a point. Plenty of horses, and a goat or two, plus a mule, had passed through Paddock A that summer. Moved in for a few weeks, and then moved on out. Not Navidad and Mouse. They remained untouched, like they was plumb forgotten or Porch's men and even Porch hisself somehow just couldn't see the horses, like the men were bewitched or the horses were somehow invisible, at least to the currents of industry that organized the comins and goins on Willow and Oak, which everyone knew, Tom especially, originated at Porch Meats across town, with the abattoir at its very center, what marked the start of the Porch fortune, where Old Porch was usually found overseein the operations of his businesses and his realty, which most definitely included Paddock A and the adjacent Paddock B.

Now we haven't mentioned Paddock B up until now, but the time has come. It weren't but a quarter the size of Paddock A and sat mostly empty, and when it weren't empty, it sure as heck was by the end of the next day.

Anythin Porch puts in Paddock B, Tom explained after a ride, *the very next day he slaughters. We never wanna see these two in there.*

But for whatever reasons, Providential or luck, if there be a difference, Navidad and Mouse stayed put in Paddock A.

There is one more matter regardin shoes that needs some quick addressin, with these shoes havin nothin to do with Kalin's. When the boys first came upon Navidad and Mouse, they was both still shoed but awfully neglected and with no sign that anyone had plans to attend to their hooves again. On one of their first rides, Tom led the way through the Tree Streets to the home of a family friend named Terrence Olsen, of Yazzie fame, who was also the family farrier, and he was happy as ever to see Tom and more than happy to reshoe those two horses, and right in his driveway too, never pausin to ask if they were Tom's horses and sure never thinkin that these here were stolen horses.

Five times that summer and in early fall they visited Terrence, and he never said more about the horses than to comment on their improved calmness and rehabilitated stature, describin them once as even tall, though Navidad was not even sixteen hands and Mouse barely made fifteen, the geldin's tanklike girth further enhanced no doubt by the ample amount of carrots and apples the boys kept bringin around. Terrence would insist on givin both horses some of his own treats and a couple of times brushin them while he told the boys stories about horses and what horses have done, which shows right there the heart of Terrence Olsen, focused so entirely on the animals he served without ever givin a hoot about such things as ownership or worth.

And then by August, it was as if Porch Meats had forgot completely the paddocks on Willow and Oak. There was still a service that irregularly delivered hay and replenished the big tub of water, but otherwise it was as if Navidad and Mouse were now permanently put out to pasture, though in truth they would've been terribly abused in that pen were it not for those two boys.

With both Tom and Kalin not blind to the horses' situation, if there was ever a time to dare the Crossin, soon began to make sense, with real soon makin even better sense. Likely Tom told Kalin then a bit more about the way there, though never on a map. They would've fer sure explored a good deal of the route first hand, enuf so that by mid-August they was startin to cache supplies here and there, the large part secured by padlock in an old miner's shack, or that's what they got to callin it, not far from the wide sandy threshold clotted with scrub oak that marked the entrance to Isatch Canyon. Kalin stored Tom's daddy's boots in the miner's shack.

Tom, whose misbehaviors never extended much beyond pranks, some ribald humor, and chewin tobacco, much to his mother's horror, plus a sip or two of beer here and there, well, he liked to call these particular August escapades their LSD trainin. Now steady there. Too many have quickly leapt to acid tabs, haunted mushrooms, and other hallucinatin trips, assertions that are staked against later encounters in order to explain all that would impossibly transpire. Some like to rejumble Tom's nomenclature to arrive at LDS, what they assert Tom really meant to say, thus providin a whole other set of explanations. However, let's dispense with that nonsense. When Tom said LSD, he was referrin to Long Slow Distance trainin, which he was a skilled-enuf horseman to know Navidad and Mouse required.

Both boys were fully determined and dead serious as well to answer this call to great adventure, and even more importantly, they was convinced that they had no choice but to answer it, on behalf of the ponies fer sure but also on behalf of their big beatin hearts, which beat bigger and bigger as the end of summer promised the fruition of their dreams.

If it's possible to imagine, there was a week there when Tom's smile grew even bigger. Kalin as well started smilin in a way his mother noticed, her not sayin a thing, figurin, maybe even hopin, that Kalin had finally met a girl.

It was while out on these rides that the two boys made lists in their heads which they later wrote down and in turn used to check against the supplies they'd already managed to gather, whether food, feed, hay nets, ropes, or tarps. It got to seemin inevitable that Tom would finally show Kalin the whole way there, and they'd get there together, and history would never forget them for doin it.

And then Tom coughed.

Tom always said he was gonna die young. The way he described it, with a glee his momma abhorred, he'd be hung up on some mighty bull, hand caught in the ropes tied by his own devisin, swung this way, that way, until he was broken, scraped off, gored, ground down, and finally stomped into an icy black dream, and in front of thousands too, maybe even on television. Gone like that and not even twenty-seven.

Instead he coughed again, and he didn't really stop after that. Tom weren't even eighteen. By late September, he was in the hospital, distant relatives comin and goin, bringin their prayers, leavin balloons, Tom callin em out for just comin around to say goodbye, which he also made sure they knew he was grateful for. *Who don't like a nice toodaloo if it comes with a balloon?* He'd say things like that and laugh even if his laughter turned too soon to more coughin.

His little sister, Landry, swore she'd overheard a doctor say the cancer was so bad, it was in his feet. Tom's momma ignored that particular bit of reportage, sidin this time with Tom, who often called his sister a fantasist with a taste too keen for every sort of exaggeration, from wingèd unicorns to horse marines. Though in this case Tom did not level any such accusations because he knew his little sis was just conveyin what mattered most: the undeterred Truth that shrugs off the nuisance of a few erroneous details like they weren't worth even the price of dust, just like Navidad had tossed off Lindsey Holt that fateful April afternoon. See, Landry to her credit was stickin to the heart of the matter. Beside the point was whatever declarations those doctors in their green smocks brought along, either tappin a pencil eraser at their results or noddin toward whatever machine was blinkin nearby. Beside the point was what their momma kept prayin for until the very end, that the Good Lord spare her second son, the only boy left to her. Tom's little sister understood: the end was comin and it was comin fast.

And Landry was right.

The last mornin that Tom ever knowd before Death took him away, Death bein too cowardly to even show hisself, Landry couldn't stop bawlin, especially when Kalin finally showed up. Kalin was so caught up hisself tryin to keep from bawlin, he couldn't but barely nod at Mrs. Gatestone or spit out a word except an odd *Hey* now and then, until Tom, who was tired enuf as it was, got particularly tired of that and singled out the boy in front of everyone there, which included two cousins that Tom didn't know from Adam.

Don't forget, Kalin, you ain't good but for two things.

Guess that's true.

So do the Good thing.

No one in that room knew what the heck Tom was sayin, which weren't a problem given his condition, except that Tom could see Kalin didn't understand either.

If Porch ever puts Navidad and Mouse in Paddock B, you swear to me that you'll do the Good thing: you get em outta there! And Tom weren't laughin then, and for the first time, maybe ever, there weren't even a flicker of a smile anywhere near his lips, and the gravel in his voice shuddered the room.

Kalin bolted from his chair like the Lord's voice was commandin him, and maybe it was, Kalin kneelin at once beside the bed and takin poor Tom's gray hand.

You take em to the Crossin, Tom managed to say, *and you set our friends free. Swear.*

Tom, I got no idea where—

Swear!

And Kalin bowed his head like some knight on one knee, only with none of the shiny armor or any magical sword, not in some grand castle neither, in fact lookin nothin like a knight, in fact still wearin those dang boat shoes, still as outta place as a donkey on a racetrack. But Kalin refused to let go of Tom, maybe not seein that it weren't a dyin boy's hand no more that he grasped but a rope of the severest kind and he was already hung up on the darkest beast of all.

Landry never stopped declarin how all the machines in that bleak little room suddenly stuttered. And they had. Or at least the light had shifted so unnatural like, though when is flourescent light ever anythin but unnatural? That little girl still sensed, down to her small stupid core, how all are finally called upon and tested before that which in its absolute Power and Fury lays bare how each and every one of us is finally placeless and unchosen, and unforgiven to boot; where every claim we might make against the future and even the past is baseless; where whatever we might swear to, whether in anger or pain, is but as worthless an act as a secret caught between the teeth of a dead man.

But Kalin still swore to Tom and Tom then whispered in his ear the way to the Crossin.

Wednesday

Chapter One

"Paddock B"

Kalin stood whiter than snow in the livin room they both called his bedroom. He slipped on his briefs first, but even in them he felt neked. It was a feelin he didn't care for one bit. Couldn't explain it none either. The cause was likely rooted in shame, but no such understandins emerged out of the gutterin surges of repulsion he felt against his own body.

He hustled on her warmest stockins next, havin already snipped off the feet without her permission, and then slipped on his jeans. That helped, but only a little. Tightenin up his belt, that didn't help at all. When he was near done puttin on a second shirt, she knocked from behind her bedroom door.

Can I come in now?

I ain't dressed yet.

His pale and frail feet disgusted him as well. He hurried them into the worst socks he had, thin and near worn through at both heels. No point wastin his good ones. Then he slipped on the gray Top-Siders. Outside it had already started to drizzle.

When are you gonna be back? she asked from the doorway. He could see she was already plenty wrecked from the day shift at the ZCMI, tryin now just to get refueled for the night shift at the University Theaters. It was always like that, long days and nights up at the Rome mall, but now whatever sleep she needed to nab had run off quick before the instincts that had kept guard over Kalin his whole life. Not that he was surprised. She had an uncanny way of sensin when things was shiftin.

Goin campin. Which was mostly true.

Oh.

I won't be back tonight or tomorrow night, he added before puttin on, for the first time too, the white wool cable-knit sweater she'd got him earlier that month.

The weather don't look so good for campin. What was breakin inside her she hid with a scowl. *What about school?* she asked when he didn't respond. *Thursdays and Fridays are still school days, ain't they?*

I'll make up what work I fall behind on come Monday. You have my word.

This ain't about makin no promises to me. School has rules.

Nobody's gonna miss me for two days, Momma, Kalin answered, slippin on his Lee Storm Rider, a blanket-lined denim jacket with a brown corduroy collar.

What about me? I'll miss you.

He didn't blame her for the gruff in her voice. Whatever all he'd never know, even if he lived longer than Methuselah, he would always carry within him as both blessin and burden the certainty that for this woman, he was her everythin.

Goin with two friends.

Two friends? You never told me you had even one friend.

Kalin didn't say nothin. He just finished buttonin up the jacket and then last of all slid on the dark green poncho.

I'm comin back, Momma. He felt heat sting both his cheeks then as he watched her tiny figure retreat, what weren't but a small step back into her dark room but movin away like he'd slapped her.

Your daddy was nothin but lies, she spat out. *Lies felt at home in his mouth. Make no home for them in yours.*

Momma, Kalin said, soft and patient, as if a tone alone might cradle her, though he already knew there was nothin he could say, especially about what he was settin out to do, that would grant her any comfort or relief. *I ain't him.*

That's the only thing that helps me sleep, she said with a sigh, and smiled too, steppin back into the light because at heart she was beautifully kind but also because she was stronger than him, always would be, and that in turn gave him the strength and confidence to smile back.

Tell me, Kalin, is it a girl? Her blue eyes sparkin in him somethin he'd never understand.

In the most despairin moments ahead, he would think again on this moment and know that his momma had already knowd he was too scared for there to be a girl. She'd just asked him such to make him blush and likely smile a bit longer, and maybe too to get him to think fer a moment more on another course of action that would've made a lot more sense than all that would instead come his way.

No, Momma, there ain't no girl.

Too bad, she said with a wink.

Kalin didn't dare look her way then, because he was in fact already smilin too much, and if there was ever a time when she could sway him, it was when he was happy because happy's sure enuf in itself to not have to be sure about anythin else.

Just headin up into the mountains for a spell, he added, pickin up the pillowcase already loaded with two halter-bridles, one set of reins with a snaffle bit, one long lead rope, and three apples.

I'm glad you're goin with friends.

Kalin's momma knew him well beyond hisself, not just what he was made of but what that all would make of him, observin in his refusal to meet her gaze how his mind was set, and worse, his heart too, and in that way that cannot be unset, at least not by the likes of her. She bit her lip and looked away. Not that her head weren't at once runnin wild with thoughts of chargin at him, slammin the door, or pullin her own hair, or maybe pullin his hair, beatin her small fists against his chest, for what he'd become right there, right then: upright, honest as ever she feared, and so of hisself that he was finally beyond seizin, by her or likely anyone else. So instead, Kalin's momma just clamped a palm over her mouth like she was stoppin a scream or at least a fit of swearin, until not even that grip could hold, revealin as her hand dropped away and her gaze returned to his lovely form that there weren't no scream or foul words at all, only her ever abidin tenderness that not even the World, in all that it was spun from and in its endin must spin loose of, will ever know an end to.

I won't ask you more then, she said as she watched him prepare to leave.

Kalin knew then that if he tried to say all she meant to him, he'd lose his bearins sure as a leaf in a wind that got no tree, and then everythin he'd set to do, mostly because of her, her profound example, built up with years upon years of travail, scootin them by on the meagerest of earnins, and never wantin no more from him than to travel no rut of the past but instead be somethin she wasn't, what his daddy never wanted no part of, somethin sound and good and worth ringin out about, why all of his plans that gray afternoon, not one hour before dusk, would tumble into dust.

Kalin unbolted the front door, and only as he took his first step into the gatherin chill did his momma make her last plea, what she would sadly recall sayin to him when the mountain finally did fall.

Promise me the only promise I've ever asked you to keep.

I ain't my daddy.

Promise me, Kalin. And for the second time that month, a young boy shiverin already before the solitary path he'd bound hisself to was again near commanded to weld by oath his Will to one he loved, as if he weren't some scrawny immaterial kid with two shirts on, plus a sweater, a jacket, and a green slicker, but Zeus hisself, who by a nod holds hisself accountable to all of time, his vow an unflinchin thing before any and every protestation, before even Change itself, immutable, irrevocable, Law.

This got nothin to do with guns, Momma.

Promise me!

There ain't no gun. I promise you.

Of course he was wrong. He didn't know it then. No one did. And he weren't Zeus either, if just because fer one thing he didn't nod at all. She did, though, and there weren't even a hint of blue in her eyes, as if a starless universe had suddenly come to settle in that second-floor apartment buildin in the flats just south of Isatch Elementary School.

Don't you forget the curse, Kalin March: you but touch a gun and what you love most will forsake you for the rest of your life. Just like that. She snapped her fingers too, and as if that one bedroom weren't dank enuf already, a darkness at once seemed to take away everythin around them, like a flash but of blackness that left Kalin blinkin. *Might as well the very hills of creation should tumble into oblivion, just like a crashin wave is lost to the sea, so Love will be lost to you. Kalin March, you heed the price of such ruinous pride.*

And while most would concede that at that moment the mountains risin up as witnesses over the valley, the peaks of their deliberations hidden in a dark crown of cloud, displayed nothin more than their own immovable indifference, especially before such a paltry scene as this, between a mother and her boy, there were a few who swore otherwise. *Why on that hour, I looked up and saw old Agoneeya herself leanin in as if to topple upon me,* Cavil Cox would swear to Howie Dirker, though it is true he was cleanin windows at the time, roped to the side of the four-story Marriott on Center. Or Dwight Ewing ramblin to Eddie Goulthrop, disbelievin hisself even as he said it, *I will never forget that moment, like a premonition, like First Nevi 12:4, how the whole range seemed to buck against the sky, even against the big storm we knew was comin. I would to this day swear it was the simple truth had I not right then looked to the bourbon in my glass and seen it was as still as the mirror on my wall.* Or even Cindi Kimber to strangers: *There was, yes, some shakes that made me doubt myself, but fever or not, I still know what I saw: I seen upon the foothills and all the slopes above a threat of such a weightlessness that not even one soul could take a step there; that the Kingdom of Daniel was at once established by the oldest instruments and undone too by the latest instruments; and it filled me with such a fright that the promise of Heaven, for what is a mountain if not the promise of Heaven?, could be removed from this earth just like that, makin of here a damnation we are already too much the fools to see.*

Whether or not the mountains truly wavered or that apartment darkened, even a little bit, Kalin still hesitated in the doorway. No question fear and doubt were at play, but mostly he wanted to linger in her gaze. She, for Kalin, would always be what a heart strives for when whatever path ahead seems cast in loss.

This door ain't ever gonna have a bolt you can't unlock.

I know it.

And that was that. Kalin stepped bareheaded out onto the balcony, into the cold and the wind, and without lookin back or even closin the door, headed toward the stairs. Maybe like the boy he still was, he hoped that his momma would come out into the wet and at least with her eyes trace his course through the small parkin lot, markin that his direction was indeed, like he'd said, toward the hills and what rose beyond, and that might give her comfort.

Only when he'd left the street for Kiwanis Park did Kalin stop and, while pullin the slicker's hood over his already wet neck and soaked brown hair, turn to see if her regard was followin him. But all he got, as the drizzle gave way to rain, was the empty railin and his own door set against him.

It was October 27. 4:07 p.m.

By the time Kalin reached Willow and Oak the rain was fallin hard. At least he'd knowd weather was on the way, that's what that green poncho was about; back in September he'd even resealed it, what was now slick enuf to bounce the water right off. She'd been watchin him put it on too, and at the time he'd thought he saw her smilin for knowin at least there was somethin of hers he'd be keepin close, her keepin him dry, but by the time the fences came into view, a sickly feelin had got hold of his guts. Too clearly he could see her seein him as a smudge of green about to trudge off in leaky shoes, with a lumpy pillowcase flung over his shoulder like a ten-year-old runaway. Which still weren't the worst of it, her smile reformin then into a recoilin hiss as he remembered that this poncho had been his daddy's first, the only thing she'd kept of his, because it did hold the rain off, and the thought of that devil on his back, again, once again in her eyes, slowed Kalin to the point that he stood paralyzed like one of them bare peach trees nearby, starin fruitless across the road at the stillness enclosed by a stranger's boundaries.

If only some movement had then stirred within Paddock A, Kalin might have hightailed it back for a hot bath, his momma's scoldin, and another try at failin his schoolwork. But only emptiness greeted him, what he'd knowd already to expect, havin confirmed so only hours earlier when the light was still hard and gray and the day was yet dry. And it terrified him, as if just one lousy paddock could speak suddenly for all graves. If fullness was an excuse to turn heel, emptiness was an even better one to run fast as a smart man can from a dumb idea. Though it weren't just an idea, was it?

Kalin pushed on ahead, through the mud, out of the orchard, dead branches trippin him some until a scatterin of brick caught his toe fer real and dropped him to his knees. He likely would've quit then too, acceptin in his heart that part of livin long means cowerin through most of it, if not from farther away, heard through the slashin flood, betwixt the crash from above and the crash upon the ruf of that sorry barn, right out of Paddock B, the call of his two friends.

It weren't no more than a few snorts, maybe a huff as well, but it was enuf. They knew he had not abandoned them.

Gettin the one halter-bridle on Mouse was hardest as that doggone horse kept nuzzlin him, rubbin the side of one cheek against Kalin's head and then tryin the same with the other side, then snortin some before recommencin this affectionate maulin.

Navidad was the opposite, like she knew there was no time to waste, the small Paddock B havin already told her what it was, years and years of it, the piss and hopelessness that had leaked into the earth, nor would be expurgated by flood or even fire, what in this newest down-pour bubbled up again like the turmoil of a premature and aborted resurrection, an eructed history of betrayal boilin around her hooves. No wonder her hind legs kept dancin side to side, though Navidad kept her forelegs rooted as trees so Kalin could all the faster secure her halter-bridle around that beautiful whiskered chin, then reins, and with one hand on her untrimmed mane, swing up on her back.

Kalin had by this point stuffed the pillowcase with the apples under his jacket. He felt bad about not givin them each a little some-thin to eat first, but the sooner they was outta there the better. They'd have plenty of time for the apples later.

Navidad, maybe for the comfort of him there, for what he'd come to mean to her, the openness to where she knew they was headed, whether that prospect of a relievin future brightened her vision or hastened her heart, why she shook her head then, stomped a hoof, and even neighed once, right as they neared the limits of Paddock B, whereupon as if to more permanently rid herself of anythin that might still dare to cling to her spirit, she threw back a kick, further wardin off what Kalin could not see, though its possibility made him shiver anyway.

Kalin with hands stayin light applied just a little pressure with his knees to keep easin her forward, though the black mare hardly needed the encouragement. With a switch of her tail she made a quick trot as soon as Kalin had swung open the gate and near dragged Kalin right off her back, at least twistin him up plenty before he could *Whoa* her to a halt, as his right hand holdin the lead rope stretched him back toward, no surprise here, Mouse, who had his own clock, near geological in perspective, and weren't finished just yet with his own goodbyes.

There that geldin stood, right in the heart of Paddock B, takin the longest pee he could muster, and makin sure to poop too, as if to add here some scent of defiance. He even looked back toward the barn as if to make sure this infernal place had registered these partin gestures.

Kalin joined Mouse's backward gaze, but unlike Mouse he did so to reassure hisself of the opposite: that no one was watchin them. Then, as they headed out onto the Willow blacktop with a steady *Clip-Clop Clip-Clop Clip-Clop*, Kalin was further relieved to find all the streets empty, with not a shadow disturbin the lit windows of nearby homes, even if Kalin also couldn't shake the feelin, *Clop-Clop-clip-Clop*, that as soon as they had crossed through the gate, somethin had at once awakened and started to follow.

And like that, in not even a minute, two out of nine gates were already behind them. Kalin did spare a glance to that first gate, the one between Paddock A and B, which he'd played no part in openin. And he beheld there a strange sight: as if instead of the various latches that locked it in place there now seethed the coilins of a red snake.

Some have asserted that it was this very same snake that had granted greater porosity between those two enclosures, between barrier and burden. Keith Lohner and Colleen Vance, at the time workin at the Wienerschnitzel at 1230 North, this was in 1987, both of whom incidentally couldn't stand Dale Laws and Joey Bird, though they still talked to them plenty, especially after the infamous snowball fight, well, they'd got to convincin each other that of course it was logical that a serpent had lifted the latch and ushered them two ponies from Paddock A into Paddock B; of course both were managin the tedium of that long shift with the help of some psychedelic mushrooms. To be fair, the snake theory isn't discussed much, and yet that possibility, alongside the more likely chance that a Porch hand had carried out the sentencin, still endures.

Anyways, Kalin only saw that snake for a blink, him blamin quick the weather in his eyes, blamin his nerves, not to mention the darkenin day that was all but collapsin around them. He closed and latched the second gate then, what in some ways had just marked their freedom and in other ways ushered them forth into a greater prison.

L ike him and Tom had done countless times, Kalin left the street for a narrow path that tonight's rain by its wash and rivulets helped hold clear. Through the low brush, he rode Navidad, stayin mostly hid from the few houses that clustered here and there as they made their way up to Oak Hills.

Riskin a shortcut through a property, Kalin slipped across a backyard that weren't nothin but dirt dreamin one day of lawn, which it finally became some ten years later. Kalin saw no reason to think he was spied until he caught against the dark windows the darker figure of a boy, little Sagamore Blanchard, not even six, standin by hisself under the cover of a back awnin, a glass of milk clutched in both his hands, gazin at this sight, mouth open, maybe questionin such a sight or, better yet, maybe grateful for the sight: a silhouette unfamiliar to these times now cast forward from another time.

From there, Kalin swung wide for the lots, keepin clear of any more yards, walkin Navidad and Mouse only where there was dirt so to further mute the clop of hooves that might even in the bedlam of such weather cause residents to open their doors or part a curtain and so behold then a rider with horses whom Porch's men and maybe Porch hisself might inquire about come dawn.

But no more inquirin shadows were ushered forth into that downpour, and soon the path departed from all homes entirely with two sharp switchbacks steep enuf to leave Oak Hills beneath them, windows no longer appearin as anythin more than tiny blurs of embered warmth in the distance, with Orvop itself seeminly buried now by a secondary storm, a dense fog risin up from the day's sun-soaked earth in answer to the cold air descendin from above, presentin a city that looked now like a wealth of Christmas lights burnin bright beneath a fresh fall of snow.

Kalin sure was grateful it weren't cold enuf for snow. He knew snow would stop them dead.

Another set of foothills waited, but there weren't no switchbacks, just one path leadin straight up and only gettin steeper and slicker the higher they got, with the water now comin down cuttin narrow grooves that made footin for Navidad more difficult. Kalin even considered dismountin. It was hard enuf that he was ridin bareback with the wet makin it too easy for his legs to lose their grip. Navidad didn't care much for him constantly havin to rescooch hisself up toward her withers, relyin more than usual on her mane too to keep him in place. Not a pretty sight, and certainly no grand example of riderly poise, especially with Kalin constantly tuggin Mouse's lead to keep him close.

Instead of dismountin, Kalin patted Navidad's neck and whispered in her ear what needed whisperin. He didn't even dig his knees in none, nor tap his heels to her side; she knew what needed doin and did it, not just for Kalin either, or even for herself, but for Mouse too, liftin up her beautiful head and juttin out her chest, if just fer a moment, to gather herself up, situate herself firmly in her hocks, before barrelin on outta there, kickin up through the mud and cascadin pebbles, until with one last lunge, she was scramblin out onto the gravel-strewn path that service trucks and park rangers use to get to the trailheads, what's rumored to mark the ancient shoreline of the paleolithic Lake Bonneville.

Mouse had kept up easily, his shoulder the whole time at Navidad's near side flank, snortin some along the way, like he was insulted she had thought to get ahead, that or troubled by what it might've meant to linger too long behind, though maybe mostly amused that Navidad or Kalin could've treated such an inconsequential slope of earth as a challenge at all.

Kalin dismounted then and stroked Mouse's neck and thanked him. Then he freed up one of them apples from under his jacket and split it apart with his thumbs. Navidad and Mouse both pulled in close to get their share of the juicy chunks.

While they ate, with Kalin sparin nothin for hisself, the boy kept his eyes fixed on the tumblin gray that marked the veil through which they'd just passed, waitin to see if whatever sense of trouble growin back there would suddenly materialize here and now. But water only begat more water.

Whatever toll this naggin feelin of pursuit took on Kalin's nerves, it weren't nothin compared to the dread he felt as they approached the old miner's shack. He'd felt somethin similar when he'd first got to the paddocks on Willow and Oak, fearin that he was already too late, the horses gone to slaughter, or a notch worse, findin some of Porch's men loadin his friends into a trailer, leavin him powerless to do anythin but watch. Now he was suddenly overtook by the fear that all the weeks him and Tom had spent layin in supplies, and Kalin in the last week alone further organizin and shorin up their provisions with additional necessities, had been found out, discovered by some thief who, takin advantage of Kalin's haste and no doubt inevitable mistakes, had carried everythin away to either own, eat, or pawn. Kalin even grinned sourly at the ironic way of his thoughts, that while he was stealin two horses, someone else was stealin his stores. If the universe or even this tellin was at heart a moral play, this should've been Kalin's discovery and undoin.

But both hasp and padlock remained unmolested, everythin within untouched and dry. Kalin first thing grabbed up a second twelve-foot lead, which he attached to Navidad's tie ring, loopin both leads around the same branch him and Tom had used all summer. Then he took out the second apple, and only after the horses had ate their part did he spare hisself a bite. The juicy sugary swallow momentarily blinded him to the rain and fast-descendin dark and even to what lay ahead.

The empty pillowcase he folded, then placed it along with the last apple in one of the saddlebags.

Kalin secured the packsaddle on Mouse fast enuf, palm-feedin him a bit of the soaked oats and raisin mix he'd brought up here just yesterday, Mouse makin clear one palm weren't enuf. Over the summer, Tom had tried out a sawbuck packsaddle but they'd settled on a Gatestone Decker packsaddle that Tom donated to the expedition. Tom had always planned to ride Mouse and bring along a family mule named Fred. Fred never knew what he missed. Lucky Fred. Kalin weren't the best with knots, whether diamond hitches, barrel hitches, or such, but somehow he managed, and soon enuf the supplies they'd need were upon Mouse and balanced right, with Mouse not seemin to mind much the arrangement, drinkin from a collapsible canvas water bowl which had collected enuf rain for a good few sips.

Navidad almost welcomed the saddle, but maybe because the rain had soaked her back or some other reason Kalin couldn't figure out, every time he tightened the cinch, the saddle pad slipped aside. No lie, Kalin near started to cry. His eyes grew blurry, and a fizzle got up behind his nose, and all over mismatchin the buckle prongs with holes he'd been matchin for months now.

Not once, not twice, but three times the saddle sat askew, Kalin wantin to blame the saddle tree or fork for goin foul, or somethin troublin the gullet, though Navidad's snorts and shuffles told Kalin who was at fault. He should've just said sorry to her right then, but instead he tried to race through a fourth try and ended up flubbin that as well, steppin back for no understandable reason, them poor boat shoes too waterlogged to serve anyone anymore, slippin right out from under him, slammin his keister down in the mud, with the jangle of Tom's saddle comin down atop him, the cantle, or what others might call that back rise of the seat, strikin him on the face, and with enuf abrasive speed, likely a quiet seam doin the actual cuttin, that a small line of blood drew up right there on the ridge of his cheek under his eye.

Kalin took a moment then to breathe, maybe some of his mother's instructions over the years finally findin purchase in his actions, so that when he rose this time, he did what was right, apologizin to Navidad first, attendin to her, so that he didn't have to think twice about what he was doin with the leather and metal that easily found then their congruence upon her back. Not that this meager accomplishment quieted the doubt that clanged Kalin's innards, doubt that he could do this, do even what was next at hand.

But done it he did anyway, like a seasoned ranch hand surveyin his provisions whether packed and balanced on Mouse or with Navidad: four tarps; a winter sleepin bag of course; two pairs of gloves; plus blankets and extra ropes, includin one long riata, a hundred feet, cotton and tawny in color, and two lariats, one at thirty-two feet, yellowish green, the other at sixty-four feet, near violet; plus waterproof matches; six tea candles; a hatchet, Swiss Army knife; canteen, pan, kettle, and bowl, and a mug; and food of course, and if things went bad, and judgin how this was all startin, Kalin better start plannin on bad, a small first aid kit for hisself and a substantial wound kit for the horses, which included sterile gauze, pads, tape, soap, scarlet oil, DMSO, disposable diapers for swollen legs, Vaseline, and ground yarrow, if a poultice became necessary.

There's little question it was this incommunicable sensation of a future wrought as nothin short of a killin trap that made of the smallest missteps and fumbles the worst of omens, weakenin Kalin's resolve and certainly his knees. But he also knew he'd better make his peace right quick with this uncertainty, or at least accept its awful company, because Doubt, whether Kalin liked it or not, would ride with him the whole way or at least as far as he could get.

Livin with Doubt, though, is a hard thing to do for anyone, especially a boy. And right then and there Kalin became certain that he just couldn't do it. He dropped his head against Navidad's shoulder, this time lettin his eyes leak all the wet they had to give. Kalin couldn't even get his breath right, havin trouble easin the panicked ache that kept overtakin his overexpandin chest. If only he could sob or at least cry aloud, how this weren't fair, how he was the fool to dare such an undertakin, an impossible undertakin, especially for the likes of someone such as him, already caught within night's desolate reach, already blasted by this life-sappin rain, and, worst of all, alone.

Of course, you who know some of this history are right to surmise that this flood of misery had less to do with a dropped saddle, and the mess that mishap made with blood and roller buckles clotted with mud, and everythin to do with the next choice that Kalin had to make. Too many too often have chimed in on this matter, whether Val Benson, HR top dog at Isatch University; Julia Barton, also at the university, as an associate professor; or Jerry Coombes, plumber at Coombes Drain, these folks often registerin to each other and friends the complex outcome that resulted out of so simple a decision, and though there weren't exactly a forked road at that old miner's shack, it near enuf amounted to the same thing: This way or that way? Left or right?

Kalin had already decided earlier to go left, the way he and Tom had planned for tirelessly, but at this moment he revisited the choice. He was surprised by how exhausted he already felt, and shiverin too, with what he'd done so far not even countin as a start of any consequence. Kalin also knew he had to get away now, and fast, or they'd be on him no trouble and the horses would be meat by noon tomorrow. But which way to go still bore him down into immobility. Even his very thoughts struggled for movement. Nor could Navidad or Mouse ease his burden with their opinions, stoic in their attendance to his decision. How their futures would now turn out was Kalin's responsibility alone.

These minutes here were all. Dependin on the direction he would choose, so much difference would henceforth unfold. And Kalin just couldn't make up his mind, so he stood there blind against Navidad's side, the rain thunderin their shoulders.

Him and Tom had discussed the merits of goin right more than a few times. It was by far the easiest route and would still lead to Tom's Crossin. Kalin would only have to retrace his path along this Bonneville shoreline path, and instead of goin back down where he'd come up from, he would just keep headin south. The way was wide too and smooth enuf to pretty much canter the length of the base of Agoneeya Mountain, and except for a few outlier residences, he'd keep well above the neighborhoods. He'd reach the Heathen-Slade Canyon Trail in less than an hour.

There was a chance he'd find a patrol car parked at the trailhead. He and Tom had noticed this on a few occasions and figured it likely pertained to the nearby and now closed hospital, which Tom was all too happy to point out had stood there since the 1850s, though back then it was called a Territorial Insane Asylum. *In other words, where we both belong!* Oh you can bet Tom had laughed plenty over that one.

For a bored officer chasin the minute hand to the hour, the discovery of a boy out ridin in the rain would've ranked up there with euphoria, worth at least a siren and maybe a shacklin, if just for the story.

But even if Kalin could get around the officer unseen, and Kalin was pretty confident that that much he could manage, it's what came next that made him the most concerned. The Heathen-Slade Canyon Trail was easy, and even if he rode all night, by which time he'd only just be startin to make his way into the convolutions of the lower steeps of the dauntin upper Katanogos massif, dawn would find his location easily pinpointed from afar. Heck, anyone livin near the cemetery could walk out their front door and spot Kalin with a semi-decent set of binoculars. It wouldn't be a pretty picture either: Kalin would have two tired ponies on his hands, with his own judgment precariously compromised by the long night, and little to show for it except more muddy trails ahead, along with increased exposure the higher he got on them wide risin slopes.

Worst of all, nothin up there would keep a jeep or maybe even his momma's own Dodge from racin up after him, right after breakfast, or even as lunch was just gettin started, and catchin him easy before lunch was finished. Nothin these two beautiful creatures could offer, with their hard hooves and outrageous hearts, even includin whatever talents Kalin might supply, would stand a chance against the mechanistic might that with just a few coughs of oily smoke would easily overtake anythin on the Heathen-Slade Canyon Trail or, for that matter, the Katanogos Aspen Roundup Route that led higher up into and around the lower ridges.

Of course, if no one thought to travel or spare the Heathen-Slade Canyon Trail a glance, him, Mouse and Navidad might just find refuge behind the occludin peaks that were waitin for them even now. And with none of the altitude to contend with, that way was sure easier, even if it was the long way around. The natural peril was also far less significant so long as the peril of human predation weren't added to the equation.

Kalin might just make it. If he got lucky. And therein was the trouble: not countin the luck he had gettin the momma he got, never in his whole life had Kalin found a good reason to trust luck. It just weren't how he was wired.

Chances were considerable that he'd be spotted at some point, and that's all it would take: he'd be helpless. Old Porch could hunt him down on dirt bikes or just send the park rangers after him.

Kalin, however, still did not quit his considerations of that direction, because, as he and Tom had also discussed, by way of that right turn there was also another shortcut to the back side of Agoneeya Mountain, and from there to Borrower Trail, which would likewise get him to the Katanogos Aspen Roundup Route with far fewer occasions for others to track his progress.

Not but a fifteen-minute ride from here, just beyond the trailhead to the great *I* on the face of Agoneeya Mountain, waited Cutter's Crick Path. It weren't much of a trail and, while not terribly steep, would still prove a hard ride. When it was dry, the way was sandy and wide enuf to make the trek almost appealin. This rain, though, would have the path lookin like a small crick and slow his progress substantially. If he ran into trouble, dawn might catch him still within view of anyone in Orvop lookin up.

The trick would be to get fast as fast could get behind Agoneeya Mountain, where there awaited what amounted to a false valley or shallow vale, what folks called Shadow's Glen, even if even here there persisted arguments over whether it was in fact really a glen, so untraveled, wooded and riverless. *Sure not no strath!* Leela White would proclaim to Robbie Bridges, Robbie at that time still pursuin a date with Leela, who agreed it was *more like a milk dish* set beneath the immensity of Katanogos risin up to the east. Robbie did finally get his outin with Leela, though as she made clear, it weren't no date just a dinner. *What's the difference?* Robbie had near wailed. Leela answered with a line she liked to repeat long after they was married: *A dinner is a dinner. A date is a dinner where anythin is possible.*

Now back to this matter of orography: in fairness to Shadow's Glen, it was hard to imbue much significance in near anythin, whether meadow or dangerous bluff, if it lay below the Katanogos massif proper, them loomin cluster of peaks so towerin, they was like skies unto themselves, each with a world of its own, not only dwarfin the likes of Agoneeya, Kaieneewa, or any of the other Isatch mountains for that matter, but encompassin too what millions of years had laid at its distant feet, includin forests and glacial lakes, ever announcin them high walls with numerous cols and jagged passages, gifts to every stronghearted interloper set on sleuthin out any number of nameless paths, which, if Kalin could just reach one, as Tom might've said, well then, all bets were off, the odds evened, and maybe in Kalin's favor, grantin him, Navidad and Mouse easy passage to Tom's Crossin.

The trouble was what waited between Shadow's Glen and the craggy-tree-filled-backcountry freedom Kalin would need to reach. That part of the journey weren't more than a series of long switchbacks that steadily rose up as they'd head east of Agoneeya, leavin behind the bouldered and walled terminus of Isatch Canyon. At any other time, that way would've presented the most appealin invitation. However, rumor was that several sections of those paths had collapsed, impedin not only all vehicles but hikers too.

Goin by way of Cutter's Crick meant bettin them switchbacks were intact and the slides were only rumors. Tom hisself was the first one to report that rumor in late September, but he weren't the only one. Kalin dialed up Park Services and confirmed that it was closed, though, when he called again last week, another ranger had suggested that it might already be repaired even if it was still officially listed as closed.

Rangers are up there pretty much every day. Better to deal with it now, when it's dry, than come spring when the snow starts meltin. Which also meant there was a good chance Kalin would come across folks who would certainly note his presence.

Tom fer sure had made all these calculations hisself, and dozens of times too, laughin his heart out over the thought of really takin the Heathen-Slade Canyon Trail or Cutter's Crick Path, even if he'd still laid out these two options for Kalin, perhaps temptin him with alternatives to the much higher and more dangerous route that they both knew was best, or just to tease him as he always liked to do, probably figurin that Kalin would also figure out quick enuf that those two options were so well traveled that Kalin could pretty much count on gettin spotted at some point and so then caught and in some dumb shameful manner too.

Besides, there's no mystery in them ways, and there sure as heck ain't no magic, Tom had declared after one such conversation durin a long afternoon ride. *History ain't ever gonna pay no mind to horses or trailhoppers on Cutter's Crick or the Heathen-Slade Trail.*

Not that Kalin gave a hoot about mystery or magic or even History. He just wanted to see these two horses get free. And in the name of that modest ambition, he had every right to select the easiest route if he thought it would result in the best outcome; just race to the back side and risk whatever eyes greeted him along the way. There might be no chase at all. Like how throughout summer and fall, Old Porch and his men had never noticed the horses' frequent absences. Kalin might just be left well enuf alone, and so by pleasant amble and sigh the three of them might arrive undisturbed at that place that lived only in his imagination, nothin but a vague reach of wild green as open as a gone gate with hinges so rusted through they was fixed, the gateless latch still there and fixed too to them two gateposts, standin firm in their denial despite the fact that the fence they had served had long since fallen down around them, or so Tom had told Kalin, rotted away, a testament to division undone by tall grass.

Might the easy way now be worth the dare? Though it weren't really a dare, was it? More like takin a chance, and chance and luck were the same thing in Kalin's book, as in not in it, not if he could help it.

Isatch Canyon then was their only option: not easy, with manifold perils, but at least the entrance was only a few minutes off. Kalin could pass into protective shadows before night had even started. Also, unlike the other routes that he'd traveled parts of, he knew this route best. And as Tom had already figured out, a good horseman with the right horses would disappear like a ghost in there.

So Kalin lifted his head from Navidad's warm shoulder and ducked quickly back into the old miner's shack, mostly empty now, sittin his wet butt down on the dry dirt, where he pulled off the Top-Siders and placed them careful at the back. Shapes of gray were all that remained of a blue that at one time seemed destined for the sea. Then he peeled off his soaked socks and stuffed them inside the shoes, like he was one day gonna see them socks or shoes again. He wouldn't.

Next Kalin put on thick dry wool socks that even if they was from this world, still felt stole from Heaven. Them black boots Tom had given him felt pretty good too. Last of all, he set on his head the big white Stetson Tom's mom had given him after Tom's funeral.

As a quick aside here, Tom's family took their hats plenty serious, Tom especially. He had straw hats, a wild fur one or two, but his black and white Stetsons were his treasures and near the best you could get: both 30X, which means top dollar because the felt has thirty times more beaver than rabbit. No question they was cruel hats from the start. They had a silk linin and a buckled band the same shade as the hat. And if the socks and boots felt like Heaven, why there's only one thing that felt better than Heaven, or so the Devil likes to sing, if you believe in that sort of thing. Thank you, Tom.

In fact near everythin Kalin had here was thanks to Tom or his family, from the saddles and tack to most of the supplies and fer sure Tom's daddy's old boots. It was all either loaned or stolen. Pretty much only the duct tape and cardboard was Kalin's, which he'd originally planned to put to use right at the start, but with the dark comin on so fast and the rain sure to ruin at once what he had in mind, he stowed those items away for another time. Which did prove a lucky thing.

After Kalin reconfirmed one last time that the hatchet and the Swiss Army knife were where they should be, in one of Navidad's saddlebags, with the binoculars in another, he rechecked her halter-bridle and eggbutt snaffle, the browband too, as well as snaps and screws, the reins, again recheckin the length of the stirrups, from wrist to armpit, and they was fine, even if fer a moment he thought to lengthen the right stirrup one more hole before lettin it be.

Where Mouse was concerned, Kalin gave the packsaddle another lookover and found the breast collar and quarter strap in need of adjustin. Dumpin all the supplies in the middle of the trailhead parkin lot would be a thing too awful to imagine.

Finally Kalin ran his hand down along Mouse's long mane and, to breathe them both into a fair place, rested his bloody cheek against the geldin's neck for a spell, rememberin again, and this time clearly, why he was here. He did the same with Navidad, and then he swung up in the saddle and headed to Isatch Canyon.

Some comfort should've come from seein their hoof marks dissolvin in the rain. If this night had been dry as last night, their direction would've been obvious to any interested party. Instead every trace left on the part of the path that was hard clay and cinder was fast washed away in the downpour, and on the softer parts the indentations quickly filled with mud.

But satisfyin as this sight should've been, as they passed behind the Sixth Ward church, Kalin still couldn't shake the feelin that somethin else, beholden to nothin a trail might hold or forget, clung to his choices and their progress. At times what was crawlin his back got so bad that, try as he might to ignore it, Kalin still had to jerk around to squint the deepenin dark for some sign of movement, first seekin out men, then lookin for the glow of some predatory gaze, maybe stalkin Mouse in back, which would've been a darned foolish quest, unless the aim was to have your wolfish skull stove in by a powerful rear kick. Unfortunately the repeated absence of nothin but rain only further unsettled Kalin, until he grew to fear more gravely beyond the fleetin streaks of fallin water the blackness itself, only just now awakenin, not so much fer takin the horses either, which he'd been takin from the Porch paddocks for near half a year, but this time for takin them for Good, and how that act alone, defined more by silent intention than deed yet, had summoned forth somethin far worse than men or animal predation, though Kalin was hard-pressed to name anythin worse than men, this presence nonetheless now installed on the heels of their journey, as if in answer to the unforeseen unbalancin caused by stealin away two creatures fated for other ends, what the Law exceedin every law scripted by human hands must redress; or as Erin Kennedy, an Orvop florist at the time, would describe it, this before she married Gus Dieudonne: *The very same Law that must offer remedy by way of a Power that stills the hearts of birds and shudders the bark from trees.*

Fer his part, Thayne Moon, an assistant basketball coach over in Pleasant Grove, would manage a pretty fine charcoal renderin, on the bottom of which he would scribble his name and the title *Rearview*, what years later none other than Cal Carneros would consider pretty darned good. It had Navidad's rump and Mouse's irreverent regard, and caught beyond them, with speckled smears of hard dark strokes worked over with striations of white chalk, the sense of the night as a

60

cage but also how that cage was imperfect or at least inadequate. Any-one regardin the piece with any seriousness, feelin like they was right where Kalin was situated, would have to wonder if they was outside of that cage or inside. Not that it made much difference. There was no escapin what was comin up from behind, jaws foul with the offal of consequences evermore upon the land.

So it was even more surprisin to Kalin, as he wound his way down a long series of easy turns to reach the start of the parkin lot, void of vehicle except for an empty service truck parked there for the night, before passin the visitor kiosk with its engraved-brass trail maps, headin then in the direction of the wide sandy threshold complicated by the scrub oak and smooth sumac that marked the start of the Isatch Canyon Trail, that he kept hearin not behind them but up ahead an unmistakable whistle, clear too, as if there weren't no racket of rain-fall, and near beautiful enuf to still the racket. As the old saw goes: *The world is best viewed through the ears of a horse.* Both Navidad's and Mouse's ears had flicked forward at once.

Them two horses knew.

Up ahead, if still in the lee of a tumble of rocks that some might call boulders or perhaps small cliffs if they knew nothin of the cliffs that waited beyond, a pale figure with a black hat headed their way. The horse he rode, what anyone would call gold if it weren't so gray, would periodically swish its long tail, snort, and shake its long white mane wild with elf knots. Mouse and Navidad in turn answered with their own head shakes and snorts, not to mention quickened their pace.

Dusk had been creepin in since five p.m. but when night itself finally arrived, it seemed to fall like an ax on the neck of the protestin day, the dark at once commandin a stretch so permanent dawn seemed a forever away.

It was 6:06 p.m.

Kalin knew at once who it was just by the way the rider and his horse moved. The way the rider talked too.

Son of a gun! Is that you, Kalin?

What are you doin here, Tom? You're dead.

Don't I feel like it too! Tom hooted with a big smile.

I stood by your grave not two weeks ago. Even threw a handful of dirt on your coffin.

Guess you didn't throw enuf, Tom said, still keepin his smile, though a darkness stole into his eyes.

Don't get me wrong. I sure am glad to see you.

Of course you are! Tom laughed, soft though, his amusement not quite riddin hisself of this darker quality that was composin his features, though even these seemed to lighten some when he turned his attention to the horses.

I know, heckuva night to set out with these two, Kalin said.

It's the perfect night.

For a bit there I thought I was bein followed. Guess it was by you.

Tom snorted, wheelin around the Andalusian palomino so they was again facin the dark breach from which Tom had just emerged. *Kalin, you should know better than that. I don't follow no one, and even if I had to, I sure as heck wouldn't follow you.* To make his point Tom even trotted ahead.

Kalin smiled, maybe for the first time since he'd started out on this crazy ride, realizin then how dry his mouth had got and even how clammy he'd been feelin all over, his breath up until then a shallow raggedy mess that now at last began to mellow and fill, aided further by the calm that Navidad and Mouse seemed all the more inclined to demonstrate with Tom's arrival.

What happened to your face? Tom asked once Kalin had caught up.

Like a darned fool, I slipped while tackin up Navidad and dragged your saddle right down on top of me. Kalin wiped his cheek with the back of his hand. Blood still swirled there.

Tom laughed some and then shook his head some too. *It's a right good thing then that I came along. If not to stop you from makin fool mistakes, then at least to laugh at you.*

They was passin under the last lamp of the parkin lot, and its orange glow seemed to suddenly make embers outta the rain. Were it not so captivatin, you might've called it the place Heaven ain't. Tom, though, in that lamplight weren't so welcome a sight, though nothin was even really wrong with him. Plus the horse he was on was plain astoundin, big and broad, with his head held high and dark green eyes fixed ahead like he was set upon this earth for only this cause, and maybe that was true. Tom's saddle was a marvel of black rawhide, laced silver and dark leather elaborately tooled with designs Kalin could somehow register if never make out. A scabbard too was tooled with more dark designs, though instead of the butt of a rifle juttin out, Kalin beheld what looked like the end of a charred branch. Tom hisself weren't close to frailin neither, not like in those final days when he was in the grip of tubes and wires. Kalin still couldn't forget how Tom had once shifted in his bed and his hospital gown hadn't shifted, exposin his side; ribs had showed forth like his skin weren't but even thicker than tissue paper, wet tissue paper, ready to bust apart. Now, though, some chunk was back in his cheeks, and, sure, maybe Tom was a little gray, but then he was also obdurate as granite, and the way he kept his boot toes pointin straight ahead showed he had some strength in his legs. You couldn't even fault his smile for bein anythin but genuine.

And yet.

I don't think you're supposed to be here, Tom.

Tom considered this. *There's plenty I'm not sure of right now, and maybe if I think too long about how I can't even remember how I got here to meet you in the first place, why I might tie up so bad I won't be any good to you. So I'm keepin to what I can recall: if you're here with these two, then that means Old Porch put them in Paddock B, and you're gettin them loose before Old Porch can put more stupid on this land.*

Right before you passed, you told me where to take them.

I don't recall that.

I do.

Isn't that enuf?

And it was, and so with no more fuss, they left the last place where, beneath the ground, pipes still carried water and cables still hummed with electricity, and they passed into the mists of what neither one of them, whether livin or dead, could know or dare deny.

Chapter Two

"A Poker Game"

Now about feelin he was followed, Kalin weren't wrong there, even if he couldn't see no pursuer. As settled as he might be on the back of the most petulant pony, Kalin had no knack for knowin how men think and see and then think some more on about what they've seen just so they can hide better their thinkin from other men and so adequately advantage themselves. Don't fret if followin that just strained your head some. It would strain Kalin's too. Life's pretty enuf without havin to lie about it. Though too often the men that mattered in Kalin's life, one man really, considered it a point of pride to do just that: lie. Not Tom of course. Tom didn't need to lie. And anyway, it weren't no man that was followin him.

Like plenty of folks have conjectured, Tom's little sister, Landry, had a head that was either full of rocks or in the clouds dependin on when you talked to her. Best to start there. Landry was the kinda curious twist of fifteen-year-old mischief that could lie on the grass for an easy hour entranced by whatever a sky had to show. How she loved to watch the high winds scrub the blue so clean the blue was practically yellow, which when she'd swear so to Tom about, and this after he was done askin if she had rocks in her head for lyin there so long, not even mindin the ants at her ankles or gnats in her ear, why he'd laugh hisself red before finally comin up for air, swearin it was true, his sister did have rocks in her head, funny rocks maybe, but rocks just the same, and then because Tom never had no beef with no rocks, he'd settle down beside her and spend the next hour arguin about the color of the sky, pretty much as caught up as Landry was in all a sky can show.

Now you can imagine for yourself how a girl who could spend an afternoon harpin on her brother about how blue ain't really just blue, or how what clouds show us is how a dream is torn apart, all while thumpin Tom hard with the back of her hand, right square in the middle of his chest, *thump!*, for teasin her one bit too much, why there is a girl who, when takin an interest in somethin, will give it a whole lot of attention and a whole lotta time. And Landry was always interested in what her big brother was up to, if only so she could do him one better. So you better believe that when he was weak in his hospital bed, not hours from death, whisperin secrets to a strange kid no one there could make sense of, Landry Gatestone paid close attention.

Not that Kalin was entirely unfamiliar to her. Let's just say her curiosity about the new kid didn't just bloom when Tom's sickness took hold. She was there the night of the one dinner and, just like her momma, was utterly mystified by what Tom had drug home.

Of course, Landry pressed her brother good afterward, but Tom only stayed wry and amused. *He's a good kid,* he'd say.

He couldn't spit out but five words! she'd replied, infuriated in fact, though she couldn't say why.

Well then, maybe I was hopin you'd learn a thing or two from him.

Tiny as she was, Landry knew how to take it to Tom too. It's hard to say where her courage came from, if that's what it were, but her big brother loved it. Landry's eyes would shine wild with what their momma called *pure undiluted impertinence,* and Tom would yip and ske-daddle as she chased after him. Fear of bein caught, though, weren't exactly an issue given as her right foot, as was indicated earlier, did swing wide in a wayward way that weren't exactly suited for reachin anyplace fast. When she was runnin, Tom liked to say, she looked like a drunk sailor on the deck of the world if that world was sinkin. No wonder she'd never gone to no dance. But she weren't bothered, or so she always claimed. She had other ways of gettin what she was after. And often that was Tom. She sure loved her big brother.

Maybe as much as Jojo.

Jojo was one impressive horse, formally a rabicano, but folks at the stables referred to him as the Big Blue Roan. His big brown eyes even had a whisper of metallic blue. Landry could ride him for days without so much as wipin a bead of exertion from her brow, teasin Tom extra when he had to mop his whole face for failin again to catch her when they was playin tag. He rarely caught her too, no matter what horse he rode, but she always caught him, showin off and crowin about it too, you can bet on that. Fer example, even when touchin the horse was what counted, Landry would make sure to tag her big brother with a big wallop on his chest, with that *Thump!,* which, however humiliatin, was always answered with his generous laughter, the two playin out on their granddaddy's fields, and bareback too, until foamy sweat ran down their horses' chests, goin in then to bathe their friends under tepid water, never too cold, as that just shuts down the capillaries you need to help spread the cool, plus you want them muscles all flushed. Just important stuff to know. She and Tom then would water them horses, massage them, brush them out, walk them some, treat them, then walk them some more, feed them, arguin the whole time over who was better at tag, seein Landry was always on Jojo, as no soul they knew could get near that big Arabian let alone put a foot in a stirrup. Not even Tom.

Anyways, Tom's gripin about what horse they was on was really just his way to admit twice to this tiny girl that he was most definitely defeated and was thus forced to beg, with a wink of course, that she never breathe a word to anyone else about his loss, which she didn't, of course, except to their momma, every chance she got.

Tom sure loved his little sister. And he didn't just whisper in the ear of only Kalin those last days in the hospital.

Landry, come here, he'd barely managed to croak out, which still provoked much objection, Landry arguin through her tears that he should come sit by her side, if he was ever a gentleman, finally assentin to sit by his side, thus provin, she told him, that her brother weren't no gentleman, which Tom chuckled over, them beautiful sparks still flyin some in his dyin eyes.

Guess this time I win, he whispered when she finally leaned down.

What are you talkin about, you darned fool?

Ain't no way in heck you gonna catch me this time.

Landry made to thump him on his chest, but of course she didn't, might've broken clean through. Just the same a fire did come into her own eyes, which by his grin showed he already understood her language of flame. *Oh, you ain't won yet, Tom. I might just come after you and tag you out there. Just you wait!*

I'll wait, but I better be waitin a long time.

Out of all of them, Landry cried the hardest when Tom died, so much and so often and for such a long time that her momma started to fear that maybe her tears would put out the fire she and Tom revered so much in each other. The only thing in truth that put a pause in them tears was when Landry started takin a keener interest in Kalin.

Thanks to the one time when Kalin had joined them for dinner, she'd begun noticin him more at Orvop High. This was before summer. He was a sophomore then, and she a freshman, so they didn't share any classes. The only time she could watch him was in the halls. She soon found out where he lockered, but he never lingered there. He had no discernible group of friends. Far as she could tell, he didn't have a single friend. Like a cipher in the snow but with no snow. She'd also witnessed how Lindsey Holt and his football buddies, like Mattock Jurgenvin fer example, didn't care much for Kalin, but also how he in turn didn't seem much troubled by them.

The big discovery had come one day after school in early May, when Tom was truckless but still turned down a ride home from Ronnie Thurgood who was drivin that white 1973 Plymouth station wagon, what they often made fun of by callin it the Great White Whale, which was still an odd thing for Tom to do since a ride was a ride. Just fer fun, Landry decided to follow him.

Tom's pale blue Ford F-250 was at the Lee Garvey Shop, but walkin still seemed a strange choice, especially as Tom was almost a senior, and, as everyone knows, what an upperclassman values most is to drive or be driven by someone other than a mom. Holy moly, though, what a crazy discovery to see her brother join up then with that Kalin kid, him arrivin by another route to Willow and Oak, where the Porch holdin pens stood, which Landry only got to understand a bit more about later, meanin Paddock A, and also what happened to anythin put in Paddock B, be it horse, goat, or mule, a place rife with enuf gory rumors to ward off any kids from trespassin there lest they get exsanguinated and sawed up too.

After that, Landry got cunnin about where she'd hide, findin better spots higher up with better views to track their rides, discoverin too that summer that they was mostly disappearin into Isatch Canyon.

How Landry didn't spill all she knowd right there, especially to her momma, who she loved like the sun, is a point of some contention. Dwanna Hales, a dental hygienist in Spanish Fork whose momma gave birth to her in a wheelbarrow, truth!, would declare to her patient and friend Hillary Osborne that Landry Gatestone *couldn't keep a secret any longer than it took for Jeananne Harvey to kiss a boy, which everyone knew took about as long as one slow dance. Not even. More like half a song!* Hillary, herself an accountant for a grain company up by way of Lindon, couldn't but agree with her mouth full of floss, though she weren't convinced neither, havin kept some secrets herself and knowin too that Jeananne Harvey sure as heck never kissed no boy while she was at Orvop High, which Cherry LaFranco and Flo Carrigan would eventually more or less confirm.

The answer likely lies with the quiet secrets Landry and Tom kept, like ridin when they should've been doin homework or eatin the last of their momma's strawberry pie, neither alertin the other but both creepin down to the fridge just past midnight. Stuff like that. See, even if her trackin was a secret from Tom, Landry still viewed it as their secret and no one else's.

She even once went after them on Jojo. Not that she ever actually laid eyes on the boys; she did find horse tracks and fresh manure, but otherwise they seemed to have vanished into thin air, so miraculously so that Landry doubted herself, finally turnin back, which was when she suddenly fer a moment heard bouncin off the shattered quartzite and high limestone walls her brother's beautiful whistle.

So you can bet your momma's best dollar that when Tom in the hospital brought up them two horses, Paddock B, and some goshdarned crossin, Landry's interest intensified more than just a little. Her momma insisted that whatever Tom was goin on about was poppycock. She even got cross with Landry, warnin the girl not to start seein what weren't there to begin with. *Your brother was very ill. Please grant him the courtesy of lettin him say whatever he wanted to say even if it made no sense at all. Lord knows he granted you that courtesy too many times to count.* After which her momma immediately burst into tears, Landry fer sure too, and then the two hugged and cried even if it did nothin to ease their pain.

Followin Tom's death, all Landry could do when she had the chance was walk to school by way of Willow and Oak. She got to know those two ponies in Paddock A pretty well. She'd tickle their noses and feed them carrots. She wondered if Kalin was still comin to ride them, but they never crossed paths there.

Then this mornin she discovered that Navidad and Mouse were in Paddock B. She at once made up her mind to tell Kalin but saw no sign of him at school. It never crossed her mind that he'd made the same discovery an hour earlier and had already got to spendin the day makin last-minute preparations.

Landry missed her after-school band practice that afternoon and near ran the whole way back to Paddock B only to find that both horses were still there! Oh how Landry fumed at this Kalin for already failin her brother. Then she snuck out after dinner, determined to do somethin herself on behalf of them horses even if she didn't have a clue what. Thank the Lord that simple girl at least dressed warm: two sweaters, her cowboy hat, wool felt, sage, with a front pinch. She even had on her dark olive ski parka that still had in one pocket the twenty bucks she'd forgotten to give Mr. Chidester that day for Marchin Band extras and such. On top of that went her raincoat, which weren't so bad, bein lined and plenty dry, if it weren't for its awful pinkness.

As she made that long jog through the Tree Streets, she got to hatin pretty fierce this Kalin for not keepin his word to her brother. So the empty Paddock B stunned her, to the point that she stood frozen in all that fallin water, mouth agape. Was she already too late? Had Old Porch already loaded the ponies onto a trailer and driven them back to Porch Meats? At least that question got her studyin the mud around the gate, findin no sign of a trailer, any tires, which is how she come upon the hoof marks first, outside the gate too and still holdin up in the rain, and then next, what raced Landry to the center of Paddock B, a set of smaller tracks! Not boot prints neither, nor big, but made by near treadless shoes small enuf to confirm the boy.

Landry's hate bounced then in the other direction, though it came back quick enuf to hate on herself, for doubtin Kalin, for bein late, though, by the look of the tracks, not too late.

Without any thought of alternate routes, Landry made up her mind right on the spot to get Jojo, even if at her slow jog it would take a good half hour and actually ended up takin her near a full hour, the whole way prayin her momma would think her asleep in her room for the night, with Landry knowin she'd need at least half the night to catch up with him in the canyon. These thoughts were good as action, just as those thoughts about what would happen when or if she actually caught up with Kalin were no more substantial than the wisps of clouds already torn asunder by the strong prevailin winds.

The only thing that kept Landry from boltin from the paddock to the street then was the sudden explosion of light comin up Briar to Oak. Landry stepped back, tiltin her hat down while takin cover by the barn. Likely the truck would race on by, except she knew the truck. It were Egan's, one of Old Porch's older sons, and her stomach got tight, then her breath drew up quicker, with a thickness near that of stone seemin to coagulate in all her joints but especially in her knees. She sure was in a pickle, eyes hungerin for a better place to hide, but the barn doors were bolted, and at the rear of the one side where she was cowerin was a steep rise of muddy hill she might've tried scramblin up if it were dry but wouldn't have managed well wet like it was. Plus it was bathed now in headlights.

Then the truck passed on by, and Landry's joints started to unlock until the truck braked hard again, white reverse lights comin on brighter than the headlights, Egan's Ford Ranger backin up fast, almost too fast, near endin up in the ditch on the other side of the hardtop.

Landry dug in her pocket for her house keys to grip between her knuckles but discovered somethin better: an old hoof pick, plenty sharp too.

Except it weren't Egan Porch who emerged from the truck. It was one of the younger Porch boys. Landry's breath returned. Russel must've borrowed the truck, maybe to run an errand, maybe this errand, to check on the horses they'd be fetchin come mornin.

What the heck?! What the heck?! Landry could hear the boy yellin as he climbed up on the fence to better survey Paddocks B and A and so behold more fully their collective emptiness. Fortunately, before he could spot her flare of pink, he got down to check the gate. Landry knew if he started explorin more of Paddock B, like she'd done herself, he'd spy her, and then worse: just because she was a Gatestone, he'd fer sure blame her for the missin ponies.

But Russel weren't like the rest of the Porches. He didn't have none of the huntin instincts of his older brothers nor any of their obvious meanness either. And even for his size, though he weren't small, he still came across as half their size and soft to boot, not to mention not quite in full possession of his speech, if that's the kindest way to say he had a stammer, nor much by way of musculature, if that's the kinder way to say he were weak. Just this past month, Landry had seen Lindsey Holt givin him a hard time, knockin him into the lockers for a laugh while Russel's own brothers, Francis and Woolsey, stood nearby supplyin the larger part of that laughter. Anyone with half a peabrain knew Russel had better start actin fast like the Porch he was and stand up for hisself or he'd get a worse beatin from his own family, which he probably did get regardless, once Francis told Kelly, or Woolsey told Shelly and Sean, and Lord help poor Russel if word reached Egan that he'd let Lindsey Holt treat him like a pinball.

Dee Wright, part of Orvop High's senior class royalty, would have this to say to the question Lolly Neilsen posed, Lolly incidentally askin the same thing of Maggie Trunnell later: *Surprised?! Them Porches got what? Twelve boys? Thirteen?* Dee Wright at this point workin a Winchell's Donuts register. 1993. *Who even knows how many! And all piled into that big house near the lake. It's like a warren in there. Nothin but boys beatin on boys, preparin and practicin all the ill behavior they're certain to visit on whatever sad fool happens by near them. And you ask if I'm surprised?!* No garden of Ashurbanipal there, as Cal Carneros would, years from then, tell hisself as his own thoughts wandered over such matters as these as well as those of Nineveh, the hunt, and gypsum lions.

In fact Old Porch had nine children, and them numbers don't even include the four miscarriages their poor momma had endured along the way to eight boys and the one girl, the very youngest and havin already fled Utah with her momma.

Anyhow, Russel took no interest in the mud he was standin in, let alone anythin other than the missin horses. He hustled his tail quick back into the Ford, tires squealin and spittin up gravel before haulin onward with yet another set of unnecessary skids at the intersection, which Landry read correctly as havin nothin to do with haste and everythin to do with not knowin how to drive.

She herself took off a moment later. She only had to get to the Gatestone barn. Russel, though, had all of Orvop to cross before he reached Porch Meats. Of course Russel could raise the alarm along the way by callin his poppa from any number of pay phones, a possibility Landry considered, though she figured Russel would treat his movin truck as progress enuf and wouldn't stop til he was pantin before his daddy with news of the shockin theft. Trouble was that Russel weren't headin to Porch Meats.

What Landry didn't know was that Old Porch weren't home that night but over at Egan's for a poker game, and Egan's place weren't but a few blocks from her own family's barn, Egan's lot once part of a forty-acre parcel Old Porch used to own, what had climbed right up to the entrance of Isatch Canyon, what Old Porch had had big plans for.

But then again Old Porch has always had big plans. Sally Boan, a fourth grade teacher at Isatch Elementary, would tell Collette Paramore, a sixth grade teacher there, along with their friend Lissa Kaynor, that *Orwin set his eye on designs that granted his pleasures greater permissions,* both Collette and Lissa made excessively uncomfortable by the way Beth had spoken the word *pleasures.* Back in the late '60s, Old Porch, schemin for greater solvency and capital expansion, had decided to give minin a go, and so without tellin no one just started to extract granite and quartzite from the canyon walls. Orvop didn't care much for that nor did the Movie Star who owned the Cassidy Ski Resort, the city finally puttin a stop to Old Porch's endeavor.

It was funny because Old Porch forgot Orvop's role in filin charges, and even the Movie Star, but came away spittin nails at the park rangers who had reported his unpermitted exercise in good ol American industry. The settlement ended up forcin Old Porch to sell the land back to the city, though he kept an acre and a half just under the Isatch Canyon Park, which he gave to Egan to build a house on along with the small stable and corral for Cavalry and now and then a couple of nags.

Russel, however, didn't head straight there. He had one detour in mind. Maybe he weren't the dolt Landry had so often figured him for, and maybe given the right chance he would've showed some real seed, even differentiated hisself some from the Porch tree, like gone off to make a name for hisself as an actor or even a pop singer. How Landry and Tom would've howled at the thought of Russel Porch becomin more famous than an Osmond.

Not that that was likely to happen. Russel couldn't sing a lick nor memorize a line, and you can forget hearin him say much of anythin aloud in front of a bunch of strangers. A kid could dream even if he was only dreamin. Like Landry, he was but a sophomore, and still as mentally unformed as his doughy body, that softness a lifetime away from findin the grit that comes from livin longer with less.

Sue Ellen Burgess, servin up ice cream at the university and good friend of Staci Lithy, would call him *pokey but not in a bad way. Like how I'd imagine Santa when he was still a boy.* Russel had sandy brown hair and eyes set a mite too close together, a fact somewhat alleviated by their clear blueness, with plump cheeks as freckled as a starry night in the Uintas.

Well, Russel raced Egan's truck beyond the Tree Streets and up into

Oak Hills, all the way to where there was nothin but new roads and dirt roads and half-finished construction, findin one lot with only the foundation poured, where he parked, hopped onto one of the pylons still bristlin with rebar, and with one hand holdin a copy of some girly magazine Egan kept half hid under the passenger seat and his other hand on the binoculars he'd been tasked that night to return to their Uncle Conrad Jewell, he carefully surveyed the streets and trails.

He'd picked a good spot too. From that vantage point he could take in parts of the Bonneville shoreline trail, and to his credit, much like an old and seasoned tracker, he was patient, and that patience was soon rewarded with the motion of shadows on shadows that Russel knew at once were horses, likely his horses, and where his horses were surely there too was the thief. The darkness, though, made identifyin the scoundrel impossible even if the direction was unmistakable.

Once again Russel didn't go to Egan's, this time headin north on 1450, along the base of Agoneeya, though instead of drivin down to Oak, which descends further to the temple and Egan's place, not to mention Landry's family's barn, Russel veered off around to Crest Lane, pullin up sharp at Bout's Park, one tire on the curb, another dented by the curb, well, you can work out for yourselves the splendid vision of Russel's exemplary parkin skills. From there, Russel blundered out across the wet grass to another vantage point he knew well enuf, and then again with those binoculars and that magazine, by this point pulped by all the water it had absorbed, freein at least them ladies from the likes of Egan, Russel caught sight again of them shadows.

The right shadows too.

Clop-Clop-clip-Clop.

Porch horses fer sure and by this point movin across the small parkin lot. Under the few street lamps there, glowin a constant orange, Russel was astonished to discover that he knew the lone rider! It was that new kid, Kalin, just one year ahead of Russel, a junior now, but still two-third's Russel's size, if that.

Russel was even a little disappointed that it weren't some proud and even dangerous man who he'd get to see run down by the likes of his daddy and Egan, maybe by all his brothers at once, though he was also glad that he could easily run him down hisself, though he'd need somethin other than a truck if he was gonna get past the park's recreation gate. Gladder still wouldn't have begun to describe Russel's feelins if he'd knowd then that Kalin was also a friend of Tom's and hence a friend of the Gatestones. How that would've tickled his daddy's malice into some kind of special action. But Russel didn't know.

M uch has been made of what would have happened if Russel had only waited but a minute longer, followin Kalin all the way to that last parkin lot lamp, where Kalin had pulled up beside Tom and declared that it weren't right that Tom was there. What might've Russel beheld then? What shapes might his sensitive nature have found there stitchin its warnins into the dark?

Joanne Willden, who thanks to alopecia would embrace a love of wigs throughout her life, even them bald wigs, would fairly render this scene in smears of ash, teal, and charcoal, and orange of course, on a letter the contents of which she didn't care for, often insistin that Russel should've intuited somethin grotesquely amiss with the number of shadows down there and so should've let the whole thing drop, leavin Egan to sort it out in the mornin, if Egan would've even cared, and likely Egan wouldn't've cared, sparin the boy and those two grand families, the Porches and the Gatestones, plus the whole city, and plenty of others too, not to mention that lone mother beaver at the top of Bewilder Crick, all the consequences slowly amassin. It's no wonder that years later Rico G. lingered for some time before Willden's work.

Russel Porch, though, didn't linger even one moment longer, and weren't that a shame. Whatever else he was gifted enuf to sense was sacrificed before this immediate discovery: a kid he could put a name to had stolen his family's horses. Truly, Russel might never have knowd such ecstasy before, and it only grew as he sped back at last to Egan's place, *like a dumb Labrador bringin home a tennis ball slathered in happy spit*, as Joanne Willden would put it. Though Seth Boss, who would among other things discuss such matters with Colby Foster, would put it differently: *More like a dumb Labrador retrievin a grenade with the pin just dropped.*

F er his part, Orwin Victor Porch was happy that night. This sure beat Lawrence Welk or *Hee Haw*. The game had started off right too, meanin the pots hadn't stopped slidin his way since he'd sat down, like the table was tilted, and maybe it was. Stake President Brother Havril Enos was also still there, standin right behind Porch watchin the cards shift around the table, around the small but growin pile of specie at the center, half disapprovin but mostly entranced.

Just a game, Havril. Ain't no serpent in the garden. Cards were a special occasion. Old Porch had even shaved that mornin, and the scent of Old Spice still clung to him.

It's not the cards, Brother Porch, that I question but rather the coin, Havril Enos answered, smilin in a way that seemed to admit he knew hisself in some Domdaniel while at the same time insistin he was playin no part in its odious doins.

Old Porch laughed, another pot startin to engorge itself on his sons' early enthusiasms, their guests' too. H.O.R.S.E. was the usual, which is just an easy way to describe a mess of poker games, the current one bein for the *O*, Omaha Hi-Lo, which, like the *H* that comes before, for Texas Hold 'Em, shares five cards at the center, though here, without gettin too lost in the weeds, the hand is often split between the one with the highest cards and the one with the lowest cards. Old Porch was already lookin good with the highest, a two pair flirtin with a full house.

As I explained, Havril, even you can play. This is what we call our Tithe Game. My own invention, by the way. Just a method of gettin the family together, see, and friends, to enjoy a bit of fun while gettin what's due to the Church to the Church.

Orwin, that's the part I'm not quite followin.

Goshdarn it, Havril! Old Porch slapped his cards down impatiently, but his smile was easy as a day off. *It's really not that hard. The last week of every month, we sit around this table with our month's tithe and use that. Winner takes all but with that all goin to the Church.*

No, I understand, Havril replied with an equally affable smile. *There's just somethin about gamblin that ain't supposed to be gamblin in the name of the Church that seems to me, how to put this?, to wiggle more than straighten.*

Ha! Old Porch laughed and stood up, and then with a big smile clapped Havril on the shoulder. *I have no idea what that means, but can I get you another root beer?*

I'm good, Orwin. I best be off.

But he ain't rang yet.

Myrna sets her table at a sharp six thirty. I've learned not to question her clock.

Old Porch followed the stake president outside and watched him secure his raincoat and resettle his hat. *Shhhhhhhh . . .* the rain seemed to say. It's hard to imagine two men so unalike sharin so small a stoop in the midst of a drench that kept gettin worse. But there they were.

Havril Enos was big as a black circus bear and wide as the rug they'd make from such a bear. He was a jovial man too, and whatever he overlooked that weren't to his likin he knew how to use to better his position. He was first and foremost a dealmaker, and the clothes he wore, especially his shoes and his watches, made clear to anyone with an inquirin eye that Havril Enos knew how to close a deal. An MBA from Darden School of Business sure helped, but it was less the degree and more the gumption that allowed him to befriend anyone, even a cuss like Old Porch. Though friendship weren't exactly on his mind. Havril already made a tidy sum managin a series of manufacturin patents in the food-packagin industry but he was still lookin to increase his holdins through real estate.

By comparison, Old Porch was shorter by an easy foot, wrangly as well, more often than not wearin that old horsehair leather vest, with mud pretty much always on his snakeskin boots if not his collar. Some said his name was of Italian origin and that it meant either mushroom or pig. But it weren't true. Sure as he weren't no Indian, there was nothin in his veins that was Italian, and he weren't no mushroom and sure no pig, though he'd gladly eat both. Old Porch was a testament to the endurin fortitude of the originless, of those always out beyond, little more than gristle, bone, and sinew, with muscles lean and tight as high-tension wires. Nothin about Old Porch was in excess, and whenever he did don somethin like a suit, that exercise in decorum was fleetin.

Porch and Enos, they was both fifty-nine, with Porch turnin sixty in a few weeks, and so edgin out his land confederate in the age department by a few months, though that had nothin to do with why Orwin Porch was so often called Old Porch. Before he'd turned thirty, or even twenty, folks had started callin him that. And it weren't because his hair had gone prematurely gray and would soon enuf turn to what it was now, white as road salt. Likely it had most to do with his voice, what was raspy, grizzled, gruff as gravel, how some say he'd talked since he was twelve.

Aside from their age, Havril also shared with Old Porch an interest in capital expansion, which also aligned with each man's correct valuation of the importance of community. *Big things won't happen in Utah Valley if you don't have the support of the wards,* Levi Powell, an insulation installer with Manning & Sons, would explain. *I'm not sayin it's sanctioned or even mentioned at church. Stuff is just talked about. Then it grows familiar. Four Summits became familiar that way.* Levi, though, never would get familiar with Tammy, Roy's daughter, though he pined for her enuf to reforest the Isatch Range, and he knew all her songs.

Anyways, beyond these two inconsequential similarities, the differences between Havril Enos and Old Porch grew grave. Havril Enos was an important Church official, whereas Orwin Porch at best went to church now and then. Old Porch had no degrees and sure as heck didn't own no gold watches. Called them handcuffs in fact. *Why on earth would a fella with limited time to his name already wanna chain his wrist to the very time that was sure as heck gonna get him?* But Old Porch was a charismatic man, and what few would admit, though most could recognize: he was also terrifyin. As Larsen Cooke, who was a manager at the Alberston's in Orvop, would put it: *Old Porch had the metal.*

Havril weren't blind to their contrastin natures, though just as his own forebears had served the Church since it settled in this valley over a hundred years ago, the Porches had been there too, servin them same folks, Havril's included, with meat. Each was as much a part of this place as the other. As Havril remarked once in an earnest effort to promote not only congeniality between the two but likely to further quell his own heart made uneasy by these dealins, if only by insincerely attemptin to bring Old Porch's jackchurch ways back into the fold: *Orwin, don't you worry a stitch; I'll make sure folks get their water,* a reference that plenty say referred to the sacrament, the Church offerin water, not wine, *just you make sure that they eat.* Some have asserted that Havril then added *and then together we'll enjoy the bread,* a double entendre referrin to the body of the Lord as well as, well, money.

That last bit there, however, is a falsity. Havril was pure in his devotion to the Church and would never have thought to sully in speech his spiritual commitments with his financial aims, even if his actions had, as he put it, started to wiggle.

Years could be spent on comparin and contrastin these two, but Karl Lamoreaux, on the back of some old drywall, did a pretty good job with just a black pencil and blue pencil. Luc Chitnis, Vanessa Clark, and Ralph Flores would sure attest to that. Lamoreaux's first try caught the blackness of the night with traces of blue in Havril Enos's hair. He got Egan's small stoop too and the way Old Porch seemed coiled and ready to strike. Lamoreaux's second try, after plenty of erasin, caught the greedy shine in both men's eyes, same shine as was on Havril's watch and wingtips and on the spittle on Orwin's lips. But the third try, what Karl Lamoreaux left alone, what was soon enuf hung in Larsen Cooke's home under Levi Powell's insulation, captured a circus bear happily balancin a ball on his nose with a rattlesnake coiled around his rear paws.

Though even this did not capture the most important difference that welded Havril to Orwin: Old Porch was way richer, with only the Gatestones bein the richest, though not by much. Where the Gatestones could oft be described as mannerly and worldly, especially where Dallin had been concerned, their big home adorned with sophisticated artifacts of the world, and of course horsely, though nothin like the ribbonned Southern set, the Porches exalted in a certain hardfisted roughness that Old Porch declared was stalwart or stoic. No question, Old Porch had the easy cash to fly all his boys to Hawaii, and first-class too, which Dallin and Sondra Gatestone had once done for their family. See, Old Porch would never do such a thing. His miserliness, along with his battered clothes and generally grobian manner, often made people peg him for some Barmecide when he boasted about his real estate deals, like to folks at Sizzler, when he was treatin his sons to butter-slathered steak and frozen lobster because of some victory on the football field. Once, though, and this because young Russel and Francis had mewled so much about it, they'd tried the fancy offerins at the Hines Mansion restaurant with molded butter and too many spoons and napkins. Old Porch had hated it. Mostly he prized eatin sloppy joes or pizzas while a poker game heated up, preferably with an old-fashioned in hand if his boys weren't near, except Egan. And either way, Hawaii would never've come to mind. Reno was the best his boys could hope for, a city not a one would ever see, a city Old Porch had spent too much time in with too many old-fashioneds and worse. Lord how he loved to find a booth where the afternoon light backlit the skirts of them fine gals enterin the diner. Sometimes them skirts got near transparent too. Sometimes you could swear you saw a bit more than the place where legs end. Or if no such young beauties were comin in, then even more fun was to be got by gettin the fat waitresses runnin around for more creamer, more Tabasco sauce, a sport Old Porch was careful not to indulge in so much in Orvop, though a few times he and Egan had had themselves a good time. They even got that one lady really sweatin. This was at The Coachman's, and the poor server was none other than Janice Brothwell, who at least in the end would find herself better remembered than either Old Porch or Egan.

Now where Havril Enos and his wealth were concerned, well, Havril did have the Lord at his table, but how he would've welcomed sittin at the tables of either one of those two families. The fact that neither a Porch nor a Gatestone patriarch would've ever been caught dead sittin at the same table with him was always lost on Havril.

He'll call, Old Porch insisted as the stake president stepped into the rain.

Havril turned around. *Orwin, I highly doubt a U.S. senator is gonna call you or any one of us, especially if it's not durin his office hours.*

Let me tell you a secret, Havril: ain't no such thing as office hours when there's real work to be done. Especially on the Hill. Hays near guaranteed me we was gonna see that bill come to a vote and that it would pass. Mark my words. And I sure hope this lack of faith you're communicatin to me now ain't your way of sayin you're quittin out of your stake in our enterprise. Because I have other people askin. Every day.

Worry overran Havril's features. *Not at all! Not at all! Quite the con-*

trary, my friend! I'm just sayin whether Senator Hays calls tonight or does so weeks or even months from now, you and Four Summits have my commitment. You can count on my money. You know that. I may never be a movie star, but like you, I'm from here, and I'd like a front-row seat for me and my family atop of one of these mountains.

Orwin, hatless and coatless except for that horsehair vest, met the man in the rain then, answerin his earnest diffidence by extendin his hand for a hard shake. Orwin's greater effort, though, was to conceal any look of disgust. Havril Enos had a grip limp as a towel. Old Porch mistrusted it, but in this case he was wrong: Havril Enos remained one of his most loyal and admirin allies.

Back in Egan's dinin room, the boys had got to orderin food. *Lots of it,* Woolsey told his father, his voice ridin high, though fortunately not near as high as Francis's regular voice. Woolsey had a rep now for toughness, Porch toughness. He was eighteen, a senior at Orvop, a better-than-average football player, with dark brown curly hair and blue eyes near mean as Old Porch's.

Who cares about food when we got cards? Old Porch said with a laugh. His good mood weren't goin nowhere. And nothin was gonna change that, especially after fillin that full house and claimin the highest hand, splittin the pot with Riddle, who won the lowest hand but not by much, barely bestin Kelly Porch with an eight under a nine.

Kelly Porch, who was twenty years old, was the one that had brung along Riddle tonight. Kelly worked side by side with him at Porch Meats. Riddle's first name was Trent, but he didn't much care for it and stuck just with his last name. *Plus, it makes me seem full of mystery, though I ain't.* Old Porch didn't know Riddle well. He seemed pretty straightedge but put in long hours and was never late. His friendliness surprised Kelly some, though not Old Porch. Old Porch was used to people takin a shine to his boys once they got a whiff of the money.

Still, Riddle didn't seem oriented that way. He was, in fact, and this despite his claim to the contrary, a bit like his name: a mystery. Sure, he was from around here, churchgoer, do-gooder, good employee, all that, but Old Porch still sensed somethin that just didn't square. Old Porch knew a lie when he told one, which was why he knew a lie when he heard one. Not that he could quite call Riddle a liar, because he just couldn't quite hear where Riddle was comin from, let alone what he'd think worth enuf to lie about.

Certainly the camaraderie with Kelly still struck Old Porch as a little odd, Riddle bein buttoned-up and gentlemanly in a way that Old

Porch knew Kelly was not. You couldn't even say it was just a young'un lookin up to Kelly to learn the ropes. Riddle was three years older than Kelly, the same age as the other hand there tonight, Billings Gale.

Those three often worked the line together, though they was as different as so many mugs in a box at a yard sale. Riddle looked a boy who should be on his mission, and frankly it was a little weird that he weren't, while Kelly was already full-grown and, as a startin varsity tight end for three years at Orvop, grown strong. Billings was a different story altogether, tan as a date, and not from Utah. He'd come up by way of Arizona, where he'd worked with plenty of livestock. Porch Meats weren't his first slaughterhouse. Billings likely knew Old Porch's life better than any of his own boys. Old Porch also trusted Billings enuf to give him the keys and combinations to the processin buildin but hadn't once invited him into the main house, what was but twenty paces away.

Francis, it's your deal, Old Porch instructed Francis, who was a junior at Orvop High and already seventeen. *Can you handle not makin a mess of it?*

Can you handle me takin your money?

Old Porch gave Francis a joyless flash of teeth, and when his son's stupid gaze faltered, he addressed the whole table. *Boys, despite what you might think, this ain't about no money. This here's about makin other men feel less about themselves. Francis, you gonna make me feel less about myself?*

On every hand, Daddy!

That's my boy.

Francis called the game, Razz, no bet limit, though they all knew that. He dealt two hole cards to each of the seven seated there, then a face-up card, or the door card, the highest card makin the first bet, which in this case was Egan with a king of spades. Then more cards face up, with more bets, and the seventh card dealt face down.

Now for folks who don't know much about cards, Razz is one of those poker variations where the lowest hand takes all and flushes and straights don't count.

Old Porch mostly kept callin the bets. He'd grown more irritated by Havril's claim that the senator wouldn't ring and irritated all over again because the senator had promised to do so while Havril was droppin by. An opportunity to further cement Havril's involvement, not to mention enthusiasm, had been squandered, and to keep the capital he needed in line, Old Porch knew he had to have enthusiasm. This weren't no quarter-acre auction. He was gonna get hisself a whole mountain, four if you was countin peaks.

Old Porch had before him an ace and a deuce, both buried, and a heckuva fine start in the world of lowness, while face up he was advertisin one queen, a five, or what he called a fever, and a three, what he called a trey. Those two visible low cards proved low enuf to get Egan to fold first and then Kelly soon after, but the rest were holdin on, likely with good reason. Old Porch knew as well as everyone else at the table that this last card was what would build or raze his hand.

He slid an edge of his mangled right thumbnail under a corner. And there it was, a four of clubs, or what Old Porch knew as the Devil's bedpost, grantin Old Porch the best hand you can get in Razz, or what everyone there knew to call a Bicycle: Ace - Two - Three - Four - Five!

Here he was then, center stage, upon the sacred boards, a performance demanded, a performance to be delivered, and with so much left to play too, the whole play, weren't it great!, before a packed house, and so what if the mountains were painted plywood?, so what if the props was all fake?, the eyes of the world was upon him, waitin on his next word, not even a word, waitin upon his next gesture, even just his next expression, and, boy, how Old Porch loved that! And so, no, despite his glee it weren't hard for him to effect a look of sourness. Not too much, mind you. A quick grimace followed by a grin flashin just enuf of the wrecked teeth he adored to conceal his good fortune with the pretense of a junk hand he'd try to sell to everyone else as gold.

Mr. Porch, Riddle said from across the table. In fact he was sittin directly across from Old Porch hisself. *That tithe stuff you was tellin President Enos, is that true? I mean, I was not made aware of that.* Riddle gave Kelly if not Billings a glance, while Old Porch only looked at Riddle, or really the cards he was advertisin: a trey or a three, a four spot, a jack, and a six. Promisin but nowhere close to his bicycle.

Of course it's true. Though not a lick of it was true, and his boys knew it too, not that that kept any of them from goin along with the claim, each one noddin. Only Billings avoided the whole thing by buryin his nose in his hole cards.

Kelly, I need a little assistance, Old Porch said then.

Of course! Kelly answered, sittin up right straight, with a voice near as straight too.

Has our friend Mr. Riddle here just called your daddy a liar?

Oh gosh, Mr. Porch! Riddle's face got beet red real quick. *I didn't mean it like that! I just didn't know, and it confused me.* Old Porch met Riddle's lamentin palaver with a coldness Riddle weren't fit for. *To tell you the truth, Mr. Porch, I wasn't plannin on givin none of my winnins for tithe. I was just kinda hopin to spend it on whatever I wanted.*

There was a long silence at that table, and then Old Porch cackled, with Egan joinin in near the same time, and then everyone was laughin, except maybe Billings, who grinned a little but still kept his focus on his cards, knowin better than to sign up for a situation that could swing easily another way, especially with Old Porch at the wheel of tonight's mood.

Riddle sure looked relieved.

Son, whatever you win, you sure as heck feel free to spend however you please, Old Porch assured the young man, a perlage of perfidy on Old Porch's lower lip, with his eyes glitterin too, especially as they surveyed all the chips this tinhorn Riddle had neatly set up before him.

Aside from Riddle's obvious excitement about his own hand, Old Porch was pleased that quite a few there thought they had a hand worth meat, a good three of them thinkin they might even have somethin with teeth. Francis, right to Old Porch's left, was showin a seven, six, and a lady with whatever he was hidin, not comin close to matchin Old Porch's hand.

Then to the left of Francis sat the eldest at the table, Egan. Egan had smartly folded and seemed to be havin hisself a good time wonderin if his old man was bluffin or not. Egan never sat too close to Old Porch because he never wanted to think of hisself as his daddy's right-hand or even left-hand man, though that was pretty much who Egan was, Old Porch's left and right hand. He was also too good a card player to sit opposite him. Whoever sat opposite Old Porch, which tonight was Riddle, was considered the fish or, in common parlance, from whence most of the night's winnins would flow.

To the left of the fish sat Billings. To his left, Kelly, who'd made sure Riddle sat at the head, and then next, closin this tidy little circle, just opposite Francis and right beside Old Porch, sat Woolsey, who after wanderin his thoughts a sec to gaze at the framed photographs on the wall, most of which were of prize bucks Egan had shot, came up with a bet that was fine but nowhere close to what Old Porch's hand deserved to earn. But Old Porch didn't wanna risk buyin the pot with too big a bet neither, nor did he want to set the rhythm of the bettin with too small a raise. So he called. It was a risk because if they all called, why then Old Porch was out of luck on a grand hand. He could all but grit them wretched teeth at the thought.

Eges, you gonna best these two bucks this year? Woolsey asked his older brother then.

You know it, Egan answered in a voice that was surprisinly soft.

I'm goin with you, right?

We'll see.

I'm comin! Francis chimed in.

Francis, don't hold up the game, Kelly growled, his voice extra nasally tonight.

Like Old Porch, Francis called Woolsey's bet as well. With Egan out, the bet moved to Riddle, who fortunately set Old Porch's teeth at ease by answerin the bet with a big bump. Billings folded at once, Kelly was already out, his dream of an easy win, buyin a good camera, gone, and then Woolsey folded too, leavin Old Porch to do everythin in his power to keep hisself from cursin Riddle out loud for bettin too much and stumpin his pot.

Of course, he'd meet and raise, but he didn't want to do it too quick neither.

That's when the kitchen phone started its clatterin like Good Fortune herself, which Egan went and answered, not sayin much but *Yes, sir, he is here,* coverin the mouthpiece then, noddin at his daddy, who was already layin flat the hole cards he'd been reexaminin to hopefully give the appearance of much tribulation and doubt.

Excuse me, creatures, while I consult Washington about this next bet.

You can be sure both Riddle and Billings drew blank stares while all the Porch boys kicked back their chairs, knowin this call was gonna take more than a minute.

Though, as it turned out, it lasted just about a minute.

Orwin Porch! roared the voice of U.S. Senator Shane Hays. *How fine it feels to participate in somethin that will do wonders for our state! I thank you for bein the stalwart citizen you are!*

Am I hearin good news?

How are your boys? the senator asked instead, with a chuckle.

Spittin and kickin and growin up like fire. Thank you for askin.

And how's our hero? I heard he left our fine state in favor of lesser territories?
Senator Hays was referrin to Hatch, Old Porch's eldest son.

You heard right. Texas now. Austin.

A Ranger?

SWAT. And far as we're concerned, overqualified for the position.

The hearty laugh that answered this observation told Old Porch that the senator was actually relishin this call.

Let's get him back to our beehive. Our state needs its good sons.

We are in agreement.

Yes, Orwin, I have good new. S 1245 has just been marked up by E and C.
E and C bein the Energy and Natural Resources Committee. *We debated the heck out of it, but there's bipartisan support, and we could see a floor vote soon.*

That's what we've been waitin for.

Oh, it was a catfight. Protests. Indian nations. The works. But we got it through on a nine-to-eight vote with the help of my good friends from Wyomin and Texas. Maybe your boy Hatch helped out a little there.

This senator weren't no fool. He knew how Old Porch could make donations flow, and that's forgettin his own check-writin; Old Porch had backed many a fundraiser, deliverin astonishin solvency to Senator Hays's campaigns as well as significantly fillin the Grand Old Party's coffers.

Senator, you've made me and plenty in this community awful happy tonight. I thank you.

You take care of yourself, Orwin, and I'll take care of the legislation. That's what you hired me for.

Old Porch hung up, grinnin like mad now. It was that kind of night.

Looks like it's happenin, boys, he announced, which would mean plenty to his sons if still leavin Riddle and Billings in the dark. Not that Old Porch minded lettin those two in on what kinda table they was lucky enuf to be seated at.

He laid it out plain as could be, how *Senate Bill 1245* had a barbed and vicious history, startin with passage of a House companion version, H.R. 2799, last spring, Old Porch offerin up its aim like the finest stage actor, *the unreserved unappropriated public lands wholly west of the one hundredth meridian.* Of course, the bill had a lot of complicated language that would doze even the most alert listeners but suffice it to say that if S. 1245 was passed into law, a large number of federal lands across the country would be made available for sale, leavin then some notable parcels in Utah free and clear for purchase and development.

Orwin Porch is gonna own hisself a whole mountain! Old Porch couldn't resist sayin aloud. A good mood can do that to you. Of course, it was a wholesale exaggeration, as the property in question didn't but hardly encroach upon the Katanogos massif, let alone get anywhere near its summit and peaks, though it did expand south of Wallsburg, past Little Hobble Crick and up Sams Canyon or Billy Haws Canyon, above Smooth Hollow and Johns Glen, and even beyond Wallsburg Ridge, Bear Canyon Pass, over Bald Knoll, which led past plenty more steeps as far as Berryport Canyon, all of which constituted a patchwork of land, some state-owned, some federal, includin some isolated rangelands under the purview of the Bureau of Land Management that for a long time now had been considered good candidates for sale back to private investors in the name of public interest. And that weren't all. Aside from the United States Forest Service and BLM, there were also additional state-owned parcels and private inholdins, especially the significant Hone family parcel, with Brother Mallory Guvin Hone, or Manic Guff as he was known, along with his thirteen children, shareholders in the family company, enthused to sell that land should the financin and resort permittin ever come together. In fact even if Senate Bill 1245 failed to pass, the sale of the Hone land alone, which included Coyote Gulch, could unite various other patches of available land and still help make Four Summits a reality, albeit a lesser reality. There was also another good-sized flat parcel owned outright by none other than Porch hisself, just east and conterminous with Pillars Meadow and extendin all the way to the Uinta-Isatch-Cache National Forest. *Good for a parkin lot,* he'd say. *A real big one.* At one time even the Gatestones had owned inholdins up there. To its credit, the State of Utah was not blind to these scattered lands and had declared that if they could ever be obtained in full, or in other words if anyone might create a contiguous property that might sustain, for example, a new ski resort equal to around 25,000 acres, why then the state would not only sanction and aid in its creation but provide financial incentives includin tax benefits for all involved.

Is that what Washington called to tell you, Mr. Porch? That you own a mountain? Riddle had the audacity to ask then. *I figured they was callin to beg you to fold.*

Ha! You got that right, Riddle! That's all any politician has ever told me to do: fold, fold, fold!

Maybe understandably, Riddle misunderstood this declaration to apply to Old Porch's cards and turned then to Francis. *You foldin too?*

Francis flared fast enuf. *Heck, Riddle, you got nothin. I'll meet your foolish bet and go all in!*

Now hold on here a minute. Old Porch didn't need to flare. *Are you suggestin, Riddle, that Old Porch takes his orders from D.C.?*

How Riddle perked up then, and Old Porch just loved to see all that greedy light rise up in his young eyes, blindin him with what he thought was already his.

Old Porch rolled back then his wrangly shoulders, some bones there crackin loud, then he cocked his head side to side, like how you might do if you were in the movies and about to start a big barroom fight, even judderin his jaw left to right, what Old Porch would never have done before a real fight, havin never lost a fight, because he sure as heck would never put on display his intentions. *Heck,* he'd told all his boys again and again, *you're never gonna win a fight if you start by tellin everyone you're gonna have a fight.* He could still see that look of surprise on the face of Cameron Eakins after he'd whacked him on the side of the head with the back of a chop knife. That was a long time ago, but it still made Old Porch smile, made him smile now. Gettin the upper hand, even if in this case it was the lowest hand, did that to him.

Porch gave his cards one last needless glance, concentratin solely on killin any reaction to the beauts hid in the hole, and was just startin to elaborately reconsider Riddle's cards, rememberin how this game weren't ever about the cards you had but how you played them best, because even the best deserved the best kinda playin, when Egan's doorbell rang.

It was Domino's with their pizzas, and that rushed everyone outta their chairs, Egan throwin down paper plates on the kitchen counter, plus extra chili flakes, then gettin the root beer out of the fridge. He also took out a six-pack of Coors Light, which Old Porch could see made Riddle immediately uncomfortable, and weren't that a funny thing to see? Old Porch thought so.

And then the doorbell rang again.

This time it was the delivery of three long hoagies with the works, which Kelly got to sawin into smaller sections with a non-serrated knife. That nearly took away some of Old Porch's smile. Kelly sure as heck knew better than that. Though maybe he didn't. Maybe he was a moron too. At one point or another, hadn't all of his boys surprised him with acts of real idiocy? Thank the Lord, Egan came over then with a real knife.

Eat up, maggots, Porch declared by way of a toast or a prayer as he raised a can of beer in the air, poppin it with the same hand too, not carin one bit for the foam that spit up and dripped on Egan's Sarouk rug. The soft aromas of garlic and burnt cheese filled the room. His boys ate and were happy, as were their guests.

Riddle and Francis stuck with root beer. Woolsey made a grab for a beer, but Egan smacked away his hand with the back of his knife. Egan knew how to use a knife. Knew how to use almost anythin.

We're still church-goin folks, Riddle, Old Porch said, takin a long gulp.

Riddle had none of the confidence now that he'd had at the table. *I just like root beer.*

Porch shrugged, takin an even longer gulp. *To tell you the truth, I can't stand this baby beer, but it still beats sodipop.*

Yes, sir. Which Old Porch had to sorta admire, because at least Riddle recognized whose house he was in and who signed his paycheck, and so long as Porch got all the winnins he deserved tonight, he might even think to see that Riddle was invited back.

You know who just called here? Old Porch asked the young man.

You said someone in Washington, I believe.

Old Porch nodded and took another bite of the lukewarm pizza, the pepperoni already a hard disk of cold congealin grease, the whole mouthful in need of somethin far better than this donkey piss. And Egan, bless his soul, like he could read his daddy's mind, handed him right then a plastic cup with a finger of brown gold.

Francis! What time is it now in Washington, D.C.?

Francis looked at the clock and seemed bewildered. It was almost six.

You're near as daft as Russel, Woolsey snickered.

Where is Russel? Kelly asked Egan. *Shouldn't he be back by now? It don't take that long to get to and from Uncle Conrad's.*

He probably wrecked your truck, Egan, and is just standin out in the rain tryin to get up the guts to call you. Francis cackled, helpin hisself to another section of hoagie, all to deflect further his father's attention.

If there's so much as a scratch on my truck, he'll die tonight, Egan growled out with a burp, and what was scary, at least to Riddle, in fact what turned his stomach, and he was real hungry too, was how Egan done said it without even the slightest inflection, like it were just a cold hard fact.

How about you help your brother out then, Old Porch snapped at Woolsey, drainin his cup and tappin it for Egan to tilt in some more.

How's that? Woolsey asked.

What time is it in Washington, D.C.?!

It's later than here, right?

You're an idjit, Kelly said to Woolsey, laughin an extra share.

It's near nine p.m., Egan said softly, refillin his dad's cup, this time with two fingers of the bourbon. *And that were a call made by a United States senator.*

Porch couldn't be more pleased with Egan. His other boys shut up, and Riddle looked noticeably impressed. Only Billings didn't look impressed, but Old Porch knew that didn't mean he weren't. He'd just lived a life hard enuf to teach you how to hide what you think.

That's right. A United States senator called to thank me! And not durin office hours. A United States senator called me personally with the good news: the Porch family is expandin! Four Summits is happenin! The time is comin soon when anyone in this valley who's got the common sense to look up will see our mountain. We might even change the name of Katanogos to Old Porch!

The boys knew that was bull, except maybe Francis, and Woolsey, and Russel if he'd been there, but a cheer still rose up, high fives in abundance, with Francis whistlin, even if none of these boys really had any idea what their pop was sayin.

Though, Egan said to no one in particular, if loud enuf for them

87

all to hear, *we do gotta ask whether Dad's really sharin some good news or just talkin on this so that he can duck clear of the big bet that's sittin right now at his front door, what Riddle here has put to him fair and square.*

And Old Porch raised his hands like he was fairly caught and returned to his seat at the head of Egan's table. *It's a good night when a U.S. senator calls you. So, Riddle, I'll call you, and I'll—* Old Porch hesitated, but that was show too. He'd already figured in that Francis's bet would top his call and give him another chance to raise again. *And I'll call you.*

I call too, Francis shouted out at once, still not in his chair, his mouth hoardin a big bite of hoagie, some of the salty vinegar and oil runnin down his chin.

Like heck you will, Porch barked, and, boy, the room grew still and cold then real quick.

Francis stopped chewin. *How's that?*

We all heard you, boy. That Old Porch wasn't even facin Francis, but talkin to him while lookin at Egan, made it that much worse.

But suppose I changed my mind? Francis asked, hustlin back to his chair, eyein again his cards, which he knew were crap just like everyone else knew they was crap.

You don't get to do that. Not after you declared to our guest here that you would meet his foolish bet, and, I think these were your words, go all in. I think I got that right? Woolsey? Kelly?

Both brothers nodded before he was done askin.

You insulted Riddle, Francis. Now you gonna back down? Egan asked.

Oh hey now, it's no big deal, Riddle spoke up then, but no one was listenin to Riddle.

I ain't backin down. Sure as heck not from Riddle, Francis spat, hatin all his brothers then, especially Egan, even if he was too afraid to hate his father, but then they were all too afraid to do that. Their hero brother, Hatch, had been so afraid, he'd run off to Texas, which is where their mother had fled to first, fleein all she'd made and all she'd lost, with their littlest and only sister in her arms. She hadn't even took a coat. All of which had, these thoughts of his mother and sister, flickered through Francis's mind as he pushed every one of his chips to the center of the table.

Egan was out, and the bet had returned to Riddle, who was rattled some by all this sudden heat but clear-eyed enuf still to see his own cards hadn't changed none. He met the raise and raised again, no doubt makin Billings, Kelly, and Woolsey grateful then that they'd got loose of this hand early on. Old Porch met the bet but this time heaved in a substantial raise.

I guess I gotta fold now, Francis said, confused, sure, but mostly shaken by the bone-grittin nastiness that had so suddenly possessed the room.

You can owe me, Egan said, meetin the raise with his own chips. And you can bet Francis weren't thankful. Owin Egan money weren't no favor a smart man accepts.

Riddle likely felt sorry for Francis then, because instead of raisin like he could've done, and surely would've done if the mood hadn't gotten so rancid, especially seein how his faith in his own cards had never faltered, he chose instead to spare the whole table yet another round of bets and family bullyin, inadvertently sparin hisself as well from a premature exit from that night's game, as he would've placed all he had left to him into that pot, a fact that Lane Granberg, Dede-lyn Matson, and Trina Pritchard would in years to come so often and poignantly reflect upon: the graciousness of Riddle's gesture as well as its awful cost.

So Riddle called Old Porch's raise and thus met and at the same time put an end for the moment to all of Old Porch's cussed schemin.

How happy Old Porch was then to reveal his winnin cards, happier still to see the middlin nothinness Riddle had staked so big a claim on. He howled crazier than an old rooster with coffee beans in his feed as he started rakin the pot his way. He was havin one heckuva night. Luck sure was with Old Porch, just as it was with Russel, who had just then started bangin on Egan's door.

It was 6:12 p.m.

At the sight of his youngest one, Old Porch's eyes glowed near febrile, his cheeks warmed and his lips gave away more of them jagged teeth in the name of gladness, which where Russel was concerned didn't happen much. This made Russel glow all the more, and he was glowin just fine already, with indignation and some lesser variety of rancor and excitement.

Our horses are gone! he cried out. *Our horses are gone!*

Cavalry?! Egan yelled, at once on his feet, chair topplin backwards.

No, not your horse here, Russel fired back quick, if at once confused.

Then whadya mean? asked Woolsey, who put no stock in anythin Russel said.

Russel ignored Woolsey as well as Egan, who was sittin back down, angered for bein angered.

Stolen! Russel declared to his father only. *But I already found out who done it!*

Old Porch's eyes never left Russel's, like he was seein somethin there he'd never seen before, somethin that measured somethin akin to hisself, somethin he was suddenly proud enuf to take credit for.

What the heck is Russel talkin about? Francis asked, maybe the most annoyed of them all.

Beats me, Kelly threw in. *Uncle Conrad don't got no horses.*

Maybe Russel's talkin about rockin horses, Francis snickered, though he snickered so alone.

Russel, did you get Conrad his binoculars like I asked you to? Egan demanded, his irritation over thinkin his horse Cavalry had been absconded with, over takin Russel seriously, still growin.

The first notes of dismay entered Russel's speech then. *I never made it to Uncle Conrad's. I was on Willow and stopped when I seen they was gone!*

Spit it out Russel! Kelly suddenly barked. *What's gone?*

Them two horses! In Paddock B!

Do we have horses in Paddock B right now? Old Porch asked Egan.

I got no clue, Egan answered. *Billings? Riddle?*

Both shook their heads.

And herein, if we might pause for just a brief spell, is one of them mysteries that's never been solved: who did move Navidad and Mouse from Paddock A into Paddock B? And it's no small matter given what all was so quickly provoked. Dan'l Leftwich, once employed at Porch Meats and by 1994 a sales rep at an Ogden Chrysler dealership, would put in quite a few hours talkin with those workin for Orwin Porch at the time and would discover that not a one knew about *or at least would confess to* movin the horses. It makes no sense to accuse Landry, which some would do, like that idjit Kurt Salvesen. Ethan Rasmussen, who would end up with Santana Rafting in 1995, would join a steadfast group convinced that the responsible party was in fact a very real snake. Such convictions do not alter that whatever it was that granted them ponies transit from one state of bein to another still keeps its silence. Of course, feel free to speculate, though seek no satisfaction other than what the deprivation of answers invariably delivers.

I seen the one who stole them! Russel erupted.

Old Porch laughed then, still warm from his victory, the good news from D.C., and a near fistful of bourbon warmin his belly. It was good to finally see his youngest pup so worked up about somethin.

Quit your yelpin, boy, Old Porch said, which weren't words exactly in allegiance with these feelins, but so it went with Orwin Porch. *They can have whatever they took for what? How much, Egan?*

Paddock B?! I'd say five bucks a head, Woolsey blurted out, not lookin at Russel, who was for him a constant source of embarrasment. *And* what I mean by that is that Russel can pay whoever five dollars a head for takin those nags off our hands.

Old Porch slapped the table and laughed with Woolsey. *Sold! Russel, you make sure whoever you're all up about gets paid ten bucks. Can you manage that?* There was a twinkle in Old Porch's eye like none of this meant a thing unless it offered up somethin that weren't yet on the table.

Ten bucks?! Russel couldn't believe his ears. *You want me to pay that thief ten dollars?!*

Rain make you deaf? Woolsey blasted out. *That's what Dad just said!*

In regards to the general temperament of the Porch family up to this point, Donald Hickman, greatly contrite in his later years about his role albeit small in the infamous snowball fight, would often point out to Guy Olsen, equally contrite about the same event, *how the mood had been mostly joshin. Just kids in the bath. You know, sinkin ships, splashin. Nothin more than a spirit of mayhem and pranks. Back then pranks were frequent too. Tom Gatestone sure managed his share, like gettin one of them cats they was dissectin in science class and placin it in, say, Liz Blicker's locker. That was worth a hoot!* And Guy Olsen would sure offer no disagreement there, though he liked to point out how pranks always walked a fine line: *When Donny Osmond had that hit song about puppy love, he weren't but fifteen. And for his success he found a dead puppy in his locker. I heard it was Egan Porch too that was behind that stunt.* Donald Hickman was sure it was Egan: *Put them Porch boys in a bath together and at least one of them's gonna drown the other. They was always about boys breakin boys. That's how Old Porch raised his kids. No wonder his wife and daughter ran when they did. They was the smartest of the bunch.*

Not that Russel Porch had any intention of lettin his family treat this moment with such frivolity. *Have you all gone plumb loco while I was gone? Like I come back to find you ain't even Porches no more.* Old Porch found hisself smilin even more because Russel now was indeed bringin somethin new to the table. *This guy didn't buy our horses. He stole them! You tell me right now, Daddy, is there anythin worse than a horse thief?*

Leavin out your mother, you mean? Old Porch answered with a tangled smile.

I ain't jokin here, Russel said to the whole room, and maybe for the first time there was some real gravel in his voice. Both Kelly and Woolsey, and at the same time too, eased back from the table, exchangin looks of amusement, whereas Egan, maybe to spare Russel what Old Porch hisself might've gotten around to, went after him first.

Then why the heck you even tellin us this for? Egan near shouted. He'd come here to play cards, not deal with his worm of a little brother. *Why ain't you already after him?*

I tried but I couldn't drive after where he went.

Why? Where'd he go? Riddle spoke up now, somewhat awkwardly but genuinely curious, his tone as if by alchemy changin some the hecklin atmosphere prevailin in that room.

He took the horses into Isatch Canyon, Russel answered solemnly.

Boy, did Old Porch lose it then. He laughed so hard, he had to spit out the bourbon sloshin around in his mouth, and right on the table too. *Isatch?! He took the horses up there?!* Bourbon burnt up in his nose. *That's a box canyon! There ain't no way through there! Not with horses! Just set up at the entrance and wait til he comes back out. You can pay him then!* Old Porch weren't gonna stop laughin either and was quick enuf joined by Woolsey, Kelly, and Francis, though Billings remained blank, and Riddle looked mystified, and Egan kept to his own fomentation of fury.

I mean to ride in there after him before he gets too far. And I don't plan to pay him a red cent. I will get back what's ours. Russel had made up his mind and weren't gonna stop. And ain't that a fact: nothin more dangerous than a made-up mind.

Boy, you see how dark it is now? Old Porch asked him then.

I do. But I seen who stole our horses, and if he can ride in there, then I sure as heck can too.

Francis spoke up again: *Who's done it then?*

That Kalin kid, Russel answered.

Kalin who? Egan demanded.

That little faggot took our horses?! Woolsey seemed genuinely shocked.

Who is this? Old Porch sat up a bit more.

He's a junior like me, Francis answered. *But he looks more like he's still in eighth grade!*

I'm gonna teach him a lesson he won't forget! Russel crowed out. So firm was he about his inevitable metin out of justice that Old Porch settled back once more and even nodded along with Russel's plan.

I think I seen him once or twice, Kelly then offered. *A little thing.* Obviously Kelly was some years out of Orvop High, but he still came around to see if Cherilyn Bacall would change her mind, kept beggin her to let him take her picture. *You better teach him a lesson then, Russel, or comin back here's gonna be real hard on you.*

Woolsey and Francis both grinned because Kelly weren't kiddin.

I'll take good care of him, Russel boasted, his own mood further inflated by his daddy's continued generosity in lettin Russel remain the focal point of so much attention.

To Russel then! beamed Old Porch, raisin over his head an empty plastic cup by way of a toast.

Go on then, Egan barked. *Take Cavalry.*

Russel sure lost his footin then. Not how he was standin but how he was braggin, struck dumb because whatever he'd got fixed in his head had never figured in a broad and powerful beast like Egan's liver chestnut Cavalry, seventeen hands tall or more.

Of course, if Russel had given it any serious thought, he'd have realized there weren't any other horse around to ride that weren't across town. Russel weren't the fastest kid. The apricot dun he most often rode, that bein Gump, was stabled over by the lake, and just gettin her to the Isatch Canyon parkin lot, why that was already two hours of work right there. Not that two hours mattered to a mind not able yet to frame time. Russel was always gonna ride Gump because Russel only rode Gump, the most kindhearted slouch more than able to get Russel up that canyon with never a mishap.

Cavalry, however, was a different story. And the reality he presented sure reintroduced time and more importantly pace to Russel's imaginative mind. Countin a quick saddlin, he was only about a half hour's trot to that godforsaken canyon. Maybe twenty minutes at a fast trot, and at a canter . . . though there weren't no need to canter because any imbecile ridin so after dark, not to mention in that downpour, weren't gonna get very far. That was if Russel could keep Cavalry from a canterin or even gallopin. Russel might could handle a trot. A trot was fine. Though even that weren't true. Even a trot on Egan's horse was a terrifyin notion. Let's face it: Cavalry terrified Russel.

I'll look after him, Egan, don't you worry, Russel said instead as he headed to the washroom.

That horse can look after hisself, Egan snarled after him. *It's you we ain't sure about.*

Plenty have discussed while plenty others have cried and plenty more have argued and shouted bitterly in both sober and drunken states, to family, to friends, to strangers, that so much of what was to follow might not have had to follow were it not for a piss, and a piss that Russel didn't really need to take. The urge was only vaguely there, but the fear over havin to even approach Cavalry, let alone get a saddle up on that high back, made Russel enact some kind of runnin away, even if it was just down a long dark hallway to the small bathroom, where he dragged out his terrified pecker and squoze out a few dribblin drops of dark yellow.

And, of course, that only got him but a few moments of reprieve. The moments that counted, though, came right after, when his fear still kept him from returnin to his family and drifted him into Egan's second bedroom, really a big closet with a futon mattress thrown down, piled up with old gear, unwashed clothes, saddle pads, and tools too valuable to leave in the garage.

It was also the room where Egan kept his gun cabinet.

Egan had built that cabinet hisself at Orvop High. It had taken him two years. Mr. Baggs taught shop class, which you could only take twice, or for one year, for only two credits, though if Mr. Baggs thought you had that extra somethin, he might invite you to come in before or after school and sometimes over the weekends to work on whatever ambitions proved worthy enuf for the use of his planer or lathe, like say if you was one of Orwin Porch's older boys workin on a gun cabinet, with racks, shelves, multiple drawers, and beveled glass. Egan won a blue ribbon for that cabinet too, in a county competition. And here it now stood, full of rifles and shotguns, even one huntin bow, while below, beneath an angled glass lid, waited a display shelf on which sat boxes of various cartridges includin those for the 1873 Colt Single Action Army Peacemaker sittin there too, atop a purple velvet pouch so dark it looked black.

This here was the same pistol their great-granddaddies had given to their sons, what Russel's granddaddy had given to Russel's daddy, which, when the time was right, Old Porch was supposed to pass along to his eldest and most revered, that obviously bein Hatch Porch. Though Old Porch had done no such thing. Two years ago and in front of everyone, except Hatch who weren't there to face this family shamin, and with Old Porch doin it so casually, too casually, *Just for safekeepin,* Old Porch had stunned them all and at the same time confused them all as he handed over to Egan the fabled firearm.

Not that Hatch didn't already have his selection of the very best and most accurate weaponry, and sure had no need for no antique like this, but like Hatch and all his brothers understood, includin Russel, this here was more than just any gun: it was one of those reverential objects, part artifact, part totem, and no doubt part killin machine, but also part somethin else. It was masterfully made and preserved, exquisitely engraved, both decoratively and ancestrally, with, in the tiniest script, the names of all the previous men who'd possessed it and, if the lore was to be believed, killt with it too.

Russel did then what he should never have even dreamt about: he lifted that angled glass lid and took hold of the dark shimmerin weapon. And that was all it took for the weapon to take hold of Russel.

Russel's palm seemed made for the thing. Already he felt at ease. No longer hastened or set upon by already diminishin fears, he could admire the long barrel, the polished cylinder, survey at his leisure all the names, names that weren't familiar at all, except for his daddy's, to the side of one ivory grip, in tiny black script: *Orwin Porch 1922* — . . . The only name without a date markin his death.

Russel didn't do much thinkin after that, except what little you need to do when convincin yourself little is all you're doin, even if it involves loadin five rounds. Russel was at least smart enuf, he did have his NRA card after all, to remove the sixth round and set that hammer down over an empty chamber before returnin the family heirloom and that last round to the velvet pouch and then shovin it down the back side of his jeans, his jacket and rain slicker coverin the bulge.

W hen Russel finally got back to the dinin room, no one said nothin about how long he was gone, but one chair stood empty.

Where's Egan?

Where do think? Kelly said without lookin up from his hand. *Saddlin up Cavalry for you.*

Russel, you're an idjit, Woolsey piled on. He also didn't look up from his cards.

You don't have to do this, you know, Francis said then. He'd meant to say it in a scabby or condescendin way but instead revealed his gen-uine worry.

Old Porch smiled before it all, glad to have an excuse to fold, happy to walk Russel out to the barn.

Egan had already brought the big horse out into the driveway, under his bright exterior lights, standin him beside a hitchin post set there for just such occasions, saddle already on. Cavalry was somethin else, proud as any bronze statue, still as one too, except for the mena-cin clouds of breath comin from each nostril. Maybe Russel stuttered his steps some when he got a real look at what he was about to do in the valley-fillin rain, in the mountain-devourin dark.

Heck, boy, I'm proud of you! Which were likely the warmest words Russel had ever heard from his pa.

Egan offered Russel his hand, but Russel ignored the help and managed on his own to scramble up into the saddle. Egan set then to bucklin around each of Russel's boots his own set of rowel spurs. Some say it was to give his brother a chance with the big horse, more say it was to insure that the big horse threw his little brother far.

You want us to come with you? Old Porch asked then, grinnin at Egan, who weren't ever gonna grin about any of this. Russel weren't taken by surprise though. He'd been expectin such a test.

You all go back inside, he told his father as he gathered up the reins. *I'll be back with them horses before you've emptied everyone's pockets.*

B ack at the table, a game of Hold 'Em had started up, with Wool- sey still jabberin to Billings and Riddle about who this kid was that done perpetrated the thievery. Kelly yawned and that made Fran- cis yawn too.

Not that you can believe much Russel says, especially when he's tryin to prove hisself, but I'm recallin better this Kalin, Woolsey continued. *He don't fit in much. It sure as heck never crossed my mind that he had any interest in horses.*

And fer sure, neither Woolsey nor Francis nor Russel nor any of them had any inklin that Kalin had been friends with Tom. That would've riled up the conversation somethin extra. Instead they was mostly intrigued by the fact that Kalin's true claim to fame through- out Orvop High was that he didn't have to take gym class.

Is he sick? Kelly asked.

I heard it's because he's afraid to take his clothes off, Woolsey said.

Kelly thought that was a hoot.

You mean he really is a faggot? Francis asked, somewhat bewildered.

Why would that make him a faggot? Billings asked, and somethin maybe cold or maybe real adult like regripped the room. *I don't partic- ularly care for gettin neked around other men either.*

You know what I heard? Kelly said then. *I heard that one out of ten's a fag, no matter how you was raised or where. All over the world.*

Huh. But if you count all of us, Francis said, *and Dad, and Ginny,* Ginny bein that little sister now in Austin with her mother, *and Mom,* which he said only after lowerin his voice, as she would always be a canker- blossom in that household, *then there's gotta be a Porch that's a faggot.*

You tryin to tell us somethin, Francis? Woolsey said with a laugh that could've outdone a wood chipper.

You callin me what you are, Woolsey? Francis shot back.

You callin me what you are, Woolsey? Woolsey mimicked back in a squeaky voice, too tired from all the eats to get up and go around the table and wrestle Francis down onto the floor, which he'd have done easily, havin wrestled varsity for three years, at 138 this year.

Francis then mentioned seein a poster of Johnny Cash in Kalin's locker, though that weren't true. He was misrememberin what he'd seen in Jay Bagnell's locker, which was right next to Kalin's. Jay Bagnell would be the one to eventually correct this tellin, recallin how Kalin's locker had always remained desolate and strange and sad. More curious was how Jay Bagnell's father, Daryll Bagnell, friends with Dr. Wyman Weitzman, had not only gone to high school with Old Porch but had lockered right next to him, recallin how Old Porch was the one who had a poster of Johnny Cash, supposedly signed as well by the man hisself. And that part was true. It really was signed by Johnny Cash.

Old Porch had stolen it from a man named Orin Pastor, who'd had it signed *To O.P.* This came out years later, though as far as that Wednesday night was concerned, Francis, for whatever reason, remained certain that inside Kalin's locker there hung a man in black.

What taste he's got in music don't make up for what taste he's got in horses, Old Porch said as he returned with Egan, swattin the rain off his head, removin his jacket. The laugh he got from the room, mostly earned, got him cravin for more drink. He was havin one heckuva night. *You, Riddle, get them two nags on hooks tomorrow. Egan will drive them over in the mornin.*

Happy to, Mr. Porch, Riddle said.

Russel ain't bringin back no horses tonight, Egan growled as he took his seat. *That idjit won't make it even one block from here on Cavalry. You'll see. He'll be back before the next hand, and he'll be makin up some nonsense about how the rain got to be too bad.*

Now, now, Egan, Porch said, pattin the table with one of his big scarred hands, fingers finally settlin in what he'd spat there earlier and not mindin it at all. *Frankly, I've never seen Russel like that. He might surprise us.*

Fifty dollars says he won't.

Fifty dollars? Against your little brother? Let's make it a hundred!

Old Porch was havin one heckuva night.

Chapter Three
"Russel Porch"

gan knew his youngest brother pretty well. Even before Russel reached the end of the first block, the boy's blood had gone cold. Hooves on blacktop seemed an increasinly dicey proposition, the wetness makin out of each successive *Clop-Clop Clop-Clop* a certainty of some slip; like they might as well already be on black ice, not but one heartbeat from the snortin and scramblin that would see them both go down or, at the very least, if Cavalry did somehow manage to keep hisself upright, still hurl Russel to the curb.

It didn't help none neither that Russel could sense pretty clear Cavalry's indifference to him, as if at any moment the monumental horse might just decide he'd had enuf of this adventure and turn to race back to Egan's barn.

My lord! Is that you, Russel Porch? Dorothy Bray cried out from her porch then, the firefly of her cigarette goin bright.

Russel had on his brown cowboy hat with that green band secured by a silver three-piece buckle set. He reached up now to tip it, because isn't that what a great cowboy on a great horse does when an elderly lady pulls herself up from her wicker chair to exclaim her astonishment before a sight such as him?

It is you, Russel! On Egan's horse! What the heck are you doin out at this hour and in such rain?

Some fool stole two of my daddy's horses from the paddock behind the Whinicam Orchard. I caught sight of him headin into Isatch Canyon. Gonna grab him before he gets too far.

Isatch Canyon?! With horses?! He must be some kind of fool.

He ain't from around here, Mrs. Bray. New kid named Kalin. Small as a mite.

You be careful, Russel. Her cigarette went bright again. *Isatch ain't no pony ring. And in this weather? My lord!*

I know my way. We'll deal with this quick.

That helped some, posturin hisself like so and boomin out his voice with a claim like he'd already done what he'd set out to do, thus further fortifyin his mission. Though by the time Russel reached the end of the Fir Avenue cul-de-sac, along the way passin plenty of jack-o'-lanterns on stoops or doorsteps, not a one lit, just gawkin out some mirthless grin composed of rot, what stuck with him from that encounter with Mrs. Bray weren't his own swagger but the way she'd emphasized the dangers of the canyon ahead. Near done him in too and proved Egan right. In the end, though, it were none other than his daddy's words, his daddy's pride, Old Porch's beamin smile with a rot all its own, that readied Russel's resolve to surpass all their expectations, not to mention this dead end, which he managed just fine, guidin Cavalry between the Mineer and Greenspire residences, across the empty lot beyond their yards, and then on through to the dirt path that ran pretty much uninterrupted all the way to the park entrance.

To Russel's credit, this ride alone was pretty bold and worthy of praise. Only just sixteen and on a strange and powerful horse, Russel still got Cavalry into a steady lope, maybe even earnin a little respect from the horse hisself, keepin their course true, keepin light in the saddle and light as he could on the reins, with now and then some taps from his toes to keep Cavalry from slowin back down into a hammerin trot.

Russel's main trouble was that darned Colt he'd stolt, or borrowed, because even borrowin, let alone holdin such a piece of angry history, should've never been on the menu for Russel. Even through that velvet pouch, the gun got to scratchin his lower back so bad that he had to fumble it free, mid-stride too, out from under his rain gear. Near dropped it too. He tried to stuff it behind his belt's front side, but when that didn't work, Cavalry startin to sense by the yanks at his mouth that this new rider was losin control, and startin to object, Russel stamped the thing hard against the pommel with his left hand and kept it there.

By the time he reached the Isatch Canyon parkin lot, the velvet pouch was soaked, and his left hand was numb. Even worse, Russel didn't have a better idea. He traded hands and tried to flex the cold from his fingers. He knew he could never drop that gun just like he knew he'd better never lose control of Cavalry. As Celia Mineer would later put it to Jared Cade: *That poor Russel was stuck between a gun and a high horse!*

Russel wound up trottin Cavalry past where he'd seen Kalin with the horses. He even paused under the last lamp, where Kalin had paused with Tom. When he seen there weren't no sign of Kalin nor the horses, Russel's determination once again started to fail. He'd already made a good run of it. And like his daddy had pointed out, Isatch was a box canyon. He and his brothers just had to set up right here, and in Egan's truck too, stayin warm and dry until that lowly fool came limpin back out.

The thought, though, that tricked Russel into goin on a little more was that the kid might've already realized the impossible path he'd picked. If Russel just went in a little ways, he'd meet him on the way out.

Again to Russel's credit, it takes somethin extra to enter the shadowy steeps of such a place, and at such an hour too, especially on a path that, while familiar to Kalin, who'd already traveled it many times with Tom, was unknown to Russel, his last time here bein when he was but ten on a church picnic, and that was only just off back at some park tables behind the visitor kiosk, which he was passin by right now.

Ahead waited the park gate.

Above Russel, the rain clouds were doin a good job coverin the moon as well as whatever light the stars might've shared. Russel sure hadn't thought to bring no flashlight. And as the darkness grew, he slowed to a very cautious walk, easin through that space used by riders and hikers to the side of the gate. Though he complained in his head about how Egan or his daddy could've at least asked if he'd thought to bring a flashlight, the fact that he hadn't was in the end a good thing. Brightness would've contracted his pupils and chained his sight to a narrow beam of nothin. Instead Russel's eyes and Cavalry's too soon adjusted to the night, somehow aided by the mass of silvery and black ledges that loomed above them, Agoneeya's walls on the right, Kaie-neewa's to the left, that face reachin both the pinnacle and promon-tory where myth and death still danced, which we'll get to later, what Orvop and even some maps for so long referred to as Squaw Peak.

Not that the path ahead even required that much visibility. It was a lot like the dirt road that Russel and Cavalry had already taken after Dorothy and George Bray's home: plenty wide, graded for emergency vehicles and park ranger trucks, with all the tree branches cut away. Russel even returned Cavalry to that big, beautiful lope. One moment Russel was bouncin like spit in a hot skillet and then in the next flyin smooth as on a magic carpet. Just Russel and Cavalry, their collective goal no more really than just this, all futures gone, the past quit too, where in this simple act of travel, they both found, that's right, Cav-alry too, a moment of great resoundin beauty in their shared solitude, their insignificance, especially before the great heaves of stone, which the farther along they got continued to rise higher and higher, and still but an insignificant architecture of time against the greater vaults that above and beyond outdistance even light.

Not that it mattered to Russel and Cavalry. They didn't care none about time. They paid the rain no mind neither nor the cold. They drank the wetness upon their lips like it was wine. They thundered the trail. They made the hardwood planks of First Bridge and eventu-ally Bridge Two sound like they was big drums, loud and reverberant enuf to enlist their hearts to join the simplest collective urge: to just Go! Go! Go!

For the first time ever, Russel knew hisself as not a Porch, no lon-ger compelled or held by brother or father or city or church. For the first time he was just there with this beautiful horse, Cavalry's stride lengthenin, easin them together upon a vastness that seemed to encourage them to just keep ridin like this all night long and all day too with never a need no more to look back.

Rumors born of that shady place still say that Russel even laughed, his first and last unfettered expression of pure jubilation.

And then he saw it. But of course he saw it. Call it fate or bad luck. Call it whatever you want. The namin won't change a thing; Russel caught it at once, off to the left, through a scramble of branches: a small peep of firelight.

And like that, everythin Russel had known about Liberty was stole away. He reined Cavalry to a quick halt. The horse obliged, but Russel could still tell by how the horse's shoulders and hocks jostled him about, Cavalry weren't too pleased. And that was the truth. Like Russel, Cavalry had been just fine ridin on and on, even if eventually, miles hence, they'd've had to face the great tumble of boulders, where now and then a fast waterfall disgorged itself into a gelid pool deep enuf for swimmers to dare high dives, a near impossible place to surmount by hoof unless your horse had wings.

Off to his left, Russel could see a mild slope leadin down to the seasonal crick bed that in early summer rackets along plenty deep and strong, even after loadin up the various pools along the way, includin the aforementioned swimmin hole kept full on the winter melt from the higher peaks of Katanogos itself. Now, though, it bein late October, the crick weren't much except for what this storm was sloughin off.

Russel pushed aside some low branches and rode down into the water, where he and Cavalry stood for a spell, barely ankle deep, slowly findin among stranger shadows another path on the far side that would lead them straight to that campfire.

I'll take them horses now! Russel cried out, still tryin to bring Cavalry to a halt, Cavalry havin reset that bit in his favor, like he'd decided he'd had enuf of this idjit on his back, and so not even comin to a full halt.

Kalin anyways just sat there, his back to them, beneath a big drift of rock anglin out from the mountainside, enuf to shield him from the worst of the rain. He didn't even turn around. He just kept pokin at the fire, what had dimmed in the past few minutes, now feedin it a bit of twig he deemed dry enuf. Nearby the two horses Russel was after stood with their leads looped over a low branch, their tack removed, wiped down, and hung up. Navidad and Mouse were nosin and nibblin at the feed Kalin had just recently set out on rocks that resembled bowls. Both horses looked freshly brushed.

The fire just needs to take a bit more, Kalin finally responded in his pleasin baritone, still not lookin up. *You're welcome to have somethin to eat before you head back.*

That relaxed Russel some, which is what Kalin meant to do.

You got some sack, boy! Russel crowed out, even louder, even as he heard his voice betray him, the pitch risin a little bit too quick. Not that it nettled him too much. He'd had a good ride, he'd found the two horses, he'd found the culprit.

Ain't much more than rice and beans, but it's sauced some and spiced enuf to keep your belly warm, Kalin continued.

Kalin tossed then somethin onto the low flickerin embers, what exploded into a fit of sparks before the rest burst into tall flames, which soon enuf brought the fire to a warm and pleasin order.

There we go! Kalin exclaimed, turnin to dig through a saddlebag set close by, not too far either from the rest of his gear, which included a neatly laid-out tarp with a sleepin bag and a blanket on top.

Truth be told, fer a moment Russel thought nothin sounded better than restin hisself beside that fire. Where better than to tell this stranger about the ride he'd been afraid to take but took anyway and why, oh my, how it had turned out finer than a heart could dream up, like nothin he'd ever done before? For that matter, when better to find out more about who this kid was and what he was fixin to do with those two horses? But the name Russel hisself had called him back at Egan's, what he was darn it!, a horse thief!, muddled him enuf that with Kalin still diggin in his saddlebag, what sprung upon Russel was some terrible jitters, got him stickin quick Cavalry's reins between his teeth so that with both hands he could draw out of that rain-soaked bag the glimmerin Colt.

I wouldn't do nothin funny, Russel said, but only because he'd heard someone say it that way before on the TV or in a movie.

When Kalin finally did look up, he had but a small bag in his hand.

Like I said: just some beans and rice.

Kalin stepped then into the firelight, studyin more closely Egan's liver chestnut stallion, and fer a moment Russel too. If Kalin had even registered the presence of the gun, he didn't show it.

Just so we manage this real peaceful like, Russel said, waggin the weapon some to make clear what he was talkin about, which only made clear that he had no business holdin the thing let alone pointin it at someone.

Kalin, though, displayed neither interest nor concern and returned to the fire, where he began to salt the pan he planned to use for dinner.

Cavalry, as if sensin that one who couldn't handle right a gun sure as heck had no right handlin him, started to back up and by his own volition even wheeled around. Russel struggled to gain control, at one point directin that pistol at hisself. Maybe again to Russel's credit, given what little talent for such things he truly possessed, he managed again to get Cavalry under control.

You best head back now, Kalin said then. *This storm's gonna get worse.*

I surely will, but I'll be goin with them two horses, Russel answered, now pointin the gun at the horses.

Kalin sighed. *You leave them horses be.*

Don't you see what I got here in my hand?! This time Russel pointed the gun at Kalin.

I'd prefer not to say what you got there. Which was an odd thing to say. Near as odd as sittin back down, as Kalin done, again facin the fire, again with his back to Russel. Now there's an Orvop sayin that warns *Never turn your back on a Porch,* but maybe Kalin already understood Russel better than the boy understood hisself.

Russel likely knew he was already beat too. He weren't gonna shoot Kalin, especially not in the back, and now he was terrified of even gettin off Cavalry. He was so sure the horse would bolt as soon as he tried to dismount that he'd likely be jumpin off anyways. And that still weren't the half of it. An unpleasant feelin had started to commandeer all he was. Somethin about how the shadows that seemed to flicker off those flames, the way they had danced across Kalin's face beneath that high-crowned white hat, before he'd turned and given Russel the silhouette of his hunched back, a shape of soot and pitch that seemed no longer human. Russel hadn't missed the seriousness in those dark eyes either, somethin akin to age, great age for which there is no accountin, born of a devout determination he'd never seen in anyone else before; if anythin similar to the rocks leanin over and shelterin them. And that still weren't the half of it. There was a coldness here too, all around and movin in closer, as if called down from the rock walls above, called up from the darker limits of the earth below, too much of it already here with more comin. Just tryin to reckon with all that made Russel's boots fidget in their stirrups, which made Cavalry dance side to side.

Boy, I'll kill you dead if you don't hand over my daddy's horses right now! Russel finally shrieked. What else could he do? Though this time the pitch in his voice really did try to shoot the moon, so unsettlin Egan's big horse that the stallion threw up his head and backed off, two steps right, two steps left, back, back, back, as if this time Cavalry had finally seen the ghost, all the ghosts.

And you know, maybe Russel had formulated after all some dim plan to shoot that gun, whether in the air or at anythin that weren't breathin, believin that simply a loud report in that early cathedral of stone might've altered somethin. He sure was tryin to raise it even as he did his best to keep Cavalry from again wheelin around. Russel managed neither. Not that it mattered.

See, this is right when the shadow fell. Though flew's probably the better way of puttin it. With perfect timin too. A blur of darkness that seemed born from the cliffs themselves. And it had in fact dropped from one of the big boulders just a little ways from the fire, right atop the slope that eased on down toward the slowly fillin crick, to where Cavalry kept wantin to head in the next second.

It ain't clear how, maybe by the sound or by the shiver of shadows cast on the cliff wall, but that sure sent Kalin into action. For all he wasn't followin, like, fer starters, how he'd been followed so easily, that boy sure caught a sense of movement right quick and knew how to react right quick too, duckin low, scroochin sideways, while still holdin down that Stetson with his right hand and for some reason grabbin up that pan on the coals with his left, way before Russel knew what hit him, and, boy, did it hit him too! Right on the side! Just around the ribs! Knocked him clean off Cavalry, who seemed as much relieved as Russel sure weren't relieved, his head takin a mean ding on some of the rock that waited for him. And that bloodied him the most compared to the hard contundin delivered next with a bony little elbow to the side of his face, which brusied at once. Not that Russel was concerned with any of these physical slights, his back already archin hard, face goin red, eyes bug-eyein, mouth suckin for the air that weren't comin in.

Kalin was already at his side, helpin Russel to sit up and take slow breaths, even if he still had the pan in his hand.

You just got the wind knocked from you is all, he kept sayin.

Kalin was right too. A moment later, albeit a long agonizin moment, Russel's breath started to return real regular, even if the rest of him still couldn't stop tremblin. Kalin saw the boy's tears and left him alone, hustlin off to fetch Cavalry, who'd got caught up in some brush around the crick that was now near knee-high, calmin the stallion before leadin him back toward the fire, clicks on his tongue, whispers on his lips, Cavalry offerin a snort back like the two was already thick as thieves.

Russel sure was gladdened to see his brother's horse return unharmed. A broke leg would've meant the end of Russel. He was less gladdened to find that the Colt pistol was nowhere near him and even more distressed to see who had it now, squirrelin it outta sight while mutterin things born out of sheer disgust.

What the—? Russel managed to croak out to the cause of his misfortune. *Landry, what the heck are you doin here?!*

It was 7:32 p.m.

M eet now the shadow that had knocked Russel off Cavalry. And not much of a shadow neither. An itty-bitty thing if surfeit nonetheless with indignant rage: Tom's little sister, Landry Gatestone, pacin back and forth before the bewildered Russel.

What the heck am I doin here?! What the heck are you doin, Russel?! Pointin a gun at someone and at someone who just got done offerin you dinner?

He stole my daddy's horses!

Them ones in Paddock B? What your daddy's gonna slaughter tomorrow for nothin? I bet he'd even pay someone to get rid of them for him.

They're still his! Russel answered, but there was no hidin the sullenness in his answer. And then, as if hearin it hisself, he sat up straight and got to tryin to better assess the state of his head, discoverin quick how the lightest touch on the bump caused him to wince hard, wince again when he caught sight of the blood on his fingers.

Ivan Dorton would spend a long, pointless evenin outside Carillon Square with Anthony Whitmer, who would have a similar dialogue with, of all folks, the sadly fated or foolish Fritz Linneman, Dorton and Whitmer bickerin about whether every now-known outcome might've changed if Russel had only got knocked out or cut up bad enuf to require that Landry personally help him back home. Whitmer would even get to wonderin what all might've changed if Cavalry had right from the outset bucked the boy off. *Russel's curse was that he'd ridden well enuf and fallen well enuf too,* Dorton would say.

Just go on and tell your daddy the truth: they ain't his no more, Kalin said, returnin the pan to the fire and finally addin the beans and rice with next a cup of water that he'd prepared earlier with the spices and whatnot already mixed in. When that was done, he came back over to Russel with a strip of cloth for his head. *Mind if I give your horse some apple?*

That would be okay, Russel answered, alternately confused by Kalin, who weren't budgin where the horses was concerned but at the same time kept provin hisself so attentive and, well, just plain nice.

Kalin had quartered the last of the three apples he'd brought that night, and after he'd fed a piece to Cavalry, who snorted with gratitude, he made sure Navidad and Mouse got their share.

Landry, meanwhile, had led Russel over to the fire to better inspect the cut on the back of his head. *It ain't much,* she announced, *but needs some pressure.* She better folded the strip of cloth Kalin had offered, Russel whinin some when she laid it hard down against the dark wet in his hair to better stanch the bleedin. For the second time, Russel failed to stave off his tears. Kalin rescued him by distractin Landry enuf so he could wipe away his shame with a sleeve.

Would your horse prefer to stand out there in the dark or get a share of this? Kalin asked Landry, addressin her directly for the first time since she'd appeared. He held up the last quarter of apple, indicatin with his eyes and a jog of his head that he knew exactly where Jojo waited.

I was sure you hadn't heard me, Landry said.

I didn't hear you. Kalin's eyes then flitted back to a spot by the fire that was empty except for a sudden bit of tremblin that seemed preserved there betwixt the idle tongues of flame. At least that's how Landry seen it, with Russel havin glimpsed somethin otherguess and altogether strange, dark twists there that should've long since been consumed. Russel even shuddered and had to look away.

Jojo won't let you get near him, Landry warned Kalin.

Okay, Kalin said with a shrug, then nodded at Russel. *That was quite a fall he took. Just make sure he's okay.* And then fixin his gaze back on Landry. *And you, did you land okay?*

I landed just fine, Landry snorted.

That's cause you landed on me! Russel balked.

Like I said, I landed just fine.

By the time Kalin reappeared, Landry and Russel had settled around the fire where it was dry and warm. The contents in the pan bubbled and spat. She and Russel both agreed that it looked horrible.

He usually don't let someone he don't know lead him so easy, Landry said when she seen Kalin was with Jojo. *Clop-Clop-clip-Clop.* And he didn't even look like Jojo had given him any trouble. Havin already anticipated that she might have to tie off Jojo trailside, which she had already done that evenin, exactly as Kalin had done for Mouse and Navidad, Landry had fit the big blue horse with a halter-bridle which maybe ain't much of a surprise given that all three sets of tack were owned by the Gatestones. Landry, like Kalin, had also packed in one of her saddlebags a lead rope, with again all the leads bein the property of the Gatestones.

What horse don't like apples? Kalin asked in order to settle the matter.

He usually don't eat nothin from strangers neither.

He was just followin your voice.

This seemed to mollify Landry some, even if it bothered her for some reason to see Kalin's eyes dart again to the spot she and Russel could both see was empty even if they'd also, for reasons unknown to both, chosen to let it stay that way, sittin instead on either side of the vacancy. Russel, though, paid no mind to such glances. He avoided lookin at Kalin if he could help it, his attention mostly with Navidad and Mouse.

Though Kalin hadn't done nothin more than you already know, Russel had discovered that he'd grown increasinly respectful of the kid. Or at least wary. If asked, he'd've sworn it had nothin to do with how Kalin had handled both Cavalry and Jojo, though maybe if pressed Russel would've come to see that the endurin calmness Kalin demon-strated in the face of a gun, a scuffle, not to mention gettin two unex-pected guests he was suddenly lookin after, four if we're countin their horses, was somethin to regard with at the very least caution if not outright admiration.

One thing Russel could've admitted, and what he pretty much ended up sayin to Landry anyways, was how Kalin had gone from this kid he felt sure he'd whoop, though Russel had never whooped any-one in his life, to feelin a little too much like when he was around his brothers, skittish and worried, like when Shelly and Sean, the two brothers who weren't there at Egan's this night, decided to gang up on him and laugh over the bruisin torture they took their time metin out.

Landry, Russel half whispered then, very much heedin these feelins. *I gotta get them horses to my daddy. If I don't—* and whose heart wouldn't break for the implorin sound in dear Russel's voice? *—they're gonna get at me somethin savage.*

Now Russel and Landry sure as heck weren't close friends, not even friends at all, but the Porches and the Gatestones still knew each other better than most families know their own kin, with what remained rancid between the older ones provin more feisty and even excitin when it came to the youngest ones. No question either, Rus-sel might've also found somethin allurin about Landry, especially that night, what with her shiny black hair, skin that glowed like them big brown eyes, not to mention her figure that was fer sure tiny but still as curved as her smile was big and long, the only attribute that some have admitted, much to their befuddlement, was near close to Tom's as humanly possible, which should've been impossible given their dif-ferences of course.

Russel, you know this don't make a lick of sense, Landry snorted, now givin her classmate all her attention, which he weren't so unhappy about. *Why's your daddy care so much about them two ponies?*

Russel hung his head and finally came clean, mostly. *He don't. He told me hisself he wouldn't value them more than five dollars apiece.*

Ha! Now there's the Old Porch we all know and love.

Kalin apologized for not havin any plates. He served Russel a good portion in the one bowl he had and doled out Landry's servin on the pan lid, eatin his share from an enamel coffee mug. He sat hisself across the fire, opposite Landry and Russel, though instead of takin that obvious empty spot, he situtated hisself right next to it, regardin it now and then as if someone was there beside him. Kalin gave Landry the spoon on his Swiss Army knife; Russel got the spork. Kalin scooped up what he could with a smooth shard of stone he'd wiped clean on his jeans.

At first Russel was determined not to touch the offerin, though upon hearin Landry's astonished exclamations, his resolve quickly failed. Soon he was stuffin his face, unable to believe that this here was just rice and beans. There were flavors he'd never tasted before, no doubt in the spices and just the right amount of butter or lard, though there weren't either of those in it neither.

Jeanna Gilson would later begin to jot down the recipe for this meal and some of the rest. In particular the rice and beans, what she would eventually share with Diane Hillam, Heidi Letham, and Olivia Chang, what she called for some reason Isatch Passover, what was, well, one of her favorites: *There ain't nothin to it, but it sure fills you up good!*

You know how to cook, Russel finally said. *That's fer sure. Thank you.*

You're welcome.

I'm sorry about pointin a gun at you too. Landry's right. That was a stupid thing to do.

Kalin nodded and maybe even smiled. Suddenly Russel wondered a crazy thing, a beautiful thing, if maybe they might become friends, if out of all this fuss, his big boasts and great ride, and it was a great ride in his mind, if none of this had been leadin toward the showdown he'd predicted and expected but simply was how friends make their first acquaintance. He sure as heck didn't behold in Kalin no Alastor nor Apollyon form of comin ruin, a creation summoned up from centuries of coincidence and consequence who would just the same too soon rise up and so alight, as if with the terrible Grace of Purpose, *and slaughter near the entire Porch family.* Or that's what Hector Angel would pretty much claim, and Gus Dieudonne too, though not to each other but to Dayton Banner, who would voice their declaration to Shaylan Chandler after she'd said near the same thing. Of course little Russel couldn't have known that. Certainly not before such obvious generosity and kind welcomin, not while there was beans and rice.

There's more, Kalin said, gesturin at the pan, which he'd moved off the coals but was still simmerin invitations. Landry didn't hesitate to scoop up a second helpin, though somewhere in there she remembered her mother's dictums on manners and refilled as well Russel's bowl and Kalin's mug. Her next bite confirmed once again her delighted surprise about how seeminly meager comestibles could continue to register such sustainin wonderment.

Of course, most of us already know that when surrounded by an endless dark and unbowin cold, when we're already good and damp from the arms the storm done thrown around us, far from home as well, anythin warm let alone edible, why then even a meal spiced with the ash from a petulant campfire is rendered greater than any banquet served to a king, president, or a monetary mogul. These three gobbled up all that Kalin's pan had to offer like they was more than three, like they was four, like they was more. Kalin had already gone to fill the teakettle with water that, once it boiled, he divvied up between a bowl, for Russel, and his mug, which he'd rinsed out for Landry, and for hisself the kettle lid. Kalin had made the switch because it didn't seem right to have Landry slurpin from the lid. The offerin also weren't anythin more than powdered cocoa, but it was the best thing Russel and Landry had ever had with a creaminess and sweetness that seemed impossible given its impoverished origins.

They all told stories then, well, Landry and Russel did, the kind that warm a belly even more than the warm food they were happy for; tales of horseflies so big, the squirrels feared them, which was one reason Russel loved this weather, basically bug free; or Landry tellin a story about Mathias Pollen, whose father was president of Isatch U and would become one of the Quorum of Twelve, perhaps one day responsible for the manuduction of the Church itself, a path that might apply to Mathias's future as well, and yet her brother Tom had still convinced Mathias to build with him a corn-mash whiskey still, for a science project of course, just for science, which Mathias, while adjustin the Bunsen burner, had so unbalanced that the entire mechanism had toppled forward, the glass parts shatterin on the floor and the hot corn muck burnin the leg of Tom, who still couldn't stop laughin even as he was yelpin and yankin his pants off. *I'm sure it was an accident,* Landry added, *but maybe also Mathias done it because deep down inside he knew that makin whiskey just weren't the right thing for him no matter what kinda grade they was aimin to get. They still did get somethin out of it that was flammable with As in Biology. Tom's only A. I swear Tom was just as proud of that as the big buckle he won for ridin Hightower.* Russel remembered a school assembly with Tom in it, wearin his big black Stetson, just strollin across the stage. That's all he had to do. Landry, who was a freshman then, chased after him wearin a lavalava, which she didn't care for one bit, but she did it because she got to swat her brother with a big Nerf bat, right in front of everyone too, except that he was too quick, even while strollin, and she never did manage to whack him. Offstage she got upset as all heck. Tom told her then that she weren't upset that she'd failed to hit him but rather because she'd quit.

Never quit, he told me. So I smacked him with that foam bat right on his forehead. Pow-Pow! I never seen him so proud. The teachers got mad because we was makin such a ruckus.

I heard you guys! Russel exclaimed.

Landry nodded. Her eyes were fillin with wet, and she had to look away. Kalin looked away too, at the darkness beside him.

Russel eventually asked Kalin where he was from, and Kalin told him.

They have horses there? Landry asked, and even if that's all she asked, her head filled with many more questions, like about Kalin's folks, or these horses in particular, or about what fool's errand he thought he was on on such a dismal night.

Kalin said they didn't have horses where he was from, at least none that he could ride, though you could see them now and then in the park or pullin carriages. He admitted that he was kinda disappointed when they'd moved west.

How come? Russel asked.

It's kinda stupid now that I've been here, but I had this idea about the West. I figured there'd be horses everywhere. Especially in the streets. But like every-where else, there was just a lot of cars. They have more horses in Pennsylvania and Maryland than they do out here.

Is that so? Landry seemed amazed by the comment.

Kalin only shrugged.

Where are you even takin these ponies? Russel finally asked. He weren't gonna let the subject go.

I'm gonna set them free, Kalin answered. *It was a promise I made to her brother before he passed.*

Russel caught then, maybe too clearly, another one of Kalin's glances at the empty seat at the fire, this time followin it too closely to a darkness that seemed to thread itself in and out of the void until it seemed somethin more than a void.

Likely Joanne Willden was right to conjecture about what sensi-tivities Russel had, how he'd even here at the first campfire started to conjure and coalesce unbeknownst to hisself what all was really goin on; the same Joanne Willden who would manage to depict this scene with thick smears of pastels that under her increasinly proficient hand somehow seemed to leave all materiality behind, renderin the blackness sat at the fire with mass enuf to bend light; the same Joanne Willden who would go on to lament near her whole life how, if Russel had only lingered long enuf back at the Isatch Canyon parkin lot to catch sight of Kalin pausin under the lamp light, *he might've sensed some spectral companion at large, even if he couldn't've known it was Tom. Might he then have just headed straight over to Uncle Conrad's with them binoculars and said nothin about the horses? Though fer sure he'd have shivered, and that shiver would've helped him stay to an alternate course.*

You was friends with Tom? Russel asked, suprised to find hisself shudderin suddenly for no reason he could lay claim to.

Kalin just sipped his cocoa from the kettle lid.

Good friends, Landry answered for him.

Huh. I sure never would've figured that. Russel rubbed his eyes then. If asked, he'd've said he done it for a whirl of smoke that got there, but really it was because nothin he was set to see this night seemed willin to stay put.

Tom used to say this canyon was haunted, Landry said then. *He ever tell you that?*

He might've, Kalin answered, his eyes stayin with the small flames.

I never heard that. And Russel did seem genuinely surprised.

Landry sure relished that moment. Oh, you bet she did! Her eyes filled then with the glow from those rubicund coals that seemed ready to welcome any fiend loose from that place devoid of grace and compassion. Landry knew bunches of stories about the canyon, about Indians that were killt around where they was campin now, their bodies deprived of their heads so the settlers that done it could show them off as trophies to anyone who dared not believe before sellin them to the U.S. Government or a museum or two to make a profit. And those heads were the lucky ones. More Indians, *the Timpanogos, the Katanogos,* Landry told Russel, tried to escape the slaughter by climbin up into the crags above. They was hotly pursued. Many were tumbled from the heights with rifles and even hurled rocks. Wild Bill Hickman was the worst offender, but he weren't alone. One band of Indians was chased along the animal trails and driven into a cave, where pursuers assumed they'd surrender and come out beggin for mercy. Or so voiced stalwart members of the Church. Wild Bill Hickman and his cohorts, however, had other plans. *They drove them deeper into the mountain, men sure, but children too, and women, some with babies in their arms. Like buffalo, Wild Bill Hickman and his men forced them poor frozen and near-starved folks into the chasms hid within. Wild Bill Hickman supposedly said that for the Lord that day he'd done not only the killin but the damnin too. And that weren't all. One woman escaped. She weren't gonna die in no hole and instead climbed higher and higher. She was the wife of the chief, who Wild Bill Hickman had already killt while he lay sick with disease, cut off his head too.*

Pareyarts, Kalin said then. *His name was Pareyarts. And that cave's a mine now. Or used to be a mine.*

We don't know her name. She ran fast and far. But they still caught up with her and cornered her at the top of Kaieneewa Mountain, what overlooks us and guards Isatch Canyon here.

That'd be Squaw Peak? Russel asked, lookin up at the stone above their heads, and the dark too that could easily devour such stone.

That's right. Rather than fall victim to their grimy paws, she threw herself off, but not before cursin them, and their families too, cursin even the Church, plus anyone else who dared come here with a heart hard as a spring pine cone.

What's that mean, a spring pine cone? Russel whispered.

Landry shrugged. *Closed, I think.*

I like pine trees. I like pine cones too. Especially around Christmas.

She's makin up a lot, Kalin interrupted, his eyes fixed on the empty space. *We don't know none of that.*

You don't know that.

Russel didn't care. *What kinda curse was it?*

Some say her rage was so distasteful to even Death that she was left to wander the space between what's now and what comes after. And because she couldn't rest, she ate them she hated.

Wild Bill Hickman wasn't eaten, Kalin objected, his irritation with Landry growin.

That there's true. So folks got to sayin she'd eat up the hope of them that she cursed.

Kalin snorted but now he was smilin a little too. And Russel smiled as well, though losin hope didn't seem like a thing to smile about.

Them that she don't like who cross the Gate of the Mountain she eats fer real, Landry just had to add, and then she stared hard at Kalin, just darin him to contradict her. He weren't that much a fool.

Where's the Gate of the Mountain? Russel asked.

Just up a ways, Kalin said.

Landry nodded, grateful that they could agree on somethin. *She's probably heard us by now.* Landry just couldn't stop herself. *Fer sure smelled us. I can imagine her right now, pacin back and forth, with nails sharp as blades and teeth too long for any mouth. I'm sure right now she's just waitin for us to cross her way.*

That's quite a story, Russel said, and he meant it, crowdin the fire a few inches more for warmth, for light, but mostly for protection. He was now even in less of a hurry to go anywhere else. And even then, the hair on the back of his neck wouldn't stop crawlin. The horses didn't seem to care for this story either, snortin and stompin a hoof once or twice, though admittedly from Mouse a stomp didn't mean much except that he hadn't eaten enuf, which was darn near never.

Sure, there is little to this bit of lore that should rattle your spine or erect hair upon whatever part of your body to warn you of trouble comin. And sure, you're likely far from Orvop and far as you can get from Isatch Canyon, though, after all, what wronged dead the world over hasn't howled vengeance after the livin? Nonetheless, do your best to imagine for yourself just exactly where these children sat, and children they most certainly were, even if edgin quick enuf toward some socially recognized maturity. Sure, they was willful, obdurate, talented fer sure, at least two of them, and maybe cursed on top of it, but the three of them still sat in that bleak rain, tormented by the cold at their backs, further enclosed by a remorseless dark, and well . . .

Kalin slapped his thighs, which Landry mistakenly read, and glee-fully too, as him bein as frighted as Russel was by her tale. But that weren't the case. Kalin was annoyed by the story, but only because he could see that Russel was shaken, and he needed the boy to be strong because he and Tom's sister was gonna have to ride back the way they come, and Kalin didn't envy either of them.

Ha! Landry laughed, still clueless. *That got you too, huh?*

Kalin shook his head. *I got enuf stuff to be scared of than to worry about stories I already know by heart. I'm just surprised you didn't tell Russel the rest. Maybe that's too scary for even you?*

Landry was sure he was teasin, and she liked that, but his comment still threw her. *What rest?*

Tom didn't tell you?

What did he tell you?

What makes that story in particular so terrifyin for you both.

How's that? she and Russel demanded then in near unison.

Why who else stood there with Wild Bill Hickman at the top of that peak? Who else did she curse?

Who? Landry couldn't be happier to ask.

Both close friends. Kalin looked first at Russel. *Garrison Porch for one.*

Garrison Porch?! Russel looked amazed, all the more so because a kid he'd knowd next to nothin about just hours ago, who he now knew as a good friend of Tom Gatestone, was tellin him about his own family history!

A few too many greats in there for me to add to grandfather but you know who I'm talkin about, Kalin said.

I've heard my daddy mention Garrison Porch before, Russel said. *He sure was proud of the Indian killin he done. Never heard no mention of a curse though.*

Who was the other one? Landry asked.

Alfred Gatestone.

You mean my great-great-whatever-grandaddy?

Kalin nodded.

Now that is a humdinger, Landry said, slappin her own thighs, shudderin theatrically, though at the same time lookin supremely satisfied by the revelation. *Guess you and me are doomed, Russel.*

Ain't that a sad thing.

Landry could see that he meant it too, and she at once felt bad for playin so glib. It hurt her heart to see Russel slump and sink his gaze into their small fire like it was his only refuge. Kalin saw it too and felt powerless before his predicament. There weren't nothin he could do to answer what Russel had come for, and he knew too well that look when you is afraid to go back to what others call so easily your home and worse your daddy. Kalin also turned his gaze to the fire, and then all three let their eyes rest in the delightful dance of those flames, the crackle, the fine smell, the glowin coals near joyful in the warmth they spared, like fer a moment this here was home, and maybe it was. Even the horses seemed to agree, murmurin up with a shuffle of sorts, no stomps needed, like they with their feet were discussin just this.

Hey, Landry, did you ever know my little sister, Ginny? Russel asked then, but Landry shook her head. *Figured I'd ask. After she left to Texas with my mom, I— Well, I miss her every day.*

Your mom or your sister?

Both of them, of course.

Hey! Landry suddenly cried out, smilin again, eyes brighter than any coals or fire. *Kalin, you got ten bucks?*

I don't even have a penny. What would I need money for up here?

Why for moments like these! She said, standin up quick, shakin her head too with disgust, even if it weren't the kinda disgust that can rob a smile from a girl. Or a boy. *I got an idea, Russel.*

What kind of idea?

Landry's smile was infectious, and as she began diggin through her pockets, he once again couldn't hold off admirin the figure before him, with obvious longin liftin his eyes from her boot tips to her widow's peak, tryin not to linger anywhere in particular on the way there, though her glare and frown that caught him by surprise quick averted his eyes back to their cozy fire. He even made an effort then to throw in some branches and was happy to see they took flame just fine.

And then Landry's little hand was right in front of him, the folded

115

green in her fingers like some beautiful night flower. *Twenty dollars, Russel!* Landry squealed in delight. Look what her parka pocket had bequeathed. Thank goodness she'd forgotten to give it to Mr. Chidester.

Russel cautiously accepted the flower, his heart already fillin and expandin in a way no amount of money can cause. Landry, though, was flabbergasted by his stupefied reaction and immediately grabbed it back, spreadin it out smooth.

For the horses, you numskull. I don't wanna see that evil old cuss you're forced to recognize as your father do you harm on our account. Kalin shot Landry a glance then. Even he weren't followin. *I'll write out the bill of sale for the two ponies on the back side by Mr. Jackson here and date it and sign it too. You do the same. This here's also double what Old Porch wanted. He better praise you for gettin such a good deal. Unless you got change. Do you got change for a twenty?*

Russel didn't.

Landry scribbled down in pen all she'd just laid out and then signed it and then saw that Russel signed it too, who then pocketed with great relief the solution to all his woes.

Now two matters arise here, the first bein Landry's mistake not to get some bill of sale that she might've retained for her own records. Plenty have said that such a document wouldn't have survived anyway, and that is a fair judgment and exculpation of her error. The second, though, broaches a subject that dozens and dozens more still discuss tirelessly: what to title this entire tale and disquisition as set forth thus far. *Paddock B* is certainly a worthy try, and while many acknowledge its aptness, few hold to it. Mike Beer, also known as Reindeer Mike, though he cared for neither beer nor reindeer, would fer his part try plenty of times to get *Paddock Omega* to hang on that Paddock B peg. To no avail. And tryin to rename Paddock A as *Paddock Alpha* didn't hang none either. *Omega Kappa Corral* was viewed as just plain silly. A greater portion of folks, though, would through insistent use lobby for the title *The Horse Thief* which, from the outset at least, still makes a whole lotta sense. No denyin there's plenty of larceny at the heart here, and the disputatious dialogues that have erupted over notions of ownership, appropriation, and entitlements of course, plus larger concerns such as liberty, seem downright endless.

The trouble, however, arrives right here with this moment when there is no refutin that the parties involved, namely Russel Porch and Landry Gatestone, had come to an agreement, and the property in question, Navidad and Mouse, whom Kalin throughout refused to recognize as property, was peaceably transferred and in apparent concordance as well with the will of none other than Old Porch hisself.

Fer sure, them three kids at that moment were mighty pleased with themselves. And no doubt their primarily capitalist enactments, if heeded, would've made the world a better place. Landry even helped Russel back through the dark and across the crick, which was rushin deeper and deeper, now above the knee, with black icy water. Kalin followed behind, leadin big Cavalry across the water and up to the main trail, where he helped Russel get his foot in the stirrup with the aid of his intertwined fingers, which Russel happily took advantage of, followed by voluminous thanks. Kalin offered his hand as well, and Russel shook it vigorously. Shook Landry's hand too. Would've shook hands with all the trees if they'd offered. His enthusiasm was that great.

Their goodbye was one of the sweetest moments really. Russel's head was already full of how he was gonna give Landry a big hug at school come mornin. At least a one-armed hug, snug around the shoulder, with a warm *Hey!* And he sure as heck would say hello to Kalin. Maybe they'd even share a private laugh about their adventure, or he'd ask Kalin how he'd cooked up them rice and beans if their conversation looked to stall, maybe ask his shoe size, if he was wearin again them weird loafers, because Russel and him might wear a similar size, even if that was obviously not so, but anyway Russel's house was full of extra boots that had fallen into disuse, and a pair could easily be spared, Russel only then recognizin that Kalin had on fine boots, black boots, that would serve him well up here, even if it snowed some, though of course Russel could also see that Kalin weren't gonna be back in school by tomorrow mornin. This wasn't just some little night-out adventure for him. This was somethin else. And Russel's back suddenly flooded cold as he thought about just where he was now and where he would have to ride to and even what waited at the end of that ride, if he made it back without failin. At which point he noticed the tug at his left ankle followed soon enuf by another tug at his right.

Please don't take them, Russel near mewled to Kalin then, who'd already quick unbuckled both of Egan's spurs. *You seen what my daddy done to that mare with wire. My brother ain't no different, maybe worse.*

I ain't takin these, Kalin said, already tyin them up to a near side latigo keeper on Russel's saddle. *Just don't want you to kill yourself. This big fella ain't gonna need no encouragement gettin home.* Which rang plenty true, and Russel was grateful then, even if he sensed it weren't the whole answer when it came to the subject of spurs. Egan's spurs also reminded him of what else weren't his.

Landry, I need that gun back.

Soon as I get back, Landry answered without missin a beat. If only she'd've answered differently, even if her reasons were sound as her reservations were deserved. Poor Pharell Rowley would write a beautiful song implorin Landry to right then and there return that cursèd Colt. He would even sing it to Monica Brothwell, no relation to Janice Brothwell, though Pharell would sing it to Janice too.

You don't understand, Landry! Russel protested, panic overtakin his features and posture.

I understand plenty. You pointed a loaded pistol at someone. I seen that with my own eyes. And you threatened to kill him if you didn't get your way. I heard that with my own ears. There is no chance I'll risk that happenin again.

Russel hated to admit it, but he could see she was right just as he could see he weren't gettin it back that night. He also believed her. Landry was a Gatestone. She'd keep her word. Plus he'd now have a reason to talk to her again. And that was a pleasant thought.

Kalin, who still had to see that Landry got on her way and didn't like leavin the horses unwatched, walked Cavalry around so he was facin toward the canyon's exit. Then with a pat on the neck, a click, and a light swat on the rear, Kalin sent rider and stallion back the way they'd come.

Cavalry couldn't have cared less about whatever Russel had in mind for their ride back, nor whether the boy stayed on or off, or yanked on the reins or threw them away; that horse just full galloped near the whole way down that Isatch Canyon trail with Russel, bless his beautiful heart, doin the smartest thing yet: he just hung on for dear life until that great liver chestnut stallion pulled up snortin and heavin in front of the parkin lot and from there on seemed at least a little amenable to a more peaceful pace home.

In Egan's barn, Russel untacked Cavalry, watered him, gave him a quick brushin, and made sure to blanket him in his stall. He put away Egan's spurs too. The tack would still need soapin and oilin, but Russel figured he could attend to that later, and feed Cavalry then too, after he'd shared his good news with his dad and brothers. Cavalry even gave him a bighearted nuzzle and Russel wondered if maybe they'd become friends as well. Weren't this the most magical night?

First thing Russel did when he got inside was throw down that twenty. Near landed it in his daddy's lap. And Old Porch sure did grin wide then because it was money and at that moment he needed more.

The night hadn't gone anythin like Old Porch had thought it was gonna go, what after rakin in so much with them early hands and the bourbon so hot in his gut, the kinda heat that guarantees no emptiness lies ahead. But nothin is ever more certain than that more emptiness lies ahead, and if you ever hear otherwise, best wise up quick before you lose your way to bad advice.

Trent Riddle had showed his calm and poise all night, foldin often, and only now and then, when he had a shot, recoupin some of his early losses. Old Porch, shame on him, never even noticed Riddle's progress. Only that his drink kept tastin worse, a bitterness buildin in his belly, in his mouth, swig after swig, hand after hand.

At one point Old Porch angrily threw away the plastic cup and demanded a glass. A real glass. Egan had retrieved for him then a Waterford tumbler with a Lismore pattern reserved only for the most special of occasions. It was so dusty, Old Porch made him wash it out first. But that was no good either. After another loss, Old Porch hurled the thing at the wall. Half-full too. Its shatters frosted the worn woolpile Sarouk rug. The base of the glass, though, didn't give up that quick, bristlin with shards thick and thin, rollin around like a fallen crown before settlin at an angle between baseboard and floor, where it stayed unnoticed, unchallenged.

Egan obliged his father by puttin the whole bottle down on the table. Egan knew better than to protest at this point. All the Porch boys knew better. Whatever was bound to happen next was gonna happen next, as if the future itself was now bound with the same immutable coils enchainin Titans in the pit of Tartarus. Or as Blake Kotter would put it: *Whatever was up next for Old Porch was already in the cards, so to speak.* Maybe Francis and Woolsey were the smart ones that night, havin not but twenty or so minutes earlier declaimed in their defense the inconvenience of state-mandated school the followin mornin, not to mention that they was both broke, and so skedaddled in Woolsey's Chevy Chevette, what Old Porch so delicately referred to as *the Gut Tub* as in *Good, get that friggin Gut Tub outta my driveway!*

Envyin some them two vacant chairs, Brother Riddle, by all appearances a good Church man, was more and more rattled at the sight of his boss drinkin so hard. A beer was one thing, but this was the kind of excess and recklessness anyone in close proximity, whether of the Church or not, knew to start plottin exit strategies around. The only thing hitchin his departure was the most obvious fact: Riddle had started to do very well. What's more, he was lookin now at the kinda pot that could and would alter his life. Or as he then lied to the table, downplayin the sum of money before him, before them all, he finally might get to take some gal out to a movie after treatin her to some of that Chateaubriand they cooked up at a fancy little restaurant not so far from the old Zurich Steel Mill. It was a misjudged bit of down-playin though. As if no one else there hadn't figured out how this pot could cover quite a few such nights. Riddle's announcement was greeted with mostly sneers, some takin it as proof that Riddle did have the cards, others takin it as proof that he didn't.

In fact Egan had better cards, though not much better, which can be the best kind. Kelly had just folded, and the bet was with Old Porch, who was so blurry with his drunk that all he thought was sure to happen was based on what he thought he was seein which he wasn't seein at all. Old Porch was likely gonna call Billings's bump, which would've likely kept Egan in, but then Russel barged in, the back of his head matted down with clotted blood, his lip cut, one side of his face startin to swell, a real horror show were it not for his euphoric grin.

It was 9:04 p.m.

Riddle thought at once that no boy could be happier than this one. He must've met someone. And then on top of it the kid had thrown down a twenty-dollar bill, and his sour old man had sweetened up as well, like his luck was finally changin, with Old Porch callin the bet as he'd planned to but tossin in as well among the chips that now wadded-up piece of legal tender. Egan didn't protest his dad's handlin of the bet and just folded, glad to be done with the hand, the game, the night if he could just get everyone outta there quick, and, turnin his back on his losses, turned his irate mood on his little brother.

What the heck happened to you?

That there money is what was owed for them horses, Russel declared proudly. *I didn't pay five for each. I didn't make no ten dollars either. I made you double, Daddy! Double!*

I'll be darned! Old Porch slurred, beamin, maybe even resemblin Russel some in his own newfound expression of glee.

You look pretty got into, Egan said, pointin out all the blood and the mud.

Oh, it was a fight, but nothin they'll brag on.

They? Egan weren't gonna let up on Russel, likely because there just weren't nothin else left for him to do.

That's right. Wasn't just the one like I'd seen. They was two.

Atta boy, Old Porch mumbled, noddin some like he might suddenly doze, even if at the same time somethin bright and wicked lit up in those hazy eyes, especially as he examined again his hole cards and began to pay Egan a whole lot of extra attention. *Egan here said you wouldn't get as far as the end of the block.*

120

Egan tried to ignore Old Porch. *Why didn't you bring them horses back like you swore you would?*

But Russel weren't thrown none. *You heard Daddy. He said we might as well pay them who took the horses for all the trouble they was worth to us.*

They weren't that much trouble, Kelly said then with a sneer.

I did say that! Old Porch seemed happy for the first time ever to agree with Russel. *I also bet your brother Egan here one hundred dollars that you, Russel, would come through. And by golly you did!*

Old Porch cackled happily as he made Egan hand over five twenty-dollar bills, all the more satisfied to see Egan lose most of what was left in his wallet. Riddle also watched calmly, distantly, again assessin his hand against the state of his competitors.

The only thing Riddle didn't notice was the way Billings was watchin him with distrust and worse distaste. Billings had over a short lifetime acquired a way of corallin expression and action into some inert and unreadable part of hisself, even if he weren't immune to the loosenin charms of alcohol, which he'd had some of, so that what might have remained unreadable at other times now lost its veil and what was inert gave way to the clenchin of fists and a grimace as well, all too recognizable as a prelude to violence, as Billings got increasinly fed up with Riddle's prim and properness, his refusal to have a drink with the rest, what Billings reduced to churchy uppity-ness he reviled. If Riddle had taken a second to observe Billings with the same clarity he was observin Old Porch with right now, he might've folded straightaway and fled.

Instead Riddle saw only Old Porch's one-hundred-and-twenty-dollar raise intended to immiserate him. Billings got so hot, his forehead might've boiled lead, hotter even than durin the more con-sequential conflicts that would arise later. But Kelly, likely because he was feelin somethin similar against Riddle and knew his friend well enuf, set a hand on Billings's shoulder, and like that the heat left Bill-ings and he folded. And he didn't even curse.

Old Porch, though, was still shoutin for joy over his pricey gambit, goadin his boys, goadin Billings, goadin Riddle, who could do nothin else but call the bet and reveal the two aces that took the hand, though he was circumspect enuf not to grab for the pot just yet. Billings was ready again to coldcock Riddle, Kelly's touch could only do so much, but was stunned into stillness when Old Porch stood up so fast and so violently that his chair flew clear back into the foyer.

At first Old Porch was just furious with his cards, like they was the ones betrayin him, what he'd believed was not just any flush but a royal flush and what was now presentin him with not even much of a hand, a jack, and a queen suddenly disentanglin into two jacks, diamonds dismergin into hearts and diamonds, until his fury was exceedin the cards, exceedin the game, if still seein red, until he was grabbin hold of the empty bourbon bottle, ready to hurl it like an ax at the shocked Riddle.

Bless his beautiful spirit, it was Russel who leapt forward, arrestin his daddy's arm before it could complete the deed and ruin hisself and Riddle. Egan, to his credit, quick as Russel, plucked free that weapon which, becomin just a bottle again, he placed out of reach. Egan then tried to calm his father, who had already shook Russel loose like it was the boy who had betrayed him. Egan gave Billings a nod then, indicatin with his eyes that Billings should flank Old Porch if his old man got worse. For Maurice Tanner, a buildin manager in Payson, this here would prove a critical moment, small as it were, when Egan recognized somethin in Billings he could use, further leveragin as well Kelly's allegiance through the most tried-and-true fraternal tool: competition for affection. And sure enuf, Kelly leapt up near fast as Billings, the two movin as one to try and restrain Old Porch's drunken temper.

Only then did Riddle rake in the substantial pot, all the while offerin up profuse apologies, Egan cashin him out and with looks severe enuf to promise more violence orderin him to hightail it outta there, which Riddle did, gladly, though not before offerin Russel a look that was both grateful and sympathetic. *Like maybe Russel was the only sane person in that blighted family, like maybe Riddle saw it, like maybe that there was a nice moment in what was otherwise a terrible night,* Patricia Dewey, at the time a registered nurse down in Salem, would say to Ronalee Golightly in 1996.

Kelly followed Riddle out to try to minimize the outburst as well as all that drunkness.

He ain't usually like that, Kelly said as they hustled through the rain, even if he knew that likely Riddle knew that that was a bald-faced lie. *You know, just the usual cowboy recklessness, thinkin Wednesday night is Friday night. It ain't often that a U.S. senator calls you.*

Already forgotten, Riddle assured Kelly with the easiest of smiles before disappearin into his brown 1970 Plymouth Duster.

Suffice it to say, as inexorable as everythin ahead seems now, with the future bein the past's unimpeachable tyrant, what happened next did not need to happen. Plain and simple. All of it could've ended right there, with whatever mess that was about to follow soon enuf forgotten with the help of a broom. All the horrors, and marvels that continue to rile too many, could so easily have been averted, and with the simplest, near effortless action, sparin the holy and unholy, the mild and the menacin, both bystanders and dreamers, even the earth itself, especially the earth, spared some the indignity of human malice that too willingly sews mild fields and glens with the teeth of Hydras.

Russel just had to shut up.

Like Tom had told Lindsey, see, Russel had already won. He'd done gone and settled the score of the stolen horses on his own, and admirably too, what in his father's own eyes was not just acceptable but applaudable. He'd even ridden a horse he had no business standin next to, almost to the Gate of the Mountain and back again, through the dark and colludin rain. Whatever his daddy was up to now had nothin to do with dear little Russel. The poker game was over, the night spent. There was nothin left for any of them to do really, except pay the deities of hangovers the followin mornin. Landry would've returned the gun, and likely Old Porch and Egan would've been none the wiser. Russel hisself would've slept like a baby.

But Egan kept gettin after him, relentless as he was bitter over the money Russel had cost him. *You sure took a lotta dirt on your back side.*

And likely because Russel, in finally havin felt the bright and warmin light of paternal affection, especially when faced now with its fadin, like a gambler addicted to the next revelation of worth or an addict hooked clear through by the promissory note of just another taste, Russel had to do whatever might incline his father to once again look his way with pride and maybe this time even with wonder.

They jumped me in the dark. Come from a ledge above and knocked me clean off Cavalry. That's how I took to bleedin here from my head. But you bet I rallied. Boy, did I ever. Showed them a thing or two.

You shouldn't have let them jump you in the first place, Egan scowled. Kelly reentered the house and at once chimed in his agreement with Egan even though he hadn't heard a thing.

Russel grinned and shook his head in the most patronizin manner he could muster, sure he was never gonna stop winnin. *They was just lucky they didn't get shot.*

Shot?! Old Porch burped out suddenly, turnin his dangerous eye from the storm of his defeat to this young struttin boy. *Shot with what?*

Egan caught on way faster than Old Porch could slur. *You took a gun? What gun?*

With Russel's one step backward, as great a retreat as the Battle of Gaixia, what Egan's predatory acumen could not miss, nor the grimace on his little brother's face either, what Egan had seen countless times

123

and what he knew meant Russel was caught lyin, not to mention the risin terror in the boy's eyes, described by too much white surroundin them dilatin pupils, Egan turned and stormed off to his gun cabinet.

The yell that followed down that long dark hallway made Russel quiver, a thing that Old Porch was likely wired to see too and to go after with punishin results, so detested was weakness or any sign of falterin in that family.

Hand over whatever firearm you took, Russel, Old Porch said slowly, the coldly wielded fury in his voice commandin then whatever drunken imbalances in hisself to cease.

I don't got it no more. I lost it in the fight, in the rain, in the dark.

It's gone, Dad! Egan roared, chargin back, standin at Old Porch's side, shoulder to shoulder, now with Kelly and Billings linin up behind. *You're not gonna believe what this maggot's done!*

Spit it out, boy! Old Porch snarled, not shiftin any the glare he'd fixed on Russel.

The Peacemaker! Egan howled.

What?! Old Porch couldn't believe his ears, even had to shift that glare around, because now it was Egan who deserved his enmity, except Egan weren't foolin around.

My Colt?! Old Porch's fury growin, Russel backin away more.

Russel, it weren't much of a fight if you soon got to makin a deal over the horses, Kelly said then, and laughed as well, though no one, not even Billings, paid much attention to this stupid arbitrary comment.

My Colt?! Old Porch seethed again, his face gettin redder, and then fast as an Isatch Great Basin rattler, he struck the boy with his right hand, his fist fortunately loose and sloppy, although the nails were plenty in play, one long thumbnail slashin down across the bridge of Russel's nose to the cheek, the flesh between his eyebrows bleedin at once, and bad enuf to get blood in his eyes, confusin and terrifyin Russel all the more, more in earnest now in his attempt to back away to the front door he should've left through ten minutes earlier.

I'll get it back! I promise! She promised!

Now likely we'll be reassurin ourselves that we wouldn't have let such a darned foolish thing slip. Guaranteed, right? In the currently cool appraisal of these events, we can see too obviously how such a divulgence, and at that particular instant too, would behoove no one, especially little Russel. But then again we ain't the ones facin off with Old Porch and his boys, with one of them boys near as mean as the old cuss hisself, in the presence of whom we'd've likely dislodged a sputterin discharge of you-know-what from you-know-where, fillin our shorts and likely spillin down the insides of both legs into our shoes.

She?! Old Porch screamed, practically bug-eyed, pawin to unbuckle his belt then as he closed in with great stomps on that terrified child in a way that sadly was not all that unfamiliar to poor Russel.

Wait, what? Who's got my Colt? Egan bellowed next, if also grabbin Old Porch's left arm to hold him back, not outta mercy for Russel but knowin the beatin would hold up an answer.

La-La-landry Gatestone, Russel managed to get out, that hesitation in his speech only drawin upon him still more of Porch's crapulent ire.

There've been plenty of quietly murmured talks about this moment as well, most reverential and amazed. Russel Porch had a terrible stammer. It was evident near every day in school, worse when he was called upon in class, until he was rarely called upon at all, but worst of all at home, where his brothers hardly tolerated the sounds jammin up in their young brother's mouth and where Old Porch, when he weren't orderin Russel to *Just spit it out!,* was shoutin for Russel to *Just get outta here!,* and regardin his fleein boy with disgust.

The thing is, as we can all bear witness to now, except for this slight hesitation with Landry's name, Russel never had a hitch in his speech that entire evenin. Margaret Wilkinson, sister to Roger, along with Brian Polson and Kirk Veach, all workin the floor at the Rome JCPenney, this was in 1988, would fabulate for hours on how, of all the nights, Russel had somehow seen his way through to clear expression, as if his small but complete adventure had relaxed in hisself a spirit free from barrier. More needs to be said about this remarkable miracle, but we, alas, must hasten ahead, for the path remains as long as it must also grow increasinly perilous.

Old Porch, for certain, had not noted Russel's profound verbal victory. Instead he stopped tryin to get loose his belt, and though Egan still gripped his left arm hard, he managed nonetheless to throw out his right hand, not missin neither, backhandin Russel so hard across the face that the boy was both stunned and knocked sideways, and even then still knocked around in a half circle, his feet tanglin on the way around, stayin tangled on the way down, his hands not quick enuf to break much of the fall, his forehead thumpin first the wall before his head twisted aside some as the rest of him toppled to the floor.

Not that that held back Old Porch any. *You let that dirty squaw—* And for clarity's sake here, Landry Gatestone made no claim to any heritage derivin her from these arid lands. *You let that dirty Gatestone squaw get her hands on my gun?!* Old Porch screamed, and kept screamin, finally gettin free of Egan, gettin free his belt too, doublin it over, and kurbashin hard as he could the back side of that simple boy, over and over, again and again, while Egan, so close by, who could've with but hardly a gesture eased that whippin, stood by doin nothin except noddin like so at each blow his dad delivered, Kelly followin Egan's example with similar nods, though he quick directed his eyes to take up interest in the furniture, while Billings watched on, laughin even, quietly but a laugh nonetheless at the sideways cruelty that weren't anythin new for him.

Russel fer his part had tried his best to handle the sudden stabs and flashes of pain. *Gosh* gurglin in his head. *Ow this hurts* and *I'm fine* also up in there, along with the fleetin peace of him and Cavalry. But all he managed to actually say aloud was *Momma?*

Who saw the blood first is unknown. It had spread far enuf to reach Egan's boots. Old Porch was so blind with rage, and high on it too, that he didn't even notice the wetness soakin up around his planted right knee. Likely, it was the stillness of the boy, the absent keenin and general flailins so typical of Russel durin previous beatins, that arrested Porch's belt, that pause drawin Egan's attention away from his own satisfaction with the scene to what was now both too quickly and too slowly unfoldin before them, that viscous fluid of iron and mystery spreadin out on the floor, startin to soak the fringe of that gold-and-ruby Sarouk rug.

Now all of a sudden it was Old Porch's turn to keen and wail as he flopped over his youngest son to find his neck, right above the collarbone on the right side, pierced deep by the base of that drinkin glass earlier thrown and shattered by Old Porch hisself.

As if to refuse the vision, Old Porch at once tore loose that piece of glass lodged in Russel's jugular. Russel's heart weren't gone yet. No surprise, it turned out that boy had a great big heart, and it was still doin its darndest to keep Russel alive, but the removal of them thick spires of crystal released his last chance, sprayin his father's face with a red splatter before returnin to a dark oozin seep.

Over the years, emergency room veterans have slowly aligned on the point that Russel might well have survived if that glass had stayed put, provided the boy was gotten to a hospital quick enuf, which could've happened, there bein a good one nearby, Utah Valley Hospital not but fifteen minutes away. Quibbles arise over whether or not Russel would've come out of it without brain damage, but the main point is still little contested: more than the awful impalement Russel suffered, it was the removal that had done the killin. *Here too,* Mr. Caracy Rudder, a composition teacher at Orvop High, would say without explanation, *is our Echepolos.* What Ms. Meredith Melson, Orvop High's AP English teacher, had no trouble followin, though she begged to differ: *Rather Russel Porch is our Elephenor;* Echepolos bein the first warrior to die in the war on Troy and a Trojan, with Elephenor bein the second to die and the first Greek, if we're foolish enuf to not count Iphigenia.

Regardless, Kelly on beholdin the state of his little brother, along with all the blood on Old Porch, at least made it to the kitchen sink before vomitin.

Billings didn't move, but he did stop laughin, even if a hint of a smile still haunted the creases of his mouth.

Egan was likewise froze as he beheld his daddy now weepin and beatin his head against his poor child's chest.

Bein as tight-knit as them Porches were, it would stand to reason that neither Egan nor Kelly would've yet started to formulate a plan on what to do next, what with Kelly throwin up a second time and Egan still froze before that slowly expandin pool of blood.

In fact it was Billings who charged suddenly into action, grabbin up towels from the bathroom and linen closet, layin them down to limit the spread of blood, plus pullin away the Sarouk rug and rollin that up. He already knew it was destined for fire. And then just as fast haulin out Pine-Sol, Lysol, and bleach.

By this point, Egan should've moved or at least said somethin, but he was still froze in disbelief, shocked no doubt by the vengeful plea-sure he'd felt just moments ago, what still had yet to abate, what was still dancin in his chest, right alongside heartbreak.

Billings weren't beholden to any father and so could implement some damage control and furthermore demonstrate his alliance with whatever direction Old Porch would choose to pursue, while Egan and Kelly continued to demonstrate their helplessness before their crumpled and bawlin patriarch until he decided for them what was to come next. And decide Old Porch finally did, risin soon enuf to his feet, wipin away, or smearin at least, the red on his face along with any expression of grief.

Get your horse out again, Eges, he snapped, Egan just as fast snappin to his senses, headin through the kitchen to the back door and out to the barn, if leavin behind a path of bloody footsteps. Old Porch next ordered Billings and Kelly to finish cleanin up, with as much bleach as they could find, *Bleach the whole house! And then bleach it a second time.* Old Porch gathered up the bloodiest towels then and piled them atop Russel, who he then carried outside into the indifferent night.

Like he'd done this before, Billings grabbed up garbage bags from under the kitchen sink. He also turned on the faucet to clear the drain of Kelly's vomit. The rolled-up rug required four bags. The towels that Old Porch hadn't taken filled another bag. Then Billings got back to the scrubbin and rinsin and, like Old Porch had ordered, bleachin every surface twice. Kelly finally got down on his knees too. The cleanin felt good to him as did not havin to say another word.

Billings, though, had noticed that where the rug had lain, the floor was lighter, but there was no cleanin away the patina of dirt and grime that had built up around it. While Kelly kept to washin the floor, and dryin it too, Billings went off to search Egan's home.

In the room with the gun cabinet he found another rug, what was also a Sarouk, both left behind by Egan's mother when she fled. This one, though, was darker and thicker, but Billings was pleased to see that it was bigger too than the first and would cover in excess time's signature of where the previous one had rested.

Out in the barn, Egan had resaddled and rebridled Cavalry. Then he and his dad had lifted Russel's body behind the pommel. They lowered his pale face toward the withers and did their best to get them stiffenin fingers to clench the reins and mane. Old Porch stood on an old mountin block, wringin out the bloody towels on his dead boy's arms, on the saddle, on Cavalry's neck and chest. He told Egan to give Billings the towels but leave everythin else as it was, the floor there bein lightly spattered with Russel's blood. Then Old Porch walked Cavalry outside to the driveway, keepin even with the horse's shoulders, with one hand on Russel, the other on the reins. He was pleased to see more blood was runnin naturally down the sides of the horse. It was some struggle to keep Russel from slidin off, but by the time they got to the front of the house, far from any street lamp and out of range of the barn's exterior lights, it didn't matter no more. Old Porch let the body fall where it might, and it thumped hard on the sidewalk.

Egan had rejoined his dad by then.

Old Porch tossed him Cavalry's reins. *Put him in the barn, but don't touch him otherwise.*

You want me to leave his bridle on?

You can halter him, but stand him where there's already blood on the floor. Understand?

Egan didn't understand but he did as he was told.

Old Porch then picked up his boy's body and carried him toward the stoop, right between them two white-faced lawn jockeys Egan loved so much, where he laid Russel in the rain, not carin no more if anyone saw, howlin like the crazed dog he was, though not a soul that night in that distant neighborhood saw a thing, or at least they minded their business enuf to convince History itself that they was all asleep.

Kelly opened the front door then. He had some ideas about leavin, about sayin he'd never been there at all. One look at Kelly's bloody knees got Old Porch orderin him down beside Russel. When Kelly hesitated, Old Porch rose up and, grabbin him by the back of his neck, near threw him down.

You keep pumpin his chest until I tell you to stop. And give him air too.

You want me to do CPR?

Until I tell you to stop.

Kelly looked about ready to puke a third time.

Don't even.

Not Medusa herself with a head of writhin serpents could've froze a man faster than Old Porch did Kelly.

Inside, Old Porch saw with great satisfaction what a good job Billings had done with the cleanin, notin too the new carpet beneath the table where they'd played their cards.

Double-bag whatever you used to clean this up.

Already done it.

Old Porch was glad to see that he hadn't misjudged Billings. *Take it back to the slaughterhouse now and incinerate it. I sent you there to check on the locks. You left right after Riddle did.*

Why Old Porch so trusted Billings, we'll get to later. Fer now, suffice it to say, unlike Kelly and even the fearsome Egan, Old Porch could see that only Billings and hisself weren't overrun by these events. Their capacity for calculation remained undeterred by violence.

Old Porch then dragged hisself to the kitchen, where he set his forehead down on the counter, even closed his eyes, before startin to beat the blue ceramic tiles with his great scarred hands, slowly at first, then faster, soon cryin out loud, louder and louder, until his voice was comin out stripped and ragged, at which point he lifted his head and called the police.

It was 9:58 p.m.

This is Orwin Porch! he wailed when dispatch picked up. *They killt my boy! They stole my horses and they killt my boy!*

Chapter Four
"The Gate of the Mountain"

Upon seein that Russel was well on his way outta the canyon, Kalin quickly ducked back under the brush without givin Landry so much as a second look. He waded across the crick. It weren't yet of concern but the depth had started to trouble him. The risin water as well as the cold spoke of more storm beyond the one directly above. Big mountains can shrug off the biggest storms but they can also hold them close.

Back at the campsite, Kalin started to puzzle over Landry, who hadn't stopped clingin to his heels. She needed to get back on Jojo and across the crick fast. But now he had to also see that she got home safe. She was, after all, Tom's little sister.

She don't belong here, Tom said before Kalin could even start warmin his hands by the campfire.

Don't look at me, Kalin snapped. *I ain't arguin.*

I ain't lookin at you! Landry fired back. *But I'm plenty glad you ain't arguin. Figured fer sure you'd put up a fuss about me comin along.*

Kalin gave her a good look now. He didn't have no energy for a fuss. Not with everythin he had to redo: strike the campsite, repack, move in the dark, and resettle somewhere that he had no plan for.

Of course, Landry had no clue what lay ahead and so remained untolled by the cost of even this immediate future. Kalin's hands trembled some, and were it not for the meal he'd just ate, felt sure he'd've collapsed into a shiverin heap.

Ain't you gonna tell her to get back home? Tom demanded, his voice near shrill.

Kalin shook his head, which Landry mistook as an agreement that her company was now welcome. After that, he ignored both her and the ghost. He had no choice. He broke down the campsite and got to reoutfittin Mouse in the Decker packsaddle, somethin Mouse weren't too overjoyed about. Landry was plenty confused and expressed her objections but quieted when Kalin laid it out as plain as he could, how easy he was followed by both Russel and her and how he couldn't chance hangin out in the same spot no more with Russel headin back to his daddy and brothers.

They might accept that twenty you gave him—

Or they might not, Landry finished for him.

At the very least they could alert some park rangers just to trouble us.

Now you're thinkin like a Porch.

Landry helped cinch up the packsaddle. Kalin felt a heave come on in his chest about havin to figure out the various ropes, straps, and knots again, again in the dark, but he tried to put it away because, like he'd pretty much just told Landry, there weren't no choice. Landry at least could help keep Mouse settled while he went back and forth carryin the loads, like the sleepin bag, tarps, and the saddlebags repacked with cutlery and whatnot. So he was plenty surprised and half-grateful to find Landry had managed to secure the rest of the packsaddle on her own. Kalin could see she knew how to rope on the loads right and her knots were good. *This ain't my first rodeo, city boy,* she answered his approvin stare, sneerin even a bit too.

He saddled Navidad next but held off givin her the bit. He was only goin to lead them farther up the way. It was too dark and dangerous to ride. He gave their campsite a last survey, not likin one bit that him and Tom's plan was already changed, and that it were easily possible, likely probable, that he'd lose somethin along the way, and they would, though not that night.

Then he advised Landry that if he were her, he'd likely head back home while the water in the crick was still low enuf to easily cross. She didn't like that none.

I thought we agreed on no fuss.

Where I'm headin is as far aways from safe as you can get.

That don't scare me.

It should scare you. It scares me.

Kalin kicked out the fire then, and the dark fell around them fast, causin Kalin to question at once whether he should've just risked the night there and tried his best to break camp before the first mornin light. But as discussed he didn't court the favors of chance, and plus he weren't too keen on the thought of some park ranger or, worse, some of Russel's brothers sneakin up on them, just for the heckuva it, or maybe because they didn't like the bump Russel had gotten on his head, fixin to return the favor. Kalin didn't think this fear made much sense, but he still couldn't shake loose of the thought of bein fast asleep while folks he didn't know gathered around with sweaty palms grippin ax handles.

By the time he got movin, Tom was already mounted and headin in the direction Kalin had settled on, a narrow path he thought he could remember well enuf, what he seemed to recall led up to a higher ledge where they could lie low, also a mite closer to where they was headed. The trick was to navigate right the branches interferin with the trail, not to mention avoid slippin off into the dark that weren't yet so precipitous but still aswarm with thick roots and bristlin with sharp rocks, all of which could seriously wound if not break one of the horse's legs and even one of his own.

A few yards in, though, Kalin could see he'd already made a misjudgment and stopped to bit and rein up Navidad.

I thought you said it was too dangerous to ride? Landry squawked from behind. Like him, she'd been leadin Jojo on foot.

It is. Kalin sighed. *But it's more dangerous for the horses if I try to lead them both on foot.* Landry nodded. *Don't creep up on Mouse too close. He don't know your Jojo, and he'll likely give a kick if just to show you he's Mouse.*

Landry snorted. *I don't see no red bow on his tail.*

I weren't plannin on no company.

You know it's a danged dumb idea, ridin like this?

I ain't arguin.

Kalin at least could see Tom up ahead by a few lengths, like a lost sliver of moonlight, pickin his way up the steep slicks amidst jagged stone. He was both a comfort and curse. Somethin to see, to follow, no question that much helped calm the risin vertigo Kalin kept tryin to refuse, his better senses remindin him that there weren't no cliffs near about, just a path of poor footin with a tangled slope above and below. Seein Tom not fall away helped grant some ease to his breathin. The curse was that Tom's glimmerin presence was only Tom, just for Kalin to behold, but beyond that Tom shed no light on anythin else around him.

And then, as if knowin already Kalin's mind and the misery of his optic desires, Tom reached down and grabbed hold of the charred branch reposin in that scabbard of black leather tooled by shadow itself. Except what he drew forth weren't no gnarled branch but a firebrand, at once aflame, the crown an awful boil of oranges and yellows and passin reds, slaggin off surges of black too, which, in their skyward flutterins, seemed darker than any black bird, darker than even the surroundin night and rain.

Kalin even had to squint his eyes some for the brightness, even as Tom's eidolon form now grew darker, the silhouette of his black hat even blacker, while his horse seemed the opposite, lighter, more a creature of ash danced with fleetin dabs of ocherous fire.

How can you even see a thing? Landry cried out from behind.

I can't.

Didn't you bring a flashlight?

Nope.

This ain't just dang dumb, this is dang crazy.

You can turn back.

And it weren't such bad advice. Charlie Burton, born in Orvop, a basketball star at Orvop High and Isatch U with dreams of a career in sports, who even played once with Byron Scott from Ogden and said hello to Jerry Buss once, only to wind up sellin cars near State Street, only to wind up years later with a career in sports after all, up in Salt

Lake City, management side this time, well, he would always have a great fondness for this moment: *The way I see it, especially when it concerns that moment when your journey really starts, those who haven't already prepared their heart for what's ahead, what it's gonna take, shouldn't even start out. You gotta prepare your heart. The heart is where what matters starts. The rest is aftermath.*

Of course, to hear Kalin suggest she turn back, why that only made Landry suck on her teeth some, and even if she did consider turnin back, however briefly, she also acknowledged that the narrowness of the path, alternately enclosed by rock or brush, would make just turnin around plenty unpleasant, with findin her way back even more unpleasant, and so she continued trudgin ahead. She'd already resolved to reconsider this outin when a wide space appeared where she could safely manage an about-face, but when the rocks finally did fall away some and the brush withdrew, Landry saw she'd never had no real intention of turnin back. She'd just been foolin herself so to keep goin. She'd come to accept that Kalin, who surely couldn't see any better than her, and in fact her eyesight was a bit better than his, still did somehow seem to know where he was headin.

Tom's firebrand had changed things fer sure, but not in the way we might expect. Kalin couldn't see the path no better. That's not how that ghostly apparition of light worked. What it did do was cast into bein the presence of their surroundins, maybe the memory of it too, but not in the way a livin eye and mind find lines and curves, edges and slopes, shades and hues, through which to achieve a recognition of shapes and patterns and so on, but rather how the dead grant no distinction to neither time nor particulars and therefore preference no arrangements once so utile to survival not to mention comprehension.

As far as the firebrand could illuminate, or maybe deluminate is a better way to put it, seein as how it also got rid of all the light that insists upon sayin it is the heart of the matter, within that eerie glow cast back about as far as Landry and Jojo, maybe a little farther, and the same distance as well ahead, to say nothin of above or below, Kalin could now behold beyond those interposed crowds of marcescent branches a great velocity no longer sustained or even ordained by roots, be they from trees or mountains, and in motion with a great emptiness, shudderin him with the realization that if such a dance were to pause fer but even a heartbeat, all would be lost, includin the emptiness itself. He, Mouse and Navidad, and Landry and Jojo too, and for certain Tom and his spectral charge, would just tumble away into an oblivion too great to name. But fortunately, it never did pause. And Kalin experienced no more vertiginous doubts either. Nor blindness.

Here was a new light, not at the expense of anythin else, no more substantial than a dream aroil with surfaces so labile, the sense of borders
and divisions vanished, until notions of place and time seemed no
more relevant than a wild breeze portendin a boundary.

Understandably more than a few have tried their hand at this
moment, be it with chalk, charcoal, pastels, watercolor, oils, saps, and
greases too dark to merely label as black. Almost invariably the pieces
bear the same title in whatever scrawl: *The Firebrand.*

Atticus Pattee, a CPA workin at Nu Skin Enterprises, would give
it a go one night with mostly oranges. It still struck his wife as a
nighttime ocean scene in which level meant aslant; that or Tom, Kalin,
Landry, and the horses were scalin the side of a wave so enormous, the
crest was beyond view, and that went for any trough as well. Breen
Lachance, a stenographer at the Orvop courthouse, would stick mostly
with red watercolors. *Sea of blood* was what her mother called it. Matt
Van Buren, the paint expert at the Lee Garvey Shop, would stick with
lemony and gold oils. It weren't no maritime vision either, and it didn't
look like night. The horses also seemed more like goats. Before she fled
to Canada in 1984, Traci Jarman, a stylist at the same salon where Lara,
Lindsey Holt's sister, practiced her tonsorial magic, would stick with
the obvious: blacks, and blacks from all kinds of materials, thick and
oily, dusty and gelid, usin tweezers too to layer in between the riotous
textures the tiniest specks of tinfoil. One of the few she showed it to,
the young man who loved her, though she thought he wanted somethin else, told her *it's like them horses are walkin on stars.*

Why'd you stop? Landry yelled up at Kalin.

This here's the Gate of the Mountain.

Tom had stopped too, that firebrand he held aloft at war with the
air, its strange brightness flickerin against the vertical slabs overhead,
where a jagged scar of ebon rock seemed to rise all the way to the
top of Squaw Peak itself, resemblin what lightnin might look like if it
burnt itself up and yet could still achieve some form of materiality; the
same bein true on the opposite canyon wall, though that sight was too
far away and too dark to see now.

Kalin hadn't known what to expect on this night, especially with
the blindin alterity of Tom's strange beacon. A difference perhaps?
But there weren't no differance. Rain fell the same way before reachin
this geological demarcation like it was fallin now beyond it. And
when Kalin shuddered, it weren't because of that wronged woman
of yore or other nearby silvicolous sprites pacin the limits of their
lore but because no line of significance ever dilineates the immediate announcement of change. The consequences that define the limit

come later. You step across that threshold like it ain't nothin. And it ain't nothin. But then the back of your neck crawls, because what haunts you now, and hunts you too, is the difference you never can quite make out. Your head will say it's all the same, nothin's changed, but your heart warns you otherwise.

You scared the Indian is waitin for you? Landry cackled.

Maybe she's waitin for you, Kalin shot back.

Let me at her! Landry cackled again. Kalin admired that even in such dark and sluicin wet the girl could still find some fun. Maybe she was right too, to keep findin fun in all of it. As Martha Dagget, who was from Spanish Fork with a hard road ahead of her, who once her dose of youth was spent would find herself too often sleepin on sidewalks countin the cracks, countin the folks walkin by, countin pretty much anythin anywhere, includin them darned gates, Martha Dagget, as if the rapture was nearly upon her, and maybe for her it had been, would on more than one occasion cry out how in no time these young riders upon their ageless horses had already passed through half the gates: *Hallelujah! Hallelujah! Four gates done with! Just like that! One and two at the Porch paddocks, the third one bein the official Isatch Canyon gate, and the fourth one bein the Gate of the Mountain. Only five left!* Which Martha knew full well weren't gonna get put behind near so quick. Not that any of our travelers, and that's includin Tom, were countin gates.

As they passed by that scar of stone, Landry marveled not at what she was finally seein, if it was what she was seein, but at what Kalin had somehow knowd to find.

How are you even makin your way? she demanded then, even as she slapped her small palm upon the rock's slick and perversely dark surface, yankin it back a breath later like if she'd left it there but one second more the mountain might've swallowed her whole. *Unless you're just foolin me, unless you're just as lost as me, makin this up as we go along.*

That was the easiest thing to believe, that Kalin was just makin it up as he went along, but it weren't exactly true.

As if in a dream we are certain we will never forget until we awake only to forget the dream at once only to recall it hours later, the path they now traveled had returned to him. *Clop-Clop-clip-Clop.* Or better, Kalin's memory of a route akin to the path they traveled now returned to him, risin up with improved definition. *Clop-Clop-clip-Clop.* Not that that should be too surprisin: he and Tom had at one time or another passed this way before. Kalin and Navidad easily knew by heart the feel of at least similar bends and jostles. And sure enuf, they managed adequately in the subsequent ravine to scamander up several inconstant switchbacks that soon, by the mildest diagonal ascent they'd encountered yet, delivered them onto a large nearly level traversal of rock, hardly a plateau but somethin a good deal more substantial than a ledge, wide enuf where they could ride side by side, though they still kept to single file, closer to the risin slope on their left, marked mostly by broken stone overgrown with lichen and in some places moss.

Not long afterward, these noctivagant numskulls passed between a stranded grove of old oaks and from there somehow managed their way down a brush-tormented declivity shielded by more Gambel oaks and Douglas firs, an easy-enuf path that finally disgorged them before a wide ring of flat boulders, enclosin what at first glance looked to be the entrance to an enormous cave but proved only a massive indentation or alcove in the high cliff walls overhangin this retreat. The ground was flat there and mostly dry, and Landry whooped at the sight of such a peaceful refuge from both slope and storm.

Tom returned the firebrand to its scabbard, with that peculiar light at once doused from perception, somehow smokelessly reconsumed. Kalin recognized the area at once, of course. He and Tom had enjoyed several lunches here in bright summer sun. At night, though, it was somethin else. The darkness and now the stillness unnerved him more than even Tom's ghostly light, and where he should've felt assured by the solidity of it all, the familiarity, and at least rid hisself of the tumblin visions that would've accompanied anyone brave or stupid enuf to dare climb a mountainside like this at nighttime, especially on a horse, even by way of so mellow a trail as this one had turned out to be, Kalin's head only gathered up more dizziness; though to be fair it was also a strange dizziness, more disconcerted than vertiginous, like how you might feel upon learnin, say, that a friend you've trusted for a long time is really a liar, not necessarily a mean one but with no regard for how events proceed from others, and yet even so you still continue to preserve the friendship, one you know now will never honor the truth, even if you keep wishin, oh how you wish it, that your friend's version might prove the truer one after all.

The feelin did seem to pass some once Kalin got around to makin a fire, usin for the first time one of the six tea candles he'd brung along for just such difficult nights. Much to his dissatisfaction, though, he found hisself forced to use a second candle before at last the scraps he'd gathered together began to smoke and bright.

This time Kalin made sure to build his fire behind a set of rocks near tall as the horses, with any illumination that might dare climb higher captivated by still taller overarchin crags and rocky sentinels, betrayin beyond such petrified bafflements no sign of their glowin presence except for the smoke, which the storm quickly consumed.

As Kalin knew to expect, sufficient scrap wood waited in the recess. The larger pieces he scavenged nearby, though plenty wet, would catch just fine once the coals got their heat up. No question the smell of that burn, along with the emergin glow and warmth, especially as the warmth rebounded off the curved walls before which he'd centered the fire, commanded immediate comfort. The light itself, though, oranges and yellows desperate before their inevitable impermanence, especially in the way they flickered, throwin about baleful shadows, seemed to unsettle the rocks themselves.

Landry, seekin to lend a hand, began to inspect ignitable offerins of yet another threshold they would have to cross come mornin. Kalin, however, quick called her off of what would've kept them warm for nights: dry as tinder, debarked by time, but somehow rendered immune to rot, what was ages old already, or so it seemed, as if brought down by some great flood, before there was even stories about floods, and thereafter bleached by sun and dry desert winds, until it seemed like a piece of ivory, an uprooted canine of the world itself, ungraven, unclaimed, unknown.

Kalin couldn't say why he regarded that easy source of timber as somethin set there for more than burnin. Landry didn't quibble with him either. She suddenly sensed it herself, and this new appraisal made her feel embrarrassed for her earlier efforts, though they weren't but moments old. Furthermore, in the presence of such ghostly remains, she felt diminished to the point of fear, but then before that fallen elm we are all of us diminished, no matter that it just lies there, wedged at an angle, to one side of their encampment, the perfect place to stand the horses for the night.

Landry untacked Jojo first, and then while she got to unburdenin Mouse, Kalin looked after Navidad. Just as he and Tom had done many times before, Kalin showed Landry which branches from this strange memory of arboreal greatness served best to tie off the lead ropes. Landry didn't voice an opinion to the contrary, seein to her satisfaction the sense of this arrangement, though she did manage to admit, in a somewhat surprised voice too, how appreciative she was that Kalin had managed to guide their willful companions through the dark and drownin drench without so much as a slip. *Tom would've been impressed too,* Landry added. In fact this comment so bemused her that she promptly produced from her pocket a small journal with thick cardboard covers and metal loops on the spine securin the pencil she used to scribble down her thoughts.

After that, and without another word, Kalin and Landry got to waterin their friends, brushin them out, after which they distributed another ration of trail mix that Kalin had carefully prepared for this journey. Likewise Tom brushed some his own horse, usin just the palm of his hand, though otherwise the strange lucent animal required no other ministrations, at ease at one end of the fallen tree, by the wild ball of bleached roots long ago bereft of any soil, now bindin the source of its history by way of air, if still clutchin too the occasional rocks to its heart. Kalin noticed how the other three horses seemed not to sense Tom's equine companion, though in Ash's presence, if it weren't a coincidence, they also seemed greatly calmed.

Kalin felt exhaustion catch up with him then, what even a few times stumbled him as he got to layin out their modest campsite. Tarps would've helped shield them more from the wind and lateral wet, but it was too much for him to figure out the necessary ropin. This mountain apse was dry enuf and Kalin needed sleep.

Instead he fed up the second fire of that night and got to preparin another round of cocoa. He had just finished fillin and settlin the kettle on the coals when he discovered that Landry had not only secured the driest place at the far wall, takin the sleepin bag along with the saddle pads, but was also already in the fit of some darned dream, legs kickin, lips twitchin into half smiles!

She can fall asleep quick as a flick of a whip, Tom muttered, shakin his head, stretchin out his legs beside the fire. *Done it her whole life. Don't wake her early though. She'll come at you worse than a rabid badger.*

Kalin took a moment then to study Tom's face. Even under the great brim of his ebon Stetson, his features did not shun the golden light. Death did not abide there. Maybe, sure, the shadows under his dear friend's eyes, as well as those creasin his brow, seemed blacker, deeper somehow, already of the night beyond him, threatenin the sudden arrival of an awful transparency, but the ruddy parts, his cheeks, lips, even his big ears, kept such extinguishin at bay. Tom's eyes too when they met Kalin's or sought out his little sister shined brighter than their fire was reflected in them, maybe brighter than a skyful of stars when there ain't no storm. Kalin had never beheld eyes so clear.

What are you doin here, Tom?

Tom laughed gently. *That's a darned good question. I figure them two is to blame.* And Tom's face lit up even more as he looked over at Navidad and Mouse, took in all the horses. Janice Brothwell, that server at the Coachman's Diner & Pancake House, would in 1986 try her best with an array of eyeliners and mascaras to get at the spirit of those four: the light-terminatin black of Navidad's coat; Mouse's burnt brown coat, lustrous and carmine; Jojo's blue; the golden ash coat of Tom's horse; and behind them all the enormous white trunk of that fallen elm.

Landry offered up then abrupt rupturin snorts. Tom laughed low and slow.

When did you know she was followin us? Kalin asked.

Only when Jojo drew near.

Kalin nodded.

Seems, though, that what's ahead ain't for her, Tom made clear.

Kalin nodded. *She also best get that—* Kalin hesitated before the chasm his speech would have to leap *—back to Old Porch.*

Tom required no clarifications. He understood what had hitched Kalin's voice. Landry, meanwhile, was now eruptin with a tumult of mumbles, like she was arguin with herself and winnin on both sides.

She'll leave at first light, Kalin continued. *I'll show her the easiest way. Far up as we've come, she won't have to cross the crick.*

That sure is the sensible plan, but my little sister don't concern herself much with sensible.

If she don't listen to me, then the mountain will tell her.

Kalin made to toss more scraps of wood on the fire but decided against it. The water was boilin. He spooned cocoa powder into his cup instead, and as the flames dimmed, with him and Tom darkenin too, Kalin finally sipped on the sweet and relaxed, maybe Tom too, chewin on a stem of dried grass he'd plucked from nowhere livin.

I don't belong here, Tom said then with a cold conviction that his prevailin smile made no sense of. *Like I'm stolen. I never felt so outta place. I can hardly remember anythin.*

Do you remember dyin?

Not a bit, Tom whispered, starin at the glowerin embers, an argillaceous pallor upon his cheeks. Kalin wondered how remembrance might transform him.

Nothin of the hospital room? Them cousins who brought you balloons? Your momma?

But Tom just kept shakin his head.

You even clear on the fact that you're dead?

They both laughed at that. And then Tom wrapped his arms around his knees, hunchin forward as if to study more closely the skein of black patternin the red coals, his face suddenly awash with infernal light.

What about your sis there? Kalin asked.

Landry?! Oh heck, I could never forget her. She's somethin else.

But nothin about the Crossin?

Tom shook his head.

Ain't that a hoot. I'm here because of you, and you got no clue.

Whereupon Tom's face began to redden, followed quick after by a sorta high-pitched wheezin sound, like how a balloon starts squeakin when the air's let out right, confusin Kalin at first until he caught sight of that big smile, a sure sign that an even bigger laugh was on the way, what finally knocked Tom over backwards, boots in the air, maybe exaggerated on purpose but heels still pointin skyward. What else could Kalin do but do as he'd always done and laugh along too? And it weren't even anythin laugh-worthy except Tom made it so.

What's so danged funny? Landry shouted, startled, shakin off her sleep but not in no happy way. Maybe she was a bit like a rabid badger.

Not that Kalin was able to stop laughin at once, truth bein that he didn't wanna stop. A good laugh is worth everythin.

You gone crazy? But her concerned look only prolonged Kalin's fit, which made Tom laugh even harder, clutchin his stomach, until Kalin was clutchin his tummy and rollin over backward too.

Landry was on her feet then and stompin over to Kalin like she meant to maul him or jump up and down on him, but that only got both Kalin and Tom goin for still another round. Of course Landry, bein Tom's sister, weren't exactly immune to such antics. She even laughed some herself, until as she was shakin her head in disapproval, she found her own laughter growin, and then they all had tears in their eyes and couldn't even say why fer sure.

I'm sorry, Kalin eventually managed to get out. *I'd got to thinkin how Tom would've seen how this first night unfolded, that Russel kid showin up, and then you knockin him off his horse, and us havin to break camp, find a second camp, and I just seen him laughin at us, and that got me laughin too.*

Okay, so you are crazy. But Landry didn't lose her smile neither.

Kalin sighed. *How are you even here?*

I never forgot what Tom said in the hospital about these horses. My momma swore it weren't nothin but Tom babblin. Just the same, I went by way of the paddocks as much as I could. Then this mornin I seen that them ponies was moved to Paddock B. I planned to tell you, but you weren't even in school. Shame on me for thinkin you weren't already at it, but good for me for actin so fast.

How do you figure?

You had a gun pointed at you, didn't you? And now you don't, and I'm even in possession of that gun. A rattler ain't a rattler even with a rattle if it ain't got no fangs.

That boy weren't no killer.

You're right there. But Russel's stupid and stupid kills more than killers do.

I'll give you that point.

Behind Landry, Tom had stood up, makin to dust hisself off, though he didn't have no dust upon him. Landry caught Kalin's glance and whipped around to find only the smokin fire.

Kalin took the opportunity to throw more branches in and blow up some flames.

So where is this crossin anyways? Landry asked.

Don't tell her, Tom said.

Do I look that dumb?

The jury is still out, Landry shot back. *How come he told you about it and not me? He told me everythin.*

He tell you about me and him ridin Navidad and Mouse all summer?

No.

Well then.

Well then, I'm comin with you to see it for myself.

That ain't a good idea.

They're my horses. I paid twenty dollars for them.

Then I guess I'm stealin them from you now.

Landry's eyes darted toward her saddlebag, where she'd stowed Old Porch's pistol. She couldn't help herself, though she didn't do so to dream of usin it but more to recall what a fool Russel had been for pointin it at Kalin, who hadn't seemed worried then and didn't seem worried now.

Take these horses where they need gettin to, she told him. *You're doin it for Tom.*

Tom grunted. *Finally, the girl gets one thing right.*

Come mornin you best take that—. Again Kalin stuttered some on the word and where his eyes went, where hers had just been, told Landry exactly what he was talkin about. *Take that thing back to Russel like you promised.*

I did make that promise, and I'll keep that promise, but I never said when.

I ain't the boss of you. Come along if you want. If you can keep up.

Keep up?! Never before had Kalin seen such a self-satisfied look. As smug as smug can get. Tom of course had seen it plenty of times. *Son, around here,* Landry said then, *there ain't no one faster on a horse than me. And on Jojo, I near fly.*

Tom chuckled plenty then, partly because it was amusin to hear his little sis address Kalin as *son* but also because he knew she weren't lyin. *She is plenty fast on Jojo. I'll give her that.*

Have it your way then, but this ain't that kinda ride, Kalin said, enfoldin hisself in the last remainin blanket spread alongside the fire, restin his head on his saddle, payin no mind that Landry, apparently blind to Kalin's miserable sleepin arrangement, had took not only all the sleepin gear but the best spot too. Not that Kalin minded so much.

Maybe fer a moment he even felt like Tom, pleased that his little sister, despite her guff, was keepin warm and safe.

Outside their little retreat the rain continued to fall, sometimes harder, sometimes harder still, but never stoppin, nor ever soft. The crick bed below, what they'd crossed hours ago, seemed now a chorus of churnin murmurs divulgin all the challenges and troubles that lay ahead. Not that the horses seemed concerned; they was fine and mostly dry and looked sleepy. Kalin was more than sleepy, but somethin about Tom now was givin him the nerves, enuf so that it was keepin at bay the exhaustion that should've dragged him fast into a dreamless collapse.

You see somethin? Landry couldn't see Tom, but she also weren't blind to the way Kalin kept starin so intently into space.

Kalin didn't answer. The fire had dimmed again, whatever risin smoke indiscernible against the drizzlin rain, its own racket loud enuf to drown out near anythin in that surroundin tomb of darkness except maybe the crick below.

You think somethin's comin for us now? Kalin eventually whispered to Tom after Landry had closed her eyes.

It does feel that way, Tom answered after chewin on the question a moment.

Is that what you're thinkin?! Landry asked, eyes open again, plenty alarmed too, which in turn alarmed even Tom, who never could stand seein his sister even a little distraught.

Kalin looked at her and smiled. *What I'm thinkin is that your momma's gonna go a little crazy if she finds out you ain't in your bed.*

More than a little crazy, Tom said.

What I'm thinkin is that if she don't figure it out tonight, if you leave early enuf tomorrow, you might just convince her how you got up to ride early, which likely won't spare you a scoldin but will spare her a heart attack. I'm figurin you ain't the type who makes her bed.

First thing you figured right, Landry said with a snort. *And I already done stuffed up some pillows under the sheets to set her heart at ease. You even know how to make a bed?*

Every mornin. Kalin suffered a pang then as his thoughts snagged up on that lump of an orange sofa where he slept, each night layin down two sheets and a blanket, each mornin foldin them back up. Sad how the ground here beat the way them old springs poked against his back like they was tryin to fly loose to other parts of the room, his momma's room, just a doorway away, her tryin to sleep there, so constantly tired and born down by the toilin she done week after week, month after month. And what for? So he could run off for this craziness?

143

Tom's downturned expression seemed to indicate he'd caught on to what Kalin meant to keep to hisself, what they was both glad to see this little firecracker of a girl had stayed clueless about.

Ain't you a peach, Landry scoffed.

I been called many a thing before but never a peach, Kalin said with a soft laugh. Like Tom, he was glad to see that Landry's alarm had passed.

Lucky you, Landry sneered, but there was a smile in there too, earnin a grin from her brother, Tom's eyes glintin bright at the sight of his little sister's unwaverin percocity.

Landry lowered her head back to her saddle, eyes at once caught in a futile fight with sleep, though she still fought. *If that Indian lady comes around, you make sure to wake me. I got some questions to ask before she gets to eatin on us or cursin on us or whatever it is she . . .* That last bit mumbled with only one eye open, and then Landry Gatestone was snorin.

Like I said, that girl sure can fall asleep fast.

Kalin set his head down too, like he might do the same, but it weren't no use; somethin kept at him, jitterin him from rest. He finally got up after a spell, this time to set the mug and the kettle in the rain, the pan too, as well as them canvas water bowls, before recheckin the horses. They helped soothe his nerves some, no question there, especially Navidad. When he got back, Tom weren't smilin, and his eyes seemed blacker than the charcoal smolderin before him.

Any sign of that Indian gal? Kalin asked.

Tom shook his head.

I guess that's reassurin, Kalin said, even if he already knew that the mainstay of his fears just came down to bein caught in a hard rain in the dead of night. He crouched down close to the fire, poked at it a bit, figurin the coals would hold til daybreak. And then the cold would wake him. Kalin was dead wrong. The cold did wake him, but well before dawn. Three times he got up to tend the fire. Fortunately, he'd set aside enuf tinder and thick branches to keep it goin right.

For everyone there is reserved a great journey.

That include the dead? Kalin asked his friend.

Especially the dead.

I'll remember that.

The journey don't count unless you finish it.

We'll finish it.

I'll remember that, Tom said.

Kalin was just resettlin hisself, and finally sensin too some notion of real sleep, when a great whisperin overhead suddenly arrested the lowerin over his eyes of his white Stetson.

You see that? Tom asked.

I do.

I guess that's reassurin. Tom didn't seem so sure.

I don't know if any of this is reassurin, I'm still seein you.

That's definitely reassurin. For you.

Both boys were focused on a great white owl that had just landed on one of the stout white branches juttin out from that fallen elm tree. Those great wings was hard to miss, though as it folded them up around itself, the owl near vanished, no longer a creature of itself but at once a thing of the wood, the stone, maybe even of the dead.

It was 11:11 p.m.

Regardless of how that owl was and wasn't there, Kalin felt glad for the company. For Landry too, the effect was pleasin, ceasin her frequent kicks and mumblins. She even let out a long easy sigh and finally embraced that place of quietude and stillness good rest requires. And while Kalin and Landry but barely knew one another, they did in that moment, if unbeknownst to each other, find shared satisfaction in sensin that they were no longer just in the company of themselves, or the beautiful horses, or, for Kalin, even those Fortean guests, because let's not forget Tom's horse, Ash, but watched over now by this feathered creature with big orange eyes, none rooted in the endurin machinations devised in the dim heads of men to achieve some perception of gain no matter how misframed, no matter the cost. Whose heart wouldn't be lifted up with the arrival of such a companion?

Tom, though, showed no sign of gladness.

While admittedly not entire, and this question of entirety will be touched on again later, at least in a way that addresses the spirit of all that must remain unfinished, and how that grand spectre of incompleteness must allways haunt every end, and the end after that, a warnin that death's truncatin powers should never be embraced too zealously; with that bein said there should nonetheless be little doubt that it is possible, and has been fairly achieved here, to surmise, conjure, re-create, at times put on display, and maybe even sing on about now and then, but mostly just relate a great deal of actions, words spoken, and even represent some the minds of both Kalin and Landry, plus plenty of others too, aided fer sure by what we best not confirm, not here, not just yet, achieved simply by continuin throughout to engage the depths of what rhymes the heart or chills it, whether, say, thanks to those long evenin discourses around a grill at Bill and Julie Evanston's house on Locust with the likes of Harmon Raster, Karen Morrell, and Terry and Jemma Bramall, or the more solemn meditations by the likes of Taft Mackey, Sheila Park, Mary Tarr, or Betsy Ballif, or even the shouts, cries of outrage, too many rants to count, most of them delivered ad hominem without purpose other than to vent a heart ill taken by bad rumorin, in short the worst kinda friends, and all of this hubbub thanks to devotees runnin the gamut from graduates of Orvop High, as well as dropouts, attendees too of Isatch University, to even many a congregant and elder from the Utah Valley Stake, be it the Oak Hills Ward, Grandview Ward, Sherwood Hills Ward, as well as the lakeside wards, and that's just fer starters, what don't even begin to address the more whimsical reflections, includin but not limited to, especially concernin that first night in Isatch Canyon, songs by Wilson Hannzer, fer example, on slide guitar and harmonica, who many years hence would sing so beautifully and plainly:

You called me from the night.
Well, here I am.
You called me to your side.
Well, here I am.

Nor should we fail to mention other works by the likes of Shawn Fentley on his beautiful guitar, Diane Hillam and Lamsyn Hayes providin both lyrics and vocals for many of these scenes, not forgettin Ruddy Hal who always had a great deal to say about the Gate of the Mountain and who over the years would share his bounty with the likes of Sharlene Kizis, Andrea Gunther, Sergio Gutierrez, Abel Ferry, and even Hal Kopeck; all of which is further supplemented by reasonable revitalization with a nod, why not?, to other wordly inspirations and knowins, thus providin ample enuf basis for all the insights and viewpoints of folks portrayed here.

Except, that is, for Tom.

His thoughts, the angles of his methods, and his unspoken opinions refuse even the most reckless speculations. To even try is to too quickly descend into shadows too cold and impossibly deep to ever ascertain some comfortin limit. The adiaphanous inscape of his reasonin, the Titanism of his mind, if what he possessed could even be called a mind, lies forever beyond our reach, opaque, cryptic, shadow-resins castin still darker shadows, which fer sure Kalin understood, the way a young'un on a bright, swelterin summer day dives from a floatin raft anchored to the bottom of a lake, determined to reach that bottom, or go as deep as that big breath will hold her, and so descends through the clear and clement top water only to find too soon the light falterin and the water coolin and then some strokes later abruptly reachin a layer of iciness that stops her dead. She can't but barely thrust her hand in there, let alone her head, and still with enuf breath, with plenty to spare, but the cold reality is too much, and her joints grow thick, and she's frantic then with an about-face to return her, lest she drown on the spot, to the green, warm, and welcomin surface.

Or if that's too childish an example, especially when scuba gear is so readily available along with wet suits and dry suits to manage the temperatures and even submersibles to endure the pressures of the very bottom of any ocean, then journey a moment far from this blue-glazed orb, past the moon and our war-weary Mars, beyond our protective Jupiter and the rings of Saturn, the icy bleakness of Neptune, you in your endless encapsulation of breath, movin farther and farther from all you once cherished and took for granted, until you're passin beyond even Pluto and whatever else rubble drifts there in those far orbits still honorin the grip of our sun, a distant star at best by then, that orderin presence you must now abdicate and abandon once and for all, castin yourself into the arms of what you will never come close to knowin but which will hold you nonetheless and guide you for near forever, forever beyond your grasp, all the while the home you once knew, even the memory of it, will be dismantled and scattered upon the void.

That right there is the darkness of a ghost's mind. That there is Tom, darkness and distance incarnate, beholden to forces beyond the reach of calculation, not to mention speculation, the ne plus ultra past which all returns are rendered impossible. Or to put it more simply: to dare close enuf to know Tom's thoughts would be to lose irrevocably our own.

Either he goes or we go.

K alin pulled down snug the brim of his white Stetson, if just to shield his eyes from Tom's, still visible behind the smoke and whatever errant light dared flare across a surface that had no business bein there in the first place. As if sensin this trepidation, Tom turned away then, his profile no less mute and cold as the limestone that towered above them as he set to watchin again that owl, as if somethin more than a creature of pale imbricated feathers resided there.

Kalin couldn't say what unsettled him more: the now obvious deadness of his dear friend or that even in death the dead might still know fear.

Chapter Five
"Allison March"

For Allison Cassandra March cleanin up after the last shows at the Rome University Theaters 1 & 2 was the best part of the night. She adored the emptiness and the quiet. Even the routine. And, yeah, sure, Clyde Hill, the manager there, might come in and get to talkin in a way that got her lookin hard at exit signs. Not that it fretted her too much. Over the years she'd handled plenty worse than Clyde, and maybe he was smart enuf to have figured that out by now, and except for when his pride or loneliness got the best of him, and maybe those two things can find their way to the same thing, and he would just have to have another go at her with some poor joke, what was really a command for her to laugh, which she never heeded, Allison could ease up and relax into this little bit of peace.

Sure, that peace did include draggin along a garbage bag, the thickest kind, enuf plys to hold easy the liquids, the half-drunk sodas that made a sound she didn't half mind when it all sloshed around with the uneaten popcorn, empty buckets, and candy boxes.

Some nights she started at the back, movin slow but deliberate, row after row to the front. Other nights she'd do it the other way around. The sticky floors bothered her some. At least moppin weren't her business. A crew came in after midnight to scrub and vacuum.

Tonight she'd started with the area beyond the front row, close enuf to see the stains on the screen where kids had thrown stuff over the years. At least she'd always assumed it was kids until she'd seen a grown man throw his Coke up there. At least she figured it was Coke by the darkness of the blemish. That was back in August. He was big enuf that no one did nothin. Not her. Fer sure not Clyde. What a thought, though, to throw a drink at a screen. What were people thinkin?

Allison couldn't rightly say what even she was thinkin. Not tonight. Her mind felt under assault, enuf so that as she walked from row to row, fillin her big bag with so much trash; about all she could focus on was to try and quiet it. *Please grant me the presence and compassion to be open to what is Good for me.* One slow syllable after another, paired with a breath, finally gettin them to lengthen, this breathin practice, which she'd been at for years now, havin taken over without much promptin. *Please grant me the strength and conviction to endure what is Good for me.* Deepenin her inhales, stretchin out her exhales, allowin the silence in that deserted place to take precedent, even findin silence beneath the low rasp of the ventilation system, if not quite beneath the chatter her thoughts seemed so determined to voice, what she kept tryin to refuse to voice, too awful to bear, worse to hear.

She'd already dropped a large cup into the bag only to see she'd missed completely. The brown stuff exploded on the floor, splatterin her black polyester pants, her white sneakers. The smell told her it weren't Coke either nor even Dr Pepper: tobacco spit, a full two hours' worth. Then Allison had gone and done it again. At least this time the mistake was Sprite, unless it was piss, though that weren't somethin you should ever come across here. Mostly the seats were filled with good church-goin folks but bein this was one of the only theaters in the area that showed R-rated movies, a rowdier bunch weren't out of the question. Tonight, though, had been quiet.

Allison returned to her boy, the singular source of meanin in her life, the only one who could make puttin up with spent chew on the floor and the likes of Clyde Hill worth it.

Where was her boy now? Would he be home before she got home? Their sofa abulge with his sleep? That was the evil hope that kept stabbin at her, like a hornet with a venom sac that don't know nothin about empty, because Allison knew he weren't comin home tonight.

Allison didn't fault Kalin's independence either. In fact she was proud of it. It kept them both goin. Without his fortitude and calm, where the heck would they be now? Her two credit cards were a heavy load, and them with interest rates over 18 percent. Kalin was left no choice but to prove hisself when she was at work. And prove hisself he had. He didn't get into trouble, so long as you don't count waverin grades, but that had always been the case.

She always knew movin around so much would take its toll. This time, though, she was determined to stay put, stick it out in Orvop, at least through his high schoolin. She dreamt of college for him, but based on last year's grades, just graduatin might prove an achievement. Allison knew Kalin had the smarts, but she also knew she'd already let that part of him down. The only hope she kept close company with was to see that she raised him to be good, and maybe in that way he'd find good people and a good job and a life Good makes possible.

What galled her now, though, wasn't just how he'd left but how he'd kept to hisself where he was goin. He'd said there weren't a girl, and she believed that. He'd sworn no guns and she believed that too. But not knowin what he had on his mind still left an impossible array of other bad choices she could too easily imagine. Had Kalin fallen in with drug users? Nothin about him, though, had seemed antsy for mischief. If anythin, he'd seemed almost resigned, takin so little with him too before ploddin out into the gray weather that had turned too quick for her likin to hard rain, wearin that slicker as well, the green one that had been his daddy's. Bad news from the start. Though what boy doesn't at some point in his life bear upon his back the burden of bad starts, of his father? As the teacher Mr. Caracy Rudder would put it: *Will Aeneas carry his pa all the way or bury him in Sicily in order to go on and found his empire?* Neither Allison nor Kalin knew much about Sicily and didn't think much of Rome. The one in Utah at least.

Allison wished there was a girl, and fer sure weren't thinkin none about the razin of Troy or the foundin of Rome, and the Carthage she knew was in New York, where she'd known some hardworkin folks who'd found themselves a good way of life, with family, and no thought of a funeral pyre. *I've had it up to here*, Mrs. Annserdodder would tell her colleague Mr. Caracy Rudder, who often dropped by her classroom, *with girls burnt to a crisp over some boy.*

Settle! the thump in Allison's heart might've declared to Kalin if he'd been there. *Put your heart before empire!* if Mrs. Annserdodder was translatin.

Because there was a girl, the wrong girl, and it was the thing Allison dreaded most, what alone could threaten to stop that thump in her chest, her dear Kalin makin a dumb choice on behalf of her, blamin hisself, intendin to relieve Allison of her tough row, doin somethin he imagined might take the hoe from her blistered hands, the worst thing she could imagine, him just runnin off, which is somethin she could understand too well, because she imagined doin it all the time.

But then Allison would remind herself how Kalin had assured her, *I'm comin back, Momma,* and she got to hopin again that he'd be there on the sofa when she unlocked the door tonight. Her little boy. Her little—

Mrs. March? Need a hand? Theater One's done. At least it weren't Clyde.

That's kind of you, Teri. I'm fine here. Do you wanna take the concession stand and I'll get to the lobby in a minute?

Teri Casper, already a senior at Orvop High, though she seemed fit for eighth grade, couldn't't've looked more pleased, what with her smile of wire, pigtails wilder than a broken hay bale, and a forehead sizzlin redder than a bad sunburn. Allison reckoned Teri spent every night soakin her pillow wet over that pimpled skin, never realizin how it kept the likes of Clyde from huffin and puffin on her doorstep.

Oh, Teri? Allison called out as the young girl headed back toward the double doors.

Yes, Mrs. March?

Have you seen this movie yet? Though she liked movies, Allison could think of nothin worse than havin to come here durin her time off.

Just parts. Too much shootin and killin fer me.

And the extraterrestrial one?

I've seen it twelve times!

One advantage, and really the only advantage of workin here, unless you're the kind who died for free popcorn, was gettin to see movies for nothin, which maybe made sense if you were young like Teri, she and her friends findin refuge or release in kids on bicycles flyin over the moon, what was playin in the bigger theater, Theater One. In that movie, as far as Allison could gather, at least someone was delivered homeward, somethin good was accomplished.

People sure seem to love this movie though, Allison shared. *That or the same ones keep comin back.*

Maybe I'll see it. Teri shrugged. *I loved him in* Rocky.

Allison understood the young girl's explanation, but it wasn't good enuf. Allison had lost patience for stories that devised excuses for violence. Where was the example Jesus set? The audience here was mostly Church folk too. It just wasn't that hard. *Clop-Clop-clip-Clop.* Enuf with the killin.

Maybe that was the thing about this picture here in Theater Two, what bits she'd caught up on the stained screen, what made her feel so wholly stripped of skin: a vet back from Vietnam come to revisit his awful lessons upon his own country. Kalin's daddy had felt pretty much the same way. Law of the jungle. Kill or be killt. Only the tough survive. All that bullcrap. He'd had her goin for a good while too, about his service in the Army. Later it was the Marines. Even the Air Force fer a spell. All of it just an excuse for anythin his hands or other parts of him did to her. He lied about near everythin to justify his actions, or sometimes just for the sake of lyin, until she stopped givin a darn about anythin he had to say and finally rustled off her boy.

Yet somethin about the parts of the movie she'd seen tonight weren't wrong either. Unlike the sweet movie next door, more black folk came to this one, and there weren't hardly any black folk in Orvop, or in Utah Valley for that matter. In fact it didn't get much whiter than Utah Valley. She wouldn't be surprised if the sum total of black folk had been here tonight, and by the way, that was near true, with Rodney Blake and his folks here for the early show, havin a good time too, all smiles beforehand, laughs while leavin too, though Allison had caught the looks on their faces durin the worst parts, and none of them had been smilin, and the boy's daddy had had tears on his cheek. Now whadya make of that? Allison didn't know except to guess. To some degree don't we all revisit the lessons we learned in the past upon the present? What does it matter, even if they really happened or not, if how they're applied makes things turn out okay? And that's what also kept worryin her: she doubted Kalin knew anythin about flyin bicycles.

Teri, you're a wonderful young lady, Allison said abruptly. *I just want you to know that. It's real nice workin with you.*

Allison's comment startled Teri, blushed her some too, at least, the girl's forehead got redder than a stop sign, though her eyes kept beamin green. She mumbled thanks to Allison and then got the heck outta there. In that way, she reminded Allison of her Kalin. Neither one of them suffered a compliment well. Maybe they were wise. Though one thing Allison knew with absolute certainty, and in the end, or at least one end, she turned out to be dead right too, the braces would be gone soon enuf from Teri's teeth along with the acne on her face, and whatever Teri did with a hairbrush would only further dazzle up all the prettiness she had in store for the world. The only question was whether Teri would be ready. She'd better get smart and fast too. Strength, as far as it meant what you weighed and what you could wield, didn't mean squat if it weren't more than what you was goin up against. Allison knew that all too well. It's what galled her most about the likes of Clyde Hill.

No question, Allison was smarter than him, quicker too, but she was also tiny. And by her boss's brute strength alone, which didn't even measure up to most of the men who came through here, he could without knowin it exert a threat she had to acknowledge as a factor in their every exchange.

Allison bent over for some wrappers when the double doors swung open again. Allison caught her breath, as if her thoughts had played prophet fer a moment, but it was only Teri again.

Mrs. March?

Yes, Teri?

I keep meanin to ask you somethin. This time Teri took a few more steps down the aisle.

Of course.

Teri's cheeks suddenly outreddened even her pimples, her voice tremblin like she was gonna ask Allison on a date. *It's about Kalin?*

Yes? Allison wondered if her own cheeks weren't burnin now.

I just wanted to know if he was okay?

How do you mean?

My Uncle Caleb's married to Mrs. Gatestone's sister. And he told me th'other day how broke up your son was at the funeral. It worried him. He wanted to know if Kalin was all right and I just didn't know how to answer.

Whose funeral is that? Allison was sure her face was burnin.

Teri's eyes widened in surprise. *Why Tom Gatestone's! About two weeks ago?*

Allison just stood there, the name hangin meaninless in the air.

Kalin and Tom were friends? Did you not know that? Are you okay, Mrs. March?

Allison had slumped onto the hard wooden arm of an aisle seat, her hand clutchin still harder that sticky spittle-wet sack of nothin.

Teri, would you think less of me if I told you I don't know any of my son's friends? Allison answered, decidin right then to take her defeat in the teeth and give this young girl whatever she might take from beholdin an older woman so in the dark about her only child that she didn't even know he was grievin. Maybe Teri would reveal herself as casually cruel, but then that would be up to Teri.

Teri, though, just smiled big as a Valentine's card. *Not at all, Mrs. March. I don't talk much about my friends with my momma either! I don't even know why I don't! I guess I just like to keep some for myself.* Teri even giggled. *Tom Gatestone was one of our school's most popular cowboys. FFA president, bullrider, all-around nuisance to anyone who wanted to keep a straight face. A real prankster but chivalrous too. I never heard of no one dislikin him. One of those guys who everyone just loves. Orvop took his dyin pretty hard.*

Cowboy?

Our school is pretty divided. There are the jocks, of course, the nerds, the drama kids. That sorta thing. And, of course, the cowboys.

What group are you in, Teri?

Oh, Mrs. March. I don't fit into any group. I work in a movie theater!

Allison smiled. Teri was just so sweet. *My son and this Tom were close?*

Teri nodded but then hesitated. *I never did see them together. At school. Or, actually, anywhere. Oh wait, that's not true. Kalin and Tom was in my home ec class, what had a whole mess of kids from sophomores on up. It's required. We mostly learned how to bake stuff.*

Home ec is a cookin class?

Hard to take seriously. Tom didn't. I mean, what kinda school grades your blueberry muffins? Tom laughed a lot. Your Kalin sat on the other side of the room in back, but he'd laugh too. I never seen him, though, say a word to Tom. I guess I just knew they was friends from my uncle.

You noticed Kalin?

How Teri froze up then! Took to scrutinizin the aisle carpet. *Aww, Mrs. March,* she finally said, still not lookin up. *You gotta know your boy is pretty dreamy, though that's a dumb word. Dreamy. Gosh.*

I kinda like dreamy. And, yes, Teri, I do.

He's so mysterious. All the girls can't keep their eyes off him.

Allison couldn't quite tamp down the wave of pride and happiness that rushed through her, enuf to return a smile to her own face.

What happened to Tom? Allison finally asked.

The girl raised her head then, even lookin disconcerted some over where her thoughts had just taken her. *Cancer. My uncle said he'd heard Kalin was there at the hospital the day Tom passed, even more broke up then than he was at the funeral.*

Now it was Allison's turn to feel broke up. What did it say about her that her only son hadn't mentioned a word about this friend, maybe a best friend, who'd just gone up and died? Maybe if she hadn't already lived near four decades and seen for herself how a person can break and break again, and keep breakin, and still keep puttin it all back together in order to try again, she might've crawled into that bloated garbage bag at her side and stayed there for good.

Thanks for askin about my son, Teri, Allison said instead. *And thanks too to your uncle for his concern. Kalin used to tell me everythin, especially when he was little. I liked to say he had the music of birds in his throat, but then as he grew up and grew bold, the birds all flew off.* Allison forced herself to stand. *It's a little humiliatin, knowin none of this about my son.*

At least now, out of this admission, Allison felt suddenly free to understand that Kalin's departure was somehow wrapped up in this news. And while it hardly resolved the question of where he'd gone and to what end, it did bring a brief spell of relief. Allison could've hugged Teri on the spot.

When did Tom pass?

Thursday, October seventh. I remember clearly because that's my sister Lorraine's birthday, and she was plenty down.

Allison hesitated then. She needed more, but she didn't know what more to ask or even say. *Was there anythin else?*

Teri shook her head. *Just wanted to check up on him.*

Kalin's a good boy.

Teri nodded and started to leave.

Teri?

Yes, Mrs. March? At least it was nice to see how thrilled Teri seemed to keep their talk goin.

Did Kalin come across, at school I mean, like a cowboy?

Teri laughed. *No, ma'am! Not a bit. Kids kinda teased him about his clothes. His shoes I think. I think they was kinda preppy?*

Allison drew a hard breath. She'd never given a thought that he could use an extra pair of shoes. It was always about keepin the car goin, and the insurance paid, and the fridge stocked, and his jeans, she'd made sure he had two pairs of them, and some nice slacks for that occasion that hadn't come up yet, all of which she'd picked up at the Desert Industries, a secondhand place that weren't so bad. He had boots for when the snow came, and he had them blue Top-Siders for school. Her stomach turned over how mean young folks can get about somethin so silly, not that Kalin had ever breathed a word.

Then how was it, would you say, that my son and this Tom were friends? I guess I'm unclear about that part.

It's a bit of a mystery to everyone, Mrs. March, but my uncle seems to think it was about horses.

This Tom knew somethin about horses?

Tom Gatestone?! Know somethin about horses? Why the Gatestones are practically made of horses!

At least now Allison had some inklin about what was goin on, *Clop-Clop-clip-Clop,* and the news of it hissed inside her like a hot iron dropped in snow, with Allison doubtin she had enuf snow for that kinda heat. *Don't you forget the curse, Kalin March: you but touch a gun and what you love most will forsake you for the rest of your life. Just like that.* Allison winced at the memory of how but hours ago she hadn't wished him well, hadn't told him how much she loved him, hadn't even hugged him for Pete's sake but instead reminded him of that curse, what he could not know the origin of because she'd made it up, out of thin air, like it was a real thing. She'd even treated it like it was a sacred thing, put there when he was not but ten, tellin him to keep it to hisself too, tellin him not another soul could ever know, meanin his daddy of course, but she hadn't needed to say that. The recollection appalled her, but Kalin's daddy, evil Connor Mayhew, had given her no choice when he'd shown her what else their boy could do at ten, *he's a natural!,* Allison answerin his awful grin with her own heart's silent resolve, knowin if nothin else that at least she'd put to work her own bleak magic, no less astonishin than if she'd've taken him down to the River Styx itself, waters more than one mother has visited with the love of her life, and on those shores, grippin him by the— Well, she didn't know how you hold a heart, but she held it anyways and in he went, in the name of keepin safe what Kalin loved more than anythin, fer sure more than his pappy, likely more than even her, maybe even more than life itself, his own too.

Does Kalin know somethin about horses? Teri asked then.

You could say so.

By the time Allison had finished cleanin Theater Two, despite the breathin exercises, her mind was racin more than ever, still tryin to figure out what she knew she could never figure out given the little she actually knew. She was even prayin fer real too, to the Lord above, that she was wrong and that there weren't no horses. Because as far as she was concerned, where horses were involved so somehow were guns.

The double doors swung open as Allison was tyin up the fourth and last garbage bag. She was glad. She liked Teri.

This time, though, it weren't Teri.

Clyde Hill stood there like he always done, smack dab in the way, like he was the door itself, and if you had to get by, it was either through him or by his grace.

Tonight he was grinnin too, with secret pleasures, his whole tongue, it seemed, wedged under his bottom lip, deep as his hands were in pockets.

What is it, Clyde? Allison snapped, sharper than she'd've liked, especially since it got Clyde blinkin, that snap revealin, and for the first time likely, a side to Allison March he had no clue about, what might make him from here on out uneasy in her presence. And there's nothin more dangerous than when a man who feels entitled to a vision of hisself suddenly grows uneasy.

Some folks here to see you.

Who? Allison weren't done snappin.

The police.

A llison still dragged the sloshin garbage bags through the lobby, two in each hand. She could only see one officer waitin by the ticket booth.

Beyond where Teri was sweepin the black-and-plum carpet waited the door that led to a long hallway leadin to the exit outta the mall, where the dumpsters stood. Allison could head out that way with an easy enuf just-a-minute excuse and then hightail it to her little Dodge Dart, and that would be that. Just take off. She saw it so clearly that fer a moment she felt confused to find herself still in the lobby. It would be so easy. Bye-bye, Orvop! Even if, at the same time, in that way that has no apparent visibility but still holds sway over impulse, Allison already knew too well that runnin no longer worked. She'd tried it so many times, her heart felt gray. Not that she could deny the feelin of her heart still thumpin to outrace the gray.

It was 11:43 p.m.

Allison dropped the garbage bags, and without meetin Teri's gaze, she already knew where Clyde's gaze was, what with him right behind her, she made a beeline for the ticket booth.

Both Marsha Naylor, a baker, and Lou Keele, a florist, would in 1985 admirably render this moment on thick sheets of cotton paper, watercolors for Marsha, colored pencil for Lou, each in their own way chartin the transformation from the Allison March inclined to flee to the Allison March tryin her darndest to stand tall, stand still, though as Marsha would put it: *Here she was still buckin hard out the gate.* These were also none other than the portraits that Shasta Roulette would see a bit of herself in. Cal Carneros too.

He in trouble? Allison barked out. Might as well get out in front of this.

Hello, ma'am. I'm Officer Poulter.

His daddy always swore to me that he were put on this earth for trouble, she said, again too loud, though for Allison fightin meant gettin loud first.

Are you Allison March? Mother of Kalin March?

I am. Is he in your custody? It was either odd or a classic case of denial, her bein so in the thrall of this maternal certainty, what most of the time weren't even right, how at this moment she never once considered that Kalin might be hurt.

No, ma'am. He's in Isatch Canyon right now. We'll get up there come mornin. What's he done?

He stolt some horses.

There it was. And it made some sense too. This business about a cowboy named Tom Gatestone. Her growin suspicions about horses bein involved. There it was. Plenty bad because it was a theft, but not bad as all that. Allison felt a deep breath come in and a deeper breath go out. *Please grant me the wit and intelligence to negotiate what is Good for me.* Her thoughts then turnin to money and the question of how all much this would cost. *Please grant me the grace and courage to love what is Good for me.* And then like that, the consequent anger that was already startin to singe her patience burnt away completely when Officer Poulter said what he said next. Allison saw his lips move. She even heard somethin of his tone. But that was it, somethin else startin to shake through her body.

She had to ask Officer Poulter to repeat hisself.

I said he killt a boy.

I don't think so.

Ma'am, we have multiple witnesses.

Multiple?

Officer Poulter nodded.

He shoot him right between the eyes? Allison weren't goin down without a fight.

No, ma'am. He cut his throat.

Officer Poulter was greener than spring onions. Allison could be grateful for that. Here was no NYPD. Nor anythin Chicago. Heck, Denver had sturdier stuff. Those pros gave nothin away.

Ha! A genuine laugh then. And loud enuf to startle Officer Poulter and get that blond moustache of his dancin. *I doubt that,* Allison added, her voice droppin to a surly hiss before throwin a glance at Teri, who was fer sure as enchanted by all this news as she was terrified by it, maybe even terrified of Allison now, seein how Kalin's mother had so quick become somethin brash and brawlin. Teri sure couldn't meet Allison's gaze, and Allison felt bad for her, or maybe pitied her, watchin the poor girl choose over a small bit of what real experience requires, blood up, fire in the eyes, the dust bunnies clottin up her broom.

I need to ask you some questions, Mrs. March, Officer Poulter continued. *Would that be okay?*

My boy's got plenty stupid he's fit yet to do, Allison answered, her voice levelin out some now, which was almost more alarmin than when she was volume-up. *But he didn't cut no boy's throat. And that means you got it wrong already. And that ain't good.*

Thursday

Chapter Six

"Aster Scree"

Dawn was still enwrapped in dark when once again the cold woke Kalin. He had to use his hands to wipe the water from his face. And that weren't nothin compared to the cold that had tormented him through the night, clawin up under his scrawny shoulder blades, between his ribs, with even more unforgivin stabs of iciness gettin after his neck. Fer a moment, Kalin wobbled so bad, he thought he might faint or at least upchuck, such was the sickness of this chill, until shakin took over in earnest, rattlin his teeth, which despite the general awfulness did seem to help some.

You're a pretty picture, Tom said with a grin. Kalin grinned back, or tried to grin, mighty glad for the sight of his friend, who hadn't moved much from his seat nor seemed much afflicted by the weather. And the rain sure hadn't abated much, though now it was mostly swirlin the air, a fine mist, which, for all its weightlessness, was almost worse, as it obeyed none of the boundaries of the various lees fortifyin their campsite.

Ain't you even a bit cold? Kalin asked through his chatters.

Not in that way.

Not wet neither. Kalin was already havin to wipe off a new film of damp upon his cheeks.

I guess there's a plus: the dead don't get wet.

You even sleep?

Not in that way.

Tom looked over at the fallen white tree. Kalin followed his friend's gaze and was surprised to find the white owl still there, still perched on the same branch, wings encirclin itself, and, like Tom, seeminly impervious to the elements, maybe even to color too.

What was left of the fire weren't much. Kalin used a stick to drag away the shroud of wet ash at the center of their firepit. Underneath was dry but still cold. Kalin started to seek out matches, likely set another candle to use, when Tom put a click in his cheek.

Stir it up some, he said, clickin again, even bendin forward, narrowin his bleak eyes, like beneath all that gray and uniform dust he could perceive somethin different.

Kalin heeded his friend and prodded more deeply the ashes until there emerged a whisper of smoke. Kalin fast dropped to his knees then, diggin out quick from the front pocket of his jeans, Levi 501s if you're curious, the tinder he'd guarded through the long night, still dry as them summer flowers Sister Avery keeps pressed between the pages of the one book she lives by but will never read, parts of, sure, but not straight through. Kalin centered this little birdless nest of leaves, branch, and lint in the palm of his right hand while with his left hand he dug on down through the ash, followin a vein of growin warmth, until he uncovered that first ember, blowin hard its orange into yellow, like a willin firefly, which he offered to his little fire-breedin nidus, what was soon set to smokin and, after more careful blowin, suddenly burstin into cracklin little wings of flame. What a beautiful sight that was! Hardly changed the temperature none, but just the promise of fire exorcised near immediately the shiverin that had up til then possessed poor Kalin.

Boilin water came next, then settin his pan to meltin one of them small pats of butter he'd absconded with from the Orvop High cafeteria, if such a small thing sandwiched between wax paper deserves even a whiff of larceny. Tom fer his part held his hands over the growin fire, noddin with approval.

That warm you up any? Kalin had to ask.

Tom shook his head. *But it's nice.*

I had too many dreams I can't remember now, but I know they weren't nice.

Then do like I'm doin and hold your hands like so. And so Kalin did like so, and it felt plenty good.

I don't think the dead can dream, Tom added.

There was one where I had wounds all over. It was awful. I don't even know how I knew this because my hands and legs and such looked fine. And then one by one these scars just started risin to the surface like dead fish in a lake.

I thought you said you couldn't remember any?

I just remembered. And this time when Kalin shuddered, it weren't from the cold.

When Landry began to stir, Kalin had just slid into the bub-blin butter two thin strips of gravlax and was now shakin up the eggs he'd brung in a jar, a dozen and some, with milk, pepper, and salt. Even a little nutmeg. It was a bit risky, seein how the jar was glass and a bad fall or even settin down a saddlebag wrong might bust it up into a big old mess. But what sustenance they'd grant him in the mornins made that risk seem worth it. The eggs was meant to last the whole journey, and there weren't near enuf for two, but seein as how Landry would only be around for this breakfast, Kalin decided to give her his share.

You cold? he asked when their eyes met. *I'll have coffee ready in a sec.*

Not cold at all! Landry declared, her eyes bright and excited. *Dry and snug! Slept like the dead! You?*

I slept like the dead too, Kalin answered, clenchin his teeth lest some of that chatterin return.

Like heck you did, Tom said, smilin, always smilin.

Kalin spooned out the instant coffee into the one mug, addin in next one creamer cup he'd got from the 7-Eleven on College Avenue and a careful teaspoon of sugar before pourin in the boilin water. Only then did he remember that folks in the Church don't drink coffee, and Landry was fer sure Church folk, her brother too, not that that had kept him from chewin tobacco or takin a pull now and then of somethin he called cough syrup. Tom did love his coffee too.

I'm sorry. Do you even drink coffee? Kalin asked her.

Gimme that! Landry said, and with such gusto and gratefulness that Kalin and Tom both grinned, watchin her hold the mug so carefully, savor the warmth. *Ha! So this is coffee! Ha! Who knew somethin that smelled so good could taste so bad!*

Tom shook his head. *The gall of this girl!*

Kalin measured out another teaspoon of coffee crystals into the bowl he'd filled with the hot water, though he added no creamer nor sugar, figurin to save the extras for when the goin got hard.

Landry didn't have much pleasant to say about havin fried cured fish for breakfast, but that didn't stop her from eatin both strips, gobblin up the eggs, and gulpin down the rest of her coffee too, once it was cool enuf to gulp. She acted insulted that the warmed bun he gave her had a quarter torn off.

You get these from the Orvop High cafeteria?

Kalin nodded.

Now ain't that a way to ruin such a passable meal, by bringin along some of the worst food ever served in all of creation. Not that that stopped her from stuffin the whole bun in her mouth, which also didn't stop her from still talkin, though at least it was pretty hard after that to understand a word she was sayin, and though it weren't silence, Kalin still cherished the peace that comes with the incomprehensible.

The kettle Kalin set on the wet ground to cool some while he turned to the little bit of nourishment he'd squandered for hisself, a bite of remainin egg, and that corner of bread, and Landry weren't wrong there, it was pretty terrible, but dabbin it in the salmon butter left in the pan helped. Kalin took the smallest bites he could manage and chewed as long as what was between his teeth still registered as food and not just wishful thinkin. What he swallowed only showed just how big the stone of hunger was in his guts. He hated bein that hungry. His face felt flush with anger, and sadness too, all scrambled up in a mess no feelin can make sense of. Or at least not a feelin Kalin could name. But he also recognized that if he couldn't handle this now, he didn't have a chance against what lay ahead. He had to focus on what needed doin and leave the feelins for some other time.

Plenty of folks, apart or together, have jawed their mind's worth on just this scene, includin the likes of Ben Carter, a seed purveyor up in Ogden, and Scott Potter, over in Vernon, servicin Xerox machines, not to mention Maureen Paulson and Tray Holmes, both workin in the same arts and craft store, Treemont's, in Bountiful. They would almost all agree that them eggs must've seemed extra yellow, extra creamy, the fried dill fish never so appetizin, and with the steam comin off the coffees and the fire spittin sparks, if this here weren't better, say, than a little July Fourth campground breakfast near Aspen Grove. However, what would get them all to quibblin was just how little food Kalin had brought for hisself. Though the reason was simple: the large part of his stores were for the horses, to make sure they was well tended throughout this ordeal, with plenty of feed and every necessary care at hand.

Got another bun? I'll take me more of these eggs too and some of that terrible fish. Landry even held out the pan lid she was usin as a plate, not even scraped clean, what little bit of egg remained off to one side waterin Kalin's mouth somethin bad. On the bright side, Kalin weren't so sure he'd ever beheld such glee. Tom fell over on his side, wheezin with laughter.

Your momma can get you a second breakfast once you're home, Kalin answered with a smile.

Why I already told you: I ain't goin home! Boy was she fast to fire, like steel to flint to gasoline.

I wouldn't've fed her a thing, Tom said, rightin hisself again, wipin the teary mirth from his eyes.

That ain't true, Kalin said to him.

What ain't true? That I ain't goin home? Landry was only gettin hotter, but she also looked confused.

A hungry dog moves along, Tom sighed. *A fed one finds a friend.*

Kalin sighed too, usin his fingers to sorta scoop up what was left of the fish grease in the pan. It was hot and burnt, but the dill still came through, and it was better than nothin. Pretty darned good if you don't mind suckin on your fingers some. That went for a slurp of coffee from the bowl, even if some dribbled down his chin.

You ever heard of manners? Landry demanded with a scowl. *You eat like a pig.*

The gall of this girl, Tom said again, this time with a low chuckle.

What even happened to your cheek?

Kalin hadn't given his right cheek any thought til then and now instinctively wiped at it with the back of his left hand, pleased at least to find no traces of blood.

Would you believe that while I was tackin up Navidad, I slipped and dragged that saddle right on top of me?

Heck yes I'd believe that! I'd assume it! Landry squealed, eyes plenty bright but still no match for her big smile that, for an instant there, almost equaled her brother's, when he was alive that is, easily bestin the smile of the Tom sittin so close now.

I landed on my butt too, Kalin added.

Landry laughed outright then.

It was good to hear her laugh.

Back when Kalin was just gettin the fire burnin again, before he'd even started messin with the teakettle, or for that matter even warmed hisself up any, he'd gone to the horses. They was fine, he was glad to see, the four of them snortin hellos as well as demonstratin, with a thump or two from a hoof, their impatience for somethin to eat, which Kalin heeded, palm-feedin Mouse, Navidad, and even Jojo. Tom's horse rewarded Kalin's offer with his backside, and a swish of his tail. Kalin made sure they got their fill of rainwater too, what he'd collected through the night. Last of all, he broke out small sheaves of hay for each. Kalin hadn't burdened Mouse too much with that necessity, knowin that higher up the wide meadows and shallow draws would offer plenty of grazin, which the extra oats and other mixes he'd keep in reserve would further supplement.

While they ate, Kalin brushed down their coats and combed their long manes with his hands. He lingered a bit more with Navidad, leanin against her. She couldn't free him from his chill, but she did give him strength. When he was beside her, Kalin felt the past weren't no place and the future weren't no hindrance. And then the cold became just cold. He stroked her neck. He tickled the whiskers on her chin. Her beautiful lashes framed a gaze that seemed to recognize his devotion or at bare minimum trusted him. Can any other look compare? Not if you're brave enuf to carry the responsibility. Many say they are; most aren't. Kalin weren't like most.

He didn't try to touch Tom's gray mount, but he did reapproach, and this time the great spectral horse did re-present his head, lowerin it some, like Kalin might just could've placed his hand upon that forehead, which Kalin nearly did, stoppin short, though, suddenly afraid to find he could feel such a creature and know hisself dead as well.

With their breakfast done, Kalin started doin the dishes by settin them out where it was rainiest. *They can soak a little first.* Then he got out the cardboard, duct tape, and knife. On the back of a tarp, he laid out strips of tape about a foot in length, the first two perpendicular to one another, then interweavin the subsequent strips until he had a square, which he peeled off the tarp, cuttin then a diagonal toward the center from each corner. Next he cut out a piece of thick cardboard that would fit within Mouse's horseshoe, Kalin centerin the duct tape square on the bottom of the hoof, Mouse's right fore goin first, then bringin the tape over the top and back, usin another strip to further secure it in place.

You can bet Landry was flummoxed! She kept demandin to know what nonsense this was about, complainin too that Mouse was already shoed and didn't need no makeshift boot. Kalin just worked on, one hoof after the next, though, soon enuf, when he turned back to start the whole process again, he discovered that Landry was already holdin up a duct-tape square, the first time without the corners cut, though by the third time she'd precut the cardboard too. Navidad's hooves were done in a flash.

Kalin had no intention of tapin up Jojo in this manner, not that Landry gave him the chance. She'd already produced from her saddle-bag two Easyboots, tossin one his way, sayin she always rode with them on hand, used to carry only one but learnt her lesson when Jojo pulled not one but two shoes on a long ride outside of St. George, forcin her to lead him eight miles back to the trailer, wrappin the rear hoof in her favorite jacket, with that big OHS badge on the left side for extra paddin, her older brother Evan's letterman jacket. Jojo's leg weren't tormented even one bit, but the jacket was holed through enuf to be deemed worthless by her distraught mother. Landry had mixed feelins about the end of the jacket but remained plenty pleased that Jojo had come out okay. Also, she and Evan hadn't had the easiest relationship.

He used to call me Laundry, Landry ended up tellin Kalin. *I didn't care for that one bit. Dirty Laundry when he wanted to get me good and riled up. Nothin riles me up more. Go ahead, call me Dirty Laundry, you'll see.*

I'd never call you that. And Kalin meant it, and true to his word, for so long as he lived, he never did call her any such thing.

Don't get me wrong. Evan weren't mean. He was the oldest of us Gatestones and carried a burden I think Tom never could understand.

Tom snorted at that declaration, then tilted his head sideways like somethin new and unexpected had suddenly appeared before his eyes. *Okay, maybe she is a little right about that.*

Or at least up until the night Evan died in that crash out near Lakeshore Drive, Landry continued. *I know you know about that. Racin Egan Porch who was twenty-two at the time. Evan was seventeen. Tom was only thirteen. Tom felt somethin different after Evan was gone.*

She's more than a little right about that.

Evan's goin was rough on all of us. And then two years later Daddy was gone. And it was just me and Tom. And then Tom— Landry shut up, and this time Kalin weren't glad to see Landry so silenced, but he admired her, beholdin how she withstood the thoughts he could pretty well imagine were avalanchin atop her, what she fought her way out of, that burial like a colt burstin back up after a bad tumble, shakin loose whatever dirt still clung to her coat, legs splayed somewhat but still ready for what comes next.

I wonder why he is now? Tom asked then. *I mean where.*

Kalin turned over the Easyboot one more time before handin it back to Landry. He knew them well. In their original plan Tom had suggested usin them. He'd assured Kalin that gettin together a dozen weren't gonna be a problem. Kalin figured Tom had included Landry's two in that count.

These, Kalin, are for when your horse loses a shoe, Landry told him, disappearin them into Jojo's saddlebag. *Not for when he's already got one.*

I'd say that was right . . . Kalin answered, his response both satisfyin her and bewilderin her, because she weren't so deaf to his unspoken *but,* which if nothin else taunted her with where he was goin, which of course irked her because she still had no clue where that could be.

Breakin camp took longer than Kalin had planned, and that bothered him plenty, especially since plannin really was what he'd done all night, step by step by step, and repeatin it too, over and over and over, until he was so tired, and still sleep wouldn't come, Kalin swearin he'd never fall asleep, and this while twistin in the wet, between the cold soakin through and the scaldin heat his jeans took in if he dared stay put too long in one position beside their fire.

By his reckonin, Kalin should've by now already booted and tacked up the horses. But it had taken much longer, from packin away their stores to tuckin away that jar of sacred eggs in the sleepin bag. Kalin was still in the midst of dumpin out the teakettle, scrapin out the pan and the dishware with a handful of gravel, and wipin that clean with a dish towel. On top of it, Landry got in the way of everythin, except where the tarps were concerned. Last night Kalin had ended up tyin up the smallest one to further shield her from the rain. Trouble was that the knots had taken in the wet in a way that made them near impossible to untie. They just refused to let go. Kalin in frustration near halved them with a knife, but Landry stopped him and a moment later had them undone and all the tarps folded.

Along with deserved castigations, Landry also assisted with the Decker packsaddle, helpin Kalin get the loads balanced on Mouse, the cinches right, fixin the breast collar too so it weren't so high to interfere with Mouse's breathin or too low to cause a sore on each point of the shoulders. Kalin could handle the ropes and the hitches, but Landry was faster and neater. In fact she was so good, she didn't need to say nothin, just whistled. Compared to Tom she whistled terrible. Compared to anyone really. But Kalin knew to bite his tongue.

Dawn had come and gone by the time Kalin had Navidad saddled up. Tom was already mounted, though when exactly he'd tacked up Ash was a mystery. Before Kalin could finish securin Navidad's halter-bridle, Landry was up and ready too. She'd bounced up on Jojo light as a grasshopper.

Good luck keepin up with me, she even dared to chide him.

Kalin found the stirrup slowly and pulled hisself up onto Navidad even slower. The cold was still in him, no doubt left there by the hunger that had faded some with the coffee but was now comin back. At least the rain had stopped, and patches of clear sky were startin to show.

Is she really as fast as she says she is? Kalin asked Tom in a whisper even though Landry was already way ahead, and ahead too with no clue where she was goin.

Faster.

Yeah well, fast don't handle where we're goin.

Just tell her to git on and head home.

Just like that, huh? Kalin shook his head. *Ain't you heard how many times I've told her to go home?* By this point Kalin was pretty much grumblin to hisself, and Tom was laughin because he could see Kalin had a point.

What's that? Landry yelled back. *I can't hear you because I'm already beatin you.* She was snickerin too.

Kalin sighed. *Where you're headed there ain't nothin but a long way to a dead end. I'm goin this way.*

Kalin eased Navidad down onto a small deer path crowded with the warnin spikes of prickly brush but which, like the paths they'd followed here last night, he knew well enuf to navigate fine. The one he'd chosen traversed along the canyon's north side, and, if divaricatin from what seemed the better route, soon descended enuf to avoid cliff walls that suddenly presented stubborn impasses to their left. It would also keep them well above the crick they could hear frothin below.

Kalin looked back to check on Mouse and was comforted to see he was comin along just fine. Landry had managed to get off the path she'd bounced ahead on and back on this one, though Landry weren't too pleased to find herself once again bringin up the rear. If the scowl on her face was any indication of the scowl workin through her thoughts, and you can bet it was, she was too caught up now in her own irateness to keep Jojo from crowdin Mouse from behind.

Watch yourself! Kalin tried to warn her.

Mouse's ear twitched once, and an instant later the blood bay was givin a good kick back, first with his left hoof and quicker still with his right. Snorted then too, a song of his own surliness at havin kicked twice and missed twice, if sweetened a bit for havin cause to kick in the first place. Jojo reacted swiftly, rearin up in the nick of time to keep clear of them shoed-menaces, though, in doin so, twistin off to the left or toward the climbin side of the hill, thrustin his chest into a nasty thicket of sharp branches, which should've spelled trouble if Landry hadn't handled Jojo perfectly. Instead of lettin him twist his way outta there, she backed him out and, upon returnin to the trail, preserved a greater distance between herself and the great Mouse, though her scowl sure worsened, and for a second Kalin thought he caught Jojo scowlin too. Weren't they a pair! Kalin smiled and caught that Tom was lookin back and smilin too, because who wouldn't have grinned at the sight of that ornery little wisp, so serious and malcontent, perched high and proud on that big beautiful blue horse, and all the while decked out in that ridiculously bright pink raincoat?

Anyway, that's how they rattled forward, unfocused, unsteady, broilin with annoyance, and in such stretched-out, ill-coordinated disarray that no soul witness to such a mess would have ever declaimed even a hint of expert presence there, not even worthy of them low and easy slopes, let alone the dangerous steeps waitin above; Kalin, Navidad, Mouse, Landry, Jojo, and Tom on his horse, leavin behind another gate, this one marked by the big fallen white elm.

It's fair to remark that nothin about that toppled testament to a different life and endurin death suggested a demarcation of transition and passage, but that's how it's come to be known as: the fifth gate.

Lydia Palmer, Orvop High graduate, eventually a gynecologist up near Layton, would create a diorama of their departure. She would swear that what she'd used for her tree was from thee Tree itself, a splinter of the original rood, as it were. She would call her delight *The Fifth*. Many believe it was Palmer too who was responsible for grantin that particular location its liminal potency through which these foolish travelers were destined to pass; though others still argue that the tree, although near horizontal, suggested more a barrier than a gate. As Jamie Jones, hisself a hospice nurse, would assert: *Didn't they just go around the thing?* But Tyson Chambers, employed at the Erville Family Mortuary in the early aughts, would object to Jones's assessment: *Seein as how the gate or the tree was already swung open like, they weren't goin around but through it.*

Likely of more significance was how, as soon as they'd got movin, that owl perched in her own white consonance had at last spread her wings wide and with two easy flaps vanished into the hard yellow light of mornin.

I guess they're comin with us, Tom said then.

Kalin didn't follow but didn't say nothin either. He was already retreatin to them circlin thoughts on how best to unburden Mouse and properly divide the supplies when the time came to carry the Decker packsaddle on his back, thoughts that were still occupyin him when Navidad abruptly stopped, Mouse and Jojo followin suit, leavin Kalin stunned before the ontic obstruction that faced him now.

See, the path was blocked by a toppled Gambel oak, piled up too with additional branches, brought down it seemed by a narrow slide of mud and rocks, days old at most.

Someone spritely like Landry could've slipped easily enuf between the gaps, Kalin too, but gettin the horses through was out of the question. Nor was clearin it an option. Worse still, Kalin had started to feel on the back of his neck time's warnin breath: he was takin too long.

Fortunately, another path opened up below this interposin mess, and Kalin could see an alternate way leadin down to the canyon floor. What he couldn't tell was whether they'd end up next to the crick or find themselves across the crick on the main Isatch Canyon trail, which, due to its windin nature, had seven bridges on the way to the terminus known as Yell Rock or Yell Rock Falls, where, when the melt-off is in full, a series of small cataracts will greet many a hot hiker, especially in the pit of summer, even if the water is icy enuf to near shake loose your teeth if it don't stop your heart first. Stewards of that dowsin experience will usually advise first-timers to cry out at once, and loud too, in order to keep hearts pumpin. Whether so instructed or not, most bathers find themselves yellin out just the same, terrifyin water shrews and bats, with this reaction supposedly bein how that barrier of boulders got its name.

Kalin urged Navidad down through the light brush, happy to see the thin branches along the way offerin little resistance, happier still to find this new path gettin wider and easier.

Yesterday, when Kalin had passed over First Bridge, that had put the crick on his right side. Crossin Bridge Two had put the crick back on the left side of the main trail. What Kalin was realizin now was that they must've passed Bridge Three last night, and along with this mornin's traverse, the crick would now be back on the right side of the main trail, meanin they no longer had the crick to act as a barrier and a blind of sorts. Furthermore, it meant that if they stayed on the main trail for the nearly two miles they still had left to cover, they'd not only be exposed but would have to cross back over the crick with no help from a bridge. And the water would be deeper further up.

Not that Kalin could see a choice. Within minutes they was off the hill and down in a narrow gully that at least offered plenty of canopy for cover. Kalin dismounted and then, without a word, handed Navidad's reins and Mouse's lead rope to Landry before creepin up to the main trail. Tom and Ash was already waitin there right smack-dab in the middle.

It was 7:58 a.m. October 28.

Kalin immediately surveyed both directions for any sign of vehicles.

You see anythin? Kalin even asked Tom.

Tom shook his head. *But you better hurry.*

Then you do see somethin?

I don't need to see it.

Neither of them liked returnin to the main trail. That had never been part of the plan. Of course Russel's appearance hadn't been part of the plan either, nor Landry taggin along. Also, Kalin and Tom had known that they'd be stealin Navidad and Mouse and so might suffer some Old Porch repercussions, even if in all likelihood such repercussions would amount to no more than a bad tantrum and maybe some gabblin on about legal actions. But Russel had queered those expectations, though not necessarily in a bad way, what with him outright sellin to Landry the horses and so negatin the matter of theft. In other words, there shouldn't've been nothin to worry about. But there was.

For one, Kalin still couldn't shake the spectral chill that had seemed to seize him as soon as Navidad and Mouse was free of Paddock B, and then Tom had appeared, and though Kalin welcomed the company, it didn't help none with this growin sense of dread. Had passin beyond the Gate of the Mountain already exacted some kind of price? Though truth be told, Kalin's jitters were diminished plenty by mornin comin on, what with the rain stopped and the air clean and frosty with pine, with now and then even great sheets of blue sky appearin overhead.

Back to the main road again?! Landry griped, at once interruptin Kalin's thoughts as she trotted up out of the gully with Navidad and Mouse, havin clearly lost patience with whatever reconnaisance Kalin was supposedly doin. *This best not be your idea of how to get me to head back home. I told you I ain't goin!*

Stubborn don't even begin to describe her, Tom said.

Kalin ignored Tom, though it took some doin, given what he was about to say, and maybe the right side of his face even flinched some, with both his eyes squintin up extra: *Landry, I ain't gonna trick you, and I ain't gonna stop you. I got enuf on my hands as it is. You can come along if you want, but only so far as you can handle yourself and the well-bein of that horse. I ain't here to tell you what you can or cannot do, but I ain't gonna carry you either. Deal?*

Goshdarn it, Kalin! Tom howled at once, spinnin around on that pale horse with a paler mane, as if that might stop Landry. *This ain't for her!*

Tom's little sister, however, couldn't've been more thrilled. *Deal!* she squealed back.

Kalin reached out to shake the hand she offered only to watch her yank it away at the last moment and cackle like a maniac, makin it clear that she sure was Tom's sister, even if it weren't clear what she meant.

At first, Kalin set the pace at a steady walk. And at first Landry didn't mind because she thought it was funny how Kalin would periodically look over his shoulder. She kept remindin him that the matter of the horses was settled and furthermore Russel weren't gonna babble nothin extra because she still had his daddy's gun, which he weren't gonna tell no one about, especially not Old Porch, lest Russel's hide get parted from the part that's under one's hide. *Clop-Clop-clip-Clop.* Kalin grunted his agreement but pointed out that Russel might still have told the story of the horses, and from his lips to more ears, a story like that might spread with unanticipated effects, especially if there were others who wouldn't be so sanguine about such venturings.

Like who? Landry demanded.

And here was Kalin's last and most pressin worry when it came down to the matter of pursuit: *Your momma for one.*

At least that stumped her fer a moment.

If she gets wind of where you've gone, the first thing she's gonna do is call up the park rangers and it won't be nothin for them to just drive up here, which both Kalin and Landry knew wouldn't take but an easy half hour.

Well then we best get movin was Landry's conclusion.

We are movin.

You call this movin?

Landry started ahead at a faster lope, but when she seen Kalin hadn't changed his pace none, she circled Jojo back around, now at a canter, until she was well behind Kalin and the horses, like she'd changed her mind and was headin back to her momma. Kalin weren't fooled though. Tom neither.

Get ready for the show, Tom even said.

Kalin didn't have to look over his shoulder. He could hear her slow Jojo, lope him around again, and this time really accelerate ahead. Kalin kept Navidad and Mouse walkin but pulled Mouse up close so the geldin's shoulders stayed even with Navidad's, now and then even rubbin against Kalin's right leg, in case Mouse wanted to join Landry's show; and fact is when Mouse did hear the hoofbeats gettin louder from behind, faster and faster too, even loaded up with the packsaddle like he was, join the show was exactly what Mouse tried to do.

Not that Landry noticed as she galloped by, standin tall in her stirrups, which really wasn't tall at all, her treatin the whole thing like it was still just one big game.

I thought you could ride? she hollered back.

And there was no denyin Landry could ride. Kalin saw it at once. And as a few will still go on about, Burnah King at Ralston's Cleaners in Rome and Grace Snyder at Hardfelt Landscapin in Orvop, both sayin as much to Claudia Bellinharp, among others, this here was a tellin moment, especially when it came to, as Grace would put it to Burnah, *them more severe choices and chances taken later on.* Landry was puttin on display her absolute ease with Jojo, but maybe more importantly, Jojo was demonstratin the same comfort. Whatever tack and bit was on him were but for show. Whatever weight was in them stirrups was for show too.

Tell her not to go so fast, Tom barked at Kalin then.

Without thinkin it through, Kalin obliged: *Slow up!*

I ain't even gettin started! Landry squealed back, and then without no wick of a lash or even a nudge from her heel, in fact all that tiny girl had to do was lean forward, hands light as humminbirds, stirrups fallin away, because she was only playin, and showin off besides, and anyways her knees might as well have been riveted to that seat jockey, fused to Jojo's scapulae, part of his formidable skeletal dimensions extendin down to the pedal bones themselves, and we're not even talkin about the big heart they was likely sharin too; they shot forward like creatures untethered from the earth.

No question Kalin recognized this easy sureness. You would too if attendin some equine spectacle, say in 1941, when you might behold, say, Lucyle Richards, a Cowgirl Hall of Fame honoree, ridin not the saddle but the belly of her horse, Chief Geronimo! That's right: ridin underneath the horse, though maybe you've already seen that picture, and if not you might even think to search around for it, but hold on a second too, because what mattered ain't in any of the pictures; it's in how Lucyle Richards moves, that's where the ease is revealed along with all its troublin consequences; because, see, Lucyle makes it look so darn matter-a-fact that we all feel we might just go and do the same thing, or at the very least think there's nothin so unusual about some lady ridin the belly underneath a horse and at a full gallop.

Not that little Landry was anywhere near upside down, nor doin anythin that came close to acrobatic, and even when she did lean forward, and Jojo took off, and his gallop was still only a hitch faster than a lazy canter, there followed them a gatherin of thunder, like they was already part of the great sky, and Kalin saw in a flash how Landry, if she'd wanted to, could've been upside down as well, or maybe standin on the saddle, maybe even standin on one leg. Not that Kalin was actually thinkin any of this, not exactly. He was just made happy to see how well Landry and Jojo moved together. Tom was grinnin too. It was beautiful, just plain joy to witness such skill and playfulness, what quiet care and quieter discipline will over the years reveal in a way that only the similarly talented and devoted are able to recognize, because when it's done right, it never looks like much, heck, it looks like nothin, but you still can't help smilin.

Fer his part, Tom had pulled back as if to check Ash lest they too fall for Landry's taunts. Kalin had also had to gather up Navidad, who, at the sound and sight of Jojo, had begun bouncin up and down on her front legs, tossin her head, whickerin gentle to make her point, waitin for the signal to barrel ahead. But Kalin kept her to a walk with Mouse's shoulder against his leg, right where he could feel him, though Mouse had already swung his rear legs wide until he was near movin sideways, like maybe he was gonna run this race like that, backwards if he had to. Kalin laughed, shakin his head some too, always amazed and warmed by Mouse's determination to go about livin his way and only his way. Kalin loved that blood bay all the more, even as he let Navidad charge some ahead and drive Mouse back to straight. And all this right as they crossed over Bridge Four.

Dagnabbit, Mouse! Kalin cried out a moment later, when this time the geldin, anythin but done with this latest bout of orneriness, decided he didn't care much for Kalin's decision-makin and, instead of just keepin straight or swingin wide again, caught up with Navidad and drove his shoulder hard against hers. What else could Kalin do? He just let the reins flow through his fingers to grant Navidad her bite, and she didn't miss the chance either, swingin her head hard around to snap at Mouse's ear, which fortunately for both of them weren't there no more, Mouse at least knowin better than to linger around after a check like that, havin some experience in this area from when Kalin and Tom used to ride the canyon together, Navidad's teeth in fact never chompin on Mouse. Kalin suspected this was Navidad's choice. She adored Mouse.

My life would sure be easier if you were on Mouse right now, Kalin said once he'd got both horses movin again at the same steady pace and in the same direction.

Your life's already easier because I'm here, Tom answered back, his eyes twinklin with somethin wild and fierce. *Now come on. Are we gonna let my sister show us up like this?*

And just like that Tom was the wind, gone ahead so fast he should've left a wake of dust, though there weren't no dust; goin so hard he should've kicked up a mess of dirt divots, though there weren't none of those either; because of course the mud weren't touched, nothin was touched by Tom, though the powerful strides of his horse briefly matched Jojo's hoove-hammerin gallop up ahead, the canyon walls alive with their echoes.

Much as he would've liked to, Kalin didn't join that race. Let the siblins have their fun. He kept both Navidad and Mouse in check, this time with a full stop, lettin both horses know that they didn't have no extra energy to spare, not against a young girl who'd be home before the hour, and especially not against a ghost, if they was sensin Tom and Ash, though the three of them could still enjoy the sight of that little girl racin her long-gone brother whom she didn't even know was right beside her, standin now in his stirrups, hootin, thumbs in his ears, stickin out his tongue at her, makin to thump her on the chest before instead hurlin up that big black hat, what rose at once higher than anyone can throw a hat and maybe even higher than a dream can throw a hat, before it tumbled back down again, landin square and snug on Tom's head, who by that point was standin on his saddle, on one leg.

The turnoff weren't noticeable, and Kalin took it alone. Tom was already waitin down by the crick anyways, and Landry weren't so foolish to get too far ahead. It weren't like she was after some place in particular, just gettin out in front of Kalin.

Hey! You tryin to lose me? she cried.

The gall of that girl, Tom muttered.

You catch on quick, Kalin said to her with a wink as she and Jojo charged down after them through the brush.

I'm not dumb, you know.

I ain't never said you're dumb.

Good. Just so's we're straight.

In the plan, Kalin and the horses should've already been traversin higher up on the left side of the canyon, with the crick here to their right servin as another obstacle for anyone tryin to catch or thwart him. Now, though, Kalin had to cross that very same obstacle, and given the storm last night, there was no tellin what he'd have to face.

Fortunately it still weren't that much.

The crick hadn't quit churnin out the noisy tale of its descent, but over the past hour the flow had already dropped enuf that numerous areas offered shallows where crossin would pose no problem. Only the jagged rocks guardin the crick banks required caution. Kalin, though, had already discovered a suitable if overgrown path parallel to the yammerin current, which he, Navidad and Mouse followed, passin quick enuf through and around brush that soon after delivered them to an open area with ample room for twice their number if still concealin them beneath a canopy of oak, alders, dogwoods, and bigtooth maples. From there it was a few strides down a mild bank to wide, fast water clear as air, the bottom aglitter with tiny yellow pebbles.

Kalin paused Navidad and Mouse there so they could drink a spell and he could better study the far side.

You even know where you're goin? Landry asked from behind, mostly to heckle him, if still addin, and with more concern: *Even I can see there ain't nothin but cliffs this way.*

Kalin didn't pay her no mind, concentratin just on the hillside, tryin to see his way through to the place he now needed to find via a different route. Eventually, with wags of their heads and loud snorts, the horses announced that they was done with this icy water and Kalin better make a decision quick. Only when Kalin twisted around in his saddle to consider downstream did he glance again at Tom, who was just chewin on some dry stalk of ghost grass, fer his part watchin Landry jitter on Jojo, she and Jojo near just as displeased as Mouse and Navidad with this midstream pause.

I won't lie, Landry, Kalin said then. *There's a helluva ride ahead. Heck, we haven't even really started. Your brother and I managed to tackle a good bit of it over this last summer but that didn't even include the hardest part, and he didn't even tell me about the very last part until, well, the end. If what he said was right, then I got at least another night up there before makin the Crossin, and that's assumin I make it.*

Assumin you make it? Landry clearly didn't like the sound of that.

Tom and I never did get the whole ride done. Some of the most dangerous parts we prepared for, but we never actually rode it through.

That supposed to scare me?

Stubborn from day one, Tom said.

What does and doesn't scare you is none of my business, Kalin answered.

Then, unlike the water eddyin around the horses' hooves that at that moment suddenly grew dark and clotted with silt and leaves,

Kalin found a clarity about how to go, and it weren't up the opposite bank, mild and welcomin as it might've seemed, but upstream, where Tom again already waited, still chewin on that stalk of ghost grass.

They sloshed for a while that way, Kalin's and Landry's noses red as Rudolph's, their lungs full with the awakenin trees and petrichor, always makin sure to keep clear of the deeper trench of flowin water that haunted the center. It was after comin around a wide and easy bend that they came face-to-face with the abrupt termination of their path, blocked by great chunks of rock stackin up into a staircase suited only for giants. Landry and Jojo stopped dead in their tracks. Havin never been this far up the canyon, and they weren't even halfway up, Landry stood flummoxed by the sight of this hindrance, or Misdemeanors, as hikers call it, another spot for a bracin dip.

Suffice it to say, Kalin weren't perplexed one bit.

Misdemeanors ain't near as big or deep as Yell Rock Falls. There also ain't no waterfalls here. The mystery of this place is really how the stream itself near vanishes. You can hear it foamin and bubblin behind you and even growlin further upstream, but right up close to the boulders the water keeps still, its arrival impossible to see. Only a faint murmurin within this geological upheaval tells one of the oldest stories: water will find a way down.

Not even a ripple now disturbed its glassy surface, bright with patches of blue sky and branches hung with red leaves and gold leaves, of air and water, how a reflection makes the same world twice, vanishin just as fast, with the mornin darkenin, heavy clouds movin in, shadows vanquishin the water's surface, revealin the movement of icy currents and lotic life beneath.

Mind yourself to stay behind me if you and Jojo don't want to go for a swim.

And maybe because Kalin weren't tellin Landry to do nothin she wouldn't have wanted to do anyway, just layin it out like he did, in that tone too that was soft and impartial, which, if she'd thought about it more, was a lot like how Kalin talked to Navidad and Mouse, Landry raised no objections and followed his path exactly, additionally demonstratin in this momentary act of obeisance her skill at keepin Jojo right where he needed to be.

Kalin fer his part followed Tom's path exactly, even as he also remained attentive to the shadows on the water, portals on the surface through which he could note a sudden steepness or preferred shallow. Maybe he recognized too that despite all Tom said he couldn't remember, his movements were a memory in itself; maybe because they had come this way before, when it had been hot, takin a break to embrace the cold waters and not shout and find themselves refreshed.

Kalin was also amused by, and maybe enchanted some too, by how Ash could settle hooves upon the water without goin deeper, makin no impression neither, as well as denyin the hold of any reflection, like they was vampires, easily forgotten too when now and then the light brightened above and this wide pool revealed only the trees again, a sudden wash of blue, until more turbulent clouds came crowdin in.

As they cautiously eased past Misdemeanors, Kalin kept returnin to that bit of grass Tom had been chewin on. Except it was gone now. Likely flung to the side. Had it disturbed the water? Or in other words, was that bit of grass from here or from the elsewhere Tom was at now? Like maybe it really was ghost grass, like where grass goes when it dies? Or had Tom instead plucked a live stalk of grass, what either Kalin or Landry could've just as easily done, the horses too, snatchin up a bite to eat, except that Tom by his claim had not only ended that vegetative life but also ushered that life into his own spectral keepin? Kalin couldn't say why fer sure, but he shuddered good then, some nascent terror brushin across the backs of his arms, maybe some ancient and vestigial reaction to take flight tinglin his spine, knowin to run when in the presence of somethin too powerful to judge.

Kalin even gave his head a shake, as if that might set him free of such useless speculations. He reasoned he was mostly tired. And that was a bad thing. It was way too early to be tired. Just goin for a swim now could put the whole venture in peril.

But there weren't no swimmin for any of them, and soon enuf Misdemeanors began to shallow more and more, and the wall of scrub oak that rose up to greet them didn't slow them down none either. In fact Navidad and Mouse began to speed up, perhaps rememberin a route they couldn't have taken more than twice, splashin out of the water, grateful to be rid of its cold hold. Kalin didn't object either, even welcomin this purposeful charge up that rock-free riparian refuge.

Jojo as well was glad to be out of the water, Landry too, though what this young girl glimpsed then, up through the dense skein of branches and leaves, troubled her more, what she had no inklin about but what she would remember later, even in the hours ahead, all that had been foretold there, a feelin voiced by the arrangement of trees, the comin and goin of the sky, those awful flesh-scrapin, bone-shatterin rocks risin high up above the thinnin canopy.

She'd've quit if she'd've listened too long to this feelin. Instead she hummed to herself and kept her focus on the distance between Jojo and Mouse. Sure enuf her thoughts and worries fell away, and she was only managin another animal trail, nothin more, up a nothin-special hillside, which pretty soon opened up even as the slope also grew steeper. Kalin didn't take it straight up but jagged right first, only to swing left a little later, before eventually executin another right, which Landry soon enuf figured out was one long switchback takin them high above the crick, soon enuf deliverin them to a grassy slope that at first sight seemed mild and welcomin. Pleasantly breezy too. Landry sure was pleased.

On closer inspection, however, the area was pocked with pale rocks big as toaster ovens, like they was hurled from above by giants, in anger or at the very minimum angry amusement, thuddin randomly around this amber brown field, there to stay for a century or two and already warnin enuf to tell any fool to turn back. This weren't no place to take a nap. This weren't no place for horses. And as far as taluses go, this one weren't much, though it was still wide and in possession of a good part of that grassy hillside. It came with more warnins too, that what had come down from above might come again.

Landry could do little but gawk at the scree, a crude ramp of broken rubble composed mainly of small, nearly polished stones, bits of limestone, basalt, and feldspar, slate too, with no doubt some pieces in there sharp as oiled knives. The scree was two hundred feet long too, easy, with its point of origin a narrow fissure in cliffs a good fifty feet tall.

For some of you that might not sound like much, but seated on a horse, and while facin such uncertain terrain, and in the grip too of a cold early mornin still cast in shadows that even the noon sun at that time of year might never get around to freein, why you wouldn't be thought less of if you determined from your fast-quickenin pulse a hard hitch in your breath.

It takes some real grit to ride even this far, Kalin told Landry then, no doubt readin right the little girl's expression.

Why you done led us to a dead end, Landry declared in response, partly annoyed but also elated, they'd gone as far as they could, as well as confused, still cranin her neck around in search of some hidden way that might further prolong their journey, all while wrestlin with Jojo, who kept jerkin his head down for some grass, now and then succeedin to snatch up a little somethin to chew.

Curiously, Navidad and Mouse didn't dive in so much. In fact both had got to poopin as soon as they'd arrived, near at the same time too, their tails risin up to rid themselves of what they no longer had use for, which weren't nothin unusual except that Landry sensed in it a kind of growin preparatory excitement about a place that was for them anythin but unfamiliar.

I reckon for you, this here is a dead end, Kalin eventually replied, even as he continued to study the spill of stones stretchin up above them.

Hold on a second. You can't tell me you're ridin up that?

Now are you gonna head home, Landry? Please? Keep your promise to that Russel kid so he don't get no more bruises than what you already handed out. Go mend your momma's heart.

Hold on, I said. Hold on, Landry pleaded, even if Kalin or the horses hadn't moved a step. In fact Kalin was dismountin from Navidad, and even handin Landry the reins, before startin to unload Mouse's pack.

If my brother said he wanted you to set these horses free, and he'd seen that this here way was the only way to go, why then I'm gonna go that way too.

Kalin had already started to disassemble the packsaddle, only now and then glancin over at Tom, findin him slumped over on his horse, lookin like a big question mark that's even more bent over than it has to be, like a question broken by its own question, just swayin his head back and forth as if to say: *No . . . No . . . No . . .*

Your brother always said you was stubborn. Does that surprise you? Kalin asked.

Tom looked up. *Hey now! Don't go involvin me in this!*

That don't surprise me one bit, Landry snorted back, watchin Kalin as he first bagged up what he could of the packsaddle's riggin, next settin aside the pack itself, which included the half breed, or canvas pad with pine board braces, two steel Ds plus the trees beneath, all like he'd planned out in the weeks before today and reviewed in his head last night, reviewin now what parts he'd need to load up on Navidad.

My momma was the first, Landry continued, *to declare that I was part donkey and with ears pinned back.*

Part?! Tom yapped. *Our momma declared her donkeyness was one hundred percent!*

Now for all her youthfulness and wild impetuous spirit, what too often gave the appearance that if her head weren't loaded with rocks it was fer sure lingerin too much among the clouds, Landry still weren't a fool. She might yet still need many years more before graspin how the world will exert its thoughtless consequences on a fragile life such as hers, but even with most of those hard and scarrin lessons still unlearned, Landry could still nose out that somethin weren't right.

She let Navidad's reins drop, them slappin Kalin on the back, not that he made any sign of needin to grab them, not that the black mare had any thoughts of movin. Landry even nudged Jojo into a wide arc around Kalin while he stayed squatted down, tyin together a series of bags loaded with feed and more feed, and then gear of course, and sleepin stuff, which he finally stopped fussin with when Landry clopped back to a halt so that she and Jojo was now standin between Kalin and the scree, Kalin at this point still assumin Landry was just gonna try to stop him and so was caught off guard some when she stabbed a finger straight at Tom, who was not even a few steps away, a few very small steps.

Why do you keep lookin right here?

Tom sure backed up Ash fast then, executin his own wide arc around until he was resettled beside Kalin, leavin Landry pointin her finger at nothin but cold air, until Kalin, not even thinkin, glanced at Tom's new position, which quick righted Landry's finger so it was once again pointin right where Tom stood, Tom this time not attemptin to escape, holdin up his hands instead like he was under arrest, like he'd done with Lindsey Holt that fateful spring day, his smile confessin that it weren't so bad a thing to be called out by his sister.

Why did you look there?

No reason, Kalin lied, ignorin Tom but findin it hard to ignore the ugly taste of even that reasonable falsehood in his mouth.

You think she sees me? Tom asked.

I ain't no idjit, Kalin, Landry growled back, squintin her eyes like such ocular contortions might materialize somethin hidden, her dead brother offerin a friendly wave. *I can see for myself when some kid's lookin at nothin and even at times conversatin with that nothin. You been doin it since I caught up with you. It's like you can see someone else here that I can't.*

She's keen too as a sharpened flint, Tom grumbled. *Smartest one in our family.*

I ain't good at lyin.

There! You're doin it again! Landry near screamed, as outraged as she was also soundin victorious.

If I told you the plain truth of it, you'd think I was crazy, Kalin said with a sigh.

Careful, Tom cautioned his friend then, maybe a little too sternly, maybe because he sensed that Kalin might do somethin truly crazy and tell his little sister the whole of it.

Think you're crazy?! Landry squalled. *Sane don't take horses up to a place like this!*

Of course, if she's convinced I'm nuts, Kalin said then to Tom without tryin now to hide his conversin from Landry, *it might make her turnin around that much easier.*

There's no tellin what that feisty sister of mine will do except confound us. That part's certain. I recommend you don't say no more.

Landry did freeze then, momentarily struck speechless at the sight of Kalin carryin on like so with the unanswerin air, not only talkin to it but payin such close attention to it, as if really listenin.

There! she declared anyways, though this time softer, and then, as if a jigsaw puzzle of partial thoughts had suddenly clicked together, loud again: *Oh! I get what you're doin! You're just jokin with me!*

Okay, I'm just jokin with you.

Like I was sayin, Tom said, back to shakin his head slow and low. *She'll go to the ends of the earth to organize her thinkin so she gets what she wants, even if she hasn't spared a single thought to figurin out what it is she really wants.*

But Landry's revelation still weren't convincin her, no matter how much she wanted to agree with herself. *No, that ain't it either.* Her face darkenin. *Now you're just tryin to get me to think that you ain't crazy!*

Tom threw up his arms. Kalin returned to orderin the load Navidad would carry and then the load Mouse would have to carry. Unfortunately just as Landry was bothered by Kalin lookin at Tom, Kalin was bothered by Tom lookin down toward the crick or farther west toward where the trees and brush concealed the main canyon trail.

What now?

Nothin, Tom answered. *Yet.*

Quit it! Landry objected. *Quit messin with me. You're bein mean now.*

I ain't messin with you, Landry. You see me talkin to nothin. I get it. But I ain't talkin to nothin. I'm talkin to Tom.

There it was, out in the open, with no bad taste sourin up his mouth anymore. Kalin felt better for it. He was tired enuf as it was, and he sure didn't care a whit for all the extra effort it took him to bend his mind this way and that way for the sake of understandin how the lyin you're doin is workin on the mind that's hearin the lie while you're still tryin to keep straight for yourself what isn't the lie in the first place. Much easier to just say it like you're seein it and leave them extra exertions to those who think Death ain't comin for them.

Now for the record, and by the way, also for the record, there ain't no record, at least not in the way we'd like to imagine one, arranged to our likin, at our convenient disposal, a footstep outside of time; anyways, for the record, there remains a sizable number of folks who maintain that Kalin was in fact crazy as a hoot. Sure, some describe his condition in kinder terms, terms like *mental instability,* or just *soft.* There are even a bunch who adamantly defend Kalin while acceptin that the predictive pensum required for such a journey, always tryin to think about what comes next and how to handle it, not to speak of the physical price such a journey exacts, nor forgettin neither the substantial pressure brought on by such solitude, might have compromised Kalin's, how shall we say, clarity of thought?

There's even some extra highfalutin cognizin goin on between some of these folks, when their dialogues start includin examples of travelers certain of an extra companion, whether they was in the deep jungles of the Amazon or out in Antarctica or even in orbit, bringin up poets and the like in defense of such hallucinatory claims, one in particular goin so far as to affirm the countin of only two before then admittin the spectral intrusion of a third, ever wonderin who it was that walked beside them? One assertion made by Joseph K. Davis, a student at Utah State, would in 2004 claim the hallucination was in response to the problem of duality, the democracy of two, a solution provided by an imagined tiebreaker, where three grants improved concord or at least a greater chance of achievin actionable resolutions. Corrina Shurtz, also at Utah State, would also in 2004 emphasize the benefits of the tetrahedron in terms of stability and out of amusement associate the four faces with the four horses. Yvette Ruffel, not at Utah State, would assert in 2032 that that sort of geometric comparative noodlin was utter verbigeration, hastenin to add that three also offers instabilities, which she refused to elaborate on except to say *ask my husband*. Yvette would also point out that when Tom first appeared, there weren't no Landry in the picture.

You see Tom? Landry asked then, her voice quaverin, the question leavin her mouth hung open as her dead brother's name was let out, her eyes continuin to stare straight ahead, upon the disquieted icy air.

It dismayed Tom plenty to see his little Landry stare at him like so, so distraught that he rode back around to stand beside her again.

Kalin answered her with a nod.

Then you're just a liar! And like I said, mean too, a mean liar, Landry squeaked out, her eyes wettin some too.

I ain't no liar, Kalin said softly. *And I hope I'm never mean. Especially to you. I do get, though, how you don't get what I'm tellin you, and I don't blame you for it. I don't get it much myself. Just, please, don't call me a liar.*

How about crazy?

Maybe that's the better truth of it. Tom just appeared out of the rain at the mouth of the canyon, grinnin too, like you'd expect, like even he thought this was the craziest thing. He was whistlin. I heard that first.

He was whistlin?

Kalin nodded. *Him here didn't make any sense last night, and it makes even less sense this mornin. But he is here. Actually, he's right next to you now.*

Landry jumped at that, and Jojo, always attuned to her movements, her mind and her heart too, sorta jumped as well. Well, not really, but the stallion did snort and initiate a sharp turn, which was in fact exactly what Landry had had in mind, endin up so that she and Jojo was now facin Tom directly; though what did such accuracy and control matter when faced with just more emptiness, what wouldn't reveal even the meagerest hint of her lost brother, not a scent nor the scantest note of his famous whistle, Landry beholdin at most her own inability to tolerate such absence, which then forced her to turn her now glowerin gaze back on Kalin.

You are an idjit! she shouted at him.

I warned you, Tom chuckled, finally amused again, especially seein his sister so caught up in fury.

Kalin shrugged. *Go on then. Figure me as one of them folks who sees the Easter Bunny or some such nonsense. I am glad for the company though. Tom's the best friend I ever had.*

Then how come I never seen you two talkin at school? Not once!

It weren't like that. We just loved ridin these two horses. Though maybe Tom loved most stealin them right from under Old Porch's nose.

I sense there is somethin to that, Tom admitted. *I still wouldn't mind ridin Mouse.* Ash neighed abruptly, in objection, and Tom had to lean forward to offer strokes of reassurance upon that proud neck.

That does sound a lot like Tom, Landry admitted. *Like you already know, Gatestones and Porches don't really get on. With me bein adopted and all, I came to that late, so I can't really say, but our momma has books detailin the disputes, and they go back a long ways.*

Kalin let her prattle on as he worked, figurin she was just tryin to talk herself away to some place that made more sense.

My momma always counsels forgiveness and if not that, then tolerance, but sometimes she still swears hate is bred into them Porches, and not just their kith and kin but them that Old Porch employs too, exceptin Tyler. Tyler's right as rain, right as sun in the rain when the rain's on the way out. Landry was really barrelin along with no speed limits posted. *A good, good man. Good as Egan fer sure ain't.* Landry stopped her yappin then. Stopped hard too. Kalin didn't miss the way she'd surprised herself with the admission, if that's what it was. She even tried to swallow her surprise. That or her throat had suddenly got real dry. *Can you really see Tom?*

I can.

Well, what's he sayin now?

He's listenin to you.

Landry snorted. *You got that part wrong.*

You remember Tyler Stokes? Tom asked Kalin then. *He's the one who ruined the Riggs's house last summer. Landry likes him cause he drives a Camaro.*

187

Tom says you just like Tyler because he drives a Camaro.

Landry smiled. *That Camaro's pretty cool. All black. Got a sunroof too. Never seen Tom in no Camaro. Unless he's in one now?*

No, Kalin answered with a laugh. *He's ridin just like us.*

Ridin what? Landry snapped.

Palomino. Andalusian maybe. Tom gave Kalin a nod. *Maybe some gold in his coat, but right now he looks grayer than old chalk.* Kalin didn't mention that the dark green eyes had started to look near black as tar.

Well, goshdarn. And for the first time Landry did look somewhat amazed, maybe even impressed. *That'd be Chubasco, or Ash as we all called him. Tom swore Ash came down upon this earth to make it better. Gosh, did Tom love Ash! I swore it made Tom better. The laugh he had, and I know you know the one, what was already big to begin with, why when he was around Ash, it filled up even more!*

Your horse's name is Ash, Kalin told Tom then.

I'm dead, not deaf, Tom snarled. *But her sayin so does bring it back some. Hello again, Ash.* Tom patted the horse's shoulder and was rewarded with a whicker soft as any lovin whisper.

He don't know his own horse's name? Landry seemed insulted, not to mention doubtful again.

His memory ain't all there. He don't even remember dyin.

I've heard it's hard to remember things after a bad shock. I guess dyin would have to be considered the worst kinda shock. Ash's departin was pretty bad on Tom. One night, and outta nowhere too, Ash's guts got all twisted wrong, and two nights later he was gone. That's about the only time I heard Tom quit his laughin. He quit smilin too. That was before you came along. Too awful a time for even me to remember right. Tom said Ash died because he couldn't stomach the world no more.

Ain't so, though, Tom said, his voice low and heavy like it was full of fallin stones. *Sometimes death just overruns you with no word on why.*

Ask him why he stolt my snaffle! Landry suddenly demanded.

He can hear you.

Tom laughed, them stones gone at once from his voice. *Her brother's dead and buried, but what's she up in arms about but a bit that weren't even hers to begin with because she done stole it from Aunt Lissie!* Tom really did sound flabbergasted.

What's he sayin?

Somethin about your Aunt Lissie bein the rightful owner of the bit.

He ain't wrong, though it still weren't his right to steal it from me, even if he was returnin what I stolt in the first place.

That works out in your head? Kalin had to ask.

Works out just fine.

Concernin the matter of Aunt Lissie's snaffle, there's little point in addin to the arguin about whether the bit was an O-ring, a D-ring, full cheek, a French link, or even a Weymouth, or whether it was made of copper or brass or rubber or even of solid gold; or whether it was the harshest of its sort, which is discreditable, or the mildest, which is most likely, given how the Gatestones trained hard to leave a horse's mouth alone, relyin on neck reinin, the proper positionin of the rider's body, and the language of legs. The greater question here was how Kalin March knew about both the bit and Aunt Lissie. After all, wouldn't this moment prove on the spot, through this imparted knowledge, that Tom was no hallucination but an incarnation of the infinitely preservin spirit world longed for by so many, especially when death and the irreversible departure from those we love seem so imminent?

Plain and simple, the amount of ridin Tom and Kalin had done together cannot be so easily dismissed, allowin for a substantial amount of time for wide-rangin conversin, which easily could have included stories about Aunt Lissie and that very same snaffle bit Landry commandeered one bright spring afternoon.

What remains of paramount importance here was how these immediate moments unfoldin before little Landry's eyes, either a miracle of weirdness or a foul conjurin that betwixt her yearnins for reunion with her dead brother and her chariness before a display of such odd pantomimes, dazzled her wits and left poor Landry stutterin some for common sense. As Hill Parmenter, a site manager with Hill Construction up in Bountiful, this was in 1991, a roofer at heart, or *a rufer* as Utah Valley folks liked to say it; as he would point out to Flo Carrigan at lunch: there was in fact a miracle for Landry to witness, and soon too, but *it didn't have nothin to do with what was known or not known about some snaffle or even with that Kalin kid carryin on with the air like there was someone there.*

Anyways, Kalin had done said his piece and was glad to be back finalizin the new load upon Navidad, hangin bags in pairs around the pommel, under the canticle on the back jockey, securin this distribution of supplies with saddle strings and rope. He struggled again with the knots, and this time Landry let him. But that weren't the worst of it: Kalin was comin to see that no matter how he laid out everythin he had, what all he desperately needed to keep if he was gonna make it to the Crossin, there just weren't no way to tackle that scree in two trips. He'd need three, and the realization drove his head against Navidad's shoulder, mumblin apologies and tryin his best not to cry, which if he had done would've been wrought out of anger with thoughts that he weren't proud of and included Landry. He didn't need to give her a glance to know that her horse could handle the scree no problem and easily manage a third of the load if not more. But Kalin knew that one, it was wrong to include her, and he felt all the more bitter for even considerin it; and two, Landry couldn't do it. Havin a horse strong enuf weren't but a small part of what was about to happen. Where he was goin needed a rider that . . . well, words just break apart here.

Hey? You okay? Landry asked, near sorry now that she hadn't helped with the ties, which, even though he'd managed fine, she figured was the source of his present anguish.

I never done it twice with her, Kalin said. He no longer cared Landry was there to witness his talkin with Tom. *I ain't never done it even once with Mouse. You was the one who rode Mouse.*

I know it, and what comes back to me now is that it weren't no great picnic.
But you made it.
If you say so.
You think Navidad can make it twice?
She says she can make it just fine.
Is that what she said?
Not exactly. Tom winked. *She says she's worried about you. Ain't sure you can make it twice. Let alone three times.*

At least Kalin laughed.

Are you sayin Tom's sayin he knows what the horses are sayin?! Landry couldn't keep herself from askin.

I think he's just tryin to make me laugh.

And Kalin did look a little relieved, acceptin now that he and Navidad was gonna have to do this twice and so startin to lighten her load, carefully layin out on the ground what he took off so it was at the ready for the second trip up. Still, he wanted the first trip to be the heaviest, with the second a bit lighter, and the third, on Mouse, the lightest. Once he felt Navidad was secured and well balanced, he rechecked both cinch and breast collar. The last thing he needed was for that saddle and everythin else attached to it to start slidin back, especially when things got really steep. Kalin briefly wondered if he should've brought a crupper, what attaches the saddle to the tail so it don't slide forward when goin downhill. Though who was Kalin kiddin? There was so little downhill where they was headin.

Kalin got down on his knees to make sure all the wet hadn't compromised his duct-taped cardboard boots. They was still holdin together.

Kalin weren't no academic, and whatever was banged out on a chalkboard, whether letters or numbers, too often befuddled him, with teachers markin him down as *dull-witted*, though one or two did recognize too late how a shyness coupled with a mind that danced everythin first into a reflective about-face made near everythin twice as difficult for him. Fortunately, though, when it came to horses, this easily fractured intelligence came together, with the sum of the parts exceedin the whole.

The final pieces of the first load, that canvas packsaddle half-breed and trees, he succeeded in securin to his back, along with the sleepin bag and other thises and thats, which he stowed in one of the larger grain sacks and tied up with the help of his belt.

You gonna get up on Navidad like that? Landry snickered. *This I can't wait to see.*

But Kalin was up in the saddle so fast, Landry near didn't see him do it. And that was the first real inclination she got that somethin she weren't really prepared for was about to happen, like a buzz in the air auspicatin lightnin. The hair on her forearms even sizzled up some, and she half wondered if skeddaddlin right now might not be the best call after all, but then Kalin asked if she'd do him this one favor, hold Mouse's lead rope, which she was more than happy to do, and in that happiness remembered herself again, that there weren't no place that Kalin was goin that she weren't goin too, and fer sure any place he could take a horse loaded up with gear she could easily reach on Jojo.

Landry was practically giddy when Kalin leaned his head down, as if to rest his forehead on the black mare's mane. Landry could see his lips movin and maybe heard somethin like words that never did quite go together, at least not in the way that makes sense with sound.

Then with a click of his tongue and maybe a rub of his heels, she couldn't tell fer sure, Kalin and Navidad took off at a slow lope around that brown grassy apron at the base of all that pebbled stone. They didn't have no problem either with them big boulders blightin the area. They knew exactly where to head and kept pickin up speed too, until, at a good canter, well above the talus now, they approached the scree from the left side.

Navidad neither hesitated nor juddered upon arrivin at that rocky slough but rather kept churnin upwards at a diagonal, if slowin some with each lunge as the steepness increased, until suddenly they reached a place where the rocks didn't fall away like water and Navidad's hooves weren't sinkin down like they was in quicksand, where without missin a beat Kalin helped the beautiful mare gather up her hocks, no doubt to maximize the purchase on that sustainin part of earth, before turnin Navidad around then, and near halfway around too, easy as a pie spinnin on a lazy Susan, to start another diagonal race, this time leftward, again churnin upwards to yet another spot of reliant stability, proceedin in this fashion, back and forth, a good half dozen times, all the way up to that narrow slit in the cliff face, where the scree began, where the real miracle took place, what Hill Parmenter in Bountiful so many years later would be referrin to.

Landry couldn't make no sense out of it, and were it not for the fact that Mouse was still with her, and presumably Tom too, or at least the possibility of him was there, she would've suffered without mitigation or reassurance the appallin shock that visits anyone who is befriended and then without warnin suddenly abandoned. Kalin and Navidad just disappeared. Landry had no clue how they'd managed to ride so effortlessly through that black crevasse without one bit of back slidin nor sign of any scramblin commotion, without even a sound. Landry just stared and kept starin, first at the pebble-like rocks still slurryin down in the aftermath and then at the fast-dissipatin dust.

It was then that Landry noticed the great white owl, what seemed to her the same one that had settled upon the fallen elm last night, now circlin above this Kalin-consumin fracture in the mountain.

Mouse then raised his head and neighed loud as he could, shakin his head as well, like he too felt, and keenly too, this act of unacceptable desertion.

Don't fret none, Mouse! Kalin yelled down from somewhere high up, his voice bouncin everywhere with reverberant clarity. *We're comin!*

And then they were back again, Kalin on foot leadin the way, half runnin, half skippin, a light hand on the reins, Navidad close behind, both of them tryin to zigzag but more than often just boundin and slidin almost straight down amidst rivulets of followin stones markin their way, as myriad as unrecognized omens.

Navidad had only the saddle on, and Kalin's back was now free of the pack. While Mouse gave Navidad ample nuzzles, Kalin carefully scrutinized the black mare for any harm, relieved to find her hooves still protected and her legs sound.

In some ways this here's the worst part, Kalin said aloud as he set to fixin up Navidad with the second load, them words tastin foul in his mouth, and anyways Landry uncertain if he was addressin her or Tom, though here Kalin was really just talkin to hisself. *Them rocks are small and smooth enuf, but just one turned wrong can give an awful bad cut.*

Sure as heck seems like a bad way to take horses to a safe place.

You ain't wrong, Landry, but sometimes gettin out of harm's way means takin the hard way.

And that works out in your head?

They say a magician should never do a trick twice because in the subsequent viewin the gimmick becomes apparent. Landry, however, watched Navidad and Kalin ascend a second time, and there just weren't no gimmick to see. Kalin even made it look easier, and vanishin through that crack where the path appeared near vertical seemed about as effortless as a yawn.

Kalin didn't take as long doin whatever it was he'd been doin up there the first time, comin down by hisself, leapin and boundin, lookin near carefree, with Navidad's saddle on his shoulder and reins in his right hand. Not that he weren't huffin hard when he reached Landry and Mouse, his face glazed with sweat. He needed a long drink of water and even rummaged around for some raisins and nuts to munch on.

I don't think I can do that, Landry admitted then, and for the first time since she'd come to Isatch Canyon, her voice was real small.

I understand.

If I hadn't just seen you do that with my own eyes, I'd've sworn it was impossible. And I just seen you do it twice. My brother did that?

He was the one who figured out it was possible.

But why? What's up past that crack there?

The way out of this canyon.

Then as if to challenge herself, or maybe to give herself the chance to change her mind, Landry wheeled Jojo around, and by an easy lope across the brown grass, findin easily too a route unmolested by dangerous rock, she ascended the hill until she too was approachin the same spot where Kalin had without hesitation rode out upon the back of those smooth shiftin stones; except Landry could already feel Jojo twistin his neck back and forth, leadin first with one shoulder and then the next like he wanted to go sideways and, if given the chance, likely pull a one-eighty.

Landry knew at once what was up: her friend weren't buyin it, and by the time they reached that large tongue of skitterin stones, Jojo had already come to a dead stop. Jojo wouldn't even step onto the surface, and Landry couldn't blame him. Even imaginin now herself halfway up scared the daylights out of her, the ever-increasin steepness threatenin to send Jojo over backward; skew him enuf to snap a leg. That said, the longer she stared at that volatile black-and-gray surface, like dark water somehow paused, the more she could make out a path of sorts, near-rockless areas clumped up with grass. If she was goin to match Kalin's ascent and reach those spots, she'd need to approach at a much sharper angle.

She managed to get Jojo to dare a step out onto the rocks, and even a second step, but by the third step he was again shakin his head and sidesteppin, demandin that Landry return him to solid ground. Not that she was done. The possible had presented itself. For her next try, she and Jojo actually made it a good ways across, but their course still weren't takin her high enuf, and so Jojo never found the solid ground he'd need to turn around on. Furthermore, the fast-shiftin stones kept denyin his hooves the purchase he'd need to maintain a good pace. Too soon, especially as Landry still tried to turn him around like she'd seen Kalin do on Navidad, Jojo started to slide backward, Landry cryin out then even as she got well away from the worst by swingin Jojo downward, straight down, the stallion almost droppin to a knee before finally kickin free of that mess with an angry snort.

Landry's cheeks was flushed enuf to outbright the sun, though in truth there was more than just anger there, a good deal of embarrassment and fear was in there too, maybe somethin else as well, as she halted before Kalin, who was already down on his knees, checkin out Jojo's ankles and shoes, relieved to find no harm, though he needed Landry's hoof pick to flick loose some small wedged pieces of slate.

You should've at least put him in them Easyboots.

I didn't know I was gonna try until I gave it a try, she answered, humbled, regardin Kalin in a new light now, marvelin at the way he'd slipped up that slide of rocks like it weren't nothin, only to do it faster the second time, a feat Landry understood all the better by how she'd just failed to manage even the first part of it. She felt both awed and broken, starstruck and inadequate, and too close to squirtin out scaldin tears for what only a heart knows when it's riled up by what it loves and what love can't do.

You sure Mouse can make it up like Navidad? she asked.

I'd say we got a fifty-fifty chance. But I ain't the best at figures, Kalin said with a smile that didn't last long. *Landry, I am glad you came along this far.*

Landry lowered her head, mostly to hide her cheeks, burnin now with nothin that had anythin to do with anger or fear, well, maybe a little fear.

I understand now why Tom picked you to ride with him in his final months. Kalin did his best to smile but failed.

Maybe I even understand why he keeps ridin with you now. Though, don't get me wrong, and Landry even raised a finger like she might wag it at him, *I ain't sayin you ain't crazy.* She couldn't help herself. She wagged that finger at him anyway.

I'd've said you was crazy if you'd've said otherwise, Kalin answered.

Landry snorted loud, if glad for the boy's words.

Is he here now? she had to ask.

But Kalin shook his head. *He's up with Navidad.*

You tell him I said to look after you.

I will. And maybe even Kalin's cheeks reddened some.

And you look after him, Landry added.

I will.

Landry smiled then and even laughed a little, but it weren't with no snort. This time it was real soft-like and wide, like the way Tom laughed when he was tellin their momma it was gonna be all right even when they already knew nothin was gonna be all right.

Kalin had finished tackin up Mouse and loadin around the saddle the remainin gear. Landry even got down to help with the saddle strings. She really was a whiz with knots. Kalin then gave Mouse's legs one last check before swingin up easy on him, at once whisperin somethin for only Mouse to hear. He'd just tipped her brother's big white Stetson, about to ride off, when Landry spoke up.

You sure you don't want to take this? She was holdin up the Colt Peacemaker, a sudden blaze of silver caught in a bar of cold mornin light.

You know who that belongs to.

I'll get it to him. I promised, Landry replied, but instead of redeliverin it to the dark confines of its velvet pouch, she shoved it behind her bronze belt buckle, the grip, big as a hatchet, pokin above her waist.

Hold on a moment! Kalin cried out. *Don't do that!*

Landry at once pulled the gun back out.

Point it way over there, please. Good. Now let's check somethin: open the loadin gate there with your right thumb.

Here! Landry said, again offerin the weapon to Kalin. But he would have nothin to do with it.

You're doin fine. Now slowly pull back the hammer spur there. Use your thumb. Two clicks should do you. See a round in there?

I can't tell.

That's okay. Roll that cylinder to the right. See anythin now?

It's empty.

Good on our boy Russel. That's what we're checkin. We wanna see that firin pin set down over an empty chamber. That's where he had it.

Kalin had Landry continue to rotate the cylinder, countin off all five rounds, until the sixth chamber, the empty one, was back again where it started, Landry slowly pullin back on the hammer so as to release it, bringin the firin pin then to rest over air. The whole process made her nervous, and despite Kalin's clear instructions, the firearm seemed only to grow heavier and more unfamiliar in her hands.

Now it won't matter even if you drop it. Just a paperweight.

Even if I pull the trigger?

Won't do nothin. But pull that hammer back again, then that trigger will tell a different story. And if you hold the trigger down, you can fire them five bullets fast as your left hand can get back that spur.

Like in the movies.

Sure.

I took this off Russel too. Landry pulled out of the velvet pouch an extra round. *Guess he was plannin on havin hisself one heckuva shoot-out if he needed all six.*

Or Old Porch keeps it stupidly loaded and Russel was smart enuf to remove the round.

Old Porch is many things, but he ain't stupid, Landry said as she stuffed the gun back behind her belt buckle.

Why don't you just put it back in its bag like you had it before?

You ridin me home?

Fair enuf.

Kalin tipped his hat, and then like that he was off at a canter, so smooth Landry had missed completely how he'd gone from a dead halt to such an even lope, once again gainin speed, with Mouse lookin dead ahead like there was nothin he wanted more of than ridin up that scree, and that's true because his heart was set on Navidad. Kalin, fer his part, gave Landry a last look, and maybe she was makin this up, but she thought she saw a twinkle in those green eyes meant only for her.

Like before, Kalin managed the ascent by way of a series of switchbacks, just a zigzag really, Mouse never falterin, just churnin away, and each time the time came to turn, he turned on a dime, barrelin even harder for higher ground, until like that they was at the steepest part, right before that jagged slit, and then like that they was through it, through it and gone. Kalin had done it! Three times! And Landry kept lookin where they weren't no more, dazzled some by beams of sunlight now and then escapin though the storm clouds above, if mostly dazed by the mountain itself, what weren't even near the real mountain yet, this small rock wall, what weren't even a tiny toe compared to the immense Katanogos, but what still commanded all her attention.

Make no mistake, Landry was sorry to see Kalin go but also plenty glad now that turnin back was her only choice. She could hold her head high and even look forward to razzin Russel some when she saw him at school later today. Other than that, she tried to keep her mind from how Kalin had said Tom was ridin beside him. That lie, for it had to have been a lie, right?, or if nothin else, real awful madness, well, that sure disturbed her. Though it weren't the impossibility that pained her so but rather how in deliverin this confession Kalin had done so so plainly, and frankly his few words on the matter were so surfeit with compassion and pain that she'd found, and for the first time since Tom's death too, an explicable harmony to her own terrible grief, which is where she was headin back to now, home, grief, where her momma would likely swat her off to her room, which sat right next to Tom's old room, to where she'd go instead, to lie on his bed and cry and cry and cry.

No question Landry had beheld three effortless ascents, but for Kalin they was anythin but effortless, especially the third one. The first part had offered no troubles. They'd gotten quickly above the larger fractured pieces of rock Kalin knew well to avoid at the bottom. A misstep there could easily cost a mean slice to a coronet or a pastern, to say nothin of havin a go at the frog, the most vulnerable part under a horse's hoof. Even with all the tape and cardboard, a sharp stone, angled just so, could stab right through. Mouse stayed close to the high diagonal Kalin had set, keepin strong and steady. When they'd reached the first bit of good ground, sandy and tufted with grass, they'd turned around just fine, again angled plenty high, again keepin the same pace, maybe even a little faster.

After that, though, Mouse began heavin and huffin as he continued to churn through what looked like gravel, or better pebbles, seein as how they was smoother than gravel and gettin smaller still the higher they got until the scree seemed more and more like dark sand. It was a hard battle. But Mouse didn't shy from the fight. True for Kalin too, also heavin and huffin, his face and back a sheen of sweat.

Kalin had only three things to do throughout, but he had to do them flawlessly: first, he had to position hisself so as to never burden Mouse excessively; second, he had to keep Mouse on the correct lead, fer example, on the right lead if the next turn was goin right. Now if you don't understand this matter, and it's a crucial one, about what a lead is, you might try now to reach your left arm out, especially if you's a southpaw like Kalin, and think how if you was turnin left, and usin that left hand, why it would be right there for you. Now, though, say you was makin a hard right; why that left hand might have a real hard time reachin across to catch you. More likely your right hand is gonna have to scramble up to help, and by then it's already too late, there's nothin to catch you, and a hard fall ain't out of the question, and you'll hit the ground with your right shoulder. Draggin a horse over to the right when he's on the left lead can result in a bad mishap, leavin you with your right leg trapped, which, even if your horse comes through okay, you can bet he'll be plenty irked.

Kalin sure honored those first two requirements: his position was good, and he knew what he was doin with a lead, though it weren't always as simple as keepin Mouse on just the one or the other. In a fight like this to the top, with the ground constantly shiftin beneath, Mouse had occasion to switch leads a dozen times.

Which leaves the third most important thing Kalin had to mind: they could never drift below them safe patches. Those little islands of surety were what made the whole climb possible. If Mouse got just a little bit too low, gone would be any solid footin, gone would be the chance to regain any speed.

Other than that, it was all up to Mouse, and Kalin made sure Mouse knew that, givin him his mouth and only usin the reins on the side of his neck, with some help from a knee, and only rarely a heel to flick at his flank if just to remind Mouse that what lay behind them now was far worse than what waited up above. A sudden whinny from Navidad, callin her friend up, sure helped make that point.

It was on a leftward zag, way high up too, where that concordance of those ever-tinier polished stones, near cemented in place by a still-more-minute sandy rubble, that Mouse's hoof landed and dislodged it all. Kalin felt at once Mouse's back hips drop down, even as at the same time his front legs sought with greater desperation to claw and scramble beyond the slip. Kalin offered clicks and raspy barks of encouragment, leanin forward, his knees in place even if his heels slipped up some, his hands never burdenin Mouse's mouth who anyways hadn't lost sight of where they had to go.

Kalin knew they had to get higher at once. If they didn't regain the ground now, they'd miss their turnin point, which meant barrelin ahead, straight to the edge of the scree, which way up here had become an unbreachable gully before which he and Mouse would have to stop. They'd likely start slidin downward then, with their only chance bein to turn down with the slippage and from there try to ride it out to the bottom.

Kalin had to do somethin, and do it fast, and in fact he was already doin it before he even got to thinkin about needin to do it, lettin his body flow to the off side, and forward as well toward Mouse's foreleg, with that right lead continuin to slash ahead in hopes of gainin better purchase, until Kalin was hangin on to the horn with his left hand and near horizontal off Mouse's right side, close enuf to the scree to scoop up rocks with his right hand if he'd been so inclined.

In this way, what Landry had completely missed, and to be fair it was high up and happened pretty darned fast, Kalin had recalibrated Mouse's balance just enuf to give the geldin what he needed to get higher up on that traverse. And it had worked, helped some by the fact that the ground suddenly and fortuitously, and maybe even *prov-identially*, as Marrot Barlow, deacon in the Eighth Ward would pro-claim, the same word he would curiously use on separate occasions and under different circumstances with both Angel Rodriguez and Hector Angel, had *providentially offered up a more congealin substantiality*, a hardness to hold them both, enuf to get them to the anticipated mound of earth up ahead, rock and grass built upon a hidden staircase of stable-enuf quartzite where Mouse could gather hisself up just fine and then, fueled some by his annoyance with the scree's bad manners, execute a perfect one-eighty, even quicker and more powerful than anythin Navidad had managed so far, speedin upwards now with even greater resolve.

That was the first of two times when Kalin had thought they might not make it. The second time, though, was the real heartstopper, right at the constricted V through the cliffs at the top, what was always a heartstopper, a steep groove bottomed with packed dirt down which stones skittered like kids on a slide but where the hooves of a horse, especially those of a stocky and powerful one like Mouse, could easily cut into and race right up. The key was makin it up through that fis-sure to the support of the narrow ledge above without slowin.

And they was in this fissure, only two strides from the ledge, where Kalin, due to the increased steepness, had to go high in the stirrups, standin up just behind the shoulders, givin Mouse the weight he'd need to help him upwards and not drag him back any. Mouse was even on the right lead and knew the way.

But the stones that now waited there, further amassed by them that had fallen behind Navidad on her two dashes up through this same crack, presented a new and terrible confusion, offerin only com-promised stability, like some terrible abacus spun at impossible speeds in the name of impossible numbers that countin fingers can no more touch than the mind can hold.

Both of Mouse's front hooves still managed to reach that narrow ledge somehow, only to slip off at once, hurlin Mouse back on his rear legs, so he was now standin near vertical, and if the slope had slipped just a bit more then, and it seemed about to do just that, the path they was on would've denied them not only their precarious position but any second chance at the ledge that would get them to the hard path leadin up to Navidad and Tom.

Mouse almost fell backwards, and who knows what would've hap-pened then, a terrible tumblin somersault all the way to the bottom, bones broken, maybe both their necks snapped.

But the ground held just long enuf, almost as if Mouse had commanded it to hold and the mountain had obeyed, the quarter horse's mighty back legs compressin again and this time flingin them well beyond that inconstant menace of unsettled rocks, even beyond the ledge itself, at last onto hard and constant earth that at once granted them pace, rhythm, breath, and, at the top, finally, rest.

Because of what nearly happened to Kalin and Mouse, Backflip Scree ain't so bad a name to attach to this ruinous place, but as you likely know, that's not the name it got. As most folks will still tell you, and we'll get to the why a little later, there ain't no other name but Aster Scree.

At the top of that path, where it leveled out, Kalin quick dismounted, freein Mouse from bit and reins and loopin the lead he'd attached to Mouse's halter-bridle around the outcrop of rock Tom and him had used the last time they was up here with the horses.

As he'd already done with Navidad, he checked Mouse's legs for injury, checked the pasterns and fetlocks for cuts, checked under each hoof, checked that the duct tape was still holdin and the cardboard weren't punctured any, checked and rechecked the cannons, knees, and hocks for any sign of injury or acute soreness, and, last of all but most important, checked the disposition of his friend, which seemed just fine, especially after Mouse got a little water in him and a chance to nibble up some feed. Navidad whinnied for the same, and she got her nibbles too. And then, while his two friends munched and enjoyed the fresh air up there, Kalin placed a gentle hand beneath Mouse's jaw and behind his knee to make sure his heart rate was good and recovered. And it was, down at around thirty. Navidad's was the same, which is to say good too. And neither needed a skin pinch. They was plenty hydrated. Mouse's petulant urine proved that point too, light-colored if so close as to get Kalin dancin to avoid the small flood headin down the way they'd just come up.

I sure am glad that's over, Tom said.

Just knowin I'd have to do it twice gave me nightmares. I'm glad I never thought I might have to do it three times.

After Kalin had once again fitted Mouse with the Decker packsaddle and redistributed the supplies, he slipped the bit and reins back on Navidad. Here was a fine place to pause, but higher up was better.

The path up from there was easy too, and they was quick enuf risin well above the cleft through which they'd just passed. Not much later they reached a flat area wide enuf to escape some the icy shadows cast by the jagged cliffs above, what rose up toward the great bands of rusty quartzite and limestone that in the right light turned the walls of Isatch Canyon to gold. Now, though, the rock seemed dull and gray, even menacin, with various outcroppins lookin like inhuman guardians temporarily petrified after some penultimate act of violence and so imprisoned until the final Act of Judgment comes due. Only a few trees grew here, though there was plenty of brush, some wayward grass, and curiously, and in bloom too, asters, which is gettin us to why the scree is named after the flower if not gettin us all the way there just yet. Mouse at once tried to eat them, with Kalin makin sure he didn't, as the flower won't do a horse any good.

Tom settled Ash by the other horses and then strolled to the ledge. From that vantage they could see the bottom of the scree. Kalin felt a wobble of vertigo, not so much because of the verticality but because of what he'd just ridden up, and though he'd just done it, it no longer seemed believable. Less believable than even Tom standin beside him. Farther down, a long line of trees rose up. Kalin and Tom both recognized them as the ones that grew between the crick and the main trail, which weren't visible except in a few places.

It was 9:41 a.m.

Landry and Jojo would have to pass back through Misdemeanors, and Kalin weren't movin until he got eyes on them emergin somewhere on the far side. He could picture her skirtin the deep water before sloshin down the crick bed, where it was smooth and sandy. He knew she'd find the turnoff because any farther down got too rocky to ride.

And yet she didn't emerge. Kalin finally went and got his binoculars, Tom's really. Kalin still couldn't see nothin but dense growth and aggravatin branches. Where he could see through, the main trail remained deserted. He got the fidgets then, returnin his gaze to where Misdemeanors lay, wonderin, and at the same time tryin not to wonder, if somethin bad or unforeseen could've already happened. What if Jojo had thrown her, and she'd hit her head and was drownin right at that moment? Such thoughts concatenated with such eidetic force that Kalin was near ready to just blindly sprint down there, when Tom cried out: *There she goes!* The ghost pointin out the blur Kalin soon had his binoculars fixed on.

There she was!

There was Jojo!

Both with their heads high, just canterin along with not a care in the world.

She'll be home before she knows it, Kalin mumbled, much relieved.

A good thing too, Tom said, also relieved. *This here's no business for her.*

Kalin knew the ghost was right, but he still followed Landry until too many trees stole her away, and even then he kept on goin until he was movin past where they'd camped last night, both the second time and the first time, without detectin a sign of either before gazin at the canyon entrance where he could just make out what was maybe the visitor kiosk and from there a sliver of parkin lot, bright now with a confusion of flashin blue-and-red lights.

Looks like police at the entrance.

I can see that, Tom said.

You suppose they're after me?

They're not after me.

All them lights for just two horses?

A big fat raindrop smacked the back of Kalin's hand. Followed by another. The rain seemed to fall slow with the drops hittin his hat soundin the loudest.

Two horses that my sister fairly bought, as I am my own witness, Tom chuckled. *Maybe she'll turn you in for stealin them. I wouldn't put it past her.*

She's gonna run into them police fer sure.

And she's got that Colt in her belt.

Kalin nodded. *It might just come to nothin more than ridin by with a wave.*

There sure are a lot of police, Tom said.

They must be there for somethin else.

Must be.

Chapter Seven

"By the gate she found a man and his dog"

The conversation with Officer Poulter at the Rome University Theaters had been downright rollickin so long as you consider a one-sided conversation the definition of rollickin. Allison March never did say much more than *It beats me* with now and then the occasional *Not that I know of* thrown in. Officer Poulter finally just handed over a card and told her that anyone at that number could help. If her son returned home, he said multiple times, she should take him to the station at once, that turnin hisself in was fer his own good. Not that that was the end of it. Officer Poulter just couldn't help hisself, his blond moustache dancin all over the place as he leavened this dung bun with the joy of one more revelation: *I shouldn't tell you this, but the boy your boy killt weren't a nobody.*

Beyond that, though, Officer Poulter refused to say more, and Allison hung in there too, even as Teri fled the theaters and Clyde finally retreated to his office. Allison could see Officer Poulter didn't really know what he was doin and felt sure he lacked the restraint to keep to hisself more details of the unfoldin events, what was likely one of the more excitin things to happen to Orvop in a long while. But as smitten as Officer Poulter was by the sound of his own voice, her obdurate silence goadin him to blather more, he did not in the end grant her the name of the child allegedly murdered by her Kalin.

On the bright side, Allison didn't end up spittin on his shoes. And she had cause. Any cop would do. Sure there were good ones here and there, Allison knew that, but she'd still had enuf of them to last a lifetime. Let's just say she was none too impressed by the persistent presence of brutes and bullies in the ranks. Call it a problem inherent in any weaponed authority. As she saw it, despite what Law Enforcement purportedly stood for, that inconceivable Good, the actual culture just didn't add up to enuf to merit that distinction, let alone warrant her respect.

Such was her distrust of police that when she finally pulled outta the mall parkin lot, she half expected Officer Poulter to follow her, to find out where she lived, but then she righted her brain, rememberin him tellin her how they'd already called and been to her apartment and the detective assigned to the case would be callin her again soon and she should pick up. This weren't no small deal.

It was 12:37 a.m. Thursday mornin. Landry by then was already snug as a bug at their second campsite, and Kalin had finally descended into a dream that was so bleak, he had no chance of rememberin it, recallin only the bad feelin that would now and then get in the way of his tryin to organize in his head how he was gonna get both horses and all the supplies up Aster Scree.

At first, habit and exhaustion headed Allison home, again pretendin that maybe she was in a dream and Kalin was already in their apartment, asleep on the sofa. She'd wake him first thing and scold him, and he'd laugh at her worry, and then she'd clear away the sleep in his eyes like she'd always done when he had nightmares. But Allison also knew, and too sharply too, that where she was at now was somethin else, somethin she'd never come up against before, even if it was also familiar, like she'd always knowd that this day would come when together they'd have to face a feast of trouble. She couldn't say why either. It was just this premonition and dread that had sat heavy upon her chest right from the moment Kalin was born. And here it was, come at last. A premonition no more.

He's up Isatch Canyon right now. We'll get up there come mornin. Officer Poulter's words stayed on repeat like a song she didn't want to hear. Turnin up the radio didn't help, what with Stevie Nicks singin about seein her reflection in the snow-covered hills, which maybe did play some part in her changin direction. Allison gave up on home then and headed to Isatch Canyon, which was a travail in itself, albeit a small one, because, truth be told, Allison had no clue where Isatch Canyon was. Of course there was no missin the mountains that rose up to the east like a great wall. Even one passin glance would reveal any number of possible canyons.

From the very first day she and Kalin had arrived in Orvop, them mountains had both stunned her and calmed her, what sleepin outside under a heap of heavy blankets on a frosty night will do. Allison knew mountains too, but in Colorado they had lived among them, while here they lived before them. Orvop and Mud Lake were situated on a wide dry plain, frequently dusty and only sporadically dusted by snow. To the west, way beyond the lake, sat more peaks, but them was milder and often obscured by a persistent haze cast up by industry.

To the east of Orvop, though, was a different story. That way rose up a sudden tumult of rock, surgin upward toward elevations often still bright with snow come early fall. Much of Utah County itself was already elevated, up near a mile, with Agoneeya and Kaieneewa risin up another four thousand feet, with those two bein some of the smaller pups in the Isatch Range, a north-south cordillera that stretched near a hundred and eighty miles, loaded with jagged crags, gorgeous saddlebacks, and numerous glens, cirques, and passes, perfect for recreatin, skiin in the cold seasons, hikin in the warmer ones, and endless explorin of the pristine lakes, rivers, and forests that extend all the way up into Isatch County, Duchesne County, and Summit County.

Orvop was generally considered the altar before the severest steeps and vertical perils, what becomes more apparent beyond Agoneeya and Kaieneewa. Unlike other areas in the state, the Katanogos massif had remained undeveloped, still under the jurisdiction and oversight of state or federal restrictions, includin the United States Department of the Interior and the United States Department of Agriculture, with the back side's terrain, which nears Wallsburg, comprised of a patchwork of state-owned lands and privately owned inholdins, an area that certain citizens have sought to convert into the Four Summits Ski Resort. Sure, plenty have called that aim a pipe dream, but the ambitious are not so easily dissuaded, especially with as precedent the nearby and very much realized dream of the Cassidy Ski Resort, situated on the back side of Mount Timpanogos and owned by that Movie Star, who to his credit did have an electric Jeremiah horse sense when it came to beautiful places, his small bucolic idyll posin as enterprise bein no exception, with just three lifts, a lodge, a big barn, and the shop where Allison worked on weekends. As the reasonin went, especially by the likes of Old Porch, *Why the heck can't you have skiin behind Katanogos if we already have skiin behind Timp?*

And maybe it's worth mentionin that a good part of the majesty of Mount Timpanogos, or Timp as it's known to locals, is due to how it stands by itself, the front side unadorned by the other mountains, hurtlin up from the valley floor to nearly twelve thousand feet, with a permanent snow field at the top, dwarfin both Kaieneewa and Agoneeya. But of course Timp ain't the only mountain dwarfin those two creators of Isatch Canyon. Phil Bauman in 1997, at that time with the Alta Ski Patrol, would say to Trisha Price how *them heights beyond were put there for but one reason: to cower your soul.*

Though before considerin Mount Katanogos, it's worth pointin out somethin else about that first salvo of mountains, in particular Agoneeya, and how a quarter mile up on its face there lies that sizable *I* constructed at the start of the twentieth century out of whitewashed rocks, hand-placed there by the early students of what was then knowd as Isatch High School, not even a college yet let alone a university. That loomin white *I* is big as a football field and for a long time generally recognized as the limit of friendly and languorous trails, after which the easy goin quickly fails, devolvin into unreliable animal paths with no certain way to any of the nearby summits. Over time, of course, carefully groomed routes such as the main Isatch Canyon trail emerged, with more to follow. Even so, there has endured a sense that the civilized front represented by both Agoneeya and Kaieneewa are but prelude to the broodin immensity of Katanogos beyond.

In fact if you lived in Orvop, you was already too close to Agoneeya to see little else than that big *I*. Folks, though, still swear that seein Katanogos isn't what matters. If you're payin attention, especially with your heart, you can always feel Katanogos back there, taste it too in the cold, clear water runnin through everyone's pipes from Rome to Orvop to all the way down in Springville. Allison liked plenty the water, but she couldn't ever claim to *feel* some bigger mountain waitin in the outback. Though just last year she had seen on a particularly clear December day them formidable peaks risin higher than even the clouds, dazzled with snow, the sun glazin them impossible ridges with rose and gold, so bright that to Allison it seemed a fire had been set there to burn down the sky.

But most of the time it weren't like that. Heck, at this very moment Katanogos was the furthest thing from Allison's mind. She was already so used to the mountains to not see them, offerin at best a place for the eye to stop its wanderin off to some too-distant horizon.

Kalin, on the other hand, weren't like her. On the first day of their arrival and pretty much every day since, he had viewed those mountains as an invitation. You can imagine what a blessin Tom was. He showed Kalin the way to answer.

Bein well after midnight, with most of the shops or eateries dark, Allison headed to the 7-Eleven just beyond Isatch University, on College Avenue, which turns into Orvop Canyon Road, one of them routes used by big rigs takin on the night, windin past the turnoff to the Cassidy Ski Resort, and then by the reservoir, which Allison and Kalin had visited once on a picnic. Fer a moment, as Allison exited her Dodge Dart, all of her drenched at once by the rain, her subsequent haste then not only stumblin her across the convenience store parkin lot, past a Peterbilt sleeper cab short of a trailer, what maybe got her mind dartin in new directions, she considered takin that Orvop Canyon Road til it became US-189 and then I-80 and why not to Wyomin?, why not even beyond?, headin her from this here known place to plenty of unknown places to nowhere altogether, hopefully, if she got lucky, just buy herself a two-liter bottle of Dr Pepper and drive, drive, drive.

You know where Isatch Canyon is? she instead asked the bleary-eyed kid at the register.

Sure, answered none other than Andy Stokes, a younger brother of Tyler Stokes, who Landry was crushin on. Not that that connection has much meanin here, because Andy would never recall meetin Kalin's mom this night. He just pointed straight out the door and told her where to take a right before returnin to his econ homework.

Funny how when it comes to entanglin events, some folks who still find themselves in it can also somehow manage to stay clear. Andy's memory of that night would come down to the difference between Giffen goods and Veblen goods.

A few minutes later, Allison was on Temple Drive. She hadn't bought a Dr Pepper either. Just a coffee. When she reached the Isatch Canyon parkin lot, she drove straight for the last lamp that Russel had seen Kalin and the two horses headin for. She parked right under it too, right where Kalin had paused by Tom and declared that it weren't right that his friend was there, which in this case maybe does have some meanin, especially seein as how Allison, as she exited again her yellow station wagon, responded at once to somethin in the light and upon the rain that made her want to shriek bad enuf to dig her nails into her palms, as if such brittle little fists could have any impact on what was amassin out there.

Still, she proceeded through the downpour, on tiptoe for some reason, the hardtop dancin with water, her tiny feet dancin too, as she kept hastenin ahead, right past the visitor kiosk, toward what she dimly considered the actual start of a trail: a big gate barrin all motorized traffic unless you had the key.

There weren't no sign of horses. *Clop-Clop-clip-Clop*. Zero sign of blood. And there sure as heck weren't no sign of her little boy.

She at least expected police here, yellow tape, lots of burnin lights, but there weren't even one patrol car standin watch.

Unbeknownst to her the police had already received a call: a horse sightin near the Heathen-Slade Canyon Trail. A quick consensus settled on the notion that the culprit, one Kalin March, had quit the dead end that was Isatch Canyon and fled south along the base of Agoneeya in a futile attempt to escape. It was in fact the patrol car usually parked by the Heathen-Slade Canyon trailhead that had called in news of the gallopin dark bay fugitive. That got everyone's attention and redirected a small brigade of interceptors. By the time the mare was finally subdued, what would be well into mornin by then, it would be determined that it weren't one of Old Porch's horses but one owned by Agnes Bonnie Hopper.

Accordin to later police department declarations, a patrol car had in fact also been stationed at the Isatch Canyon parkin lot, but, the way things can sometimes unfold sideways, there was an hour there when reports were comin in of not just one horse but a second too, what proved a phantom horse, and with a rider as well, what also proved to be a phantom, but what got that lone patrol car speedin off in the direction of the hospital.

Not that the absence of police did much to steer Allison toward brighter thoughts. She kept takin in the loomin blackness of the canyon itself, made even blacker by the comparative alchemy of all them gray clouds fulminatin overhead. However much the light of the sleepin city of Orvop, the always glowin temple just down the way lent its shine to the immediate high walls of limestone, dolomite, and sandstone, what lay beyond that heavy steel gate, where Allison now stood, no longer on her toes, remained so dense and obdurate and heavy as to seem in its lightlessness to outweigh the very mountains themselves.

Joanne Willden, who you may recall had brought her smears of ash, teal, and charcoal to render Kalin in this same parkin lot, would also apply her imagination to settin Allison in the same place. Though an exemplary artist, this would prove one of her lesser pieces, especially when compared to a work on the same subject by Les Fadley, at the time an art teacher over at Timpview, who, with a lot more oils and maybe a smidge more patience, would bring more life to Allison March's rent features as she failed to rend the dark, a piece he would show to Joanne, who fell in love with it, as well as to Dorothy Meyers who would discuss the work with Lewis Lang at a bus stop.

By this point even the coat collar Allison had pulled over her head had begun to soak through, the water slippin through her hair, congregatin around her neck and shoulders, the cold shiverin her somethin terrible, no question abetted further by that implacable vacancy ahead, what even backed her off some as she cast a fearful eye up toward what Andy Stokes, that bleary-eyed kid back at the 7-Eleven, had referred to as Squaw Peak.

Is here really where her only child had come? On such a night too? Gone by hisself into this place? Was he really up there right now? What on earth for? Horses? Even she could see this was no place for horses.

That shriek she'd continued to keep buried wanted even more now to assert itself against the racket of fallin rain. But even as Allison opened her mouth, no sound emerged. Instead she could manage only a defeated head shake. She couldn't even cry. And then a dull ache concentrated this feelin of woe and fear and desperation and powerlessness so that even as she walked back to the car, if eyes had been upon her, though there were none, she would've seemed somehow compromised, ill-coordinated, a jumblin amble of loose limbs short of a reason to go on. Such is the cost when you are bereft of any response, a cost that won't cease its demand for payment. Allison couldn't even pound the steerin wheel, so she just drove off, away from the canyon, along too many dark and empty streets, returnin to their tiny apartment where his sofa waited, empty, upon which she lay herself, like he was her only wish, and he was her only wish, and if it was to be an unanswered wish, then let this sofa be her coffin.

Detective Peters woke her just before dawn. Actually well before dawn, right in fact as Kalin was wakin up to face his day and with Tom's help revive the fire. Allison answered the detective's questions with only the dull truth. She'd heard nothin from her son. When she in turn asked him if he'd heard anythin, he regurgitated somethin about bein unable to divulge details in an ongoin investigation. Allison could tell he weren't nothin like that Officer Poulter. His voice was steady though not unkind, evened too by a good deal of experience. She hung up on him.

Allison hadn't taken off her wet coat when she'd come in, and the sofa felt damp through. She shed her theater uniform, black polyester pants, white polyester shirt, and turned on the shower to warm herself and clear her head. It did warm her but did nothin for her head. It was hard enuf to drag on some clean underwear, dry faded jeans held up with a faded rainbow belt, and a white long-sleeved shirt, over which she put on a light sea green sweater. She was at least thinkin clearly enuf to put on thick wool socks, though not so clearly when she then put on her plenty thinned and scuffed Stan Smiths. They was comfortable. She could hardly brush her hair, let alone her teeth. She left the specks of turquoise in her ears, tyin her blond hair up in a shaggy ponytail with a black hair tie.

A stranger had once described her as a riverbed long since panned of gold but with enuf twinkles of brightness left to if not buy somethin special then remember what special could mean. She'd thrown her drink at him, but he'd bought her another one before he left. She'd known too many mean men to understand one who wasn't. She wondered what he'd say now, all these years hence. Were any twinkles left? Not that she'd ever run into him again. She'd long since given up goin to bars. In fact that one had been one of her last.

Coffee. That's what came next, and she could manage that, even if she didn't manage, because before the water could boil, she had a plan.

Allison March didn't park in one of the school's lots but in front of Meaai Lelei, a Samoan eatery that still hadn't opened.
It was now 7:32 a.m.
Light was only just now challengin the storm. It weren't winnin either. School buses had started to arrive, and car pools were droppin

off kids. At least fer a moment the rain had paused. Out in front of Orvop High kids took advantage of the lull and loitered around on the steps for a few more unmonitored moments before headin inside. Allison adjusted her gray winter parka and pulled down snug her rosesable cable-knit wool hat as she crossed the street and cut through as many groups millin about as she could, her ears open for anythin to make her pause. But there was nothin. A few students noticed her, and though it was likely harmless curiosity, that hurried her along.

As she approached the school's main entrance, she was determined to ask Principal Furst about Kalin, whether he was there, though right before the glass doors, she stopped, lettin more and more students cut in front of her, and interestinly enuf one of them was none other than Woolsey Porch, who knew nothin yet about his youngest brother Russel, in fact none of his brothers had heard the news yet except, of course, for Egan and Kelly and their old man, who had yet to return home. Of course, Woolsey's innocence was about to change, and in the next few minutes too: news of life's sudden demise, cruelly delivered by none other than the voice of rumor, was already mummerin through the school hallways.

Regardless of what was to come, though, at this instant Woolsey could only see an older woman in his way, while Allison could only see a glass door swingin wide open to a dumb idea. Principal Furst or the vice-principal or whoever she finally got to see would only confirm what she already knew: Kalin had not turned up at school that mornin.

Allison retreated back to her car, and at least by then Meaai Lelei had opened. They didn't have coffee, but they served up an egg dish with pineapples and somethin called panikeke, what was fried dough as far as she could tell, but it was sweet and felt fortifyin.

She bought a paper. Local news was mostly about the storm system comin in, stacked up and relentless, expected to last well on through the weekend, joyous news for skiiers in the area. There was also some stories about a bill in the senate, *Senate Bill 1245*, which could see a vote soon, somethin about the federal government cedin federal land back to the state to manage as it saw fit, which as far as Utah was concerned was considered good news.

It was 8:33 a.m. when Allison stood up to pay the bill. In her wallet she found the folded postcard she'd kept for she-didn't-know-how-many years. It was of the tombstone of someone named Nikos Kazantzakis. She'd never heard of him, much less read him, and the epitaph was in Greek. But she knew what it meant: *I hope for nothin. I fear nothin. I am free.* She liked that plenty, though not nearly as much as Kalin did. When times had been hard, with his daddy gettin worse and worse, when she and Kalin had had to run out in the night, then find a new place, and another place after that, Kalin would ask her to take it out. When they'd settled in Colorado she'd pinned it up above his desk. When they'd left Colorado she'd folded it up and kept it in her wallet. She'd meant to pin it up in his room here, but there weren't no room for him yet and no place to pin it up above the sofa. Kalin hadn't minded. *Nec spe, nec metu,* he'd told her with a hand on his heart, somethin a teacher here had taught him. On the other side of the card, the dark side of the moon so to speak, there were words from her sister, the kind that burn the bridge, though that was some time ago and there weren't no more bridge left to burn and no more fire neither. Allison tucked the postcard away and found the cash she needed.

Tryin her best then to rally up the energy pointlessness requires, startin with just movin toward the door, and then likely movin on to that dumb idea after all, seekin out Principal Furst, if only to confirm the worst, her determination was checked as some students suddenly roared into Meaai Lelei, loud, thrilled, likely cuttin first period, which Allison knew for most of them was seminary. She could see they was psyched to play the arcade games there, maybe psyched to sluff the whole day.

But murdered?! one shouted, that would be Doug Harwood, already stuffin quarters in the machine called *Centipede.*

Cut Russel's head clean off! said another, that would be Larry Ashby, him stuffin quarters in the machine called *Missile Command.*

You know that's all bullcrap, said the last one, him bein Rick Ramsey, the most sensible of the three. They all played soccer together and smoked pot together too if Doug Harwood could get some off his older brother. Though they weren't stoned now.

I'm sorry for interruptin, but did I hear you just say a boy was killt? Allison asked.

That's what we heard, said Larry Ashby, the one spinnin the ball on *Missile Command.*

Who? Allison asked.

Russel Porch, said Rick Ramsey, the one waitin his turn.

A kid at Orvop High did it too, Doug Harwood added, spinnin the ball on *Centipede,* firin fast as he could.

Keelin I think is his name, said Rick Ramsey, shiftin the quarters from one hand to the other.

Did you know him? Allison asked.

Rick Ramsey shook his head. *You guys?*

They all shook their heads.

Any of you know Russel's folks? That's what Allison really wanted to know, but she was already feelin like her question had come out wrong.

The two playin just stopped and looked at her.

His folks?! said Doug Harwood, the *Centipede* machine groanin then with the sure sound of some kinda defeat.

Rick Ramsey gave her a good look before steppin back.

Maybe I know them? Allison said, gettin that wrong too, and wincin too.

Are you a reporter? asked Larry Ashby, steppin away from *Missile Command* but, unlike Rick, steppin toward her. He was the biggest of them by far. *Everyone knows who the Porch family is here. Why you askin these questions?* He gave her a hard look, and even though he weren't much older than Kalin, he was big as a man.

How badly did she want to turn tail, and nothin was stoppin her either, but if she had a chance of findin anythin out, it was here, and now, from these three.

His name ain't Keelin. It's Kalin. And I'm his mother.

That changed things some.

The one they say killt Russel?! asked Doug Harwood, lookin at her now like she was famous.

Allison nodded. *I need to find Russel's folks.*

I f it weren't for the large sign, PORCH MEATS & CO., posted on Zurich Road, Allison would've assumed she was lookin at a home, and in fact it was the Porch home, a two-story spread of brown bricks and big windows hidin their withins with brown curtains. Down one side, beyond a wide gravel driveway, she spied a shed of sorts, with broken bales of hay in front and a general disorder extendin from there that included a rusted tractor and a truck on blocks. Farther back waited what looked like a much bigger buildin.

Not that Allison was gettin a good view of anythin. Even inside the car, and with the defrost on high, the windows wouldn't stop foggin up, given extra substance she felt by mustiness in the air, some of that no doubt due to Mud Lake bein so close by, and of course the refinery too, but also because of the unmistakable sweet stink of manure nearby minglin with the smell of peat, lye, and smoke. For Allison, from their time in Colorado, it weren't an unknown mix of things to find on the mornin air. *Smells like Greeley,* Allison thought, makin too a deeper and much more unsettlin association: for all her travels, for all her drivin desires to escape, she was still somehow findin herself in the same place.

Then she saw them, far in the back by what looked like dog kennels:

two horses, a buckskin and a pinto, bein led by a man with long black hair. That would be Billings. He'd already noticed the yellow station wagon and the dirty blond-haired lady at the wheel but gave her no more thought than that. Weren't the first time he'd seen some distraught woman in a rusty car pull up in front of the Porch residence. He focused on loadin the ponies into the trailer.

It was 8:49 a.m.

Somethin about the horses really put the terror in Allison then, and she hadn't even locked eyes with Billings. Their manes, their beautiful necks, their proudly thrown heads, they recalled for her what quailed her heart. It was the terror only a mother can know, as her only son grows into hisself, in a way that goes beyond hisself and easily beyond herself too. The pinto went up the ramp and disappeared into the trailer, followed by the buckskin, likely a mare, who pinned her ears on the ramp and gave the fella at her halter one heckuva hard time, what Kalin wouldn't've had no trouble with. Such were his gifts. How many times had she studied her boy in his sleep, askin the same questions: Who are you? Where did you come from? How did I get so lucky? If the world only knew . . . But then again, the world likely did know; it was just these folks here who hadn't figured out yet who it was exactly that walked among them.

Allison fluttered her lips. She wanted nothin to do with any of this, but she also knew when what she wanted or didn't want didn't mean diddly against what she had to do. She figured she'd start with the front door and, if there weren't no answer, there decide if she had the courage to approach the big buildin in back or fer starters that man by the banged-up trailer. Not that that plan moved her any from the driver's seat, engine still idlin, her hands near fused to the wheel.

In many an AA meetin over the years, part of what had helped her escape Kalin's daddy, Allison had spoke plainly about her fear of confrontation. She'd meant to find a meetin in Orvop but had yet to hear about one closer than Salt Lake City, which was a good forty-minute drive away. Time she didn't have. And besides, she weren't so sure how sayin aloud what she'd already said aloud so many times before could help. She still remembered clear as a day without a cloud, as if it was still on her lips, what'd filled her with shame when she'd first gotten it out, and this was years ago: *I'd rather run than face a thing head-on* even as she'd at once vowed right then and there that if she was gonna change one thing about herself, what she'd had limited success with at first, but since Kalin's daddy was now in jail for good she had a better chance at, sayin it aloud even now in the car: *I wanna face a thing rather than run from a thing.*

Allison settled herself further with some long breaths, nose only, and then, because she kept eyein the front door across the passenger seat, she didn't see what was comin for her driver's side.

The rap on her window near made her scream.

We're closed.

Allison, of course, didn't know this here was Kelly Porch, up the whole night long, eyes and head full of the kinda awfulness that won't leave no one unchanged. She just saw a tall, powerful young man, shoulders wide as his eyes were wide set, cheeks freckled, with only his lips, unusually soft and big, betrayin some sense of early youth. He had on one of them big rodeo buckles too, silver mostly, with a gold bull at the center, on the run. A light brown hat kept the drizzle off his face.

I'm here to speak to the Porches? she said as she cranked down the window. *Is Mrs. Porch in?*

She don't live around here no more.

Mr. Porch then?

My daddy's with the police. We've had quite a night of it. Kelly bent down then and gave her as much a look as he did the inside of her car, like he was lookin for somethin to want. *What can I do you for?*

I'm here about Russel.

Kelly stood bolt upright then, like she'd done kicked him. *Who are you to Russel?* Asked in that way that ain't a question, too much bite in his words, too much bright on his buckle.

Allison's hands started shakin so bad, she near cursed them as she dug out a pen from the ashtray and retrieved a crumpled receipt off the floor.

My name's Allison March. This here's my number. If your father's willin, I'd like to talk to him. I'm the mother of the one they're sayin killt Russel. Are you his brother?

Kelly didn't nod or offer up his name, but he did take the phone number.

Allison headed the Dart station wagon back to the apartment, again thinkin she might find Kalin on the sofa, again thinkin all this was a terrible misunderstandin but knowin at the same time, again, that Kalin weren't there, what knowin made returnin to too much to bear. Returnin to Orvop High, though, was still somethin worse. Principal Furst would only say Kalin was truant, and whatever he said after that wouldn't matter. Allison changed course again, this time headin to the police, intent on findin this Detective Peters if for no other reason than to beg for some kinda substantial news.

At least at the Orvop Police Station Allison managed to get out of her car, but that was about it. A few officers goin in gave her a look, but no more than that. In fact this was Allison's first glimpse of Detective Peters, though she didn't know it. He was headin out, in a hurry, though the manner of his pace hardly betrayed the state of a mind that yesterday was plannin out with his wife's family a vacation down to Moab and now was dealin with immense pressures that required unerrin focus. Allison figured him for a former athlete, and she was right, and though he weren't in uniform, she didn't miss the badge on his hip. Maybe he was Hispanic, Hawaiian, or even Tongan, or maybe just very tan; either way he was immediately noticeable given the prevadin paleness that defined this here community, what Carey Boone described as *havin about as many shades as cottage cheese.* He noticed her too, they exchanged nods, and he even complimented her car, *Nice Dodge,* said with an easy-enuf smile. Though it's true that she'd spoken with him just that mornin, his voice at that moment did not ring familiar. She gave him a tight-lipped smile and thought no more of the man who would become so important to her in the unrevisable future that awaited them both.

Can I help you? another cop asked her, this one a woman. Her name was Tish Haggerty, who years later would revisit this moment with Misty Blue Whitlock, Roper Brunsen, and Jo Ellen Shrapernell.

Allison nodded. She needed help. *I'm lookin for a pay phone.*

One right through those doors, Tish Haggerty said with a smile. *Or you can use the one on the corner over there if you need more privacy.*

Allison thanked her and picked the pay phone on the corner. She set as much change as she'd dug out of the car's glove box on top of the phone. And then she just stared at the keypad. She needed help. She needed to call someone, but she had no one. She'd lost her parents years ago. She had no siblin who wouldn't hang up on her, no friends who wouldn't hang up on her. Fer a moment she even considered callin Kalin's daddy. Of course, she'd rather be dead than do that, but the thought did cross her mind.

She repocketed the change. She didn't know what to do. When tears threatened she knew she wanted nothin to do with them either. What she wanted was her boy, and so she returned to Isatch Canyon.

The presence of the empty horse trailer surprised Allison more than the number of police already there or the patrol car she'd followed in, lights a-goin. In fact Allison dismissed near at once her conclusion that this here was the same trailer she'd just seen over at Porch Meats. Orvop weren't exactly a horsey town, not when you compare it to places like Brandywine, Pennsylvania, or Lexington, Kentucky, or so much of Maryland and so much more of Texas. But there were horses in Orvop nonetheless, and a trailer on the road or parked up next to a house, even if that house didn't have no barn, weren't so unusual. Maybe if she hadn't've seen the truck haulin the trailer, a 1978 Chevy, coughin diesel pretty much as soon as you turned the key, what from Allison's perspective had stayed hid behind the main processin buildin, she'd have knowd at once this trailer here was the same one from Porch Meats. The Chevy was likely what threw her, the red, the white; it seemed obvious there, so blatant and unencountered. She at once discounted her better instincts and instead returned her gaze to two Orvop patrol cars, two Utah County Sheriff cars, all their lights still goin; and then a fire truck, them lights also goin; a park ranger truck too, no lights there; and last of all the yellow police tape put up by the visitor kiosk, like that was where the crime had taken place. Had it?

On closer inspection, Allison discovered the tape was up mostly to keep curious folks like herself away from the white canopy tent gettin set up at that moment, with three card tables already standin underneath. Someone nearby wondered aloud if that was where they'd put the bodies. This prompted a discussion among strangers about whether there was more than one body? Most confirmed there was only the one, but they still waited like maybe more bodies would appear any second.

Allison was most surprised to find out that despite such commotions, Isatch Canyon Park was still considered open. Not that there was so great a risk of lots of hikers headin out on a cold Thursday mornin in the midst of a rainfall that seemed only to be gettin worse. The canyon itself still had on display the same endurin emptiness she'd beheld so many hours ago in the dark. Not even her glimpse now of the quartzite and limestone cliffs risin toward the summits of Agoneeya and Kaieneewa did anythin to lessen her experience of immense absence, though even that was immaterial given how Katanogos itself and even its lower ridges and descendin spurs remained invisible from here, what Allison then, if she'd paused to ask herself, might've admitted, yes, she could feel it in her chest. And it weren't a good feelin either.

By the gate she found a man and his dog studyin, just like she would do in a moment, the main trail that runs the length of the canyon floor, across seven bridges, all the way up to Yell Rock Falls. Allison had no way of knowin that this here was Orwin Porch hisself. Of course, in turn, Orwin Porch had no way of knowin who she was.

He marked her arrival first with a grind of molar dissatisfaction, and even took a light swat at his face, as if a mosquito had alighted there. Then upon gettin a full view of her, Old Porch takin in her figure, her approximate age, and givin her hands a good glance too, her narrow waist, plus everythin else on the way down to her knees, where he lost interest, his features lightened some, maybe with even a blink of blue enterin them gray eyes and a smile of sorts appearin on his lips, the same one he'd share with anythin deservin of his desires.

That look weren't lost on Allison, but it weren't so big a bother either. She'd outlived the spell of her youth. She'd almost forgotten those young years when she'd grown long, when even a shallow inhale could bring a fullness to her chest that stirred up the wild in boys' eyes, and her breasts had had nothin on Mel Marshall's, who, no matter how hard she'd tried to hide them, had known wildness her whole short life. But Allison weren't a cub no more, when such attention might've seemed like flies worth playin with or swattin at; now she was more the mother lion, payin no mind to bees beardin her jaw as she kept an unblinkin eye out for her cub upon the savanna.

Allison smiled back easy enuf before turnin away, both of them keepin their respective peace with the manifold destinies laid out before them in the language of rock and storm-soaked bark.

Not that Allison could dismiss the old man entirely, who gratefully seemed apart from the municipal commotion not even a hundred steps away, even if at the same time somethin about him provoked in her an immediate wariness that she could not understand. He was to be avoided, and yet he seemed so bewildered and even frail. Curiously, especially given the weather, he didn't wear but rather chose to carry in his big hands a charcoal cowboy hat encircled with a bruised-plum-colored ribbon, leavin exposed to the relentless slap of rain his liver-spotted scalp and the straggly remains of gray-and-white hair. A life in the sun had creased, cracked, and leathered his features to no betterment, but Allison could recognize that more than just the harshness of light had written its speech upon his face. Perhaps what disturbed her most was how undisturbed he was by all the police. Maybe he was one of them? Just out of uniform? Did his coat conceal a sheriff's star pinned on that raggedy horsehair vest he wore beneath?

Allison kept her distance.

It's somewhat amusin to consider how, fer all their substantial instincts and in some areas superb attunements, neither Allison March nor Orwin Porch, as they took private measure of each other, could succeed in sensin how that great gap before them now, built by two lesser mountains, was measurin them; how out of two impersonal elevations a grand conspirin continued, inhumane in its architecture, expectant and unfazed, protean, protonic and strange; havin already conscripted into its unfathomable Service, its measurable boundaries, everythin from lichens to moss to broken leaves to great blocks of ancient stone to even this latest storm. And this influence was nothin compared to great Katanogos beyond. For even as everythin would change, nothin could change except as ordained by the obscure tenets of such lithic Absence and Judgment bindin not only this woman and this man but many others already caught within that cradle and crucible of what the future would in regardin the writ past come to call Destiny.

That bein said, and not givin a hoot about mountains or who was or was not guarded over by unreadable Providence, Orwin Porch's Rottweiler trotted over to sniff up Allison's sneakers. The old man did nothin to stop him. Allison gave him a pet. She couldn't help herself. The dog's tail had started to wag. He was nice.

Seems your dog likes me.

No, he don't. He don't like anybody. He don't even like me, the old man said, keepin the same smile he'd already shown her, maybe because he didn't mind so much lookin her way again, not that Old Porch needed a reason to look any way he pleased. He was always on the lookout for a nurse or a purse. Even an empty purse could do for a night. *He's just hungry. I guarantee it.* And to prove the point, he produced a small piece of Porch jerky from his pocket, which he took a bite from first before offerin the rest to the Rottweiler, who didn't budge from Allison.

The old man cocked his head, finished the jerky hisself, and finally gave an approvin nod: *Okay then, maybe Mr. Bucket does like you.*

Mr. Bucket? That's his name?

Mr. Bucket Number Five.

I'm guessin he was preceded by one through four?

You'd be guessin right. As far as I'm concerned, they're all the same dog.

Allison forced a congenial smile, though his explanation didn't sit well with her. She returned to regardin the canyon ahead, unaware that at that exact moment, a good four miles up and then some, her Kalin and Tom were standin atop Aster Scree lookin anxiously down for some sign of Landry and Jojo, who, under tree cover, had just left the crick and were now headin up the slope leadin to the main Isatch Canyon trail, what Allison and Old Porch were now contemplatin.

Where would this take me? Allison asked, realizin that despite her better instincts she was cravin some small talk. *If I went the whole way?*

Maybe the old man needed some of the same, because he was game to keep their chitchat goin. *You'd get a good half day's walk in and then, unless you brought ropes and knew how to use them, you'd have to turn around and come back out.*

It's a dead end?

Isatch here is a box canyon. He squinted his eyes then to study her more closely, or anew, this time notin her waterlogged Stan Smiths. *Not really a day for a hike, but you don't look like you came here to hike.*

I heard a boy was killt up there last night.

You heard right. His throat was cut. Bled out on the way home.

Russel Porch?

He was my youngest.

Allison made a sound then that even she didn't understand. Maybe it was a cough or a groan or a gasp or all that combined. Either way it lurched out of her unbidden. Orwin Porch didn't seem to notice.

The one who done it is still in there, he continued, *and I mean to be here when he comes out.*

Despite havin so fortuitously stumbled upon her goal, Allison at once wanted nothin more to do with it. She wanted to run, just excuse herself and then drive, drive away. Just drive, drive, drive.

Mr. Porch, she said instead. *My name's Allison March.*

Old Porch showed no sign of recognizin the name nor givin a hoot that he didn't

I'm the mother of Kalin March. The one they're sayin killt Russel. I've been lookin for you. Went to your home earlier. I just wanted to meet face-to-face and let you know that my boy, well, he wouldn't do no such a thing.

Orwin Porch yanked up Mr. Bucket #5 sharp then and didn't stop there either, kept yankin him by the leash until the big dog was close to his leg, that metal prong collar no doubt helpin him get his way. Then Old Porch stepped back from the gate and put on his hat, castin his already darkenin eyes into even greater shadow.

You got some sand, lady. I'll give you that.

I'll do whatever it takes to help you find your boy's killer. And I'll stand with you the whole way until the one that's done this stands trial.

A trial? Old Porch's voice rose with a question, though there weren't no question, him smilin now too, this time a real smile, puttin on display all them shattered teeth, maybe his diversivolent nature too.

For whoever done this to your child, Allison still answered.

Boys will do things you can never expect, what even they themselves can't know to expect. They're still drunk on their youngness, with anger in their hands. And what it takes to set them off is near nothin. And if there's a knife at hand . . . Ma'am, you've got no idea what your boy is capable of. I'd say the same for my boy Russel, except that Russel wouldn't know how to fight his way out of a paper bag.

Kalin neither. And he sure don't got no anger in his hands.

Old Porch spat. *I appreciate your directness, and maybe I can even sympa-thize with you bein his mother and all, but last night my boy came to me drenched in his own blood, and he named your boy as his killer.* Old Porch spat again. *My Russel caught your Kalin stealin my horses, and he paid for it with his life.*

Allison had no words, not that Old Porch, if she'd had any, would've stood by to let her speak them.

Yesterday, he continued, *I had eight boys. Today I got seven. Some are already up there, lookin to make right what was made wrong last night. You best brace yourself for how this is gonna end. One way or another, your boy will be found, and when he is, he won't have no life left to live. I guarantee it.*

It was 10:04 a.m.

Chapter Eight

"Cavalry"

ow we got to address here even more ugliness: murder. And in some ways worse: the intent to murder. And then even worse on worse: an agreed-upon intent by several individuals without one word said, forget whispered, not aloud ever, what any court would have difficulty prosecutin: no verbal ledger to connect the dots, nor no obvious purchase or gatherin of weapons or some other implement suited for awful violence. Which also begs an awful question: if intent was in no way apparent, was there intent at all? But of course there was, no question.

Because it was intent alone that began its fuliminatin, and near at once too, in front of Egan's house, out on the sidewalk, and we're goin back here to that moment with the youngest Porch only recently demised, just after midnight, with Kelly, crouched in the rain, perseverin with pointless CPR on his dead brother Russel, until the ambulance finally arrived, followed soon after by a fire engine, then Orvop City police to whom Old Porch, Egan, and Billings dutifully relayed the events of the evenin: a friendly game of cards, word of stolen horses, Russel settin out on Cavalry to retrieve them, Russel returnin with his throat slit, fallin sideways to the sidewalk, and then Old Porch callin 911 while Kelly here, the true hero of the night, never ceased his attempts to resuscitate his youngest brother.

The police asked why Russel wasn't taken inside and seemed satisfied when Kelly explained he feared movin Russel, even a little, as it would've caused a cessation in the chest compressions he was administerin betwixt puffs of fraternal air upon them coolin lips, actually cold lips. Kelly worried aloud that he also feared Russel's neck might have broken with the fall, or some part of his spine fractured, though he admitted in retrospect that that was a stupid thing to go on about, as he'd seen with his own eyes how Russel merely slid off Cavalry. *We rushed out soon as we heard that big horse clatterin on the cement.*

The police asked if anyone other than those here present were there when Russel had returned. Egan shook his head. The police still wanted a list of those who'd been at the house earlier, and Old Porch obliged them at once, startin with Havril Enos and then Francis, Woolsey, and last of all Trent Riddle.

Now a good bunch of smart folks have reckoned that this was an error right out the gate. Old Porch could've omitted Riddle's name and claimed reasonable forgetfulness due to the tragic events of that night. Though as Cliff Woolf has pointed out: *One way or another the Porches was gonna have to deal with Riddle. Riddle alone knew what could not be made known if Old Porch's version of things was gonna hold up as the truth.*

Old Porch even offered up how Riddle drove a brown Plymouth

Duster. *Maybe 1970?* Which was true, the date too, followed then by the big lie, why blood often compounds with more blood, the erasure of its spillin demandin still more spillin, and so on, which we'll get to soon enuf.

Like sleepin pills powdered up in yogurt, Old Porch knew just how to mix up mostly the truth in order to get the lies down untasted. He declared apologetically that he didn't know Riddle's address or number, but he'd be happy to get on over to Porch Meats and dig up that info for them or send one of his boys here over if they was in a rush. Not that he paused for a response, makin it clear that he hoped the real rush was not to find Riddle but the Kalin boy who'd done killt his son. The police assured him at once that locatin the killer was the only thing that mattered. Officer Willard Mildenhall then mentioned that Detective Peters was on his way and the Porch family could rest easy knowin he'd be in charge. *One of our best,* Officer Mildenhall added, his eyes fer a moment settlin on them white-faced lawn jockeys Egan loved so much.

Years later, Officer Mildenhall would recall the deafenin uneasiness provoked in him by those two statues that back then weren't worth more than twenty bucks, what he hadn't even really understood, repainted the way they was, though with some of that pale paint now flakin off, warnin him for reasons he could never have explained then, nor later: to be careful, a cautionin he felt but didn't heed. None of them did. Except maybe Detective Peters.

That Egan hadn't pulled right then from his wallet the folded card listin most Porch Meat employees with their numbers, includin Riddle's, plain as day, in black ink, or that Kelly didn't just rattle off the number that he knew by heart illustrates just how quickly and seamlessly these boys closed ranks behind their daddy's misrepresentation. Billings too gave not a sign of knowledge. And though nothin more was said really than this display of ignorance, it was understood that when Old Porch asked Kelly to stay with him, and when Egan right after volunteered to drive over to Porch Meats to get Riddle's contact information, the police raisin no objection, most of them just circulatin around Egan's house, now and then pokin their heads into the barn to dry off, warm up some, but also to ogle the bloodstained Cavalry, somethin terrible was by then already in motion, invisible to all but Old Porch, Egan, and Billings, and maybe Kelly, though that Porch boy was sufferin enuf gastric objections to keep forcin his eyes closed with every cramp.

You're the real horseradish, Old Porch had told Egan before he drove away.

That was the most said. Even when Egan and Billings was alone, they didn't say nothin about where they was headed. Egan just punched in that 8-track of Nazareth, Dan McCafferty at once singin *A world all for free* as the Ford Ranger roared away from Isatch Canyon.

There are ways we know things. Sometimes it's laid out neat and clear, how somethin happened, how somethin's gonna happen, like an itinerary or, in the case of who someone is, like a yearbook picture with a résumé stapled behind. But as you've likely figured out by now, that's not generally how things unfold in the thick of things. That first impression is too often just a way to not see what happens next. The clearest view, on the other hand, demands an awareness mindful of the slow but uninterruptible accretion of detail. But that is a process that tolerates no rush. This is what some might call slow time but is really just time in all its fullness, especially when the matter at hand is real friends, which is perhaps our greatest try at fullness.

Fer now, let us agree that this recountin so far does require some effort to coerce from memory and instincts a reasonable assessment and picture of those involved; though quite rightly it seems equally fair to expect now and then some effort here to refresh our collective understandin of folks depicted here.

Fer example, Kalin has only partially come into view, his brown hair, green eyes, and scrappy build, what some might've described as lanky if he weren't so small, if while on Navidad comin across as lithe and nimble from smile to bootheel, though clumsy as all heck when he weren't around a horse, and whether it's important or not, with hardly a shadow about him either, even if there was at his core a bafflin darkness thicker than anythin musterable with the tarriest oils. Or take Old Porch, also a partial portrait, typically armored in that horse-hair vest with those snakeskin boots on, and them icy gray eyes and shattered teeth colludin into a cussed face and form that, whether by harsh daylight or cold moonlight, will at once demand of any skilled assessor of character a quick step back, if only because any proximity to them cruel scarred hands might seem too close for comfort. However Allison March, Kalin's mother, by this point might seem fairly well composed even if that is hardly the case. That goes for Egan too, and Kelly with them wide-set eyes. Even poor Russel has more to tell, though not much.

And then there's Landry Gatestone. Why at this point she ain't even half-sketched. Her fire and will, certainly her skill on Jojo, not to mention her aptitude with ropes and knots, fer sure that all's plenty apparent, but what vitalizes her has not yet made it into words. And then, of course, what do we do about Tom? He's perhaps the most vacant of all, a ghost, and yet not even that, hardly even a ghost of his former self, even if he does got his laugh, or some of it. His full laugh, why that would shudder mountains if not make them tumble.

And then there's the various commentators whom we can never really behold, a Greek chorus of sorts, but only if we accept that at one point or another we are all of us a member of such a chorus, conscripted by tales told. Fer example, in another tale, Kalin and Tom might serve as mere commentators with not even hats on.

That leaves the horses, the heart of this here, without whom all would collapse. What do we truly know of them? Navidad, the mustang, a black mare with a white star, swifter than an arrow? Or Mouse, mostly quarter horse, a blood bay geldin with a white blaze, the destroyer, or at least as ornery as a grizzly outside a honey shop? Or Jojo, an Arab, blue as a dawn sky that ain't never gonna set the sun free? Or Ash, well we got some notions already about Ash. But of their histories, their quadrupedal lives, their moment-to-moment thoughts, their sufferin and delights, what immediacies they prefer, what impressions they guard, what do we know of these?

Some no doubt will replace these equine friends with images they've encountered in a movie or on a postcard or perhaps, if encountered beyond representation, substitute in an animal slavishly led forth at a pettin zoo or for a sunset ride, near hobbled with saddles big as sofas. Them, though, that are more horse inclined, with the experience to prove it, heartside and back side, will have already noted the absence of those distinctions that comprise a personality and define a friend. Fret not; these will come and by the end will be enuf to fashion a serviceable tableau befittin our four horses. For they remain, after all, lest we ever forget, everythin here: what Kalin confined hisself to both in deed and declaration, *Just the horses,* and what Tom reached for most in death.

Finally, what's hard at work beyond the individual, emergin as collective intentions, no matter how subsequent articulations foolishly refuse the larger contexts that encapsulate further all animal spirits, these confluences of actions, patterns, human enterprises materialized, call them even schemes, do not arrive fully formed, even for primary participants, no matter how confident they remain with the whole; after all it is only their whole, what is often mostly imagined, strugglin throughout to accommodate inconsistencies, ambiguities, alterations, until finally the deed it is, like a punch line to a joke, at last announces itself and so defines, and to most folks' satisfaction too, the causal formulation that preceded it.

Observe how Egan and Billings weren't sayin diddly to one another, even as they was tearin straight across Orvop to Riddle's place, with each in their own way still convinced that they intended only to have a good sit-down with Riddle, to just talk to the boy, explain the situation, in the same way that some horndog might tell hisself he just wants to talk to some lady, so it don't matter that she's married or even that he's married, he just wants to say hi, and he means it too, even when that hi turns into an afternoon stroll, then a lemonade, then a kiss that's not only about a kiss but how a hard place needs a wet place; how, say, for example, the likes of Jordan Heaton and Nadeen Garriman ultimately proceeded to connect. In the same way, and yes this might seem a perversion of the most biological prerogative, especially such natural bodily orchestrations, anticipatory of bondin, love, and family, when compared to that foulest deed, what breaks the sixth commandment: the killin of another. And then to trouble this opposition even more, for some such acts of violence can offer similar if not greater satisfaction than mere physical desire and congress.

Billings had some experience with violence but unlike Egan found no exhilaration in it. For Billings violence was a necessity. For Billings violence was only needed if it helped guarantee survival. For Egan, however, violence already existed within that tinglin zone that promises renewed statisfaction, growin only stronger as he pulled into the parkin lot of Riddle's buildin, like he was on a hot date, even as he kept tellin hisself how they was only gonna tell Riddle how there was an emergency at Porch Meats, somethin to do with an early delivery of livestock in need of immediate processin, which was how they'd get him to the kill floor, all while sayin that of course he'd be nicely compensated, they all would be, which, along with Riddle's poker winnins, would make his night that much more exceptional.

You'll recall that Riddle had not witnessed Russel's tragic demise, but unlike Woolsey and Francis Porch, both of whom had left earlier, Riddle had seen Russel arrive not only boastin of his accomplishment but helpin too to grow the pot that Riddle would finally take. In other words, Riddle had seen for hisself Russel's neck intact as a newborn's; he knew full well that Russel hadn't bled out on the sidewalk beside Cavalry. Given the story that Old Porch, Egan, Kelly, and Billings had lined up behind, that remained a big, big problem.

Egan had only once before handled such a problem, and he hadn't even really done the handlin part, as it was Old Porch who serviced the end. This was three years ago, when Egan was twenty-three. The man's name was Brad P. Hone. He'd been the one to approach

Old Porch with an offer of assistance, part of the ongoin wranglins that concerned Four Summits. As Egan heard it explained, Old Porch figured the apple knocker would either try *to gazump or gazunder us* accordin to what benefitted him most. With that strong possibility in mind, Old Porch had decided it was about time his son get in on some man-moldin labor and so had told Egan to come along. Egan was thrilled by his father's confidence in him and then bored stiff. The three had met one afternoon at an Arby's in Midway. At least Mr. Hone didn't bring up at once the Hone family landholdings southeast of Heber. He mostly talked about some other property he had inherited up near Coalville and then got goin about horseradish, what was good horseradish, what wasn't good horseradish, and Arby's had the kind of horseradish that wasn't good, though Old Porch's Four Summits dream was the real horseradish. Egan just kept his straw stuck where his front tooth used to live and slurped on his Mountain Dew and didn't say a word. Old Porch didn't say much either. Didn't eat neither. Only in the parkin lot did Egan understand that this Mr. Hone was also one of them politically involved men that his daddy frequently had dealins with in Salt Lake City. Maybe a lobbyist, though Egan couldn't be sure of that. Egan weren't even really sure what a lobbyist was if it didn't have nothin to do with the entrance of a hotel.

Then this Mr. Hone, wearin his light green polo sweater and the jeans he'd maybe worn twice, started bringin up the name of state representatives and senators and the folks he knew at the Bureau of Land Management, and then finally the Hone family's inholdins, *etc., etc.,* crucial to Four Summits, sayin, well, how there were things he knew that might not make the Hone family particularly happy, especially the Hone patriarch, that salty nonagenarian known as Manic Guff, if they heard what Brad, the thirteenth child, could and would tell them, what might very well disincline anyone else to keep conductin their business with the likes of Orwin Porch. *The family will vote, and I'm your key to Hone family consensus.* Of course, Mr. Brad P. Hone had no intention of disturbin that consensus. *Consider me like a son, Orwin,* he even said. Because he was gonna be Old Porch's right-hand man, at-large, takin care of any indiscretions that might slip from the lips of others, *But not my lips, Orwin,* disclosures that might spoil the delicate relationships necessary for Four Summits to move forward.

Egan didn't follow none of it, and his takeaway, what he later recognized was a real stupid takeaway, was that Brad P. Hone wanted a job, and that's just what Old Porch seemed then to offer him, with a big handshake and a flash of them ragged teeth, plus pourin on thick the thanks, with promises to not only salary the man but offer points as well, on the whole operation, that would surely be in order, which Mr. Brad P. Hone admitted was how he saw it too.

Old Porch never said a word as they drove up south of Wallsburg to one of the service trails that climbed farther up toward the Kata-nogos back side and would grant them a sliver of a view of a small portion of the land in question. Old Porch wasn't in no hurry either. He just rambled the pickup along the dirt roads, stuffin his lip with Copenhagen, playin the same Johnny Cash 8-track he always played: *At Folsom Prison.*

When they at last got to a rise that he deemed fittin, with the afternoon light just right, Old Porch's smileless disposition shifted to one of amiable excitement as he got out to greet this Brad P. Hone, who behind them was also just gettin out of his car, equally thrilled it seemed. Old Porch pointed up to some peaks, and to be clear what he was referrin to was but some low-lyin if jagged sentinels standin promontory before the mostly cloud-concealed Katanogos, and asked Mr. Brad P. Hone if he considered them the real horseradish? The man nodded vigorously, sayin that surely they was. But his expression paled and then reddened when Old Porch raised the followin conundrum: was it possible for real horseradish to be real horseradish if it was also balderdash? *You got no idea where you are,* Old Porch snarled. Mr. Hone looked pretty confused then, nor did his expression change much when Old Porch explained that the hills he was pointin out weren't even close to where Four Summits would inevitably reside, a resort that would eventually draw international interest on behalf of their fine state. Might Utah even host the Olympics right here some day? *To heck with that Cassidy Ski Resort and Little Cottonwood Canyon!*

Old Porch then spawled out some tobacco near enuf to Mr. Brad P. Hone's worn tassled loafers to get the man to jerk back. That made Egan growl inside hisself, always bated by any sign of fear. But Mr. Hone still tried to play it like he held the better hand, sayin how Old Porch better watch where he was spittin or he could kiss Four Sum-mits goodbye, though, before he could stomp back to his sorry little green Datsun, Old Porch told Egan to punch Mr. Hone's nose. Egan didn't do nothin, a reaction he still detests in hisself, whereupon Brad P. Hone, afraid at first, started to laugh, and then Egan did punch his nose. And when Old Porch told him to make sure it was broken, Egan punched him again. Then Old Porch ordered Egan to kick him and keep kickin him until he was curled up like a roly-poly, which Egan did. Now Old Porch was chucklin fer real, tellin this Brad P. Hone how he was a fool to threaten his family, which made Egan kick harder, as he at last understood that all this had been a shakedown, this idjit tryin to blackmail the Porches and now gettin a boot tip for it. Old Porch chuckled some more and spat more of his tobacco but never anywhere near this wailin man, like even his dirty spit were too good for the likes of him.

Now, son, Old Porch said to Brad P. Hone, *I'm gonna take this here piece of rebar,* what Old Porch after puttin on some gloves had retrieved from the flatbed of his truck while Egan was still kickin, *and I'm gonna stick it up your bunghole and there's nothin you can do about it.* Egan stopped kickin. Brad P. Hone started to bawl then, with the blood gooped on his face just runnin more. *Just kiddin, Brad! Sheesh!* And Old Porch threw the rebar in the back of Hone's Datsun. *Consider that a gift, a memento of construction soon to be,* though Old Porch didn't take off his gloves. *Brad, I got zero interest in your bunghole.* And then Old Porch pulled out from the back of his truck one more thing, an old baseball bat. By the look of it, the very one Hatch Porch had prized durin his Orvop years. Except it was modified now, drilled through at the end, an old horseshoe bolted in place. Old Porch offered it to Egan, but again Egan hesitated. Old Porch didn't.

At first, Egan thought his dad's purpose was to make it look like Brad P. Hone was kicked by a horse, like he wanted the man to bear the welts and bruises of some equine war he'd lost. Egan thought that was funny. He even laughed some. But Old Porch rotated the bat so the horseshoe weren't anywhere near the side facin Mr. Brad P. Hone.

Old Porch not only didn't hesitate; he didn't miss either. His sons didn't get their athletic talents from nowhere. He smacked the fingers Brad P. Hone managed to flail up right on through to his forehead.

Hone flipped back, out cold it seemed, but Egan could see he was still breathin, and groanin some too. His daddy fixed that by puttin a ziplock plastic bag over Brad P. Hone's head and, with his hands around his throat and one knee on his chest, steadied him unto death.

Egan was pretty dazed after that. Old Porch only said, *He was gonna take everythin we had.* Egan drove their truck, followin his dad in Hone's sorry Datsun. They drove easily enuf down the dirt roads and then along the paved ones and then down the busy ones and past even a cop. Egan's drivin must've been off because the officer pulled him over quick, sayin it was because of a busted taillight, and it turned out there sure was a busted taillight. Egan even apologized, findin his calm again, and it weren't no big deal. The ticket weren't no big deal. None of it was a big deal. Even if his daddy was long gone.

At break of dawn the followin day Old Porch was already at his little wooden desk in his little office in back of Porch Meats. Business as usual. He sure didn't indicate to Egan that anythin out of the ordinary had happened, though he did seem more openly pleased and made sure the Porch boys beheld his new affection and approval for Egan.

Some weeks later Egan happened to catch in the paper news of a Brad P. Hone dead in a car accident up near Coalville, apparently impaled by loose rebar in the car, survived by a wife and four daughters. That was it. For months afterward Egan expected the police to come and arrest them or at least ask him a question or two, but that never happened.

Some have maintained that Egan weathered this incident just fine because, as Old Porch often made clear: there was a big difference between uppity Salt Lake City Church folks and the Church folks further south who made the state of Utah great. How that makes a case for killin was never made clear.

Plenty of others, though, sidesteppin such ludicrous justifications, have simply expressed sympathy for Egan, and that ain't so unjustified. No question the consequences of witnessin The End of Brad P. Hone must have been severe. Nonetheless, Egan weren't so young a pup then, and really any sympathy for him should be directed to earlier scenes in his life, even as far back as when as a toddler his momma weren't able to shield him from the influences of so brutal a man as Old Porch. Truth is that by the time he was swingin at and kickin Brad P. Hone, Egan was already brutal, and in fact what had bothered him most about the incident wasn't what had been done but that he'd hesitated not once but twice. Despite Old Porch's public display of appreciation, Egan sensed in his daddy a low-simmerin disappointment.

But then not so long after that Old Porch brought out the family Colt. He explained to Egan that it was a testament to how life lives and not to how men think it should be lived. It was both an antique and the Porch future. He then ran his finger along the barrel and swore how only he was strong enuf to wield it. For Egan the metal seemed to shine both bright and black. The stocks, Old Porch claimed, were not some prissy pearl but polished ash, what Mr. Caracy Rudder would claim, with a wink, was took *from Mount Pelion in southern Thessaly.*

Old Porch also clarified for Egan, and in private too, that this weapon was not for the eldest son or even a son for that matter. It only and always had just one legitimate heir. Old Porch explained then how every name engraved on the weapon had taken the life of another, *some havin taken more lives than just one.* He looked Egan hard in the eye then. *Out of all of your brothers, your name is pretty much already writ here, if by attitude alone, but I need to hear it from you, you need to tell me yourself, that you are deservin of this. Are you?* Egan didn't hesitate. *I am!* But Old Porch shook his head. *The heck you are.* Might as well have just slapped Egan like some flimsy girl. *Until that day when you are,* Old Porch continued, now, though, almost kindly, *you keep this family heirloom at your house.* Then he made the same announcement to all his sons, except Hatch, who by that point was in Texas. The boys went slack-jawed, havin always assumed that it belonged to Hatch. Old Porch didn't mention nothin about the necessity of killin someone with it. He merely tossed it onto Egan's lap like it weren't nothin more than a bag of beans. *Just for safekeepin* was all he'd added. Whether a tactic or habit, Old Porch built many an alliance by keepin secrets; it was a way of creatin a false sense of intimacy by givin whoever he was dealin with the sense that they was special, and wasn't that a good feelin? Useful too.

Egan had taken the gun home, oiled it, polished it, and then placed it in his gun cabinet, only to take it out a minute later to practice with it, sight it, polish it up again. He couldn't wait til he could use it fer real and add his name there, right beneath his daddy's. Like Old Porch had said to him in the stillness of his dark little office: *After I'm dead, you're the one who's gonna make sure Porches keep what's theirs. You're it, Egan. The real horseradish.*

A fter knockin a while on Trent Riddle's door and then searchin the parkin lot again as well as the nearby streets for Riddle's brown Plymouth Duster, both Egan and Billings accepted that Riddle just weren't there. It bein 4:00 a.m. by this point, with Thursday mornin's first light still some hours off, the clouds broodin above, now and then sheddin great surges of clatterin wet, with no moon in sight. They came to the uneasy conclusion then that Riddle had either come home only to leave again or hadn't come home at all. Though where he would've gone off to at that hour remained a mystery.

So Egan and Billings just sat in the idlin truck and waited. The only thing they discussed openly was how Riddle might go from wherever he was now directly to work, and that caused a somewhat long debate over whether or not one of them should head to Porch Meats in order to be the first there to greet him. At least they was both calmed by the reasonable assumption that Riddle weren't about to head to Porch Meats at that moment. Where was the sense in that? Besides, as Billings recalled, Riddle always got to work just shy of 8:30 a.m. That point provided a little light on their future doins. If Riddle didn't show at his apartment by 8:00 a.m., then they'd hightail it to the slaughterhouse. That did in turn lead to another conversation that weren't nearly so voluble nor high-volumed: how was they gonna have that *private conversation with Riddle* with others likely startin to arrive at the plant? *We'll figure it out*, Egan said softly, and Billings was fine not sayin more.

When a gray and rainy light at last began to remake the sky, they both went to Riddle's door one more time in case they'd somehow missed his arrival, but there was no answer and still no sign of his Duster.

Old Porch meanwhile had stuck it out with the police, keepin Kelly tight at his side throughout. Once Russel's body was hauled away, the officers who stuck around seemed to have forgotten the matter of Riddle's contact information, and Detective Peters, when he finally showed up, didn't ask about it neither. He just gave the coroner permission to do his job, and in fact didn't much linger over Russel. To Old Porch it all seemed a matter of routine in the face of a foregone conclusion: just makin sure necessary evidence was collected correctly, photos taken, statements taken, nothin of interest left behind, that sorta thing. Standard procedure for a homicide.

Old Porch didn't like Detective Peters much, but he didn't not like him neither. The man came across as a bore, and his ho-hum manner of askin questions and scribblin down the answers struck Old Porch as dull and inconsequential, even when he offered his condolences over Old Porch's loss. But when he apologized for bein late in the first place, explainin how his Mustang had broken down while he and his wife, Elizabeth, had been up in Bountiful visitin with her family, why that part had surprised the heck out of Old Porch. He just couldn't see the detective in a Mustang. The Honda Civic hatchback he'd arrived in, purple as an eggplant set too long in the sun, that seemed a better fit.

Detective Peters had suggested they conduct the interview out of the rain, recommendin inside the house when Old Porch didn't offer. Old Porch explained that the house weren't his but his son's and Egan had left to track down some information for an officer here. Old Porch didn't have the key. And that was true, though the front door was unlocked, as was the back door. Not that the detective had been inclined to check.

They stepped into the barn instead. Old Porch told him the same version of events as he'd told Officer Mildenhall, and then Kelly did the same. For Old Porch it was easy, though his minimizin of Riddle's presence there made the path ahead all the more certain and necessary.

To his surprise, Kelly discovered he could handle the questions just fine, with even his guts easin up some. In the end, Detective Peters had seemed mostly concerned and finally irate about the fact that the saddle pad Cavalry had had on him when Russel rode back, what was a rose pink from the blood as well as spattered with darker matter unknown, had still not been gathered up as evidence but left flung over a saddle stand to dry. That was taken care of quick, and Detective Peters hadn't had to raise his voice one bit nor hurry his tempo any, and Old Porch did take note of that.

Once that was done, Old Porch and Kelly headed back to Porch Meats. They was just through the door when the phone rang. It was Detective Peters again, and Old Porch's hackles went up fast, fer sure expectin some *Columbo* bullcrap, some last thing he'd just happened to have forgotten to ask, or worse, some mention of Riddle, like maybe the detective was with Riddle at that very moment, these thoughts palpitatin Old Porch somethin fierce so that he had trouble fer a moment makin sense of what the detective was tellin him: a horse, a black one, or at least a dark one, and in fact maybe two horses, had been sighted down near the south side of Agoneeya, headin toward Springville, with everyone thinkin that maybe the one who stole Old Porch's horses had finally figured out that Isatch Canyon was a dead end and had somehow managed to scurry out and let those horses go, horses that were now runnin free in the streets of south Orvop. The detective seemed certain the horse or horses would soon be caught, whether with the thief around or not, and it would be awful helpful if Old Porch could come and confirm that they was his.

Old Porch repeated aloud the address where the horse or horses had last been seen. Kelly wanted to come, but Old Porch ordered him to sleep and keep his mouth shut when Francis and Woolsey woke up for school. Kelly said he weren't tired but was snorin on the couch when Old Porch and his Rottweiler, Mr. Bucket, headed out the door.

Old Porch grabbed hisself an apple, though instead of headin straight to his truck, he went around back to one of the rear paddocks. She was already amblin his way. All black with a white star and stripe. His mule. His Effy. That was her name even if it had taken a bit to set-tle there. For a while Old Porch had called her Effin because she was his Effin Genius, a mutterin now decades old. She'd actually got loose from her paddock just yesterday, again, as she'd done plenty of times before and could likely do plenty of times more, even if, despite findin herself free to wander anywhere she liked, she just strolled on around to the front of the house and ate up all his flowers and then rolled around in the flower garden and finally pissed voluminously on Egan's truck. Old Porch had gotten a kick outta that.

He fed Effy the apple now, and she ate it all and welcomed too his rubs and scratches, the soft words he reserved only for her, with no understandin neither why she alone received such affection. No friend of Old Porch's, none of his boys neither, no woman even ever got anythin close. Mr. Bucket weren't in the runnin, maybe because Mr. Bucket was Mr. Bucket #5 and easily replaced. Not her. There was no replacin Effy. In fact Effy provided the sole place left to Old Porch where he could spend the kind of attention that requires nothin in return, and spend it he did. And while he never did give it much thought, he was always surprised by how much lighter he felt and at ease every time he'd given his Effy his time. Like he could forgive a world, forgive hisself, forgive his desires, and finally get around to maybe even meetin the world fairly. Even at this moment Old Porch smiled and laughed softly and patted her side and accepted her snorts as a sign equal to his own melancholy sighs, where he could here feel so alone with only her, and yet at the same time feel so favorably met by so much more than her.

After that, Old Porch drove by Riddle's apartment and saw Egan's Ford Ranger and knew there was nothin more he could do there except keep goin. For a while the horse or horses that were supposedly his seemed but a rumor, and Old Porch nearly returned home, but then a confirmation came that a horse had been sighted trottin down Center Street. Two patrol cars and Old Porch in his truck took off then, and around sunrise they located the mare.

Fer one thing she weren't black. She was a dark bay. Poor conformation didn't begin to describe the swayback, high withers, short pasterns; an otherwise mess from pig eyes to mangy coat to split hooves. The only thing this creature had in common with Porch's is that she too belonged in Paddock B.

Mrs. Agnes Bonnie Hopper arrived right around eight to lay claim to her beloved Ariel. She still had her gray hair tucked under a net and wore her bathrobe over a pair of baggy jeans. She apologized profusely at the same time as she expressed an equal amount of confusion over how it was that her wanderin horse had generated so much attention.

It's important to mention this little moment because when she was told by Officer Poulter that they'd thought hers might've been one of them stolt from Old Porch's Paddock B, she at once responded: *What's he care what got took from there?* She said it too in his presence without sharin with him her eye, her scowl carvin up her cheeks better than a pumpkin. *Everyone knows that what goes in Paddock B he renders the next day,* she even added. Old Porch gave the old lady a wink. *Agnes, give me five bucks and I'll let you lead this bottle of glue in there yourself.* She looked at him then with such disgust and pity that even Officer Poulter dropped his gaze.

Old Porch left and under the impression too that he'd lost that bout, what he didn't care for one bit. Not that a shack dweller like Agnes spendin her social security on hay and oats could really spark him, but she'd still got him thinkin on how he'd lost a mighty lot this night: two horses, a pot of dough, his boy. Old Porch didn't like losin.

From a pay phone near the Paramount movie theater, he called home and, good for him, Kelly picked up on the first ring. Woolsey and Francis were already off to school. *They don't got no clue.* That was okay, Old Porch assured him. Kelly said then that Egan and Billings had just pulled up. Old Porch weren't gonna bring up Riddle on the phone. Instead he told Kelly to load up two horses in the trailer, one for Kelly and the other for Billings, and *then get the heck over to Isatch before the whole circus sets up there. I want them stolen horses back. Tell Egan to get Cavalry. I'll meet you at the entrance.*

At this point Allison had just settled into her breakfast at Meaai Lelei. Kalin, Landry, Tom, and the horses was ridin along the main Isatch Canyon trail above Bridge Two, soon to descend back down into the crick, which they'd follow to the Misdemeanors swimmin hole. Riddle was still nowhere to be found.

It was 8:13 a.m.

Egan was bothered plenty by Riddle's disappearance, but there weren't much else to be done at this point. Billings decided to hoof it back to Porch Meats. Egan had near forgotten his home was a crime scene. He couldn't even park in his own driveway. Yellow police tape hung across his brown lawn, wrapped around them lawn jockeys. Fortunately the house itself weren't part of that sequesterin, and Egan could have hisself a hot shower, scrubbin so hard that his bar of Irish Spring busted apart; after which, with coffee good and brewed by then, he fixed a mug of that black and got to figurin out what guns to take.

Officer Poulter had just arrived from downtown Orvop to check on Officer Mildenhall, who'd also been up all night. When Egan had emerged from the house, both officers had followed him into the barn. Egan snapped at them then, wantin to know if his barn was part of the crime scene too? That caught Officer Poulter off guard.

Not at all, Egan. Officer Poulter actually looked hurt. *I just saw your dad is all. We thought we'd found your ponies, but it weren't nothin but a cranky old mare got loose from Agnes Hopper. I'm guessin you're doin what you've right knowd from the start: headin up in the canyon to see if they're there?*

Egan didn't respond but picked up his saddle, and when he couldn't find the saddle pad, Officer Poulter remindin him how it was entered into evidence, *because, you know, of all the blood,* it hit Egan hard, Russel

236

gone, his little brother dead, hittin him in the chest, his heart bangin with alarm. Both Officer Poulter and Officer Mildenhall had to keep Egan from reelin over backwards.

There, there, I got ya, Officer Poulter soothed while Officer Mildenhall took the saddle from Egan's limp arms.

I'm okay, Egan mumbled, squattin down, though he was clearly still a dizzy mess of confusion, now with his head down between his knees. He could've stayed like that forever. Become a statue for quittin. Only the thought of Old Porch and what he'd've done beholdin such a sight got him standin again and saddlin up Cavalry.

You just lost your brother, Egan. No easy way about this.

Egan thanked both officers for their concern, and they responded with more consolations and stalwart declarations about bringin to justice the heinous criminal responsible for such awfulness.

It was just after nine by the time Egan rode into the Isatch Canyon parkin lot. *Clop-Clop-clip-Clop.* His daddy and the dog was there to meet him. Egan had on rain gear, but it didn't seem near enuf to keep the wet away. Through the rain he could hear the crick gushin with runoff.

Any idea what time it is? Old Porch growled. *I told you boys to hurry!*

I know exactly what time it is. Egan weren't afraid of his old man's growl nor anybody's growl for that matter. *The popo are still at my house in case you forgot.*

Where's Kelly and Billings? Old Porch was still growlin, givin Mr. Bucket a yank too, hard enuf to earn a whimper from the big Rottweiler.

I imagine they're on the way over, Egan answered, shiftin slightly on the big liver chestnut horse, who showed no interest in any of this, jostlin the Weymouth bit around in his mouth, throwin his head some toward the gate and the main trail like he remembered it, remembered his good ride with Russel last night, and he did remember it, feelin fine at the thought of havin some of the same again.

Old Porch told Egan then about Agnes Hopper's loose horse and how everyone fer a moment had thought this was gonna be settled before dawn.

Poulter said he'd seen you downtown.

Porch grimaced, maybe because his news was old or he had to keep lookin up at his boy. *He's still up there. Best bet is that he's stuck.*

There ain't been no sightins? Egan asked, scannin the municipal vehicles that kept arrivin, includin two more Orvop City patrol cars parkin near the visitor kiosk.

Oh, them boys haven't been up there. They're still tryin to figure out who's gonna tie whose shoes. They see the crime as not happenin down here but up there, and up there is no longer Orvop City's business. That's the county's. That's Sheriff Jewell's jurisdiction.

The first bit of good news.

Undersheriff Conrad Jewell was married to Old Porch's sister. Russel had been tasked with returnin his uncle's binoculars when he'd stopped at Paddock B last night, the very same binoculars Egan had with him now.

And Riddle? Old Porch asked, a question followed quick with a low grunt or cough.

Egan shook his head. *He never showed at his place.*

That took some stomachin, and Old Porch had to take his time with this news. When he finally did speak, his voice hung just above a hoarse whisper. *I'll get to Riddle. Fer now, we need to get back our horses. And we need to make a show of it. They're important to us.*

And that Kalin?

It's a heckuva mess we're in, Egan. Old Porch set a big scarred hand then on the scabbarded rifle at Egan's left leg. *That kid's got a story to tell that won't do us no good if he tells it.*

Didn't Russel say Landry Gatestone was with him too?

I'm sure she'll have the same story. If it were only summer, Mr. Bucket could've found her blind.

What's summer got to do with it?

She'd stink to high heaven from the heat. We'd probably smell her from here. Old Porch tried to chuckle.

I can round up more dogs, Dad, Egan said. *If that's what you're anglin for?*

Old Porch waved the idea away. *They'd just cause more trouble, gettin lost instead of findin what we cannot let stay lost. You hear me, Eges?*

I do.

This here's the real horseradish, Old Porch said then, with them gray eyes focused hard on his boy, somethin proud and real there, what tightened up inside Egan like a wood screw drawin a joint in true.

There's your brother, Old Porch said then. *Finally.*

Egan twisted around and at once saw the family's red-and-white Chevy belchin up big clouds of diesel as it lumbered up the hill, haulin along their trailer. When he turned back around, he seen that Old Porch and Mr. Bucket was already headin over toward a sheriff's car parked among the police cars. Egan waved when he realized his Uncle Conrad, uniformed up with a clear rain guard over his brown felt cowboy hat, weren't just wavin at his old man.

Egan trotted Cavalry over then, dismountin quicker than the fallin rain, and gave the big man a hug.

Egan, I am so sorry.

Egan could see his uncle meant it. He was a good foot taller than Egan, wider too, but also softer, with sandy hair, a narrow nose, and light brown eyes. A lot of years had slipped by since he'd made all-state as a center for Mountain View, but for whatever burgers and fries had done to his girth, few doubted that he still had plenty of fight left and, if nothin else, raw holdin power. If you weren't huggin this man or at least givin him a handshake, you was lookin for the long way around.

Thanks, Conrad. We're pretty shook up. Egan handed over then the binoculars.

I was just tellin your dad how we got the right folks on their way. We'll find the one who done this to your brother. I'll be right here in case that ne'er-do-well decides to come out first. There ain't nowhere he can go.

I already told my boys he's likely stuck somewhere, Old Porch said.

Darn foolish, takin animals in there, Undersheriff Jewell grunted. *Kid strikes me as a real knucklehead.*

Got any problem, Conrad, with Egan takin the trail to look for our horses? Old Porch asked then. *We don't want to get in your way.*

Until we've got a confirmation he's in there, the park's still open, and heck, I'd think less of your boys if they weren't up there lookin.

They all smiled a little, or tried to smile, the reason for this gatherin there not lost on a one of them.

How's Aunt Kip? Egan asked.

My wife won't be anythin but displeased if she hears I'm anywhere near your dad here.

Old Porch smiled some and then gave Undersheriff Conrad Jewell a strong pat on the shoulder. *You're the only good thing that sister of mine ever done. Give her a hug from me.*

Egan brought along not only that scabbarded .30-06, a Winchester Model 70 with a Leupold scope, but a second scabbard as well, heavy with his 12-gauge, bought at Wolf's Sportin Goods when Egan weren't but twelve, an Ithaca model 51 Featherlight, gas operated. He didn't know what to expect, but he was comin loaded for bear. He'd also brought two boxes of 150-grain bullets with boattail soft points, and in a pack behind the cantle of his saddle, two guns, the Smith & Wesson .357 Magnum he'd got for graduatin from Orvop and a double-action 9mm Smith & Wesson Model 59, aluminum frame with all identifyin numerics filed off. Other than that he had just a canteen of water and one bag of Porch jerky.

When Kelly and Billings rode up, Billings on Gads, the pinto, and Kelly on Barracuda, the buckskin mare with an uncentered snip, Egan was pleased to see Kelly had hisself a scabbard too, likely carryin his Remington 700 BDL, a .270. No matter if Billings had come unarmed.

Park Ranger Emily Brickey intercepted them in the middle of the parkin lot. The rain had at that moment started to dump again, and it was hard to see her face, let alone gauge her excubant expression. Her hair was mostly tucked up under one of them light brown park ranger baseball caps, her face lost under the brim, with the rest of her buried in an oversized dark park ranger raincoat, standard issue. Egan might've not even seen her if she hadn't waved them over. She told them that First Bridge was underwater and Bridge Two was likely even worse, and how she knew this we'll get to in a second. It partly explains her gaunt appearance. Egan politely thanked her for the information and asked if she'd seen two horses on the loose, and she answered that she hadn't, and that was that. He gave her a wave as he continued on by and, in lookin back, caught sight of the lights of yet another Orvop patrol car speedin up 2300 North, lights a-goin, and behind that a dirty smear of yellow, that Egan had no way of knowin was Allison March's Dodge Dart station wagon on the way.

The trail gate was locked, but that didn't matter. The horses were walked easily enuf through the side pass set there to accommodate hikers and riders like themselves. A sign made clear how dirt bikes and even bikes were strictly prohibited. Once on the other side they took off into the mist at a hot canter.

It was 9:47 a.m.

Let's return now fer a moment to Park Ranger Emily Brickey, who, after Egan and his crew had departed from the lot, headed to Undersheriff Jewell to relay news that the key to the main gate had still not been located and a locksmith would have to be called. It was a burdensome admission, as she herself had had the key last night. Around 11:00 p.m., she'd learned that two horses were supposedly runnin around either near or in the canyon. The version she'd heard was stripped of its more odious elements: theft, murder. Bein the go-getter she was, and a night owl at that, Park Ranger Brickey had volunteered to take a look.

For this late-night outin, she had taken along Rumi Plothow, who at the time was workin at Carillon Square, savin money so he could get a degree at the School for Environment and Sustainability in Michigan; Park Ranger Brickey planned to follow him once she graduated from Isatch U. It was an odd friendship. She and Mr. Plothow were close and with plenty in common, except that she would never, not for her whole life, return the affection he for his whole life would reserve for her. Rumi Plothow had insisted on drivin. He even put on a cassette of her favorite band, The Doors. When Park Ranger Brickey exited his truck to unlock the main gate, Rumi had even fast-forwarded the B-side. As he'd recall later on, and in the company of Berrid Dwyer, a proud fisherman most of his life; Barbara Frye, a masseuse, also for most of her life; and Missy Yamazaki, a concierge in the early '90s: *I don't know, it just seemed weather-appropriate, and she liked the song, and I didn't mind it, but it did make that drive extra spooky, and me and her never could listen to it again without thinkin of that night.*

At that point, First Bridge was fine, but the crick just below Bridge Two was startin to clog with loose branches and so on, and water was risin over the slats. Jim Morrison was goin on about a killer on the road and sweet Emily about to die right when Park Ranger Brickey, just as they was comin around a bend, beheld the giant.

It was silly of course, she would later recall. *We had gotten up to around what Orvop folks call the Gate of the Mountain. That's where I seen that nightmare. I know there ain't no such thing as a man that big, but my instincts took over. I just screamed. Poor Rumi hit the brakes and that made it worse. I figure now that the brake lights must have somehow cast a shine of red out there, and that made me scream again. Of course, it weren't nothin but a big broken tree with torn limbs danglin off the side of the trail. I had a good laugh at myself then, and not long after we headed back. Buckets of rain was comin down, and it cut our visibility to pointless. I'd realized by then we might get stuck above Bridge Two if it fully flooded. I thought it was hilarious, what a scaredy-cat I'd been, though later, what with all that happened, I see it weren't so funny. Like the mountains themselves had tried to scare me off, and I'd failed to heed their warnin. Or, I don't know, maybe I did heed it, or just enuf anyways to still be here tellin you this. I can't even see anymore what I'd seen so clearly that night. I do remember swearin it was a giant of a man with hands raised in anger. Later, though, I remembered it more like a towerin woman, black as her heart, with hands cast down to curse the earth. Later still, what I recall even today, and I can see it right now, well . . . it's a horse, black as soot with eyes of fire. Funny thing is how when I did get up around Bridge Three again, I looked for that broken tree but couldn't find nothin like it around. It was weird. Maybe that scares me the most. Still.*

Upon exitin the canyon, Park Ranger Brickey had made sure to lock the gate and somewhere after that lost the key. She'd find it a good year later. It had slipped through a hole in her raincoat pocket and settled down in a seam between the outer shell and the inner linin. Its absence she discovered in the early mornin when she'd walked the trail alone, partly to confront the fear she was tryin hard not to accept, mostly to report what bridges were flooded. She never got that far.

First Bridge was under several feet of water. She at once called that in, figurin she'd be told to close the park at once, but there was a delay and a tangle of miscommunications. Orvop Chief of Police Wilson Beckham wouldn't officially close Isatch Canyon Park until later that day.

As was already briefly touched upon, one source of trouble was that only part of the park was within the Orvop city limits. At around Bridge Three the city of Orvop ended, and what followed became part of Utah County and fell under the jurisdiction of the sheriff's department. Park rangers under the Utah Division of Wildlife Resources, itself part of the Utah DNR, or Utah Department of Natural Resources, saw to the upkeep of the park that went on from that third bridge to encompass the whole of the Katanogos massif. Technically the city of Orvop was responsible for the maintenance of the park's entrance, but the park rangers, even if their main office weren't in Orvop but down in Springville, frequently pitched in, mostly because the rangers loved the park.

Further complicatin matters was how to determine the jurisdiction of the unfoldin criminal investigation. While Russel died in Orvop, makin it a matter for the Orvop police, the attack upon him, as far as both the Orvop police and sheriff's department were concerned, had likely occurred beyond the city limits, thus makin it a county affair. Either way, the park rangers were needed, rangers like Brickey, for assessment of the trails, as well as law enforcement rangers who were on their way to assist with apprehendin the primary suspect, Kalin March, if he was indeed beyond the Gate of the Mountain.

To be clear, everyone involved knew this matter of jurisdiction was really a budgetary concern. Police, sheriffs, and rangers all got along just fine and, with most if not all bein Church members, were extra inclined to help each other and thus deliver upon this abhorrent act a swift and conclusive response.

Undersheriff Jewell was stuffin more quarters into the pay phone at the visitor kiosk in order to initiate another round of calls to clarify duties in multiple departments when Woolsey and Francis came haulin into the parkin lot. Woolsey was in his Chevy Chevette with two older Porch brothers right behind him on dirt bikes.

Orvop Chief of Police Wilson Beckham had just picked up, and he'd just gotten off the phone with Jewell's boss, Sheriff Hiram Brunt, both agreein that Orvop should continue its investigation locally while the Utah County Sheriff's Office, and in this case that meant Jewell, should handle the investigation beyond the Isatch Canyon main gate, in coordination of course with the law enforcement rangers, better equipped for such excursions, especially given what weather was on the way. Which was all fine and dandy, except the gate was still locked, and no one could find a locksmith, and Undersheriff Jewell had finally sent one of his deputies out for a bolt cutter, even if Park Ranger Brickey, the one who'd lost the key in the first place, was now sayin the gate didn't matter since First Bridge was too deep underwater for any truck.

Francis Porch rushed out of the Chevette first, his face aboil with anger, steamin with tears, runnin to his father, still at the park gate with Mr. Bucket, Allison March havin departed from his company but recently.

Rumors about the killin of one of its sophomores, Russel Porch, had overrun the halls and classrooms of Orvop High School. Principal Furst had tried to call to his office both Woolsey and Francis so they could hear from him what he still could not confirm, but both boys had already abandoned the school grounds. When Woolsey and Francis had then discovered their house deserted and Porch Meats closed for the day, they'd called Sean and Shelly, who'd also heard no such news but were fast enuf on their way to Isatch Canyon.

Is it true? Francis yowled at the same time that Woolsey was screamin, *Russel's dead?!*

Old Porch just crossed his arms and nodded to them both.

Francis looked like he was shot straight through the heart. He just dropped to his knees to cry or beat the ground in rage or just beat the ground to hide his cryin. Woolsey made fists, pacin back and forth.

Was it that Kalin kid like they's sayin at school? Where's he at?

Again Old Porch nodded and this time pointed to the canyon.

Woolsey made to start runnin that way. *Look at me, boys,* Old Porch hissed, Woolsey haltin his bum-rush, Francis liftin his eyes like a persecuted saint. *I need you both now to man up. Your daddy here needs you by his side.* Which worked at once on both these young boys. Shelly and Sean, however, didn't even pause for any words of clarification, let alone for that sign that prohibited dirt bikes on the main trail. They just tore off through the side pass, gunnin their bikes for the straight ahead.

Undersheriff Jewell had to hang up with Chief of Police Beckham when he seen that flagrant disregard of park rules. Not that he was so surprised. He knew all the Porch boys.

Oh heck, he still groaned.

They won't get no further than First Bridge, Park Ranger Brickey reminded him.

That at least was some relief.

Orwin! Undersheriff Jewell yelled. *Given the circumstances, your boys might get a pass when they're back, but just this once. I don't want to see no more dirt bikes unless they're in this parkin lot.*

Old Porch gave Undersheriff Jewell his word, promisin to scold them both first thing. Park Ranger Brickey had other ideas.

By this point, Allison March, after her shockin interaction with Old Porch earlier, had retreated to her yellow Dodge Dart, determined to depart at once only to again question where she would in fact go. She didn't know anyone that well but also lacked the fortitude to engage next the continuously expandin police presence around her. As another fire engine pulled into the parkin lot for no understandable reason, given the weather, she was tryin to meditate, carry out some breathin exercises. A hard day was still awaitin her. She knew that much. She also knew she'd eventually get back out there. She'd even manage to talk to Undersheriff Jewell, though she'd find only coldness and learn nothin new.

Meanwhile, Landry was back on the main trail, canterin toward the canyon entrance. She'd started off fast, just for the heck of it, mostly because she could tell Jojo wanted to run, but the more she thought about what her momma was gonna do to her once she got home, the more she slowed Jojo, until they'd settled into an easy lope that was still pretty swift. Landry had no police in her eyes, no sense of the risin confusion about to greet her. She saw only the wet, wide trail ahead, overhung with branches. She heard only the chatterin crick full with the memory of last night's storm and maybe the story of a new storm on the way. Though at that moment the rain abruptly stopped. Landry inhaled the soft air and smiled. She'd had herself a fine adventure.

On the way down, the main trail between Bridge Three to Bridge Two began to rise and pretty steeply too, so that as Landry reached the crest, despite wantin to race the downhill that now awaited them, she pulled up hard, Jojo snortin partially fer the surprise halt but mostly because of what waited below. And for Landry the surprise was twofold: not only discoverin Bridge Two under water but also spyin the three horses waitin on the other side.

It was 10:17 a.m.

Nothin about this sight pleased her, and you can forget the flooded bridge. Just the way the riders was spread out was cause for alarm, their arrangement makin clear their aggression. There was no way around them, and the gaps they maintained between each other demanded either that she stop or try to race through. Landry eased Jojo down the slope a few steps before stoppin again, this time makin another unhappy discovery: one of the riders was Egan Porch. Egan Porch anywhere near her was never a good thing. And he was on Cavalry, whom she'd recognized first, snortin and beatin the ground with a hoof. Cavalry weren't faster than Jojo, but he was still mighty fast.

Landry's face twitched, and even her jaw got to joggin senselessly left and right. Egan, of course, stood smack-dab in the middle, with his brother, Kelly Porch, on his right, and someone she didn't know on his left, someone she wisely feared at once, maybe even more than Egan, maybe because she could see that for him there weren't nothin personal here. Landry ground down her teeth then to stop whatever nonsense her face was givin away, though she couldn't keep her hands from white-knucklin the reins, not that her hold jerked on Jojo's mouth any. Landry knew better than to visit these troubles on him.

The three started wadin easily enuf through the water coverin the bridge. But when Landry backed up Jojo to the crest again, Egan stopped in the middle, the icy water rollin idly around the knees of all three stationary horses.

That you, Bowlin Ball? Egan hollered out, lookin up at her with that awful smile, if also havin to shield his eyes, as at that very moment a bar of sunlight had broke free of the churnin storm clouds above.

No doubt you've already heard plenty of what's been said about the light that stung Egan's eyes, stung the eyes of all them boys. Hollis Robertson, owner of LR Feed Company in North Logan, would dryly swear to Duwayne Small and Dahl Horton that it *weren't nothin more than a blindin coincidence, excuse the pun, that had no consequences other than to give that poor girl another moment to take in all that was set against her.* Harlan Webber, though, who at that point still worked for Hollis, would never shake the sense that there was somethin preordained about its arrival, notin the unusualness of such an occurrence given the storm overhead, which incidentally is not true; plenty of lulls in the weather had occurred with patches of blue regularly appearin. Nonetheless, you can see his point, especially if you've spent a moment starin at Thegan Olson's paintin of Landry up on the hill, she and Jojo in silhouette, immense shadows cast by the both of them, their outlines auraed in light, all with a backdrop of boilin clouds; while down below in the foreground, the three men stalled in the water are flingin up their hands a little too dramatically before their eyes. Accordin to Pril Neihaus, Zack Solomon, Juzo Racer, and Claire Colter, Thegan Olson managed to capture, with oils and metals and shreds of all sorts of stuff he often scavenged from the hardware store where he worked in Sandy, somethin that made that particular canvas seem warped with an energy far surpassin even the most elemental human concern.

You know darned well who it is, Egan! Landry shouted back. She weren't no fool, the gun at her waist waitin heavy there with announcement of what could happen next.

You see that Kalin kid around here? Egan asked with an easy smile, turnin Cavalry sideways to make extra clear that her way was blocked. Kelly followed suit. The other one, him bein Billings, didn't move at all, which only further amplified Landry's fear of him.

What business is that of yours? Landry hurled down at him. *Ain't no stolt horses this way if that's what you're in a fuss about. That was settled last night. Them's my horses now, and Kalin can do with them what he likes. Your little brother sold them to me last night. Twenty bucks. You go on and ask him.*

Russel's killt.

How's that?

Your boy Kalin cut his throat.

Landry guffawed. *Now ain't that the stupidest lie I ever heard.*

Morgue don't lie, Bowlin Ball.

Don't you dare call me that, Landry snarled back. She was about fed up. She didn't like this talk about Russel, she didn't like Egan callin her no bowlin ball, and she sure as heck didn't like watchin Kelly and the one she didn't know start advancin on her.

That looks like my dad's gun you got there, Kelly said then, disapprovin of the asportation so casually on display.

Russel came armed, and I whooped his butt. Didn't want him to shoot hisself.

Give it here then, Kelly said, even extendin one hand while his other continued to shield his eyes from that persistent sunbeam.

I aim to give it to Russel myself. Just like I promised.

You don't hear so good, BOWLIN BALL! Egan shouted then. *I SAID RUSSEL'S DEAD!*

Landry flinched. She couldn't help it, even if she still couldn't make no sense out of what Egan kept insistin on, and then the cold sweat that in truth was there the second she'd laid eyes on Egan made itself known to her.

Then I'll give this old gun to Old Porch directly.

That there is my gun, Egan growled. *Russel stole it from me. And now you can give it back to me.*

Landry caught the way Kelly glanced at Egan, not in agreement either.

I said I'll give it to Old Porch directly, Landry said again.

Fine, Egan answered, but too quick, his smile makin the lie all the more apparent, even as he eased Cavalry back to make more room for her to pass. *Ladies first.*

I ain't no lady. You dingbats can go first.

Neither Kelly nor Billings moved much then, though they did turn their horses' heads back toward the Isatch Canyon entrance, the horses plenty relieved to not be facin the sun no more. Egan kept his eyes narrowed, with any effort at a smile long gone. Landry felt sick with fear, and in fact one of her legs, the right one, started to shake on its own. It kinda stunned her to just watch the thing jangle and jerk in the stirrup, causin even Jojo to look back with some alarm, shiftin away his flanks some from her bodily insurrection and racket.

Landry didn't exactly plan on what she'd done next. It was a combination of this overall dread drenchin her body, with that shorter leg of hers betrayin her like it did, as well as a sudden hot discomfort in her crotch, somewhere between mad itchin and an itchin already scratched, scratched wrong, plus the general disgust she felt bein even proximal to the likes of Egan and his kin and kith, but what also included a growin awareness that if she didn't set herself into action quick, she was gonna seize up. This was Landry Gatestone's greatest shame: when the whole of her might just turn to stone. When that had happened she weren't worth even spit in a wallet. *Useless* was what she'd called herself, a cumberworld, a burden to others, especially that afternoon outside Regal Lanes, after which, when Egan had offered her a ride home, she'd accepted!

But Landry weren't no *Susanna and the Elders*, set in ivory, as Cal Carneros would one day say, and so against such closure of her joints and the loss of any future agency, Landry gathered in her knees, just a tiny bit but what was more than enuf to alert the Big Blue Roan that she was back, and then with the slightest lean forward and the lightest draw on the reins, what given the distances here was noticed by neither Egan nor even Billings, and you can forget Kelly, who was lookin back down the main trail like they might actually head that way, Landry brought Jojo to the sky, knowin the turn to follow like a top knows to spin.

Before these men Landry and Jojo at once became an immense shadow, as if that girl and her horse were suddenly a part of the glowerin storm clouds above, until like that their collective silhouette vanished, might as well say in a flash, that sunbeam behind them, no longer mitigated by their presence, blindin all three men, like she had become lightnin itself, followed at once by thunder, what was the sound of her hastenin gallop givin away her flight.

Not that Egan, Billings, or Kelly even thought to race after her. In fact Egan laughed. In fairness, it weren't pure arrogance what he done next: just nudgin Cavalry forward at the most leisurely pace. Kelly, more willin than most of his brothers to challenge Egan, this time did the same. Both Porches knew she had nowhere to go, and there weren't no point runnin their own horses ragged. She weren't even their main concern.

Once out of the water, Egan gave Cavalry a flat kick and took the rise at a brisk walk. At the top, he stopped and studied the way the trail dipped ahead. Landry was long gone. Egan then clamped his thumb on his left nostril and blew the right clean of snot. Then he did the same for the left nostril. After that, he dug out a plug of tobacco, settled it under his gum, and spat once. Above them the sky seemed to grow darker even as it continued to hold back most of the rain. Egan treated that as some good luck, as if the sky the whole valley wide was on their side, though nothin could've been further from the truth. The sky weren't with them, not with any of them, not even with Tom, and worse, it had plans only them mountains would ever understand.

Landry gave Jojo the trail, let him unfurl, and with every stride he lengthened even more, relaxin, in turn relaxin Landry, the fear evaporatin off her, lost to the day, a day already left far behind her, leavin both her and Jojo free to pursue the intangible future ahead, even if that didn't matter either, not compared to this ride right then. She couldn't know it, but she felt much like Russel and Cavalry had, only instead of night, rain, and mud, she and Jojo was enjoyin a trail that had hardened some throughout the mornin and now presented the smoothest ingress back up into the canyon. Jojo's hooves practically sprang up from the earth as soon as they touched down, the soft thuds of his unrelentin pace further calmin them both, as they drank in air pungent with the delights of wet trees, moss, and river mist.

Landry was even smilin, and we might as well say Jojo was too. Of course, that smile weren't gonna be worth even a giggle if Kalin didn't help her, the thought Landry was most tryin to outrace even if where she was runnin straight to was where that thought lived.

If only he wasn't too far up them bluffs yet.

And lucky for her, he wasn't.

Though was it luck? Some have said it was just plain good manners, Kalin keepin an eye on Landry to make sure she got outta the canyon safe, and it's a valid point. True, Kalin was also takin a little breather after finally gettin hisself somethin to eat, Tom near demandin that he get some sustenance inside hisself. He tried first to get out the Dorf jerky but couldn't find it quick enuf and ended up with one of the Orvop High buns, a palmful of raisins and nuts.

She's comin back, Tom said.

I can see that much myself.

She's comin back fast.

I can see that too, Tom. Ain't no one behind her. She's scared, though, ain't she?

She's sure in a hurry.

Do you know why? Kalin lowered the binoculars to take in his ghostly friend's expression.

Just because I'm dead don't mean I know what she's thinkin. Even alive I didn't know what she was thinkin.

Kalin raised the lenses again. *But where's she goin?*

Landry had raced past their turnoff. Fer a moment both Kalin and Tom were certain she'd missed it. She flew Jojo up a good ways too before she finally stopped.

She figured out her mistake, Tom said.

Except instead of turnin around she backed up Jojo a good ways before headin off on a skimpy animal path on the Agoneeya side of the canyon, what quick enuf joined a rocky patch, from where she also backed Jojo down the way she'd come, lastly backin him up even more.

She's tryin to trick someone.

Then she's bein followed.

But is she? Tom asked.

Kalin scanned the trail as far back as he could before trees over-grew the view. He could still spot no one. Landry by now was lopin on the side of the main trail, back to the right turnoff.

Kalin tucked away the binoculars in one of Navidad's saddlebags before untyin her lead.

You takin her down? Tom asked.

Kalin shook his head. He was only resecurin the lead around the jagged set of rocks that rose above this back part of the ledge. He did the same for Mouse. *This ain't on them. Just makin sure they're settled plenty while I'm gone.*

Don't you trust me? Tom asked with a wink, eyes bright as a glitter of stars at midnight.

Put that on my tombstone: Never Trust Your Horse to No Ghost.

Now that's just unkind, Tom answered but chucklin just the same.

Instead of usin the shorter lariat, a thirty-two footer, Kalin slung the sixty-four footer over his shoulder; then he took three long replen-ishin gulps from his canteen, wiped his mouth with the back of his hand, and before headin down hurried over to where the brush and wayward grass was thickest, where he plucked up as many asters as he could hold in one hand.

Listen here, Kalin! Tom yelled down. *You got no moves! Jojo won't let you near him!*

Except for a few steep spots, the first part of the path was an easy jog down. When he got to the narrow area where he'd tied off Navidad after her second ascent, before he'd gone to get Mouse, he used a crack in the rock to fix one end of the rope before slippin for the third and last time down through the fissure to the scree.

Mostly he handled the sheerest part with his feet, but he still arranged the rope so he could rappel down somewhat. Though this he did only to gauge how he should handle the rope on the way back up. Gettin down was the easy part.

Kalin had never tried to get up through the fissure on foot. The steepest part weren't even half a horse length, which is why both Navidad and Mouse got up over it just fine. Kalin weren't no rock climber, but he could still tell there weren't much by way of hand- or footholds. It weren't hard to imagine gettin jammed up there in the middle of that narrow gap. Still, Kalin figured clamberin his way up, either grippin or wrappin the rope around a forearm, should get the job done. It pained him, and he at once called hisself stupid too, when he realized he'd left his gloves behind with Mouse. Already his palms were raw from just handlin the rope.

Once down that wall, he could've abandoned that tether and just jogged straight on down that slope of slippery pebbles like he'd done before. The reason, though, that he'd taken the longer lariat was to manage, without losin any ground, lateral movements closer to the top.

Here his left hand caught fire, in the crux of his thumb and palm, with his lifeline also sufferin striated tears upon the spirallin ridges of the rope's cuntline. Kalin still held the rope tight, bound it down around his elbow too, that helped some, as he managed to swing over a little to that part of the scree where the rock was solid, where both Navidad and Mouse had propelled themselves straight up and through the fissure. Here, with the help of loose rock, he set some asters.

And so it went for the rest of those secure spots hidden upon the scree, Kalin slowly descendin, skippin from one side to the other, markin more patches of sure ground with flowers. Less than a third of the way down, to the great relief of his left hand, he no longer needed the rope and could manage the zigzags on his own. Providin you knew that it was the asters that mattered, you could now gaze up from the base and behold the key to this challenge.

Kalin was only just then steppin out onto that wide grassy area strewn with those large rocks when Landry broke through the brush, water from the crick below still streamin off Jojo. Even Landry was wet from the waist down. In her haste, they'd slipped from the shallow ground into the deep. Fortunately Jojo had managed to swim and scramble back to sure footin, but the Big Blue Roan weren't too happy about the dunk.

Landry was fer sure surprised, and super relieved, and plenty happy as well, to find Kalin waitin there for her, but Landry bein Landry also made sure to pay Kalin no mind, ignorin him in fact, cryin out for Jojo to fly, her mind set on the belief that her best option was to this time race Jojo straight up the scree, which, considerin the elation she was still feelin from their sprint along the main trail, now further magnified by the presence of Kalin, seemed a sure thing.

But Landry didn't even get a few strides in before Jojo revealed a different mindset, stoppin quick, near trajectin Landry over his neck. Landry went pale then over her misjudgment. She weren't alone. Kalin was even whiter at just the reckless sight of it all.

Landry dismounted, the disgust in Jojo's eyes only exceeded by the fear in her own.

I can't do it! Landry kept shoutin. *They're comin! I can't do it! They're comin after me! I'm trapped!*

Breathe, Landry. Breathe. Who's comin?

I should've just walked him up. Landry even looked like she was gonna try just that, at a walk, but Kalin stopped her.

Walkin don't work. You think Tom and I didn't try that first? You get stuck about two-thirds up.

Maybe Jojo will be different?

If you try the gap up there from a standstill, Jojo will either throw you for your idiocy or you'll both go over backwards. And you will go over backwards because all you'll have is a wall of rock on either side.

A mechanical whine began to fill the canyon. This time Kalin caught the panic in both Landry's and Jojo's eyes.

They're almost here! Landry cried.

Kalin already had three options figured out: for number one, he felt pretty sure he could get Landry up above the scree by foot, but that meant abandonin Jojo, which he knew Landry wasn't gonna tolerate; he weren't gonna tolerate it either. For number two, he'd ride Jojo up hisself, which he felt pretty sure he could manage despite Tom's earlier protestations, maybe even with Landry in the saddle too. Kalin didn't even want to consider the third option.

Since that first option was outta the question, Kalin figured he'd start with just mountin Jojo. He hadn't even moved, when Jojo, like he'd heard too clear Kalin's thoughts, started flarin his nostrils. One small step and Jojo's ears were pinned. By the time Kalin had got to the nearside, the big blue horse was throwin his head left and right, tryin to knock Kalin away for darin to even share the same air.

He won't do it! Landry cried and she weren't braggin.

Give me a chance.

Landry handed Kalin the reins and stepped away. Kalin stood perfectly still, whisperin and hushin, eventually managin to get in close enuf to stroke the horse's neck. Kalin even managed to get his left foot in a stirrup and even had his right leg swingin over the saddle, but Jojo was already movin by then, swingin his haunches outta the way, ears all the way flat, tryin at the same time to both bite and buck Kalin, who had landed soundly back on the ground.

On any other occasion, Landry would've taken pride in her horse's loyalties, but Kalin found only terror on her features, chalky pallor, her lips drawn back in a grimace, them small white teeth clampin down as that high, metallic whine kept gettin closer.

That left what Kalin had hoped not to consider, though in fairness to both him and Tom, in some way he'd always known the third option was their only option, why he'd placed the asters where he had on his way down.

What am I gonna do? Landry asked, back again on Jojo.

You sure you got no way back the way you just came?

Landry shook her head.

Where we're goin ain't no safer.

They mean to harm me, Kalin.

She didn't say who, but Kalin didn't need to hear more.

This is how it's gonna go. Kalin was glad that at least Tom weren't down there with them. *You're gonna ride Jojo right to where I show you to ride, and you'll do it better than me because you're one heckuva rider.*

Landry nodded.

See that lowest bunch of flowers there? Landry nodded again. *That's where the ground is solid enuf and wide enuf for Jojo to turn around and get a good start for the next leg up.* Kalin then traced out for her the back-and-forths zigzaggin up the scree, from aster bunch to aster bunch, all the way up to that jagged V, high above, cuttin through the cliff walls.

Now while you get them Easyboots on Jojo, and put them on the front hooves . . . Kalin trailed off. That metallic whine had got even louder. Dirt bikes fer sure. Jojo's ears had perked up too, twitchin now like they was loaded with flies.

The front? Landry already had the hoof boots out, but she'd also caught his hesitation.

I don't know, Landry. And Kalin didn't know. *Maybe the back hooves are better. Yes, the back hooves!* That last bit blurted out, loudly too, decisively, though it still was a guess. *He's gonna need everythin his back legs can give him to get through that crack. And go throw that gun in the crick. You don't need it jabbin your ribs.*

Landry had no intention of tossin away so fine a piece of metal. Plus it made her feel good. She stuffed it back in its velvet sack, askin while she hid it away in one of her saddlebags: *Tom got up there?*

Easily. Kalin didn't tell her Tom had also tried half a dozen times before makin it up the once, swearin then to do it only one more time.

Well, he ain't half the rider I am, so I should make it.

You'll do just fine.

Landry looked somehow disappointed. *He didn't comment that I said he was half the rider I am?*

Tom's not down here. He's up with Navidad and Mouse. And Ash.

He's gonna love this surprise! Her smile was back.

Whoa! Hold up there! Give me a sec to get to where I can do you some good!

As that horrible whine of engines grew still louder, Kalin scrambled up the scree. He demonstrated by foot the path Landry would need to follow, what at first required of him no more than a hurried amble. But as the steepness increased, Kalin was forced to crouch down more until he was on his hands and knees, strugglin plenty against the backward-slidin debris that each lateral move upward created. At the next bunch of asters, still well below the fissure, he had to pause just to catch his breath, eyein the danglin rope. Even that was still a good ways above him.

Landry, who had with her own eyes beheld Kalin ridin up this spill of shattered stone not once but three times, makin it look no harder than a lazy lope around the ring, couldn't help but notice thanks to the benefit of contrast, what has already been more generally mentioned, how ill-suited for motion and bereft of coordination Kalin seemed when he wasn't on a horse. Was it any surprise that he'd dragged Navidad's saddle down on his face when he was first startin out? Even when breakin camp, he seemed the buffoon. And this vision of general ineptitude clouded Landry's sight and judgment, as she began to wonder both how she could've ever thought herself incapable of managin this ride, because of course she was a better rider than him, while also at the same time wonderin, since he was a buffoon, how she was supposed to trust his instructions. Jojo then, likely because he was feelin Landry's conflictin confidence and doubt, threw his head up and even

253

tried to back away from the scree, which Landry put a stop to, causin Jojo to at once neigh and neigh loud.

Navidad came to the rescue then, and in fact she right there might've altered the outcome of this whole tellin. For Navidad had heard Jojo's cry and answered from above with her own loud reply, reverberatin down through the split in the crag, followed not a moment later by Mouse's less imposin vocalizations, all of which not only confirmed that the two horses were up there but that *up there* was possible.

Kalin smiled at these announcements and was further encouraged by the fact that, just as the shriek of the dirt bikes got to their very loudest, their engines did not then quiet with news of their arrival, but rather continued whizzin on by as they raced higher up into the canyon, gettin softer and softer.

Landry didn't waste a moment, urgin Jojo with a strong slap of her heels, for the first time situated at the right startin point, pointed in the right direction. She didn't race him either but kept his pace steady; strong, yes, but not lungin, so Jojo moved evenly up against the skitterin stones, which, when unsettled, slid at once downhill.

Just as Kalin had showed her, and he kept hootin too his encouragement from above, she made for that first bouquet of asters, where the patch of ground at once renewed both her and Jojo's confidence, especially as they executed a near perfect turnabout, Jojo findin enuf solidity beneath his back hooves to initiate the powerful charge necessary for the next leg of their run up the scree.

But as they got higher and higher, Kalin could see how Jojo had started to slow and even worse drift down some upon those evercollapsin stones. Kalin at once abandoned his perch, scramblin down and to the next batch of asters that Jojo and Landry would need to reach.

Aim above the asters!

Landry urged Jojo higher, while Kalin, aside from wavin his hands and demonstratin a whole array of clicks and guttural exhortations, mainly used Jojo's dislike of him to motivate the horse to get as far away as he could. By the next turnabout, Jojo was chargin even harder, faster too, even as the steepness continued to increase.

There's little doubt that Kalin's multiple times up the scree had helped, however impermanently, to compact the path enuf to make Jojo's ride easier. That bein said, they was now reachin one of the trickiest parts, namely because there weren't much more Kalin could do until they got to the fissure except yell.

The apex of the scree was bordered on either side by an unassailable barrier of rock. If Landry didn't make the next group of asters, where she could once again safely turn around, she would reach that wall and, with nothin solid underfoot, would either fall or, if she could keep Jojo upright while he tried to catch his legs, head straight down, which, at that height and at a speed commensurate to that kind of steepness, might easily lead to an even more severe fall.

Aim above the asters! Kalin was yellin again. *Get above me!*

Who knows if it helped. Maybe it weren't but noise that makes no difference. Whatever the case, Landry did keep above the flowers, and Jojo made the next turnabout look easy as a child spinnin around on a merry-go-round.

With more stones now givin way, and each slippage remindin Kalin that the whole thing could avalanche at any moment, he followed his own advice and made a mad lateral clamber toward the middle, the most unstable part, but well above where the rope ended. With that shattered slope of rocks draggin him down more with every lunge, Kalin still just managed to grab hold of the end just as the rock beneath his feet completely abandoned him. Then by alternately coilin the rope around one wrist and then the other, and in both cases grippin as hard as he could, he found the right rhythm to see him up that final part, closin in on Jojo and Landry from below, because he was now goin straight up and they still had one more zigzag, and all the while hootin and yellin to urge them constantly upward. At one point Kalin hung on with just his left hand while his right hand frantically waved overhead that big white Stetson, a bit dusty at this point, to further goad Jojo from the likes of him.

Only one last section remained: through the fissure itself that was darned near tight as a rodeo chute. It was by far the most dangerous part of the whole endeavor because here there was no room to turn out. And steep as heck too. If a horse stalled there'd be no choice but to go over backward. After that only badness would follow. Worse still Kalin intended to be right behind Jojo. He'd fer sure be crushed if Landry and Jojo didn't make it.

Kalin was already soaked in sweat and shakin, and his palms hurt like they was burnin on the inside, like the bones in his hands had caught fire, but he still couldn't let Landry risk it on her own. Tom and he had spent the good part of a summer figurin it out, and even so, they never really figured it out.

And so, though his breath kept comin out ragged and his thighs burnt like his arms were burnin, Kalin kicked and dragged his way up the last of it, and right in time too, comin level with Jojo fer a moment, as the Big Blue Roan with Landry perched on top like a leaf on a wave, reached that last bit of solid rock, readyin for their last leap upwards, or a bad scramble if they had to, Kalin then landin his big hat on the horse's back side with a loud swat, which Jojo did not appreciate one bit, kickin hard away even harder, and with an angry snort, and if you'd been there you wouldn't've been faulted if you'd've sworn Jojo and Landry had flown the rest of the way up, as if more than mere equine muscle and determination had defended itself against gravity, as if constellate Pegasus hisself had right then and there bequeathed upon this heir with so humble a name as Jojo not only wind and lift but actual wings with the hooves too to rise up against any Chimera, facilitatin a careenin upward that was even spied by that white owl just then settlin on the rocks overlookin Navidad and Mouse, all the horses, maybe even Ash too, the lot of them soon greetin Jojo like an old friend who seemed to have knowd already just where he'd be welcomed, not pausin at that first shelf of suitable rock but continuin upwards, followin the slowly mellowin path until he had reached that more substantial slab where Landry first regarded Navidad and Mouse with great relief until she'd looked around a bit more and seen how she'd wound up in a worse place than below.

K alin was still on his belly, still hangin on to that rope. After spurrin Jojo onward he had immediately flattened hisself against the slope, not so much to help hisself in the event of an accident, for no positionin of his body would have spared him if Jojo had tumbled on top of him, but rather to make certain that the rope was held down low so as to not in any way trip Jojo by accident.

Once they was gone through, though, leavin a cloud of lingerin dust in their wake, with even a drizzle of rain now and then slappin down on him, Kalin hauled hisself back up on his feet and then dragged his way through the last part, his hands howlin, his head throbbin, and while maybe there was some immediate relief in knowin Landry and Jojo were now safe, knowin too what lay beyond this modest victory, still only the beginnin, stirred somethin terrible in his heart.

Kalin is often depicted as stoic and calm and plenty gentle, and these things he most certainly was, especially when he was around horses, but what probably also won't come as no surprise is how more than mere placidity resided in his core. Kalin weren't never no saint. Even here in this short albeit challengin climb through a steep chute of rock, his mind had erupted with curses. Perhaps the anger helped him dig deeper for resources he desperately needed in those minutes, to grip harder, lug hisself faster over them last high steps, but you might also be surprised to learn at whom he directed his ire: his mother. In his head she castigated him for puttin that young girl into such a dangerous position, and in his head he squalled back at her about havin no choice even if none of his obstreperous objections managed to still the hard condemnin shake of her head. *What have you done, Kalin?* that shake seemed to say. *What have you gotten yourself into? What have you gotten her into?!*

When he finally made it back up to Tom and the horses, rope coiled again and slung over one shoulder, dusty hat in place, Landry was still down around Jojo's legs, carefully studyin each hoof for damage. So far it was all good. She was even replacin the Easyboots, if still tenderly runnin her hands over Jojo's rear tendons, as Kalin stumbled over to have hisself a well-earned seat.

Navidad and Mouse both jerked their heads up at his arrival, snortin either with relief at seein him in one piece or disgust for havin wrecked hisself in order to reappear without extra food. Kalin's breath at least had slowed some, and he no longer felt the angry heartbeat in his chest, but he still needed to drop his head between his knees, concerned plenty with how his lightheadedness and general dizziness was refusin to quit.

You brung her up here?! Tom weren't hidin his fury.

I don't feel so good.

Landry fetched him his canteen and made him drink.

You okay? she asked.

I will be. Thank you. How's Jojo?

Likely hates you more than he did before.

Smart horse.

I can't believe we just done that. That's the craziest thing, and I mean thee craziest thing I've ever done! I know that because I'll never ever do it again. Ever. And you did it three times!

And I'll never ever do it again either, Kalin said with at least a hint of a smile.

You need to get her down from here! Tom weren't lettin up. *Now!*

And how am I supposed to do that? Kalin lashed back at the air.

Oh Lord! What's he sayin now?!

He don't like that you're here. And frankly I can't totally disagree with him. But while gettin up here is scary, it ain't nothin compared to goin down with a horse.

How many times you done that?

Tom and I managed it just the once togther. And then I did it with Navidad the once like you already seen, and I thought— Well, you don't wanna know what I was thinkin. Let's just say I ain't ever doin that again either.

Kalin said no more on the subject, focusin instead on how to do just what Tom wanted, what Kalin wanted too, even if tryin to think it through made his temples throb. Kalin had to press his index finger and thumb into his eyes to blot out the predicament, which fingers-in-your-eyes never succeed in doin, Kalin just givin hisself them blotches of black and sparkles to blink away. Who was after Landry anyway? Who was she so afraid of?

Kalin! Landry suddenly squawked out. She was hunched over Jojo's right front hoof, and Kalin could see her shoulders were shakin.

Maybe because Jojo's hoof was restin in Landry's hand, Jojo didn't at once object to Kalin movin close to her side, though the big blue horse did still feign a couple of disinterested snaps at Kalin's hat.

There it was: a black piece of jagged rock on the underside, wedged between the frog, what looks like a *V* extendin from the heel of the hoof into the sole, and what's called the bar, a part of the outer hoof that juts in close to the frog and creates what's called the collateral groove. It's not unusual to find mud or manure compacted in there, and it's easy enuf to get out with a pick. But other stuff, bad stuff, can find its way in there too, like a nail or this here misfortune.

Kalin lightly prodded the edges to see how much it would stir Jojo. It was a good sign that Jojo didn't object none, but it also weren't proof of anythin either. Kalin and Landry didn't give words then to what both of them couldn't stop picturin: pullin that stone out to reveal a deep gash or puncture bubblin with blood. Such an infliction up here would prove a death sentence.

Go on, Kalin said soft then. *Do it.*

Landry gently slid her pick under the rock and popped it free. There weren't even the slightest sign of an abrasion, let alone a cut beneath. Both Kalin and Landry gave a big sigh of relief. Tom too.

Fortunately, Kalin also had extra cardboard and more than enuf duct tape. Like they'd done that mornin, he and Landry got quick to further protectin Jojo's front hooves with makeshift boots. They also further reinforced the makeshift boots on Navidad and Mouse.

Only then, maybe because these preparations had put in her mind the question of what was next, did Landry give their surroundins the closer look they deserved. Landry at once wished she hadn't.

Fer starters her ears went funny. She felt upside down and wobbly. And to be clear, there was plenty of room on this shelf, but in comparison to the mountains that rose above them and the lethal heights below where they already stood, this tiny sliver of levelness suddenly felt as insubstantial as a soap bubble dancin with a porcupine. Landry tried to look up again and again felt struck dumb by the sight, so precipitously and unquestionably did the walls of the canyon rise up around them that an end to them seemed called into question, disappearin as they did into the dark churnin clouds no longer dolin out patches of sky or errant wands of sunlight.

And that was up. Below, what Landry had moments ago tried to convince herself was a scalable slope, she'd gone up it after all, fear had altered into a vertical face. Leadin Jojo back down that way seemed the greatest fiction she'd heard so far, and that included Tom's presence beside Kalin, or Egan Porch's claim that Russel was dead, somethin she figured she'd better relay to Kalin now, the reason why she was openin her mouth now, which was when the sky opened itself up too.

What had for a while remained an on-and-off drizzle they had all but managed to forget, now became a tumble of water, suddenly releasin cold sheets that at once drenched them all, maybe not Ash or Tom, but to Kalin's eyes even Tom looked out of sorts.

The rain fell so hard that the mountain itself seemed incapable of accommodatin the offerin, gatherin it, almost as if to weave its myriad rivulets into bigger braids, or in some cases sayin to heck with weavin and just pourin down little rivers, the biggest one floodin down now through the very gap they'd just come up through, creatin there a cataract batterin the scree below.

It was 11:09 a.m.

What now? Landry gasped, for she had still failed to locate a single way off that ledge aside from jumpin.

I don't know, Kalin answered.

Whadya mean you don't know?

I'm thinkin! The hard rainfall was changin things fast.

You darned fool! Landry hollered at him. *Look around! Look where you've gotten us! I wouldn't want to be up here on even the sunniest day. Certainly not with three horses!*

Four, Tom corrected her.

Four, Kalin repeated. *Tom don't like you forgettin Ash.*

Landry looked appalled. *Where we're standin now, you know, could just give way? How do you think screes get made?*

Like Landry, Kalin had also retreated as far from the edge as he could, back among the horses, where at least Navidad gave him a nuzzle, which given the circumstances felt mighty good.

What else is Tom sayin? Landry croaked out. *Aside from pointin out how well he can count.*

Tom hadn't left the edge. He stood there, surveyin the canyon floor. Somewhere down there the scream of dirt bikes had started to grow louder again, even in this onslaught of rain.

Whadya see, Tom? Kalin asked.

I don't see no police.

He don't see police, Kalin relayed to Landry.

Police?

Weren't police chasin you?

What the heck are you talkin about? Why on earth would police chase me?

We saw police lights at the canyon entrance. They're still there.

I weren't runnin from the police! That'd be a darned fool thing to do! I was runnin from Egan!

Egan? Who's Egan?

Tom shifted uneasily then and wouldn't meet Kalin's gaze. Even Ash lowered his head, shakin his white mane, swishin his white tail, like he too felt the same discomfort.

He's one of the Porch brothers. One of the oldest, Landry answered before addin real quiet then: *There ain't nothin he ain't capable of.* Then, like Ash, she too hung her head.

He's the one who got you so shook up you managed the impossible?

At least that got somethin like a smile out of her, but it didn't last. *I ain't ashamed to say it: I'm more afraid of him than that craziness we just got done with. Tell Tom to stop smirkin. He don't know the half of it.*

Tom ain't smirkin.

Tom weren't either. He was starin back down at the canyon floor. *They're comin,* he said.

But not fast. Egan, Kelly, and Billings had never quit takin their time. The path was soft, and followin Jojo's tracks weren't no big deal. Each hoof made a clean mark if it weren't kickin up a big divot.

But then they got company. Sean and Shelly, undeterred by signs prohibitin dirt bikes nor by the submerged state of First Bridge and Bridge Two, roared up to join their brothers.

Sean and Shelly were younger than Egan but older than Kelly; Sean bein twenty-four, Shelly twenty-five. They lived together in one half of a duplex near Westridge Elementary school in Grandview. Whether you called it income or appanage, they was both technically on the Porch Meats payroll, in the truckin division, even if they rarely hauled squat. They sure had money, though, what they spent on whiz-bang trucks, BMX bikes, snowmobiles, and too many skateboards, which neither one rode well; in fact none of the Porch boys could skateboard except for some reason Russel. Guns too. They had lots of guns. And now and then they liked to blow up things. On the Fourth of July they'd built some pipe bombs, big ones, big enuf to blow loose the stump of an old cherry tree. And to think Shelly had once upon a time wanted to write plays and Sean had wanted to be a painter or a surfer.

They was big boys too, and size had no say in slowin them down.

They was both real fast. Sean had been a startin outside linebacker, and Shelly a defensive tackle. For two years they'd played together. They each had brown coppery hair and big hands like their old man, though without scars. Sean's eyes were hazel, gold even when the light was right, while Shelly's were dark brown, real dark, no matter the light. On this day Shelly had a sty in his left eye that was swollen and red but somehow seemed to soften a bit what was otherwise his dead-eyed glare. Sean weren't whole neither, sufferin from a bad cold, which at least gave him the opportunity to gleek on or hawk loogies at Shelly.

They arrived on Honda CR250s. Shelly's dirt bike was green and black for Orvop High, Sean's red and black. The water over First Bridge had already started to lessen, with a storm-created dam of branches and sand havin washed away earlier. Not to say that the traverse was easy. The water was still waist-high for a good dozen feet over slippery boards. For these two boys, though, that weren't nothin. They hauled Sean's bike over first, and when they brung over Shelly's, they weren't even a little winded. Same went for Bridge Two, which was wider and not near as deep.

After that, they caught up pretty quick with Egan, Kelly, and Billings, spookin the horses some and earnin curses from Egan, who could already see that their appearance was gonna accelerate a response from the police back at the entrance. And even if their Uncle Conrad did let it slide, the Isatch park rangers were under their own authority and wouldn't tolerate one bit unpermitted motorized vehicles in the park. And that was just what was in store for later. Now Egan had to deal with their stupid anger that weren't doin nothin but gettin in the way.

A lifetime of boy-maulin-boy, which pretty much summed up the Porch family, kept Sean and Shelly gougin wide mud-spittin circles around their brothers, clutch-poppin wheelies this way and that for show, further jitterin the horses and even worse, wreckin Landry's tracks. Egan briefly considered shootin Sean and Shelly right on the spot. He even thought he could blame the Kalin kid for it. For Egan, killin these two weren't no unfamiliar thought.

Kelly answered his brothers' scowled faces and angry shouts with a finger that at least sent them racin off in the right direction. Why not get them spookin Landry's horse instead? Egan gave Kelly a nod of approval. They would handle the Kalin kid.

It was all throttle then for Sean and Shelly. They headed fast as they could up that wide trail, screamin Lord knows what, still poppin wheelies, showin off to Lord knows who, the quartzite gates and perilous limestone walls reverberant with their intrusion, a ruckus perhaps judged higher up by juries of aspens, maples, and birches.

Bart Roskelley, a research hydrologist at the Glen Canyon Dam in

Page, when he weren't talkin about the summer of '83, loved to bring up how both Sean and Shelly had, whether consciously or not, lined up their tires on Jojo's hoof marks *and like Pac-Man, ate up what they was after.* Horace Montgomery and Lauren Barnes, both at this time workin at Bulk Fertilizers in Gunnison, also liked to toss around these moments. *They had no clue about Landry,* Lauren Barnes would assert. *They just knew about Russel's death. Might not've even known about the stolen horses. If they had, they'd have noticed there weren't but one horse ahead.* Horace Montgomery would agree: *They had no idea what they was lookin for. Their anger was just takin them ahead as fast as possible, way past the actual turnoff, past Landry's bluff, and even past where Jojo's tracks stopped.*

Nahi Pasket, an engineer at the Space Dynamics Laboratory in Logan, would believe his whole life that all that was really holdin the attention of these ultracompetitive young men was outracin one another, an opinion she repeated to Duane Newren and Guy Olsen and Tamara Harward too.

It is true that as the two brothers tore across the last bridge, Bridge Seven, Shelly was already screamin his victory, with Sean at his side, hotly screamin his objections, even as they brought their machines to a thumpin idle before the immense boulders and stone walls that declared Isatch Canyon the dead end it was: Yell Rock Falls, what at that moment was pretty much just one big cataract, beautiful and scary too, goin like mad, fillin the upper reaches of that narrow canyon with the roar of rapids, above which hung a gentle mist.

One thing fer sure, there weren't nothin here that those two brothers could pair with the death of their little Russel.

And as they headed back, the rain really let loose, the same downpour that had soaked Kalin and Landry up on their ledge. The crick came to new life as well, as more runoff descended from all sides of the canyon, the heavy turbulence churnin even harder toward the canyon entrance, an engorgement that would soon enuf submerge more of the lower bridges, spill out onto the park's parkin lot, and finally flood the streets below, threatenin even the Orvop Temple.

Billings was the first to discover Landry's ruse, by fallin for it first, at least for a few minutes, followin the diversion until even in the downpour, with more and more wash and condensin rivulets turnin the trail into a slop of mud, he divined how the brush and tall grass dancin ahead were neither snapped nor even convincinly parted like they had been a few strides back. From there it was easy to see how Landry and Jojo had backed their way outta there.

Billings was pleased with the discovery, but also, for just a moment, set on edge, because if that little girl had already gone to such efforts to mislead Egan, she weren't just playin out here but feared them fer real. And fear can change things up fer real.

Landry, of course, was right to fear them. Billings knew that. But it also meant she wouldn't be caught unawares again and furthermore would get across to that Kalin kid, if that's where she was headin to, that he had real trouble on his hands, so he likely wouldn't be caught unawares either.

It took a while longer, but both Billings and Kelly finally spied out below Bridge Five the correct turnoff, which was revealed not by the tracks, which the water now sheetin the main trail had effectively erased, but ironically by the branches that Landry had hastily cast behind her in an effort to further hide her tracks.

Down near the crick, which was amply sheltered by the canopy, plenty of hoof marks revealed themselves, and here for the first time it was apparent that there was more than just Landry's horse. Three at least, though Billings thought he counted four.

Crossin the crick in such conditions should've proved near impossible but the Porch boys had some luck on their side. The Misdemeanors swimmin hole served as a dam of sorts and at least for the moment was mellowin the current. Though it was deeper than before, Egan, Kelly, and Billings made it over to the other side in no time.

Sean and Shelly both hesitated before the water, and maybe they weren't entirely the kind of beef heads folks generally view them as, because instead of attemptin to once again carry their bikes across water, this time deeper and more dangerous, they drove back up the canyon, above Bridge Five, where the crick switched to the Agoneeya side of the canyon.

There they attacked the hillside at different places, but only on the fourth try did they find an animal trail that led them back to the base of Aster Scree, arrivin there pretty much at the same time as Egan on a soaked Cavalry, Kelly on a soaked Barracuda, and Billings on a fairly dry Gads, all trottin up to that small meadow abundant with them large, strangely scattered rocks, white as faceless dice.

The talus warned the dirt bikes to a halt and slowed too those on horseback to a cautious walk. The lower part of that stony barricade was also cloaked in mist now; what waited higher up, what was water-battered by the cascade that spat forth from that narrow fissure in the cliffs, hardly drew anyone's attention.

It was 11:27 a.m.

But even though noon had nearly arrived, the canyon continued to grow darker, shadows slidin down the canyon walls as if their creation no longer depended on the sun.

Egan had already dismounted and, walkin Cavalry to that slope of time-polished rubble, at once deemed the scree unassailable, especially by horse, and so not even worth his consideration. Not even in better conditions would he have regarded this place as anythin but a terminus, even as animal instinct kept tryin to rouse him from this supposition, what held him there both mystified and enthralled.

Impossible to ignore were all the hoof marks disappearin onto that easily shiftin surface of stone, what Egan forced hisself to keep regardin if just as another bit of subterfuge that would with enuf scrutiny reveal its gimmick. However, in his widenin search, Egan had yet to find even one hoof mark exitin that river of rock, nor could he locate an alternate path of stone to explain this disappearin act. The easiest bet was that they had somehow retraced their steps back to the crick and from there retreated to the canyon entrance.

At least that's what Egan kept insistin to hisself: one big doubleback. He blamed Sean and Shelly for tearin up the telltale equine signatures that likely would've made such an escape evident. It weren't hard to imagine the whole lot somehow returnin to the crick, timin it right so that once Egan, Kelly, and Billings had passed by, they could retake the main trail. Maybe they was gallopin back right now. He could picture them laughin as they rode, makin a fool of him, with maybe Landry's momma, the fearsome Sondi Gatestone, waitin off a trail that deviated north of the entrance, parked on a quiet street in Indian Hills with one of her big fancy trailers at the ready.

But even that explanation wasn't pullin Egan's eyes from the scree, what no longer interested Kelly or Billings, who just figured they'd escaped some way they hadn't happened on yet, Sean and Shelly just revvin their bikes and chokin the air with their exhaust. Egan even kicked at the tiny rocks. How had Landry, the kid, and all their horses stepped onto the tongue of the mountain and just disappeared?

And then Sean, of all people, suddenly let out a shout.

There she is!

Landry just couldn't help herself. Like Tom always said, *Rocks in her head!* Maybe he was even sayin it right then too, when she chose to reveal herself in the name of a good goadin.

Kalin had only just finished askin Landry to keep the horses calm while he crept out to the edge to see exactly who they was up against. He'd even crept out on his belly. Not Landry. Who knows what she was thinkin; she just strode on over, standin tall, if her little stature could ever be called tall, with that awful pink raincoat glowin in the rain, and wavin around her sage cowboy hat too, all the while hurlin down insult after insult, ire she was helpless to tamp down risin up in her like all the earth vomit that had disgorged from Mount St. Helens but five months earlier.

I'm up here, Egan! You yellow-bellied sonuva dick-swallowin sow! Which Landry later regretted because she had unfairly impugned his poor mother, not to mention all varieties of wholly innocent sows. *I rode up here on Jojo too! You ain't even half the rider I am! Pow-Pow! I dare you to even try! Ha!*

She even took another step closer to the drop-off, which, if she'd carelessly overstepped, would've seen her tumblin down a bad ten-foot drop onto a brief but very steep slope, which would've spat her into the air before droppin her a good fifty feet down to the scree.

Get down! Kalin hissed at Landry, but she only stepped away. He followed her, still prone, Tom beside him.

Why are you on your belly? Kalin then hissed at Tom.

Seems wrong not to be.

Down below, Sean and Shelly was goin plumb crazy, drivin their dirt bikes to the edge of that pebbled river, close as they could, before veerin away to have another go, like dogs who've cornered a baby bear, except in this case it weren't a baby bear but the mountain itself.

Maybe because Sean had been first to spot Landry, Shelly took the widest loop yet and this time, fueled by pure competitive fury, accelerated straight at the scree, and to be fair he got pretty far up before the tires started spinnin out and he had to drag his bike around and sorta skid sideways, which was when the engine stalled.

Not to be outdone, Sean took the same approach but with more speed. And that made all the difference. He flew straight over the handlebars.

Tom laughed pretty long over that one, rollin around on his back, offerin his hands up in prayer. Landry was doin the same thing.

I am so content to have just seen that! Tom finally said, tears streakin his face. *And I just had me a thought, Kalin: what if where I am now is some version of Heaven that I couldn't have dreamed up, bein as stupid as I was in life? I mean, look around: I got horses, folks that mean a whole lot to me, and laughs, good laughs.* He peered down on Shelly, who was now kickin his bike like that was to blame, and why Tom started laughin all over again, just like Landry started doin again, just as hard, and why the pair of them laughin like that, that was pretty heavenly.

Kalin couldn't say what caught his eye then, but it inspired him to move quicker than his own thoughts could follow, rollin him hard sideways, knockin Landry down at the same time as a rock exploded behind them, the ugly shot ringin out through the canyon.

And that was just the first one.

Here's what happened: Egan, havin forgotten to bring binoculars, had unzipped the scabbard with the .30-06. He just wanted the Winchester for the Leupold scope to get better eyes on that petulant girl spoutin off about ridin her horse up the side of a mountain and through a waterfall. But when he'd got her fixed in the crosshairs, his index finger couldn't help but curl under the guard, just drift a little over the trigger, near caressin it. His thumb even nudged off the safety, what eased away his breath.

There in the crosshairs was her dark little mouth. There was her small chest. And there, just a little lower . . . which is when his hand wobbled as he caught sight for the first time of the one they called Kalin. It had to be him. Cowerin at her feet. And this combination of present and past desire, anger as well as satisfaction with the discovery, not to mention the turbulent sense of his brothers nearby tryin at every moment to best him, somehow took his finger all the way, firin at what was by then not even a blur, not even the ghost of a shadow, gone entirely from the scope.

Now of course, if Egan was shootin, Kelly sure as heck was gonna shoot too. Sean and Shelly, even faster than Kelly, dug out what they'd brung, Sean a shotgun, Shelly a revolver, both of them just firin at the cliffside while also duckin behind their dirt bikes, like them was suitable cover, yellin all the while how they was bein shot at, which was hogswallow, as well as yellin how Landry and whoever else was up there couldn't shoot worth a darn, which was kinda true, given as how both Landry and Kalin weren't doin nothin more now than cowerin behind a wedge of rock.

Did they just friggin shoot at us?! Kalin barked up at Tom.

I think they're still shootin at us, Tom drawled back. He'd resettled his hat and was now standin up like he needed to stretch legs that would never need stretchin again. That or he'd just got bored pretendin bullets mattered to him.

This don't make a lick of sense, Kalin rasped, so befuddled he not only failed to grasp what was goin on but consequently couldn't think of what to do next. *Unless they're plain crazy?*

Oh they're crazy! Landry chirped back, not a stitch of amusement on her face. *All the Porches are crazy!*

An immense flash suddenly warned the mountainside, followed soon after by, give it a count of twenty, what at once put the present fusillade in its place, the fulfillment of that prophecy and promise, a breach of thunder growlin through the canyon.

Whether coincidence or not, that seemed to call an end to the gunfire below, just as it also further jittered the horses, who, while well out of reach of any direct fire, were none too pleased about the gunfire, their twitchin equine ears and stompin hooves makin that all too clear. Kalin and Landry scrambled back to them, doin their best to calm their anxious steps and troubled head shakes, mostly succeedin too, though Jojo did persist in pullin back against his lead. Landry quick as a thrown knife took the rope in hand and gave Jojo the room he needed to turn around so he was finally facin Navidad, Mouse, and Ash, who durin all this had done nothin more than flare his nostrils.

Landry's resituatin of Jojo did briefly bring him into view, and the effect below was astonishin. Egan's lens filled with the horse's head, and even when he looked up without the scope Egan caught a glimpse of that big Arab with a black mane. Egan was gobsmacked. Had that little girl really ridden her horse up there? He still couldn't believe it, and he put that disbelief to work, searchin again for an alternate route, even as his eyes kept returnin to the scree and then, higher up, to that fissure still gushin water. He even spotted the asters. They was sayin somethin all right, but he couldn't for the life of him understand their speech.

Meanwhile, Kalin had retrieved his binoculars as well as an oat bag. After he'd palm-fed the horses with what little nibbles remained there, he cut off the bottom of the sack, and then proppin it open with twigs so it weren't nothin but a canvas tube, he recessed the binoculars in the shade of that makeshift blind. Then, once again on his belly, positioned between a gap in the rocks, this time scrabblin as far right as he could get so everyone below was pretty much in profile, especially seein as how they weren't lookin his way no more, Kalin at last got hisself a good long look at the folks who had just tried to kill him. It's a moment that Ms. Melson would now and then refer to as *the first teichoskopia, or view from the wall, in this case a cliff, but the action is still the same.* Neither of her friends, Mrs. Annserdodder nor Mr. Caracy Rudder, would quibble with this claim, and in 2001 Ms. Melson's AP English class would dutifully write down *teichoskopia*, though they weren't then discussin Aster Scree. Not back when Ms. Melson still wore her hair like a gold beehive, with hair spray so shiny it looked liked sugar.

Landry, suffice it to say, refused to leave Kalin's side, and Kalin didn't deny her a place, though he weren't hidin either his saltiness over what she'd done.

Do me a favor and try not to stand up so they know exactly where to shoot.

I deserved that.

I'd like them to think we've left.

That there's Shelly Porch, Landry pointed out then. *He's the one on the green-and-black bike. Sean Porch, there, he's the one who went over the handlebars.*

Kalin studied them both. He didn't need to know Sean was a former Orvop High football star who hadn't stopped pressin plates when school ended, though Landry made sure to tell him. He had a face as blunt and near as narrow as an ax poll. But there was somethin soft about him too, at least compared to his brother, who Landry said was the meaner one. Shelly had them black eyes and a scab of scar tissue on his cheek, like he'd fallen asleep on a belt sander. His scowl weren't helpin none, nor his split lip and swole eye.

Keep clear of Shelly, Landry whispered.

Either way, it weren't the size of their arms that worried Kalin but the potency of the armaments they was wieldin. Sean had by then lowered his shotgun, but Shelly was still wavin around a .38-caliber Ruger Service-Six, though with nothin now to aim at he finally just shot at the sky, and this time, instead of near all his brothers joinin in, he got the stink eye from everyone, includin Billings.

Kelly's there, Landry said as Kalin panned the binoculars over to the buckskin. *He'll do whatever Old Porch sends him to do. He's a couple of years outta Orvop and maybe knows a thing or two. Not the right thing or two, but there you have it.*

Kalin studied Kelly. He had none of the bulkiness or brute energies of Sean and Shelly, but his presence demanded of Kalin an uneasy alertness. Some of it had to do with the way he sat on his horse, patient and relaxed, even as more thunder rumbled through the canyon. Some of it also had to do with them easy broad shoulders; he was tall too, and with wide-set sharp blue eyes glintin from under the brim of his brown hat, along with havin the whitest and maybe straightest teeth of the bunch. Like his brothers, he had similar sandy brown hair, but his cheeks was also freckled lightly, and he had big, soft, almost pouty lips. No wonder he was considered the best-lookin Porch, though Kalin had no idea about that. What struck him like a knuckle-hit to his sternum was the sickly anger that was now at work foulin up those pretty features.

Kelly had at the ready a Remington, which as Mace Rogers once put it, was *beat to heck by horses and mountains*. Kalin had no doubt it shot fine and was also pretty sure this fella Kelly could reach the center of a target just fine too. He had a despairin determination that was surpassed by only one other.

Too much to say about Egan, Landry hissed.

You can see for yourself who he is, Tom said, back down on his back, starin lazily up at the clouds and the fallin rain they was emancipatin, such freedom touchin him none.

Kalin lingered the longest on Egan. No knock on his sternum was needed to warn him that this Porch son was who you'd best keep clear of. Unlike Kelly, there was nothin pretty about him. The gap in his teeth weren't the heart of it either. There was somethin else, somethin angrier, mashed up and concentrate in his features and movements. He weren't near as big as the other brothers, but Kalin didn't doubt he could take on any one of them, maybe all of them at once. Kalin also saw how Egan's horse obeyed him as much as he feared him. Kalin didn't miss the rowel spurs on his boots. He didn't like that.

I'm surprised he let Russel ride his horse.

Cavalry, Landry and Tom said at the same time.

Cavalry, Kalin said a breath later. *Russel had no business on that horse.*

Russel had no business comin out last night, Tom said.

Russel don't even look much like these boys here, Kalin added.

Russel's different. He's a pain in the keister but he's sweet, Landry said, realizin as she was sayin so that she'd also just been presented with another perfect moment to tell Kalin what Egan had said about Russel, his throat gettin cut and all, but Kalin had already raised his finger to his lips.

Egan's the one that fired first, Tom was sayin.

I know it.

That Russel's sweet? Landry asked.

That that there Egan took the first shot, Kalin whispered back.

I don't doubt it, Landry said.

But guess what?

What? Tom and Landry both asked.

He also missed.

Yeah, he did miss, Landry echoed.

Tom got to laughin again. *Kalin March, ain't you a miserable rooster without a hen, but you are right!*

Who's he? Kalin asked Landry then, pointin out Billings.

Landry belly-crawled behind the binoculars. *My guess is he's someone who works at the Porch plant.*

What about you, Tom? Kalin asked. *You know him?*

Tom shrugged. *What does it matter? He's as dangerous as the rest.*

More, Kalin said.

More what? Landry asked.

More dangerous than the rest.

I dunno. Egan's pretty bad. But then they're all bad.

You'd know better than me, Kalin said.

A good time for these boys was goin over to Kenny Lithy's house to help with his rat problem. Rats was all through his backyard. In tunnels, in woodpiles, under old boards just left there to rot. The Porches didn't bring no traps. They just came over with pitchforks and shotguns, and they had a blast. Just killin rats all afternoon. I know this because I saw it. The whole thing. At the time I was friends with Kenny's sister, Staci. We was in fifth grade! We hid the whole time in her basement. Staci didn't end up at Orvop High, so I ain't seen her in a long while.

Kalin listened, but he was also back behind the binoculars, studyin Billings. Ample violence waited there, but it weren't in the black hair or the dark ruby cowboy hat or even them black brows castin further into shadow them dark eyes. What unsettled Kalin most was far simpler and clearer than any question of appearance: Billings hadn't drawn a weapon, and Kalin could spy under his jacket the grip of a revolver. And Kalin knew why there weren't no gun in his hand: because there hadn't been a shot to take.

I'll be glad never to see him or that Egan again, Kalin muttered as he at last put aside the binoculars.

You'd think dyin would've at least removed from my sight the antics of these Porches. Tom sighed. *Makes me rethink my idea of me bein in Heaven.*

At least they're turnin back, Landry said. And that did seem to be the case. Partly. Kelly had moseyed the buckskin pony back toward the brush where they'd come up from, still tryin to get an eye on what was goin on up on that ledge, though even from that far away there weren't no view, though what finally grabbed all of his attention was the growl of the crick.

Despite noon just comin up, the day seemed to grow only darker, them breathtakin columns of cumulonimbus and nimbostratus, hoverin around since yesterday, now compactin down into severe densities of weather, intolerant of light, pourin forth more and more soak, enlargin the streams of water sluicin down wherever there was a slope, as if to demand that even the notion of dryness should be stricken from understandin; water off the mountains, water from the sky, water from the air itself, as if to presage another biblical flood contrary to any covenant in favor of fire, so that the crick not only filled but overwhelmed itself. Not even Misdemeanors could retard any longer the growin flood, the lastin covenant with gravity draggin downwards this devotion of water at the cost of the banks and anythin else in its way toward Orvop itself, the temple first.

By this point, Sean and Shelly had ridden their bikes over to Kelly, but, unlike Kelly, were not dismayed by the impassable crick. They indicated that the way they'd come in didn't necessitate a crossin.

Kelly followed the dirt bikes without lookin back. In fact in the days ahead, it was one of the few times when Kelly would feel good about hisself: in control, in charge some, enjoyin the rewards of free will dosin his system with feelins good enuf to settle his guts and his conscience. He liked leavin Egan behind.

That new direction didn't worry Kalin and Tom none. They knew there weren't trails there. The way Sean, Shelly, and Kelly was goin would only reveal cliffs growin higher and higher until up past Bridge Five they'd have no choice but to turn around again or drop down to the main trail.

But Egan and Billings weren't in no hurry to get to nowhere that proved nothin. Egan's focus was now solely with this curse of shattered stone. If it had just been Landry yellin down that she'd ridden up it just fine, he wouldn't have believed her. But then he'd seen the Kalin kid, and then the blue horse. Egan knew he could likely manage the scree on foot, but on Cavalry, it still struck him as impossible. There had to be another way up there, what finally got him scabbardin the Winchester. Maybe his brothers had already found the trail they'd need.

And then Billings came over with a story about them asters.

Kalin, Tom, and Landry watched the two conferrin, and then they seen Billings with an outstretched arm draw a zigzag up the scree. It had taken a while, but he'd finally seen the order that them clumps of fadin flowers had imposed upon the slippery rocks. Kalin was surprised how the rain hadn't washed them down, cursed hisself too for not grabbin them on his way up. Or rather Tom cursed him.

You shoulda grabbed them on the way up.

I can see that now.

See what? Landry demanded.

I should've got rid of them flowers when I had the chance.

You think he's gonna try to ride up here? she asked, already too much fear in her voice.

He won't try if he thinks you're a better rider.

Egan don't think anyone is better.

Then I reckon he's gonna try.

Should I get that gun?

Sit still, Landry.

Like that's ever an option for her, Tom scoffed.

Let's just watch, Kalin said real gently.

That is definitely not an option for her.

I'm gonna get the gun.

Please, Landry. Don't do that. Don't even say it. This Egan ain't gonna make it up. I just wanna make sure Cavalry comes through okay.

But Cavalry didn't come through okay. And if you're the kind who might get squeamish or, worse, soul-hurt about a moment that necessarily points out not just the sublime endurance of these beautiful creatures but also their frailty in such conditions, conditions in case it weren't glarinly obvious that they ain't in any way suited for, you would not be faulted for briefly divertin your attention elsewhere. Violence, when it arrives unmitigated by play, posture, or irony, will bruise in the tellin as well as the hearin, which is why we also won't linger. Though let the facts be laid out plainly.

Egan, before he attempted the ride, retrieved his .357 and stuffed that behind his buckle similar to how Landry had carried the Colt. Then he conferred one more time with Billings.

Egan did pretty well on the first couple of switchbacks, and then sadly, he did far better on the next few, even findin a certain cadence that kept takin him higher and higher up that shiftin slope.

The trouble, though, was with the path. As has been mentioned once already but bears repeatin, Navidad and Mouse on their rides up, by the variance of stride and impact crucial to the subterranean logic of loose stone, had helped secure the path that Landry eventually followed. Her ride, however, had achieved two things unnoticed by either Kalin or Landry: the lower switchbacks had been rendered even more solid, while those two-thirds of the way up were additionally destabilized and made even more fragile by the water now disgorgin itself from the fissure above.

Egan was oblivious, though if he'd cared enuf about Cavalry to just listen to that powerful steed, he might've picked up on the growin confusion becomin more apparent in his stride, especially as more and more stones started to give way. Egan just kept thunderin higher and higher, blinded by his early success, so much so that he could see only how one success must determine a subsequent success, all the way to the top.

Egan and Cavalry even made it to the fissure. And after that not even Kalin could've done better. A horse can learn to enter water just fine, and swim fine too, but to take water in the head while gallopin up an unfamiliar and near vertical slope is just plain askin for it. Egan was askin for it. He beat at Cavalry's back side with his hat and dug them rowels into his flanks, severe enuf to demand blood, and miraculously he made Cavalry take the plunge up through the water.

Who knows what Egan expected past all that spray, but it weren't the walls that greeted him on either side. Cavalry balked at once and, losin momentum, tried then to turn out, but in that chute of rock there weren't no room to turn out, and so Cavalry slammed into the wall, and given the grade and the slipperiness, with no option to slowly back up, it weren't but an instant more before horse and rider were topplin over backwards.

Egan heard the pop and swore it was his own back breakin. He saw the blood next and swore it was some deep artery in his pelvis that would see him lifeless before he stopped rollin. But it weren't him that was broken and bleedin.

Egan didn't rush to the action, but he also knew he shouldn't tarry. Billings was already there to offer Cavalry the misericord of his own .44 Magnum, a Smith & Wesson Model 29-2, the sight of which surprised Egan. Egan shook his head, though, drawin out his .357. The bone that burst through Cavalry's back leg showed there weren't nothin else he could do. He shot the horse through the temple. He didn't mind the sting of bone particulate or the spray of blood on his face. His mind weren't anywhere near to what he'd just done. It was workin on somethin else, which is why we can't dance away just yet from this awful scene, with just that lone shot echoin through the canyon.

Up above, Landry covered her face and started to cry. Even Tom had to look away. Kalin felt his own face flush and his eyes burn, and only when he was sure that Calvary had no more sufferin to give the World did he too look away.

But then all three did look down again, wonderin what the heck that was all about when they heard a second shot. Egan and Billings was by then unsaddlin the dead horse, haulin off the pack and the scabbards, and finally and at long last retreatin.

Billings offered to let Egan ride with him on Gads but, with no thought to further burdenin that poor pinto, Egan refused. He did allow Billings to handle the rifles and the pack but insisted on walkin out and carryin his own saddle too. The .357, he kept that behind his buckle, while the blood on his face he let make its own deal with the rain.

Egan was a thing of horror when he reached the main trail. Kelly even grew noticeably pale, and Sean and Shelly got a little slack-jawed.

Aside from the blood on his face, Cavalry's blood was also on his jeans and shirt. The water around his boots ran rose. Egan, though, still looked plenty glad to see his brothers. On the hike there he'd mostly stewed on the possibility that Shelly, Sean, and Kelly had not only found a better path but already done away with Kalin and maybe Landry too, plus retrieved the Colt and who cared about the horses, and how from then on Egan would be known as the Porch who couldn't ride and got his horse killt doin somethin extra stupid. But when he saw that that weren't the case, why he even smiled some, which made his blood-slopped form that much more gruesome or *unholy,* as Lee Peart, workin at a Gas N Go over in Willard, would describe the moment years later, in 1998 to be exact, in fact titlin a minature oil on plywood that he'd painted *Unholy Us.* It was a piece that would later be discussed quite often by Glenn Taylor, Martine Sahu, and Kiki Hart.

What the heck happened? Sean finally demanded, Shelly too, with only Kelly askin if Egan was okay.

Egan told them how he'd seen a way up the scree, describin without creditin Billings the path marked by asters, and how, as he neared the top, the Kalin kid had shot Cavalry in the chest, who'd toppled backward, throwin Egan clear, but bustin a leg so Egan had had to do the big horse a kindness with the very same .357 now on display at his waist. Billings nodded all the way through this retellin and thus cemented his bond with Egan.

That was the story they came out of the canyon with too, with gettin out bein no small adventure either, worthy of another story that there's no need to dwell on here, except to say that Barracuda and Gads did live to see another day after makin it over the flooded bridges, though, with the risin waterline and them slippery boards, the dirt bikes had to be abandoned just above Bridge Two, where Park Ranger Emily Brickey happily impounded them the next day. Sean and Shelly Porch were both ticketed too, though that was the worst of it.

Egan got nothin but sympathy, and, thanks to his story, Under-sheriff Jewell now knew, and in turn Orvop municipal police now knew too, what kind of dangerous and cruel criminal they had on their hands. This Kalin kid was a killer. And even though it clangored somethin awful, and in nonsensical ways too, the précis on Kalin March that swiftly circulated through Orvop came down to pretty much this: *he stolt some horses, and he killt some horses.* The fact that only one horse had died was lost in these retellins.

Also worth mentionin, Egan by this point pretty much believed what he kept tellin folks to believe, until soon he could barely remember what had really happened, how he'd taken out of his pack that second gun, the semiautomatic 9mm Smith & Wesson Model 59 with its bright aluminum frame, with all identifyin elements filed off; clearly not carried forth into the canyon with anythin but murderous mal-intent. Egan then had lined up a shot below the dead animal's shoulders. Billings had once again offered to do that work, but once again Egan refused him, though he did accept the recommendation that usin a glove was a good idea, especially if there was somethin to that stuff on TV about powder burns. Egan also agreed to dispose of the gloves in his daddy's incinerator.

Egan puttin a bullet in Cavalry's chest was the second retort Kalin, Tom, and Landry had heard, to their bewilderment. Egan knew too that he'd got the order wrong. He cursed hisself for not firin the 59 first and then finishin off Cavalry with the .357, but he was also confident there would be no forensic examination of the horse, though if it came down to it, diggin out that parabellum would still prove beneficial to the Porches.

The last thing Egan did to really distinguish hisself in the eyes of the mountain was stand on Cavalry. He'd seen how the wound to the chest had bled very little, seein as how the great animal's heart had already ceased its indomitable tempo. Egan grew concerned that it might present obvious evidence to the backwardness of the shots and so subvert his tellin of events. So he climbed atop Cavalry and soon after, assisted by Billings, began to jump up and down on the body to squeeze more blood from the hole. That's somethin to picture: Egan and Billings jumpin up and down on poor Cavalry.

Curiously, in the moments before his death, Cavalry's mind in the crucible of all that awful pain, a writhin further intensified by what no one knew or cared to know, how along with his leg his spine had broken too, Cavalry still found for an instant that moment of peace and freedom when he was with, of all people, young Russel, the two of them just ridin along, free from the past, free from the future, free.

For Kalin, Landry, and of course Tom, there weren't no choice now but up. Tom led the way, followed by Kalin on Navidad, Mouse next, with Landry takin up the rear.

Landry fer sure was amazed to discover how Kalin, like he was partin the waters, if them waters was made of stone, just stepped up onto the hillside, revealin with each successive step a path that grew more and more accommodatin to a horse. Soon they was makin steady progress, and if they feared a rifle shot to the back, it was a fear put to rest whenever one of them, mainly Landry, looked back to discover little left of the canyon below but a tumult of cloud and rain that only seemed to increase as well as densify the higher up they got.

Not a word was said, nor a pause taken either, even when the trail began to widen, finally comin to an end at a juncture of sorts, kinda like a big *T*. However, instead of the fingerpost that would declare the importance of that spot many decades later, the place now was marked only by a natural pile of rubble that anyone passin wouldn't fer a moment have thought to be a cairn, though it was, of sorts, built by time itself. Kalin didn't hesitate here, headin right at once and so commencin with the next part of this journey, a long traverse headin east across the north or left side of the canyon wall, the elevation slowly risin the farther along they got.

Kalin knew full well that this way up to Mount Katanogos was not without risk, but if they made good time now, and given how early afternoon was already upon them, they'd better make good time, then they'd free themselves of the slopes off to their right, which would only continue to steepen until they was so steep, you wouldn't be faulted for callin them cliffs, though they weren't, the termination of their grade marked by actual cliffs gettin taller and taller until they was hundreds of ragged feet above the canyon floor.

That said, if they could reach the tricky turn away from such perils, still some distance away, why that would deliver them to a wide and grassy passage that rose more amiably beside a wanderin stream that now and then turned into small waterfalls splashin idyllic little pools. It was an ascent that not even a hard rain could much impede. For even in dusk, or scratch that, even if they was in the folds of night itself, the trail was so forgivin that one could easily, no question about it, make the cirque meadow and behold what held the origin of the stream they'd just paralleled: Altar Lake, an icy, virid body of water born of the near year-round snowfields beneath Mount Katanogos's summit ridges. From there, even in the pith of blackness, Kalin could with not too much duress get them to any number of locations where they could escape the rain, build a fire, and finally rest. The horses would find not only plenty of mountain water but grass to graze on for days. Even Mouse would have a hard time stayin hungry.

In fact it was this thought of a serene refuge that kept Kalin leanin into the rain that only seemed to fall harder and harder, with now and then enuf wind to turn each stingin impact on his cheeks into a reminder that whatever calm awaited them far ahead was no excuse to forget the increasin danger they rode beside.

Up ahead Tom once again drew forth his burnin brand, which for a while seemed to clarify the path, until even its yellow-and-orange flames looked to be consumed by the fallin gray clouds or mists that constantly whipped by. Not that it ever failed. At least by its beacon Kalin could set a course, even if he was never certain if what he beheld was light or the memory of light or somethin else. Look there! Is that a person?! A child?! More horses?! Eventually, though, these imaginative shadow shows by way of rock and brush began to fail, until Kalin found hisself beside Tom, the ghost scabbardin the brand, him and Ash standin still as trees before the first of nine screes.

Kalin didn't stop, passin without reflectin on the ghost on his ghost horse, determined not to succumb to the same overwhelmin desire to quit, even if he and Navidad managed only a few steps out onto the wide gray back of that uncertain way, Navidad jitterin so bad that Kalin had to stop. Mouse had refused to take even one step upon that back of broken rubble and near jerked Kalin right back over Navidad's rump.

Now this weren't like Aster Scree. It weren't anywhere near as steep, and there was a path too. Sure, farther down it got pathless and slippery, but they weren't goin down there, so it didn't matter. At least they better not go there. Big cliffs would take them if they did. Up weren't an option either, as that way also terminated in cliffs. Straight across was the only way. And that weren't no real task. Kalin was provin it already, still standin steady on the path, horse-wide at the narrowest, likely forged over centuries by elks, mountain goats, and plenty of other creatures rightfully heir to this place.

Kalin considered testin Mouse's beef but then figured to back up and start again this time with Mouse at Navidad's shoulder. Instead he rode Navidad up the slope a few steps, turnin her around that way, and then rode past Mouse, who fast enuf followed suit.

Landry by this point had caught up, near as jittery as Navidad had been before the sight of what lay ahead. She had no clue that Tom was right beside her, also lookin plenty bothered.

Kalin patiently explained to her how this scree weren't nothin like Aster Scree, how the path was solid as a sidewalk. But he weren't all that convincin, given how the rain kept fallin harder, with too much of it fallin sideways, and the clouds continued to get lower like they was plannin to close in on them, and now and then, unannounced by any promissory flash, a peal of thunder would rumble the distance, fortunately soft enuf to earn only the twitch of an ear from Jojo and an unhappy whicker from Navidad. Mouse weren't scared of no thunder. Ash, though, seemed the least pleased.

And that still weren't the all of it: farther off, in fact right where they was headin, the sight of which was buried beneath still more weather, another kind of low rumble seemed to answer the thunder. It weren't a sky-born sound and it backed off the horses quick. It also didn't taper away like thunder but endured, even growin louder, like the mountains were challengin thunder, until that long guttural growl finally relinquished itself to a long angry hiss that Landry and Kalin figured was just the wind pickin up, though Tom weren't so sure.

This the only one of these we have to cross? Landry asked.

There's a few more.

This the widest?

There's wider.

Then is it at least the steepest?

They get steeper.

You think maybe we should wait until the rain stops some? At least so we can see where we're goin? Kalin hadn't missed that Landry was bein awful brave, seein as how bad she was shiverin. Even he was shiverin.

You know my little sis ain't exactly wrong, Tom said then.

Landry caught Kalin heedin the emptiness. *Now what's he sayin?*

He agrees with you.

Kalin dismounted then, handed Landry Navidad's reins, and walked a ways out onto that first scree. The path remained solid, but the farther along he got, the more uncertain everythin seemed. The canyon was barely visible, with what was visible continuin to shudder off great heaps of water, with rock goin with it now and then, earth too. Ragged cuts in the path had already appeared, rivered up bad by the sluicin wash the mountain refused to accommodate. They looked like the marks of giant claws or teeth. And that was only what Kalin could see. He knew it would get way more minacious beyond the spurs of rock obscurin what they'd have to get by next.

There's no sayin how badly Kalin wanted to keep goin. If it was just him on foot, he'd have gone for it. But these conditions weren't fair to Navidad, Mouse, and Jojo. Maybe not to Ash neither. Might kill Landry. It weren't freezin, but the cold cuttin through them had a feel of ice. The wind weren't lettin up none neither, and any way forward was gonna have to be met with mostly closed eyes. The shriek of it too was somethin else, a thing of fury so loud Kalin couldn't even hear Tom, like the wind was darin the mountain to just try to keep standin, unless it weren't the wind but a big white cat out there warnin them away from whatever ideas Kalin had about the future.

Kalin let out a groan and even set one knee down, even bowed his head before the boom of the conspirin elements, and for what all confusion overtook his heart then, at least this much became clear: the storm weren't fadin; the storm was only gettin worse. Fer now the way ahead was outta reach. They'd better get to cover.

The trouble was that the only cover Kalin could think of was back the way they'd come and then some.

Low to ground and bent over like he was right then, Kalin lacked all resolve, but as he dragged hisself upright and shook off best as he could his shivers and doubts, returnin his mind and heart to his friends, Navidad and Mouse, Tom on Ash, Jojo, and even Landry, he found again in their presence the purpose he'd require to get them through this.

Landry didn't complain none when they turned back and was doubly grateful when Kalin dug around in Mouse's pack for the sustenance they'd all need. The horses got their share of oats and apple-sauce plus a little more. Then Kalin dug up a bag of nuts, raisins, and peanut butter rolled up into balls and coated in oats and such, which he made sure Landry got three of, two fer now, one fer her pocket. He gave hisself just two. If he didn't limit their nutritional fortifications now, they'd end up with nothin when they needed it most.

It was 3:09 p.m.

As they rode back to the *T*, Kalin began to fear somethin new: maybe Egan in the company of that other fella had returned and managed the climb on foot. Maybe they was waitin for them now, this time with gunshots him and Landry couldn't hide from. Spurs of ratchetin mountain prohibited any view. Only when they came around a final interposin bulge of canyon wall could Kalin finally gaze down on that juncture and find nothin more than that cairn of rocks assembled by the mountains themselves and big sheets of rain tossed this way and that by the storm.

He'll be back, Tom said, ridin beside Kalin but up on the hillside like it was level as a pool table.

I know it, Kalin snapped. *I just got no idea why.*

There I can't help you, Tom answered.

Why the heck not? You're the one who just now said he'll be back. Kalin even tried to imitate Tom in a way that tickled Tom into a little giggle. *Come on now: what exactly do you know?!* Kalin demanded.

Easy there, Mr. Snappy. Tom even raised his hands, leavin them up a bit too long, his smile gettin a bit too wide, even if he did seem to want to answer Kalin's question sincerely. *What do I know? Well, first off, I reckon you'd have a hard time answerin that question yourself: what exactly do you know—*

The heck I would!

279

Hold on there, cowboy. Let me finish. I'm just sayin it's a harder question than it looks. Ask the same of my sister back there and I reckon she'll dive right in, and day and night will be over before she's even reached the end of her first year on this earth, and she don't even remember that part. But puttin aside that abidin trickiness, I'll answer what I think you're gettin at: what do I know now that I couldn't have known when I was alive? Well, fer starters, only a few things are clear. Tom looked around. *The horses, you, Landry, and this trail. Sometimes more but that just might be the gift of reason. Like I seen how Egan shot at you and meant to hit you; so he probably means to shoot you again.*

Now that weren't so hard, was it?

I ain't done. There's more. It's like this gatherin of weather around us; I can see it too, but I also see out there a gatherin of meanness headin our way.

For Navidad and Mouse?

Ain't nothin here that matters except them horses. I think you know that.

I can live with that.

And I guess I can be dead with that, Tom chuckled.

Holy cow! Landry cried out then. *Look at that!*

They'd just reached the *T*, and maybe because Kalin had been so ready to find Egan and Billings, he couldn't rightly frame what else now stood before them.

Ain't he just somethin beautiful! Landry was dazzled.

Such size and magnificence that Kalin near forgot the situation they was in, Landry fer sure did, maybe even Tom too. Tom did sit up straighter. Mouse couldn't be bothered, but Navidad sure came to attention before that extraordinary creature. Such antlers on his head with near too many points to number. What Tom's brother, Evan, would've called a giant thirteen-by-twelve bull if he didn't say to heck with countin and just call him a cactus buck.

A bull elk, wreathed in mist, his back big enuf to carry mountains. And he just stood there, like he'd been waitin for them, eyein them in a way that enchanted Landry and warned her too, warned them all, with a snort of breath to remind them that storm clouds weren't just in the sky.

The elk considered the path that led down to Aster Scree, but instead of goin that way, or toward them, or at the very least away from them, he just took off straight up the mountain, lookin lighter than a snowshoe hare outracin a coyote, finally vanishin into the descendin cloud.

I feel blessed! Landry cried out with delight, and this when every exposed part of her was drenched, with wet startin to sneak down around her neck and in by way of the cuffs of that pink slicker, all while an unkind cold continued to gnaw at her fingers and toes, determined to lay hold of her bones. Kalin weren't doin much better, too often tryin to shake the rain off hisself like some starved and sickly dog. But while he had settled for a grimace, here was Landry suddenly lookin like she was at a Sunday picnic at Kiwanis Park, just cooin away over a plump little May baby, what in this case happened to be a formidable creature with a rack as big as a Christmas tree. Even Tom was charmed by Landry's jubilance. And maybe Kalin's grimace did lessen some too.

It was about then, as they pressed onward, traversin west now, back toward the entrance of the canyon, toward a sunset the storm would never let them see, that Tom's smile seemed to grow dull, to the point that it almost looked inauthentic, which had to be one of the scariest things Kalin had seen so far.

What's wrong with you? Kalin demanded.

You know I can take about anythin.

I do.

She weren't never meant for this dare of ours. I know that much. You know that too. You also know where we're headed now.

Kalin didn't disagree but there weren't much he could do either. *She can't go down.*

I know that.

Then what are you tellin me?

I wish I knew.

Are you tellin me anythin?

I wish I knew.

Kalin looked back on Landry. He could see the shake on her shoulders, the chatter on her lips, as well as the alert that weren't wanin from her eyes, still keepin Jojo clear of any churlish kickin Mouse might get up to, even as the rain hammered down on them, forcin her to keep wipin away the wet despite the good-sized brim on her hat. She'd be cryin, Kalin was sure of it, if she weren't still smilin.

Check your cinch! Kalin yelled back at her.

How's that?

Check your cinch! We're wetter than beavers. I don't want your saddle slippin off.

She was sittin strong but her saddle leather was fer sure still swollen with water. That can change how your saddle sits.

Lordy! Landry yelled. *I check my cinch regularly. I hope you're not just figurin that out right now, cowboy!*

I am just figurin that out right now, he yelled back.

Ain't that a comfort! Landry yelled. *At least tell me you know where you're goin.*

Kalin turned to Tom, expectin him to say somethin about the gall of that girl, but he said no such thing, his smile even duller, that familiar twinkle leavin his eyes.

I don't think I ever said so, Tom said now, and in a voice that Kalin weren't sure he'd ever heard before, not comin from his friend at least, and somehow wailin his heart. *No, I never did say so. Not to you, not to my momma, and fer darned sure never to her. My little sister, why Kalin she is my every joy. Might be my only joy. And nothin will ever change that. Not even death. If bein here ain't proof of just that.* Tom tried to chuckle but could barely muster a grin. *No matter if she cusses my guts or that she stolt Aunt Lissie's snaffle, I love her, Kalin, more than I could ever know love in life. If somethin were to happen to her—* Tom's voice broke, and that, fer sure, was a first.

She don't cuss your guts. Not that I've ever heard.

They'd come out upon a wide area in the trail, and Tom had slowed until Ash finally just stopped.

Ever heard what? Landry asked. *Oh, are you talkin to him again?*

Kalin sighed. *I don't know who I'm talkin to, Landry, and we've got some distance to cover yet. After this spot here, there's only one more place where we can take a break.* Kalin's voice trailed off, his mind dark with the thought of where he was takin them.

What's my brother sayin? Landry asked again.

Check that cinch.

A t the next rest stop, where the trail widened out into an area crowded with enuf juniper trees to keep some of the wind off their backs, they stretched their wet legs, checked the horses, and refreshed them best they could.

So reluctant about what lay ahead, Kalin briefly considered tyin up tarps and campin right there. They had enuf daylight left to see that through. The problem was the temperature. All their breath was on display. Even startin a fire would be near impossible, and then there was the trouble of thunder that had once again recommenced, this time with greater ardor, distant flashes givin shorter and shorter notice. Out here they'd have no way to shield the horses from panic if lightnin and thunder ever fell directly upon them. Just one frenzied bolt from here and they'd be on their own tryin to outrace the mountain. And no one, not even a horse, can outrace a mountain.

There was also the question of the other side of the canyon. They was plenty exposed here. And a fire, if they did get one goin, would only announce their position at once. Kalin dug out the binoculars. Just as he'd dreaded the appearance of Egan at the *T*, Kalin now had a new dread: he hadn't forgotten Egan's rifle.

Once again, Kalin used the empty oat bag to recess the lenses.

What are you lookin for? Landry asked.

Trouble.

Kalin crouched down amidst the low juniper branches, methodically scannin the far canyon wall, what was the north side of Agoneeya Mountain, a generally more mellow series of slopes, spurs, and corridors, more populated with trees than this side.

The good news was that the gray veil of the storm mostly obscured the far side. The bad news was that Kalin didn't trust the good news. With a powerful scope a good hunter might make such a shot. Even close enuf could be deadly. It weren't just thunder that could spook the horses.

In the end, though, Kalin caught no sign of movement.

You see anythin? Kalin still asked Tom.

I'll need them first, Landry answered, grabbin the binoculars like they was hers, and in many ways they was hers, more hers than his: Gatestone property. Landry was about to yank off the oat bag and even step clear of the juniper branches, when Kalin stopped her and explained how he was shieldin them so as not to inadvertently give away their position with a flash of light on the glass. She looked at Kalin like he was crazy.

Light from where?!

I see hunters over there, Tom suddenly said. *They ain't lookin this way. See the smoke of their campfires?*

Campfires? Kalin asked.

What's he sayin?

He says he sees campfires, Kalin told Landry.

Where?

Kalin told her where Tom was lookin, but Landry saw nothin, and when Kalin took another gander, he didn't see nothin either.

It's nice over there, Tom continued. *I can see deer, birds in the branches. One hunter's smokin a pipe.*

Tom, you're seein somethin we can't.

I reckon that makes sense.

After that, there was a discussion about whether or not to lead the horses on foot. If and when thunder came and the horses did try to bolt, they had a good chance of shakin loose of Kalin and Landry, who would have only wet leads to hold on to. Up here in the fury of this storm the horses wouldn't have even a minute before they was fallin off the cliffs below. On the other hand, with Kalin and Landry ridin, they had a shot at quietin and reassurin the horses before they was in full flight mode. Mouse wouldn't have that advantage, but Kalin weren't worried about Mouse. Almost nothin spooked him.

Like before, they headed out single file, Kalin and Navidad leadin the way, with Mouse right behind, followed by Landry on Jojo. At first Tom rode right next to Kalin, again on the hillside like there weren't no grade at all, though by the time Kalin had got to wonderin about the torch, Tom had slipped back beside Mouse, which maybe was also a good thing, until he was too soon trailin Landry, which was where he stayed, him and Ash, the two of them like a sliver of moon set free to wander the dark, a thinnin harbor of light, whether there was sun or not.

Kalin didn't like not havin Tom within earshot, but he did like that Tom was close to his sister. One thing Kalin had asked Landry before they'd mounted up: *Can you do me one favor, Landry?*

It depends, she had still sassed back.

Don't look up much, and definitely don't look down. Just keep your eyes on Mouse the whole way.

To her credit, Landry didn't look down at once to make the point of just how big a snot she was. Likely she had started to trust Kalin some, at least when it came to the horses and ridin. It helped that she could also see that Kalin weren't lookin down either. Or up. The back of his head was always in line with the way ahead, which only seemed to get narrower and narrower as it wended over and around the various spurs, past ribs of orange quartzite or black varved slate, the path mostly solid if now and then challenged by a scare of gravel that required extra care lest the horses lose their footin.

And throughout it all the rain never ceased, continuin to slice down, the cold in the air burnin their ears and cheeks, the clouds crouchin still lower, darkenin still more. Though maybe at least those dense calamities of brume did help in one way, by mostly renderin invisible the perilous steeps that fell away but one step to their left.

Kalin never once gave the slightest indication as to just how terrifyin their position had become, so whipped with water and prowlin mists that not much was ever plainly revealed except here and there a patch of brush or some petulant scrub oak. Now and then the trail seemed to lose all substance, as if animal transit had momentarily ceased there or the animals had given up and turned back. Navidad and Kalin would just plod right on through such unchartered territories with only his faith in the destination to keep them on *the windy and narrow,* as Annie Miller, from St. George, by then flirtin with a job in public relations for the Church, would say to Cheyenne Riddaway and Daisy Fitzgarbie, until some recognizable form of pathway reasserted itself, even if where it ultimately led, what faith alone could not reveal, only History, was either to a place of refuge or their end off a cliff's edge.

Kalin felt Tom's absence more and more, especially as the path grew more uncertain; but even that didn't compare to somethin Kalin could never have predicted, revealed whenever he spared a glance back to make sure Mouse, Jojo, and Landry were okay, Landry's eyes so fixed on Mouse's tail that she didn't catch Kalin disobeyin his own rule: the farther west they got, the more Tom lagged behind, until in the end the storm seized him entirely.

When Kalin lost sight of Tom, the lightnin came for them; through those curtains of gray, great sheets of blindin rage were unleashed upon their tenuous traverse, followed too soon after by thunder, closer and closer each time, until every crack and rumble seemed set on achievin only one thing: shake them from the mountainside.

One time, in the throat of such a roar, Navidad suddenly reared up, Landry havin just lifted her eyes from Mouse in fear of the light that had just flashed about them, and in anticipation too of what already answered that light, beholdin Kalin perched, inconsequential as a prayer, on the back of that beautiful and near vertical animal. Had he but pulled his hands a little to the left, they'd have both dropped from the trail like a stone down a well. Had he pulled his hands a lit-tle to the right, toward the presumed safety of the risin mountain, Navidad in findin no purchase there would've spun backwards and either kicked loose of the trail with her back legs and fallen away or in turnin around overshot that thin margin of preservation and gone headfirst into the same tumble unto death. But Kalin's hands, like the rest of him, stayed perfectly still, in concord with Navidad, who, understandin such poise, presence, and calm, especially in the face of such immense natural injury, did not veer one way nor another, and finally, and slowly too, very slowly, floated straight back down to the earth, gentle as the prayer that does have consequence, makin even less of a mark upon the earth than Tom or Ash could, only to immedi-ately resume again this trek through the perils of night's fallen clouds.

Chapter Nine

"We in it now"

*S*ondi, you in there? Old Porch yelled, poundin the palm of his hand against her door. Sure, he hadn't gotten what he needed today, not yet, but he had in his belly once again the feel that rides up warm when what you're huntin goes to ground it can't defend or escape. It settled in him somethin good too, the taste of somethin close, what no amount of bourbon can match, though he still welcomed the slugs from the flask he carried in his jacket pocket.

I know you're in there, Sondi! He banged again on her door, this time hard, with the heel of that big scarred hand. When that brought no results, he went in again, this time with a fist, but the door swung in first, stumblin Old Porch forward.

It was 7:33 p.m.

At any other doorway, timin like that woulda been a thing of chance. Not here. The brutish nature of the knock had already ruled out an emergency. With an ear for the cadence of aggression, a rightly timed openin on the downbeat might just take away any advantage the knocker presumed. And since this was most definitely a musical household, with not a soul under that ruftop lackin a beautiful ear and formidable sense of timin, chance had nothin to do with gettin that good stumble forward, right across the threshold.

Though it could at times be called her favorite instrument, tonight Sondra Gatestone, mother of Evan Gatestone, Tom Gatestone, and Landry Gatestone, had no need for her .410 shotgun. She was gauge enuf herself, just standin there, tall, with jet-black hair she dyed or didn't dye, she'd never tell, hands as wrinkled as they was cracked as they was strong enuf to twist off the cap of a batch of cherries she'd canned months ago. Her eyes too didn't hide their fractures of hardship either, even if they was greener than Altar Lake on a bright spring day. Like them glacial waters too, they winked of somethin unearthly set free upon this land, amused by the folly put into daily practice across this valley by proud and vainglorious men. Her gaze, not to mention her big chest, to where most men's eyes fled when they couldn't meet that gaze, was the gall of every man who couldn't have her, especially after her husband, the good Dallin Gatestone, passed some three years ago, one errant kick by a horse stovin in his head much as it had stove in her heart. *Clop-Clop-clip-Clop.* Suffice it to say, Sondra Gatestone didn't care a whit for subsequent suitors and would've turned them all to stags, consumed by their own dogs, or hers, Mungo, her big St. Bernard, if she also hadn't found it so funny. No doubt here's where Tom got some of his mirth, Landry too.

Even now, standin so imperious in her own doorway, she couldn't quite suppress the tiniest of smiles as she watched Old Orwin Porch

throw his arms back to keep from scootin even a toe over her threshold. He had some balancin skills that not even bourbon could best.

Sondi! Had Old Porch ever seemed so pleased though? *I am so sorry! I truly am!* A sentiment he continued to express, though it was unclear exactly what he was on about and none helped by the expandin size of his own grin.

That makes two of us.

Old Porch laughed then, the cold cloudin his breath plenty, as he slapped the rain off his shoulders and made a big show of admirin her wide array of pumpkins, enormous, squat, stippled, bright orange, and jaundiced, one even white as a turnip, in preparation for Halloween. Old Porch's good humor didn't fade much either. That's where he was at. The jarrin results of last night's poker game, not to mention the drunk he'd been on, had over the course of this day transformed him, until not a glimpse of his poor Russel lyin on Egan's floor intruded on his thoughts. Yes, Russel was still dead, but what mattered now, the only thing that mattered, was that the one responsible was on the loose. Not that Old Porch had actually forgotten his own hand doin the doin or that he actually believed the newcomer had done the killin, but rather he understood it like this: if this Kalin kid hadn't messed with Paddock B in the first place, then Russel would still be alive. What did one later moment matter if the moments before bore the blame for their consequences? Soon enuf Riddle's end would hang around Kalin's neck too. In fact whatever Old Porch had done or would do from here on out was irrelevant. He was playin out the role demanded by another's actions. He could smile, he could drink, he could take his time gettin to his point. His guiltlessness now as plain as Sondra Gatestone's allure.

And Old Porch still had no clue yet that it was none other than Tom Gatestone hisself who had first introduced this Kalin kid not only to Navidad and Mouse but to those trails where they would go in order to escape Porch's jurisdiction and verdict. Nor would he ever guess that Tom was still involved, perhaps spurnin the grave so that his plans might be seen through.

Vernon Mattson, for a good while an REI clerk in Fairbanks, Alaska, would over the years speak extensively to the likes of Dirk Meyer, the future mayor of Orvop, the trippy and adorable Florence Gibbs, Roger Kelsch, and even the ever-longin Julianna McHenley to name a few, about what change Old Porch might've permitted his-self had he understood the awful symphony of repercussions he was already abettin. Also privy to Vernon Mattson's long ponderances was an ex-girlfriend, Lisa Talbot, who'd spent a good bunch of days and nights in Fargo, North Dakota, datin a fella named Jon Bush out of Rapid City by way of Deadwood, South Dakota, who'd just broken up with Kara Ongg. Anyways, Lisa Talbot would be inspired to start, even if she would never finish, the *Porch Cycle,* what would imagine with stirrin recitatives Old Porch kneelin before Sondra Gatestone, this time gettin a glimpse of the Erinyes set loose upon too many involved in these colludin events:

> *On my knees I'd've gone if I'd've known*
> *what Furies chased me. I'd've ceased my accusations;*
> *thrown off my entitlements; whatever else I blamed!*
> *Succored the dead! Erased my name! Prostrate*
> *and repentant, I'd've even begged! If I'd've known then*
> *what Heaven forbade and Hell had freed instead.*

But Old Porch was nowhere near his knees, nor any more aware about how the success he felt certain to secure was but a small tip of the tail of a beast whose immensity he could not fathom. Instead Old Porch just burped before uppin the ante with a belch that had him lickin his lips and swallowin somethin hot enuf to scald the back of his throat.

That it had to be on such a night, Old Porch croaked. His throat did feel scarred. *So cold and wet and gettin colder. And that I have to come to you, who's just set her boy to ground.* Old Porch even had the gall to drag from his head that charcoal felt hat with its plum-colored ribbon, like he could ever be repentant or even genuinely polite. *Me of all people! Here on your doorstep with you and me never seein the same thing the same way once.*

You drunk, Orwin?

My boy's killt! he near wailed then.

That is bad news, but you always bring bad news.

I guess that's so. And like that, whatever wobble Old Porch had had about him was gone. *Some new kid done cut my Russel's throat.*

Name's Kalin, Egan added, emergin from the rain. At least he had the decency not to take his hat off. *Stolt two of our horses and shot mine.*

Since quittin Isatch Canyon, Egan had been pleased to see how well his tellin of things had caught fire. He'd played up plenty his pain over losin that great horse, how he'd had to put Cavalry down hisself. *There's a vicious killer trapped somewhere in our canyon,* he'd told Ilene Clayton, a reporter for KIUB. He was thrilled to learn they'd aired that.

Egan meant to join his old man now, but before even one boot could find the first step, Sondra clucked sharp and shook her head.

You stay out there, Egan.

Old Porch swung a look back Egan's way and nodded for his son to keep off.

Sondra Gatestone weren't ever gonna forget seein her Landry emergin from, of all places, Egan's truck. She'd looked gray as a ghost, Egan laughin her away, sayin loudly he was happy to give her a ride home anytime, *least I could do,* them words seared particularly in her mind, more than even the bruised forearm Landry refused to talk about, the silence that had endured too long, puzzlin even Tom, until days later the silence seemed to catch hold of Tom too, with Tom's broodin then makin somethin extra awful out of their already barren home. Sondra Gatestone had cursed the Lord then that her Dallin weren't with them and thanked the Lord that Evan weren't with them, Lord knows what he'd have gone and done, her curse and thanks zeroin out the Lord's obligations, leavin Sondra on her own to figure out what to do, realizin at some tragic moment what all parents must one day recognize, if they're fit to be parents, that the answerin has started to fall from their shoulders and onto their children's. Not that she'd accept so easily their complete independence, likely not until she was in the grave, especially where her little Landry was concerned. Sondra half wished Egan would come knockin on her door if just so she could see him set one foot over her threshold. She had a 12-gauge too. Her other favorite instrument.

No question, hearin these low voices, and likely scentin her mood too, Mungo came around from back and stood facin them two men, big as a house, a growl in his throat bigger than any house.

Egan backed off more, but the big St. Bernard didn't faze Old Porch. Not much did.

You remember Hiram Brunt's dog? Old Porch asked. *Oh heck, this was years ago. Nasty shepherd. Used to come racin after my tires whenever I drove by. I was fine for a while, but High-and-Mighty Mr. Brunt weren't doin nothin to check his animal. I got fed up. Got myself a long rag and knotted one end and then secured the other end under my hubcap.* Old Porch grinned. *Drove by real slow one day, and when that dog got hold of that rag why then, boy, did I speed up. Dumb dog didn't know how to let go fast enuf. Thump. Thump. Thump.*

Mungo ain't the one you have to worry about here, Sondra said.

And she was right. At the sound of her voice, with his name upon it, the St. Bernard wagged his tail. Both men smiled. Sondra clicked her tongue, and the big dog stopped waggin his tail. The men stopped smilin too.

Egan was the one who set eyes on this Kalin, Old Porch said then. *Why I brung him along. But he set eyes on somethin else too. Go on, Eges. She won't bark no more. Sondi here ain't nothin but bite.*

The Kalin boy has got Landry with him, Egan said, spittin tobacco juice on her porch.

What's that supposed to mean?

He's took her, Sondi, Old Porch grunted. *No other way to see it.*

Them's the appearances, Egan confirmed, spittin again on her porch.

Spit one more time on my porch, Egan, and I'm gonna tell Mungo here to take that tobacco right outta your mouth. It'll be like he's kissin you, only afterward, you won't have no more lips.

Knock it off, Egan! Old Porch roared. There was only one Porch allowed any posturin, and it sure weren't this second son. Old Porch even dragged his boot over the mess like smearin it was clearin it. Then Old Porch put on a sickly smile. *Sondi, whether we like it or not, we're in this together now.*

What are you goin on about, Orwin? Out with it. It'll take a heckuva lot more than some boy to kidnap my Landry.

Beggin your pardon, ma'am, even your Landry can be hog-tied by just about any man who's got a reason to swing his legs wide when he walks, Egan said, grinnin enuf to show off that missin front tooth, out of which he sent a stream of more brunneous spit, though this time in her flower bed.

Is that so, Egan? The sight of him turned Sondra's guts.

Law of biology, ma'am.

And you saw her bound up?

Sure as the Lord is my Savior.

And Jojo too?

Jojo? Egan said it like he didn't know what Sondra was sayin, though she hadn't missed the shift in his eyes.

The horse she rode off with yesterday?

I ain't seen no horse.

Sondra nodded fer a moment, lookin over at Mungo, who'd by this point stretched out on the porch; her look quick gathered him up to his feet. She took another moment to reconsider the two men. *I think you're both lyin sacks of pig guts.*

Just a courtesy call, Sondi. Old Porch weren't bothered none. That sickly smile even grew as he returned his hat to his head, noddin like he was the gentleman of some manor he'd only ever dream about. *Police already know. They're coordinatin with the sheriff's department.*

Notified by you I'm sure.

She sure is a cranky cooter, Old Porch said to Egan then, now flashin them broken teeth, before returnin his cold eyes to Sondra. *Just takin the high road here.* Old Porch even threw in a wink and then coughed and kept coughin until his hands were on both knees and he was pukin up the day right there in front of the Gatestone's front door.

Sondra quick strode to the side and turned on the garden hose. *How's about some water?*

The jet of water blew the vomit Orwin's way, who fast as a rattle-snake stayed one step ahead of his own effluence, flyin off them three porch steps and out into the rain. Egan weren't near as quick and paid the price: some of his dad's leavins splatterin his boots and jeans. And then just as fast as they'd come, they was gone, slippin into Egan's Ford Ranger, skiddin off without turnin on the headlights.

Sondra took a moment to finish sprayin off her porch, the steps too, and the walkway. Her hands still had some shakes, but those passed. She let Mungo enter the house first, next lockin the door before followin the dog through her dark home to the kitchen.

I don't know what them two are up to, but it's trouble fer sure, she announced to the shadows. *Shield your eyes before I turn on the lights.*

Allison March sat at the kitchen table with her eyes closed. Mungo was already beside her and with a yawn and a big sigh settlin his back against her legs.

I'll brew us some herbal tea, Sondra said.

Kalin would never cut no boy's throat. I know it.

Sondra near guffawed. *Porch is somethin else.* She filled the kettle and lit a burner, checkin too the oven, already hot with somethin sweet risin up in there. *He had an Easter egg hunt for his stake, charged ten dollars a head. He said the proceeds would go to the Church. He does that a lot, tellin folks who give him money that it's tithe for the Church. Anyway, he was in a costume, not a bunny like you'd expect but a pirate! Can you believe that? On Easter, dressed up like a pirate! Had the eye patch, tricorn hat, gold tooth. That's when he told everybody again that one egg had a thousand dollars in it. A good three hundred folks had showed up for this hunt of his. But no one ever found that egg. Old Porch, though, swore someone had, said they wanted to remain anonymous. Since everyone there were Church folks, no one doubted him or had the gumption to question what had just occurred. It's not even like Old Porch needed the money. He just does stuff like that to get away with it. That's who he is.*

Kalin wouldn't kidnap your girl, any girl, Allison said then, still appalled by all she'd overheard on Sondra Gatestone's front porch. Her eyes were by now too spent to well up anymore, though her cheeks weren't near done with their reddenin and splotchin.

Oh hush, Allison. I know that much. My gosh, Landry could dream up nothin better than bein kidnapped by your boy. I'd be more believin if I'd just been told she kidnapped your Kalin. She's been moon-mad for him from, gosh, pretty much the moment she laid eyes on him. Sondra set out cups and saucers, spoons too, some honey and lemon, then took out from a big bread box on the counter half a lemon cake drizzled with sparklin white glaze. *I saw her eyes shinin large the day my Tom left us. Kalin was at his bedside, Tom whisperin Lord knows what kind of foolishness, and Landry holdin her breath like here was some god come to earth.*

Woe to the mother who gives birth to a god, what Allison nearly snarled out.

Aren't all our babies gods? Sondra asked and she meant it.

Allison managed a little smile then. *Kalin's just a boy, my boy. Though maybe you're right; maybe in the eyes of any mother there ain't no difference.*

Ha! Sondra laughed, retrievin a pie server from one of the many drawers in that enormous kitchen with two stoves and two fridges and an island in the center along with this old wooden table that probably set dinner before the Civil War was done or Utah even settled. *I know that to be true. I do. And I thank you, Allison, for findin me and comin to visit.*

I'm sorry we didn't meet earlier. I would've liked to have met Tom and you under different circumstances. My son never spoke of your son. I can't say why that was so, though, in his defense, he didn't speak much about any of his doins. At least not to me. There was a time when he told me everythin.

It's called bein a teenager.

Allison liked this Sondra Gatestone. She was glad to have found her. Seemed about the only right thing she'd done all day. Mungo groaned, half in a dream, and Allison absently gave his head and shoulder a good pettin. *I know there's a fierceness in Kalin he's afraid to let out, but he has plenty of good magic in him too. He's gentle. Especially when it comes to horses.*

I imagine that's what my Tom and your boy had in common. Tom was an unparalleled rider. I hope wherever he is now, he's still ridin.

Allison excused herself to use the washroom. Like the rest of the house, even here had high ceilins. There was intricate herbal-themed wallpaper too, sage and thyme. The soaps were scented, the hand towels a lavender hue so vivid they might as well have been scented. There was a Canterbury of gardenin magazines. On the wall was a sampler with colorful needlework that included horses and an Emily Post quote: *Manners are a sensitive awareness of the feelings of others. If you have that awareness, you have good manners, no matter what fork you use.* A few framed pictures of ancestors in front of the state capitol or the United States Capitol hung on the wall, evidence of centuries of belongin.

Funny how Sondra had felt it necessary to apologize for such a grand washroom. She'd warned that the sink's hot and cold porcelain faucets were reversed, and the only way to correct the error would be to banjax the fixtures. They was that old. *But I love them so much, so I leave intact their confusion.*

When Allison returned to the kitchen, Sondra had already poured

293

their teas, cut each of them a sizable wedge of cake, and was in the process of sittin down when midway she leapt back up to retrieve some milk. *In case you don't like lemon. I think chamomile works best with lemon, but I seen some around here take it with milk.*

Sondra also set down a bottle of Hearth Honey. Allison could see Sondra was one of them blessed or cursed with boundless energy, one who would never settle no matter how you drank your tea.

A young girl I work with over at the cinemas, Teri Casper—

Oh we know Teri! Her Uncle Caleb is—

Married to your sister?

That's right! My sister Lisbeth. See, you're catchin on just fine as to how everyone knows everyone else here in Orvop. For better or worse. Sondra was up again to recheck the contents of the oven, both ovens. A beautiful smell flooded the kitchen. *Allison, you have brothers and sisters?*

I have a sister.

Sondra might've been checkin on her pies, but she still didn't miss an off note. *Are you not close with her?*

She turned her back on me some years ago. No reasons I could tell you except the stories she keeps in her head, I don't know, so warped of this world, they gall her into a solitude of . . . strangeness.

That's beautiful, Allison! Sondra suddenly exclaimed. *I do like you! Oh I do! Warped of this world! Solitude of strangeness! Is that yours? That is just gorgeousness itself. Even if what I imagine you're gettin at isn't so pleasant.*

Sad.

I understand. Maybe that's why we need some beauty, beautiful words at least, to counter some of that sadness. Remember time is big enuf to mend the worst breaks.

Or keep them broke. The women in my family live long. Ninety-four. Ninety-eight. Even a hundred and six. But they grow cold too. Allison took a deep breath to free her from that other world of pain. The rich sweet smells, crispy and buttery bubblin, came to the rescue. *What are you bakin in there?*

Cherry-rhubarb pies. Was in the mood. Used some of what I canned last summer. I love the way the smells fill the house. It's like you have visitors. Visitors you hope will stick around. She ran both her hands down the front of her long, dark blue skirt, though it was already plenty smooth.

I never heard bakin described that way. It's true though. It does make your home feel happily crowded.

Happily crowded. See there, you've done it again. It is a big house. It can feel empty at times. Sondra caught how Allison was lookin for somethin right to say and was now at a loss for words. *Eat some of that lemon cake. It's a good one. I promise.*

Allison took a forkful, and, yes, it was astonishin. Her mouth exploded with citrus, while the sponge had an almost creamy texture. She also realized she hadn't eaten anythin since breakfast.

I told you, Sondra said with a wink, her fists on her big hips like she'd just seen a war won. *If only that was true.*

Allison set down her fork. *Teri was the one who gave me your number. She told me about Tom's passin and his friendship with Kalin. After the police, I went to see that Mr. Orwin Porch—*

You went to see him? On your own?

Allison nodded. *Not that it helped any.*

That took sand.

That's what he said. When I ran into him at the entrance to Isatch Canyon.

By chance? Did he have anythin to say?

He means to personally see Kalin in a grave.

Sondra nodded. She didn't doubt that one bit.

Afterward, Allison continued, *I didn't rightly know where to turn or go. I even began to doubt myself. Maybe I was wrong about Kalin.* She hung her head. *Somethin even Mr. Porch suggested. Parents do often misjudge their children, blinded by their love.*

Orwin Porch used the word love?

I'm guessin that was his meanin.

Guess away, but don't use the word love where he's concerned, Sondra snorted. *Let's just say you went to the wrong house first. But you came to the right house eventually. Oh, and if it makes you feel any better, Tom never talked much about Kalin either except to say he was new and weren't in the Church and he'd overheard too many students invokin Third Nevi 11:34. We don't take kindly to scripture used like that.*

Nevi 11:34? Allison looked confused.

Sondra in turn looked uncomfortable. *It ain't a welcomin passage. Basically if you ain't in the Church then you're damned.*

I see. Kalin never told me.

Your son did come by here one time, Sondra said then, smilin a bit now.

You met Kalin?!

Tom brought him for dinner. Your boy hardly said a word. He was very polite. In fact that was about the sum of him. Just thank-yous and yes ma'ams. I could see he and Tom were close, but why remained a mystery. Now, though, I understand it was about ridin. You come from horses?

Oh no, not at all.

But your son knows how to ride, right?

He does.

How'd he learn?

That is a story fer sure. And one that clearly weighed on Allison

March. *When we moved to Colorado, Kalin weren't but five, but there was some horses nearby, and he sure took to them, and they took to him. I loved to hear how he'd shout out their names, names like Sparkle, Flame, Blondie, and even Honey. His daddy thought it was a hoot how they'd just saunter up to Kalin. Like he was a sugar cube. I paid it no mind, but his daddy got him up on their backs. Kalin would muck out stalls and dole out feed and in return get time in a saddle. He learned fast. Soon he was makin some change exercisin the horses.*

Well, ain't that a pretty story! He sounds a lot like both my kids. Naturals. Evan, though, weren't really much with horses.

I didn't like it. Allison sounded ashamed. *He was ridin thanks to his daddy, and nothin ever good came from that man. Well, except Kalin.*

You're not together?

No, ma'am. He's in prison. Fer killin a cop.

I see.

Connor Mayhew. Allison wanted to make it clear that she hadn't taken his name. *He's in for the rest of his life.*

Is that a relief?

I used to keep this calendar on my table. You know, big and wide with one month per page. I got to markin the days that were bad with red and the really bad days with purple. Soon enuf I got to seein that every month with him was too bruised to stand anymore. So, yeah it's a relief, but it don't do nothin for the badness you feel for bein with his likes in the first place. I think I'll carry that until I die. Maybe I'll carry it a little less if I can see Kalin not go walkin in his daddy's footsteps.

You'll make sure he don't.

To be fair I don't know if Kalin's daddy ever had a chance. His momma pretty much ignored him his whole life, and the life he got taught him cruelty. Booze didn't help. I walked some of that road with him. Maybe that's why we got on like we did in the beginnin.

Sondra cleared her throat and went to check on her pies. Allison knew alcohol was strictly forbidden by the Church and that even the subject could spook members.

Don't worry. I'm done there. I learned the hard way. Who'd think learnin gratitude for what you already have can be so hard? I guess I'm still practicin. Sobriety ain't a destination; it's a journey. Or so they say in the program. Appreciate what matters: good health, my beautiful boy, you, this lemon cake. It's hard though. Sometimes real hard. Allison laughed. *You know sometimes it gets so hard I leave a shred of somethin stuck between my molars, on purpose, just so I can look forward to a little relief at the end of the day when I finally get out the floss.* Allison weren't laughin no more. *I've had to come to grips with who I am. See, I'm always able to imagine an excess to my good fortune that in turn always guarantees my disappointment. Disappointment is not a good recipe for happiness. I don't wanna grow old just to grow cold.*

How old are you, Allison? If you don't mind my askin.

Almost forty.

You won't grow cold.

Thank you. I was cold, though, about Kalin's ridin. I didn't take no interest in it. I guess it was fear. His daddy saw it as a way to make us money. Put on a show. That was his plan: little boy wonder on a horse. Or a pony. It didn't matter. Anythin with hooves, my Kalin can ride. His daddy acted like we was already rich. Money, money, money. He kept callin Kalin Our Great White Hope. Frankly it was sickenin. But then when Kalin turned ten, we discovered horses weren't his only talent.

I am intrigued. Sondra sat down and for a moment stayed there. The focus disconcerted Allison enuf that she suddenly didn't want to give voice to what she'd seen, to what she'd done.

I remember when he was just a few months along. It was before dawn and he was babblin on and on. Chirps and songs. You never heard such a happy baby. I was laughin just to hear them crazy sounds comin out of him for no reason. I thought he was talkin to the walls. Funny, I got no recollection where his daddy was that mornin. He was gone a lot. Anyhow, I stepped outside for, you know, a taste of the cool air. We was in Vermont then. Right around South Royalton. And that's when I heard it. The trees were full of birdsong. I hadn't even been aware of it. But my little Kalin was—

He was answerin back.

That's right! He weren't chirpin for the heck of it. He was talkin with the birds.

Then this other talent of Kalin's, it concerns birds? Sondra asked, tryin to connect the dots.

Oh, no, that weren't a talent. He was just listenin.

Sondra was startin to see more clearly how fear was curtailin Allison's speech. *You don't have to tell me, Allison. You know that, right?*

I'd like to though. My boy, see, is a bit odd. Even to his mother. Fer example, he won't get neked around me, not around anyone. And I mean not at all. Not his shirt off. Not even his socks. And he's been that way since he was about ten.

Then his talent has somethin to do with clothin? Sondra laid one hand over the other and pulled her shoulders back.

I cursed him.

You cursed him because he was talkin to birds or wouldn't get neked?

I'm sorry. I know I'm all over the place, Allison said with a sad little laugh and a sadder wave of her hand. *His real talent scared me so much that, like a witch, I set upon him an awful curse. I told him that if he were to ever do this thing again, he would lose the horses he loved. They would shun him forever. All of them. I just made it up. I did it to spite his daddy fer sure. But I also did it to protect Kalin.*

It can't be a real curse if you just made it up, Sondra said, maybe with a touch of sarcasm, mostly to free Allison from whatever guilt this was.

The thing is, maybe I am a witch, because when I said it to Kalin, and I josh you not, Sondra, and it was an awful night of storm and bellow, somethin like tonight is, and though it was also only a storm and I was only lyin to a child, I still felt then like somethin else was suddenly speakin through me, bigger than me, bigger than any mountain, and in fact the moment I laid that curse upon him, I even saw in my mind's eye mountains fallin. Maybe I saw it in his eyes too. I can't remember. Allison's head even briefly fell, but she forced herself to lift it up again. *I'd already got wind of what Kalin's daddy was up to: he was teachin Kalin to shoot.*

Sondra had grown more and more tense with this near-incoherent talk of birds, nekedness, curses, and witches, and now fallin mountains, all of it no doubt further charged by mentions of alcoholism, murder, and prison. Nothin worse than when a possible friendship rots right out from under you with a sudden revelation of severe differences. Allison, by comparison, was somewhat gladdened by this evident reaction, or at least she found it a relief to see this elegant beautiful woman seein her as the convoluted white trash she was. The Gatestones were pratically royalty. Allison was lucky to have an address that lasted a year.

That said, at the mention of shootin guns, Sondra at once relaxed and even smiled like she was genuinely amused, her turn to be relieved.

Why, Allison, all my kids know how to shoot! It's practically a religion around here. Tom and Landry both got their NRA cards when they was around twelve. Ain't a home here that ain't armed.

Allison nodded. *But, see, when Kalin shoots, it ain't just shootin. It's somethin else. Chilled me to the core. I still shudder at the thought of it. His daddy, though, was so thrilled. From that point on, he was to heck with horses. Guns are way cheaper, and they don't eat nothin either. Except gunpowder. That's what his daddy used to say. He had all kinda schemes and meanness in store for my beautiful boy. I cursed Kalin as soon as I found out.* Allison really did shudder then, and she was warm as a house mouse under a stove. *But who believes a curse?* she still asked.

I've cursed my kids plenty of times, Sondra responded, *and told them not to do what they went on to do anyway.*

I figured the same too. Kalin, I know, wanted to honor my prohibition, but he also wanted to please his daddy. Allison went on to describe how Kalin was exercisin some ponies. It was a clear afternoon at a farm where the owner was just delighted to watch this ten-year-old kid ride the way he never could. And then Kalin's daddy told him that he should see his boy shoot. *At the same time?* the owner wanted to know. *Well, no, we haven't gotten to that just yet, but we will,* Kalin's daddy had answered. The farm owner offered a .22, but Kalin's daddy wanted a revolver. The smallest the owner had was a .38, and Kalin's daddy said that would be fine. The farm owner had then pointed to a post twenty paces away and said to shoot that. But Kalin's daddy said he hadn't brought up the subject to waste the good man's time with somethin most men familiar with firearms could handle. He asked the man for a pack of cards and then asked for an ace. The owner handed him an ace of spades. *Now do you think my boy, only ten, mind you, can shoot this card with a gun he's never used before?* Kalin's daddy asked. *Where you gonna set it?* Kalin's daddy had shook his head. *I'm gonna flick it right up in the air.* The farm owner did not believe Kalin could do it. *And I should tell you, Kalin's daddy was havin a good time now,* Allison continued. *This was what he lived for.* The farm owner said he'd wager one hundred dollars but Kalin's daddy refused. *Kalin's daddy never wanted just some of the money. He wanted all of the money. He told that farm owner: My little boy will shoot it right through the middle, and if he don't I'll pay you a hundred bucks just for takin up your time.* The owner thought that was a hoot and likely expected to make some money now too; more so when Kalin's daddy flicked that card high in the air but did so so badly, it tumbled head over heels. *I thought the whole thing was a big bunch of stupidness, and then Kalin fired. He moved like water. He was so fluid and quick that it didn't seem like nothin, like it was over before it started, though now up in the air, just driftin down, was two cards.*

Two? Sondra asked.

Kalin had cut that card clean in half. Right down the middle. His daddy loved that Kalin was left-handed too, said it was extra theatrical, sinister. He'd tell me later that if this circus act didn't pay, Kalin could rob banks. And he'd meant it too. The farm owner was thrilled and, though he held both halves, declared it was still impossible, a trick, a dash of luck, and that he would hand over to Kalin's daddy one thousand dollars if Kalin could do it again. Dig out another ace, Kalin's daddy had told him. And Kalin did it again, this time through the center of the ace of clubs. Ten thousand dollars. Kalin put a hole right through the ace of diamonds. All or nothin, if he puts a hole through the ace of hearts, one hundred thousand dollars. Kalin's daddy threw up the card, but this time, bless his heart, Kalin didn't shoot. What neither men were aware of, though fer sure Kalin was, was how with each firin of that gun, them four ponies Kalin had been exercisin had grown more and more irritated, until, with the third shot, they had just done reared up and run. And Kalin started cryin, tryin to apologize to me. I'm so sorry, Mommy! He kept wailin. Just broke my heart. But you know what,

I was half ready to side with the men and tell him the horses was just scared of the gunfire and everythin I'd said the night before, that curse, was just rubbish I had no business sayin, drunk business at that, but then I seen how when Kalin ran back over to them horses, they shunned him. In fact no horse would come near Kalin for almost a year. And by then everythin had changed in the home. Kalin had refused to touch a gun again, and that pleased me, but Kalin's daddy had lost out on one hundred thousand dollars. He took that out on me, and when Kalin tried to stop him, he done it to Kalin too. That was that. I grabbed up Kalin and we ran. Different places, different towns. My own boozin ended at least. Then for a while I thought another man, other men, might shield me from Kalin's daddy. That ended too. Cursin as well. No more excess. But I never could stop runnin. And Kalin's daddy hunted us until the worst of him got the best of him and he wound up behind bars for longer than even he can survive.

Sondra tried to take that all in, wound up standin again, pourin more tea, though their cups were more than half full. *That is quite some— That is quite somethin. Do you think your boy has a gun on him now?*

I'm sure he doesn't. I asked him before he left if what he was up to involved guns, and he said no. I believe him.

You heard Egan, Orwin Porch's son. He said your Kalin shot his horse.

Kalin would never hurt a horse. Ever.

Maybe he missed?

Kalin don't miss.

Sondra didn't look convinced.

He don't have a gun, Allison said again. *Whether you believe the curse or not, Kalin believes it.*

Sondra said she needed to think on this more, returnin to her ovens again, but this time, satisfied, she put on her oven mitts and then proceeded to take out, one after another, with lattice crusts browned to perfection, not one, not two, but four cherry-rhubarb pies!

Good gosh! Are you throwin a party?

Mungo stirred some, like the question itself provoked some antic- ipation, and then resettled hisself again.

I do like to bake when I'm upset. It calms me. I'll give most of these away. I did want to try out some new things. You see in a week this house will be filled to the rafters with college girls. A church function. Charity in Practice. That's what it's officially called. I'm the president of the Orvop Relief Society, more like the wheelhorse if I'm speakin frankly, but I love doin it. Sister Dowdell helps out. Judy's our vice president. No one's better at keepin lists organized and sendin out reminders, though everyone knows she ain't in charge. Don't get me wrong; I love Judy. But by herself, the girls would overrun her like raccoons loose in a pantry. How I adore the girls. I love their precociousness. We gather, we talk about bein purposeful in our welcomin and attendin to those we don't know, who aren't close, who are strangers. Everyone tries to put back into focus how to help others. And I try to make sure everyone gets a little fatter. Allison, are you a Church member?

I was. I haven't been back for some time.

I hope you don't mind my askin.

Holdin down three jobs don't exactly make for time.

You have three jobs?

Allison nodded.

Well, Lordy. The Church don't like to see its Sisters workin. In fact that was the gist of General Conference early this month. Our duties are with our family.

Conference?

Church affairs. Dallin and I usually went, though on occasion he'd take Evan and Tom huntin, and they'd listen to it on 1160 AM radio. These days I have it on at home, KSL, the TV.

I'd love to not have three jobs. I do it for Kalin. And ain't that the pickle, when you gotta leave the one you love to love the one you love?

The two women shared a cordial smile that conceded in silence a willingness to leave alone any more conversin about the Church.

I'd offer us both a slice, but these pies still need to cool awhile.

Sondra, when I called you, I didn't know that you was in any way involved in this. I had no one to turn to. I just needed some perspective, at best some advice. I had no idea that my son had somehow involved your daughter!

Oh hush! When Landry went missin last night, my heart went missin, but when I seen she was gone with her horse, that'd be Jojo, then I knew she was up to darn stupidness, but at least my heart came back some. If there's one thing that girl can do, it's ride. Fantastic riders, her and Tom. Oh dear. At the thought of them, Sondra had to steady herself with a fist on the counter. *I'd offer you a piece of pie, but these need to set an hour before they're any good.*

Oh, that's quite all right.

I already told you that, didn't I? Oh dear. Sondra looked around to gather herself, start things anew. *Allison, where are you from?*

North Carolina, but by now I've been more years elsewhere than all the years I spent there.

Do you still have family in North Carolina?

Allison shook her head. *My sister lives in Delaware with my mother. My father passed a long time ago.*

That must've been hard.

I'm sure it was, but when you're young you don't always understand so well how much you've lost.

I guess you already know big families are the norm around here?

I think it's crazy but it's nice.

It is crazy! My sisters each have eight. My brother has nine. I got nieces and nephews galore. You'd think with hips this wide I'd've been right up there with them. And we sure tried. Heavenly Father saw fit to give us Evan but then took him away. Heavenly Father saw fit to give us Tom and then took him away too. I went out and got Landry on my own. We adopted her when she was but barely six. She was born in Samoa and then kicked around the United States. Lived on pretty much every street that's a one-way to a dead end. Then I grabbed hold of her and wouldn't let go. A fit all right. Or a fight dependin on what day you was visitin. Dallin called us Feisty and Fire, though he never did make clear who was who. Sondra smiled, fussin the pies into an arrangement on a rack for coolin, then rearrangin them again so they sat in a way that, if it didn't better them none, eased somethin in her. *I like to keep busy. When you're doin nothin, it's harder to do anythin.* She eyed the pies but without any sign of satisfaction or desire. *Dallin and I figured Landry would eventually find her way back to the sea she was born next to, but the sea turned out to be her Jojo. She's like a wave on that horse, and he's like her ocean, and when they're together, they can go forever.*

I'd like to see that sometime.

Landry's got a gift all right. Maybe like your son. Especially on Jojo. No one can ride him but her. Not even Tom and he could ride a bull big as a mountain. You should've seen him on Hightower.

The thing I still don't follow is why she would've taken her horse at all?

Oh you poor thing! At least there I can help out! Sondra put on a new kettle and insisted as well that Allison have another wedge of lemon cake. *Eat! We are gonna need our strength!*

Allison did as she was told and was embarrassed by how quickly the second slice vanished. Sondra looked pleased.

To take the long way around, since we have time, let's start with Orwin Porch. His money comes from Porch Meats, generations of butchers in that family, but he's also got trucks. Hauls all over the country. And that ain't the end of it. Not even the start of it. He'll do anythin for a buck, includin that Easter egg hunt I was tellin you about, though that was twenty years ago. He's still a kill buyer too I hear, operatin out of Willard with a fellow named Elster Bundy.

What's a kill buyer?

Someone who gets abandoned and generally misused horses on the cheap and sells them in Canada and Mexico for slaughter. Though what Old Porch loves most is land. Sondra's eyes gleamed as she told Allison about the properties he owned, like they were her own, fields for grazin, stables and paddocks, plenty of lots with businesses on them, warehouses, storage facilities, landfills, and even apartments he rented out. All over the valley and state. *Which brings us to a barn and some holdin pens not so far from here over on Willow and Oak. I only found out about this after Tom was gone. Apparently there's this Paddock A where Old Porch keeps horses he's movin* around to Lord knows where. But there's also this Paddock B. Whatever winds up there, Old Porch supposedly renders the next day.

He does it hisself?

Sondra shrugged. From what I can gather, Tom and your Kalin used to ride two horses from Paddock A.

Without permission?

That's the sense I got. Now rest assured that was my Tom's doin. He was a prankster at heart, and any chance to thumb his nose at Orwin Porch, he'd take. Us Gatestones and Porches have a long history. But at the hospital, Tom involved your son. He made Kalin swear that if those two horses ever got moved to Paddock B, he'd take them to the Crossin and set them free.

What's the Crossin?

You got me there. Those details he whispered to Kalin, much to the consternation of my little Landry. After Tom passed, I drove by them holdin pens, and there in Paddock A, Landry and I made the acquaintance of Navidad and Mouse.

Those are their names?

Those are the names Tom and your Kalin gave them. The kettle was hissin now. Sondra looked relieved to have somethin else to do. She refreshed the teapot, considered sittin down again only to start wipin down the counters, though they was already pristine.

When I found out Landry had took off on Jojo, Sondra continued, I drove to Paddocks A and B. They was both empty. Mouse and Navidad were gone.

You figure they're the horses my son stole?

I'm sure of it.

I'm still confused. They were in Paddock B. Weren't they meant for slaughter? Are they worth somethin dead?

Those two?! Around here you'd likely have to pay someone to get rid of them.

Then why does Mr. Porch care so much?

Now you're startin to get a sense of the man you tried to get out in front of it all with.

It don't make any sense.

No, it don't.

And what's his boy Russel got to do with this?

That part is still a mystery.

So your best guess, as far as your daughter's concerned, is that when Landry got wind that the horses had been moved to Paddock B, she knew my son would try to take them to this Crossin, wherever that is?

Sondra nodded.

And likely your Landry wanted to go along?

I think that's the rough of it.

Up Isatch Canyon?

The mysteries keep propagatin. That canyon sure as heck is no place to ride a *horse, let alone a place to set them free. It's a dead end on a dead end, endin with a heap of boulders piled up all the way to the foot of Mount Katanogos. Another dead end.*

That's what Mr. Porch said too. I'm still not gettin this. Why then would he come here tonight to tell you that my Kalin had kidnapped your Landry? What was the point? He said he already told the police. What was he doin?

That's maybe not so big a mystery. Sondra sighed, clearin the plates, includin the rest of the lemon cake, what she figured she'd marry with a cake she took out of a cupboard. *Well, will you look at that!*

You found a cake you forgot about?

Very funny. I know where all my cakes are! Sondra showed her the orange cake. It even had them candied curls of orange rind on top. *There was more than half, but now, see, there's only a quarter left. Landry took some. I can't tell you how that warms my heart.*

Mine too. Maybe they're sharin a piece right now?

That is a lovely thought. Then let's you and I share a little. For them.

Sondra didn't wait for an answer, not that Allison objected, Sondra cuttin up a slice, which, since she'd already cleared the plates, she placed directly in Allison's hand, which Allison also didn't object to.

Your son, Kalin, Sondra began again, *honored my boy's last wish. And my frenzy of a daughter followed after your boy, fer sure because she had a crush on him but mostly because she loved her brother more than the moon can love the sun. And that leads me to a more serious apology to you for involvin your boy and even involvin you now in somethin that has nothin to do with either of you.*

Which is how Sondra then started to further detail the two families' disregard for one another: Porches versus Gatestones. She spoke about crimes near a hundred years old, when they was all but ragged pioneers, and them weren't as bad as those that happened fifty years ago, when they was civilized, or even twenty years ago, when they was all prosperin. Indecencies ranged from Halloween pranks involvin toilet paper and cow manure to property destruction involvin a burnin barn and a slurry of toxic waste bequeathed to a field. There were also brute acts of harm and, in some cases, accusations of murder.

Sondra, to her credit, didn't always claim the higher ground. *The Gatestones enjoyed a fair amount of pecuniary advantages from the outset, and with that came a compoundin power that easily outbalanced the angry energy of the Porches.* Unlike the Porches, the Gatestones were lawyers and judges, some doctors, a few academics, with many in the higher echelons of the Church. Where the Porches would happily wield a firearm or ax, the Gatestones could wield the courts and secure a death sentence or two. *One Church elder swore our conflict was older than Cain and Abel. A likenin I did not care for.* As Sondra made clear, to her mind the start of this

304

rancor is forever lost in the smolderin ruins of a history that still now and then spits forth like a devastatin spark a new origin story of some swindle for an unremarkable plot of earth or a horse.

Both Porches and Gatestones are entwined with horses, and horses aren't even that much a part of Utah, Sondra explained. Not like Montana, Colorado, or Wyomin, and of course vast stretches of Texas. *But they're around.* Sondra described the wild herds of Onaqui, Winter Ridge, and Tilly Crick. *Many folks still see them as just the beasts of burden that the settlement of the West required. That would be the Porches. Others treat them more as a religion. That would be the Gatestones.*

With horses always comes the necessity for land and the right to graze. And the Gatestones were like the Porches in that manner, as they too coveted territory. *This house is but a small example of the fortune that extends well beyond these walls.*

You say that with some doubt.

Do I? Not so much doubt as maybe distance?

Sondra, see, was not a Gatestone. She was a Hearth, and she came from no wealth at all, though, perhaps to the gall of both Porches and Gatestones, who were earlier settlers in this valley, her family had arrived before them both. *We were one of the Utah originals. Peaceable bee-keepers devoted to honey and wax, what we sold in the local shops, traded with the Indians and, if rumor is to be believed, we even spoke their language, with one of the Hearth girls even runnin off with a young chief, never to be heard from again. The family lore said she was scalped and buried under a river log, but I like to think both of them escaped to San Francisco. Maybe all the way to Hawaii. I think when I die, I'd like to know their story.*

That'd be your first question?

Sondra laughed. *Well, maybe not the first. But high up on the list.*

They continued to talk like this for such a long time that Sondra announced with delight that the cherry-rhubarb pies had set enuf and required tastin, if just on behalf of the young ladies comin over next weekend, as they would require the absolute best cookin, *because to inspire high acts of charity requires high acts of deliciousness.* Sondra was plannin to muster up pumpkin pies too and pecan pies and sweet potato pies. She cut two big wedges of the cherry-rhubarb, which she served with glasses of cold milk.

Allison marveled at how, with the worry and grief eatin away at this woman over her missin daughter, her lost son too, her two lost sons, Sondra still kept battlin on with activity and optimism. And lots of sugar. Allison weren't that strong, and whether that was true or not, and it wasn't, believin it so made it so. She slumped in her chair, borne down by the thought that Kalin might soon join Tom. It was just too much. Though the cherry-rhubarb pie was impossible to resist, even if all the sweets combined with exhaustion had started to static up her nerves.

Allison rose and apologized. She didn't say she'd had enuf tea, enuf cake, enuf pie. She didn't say that she needed to starve. She just said that she needed some air.

Sondra at once led Allison through a sittin room, which she left dark, out onto the back porch. Mungo followed close behind.

The cold shocked Allison, but it also felt good, joltin her awake and aware, their breath foggin thick. Even Mungo woofed out small clouds.

The yard itself was beautiful and large, the gardens lit, most amassed along a gently slopin hillside of lawn that ended with a grove of fruit trees. Sondra told her about the bear that had once walked right across. She told about a homeless man livin in her cherry orchard whom she soon discovered was there with his wife and child. *The Church took care of them. They have an apartment now on 900 East, and a job, and their kid goes to Isatch Elementary just like Evan, Tom, and Landry did.* Sondra pointed out her blackberry bushes. Back in August and September she'd managed to fill three buckets.

It was 10:33 p.m.

But Allison pointed beyond the orchard. *That's Isatch Canyon there, ain't it?*

That's where our children are right now.

Both women shivered together, also noticin together how since the rain had quit, the cold had gotten worse. A silver shimmer now spread over lawn and trees.

Isn't there some way we could just go up there and get them? Like right now?

You'd do that? Sondra studied Allison, maybe even anew.

Do I have a choice?

Unfortunately you do. We both do. There's another storm comin in, and the terrain in the best of conditions is too much for the likes of us. If Egan couldn't catch them, we don't stand a chance.

We still gotta do somethin.

We will.

Sondra's conviction helped beat back some the cold.

Your Kalin, when he and Tom became friends, became part of the Gatestone family, Sondra added.

Thank you.

Don't thank me yet. If, like Old Porch and Egan are sayin, Kalin's with Landry, then that's how the Porches will see him too. As a Gatestone.

Shouldn't the police hear from you? Allison was surprised at herself for not askin this earlier.

Oh, darlin, I've already told them everythin! Called a dozen times at least. And other folks as well. Don't you worry. Things are in the works. But it won't clear up much fast. At least not yet. I expect Old Porch will call Child Services to report that I got a runaway kid or am neglectin his testimonial of a kidnappin in progress.

He'd do that?

This afternoon I went ahead and called Child Services myself, just in case, but muddy water stirred don't get no less muddy.

Allison folded her arms across her chest. *Mr. Porch still has hisself a dead boy.*

He does.

Maybe your Landry can shed some light on that.

Sondra nodded. *We can hope.*

I sure hope she'll put an end to this business about her bein kidnapped.

But Sondra didn't nod then. Instead her gaze dropped to the worn wood under feet. *If that don't point to the trouble in this all. You asked me earlier why Old Porch came here, and I didn't answer you. I could say I lost track of my thoughts, but that ain't exactly true. I think I just didn't want to face my thoughts.*

Oh.

You see, Allison, if I read Old Porch right, he only came here tonight to tell me in his awful way that my little girl ain't comin home and that he intends to make sure your boy takes the blame.

He means to do somethin to your little girl? Allison was outraged.

We in it now. We are in it now.

Chapter Ten
"The Awides Mine"

The gouge of darkness at the top of a fast-mellowin slope seemed as abhorrent as it was an offerin near miraculous, at least for Landry, who thought their trial would never end, and for Kalin too, and he'd been here once before and swore then that he'd never come back. The promise of shelter had overruled any trepidation he hoped he'd misremembered.

When the horses finally reached a wide-enuf shelf of levelness to stop and turn about on without riskin some awful tumble, Kalin slipped off Navidad, handin the reins and Mouse's lead rope to Landry. Though instead of headin for the mine entrance, he at once stumbled back the way they'd come. Landry could see he was plenty pale but more obviously in a panic.

Tom! he kept screamin. *Tom!*

Landry still sat atop Jojo, and yes, though she already knew about what she mostly deemed a hallucination of her brother, her mouth still fell agape, maybe Jojo's jaw dropped some too, at the sight of this boy yellin after the clouds and rain-whipped darkness.

He's gone, Landry! Tom's gone!

Landry felt sure Kalin would start to sob. His body was tremblin as he stood so paltry in form, inconsequential before the Gallionic elements surroundin them, beholdin a departure only he could register, like some reversed tale of Orpheus, a Eurydice with her back to the underworld she'd yet to breach, beggin for a glance, any glance, which might betray back to life not her but him, Orpheus, which only makes sense if Orpheus is the dead Tom still of the world above and Eurydice is the much-alive Kalin, only now about to head below, which was this zany notion Caracy Rudder would pursue in the company of Mrs. Annserdodder and Ms. Melson, the two women chalkin up Rudder's dazzlin back-and-forth confusion to the start of an anguished divorce he would suffer through for three years. Caracy Rudder sure played a lot of slow songs durin those days, which kept his sadness-mug full. Mrs. Annserdodder would bring him pumpkin bread, and Ms. Melson would send him different translations of Homer.

No matter how hard he yelled, Kalin could see Tom was gone, and Landry could see Kalin could see Tom was gone. In fact except for Tom, they suddenly could see everywhere and everythin with unparalled clarity. Stars kept amassin above, and of the clouds that refused to budge or offer translucency, they was auraed by what was no doubt a big moon. There was a relief here to see so well, though it was a relief rimed by defeat. After all, they had backtracked so much, they was now even beyond the official entrance to Isatch Canyon, if

309

high, high above, nearly on the face of Agoneeya, though still hundreds of feet below Squaw Peak. Of immediate concern was how this increased pellucidity was commensurate with a plunge in temperature.

Kalin and Landry was both shiverin bad, and the horses didn't care none for the cold either. Worse still, what weren't thunder and seemed born of all directions was this awful crackin, like the mountain itself was made of glass and here was the music that preceeds the shatter.

Kalin! Where are we headed? Up there? Landry pointed at the hole in the rocks.

Kalin nodded, though he still seemed chained to his vision of an absence that had refused to follow. *I can't believe he's gone.*

If we don't get us to some warmth, we'll be gone too!

But Kalin still didn't move, seemin then to Landry too greatly diminished, the way the defeated look when they've not only quit the contest but forfeited as well any sense of larger purpose, free even of bitter regret and certainly obligation. It was a look that would break anyone's heart. He was just helpless, moored between what he'd lost and what he now had to engage.

Maybe sensin this growin rigidity, Navidad butted her head against him, as if to help him along, at least get him movin again, and maybe that was all Kalin needed, because he did start movin again, step by step toward all the darkness the earth can conceal.

Not that Kalin seemed any better when he reemerged from that puncture of blackness some minutes later. He still appeared bereft before the sight of his missin friend, even if his steps no longer seemed to be draggin through thickenin mud.

Kalin already understood that in order to enter that damp tunnel, the horses would need to duck their heads. And that was just the first challenge. Once within, peculiar echoes would accost their sensitive hearin and dare them to respond with fright. But Kalin also understood they had no choice, and that afforded some relief.

He gathered from Mouse's pack the necessities they'd need, the primary one bein a long-sleeved shirt, the only extra he'd brung. Navidad's nose went through the head hole and the rest covered up both her eyes and ears, usin the sleeves along with some saddle string to tie the shirt in place.

A palm of that oat-applesauce mash helped coax Navidad to lower her head as they disappeared together into that hollow of perfect shadow.

I'll hurry, Kalin let Landry know, though there weren't no hustle in him, not even in his voice.

What comfort Landry expected would follow the sight of such progress, soon she'd be out of this storm!, was too fast countered by the weird sense that they were right there already seized and forever undone, and she was now, this part accordin to Rudder, Melson, and Annserdodder, the musically inclined Orpheus, and here was the end of her Eurydice, that bein Kalin, swallowed by what commands every grave. Not that Landry was puttin any names of myths to the awful panic that had begun twistin through her, cuttin away her breath, while knuckles whitened around reins and Mouse's lead.

Many years later, Mr. Rudder, with crumbs of pumpkin bread collectin in his beard, would even remark that his choice of myths, if momentarily resonant, was still wrong: *Kalin weren't never no Orpheus, and he sure as heck weren't no Eurydice either.*

Bear in mind, though, that Landry did in fact know the Orpheus-Eurydice myth well enuf to think of it because her sophomore English teacher, none other than Mrs. Alice Annserdodder, had not but weeks earlier taught this very story to her class, Landry listenin if indifferent then before the recountin, despite havin just lost her brother Tom, and her daddy Dallin three years before him, and her eldest brother Evan two years before that, and earlier still, her biological daddy, Langston Cope, who'd made it back stateside, to his hometown in Arkansas, not far from Monticello, a beautiful man blacker than midnight is blue, with a mind clearer than a winter sky, who by hand continued to free from raw wood violins of the greatest lightness til he was felled by somethin brutal if swift afflictin his chest, and this when Landry was not even one, losin him in life as well as in memory. Landry's birth momma had lasted until Landry was five. She weren't no happy story either, but she was more beautiful than the sea is dark when the day is gold, and she'd delivered Landry unto a world in which horses galloped the earth with the wind forever in their manes, or so Landry still liked to believe. And that's where Landry's mind was too when Mrs. Annserdodder was goin on about love lost.

Kalin incidentally had had near the same experience, havin taken Mrs. Annserdodder's class the previous year, where he'd also heard the same story, followin along even less than Landry had that day, as he'd also been daydreamin about horses, lamentin how few of them he'd seen since movin to Orvop.

Though in fact on Agoneeya Landry's feelins if not memory did find the story of Orpheus, of that musical one who'd lost his love, who'd gone to reclaim her from the place where the dead linger only to lose her again, the second time time to impatient longin. Suddenly Landry experienced the end of a story that was thousands of years old.

Kalin was gone.

Kalin was still gone.

Sure, there weren't no confirmed death, no finality of the grave. Yet. Instead there was somethin worse, emergin foul and repellent, a sense of sufferin that in its remorseless unfinishedness presented, at least to Landry, the signature of Damnation itself: *Abandon All Hope* would never adorn this gateway but rather *Hope Will Forever Torment Whomever Enters Here.* Or as Gillian Orr would say of that place: *Where Curt P. Richter was a presidin devil.*

Suffice it to say, Landry realized in this bitterest of moments that she was a sophomore in high school who had no business bein out so late, let alone in such threatenin conditions, let alone by herself, let alone on horseback, let alone so terribly high up on this canyon wall, let alone perched right above a slope so stupefyinly steep, what so quickly ended with ragged and fractured quartzite cliffs ready to embrace her and Jojo into a finality that was only just a hair more abhorrent to where Kalin and Navidad had disappeared.

And Kalin was still gone.

Landry started then to shiver harder. Too hard. She could feel how the cold that had been gnawin on her peripheries had finally penetrated deeper, into her marrow even, in a way that no shiver or convulsin would combat. Anyone who'd've come by then would've caught upon her cheeks and lips a hue of surrenderin gray. But no one was there. Not even Tom.

And Kalin was still gone.

Landry might well have done somethin stupid then, some last-gaspy titubation for action, if just for action's sake, if it weren't for Orvop itself, all laid out below, just aglitterin like a bowlful of gemstones tryin to mirror the great bowl of gemstones above. And, she thought, well, if the one down there could hold her home, why couldn't the one above do so too? And that was all, a tiny moment of reflection that warmed away her fear if it didn't exactly warm up her blood. She missed her momma somethin awful. But she missed Tom most.

And then Kalin was back.

Without Navidad either, and already movin quick to blindfold Mouse, now with his only sweater and, like he done before, lowerin the geldin's head with a handful of treats before vanishin again into the black. This time, though, he was back quicker than a count of ten.

Landry couldn't keep away her smile.

I never thought much of Orvop, she chattered out, because the heck if she was gonna tell Kalin about her frights. *But from up here it's pretty darned pretty.*

She figured Kalin would make fun of her for sayin so, but he didn't. *I see what you mean.*

Kalin had stopped shiverin, and Landry knew he hadn't got on but maybe a shirt or two and his Lee Storm Rider under that green poncho. They used her pink raincoat and more saddle string to blindfold Jojo; Kalin gave Landry enuf oat mix to lower Jojo's head. But Landry hushed Kalin as soon as he began to explain how to proceed, reprimandin him for thinkin she was fool enuf not to have observed his doins the first two times. *I know how to lower my own horse's head.*

And that was true. Jojo obliged just fine, and then with her right hand gatherin the reins under the bit rings and her left hand holdin Kalin's, they stepped together into the black.

For Landry it seemed like miles. *Clop-Clop-clip-Clop.* Her absolute blindness makin of distance somethin she had no hold on. She doubted the ground; she would fall away. Jojo would fall away. But her ears came to the rescue, sharpenin on the clop of Jojo's hooves, his occasional snorts. But when her nostrils flared with the tingle of smoke, even a suggestion of warmth, she doubted herself. Even when her blindness began to retreat before an orange glow up ahead, she doubted the vision. Only when they rounded a bend in the passageway did her eyes blink with amazement before such a sight: here was a large chamber with a ceilin at least a dozen feet high if not more. A cave-in to the left, who knows how many decades old, marked the limits of one side. That's where Navidad and Mouse stood; their leads loosely tied off on some iron railins, twisted and rust-bit. Navidad was unsaddled; Mouse still bore the packsaddle. They was also still blindfolded. Opposite the horses, to the right, burnt the small fire. Smoke, however, weren't fillin up the room, and Landry soon discovered there was a tunnel directly above the flames that may have at one time been used to reach other parts of the mine overhead. Though there was no sign of a ladder.

Near opposite the entrance through which they'd just entered another passage presented itself with an obsidian opaqueness Landry didn't care for at all. Kalin had already taken the shorter lariat and, usin the rustin twists of steel already in the walls, what might've once supported a gate, ran the rope back and forth until he'd managed to create a barrier of some sorts.

Just a ways in from here, Kalin said while recheckin the lariat, *there's a shaft that goes a long ways down.*

Landry uncinched Jojo and at long last dragged down his saddle.
We gonna leave them blindfolded?
You know, I ain't sure. Whadya think?
Inside here just seems just like a weird barn.

You think?

We'll tell them it's a barn.

The horses seemed hardly perturbed by the sight of this new locale, which, with all of them there and that small fire goin, was startin to actually warm up.

They'd soon freed the horses of all their tack, and Kalin laid that and their supplies before that roped-off passage for reorderin later as well as providin more of a barrier against an unnecessary mishap. The saddles, though, he lugged close to the fire.

Landry, meanwhile, saw to waterin and feedin the horses, with both of them brushin out their coats and inspectin their legs and checkin their hooves and generally makin them feel at home.

We're gonna need more wood, Kalin announced then, but he didn't head back outside. Rather takin a small burnin spear of wood and steppin over their supplies and then under the lariat, he once more disappeared into blackness.

I bet you wished you'd brought a flashlight! Landry yelled after him, half-pleased with herself for musterin a taunt.

I didn't think I'd end up here! he yelled back. He seemed suddenly far away again, his voice reverberant if also swallowed too quickly by spaces that Landry didn't like one bit. Gone was the smell of the mountains; instead a singular dampness, gritty with mineral mustiness, pervaded everywhere. Landry didn't like that either.

When Kalin returned he was draggin with him some old wooden chairs, or parts of them.

You find a town hall back there?

We aren't the first to come by here. You should see the old beer cans lyin around. Too bad we can't burn them.

I bet we're the first to bring in horses.

Kalin set to breakin up the backs and the seats and soon they had a suitable pile of wood that, after a few trips, proved promisin enuf to last them til dawn.

There's even a desk if this runs out.

How about a bath? And a bed? And an oven. My momma bakes the best chocolate chip pancakes. Actually everythin she makes is the best. You should taste her cherry-rhubarb pie! That's one of my favorites.

They sat around the kettle, waitin for the water to boil, and while it weren't no Sunday brunch at the Gatestones' it was still sublime. Fer starters, they had more cocoa. Kalin said he was gonna divide just one packet but, finally registerin the state they was both in, dumped two in and stirred until the mixins was bubblin and creamy. Landry, as she expected, got the mug again, and Kalin poured his share into the bowl.

After they'd helped themselves to the sips needed to still their shakes and put some warmth in their stomachs, *Not too fast!* Landry had exhorted Kalin and probably herself too, *Or your belly's gonna cramp up fast!*, Kalin got to makin them one heckuva meal. No doubt one can of mushroom soup, ramen, some diced potatoes, plus two of them Orvop cafeteria buns might sound to most as pretty darned paltry, but for them two it were a feast. Kalin added in extras too, spices, bits of cheese, and other stuff that no doubt elevated the culinary experience enjoyed in that dank mine. Kalin, though, never considered tossin in some carrots; he and Landry both agreed that they were for the horses, and that was their dessert, watchin Navidad, Mouse, and Jojo chow down on the carrots.

For reasons she couldn't quite follow, Landry felt good watchin Kalin go from chatterin and shiverin to calm and, after a while, even rosy-cheeked. She relaxed, seein him return some to hisself, and her own jitters vanished.

While Kalin cleaned up, Landry repositioned the saddles so they was near the fire but not too near. Then, after arrangin the saddle pads to serve as a bedroll for herself, she gave the one horse blanket to Kalin and then the one sleepin bag to herself, without thinkin twice, which, yes, does come across as selfish, because, well, it was selfish, also indicatin how Landry was either entitled beyond the reach of a good conscience or entirely thoughtless. Rocks in her head or head in the clouds, it don't matter.

That said, Landry at least noticed that Kalin, who was left-handed, was mostly usin his right hand. Soon she had him lyin down with his back against his saddle, under his blanket too, while she went out the mine entrance fer a moment.

Now the way out seemed no great distance; to her mind but a few steps. She was thinkin of only findin the coldest stone but in fact wound up with somethin better. The temperature outside was well below freezin, and with that plummetin mercury came new benefits: ice. In fact thin sheets of ice had already formed near the entrance. She broke and stacked as much as she could carry. One piece she made Kalin hold, and the rest she placed in the two collapsible canvas water bowls as well as in the kettle. The horses could drink the melt, and she and Kalin could boil it to drink and refill their canteens come mornin.

But Kalin's palm needed more than just ice. Landry's momma would have bit her lip at the sight of them rope burns. They was bad, all red and blisterin with the skin tore open in too many places, but her ma would've also knowd what to do: aloe vera and maybe even gauze lightly wrapped around the palm.

A lariat's a stupid thing to use for a climbin rope, Kalin grumbled. *Especially without gloves. What was I thinkin?*

You weren't is all. Landry said it as a fact, not as a barb.

You think some butter would help? Kalin asked. He knew his hand was in bad shape. If he'd've just put on his gloves, he'd have spared hisself so much pain. *I heard butter on burns is the best thing.*

There's another stupid thing. You can be glad I'm here. Butter traps the heat and might even worsen the infection. You bring along any aloe vera?

I don't even know what that is.

The next best thing I can think of is to pee on your hand when you go next.

Seriously?

That's what Tom told me.

You believe him?

No.

Thanks for the ice.

Landry liked gettin thanked. *Does this place have a name?*

Awides. Kalin said it like *widest* but with an *a* in front and without the *t* at the end. *It's also been called Eighties but I don't know why.*

Tom showed you the way here?

Kalin shook his head. *I found it myself. Heard stories. These mountains are full of lore. When me and your brother weren't ridin, I'd still come up here on foot to just poke around. Things made more sense to me up in the mountains than they did down in school. My momma wanted so bad for me to just fit in here and get along.* Kalin shrugged and shut hisself up, even if it looked to Landry like he was still havin words with hisself, what he weren't willin to share no more with her, which made him seem only that much more lonely and maybe even crazier than she could take. Landry felt bad for him, no question there, but if he hadn't been Tom's friend, she might've felt pretty uneasy about findin herself so close to him now. He sure could ride a horse though. There was that.

Where'd you learn to ride anyways? she asked.

Tom used to ask me the same thing.

You ever tell him?

My momma.

Your momma knows horses?

Never even been on one, but she taught me everythin I needed to know.

You know that don't make a lick of sense, right?

Tom said the same thing.

I sure do miss him.

My momma knows how to listen and how to find where there's stillness, stillness even in her own breath. That's all I really know how to do: just listen to my friends. I got no interest in makin them do what they don't want to do.

316

You think a horse wants to be in a mine?

Kalin smiled, and Landry realized it had been a while since she'd seen him look even a little amused. *You make a fair point, though I'd say these horses don't look too bothered.*

In this odd barn, Landry added, answerin Kalin's smile with hers, both of them laughin when Mouse upped his tail and let plop some juicy manure. Not to be bested, Jojo went ahead and did the same. Navidad whinnied as if to object or approve or just join in on the laughter.

I'll tell you somethin I ain't ever told Tom, Kalin suddenly announced.

Tell me! Landry was thrilled at the thought of learnin somethin her brother didn't know.

Them first weeks when we was out on Navidad and Mouse, I got super bad blisters.

That ain't nothin. Your fingers or your calves?

Both butt cheeks. Big ones. I couldn't hardly sit.

Landry giggled. *That's nothin new neither. Especially if you're used to ridin a lot and take a break and then come back at it again.*

Tom kept sayin I was a good rider, and there I was with a near-bloody bum under three pairs of underwear. I was so embarrassed. I was even embarrassed about bein embarrassed.

I guess I'm guilty of that too. Like all them cliques at school that I feel bad about not bein part of, though I wouldn't want to be part of them anyway.

Kalin didn't say nothin.

Life sure is perplexin, especially when people are involved, she went on. *The way I figure it, you just have to know how to tell the difference between them that have somethin to say and them that don't. Like when you're listenin to some jibberjabberin, that you might even get swept up in it, believin it, until you, I don't know, start to get wind that that jibberjabberin isn't gonna do no one any good because those doin the jibberjabberin ain't doin no one any good, they're just, you know, jibberjabberin.* Landry paused. *Not that I'm an expert in determinin what's jibberjabberin and what's not.*

I guess that's one way to put it. Me, I think life comes down to whether you stay on or get bucked off.

Landry liked that. *Nice and simple.*

But that ain't quite right either, Kalin added.

Oh.

Because when you do get bucked off, and we all get bucked off, what matters most is gettin back on.

Tom rode this bull named Hightower, Landry said then. *Maybe he told you about that?* Tom had but Kalin wanted to hear Landry tell it. *Hightower was just huge, and Tom rode him longer than anyone. Won that big belt buckle to prove it. But thems that rode before him, and likely after him, Hightower threw hard. Some barely got up. Some didn't get up. Some got hurt real bad. What if that happens? What if you get so hurt, you can't get up?*

Kalin thought about that fer a moment, and his mood darkened some, and the fatigue that he'd somehow held at bay began to re-etch its cost upon his face. He threw on a little more wood and prodded the pieces until they rested where the coals were hottest. Flames emerged, but they didn't spring much to life. Rather, they kept close to the fuel, dark tongues occasionally tinged with yellow releasin their melancholy smoke to the shaft overhead. Though not all the smoke. Enuf black air stayed behind to keep Kalin's and Landry's noses runnin, puttin a sting too in their eyes. Were it not for the warmth, they might've done without the fire altogether, like there was somethin wrong with it, wrong with even its light, a dullness and odor vergin on extinction.

After Tom died, I didn't ride Navidad no more, Kalin said, pokin the fire with the leg of a chair. *Not Mouse either. I'd go by the paddock every day, but I lacked the courage to sneak them out. I missed Tom for the friend he was but also for how he made possible who I could be just by bein around him, laughin at all the stupidness that goes on. And he sure was one heckuva rider. He'd say the same thing: you get bucked off, you get back on, and I guess when you can't . . .* Kalin still didn't finish his thought. He tossed the charred chair leg into the fire instead.

Then you're dead?

Yeah, I think so. Then you're dead.

It was Landry's turn now to brood over the black stir of smoke that continued to devour the low flames.

Poor Cavalry, she said after a while, and at least that was out, what had privately plagued them both since they'd heard the gunshots.

Useless, Kalin grunted. *A useless killin.*

I can't believe we even saw what we saw, Landry continued, her eyes waterin not just from the smoke, smearin the disappearin flame.

That's your problem, Kalin said gruffly, his eyes blacker than smoke.

I guess so. It weren't lost on Landry how upset he was.

I didn't mean it harsh like it just sounded, Kalin added. *I only meant that sometimes not believin what's right there in front of you can be a problem.* Kalin stood up abruptly. *Back in a sec.*

Bring more ice!

Kalin didn't respond. Again Landry took note of how he moved, how he'd even drank his cocoa, fed the fire: clunky, like his limbs couldn't carry on the conversation they was intended to have with each other.

When he returned, he brought no ice. Landry asked him if he'd seen Tom, and Kalin grunted somethin she took fer a no before turnin to his sovereign cause: the horses, massagin them, goin over their backs and legs for sores and wounds, checkin the water in their bowls, layin out handfuls of timothy and alfalfa, some bran mash with molasses and salt too, usin his right hand to brush them out again, seein how his left hand remained a mess, even attendin to Jojo, and talkin to all of them throughout. It takes a special kind of creativeness to know how to talk to a horse in a way a horse can hear.

And exhausted as he was, that much was obvious, Kalin still wouldn't lie down. He'd get as far as sittin down on his blanket and then he'd just dart out of the mine again, more and more worried about Tom. Exhausted as she was, Landry couldn't help but stay awake too, gettin more and more worried about Kalin.

Maybe the storm took him? he said one of the times when he returned.

You think a storm can take a ghost?

Maybe I should go after him.

Don't you dare.

For Landry, it was somethin awful and odd to see this kid so bereft over her dead brother, especially when set against her own grievin over Tom's passin, what seemed a long time ago though it weren't but weeks, and then, like that, to see Kalin return no longer agitated, just tired, and plenty relieved.

Tom's back.

Right here, right beside you? Landry sat up.

He says he don't like mines. He's by the entrance.

He's dead! What does he care about mines?

He looks cold too.

Then tell him to come sit by our fire.

Tried that. He says that's a different kind of warm that don't work on him.

You're just makin this up as you go, ain't you?

Pretty much.

I believe that.

You catch on fast.

Kalin, there's somethin I haven't told you yet, but I need you to believe it because I don't believe it, and I swear I ain't makin it up.

Go on then, Kalin said, flutterin his lips some as he squatted down close to their smokey fire, hands out, no doubt to recoup some of the warmth he'd lost by leavin the mind, the mine!, but also likely to let whatever Landry had goin on in her head seem more bearable to share if he weren't too focused on her. Kalin even lowered his head and rubbed the back of his neck, and why Landry, she did like the way the back of his neck looked right then, and his hands too, Kalin had beautiful hands, even the one that was all blistered. And just for this sight of him, Landry near didn't bring up what she knew she'd better bring up; fortunately, and this is thanks to her momma and her departed daddy and her brothers, she also had enuf understandin of the truth in her young heart to know that when the truth comes, it always comes first, and often with loss too, before it offers any gains. Still, Kalin sure did have beautiful hands.

Russel's dead. There, she'd done it.

How's that again? And Kalin sure looked up hard then. Gone was the pretty sight of his neck, his hands. Landry had even sighed a tiny bit as their softness departed; she couldn't help herself and for some reason even got to thinkin of the Porch paddocks where all this had started, and then of that delapidated barn, imaginin the doors blown off, the ruf too, and then all the railins shocked down, and the place made a field again, with tall grass, so tall you could hide in there as long as you liked, where no one would see you or anyone you was with, with somethin like a moan rollin along with the breeze. But Landry's little sigh and whatever thoughts were mingled in with it, maybe her way of tryin to run from what she'd finally brought up, was cut short by the severity of Kalin's stare, now near brighter and blacker too than the fire smolderin between them.

That's what Egan told me, she stammered. *He said you and me was wanted for cuttin his throat.*

He said you and me cut Russel's throat?! That's what he said?!

I didn't believe him.

Why on earth would we do that? Cut the throat of that bewildered boy? He said that? Now Kalin looked confused.

That's why I ran like I did, why I was so darned scared. They looked like they was gonna do to me what they said you'd done to Russel.

Me? I thought you said he said we did it?

Egan did single you out. He figured you was the throat cutter. Though I guess that might still make me an accomplice.

Kalin then seemed to relax some. *That explains some them shootin at us. Shootin at us over Navidad and Mouse never did make sense.*

Mouse snorted then, like he'd heard and understood what Kalin had just said. And maybe he had. Mouse was full of ornery mysteries. Then Navidad and Jojo went ahead and snorted too because they sure as heck understood Mouse.

Sorry, friends, Kalin even said to them, and Landry shook her head, smilin some, as the craziness of this Kalin kid struck her all over again.

I told Egan he was lyin, but he sure seemed dead set on his version of things.

Even if it is true, how did it come to be true? We sure didn't do it.
Ask Tom?
He'll tell me it don't work like that.
What if I ask him?

Kalin never did understand the feelin that came over him when Tom had vanished. He'd gotten tenser and tenser, while at the same time feelin increasinly detached from everythin in a way that left no space fer anyone else, not Landry, not even hisself, maybe not even the horses. Now, though, standin at the mouth of the mine, even in that cold, made colder by a continuous boreal breeze, Kalin could at last relax some. He was beside his friend again. Well, technically Tom was squattin beside Ash, the two of them balanced easily enuf on the dangerous slope rushin away from the mine entrance. He was either surveyin the far side of the canyon or scannin the canyon floor below. The valley, though, where Orvop lay, held no interest for him.

Landry would like to know—

I heard her, Tom snapped back. *You was right: it don't work like that.*

Kalin watched Tom remove his black hat then, like there was still rain clingin to it, though Kalin had never seen anythin earthly cling to Tom, and anyway the rain had stopped hours ago, and the air kept gettin crisper and clearer, and everythin that was nearby, from rock to tufts of determined grass, sparkled in the cold.

What is it? Kalin asked.

Tom was now studyin his hat, and fer a moment Kalin thought he detected there a delicacy of blue-gray frost, but then it flickered away as Tom resettled it back on his head, right as a blast of lightnin seared away everythin, a reminder of what the heavens can at any moment take, and easily too, followed not long after by thunder underscorin that point.

Landry arrived only to jump back.

It's just weather, Kalin reminded her.

I got real worried, Kalin, Tom said then. *Slippin behind like I did.*

Tom, you know where we was. We had to keep goin.

I know it. Tom slapped the air for no reason Kalin could make sense of. *The farther from the horses I got, the less I could remember. But I couldn't go no faster. It was like Ash and me were wadin up a river set against us.*

What's he sayin? Landry demanded.

Hush a moment! Kalin snapped. *Tom, what couldn't you remember?*

Where I was. What I was doin. Even who I was. I felt sure me and Ash was gonna fall off this mountain. Tom paused as if to gather up the words or

321

his courage for the next part. *Down there* . . . Tom extended a long finger aimed at the bottom of the canyon. *There ain't no ground to stop me.*

How do you mean?

It goes on forever.

The vision chilled Kalin worse than the cold. He told Landry then how the farther Tom got from the horses, the worse it got for him. Tom nodded at Kalin's assessment.

You mean from Navidad and Mouse?

What else other horses are we talkin about?! Tom snapped at his sister. And Kalin repeated for Landry what her brother had just said, minus the snap.

But what about Jojo?! Landry seemed pretty ticked. *Or me for that matter?! And what about Egan sayin Russel is dead?!*

He didn't mention Jojo or you or even me.

How come?

The gall of this girl, Tom groaned. Even Ash seemed to whicker in agreement.

You know how you can see and hear me but Landry can't? Tom asked Kalin then.

Kalin nodded.

Well, I see things you can't.

Kalin didn't think Tom just meant stuff like the hunters he'd seen across the canyon earlier. *Bad things?*

Tom nodded.

Now what's he sayin? Landry weren't gonna let up.

He's tellin me he sees things we can't, he told her.

Bad things? she asked.

Scares me almost as bad as fallin, Tom responded, tryin to force some kind of smile, which weren't a pretty sight. *And the torch you seen me carry?* Tom continued. *By its light I can see even more things.*

Beyond the canyon, well south of Orvop, another flash suddenly cast into silhouette distant crags and peaks, seeminly caked in ash, until darkness again stole away this vision, with thunder, many moments later, assurin them that what they'd seen weren't no dream.

At least the storm's headin away from us, Landry whispered.

Another's on the way, Tom said, which Kalin passed along to Landry.

Landry thought that over. *Tell him he better come on inside with us. Sit by the fire. And even if the fire don't help and we don't matter a stitch, that's where the horses are at. All the horses.*

Tom peered over his shoulder at the entrance of the mine but didn't budge much.

What? Kalin weren't no idjit. *Out with it then.* Kalin could see plain and clear by Tom's expression that what was terrifyin below weren't nothin compared to what waited in the mountain.

How'd you find this place? Tom asked.

Whadya mean how'd I find this place?

He wants to know how you found the mine? Landry demanded. *Why?*

I was just explorin, Kalin answered Tom.

But that ain't the all of it, is it?

Tom was right, but Kalin had to think about it a sec before he remembered. *I heard a story about a cave that became a mine that was haunted.*

Cannon Cornaby, self-billed as an amateur historian when he weren't managin the Payson Smith's Food & Drug, would take a great deal of pleasure in recountin the various stories that circumambulate this particular location, especially to Ron Welch, Gladdis Beaumont, Christi Call too, and Veronica Lasseter, not only recallin the first year of production, 1902, as well as the last, 1917, but detailin as well the ore body, tabular, the materials, smithsonite and sphalerite, if mainly dwellin on why it had closed, what many miners had begun to sense. Shelby Jensen, on the other hand, also in Payson then, and also at the Smith's Food & Drug, this in 1999, would happily tell Cannon Cornaby whenever she saw him, and she saw him quite often because they was married, that the only reason the Awides Mine shut down was *because there weren't nothin of worth in that crumbly part of the mountain.* Shelby Jensen was a geologist. *The thing is, Shelby,* Cannon Cornaby would still gently object, *just like Payson can't, just like Orvop can't, when we're talkin about Isatch Canyon, Kaieneewa in particular, what with Squaw Peak, we too can't get away from the Timpanogos Indians, the Katanogos Indians, and what was done to them.* Shelby Jensen didn't quibble with that. Nor would her various friends includin Kali Morales, Naomi Dennison, and even Sharon Aldonas. We'll get to Sharon Aldonas later.

You didn't tell me this place was haunted! Landry looked pretty aghast too. *Answer me, Tom Gatestone, is it haunted?*

Makes my skin crawl, Tom answered her. *And I don't even have skin.*

Tom says he just don't wanna go in.

Hmph. Landry weren't havin any of it. *I don't give a fig if it's haunted. It's warm, and I'm too tired now for fear.*

Over Tom's protestations that he could hear her just fine, Kalin repeated Landry's words, exactly like she'd said it, even as Landry was turnin to make good on her declaration and head back inside, only to abruptly turn back.

Tell him too that I miss him, Landry blurted out then, like sayin so was really the most terrifyin thing about that night, and for Landry maybe it was.

She misses—

I told you I can hear her.

I get it! You can hear her! Kalin suddenly barked back, loud enuf and sharp enuf that even Landry flinched, and Tom fer sure flinched. *But your little sister, whether you like it or not, likes to hear me askin you the question like she asked it. It allows her to see that what's on her mind is gettin communicated right, and so in turn it lets her see that what's on your mind is gettin communicated right back to her. Is that so hard for you to understand?*

Tell him to get in here with us now, Landry ordered Kalin then, no doubt emboldened by Kalin's words, words that had nailed near perfect how she was feelin about the whole matter. *And if he don't come with us then I'll know him to be a nidderin ninny even when he was dead.*

My lord and Savior, that girl! Tom howled. *The absolute gall!*

Your sister says—

He heard me, Landry said with a scoff.

And Kalin stumbled after Landry as she retreated to their chamber, still abright with that glowerin firelight and oily smoke, made warmer still, and more welcomin too, by the horses' calm.

He comin with us? Landry asked in the softest whisper.

Yeah, he's comin.

And where it could accurately be said that Tom's step did fer a moment stutter upon the threshold to that place, Ash went right on in. Didn't need no blindfoldin neither, nor a treat. He just lowered his magnificent head and plodded ahead, beside his Tom the whole way, until a moment later Ash was standin beside Mouse, Navidad, and Jojo, and Kalin was pointin out to Tom a place by the fire that Landry was already happily arrangin for her dead brother.

But Tom wouldn't sit down. Instead he reached fer that scabbarded brand that once again, as he drew it forth, immediately burst into a strange ocherous blaze.

That's when Kalin saw for hisself why Tom was so afraid.

Friday

Chapter Eleven

"Not even the dead could get their stories straight"

WWhatever you've heard about what happened next, one thing's fer darned sure: consistent with her natural inclination as well as talents, Landry, as midnight fell, fell too, fast asleep. Exhaustion far outweighed any stories of phantasms relayed by a boy spattin with the air, with any lingerin fears put to obeisance by the knowledge that Landry's beautiful and fierce Jojo would alert her should any spectral or otherwise mischievous misdoins intent on doin her harm show themselves. Sure, while restin her head upon her saddle, Landry had still kept one eye open so the other could rest, switchin them up every few breaths, so the one that was just open could rest, and the one now open could stand guard, even if somewhere in between both stayed closed, and that was that, how we all fall prey to sleep's beautiful betrayal.

Did Landry dream? It's a fair question, and while somewhat debated, the answer's a resoundin *Heck yes!* She twitched her way through the night, sometimes peelin back her lips to snarl, sometimes gnashin her teeth, though her arms and legs remained frozen, bound in coils of constrictin dark, even if her fingers still tried to claw at somethin too near and complicated to merely weaponize. When the liberation of mornin finally greeted her, aside from the cause of her abrupt awakenin, her stiffness, the pain in her cheeks, her tongue feelin briefly scalded too, which we'll get to soon enuf, she with great smiles indicated she'd had the most restful sleep and recollected no disturbances.

Later, though, she would come to recall with near-violent astonishment the siege she'd endured durin those long hours. One memory commenced with a wrong turn, the worst possible wrong turn, the result of which found them all lost. Gone was Kalin. Gone were the horses. Gone was even Jojo. He'd got loose, and instead of thinkin to liberate hisself by followin where the frosty canyon air was clearest, he'd wandered deeper into the mine. The rope gate that Kalin had fashioned weren't there no more. By agility, luck, and most certainly instincts of self-preservation enacted by the dreamer's mind, Jojo eluded the immediate vertical shaft, wanderin still deeper into the mine, growin more bewildered at each new branchin passageway until he was finally compressed to a shiverin halt by no wall nor overhead limitation but by a lightlessness that would not, could not, relent.

Into that labyrinthine trap Landry had hurled herself, yellin for him, even as she also found herself more and more turned around. In the dream, she did find Jojo. She sobbed at his touch, his warm breath on her hair as she clung to his neck. On his back, she was determined to ignite a flare, flick on a flashlight, strike flint to steel. But though she'd imagined each of these options to the point of solidity, her hands remained empty. And so, given no choice, unless you count stillin yourself until such a time that you and your hooved friend become a figure of stone, a petrified monument to all that cannot be traversed, ascended, or navigated, forever imprisoned amidst the rubble of that long lost enterprise of ore, Landry and Jojo struck out down them black passageways, slowly at first and then pickin up the pace, defiant in their collective will to break free of the darkness and confusion, if panic still found them, ready to take them down, which was when Tom's whistlin, the most beautiful sound you've ever heard, suddenly appeared to guide them home.

And that was just one of Landry's later re-encounters with her own capacity to invent things when fear's begun to prevail but where love is not absent either.

Not that most folks take much interest in Landry's noctural inventions. After all, what generally gets the most attention is what Tom with that fiery branch of his revealed to Kalin, and how soon after they was surrounded.

Jobie Leveridge, from St. George but on this occasion in Las Vegas enjoyin the Circus Circus Hotel & Casino breakfast buffet, would declare, what he would also eventually insist on to Stuart Rasband, Rusty Glasset, Cary Swindle, and even to Sherry Hindmarsh, and with his fork stabbed through not one, not two, but three sausages, that it was at best speculative, what *Kalin hisself must've dreamt up,* because there was no question Kalin was on the brink of exhaustion, twice that of Landry Gatestone's, at least, given the number of times he'd gone up and down Aster Scree, sharin too much of his food too, *plus the awful burden of leadership.* Shawn Winnie Dulle, from Carson City and at that very same table with Jobie, would find hisself inclined to agree that Kalin was surely fit for sleep, but he also had to say that *real fear, the kind that squeezes out whatever adrenaline you possess yet,* why that might've helped drag him into a reckonin sleep couldn't contain. Matty Goforth, also from Vegas, also at that table, would cluck his tongue and, drinkin more of his coffee, hold forth that *what Tom was seein in them chewy minutes, what Kalin then was seein, was in itself proof of what was bein seen.* Jobie Leveridge, who by this point had stuffed all three of them sausages in his mouth, would stop chewin then and give Shawn Willie Dulle a look that might as well've been an eye roll, though it was more vulgar. Shawn Willie Dulle, however, paid Jobie no mind: *Matty's talkin about the Riggs boy.*

Though before gettin to that, *the Riggs boy,* it's perhaps worth an extra second to consider a different kind of gatherin, a different kind of dialogue, what has been thrown around plenty by them wild, fluent artist types, like Nastasia Claybaugh, Melissa Grant, Mina Berry, Carla Leffert, and Justin Voight, with this particular gettin-together-to-mostly-talk takin place on the shores of Bear Lake in 2002: two couples, four colleagues, all from Draper, all graduates of the University of Utah, but by the time of this vacation already profession-scattered to Dallas, Palo Alto, Cambridge, and Princeton. Kim Kapp was goin on about how *those gates gaze upon you, no matter the manner of your journey, whether through sleep, hallucination, misery, a ghost, or your own death.*

Her husband, Hyrum Kapp, would prove more interested in the greetin: *Instead of a Sibyl of Cumae or Tiresias or Virgil, or even a Dante, lore guided Kalin's footsteps—*

Don't forget Tom, his wife would interrupt. *Tom lit the way.*

That's true, Hyrum Kapp would concede incorrectly. *What intrigues me, though, after all these years, is how the one to step forth and translate the passages of that place, that place apart, I think you called it that, Kim, was no part of a tradition we are comfortable with in this country.*

Tilly Syme would speak up then, sensin the conversation headin toward her neck of the woods: *You're referrin to the oracular?*

Hyrum Kapp would nod. *The lost stairs of speech.*

Karlin Syme would join in now: *But for whatever insubstantiality surrounds the spectral congruence about to amass, especially when we consider the known and or altered personages about to come forth—*

Includin Tom's father, Tilly Symes would interrupt.

—what's of note is how the cost of speech was not blood, Karlin Syme would continue.

Per Homer or Virgil, Kim Kapp would add.

Right! Karlin Syme would exclaim. *That place took no interest in sacrificed bulls, lambs, or an infertile cow.*

The price of speech was passage, Karlin Syme would finish. And they'd nod some more, drinkin their beverages and starin at the clear blue waters. How was it that none of them had had children?

Ms. Melson, who'd earned her PhD at Isatch U, with her dissertation on Thamyris bearin the fancy title *The Greatest Art Forgets,* would one day in the company of both Mr. Caracy Rudder, who had also earned multiple degrees at IU, with one of his dissertations focusin on huntin and field dressin as depicted by Homer as well as contemporary Utah sages, and Mrs. Annserdodder, who'd gotten no such degrees but remained a much-loved high school teacher throughout her life, partly because she was such a carin listener; to these two Ms. Melson would point out that to summon the dead, Odysseus had had to dig a well shaft with sides a forearm wide and surround it with milk, honey, wine, water, and handfuls of white barley. *The dead are attracted to milk and honey, but to speak they must delibate animal blood,* Ms. Melson would explain. Odysseus was required to fill his pit with the blood of a sacrificed black ewe and ram. *Kalin, though, had to pay a different price.*

Whereupon Mrs. Annserdodder would interrupt her friend: *Wasn't Tom the one who paid the price?*

But Ms. Melson would wave away the objection: *Landry, Tom, Kalin, they all paid a price.*

And Mr. Caracy Rudder would nod: *No one talks to the dead for free.*

It's hard to say whether the light thrown from Tom's brand was orange or red or by that point somethin darker. Kalin would describe it to Landry as all of those hues but also as an illumination that was without origin and unnaturally clear. Or as he put it: *There but not there. The color shiftin.* Partly this distinction between the light we know and the light Tom's brand cast is due to how what boy and ghost were seein was different even if the two experiences were still compacted into one.

As Tom described to Kalin what he was seein, Kalin beheld their surroundins expand, the walls fallin away like black mists, the ceilin risin into nothinness, with those unfathomable depths presented soon after offerin no hint of a moon or celestial history; the ground beneath their boots beyond the reach of texture. No Goshen here.

Kalin, though, could still see Landry beside their miserable fire. Though where Kalin should've slept, there now stood an enormous elm tree, with large boughs overhangin all, crowded by a risin confusion of smoke, the near immobility of its dark leaves warnin Kalin that he was far from any Outside his dreams were better off pursuin.

Nor did the strangeness stop there: beyond the sleeper, beyond the tree waited a crick bed awash with waters as black as the remembrances its endless ripples preserved, matched only by a more entire darkness risin up beyond, like an immense mountain you'd've called an abyss if it weren't already surpassin heights far exceedin any imaginable sum. It were no comfort, either, that in the shadow of this obvious apparition the tree appeared dead, and Landry seemed paler than snow, colder than marble, somethin amiss too with her face, particularly her temples, as if in this grave stillness she was already perforated by an emptiness that grew only more profound, with every breath that she seemed less and less capable of takin. Was that a red squirrel beside her?

Keep the horses close to you! Tom warned Kalin. *They're too much of life for what's here!*

The horses had already begun to shuffle around, either to run from or face what they could not see. Only Ash turned to regard the passage that Kalin had roped off. Except the ropes were now gone. Furthermore, the passage weren't much of a passage but rather a great arch, as if fashioned out of generations of tusks.

In 2027, in a Boise breakfast spot called The Jupiter, Holly Brereton and Reen Nakamura would argue inventively, obstreperously, about whether, to their minds, the gateway was a thing fashioned out of ivory or antlers and would nearly come to blows over whether the tree was really an elm. It's maybe of some inconsequential interest that on that day above the counter hung a placard with a quote by a fella named Ogden Nash: *The door of a bigoted mind opens outwards so that the only result of the pressure of facts upon it is to close it more snugly.*

Pointless as this aside might seem, concernin a dispute over the nature of an arch and a tree, it does get a little at how, outside of the mine, Tom's brand had provided for Kalin a beacon, a source of confidence, inspiration even, and fer sure a way to remember, while within the mountain, its increasin dimness only served to conjure doubt, forgetfulness, and finally despair.

And that was just fer starters: inexplicit movement had begun to whirl around them. Some would've felt nausea, as if deep in the bowels of a lightless hull tossed about by an immense storm; others would've surrendered to a sense of escalatin dizziness culminatin in unconsciousness.

In Kalin it stirred up somethin even more unfortunate. Paul Pace, from Ogden but by this point at Columbia University, would say only that *It's not a bad idea to remember feelins are an experience of deep ancestral time. The primal feelins exceed what even a century of life can explicate. The ancient ones have roots millions of years old.* Fer sure Kalin was overwhelmed by what was tryin to possess them, but he didn't get lightheaded. And that's because in some ways Kalin felt right at home.

The horses had started throwin up their heads then, but Tom's subsequent calmin of Ash, because even Ash had grown upset which incidentally took him some steps away from Kalin, had the added effect of helpin to calm both Navidad and Jojo some. Or so it appeared to Kalin. Mouse weren't all that bothered. He was just hungry again.

Veldon Brower, originally from Lehi but eventually landin in Caguas, Puerto Rico, partly in response to Paul Pace, and overdiscussed in a number of phone calls with Gaylene Zobell and Phenprapa Devey, as well as LeRoy Kriek and Nicole Beesley, would in 2006 wonder aloud about the cost of emotional perception. Any perception. What do we pay for just seein the path ahead? What do we pay for just seein our reflection in the mirror? What do we pay for somethin that's not ahead but will nonetheless traverse the approachin intersection at any given future second? What for that matter do we pay for seein somethin that's not there at all? And in turn what liberties do such inventions gain us? Or take from us? *What do we create when we know the voice informin us is not our own? Beauty or Horrors?* Veldon Bower would ask. *Or both?*

Fer sure both beauty and ample horrors confronted the boys now. We'll never know how Tom experienced that place, and we can fairly say that Kalin, even if he'd been vested with a firsthand vision of the dead, would not likely have been able to meet their parley alone. That said in the moments that followed they would together grasp the dynamics of the comin assault: Kalin quick understood that only his corporeal presence could part the siege, with Tom, by the movement of his infernal torch, directin Kalin to where he should stand next.

And if that weren't enuf, Kalin did in fact begin to glimpse for hisself, here and there, molderin shapes reachin out to him.

The Dead had arrived, and more were on the way. It was as if the darkness itself were now porous, and through such infinite stomata there now squirmed the aftermaths of so many lives. The air itself trembled to accommodate so desperate an incursion.

What do they want? Kalin hissed in disgust.

The horses!

Someone now emerged, and Kalin felt firsthand then how absence can give way to form. Kalin's heart pounded harder as if in response to how easily the rivers in his own veins could cease to flow. And then Tom's brand failed completely, the dark red flickerin away like the last drops of blood drawn down into a black devourin sand.

Tom declared that there was a woman before them. Her name was Pia Isan. At least that was one of her names. Isan worked too. So did Isa. She was tellin Tom that they'd never had horses in here before. Tom told Kalin that a little chipmunk sat upon her shoulder.

They think we've brought the horses for them.

You mean like a sacrifice? Kalin asked, alarmed. *Like heck they're touchin the horses!*

She says only horse meat will get the dead to speak.

She's a liar. Kalin was already drawin Navidad and Mouse closer, tryin to leave. *She's talkin to you, ain't she? And you're talkin to me.*

Hold on, Tom said. *She says there's another way to hear what the dead have to say.*

We're leavin.

She says your momma's here.

Kalin's blood froze up somethin awful then as he twisted hisself around in every possible direction to see somethin he'd never see, to awaken hisself, to free hisself from that ugliest of thoughts.

She sees my mom? Kalin finally begged of Tom.

Your momma's tryin to tell you somethin.

What?!

Isa needs somethin from us first.

She can't touch the horses! Kalin near yelled, exasperated. He felt both at liberty to sprint free with Navidad and Mouse as well as nailed to the ground, the horses too, all of them welded in place through boots and hooves.

After a bit of mumblin on Tom's part, which at least gave Kalin a clear idea of what Landry had had to put up with, with his own mumblin with Tom that is, Tom laid it out plain and simple: Tom and Kalin just had to promise to take Pia Isan to the Crossin.

She says her way is with the horses, Tom said.

That's it? That's fine. We know this mountain. We know the way up it. Now tell me why my mom's here. Tell me what she's sayin.

Isa don't believe you. She's already lived one life of broken promises.

I don't break my promises.

She says this time if a promise gets broken . . . Tom's voice trailed off.

What?

I'm not sure her deal's worth takin.

Despite the pit in his stomach, that his momma might be dead, that there was a deal he could make to hear her speak, Kalin had had enuf of the unseen. *Then we're not takin it.*

She can hear you.

You're welcome to come, Kalin addressed the air. *What's one more ghost among friends?*

Very funny.

But that's it.

She says death don't work like that.

Don't you two make the perfect pair.

My brother Evan's here! And my daddy too!

Tom, Kalin warned his friend. *Don't let that make a bit of difference to you.*

But it does.

Tom held up his hand then. More was happenin. Kalin's ears couldn't catch nothin, and even though it served no purpose, he was squintin extra his eyes.

*U*h-huh, Tom grunted, and then after a moment asked the air: *How's that again?* A bit more mumblin followed, then some emphatic nods, before Tom declared loud and clear: *I do. Yes, I do. I make that promise to you.*

Suddenly Tom's brand was alight again, still but a flicker, except this time it weren't no red nor even orange but a dark and perilous violet. Meleager's brand. And then like thunder answerin lightnin, an awful crack briefly sundered the dark.

Tom, what did you just do?

Tom seemed extra ashen, his eyes pools of black.

She's comin with us.

What did you promise her?

She gets the freedom she deserves when the horses get theirs.

Kalin wanted to know more, but Tom's eyes went wet, or looked wet, and then he either coughed hard once or it was a sob. *Evan! Dad!*

Kalin learned near nil about his friend's sciamachy with the souls of his unspent heart, if souls is what they were; though accordin to Tom, a flood of early settlers had already got in the way of his family reunion, them original Utah pioneers, ebbin and flowin around them before givin way before the Indigenous people of these lands, who seemed at once mournful, amused, desirous, scornful, and even curious. Even if Kalin couldn't keep up, Tom somehow knew them all by name.

There was Briggham Young. There was Captain Howard Stansbury and George A. Smith and Barney Ward. There was also the likes of Isaac Higbee, General Daniel H. Wells, Captains George D. Grant and Andrew Lytle, Captain John Scott, Jehu Blackburn too, and Jim Bridger and Dr. James Blake, plus Alexander Williams, Sorenus Taylor, Frank Woodard, George Boyd, Hosea Stout, David Fulmer, plus Dick, Judson, Shell, and Irwin Stoddard, and William G. Pettey. Someone named Dimmick Huntington claimed he didn't want nothin, just to open their ears, which he shouted. Others too started shoutin about how they weren't there for anythin either, men like John Rufus Stoddard, Richard A. Ivie, and Jerome Zobriski, and to prove their point they even tried to spit on the horses.

There weren't no Joseph Mith. Tom would've noticed him, but before he got a chance to ask one of the many Church elders who'd appeared, who showed nothin but kindness toward the horses, they was all replaced by the simpler folks who'd planted fields and woven fabrics and built homes and taught in schools. Some talked of pantaloons, shawls, and percussion caps. Others bemoaned the absence of lead balls, kegs of powder. One just wanted a badger-hair shavin brush.

Then came the dairy farmers, the honey farmers, them poetic hearts who tried to harvest a mood and bake the best bread with it. Until out of the moldy dark plodded forth two who seemed to crave Tom's attention as much as they also seemed driven toward him like petulant third graders approachin the principal.

Here before Tom stood none other than Garrison Porch and Alfred Gatestone, as hardy as they were scarred, in the full of their lives but burdened by the untold consequences of those lives. Their hats they wore level, but their vests were unbuttoned, and their pants, like their gloves, were rent here and there even if the holes offered no glimpse of flesh. Soon they was joined by a third, none other than Wild Bill Hickman, killer and decollater of men and women, maybe children too.

They each stepped forward to lament what a foolish thing Tom had just done, to bind hisself to an Injun. Tom, to his credit, smiled first, then laughed a little, then laughed outright.

I'm so darned tired of your bullcrap, but even you three are welcome to come along. If you dare.

Garrison Porch tried to say how it was awful that such small enmities had produced such long-lastin hateful behavior, *but you can never trust a Gatestone to do the right thing.* Alfred Gatestone also lamented the animosities constantly curdlin their friendship, similarly suggestin it was them Porches to blame. Wild Bill Hickman swore only that he would never follow no Injun, even if that Injun was only followin horses, which if he couldn't ride, he might as well eat.

More Porches and Gatestones came forward then, complainin about the poor qualities of the other, bringin up all sorts of stuff, includin that Applebaum Snake Altercation as well as that damnable cherry orchard, which was really an apricot orchard until it became an apple orchard, and so on. Not even the dead could get their stories straight or release themselves from the foul bonds of disagreements as recent as the Gatliner Realty Dispute, the Harvest-Meadow Development, and the Ridgeline Meadow Estates Claim and so on and so on.

Then more tribespeople stepped forward to gaze coldly in Tom's eyes, whether persecuted or not by Gatestones, Hickmans, or Porches; or victimized by each other or subsequent others, generationally; whether they was the Lagunas, bearded ones, the Arrow Reeds, Timpanogos, Katanogos, Snake Shoshone, and eventually the Utes, though they was more Colorado folks, wantin to get the heck out of Utah; with the likes of the Capote, Grandriver, Mouche, Tabaquache, Uintah, Weeminuche, and Yampa offerin their thanks to Pia Isan before regardin the horses, those equine intelligences bein the only reason they'd come forth, to get some glimpse of beauty in that black pit.

Many more followed, includin the one hundred and two killt at the Battle Crick Massacre on March 5, 1849, though at one point ninety-eight was declared the number and then later one hundred and forty-nine, includin women and children. Tom couldn't keep up with who came after that, describin them only as folks cravin the sight of Navidad, Mouse, and Jojo and even Ash. Enslaved Indians still lookin for their mommas and daddies thought the horses might tell them where to look. Their names flowed by like water, and maybe that was an okay thing. The names Tom could account for included Turuni-anchi, Walkara, Sowiette, Kanosh, Tabby, Arropeen, Washakie, Tintic, Sanpitch, as well as Kone, Blue Shirt, Ankartewets, Pernetta, and Pick. Old Bishop, he was laughin about sometimes wanderin the banks of Orvop River until the horses got him back here, with Bishop Whit-ney standin by him too, and then more folks with names like Kinead, Reese, Rockwood, and Moorman swept by. Juan Rivera was in there too, as well as Domínguez and Escalante.

Those who wished Tom to fail refused his invitation to join him, while those who wished Tom to succeed said that the horses had no chance and they would not risk what was familiar on a chanceless journey. Some refused because the torments that Tom had chained hisself to might in turn apply to any who accompanied him. Even here consequences continued to shape the course of their bent eternity.

Tom grew more resigned before such insubstantial appraisers of his character and vow. Kalin felt like he was at a weddin, or really the aftermath of one, where Tom was the groom. Fer his part, Tom looked thinner too, more drawn out, maybe even taller. And that hubcap of a buckle he wore seemed oilier and blacker, aboil with bright slashes of serpents born of indeterminate silver. Even Tom's hair and boots seemed blacker, and that went for his brows and eyes too, though his Stetson seemed salted with gray. At certain angles Tom's face seemed older, how he might've looked if he'd been afforded a life where older was an option. It was eerie to behold how not even the dead were beyond the reach of age.

Not that Tom's new look slowed down the parade any. Like his own voice, small and fast, they clamored dense and deliberate, carryin between them the agony of a present they'd lost sight of. Not that some folks didn't arrive calm and wistful, grateful just to glimpse the horses. Others, however, wavered so badly, it was like they was drunk on the same loathsome box of wine. Still, more came heavy with anger and violence in their hearts. The worst came in confusion. Plenty came longin for love. These, though, came because they were loved:

Eden, Tom Simon, Martin Levey, Kenneth Levey, Pat and Vicki, Sara Mehan, Rory Mehan, Layton Kesner, Waltraut, Otmar, Winona Kay Howard, Adrian Gaskins, Steven Genard, Reat Underwood, Harold and Martina, David, Guacolda and Edmundo, Carl Schmidt, Audrey Schmidt, Beverly Schmidt, Harvey King, Faye King, Katya Mehdi, Darius, Sylvia and Robert Lindsay Lewis, Jenji, yoda baby and Chris, Kona Hoffert, Mary Alice Schooley and James Schooley, Wesley Gagne, Delores Lang, Sthephany, Elliott James Smith, Sandra Williams, Dot Buckley, Benjamin Dylan Harper, Jamie D. Frisbie, Jasper Nouzovsky, Elisabeth Bell, Amy Youmans, Murphy, Nunu, Roxanne and Michael Shepish, Charles Caton, Andreas Bilger, Roy Turner, and Bubba too, Franklin D. Mapes, Neal Turner, Pamela Parker, Georgia Mendoza, Bob Glaberson, Greg Sanders, John Wilson Cumming, Morag Campbell Donald Cumming, Vern Habeck, Bev Schmidt, Leona, Brian Kelly, Terry Fain, Davis Graham Anderson Jr., Cody Randall, Little P., Morris, Sam Hoff, Claire Adema, Justin Denman, Valois, Peggy Ethel Hooper, Glen Hamilton, Steve Muir, Wanderin Stars, Zişan Yazak, Dolores Marie, Esperanza C. G., Billy F., S.A.M., Jimmy L., Gregg Wadley, Grasso and Frank, Tim, Janusz, Bogusław, Phil Toone, Gary Langhans, Kathleen Shea, Andrew Phillip Owen, Haigen Terrence Pennycuick, Leila Tina Doan, Henryka, Teofil, Trixie Tumbleweed, Tad, Ralph Gervasio, the Rays, Don Behrstock, Claire E., Tristan Haegar, Jack Springer, Haley Shea, Matt King, Jay Deng, Michael Babaian, Gary, the Shirleys, both Shirleys, Stephanie too, Dolores Modine, James Kenneth Johnston, Helen Panaia, Daniel Clarence McDougall, Kelley Given, Stephanie, Jay Kirkpatrick, Koah Pelletier, MeMe, Bernie, Tony Ligl, Kelly McConahay, Dan McConahay, Bud Army, Bill Steptoe, Barb Steptoe, Audrey Blaine Magaña, Mihaela, Lucy Patterson, Gregory Eidson, Emma Allen, Jennifer Connelly, Elena, George Rosatone, Reveila Sovindotter, Ermila Nuñez, Pachita Pantoja, Celina Denogean Arredondo, Patty, Cozmo, Robert Rienstra, Mary Talerico, Amiel Giampapa, Billy P. Hutchisson II, Ian Goddard, Kelly King, Joanne, Dana Dickson, Marilyn Daskiewich, David Daskiewich, Alice Elizabeth Gracia, Hosler Lee Wall Jr., Artie Garcia, Jack Robinson, Max, Morgan, Grace, Erin, Arden Pepion, William Joseph Copson, Cassie, Tony, Edward, Beryl, Teresa, Micki, Ana, Miguel, Ricardo, John Lee Hamm, Tamar Hoffman, Nel Raymundo, Sven Gustafsson, Ingrid Weylerz Gustafsson, Anki Sundberg, Arne Larsson, Lars Gustafsson, Daniel McNeme, Candi Holzer, Rachel Stahler, Teague McCarthy, Anne Chimenti, Big Dan Pederson, Gabe Rodriguez, Red Pederson, Uncle Bill, Clint Rickman, Carson Hunt, Andres Cabrera, Monroe Aboyoun, Eugene Fest, Crockett and Blake, Kenneth Roman Range, Sean Philip O'Malley, Luiz da Silva, Luiz Vieira Faria, Bob Lorain, Ron Bartholomew, Qwysa bolti Rivera, Wybie Watson, Nevaeh Young, Jillian Nunley, Cooper Horton, Joseph Sharp, Eli Bryant, Rumor Olivier, Thia, Jesica, Adela, Charlie, Noemi, Adam Cope, Gabriel Benson, Karen Thompson, Cecilia Bruton, Landon Sommerfeld, Zach Rodgers, Joe, Ruez too, Joanne Peuser Dunkin, Henry Julius Kokosenski, Sheila Marie Kokosenski, Rachel Stella, Danielle Yost, Barbara Katz, Morton Singer, Hendrick Willem Tak, Rebecca Roberts, Kevin Crank, Roger Begay, Spencer, Richard Aaron Leeper, Isaac Michael Bartkovsky, Lilian Ruskin, Natasha chichilnisky-Heal, Sarah Sprinkles, Keith and Amy Sprague, Ava Mick, Ryan McBride, Roberto and Agrippino, Caitlin, Roland, Bones Jones, and Jack, Sævar Þór Carlsson, Þór Sævarsson Carlsson, Louis Jurney, John Hatch, Thomas Wyatt, Dan too, Cameron, Andrew Jamison, Mark Thomas, Clyde Ward, Julie Ritchie, Renee Frederick Krites, Drake Kent, Ronny Kaiser, Bernard Pierre, Kathleen and Richard Fudali, Pam, Des, Ken and Mary, Tinman, Alice and Jim McCormick, Keith and Carol Cutbill, Brittany Knupper, Buck Paul, John, Mitzi, Rosser and Mabel, Alisa, Julie, Asri, Angela, Lee, Trigger, Karen Felicity Angelillo, Roberta Prindiville, Marco Leon, Janina Kvedarienė, Zeferinas Jonutis, Kęstutis Nastopka, Virgilijus Dudonis, Zbignevas, Silkė, Jonathan, Enedina Maria da Silva, Cavendish, Hillary, California, Ms. Mason, Tommy, Dorothy, Adella, Edward Walker Cowell, Sadie Carcione, Wilma Cley Cerullo, Maria Aparecida de Oliveira, William David, Hulda Sjöström, Hugo Fernandez, Esther Veunes, Robert and Minnie, Emily Rose, Wayne Stuck, Lance Doeden, Jillian Pedone, Karly Chiappetta, Carolyn Mathabel, Clair Mathabel, Laverne Belk, James Homer Day, Ruth, Ercilia, Joyce, Frank, Colby, Sheela, Martín, Baby Hoffert, Harold Brown, Ian Kubik, Darin Eppler, Mara Schwartz Kent, Christopher Norris, Natalie Norris, Zak, Sandie Ryan, David Leo Pike, Fanny Lou Pike, Buzz Seaton, Harold Seaton, Simon, Melody and Sherman, Badia, Elsa, Roberto, Martha, Samuel Vega, Dan Vega, Cosmo Maxfield Felton, Roy Delbert Nelson, Myrna Loy Knight, Calvin Chamness, Toby, John Sarao, Tommy Murphy, Evan Michael Line, Alexander Sebastian Javierto, Carolina Señoron, Cody Randall Thomas, Great-Grandpa Jack, Steve Hiles, Annette Nathanielsz, Maxine Davies, Joe Lill, Matt Enright, David Feldman, Margaret Purcell, Shelly Kay Bohannon, Harriet, Vincent Devlin, Tabea, Austin Vines, Hutchie, Elizabeth Sneddon, Raymond Field, Evelyn Field, Karen, Giana, Abi and Matilda, John Arther Kendall, Nurse

Jakey, Arora, Seth, David L. Porter, Sue Hebert Porter, Irene Porter, Lewis Porter, Thelma Barker, Yoka Luelsdorf, Johnny Johnson, Rosemary Johnson, Gustavo Guarino, Jim Brinkerhoff, Rick Robertson, Naomi Smith, Thomas Conrad, Jonathan Robertson, Skittie Oi, Pamela Fabrega, Sam Turner, Richard Tardif, James Shelton, Byron, Renly, Lee Gerstenberger, Rubi, Mariquita Bontia Capuno, Betty Salerno, Kendon Parker, Dan Adams, Jesus Capuno, Reuben Galindo, Tony Micciche, Brett Bartlett, Rusty Cornelius Solvay, Soledad, Salvador, T.J., Christine and Ronald, Don and Frankie Bassin, Kay Coleman, Geoff Shatz, Paul Pokorny, Viola Freed, Hermenegildo Oliva, Geovani Padilla, Penelope Salamon, Betsy Bounds, Tim, Gerald Czerwinski, Garrett Trongo, Garett S. Sinclaire, Dale Robert McCracken, Robert Roy Rosenberg, Steven Gutt, Samantha Houlias, Shera Jean Dougherty, Jarden Troice, Scott Yeffet, Maggie, Roy Potthoff, Pop Filla, Betty Cooper, Curtis Wheeler, Bernard Jones, Michael Payon, Jacqueline Sanford, Grampy, TV, and Taylor, William Grennan, Betty Smith, Tunie Burns, Joy, Dank and Angel Beverly, Larry Meile, Angela Grace Flack, Stanley Hunter and Elva Bernice Reed, Joye Ellermeyer, Julie Turner Jacobson, Lauren Sanday, Amanda Marie Bauer, Augusta Bauer, William BAJ Bauer, Jean Lieser, Jim Lieser, Maurice Cartney, Harry Ohlfs, Heather Ohlfs, Brian Stiner, Reid Jessen, Vinson Ya, Aaron Bauer, Nina, Phillip Grace, Yolonda Bernal, Barbara Yvonne Mitchell, Lucy Rowntree, Dee, Don, Eileen, Thordis Andreasen, Jon Kristjan Simonarson, Chuprina Andrey, Nikolay, Danilov Pavel, Uncle John, Auntie Pam, Tony and Jean, Alan and Maisie, Thaxter Trafton, Clay, Stephen, Bonnie, Mary Catherine, Kelly O'Leary, Michael Silverblatt, Chelsea Smith, Mandi Webber, Ashley Eugene Lindquist, Maria da Conceição, Clifford, Stephen, Ellen, Deshka and Robert, Lynn Wood, Justin Sena, Rosalinda Castillo, Francesca Puentes, Mary Beth Cole, Delicia, Robert Hochman, Alan Keith, Ant, Jennifer Kelley, Sean Hamby, Garren Fry, Troy, Mary Reilly, Kassidi Kryzkwa, Guy Phillip Karkeet, Donna Marie Lubiarz, Scott Gerard Evans, Delphine Lubiarz Karkeet, Katrina Lubiarz Perrault, Sue, Jeremy Bacheller Sr., John Guy Bacheller, James Gay Jones, Jahseh Jeremiah, Sean Lamb, Mitzy, Cookie and BigWig, Archie, Lewis, Sheilah, Monty, Margaret Thompson, Christina, Sean, Brian, Deborah, Thomas, Linda, Louise, Poppy, Caleb, Lyndon, Liam, Danny, Felippe, Mergo, Logan, Keegan, Yordy Coste, Lois & Matt, Ann Wise, Lee Joy Davis, Oscar, Alma, Cardoza, Gabriel, Isabel, Kris, Lucas, Shannon Callahan, BJ Crawford, Carl Henk, Janet Mischianti, Scott Magill, Antonio Herrero, Joseph Pettit and Susan Tasson, Kat Paled, Oma, Vanessa Booker, Jane Flynn, Anna Odeh, Farouk Odeh, Clifford Poncho Scites, Tristan Rochelle, Herb Shaffer, Joseph Anthony Kennedy and Virginia Ann Kennedy, John Villarreal, my dad, Bjorn, Glenn, Abacus, Tylus Hoagland, Paul Armitage, Daniel Melville, Bruce Beiderbeck, Beverly, Stevie, Betty, and Walter Blodgett, Elsie Wilde, Mario Calabrese, Carlton and Leah LaGrow, Brian Stephen Johnson, Kathleen Austin, Consuelo Elliott, Marcus Almon, Max and Koda, Zarmaine, Carmine Demarco, Rocchetta Paris, Shirley Imes and Charles Imes, Jonathan Thursday Youngs, Kafka, Pamela Jenkins, Robin, Alta, Matt Butcher, Jerzy Senger, Frederick & Ruth Abbott, Tully, Steven, Tyler, Romulus, Delores, James, Peter, Syble Sue Coley, Debbie Ishie, Myrtle and Pete Samko, Tony Trimarchi, Tom Jordan, Aggie, Papaw Tommy, Joseph Arnold Harshman, Roger G. Harris and G. Quezon DeGuzman, Taylor Strait, Leah Grant, David S. Molotsky, Michael Black, Walter Wood, Pierre Gerber, Kalli Nowell, Armen Kocharian, T.J. Levey, Bonnie Brunken, Uncle Sonny, Sandra Lee Ramler-Rush, David Dufresne, Linda Sullivan, Jeni, Julie Albert, Marguerite Darmenton, Bruce Smith, Xanthippe, Stefanos, Maria, Salvatore, Carlos Castro Barahona, Frank Glover, Jr., Jim Firth, Park Don Hee, Sky, Paul, Emily, Chloe, Nathan, Edward, Paul and Dolores Proch, Gordon and Evelyn Rose, Jamie Topham, Hayley Conklin-McElroy, Ian M. Keene, Luka W Noll, William Kennedy Hastings, Wanda Ruth Brouillette-Hastings, Kyle and Elizabeth, David Kocienda, Darian Kyle Jackson, Manuel Corpuz, Ananke, Werner, Margot and Horst Clobes, Madonna, Junior and Randy Dubay, Minnie, Sylvia and Robert Lindsay Lewis, Luna, Daisy, Danny, Kenneth Recio, Mary Nunez, Marion, Milton and James Busby, Melissa Nicholas, Ax, Adam, Finn and Shrimpo, David Allen Usher, Devon, Lain, Ruby, Seth, Franky, Erin, Nova, and Karime, Phyllis Senkarik S Toad Martin, Odette O'Brien, Joan Devin, Dave Hanratty, the Maggies, Leionell Wells, Charles, Elijah, Rhea, Hugo Pereira, Marion Field, Tom Harboard, Luuk Wagner, Laika, Katherine Yerke, Crystal Bernstein, Ryan Bernstein, Kaye Bernstein, Jakub Stather, Charles W. Nolan, Eric John Wilmshurst, Barbara Thom, Teresa Loughran Whitely, Elmer Higgins McCusker, James Patrick McCusker, Seamus Goldie, Merlin, Cynthia Hughart, Dolores Marquez, Nazia Cassim, Imaan Davids, Tiger-Anne Cupido, Roderick Franklin Jones, Dan Freedman, Michael Bacon, Aron Warren, Lottie Warren, Tim Noonan, Gianna, Alfie, Koda, Lieonel Wells, Charlie Morgan, Elijah Wallace, Aurora, Radosav and Mirjana, David Mycoff, Bobbie too, Lori Ann Harris, Ann Wise . . .

And those names were just an itty bit of a much longer, impossible list, as even more flooded by, amazed by the risk Tom was takin, amused that the guarantor of Tom's wager was the scrappy kid beside him, and otherwise grateful for the presence of the horses. For their part, Navidad and Jojo and even Ash had come around to revel some in all this sprectral attention. Mouse alone stomped a hoof as if to say: *Keep movin!*

Tom always made sure Kalin stood between the dead and the horses. Fer whatever reason, somethin about Kalin kept them at bay. Tom couldn't even guess as to why. Maybe simply because Kalin was alive. Even Pia Isan made sure Tom stood between her and Kalin.

One figure who emerged looked like he'd come to the wrong place and just couldn't figure out what to do. He stood before Tom, just a-quiverin with nothin to say.

Who is he? Kalin asked.

I got no clue.

What does he want?

His name was Brad P. Hone, and he eventually got around to sayin how his bones weren't restin right in their journey toward dissolution and star-flung journeys, and would they go to his wife and children and tell them somethin . . . the details of which were lost on Tom and so lost on Kalin, though Tom still promised that Kalin, should he survive, would convey a message to Brad P. Hone's wife and children. Brad P. Hone thanked them and in return offered up to Kalin a warnin.

Tom was unclear, though, what he'd said. *Far as I can tell, he's sayin not to mess with Godder Ford.*

Who the heck is Godder Ford?

Beats me.

It seemed that Brad P. Hone wanted to linger, but like an oak leaf spun about and swallowed by nearin rapids, he was swept away as more dead arrived, includin one man named Cameron Eakins, followed by names that stayed about as blurry as the faces Kalin couldn't see anyways, followed by a young man, about Kalin or Tom's age, who called hisself Robert Gaff. Tom told Kalin that he looked like he wanted an autograph, and not from Tom, nor even the horses, but from Kalin, who he was claimin was his last chance to rest. He carried in his hand a bowlin ball of all things. He too had things to beg of Tom, which Tom again promised Kalin would do, should he survive, which charmed the young man. *He made it this far, didn't he?*

Kalin, fer his part, had begun to ponder more deeply the significance of that *this far*. How was it that right above Orvop lay the very threshold to where the dead gathered?

Which made Tom laugh plenty. He chided Kalin for thinkin that a place as immense as the chambers holdin all of history should have but one entrance. *I'm livin proof that the way in lies everywhere,* Tom surmised, his laughter fadin.

Also worth notin, certainly for those who are countin, this here marks the sixth gate, either at the entrance to the Awides itself or within the Awides, or wherever folks like to put it, and there's quite a range, with some like Callista Toone and Morgan Harris, both up in Malad City, Idaho, goin so far as to suggest six hundred and sixty-six possible locations in and around the Awides, which is the kind of numerology stoned idjits get caught up in because they're too afraid to look up and start countin stars, though neither Callista nor Morgan were stoned when they came up with that number, 666, though Charlie Burton, Martha Dagget, Reen Nakamura, and Vernon Matson sure thought they were.

Kalin didn't give a hoot or holler about such countin games, but nonetheless somethin didn't square right, his suspicions and doubts only deepenin when he demanded of Tom if out of all the dead folks there was even one dead animal, not countin their Ash. Tom admitted he hadn't seen a single one. Not a mouse, not a worm, not the smallest scuttlin thing. You can forget a goat or an elk or even an owl. No dogs neither nor cats. And there sure as heck weren't no horses. Weren't even a blade of grass or whisper of moss. Not even a patch of lichen to ease the eye.

Pia Isan does have that little chipmunk on her shoulder, Tom said.

I guess that says somethin about her. Though Kalin's mouth dried as he wondered again about what deal Tom had made with her.

If you don't get Navidad and Mouse to the Crossin, Tom finally admitted, *why then I'm bound to this place.*

That sure left Kalin speechless. He couldn't imagine a greater torment than to find hisself where there was such an unholy absence of furry and feathered and even slimy creatures. Wasn't it in their presence that the sky was lifted and the world breathed? Just watch for a spell a colt tryin to outrace a field or a red hawk soarin on a west wind, you'll see what happens to the sky. You'll know how the world sighs.

Tom, though, paid no mind to such consequences, continuin to swing around that bruised torch, cranin his neck some in an effort to discern now what his terrible risk had guaranteed him: gettin to talk to his brother and father. Except the dead were now withdrawin, like the way the sea retreats before a tsunami arrives, leavin the sand bubblin with fish floppin for water.

Tom's torch flickered then, catchin hold of a figure headin their way, immense in the distance but never gainin in size either as it continued to approach, at great speed too, until before them stood someone Tom could not understand. Forget gender or size. Here appearance itself was incommunicable. Not even its language was intelligible.

And so from this figure whom the dead had fled, like moths from a dead lamp, came utterances meaninful to only Pia Isan, who passed them along to Tom, who cajoled what sense he could from her speech, which he in turn passed along to Kalin.

It was the Future that now stood before them. And the Future declared that if on this day Kalin managed to pass over the greatest altitude of his journey, with all survivin, the girl too, for she now figured mightily in the events to come, then they would know no resistance and without fuss reach the Crossin and Tom's agreement would be fulfilled and the horses would be free and Pia Isan would be free, as would anyone else brave enuf to accompany her. Even on their way home, the mountain would not interfere. They just needed to be on their way before dawn touched the mine entrance.

But . . .

If they was delayed and the sun did kiss their path before they was on it, why then the mountain would oppose them, and no matter how much they struggled, they'd never triumph.

But why should they be opposed in the first place? Kalin wanted to know, but Tom said Pia Isan said the Future wouldn't say.

You get what you deserve if you ride with cowards, was all the Future would say.

Kalin thought this Future was full of rubbish. For one thing, he weren't ridin with cowards. Secondly, he'd always planned to leave early, which thinkin on it now stirred up an even greater desire to quit this place; except like a sleeper tryin to end a nightmare, Kalin discovered the exertion necessary to even yell out for Navidad was impossible, an impossibility that reassured him that this really was just a bad dream and he had to but wake up and rouse Landry and they'd be free of the mine in no time.

I see Bayson Riggs, Tom said then. *He's with his mother, Mary, and his father, Leland, as well his brother, Shawn.*

Now Kalin knew that weren't right because Bayson Riggs sat three desks away from him in Mr. Banner's math class. In fact he'd only this year taken note of Bayson because he sat adjacent to other football players in that period, and when Mr. Dayton Banner had got to joshin with the players that there was no way the Orvop football team would take State, and statistically he was right, the players, and that included Bayson Riggs, demanded a bet: if the team lost, the players would stay after school for a whole semester to study math with Mr. Banner, but if they won, they'd earn the right to dogpile on Mr. Banner right there in the center of the class.

Now as it would turn out, on November 19, not but a few weeks away, Utah's oldest high school would defeat Pleasant Glade in the finals for the State title, and Mr. Banner would have to submit to the beatin.

It should be noted that Orvop weren't like plenty of high schools across the country with kids only posin as players when in fact a strong wind would've knocked down any one of them. Many of these Orvop kids were big enuf to start next year for big college teams, and some would do just that and even go on to play pro. They did not blow away in the wind, and adults had a right to fear their collective energies.

To his credit, Mr. Banner would not shirk from his oath. He weren't tackled or nothin either but quite decorously submitted to the carpet floor where some of the larger boys, includin Mattock Jurgenvin fer one, surrounded him first in order to somewhat protect him. But big as they was, they was no match for the avalanche of young bodies that flew at the pile. Some of the smaller kids even launched themselves from atop desks, hootin for attention as they outdid each other with aerial displays. Mr. Banner would emerge dazed with a bead of blood rollin down his forehead, but true to form he fished from his pocket a sable-brown sudarium to staunch the injury and then resumed class.

Lindsey Holt would prove far less decorous. He emerged from the pile with his hair badly a-mess and none too happy about it. Like Jurgenvin he too had applied his considerable strength to help shield Mr. Banner and later frogged into near paralysis those littler kids who outed themselves for havin jumped on the very top. They weren't even on the team.

One nice thing that did come out of this was an extended conversation after class between Mr. Banner and Lindsey Holt. Lindsey was terrible at math and nearly every day sought to escape the room as soon as the bell rang, but this afternoon, with Lindsey checkin on Mr. Banner's well-bein, Lindsey learned that Mr. Banner played the drums. Mr. Banner in turn learned that Lindsey Holt was a gifted bass player with a wonderful ear and a near-flawless sense of time. The two would eventually jam together and even record some songs.

But all this, yes, is to drift a bit from the point: Bayson Riggs would be in that dogpile too, right in the middle, happy to savage those below him as he took whatever pummelin those above dared to deliver to his back. He would emerge fresh and amused with a radiant smile that the world should never have dimmed but did anyways on the early mornin of December 28, 1984. While takin Spanish Fork Canyon to Vail for a ski vacation, about a dozen or so miles east of the Billies Mountain cut, the Riggs' family Jeep Wagoneer hit black ice and suddenly found itself slidin out of its lane and, as the awful coincidence of things sometimes arranges outcomes, right in front of an eighteen-wheeler. The impact killt Bayson and every other Brigg in that vehicle except Mattock Jurgenvin, who was in the back. Bayson's mother's shoe was found in the snow just outside of that mash of disfigured metal.

It was an awful tragedy that would reverberate throughout Orvop, still reverberates, but it also wouldn't take place fer another two years.

That don't make any sense, Kalin told Tom, explainin how he'd seen Bayson alive just a few days ago in Mr. Banner's class.

Maybe he and his family died since then? Tom wondered aloud, though he hardly seemed convinced hisself by these speculations.

What about Russel Porch? Can you see him? Kalin asked.

But there weren't no sign of Russel. Neither Tom nor Kalin could say what that proved. Fer example, if Bayson was here, but he was still alive back in Orvop, did that mean that Russel, who wasn't here, was dead? It didn't make no sense no matter how you figured it. Tom tried to motion Bayson and his family closer, but they seemed unable to see him and retreated. The Future proved useless in explainin why the Riggs were there and knew nothin about Russel. Even Tom was startin to get fed up with the Future.

And then the Future pointed to someone who proved Pia Isan was wrong to think she'd been mistaken earlier: Kalin's mother was indeed there and, even worse, she was with Tom's mother who had rocks in her pockets, leaves tanglin her hair. Now that upset Tom to no end, but no amount of pleadin with Pia Isan, who in turn did what she could with the Future, who apparently was equally fed up with Tom and Kalin, would draw the mothers closer. Pia Isan did impart one last unpleasant detail: Tom's mother had small fishes in her guts, and Kalin's mother had what looked like rebar through her sternum.

At this point, Tom's father, Dallin Gatestone, and his brother, Evan, finally managed to make it up to Tom, but Tom fer his part was only yellin at them to go talk to his mom, and they in turn were yellin at him for makin such a stupid deal with Pia Isan. What had he done?! And fer what? *Fer nothin!*

And then they were gone, and Tom suddenly beheld Landry. Tom's smile vanished completely, along with even the tiniest glint of mirth, as he beheld his little sister curled up on the floor, outdoin the dead in her deadness. Tom kept pointin to her corpse too, and only Kalin could calm him down by pointin to the Landry who was also curled up but very much alive. The big elm had vanished along with the crick awash with its black water. The arch too and all the dead. Not even the Future had lingered. What remained was the awful smoke from their dull little fire that was at least keepin their chamber warm as a kinder and more forgetful darkness fell then around Kalin.

As numerous as they already are the many commentators mentioned thus far are not entirely on their own in their creative retellins, rants, iterative speculations, and musins regardin the events that transpired in and around Isatch Canyon and the Katanogos massif that late October in 1982. There are in fact three occasions that brought together many of these disparate voices, the first bein the largest of such gatherins and also the most tragic.

The second, though, was mostly a frolic takin place in 2013, durin an Orvop High reunion in fact, though not part of the sanctioned events or on school grounds; rather this impromptu coalescence occurred durin the July Fourth Orvop City parade. Folks from the reunion, locals as well as those comin in from out of town, relaxed along University Avenue, with the group in question enjoyin a good patch of shade on the lawn of the Orvop City Library, takin in at a distance the sights of llamas draped in American flags, inflatable Smokey Bears aloft on the updrafts of civic pride, with the local Elks Club scootin along on what looked like skateboards nailed together with small rugs atop to affect an appearance of flyin carpets, while not far behind them military trucks hauled weaponry led of course by the Orvop High Marchin Band, earnin raucous cheers.

Not that anyone was talkin about either the parade or the reunion but rather Pillars Meadow and soon enuf that night in the Awides Mine.

An early argument erupted over whether the Awides was in fact Buckley's Mine, as there are certainly some similarities with that hole in the mountain and its endlessly runged ladder. But that unresolvable question was but prelude to what would take hold of the rest of the night when a question was posed by Gia Rockit and later restated by both Fali Nihonmatsu and Cabbot Kaprielian as to where exactly Landry was lyin beside that elm tree, and where in relation to her was the arch, and in relation to the arch where exactly did Kalin, Tom, and the horses stand.

Steve Harrin and Orlando Banuelos took on the roles of Kalin and

Tom, with Shawna Chen sittin down where Landry was supposed to be, though Shawna refused to sleep, enjoyin instead a big cup of the homemade root beer Dalton Fossum had brought along. Thayne Moon, still a coach, and one of the best too, with Billy Biddulph and Haddy Visick happily acted as the horses by, well, horsin around fer one. Admittedly there was bickerin over where the mine entrance should be or the tunnel that headed deeper into the mine.

Rita Christleib played Pia Isan and stood beside Tom, still Orlando Banuelos, and Boise Bond took up the role of the Future but quickly swapped out with Don Bearman, who was soon replaced by Boyd Trammel, Kay Shroeppel, and even, believe it or not, Cathy Windell, later replaced by Ruth Ann Heimdal, Sarah Caulson, and Pilar Hinckley, and, well, you can see how this played out, with more and more folks takin on the roles of the various dead.

Nor did this curious reenactment end there. The official July Fourth parade was over but a new kind of involvement had energized this slowly growin group. Around twilight some folks went off to get pizzas and on their way back wandered into the old Womens Gymnasium across the street, where plenty of bands had played in the '80s, and what had been subsequently put to use as a boutique, a charity center, and even a trampoline fun house. On this day the space was bein prepared for a hush-hush musical event takin place the followin week. The doors stood wide open with no one around to mind the intrusion.

As the group relocated inside, word spread, and soon more folks were strollin on in, with most everyone talkin to most everyone else about what's already been related thus far, as well as a lot of what waits ahead, though by this point they'd somehow moved collectively beyond such chatter to somethin far more performative, devotedly so, turnin their passions into a pageant of sorts, the second parade of the day, or better, a night parade, a parade of the dead, with some folks declarin themselves the anticipated pioneers and settlers, others takin on the roles of the Indigenous folks, others gettin lexiphanic and pretentious, which is to say highfalutin, appearin as Homer, Aristotle, Sappho, Virgil, and Dante, with still more castin themselves as local heroes, for example, Ogden-born John M. Browning. Meanwhile, Logan-born Elaine Bradley of Neon Trees supposedly showed up. Daniel Wayne Sermon of Imagine Dragons supposedly came by too. The dead always need a stand-in.

Likely charged up on all the sugar in Dalton Fossum's seeminly endless supply of homemade root beer, folks like Vernon Mattson; Chelene and Denise Jasperson; Nathan Nibley; Erin Kennedy, startin

348

to think seriously about Divinity School then; Zarli Washburn; Ilene Clayton in the flesh; Alisa Groesbeck; Breen Lachance; Bryce Stewart; Julaine Jentzch; Harvel Kurst; Ladawn Crosset; Lee Peart; Dawn Brummett; Pharell Rowley; even Colleen Vance; Marcee Falgoust; as well as Pinegar Nelson, who painted the lemon cake on a paper plate; Lou Keele; Jenny Frampton; Cliff Woolf; Jody Leitus; Lela Schneiter; Leon Walser; and Koji Rangroo; as well as Bhanu Irarte, Nikki Cliff, and Shana Whiting; and that's still namin but a few, got good and giddy on persona. Robert Leroy Parker, Loretta Young, and Big Bill Haywood were just fer starters. They performed Neal Cassady too. And Frank Zamboni. Then supposedly Brandon Flowers arrived and took over as Tom and shortly thereafter switched it up and took over as Kalin, even singin out somethin like *I will walk with the dead and the dyin where I used to live,* which whether he did or not, he weren't gonna sing publicly until 2022, though in fairness it's also been suggested that it weren't Flowers there at all but Gary Allan with David Archuleta standin in for the Future unless it was Dan Reynolds or Roseanne Barr or even Payson-born Jewel Kilcher? Marie Osmond also supposedly dropped by, as did Tracy Hickman, Brian Evenson, Chris Conkling, Jenny June Oaks, John Warnock, Nolan Bushnell, Don Lind, and Gifford Nielsen of all people, but he was just havin a chuckle, and that went for members of the bands The Klick, Act Five, and The Rude Boys, as well as for Donny Osmond, who was just there to find his sister and ran into Steve Young.

It was that kinda night, mostly a goof, but there were moments too when some folks began playin the ones they lost, the dead they thought of often, missed too much to think about for too long. That's when the more musically inclined brought out their instruments and shared their willin voices, eventually findin the needed melodies and lyrics to accompany that night and comfort the bereaved.

Eventually Eldon McKennan; Frances Cassius Cowderry; Annie Miller, who'd recently been accepted to the University of Chicago; Caracy Rudder; Doran N. Tolan, who sculpted the much-discussed *Old Porch in the Rain*; and Lorenzo Swapp, with Daron Mooney there too, as well as Janet Hawks, Bart Roskelley, Teresa Cloward, Demming Despain, Lanise Parcell, Clint Hoffer, and Lydia Palmer, all found themselves on the steps outside, with Shen Dean comin along with Joanne Willden, who on that night had on a bright blue wig, smokin cloves too, just for old time's sake, starin across the avenue at far-bleaker thoughts, beyond the hold of their insubstantial spectral whims, ponderin somethin different, somethin else, time-broke, unable to quit sufferin the knowledge of ends, blood-drenched.

Some still say the Movie Star who owned the Cassidy Ski Resort dropped by then. It weren't an impossible thing. Cary Swindle had once gone to a party up at the resort thrown by some guy named Mike Medavoy, where Barbra Streisand was playin charades, Goldie Hawn too, and Cheryl Ladd, while other famous folks talked about Natalie Wood, and Martin Sheen's son told Cary that he was pretty freaked out by Utah in general: *This place is weird.* Plenty swore the Movie Star had lingered outside the Womens Gym, talkin about art and horses and what he loved. It was possible. He loved the canyons. He loved the mountains. He was devoted to them. So were most of the folks there that night, in spirit or fer real.

It's hard to say what such a spontaneous theatrical gatherin accomplished, even if it also included the likes of Jonathan Nez Paine, Ross Killian, Cyndee Francom, as well as Lyric Loveless, yes Lyric Loveless; Dealynn Gagnon; Juval Harmon; and Orly Vanleuven.

Chalise Brimhall, who was pretty good on a tightrope so long as it weren't but a few feet off the ground, and who that year would leave Spanish Fork for Orleans on Cape Cod, and who was nowhere near Orvop that July Fourth, still did hear from friends of this strange happenin. Decades later she would declare that what did or didn't happen that night was beside the point. Of more interest was how the entreatments of the dead skewed the obvious precedents. *In The Iliad, she would tell her sister one bright mornin as they strolled beside Atlantic waters, the dead Patroclus begged his hero-beau, Achilles, to bury him so his insubstantial self might pass through the gloomy gates and reside in Hades. In Hamlet, though, Hamlet's father's ghost wants more: he commands his son to vengeance. And then there's Tom's fortean presence, who asks no more of Kalin than his company. The numerous dead, however, are a different story: they demand Tom's presence be consigned to their ranks. And one senses there is no such thing as a nudum pactum among these dead. The horses, though, offer somethin new: if they're freed, there's freedom for the dead too. We don't know what freedom for the dead constitutes, but we do see that what matters here isn't how the dead deal with the livin but how the dead deal with the dead.*

It sure doesn't help those inclined to speculate that when Kalin awoke he had nothin in his head but shreds of panic and dread. Tom weren't around. Even worse, Kalin was drenched in sweat, his mouth was dry, and he couldn't see nothin. At least the coughs that followed helped straighten his thoughts some. The fire was out, and smoke had spread throughout the chamber. Kalin fetched more wood and blew splinters and embers back into flames, which soon were blazin big enuf to get that shaft that was servin as a flue overhead suckin up the smoke again.

Landry didn't wake, but her own mumbles and kicks told Kalin that she was fine. Next he checked on the horses. They was annoyed, though at least since they was standin on the opposite side of the chamber, they weren't near as eye-stung by the smoke. After checkin their water, he drank some for hisself and then headed out to relieve hisself.

Some have anticipated that Kalin would find the day well upon him and the easy path described in his nightmare already lost. But that was not the case. The canyon still seemed held in the frozen pit of night. Tom was there, gazin out over the blue dark. Kalin felt sure there was somethin important to talk over, but what exactly that was didn't come to him.

Do you still need to piss? he asked Tom instead.

I guess I don't.

Then that right there's a positive side to bein dead.

That I don't have to piss? Tom asked.

Sure.

I sorta miss pissin. Especially on Kyle Orlando's car door handle. He was talkin bull about the FFA. Do you know he even talked bull about Hightower? Hey, you think that's why I'm here? Like this is punishment for pissin on Kyle Orlando's car door handle?

So you do think you're bein punished?

I'm with you, ain't I? Tom laughed, the sound glidin down among the low pines, drawin from Kalin a smile that might've also turned into laughter if he hadn't noticed Tom noddin at the air, an act that seemed to recall for Kalin somethin vivid and urgent he had to discuss with his friend, even if he still couldn't arrive at any details. Sometimes we remember only the feelin attached to the clarity we once knew even if we no longer possess the clarity itself. That was Kalin right there: oblivious to the halls of the dead if nonetheless aware that somethin about Tom had changed.

Kalin returned to the fire to doze. Again, some anticipated Kalin would find a sleep so deep, he wouldn't wake til noon. It was worse than that but in a wholly different way. The fact is Kalin couldn't sleep for long at all. He was plagued by scenarios of Egan and his brothers reachin the *T* before them, or even gettin there so quick that they were already followin the path here where with weapons drawn they'd stream into this chamber, their awful shadows ablaze with

351

report, killin the horses, killin Landry, killin Kalin last by throwin him down that awful shaft beyond the roped-off passage. One dream had Old Porch slaughterin the horses by hisself.

Well before dawn, Kalin nudged Landry awake. She didn't care for that one bit and gave him one heckuva growlin. Rabid badger indeed. Kalin could hear her brother laughin, though he was still outside by the mine entrance. Fortunately a breakfast of eggs, the last of them, some shredded cheese, more of them Orvop cafeteria buns, what quick gave up their freeze in a bubble of butter, plus the last of their cocoa and coffee crystals calmed her down some. Not that Landry was even one bit thankful, shovelin down what he offered her with maybe a grunt, now and then a burp, but never an appreciative word to the one who had not only so kindly prepared her meal but due to their limited stores had reduced substantially the size of his own portion. At least she helped a little with cleanin up the cutlery.

Kalin hadn't brought along no curry comb, and so after breakfast he used the edge of his right hand to wipe down the horses and then his whole right hand to in effect brush them. The blisters on his left palm kept him from usin both hands. Next he gave them a good massagin and talkin-to, which he always did before and after every ride, again makin sure there weren't no saddle sores or sores around the cinch and that Navidad's mouth was good, recheckin and double-checkin all their legs and hooves. *No foot, no horse,* as the Gatestone farrier, Terrence Olsen, would so often say.

In the collapsible canvas bowls Kalin added some of his sloppy oat mash, along with some molasses too and salt. Maybe even Jojo found a tiny bit of tolerance for the kid then. Mouse headbutted Kalin with obvious affection but Navidad always seemed the happiest when Kalin was around.

Once that was done, Kalin, as soft as he'd been with the horses, let Landry understand how they'd need to make good time this mornin. Today was the day that would make or break them. But Landry still weren't quite through with her growlin, nor her burpin either, though the burpin was a good sign, a sign of satisfaction. She also wanted to settle her own impressions of the night they'd just survived. It's true she'd slept like the dead, but even the dead have dreams.

The goat was white. Or gold. And stubborn. I somehow knew he was seventy-nine years old. Every year he'd go for this swim. The stream isn't much. These little brown leaves float on the surface. The water is icy and clear. I can see the rocks on the bottom and small fish flashin by. Then the goat jumps right in, and he's, well, he's wonderful, and then he just trots on out to a heap of ash, which he starts rollin around in. Then all of a sudden I'm in the water, squattin down, up to my neck, and it's freezin! It hurts! I'm so cold, I can't even move! But I'm also thinkin to myself: I can do this! I can get out and go roll around in that ash too! It don't matter that he went first.

Kalin didn't have no response.

Well? Landry still prodded him. *Whadya suppose that's about?*

Kalin still didn't have a response.

The water was just so clear.

That seems like a good thing. Kalin was mostly focused on packin up their gear.

You sleep okay? Landry asked.

Not really. The fire went out. I kept worryin we'd sleep too long. I kept worryin that the horses would get up to somethin. I also kept havin this feelin we weren't alone, this feelin that Tom was tryin to tell me somethin that I can't remember no more, though I guess the gist was obvious: we'd better get movin.

Tom, what did you wanna tell Kalin last night? Landry asked the air.

He's outside with Ash. Whistlin too.

I wish I could hear that. What song?

I don't know it.

Hum it.

I can't hold a tune.

Blue dawn come console me, I lost who I was with, she sang. *That one?*

Kalin nodded. Landry had a beautiful voice.

They was in the midst of layin out their supplies when they heard an awful hiss comin from outside. It was loud too, so loud there weren't nowhere to hide in that chamber. Mouse swung hisself around and backed straight into rock. Both Navidad and Jojo reared up and whacked themselves on the top of their heads, which got them swingin around and foulin some of the gear laid out nearby. Had the sound kept comin, fer sure the horses would've kept gettin wilder and maybe even have broke loose. There was no worse imaginin than them horses undertakin a panicked scramble out the mine entrance, where they'd lose hold of their footin and tumble off the cliffs below. And if they somehow got loose in the mine itself . . . Kalin and Landry just couldn't think on that.

Fortunately, Kalin and Landry were immediately among them, with hushes and pats, some hay eventually, more strokes, easin all three back into a state of repose and chewin. Kalin dug up a carrot.

A quick inspection outside revealed only a purplin dark. Tom had no answer either. Ash held his head high, ears straight up at alert.

The good news was that thanks to their feastin and the horses' eatin, their load was much reduced. The bad news was that there weren't much left to eat for even later that day. Landry was particularly displeased to see there weren't no more cocoa. No coffee neither. Gone were the eggs, cheese, the foil-packed dinners. No more butter or salmon. No more cans of mushroom soup. Four cafeteria buns remained. Some sugar, some spices. There was some dried fruit and trail mix, as well as a bag of Dorf jerky. Landry knew Russel Dorf. He was an Orvop High student and, like his brothers and sisters, worked for his dad. The horses didn't have much left either. The hay was mostly gone or would be gone by the time they finished this round of eatin. At least there were still bags of sweet feed, loaded with oats, corn, molasses, and a mash of other good stuff includin extra vitamins.

Kalin explained that by early afternoon they should reach Altar Lake, where the surroundin meadow would offer plenty to graze on *provided there ain't no trouble.*

Landry got out her hoof pick and scratched a big *V* on the dusty rock floor. *This here's Isatch Canyon, and this here's roughly where we're at. Now show me where we're goin. Please.*

Kalin took the hoof pick. He first managed a wobble of a line from the Isatch Canyon entrance to the *T* above Aster Scree. From there he dragged that hoof pick east, high along the north wall of the canyon, a wiggly line that eventually led up to what Kalin assured her was *a mild and grassy draw* with plenty of streams and even a few small waterfalls. Toward the top waited the most beautiful sight, what's now known as Mist Falls, where they would water the horses, fill their canteens, and take a breather.

Wait til you see it, Landry.

Anythin beats this place.

The way the water falls is somethin else.

From there they would have to go only a bit farther to Bewilder Crick and then Altar Lake, fed by a near-permanent body of snow that stretched up toward the high steeps of Mount Katanogos. Kalin didn't bring up Kirk's Cirque or what waited beyond the lake.

Along with Henry Tabori, Debra Loveridge, and Nancy McClanahan, Trevor Bell and Emerson Nation would consider this a moment when the prevailin image of Kalin the Truth Teller falters, both of them rightly pointin out his obvious lie of omission in a high-spirited debate with Sita Houtz and Miranda McCay, all of them in Anaheim, Orange County, at that point, quarrelin after a No Doubt concert at the Inn at the Park. At the time, they were all workin together at Zeed Records. Both Sita Houtz and Miranda McCay would hold steadfast to their claim that *makin too clear the whole journey might've messed up Landry.*

Kalin knew she needed somethin to look forward to, and what he shared with her was absolutely true. Mist Falls is a gorgeous place.

There's also no denyin the pure and simple pleasure found in seein ahead clearly. It matters little if the endeavor is flawed and even endlessly incomplete. A carefully prescribed future leads away from uncertainty and introduces calm.

Then Tom's Crossin is somewhere around here? Landry's hand hovered over a big patch of nothin northeast of Altar Lake.

Kalin nodded. *But I ain't even tellin you the best part.* Kalin returned the hoof pick to another patch of nothin, what at least was closer to Altar Lake. Not that Landry could know its perils. *Like nothin you've ever seen before. I promise. It'll change the way you see the whole world.*

It did that for you?

It sure did. And I wasn't even on a horse.

Their gear came down now to one canteen; the kettle; the pan with lid; the one bowl, the one mug, followed by the one spork; a Swiss Army knife; a hatchet; three remainin tea candles, Kalin havin used another one to get and keep goin the fire in the mine, along with the waterproof matches and a flint-and-steel kit; then there was the sleepin bag; the saddle blankets; four tarps; a first aid kit and wound kit; two saddles; the one Decker packsaddle; three leads; two sets of halter-bridles, reins, and bits; the two collapsible canvas water bowls; Landry's hoof pick; duct tape and cardboard; and then two lariats, the thirty-two footer, yellowish green, and the sixty-four footer, near violet, plus a hundred-foot tawny cotton reata; all of which they tucked away in assorted saddlebags.

On her person, Landry had boots; one pair of black socks; underwear; jeans; a bra; a shirt; two sweaters, one marl-colored, the other sable; plus her dark olive ski parka; her sage wool-felt cowboy hat; and last of all that pink raincoat. Kalin had on his person his daddy's green slicker, the Lee Storm Rider, one cable-knit sweater, two shirts, jeans, his mother's hose, briefs, socks, and the Gatestone boots, and of course Tom's white Stetson, stained a bit by the journey. Kalin had also finally found, under some vegetables and fruit for the horses, those darned gloves, what would've so easily prevented the hurt inflamin his left hand, though he grimaced more over the rations left for the horses, not to mention for him and Landry.

Didn't count on Jojo, did ya? Landry asked as they saddled up.

I did not.

Or me?

We'll make it figure out okay.

How? Landry sure was good with the hitches and knots.

We'll make it figure out okay, Kalin said again, like repetition could prove somethin; it don't but now and then it can prove soothin.

Then Landry pulled out from under her pink raincoat the velvet pouch holdin the Colt Peacemaker. For some reason she hadn't thought to repack it. Like she wanted it near, like she wanted to hold it, like she wanted Kalin to hold it.

We can go huntin, Landry announced, removin the weapon from the bag, free at last. And oh, how it glimmered. Poor dumb child had no idea what she held.

Kalin, though, was already scramblin backward, and didn't stop retreatin neither, not until he was enfolded by the horses, who, detectin Kalin's upset, commenced snortin up their own fuss, stompin hooves and generally shiftin this way and that like suddenly no place they could stand was safe.

Whoa, there! I ain't pointin it at you! Landry exclaimed, lowerin the weapon.

Put it away! Kalin yelled from as far away as he could get in that chamber.

And Landry did at once do just that, puttin it back in its bag and then in the saddle satchel where it belonged.

I didn't mean nothin. I'm sorry. And Landry did feel bad for causin such a reaction. *I can see guns bug you.*

They don't bug me, Landry, Kalin answered, still stayin as far away as he could. *They flat-out scare me.*

You're a funny one, Kalin March, Landry sighed, plenty confused but willin to slough if off. *No wonder Tom liked you so much. You must've made him laugh pretty much around the clock.*

Kalin felt even worse after that. Partly he was confused by so visceral a reaction. Earlier appearances of that gun had put him on alert some or just annoyed him. This time, though, his movements were way ahead of his thinkin. Maybe somethin about this place, what he'd experienced there overnight, had rendered the gun's potential energy somehow disproportionately kinetic. In Landry's hand the black flash of that weapon had seemed to writhe like entwined serpents of mercury and tar, fanged as well, and where there was an absence of inscription, that's what drew forth from Kalin a cold curl on his lips, a look Landry didn't care for one bit.

Even put away now, buried deep in its damp velvet, the memory continued to chill Kalin's skin, sweated it too. His mouth only got more parched. He couldn't stop seein his mother, her silent judgment, that curse in her mouth somehow amplified here. He'd sworn to her that there weren't no gun. No girl either.

What weren't as obvious was another aspect of Kalin's confusion: given how far away he was from his mother and her curse, from Orvop, from civilization, would it really matter if he'd just handled the thing fer a moment? The thought didn't attach itself at once to dread but rather, if he could admit it, to delight, maybe even desire.

Get back over here, Landry said then, oblivious of what she'd just provoked. *The gun's away. I ain't gonna hurt you.* She spoke too in the same way she would to Jojo when that big blue beautiful horse needed coaxin through a rough spot. And it worked. Kalin returned, back to her side, back to double-checkin the packsaddle on Mouse.

My momma warned me that if I ever touched a gun, no horse would ever come near me. Might as well get it out in the air. Maybe the air would kill it. Or better, Landry could laugh it into oblivion. *She said it was my curse.*

Your momma told you that?

Kalin nodded.

You sure she weren't just makin it up? Like the way some folks say if you do some bad thing, you ain't gonna go to Heaven? Except like for you, horses are Heaven? By the way, horses are Heaven for me too.

Kalin chuckled at least. *When we get back, you can have that conversation with her yourself.*

Landry blushed. *You're gonna introduce me to your momma?*

I figure I got no choice. She's gonna wanna know who I got stuck up here with. Kalin even felt his own cheeks strike heat some.

Landry, maybe for the first time, was speechless.

We got some miles ahead of us today, Kalin followed up quickly. *But you're one heckuva rider, and you're on one heckuva horse.* Navidad snorted at that and Mouse promptly released a prelapsarian flood of urine. *If we keep a good pace like I know we can, we'll be fine. We'll be better than fine. You'll get to see that waterfall and then about when the sun is settin I'll keep my promise and show you thee most beautiful sight in the world. By tomorrow we'll be at the Crossin, settin Navidad and Mouse free. We'll travel hungry after that but we'll get home just fine.*

Navidad needed no encouragement to lower her head. Despite its darkness, the passage was still bright with the smell of cold mornin air. Mouse followed Navidad at once, now and then buttin her flanks with his wide forehead, which only seemed to reassure her. *Clop-Clop-clip-Clop.* Jojo followed along at an almost casual pace.

Landry gave their chamber one last glance, already greatly dimmed by their dyin fire. Rope no longer barred the passage deeper into the mine. She was glad to be leavin. They all were.

Up near the entrance, they were once again accosted by that strange hiss that had so upset everyone earlier. This time it was preceded by a series of cracks, as if enormous sheets of plate glass were breakin. Fortunately, the horses were not as disturbed, likely due to the sharp clear air as well as the vast vista, still cast in dark purple light, of black tree lines and high rock walls.

Tom and Ash were already there waitin, Ash lookin toward what Tom was pointin out for Kalin, what Landry had already spotted: high on a ridge on the south side of Isatch Canyon, toward the summit of Agoneeya, where dawn's first rays had just begun to strike, there bloomed a great eruption of orange and rose, as if ice could be set afire, tearin downward, like a comet hurled either by indifferent distances and ratios above or Titans, if there is a difference, determined to undo the world below, a prologue to extinction. Mr. Caracy Rudder, post-divorce, reacquaintin hisself with loneliness and findin it sufferable, would treat this scene as a depiction of an endlessly reiteratin Lucifer, Promethean at the outset, if Stygian in outcome, at once diminished upon reachin the shadows below, gatherin then unto itself all that was left after such a fall, such a song, a growin rumble, the music of bro-kenness, discontent, which nonetheless in this moment of dispelled wonder and allusion still made apparent, through those great clouds of ice particles thrown up behind, one more act of brilliance, a blindin halo of light, even as that darknenin avalanche fled farther from such rainbows, plowin through trees, down steep ravines, too soon a new cloud upon the canyon floor.

Landry and Tom both turned then, and at the same time too, to survey the steeps above the mine entrance, wonderin whether or not the north side of the canyon might answer now that minor cataclysm with one of its own.

Not Kalin. He was already beholdin somethin far worse, though to be sure it was also a wonder.

Here, already upon them, encirclin them with its glossiness, was an impasse far graver than any worries Kalin might have had about avalanches. It was what made sense of the persistent cracks he'd heard throughout the night, sometimes no more than a click of stone upon stone, like the mountain was tiptoein, at other times like the moun-tain itself was startin to shatter.

Holy cow! Landry exclaimed, now seein it too, her breath a thick billow of cloud.

Some areas were thick and gray, other areas no more than a silver-blue verglas. But no matter where they looked, everythin was lac-quered in such perilous beauty.

Ice!

Everywhere!

Visible nearby were collections of the tiniest beads, as if the rain had frozen midair in order to enter this new marble game upon landin. Brush and small huddles of trees were equally enclosed. Nor was the entrance of the mine any different, filigreed with pathways of frozen water. Where they needed to go waited slopes rimed in pale slipperiness, with some parts of the path appearin far glossier, blacker too, and by Kalin's reckonin a whole lot meaner.

Landry made to take a step beyond their rock threshold, but Kalin blocked her fast, used his arm and a leg too.

Watch, he said as he pointed to the way they'd have to ride. He picked up a rock near big as a toaster and fer sure a lot heavier. His left palm screamed with pain even as the cold stone also helped alleviate the pain. No matter. Kalin needed to make a point, for Landry but also for hisself. A pebble might imply that somethin heavier wouldn't be subject to the same consequences.

Kalin hucked the rock out onto the path. Landry expected it to break through the ice and settle, but instead it skipped off easy as a tiddlywink, and down the slope it raced, gatherin speed until it was flyin over them cliffs below.

The horses weigh way more than that rock, Landry tried to insist, though she couldn't hide the doubt in her own voice. *Won't they just break through?*

Kalin snugged on tight his Stetson, what in the light of the comin day was lookin plenty smudged-up by the smoke they'd suffered throughout the night, to say nothin of whatever grit the mine itself had had to offer. Then he squatted down and picked up an even bigger rock. His strength surprised Landry.

This one fared no better. It just bounced higher and vanished over the cliffs even faster, the rest of its journey reverberant upon the canyon walls.

Almost sounds like it's sayin somethin, Landry observed.

It's sayin we're stuck.

Chapter Twelve

"Ice!"

The single-engine 1979 Beechcraft A36 Bonanza juddered in the crosswinds bickerin between Kaieneewa and Agoneeya. However, a headwind floodin down off Katanogos, either born from them glowerin clouds right above or from somewhere farther away, steadied the plane.

Not that the pilot, Tucker Wyatt, was bothered by any of it.

I'll bring us in lower for the next pass, he yelled. He recommended startin without binoculars or they'd get lost in the closeness, and it might unsettle their guts some too.

Sondra Gatestone sat up in the copilot seat while Allison sat behind the pilot seat, her face at the window, clutchin the binoculars that had already given her a taste of airsickness when every little bounce up here danced the view down there by hundreds of feet.

Allison knew they'd be flyin into weather. What she hadn't expected was the noise, the rattle that she felt in her teeth. Whatever lightness the small plane achieved up here, it weren't by magic. The turbulent pathways of air made clear that they was only guests, held in the thrall of forces far greater than aluminum and steel.

Without warnin the plane slid wildly to the left, then just as suddenly slid right, only to then bounce straight ahead, like a sliver of the smoothest stone skippin across a glassy pond.

Sondra yipped, her friend, Tucker Wyatt, joinin in, puttin a bit more heart into the throttle too. Allison swallowed hard, and when they both turned around to check on her, she did her best to grin.

Once free of their gaze, she began draggin in as much breath through her nose, as slowly as she could, holdin it, before releasin it out even slower. Again and again. Tucker had already started a high-bankin turn, right behind the back side of Agoneeya, until he was lowerin the nose and speedin downward toward Mud Lake, one big U-turn, with another one over Orvop, until they was again roarin back toward Isatch Canyon, and just like Tucker had promised, lower this time, and slower too.

On their first pass, when they was higher up, the area hadn't seemed much more than an elaborate map, still dazzlin but somehow flatter, enuf so to conceal the heart-wrenchin challenges posed by a few feet of such terrain, what was now on this pass all too evident.

My gosh! My gosh! Sondra kept cryin out. *It's all ice! It's all ice!*

Allison hadn't quite got there yet. She could see the sparkle and hyaline glossiness on the great walls of crumblin stone, and, sure, she'd noticed the frost captivatin everythin from them pine trees, birches, and aspens on the higher ridges to the scrub oaks and brush below, all of it colored up beautifully in the mornin's violet shades, but it was still nothin but a pretty postcard you'd find the back of quick enuf to scribble down that fall's russets and golds was endin, tellin whoever was on the receivin end that winter would soon be here.

Nature's Beauty has a way of arrogatin the future, assurin the beholder that as it is it was and so it shall ever be. Allison did find herself pretty gobsmacked too before the sweep of those great surroundin walls, and them still nothin compared to the heights of Katanogos itself, still buried from view by the storm. Even the brave stands of trees, with their perched verticalities swearin on every moment that there they would no longer stand in the next moment, but still did stand, for a century or more, why that sundered Allison's heart.

The Kaieneewa side of the canyon gave up a sharp crack then, and Tucker Wyatt bucked the plane off to the left, pointin and yellin out the avalanche of stone now racin down a narrow chute, soon expandin beyond that deep geologic crease, wipin out whatever trees and brush had dared to live in its way, kickin up more and more dust, some of it bright with blinks of ice, the rest darker than blind rage.

Allison didn't like much that her dear Kalin and Sondra's dear little girl had chosen such Beauty for their refuge. What Sondra had spotted at once, Allison now studied with greater focus, a terrain bright with silver and dark blues, stalactites of frozen water markin every elevation, on every boulder and branch. And that was just the start: great caps of nearly transparent ice covered the largest slabs of rock as well as the smallest pebbles. Some ledges glistened blacker than the night that had just passed.

Even Allison knew such conditions required ice axes and crampons, special pitons and miles of rope. Just last winter, she and Kalin had drove out to Bridal Veil. The falls had frozen solid. Of course water still descended within, but the outside was the memory of that fall, a column of immense white, trappin within a glow of blue, like shards of the sky, and in some places even a coppery yellow light. Every year climbers would dare the ascent, and though she and Kalin had only witnessed triumph, onlookers nearby warned them that the worst could happen, the ice could prove foul, and then a climber would fall, their pitons fallin away too, which neither Kalin nor Allison felt was a price worth payin for such an adventure let alone a view.

But now her Kalin was supposedly down there, at heights greater and far more dangerous than Bridal Veil Falls. She doubted he had the gear, and any idjit could see a horse wouldn't last even a minute on such slippery steeps.

There was another crack, and Tucker Wyatt pointed to yet another cascade of rock and ice.

There's enuf sun pokin through these clouds to warm the ice on the high ridges, Tucker yelled. *What the freeze last night split apart or dislodged is now free to kick loose with the thaw.*

Allison shuddered again for their kids. Her beautiful Kalin! Sondra's little girl! Horses! What had they gotten themselves into?

Tucker Wyatt eased the plane deeper into the canyon. *This is as low as we get!* He weren't gonna let the terrain outclimb the plane. *Ever since that darned movie Star Wars come out there's been some fool pilot who thinks he can fly through about any canyon. Just ends up a burnin mess on a rock pile. Ain't happened in Isatch Canyon yet, thank goodness. Maybe it helps that enuf folks think it's cursed. I don't think it's cursed. But I don't mind it none if that keeps the knuckleheads away.*

Tucker patted Sondra's hand some and then even left his hand on hers fer a moment, and Allison suddenly beheld these two anew. She'd taken Sondra at her word when she'd introduced the white-haired gentleman in his calfskin boots, faded Levis, and brown bomber jacket as no more than a friend. On the tarmac, he'd remained cordial and mannerly, with handshakes for both, and except for somewhat rapturously pointin out the qualities of his beloved plane, had demonstrated no such familiarities with Sondra. Likewise, Sondra had showed no closeness nor warmth. In fact whatever verbal declarations of amity they'd mustered ran contrary to their otherwise chilly physicality toward one another. Even when standin side by side on the tarmac their body language somehow put on display a spectacle of distance.

Their affection now, though, even if it didn't go beyond those hand pats, was tender and compassionate. Allison couldn't remember the last time a hand had caressed hers and assured her that livin was still worth the pain.

Allison was already in awe of Sondra's strength and determination, how she'd handled Old Porch at her doorstep, organized their own search and rescue, this flight for example; and yet in lookin at her now, lookin for some hint of optimism, Allison glimpsed Sondra as harrowed and gray enuf to return her to her own window, only to find there, in the glass, her own harrowin reflection floatin like a ghost above the icy trap below.

On the next pass up the canyon, Allison alternated between what she could see of the left or Kaieneewa side of the canyon without binoculars and what her instincts demanded she study more closely, what each time revealed just more untraveled ice. And in either case, both vantages proved too much. Without lenses, what chance was there to glimpse anythin so small as a person or a horse? The sides of Isatch Canyon were too immense: tiers upon tiers of vast balconies and screes, sheer faces, itinerant woods, the penetralia of its various recesses? Just the hope of glimpsin two foolish kids with three horses seemed folly, especially if they'd already fallen, were already entombed within the rocky jaws of some deep crevice, a sight she could no more seek out than resist conjurin. With lenses it all seemed even worse, a blurrin shudder of too much detail on one tiny patch of terrain. Was that a path or an animal trail or just a ridge of narrow rock elevatin the ice to make her think fer a second that here was a route their children might follow?

Why?! Sondra suddenly screamed out, though in fact she weren't screamin, only yellin, same as Tucker Wyatt had been doin the whole trip, above the roar of the engines, the constant molestation of racket and rattle. But screamin or yellin, Sondra still was entitled to anguish and rage. Even toward Allison herself. After all, weren't it Allison's boy who had dragged Sondra's last livin child into this mess? Allison even flinched, as if Sondra had suddenly just reached back and struck her in the face.

In fact Sondra weren't givin Allison a second thought. *Why this way?!* Sondra demanded. *Look around! It don't make a lick of sense. There ain't no darned place to go! And fer sure not on a horse! A horse can go plenty of places, and fast too. A horse can cross this frickin country, but a horse still ain't no goat. A horse cannot go up a rock wall!*

I can't even give you a guess, Allison yelled back. *I'm just as confused as you. I can't even get past my boy takin two horses that weren't his.*

Sondra nodded, and while it's doubtful she'd caught much of what Allison had yelled, it also weren't lost on her then how this tiny woman, her face pale and fadin beneath a mess of beautiful auricomous curls, was as bewildered as she. But weren't that the very definition of bein a parent? Hadn't Landry already taught her how the mind of a child can quickly outpace the one who feels entitled to form it?

Tucker Wyatt made six more runs at about the same altitude, but each pass only further cowed the two mothers, with only their sense of futility near matchin the immense slopes below.

Can we go that way this time? Allison yelled up at Tucker, pointin left toward the cliffs that rose up above Isatch Canyon, toward the hidden Katanogos.

Tucker shook his head. *Not in this weather.* The way he looked, there was more than just weather up there to fear.

Durin a conversation at Trolley Square, while takin down a Kitchen Sink Sundae, Auris Satterfield would point out to Jolene Johnston that Tucker Wyatt's Bonanza had a cruisin ceilin of near 25,000 feet, which tops Katanogos easily. They was both from Bountiful and at the time workin at the Salt Lake City International Airport. Auris Satterfield was studyin for her pilot's license. Jolene Johnston was at the MTC in Orvop. She'd already hiked the Katanogos massif many times. *It weren't just about altitude,* she'd told her friend. The great bowls of rock up there, plus the ridges and deep gorges, not to mention the positionin of the summit headwall itself, created all sorts of *tight spots and gusty commotions that ain't the easiest thing to wrangle in a small plane.* After all, up by Kirk's Cirque, there still lies the remnants of a B-26 bomber that had crashed there in November 1959.

Of course, laid out on a map the Katanogos massif ain't but a few inches of wobbly lines. As the crow flies east from Isatch Canyon to the Tabiona Rodeo Grounds, there ain't but seventy-five miles. Thirty-nine miles northwest to Wallsburg. Of that, a good twenty-five miles, plus a quarter, is wild terrain with no formal trails except animal paths. And these distances, while vast to even the most experienced hiker, what on a bad day can feel about as far as Orvop is from Perth, still don't take but a small chomp out of a ruler slapped flat on a map. The way from Isatch Canyon to Kirk's Cirque don't even rate a handful of inches and gets you squintin hard at them finer lines. Locate Isatch Canyon on your own map, and what these ladies flew over you'll traverse in not even a blink. It won't seem like nothin. Not that you'd be markin the first time, or the last time, folks have mistook a flat space spread out on a table for a livin place.

After all, there's a long history of substitutin real terrain with confoundin squiggles on paper. Generals are often the worst offenders, from Troy to Thermopylae, Waterloo to Gettysburg, Ypres to Afghanistan. Vietnam, a country that ain't much bigger than the state of California, presented on paper no more of a military endeavor than some afternoon picnic at Fort Sumter. Miles are surveyed near as fast as the speed of light, hardly provokin any warnins of resistance. Measure, though, such narrows and fields by the dead that covered them, and we're quick to apprehend the loomin infinities territory commands.

Strange then how, despite their frantic attempt to comprehend what ain't even worth a fingernail on a map, not once did Sondra's or Allison's or even Tucker Wyatt's eyes ever drift over the entrance of the Awides Mine; and yet from just within those hollows both children noted the repeated return of that plane without once thinkin that there flew two women who loved them more than life.

Back at the airport, Allison resolved to again disgorge the contents of her heart, but her resolve stuttered some as she stepped out onto the tarmac. Her legs felt unsteady, her stomach unsettled, her

365

head light. The rain had even ceased some, and even with more clouds continuin to pile up over the mountains, over the lake, some would still part and let through bright scattered beams of light, which while brightenin the day some still did nothin to cheer her up.

It was 10:18 a.m.

No longer side by side in the plane, Tucker Wyatt and Sondra Gatestone had resumed their formal attitude toward one another. Tucker wished that they'd accomplished more, which upon sayin caused him to offer up his plane again. *Anytime. I don't even need much notice.* He and Sondra did exchange then a quick hug.

I have to say it again, Allison said once they was back in Sondra's dark blue Ford Bronco, with Mungo offerin them wet nuzzles from the back seat. *My boy's the one that got your Landry involved in this, and I have to take responsibility for that fact. I am so sorry.*

We've already been over this, Sondra answered, her eyes stayin with the road.

That was before I had any idea where Kalin was goin.

I doubt he understood where he was goin. Best as I can figure, my Tom and your Kalin did a lot of ridin in the canyon. Maybe your son figured he could hide there. Now, though, with this freeze, that canyon's a whole other place.

This latest apology didn't help Allison feel any better, but at least she also saw how continuin to apologize weren't gonna get a different result. The only way through this was to get Kalin and Landry back to safety. Through her window, Allison could see Squaw Peak off in the distance, all salted with frost. Somethin about its smallness defeated her. Behind her finger, behind even a sliver of fingernail, not even Kaieneewa existed.

You know when the plane was takin off, I felt like our kids were within our reach, Allison said. *That we were gonna spot them on the first pass. Now, though, they seem permanently beyond us.*

Hush that, Sondra snapped. *You don't have a mind for mountains, but that doesn't mean your boy is the same as you. I know Landry's got some sense of that canyon. And she sure knows how to ride her horse. And she will do everythin in her power to keep him safe and sound. Just because they did one thing stupid don't mean they'll do everythin stupid. Let's have some faith in them.*

You have that faith, don't you?

I do. And that faith is yours too if you want to borrow mine.

Sondra took a curvin and soon forkin road away from the lake and the airport and in a short time was drivin on Zurich Road right past Porch Meats. Sondra made sure to slow too. Allison at once began to slide down in her seat.

Don't do that. We don't hide from Porches.

Mungo sure didn't slouch. But if Allison feared seein Old Porch again, or the one who'd rapped on her window when she was parked there, that would've been Kelly Porch, all she saw were Porch workers millin about. Trucks had overwhelmed the driveway, with plenty more parked on the street, dirt bikes too. Some of the men were smokin cigarettes, pretty unusual in Orvop. A few gave the Bronco a hard stare. Allison didn't see a single woman.

Sondra laughed.

Looks like Porch is marshallin hisself a little army.

Next they drove to the Orvop Police Station. Allison had assumed for some reason that Orwin Porch had been holed up in the main house, probably sunk down on some old livin room couch with the TV on, or back inside his plant, with more of his men, in some room where above concrete floors carcasses hung on hooks, but in fact Old Porch had only just left this very location. He'd intended to go inside, but like Allison earlier in the day, he'd changed his mind and sped back to the canyon entrance, just missin the women.

It was 10:41 a.m.

The ones directly handlin the case weren't there, but Sondra weren't bothered. She hadn't come for them. And she found who she was after quick enuf, Chief of Police Wilson Beckham, who even came out to greet her, and in turn Allison, before usherin them into his office with the offer of somethin to drink, which they refused, and some downright comfortable chairs, which they accepted. Instead of returnin to his seat, he sat right down on his desk, expressin first his condolences over Tom's passin before admittin how *this whole thing is a real good mess, and it ain't gonna get no better until we get your kids out of that canyon.* Seein as how the large part of the canyon weren't part of the Orvop municipality, he explained, the sheriff's department had to be involved, along with, of course, the park rangers. That bein the case, the alleged theft of the ponies had still taken place in Orvop, even if the alleged murder hadn't, and that meant the Orvop police were still involved.

Heck, I don't need to trace that out for you, Sondi. We're all in this together, and we'll get it straightened out.

I'm glad to hear that, Wilson. Sheriff Jewell, as you and I well know, is married to Kip-Ann, Orwin Porch's sister. I'd like to hear from you that that won't be cloudin his judgment.

Chief of Police Wilson Beckham carried on for a minute with the nececessary assurances, but he also weren't no small man seekin to hide from directness. He made it clear that the Russel boy had been cut down and had bled out and there were witnesses confirmin how he'd named Allison's boy as his killer. He looked Allison in the eye then and told her that either way, disregardin some radical realignment of all these facts, whatever department caught up with him first would arrest Kalin. He was advisin her now to secure legal representation. *We have folks who can help you with that, but seein as how you know Sondra here, she's got a Rolodex of lawyers she can introduce you to.*

We're on our way to Holly Feltzman's office next.

Like I said.

Sondra then made it clear that she was certain Landry had not been kidnapped by Kalin. She emphasized that Kalin had been a close friend of Tom's and had been at his bedside at the hospital.

That paused Chief of Police Beckham. *I did not know this, and that, yes, does call into question other claims recently made.*

And I hope calls into question those makin such claims, Sondra said, crisp like, like she was takin a bite out of a green apple.

Would you mind repeatin this to Detective Peters? He's overseein the case.

On their way to findin Detective Peters, Allison near ran into Officer Poulter. The sight of her snarled his lip, his blond moustache twistin up in a most unpleasant way. Musterin what menace he could, he tilted his body toward her, spreadin his legs more to block her path. That was before he saw Sondra Gatestone comin. It was a pretty extraordinary transformation, what happened next. Allison felt like she was with a celebrity or a figure of power, a president even. Officer Poulter was suddenly stumblin to get out of the way while still tryin to mumble pleasantries at Sondra, who had missed nothin and made sure he didn't miss her scowl.

Detective Peters was out in the field, but Officer Naomi Unga took Sondra's statement. Officer Unga was matter-a-fact and besides takin notes on a yellow legal pad with a stub of a pencil, what she'd type up soon as they was done, she thanked Sondra for her time and said little more than that.

On their way back to Isatch Canyon, Sondra did like she said she was gonna do and stopped by at the offices of Feltzman, Oglewrench & Davis located off Center on a small street crowded with jack-o'-lanterns and Halloween skeletons. This time Mungo didn't wait in the Bronco.

The receptionist there, obviously new at her job, made it clear that no dogs were allowed inside, especially one near as big as a horse, addin that Holly Feltzman had no availability until January 1983. Sondra ignored the poor lady, and anyway Holly Feltzman was already racin their way, like Mick Jagger hisself had just come knockin, and him she'd probably have made wait at least a breath. Allison felt a funny feelin then spread across her face, like she was blushin, though she weren't, just the bloom of a smile, over her good fortune that she'd somehow wound up in the company of such a good and important person. When had that ever happened? In her whole life?

Holly Feltzman was somethin. She had red hair so bright and lustrous Allison assumed it was a wig. And, okay, it was a wig. Her eyelashes were thick as a rake, and she wore lipstick even thicker. She got them mugs of cocoa. She offered coffee too, and much as Allison was cravin a cup, if just to ease up the poundin headache that kept comin and goin, she followed Sondra's lead. Under her desk Holly kept a jar of treats just for Mungo.

How are you? Sondra asked, givin the attorney a big hug.

Down, Sondra. I'm down, Holly Feltzman answered, but she was still grinnin.

You don't look down.

Oh it's not a big D like Depression or Despair. More like a little d. Somewhere between despondent and disappointed.

That still sounds serious, Sondra replied with a wink.

Oh, it is. No one in this town seems to wanna talk about the royal family and the new Prince of Wales. It's a shanda. Princess Di, anybody? How am I to go on? These last questions were mostly addressed to Mungo who she'd got down on her knees to hug. *I was expressin just this to Brother Ewing, and why if he didn't say I sounded like a drunk in a bar.* How Holly Feltzman squealed with joy over that description.

Their meetin weren't long. Once Holly got back behind her desk, she got real steely real quick, listenin carefully to what Sondra had to say about the ugly events unfoldin, and then in turn listenin to Allison's version of the same events, pretty much echoin Sondra's tellin, except for how she was sure Kalin had nothin to do with the death of Russel Porch's boy. *Not with a knife.*

Holly was real busy. She made that clear. But she was also a big fan of the Gatestones and no friend to the Porches. Along with her regular caseload, she was representin the Wongs, who were strugglin with a daughter with ALS as well as various liens against their property, some of which seemed fraudulent, designed purely to harass the poor family, and on top of all that havin to file multiple restrainin orders against Woolsey Porch, maybe Francis Porch, Russel Porch if he'd been alive, *and that darned fool, the Darren Blicker boy,* all of whom allegedly continued to pepper the Wong's property with BBs, *includin the side of the trailer where they sleep because they can't afford right now to get the asbestos removed in the main house, what was discovered when they was repairin some drywall around the chimney. They don't have a cent but what am I gonna do? It's a tzedakah. They need my help.*

Next she addressed her fees, which Allison could not afford even one small part of but which, thanks to Sondra's vague insistence that they would reach a suitable and satisfactory agreement, got Holly to put aside for the moment the question of her retainer. After that, she walked them through what they'd do after Kalin was brought in and arrested, an outcome she wanted to guarantee by exhortin both women to make sure *every officer you meet knows Holly Feltzman is with you. We don't want some fool shoot-out. Orvop police know I can cost them plenty, but I want to make sure the sheriff's department knows I'm happy to get a piece of them too!* Holly was pleased to hear Sondra say that they'd just said as much to Chief of Police Wilson Beckham and she was extra tickled by his reaction to Sondra's assurances that Landry weren't kidnapped, though what legal significance that had was lost on Allison. Of course, she only had to look to Holly Feltzman's walls to behold what her expertise could amount to: Holly framed and hung up her settlement agreements like most folks in Orvop hang up antlers.

Sondra made some small talk then that had nothin to do with either Landry or Kalin, usin names like *the Harvest-Meadow Development* or *the Ridgeline Meadow Estates.* Old war stories. In one, Sondra's deceased husband, Dallin Gatestone, had wanted to hold on to certain allotments because he knew that Old Porch just wanted to build on them and he wouldn't be able to do any such thing given the municipal restrictions already in place, not to mention multiple easements. Old Porch was such a liar, he could only assume Dallin Gatestone was lyin too, so much so that, despite his own lawyer's cautionary advice, he grew even more adamant about the purchase, arguin obstreperously that he'd just permit away the restrictions, fence off the easements.

The storytellin put Holly in an even better mood, and by the end she was pledgin to do whatever it took to get their kids out of this alive and see that justice was served.

Afterward, the two mothers went to a little shop next door and ordered sandwiches. Sondra reassured Allison about the legal fees. *This all's gonna cost us somethin awful, but the measure of that awful ain't nothin compared to the awful we'll have to pay if even one of our children is lost.*

I don't know how to thank you.

Here's to makin the right choices, Sondra said then, raisin her can of orange soda.

And to makin the right jokes when we make the wrong choices, Allison answered. The joke fell flat.

Let's not make wrong choices.

370

Undersheriff Jewell hadn't budged from the Isatch Canyon trail-head. Two big tents granted shelter to several whiteboards, long card tables, plenty of chairs to go around, and in the second tent a big thermos of hot water, with Styrofoam cups and a bowlful of herbal teas and instant cocoa. There were Pop-Tarts too. A table in the first tent held the radios. In both tents space heaters kicked out gusts of warm dry air; power cables snaked out to two gas generators putterin away near the visitor kiosk. Pretty much anyone who dropped by got a handshake and a smile, but Undersheriff Jewell offered no such thing when the mothers of Kalin and Landry approached. He recognized Allison March from their brief interaction yesterday, and seein her with Sondra Gatestone put him on alert.

Sondra didn't disappoint. With Mungo leashed at her side, she came in blazin, straight to the point. Not that she was loud though. Her voice stayed plenty soft as she made it clear that they'd just come from a sit-down with Chief of Police Beckham. Softer still when she made clear the legal representation she'd just secured for both kids *and anyone else who's on the other side of your guns.* That was a bit sharp. Then she dropped Holly Feltzman's name, and boy did that sour up the sheriff's face real good. Once again Allison had that feelin of bein in the company of folks she'd only seen in movies. Though this here was like no movie she'd ever seen, and to be fair Allison didn't go much to the movies, except the bits and pieces she caught at the University Theaters.

Park Ranger Emily Brickey arrived soon after, and Undersheriff Jewell welcomed the intrusion. Since yesterday, under a tentative agreement between the Orvop Police Department, the sheriff's department, and the park rangers, Isatch Canyon had been temporarily closed, but word had just come down from Salt Lake City that now at last the state park was officially closed.

It was 12:19 p.m.

Not that it mattered. Due to the weather no hikers had come along. And since the alleged shootin of Egan's horse, the park had stayed deserted. Other than a truck to salt the main trail as far up as Bridge Four or Park Ranger Brickey's earlier excursion that mornin with three other rangers to impound Sean and Shelly's dirt bikes left by Bridge Two, both bridges froze solid, no park ranger or officer had ventured in since.

Park Ranger Brickey smiled warmly at both Allison and Sondra even though the women were strangers. She was happy as well to pet Mungo on the head. She and others like her were part of the reason Allison had brung Kalin to Orvop in the first place. Allison thought the ranger was pretty as a penny. She had clear skin, dimples in both cheeks, thick brown braids comin out from under a light brown park ranger baseball cap. Half her left ear was gone, savagely too, like it had been eaten by a bear, and her not hidin it, like it weren't nothin to give half an ear to a bear, made Allison smile all the more warmly back.

Folks are sayin we're triple-loaded with storms, Park Ranger Brickey told Undersheriff Jewell then, though she addressed Allison and Sondra too. *What's up there now is already bigger than what came through yesterday. Snow's a certainty at the higher elevations. Maybe even a dustin in the valley. Whoever goes up there lookin for that piece of trash aside from—*

That trash is my boy, Allison cut in real quick. *His name is Kalin. Kalin March. He didn't kill nobody. You're after the wrong person.* Allison couldn't help herself, and Sondra didn't blame her either, givin her arm a squeeze.

Undersheriff Jewell and Park Ranger Brickey shared an uncomfortable glance.

My apologies, ma'am, Park Ranger Brickey responded.

Sondra, I'll let you know if I hear of anythin of substance, Undersheriff Jewell said then. *So far we've seen nothin of your kids.*

I thank you for that, Conrad, but I haven't said what I came here to say. And I'm glad too that this park ranger— Sondra read the badge on her jacket, *Park Ranger Brickey, nice to meet you, is here too.*

Sondra then made clear that Kalin had not kidnapped Landry, and if they was really tryin to contrive in their feeble minds that a sweet fifteen-year-old girl like her daughter Landry was involved with this bloody business about Russel, as put forth by a snake like Orwin Porch, then they was gonna get bit too.

You threatenin me, Mrs. Gatestone? Undersheriff Jewell growled, if keepin his eye on the big St. Bernard too.

You bet I am. Sondra didn't flinch. Mungo yawned. *To the full extent of the law. I will not tolerate one single misstep. Keep that pretty career of yours in mind as you go after our children. That goes for you too, Park Ranger Brickey.* A colder blast Park Ranger Brickey had never knowd before, and she'd been to the base of Katanogos once in the heart of winter.

Get outta here! Undersheriff Jewell said then, wavin them away.

You tell us first: who's up there lookin for our kids?

That's the department's business.

There was no mistakin the distant whines now bouncin around the canyon walls, a good ways up too, but in this cold clear air the sound of engines seemed right around the bend at First Bridge.

Dirt bikes?

ATVs. Park Ranger Brickey's correction earned an eyeful from Undersheriff Jewell.

The sheriff's department has ATVs? Since when?

Willard! Undersheriff Jewell roared out for a deputy who was at that moment sendin away a reporter nosin around the tents. *Escort these ladies out, please.*

Park Ranger Brickey seemed embarrassed, but in avoidin the undersheriff's stern glance wound up lookin at Sondra and Allison. Allison didn't squander the opportunity.

My Kalin didn't kill Russel Porch. Remember that. Someone else has done somethin foul, and they're tryin to say it was my boy.

Willard! Undersheriff Jewell yelled again.

Am I gettin the sense that your men are not on those ATVs? Sondra weren't gonna let this go. *Are they park rangers then?* Her voice perhaps elevatin just a little bit.

Park Ranger Brickey couldn't meet Sondra's glare, but she also couldn't keep from shakin her head.

Though near everyone saw it happen, plenty forgot too how first a small dark bird soared above the parkin lot with a snake in its talons only to lose the writhin thing when an eagle charged downwards. The dark bird had dropped away, as if mortally struck, but the snake did not reach the ground. Instead the eagle seized hold of that red signature upon the air and without so much as a peck tore it in half. By then the dark bird was above the eagle, and together they flew off. And likely because it had happened so fast and folks weren't sure if maybe it had just been a branch, because they couldn't believe it had really been a snake, just like they also couldn't determine if the small bird had been with or against the eagle, everyone dimissed the visions already disturbin their memories. Besides what did these folks or any in their time know about the warnin of birds?

And while neither of the mothers beheld that spectacle, they were still inside the tent, Sondra never forgot Park Ranger Emily Brickey's headshake, nor did the park ranger ever forget the question asked by Tom and Landry's momma. Months later in her deposition, and later as a witness for the courts, Park Ranger Brickey with her half-eaten ear, and by the way it was an infection that had done it to her, when she was eight, though it was implied in the trials that this affliction had rendered her deaf and stupid, Park Ranger Brickey showed how she not only could hear just fine, she could remember important matters with unusual clarity.

She would dutifully recount how but an hour earlier, about when Sondra and Allison were tryin to refortify their achin hearts with sandwiches, Orwin Porch, Egan Porch, Kelly Porch, and this fella named Billings Gale had huddled around the very same card table the mothers had stood before. Sean Porch and Shelly Porch had remained outside the tent, not far from the teenagers Francis and Woolsey Porch, joined there in the parkin lot by friends, includin the acne-scarred Darren Blicker, who at once started blastin REO Speedwagon from his car, *Waitin for the thaw out,* and later on Tom Petty, *Everybody's had to fight to be free,* The Charlie Daniels Band too, just the one song most everyone in Orvop knew. Styx's *Renegade* got played too many times to count, also *Great White Hope.* No one wanted to hear *No One Like You* by the Scorpions for the fifth time, but Darren still played it a fifth time and then a sixth time.

Darren Blicker and Woolsey Porch, who Darren considered his closest friend, mostly hung out by Darren's car. Now and then their talk and music would get loud enuf to earn shouts from Egan, who just as fast as he appeared would disappear back inside the tent.

That's where Old Porch was, by the radios, stabbin a map of Isatch Canyon with the thumb of his right hand. In fact on one such downward strike his thumbnail, what was already split and yellow with rot, came apart, half of it suddenly juttin out at an absurd angle. Park Ranger Brickey recalled the sight as bein so jarrin, this absurd anatomical geometry, that she felt as if she'd just witnessed a femur poke out of someone's thigh. Even Undersheriff Jewell and Egan Porch recoiled at the sight. Old Porch didn't care one lick.

You explain to me where they go from here?! Again Old Porch's thumb stabbed the spot where Egan and the rest of his brothers had claimed to have *cornered* Kalin, Landry, and the horses, *cornered them too on a narrow ledge* from where Kalin had shot at Egan and put a bullet in Cavalry. *There's nowhere to go! Especially with goshdarn horses!*

There's a scree right below, Egan said, pointin to a place on the map that depicted no such thing. *If they could ride up that, maybe—*

Maybe what?! Old Porch's breath boiled out his nostrils. *These here are cliffs. Unless them horses can fly, and they cannot, that is one thing I am frickin sure about, then they're stuck.*

Or there's a lateral move this map don't show, Undersheriff Jewell said, usin a capped BIC ballpoint to trace an alternate route. *Along here, deeper into the canyon, or back toward the entrance, though in either direction, up that high, they're still stuck. There ain't no way down.*

They also couldn't've got far in this weather, Egan brought up. *They spent the night somewhere.*

If they tried to stick it out on the mountainside, they'd've slid off by mornin, Kelly said then, speakin up for the first time.

Undersheriff Jewell grunted in agreement. *There ain't a crevice in this canyon that ain't at one time been a grave for a horse.*

The warmest we'll get today is in about an hour or two, Park Ranger Brickey said then. *If we get above freezin, maybe we'll see some of this ice melt. I'd say that's our window to get up there and find them. If they survived, they'll likely be huddled up somewhere near froze to death.*

Undersheriff Jewell gave Park Ranger Brickey an approvin nod. He even repeated her caveat: *If they survived.*

Old Porch had every reason to underestimate Kalin and Landry, but it wasn't lost on him either that those two kids had somehow managed to elude Egan, the very best rider in the Porch family.

Usin that same mangled thumb, he turned his attention briefly to the entrance of the canyon; in fact his nail scraped right past the Awides Mine, unmarked, before headin back to Aster Scree, then past it, followin the same path Kalin, Landry, Tom, and the horses had tried yesterday before the weather had turned them back.

You're sayin they got that far yesterday? Egan was askin. *I don't think so.*

This is precipitous, unstable terrain. Steep is an understatement. Park Ranger Brickey was continuin the line Old Porch had started, what in fact was the exact same route Kalin was plannin to take if the ice ever thawed. *And with the freeze, this here, here, and here—* And the *heres* kept comin as Park Ranger Brickey pointed out numerous places that were in her assessment *like bobsled runs straight to the bottom. And when it thaws there's no tellin what the soil saturation will be. Could settle like concrete or give way like wet cement. We've been hearin slides all mornin.*

Old Porch kept draggin his nail all the way to the end of the canyon, where still more cliffs waited, a part of which was called Cahoon's Staircase because it led either up via a sketchy trail to a part of Katanogos called Halo's Hollow, adjacent to Kirk's Cirque, or down to an area above the high bluffs of Yell Rock Falls called Tiffany's Vista, where manageable trails around to the back side of Katanogos were abundant. Though why not take the Heathen-Slade Canyon Trail, which Old Porch knew was the easiest route, or head up past the big *I* on Agoneeya to Cutter's Crick Path? Wouldn't either of those have made more sense?

Old Porch was only just now startin to realize that he'd lost sense of who exactly he was up against. At first this Kalin kid had been some lone idjit, not from Orvop, who'd made one heckuva mistake. But now somehow he'd managed to kick free of Egan and his boys, and on a horse too. And then it turned out he was with a Gatestone. Weren't that the darndest revelation!

Conrad, if they got this far, do you think they could make it down to here, by way of Cahoon's Staircase, *on horseback?* Old Porch's awful nail was stickin with Tiffany's Vista.

Park Ranger Brickey didn't wait for the undersheriff to respond. *Cahoon's Staircase is closed. Even on foot it's impossible. If that's where they're headed, they'll have to turn around.*

Old Porch ground down his ragged teeth so hard, his jaw muscles bulged out in big ugly bunches. He hadn't asked her opinion, and he didn't take to her talkin so open and uppity at him. But he still nodded.

What no one gave a notice to was that tiny fracture of map accountin for the area between two interlockin spurs, where the water from high Altar Lake wandered down in the form of a line thinner than a hair. It was the same with the map Tom had consulted many months ago because Tom's map was the same as the one in that tent. Pretty much everyone in Utah County, if they was interested in this area, had this map and so would've encountered too, if they was lookin, the same barrier: cliffs. And even if Old Porch was to disregard them cliffs on the map, followin that hairline stream, and whatever other hazards were thrown in the way, right to where this map ended, to what Old Porch still knew was there, Altar Lake, what then? Even if a horse could get up that high, only worse waited, because that's where the full might of Katanogos waited.

It just didn't make any sense. None of it. And Old Porch's frustration only continued to grow.

Park Ranger Brickey weren't helpin either with her yabberin. *If they was seen here, then they're likely stuck at this elevation.* She was back above Aster Scree.

The point's been made, Old Porch growled at her.

Undersheriff Jewell had some sense of his brother-in-law and stepped in quick. *Orwin, what Emily's gettin at here, and I'm inclined to agree, is that if they did try this crossin, whether at night or even this mornin, we should likely start lookin for their bodies down here.*

Even Egan agreed with that assessment. *Dad, we can start right now. We don't have to wait for no thaw. And if there ain't bodies, we can get up after them when it does thaw. Either way, they're dead or trapped.*

I'd say that's so, Kelly chimed in. Billings kept his lips buttoned.

We have the ATVs, Egan continued, keen to get the talkin part done with so they could get to the doin part.

Ice won't matter, Kelly added. *Not on the main trail.*

Old Porch straightened up some, disregardin whatever consensus his two sons seemed pleased to settle on, glarin only at Undersheriff Jewell. *Conrad, I still want to know, if they did make it down Cahoon's Staircase, where then? Maybe you should send some folks around the back side of Agoneeya to at least check out Tiffany's Vista for any sign of them?*

Sir, with all due respect, Park Ranger Emily Brickey again spoke up. *No horse is gettin down Cahoon's Staircase. Like I said before: it's closed, it's a dead end.*

I weren't talkin to you! Old Porch lashed out at her, loud too, too loud.

Whoa, Orwin! Whoa! Undersheriff Jewell responded fast, even leanin his big frame over the table if just to block Old Porch's view of the young park ranger. *This is my call!* And Undersheriff Jewell was dead serious. *I've done nothin but think on this all night and mornin. Wherever the kids got to last night, they didn't get further than here or here. Even if they abandoned them horses, even on foot.*

I know Cahoon's Staircase, Egan added in a matter-a-fact tone to resettle his dad, somethin he'd got expert at over the course of his life. *No horse is goin up or down that. You're givin these two too much credit, Dad. They don't know what they're doin.* Egan here was also communicatin somethin else: that Old Porch best let calm prevail so they could get the heck into that canyon before anyone with a badge did.

Oblivious to any subtext but still adoptin Egan's tone, Undersheriff Jewell made it clear then what they all could expect from here on out: *Right now I've under my orders a team of law enforcement rangers assemblin the ice gear they'll need to head up the scree where Egan's horse was killt.*

Which was true, even if by this point that team of law enforcement rangers amounted to just two. There were supposed to have been eight. To be fair the two men sent for were highly adept in such conditions as well as armed. In fact Corbet Wadley, from Sandy, and Bren Kelson, from Park City, had reached the park before dawn. The two had almost taken off too, their gear slung over their backs, a thermos of hot coffee for each, ready to get up into the rocks and see what was what. But in checkin in with their own superiors, who checked in with Undersheriff Jewell, it was clear that they were under no circumstances authorized yet to proceed until proper backup was in place, which would turn out to be hours away. Undersheriff Jewell didn't want those two scalin up the side of the cliff if there was some crazed teenager willin to fire potshots at the helpless climbers.

It's somewhat ironic that if these two law enforcement rangers had ascended Aster Scree in the early mornin, they quite probably would have altered this entire history.

It's also worth notin that while proceedin with great prudence, Undersheriff Jewell mostly thought this was all theater. He had made a worthy career out of demonstratin patience, calm, and unrelentin tenacity no matter how slow his progress might at times seem. People didn't get hurt under his watch and people still got caught. Undersheriff Jewell understood that waitin for the canyon to thaw some would turn highly dangerous circumstances into easily managed ones. He also understood that the kids above, if they was alive, had nowhere to go and would only be losin resources with every passin hour, growin weaker and more scared. He wouldn't be surprised if they soon tried to signal for help. If they was alive.

Though, also, truth be told, Undersheriff Jewell didn't believe that was gonna happen. Fer reasons he couldn't point to and wouldn't rely on, he'd already started to assume that the kids weren't alive, the horses dead too. It was just a gut feelin. Death was up there doin its work. And in some ways he weren't wrong.

If anythin kept unsettlin this picture for Undersheriff Jewel it was them shots fired at Egan. It was considered a fact by this point, but it was a fact that provoked in him this impossible-to-dismiss sensation that somethin just weren't addin up right. That armed confrontation was an escalation he'd mistrusted from the get-go.

These rangers are already up there? Old Porch asked then.

Undersheriff Jewell didn't miss the alarm in his friend's voice. *They'll head up soon. I'm waitin on some men to provide cover from below. I wish your Hatch was here. We need a good sniper.*

I'm glad to hear it, Old Porch grunted. *I was startin to believe you was all just sittin in this tent.* Old Porch forced a smile, and while Egan and Kelly knew to chuckle, Undersheriff Jewell did not join in.

The only trouble we'll get is if this storm starts dumpin snow. If we find them hunkered down then, even right above that scree, why we're gonna have one heckuva rescue on our hands.

Old Porch lost it.

Rescue?! Old Porch was incensed, if he weren't just outright crazy, some old-world claim on lynch law alight in his eyes.

The courts would later object to Park Ranger Brickey characterizin her own reaction as one of fear, the argument bein that she was arrivin at the state of her emotions based on events both prior and subsequent to this particular encounter, the prior events includin the terrifyin giant she'd encountered the previous night when she was on the trail with Rumi Plothow, and the subsequent events, well, we'll get to them soon enuf. Park Ranger Brickey heeded the objection and recharacterized her impressions for the court, though it hardly altered her narrative, her understandable trepidation eventually becomin part of the public's general squibblesquall.

The record states that Park Ranger Brickey then recounted how after shriekin *Rescue?!* Old Porch had with his other hand gripped that piece of nail still hangin off his thumb and ripped it off.

And it weren't just the little piece, she would say. *It was the whole nail!*

The whole thumbnail?

A query Park Ranger Brickey would answer with a nod, whereupon she was instructed to voice the affirmative or the negative.

Did Orwin Porch rip off his whole thumbnail?

He did. And then he threw it at Sheriff Jewell.

He threw it at Undersheriff Jewell?

Yes.

Did it hit him?

No. It didn't go that far. It landed on the map. Right on the bluffs of Isatch Canyon. I still see it so perfectly. There was a spatter of blood. Not too much, but the blood was bright. If that weren't a sign we should've heeded.

To his credit or not, Undersheriff Jewell just shrugged off the behavior. Old Porch weren't no stranger to him. *That's right, Orwin, we could very well end up with a rescue on our hands.* The undersheriff even swept aside that nail like it weren't nothin but a chip of wood or an errant bit of leaf, even if it did leave behind a smear of red. *I can't even imagine how we'll get those horses down if it snows.*

Rescue my boy's killers?! Apoplectic don't begin to describe Old Porch then. Park Ranger Brickey speculated in court that she feared he might try to discerp his whole thumb, though she didn't say *discerp.* That got a big laugh but was still struck from the record.

Undersheriff Jewell had had enuf. He weren't undersheriff because he spent his days on his back suckin on milkweed, tryin to convince his thinkin that the sky weren't blue. He raised hisself up tall and squared his shoulders against his brother-in-law.

The law is to take them in and let due process carry on with the rest. And that's what we'll do. We will first locate them, and then we will bring them down. Alive. Do you understand me, Orwin? Those kids are minors, and until the Law determines otherwise, they will be treated and protected as minors.

Fer his part, Old Porch weren't Old Porch either because he spent his days suckin on the same stupid milkweed, havin the same argument with the sky. He knew when blue was blue and knew a thing about what red looked like too. And the undersheriff was near red as he would get that mornin.

Likely to both conceal his own undimmin rage as well as grant Undersheriff Jewell his moment, Old Porch snatched off at once his hat, and near crumplin it with both hands, bowin his head too to hide his face, apologized for speakin so rashly and inconsiderately, not failin to mention either how his heart was possessed by only one thing, the loss of his dear child, his youngest child, his dear Russel, and the sooner this matter was done with, then the sooner he and his boys could get to grievin. Undersheriff Jewell was moved. Even Park Ranger Brickey was moved. And when Old Porch at last lifted his head, his face seemed to comport to these expressed sentiments.

I know it's a big ask, Conrad, but will you allow my boys to search for our horses? We won't go anywheres near where your men'll be. Just take the ATVs up the main trail to Bridge Four, maybe Five, unless that's too far?

Be my guest! the undersheriff roared, no doubt happy to see that they'd got through the previous stickiness.

Sir, ATVs are strictly forbidden within the park, Park Ranger Brickey at once objected, though she didn't like much havin to speak up again. When asked later why she had, and she was asked later, and in court too, she replied that it was her duty.

Oh heck, Emily! Undersheriff Jewell erupted. *Orwin's just lost his youngest child! Murdered! Fer Pete's sake, let him at least have a go at findin his horses! We could use the help!*

Is that an order?

Undersheriff Jewell looked in disbelief at the young park ranger.

You're goshdarn right it is!

As most are aware, there's been plenty of debate over this exchange. Did Undersheriff Jewell really order Park Ranger Brickey to overlook the laws of the park grounds, which categorically forbid the use of motorized vehicles by civilians? As we've already seen, Sean and Shelly Porch were both ticketed, with their dirt bikes impounded. To homologate such an incursion was a career risk not undertaken lightly. But Undersheriff Jewell did do just that. Risks be darned, if they were ever rightly considered.

Anyways, plenty in Orvop, includin some of the park rangers themselves, have since testified that the intermittent presence of dirt bikes or ATVs was not uncommon. There just weren't enuf park rangers to even note all the infractions, let alone catch and ticket such scofflaws. Utah's a place where the laws of the State, the laws of the Church, and the laws of the Land don't necessarily align, but its in the variance of the in-betweens where most folks live.

After that Park Ranger Brickey did what she was told. She unlocked the gate, now secured with a new chain and combination padlock, and stood aside as Egan, Kelly, and Billings, each on a three-wheeler ATV, roared into the park, all of them armed with rifles and likely other firearms.

It was 12:02 p.m.

Not long after that she did the same for an Orvop police vehicle driven by Officer Poulter, with Officer Mildenhall in the passenger seat, both of whom were there to assist two law enforcement rangers, Corbet Wadley and Bren Kelson. This too was a mistake, but no other officers who were first of all plenty rested not to mention trained for this kind of work were available. Poulter and Mildenhall had rallied with the help of ample Mountain Dew, scrambled across the crick, and caught up with Wadley and Kelson by the corpse of Cavalry. Everyone could see the horse had been shot in the head. The law enforcement rangers also noted a gunshot to the chest with any leakin blood long since froze up. Durin the night animals had gotten at the flanks and the belly. It was a sad sight.

Bren Kelson took the lead climbin up to the fissure. It weren't no big deal. He was made for this job; though it's true, his square jaw, wavy hair, and, except for some scars from acne and a nose curvy as the Orvop Canyon Road, the rest of his features made him near good-lookin enuf to make actin seem a viable option, or politics. He weren't against the idea either. He'd also been one heckuva wrestler at Orvop High and Isatch U and had never stopped stayin fit. Corbet Wadley was equally fit, from swimmin, with green eyes and black hair and had an easy disposition void of ambition except to excel at this career, which he adored.

Aster Scree presented no problem. The ice had fixed the slippery stones better than bedrock. The fissure, though, was no longer pass-able. Fallin rocks had sealed it up. Bren Kelson and Corbet Wadley decided to just climb over the whole crag and would've too if right before hammerin in that first piton Wadley hadn't lost his footin and sprained his ankle. Poulter and Mildenhall did come in handy then, helpin that cursin ranger back to the truck.

Law Enforcement Ranger Kelson, nonetheless, still made a go of it hisself and did in fact reach the top of the crag, though the goin was slower than he'd anticipated. First the temperature started to rise, meltin a lot of the ice. The rocks began shiftin. Kelson shed the gear he'd brought to handle the ice, gear he'd used plenty of times on Bridal Veil Falls in fact. Unfortunately the rock underneath was lousy, and he had to be extra diligent about each and every move.

When Kelson finally did reach a point where the fissure was no longer blocked by rock, he discovered beyond there another wall of tree limbs and debris. By the time he'd surmount that, any oppor-tunity to impact the future would've long since passed. Not that he knew it.

When he at last radioed in his location, he was told to return, though before acquiescin he did take a moment to enjoy the majesty and clarity of the canyon, what he'd share that night with his fiancée, Brooke Young.

Back at the Isatch Canyon entrance, Park Ranger Brickey was the one to help Ranger Corbet Wadley to a medic. The sprain turned out to be far worse than expected: the ankle already looked like a basketball, if basketballs were purple. Wadley shed hot tears that hour but not over no pain. He hated desks, but to a desk was where he was headin. At least for a few weeks. In fact he didn't get back into the field until well into the followin year. Wadley wondered for the rest of his life how things might've come out different if he hadn't slipped. The tears he shed then were from pain.

Park Ranger Brickey had offered to go up and assist Law Enforcement Ranger Bren Kelson, who she didn't know well but was familiar enuf with to like and respect. Undersheriff Jewell denied her request, orderin her instead to radio Kelson to return at once. The last thing Undersheriff Jewell needed was to coordinate another rescue operation for a ranger out on his own. It took Park Ranger Brickey hours to hail Kelson on the radio. When he finally called in, he explained how the crag and the canyon walls had prohibited a decent signal. He also noted, for the record, that there weren't no sign of the kids. *Just elk droppins, likely from a big old elk.*

The only satisfaction Park Ranger Brickey derived durin those hours in the parkin lot was seein the two Porch brothers just as stuck as she was because she'd seized their dirt bikes. At one point she was sure that the older one with dark eyes, the one with a sty, that would be Shelly, seemed ready to charge on over, but the younger one, that would be Sean, still coughin some and spittin more, intervened. They started yellin at each other then until Old Porch came chargin out of one of the tents and told them to get the heck outta there. They didn't like that, but they obeyed.

As Park Ranger Brickey would later testify, she had failed to include in her initial report on those events occurin on Friday, October 29, any mention of Old Porch's gruesome nail-flingin tantrum nor Undersheriff Jewell's willingness to allow Egan Porch, Kelly Porch, and Billings Gale to enter the Isatch Canyon Park on their ATVs. She was mortified to realize she had no recollection as to why she hadn't included even the briefest mention of that scene, except if perhaps the distaste over what had transpired had somehow erased the offendin minutes from her head albeit impermanently.

Throughout her life, though, Park Ranger Brickey would wonder if perhaps a more illuminatin description of how Undersheriff Jewell and Orwin Porch had interacted that freezin midday might've saved many of the lives the ensuin days would see lost. Might not her supervisor, Mavis Blackledge, have taken immediate offense over the matter, and likely, because he respected Emily, given her an earful for not tellin him sooner, while sparin the worst for Undersheriff Jewell, who had no business handlin the Porches like he'd done?

That elision would never stop tormentin her: *It haunts me.* She would even claim that she had a ghost who would come at night to sit in her shadows. *Just eyein me, waitin for my time to come. Not that ghosts care about time. Forever makes even the longest lifetime worth not even a blink.* Not all ghosts are like Tom.

By the time Sondra and Allison had made it to the Isatch Canyon parkin lot, anyone there could hear in the distance them ATVs. Sondra spied out quick enuf Sean and Shelly Porch, who did look like they was in a mood foul enuf to charge a pretty park ranger, but she also saw no sign of Egan or Kelly. It weren't so hard then to put two and two together: Egan and Kelly were up in the canyon, and Sean and Shelly was pissed that they weren't.

Sondra also spotted Woolsey and Francis. They was surrounded by other Orvop students, all of whom should've been in class. Lindsey Holt had also spun by, though as soon as he saw everyone congregatin around Darren Blicker's car, he turned his truck right around and skedaddled back to Orvop High. Despite his size and indisputable strength, Lindsey still shied from any Porch.

In fact one time Woolsey had saved up spit in his mouth through the course of two periods. He'd done this skiin before, storin up saliva the whole lift ride up and then deliverin that mess of wet on the back of one of his buds or brothers before tearin off down the slopes. But this weren't ten minutes on a chairlift. This had been two hours! And in the lunch line Woolsey had drenched Lindsey's letterman jacket. The guys howled with laughter, Tom too. One girl behind Lindsey gagged so bad, she near threw up on him. You can bet Lindsey gave chase and even cuffed Woolsey hard across the back of the head, but that was the sum of it. Lindsey would always have to weigh hard the other Porch boys who stood behind Woolsey.

Not that Lindsey was missin much here. There was little laughter, mostly just a bag of Red Man or a can of Skoal Wintergreen passed around to keep lower lips packed. A grim gatherin fer sure, and the surliness weren't helped none by the sight of Sondra Gatestone, because every Porch knows every Gatestone, and vice versa, and, yes, scowls were expected, but Sondra sensed quick enuf how that cluster of millin-about angry boys was about to turn into somethin else. Francis Porch stepped forward first, his face blotched with a red agony that too soon dissipated to a chalky palor as he just as fast withdrew to the scrum.

Woolsey Porch, though, when he emerged did not withdraw. He kept right on marchin her way. He was a regular hotspur fer sure, happiest when he was in the heat, further fueled no doubt by the stereo in Darren Blicker's car, now crankin AC/DC. *You're only young, but you're gonna die.*

You this Kalin's momma? Woolsey had chosen to address Allison first, and at once Sondra felt her own position improve some.

I am, Allison answered, steppin forward. She did have sand, Sondra noted, as she readied herself too for whatever was to follow.

Woolsey first tried to spit tobacco on Allison's Stan Smiths, but somethin about the mix in his mouth didn't coalesce, and he mostly sprayed his own boots.

My boy didn't kill your brother, Allison told him, like she knew she'd have to keep on sayin until it finally got roots enuf to take hold.

You don't got no boy no more. Best get to them side of the facts now.

By this point the scrawny, straw-haired Darren Blicker had hustled their way too, his hands on Woolsey's shoulders, tryin to guide the belligerent boy back to the group. Blicker wouldn't look at Allison none, but he nodded at Sondra, explainin that the situation here *is just real hard to take,* which Sondra accepted as a kind of apology, thankin Darren Blicker, which Woolsey didn't like one bit, shakin off his friend as they walked away, *Don't take her frickin side! She's as much in this as her!* pretty much audible to everyone in the vicinity.

Let him spit on hisself, Sondra snorted. *Let them all spit on themselves.*

A reporter from KIUB scurried over then, as in the Isatch University Broadcast program, which could be described as local as local can get. Ilene Clayton, from Carthage, Illinois, a senior at this point at IU with a major in communications, who you might recall would appear at the Womens Gymnasium in 2013, wanted to get on tape a general statement. Allison was all too happy to repeat what she knew to be true: someone was to blame for this terrible loss of life, but it weren't her son, Kalin March.

Sondra waited until the fella recordin Allison, Steven Hensel from Waterloo, Iowa, had lowered the camera before she told Ilene Clayton how *the only one sayin this stuff about who killt Russel Porch is his father, Orwin Porch, and it's best to treat whatever he says with a grain of salt.*

What Allison had said played well when it was broadcast that afternoon and evenin, but largely because Ilene Clayton also got Old Porch on camera.

To be fair not even the recountin to follow will do justice to the great unmapped expanse that marks the mercurial talents of Old Porch. Half the stories about him ain't true, and the other half ain't true enuf. He's squirrelly, swift, violent if need be, a bawlin baby if need be too, and otherwise a nasty survivor with a taste for what it means to live longest without livin a bit by the prescriptive notions of others, whether put forward by kith or kin, the State, the Church, or whatever befouled societal norm, in Old Porch's eyes, has clawed its way up on the rocks of these lands and declared itself Law.

When KIUB reporter Ilene Clayton and her crew turned the camera on him, Old Porch's eyes at once softened and glistened. Like he'd just done in Undersheriff Jewell's tent, like that was a rehearsal, he again snatched off his hat, them scarred hands grippin the brim, his head bowed, like he was standin before the Lord Hisself. Gone was the Old Porch who yesterday mornin had told Allison her Kalin had no life left to live, *I guarantee it*, or last night had puked on Sondra Gatestone's doorstep. Here instead stood the sweetest, frailest man you ever seen. Darned near decorous too. To them who would see the televised clip, and there would be many, Old Porch seemed Church-like if not outright saint-like, and downright iconic too, from them old snakeskin boots to his faded Lees to that old horsehair vest. The kind of cowboy the nation had just elected to the presidency, except Orwin Porch weren't no actor, he was the real thing.

Old Porch spoke with wilted words about how, what with the loss of his little Russel, his heart was busted for good, except now it was breakin all over again, and who for? *Why this Kalin boy! I know nothin about him, but here he's gone and thrown his life away. Don't fleein into a canyon that's a dead end say it all? How sad is that?* Old Porch's forgivin tone never faltered as he described Kalin keepin at bay them folks who was tryin to help him. *But what did he do? Shoot at them! Even killt a horse!*

Whether it weren't no more than some condensation twinklin on the edge of his eyes or actual moisture conjured by his devisin heart don't matter. On TV, Old Porch was quiverin, teary, a feeble old man. *Maybe at least I can get back my two horses. Keep them in your prayers. Please.*

For weeks afterward, Porch Meats was innundated with pies, casseroles, breads, canned fruit and jams, some jars lavishly bound up with ribbons and pink-scripted cards offerin sympathies and telephone numbers, with a little heart drawn over whatever *i* needed dottin.

To Ilene Clayton's credit, KIUB sure got the scoop of the day. The interviews even got picked up by KSL and were later rebroadcast throughout Utah and even in Idaho, Nevada, and Colorado. And why not? On one hand there was a bereft father shattered by a terrible loss, a murder in fact, while on the other hand there was a mother swearin it weren't her boy that done the deed. Who was to be believed?

It was quite a story, and from then on its appeal would only grow.

Somethin should probably be said about whether or not Old Porch hisself had come to believe Kalin was the one who done in Russel. See, the more times he told the story of how Russel bled out before his eyes, died right there in Old Porch's arms, but not before namin Kalin as his killer, the more Old Porch hisself saw only that. You too might find yourself susceptible to this kind of picture paintin. It might even make the most sense too: just a father sufferin the sight of his blood-drenched child, clutchin that failin life, bawlin, breathless, his sons bawlin too.

And Old Porch didn't stop either, convincin folks who was to blame every chance he got, even if he also never ceased thinkin about Trent Riddle. There was the real trouble. A thorn in his side, a thorn big as a bayonet. Because, see, fer the second mornin in a row Riddle hadn't showed up at work, and neither Egan nor Billings had seen anythin to indicate he'd returned to his place. The guy had just plain disappeared, without tellin no one where he'd gone or when he planned to be back. And now with Egan, Kelly, and Billings up in the canyon dealin with Priority Number One, it was left to Old Porch to handle the one witness who could challenge his story.

Somewhat foolishly, Orwin Porch even drove by Riddle's place hisself, checkin the parkin lot for Riddle's brown Plymouth Duster, only to think better of what folks might say if he was spotted there, and he was spotted there, by Corrie O'Brien, Leo Gans, and Daniel Leishman. Orwin Porch should've at least caught sight of Leo Gans. Poor Leo, always carryin around a basketball, always with the same Philadelphia Flyers jersey on, never with a place to go.

It was 1:17 p.m.

Next Old Porch returned to the police station. He'd already been there earlier that mornin, a little after 10:00 a.m., before he'd thought better of the idea and took off just a few minutes before Sondra Gatestone and Allison March arrived to do what he'd been unable to see through: sit down with Chief of Police Beckham.

This time around Old Porch made it into the buildin, but before he could reach the chief of police, he was buttonholed by Detective

Peters, who sought to revisit some minor details pertainin to Wednesday night. By the time they reached the detective's desk, Old Porch was already deep into a retellin of the gruesome events, heapin praise on his boys, like Kelly givin Russel CPR, or Egan givin Kelly support by just bein there. *He's got so much backbone, he's got extra to share.* Detective Peters at once mentioned that he still needed to talk with Egan *and that goes for your man Billings Gale,* somethin Old Porch assured him he'd help facilitate.

Throughout, Old Porch worked hard to create an impression of unwaverin generosity, thoroughness, thoughtfulness, and whatever other rubbish word one can arrive at to gild manure. Old Porch even brought up Riddle, notin that the young man had missed two days of work in a row, which weren't no big thing, seein as how Old Porch had shut down his facility yesterday, except that Riddle was an *on-the-button on-time kinda guy and should've at least called in. This absence just ain't in character.* Of course, Wednesday night Riddle hadn't exactly been in character, Old Porch made sure to add. *He got really drunk.* Old Porch even managed to look discomfited for havin to divulge such uncommon behavior. *Detective, I'm not one to judge. I did my share of misbehavin in my younger days. It's just that Riddle went a bit too far if you know what I mean.* But Old Porch was unable to sense whether Detective Peters knew what he meant; maybe he was one of those devout spic types. Old Porch decided to treat him as that.

Riddle had a bad headache comin. I didn't cast no stone. I kept my peace. By the end, though, well, it got pretty bad, like he was near hallucinatin.

Thank you, Mr. Porch. Is there any reason you didn't mention this Wednesday night when we spoke?

I don't know. I didn't think of it. What happened didn't concern him. He was long gone by the time Russel made it home to die. Old Porch dragged the back of his hand across his eyes, though they was dry as Moab in the summer.

Of course, I understand, Mr. Porch. I thank you just the same for bringin this to my attention. It's always best to get the full picture.

Old Porch nodded, pleased to see Detective Peters takin so many notes.

Is that thumb of yours okay? I can get you a Band-Aid?

The inquiry surprised Old Porch near as much as the sight of his thumb. Had he even given it a second thought since he'd ripped off the nail? It sure was a swollen, bloody mess. Old Porch declined the offer, sayin how he was headin home and had plenty of remedies there.

Did Trent Riddle drive home on his own? Detective Peters asked then.

Old Porch might have blinked extra then, recognizin his mistake, or at least what he hadn't thought through, grittin too his teeth to hide whatever his face had likely already given away.

I don't recall. I hope not. The night's already so . . . by everythin that happened. Old Porch hung his head, shook it some, commanded his eyes to abandon their desert, and they obeyed, his cheeks streaked when he raised his head again.

Detective Peters fumbled around for some tissues. *Don't you worry, Mr. Porch. I'll sort the rest of these details when I talk to your son Egan.*

That's the right thing to do, Old Porch said, snortin his nose in one of the offered tissues. *He and his brother Kelly are tryin to find our horses now.*

Detective Peters came around his desk then to pat Old Porch on his back. *We'll get your boy's killer. And for what it's worth, Riddle's folks and friends are just as concerned as you.*

Outside the police station, Old Porch retrieved Mr. Bucket from the red-and-white Chevy diesel. He didn't want to seem happy to get outta there. Not that the encounter hadn't been friendly enuf, though he still had a nasty knot in his chest. No doubt he'd just upped the ante to this mess. But nothin he'd said to Detective Peters would misalign with what he'd already prepared his boys for that mornin, and by boys he meant Egan, Kelly, and Billings. He trusted Billings most of all. The guy knew how to keep a story.

They'd stood around in the kitchen, drinkin black coffee and watchin the mornin drift in. Old Porch had brought up how strange it was to see Riddle drinkin so much after Francis and Woolsey had cut out. That caught Kelly flat-footed with Egan doin no better.

Billings, you recall what Riddle was beltin down?

Jack Daniels. Billings hadn't missed a beat. Cold-blooded joy to Old Porch's heart.

Egan caught on then. *Straight. At the end.*

Kelly, how'd he get the bottle?

No idea. Brought it with him. Better.

Egan, what kinda stuff was he sayin?

He was in slursville. I couldn't make heads or tails of it. He'd won that big hand and I guess was just dumb happy.

Old Porch had left it at that, even if he hadn't liked it much then and liked it even less now. Riddle was gonna turn up eventually, and if Detective Peters or even one of them numskull officers got to him, he'd sure as heck deny drinkin and then draw a picture of Russel walkin in on them, so pleased with hisself, even tossin some cash into the pot. Old Porch sucked in both lips, tugged Mr. Bucket closer to his side, his steps falterin some on that wide sidewalk, gettin served now with a vivid image of that pot he'd lost, the blur of Riddle gettin the heck outta there, followed by the biggest blur of all.

Old Porch knew it wouldn't be hard to find churchers willin to vouch for Brother Riddle's character. Old Porch's story might rag up and tatter pretty quick then, which would turn the scrutiny on Old Porch and his family, the kind of scrutiny the Porches might not survive, not if Riddle survived, if that Kalin boy survived, especially if Landry Gatestone survived.

The thought of those voices tellin their side of things slammed into Old Porch then, stopped him dead in fact, what no average man could take standin, and add to that a rotten thumb, nailless now and swellin with pain and infection. But Old Porch took it standin, tellin hisself he'd met worse head-on, though he hadn't. Then he swallowed once, pounded his chest once, and, draggin Mr. Bucket with him, got back to walkin.

The news was even better than Old Porch might've imagined: Senator Hays was happy to report that Senate Bill 1245 had been scheduled for consideration on the Senate floor next Thursday, and the senator was convinced it had the votes.

The bill's got a positive score in the millions. Always nice when Federal coffers see some gain. Before Thanksgivin we could have the president's signature on it.

Old Porch could hardly speak.

You all right, Orwin?

Some dark calculus that went far beyond mere impulse spurred Old Porch then to do what he did next: he told the senator about how his youngest boy, Russel, had been murdered and by a horse thief no less. Wednesday night in fact, not long after he and the senator had spoke last.

Oh heck, Orwin, I am so sorry! I was gonna suggest you be here for the vote, but now—

Old Porch cut off the senator. Now he had to be there. He'd come right after the funeral. Because in the end weren't this all about horses? Acquirin land and managin land *to serve our heritage, to serve our great state.* Old Porch didn't mention Four Summits and the ski resorts. *Russel loved horses, and he died defendin them against an outsider. More than ever now, this bill is about him.*

Senator Hays listened carefully and no doubt saw how dedicatin this bill to a fallen boy devoted to horses might not be such a bad idea. The Capitol could use a good dose of the likes of Old Porch.

Senator Hays's secretary, or whatever you call them helpers in

D.C., got on the line to schedule an early lunch on Thursday, November fourth. Would Old Porch be free to meet with several other folks before the vote?

That's what Old Porch wanted to hear.

Next he called back three state senators to endure their words of solace and outrage as well as every offer of help that weren't worth a tin quarter at the bottom of a crap heap. When they finally took a breath long enuf for Old Porch to get a word in edgewise, he repeated what he'd told Senator Hays: how Senate Bill 1245 was for Russel, how they'd dedicate Four Summits to Russel and *any other young man whose life was cut short in the pursuit of our state's environmental grandeur.* Generalizin usually worked when dealin with politicians. He made darn sure, though, that each knew how keen the senator was to see Senate Bill 1245 through. *Let my son's death serve this great country of ours! That's what he said to me on the phone just now!* And those three Throttlebottoms ate the lie right up.

Old Porch's eyes even watered some on their own, thinkin how his boy's end was provin the catalyst these past years had required all along, the blood sacrifice without which no abstract notion can survive, what every great deed requires if they are to become a part of the physical fabric of this World and its History. Might not even Divine Providence be at work?

Old Porch called up Custom Enterprises.

Meanwhile, Sondra Gatestone and Allison March had left the Isatch Canyon parkin lot, a hard choice seein as how despair kept demandin they keep to the entrance, which was accomplishin zilch, though to be fair Sondra had secured assurances from Park Ranger Brickey to call her if there was any news, the two mothers now headin to the Utah County Sheriff's Office in Spanish Fork. As Sondra explained on the way there, the closer they stayed to Undersheriff Jewell, the less leverage they had. However, a good sit-down with his supervisin officer could put them in a whole different situation.

Upon their arrival, they requested a meetin with Sheriff Hiram Brunt in order to communicate their displeasure that Undersheriff Jewell, given his close family ties to the Porches, hadn't yet recused hisself from the investigation. Sondra didn't know Sheriff Brunt like she did Chief of Police Beckham, but suprisingly enuf Sheriff Brunt still welcomed the women into his office.

Sheriff Brunt was a no-nonsense fella, born and raised in Rome, educated at Isatch University, servin his mission in Peru. He was squat as a wood barrel full of concrete. He didn't budge much, but he was also so confident in his station that he didn't put up a fuss either. He listened for two minutes and then cut them off. He was confused. The Utah County Sheriff's Office was not handlin this matter. He directed them then to see his operations chief, Deputy Dana Angerhofer, who was out but due back soon.

Sondra and Allison waited. And then waited some more.

When Deputy Dana Angerhofer finally did show up, she sure presented a towerin figure to contend with, even less likely to get pushed around than Sheriff Brunt, though like the sheriff she too was at ease with herself, kind as well, and clear-spoken. She understood the mothers' concerns but assured them that the only involvement the sheriff's department had at present was to serve as support for the Orvop City Police and the park rangers, especially the law enforcement rangers who despite any setbacks would be spearheadin the effort to locate the children and the horses. Deputy Angerhofer thought it would happen that day. She didn't pay the weather no mind.

If I believed every forecast, I wouldn't get half of what I get done every winter.

Undersheriff Jewell, she reiterated, was only at the Isatch Canyon Park entrance to assist with logistics. There would be other sheriffs in the field handlin any engagements. She urged them to seek out their ward bishops for counsel.

It was 2:26 p.m.

At least both mothers felt relieved enuf to head back to Orvop, stoppin first at Allison's place. Allison ignored the empty couch and went straight to her bedroom, where she pocketed a rock she kept next to the lamp by her bedside, a smooth gray stone encircled by a white line, what she called a Nightmare Stone, because if you put it under your pillow or held it close, it kept the nightmares away. At least that's what she'd told Kalin. Next she checked the answerin machine, still hopin with each message that she'd hear Kalin, his soft voice with only a few words needed to explain this bad dream away, tellin her how he was just stranded at the mall and could she pick him up? Two of the messages were in fact from the mall, her manager at ZCMI and Clyde Hill from the University Theaters, both complainin that she hadn't showed up for work. She quickly dialed both places and left messages that she was out due to a family emergency and would not be able to come back in until the followin week. She was stuffin a bra and a clean shirt into a bag when Clyde Hill called back and fired her.

Allison resolved not to tell Sondra that last part, but by the time they was back at the Gatestone residence, feedin Mungo, feedin themselves, she let it out anyway. Sondra snorted and muttered somethin along the lines of good riddance, and it was all goin to be okay, even if she couldn't hide the distress knit across her brow.

They then drew up lists of what they'd need to last the night in the canyon parkin lot. They refused to sleep in a bed until their children were freed from the jaws of the mountains. They needed to keep vigilant, a constant reminder to Undersheriff Jewell and whatever Porch was loiterin around that they would suffer no abuses of the law.

If their children didn't come out of this alive because of some careless shot, someone there would pay. It was that line, their own retaliatory justice, no more real than Old Porch's belief that Russel's death was now servin some grand purpose, that helped the mothers find for at least a few hours some faith in their actions.

Allison did wash up then. A long, hot shower in an immense guest bathroom that did her a great deal of good. She took her time too, afterward puttin on as many layers as she could find. Even with the heater runnin all night in Sondra's truck, the Istach Canyon entrance was gonna be freezin. Allison's feet had suffered plenty in the Stan Smiths, and Sondra had insisted she try on the plenty of extra boots lyin about. Tom's winter boots fit Allison perfect.

Next they arranged and packed up the gathered blankets, thermoses full of hot cider, sandwiches, candy bars, gummy bears, cakes and pies, not just for them but for the deputies and rangers on duty. Plus extra socks and gloves.

Throughout these preparations, Sondra helped herself to slices of cake, which Allison politely declined, claimin to have no appetite, which was partially true. She'd started to feel how the excess of sweets she'd already indulged in around Sondra had given her what felt near like a hangover. What she really needed was some good ole chicken soup, and she did manage to arrange for that, for both of them in fact, though Sondra wouldn't touch the salad Allison had made for a side.

Secretly at first, and then more openly, the two mothers hoped that these preparations for an all-night vigil would prove unnecessary, with their kids reappearin before the day was spent. They did take as a sign and rejoice some when Chief of Police Beckham called. While there still weren't no sign of the children or the horses, he'd gone ahead and stationed not one but two more of his officers at the Isatch Canyon Park entrance to help further guarantee the success of the operation. He'd also spoken with Undersheriff Jewell and made clear that, due to the fact that he was married to Orwin Porch's sister, and since the Porches were very much at the center of this matter, in order to avoid even the slightest taint of impropriety, Undersheriff Jewell's participation would have to be limited to logistical support.

I warned him to stay out of the field.

Sondra thanked him but also didn't let him get off the line so quick. She wanted to know what was bein done about them Porch boys on their ATVs.

That's also been taken care, the chief of police responded. *I've ordered both Jewell and my men to get them the heck outta the canyon.*

It was 3:39 p.m.

What neither Sondra nor Allison knew was how on that very afternoon Russel Porch's autopsy was finally underway.

Early yesterday mornin, Russel's body, embraced in a nonporous bag with one zipper, had been whisked off to the Utah Office of the Medical Examiner. A series of delays no more significant than postponed deliveries of swabs, antiseptics, and scalpels, a rushed reexamination ordered by a Salt Lake City judge, and the absence of several personnel due to truancy, food poisonin, and the flu, not to mention a power outage that left the buildin strugglin on backup generators for nearly three hours, served to backlog many cases as well as bug the heck out of folks there tryin to get their work done.

Today, though, was a different story. And as has been talked over plenty by the likes of Dixon Walters, Blaine Todicheenie, Glendon Hoffman, and Kristy Coulson, by 9:00 a.m. three autopsies were already in progress. Russel's autopsy commenced at 3:49 p.m., performed by Assistant Medical Examiner Annabelle Kasey, MD. Annabelle Kasey weren't the top forensic expert there, but she was still tops, with degrees from IU, the Unversity of Utah, and Stanford. Though her education had little to do with her finest quality: a steadfast commitment to discovery without prejudice. Dr. Kasey knew full well the dangers of installin patterns beforehand. *Installin.* Dr. Kasey had spent a good two decades learnin just how to uninstall patterns. Much of the satisfaction she took from her work derived from not knowin a thing before she began lookin for the thing. The joy came from lettin a pattern emerge where before there'd been none. Now that might seem an odd way to describe a profession that most consider gruesome. But Dr. Kasey had learned this delight throughout her life, whether with her herb garden or astonishin progress made by her son with autism.

With Russel Porch, though, she'd already heard too much. *You've got the boy that got his throat cut!* Or: *Poor kid was sliced ear to ear and bled out like a steer.* Or: *Knifed in the neck.*

After first surveillin and recordin the overall condition of the body, notin several abrasions on the knees and elbows, as well bruises and welts on the back suggestin possible strikes, with more contusions on his head consistent with a fall, those from when Landry knocked Russel off of Cavalry, Dr. Kasey focused in on the laceration above Russel's jugular. He weren't cut ear to ear, and whatever had stabbed him weren't from any knife she'd seen before. The cut weren't more than two inches, 5.52 centimeters to be exact. Dr. Kasey might've categorized it as a puncture were it not for the lateral striations, perhaps suggestin some cuttin, though those could very well have been caused by the acute angle of entry.

No doubt due to the chatter precedin the exam, Dr. Kasey's head wouldn't stop orbitin a knife as the instrument responsible for the wound. Maybe a dull knife? Finally, though, she managed to *uninstall that pattern.*

At that moment, she was listenin on her Walkman to *9 to 5* by the inimitable Dolly Parton, a song that for some reason, despite its repetitions, or maybe because of them, freed her thoughts from predicatin themselves on other thoughts, and so with that space finally achieved, Dr. Kasey could recognize that the injury before her had more to do with glass than steel. Broken glass. Maybe a beer bottle?

Dr. Kasey grumbled audibly as now even that pattern undeservedly tried to install itself in her head, once again organizin her thoughts around a conclusion she had no right yet to make.

Her sister had recently given her this mix-tape, and the next song made her laugh: Van Halen's *And the Cradle Will Rock* . . . Her sister was due to give birth any day now.

Next Dr. Kasey inspected the torn jugular and superior thyroid vein, as well as the common carotid artery, also perforated, when a tiny glitter drew her tweezers toward the partially severed sternocleidomastoid muscle. She might as well have found a diamond. She hummed some as she delicately plucked free the tiny shard and placed it into a specimen dish.

For the length of *Roundabout* by Yes, she studied the iridescent splinter under a microscope.

Long gone was the notion of a beer bottle, or any bottle for that matter.

She returned to the body, and a few minutes later was hummin again when she discovered buried under the digastric muscle a larger sliver. Opposite the razor-sharp edge on this shard appeared to be a machine-cut indentation with beveled edge.

No question the cause of death was from this cut, but it weren't made by any knife. *Spirits in the Material World* by The Police was now playin. Dr. Kasey eased the volume up from six to eight as she contemplated what chaos had surrounded this killin. Chaos usually played a part in most killins. Her hummin turned to a growl as this time she rid herself of the idea of a killin.

To two evidence bags Dr. Kasey applied stickers with her name, case number, the date, and the time, October 29, 1982, 4:51 p.m., addin to the first bag *SHARD #1* and then *SHARD #2* to the second bag, where she also wrote *WEDGE CUTS?*

A little later, while she was typin up the report, her brother-in-law called with news that her sister had just been admitted to the hospital. She was already seven centimeters.

In a hurry now, Dr. Kasey called over Chester Walheimer, an intern from the U of U. She asked him to file her report and enter into evidence the two bags. He was more than happy to help.

It was a glass, not a knife? Chester Walheimer asked. She nodded, and likely because she wanted to share with her loyal helper some of the thrills this line of work could offer, she fetched some tweezers and held the biggest piece under her lamp. The spectrum immediately dazzled her desktop.

What does this little rainbow tell you?

It's rainin in here?

Funny.

I dunno.

It's not glass, Chester. It's crystal.

Chapter Thirteen
"That Traverse"

For Kalin and Landry, the passage of mornin was tolled out by collapses on far ridges. It was in fact a new amassment of storm clouds layin siege to the Katanogos massif that had helped lurch temperatures above freezin. The insulatin closeness of more clouds pushin down into Isatch Canyon had warmed some the air, the thaw further hastened by periodic rents in the clouds.

Often the slides were beyond view, a distant crack followed by a sudden hiss, soon after answered by echoes of its long fallin.

A lotta ice and rocks come loose when the sun gets through, Tom declared, which, though it weren't news to him, Kalin still related to Landry.

Like that ain't obvious to any idjit with half a toad's brain, Landry remarked with a scoff, her own clouds puffin forth from her nostrils.

I'm so glad she came along, Tom said, and even spat too, though Lord knows what he was spittin.

Not an hour later they took heed of another crack, this time observin just opposite where they stood great plumes of frost risin up above one of the high Agoneeya Mountain spurs, markin the course of debris, swift as a trail of black powder alight, finally explodin over a bluff, if obscured the rest of the way down by dense groves of trees. More than enuf ice particles stayed aloft to play a ghost adrift above the aftermath of its own end.

Landry noted that just by holdin up her little finger she could blot out the whole event from top to bottom. *It weren't nothin but that.* But Kalin shuddered at how much rock and ice had roared down the narrow chute, obliteratin whatever had stood in its way, fillin the canyon with that low predatory growl, what even set to shiftin uneasily the horses, and that included Ash.

We best keep back, Kalin said. *The sun's already on our side of the canyon. Who knows what could come down above us.*

Landry tried to crane around to see what loads above the mine's entrance might suddenly collapse with commensurate fury, but no angle provided her with anythin more than the sight of rough quartzite and limestone.

Tom looked uneasy too but for no reasons that had anythin to do with what waited above. His glances kept returnin to the depths of the Awides.

A couple more hours and we should be good, Kalin said to settle both sister and ghost brother.

Far away another crack warned them that the canyon was anythin but settled.

In those early hours, because it weren't fair to leave the horses in the dim, Landry and Kalin took turns leadin them up to the entrance and back. Fresh air ahead got them trottin every time. The horses were also sick of the mine. And they hated goin back. Kalin and Landry kept them watered, fed, and groomed, and maybe these attentions bettered their stays within. Kalin had tried to improve their fire too, but no manner of new design or adjustments would lessen within that chamber its overly sooty and insufferable nature. At least it was warm though. Tom never entered the mine again, even for the horses. Ash was of the same mind.

Now at the entrance Kalin and Mouse played the game of *which hand?*, Mouse still bumpin his great obdurate head against Kalin's chest, offerin up too a concert of snufflin snorts, before returnin to Kalin's fists, Kalin eventually revealin the piece of carrot, strokin Mouse's broad neck and long tangled mane while the cracks born from his carroty chomps rivaled the canyon's unsettlin disposition.

Once that was done, Kalin's palms confirmin emptiness, Mouse still didn't cease to bump Kalin with his head, like a cat on catnip.

What is it about you that horses like so much? Tom asked then, makin no attempt to cloak his exasperation.

Kalin shook his head. *Mouse just tolerates folks.*

He sure likes to tolerate you. I'll tell you this, Kalin, no one born in a place where trains go underground should know the first thing about horses, especially how to ride one on the side of a mountain. And to think what I'd've missed if I'd've let Lindsey keep on kickin you.

Why did you stop him? Kalin had never asked Tom this before.

Seemed unfair. What with him the giant and you not even a roly-poly. Tom smirked.

The sun had gotten higher. What patches of sky were visible were near gray as the clouds, a gray without even the memory of blue, lifeless and disheartenin.

This storm's just gonna keep on comin, ain't it? Kalin asked then.

I don't see no other way around it, Tom answered, eyein where they'd soon have to head, his smile dimmin plenty.

Landry appeared then with Jojo. They gazed together at the wisps of mist racin out of the canyon. Kalin offered to walk Jojo back inside, and Jojo went with him. Landry was impressed until she convinced herself that he'd had a carrot to offer. She gave the one she had to Mouse.

When Kalin returned, he had Navidad. Tom's smile brightened some. Though she was generally calm, the air and the sight of the canyon, brightenin more and more with the mornin, got her noddin her head so hard, Kalin had to grip pretty hard her halter. He even slid his right shoulder under her head, steppin in front of her chest too, lest she try to leap forward. As Jordan Heaton would assert, and this bein the very same Jordan Heaton who was a personal liability lawyer, one of Orvop's best too, until he was proved a faitour and arrested for embezzlin from the firm: *That mare just wanted what all of us want: to run.*

Though what helped Navidad most to contend with her better instincts for freedom was not Kalin's grip but him describin in his hushed way the details of their predicament, the steeps ahead draped in shadows, still grizzled by ice, the ice that would soon enuf give way as the sun continued its ascendency, releasin them to a path that would take them past flowin brooks to meadows where she and Mouse could graze to their hearts' content, and from there reach a place where their tack would fall away forever.

You do know she don't understand a word you're sayin? Tom said then, his grin back to full, eyes sparkin more than this palace and prison of ice.

That's what bein dead tells you?

Dead got nothin to do with common sense.

She understands the music, and I couldn't give her that music if I didn't find the words first.

Ha! If that don't say the thing without sayin anythin.

Tom, can I ask you somethin?

Tom nodded but like in a way that made Kalin think Tom already knew what he had in mind to ask. *Did you just spring up from my own head because I couldn't see myself through all this without you?*

I've wondered that too. Only the other way around: that you's the one who sprung from my head because I couldn't see myself through death without you.

I don't believe that for a second.

Me neither. Tom laughed. *I'd surely have picked Eva Thorn over you!*

Tom had been all set to ask Eva Thorn to the prom he never lived to see.

Kalin laughed too but real quiet.

Not that I spend any more time than this thinkin that way, Tom continued. *It gets me too dizzy. Navidad here never gets me dizzy. She and Mouse are enuf.*

Back in the mine, Kalin found Jojo and Mouse grazin on scat-tered remnants of feed strewn on the floor, which Navidad was eager to get in on.

Landry was nowhere in sight.

Kalin knew at once she must've slipped beyond the ropes he'd put up to block the passage that led to that vertical drop. And when she didn't answer his call, he went that way too, heart sinkin when he reached the vertical shaft and she weren't there.

Across that bottomless pit of blackness ran a beam that was wide as a divin board. Still, it was long enuf to make doubtin your steps, let alone the beam, more than likely. Kalin weren't sure what to do. Again he cried out for her, readyin hisself to dare that beam.

Then her voice reached him, his name in his ear, though it weren't ahead of him, nor behind neither, and definitely not from below. Kalin looked up then and by the glow far above spied the silhouette of steel rungs in the wall. They went up about a dozen feet. From there it weren't but a small lateral move to what looked like a wooden ladder risin directly above this bottomless pit before him.

Climb on up! Landry cried. *Been yellin for you for the last ten minutes!*

Kalin weren't sure how that was possible, but he let the delight in her voice goad him into action, even as he feared each step on them rungs would reveal the erosion that would cast him down. Not that he'd fall that far. The tunnel's rock floor would catch him, though at fifteen feet, break him was a better expectation. Below the wooden ladder, though, waited a depth he had no answer for, and it was then too, as he managed the rungs, his left hand flarin with pain, that Kalin suffered an uncomfortable flash of faces he'd confronted durin the night, dreams they were, if they was also warnings, of the cost of things, of deals gone sideways, of perils he was already misplacin again.

Landry didn't quit titterin with glee over the misery he announced with every grunt, which really were just disguised curses, him cursin his foolishness for followin her up here, cursin his own clumsiness when twice his feet slipped before he finally figured out how to lodge each rung in the arch of his boot, the whole way up countin out his progress to keep him from cursin her name aloud.

Seventy-eight, seventy-nine, eighty, eighty-one, eighty-two . . .

Until at last Kalin emerged into a small antechamber with one passage that after a mild bend arrived at a room bright with the risin day. There was an old firepit at the center surrounded by unburnt cardboard, maybe used once as sleepin mats. Empty and very dusty Coors cans were scattered about. Dark passages went off in every direction, but what arrested his breath was the great openin through which he could behold the whole valley.

Ain't that a sight! Landry squealed.

And it sure was a sight.

I figure we're just under Squaw Peak. And look, you can see the Isatch Canyon entrance perfectly. Landry handed Kalin his binoculars, which were really her brother's and so really probably more hers than his. *The good news is the freeze has stalled them too. The bad news is that they're still there.*

Kalin studied for the first time the commotion below, fire engines, police vehicles, park ranger trucks, tents by the gazebo, a news van, maybe two. Kalin couldn't help but look for his momma's yellow Dodge Dart.

You're tryin to find your momma's car, ain't you? Landry asked. *It's okay. I did the same for my momma's truck.*

Kalin then sought out them ingressin trails that he might now have a better view of, but the one that mattered most, the trail up to Aster Scree, was blocked by rock just as the crick and most of the main Isatch Canyon trail stayed hidden beneath the dense canopies of trees.

Your friend Egan and his brothers could already be makin a go of it.

Don't you ever call him my friend.

Kalin could see Landry weren't foolin and apologized at once. But that's not what made him lower them binoculars. It was a buzzin that sharpened as it grew louder. He and Landry spotted soon enuf then the small plane.

It was 9:09 a.m.

Both Landry and Kalin stepped back at once.

Crap! You figure that's police?

Maybe, Kalin answered, steppin farther into the chamber, though they was already well concealed within shadows.

You know we can't outrun no plane.

We cannot. But we'll get to where no plane's gonna think to follow us.

You sure got a lot of faith in my Tom's Crossin.

I don't know that I'd call it faith.

What then?

I just took him at his word.

The plane disappeared along with the buzzin that had announced its arrival.

Landry gave a sheet of cardboard a kick. *I think I'm less scared that you're crazy, and for the record I'm pretty sure you're crazy as a hoot, and more afraid that you're just plain stupid. Or, if that's unkind, then too much the fool to realize my brother was pullin your leg.*

That's a possibility.

You do realize, right, how lettin Navidad and Mouse loose in some wild place will likely be the end of them?

There weren't no dream of a better place in Paddock B, Kalin replied. *At Tom's Crossin there is. Those are your brother's words.*

Out in the canyon, the Beechcraft had returned fer another pass.

Back by their fire, Kalin and Landry repeated pretty much what they'd done yesterday, fashionin duct tape boots, this time with extra cardboard. Kalin got out the Gatestones' farrier kit in case an errant nail needed attention, but the horses' shoes were all good.

Bored, Landry gave the tools a good once over, the clinch cutter, the pull offs, the crease puller, the rasp, and the hammer, before spinnin the hammer up in the air and catchin the handle on the way down, at least catchin it most of the time. Kalin eventually joined in, catchin the handle on the way down, every time. He'd also hold the head and spin it up that way, grabbin the head too without hurtin hisself on the whirlin claws. But that weren't nothin compared to the involute mischief he got up to next: somehow Kalin hid the entire hammer behind his right arm, or rather behind his upheld hand, the claws somehow wedged in between his fingers, with the handle runnin down the back side of his forearm.

Landry couldn't follow fast enuf to understand what dexterity was really on display, and it didn't help that Kalin did it only once, because somehow from this position of absolute stillness he chucked the hammer upwards, settin the thing spinnin too, even faster than before, dangerously fast, around and around in a blur that negated its own-hammerness, all while Kalin at the same time lowered hisself just a bit to match the descent, and then like that, like it was nothin, snatched the thing outta the air, right where you'd want to snatch it too, right by the handle, ready to strike, ready to hammer home a nail.

Landry whistled and clapped, Tom suddenly beside her, neither whistlin nor clappin, though there was no denyin his smile, and Kalin didn't miss that somethin else in his eyes, not just black, but black if black could flicker with satisfaction.

I'll be damned, the ghost even whispered.

Where'd you learn how to do that? Landry asked.

That, my daddy taught me.

I'll bet he did, Tom added, and then like that he was gone again.

And you ain't even right-handed! Landry noticed then how Kalin weren't usin his left hand at all, just lettin it hang at his side, fingers loose, thumb through a belt loop. *Let's have a look at that.*

One advantage of resortin and repackin everythin was knowin where everythin was. Landry fetched the first aid kit. Kalin made clear that he weren't usin nothin that the horses might need later on.

You ain't helpin them one bit if you're disablin yourself.

And just like she was good with knots, Landry wrapped right Kalin's exuviatin flesh, across one way, across another, between his fingers, never too tight, but also never so loose that it would clump up when he put on his gloves, and Landry made sure he put his gloves on right then and there. Kalin was mighty grateful and said so twice.

Durin the whole ordeal, Kalin had stayed squatted down between the horses, and though they couldn't banish his pain, Navidad and Mouse did help some with their distractin nuzzles and nibbles, and when he finally stood back up, they nickered together, and that got Jojo sharin a soft whinny. Even out by the entrance Kalin heard Ash whinny, though his was louder and carried a different message.

Fer the first time since they'd arrived, Kalin stepped out onto the path, still cautious as heck, keepin as low to the ground as he could in order to splay hisself out if he slipped and started some irreversible slide. He continued like that a good ways, now and then crouchin even lower to poke at the ice. On the way back, though, he walked tall, here and there stompin a bootheel into the slosh, concerned now with how well the rocks beneath were holdin up.

Kalin licked his lips then, even made like he was eatin the air, like it was some caramel apple just danglin before him, which Landry smirked at, only to do the same a second later. To her surprise she could taste how the iciness was gone, and the slush on the air had a taste she was just startin to learn. It was similar to the smell dirty snow gives off if you've ever had your face rubbed in it, which both Evan and Tom had done to her plenty of times until she'd learned to stand up for herself with a squall of kicks and bites.

Back at the mine entrance, Kalin threw out some rocks. Landry did the same. Both were pleased to see the rocks didn't go far. Where they landed, they stuck. No matter their size. The cliffs below, which at dawn had seemed but a skip away, now seemed blessedly out of reach. Landry and Kalin even shared a smile.

Should we lead them or ride? Landry asked as she brought out Jojo behind Navidad and Mouse.

I trust Navidad's steps more than I do my own. And like that, with an easy click in his cheek, a kiss in his calves, Kalin, Navidad and Mouse headed out onto the trail and left the Awides Mine behind.

This was also about when Old Porch was gettin frothy with Undersheriff Jewell while Allison March and Sondra Gatestone were sittin down with Holly Feltzman.

It was 11:11 a.m.

Landry surprised herself then when she realized she still needed a second to reconsider what Kalin had just said. At first she lied to herself about needin to give Mouse extra space, but really she was squirrelin around the question of whether or not she trusted Jojo's steps more than her own. Not that she didn't get around that one fast enuf, scoldin herself for dillydallyin, under no illusion about her own condition, no Olympic track star in her future, not with that wide swingin leg makin her *just a hair's length from lame* as Doctor Hafen once put it to her momma. By contrast Jojo's step and stride was a lesson in magnificence. Landry could never afford to abandon her trust in him, not up here, a realization that finally got her out on the trail.

Though, yes, even here there's some debate. Tabitha Karush, a coffee slinger in Flagstaff who loved to cry out whenever she could: *I'll muck stalls for free,* would claim that Jojo's gettin goin had zip to do with what Landry was frettin over at that moment. Merril Chance, at the time also down in Flagstaff, a devout drinker of the coffee Tabitha would sling when he weren't on the clock as a rail worker, would argue that Landry must have, however slightly, signaled the horse. Tabitha Karush, however, remained convinced that Jojo had done the decidin: *He was in charge of his own fate like we is sometimes of our own actions no matter if whoever's ridin our back says otherwise.* No agreement was ever reached between Tabitha and Merril, though there was a kiss, and the two friends would continue to enjoy such discussions, pleased to learn over the years that between them they knew Ethan Rasmussen, Bill and Julie Evanston, Dane Barlow too, and even Tyson Chambers.

To comfort herself, Landry noted how in some places the ice was completely gone. Unfortunately she also noticed how in other places, especially where shadows refused to retreat, warnin tongues of gray still awaited them, hard too and slick. As if sensin Landry's trepidation, the great blue horse suddenly stopped right where the slope appeared steep enuf to be sheer, plenty shadowed too and icy, which Landry was foolishly takin in. In other words, in the worst possible spot.

At once, Landry's whole self started to seize up. Jojo snorted then and even shuffled his legs some, sensin Landry's worsenin condition, likely smellin it on her too, for a horse has a special sense for human fear, and nothin you can do will hide it except gettin rid of it.

Where we're goin now you've already been, Kalin hollered. He'd stopped too, lookin back at her with a big grin, almost too big for him. And though it was to her disadvantage, Landry knew at once that Kalin was just tryin to smile like Tom would've done in spots like these.

Don't talk to me like I'm an idjit! she still yelled back, like maybe a little anger could help her forget the perils one misstep away. Why had she looked down? She'd be mad at herself if she weren't so afraid.

And last night you were in the middle of a thunderstorm! Kalin didn't let that grin dim one bit. *This is gonna be easy.*

But try as he might to help her, Landry and Jojo still weren't movin.

In fact she was now so locked up she couldn't even fake a grin, let alone nod. But she also realized the peril she'd put Kalin and the horses in if he tried to get back to her. Only her fingertips had any freedom left, but she used that to signal Jojo through the reins to get movin. And it was by his steps forward that her beautiful horse managed to unlock Landry, joint by joint. And that weren't the end of it either. As Jojo's pace quickened, and his whole form loosened, no doubt aided by the confidence in Kalin's voice, still callin out to them, and by Kalin's ease atop Navidad, with Navidad even more relaxed, and Mouse the most relaxed of all, Landry continued to ease up on herself, which helped Jojo relax even more, in his haunches, his great shoulders. He even lifted his head higher, took deeper breaths, now further refreshed by the crisp and clear air but most of all enthralled by the prospect that will motivate pretty much any horse: to just move.

Their path hadn't even changed none. It still seemed no wider than Landry's waist, but it granted her a feelin of breadth, like it was also wider than some service road. A few minutes later and Landry wasn't even givin a second thought to their progress. And after that they moved at a near-unwaverin pace.

Is Tom up ahead? Landry yelled out at one point. She was just curious.

Kalin didn't look back, but his smoke-stained Stetson rocked up and down.

Tom wearin a hat? Landry yelled up again a little later.

Again Kalin nodded.

Is it the nice black one?

Which is when Jojo's next step suddenly lost its hold. Whatever cloud Landry's head was keepin company vanished as soon as she felt that sickenin weightless drop as Jojo's right forehoof slid off the frozen surface, followed by his knee bucklin, what, maybe, would've dropped him all the way to that awful slope on their right had not his rear legs at once compensated, lungin the left foreleg ahead, at once findin solid ground, what righted this stumble quicker than you can say bumble, leavin Jojo not a bit concerned, amblin ahead again just fine, with Landry suckin in a mess of air too fast, now beholdin icy patches everywhere, her hands worse than clammy.

Hey! Kalin yelled. Navidad looked back at her too. In fact even Mouse was lookin back. If she weren't so surprised that Kalin had registered Jojo's slip, she'd be even more so by this collective regard.

Hey is for horses, she managed to snap back, startin to breathe again. *You okay?*

You ain't my momma, you know!

Landry's focus on the path ahead never wavered after that. Only when the immediate steepness down on their right had diminished, only when they'd passed beyond them great horizontal stacks of golden rock to their left, striated with castaneous streaks, too much still curtained with hard sheets of ice, above and below, did she twist around in her saddle to see better where they'd just been.

Had they really come all this way last night? Through sweeps of hateful rain and fog thicker than blindness? Landry had cursed it all to heck and back, that nothin could ever be worse. She knew now that weren't true. Takin in the switchbacks they'd just traveled, thin as the thinnest crack wanderin across a plateglass table, she was humbled enuf to offer a silent prayer of thanks for havin been spared even once last night the sight of their impossible journey.

Landry accepted then a couple of things about herself: yes, she was molten sun when the moment was right, and, yes, anythin in her way better look out! Landry was comin through! But she also weren't always so bold. Fear could betray her, fear could freeze her up, even steal away her voice, so bad she couldn't squeeze out one peep.

That had happened only once before and it still haunted her.

The shame of it.

Landry spat at the memory, tried to spit it out. But spittin never helped. She cracked her little knuckles then. That didn't help either, but it felt good. She wriggled around her ankles some. Anythin to keep herself in motion. She shouted out to Kalin again.

Tom can ride back here if he wants to.

Kalin didn't nod then or shake his head or even look back.

He says he'd rather be dead, he finally yelled out.

Landry laughed and then yelled out somethin snarly about how she'd expect nothin less of her brother, until she also began to puzzle over Tom's response a bit more, or at least the one that Kalin had relayed. What she arrived at startled her so much, she actually jumped in her saddle, which then startled Jojo, especially with her now jerkin around left and right.

Oh my heck, is he already back here? she finally managed to squeak out.

Kalin's hat rocked slowly up and down.

They made good time coverin the challengin and often heart-thumpin terrain, real good time. Nothin near the dreadful pace they'd suffered in the howl of a storm. What took them hours last night didn't cost even one hour today.

Kalin was still plenty relieved to finally halt above the windin path that descended down to the *T* above Aster Scree. From where they was perched, it didn't seem nothin but a scratch in the steep, but it was

at least familiar, and for Kalin this place of three directions, so designated by that mountain-assembled cairn, built in his heart another
cairn comprised of what they'd survived and where they now headed,
that palm of purpose extendin toward what he must not, could not
waver from except in profound injury or death.

Sure glad to find no Porch boys around, Tom muttered, givin voice to
Kalin's greatest worry.

No argument there. Kalin had dreaded reachin this very rise only to
find camped below an armed party, somehow immune to the ice, smug
in their willingness to do harm. Not that their absence kept Kalin
from scannin the highs and lows of their surroundins for some out-
of-place detail that might betray an ambush. But only brush, a few low
trees, and more scarps of ice here and there greeted his inspection. The
whine in his ear, though, what was buildin too, warned them all that
engines were once again back in the canyon below.

It was the one thing that checked Kalin from outright insistin
Landry risk descendin Aster Scree.

She has to go, Tom growled just the same.

She can make up her own mind, Kalin growled back.

F er Landry, reachin the *T* was pure relief. She'd had her share of
cold, hunger, and harrowin heights she weren't meant fer and
what fer sure weren't meant fer Jojo. She'd also already glimpsed yesterday, in the foulest weather, before they'd had to turn back, where
they was headin back to. Landry missed her momma somethin terrible
too, she missed her own bed, but she also couldn't shake from her head
the pictures Kalin had painted, of that misty waterfall, of some great
wide meadow, of a view he'd promised would change the way she'd see
the whole world. That too was worth somethin, right?

It's your choice, Kalin told her. *If you're ready to get home, I'll help you
with Jojo goin down the scree.*

It gets worse ahead?

Kalin nodded.

Worse than what we've just been through?

Kalin nodded again.

What's Tom say?

He wants you home, home now, home yesterday. He don't want you here.

Well then tough.

Though to be fair, Landry's choice weren't near so glib. The whine
of ATVs meant Porches to her, even if, as Chalise Brimhall loved to bal-
lywhoop about with Aloe Malafa, a veterinarian in Jackson, Wyoming,
who was right then below them were those law enforcement rangers,

Corbet Wadley and Bren Kelson, along with Orvop Officers Poulter and Mildenhall. Kalin never did see them, but he did scramble down enuf to discover the fissure was impassable, stacked high with rock and debris.

Still, it was more than just the Porches and even their choicelessness that moved Landry east on that traverse, ahead even of Kalin, Navidad and Mouse, ahead too of her ghost brother on his ghost horse, and with not a clue about where they was goin. Sure, yes, maybe it was just Landry woolgatherin, head in the clouds, rocks in her head. Maybe it was that wink in her heart again to just dare somethin insensible. Or not. Maybe this time it was Kalin, this boy catchin up with her now, who'd already made for her lifetimes out of hours.

It was just a case of teenage hormones stirrin that stupid girl toward unreason, the often captious Connie Snell would assert, at the time livin in Eugene, Oregon, employed at a tile-makin factory. Ladawn Crosset, out of Cody, Wyomin, though she liked to say she was from Big Whiskey, would back her up too: *Landry was done in by the sight of one pretty boy, though any pretty boy would've done*, which Gabe Bangerter agreed with along with Keeley Wilde, Oscar Rollins, Betsy Ballif too, Cannon Cornaby, and Hill Parmenter.

Likely, though, the prevailin spirit that urged Landry onward was the horses and Tom, in that order. First of all Navidad and Mouse were technically hers. She would've felt obliged to look after them. Second, she'd gotten quite close to them. And nothin sounded better than to see them through to someplace better.

And, yes, she accepted that her brother's idea of someplace better could prove a big joke. She hadn't forgotten how Tom's idea of fun was spendin the afternoon with her crank-callin. They'd pick numbers out of the white pages, sometimes even out of the yellow pages, and soon as someone picked up start holler-singin *You Are the Sunshine of My Life* until they was hung up on. Landry loved those times. In fact it was on one such afternoon when Tom shared with Landry how he'd swapped in, for the one slow song allowed at a school dance, *Mountain Jam*, which ran over a half hour. *That way Dwanna Hales could get her kiss, get married too, and pregnant, or the other way around, all in one song*, Tom would joke with his pals, and he didn't even know Dwanna personally but fer sure had heard about the unkind things Dwanna had said about Jeananne Harvey. Not that Tom shared any of that with Landry, though he did tell her how he'd landed hisself in the principal's office for *Interferin with the Dance Committee's playlist*, though Principal Furst loved Tom and just wanted to hear what it was like to spend more than one second on Hightower. No question Tom adored pranks but, also no question, he weren't ever cruel. Especially to horses. Tom's idea of someplace better for Navidad and Mouse probably was better.

When they first opened up on the main trail, Egan and Kelly, so eager to outdo the other, near rolled their ATVs. Lance Mecham and his brother Jode, both from Santaquin, both in Kent, Washington, both at REI, would speculate endlessy about how everythin could've ended right there *if those two would've just crashed.* And there were many opportunities. By noon plenty was meltin, but you could still be haulin along through some slush, gunnin harder to get through it, only to hit ice as hard and slick as it was at dawn, and why then, all bets was off! Them wheels would lose hold and whirl both brothers into a series of spins that looked fun if there weren't anythin in the way, Kelly only just missin a tree, Egan near plungin into the rumblin crick. Only Billings knew better, holdin his pace steady.

At least after his close call, Egan slowed down. Kelly kept roarin ahead, but seein Egan pokin along killt the fun, and he fell back to drive beside Billings.

From then on, they searched the low ground for signs of dead children and dead horses. Egan revisited Aster Scree, facin again the awful sight of his Cavalry, still lyin there above that ice-decked talus, some mix of love, spite, and shame shiftin around within him until anger overran such ambiguities and like lightnin to copper quick flew to the Kalin kid, with Landry not escapin his ire either.

Egan then considered the ice column descendin from the fissure like some white-haired Rapunzel darin a fool to try her glitterin tresses, some of which even cracked loose right then, landin not far from where Billings was also studyin the challenge. Billings said they should return in a couple of hours if they didn't find any bodies, and here was their last resort. Egan agreed. Kelly had stayed on the main trail and was glad to hear they weren't goin that way again.

Neither Egan, Billings, nor Kelly could know that they had already overtaken Kalin and Landry, who were still makin their way toward the *T*, not even fifteen minutes away or so. Of course if they'd waited there, they'd've soon seen Officers Poulter and Mildenhall drivin Law Enforcement Rangers Corbet Wadley and Bren Kelson. Who knows how that would've gone.

It was 12:31 p.m.

Back on the main trail, Egan welcomed some sense of control. And at least headin up the canyon felt like progress. But an hour later, when they still hadn't found anythin, the only sign of progress was their low gas tanks. They hadn't even secured one decent vantage point to sight the cliffs above.

Billings was the one to first wise up and suggest findin a route on the mild Agoneeya side of the canyon to their right. From there they could better survey the Kaieneewa side.

Funny or not, they ended up takin the very path Landry had started up yesterday to mislead these very same men. Now, though, Billings kept on drivin, gettin them a good ways up too before they had to park the ATVs and then by foot head up among the serrated spurs and ridges, which weren't near as mild as they'd hoped.

This is goshdarn pitiful, Kelly said after another hour of followin trails that kept promisin a view only to prematurely drop down again into thick and relentless brush.

Egan reupped some tobacco in his lip, spat, and grinned. *We'll get where we need to be. Won't be anythin on the other side that can't be got by what's on your back.* He meant Kelly's Remington 700 BDL.

At one point they did stumble upon a pretty decent clearin from which they could see some of Aster Scree as well as the main trail, where Orvop police was headin back to the Isatch Canyon entrance. They had no clue that Officer Poulter and Officer Mildenhall were lookin after Law Enforcement Ranger Corbet Wadley, who'd just sprained his ankle. Though, if they'd looked a little harder, they'd have also spotted Law Enforcement Ranger Bren Kelson startin to make his way up that dangerous crag. They might even have glimpsed nearby the *T* an enormous elk.

By then, though, Kalin, Landry, and the horses were long gone.

It was 2:38 p.m.

*A*in't them the same owls we seen the first night? Tom asked Kalin, laggin up some to ride even. *I thought owls slept in the day.*

You see more than one, huh?

Landry, after doin an admirable job leadin the way, had finally admitted that she didn't know where she was goin and ridin point was exhaustin, especially as the trail presented more and more loose stones and the drop-offs to the right had once again grown more precipitous. And they hadn't even reached the screes yet.

You lookin at that white owl? Landry yelled up from the rear. *Looks like the one we saw the first night.* Then added: *I thought owls slept in the day,* just like Tom had said it.

Kalin told her how Tom was seein more than one.

How many? Landry yelled again.

Kalin held up three fingers.

Huh.

One or three, Kalin welcomed the sight. Just beholdin that creature of feathers and talons aloft in the cold air did somethin to him. He marveled at its silence, its calm, how what plenty have called a dumb creature, dumb as history, mute too as history's final pronouncement, could navigate so gracefully these high places of rock and wind. Kalin and Landry both smiled. Tom, though, had to avert his eyes.

Then a little bit later they came across a big plump yellow-bellied marmot, just waitin out on a big gray rock above them.

Ain't he enjoyin the sight of us! Landry yelled. *How many does Tom see?*

Four, Kalin yelled back.

Your ghost needs glasses.

He says the same of us.

Our momma, Tom said, *always told us that we should never begrudge company that's got more than two legs.*

Does that mean I can begrudge you? Kalin chided his friend.

Tom laughed, but his laugh came up short, especially as he looked off to his left, where nothin with any legs sat, not even a big old mountain mouse.

Now what are you seein?

But Tom shook his head, his face darkenin like the clouds above. Then a moment later Kalin near had to shake his head when he found hisself lost in a slew of incoherent impressions from last night in the mine, what filled him with dread.

I can't tell if I had a dream last night that I can't remember or if it was somethin else, he told Tom.

You don't remember?

Kalin shook his head. *Or maybe just little bits that don't come together in ways that makes sense. I think I saw my momma. Yours too. What was that place?*

A wrong turn.

We had no choice. We needed the shelter.

You did see your momma and mine too.

Go on, Tom. Tell me.

Maybe Tom meant to smile, but instead a grimace fouled up his lips.

What are you two gabbin about now? Landry demanded from behind, and even Jojo threw in a snort. Mouse lifted his tail and pooped.

Give me a moment to get the whole of it, Kalin said, lookin then to the sky like maybe up there he'd find some way around what needed sayin. But up there was just more bad news.

You know how I'm here with you? Tom finally asked.

411

Of course.

But how Landry can't see me, right?

So she says.

Well, I ain't alone no more, though you can't see her.

I can see Landry just fine.

Not Landry.

How do you mean? Somethin jostled real familiar then in Kalin's memory, though it still failed to arrive as anythin more than a wary feelin.

Right there, Tom pointed off to his left, *walks Pia Isan with a dang chipmunk on her shoulder. She's comin with. When the horses go free, she'll be free too.*

Kalin shrugged. *All righty, then. The more the merrier.* But Tom didn't look too merry.

Goshdarn it, Tom! Out with it!

Tom swallowed hard, though who even knows what it was he swallowed. Ash tossed his head a couple of times, like he was tryin to help Tom get out what he couldn't. *You really can't remember?*

Kalin shook his head.

See, if these horses don't make it to the Crossin, then I'm bound to her.

I'm takin that's a bad thing.

It ain't a good thing.

We're gettin Navidad and Mouse to the Crossin. Your friend will be free soon enuf. Tell her that.

She can hear you.

Kalin tipped his dusty Stetson to the air.

Now what you doin?! The deaf could've heard Landry's annoyance.

Don't tell her, Tom pleaded.

Of course I'm gonna tell her.

And Kalin did just that.

Will you ask the lady a question? Landry asked when he was done.

She can hear you! Kalin and Tom said at the same time.

Are you Pareyarts's wife?

Her? Kalin and Tom said, again at the same time, though after Tom did some of his own talkin with nothin, him and Kalin learned that Landry had asked the right question.

Kalin told Landry that Pia Isan was Old Elk's wife.

Well then, does she have teeth like knives and fingernails sharper than knives? It was a little disturbin to see Landry look so gleeful about such questions. *Is she gonna eat us?*

She's got beautiful teeth, Tom said with a sigh. *But she don't smile much. She carries an ax-head. Rusted.*

You didn't mention that part, Kalin said.

I'm sorry, Isa, Landry chimed up then, *for what our ancestor Alfred Gatestone done to you, if that part's true.*

Kalin relayed back to Landry how Tom was sayin how Pia Isan had indeed thrown herself from the high cliffs to escape the likes of Alfred Gatestone, Garrison Porch, and Wild Bill Hickman. Pia Isan also wanted to make clear that Landry weren't really a Gatestone and so didn't need to worry.

Worry how?

Kalin watched Tom listenin to the space beside him. *She says she'll eat me if the horses don't make it,* Tom finally admitted. Kalin couldn't tell if he was jokin. *I can't tell if she's jokin either,* Tom continued. *To tell you the truth, she don't seem the jokin kind.*

After takin several more switchbacks, they reached the base of a new span of cliffs that would mark the end of their ascent of the south side of Kaieneewa. From there, *Clop-Clop-clip-Clop,* they rounded up over an immense spur headin them now to the northeast. They lost sight then of the main trail as well as the Isatch Canyon entrance. Katanogos stayed hidden, still robed in clouds, but for the first time it also seemed approachable. In between the mists that haunted the ground and the weather obscurin its limits ranged new horizons of saddles, peaks, and ragged arêtes.

Not that Kalin paid any attention to such sights. The trail they now followed weren't even a trail, more like an ancient ribbon of stone that had achieved some levelness beneath risin faces often with terrifyin overhangs. Below them the scarp had steepened too, abruptly endin with a band of cliffs that plunged to the canyon floor.

Kalin told Landry not to give them hundreds of feet a second thought. *Fifty feet will kill ya.*

Twenty feet, Tom added with a laugh, which Kalin dutifully relayed to Landry, laugh and all.

Landry didn't laugh, but she agreed with the logic.

The horses remained unbothered. Navidad liked the air up here as well as the occasional tufts of grass, which Kalin let her dive for. Mouse never waited for permission. Swished his tail too to remind Jojo to keep his distance. Jojo knew better than to challenge that swish.

At times they knew themselves enfolded by the mountainside, and the goin was easy and felt safe. At other times the mountain seemed to expand and push them right to an edge where they fought desperately to remain until the mountain drew them back in again, like the mountain was breathin in and out, though the higher they got, the more ragged that breath got.

No matter that they'd got this far yesterday before turnin back, the sight now of that first scree still rattled, or re-rattled, all their nerves, even Kalin's, and he knew it weren't no big deal. Fer all it threatened, and to be fair it was a lot bigger than Aster Scree and seemed steeper, and it weren't hard to imagine them countless little stones suddenly shakin free and spillin downwards like sand in an hourglass, or maybe like sand through a busted hourglass puts it better, Kalin knew better than to dwell on such concerns: he knew the scree was solid.

Not that Kalin and Landry didn't hold their breaths as they crossed. Even Tom did, which was a feat unto itself given he didn't have no breath to hold. Neither Navidad nor Mourse showed any concern for their circumstances. Maybe just to nettle Jojo behind him, Mouse even pranced some at one point. Not one pebble tumbled loose. The rocks and dirt had settled in hard as a wide sidewalk.

Still, Kalin and Landry couldn't help but trade relieved smiles as they reached the other side. They even dismounted to pat the horses and give them water. A hawk flew near level with them then, and Landry swore she glimpsed higher up on nearby peaks, amidst the swirlin clouds, mountain goats starin down on them. The air sparkled with ice and brightened their noses with the scent of fir trees.

Landry wanted to know how many more screes they'd have to cross. *I don't like them. I'm gettin to not even like the word.*

We got eight left. Right in a row. The last one's even easier than this.

And while their confidence in the trail only grew, a very different kind of doubt still had a go at them, sometimes at the same time, even if neither of them were aware of this shared trepidation, that they would come over the next spur or manage their way around another bend only to find, of all things!, a Great Basin rattler curled up before them, or a trio of coyotes, or even one bellicose cougar, either way some unanticipated creature to spook the horses into a turmoil that might end them all. And even when those thoughts were finally swept aside, because weren't it too cold for rattlesnakes?, and they was way too loud for coyotes and cougars, the memory of those mornin avalanches would once again return.

The trail was one thing, but the screes remained especially hard for Landry, even if the path across the first three was just as solid as the trail, maybe even more solid. It was the imaginins, the pulverizin of over articulate rocks into motion, how it could all just give way, that threatened Landry. Were it not for Jojo's resolute pace and calm, she might've froze up bad.

Kalin at least had Tom to talk to.

At one point, Tom reminded Kalin how it weren't just Pia Isan strollin beside him since the Awides Mine, how there were others, *who I can't see same way as you can't see her. I keep seein things differently too, what don't ever seem to settle.* Kalin didn't understand this but figured it had somethin to do with how Tom and Ash passed through grass that was there as well as through grass that was almost there as well as through grass that was not there but out of which Ash could still snag a bite. Kalin's momma had told him that the spiritual was just a conversation with what's unseen. Or as good old Marty Hogencamp would later joke, once he was married and settled with ten kids, if a fella can ever settle when he's got ten kids: *John Steinbeck said a man on a horse is spiritually, as well as physically, bigger than a man on foot. Ha! But what of a ghost? And a ghost on a ghost horse?!* This amusement got around too, even if it weren't all that amusin, but Dwight Ewing would still retell it, as would Ben Carter, Heath Bills, and Beth Crown, along with near every Greenspire.

Had Kalin also started to see things differently because of what he couldn't see? And how was that also changin how he felt about what he could see? Ever since the mine, this way of notin what was there and might've been there had grown stranger. It was similar to what happened whenever Tom drew forth that fiery brand, makin their surroundins even more intense, if vague too or likely. Kalin suddenly recalled that Tom's torch had gone out in the mine, died in fact, only to, yes, that's right, sputter back to life, though this time instead of orange, or even red, the flame had been violet. Anyway, regardless of that brand's strange thanatoptical deliverance, Tom's presence in the world seemed to gift it an extraordinary if unsettlin vividness.

Kalin even shared such reflections with Tom.

It goes the other way too.

You mean around me everythin gets brighter? Kalin asked.

Heck no. It gets worse around you. Around Landry too. Though more worse around you.

Glad to be of service.

But I can understand the horses more.

Like they talk to you?

They don't talk, but I know what they're tellin me.

What are they tellin you?

I dunno. Their lives.

And it weren't just the horses that was here either. Tom told Kalin about Ariel, a dark bay who was a mangy mess but whose heart got young and calm whenever Mrs. Agnes Bonnie Hopper came around with feed and a brush, a heart that also beat too hard whenever Agnes was gone. But what Ariel wanted most weren't Agnes but a meadow she'd knowd once before and hadn't stopped lookin for around every street corner in Orvop, a meadow with horse-kind friends. *Troubles is that meadow ain't in Orvop. It's up near Bozeman.*

Tom also had things to say about two horses Kalin had seen real recent, ridden by Kelly and Billings: Barracuda, the buckskin mare, and Gads, the pinto. Barracuda liked apples and carrots but Gads went bonkers for grapes. And then there was Cavalry, Egan's big liver chestnut stallion. *Cavalry has a story that goes well beyond the five or so years he was with Egan. Starts in North Dakota. He had a good life there. His name weren't Cavalry either. It was Doodles.* Then Tom told Kalin that the happiest that horse had ever been was just this last Wednesday night, when Russel was at the reins. *Not the whole ride, mind you, but there were a few moments there when they was both in perfect sync. I can't speak for Russel, but Cavalry had never felt so free.*

Then you can talk to dead horses too?

And that's when Kalin learned about Ash.

Not that Landry took too kindly to bein left out of a conversation she'd've had to be blind to not see, what with Kalin up ahead mumblin this and that, shakin or noddin his head.

What's Tom tellin you now? Landry had finally squawked out, her irritation not lost on Kalin, nor the notes of desperation likely havin to do with feelin alone with her own fears back there.

So Kalin helped Landry get her mind off where they was at, because sometimes thoughts need a break, the heart too, crossin the fourth and fifth scree without a second thought, not much of a rise in pulse either, as Kalin relayed what Tom was tellin him, which was how they made their way from one stretch of mountainside even a fool could travel to another stretch that even a fool would know to avoid.

Here then is The Story of Ash.

Ash was born south of Moab. He still remembers his first two years. He was a stumblin wonder over anythin higher than his knees. He remembers his momma as the singular joy he returned to every time he finished puttin them long legs to the test of outracin the clover beneath his hooves. After she was gone, he never did experience that joy again. Not even in death. That didn't seem fair. Seems a warnin too.

In the beginnin Ash loved the fence. He would run alongside the rails. Sometimes he'd just hang his head over for a scratch or a nibble. He loved apples too. Granny Smiths especially. He also loved the tall grass that grew by the fence posts. And then one day he and the fence got themselves into a disagreement.

Ash charged the fence, as if the fence might do the smart thing and turn tail and, well, you know, run off. But that fence did no such thing, and Ash had to pull up short with a snort. Not that Ash gave up. Next he tried leanin on the fence, as if he could get that fence to act like other horses did: lean away or move away or at least lean into him like his mother would. Ash even tried some kicks that landed fine but didn't do much but scuff the fence.

Not only would the fence not move, but the fence made sure that Ash couldn't move on by. Finally one day Ash charged faster than ever. He'd already grown taller and stronger, and this time as he reached them forbiddin rails, his long legs just left the ground. It weren't even hard. Ash just abandoned the earth, and then there was no more disagreement. Ash landed on the other side. It was near magical.

The only trouble now was that the other side didn't matter nearly as much as that fence. Ash trotted the length of its other side. Already a new disagreement was in the air, but that weren't nothin compared to the sound of his momma neighin for him from across the corral, reachin that part of the fence a moment later, her arrival preceded by thunder. Ash jumped back over to his momma. Like there weren't ever a fence. After all she was his singular joy. And that was that as far as the fence was concerned.

Now no one, not even his momma that day, had seen Ash make his jump, but maybe because Ash knew he could jump so high, so far, and most of all so easily, he had no need to demonstrate such flight again.

Ash has no memory of his daddy and likewise has no memory of what happened to his momma. He remembers standin in a trailer for a long time with the world blurrin by outside like he was runnin fast and without stoppin, though of course he was already stopped, in fact he was near still as the fence he'd never forgot, and it was now the world that was runnin, and Ash wondered if the world might soon challenge him too and jump over him, and maybe it finally did, but Ash weren't sure.

When eventually he got free of that metal box, he was both a horse and a fence. And then Tom came along. He was barely able to toddle, but toddle he did, right on over to Ash, chirpin like a bird that can't fly. His hair smelled better than grass. Ash nibbled at it, and Tom chirped like maybe he could fly. And from then on Tom was always there.

He would sit on Ash's back, sometimes with his momma holdin him, though mostly it was his daddy doin the holdin. Tom's daddy laughed a lot. Soon enuf Tom could sit on Ash without either his daddy or his momma, and instead of chirpin he laughed loud like his daddy.

Ash could hardly feel Tom, he was so tiny, but even when Tom got to gettin tall, Ash could still hardly feel him, because by then Tom was a part of him, and as it turned out, Tom reflectin on this now, pausin too so Kalin could pass it along to Landry, who nodded hard like she'd knowd this part all along, and of course she had, even if she'd never put the words together to say it like so, yes, yes, yes, of course, of course, Ash was part of Tom.

The two were inseparable. Tom rode Ash with saddle and reins. Tom rode Ash without a saddle, without even reins, sometimes with just a halter, sometimes not even a halter, just lopin around with a handful of white mane, sometimes with arms outstretched, just laughin in the heart of a big canter that smaller horses would have to gallop for.

And if Tom did slip off, and he slipped off plenty, why he'd just roll off that big horse's back with a hoot, and Ash would stop and trot back to nuzzle Tom and nibble at his hair.

Hardly a day went by when Tom weren't with Ash, ridin him, groomin him. And when now and then Tom didn't show at the barn, Ash was unsettled, even if Tom's dad was there to ride him or Tom's momma was there to bathe him and clean his hooves. Landry made Ash's tail switch back and forth.

Hey now! Landry yelped out, but Kalin's glare reminded her that this weren't his story, and any beef she had she'd have to pick with the dead later, which in this case weren't Tom but rather Ash, and if Ash considered Landry a horsefly deservin a tail lashin, why that was between them. Kalin didn't mention that even now, in the midst of Landry's fussin, Ash's tail had started swishin back and forth like mad.

When Tom started enterin them youth rodeos and attendin FFA events, what sometimes took him away for a whole week, why poor Ash would keep to the back of his stall, even his guts objectin to this absence. He shat more and ate less and even drank less. Even when Landry, that little horsefly, chased him out with a hoot, Ash trotted around the corral just once, stoppin in the middle, where he just stood with his head hung.

There are sadder sights in life, but pin that one up on the cork-board just the same.

The horsefly did her best to caress his neck, and to be fair Ash was surprised to find out a horsefly could do that, though it still better keep its distance around his backside.

It was durin such times that Ash reconsidered the fence.

After all Tom was on the other side. Somewhere.

But then Tom would return and there weren't no disagreement

anymore between Ash and the fence, and anyways Tom would swing that fence out of the way and together they'd head up into the hills like they'd never be apart again.

Usually they'd take the main Isatch Canyon trail, ride all seven bridges, right to the end, right up to Yell Rock Falls. Often they roamed the crick bed when it was dry. That's how Tom discovered Aster Scree. A few times they took long rides around the back side of Agoneeya. They tried both Heathen-Slade Canyon Trail and Cutter's Crick Path and by way of Shadow's Glen managed to reach Tiffany's Vista, over-lookin Yell Rock Falls far below.

His whole life Ash only jumped a fence twice: once away from his momma and the other back to his momma. Tom never once thought Ash could jump a dandelion let alone a fence. To be fair the Gate-stones had no interest in jumpin, though Landry had jumped Jojo a few times, if just to make mischief.

Get outta here! Landry cried out then.

It's not true? Kalin asked, genuinely surprised, perplexed some too, as Landry now looked fairly ill or very frightened or both.

Tom really is up there with you, isn't he? And on Ash too!

Kalin nodded. *That or Tom knew his sis well enuf to figure she'd jump Jojo at some point and told me so over the summer.*

That also makes sense. Even if the effect felt more like confusion than the resolvin pleasures of reason.

They was right then in the middle of another scree, number six in fact, a big slide of busted mountain, which upon reachin looked loose as cereal on a playground slide and terrified them both, but upon fur-ther inspection proved once again set as concrete, and wide too as a dozen playground slides side by side. They could have trotted, even cantered, but Kalin kept them to that same slow walk, Tom on Ash to the left, Mouse behind, with Landry on Jojo in the rear.

Now and then Tom would droop his head extra as if to listen to Ash more closely, even if Kalin never could hear Ash make a sound. Tom would nod and, before continuin on with the story, pat the palo-mino's great gray-gold neck.

Ash could still recall the night Tom's father died. Dallin Gatestone was just laid out right in front of Ash's stall with blood on his head. Many men Ash had never seen before kept arrivin to fuss over the body before they finally took it away. Tom didn't come by but once that whole month.

Oh, Ash, Tom started to say now, and more than once, often like he was gonna cry, until he finally just set his forehead against Ash's white mane, and if he was cryin, he hid that from Kalin.

It was in Tom's absence that the pain in Ash's guts started up, at times feelin like he was struck through with a spear. Even when Tom was with him, the pain still winched around inside poor Ash, and the more it grew, the more the great horse's confusion grew, until Ash couldn't eat no more nor even drink.

On the night Ash died, he did manage to walk hisself from his stall into the Gatestone corral, like he was gettin better, when really he just wanted to get to the fence. He thought that if he could just jump over it, he might, well, you know, *Clop-Clop-clip-Clop*, jump free and get clear of this pain. But the pain was too great, and he fell to his foreknees. Tom stayed with him then, and Ash remembered Tom's head against his shoulder, the way he shook and sobbed, and then the pain was gone and Tom was gone. Everythin was gone, and Ash realized too late he would've gladly taken more of the pain if he could've had just a little more time with Tom.

And then, like that, Tom was there again, and they was ridin together through the rain and comin upon two horses Ash had never knowd before, though Ash seemed to recognize the mare.

Kalin gave Tom a moment after that. His friend seemed shaken, havin to relive them events.

You never did speak much about the night your daddy died, Kalin said when Tom finally looked his way.

I'm sorry, Kalin, Tom answered. *I can't remember that night. I can't even remember my daddy much. It's hard to even get hold of what my momma's face looks like.* Tom squinted like that might help.

What did happen to your dad? Kalin asked Landry.

They said it was Ash that kicked him in the head. Just one of them tragic accidents. We was replacin the stall doors with stall guards until the new wood ones was ready. The story that took was that daddy was bendin over when Ash just let loose a kick. Caught him right smack in the back of the head. Dead as sand. Though a coroner said it was a heart attack that killt him.

Ash was a kicker?

That's the thing: Ash never kicked. But no question it was a horseshoe that done the dentin. There was horse hair in it too. Barn accidents happen all the time. Momma always said Tom was a barn accident.

Tom laughed loud then. *Listen to my little sis. Crackin jokes whenever she can. Ain't she a treat.* And he said it ironic but meanin it too.

You would've liked my dad, Landry continued. *What does Tom say?*

Kalin didn't know how to say it kindly.

Speak up! Landry hollered.

He says he don't remember your daddy. Not even your momma.

Well then, ain't bein alive in death the saddest thing of all.

Landry did the talkin after that. And Kalin was glad for it, Tom too, and maybe even Ash, as Landry conjured up a fine picture of the benignant Dallin Gatestone, an older gentleman who was as easy on his horses as he was on everyone he liked. And those he didn't care for he didn't involve hisself with much. Of course, no good life led allows one to be that choosy.

Dallin Gatestone had served with the Navy in Korea which was where he learned the ropes and the knots that in later years he'd teach to Landry. He lived in Hawaii for a year after that and then in California for a month, where he worked as an extra ridin horses in the movies. He met Sondra while at Orvop High and married her when he got back from his mission in England. Sondra wrote Dallin near every day. His law degree from Isatch U came later. *He always told us he was okay with words, but they wasn't what he loved most.*

Dallin's oldest brother had been born when the Gatestones opened the Orvop feed-and-tack stores. Dallin's oldest sister was born when the Gatestones were messin around with a trail-ridin service. By the time Dallin was born, the Gatestones were richer than ever on land investments throughout the state. Neighborhoods that weren't but dusty parcels in the foothills or discouraged plots out by the lake were either built upon or leased out to the municipalities of Orvop and Rome as they expanded. The Gatestones spent most of their money and time on horses. They didn't care for cars or even Philo Farnsworth's invention. Dallin Gatestone loved pointin out famous Utah folk, and Farnsworth was one of his favorites, Beaver-born, helped invent the televison. They did get an old black-and-white one but seldom turned it on. Not even *Gunsmoke* did it for them.

Maybe it weren't so bad that our daddy died because of a horse, Landry concluded. *How Tom died, eaten alive by cancer, that's an awful way to go. There's somethin to be said for goin quick.*

Kalin had no response.

What does Ash say about kickin our daddy? Landry asked then.

Kalin turned to Tom.

Well? Landry said.

Tom says Ash did no such thing.

They passed over the seventh scree without comment, and it was the biggest one by far. Maybe they was too spent for jitters. Landry weren't even grittin her teeth no more.

There are a few who like to imagine this little-remarked-upon crossin was when somethin changed in Landry. Fewel Marcondes, a dancer in Phoenix by way of Tombstone, this in 2018 outside The

Twenty-Seven Veils, where she'd just quit, would claim that here Landry had first understood the cost of change: *Because the price we pay for experience, the price that alters us permanent, can be paid only if we go beyond the limits of who we thought we were. Only then can we realize how we were all along someone else.* A realization Fewel Marcondes would share over the years with Ingrid Harbor, Lyric Loveless, Trina Pitchard, and even Jerry Coombes. Whether accurate or not, when Landry got to the other side, she yawned.

Kalin weren't worried about the last scree. It was the one fast approachin that caused him the most consternation: by far the narrowest, which should've been good news, except it weren't laid back at all like the others. In fact the eighth scree was almost too steep to support its own rocky composition. Almost.

Before Tom and Kalin had crossed it, and they'd done it only once together, Tom had demonstrated how just one sharp kick loosed a fast stream of gabblin stones that when they shot off the cliffs below, sounded like a cough. *Like the mountain's clearin its throat, except it'll be us that gets hocked up and spit over the ledge.* Worse still, after a few steps the way forward lost clarity; you'd hit a patch of sandiness that seemed better suited for a dune buggy, followed by a bit of rockiness better suited for a piton. Tom on Mouse had handled it fine, Kalin and Navidad too, though Kalin had needed Tom's example. They even laughed on the other side over havin feared what hadn't cost them half a minute, though they got scared all over again on the way back. Again they started high, again they finished low, because, see, there weren't no place on them sandy patches that a hoof weren't gonna slide. Ridin out into that terrible chute meant slidin for too many breaths before reachin solid ground again. Their nerves had shook for days.

Kalin chose not to share such recollections with Landry and even avoided lookin at Tom, who'd already gotten extra ashen.

This here's the last of the worst of it was the sum of what he told Landry.

We're almost done?

There's one more after here, but that one's a cinch.

This don't look bad.

It won't even be a thing if you do just what I do.

I got a question.

Of course she does, Tom groaned.

Go on.

What does Ash say happened to my daddy? I mean if it weren't his hoof, whose was it?

He don't know.

You think it could've been Jojo?

Ash don't know.

Same as he'd done with the previous screes, Kalin dismounted and, with one hand still loosely holdin Navidad's reins, tested the way ahead with the heel of his boot. Then he stepped out a bit, waitin for that sickenin feel when the ground beneath your feet starts to give way. Only on this afternoon nothin budged. Of course, that was just for Kalin. The way ahead would have to handle horses.

Kalin went first, Mouse in tow, but they didn't slide one bit. Landry followed their example and also didn't slide. On the other side, she yawned again, but smiled too. Kalin realized then just how much he loved seein her smile, and how much less everythin seemed without it, and how in fact she'd hardly smiled at all over the past hour. Kalin also realized then that Tom was no longer at his side but had fallen back beside Mouse. Still, Kalin was elated.

The last scree is just over that spur there. It's wider than all the rest, but don't worry, ain't a bit of it's loose. The path's wide as a highway. You'll see. There's grass. Even trees.

I'm hungry. My belly's talkin about as much as you talk with Tom.

On the other side we'll pick up a trail that takes us to that waterfall I was tellin you about, and from there it's an easy walk to the meadow and the lake. We can eat then. We can have a picnic right on a little pebble beach.

Altar Lake? I didn't know you could reach it from here.

Most people think you can't.

That's not the Crossin though?

Kalin shook his head. Tom had eased Ash closer to Landry, givin her a smile that weren't ever gonna be a laugh. The dead don't stop breakin your heart.

You and Tom made it up to Altar Lake? Landry asked.

Kalin shook his head again. *He and I never made it much farther than here.*

Landry's smile grew.

Yeeehawww! I love beatin my brother! Let's get to that picnic!

Just like Kalin had said, from the top of the spur ahead they got a good look at the Ninth Scree. Unlike what he'd said, there weren't no path wide as a highway, there weren't no grass neither, though to be fair there was a tree. Even worse, what they now faced seemed multiple in its appearance, as if enormous claws had had a go at the soft flank of the mountain, gougin out new channels and chutes.

This is the cinch you was talkin about? Landry asked, her face tight, smile long gone.

It's changed.

You think maybe here's what we heard yesterday or even early this mornin? Maybe.

It didn't help to see that Tom was now laggin behind Landry, far behind, and slunk over on Ash too, just shakin his head. And that weren't even the spookiest part.

What is it, Tom? Kalin yelled. *Ask Tom what he's lookin at,* he yelled at Landry next.

Landry did as she was told.

What did he say? Kalin asked her then.

You better be kiddin.

I am. Mostly.

Kalin handed her Mouse's lead and rode back to Tom.

We best get across this thing quick, Tom said before Kalin and Navidad had even stopped.

Your brother says we better get across this thing quick.

Is Egan comin? Landry asked Tom directly.

I don't know, her brother answered.

He can't say, Kalin said.

Like he won't say?

Like he don't know, Kalin told her. *How much time do we got, Tom?*

I know even less about time.

What's he say?

He don't know anythin. Kalin then added by way of interpretation, *He's just got the willies.* A characterization Tom didn't object to. *It don't matter. We ain't goin back. We just have to deal with what's ahead.*

Not that Landry didn't start sneakin looks over her shoulder, even though she was mostly checkin on Mouse.

Once they got to the edge of the Ninth Scree, Kalin and Navidad rode up alongside it, lookin for where stones were small enuf for a horse to easily manage or were flat as pavers, or, even better, presented a path of sandiness however meanderin. As best as Kalin could figure, the vast rearrangement here was the result of all that gushin water last night.

It could've happened a week ago for all we know, Tom yelled up.

Tom weren't wrong. Kalin hadn't been up here for weeks. Not that the when really mattered. Kalin just had to get them across safely. He also weren't sure it would prove harder than what he'd told Landry. Sure, it looked different, but maybe like the eighth scree this one too had settled into solidity. Yes, there were rivers of rocks that had wiped out whatever grass and trees Kalin remembered, but those they'd avoid. Other areas seemed soft and accommodatin. One point in the middle looked like an especially good place to aim for: where the ash tree, in fact the last tree, still stood.

Kalin rode to where the ash was straight ahead of him. Even half-way across, the scree seemed monstrously wide. Kalin still feared testin the stability with his bootheel. But he did. The stones at once gave way with a serpentine hiss, and, yes, while some of them stones settled at once only a few feet down, plenty more just picked up speed until they was disgorged off the edge of them tall cliffs below . . .

It was 3:08 p.m.

On top of everythin else, it was gettin colder, maybe even dimmer. Kalin blew clouds of breath on his hands. He knew the day weren't done yet, but clouds above kept tellin a different story. It panicked him to feel hisself so trapped, but no matter how hard he dug down inside hisself for some answer to this predicament, what come up was as scaldin as bile and about as articulate too.

What's the plan? Landry finally yelped, also feelin that they was waitin too long.

I can't even walk across this.

I don't even think I can, Tom added. He could walk Ash to the edge, who would paw a leg over the scree but refused to set a hoof down.

It was plenty disconcertin to see Tom and Ash halted like that. Landry's goadin had gotten Tom into the Awides Mine. Would that work here? Could he even goad his own self out onto this river of rocks that might at once accelerate him to the bottom?

We'll use the ropes then? Landry now was gettin irate.

What else was there to do? Kalin would nod at anythin she said.

But we don't got the one length to match that distance, right?

Again Kalin nodded.

Even the reata and lariats together won't do it, right?

Again Kalin nodded.

Goshdarn it, if this ain't like one of them dang word problems I can't ever figure out in math. If one horse carries one person—

No horse is carryin anybody out there. The scree won't hold. I'll go first. We'll use the ropes. I'll go for the tree.

Landry eyed the ash. *How far do you think that is?*

Kalin figured it was about fifty yards, but he didn't trust his figurin.

We can use the leads too, Landry said.

Shoot! I clean forgot about the leads!

How are you gonna get the horses over? No rope we have is gonna stop a horse from slidin off this mountain.

The only answer Kalin had right then was to tie one end of the long tawny cotton reata to Mouse's Decker packsaddle. Landry, meanwhile, put on an easy display of magic, executin loops and interlockin overhand knots to add next to the reata the three leads and, when that didn't seem enuf, the two lariats. Over two hundred feet. Not exactly light though.

Do your best to pay it out, Kalin told her as he tied the end of the lariat around his waist. *You ain't big enuf to haul me back. Only Mouse is. Just back him up fast as you can and hope that gets me out of trouble.*

You do realize this ain't a good plan.

Tom won't abide the better one.

I'm not sure that even counts as a plan, Landry continued.

What better one? Tom asked.

It don't matter, Tom, Kalin gruffed out.

He ain't even come to it on his own?! Landry smirked. *A scared ghost AND a dumb ghost. I can't wait to see the look on our momma's face when I tell her what's become of our Tom.*

Landry didn't approve of the square knot Kalin had used to attach the reata to Mouse. She redid it quick. She felt the same about the square knot Kalin had used to tie the lariat hisself, untyin that as well, though instead of retyin it around him, she executed her magic to secure that long knotted prayer to Ariadne around her own waist.

Whoa! Tom, of course, erupted at once.

This is the better plan, Landry at once addressed Kalin and the air. *I'm the lightest!*

You can't let her go first, Kalin, Tom groaned. *You just can't.*

Tom— Kalin started to explain.

I'm goin, Landry cut them both off. *And my brother best quit his ghostly whinin.*

And like that, Landry was headin a dozen or so feet above them, where, without so much as a pause, she headed out upon that skein of intolerant stone.

Don't let me down, Mouse! was the only thing she hollered back.

And for a while there she made Kalin and Tom feel sheepish about their worries. This weren't no big deal. Landry hadn't lost but a few inches of ground. Both Tom and Kalin even got to talkin about how she'd likely have to scooch and slide her way down some to reach that big old ash still below her. Now and then she'd pause to drag her way more rope, to keep some slack in it.

About then Kalin realized what a dumb idea it had been to plan on backin Mouse up if there was trouble. Why hadn't he just positioned Mouse so he was facin away from the scree? Kalin was standin on Mouse's off side, uphill from the quarter horse, facin the scree; after payin out more rope, he pressed his right shoulder against Mouse's left shoulder, and with his right arm under his neck, holdin the halter-bridle with that hand too, readied hisself if they needed to walk Mouse back and drag Landry to safety.

In his wounded left hand, Kalin held the reins to both Navidad and Jojo. Here was another dumb idea too late to fix. Like Mouse, they too were facin Landry.

You could've told me to face them away from the scree! Kalin even snapped at Tom.

Huh? I thought I did. Tom looked genuinely confused too, just sittin there on Ash, paler than ever, unblinkin, watchin his little sis traverse what for decades, centuries maybe, had remained just more rocks upon rocks, *solid and unmovin as Stonehenge, the pyramids, the Parthenon,* as Mr. Caracy Rudder would put it in 2010, makin the idea that they could just give up their hold on a place, on this very day, this very hour, and all at once too, seem as fantastical as an Iberian horse with wings.

And then Jojo started to whicker. By the time Kalin registered that Landry was startin to slide, Jojo was already pushin toward the scree, draggin Navidad along, with Mouse, of course, doin the opposite, dig-gin in at once, and so dividin Kalin, drawn if not yet halved.

Kalin tried flingin his left leg out to block Jojo, and when that didn't work, used them reins to pull both Jojo's and Navidad's heads down, and all the while still keepin a hold of Mouse.

It didn't help none that Kalin's left palm was screamin again. What terrible pain was burnin there! Even gauzed and with gloves on. But he had no choice. He had to keep his grip tight. He even kneeled to pull Navidad's and Jojo's heads down more, addressin them with what stern-soft words befitted this predicament. Kalin thanked his lucky stars that at least for the moment the contrarian Mouse had chosen fixity over departure. Why hadn't he faced them all away from the scree? What kinda idjit was he?

To make matters worse, Kalin realized he had no choice but to reorient the horses now, and fast, because what he knew with stomach-flippin certainty was that Landry was about to need their help.

Even as he kept cursin hisself, feelin the confidence in all his choices hollow out, Kalin still managed to swing Navidad and Jojo around, and then somehow swing Mouse around too, so now at least all three ponies faced away from the scree, with Kalin still between them, still facin the scree, still lookin out on Landry's traverse, with his right arm under Mouse's neck, his left under Navidad's, with Jojo slightly above Navidad on her off side, both their reins in his left hand.

Landry, fortunately, weren't sufferin no indignations of doubt. In fact out there on that oblivion of shattered limestone, even as its shifts beneath her boots continued to communicate a downward devotion she was powerless to prevent, Landry's confidence only grew. She moved lightly and steadily, and whatever ground she set in motion moved her in the right direction. And then it was over: she'd reached the ash where she raised her arms and hollered out a relieved hoot.

Kalin hooted back at once and Tom whistled. Tom even looked a little less ashen. The horses swished their tails and snorted as if glad to hear her voice on the wind, though that also got Jojo wantin to turn back around her way, which took some gentle wrestlin from Kalin to secure just a little more patience from that great blue horse.

Now as easy as that was, and Landry hadn't even run it, she was still pantin pretty hard, and sweatin too, sweatin enuf to at once loose herself of that lariat and even shed her pink slicker.

Landry felt better at once, even as she also noticed a strangeness about this tree. Given the time of year, the absence of leaves weren't so startlin, but there was also a grayness about its bark and a brittleness to its branches that Landry should have recognized at once as dead.

She was more elated knowin that crossin this thing was possible and would also present a barrier to whatever Porch or other dang fool was tryin to catch them. In a minute they'd take the horses along the path she'd found and then from here manage the rest in a similar way. Landry also realized she had work to do: they'd overestimated the distances; the reata and the three leads had sufficed. She expertly sep-arated out the lariats, coiled them up, one for each shoulder, and then retied one end of the three leads around the trunk.

You see that? Kalin asked Tom.

I see a lot of things.

I swear that tree just moved, Kalin said.

Tom weren't so sure. *Maybe just the rocks around it shifted some?*

Kalin studied the rocks. They weren't movin. Worse, the rope in places had started to lift off the ground. Fer a moment longer, Kalin tried to convince hisself that this was due to how Landry had tied off her end.

Landry! Kalin finally started screamin. *The tree's slidin!* Which was right when Kalin felt Mouse heavy up beside him as the reata grew still tauter, beginnin to exert a future promise of a weight and drag that not even Mouse could defy. Mouse was tied to the ash which was now headin downward thanks to who knows how many tons of debris pushin against it, shearin off its broken roots. Not that Mouse submitted. Mouse bein Mouse defied it, diggin in against the pull con-centratin its demands across his chest. Mouse not only didn't back up, he even stepped forward.

Kalin, of course, knew this was one tug-o'-war Mouse could never win. Even if it had crossed Landry's mind, it had never crossed Kalin's that he might need to rapidly release the reata. Consequently he saw only one option: diggin out his Swiss Army knife, gettin a blade out big enuf to cut the rope, all while shakes and ill coordination made a mess of his action. To his credit, Mouse held his own. Some have even written songs about this moment, when Mouse took on the mountain and even, fer a moment, won. Whether to Collette Paramore, Tray Holmes, Arlyn Roberson, Phil Bauman, or often a roomful of strangers, churchgoer Apryl Weber from Hanalei, Hawaii, would often sing on her uke a ditty she wrote that became quite popular: *Mouse, What Mountains Did You Bring Down?* Reny Isom, from Fullerton Nebraska, also a Church member, would sing on his guitar a song that weren't ever popular but good nonetheless: *Mouse Don't Back Down.*

But Mouse did back down. And he groaned somethin terrible as he was dragged back toward the scree, Navidad and Jojo backin up with him, with Kalin doin his best to keep sawin at the rope.

Tom got real worked up then. *Just pull the end!* he howled, Kalin still not understandin because he hadn't grasped that Landry had smartly used a Riverman's Bend with a bight, mainly because it offers what he needed, what Kalin finally did somehow come to understand, stoppin with his knife antics and yankin hard the rope's workin end, immediately releasin Mouse from his bondage, and not a moment too soon.

Landry, on the other hand, didn't fumble around none. Before the tree started to really slide, she snugged her hat down around her ears and, still carryin both lariats, skipped away from the tree. Well, that's not exactly right. She'd used a Highwayman's Hitch to secure the last lead around the trunk and, unlike Kalin, knew to go for the workin end. It weren't even a thought. Not that her performance was near as smooth as her not thinkin, but in her defense, the tree had also started to spin around.

Whether because of luck or more sensible reasonin, Landry leapt to a pile of rubble that didn't at once collapse. That's when she realized she'd got turned around by the rotatin tree; she weren't headin back to Kalin but toward the other side. To her credit, she never considered reversin course. Scramble on she did.

Unfortunately the more progress she made, the more the rubble drifted her down, the speed of her descent only increasin the closer she got to the other side, though the refuge offered there, almost within reach, made her kick and claw that much harder, even while beneath her a widenin stream of stone and dirt kept flyin off the cliffs, blossomin more and more halos of gray dust.

And Landry didn't stop until her boots knew unmovin rock and her face was feelin the stingin lashes of the tall brush she hurled herself through, hands grabbin at whatever branches were near, no matter what thorniness greeted her palms.

True, she'd left the last lead still coiled around the tree. True, she'd left behind her pink slicker. But she'd made it to the other side. That's what mattered. Landry threw up her arms fer another victory hoot. And Kalin at once answered her back with his own weak hoot, Tom too, doin his best to whistle, though it weren't much of one.

There was some good news too. The tree had not only stopped and resettled but in its slow wheelin around downward had shed the leads so that all the knotted rope now lay stretched out upon the scree like the molted skin of a long skinny snake. Leadin the three horses down alongside the rocky debris took some doin, but Kalin finally reached a place where, with the help of a scrappy branch, he could retrieve it.

Landry had disappeared. Kalin figured rightly that she'd dipped out of sight in order to seek out a route to get her higher up again on the scree. Nonetheless, her absence disturbed him. It was bad enuf that she was now a good distance away.

Kalin was still tryin to work out a new plan as he led the three horses back up to where Landry had started her traverse, and even managed to get up a little ways higher until the grade said no, when Landry finally reappeared on the other side, near opposite them, and what a beautiful sight she was. Whatever math they had or hadn't learned yet, they both understood the need to get as high up as possible in order to shorten the distance they'd have to cross.

Landry had managed to find an easy trail up around some scrub oaks and fir trees that eventually delivered her into the protective custody of some Engelmann spruces. She at once knotted the lariats together, tyin one end around the trunk of the tree closest to the scree and then the other end again around herself.

Kalin was takin a moment to feed the horses some nibbles and as much water as they needed. He needed water too. And while he rechecked Mouse's packsaddle, it kept botherin him that he still hadn't arrived at a neat solution on how to get across, in fact spendin most of his mental energy tryin to shunt away the naggin declaration that there might not exist a neat solution.

She's comin back, Tom hollered, and that sure got Kalin's attention.

Landry seemed to have learned a thing or two from the first crossin. Fer one, she was better at findin the right places to step, them elusive solid spots, not even marked by asters, and so hardly slippin down nor even settin loose any stones to remind them of what waited below. Fer another, she'd also done some thinkin on what needed to

430

come next, and she let Kalin know it too. Kalin didn't put up no fuss. He did exactly what she said. Or rather he did exactly what she yelled. She was still a good ways off.

First, he tried rodeo-style to throw the rope he held out Landry's way. He didn't get close. She'd reached the limit of the lariats by then and was now sittin down on them barely stable stones. Kalin could see her snickerin.

Tom wasn't. He was howlin mad. *Don't tell me we's doomed because you never learned to throw a rope!*

Just watch, Tom, Landry shouted out to her brother. *Next try Kalin's gonna send it back the way we come.*

That startled Tom. *Oh boy, if that don't shiver me some. Like she could see me fer real.*

What's he sayin? Landry demanded of Kalin. *Is he afraid I can see him?*

Kalin weren't gettin in the middle of that, and he did finally manage a decent throw, and right on target too. Sure, it came up short, but it was somethin, not enuf of somethin but still somethin. Kalin regathered the ropes and readied hisself fer another attempt, except this time Landry yelled out for him to stop. She had another idea.

Landry asked Kalin to clip the bull snap at the end of the last lead rope to the tie ring of Jojo's halter-bridle. Kalin at once felt dangerously ambiguous about what was unfoldin here, but he still did like she asked. They briefly debated whether or not to leave the saddle on Jojo, Kalin bringin up how any additional weight might disadvantage the horse, but they both agreed it weren't gonna prove the difference.

Okay, Kalin, Landry yelled at last. *Send Jojo my way.*

Kalin had positioned Navidad and Mouse farther up the slope, standin pretty much right in front of them too. That meant handlin the reata and the leads with just his right hand. There weren't no other choice. Then he whispered to the great blue horse how much Landry needed him, how he should get on over to her, get over as easy as possible.

Kalin was sure it was gonna take more than that, but Jojo headed out onto the scree at once, eyes fixed on Landry, who was already callin him by name, also with clicks and other sounds Kalin was sure he'd never heard her make before.

Thanks to a patch of stable rock, Jojo got a good start and continued to make good progress until Kalin noticed first how Jojo's ears kept flickin all about and then seen how his hooves were strugglin more and more to find solid ground. Kalin did what he could from his side to keep above Jojo, tuggin on the rope so the horse's head stayed headin uphill. To let Jojo turn downhill would doom the horse. Kalin in fact was so fixed on Jojo's traverse that he missed what Landry had gone ahead and stupidly done.

Tom hadn't. *She's untied herself!*

Landry had seen no other way: in order to close the gap, she had to abandon the lariats. Jojo, at least, upon seein Landry scramblin his way, struggled that much harder to head up against the rocks now startin to cascade against them.

Kalin could do nothin but let go of his end of the reata and watch.

There was some relief when Landry got close enuf to Jojo to get hold of a lead rope, racin alongside him then, urgin the horse on as she did her best to gather up the rope draggin behind, lest it foul up Jojo's legs or even hers.

For the most part they kept ahead of the slides startin in their wake. But even though Landry aimed to keep their angle high, their trajectory soon knew only descent.

The hiss and clatter of stones flyin over the cliffs below continued to grow. At one point scores of moths shot up into the air to join the clamor and confusion. Landry and Jojo could do nothin but push on, hopin not to find themselves in the middle of a fast-collapsin river of rubble that would hurl them to the canyon floor.

Kalin and Tom were beside themselves, but Landry only grew calmer as her focus on Jojo continued to increase. Time had vanished for her, maybe for both of them, as she kept the big blue horse on a path of flat rock or small pebbles or sandy earth.

They had started a good ways above where the ash now stood, above even where it used to be, but as they crossed the halfway point, that awful aggregation of deceivin stones had already delivered them to near level with the tree, and worse, Landry's and Jojo's descent had started to accelerate.

What up above appeared as minor grooves had down here become chutes, which Landry was doin everythin she could to avoid. The problem, though, was that the way they was movin weren't workin. Finally Landry, with a shout at Jojo to follow, bolted ahead, sprintin and stumblin across the last section. She'd let go of the rope. It weren't the rope that mattered anyways. It sure weren't what bound these two together.

Seein Landry make her dash away from him sure put the spirit in Jojo's hind legs. He charged and he kept chargin against the dissolvin ground. Jojo's first kick, though, only slipped him farther down, drawin him perilously close to one of them gouges wide enuf to swallow them both. But the great blue horse recovered quickly, and on the next kick he lunged well clear of the collapse, propellin him forward fast enuf so that he reached the far side just ahead of Landry.

Fer the third time that afternoon, Landry raised her arms, though she was too bad for breath to manage even a little hoot.

Kalin and Tom threw up their arms but also couldn't hoot, breathless as well, not from exertion but for the sight of Landry and Jojo near stolen away by a river of stone.

As they watched her disappear into the brush again, Kalin felt an impulse roll through him: to just go for it, right then and there, just lead Navidad and Mouse out upon that tide of unsleepin stones and outrun whatever failure the ground offered them, just scramble through it, until they was on the other side, over there with Landry and Jojo. He just had to believe. He just had to have faith. He just had to go ahead and do it.

Tell me you don't mean that, Tom demanded just in time.

I don't know what I mean.

Fair enuf.

I might though could outrace the worst of it like Landry just done?

You might get lucky.

Kalin didn't like hearin that. *I'm not the most coordinated when it comes to my feet.*

You ain't.

But I sure as heck would like to get this over with.

You'd be doin it with two horses. And one with a packsaddle on.

Kalin nodded.

She's got the leads now.

She's got all the rope now.

And like that the impulse to head recklessly out upon the scree left Kalin. But the dread also grew. What lay ahead now seemed even more fearsome. Even the faint haze of dust that floated above the settlin stones drifted toward him like a threat. Furthermore, the various slides within slides, along with these emergent narrows devourin up such a wide swath of crumblin mountain, what *should never have been confused with the architecture in Salisbury Plain, Giza, or Athens,* as Ms. Melson would quip in 2011, provoked in Kalin enuf dizziness to force him to throw his head back, the turbine of clouds above then disorientin him even further, forcin him to squeeze his eyes shut.

And when he returned again to the challenge, the circumstances seemed even worse. Nothin moved, and yet now all of it seemed ready to move at once, at any moment, sweep everythin away, even that strange mountain ash tree.

At least Landry and Jojo were safe.

That was somethin.

At least Landry and Jojo were safe.

What Kalin didn't know, what none of them could know, was how at the base of the Ninth Scree, where the cliffs waited with their vertical offerin of a three-hundred-foot drop, there was also some levelness to be found due to a wide overhang. Loose rock had built up there over centuries, and though, as we've just seen, plenty could still skitter forth beyond the edge, plenty more would join the amassment servin as an effective buttress against all the shattered rock that rose above it. In this regard, maybe Mr. Caracy Rudder was right to mention monuments that had survived for millennia, or so Mrs. Annserdodder was kind enuf to suggest to Ms. Melson.

However, yesterday's rains had altered every stony claim on the future. The water had channeled through the turmoils of rock and earth, in some places further settlin and compactin the debris, in other places further clearin away the particulate hold of sand and ragged chips. The water had not only worked its way through the pile upon the overhang but had also seeped down within the overhang itself, findin fissures to pulse through, carryin along flecks of the above shatter, cloggin some areas in ways that created pools of water within, in some areas substantial pools. Then when the temperatures began to plummet, the power of ice demanded, as it always had, the price mountains must always pay.

Landry had put the scree behind her. She was first makin sure that Jojo weren't hurt, and by some miracle he wasn't, and, second, that he had whatever water still sloshed in her canteen. What she'd have given for even a small wedge of apple to offer him. The gold grass fightin up through the pine needles would have to serve. She then unclipped the lead and looped his reins around a branch low enuf to give his head room to roam the ground.

Next Landry hitched one end of the reata around the same trunk she'd relied on before. Then she separated out the three leads and coiled them and flung them over her shoulder. The reata was now tied to the lariats, one end of which she secured around her waist.

She didn't alert Kalin that she was headed back his way to get Mouse. Instead Landry practiced light steps, particular steps, and except for one bad moment when the stones gave way, she managed again to reach the limit of the rope.

This time she didn't sit down but looped one end of the three leads around and in on itself a bunch of times, usin the bull snap to clamp hold of the rope and so secure the knot.

With expert handlin and what Tom confirmed was the result of loads of practice, she began then to spin that weighted end above her head, slowly feedin out more and more rope. She sure did put on a show too, at first just to tease Kalin some, demonstratin how you was supposed to really handle a rope, soarin it above her head, at her side, behind her back. Weren't that somethin? Weren't she somethin? Just look at her! Perched in the middle of such awful danger and still havin herself a blast. And maybe the mountain didn't at once toss her into oblivion because it too was enjoyin the show.

The sheer impudence of that girl, Tom drawled, though he was smilin.

Kalin was just mesmerized.

Truth was, though, that how Landry finally did manage to get Kalin that rope didn't happen on the first throw or the second or even the third or fourth, and it didn't require no fancy loops above her head either, nor dancin eights at her hip. In the end, she had to resort to securin rocks with her knot, and only then, by swingin that bit of heaviness around, did she get off a good-enuf throw.

The rope didn't fly so far that Kalin was absolved from havin to risk an incursion. He also had to make peace with leavin both Navidad and Mouse, usin his belt and long-sleeved shirt to hobble them both, while still implorin them with murmurin calmness to stay put.

At first Kalin tried to light-foot it like he'd seen Landry do, but the stones immediately betrayed him. For a while Kalin managed to keep ahead of the unleashed currents of erosion but all too quickly saw how he'd soon be caught. He leapt then, kinda like he'd seen Jojo do at the end, though in Kalin's case he looked more like a frog hoppin off a hot grill. It weren't pretty but it did work. He got lucky too, because where he landed proved solid enuf to pause. He had to pull up his pants. He'd lost weight. He needed his belt.

Then on all fours Kalin angled up enuf to grab the weighted end of the leads. Instead of tryin to light-foot it back, though, Kalin mustered a series of long jumps that carried him down a ways but still returned him to solid ground, where his hustlin didn't end, racin up just as hard to Navidad and Mouse lest the racket of so much skitterin rock spook them into a bad decision, with Kalin's race impeded somewhat by the need to keep a thumb through a belt loop lest his pants fall down and expose his under clothes which sure would put a burn on Kalin's face. Not that Landry would've seen much at that distance. Landry was clappin and hootin.

Once the horses was unhobbled, a lead snapped to Mouse's halter-bridle, and his belt back on, Kalin finally sat down.

I thought I was a goner.

Mouse leaned down and gave Kalin's head a hard nudge, with a wet snort too, what helped further calm Kalin.

I thought we was too, Tom answered.

Kalin readied the rope so he could pay it out smoothly once Mouse got goin. He and Landry both knew there was enuf to get the quarter horse on his way, but Kalin would still have to let go of the leads, leavin poor Mouse to face yards and yards with no one at his side. As if it ain't already obvious, none are spared from havin to dare at least one passage without assistance. Only what we keep alight in our core will favor us onwards.

To be fair, a good many folks have objected to this fragile notion that were the Ninth Scree to give way beneath hooves and boots, the ropes these children had used to span its dangers might save their lives. They'd do diddly-squat is the general consensus. Like a rope stands a chance against a thousand pounds of horse gettin dragged down by thousands of tons of rock.

Perry Metz, at the time a bartender at the Kaktus Glass in Bernalilo, New Mexico, who liked to say he was born in Hadleyville, who'd also once brought Sister Avery some flowers to press in her book as well as hung out with the likes of Yash Rocker and Janeen Ewell, well, he often flew in the face of sense, arguin that ropes did offer invaluable assistance: *If the dirt's slippin out from under you, you at least got somethin to help haul your dang butt over to where the ground is more secure.*

Wendy and Bruce Oldroyd, both in Iowa City, at the university there, though plenty familiar with the Isatch mountains, havin grown up in Pleasant Grove and Spanish Fork, would in the company of Ronalee Golightly, Alexa Ussachevsky, or on the phone with Haru Taguchi and his husband in Japan, or with Jamie Jones, Maureen Paulson, or even with Tyler Stokes, who'd done the job on the Riggs home and wound up workin for a spell at Porch Meats, as well as with Jobie Leveridge, emphasize how ropes were beside the point, with such treacherous accumulations of loose stones provin *harsher than a hillside of broken glass you'd never want a horse to go anywhere near.* Though as Wendy Oldroyd's brother, Tatum Watkins, who was teachin kayakin on the Arkansas River, at this point livin in Denver, though he liked to say he lived in Shinbone, would bring up just to hear hisself speak: *Ain't a scree I regard now, however mild, that in my mind can't just give way.*

Bruce Oldroyd's sister, Emilee Oldroyd, an art teacher in Janesville, Wisconsin, would create an astonishin tableau of the Ninth Scree, evokin the immensity of the disruptions occurin that day along with the many pathways of easily navigated stability. Todd Stevens loved that piece, as did Emanuelle Bucks, Miles Daley, Dan'l Leftwich, Grace Snyder, and Larsen Cooke.

Same as he had with Jojo, Kalin positioned hisself uphill to better keep Mouse's head set against the slope.

Get ready! Kalin shouted to Landry.

Come on, Mouse! Landry yelled and kept yellin.

But Mouse weren't movin. He just stomped a back hoof down hard. Stomped twice. Kalin tried an easy tug. Mouse tugged back harder. Kalin tried to lead him onto the scree by the halter-bridle. Mouse still didn't budge.

Mouse has gotta be the smartest one here, Tom said from atop Ash.

Kalin tried talkin more to Mouse, lowerin his voice so low that not even Tom could hear. Mouse nickered back but remained rooted. As a last resort, Kalin took off that dirty Stetson and gave Mouse the hardest swat he'd ever given a horse. That sure got the surprise it deserved. Mouse kicked back and gunned hisself forward, further warned to keep goin by the collapsin rock.

Maybe if he'd just stayed at it like that he'd've done fine, but with Mouse bein Mouse, he slowed too soon. At least Kalin didn't have to correct his course none, but he sure did start hollerin. Tom yowled too, like that would do any good, though you can't fault a ghost fer tryin. At the very least, Tom's urgins urged Kalin to keep his urgins goin strong.

The very worst thing Mouse could do now was stop altogether, or even start turnin back around, for then, like the creature of prey he was, if he got wind of his predator, what here was the dissolvin mountainside, he might try to flee straight down and all too soon depart their company.

What also weren't no good thing was how them leads, now gone from Kalin's hands, kept bouncin along the rocks, one of the two knots, and on one occasion both knots, catchin here and there on a sharp outcroppin, jerkin Mouse's head down or to the side, pesterin him with misdirections as he still endeavored to reach Landry.

Though hold that line he still did. Mouse even picked up the pace. And somehow, through that labyrinth of wrong turns, where just one bad step could've found a rock to stab through them improvised cardboard boots, or even worse, trap a hoof, even crack a leg, Mouse somehow intuited a path of smooth stones and soft dirt, which, yes, was still givin way but not enuf to take Mouse away.

Tom hooted so loud, Landry should've heard him. She couldn't, but she could almost reach Mouse; he weren't but an arm's length away, which was when the biggest swath of rubble so far collapsed.

Boy, that killt Kalin to see. There just weren't a thing he could do. It was all up to Landry. She had to grab that lead; she had to get that horse to higher ground. And Landry near did it. Aided by the taut rope at her waist, she flew toward him in a smooth arc, takin big leaps until she was near on top of him, even if the shiftin angles and speeds involved in this near collision kept the leads just out of reach.

Landry did, though, manage to grab hold of the packsaddle, clawin at the bindin ropes in a desperate effort to stay with Mouse. But that was not to be, and the geldin lurched on, still headin for the far side, thank goodness, if also still driftin downwards.

At the sight of Mouse heavin hisself forward, Navidad lurched forward too. Kalin had his hands full then, bringin her back to a standstill.

By then Mouse was well beyond the ash tree, still above it too. Unfortunately, and this likely due to the horse's frantic struggles combined with whatever Landry had grabbed for earlier, items from the packsaddle had started to come off. There went some food, a tarp, there went the sleepin bag, with still more items strewn upon that movin rubble.

Mouse kept pursuin the far side, with now Landry also scramblin in the same direction, usin the lariats to keep herself headin uphill. To her credit, despite the significant energy demanded of her scramble, turmoiled additionally by her risin fear that she might not make it, that the mountain might just bury her, Landry never quit urgin Mouse to keep goin, hootin at him with her beautiful voice to buck free of this maw set on consumin them both. And buck he did, buck she did, both of them kickin their way forward like hornets were at their rears.

Landry knew herself then as nearly dead, which she very well might have succumbed to had it not been for her determination to see this crazy adventure through, in the name of her brother, but mostly in the name of the horses, and at that moment in the name of Mouse.

In the final stretch, the rocks seemed to behave strangely around Mouse, or at least that's what Landry seen; as if anticipatin each furious stride, a mutiny of stone sought to refuse this gambit; as if Mouse was a Killer of Mountains and this mountain wanted nothin more to do with him except see him on his way.

Maybe why Mouse reached the other side first.

Landry came in a respectful second, with her final sideways dash relyin on the rope at her waist to swing her above the chaos fallin away beneath her boots.

Not a moment later she was with Mouse, and then Mouse was with Jojo, Jojo sure glad to see Mouse, shakin his big beautiful blue head and long mane. And Mouse didn't complain none about the attention, acceptin the nuzzles, the welcomin snorts, while Landry watered Mouse from the palm of her hand.

Some folks, like for instance Zarli Washburn, in Owings Mills, Maryland, an equestrian instructor at Garrison Forest School, would often invent in long calls with friends back in Utah, includin Lolly Neilson, Lane Granberg, and Howie Dirker, that this here was the moment that ended all threats of kicks from Mouse should Jojo ever ride up rearside too close. From this point on, Mouse never again snapped at the air if Jojo jostled his flanks. As Zarli Washburn would keep sayin: *Here was the start of the closeness that would play out so significantly above Kirk's Cirque.*

At which point an immense crack rent the whole canyon, somehow born of the scree but eludin any precise sense of origin.

Kalin froze.

Tom froze.

Landry froze.

Even the horses froze.

They waited upon a tumult that none of them, not even the ghosts, could survive. But whatever collapse that calamitous utterance had seemed to portend, nothin more happened.

Landry headed the horses deeper amidst them Engelmann spruces, where the ground continued to soften and darken until it was covered by a thick carpet of dried needles. Fer a moment Landry thought she'd reached a place no longer concerned with the sharp angles of upheaval, the staggerin consequence of potential energies, the price of altitude, a place no longer under the influence of Katanogos. She wanted to stay there forever.

When Kalin saw her emerge from the trees, she had all two-hundred-plus feet of rope with her, already tyin one end around the nearest spruce, the other end around her waist. She was doubtin then her decision to leave two leads with the horses. It was for their safety, but maybe she should go back for them? She started headin out on the scree, except she weren't headin out on the scree, in fact she weren't movin at all. In fact her legs had locked up so bad, she had to sit down. And she feared if she stayed seated too long, her arms would lock up as well, like they was already startin to do, her fingers too. Next she'd lose her voice.

I can't go out there again, she managed to shout to Kalin. And kept at it, because even through her cupped hands, it took two or three times before Kalin understood her meanin. *But I will get out there again! I will!* Though she was still sittin. *Just give me a sec.*

Confound her! Tom grunted. *Does she ever mean anythin she says?*

Sure she does, Kalin said in tones intended to soothe the ghost. *Sometimes sayin a thing you can't do is a way of findin your way to doin it just the same.*

Confound you too!

Kalin started yellin for Landry to stay put. *Maybe I can think of somethin else!* Which got her legs to loosen up enuf so she could stand again.

What somethin else? Tom demanded.

I don't know! I have to think on it! Kalin yelled with more than a little cross in his voice.

She's comin our way again! Tom yelled.

This time, though, there weren't no way to light-foot across the top half of the scree. Everythin had changed, and Landry was no longer welcome. She knew it too and screamed as the rocks poured away from beneath her. The snake had awoken. She retreated at once, runnin harder than she'd already run with Jojo and Mouse, doin everythin she could to get loose of that undulatin uncoilin, at one point fallin to her knees; she fell twice before throwin aside the rope, what was now slowin her down, her eyes locked the whole time on the spruces ahead. Only when she was a few paces from solid ground did Landry spare a glance back at what was clawin up after her. And that look near cost her her life. Her throat constricted so bad, no breath could get in or out. Then her legs started seizin up again, and she toppled forward. Her elbows sure got bloodied then, but her arms did not desert her. She clawed at the rock and kept draggin herself away from the envelopin slide until her legs finally got back to doin what legs do best: kickin and runnin.

Landry reached safety right as the area she'd just crossed shrugged loose tons more debris, rivers within rivers of stone hurtlin toward the edge of the cliffs below, where everythin would once again settle, *still in Medusa's thrall,* as Mrs. Annserdodder would mutter years later.

And herein lies a fable pertainin to our frequent misjudgments, missteps, and failures: had Landry not dared this last and apparently futile attempt, what had nearly undone her life, the next few moments fer sure would've seen Kalin murdered right there.

For at that moment, with dust still risin up all around, a rifle shot cracked across the canyon, strikin rock not a dozen feet from Kalin and Tom, at once stirrin Navidad into backsteppin bewilderment, Kalin followin her just as fast, until with calmin hands and an even calmer voice he regained her side, swingin up into the saddle then and with a hard click headin them straight up the steeps alongside the scree to as high as he'd ever got on foot, even higher, until they were hid within the heaviest billows of dust risin up off the multiple rockslides still in motion below.

I think someone shot at us! he yelled at Tom.

I figure that's right, Tom said, ridin up beside Kalin and Navidad.

You figure it's the Porches?

I reckon they ain't yet given up.

Another shot cracked across the canyon. This time the impact was far below them, rock still shatterin into a swarm of nasty ricochets.

There's some good news, Kalin said.

Gettin aimed at is good news? Tom asked.

They don't know how to shoot.

Ha! Ain't you a rosy one!

Thank heavens one of us is! Kalin even managed a grin.

But Tom didn't grin back. *Heaven's got nothin to do with where we're at.*

Kalin nodded. He thought that was about right. It also weren't lost on him how Tom in sayin so had suddenly seemed void of mirth, his eyes hollow and dark, sinkin into shadows that play no part in this world, makin of Tom someone who weren't even Tom.

And then somewhere in the lashin clouds above a low rumble murmured as if to remind the mountain that whatever it might bring forth weren't nothin compared to what a sky could command.

Kalin urged Navidad higher.

You know horses can't fly, right? Was Tom's response but he followed.

Who needs wings if you know how to ski! Kalin said with a laugh, his grin postively alarmin, partly because it was also so darned relaxed.

A third rifle shot tore past them, this time close enuf for Kalin to taste the burn on the air.

Not that Kalin cared a lick.

It was just Navidad and him now.

And this here was what he was meant for.

Like his shoulders, Kalin's smile continued to broaden, and, well, seein that, Tom's smile returned, and Tom was Tom all over again. The ghost even raised his dusty hat in the air, his eyes afire now with the darin of it all. He hooted them on, loud too, though his whistle, when it came this time, was louder, so loud it seemed for a second that Landry had heard her brother on the other side, because she joined right in, with her own hootin and hollerin, for all she was worth, as Kalin and Navidad rode out onto the collapsin scree.

It was 3:52 p.m.

End of Part One

Part Two:

The Mountain

Chapter Fourteen

"The Great Rockfall"

ow to back up just a bit, above the timberline, the north side of Agoneeya, or what is the right side of Isatch Canyon if you're headin in, made good on its reputation for mildness. Even the few limestone faces toward the summit, with them slopin like gentle slides for giants, weren't nothin compared to the loomin cliffs and screes so afflictin the left side of Isatch Canyon, or what is the south side of Kaieneewa. Unlike the astonishin and terrifyin Katanogos massif to the northeast, Agoneeya seemed indifferent to altitude, an old mountain, a forgivin mountain, glad for company, even if that included the likes of Egan Porch, Kelly Porch, and Billings Gale, who'd continued to sleuth out the right meanderin animal trail to get them high enuf for a clear view of the Kaieneewa side of the canyon.

Egan cursed their lack of machetes. Whatever pocket knives they'd brought were inconsequential before the brambles that constantly reimposed their prickly walls whenever they thought to abandon, say, the elk path they was on. Sometimes, though, when a narrow trail started to dip back down, Egan could shove aside some branches and break on through to another wanderin path higher up. Sometimes they crawled, too often they erred. Distances that a straight trail or even a semi-decent switchback would've covered in less than a half hour took them hours to cross.

It got to where it felt like sweet Agoneeya was goadin them. The trio would reach some clearin only to realize that they'd descended! On one occasion they'd even gone backward some.

Not that they gave up. The three men continued to take turns assaultin barricades of tangled branches and boot-grabbin roots. No one got through without at least a few substantial scratches. Egan took a bad one over his left eyebrow and down his right cheek. Kelly earned a gash across the bridge of his nose. Even Billings, who was the nimblest and moved ahead with the least amount of resistance, wound up with several small punctures along his jaw, resultin in a slow drip of blood from his chin which only started to clot up when they finally got above the brush and at last could take in not only Aster Scree and the *T* above it but the first few screes Landry, Kalin, and the horses had crossed earlier that day.

Egan unslung his .30-06 Winchester Model 70 and puttin the Leupold scope to work took in first the body of Cavalry. Seein his dead horse again finally got at him. Egan felt briefly dizzy and hot as well as blue. Over and over he'd described for folks how that Kalin kid had shot his dear horse, with Egan then havin to put a round in Cavalry to end his sufferin, and at least that last part was true. This version had grown so convincin that what had really happened yesterday had slid behind Egan's words and hid. Say it like you want it, and the truth you need is yours for free. *Three T's and the truth,* as Orly Vanleuven would put it with a big laugh.

Except seein Cavalry now, and from afar, for some reason routed those lies, and Egan found hisself shakin his head like his ears was full of red ants for the shame of havin ridden the animal so badly.

And then Egan caught sight of the law enforcement ranger, Bren Kelson, roped up, on the top of the crag, startin to make his way past the collapse of branches and rocks lodged in the fissure.

Heath Bills, at the time in Kansas City, Missouri, employed by Hallmark Cards, would speculate with Merijo Jarvis, still in Salt Lake City, workin up at Gold Miner's Daughter, how here was one of them awful moments that was too little remarked upon when it came to Egan. *How so?* Merijo Jarvis would ask. *I hope your kiddin?!* Heath Bills would reply. *Because no hunter I know has ever settled his aim on a person.* He was referrin to the fact that while Bren Kelson was thinkin of his fiancée, Brooke Young, and the date they would have that night, *he sure as heck weren't thinkin that crosshairs might be hangin over his chest,* as Levi Powell would say to both Matty Goforth and Trevor Bell.

Egan didn't linger, though he did feel charged up by the shot he could've taken and equally disappointed because he hadn't taken it. He'd never tell nobody, but he'd even got a rise in hisself when he'd clicked off the safety just for kicks.

Billings and Kelly had already pushed on ahead, happily takin advantage of the now-easy way east across brown grass and soft stumbles of stone. Here and there a cairn emerged to mark a trail of sorts, likely built by some Isatch U students enjoyin the pleasantness of Agoneeya on some sunny afternoon as well as the breathtakin views to the north, where now and then sections of the upper ridges broke free from the clouds, if still leavin the Katanogos summit to carry on its unwitnessed consort with the storm.

Revealed beneath the canopy of clouds, only partially obscured by spindrifts of mists, were those uplands and steeps of the massif, thick with groves of aspens, birches, fir trees, and maples, where coursed a multitude of streams, intermittently cascadin over bouldered drops before resumin their flow down grassy hillsides, gold now with fall but come spring bright with blooms of sticky purple geraniums, skyrockets, and sugarbowls. Golds, reds, and the blue-green shades of thousands of pine trees already awaited anyone willin to absorb the magnificence there, but neither Egan nor Kelly gave it a glance, nor even Billings, who still had the place and space within hisself to register such instruction. Mostly they focused on this latest path, gainin greater definition as they pushed faster ahead.

Egan did at least note how the sun's march west, though occluded by clouds, was now quickenin its descent to the south, foldin this side of Agoneeya into a deepenin indigo, which too soon would turn to an even darker shade of violet. The temperature was already droppin, and soon all that had thawed would likely refreeze again. Egan's hands had already stiffened and reddened, and only his exertion kept the cold at bay. Egan didn't let up and soon passed Billings and then Kelly. By the time they reached the top of the next spur, they were all winded, but Egan still wouldn't pause, pushin higher and higher.

Much to Egan's surprise, Kelly eventually overtook him. For Kelly, that's all that mattered, bestin this older brother. But Egan denied Kelly any victory by stoppin at once. Kelly had no choice but to stop. Billings was already sittin.

From where they stood now, each could take in that vast Ninth Scree, which Landry had already crossed three times, the one by herself, the second with Jojo, *Clop-Clop-clip-Clop,* and the third helpin Mouse, though by this point both horses were out of sight, hidden in that clump of spruces that neither Egan, Kelly, nor Billings even considered.

Kelly felt pleased to have his rifle out before Egan, shoulderin fast that Remington .270, eye at his Vari-X III scope. In his rush to overtake his brother in somethin, he hadn't taken the time to support hisself, and so from that distance the canyon jumped and danced in the lens with every adjustment he made or breath he took. Though Kelly still found her, even if he never did notice the rope around her waist. Maybe that was because he weren't lookin for a plan, the designs of an ever-workin intelligence; he saw only the Landry he was familiar with, her incompetence, idiocy, misfortune now, the terrible flailin of a child caught in the worst of places, leapin around like a tiny desperate animal lost in a river of earth, the flow continuin to widen and deepen, and with her clawin to get up the banks that would each time break away enuf to deny her safety, leavin her to achieve no more than a sickenin pantomime of success, endlessly incomplete, unfinished, as she tumbled down and down into the maw of that failin churn of stones, swallowed whole by it, by the mountain, already eructin in its collapse the coverin signature of this cost: them thick billows of dust, gray, brown, dull yellow, what some folks, whose names you can probably guess by now, would describe as *the coverin Cherub of History,* or at least coverin this history, with Kelly trackin the debris sluicin over the cliffs below, where of course Landry was headin, had to be, even if he'd already lost her, if thinkin he was still followin her shadow, in the midst of so much rock and dirt, flyin over the edge.

The Gatestone girl just fell! Kelly cried out without lookin up, continuin to jerk his rifle and scope around, like he needed to confirm what he was already sure of. *She's gone! I can't believe I just seen her die! She's gone!* Weren't it awful? Weren't it spectacular? Who else could he tell?

Until Kelly, by sheer luck, managed to also glimpse none other than that Kalin kid.

Kelly was gobsmacked.

I see him! I see him!

The one who'd done in their baby brother Russel! Unprepared for the waves of nausea that followed, this time as sudden as he'd once felt flyin around on the Zipper carnival ride, goin forward in turns, with a belly full of cotton candy and soda pop that weren't gonna stay down for long. Not that Kelly gave in to that desire to puke. He even managed to get Kalin in his crosshairs before more risin dust wiped the boy from his sight.

Kelly still fired.

He fired twice.

It didn't help that he was shootin 90-grain shells or that he hadn't sighted his rifle since last fall. Though even with the right rounds and a sighted rifle, Kelly still wouldn't've hit diddly, not at half a mile away. Not that that stopped him from declarin differently.

I got him! I just put that boy down!

Egan by then had found Kalin, on a black horse, ridin uphill, dust condensin around him, shadows too, almost so dense to warn him from the sight.

But Egan didn't fire. Not yet.

He led the boy higher and higher until steepness ordered the horse to stop or start demonstratin some equine talent for pitons and rope, boy and horse wheelin around then to face that immense scar of broken rock.

To Egan, Kalin weren't much more than a grainy blob: pallid and scrawny, even at that distance. Egan might've at least admitted the kid wore his hat well, tilted right, catchin what light was out there, where shadows sought to permanently reign. But what did Egan know of shadows? Egan settled them crosshairs right on the shiftin blob that was the boy's chest, unless the shiftin was just his own breath. Then, right as another gust of dust began to steal Kalin away again, Egan clicked off the safety and fired.

Whatever penetrative elation Egan then experienced with the

eruption of his firearm, coupled with the subsequent hiss across the canyon, a music of velocity that at once places great distances within reach, just as fast retreated into a disappointment, struck through with longin, when the result of such impetuous desire makes clear that not everythin is available, within reach.

Though Egan's shot did still come close, and plenty's been said and over-said about that. Gabe Bangerter, a UPS driver in and around Three Forks, Montana, who often said he loved drivin on empty, would in 1990 blame the temperature differential between where the shot was fired and where the shot ended up: *Fired from the south side of Isatch Canyon, what at that hour was in the shade, and then hittin the north or south-facin side of Isatch Canyon, where it was warmer, Kalin and Navidad in a patch of sunlight, that can change a lot of things.*

Though it weren't like Egan was so inexperienced to have failed to note the risin air and calibrate his shot accordingly. He was loaded too with 130-grain rounds. And unlike Kelly, he'd recently sighted his Winchester.

Shawna Chen, in Spokane, Washington, an asset protection specialist at Home Depot at this point, wouldn't dispute Gabe Bangerter's assessment but would contend that even with Egan takin *a measured gander* at Kalin, he was still *jittered plenty* by the prospect of Kelly gettin off a third shot: *Egan weren't gonna let his younger brother outshoot him!* Egan at this point was more in a contest with Kelly than he was committed to fulfillin the death writ their father had issued.

Of course, as Jeff Cannon, from Orvop, livin out his life in Orvop, workin at Allen's Camera, would point out: *Six hundred yards is a long, long shot.*

Others, includin Albacely Bennion, at the time in Martinsburg, West Virginia, employed at the county assessor's office; Wendel Moore, in Seacry, Arkansas, a pediatrician; and Kandie Moore, wife to Wendel, herself a radiologist, would insist that first and foremost one must not disregard what it means to actually try and kill someone. As Albacely Bennion would put it, and she was a skillt hunter herself with plenty of brothers and cousins who loved to hunt: *It weren't no matter for Egan to drop a young buck or, knowin Egan, a doe of any size. That's way different than gatherin up in your eye the viciousness needed to kill a young boy who incidentally you know had no hand in killin your brother, who did not harm your horse. That might just put a little kink in your aim.*

Melvin Athaiya, a likeable-enuf handyman in Asheville, North Carolina, would add to this train of thought by reiteratin that the chances of makin such a shot was at best unlikely: *It's easy to fire at someone if you know you ain't gonna hit them. Except for Hatch, none of those Porch boys were gonna get close.* The theory here bein that Egan was just gettin an early taste of it. *Like he was praticin maybe,* Keeley Wilde would say to Emily Larsen, Kelsey Selva, and Nahi Pasket after she'd relocated from Orvop to Milford, Delaware, where she would manage a local gym for years.

The general consensus holds that here was another example of Egan circlin heinous acts. He was on the front row when Old Porch put down Brad P. Hone. He'd gotten closer with Robert Gaff.

Robert Gaff was a student at Orvop High. Kalin had never noticed the kid, but Landry knew who he was well enuf to feel the smart of his unexplained disappearance months later.

Egan had disliked the boy at once. Robert Gaff was the weak sort, kinda pretty too, and to make matters worse smiled at Egan whenever he dropped by to pick up Francis or Russel from school. *What's his problem?* Egan would ask when he seen how the frosh wouldn't quit with his stares and smiles. *Aww, he ain't bad,* Russel would say. *He's a little touched but he's okay.*

The opportunity presented itself one Sunday mornin. On his way to Rome, Egan spotted the kid walkin along the shoulder of Route 256, what everyone called the Diagonal. Egan pulled over to give him a hard time but was met once again with that strange smile.

Ain't you a fine sight! Robert Gaff even crooned, though to be fair he hadn't meant it how it come across, only that he was tired, and it was hot, and this here was none other than Egan Porch stoppin to help him out. He didn't even hesitate either. Just climbed right in.

Shouldn't you be in church, Gaff?

Robert Gaff blushed. Egan Porch even knew his name!

Guess we both had the same idea!

What idea is that, Gaff?

Why livin a little, I guess.

It don't matter in the end what Robert Gaff said that finally set off Egan good enuf to punch the boy so hard, he near flipped over backward, slammin into a dumpster behind a strip of stores with a pizza shop. From the moment Robert Gaff climbed into Egan's truck, Egan was lookin for somethin to go off on, and likely in the back of his head he also wanted to finish what he hadn't finished with that Brad P. Hone. Demonstrate some real horseradish, which even in this case, where there weren't no contest, Egan still couldn't pull off.

Sure, Egan beat the boy bad and even threw him in that dumpster, where he'd meant to finish him off fer real, except Robert Gaff's long eyelashes and smile had proved too much. Egan just left him there in the trash, and it took a good number of blocks before Egan realized that it weren't over. Far from over. Now that touched kid would go to the police, or if he didn't have the wits to do so, whoever got to tendin to his wounds would go for him, and then they'd come for Egan, and why? Egan could just hear his daddy sneerin out the why: *Because you couldn't finish the job!*

Trouble was that when Egan returned to the dumpster, it was empty. Except seein that it was Sunday Egan knew it couldn't've just been emptied, so fer sure, he was at the wrong dumpster. And so Egan spent the rest of the mornin searchin dumpsters. Here, though, comes the weirder part: Robert Gaff still went missin. Didn't show up no more at Orvop High. His guardians put up signs and printed stuff in the papers and even got him on milk cartons.

And this troubled Egan because he'd earned his name on that Colt now except there weren't no proof. He couldn't even bring it up to his daddy. What was he gonna say? All Egan could tell his daddy was that he was good and ready for the real horseradish, and earn hisself a scowl. *We'll see . . .*

To this day no devoted and practicin member of the Church can understand how Egan Porch was so lost in the thrall of his father's light, a dim light at best, dark even. Especially since Heavenly Father offers such resplendent and infinite brilliance, such undiminished Love. It just puzzles the soul as much as it breaks the heart, Joseph Wooton would say many years later, while he was at the MTC in Orvop.

Maybe it was Clarence Crossman, at the time workin at the Caneel Bay Resort on St. John, who would make the best case for Egan's missed shot, arguin his position before both his wife, Radwan, who was sittin at his side, and her brother, Broze Bearden, on speakerphone, who was back in Spanish Fork, coachin baseball. Clarence Crossman would claim that Egan must have seen the real light at the last instant and *it hadn't had nothin to do with the Church: a bull's-eye would not only have killt Kalin but done in Egan. Ain't it obvious?* The Kalin boy's body would've eventually been found lyin cold and stiff on the mountainside, cut down by a .30-06 matchin what plenty of folks had witnessed Egan carryin into the canyon. That would surely have raised suspicions and, as Clarence Crossman would conclude, *no question that understandin would've flinched Egan plenty when firin off that round.*

What else explains why Egan didn't fire again? Egan had plenty more opportunities. In fact they all could've kept shootin, but they didn't. And fer sure that choice was further reinforced once Kalin and Navidad rode out onto the Ninth Scree and it started to collapse. Egan, Kelly, and Billings likely considered him a goner. And whatever feelins the missed shot stirred up in Egan, he was likely most glad to realize both his Bowlin Ball and the kid were dead. Egan even regretted wastin a shot.

In fact in retrospect, the whole thing put a frost to Egan's marrow, enuf even to make Egan want to throw his rifle down, step away, turn his back on whatever happened next. In truth, though, he couldn't take his eyes off Kalin, just like he couldn't admit to hisself his amazement, awe too, and even curiosity, as he beheld the slow and unfazed manner in which this boy, whom it's important to recollect Egan had never met nor even set eyes upon, not until now, not countin the blur he'd encountered in his scope at Aster Scree, astride now on a horse no one had spent so much as a penny of a thought on, started to descend a field of rock riverin with serpentine paths of sand and stone.

Or was he just slidin or even fallin?

Did the distinction even matter?

Furthermore, what had moments ago seemed forever cast in an afternoon gray the color of pewter was no longer so seized; the clouds had reconfigured themselves as easily as blinks of light on a breezy lake surface, fer sure in some places compoundin darkness blacker than charcoal but in other places partin and so releasin great beams of sunlight upon that fearsome scree.

Egan's eyes watered some before the sudden brightness, forcin him to blink extra and resettle his vision behind the scope. When he located Kalin and the horse again, they was farther down, as if on the most direct path to that edge where they'd surely fall off like the buffalo Egan had seen in history textbooks, with Indian folk or frontiersmen racin such quarry off cliffs.

Egan couldn't stop lookin, now and then even murmurin to Kelly and Billings, who were watchin as well: *Ain't this everythin!* Just the stillness of Kalin surrounded by all that chaos seemed an impossible display; as if that poise or posture, or whatever you wanna call it, the very lightness of his hands upon the reins, his fixity in the saddle, the way even the toes of his boots hardly wandered, seemed to bust up for good countless laws of physics. And that's still not addressin the blindin clarity of it all, attributable of course to the appearance of some sunlight, fer sure, but not what kept arrestin Egan's breath, confusin his aims, and most of all amplifyin his longins: to one day achieve such uniquity, to be like this kid, on so rare a horse, who with each downward step both was summonin and becomin a great pillar of fire; what still weren't the most of it, as what accompanied this feat, that terrible sound of accumulated time, too heavy fer time, lettin go of time, finally rumbled the far slopes of Agoneeya with a music voidin a previous era of geological stillness, comin apart, comin down.

Lore, myth, legend, that's what Egan finally saw, what he'd half imagined once when he was but ten, starin at old postcards of cowboys ridin down a hillside at the end of the day amidst Pactolian hay or at least gilded in dust, them postcards bein what he'd stole from Hatch's shoebox; or even these days when he'd wind up gazin at his father's Frederic Remington sculptures, authentic ones too, Old Porch havin showed them all the receipts, thousands of dollars' worth, tens of thousands of dollars' worth; or when Egan had watched John Wayne in *Red River* or even paused over a picture in a magazine of the Marlboro Man, where cowboys rode surrounded by vast herds, sometimes in a stampede, a storm upon the earth that only a few men knew how to live above. And that was still only some of what Egan saw in Kalin. He wanted to slow it down all the way; he wanted to smoke a cigarette.

Treesje Treeangle, an installation artist in Jersey City, would wind up creatin the stunnin piece *Down Through Clouds,* composed of numerous semitransparent screens hung at various heights and angles in a dimly lit room already suffused with fog. What made it especially exhilaratin or terrifyin was how the artist had somehow managed to cast upon every screen the shadow of an unnamed figure, the shadow of an unnamed horse, growin progressively larger and darker the farther back the screens went, and those at the very back were a good thirty feet tall. Furthermore, it seemed that the figure and the horse castin the silhouettes should be at the center of the piece, in the center of that warehouse, where onlookers were warned not to go, even though everyone could see that except for an assortment of lights there weren't no rider there and certainly no horse.

For Egan, the persistent illusion was that Kalin wasn't even movin. It's what made this vision so unreal and yet what conversely increased Egan's fascination with what he knew was of course happenin. Then he spotted that mountain ash on the move again, how could that be?, slidin closer and closer to the edge, and by its passage further addin to the accumulation of dust risin to the top of the scree, where Treesje Treeangle likely got her idea, sunlight castin Kalin's and Navidad's shadows upon that impermanent screen, a concordance of absences that seemed in those moments the measurement of what not even the mountains could answer.

Egan should've shuddered. Egan should've seen then that this weren't just about him, nor about Kalin, nor even about Russel. But Egan could not read such script. None of them could. Not even Navidad, though she didn't need to, even if both her and Kalin were coauthors of this moment along with the rock and the dust and the sun and time.

And then Kalin was gone.

Egan at last lifted his eye from the scope to reconfirm that the Ninth Scree was consumed by dust even as that low and continuin rumble warned him of more to come.

Egan and Kelly stayed put, but Billings had scurried higher up where he could draw the best bead on Kalin. Who knows if the .30-30 Savage 170 would've gotten there. The 35 Remingtons, 200-grain, would've made it close; the Nikon scope would've seen to that.

But what not a Porch knew, includin Old Porch hisself, was that Billings was quite the game player. Board games in particular, but especially chess. In fact the only one who knew just how good Billings was was none other than Trent Riddle, who'd won his fair share of chess tournaments throughout the state and yet had never once beat Billings. More importantly, Billings could translate those skills onto the board he recognized as his life. If he made the shot, which he understood quite literally was a long shot, he'd be 100 percent sentenced to death by a judge and jury with not a single Porch standin up in his defense. Old Porch valued loyalty so long as it ran his way. Billings also figured, and probably correctly too, that Old Porch knew Billings knew this, which is why perhaps their relationship seemed so easy, Old Porch frequently allottin Billings special dispensations that got him his used truck but with not even twenty thousand miles on it, plus them good stacks of bills he'd hide within the wall right beneath the medicine cabinet in his bathroom, what Billings planned to use when he quit Orvop in a week or so.

Billings had originally thought to skip town this weekend, but with the Russel business goin down, if he got outta there now, fer sure he'd get the blame. He first wanted to see the blame land on this Kalin fella. Billings also needed to keep an eye on Old Porch lest Old Porch get the idea that Billings wanted to use what he knew for his gain, which Billings had no desire to do. At least not yet. Not that maybe years from now, if he needed a favor, mind you without nothin bein said, Old Porch might prove more obligin because he'd want to do right by Billings, on his own volition see, to appear magnanimous, even if what was proddin him was the certain knowledge that Billings had witnessed a death History had got wrong. Old Porch would know that his boys could perish because of what Billings knew, if Billings turned. Loyalty is but a shade off from a threat. But Billings wouldn't turn and the more Old Porch saw that, remembered Billings doin what needed doin, the more he'd happily reward him.

Fer Billings, headin back to Porch Meats with news that this was now all settled was the best possible outcome. He'd be free with no claim on the future other than his own capacity to reinvent hisself.

So Billings just settled in, enjoyin the show, a boy and a horse with nowhere to go but down and down and out. Yet the more he watched, why the more closely he watched. One immense boulder bounced right over them. Billings doubted he'd ever seen such a rider, or for that matter such a horse, like they was one and the same, treatin such terrible circumstances of churnin collapse like it didn't concern them, casually weavin and slidin where just one misstep would have resulted in both horse and boy borne under, entombed at once beneath a debris flow comprised of tons and tons of wet, movin rock.

But Kalin and Navidad were not borne under, and Billings continued to marvel at how they managed a lope here and there, at one point even sidesteppin but always downward. Not that through that Nikon scope, tight as it was on Kalin, Billings didn't keep anticipatin the moment when kid and horse would just drop from sight as they went over the cliffs, and so he was greatly surprised when Kalin instead reached that rootless mountain ash, it too also continuin to slide, if at a much, much slower pace than everythin else.

Billings didn't know what to expect then, but it sure weren't what happened next: the black horse suddenly reared up. What's more, the kid's hands stayed near motionless; even the reins retained that slight curve of slack. Then both rider and horse spun around to face the tumult they'd just run with, run from, and now challenged head-on, challengin the collapsin scree, maybe challengin the mountain itself. The kid even lifted away that grimy Stetson, and though it weren't for show, because fer sure it had a purpose of balance, it also was a sight: that horse up on his back hooves, right beside that strange dead tree, with the boy perched up easy in the saddle, the stirrups, with one hand high in the air holdin one misused cowboy hat.

Quick then the Kalin kid swatted the horse's flanks with the hat, both sides fast, before hurlin hisself forward toward the horse's black neck, holdin tight to the mane, as that great animal leapt upwards, against all that crashin rock, a tide of earth the horse refused, at once in its midst, at once apart, at once devoured by great plumes of dust, darkness too, whereupon the storm clouds above refused the sun too, and shadows and bitter cold again overtook the canyon.

On the hike back down, the three were practically giddy, though the true reason for that, the beauty of the horse and rider, was never mentioned. Mostly it was crap talk. Kelly couldn't stop sayin how Landry was eaten by rocks, and by that point, havin heard Kelly tell it so many times, Egan was convinced Kelly was tellin the truth.

Eges, why do you always call Landry Gatestone Bowlin Ball? Kelly asked outta the blue.

Both take three fingers in three different holes.

How does that follow?

Behind Regal Lanes. Landry loved it so much, she begged to lick my fingers.

Later, when they got to talkin about Kalin, the more they chattered, the more they convinced themselves he'd done killt hisself on purpose. Billings brought up how he'd seen both horse and rider slide all the way down to that strange tree in the middle, though whatever happened after that, he left it alone, though the longer they talked and the longer they walked, the more it seemed to Billings that what Kalin had done next was an impossible thing, which didn't sit well with Billings because everythin he'd seen Kalin do up to that point, before it was all obstructed by dust, had also seemed an impossible thing.

Fer his part, Kalin knew no difference between hisself and Navidad as they approached that deracinated mountain ash afloat upon the Ninth Scree. And while Kalin on some other occasion might've admitted how this here was yet another thing made up in his crazy head, he still felt by tremendous waves of delicate sensation Navidad's hooves upon the rock. Even more curious, and we can add this here with 100 percent certainty, was how the same can be said for Navidad: she knew Kalin's way, beyond merely his hands, his narrow knees, even the angles of his bootheels, but rather through his calm and surgin heart, his simple breath, his regard for what lay ahead and what path would deliver them without injury from the roar that deafened their ears. They heard only each other, they knew only each other, they rode upon the back of thunder, and the thunder welcomed them, and they were the thunder and the mountain too.

Beyond the tree, upon a coilin path of soft sand, Navidad was borne down by the onslaught descendin around them, the mountain's wholeness dedicated now to this new future, *disjecta membra,* as Cal Carneros would years hence declare. Kalin didn't blink though. Nor did Navidad. They knew the backward steps necessary to find the way ahead. And they knew the moment to wait for, until like that they was gone, kickin hard away, flyin finally above and beyond these awful currents of degeneratin territories.

And it was enuf.

Just.

Only Tom saw how close they'd come, one back hoof on the edge, where one slip would've seen them fallin off them cliffs, but Navidad never drifted back again, and together they angled up and away, reachin the far side in a cloud of dust, scramblin into the tall brush, and not long after arrivin within that copse of Engelmann spruces where Landry greeted them with a mixture of joy, confusion, risin anger, but most of all great relief.

You look more like a ghost than Tom! Kalin even chided her, though he was also shakin pretty badly.

I was sure you was a goner.

It was close.

And they was shootin at you too! Pow-Pow. Though this time said without no rousin conviction. *I don't think they saw me. If they had, I would've got some shootin at too.*

Kalin nodded. *Rifles. Three shots. From the other side of the canyon. Whoever got off the first two had no business behind a trigger. The third one, though, he knew what he was doin.*

We made it.

We did. Kalin allowed hisself a smile then, and that seemed to help ease away some of his shakes, what looked more like tremblin now. Landry got him a canteen then, and that helped persuade away even the tremblin. Kalin gulped and gulped, realizin only then just how thirsty he'd got. Navidad was no different, and Landry made sure the mare got her fill, rubbin her neck as well, and shoulders, before hoppin around Navidad's legs.

Some cuts here are gonna need our care.

Kalin nodded. *Hey! Where's Tom?*

Landry looked up. Gobsmacked, she was. *You're not seriously askin me?*

Despite the already dim light, Kalin still made sure to shade the binoculars with various boughs. He eventually caught sight of Egan, Kelly, and Billings headin back down. And that was a glad sight.

They must figure we're dead.

Who is it?

Kalin handed her the binoculars. *That's Egan and Kelly. With the one I don't know.*

They watched until there weren't no more sight of them, and then they watched a bit longer. Kalin went searchin for jerky, but Landry came back first with a carrot, which they cut up five ways, givin the horses their share first before gnawin real slow on what was left.

We'll get a good dinner tonight. Kalin tried to keep from his head how much farther they still had to go.

After they'd done what they could for Navidad's legs, and Jojo's too, with Kalin and Landry both agreein to poultice them once they'd camped, maybe even poultice Mouse's legs too, though, Mouse bein Mouse, he didn't have one nick, Landry set about checkin and resecurin the saddles and packsaddle while Kalin crawled up as high as he could, farther than Landry had gone, farther than there were trees. Without no trunk to anchor a rope, Kalin wound up usin a big boulder to secure one end of the reata. It was bad enuf that he was headin out on that scree again, but this time for a ghost?!

Tom was still on the other side.

Kalin first tried yellin and motionin for Tom to get his keister movin, but Tom just sat there on Ash, either shakin his head or offerin up that helpless display of hands out, palms up.

One bit of good news was how many of the little slides released within that immense triangular swath of broken stone resulted in large areas of stable ground. Like snowy slopes safe to traverse after an avalanche, Kalin's steps were rewarded again and again with solid footin. He felt nearly like Landry earlier on when she'd made it a good ways across without slidin one bit or even kickin a stone loose.

Of course, no one knew, not even Tom, how that sizable overhang at the bottom had grown even more fragile followin Navidad's and Kalin's escape.

But as Beth Crown with dusky blond hair, a retired public defender livin out her winter years in Greenwood, Mississippi, would put it: *Sometimes it's better not to know.* Tom had told Kalin on one of their rides about Beth Crown, how at Isatch Elementary he'd taken a shine to her. When she told him in sixth grade how she'd show him what was beneath the bushes out in front by the flagpole, why Tom thought he was gonna get kissed fer sure. Beth Crown did no such thing, but she did show him tunnels and little rooms under them juniper boughs. *Here's where I like to come after school to hide.* Tom should've understood that. He should've done somethin. He should've helped her. He'd even told Kalin a longer version, but Kalin hadn't understood either. Sometimes stuff is just too private to really get across. And besides, what could Kalin do? Was savin the horses gonna help Beth Crown?

You wanna explain yourself? Kalin yelled at Tom, the ropes paid out to their limit.

Beats me, Tom answered with a shrug. *I can't move no further. I'm stuck.*

What's that supposed to mean?

Tom, in an effort to demonstrate what not even he could explain, nudged Ash forward. Ash took one step and then stopped, forehoof hung in the air. Tom had to back up in order for the horse to lower his leg again. *It's the same with me. I just freeze there.*

Kalin was as unnerved as he was stumped. He even plopped hisself down to think on it, which, glassin him from the copse of spruces, Landry didn't like one bit. They'd seen the Porch crew leave, but that didn't mean they hadn't set up somewhere else. She also wouldn't've liked learnin that Kalin right then was thinkin of losin the rope and makin a go for the other side.

Maybe it's a dead thing, Tom yelled.

Now that's bullpucky and you know it. What makes this godforsaken scree any different from the eight others we crossed today?

You figure it is godforsaken? Tom even looked scared at the thought.

Kalin scowled. And then it hit him, and he smiled.

What? You think of somethin? Even that far away, Tom couldn't miss that grin and even smiled a bit hisself.

How far did you and me actually get to explorin this route?

I'm sorry I don't recall. Tom looked over to the air then, and only after a bit did he return his gaze to Kalin. *She says it's like that. Now and then you get to glimpse what you used to be, but those moments happen less and less.*

Stop with Isa for a moment. Look around you. Just look.

Tom did as he was told, and who knows, maybe even Pia Isan with her chipmunk and ax-head did the same. The views of the canyon and what was to become Katanogos had an astonishin capacity to stagger both the livin and the dead, but that wasn't it.

Don't you see? Kalin even stood up to make the point. *This is as far as you and me ever got!*

Tom seemed to relax a little and even laughed some. *That makes some sense, though I don't reckon I know why.*

Kalin was glad at least to see Tom more at ease, not to mention plenty pleased with his own figurin, even if it didn't take but a moment longer, perhaps hastened by the cracks of some tumblin rocks below, to realize that this revelation didn't change squat.

Tom, I'm not leavin you. Kalin suddenly coughed, his eyes burnin, his face wet.

You got the horses across, Kalin. You have Landry to look after. Then Tom stared at the empty air beside him, and his smile faded.

Kalin turned around. Landry was yellin at him. She'd edged up to where the rope was tied. She yelled some more.

She says she'll live the rest of her life knowin her brother was yellow-bellied, Kalin relayed to Tom.

I ain't.

I might just have to agree with her this time.

Tom tried again to get that beautiful palomino movin forward. Ash wouldn't budge. Tom dismounted and tried to move Ash with urgins and even swats but that weren't no good either.

You got a rope? Kalin asked then.

Tom did.

Try throwin me the end.

I don't think you can pick up this kind of rope.

Just try.

I don't think you can pick up this kind of rope, Tom said again.

You got a better idea?

Unlike Kalin, Tom knew how to spin a rope, better than Landry too, and in death maybe even better than Allen Bach. He weren't shy neither about puttin on his own show, gettin that rope whirlin above his head, so high and so fast, Kalin was sure he could throw it clear across the scree if he'd let go. Maybe even across the canyon. Maybe he could've even lassoed Mount Katanogos. Instead Tom executed his version of a Johnny Blocker. It weren't like the rope hit a wall, but it did seem to collapse and drop straight down not even a foot from where Tom and Ash stood.

Tom was right. It weren't the kind of rope Kalin could pick up.

The journey don't count unless you finish it! Kalin yelled.

This is as far as I go, Kalin.

But Kalin weren't stoppin. He untied the rope at his waist and started joggin Tom's way, but he didn't manage even a dozen steps before somethin strange suddenly erupted from amidst that isolated group of Engelmann spruces.

Fer reasons still unknown, all three horses had started to neigh. Jojo had kicked off the first round, followed soon after by Navidad; only then did Mouse deign to join the ruckus. Fer a moment they didn't even sound like horses, more like a drove of brayin donkeys.

That's when Ash, to Tom's and Kalin's surprise, responded in kind, throwin his head up and down a few times, neighin loud as he could, which only got Jojo, Navidad and Mouse neighin even louder.

Either they felt that by securin the accompaniment of this equine ghost they might also guarantee their own passage through whatever lay ahead, or they loved Ash, Yvette Ruffel would in 2014 remark to her friend, Kim Kapp, who would reply: *Whether they knew it or not, up there they were the embodiment of those spirits that walk with mountains. And not just the horses but the children too. All of them.*

And so Ash continued to neigh, until eventually, while still throwin his head up and down, he stepped forward, then stepped yet again, until he was well on his way across the scree.

You can bet Tom's eyes went wide then, Kalin's too, but Kalin didn't forget hisself either, at once urgin Ash to head his way, with Tom keepin pace behind the palomino, until he too was well on his way across the scree, and by that point startin to whistle. Kalin sure missed that sound. Tom whistled pretty as any bird.

Kalin kept on scurryin backward, low and just so, to keep Ash strivin for somewhere to get to, just ahead, even if Kalin also knew it weren't him drawin the ghost horse on. Navidad and Mouse had stopped neighin, but Jojo wouldn't quit, and Ash wouldn't quit answerin Jojo. They was quite the pair in life and death, between life and death.

Tom followed, and now that he was upon the once-turbulent rock, he again moved easily and freely, all leisure and pomp. He even paused a third of the way across to remove his hat and, like some ghostly gentleman, bow low with one arm extended as if to let the invisible Pia Isan and her multitude of invisible charges go first. Tom was smilin and laughin, a new blade of grass again somehow between his teeth.

Landry had reemerged from the spruces, this time with Jojo. Just the sight of the horse spurred Ash to a canter, and like that he was across the Ninth Scree with Kalin right behind, arms loaded with rope he blessedly hadn't had to rely on.

Ash is right here! he told Landry. *And Tom's right behind!*

And Landry reckoned that made sense given how Jojo had abruptly stopped neighin and started nosin the air. Landry tried hard too to keep her smile, but the sight of Kalin's tear-streaked cheeks unsettled her. She'd also just watched him, this boy heart-struck over the brother she loved more than life, out there by hisself, pleadin and pleadin with a vacancy she still couldn't comprehend, until he was finally doin the stupidest thing a person can imagine: abandonin his only hold on a real-life lifeline, the only stability this side of the scree, this side of the mountain, this side of reality. Of course Kalin was mad, mad as any mendicant cryin the end of days. It almost made Landry start sobbin right then. But she wouldn't allow it. She'd already chosen to be a part of this ill-fated brigade to a place that still didn't make no sense. So she kept on smilin and led Jojo and, she guessed, Ash back to the refuge of them spruces.

Except Tom weren't right behind. Though he'd continued his stroll, he'd done so at an increasinly testudinal pace, appearin both shocked as well as amazed by how and where he found hisself now, marvelin at his own arms and legs like they was limbs born anew. Even his surroundins must've appeared new because he kept reconsiderin them, bemused as well as surprised, as if the whole world seemed altered enuf to defy any crutch of familiarity. Until finally he just stopped, smack-dab in the center of that megalithic snake of yet unfallen parts, just takin in the view, where he then spit free that piece of grass that anyone would be hard pressed to say was livin or dead let alone weighin a thing.

As Kelly, his older brother Egan, and his pal Billings tramped down across the last clearin that would still afford them some view of the Ninth Scree, Kelly glanced back. They was about to enter the high brush that would swallow them up until they reached the ATVs, at which point night would be on them.

Fer some reason Egan and Billings also paused to look back at that wide gray scar of broken angles and shattered stone in the distance. The dust was gone by then, if somethin else still seemed to linger in the air, especially toward the middle, where the glint of somethin contrary to any claim of transparency focused their collective attention.

Though of course not one of them could actually see that revenant figure called forth in the howl of that rainy Wednesday night to register his presence upon the narratives of a boy's heart and a girl's heart too; who now on this Friday afternoon found transit across what earthly experience had sought to disallow; a figure of imagination and what must necessarily exceed imagination released from the generative prison of memory, and not through the lovin insistence of his little sister or those urgins by a cruelly gifted outsider but rather through the cry of the horses, the livin ones, and the dead one too, decreein by their illegible desires the right to exceed in death every limit decreed by life.

No, Kelly, Egan, and even Billings beheld no such spectral authority, their minds at once concludin that out there was a bighorn sheep or a Rocky Mountain goat or a mule deer or maybe even a big elk. Fer sure if either Egan or Kelly had got beyond their hunter's zeal, next might've come a willingness to render out of that fleck, that weren't even a fleck, a man of the palest sort. But not a one of them got that far. The only sensation afforded them as they began to abandon this notion of an animal was that whatever was paused out there, some turbine of nothinness, whether compiled by the wind or already burnin, a pillar of atrocious fire castin no light, it weren't to be viewed by them, but rather, and quite conversely too, there to view them, and neither with curiosity nor concern but rather in judgment that elicited in all of them a shudder they each in their own way rushed to deny.

Only as they turned away did that terrible crack heard all the way back at the entrance of Isatch Canyon, and some say as far away as Rome, fer sure in the very vaults of the Orvop Temple, that trumpet mute, seem to cleave the mountains themselves. So loud it was, like the breakin of a great branch above their heads though no great tree stood anywhere near them, Egan, Kelly, and Billings threw their arms up and ducked.

The thunder that followed seemed to announce the fellin of every tree, the rendin of every canyon wall, the collapsin of every mountain, when in fact it was only that compromised and overburdened overhang at the base of the Ninth Scree that was finally givin way.

It was 5:13 p.m.

Balanced on a curb outside of Independence Hall, drenched in Philadelphia rain, Durry Zug would belt out the improvised ode he would later call *When Waitin Here Weighs Nothin at All,* which really weren't no good. Boise Bond and Tamsyn Horrocks would do a better job with their duet *You Never Stood a Ghost of a Chance,* which they'd sing twice to an appreciative crowd at the Grog Shop in Cleveland, Ohio, with some folks from Kirtland also in attendance. Both songs sought to capture the price of emptiness. *Sure, a bunch of folks focus on the mountains tumblin into pieces, that's pure First Nevi 12:4 stuff, but such scripture-battlin ain't our jam. Boise and I was more interested in what weren't there,* Tamsyn Horrocks would say. Boise Bond would recall without attribution the lines: *When suddenly, like a thing that falls, the mountain trembled.* Durry Zug couldn't put it much better, addin only how he *was just standin on the curb makin stuff up.*

With much of the overhang suddenly in freefall, the aggradation above also collapsed, initiatin a mass movement and a lateral spread that accounted not just for the fall of the Ninth Scree but substantial margins of the perimeters as well, which included even them Engelmann spruces where Kalin, Landry, and the horses hid.

Fer a moment, though, even as the first surge of dust rushed skyward to challenge the storm clouds, the greater part of the mountain still seemed to hang back in defiance of what had just been ordained; as if centuries of creation could outweigh the significance of gravity.

But of course gravity grants no tokens of exception.

Kelly, Egan, and Billings watched as the Ninth Scree began to surge downward, like a great serpent, pursuin its escape in the abyss openin below, the ensuant avulsion maskin evidence of its own end with more towers of risin dust.

And yet, even so, by some strange magic, for what else to call the conspirin laws of physics that must defend the last straw that broke the mountain's back, even if it were a piece of ghostly grass?, that solitary, rootless, and dead mountain ash, still vertical upon a plinth of its own gatherin, not only continued to slide closer and closer to the edge, part of its base finally exceedin that edge, but then also abruptly stopped, and there it stayed too, even as the surroundin tumult continued downward, half on one side, half on the other, partin the mountain itself.

465

And there it still stands. Go see for yourself. You won't be alone. Too many are eager to confirm the rumor of its persistence, this monument to futility, built by Glory, its lifelessness beside the point before the arrangement of its strange, leafless limbs.

Egan told Undersheriff Jewell everythin, except, of course, the part about shootin at Kalin: how they'd seen the girl go down followed by the kid on the horse and then the whole side of the canyon.

Word spread from there. No one doubted the report because no one at the canyon entrance missed the roar that uttered forth. Some swore Squaw Peak herself had shuddered. Others swore they'd seen Agoneeya shake. Plenty were convinced that an earthquake had just occurred. *An earthwake!* one child cried out. Plenty more reported seein fire or at least smoke, too much of it, suddenly coughed up high enuf to be seen from many parts of Orvop, *An A-bomb!, A volcano!*, until what rolled on through to the entrance made clear it weren't smoke.

Undersheriff Conrad Jewell notified park rangers that they were gonna need a lot of help recoverin the bodies come Saturday mornin. Chief of Police Beckham suggested they start canvassin the university for volunteers. Sheriff Hiram Brunt was already in touch with Orvop's fire chief, James Hammer, charged with assessin the risks involved in searchin the rockfall. Orvop's mayor had a call into Governor Matheson's office. And that was just the official side of things.

Word was already percolatin through the wards.

Horses were dead. Landry, the adopted daughter of Dallin and Sondra Gatestone, was dead. The new kid, Kalin March, was dead.

And then it started to rain again, hard too, so that by the time Egan, Kelly, and Billings was back at Porch Meats, back in the main house, seated around the big table in Orwin Porch's dinin room, water kept hittin the windows so hard sideways that from the inside, the house looked near submerged.

It's a curious fact that this very table they was organizin around, stained dark, lacquered thick, wide and round enuf to sit a whole quorum and still have room for antsy elbows, was in fact the exact same table that occupied the Gatestones' dinin room, which Allison March had already walked past half a dozen times, admirin its grandeur if preferrin the kitchen table. Not that either family ever found out about this commonality, maybe somethin worth notin, even if it's never mentioned again.

Sean was seated as far as he could get from his daddy's bad mood, kickin back in his chair like that might get him even farther away. Now and then, though, he'd rock in to swipe a tissue from the box in front of him, snortin and blowin away until the wad in his hand was wet enuf to merit a toss to the floor.

Shelly, on Sean's right, stood up then, partly because he was sick of Sean's snottin, not to mention still irate about the stye still troublin his left eye, but also because he intended to settle what his mind had been set on doin for some minutes now. Frankly it was a relief to quit that room too. Dinner had been an awful thing of cold sandwiches, Bumble Bee tuna with too much mayo, served with tasteless chips and orange juice in paper cups. Though he could easily afford better, Old Porch insisted on Minute Maid frozen concentrate, what he kept loads of out back in the chest freezer alongside the venison and gallon tubs of ice cream. What's more, Old Porch made sure to water it down six parts to one. God-awful stuff that their mother would never have tolerated but the boys had learned to chug down without complaint, which apparently was the lesson. Shelly was gonna have hisself a beer.

What the heck you think you're doin, Shelly? Old Porch snarled at once from the dinin room when he heard the pop of the can.

Shelly actually looked at the Coors in his hand like he was suddenly unsure. *Havin a beer?*

No, you ain't. And it was how Old Porch's voice got real soft and low that kept the can from reachin Shelly's lips.

I'll pay you for it, Dad, if that's what you want.

Dump it.

Shelly did hesitate but that hesitation was all he had in him. He poured the beer in the sink even if he did steal a gulp from the stream, like a dog from a hose, wipin the foam from his face in his elbow. In the dinin room, Sean snickered at his brother, blew his nose some more, snickered again, until Old Porch slammed the table hard with his right hand, his infected thumb on display and sure not gettin any better. Old Porch even winced but not enuf to diminish his glare none.

Sean rocked his chair back again, though now Egan and Kelly were also givin him hard looks. Sean didn't care for that. Kelly was four years his younger and had no business lookin his way like so, but Sean also couldn't shake how different this younger brother seemed now, meaner, much meaner. Sean blamed his cold and the ache in his sinuses. He'd deal with Kelly later. Not that Kelly cared, already back to his *Popular Photography*, the September issue, the one with clouds, peaks, and pines on the cover, which Kelly eschewed in favor of an ad for the Canon F-1. Sean considered walkin over and grabbin the magazine, though he knew there wouldn't be much by way of bikinis. Though that weren't why he held off.

Then the front door burst open, and Old Porch turned around to

467

see who it was, already smilin, a look of joy that soured near as quick when he seen that it was just one of his teenagers trompin in like a soaked rat.

Is it true? Is he dead? Woolsey demanded of the room before even shakin one arm loose of his raincoat. He again looked near as mad as when he'd gone at Allison March in the Isatch Canyon parkin lot.

Where the heck have you been? Kelly asked, eyein Woolsey's taped-up hands.

He just beat South High School, Francis said, enterin the dinin room so slowly he looked like he was drugged or somethin. He'd just been on the phone with Preot Ackley, who'd told him about the Orvop High victory and his brother's success, and it had made him briefly happy until he got upset with hisself for not havin supported Woolsey, especially since stayin in his room had turned out to be just more of the same body-eatin misery that showed no sign of lettin up. *Coach Pailey named Woolsey MVP. They beat South forty-one to thirteen.*

I heard that, Sean said by way of congratulations.

I heard it too, Shelly yelled from the kitchen, though he hadn't.

Old Porch didn't care for either Sean's or Shelly's response.

Who went with you? Old Porch asked Woolsey.

No one, Woolsey answered.

You went by yourself?

Woolsey nodded.

Well, ain't you about the only Porch left worth talkin about tonight!

Old Porch even stood up and, surprisin everyone, the Orvop senior most of all, clamped a big hug on Woolsey. Mr. Bucket, who'd been cowerin under the table, stood up too as if drawn to the warmth. Even more surprisin, Old Porch then began to carry out a gentle inspection of his boy's hands. *These are taped up good.*

Coach Pailey wrapped them hisself.

You okay?

This ain't nothin, Dad.

Shelly! Old Porch barked at his big boy, who was still loiterin between the kitchen and foyer. *Bring me one of my Coors and a frosted glass from the freezer.*

Yes, sir!

Shelly seemed a little pleased, maybe expectin Old Porch to give him the beer or at least share the beer. Instead Old Porch had him fill that glass and hand it to Woolsey. That got Shelly frownin. Not Woolsey though. He drank it down in three big gulps, which got everyone laughin. Except Shelly. Old Porch ordered Francis to go get an Albertsons apple pie out of the freezer and throw it in the oven.

Did Coach Pailey finally bench that Rodney Blake like I've been tellin him to do this whole season? Old Porch asked Woolsey.

Woolsey shook his head. *Rodney did great.*

That's surprisin, Old Porch grunted. Though he'd never be caught dead sayin it outright, Old Porch never ceased implyin that Rodney Blake started only because of what he'd overheard Principal Furst tellin Coach Pailey, how he was doin the right thing, meanin because of what the Church had ordained by revelation four years earlier, in 1978, how black folks was now to receive the Holy Priesthood. It only followed that the quarterback position should fall next. Old Porch didn't care one bit for that kind of decision-makin. This was not how excellence emerged. This was how the whole darned state was gonna go to seed.

You'll like this, Daddy, Woolsey said then. *They had to carry the quarterback from South off the field in a stretcher. No jokin. They said I hit him so hard, he went deaf.*

It's true, Francis added, givin everythin he had to just surface a voice from hisself. *That's what everyone's sayin.*

Why weren't you there? Old Porch suddenly growled at Francis, Mr. Bucket retreatin at once beneath the table. *Why do I got to hear what everyone's sayin? Why didn't you see it for yourself?*

I should've gone, I should've, Francis answered, once more collapsin, rememberin then, for some reason, Boys State, of all things, last June, up at Weber State, when he'd got up in front of all them boys to propose a law protectin horses and found his voice had quit on him. A lot like he was feelin now. Except worse.

Why didn't any of you go?

No one there met Old Porch's eye.

Woolsey, you're gettin the full treatment. Not just a beer and some frozen pie. Tomorrow night, no, make it Sunday night, Sunday night we'll go up to that fancy restaurant at the Cassidy Ski Resort, the one with the dead tree in it, and we'll have us a real celebration. Steak, corn, the works. You like that?

Woolsey swallowed, nodded. *Sure, I do. That would be awesome.*

Then that's what's gonna happen!

But is it true? Woolsey still wanted to know. *Is the Kalin kid really dead?*

That's what your brothers say. Saw it firsthand.

Not just him either, Francis added, though with little joy.

Talk about a compare-and-contrast assignment in Mrs. Annserdodder's class. Woolsey, who'd eased up when granted Old Porch's attention and care, had with this return to the subject of their little brother's killer reverted to his initial bellicose state, his face goin red once more, eyes squintin, voice soundin like the BBs he rattled the aluminum sidin of the Wongs' trailer home with while he cursed their Japaneseness and what they'd done to Good Americans in World War II, even though the Wongs were of Chinese descent and had been in this country near as long as Porches had been in Utah Valley. How Woolsey loved shriek-singin out *They're comin to America!* whenever he saw a Wong. He loved that song.

Francis, on the other hand, couldn't get much beyond sallow and withdrawn, and when he spoke, his words came out in drips, dull, with none of the bright notes normal for him, especially when Russel had been around, feelin his oats, flauntin his certainty about his grand old future, about how he'd become so famous and so rich, he'd give Francis all the money he'd need to start a restaurant. Francis could barely handle ploppin down in his chair. Even Shelly, who was still pissed about the beer, spared Francis a worried look.

Who else beside the Kalin kid? Woolsey demanded.

Kelly says Landry Gatestone's dead too, Sean said.

That damn Liminite got what was comin for her, Old Porch growled. *And I ain't swearin neither.*

Egan grunted his approval.

They both got got. Kelly was sittin right to the left of Old Porch, back to the foyer, opposite Egan, though he weren't lookin at Egan nor his younger brothers, only at his dad, who'd eased back some on his scowl.

Okay, okay, that's enuf, their daddy said. *I don't want to hear no more on this. Not yet at least. Billings, you mind checkin about a pot of coffee?*

Yes, sir, Billings answered, glad to be set free of the dark gravity demanded by that big table. He moved faster than usual while showin no effort. By the time Sean had rocked his chair in to let him pass, Billings was already by, headin for the kitchen. Old Porch's glare got Sean outta that chair to help with coffee cups.

Coach Pailey said there was one heckuva rockslide up Isatch Canyon, Woolsey added now, sittin down between Francis and Egan, opposite where Billings had sat. *Darren Blicker said the same. Is that what got them?*

You heard true, Egan confirmed.

We were the ones that seen it! What a sight Kelly was: a scabbed stripe across his nose lookin bright red enuf to start bleedin again, his lips cut up too from lashes he'd got on Agoneeya. *The whole mountain near—*

Goshdarn it! Old Porch snarled at Kelly. *What is it about that's-enuf-for-now that you don't understand?! And what the heck even happened to your face? Did you try to tongue a porcupine?*

Sean, Shelly, and Woolsey loved that. Even Francis snickered.

Not Egan though. *What is it, Dad?*

Old Porch turned now to scowl at Egan's bloody eyebrow and cheek. *You get in on that porcupine too?*

470

Now it was Kelly's turn to laugh.

Egan ignored them all. *Why don't you wanna hear what we seen?*

Egan was the only one, with maybe Hatch bein similarly blessed, who now and then could dial down some of their dad's innate petulance. *I do,* Old Porch declared. *I wanna hear every last bit. From the very start to the very end. Just give me a minute. We're waitin on someone. Be here soon. Where's that dang coffee, Billings?* But Old Porch didn't turn toward the kitchen, checkin his watch instead.

Shelly and Woolsey exchanged glances. Francis didn't care. Egan shot Kelly a look across the table before returnin to his dad. *Who else is comin?*

Just a few on the coffee, sir, Billings hollered from the kitchen.

Old Porch said nothin more, and the room fell into silence, Old Porch's sons waitin then, just watchin their old man close, fearful a bit, hopin that somethin about his manner or even his dress might give away somethin. But they saw nothin new, same old dad, same old horsehair vest, soaked through, givin off a musky scent brawlin to the corners of the room. That vest deserves its own moment, but not even a small part of that story will be told. Peace be with you, Morit.

I ain't sayin anythin I'm not willin to say a hundred times again, Egan finally dared to continue. *Kelly ain't lyin. We was sure the whole of Kaie-neewa was comin down.* Egan figured hisself exempt from his old man's mood. Egan figured wrong.

Goshdarn it! Are you deaf or just frickin simple?! Old Porch roared. He even stood up this time and slammed both his hands down on the table. Egan failed to meet his father's glare, and throwin Kelly a look proved another bit of poor figurin. *If you don't understand what I'm sayin, Egan Porch, Kelly there sure as heck ain't gonna understand either. I said I don't wanna talk about this right now!*

No one now could ignore this fury, clearly edgin toward violence too, but ignore him they still tried to do, if just by recoilin from the sight of their father, except for Francis, who, unlike his brothers, didn't look to the floor or at a wall, his own grievin more than enuf to remove the sight of such familiar outrages. And in fact it was Francis who spoke up next, his voice finally risin above that low drone to somethin screechier: *Don't you all get it! Russel's dead! Russel's gone! He ain't ever comin back!* Woolsey put his arm around Francis then, doin his best to give that boney little shoulder a squeeze, and with them jammed-up and sprained fingers too, which hurt plenty.

Listen, maggots, if you can't figure out what I'm askin of you, then maybe you can listen to Francis! Out of all you numskulls, he's about the only one here with any sense! Old Porch nodded at the stupefied boy.

Billings brought out a big mug of coffee then, though before settin it down for Old Porch, he used his free hand to cover them scabs on his chin lest he get dragged into them porcupine accusations. He returned next with more mugs for them who'd raised a hand for some joe. Sean carried the pot out and set to fillin the mugs. Only Francis had no interest in coffee and with a sigh got up to fetch the apple pie from the oven, bubblin up and oozin now. Woolsey got the first piece, his dad the second, followed by everyone else. A grateful hubbub followed then.

But Old Porch left his coffee untouched as well as his piece of pie. When he checked his watch again, it seemed he was givin up on an idea, and then he stood up and left the room.

As he stormed away, Old Porch was struck by how much of his life seemed unfinished. Even this house, his house, what he stomped through now, appeared to him as a monument to that unfinishedness. He'd lived here near three decades now, even built some of it with his own hands, dug ditches, set fence posts, poured the concrete floors of the processin plant, as well as seen through by charm and bribes the permits grantin him the Orvop business and his Orvop residence on the same expandin parcel. So much he'd got done, so much!, toil on toil, but for what? The water pressure was still near as moody as that crap Edelbrock carburetor on the red-and-white Chevy, half the windows in the house had cracks, the northwest corner of the foundation had a bad rot crumblin through it, and that was right below where he slept! Gutters needed fixin, the chimney had started to torque on its own accord, and these were just basic structural concerns. Inside was its own disappointment. The ceilings had always been too low. The rooms too dark. Curtains weren't for crap; one room still had rugs flung over cheap rods bought at Sears. Also, near every room was haunted by boxes, them that needed to be unpacked or them that should've been hauled away years ago. Stuff that asked only for a hammer, a hook, and some hangin wire still lay on the floor or rested against the wall they'd never climb: an elk Old Porch had shot when he was twelve, a five-by-four buck when he was fourteen, foxes, a boar, even a mouse he'd killt and had taxidermied for a laugh when he was fifty. He'd always sworn he'd have at least a black bear by the time he turned sixty. November was gonna reveal another failed plan. Not even his own rodeo buckles, back when tickets and bones were cheap, got anythin but an expensive frame and one of a dozen closets. Even them orginal Remingtons didn't belong where they was set, on a table best used for a lamp or house keys; there was even one in the garage. Or what about at the end of the house, near the driveway, the wall that Shelly, that maggot, had backed his truck into, blowin bricks clear across the family room, what might've killt Russel right then and there if he hadn't been in the La-Z-Boy readin Egan's *Heavy Metal* comics? Three years goin on four and that mess was still there, barely patched with Sheetrock and paint, with an outside brick job worse than a scab on a nipple.

It even galled him that he still had a bronze wolf knocker for the front door that had yet to leave its shippin box. It didn't even go with the cobra door handle. And by the way he hated the cobra door handle. Maybe he hated the wolf knocker too. Maybe he needed a whole new door. Often he thought the best plan was to demo the whole place.

The Porch house would never amount to more than an idea its own reality could never match, and so to Old Porch it always felt unsatisfactory, maybe even shameful, like a marriage gone dead. He had even come to accept that the only finishin line he'd ever know here was when he sold this dungheap and built fresh in Indian Hills the mansion the Four Summits business would finally pay for.

In his bedroom now, Old Porch realized what he'd come for weren't there. Why he then threw open her bedroom door, what used to be her bedroom, he couldn't say. At least Old Porch had come to accept that every act of hurt he delivered upon others often first necessitated some cost of hurt upon his personhood. It was just how the world worked. A blood sacrifice was always required. He'd never heard of Agamemnon, but he would've agreed quick upon the price the old king had paid to sack that city across wine-dark seas. Though at this moment, standin in the doorway, whatever registry he kept within hisself on pain received against pain allotted seemed badly errant. What was his throbbin thumb to any of this? Or seein Francis wail over his brother? Or even this room where he never went? Was it too much or not enuf? What would his mansion in Indian Hills finally cost him? Old Porch didn't know except that he'd have to hurt more. That was what great gains always required: hurt and more hurt.

So Old Porch took an extra minute to stare at the king-sized bed, where she'd slept before she left, sayin it was because he snored, because he moved too much, because he confessed in his sleep the most awful deeds, because even his dreams smelled vile.

On his way outside, Old Porch made sure to slam the screen door. He didn't pay no mind to the downpour that at once soaked his shoulders and ran down his back, streamin down his butt crack too before it got to soakin his socks and fillin his boots. He did fer some reason notice the zip line that ran from the ruf of the main house to a shed close to the plant. Hatch had put it up with Egan's help, but only Russel and Francis had ever used it more than once. Old Porch had loved it back then. Like he might try it hisself. He didn't like it no more. Let Billings take it down. If he could've jumped that high, and if he'd weighed as much as a loaded gravel hauler, he'd have torn it down right then with no thought for his ruf.

Effy trotted over. The mule was dependable like that and welcome. It was funny to Old Porch now, seein how's when he first got her, before she was his Effy, before she was his Effin Genius, how he'd called her Iffy because he wasn't sure he'd let her live to the end of the day, and then to the end of the week, and then to the end of the month, by which point she was always escapin, Old Porch acceptin she weren't ever leavin.

One time he woke to find her nuzzlin him up from a nap in the livin room. She'd come right into the house for no reason he could discern except to knock over the chair Egan's coat was slung over and piss on it. She was his kind of mule.

Old Porch had no treats with him, but he still drug up a handful of brown grass, which she accepted happily. He then got down on his knees to peel away the muddy wrap on her back left leg, plenty pleased to see the abscess he'd drained hisself a week ago was now near healed. After he'd retrieved the map from his office, he made sure to give her a bucket of feed and share with her a happy secret none can know.

Back inside the main house, Old Porch wiped the rain from his face, and then after takin off his hat, finally, he shoved away whatever stuff was crowdin that dinin room table, mostly them paper plates gobbed with crumbs of pie, some of which went flyin to the floor to make another mess he cared not a wit about. Near delicately then, like it was some ancient lingerie, he spread out the map, usin coffee mugs to hold down the corners and the sides, markin the entrance to Isatch Canyon with his own mug, the coffee sloshin over the lip, which Old Porch wiped away with his wet forearm, coffee and water fleein the paper like even they was scared of Old Porch.

Egan kept his peace throughout. He weren't a complete idjit. Maybe he even took some comfort knowin that at some point his daddy would need him. After all, only he, Kelly, and Billings had witnessed what had happened up in that canyon, just like they was the only ones here who'd witnessed what had happened to Russel. Neither Sean nor Shelly nor Woolsey nor Francis knew anythin about any of that. Egan even shuffled closer to Old Porch so that when the old man finally did ask for the story, why he'd be right there to point out on that map where the slide had happened.

Outside it had started to rain even harder. The rain slapped so loud, it made Shelly jump twice. That second time made Sean laugh like there couldn't be anythin funnier. Francis, though, didn't laugh. He just asked his dad if he needed a dry shirt. Old Porch ignored him.

Everyone jumped when at the front door someone, or somethin, started bangin. Mr. Bucket went berserk with barkin. Only Old Porch didn't startle. He even looked struck through with joy. He gave a boot toe to Mr. Bucket, though.

It was 10:36 p.m.

Hatch Porch come in bigger than that room or any room. He had that effect. Things always looked small around him. Dimmer too. He left folks breathless. He had that Porch jaw, big, square, strong. Only Francis had a droopy little chin. Hatch also had them gray-blue eyes similar to their old man's. Only his hair was un-Porch-like, gold, even reddish, enuf so that as a fifth grader at Isatch Elementary, kids called him Pyro. It sure beat Tinkerbell, which was given to Oscar Rollins, who'd rightfully ended up loathin the name even if he would prove hisself one of the brightest to emerge from Orvop. It's a fair question to wonder if Oscar Rollins ever did refind the joy of the name he'd leapt out of his seat to call hisself that first day at school, earnin a big laugh as well as a curse. Hatch, on the other hand, had been caught playin with matches, declarin joylessly that he was *born to burn somethin down.* Julia Barton was the one who called him that, which was shades of fittin and ironic given that she herself became a *burner,* a variation of a cutter who instead of usin a sharp edge to locate pain seeks out flame to bubble the flesh, and in Julia Barton's case, all in the name of a name she would not speak. In fact it was two names: Coach Pill of the Orvop gymnastics team and Egan Porch. Egan Porch had done a lot of damage in his days.

Hatch also had somethin else about him, and not just a voice that was warm as honey, or his other parts, like them lips that was even fuller than Kelly's, or that Sundance Kid thing goin on under his nose, thick as a raccoon tail, only sunnier. Hatch had this crazy alignment, and we're not just talkin symmetry; it was more than that. His features sat just right, cheekbones, that broad forehead that weren't too big, just right enuf to give them dazzlin eyes all the shine they could deliver, and they delivered a lot.

Hatch should've been a movie star, though no one ever quite put it that way. At Orvop High, and more generally around Utah Valley, folks loved sayin that Hatch was so pretty that, if he weren't a Porch, he'd sure as heck be singled out as *a fag*. Not that anyone called him that to his face, fer sure not when he was the mauler on the grid-iron at Orvop High; or while at Isatch U, in the ROTC and an All-State linebacker for three years until he was injured; fer sure not later when he was an officer in the United States Army Rangers, a sniper who won numerous contests, though spent only four weeks in Saigon before bein redeployed to Germany for more trainin for reasons no one understood, though it earned him rank, commendations, and even an investiture with champagnes and espresso truffles, neither of which Hatch touched. He did parachute into Fort Stewart, Georgia, in the summer of 1974, after which he ended his service in the military and went off to serve his Church mission in Samoa, the only one among his brothers who did a mission. Everyone figured he'd return to Utah to run the family business, but Texas got him. Hatch pursued a career in civil enforcement in Houston before finally endin up in a SWAT unit newly formed in Austin. He was praised for puttin down an armed and dangerous fugitive named Tennis Nemon. Hatch Porch, however, corrected the record, sayin it was another officer who took the shot.

Anyways, the first thing this big man did after walkin through the front door was grab hold of his daddy and cry on his shoulder. Hatch wasn't gonna let go of Old Porch either. Egan, Sean, and fer sure Francis swore there was tears in both men's eyes. At least both men wiped their faces soon as they stepped apart.

That got everyone goin, like they finally had permission to cry. Francis just dropped his forehead to the table and sobbed. Woolsey, Sean, and Shelly welled up. Egan and Kelly kept dry eyes but gave no looks of disapproval. Who knows what Billings was calculatin. He kept his face flat, and them eyes under them black brows stayed still and inscrutable. Mr. Bucket wouldn't quit Hatch's legs, now waggin his tail, squealin for attention.

Hatch didn't disappoint the dog either. He got down on his knees to trade kisses for pets. Hatch weren't afraid to cry, but he also weren't one to linger in such moments either. Like some tropical cloudburst, he could be all rain one minute and in the next bright with his own agency and purpose. One thing that freed him from the influence of his brothers was how little he cared how they might judge him. They, on the other hand, paid close attention to his every action and by those actions organized themselves accordinly. If he cried, they'd cry. If he laughed, they'd laugh. If he believed this was all gonna turn out all right, then they believed the best too.

Hatch next bear-hugged each of the teenagers. He even grabbed up in the same way both Shelly and Sean, Kelly too, and even Egan, with whom he'd shared the most adversarial relationship, the friction mostly comin from Egan, who never could stand the reverence accorded to a brother just a handful of years older than him.

Hatch cried like a big baby on Egan's shoulder.

Russel couldn't hurt a fly if he tried, Hatch wept.

I know it, I know it, Egan somehow managed to cough out, disturbed both by Hatch's outward display of sorrow as well as his own inability to join in on that grief.

Only Egan weren't red-eyed and cheek-wet, but at least when his brothers finally got to smilin a bit, well, he could manage that much. Billings had to keep his head down. Like Kelly, he too must've felt the cause for this outpourin of familial anguish slappin up against the tiller of his thoughts, what kept steerin him toward greater and greater dissonances.

But Old Porch somehow managed it all: tears, smiles, regrets, joy even, like he knew what Hatch, Sean, Shelly, Woolsey, and Francis knew to be true, just as he knew too what Egan, Kelly, and Billings knew to be true. He held it all.

I want every detail, Hatch declared, standin beside Old Porch, acceptin a mug of coffee from Kelly, which he set down at once and never touched afterward. He didn't sit either. About the most he did to settle in was drop his ruck and rifle case in the foyer.

He'd driven up from Austin near straight through, left pretty much right as soon as he'd heard the news yesterday afternoon, The Eagles keepin him company, a lot of *Desperado* repeated, and Merle Haggard too singin *Good dogs and all kinds of cats* or *When I first heard a lonesome whistle blow.* All of Willie Nelson's *Red Headed Stranger,* with *Hands on the Wheel* played extra times. Then *Waylon & Willie.* Hatch also spent a long spell with Crosby, Stills, Nash, and Young, mostly *So Far,* laughin some at the memory of Egan drivin them back from Lake Powell one summer, in fact with that very same cassette on, because all the brothers had refused to listen to Egan's tapes of Nazareth, Black Sabbath's *Paranoid,* and Grand Funk Railroad. At one point Egan had gotten so frustrated that he pulled over on the side of the road, even got outta the dang truck, yellin *How long do I have to listen to this frickin chamber music?! CSNY, chamber music?!* That was some funny stuff. Of course, that was back when Egan was still afraid to touch a dial if Hatch was up there in the passenger seat. Things had changed since then. Hatch knew Egan was fierce, but if there was a reckonin to be had, Hatch knew he was still the one who would deliver it. Handily. *Find the cost of freedom buried in the ground* had been on about when a radiator leak near

Albuquerque waylaid Hatch some hours. Hatch paid it no mind, and while the shop got to work, he took hisself a nap under a New Mexico bench, ready for more road when he woke, ready for the Isatch hills.

Erase from your mind too any expectations of what a Texas SWAT officer might wear. Hatch had come geared up like the army sniper he was at heart, from field boots to camo, even a tactical vest. He didn't take off his winter coat either, nor touch his hat, a black baseball cap with black embroidered letters no one cared to read.

You look like Rambo! Woolsey even yelled with a big happy grin.

No, he don't, Francis snapped, surprisin Woolsey with the objection.

Who's Rambo? Shelly asked, diggin a knuckle in his eye.

It's the movie that just come out with Rocky, Sean explained, his nose red from all the blowin.

Hatch couldn't give a gnat's fart about who he looked like or what-ever else his little brothers were chatterin on about. He was Hatch Porch, and that was more than enuf. Even just takin the map in, the way he set his fists on the table, nothin about him movin except them frosty eyes, he was both a statue and not, just as accustomed to bein looked at as he was ready to deliver violence. Egan stepped back. Not even Shelly could meet Hatch. Hatch made them all look frail. Espe-cially Old Porch.

I'm guessin this cowardly infidel hauled his butt into Isatch Canyon with some boneheaded notion of refuge?

That's where he's hidin, Egan said flat as a skillet, feelin in his arches, under his fingernails, the annoyance Hatch always drug up in him.

We saw them right— Kelly jumped in.

Them? Hatch was already confused.

This Kalin kid and Landry Gatestone, Egan answered.

Hatch looked at Old Porch. *We got a Gatestone involved in this?*

Old Porch nodded.

Right here's where we saw the biggest rockfall anyone's ever—

But Hatch cut off Egan right away, and that was lucky for Egan, because Old Porch had a mind right then to throw his boot at him.

I wanna hear it from the very beginnin, Hatch said as he scanned his brothers' faces in search of the one to take on the hardest part.

Go on, Kelly, Old Porch grunted.

That sure as heck caught Kelly off guard, but he took fast to the command and the duty.

We was playin poker, Kelly began.

Here? Hatch interrupted.

Naw. We was over at Egan's. Russel burst in—

You were all there?

Me and Shelly weren't, Sean said, blowin his nose.

Who are you? I don't know you, Hatch said outta the blue then to Billings, and boy did he sound like a cop then. Egan's neck hairs bristled, Old Porch's too, not that he'd've admitted so. Billings, though, met Hatch's gaze with bland contempt. He was the only one there not bowled over by this legendary firstborn.

This is Billings, Old Porch answered for him. *He works for us, and he's been good by us.*

All right then. Nice to meet you.

Billings, go kennel Mr. Bucket out back before he gets Hatch's leg pregnant, Old Porch ordered then.

Billings obeyed at once. He didn't kick the dog, but he didn't give him no snack either or think to freshen his water bowl. Fer all the involvement Billings didn't want, he needed to understand how this new arrival was gonna play out. If the Porches decided to feed Billings to the Texas cop, he needed to be ready.

Job's fine. Sometimes it's worth the hours, other times you feel like you just spent your whole day killin ants, Hatch was sayin as Billings returned.

Go on, Kelly, Old Porch grunted once Billings was seated again.

Kelly took a long look at Francis and Woolsey first. They had no clue. That went for Hatch too. Kelly weren't worried about the teenagers, but he had to make sure Hatch believed every word. He started with the truth, how Russel had barged in all hot and bothered about two horses someone had stolen from Paddock B on Willow and Oak. Francis and Woolsey nodded. They'd been there for that part.

But again Hatch looked confused. *Paddock B? You mean where we put animals we plan to render?*

That weren't the point, Old Porch snapped, though he kept his steely glare locked on Kelly.

Kelly's stomach turned under the scrutiny, but he didn't buck the challenge either, gettin to how Russel had spotted the culprit leadin the two horses into Isatch Canyon.

Again Hatch broke in. *With horses? Isatch Canyon? I just don't get that.*

He's an idjit, Shelly snorted, Sean sayin the same thing, a repeated declaration that got lively nods from Woolsey and even Francis.

Kelly resumed, this time heatin up the pace some to avoid further interruptions as well as to get his part over with. Sweat had sprung up on his back, and he feared it might show through his shirt.

Egan then gave him Cavalry to ride, saddled him up too, and off Russel went.

Hatch couldn't believe his ears. *I didn't think Russel had that much sack to set hisself up on Cavalry.*

We cut out after Russel left, Woolsey said then.

It was pretty funny at that point, Francis added, if still solemn as heck. *Russel was actin like some old cowboy sheriff, swearin he'd be back with our horses before the poker game was done.*

We figured Cavalry would toss him before he got to the end of the block, Woolsey added.

Cavalry did no such thing, and Russel found what he was lookin for, Egan said then, and the room fell into silence.

Wish he hadn't, Old Porch whispered.

And then Russel came back? Hatch asked, lowerin his voice too.

Egan nodded.

And at this point there was just you, Eges, and Kelly, Billings here, and Dad?

That's right, Egan answered, again noddin.

Riddle was there too, Kelly said, speakin up. *He works with us. Mostly in the trap room.*

Where's he at?

Egan and Billings shared a look across the table.

Kelly shook his head.

Darndest thing, Old Porch said then. *The kid disappeared that night. He was wild drunk.*

Wait! What?! Woolsey interrupted. *Trent Riddle was drunk?! That don't make no sense! Riddle don't even drink Mountain Dew!*

Well he was drinkin more than Mountain Dew that night, Old Porch gruffed back. *Got so hammered he didn't know who was comin or who was goin. At one point he thought Kelly here was Russel.*

Kelly nodded, relieved to finally have some instruction. *I'd stepped outside to look for Russel, he'd been gone awhile, and when I walked back in, Riddle was goin on about me bein Russel. It was pretty funny. At the time.*

Ain't it the ones who never drink who get the craziest when they finally do, Billings added. Hatch approved of that observation with a grunt. Old Porch couldn't have looked more pleased with Billings, and Kelly, though he showed it only with the barest tremor of a grin.

I'd like to have a word with this Riddle, Hatch said. *We got an address?*

Anythin you need, Old Porch said soft-eyed and near obligingly, before turnin an expectant gaze to Egan.

Egan ignored the look. To him, both Kelly and Billings seemed wobbly in their tellins. They needed to see how it was done. Egan laid it out then how he'd been the first to hear Cavalry through the rain.

What time was this?

I don't know. Headin for midnight?

How about an actual time, Eges?

Egan gave back a grin that anyone who knows Egan knows ain't about makin friends. Hatch weren't bothered. He liked findin where the fight was, and with his little brother there was always a fight, unless he was already beat, and why then Egan just had to grin and bear it, which is what he better do now. Or at least that's how Hatch saw it.

There weren't no clock or watch about? Hatch even pressed.

Why, Hatchy, I was playin poker. I weren't watchin no clock, and I don't wear a watch. Egan sure liked the squirt of joy he got outta seein Hatch flinch for gettin called Hatchy. *We all headed out,* Egan continued. *And there he was, still on Cavalry, paler than a ghost. Russel had the mane in one hand and his throat in the other. Blood was everywhere. He fell right as we got to him. Pa kept askin who done it, and we was all there when he named his killer.*

This Kalin kid? Hatch asked. *Kalin March?*

That's right, Old Porch said, pleased as plum punch spiked with rum. *Kalin March.*

And then, though it weren't necessary, Kelly and Billings said it too. And then everyone was sayin it.

Kalin March.

Kalin March

Kalin March.

Kalin March.

Maybe they'd've kept on sayin the name too if Old Porch hadn't spoke up, his voice now a mess of quaverins and hitches. *I mostly just remember holdin little Russel. I seen that jagged cut across his neck, and with my bare hands I sought to seal it up, keep any more blood from spillin out, but he didn't have much more left in him. It was on that brute horse's back, gone in the rain. Your dear little brother. My dear little Russel. My little boy.*

Old Porch sobbed openly then, unbridled, like he'd never done or would do again before his sons. They in turn seemed collectively stunned until they was just as moved. Like he was showin them how to grieve and they was heedin his example. All their eyes grew red with wellin. Kelly's too, even Egan's. Billings had no tears, but he still lowered his head and shook his shoulders lest the rest come to know just how indifferent he was and different from them all too.

Puttin aside what statements Old Porch had given the police Wednesday night, which were flat if undeviatin from what he'd just now said, except for the part about Riddle's drunkenness, or how he'd acted all frail before the news cameras, this performance was one of his best. And it communicated somethin actionable too. His sons knew what had to happen. Billings knew what had to happen. Even the hero lawman Hatch knew what had to happen.

Alexa Ussachevsky, by the late aughts at DecisionsMark, in Springville, is not alone in claimin that this was in fact Old Porch's second real performance, the first bein with Allison March at the gate to Isatch Canyon: *In that one he reveals too much. Just listen to him!* Quotin Old Porch verbatim, what was hardly verbatim: *Boys got no clue. They're drunk on anger. It takes nothin to get their fists goin.* Alexa Ussachevsky would set her own fists on her waist then, her feet apart, chin high, like she'd just solved cold fusion with an eyedropper and wad of tin-foil. *You see it, right? Old Porch ain't talkin about his sons! He's talkin about hisself: unpredicatable, drunk, ready to fight. He's confessin to Kalin's momma everythin she needs to know.*

However, for this second performance Old Porch had positioned hisself at the center of the story, martyrin Russel and to a great extent martyrin hisself too. *Why they might as well both be up on the cross,* Arlyn Roberson would quip in 2024 outside the Folger Shakespeare Library in Washington, D.C.

When Old Porch's bawlin finally abated, leavin him near prostrate on the table, Hatch was still pattin his old man's back with one hand while continuin to wipe his own eyes with the other. Egan did the same from the other side of Old Porch, though there weren't but dry-ness in his eyes.

That's when Kelly felt his guts go from complainin to wrong. He thought fer sure he was gonna puke right then if he didn't do worse in his briefs. Kelly even lost hold on where he was at and who he was. Was his name actually Kelly? So unusual and unceasin was his daddy's display of anguish, Kelly even doubted what he'd seen that night at poker: Old Porch drunk, brawlin with anger, beatin on little Russel, then little Russel with a broke piece of glass stuck in his neck, bleedin out right there in Egan's livin room, visions now replaced by the sight of his daddy, Egan, and Billings helpin poor Russel down from big old Cavalry, their little brother now a ghost in their arms with, in this vision, weirdly, more and more color returnin to his face, until Russel was speakin the name of his killer, *Kalin!,* whereupon death snapped back into place, swift as a blown bulb, extinguishin color, light, and life, even the dream of a ghost.

Kelly bolted for the bathroom but only got as far as the kitchen, and this time he didn't even make the sink, throwin up on the counter, the floor; he even got some on a cabinet. About the only thing he did spare were his briefs.

Egan's own discomfort came down to nothin more serious than a small canker under his lower lip, what he prodded some with his tongue, until he put any thought of it aside like he put aside how Russel actually departed. Them details was irrelevant, especially given what the future still had in store for them, what they'd better navigate right if they wanted to keep their lives beyond the bars of a jail cell.

Old Porch demanded somethin to eat then. Beef broth from one of them foiled cubes would do. *Put in some onions and carrots. Potatoes.* Hatch would take some too. Francis at once quit to the kitchen.

Who can tell me about this Kalin March? Hatch asked then.

What followed next made everyone feel good, even if what all the brothers proclaimed, and felt even more convinced by the more they carried on, wouldn't in the end make a difference to a one of them. Even Francis returned to the dinin room to join in.

He's a nobody.
He's a pussy.
He's not from around here.
A loser.
A wuss.
Scum. Everyone says that.
He's trash.
A moron.
He's a spaz.
He's an idjit.
Dirty.
He don't have more than just the one set of clothes.
Stinks worse than the Tongans.
The Wongs too.
Greasy.
Don't shower.
From the city.
I heard New York.
I heard Boston.
I heard Chicago.
I heard Brooklyn.
Isn't Brooklyn New York?
No, Brooklyn ain't New York.
Sells drugs.
That's what the stoners say.
He's a faggot.
Of course he's a faggot.
Seriously?
He don't hang with the drama fags.
He's always alone.
Real quiet.
Just kinda drifts from class to class like a ghost.
Exceptin he's a ghost you can see.
Barely. I barely remember seein him at all.
You know he don't even have one friend?

Old Porch busted in then. *What about Landry Gatestone?*

Woolsey and Francis exchanged wide eyes of confusion.

Whadya mean? Him and Landry is friends?! Woolsey seemed astonished.

I thought the Kalin kid kidnapped her? Francis asked, parrotin back what Old Porch and Egan had told him last night when they'd got back from wherever they'd been. And just to recall this part, they'd been at Sondra Gatestone's. *Ain't that what folks are sayin?* Francis looked to Woolsey.

Old Porch ground down hard on his teeth then, avoidin whatever looks Egan had for him, which Egan weren't givin him, smart enuf to keep his focus locked on the teenagers.

We don't know what the heck she's doin up there with him, Old Porch said.

Unless she was doin the obvious thing? Egan added then with a salty leer. Kelly laughed as he returned from the kitchen after cleanin up his mess. Sean laughed too behind another snotty tissue. Shelly whistled happily through his own gapped teeth.

Hatch weren't amused. *Sondra Gatestone and the Kalin kid's mother, Allison March, are a team now. Sondra Gatestone has retained on behalf of Mrs. March legal counsel. Holly Feltzman, I believe.*

Old Porch cussed a blur then. *Feltzman?! Holly Feltzman?! Ain't that just more poop in a poop pile I can't take! Goshdarn it!*

You know Holly Feltzman? Francis asked.

You all know her. She's the same legal counsel that's given us such headaches whenever the Gatestones start puttin their noses in our business.

Then this Kalin March is tight with the Gatestones? Hatch asked.

Not that we can figure.

Like I said: maybe Kalin and Landry was just doin the obvious thing, Egan said again. Though this time he was ignored by everyone.

How the heck did you find that out? Old Porch asked Hatch. He hated surprises, but at least this one was comin from his firstborn.

When I was hung up in New Mexico, I gave Sheriff Jewell a call. He and I had a good long talk. And I'm expectin a longer one come sunup.

Old Porch gave Hatch a hard pat on the back then. He was impressed. Maybe for the first time that night. Maybe even grateful.

I know Conrad's gonna be out searchin come dawn, Egan said, steppin closer to the table. It was a lie but Hatch needed checkin.

He's overseein the search, Eges, was how Hatch checked Egan. *He ain't gonna be out there hoofin no ravines.* Even Old Porch checked Egan with a glare, no tenderfoot when it came to knowin how his two boys could get to windin themselves up for a fight.

Good, then we're all up to speed, Egan said then. Another thing that weren't true.

I'd still like to hear the rest of it, Hatch added easily, even smilin some, this relaxed manner of his flusterin Egan more and more.

It was Kelly then, not payin close attention to any of this, who started to answer Hatch's question about the rest of it, gearin up for what all happened on what would come to be known as Aster Scree, when Francis suddenly spoke up, loud too and real abrupt, so much so that he startled hisself.

There's somethin else about this Kalin kid that ain't been said yet.

Woolsey looked at Francis like what could Francis know that he didn't know? Francis didn't heed the look.

Teri Casper's been sayin somethin funny.

Teri Casper? Woolsey exclaimed. *You talk to her?*

Preot Ackley's in her math class, Francis continued. *Preot called me tonight to tell me about the game. She also told me how she'd overheard Teri talkin with her friends about the funeral and how her Uncle Caleb had seen the Kalin kid there and how he was awful broke up.*

What funeral? Old Porch demanded.

Tom Gatestone's.

Tom Gatestone?

Francis nodded. *One of Teri's friends said she'd heard the Kalin kid was even at the hospital the very day Tom had died, right at his bedside.*

Tom Gatestone and this Kalin kid were friends?

It appears so.

Old Porch nodded at Francis with the kind of approval that made Egan beat the floor with his bootheels for no reason he could name. Egan wanted to spit too, but he just kept kickin the floorboards until Hatch looked at him like he was crazy, and maybe he was, just a little, just for that moment.

Old Porch recognized how there was importance in this news, but he couldn't say right then why. Somethin about it made sense. Somethin about it also seemed to darken the room. Even Billings looked up from where he sat and squinted at the chandelier like he'd just felt it dim. But it hadn't. The room felt colder too. But it wasn't. The rain seemed to drum down harder upon the ruf. That wasn't true either. But there was no denyin that some shadow had captivated them as soon as these Porches recognized that Tom Gatestone was now somehow involved.

Maybe because he recognized there weren't nothin he could do with this latest revelation, Kelly resumed tellin Hatch how yesterday, he, Egan, Billings, Sean, and Shelly made it about five miles up into Isatch Canyon, just shy of Bridge Five. Kelly, Egan, and Billings came on horseback while Sean and Shelly took dirt bikes.

485

Shelly couldn't contain hisself here. He just had to interrupt. What good was the world if Hatch didn't know how him and Sean had carried the bikes over the flooded areas? They'd figured out too how to get over the crick without gettin wet, though they was plenty wet anyway with the rain comin down like they was under a waterfall. *We rode past Bridge Five where the crick is on the Agoneeya side, and from there it weren't no big deal gettin back down to the scree. We near beat Egan and Kelly.* Maybe because Shelly also hadn't fared so well tryin to ascend the scree, he didn't bring up Sean goin over the handlebars. Neither could resist, though, sayin how everyone took shots.

Hatch at once looked concerned. *You were firin at them?* Maybe concerned isn't right; maybe appalled is better. *Did you hit anyone?*

No, Shelly added quick. *They was too far up. Behind the rocks.*

I wouldn't've missed, Woolsey said, hangin in the doorway, with Francis back in the kitchen still fixin that bowl of broth for his daddy.

You wouldn't've even got your gun out, Shelly said to set the boy straight. *We was gettin fired on.* Which was a lie. *You'd've turned tail and crapped yourself on the way out.*

Sean liked that one a lot and laughed til green snot bubbled out of a nostril. Then he yelled for Francis to make sure he made enuf soup for him too.

They was firin at you? Hatch asked.

The Kalin kid killt Cavalry, Kelly explained.

I'm so sorry, Eges. I hadn't heard that part.

Egan nodded.

Kelly continued, *Egan was tryin to ride up the scree just like they'd done—*

They rode up a scree?! Hatch interrupted.

They got three horses up there, Shelly added.

My lord, three horses? Was it really a scree or just mostly dirt?

Naw, it was rocks, Sean spoke up. *Slippery sums-of-you-know-whats. Sucked down our tires right quick. Shelly and me couldn't make no headway on bikes.*

Sean went right over the handlebars. Egan sure as heck weren't gonna leave that juicy tidbit untold.

Now hold on— Sean started up.

Enuf, Old Porch barked. He knew where this was goin.

Kelly speculated that there'd likely been an easy path up to the crack in the bluffs before the rain got outta hand. Night had been comin on too. They'd no choice but to retreat.

They got lucky is all, Kelly said to finish up.

Billings was the only one not to answer that observation with a nod. Hatch noticed it too. Billings's attention had wandered from all this familial theater to the Frederic Remington on the foyer floor, still waitin on the day it would get the right table suited for its display, a day that would never come. The sculpture depicted a bronze rider amidst a turmoil of angry steer. Hatch also noticed a look of disgust on Billings's face.

Egan, meanwhile, was describin how late in the night, after the rain had finally stopped, the temperatures had plummeted so that by mornin Isatch Canyon was covered in ice. Uncle Conrad wanted everyone to stay off the mountains until the day had warmed some. There were also journalists around. And TV crews.

Serious?

Heck yeah! Woolsey told Egan. *This is all over the news now!*

Local, Shelly growled, and he did seem angry about it.

KIUB, Sean added with equal disdain.

But Woolsey didn't mind standin up to his big brothers. In fact he lived for it. *It's on CBS now.*

CBS? Even Old Porch seemed amazed by the growin national status of this unfoldin story, even pleased, his thoughts racin to how that might help further secure the vote on Senate Bill 1245.

Though it weren't true. CBS had not picked up the story.

Egan continued on with how Uncle Conrad and the park rangers figured that if Kalin and Landry had survived the night, they'd be trapped, unless they'd brought crampons, and crampons for the horses too, without which they'd all slide right off the mountain. Egan vouched for the slipperiness of everythin, remindin Hatch of one year when the streets of Orvop were so sheeted with ice, they near could skate to school. At least the sheriff's department and park rangers agreed that while they waited for things to thaw, they could search the canyon bottoms for bodies.

Which you participated in? Hatch asked.

Uncle Conrad let us in with the ATVs, and we got up there pretty quick. Where we lost them the night before, above Bridge Four, was still ice. It would've taken us the rest of the day to get up past the scree, above the cliffs and we'd still've needed to go back for ropes and gear that to tell you the truth I don't know a heckuva lot about.

Hatch seemed to appreciate Egan's admission of inexperience, but he was also Hatch. *That's why I'm here.*

Egan got some teeth chewin on the canker as he smiled. *They had some law enforcement rangers scalin the ice. One messed up his leg, and the other didn't reach the top until much later.*

Egan described then how they figured the best bet was to climb the Agoneeya side of the canyon. Hatch softened Egan some then with his approval of the tactic.

Egan then pointed out on the map where the scree was, what was still not known as Aster Scree. From there he drew his finger across to the opposite side of the canyon.

We come over this spur, and then in a clearin about here we found ourselves a good view of the Kaieneewa side. See?

Egan, I know how to read a map.

That may be, but the map don't show none of the screes they was crossin. And there ain't no sign of the biggest one. From about here to here.

Good size, Hatch grunted, puttin down his fingertip as if to confirm the distance.

Yup.

Old Porch pushed his way in then with his own big fingers. *Here? You sure?*

I know how to read a map too. If he weren't scoldin Old Porch, Egan sure was scourin him with sarcasm. Scourin them both.

But Old Porch didn't hear none of that. He was too knotted up in consternation, disbelief fixin all his attention on that map.

What is it, Dad? Hatch asked.

I just don't get it! Where the heck do they think they're goin?

They's idjits, Woolsey declared, loud as he could get away with, and at that moment he felt he could get away with anythin. Sean and Shelly sure laughed, and that made Woolsey beam.

Fine if this boy who's not from around here heads into Isatch Canyon with ideas about where it leads even if it don't. But now it turns out— Old Porch looked over at Francis —*that this boy was friends with none other than thee Tom Gatestone, who sure weren't no idjit, especially when it came to ridin horses and bulls.*

Naw, Tom was an idjit too, Woolsey again declared, again loud, still beamin, but what ended fast when Sean and Shelly didn't laugh with him, didn't even look up.

Billings stood up then and leaned in over the map. Hatch, actin like the map was his territory, didn't budge none, but Egan did, and Old Porch actually gave Hatch an elbow to back him up. Billings paid no mind to any of this fuss. With a long fingernail he traced the route Kalin and Landry had taken from the canyon entrance to Aster Scree to the *T* above, then up and over numerous spurs to where the great rockfall had occurred. But he didn't stop there. He also didn't keep headin east to the supposedly closed Cahoon's Staircase, what either ascends to Halo's Hollow or descends to Tiffany's Vista, how Old Porch had done it in Undersheriff Jewell's tent. Instead Billings stopped on compactin elevation lines marked with a series of consecutive ticks.

These cliffs ain't drawn right on this map, Billings said then. *I got a good look at them. They're broken in places. Might even hide a path up to here, where the goin would get a lot easier.*

Old Porch grunted like somethin was finally startin to make sense, especially as Billings kept tracin out with that long fingernail a possible route leadin high up into Katanogos itself, to Altar Lake, to Kirk's Cirque, whose headwalls, especially the Upecksay Headwall, rise up to create the summit ridge, which from sea level puts the mountain at near three miles high.

Old Porch jammed his sick thumb into the center of Kirk's Cirque. What had started to make sense had now just as abruptly ceased to make sense. *Them walls are near vertical. Another dead end.*

I think that is the case, Billings said, though he still gave the area a longer look, as if he might detect porosities the compaction of black lines refused to reveal.

However, the cirque is still high enuf and by its entrance oblique enuf to avoid easy observation, Hatch said then.

You think they planned to hide out up there? Old Porch asked.

Hatch shrugged. *If they brought the right supplies, they could stay for a while. With a gun, they could hunt some too.*

They've got the Porch Peacemaker, Kelly broke in, insistent on stayin in the conversation. *Won't have more than five or six shots, though, and that's not countin them that was used on us and Cavalry.*

Well, that sure got at Hatch. *You mean the Porch Colt?!*

Dad gave it to Egan, Kelly clarified.

You gave Egan the Colt Peacemaker? Hatch was incensed.

I let him keep it is all, Old Porch said but like he was sneerin.

Why? Hatch now seemed genuinely perplexed as well as hurt.

Russel stole it anyways. Kelly wasn't shuttin up. *And then Landry Gatestone stole it from him.*

That little spit took our family heirloom? Hatch had to step away from the table, shoved back by shock as much as disgust. Not that he let more than an instant pass before he was turnin on Egan. *How'd you even let Russel get at it?*

Egan weren't gonna stand down. He knew full well why he deserved the gun and why hero boy here, who'd gone to Vietnam by servin in Germany, didn't. If Old Porch hadn't stepped in, they'd've gone at it fer sure. These two had fought more times than there were hairs on their daddy's horsehair vest.

Russel paid the price for handlin that gun, Old Porch said and ended for the time bein whatever moves these two were gearin up to try. Out-wardly Old Porch looked real displeased, but inwardly somethin about their friction felt like he'd been dealt aces down. *That gun was never for children.*

How do you know Landry even has it? Hatch asked then.

We seen it in her belt, Kelly answered.

You mean you seen her with this Kalin kid?

Naw, she was by herself. Must've left him behind.

When was this?

Thursday mornin first thing. She came ridin outta the canyon like it was nothin and she was just enjoyin a ride. We all saw the piece in her belt. But when she saw us, she hightailed it back the way she came.

At this point Francis came out with bowls of broth for his daddy, Hatch, and Sean and, given the mess Kelly had made of the kitchen, for him too.

There's more if anyone wants some, Francis announced, but no one paid him any mind.

Kelly did give the broth a quick slurp, and it was good, good enuf for a second slurp, but that still didn't keep him from blatherin on. *No question the sight of Eges got her runnin, especially given their history.* Kelly yucked some then, in that salacious way that's way too obvious, how men will do when they wish to say a thing in hopes of impartin to other men a similarly salivatin disposition, though why men would like to be united by their drool is an unsavory image of allegiance not worth dignifyin here.

Old Porch didn't like it none either.

What history is that? he snapped.

Kelly blinked hard then, startled by the sound of objection, tryin then to review what he'd just said and figure out a way to either back it up or recant. Kelly weren't ever the quickest in such situations.

What history?! Old Porch roared again.

Nothin, Pa. Them two just had dealins. You know, the obvious kind.

I've no idea what sort of dealins you're referrin to. Is she even sixteen? Egan?

Egan shook his head real slow, his calculatin goin fast toward how best to blow Kelly's brains out. *I got no idea what Kelly's sayin.*

Kelly? Old Porch asked again.

Just Egan shoutin stuff from his truck. She's a Gatestone, ain't she?

Nope. Never did that, Egan lied.

That pissed off Kelly. *Like when Russel in the fifth grade, when he got in trouble, and Dad sent you down to pick him up and you saw Landry Gatestone's toy horse, what she'd brung for some show-and-tell, and you went and snapped off each leg just to see her cry?!*

490

Never did that either, Egan lied again, and now it looked like it was gonna be Egan and Kelly goin at it, with Egan even rotatin his shoulders to load a fist; not that Kelly responded in kind because he understood somethin the others didn't: Egan weren't signallin a fight here but rather warnin Kelly to lie and lie better this time.

Francis! Kelly suddenly yelled out with the best grimace he could muster. *This soup or whatever you're callin this slop is just plain awful!* Which was the best lie he could come up with given such short notice.

This family's always had issues with the Gatestones, Old Porch growled. *They steal from us. They never tire of gettin in the way of our successes. Heck, they've even tried to kill us.* These were mostly lies as well. *But at no time do we make our point by goin after a child.* This was also a lie. *Do you hear me?*

Kelly's up his own butt, Dad, Egan said then. *Or he's talkin about hisself.*

I just misspoke, Kelly admitted then, sorry to see Francis take away the soup, though Sean quick signaled Francis to bring Kelly's bowl over to him.

Old Porch nodded.

Russel's been on my mind is all, Kelly continued to clarify. *Egan's right. I'm just makin things up.* Was he makin it up? All of it? At which point, if it was possible for a mind to feel sick as a belly, Kelly's thoughts begged for him to throw them up. And then just as quick that settled. His belly too felt better, though maybe that was because of the broth. Because: none of this mattered, Landry Gatestone was dead. The Kalin kid too.

Old Porch pushed aside his broth without givin it a taste and ordered Kelly to get him some chew.

Meanwhile, Hatch had begun to feel the instability in all that had been laid out about these events. He just didn't know how to get at what was square and what was skewed. He also knew too many consequences would come from drivin too hard at his daddy for facts. The same was true for Egan. Kelly was softer though. Hadn't he just puked in the kitchen? Hatch could go after him. Just not yet.

Kelly, Shelly spoke up then. *Did I hear you right? Did you just tell us that Landry Gatestone outran you and Egan on her horse?*

Billings got out in front of that one. *She did outrun us. Easily too. That's one beautiful horse she's got. I reckon even if we'd started even-on-the-line she'd've bested us. She also laid down a false track before doublin back, which kept us occupied until we spotted her trick. By then she was already up the scree with the kid.*

Well then fer sure Landry weren't kidnapped, Francis said. *Right?* He looked puzzled.

So there was another way around the scree? Hatch asked.

Billings shook his head. *She rode up the scree just like we tried to. She's a great rider. And fast.*

Of course she is, Old Porch confirmed. *She's a Gatestone.*

Does Conrad know about Landry runnin away like she done and with our gun? Hatch asked.

Son, Old Porch said then. *I don't know how Landry or for that matter Tom Gatestone fits into all this. Here's what I do know: this ain't about either one of them. This here is about us Porches and that Kalin kid who killt your little brother Russel. Heaven forbid if Uncle Conrad, the Orvop police, and Lord help us the news start seein this as some continuation of our long history with the Gatestones. Why then justice for our Russel will get lost in all the proceedins and cross accusations that will follow. Hear me now, Hatch: I swear on whatever grave or good book you set before me that this has nothin to do with the Gatestones.*

That got big nods from all the brothers: from Francis, Woolsey, Sean, and Shelly, who knew no better, to Kelly, Egan, and Billings, who knew it all.

Then what do you make of Sondi helpin out the mother of this Kalin kid? Hatch still had to ask. He was in fact a good cop. A very good cop.

Old Porch waved his hand like a fly were in his face. *Ain't that just a Gatestone seein a chance to get our backs up against a wall?*

I can believe that, Hatch murmured, and he could. Such Gatestone meddlin weren't out of the question. Like most Church members raised on a history of Gold Tablets and Angelic translations, Hatch and his brothers had been raised on a history of their feudin. The Gatestones weren't any different. First day at Isatch Elementary and they was at each other. First day at Farrer Junior High was more of the same. By Orvop High they knew where they stood.

When Evan Gatestone had died in that awful wreck, that weren't anythin more than boys gettin dumb behind a V8, intoxicated on the notion of no speed limit. But his death was still added to the list of Porch-Gatestone grievances. Hatch would never forget Tom Gatestone watchin Egan go on about his victory because he'd survived and Evan hadn't. Tom didn't so much as raise an eyebrow. But he sure weren't smilin neither. Hatch could still see them eyes blacker than cold coal.

Francis! Sean yelled out then because someone needed to say it. *What the heck you put in this soup? It's goshdarn amazin!*

That was near the only time since Russel's death that Francis's cheeks felt the warmth of a big smile comin on. Color even returned to his cheeks.

Aww, it's just bullion is all, Francis replied, even if that too was a lie. He'd been makin bone marrow soup for some time now, and he'd added some of that to that lone bullion cube, mincin up as well some onions, tossin in spices only his mother and him had ever touched along with diced potatoes, carrots, and celery. The ingredients weren't much, but the balance was everythin. Francis was one heckuva chef. Not that many knew well enuf their own tastes to say so.

It ain't but hot water and salt, Old Porch growled at Sean. He still hadn't tasted it. *Don't put a head on the boy for doin more than that. And pick up them tissues. You look like some granny proud of makin fart syrup.* No one knew what that meant, but Kelly laughed anyways. Old Porch didn't like that. *Where the heck's that chew?* At least there Kelly was ready. He slid over his bag of Red Man, which Old Porch quick got to, deliverin his first spit into Francis's bowl of untouched goshdarn amazin broth.

Hatch had returned to the map, studyin the cliffs Billings pointed out as well as the cirque far above.

With a gun, yes, they could hunt enuf to last a little longer, Hatch mused. *Egan, do you think Russel grabbed extra ammo before he left?*

I know he didn't, Egan said defiantly and proudly too and so givin no thought to what he was revealin. *Weren't nothin missin but the Colt.*

Then we've got shots fired includin the one that killt Cavalry and the one meant for you, right?

Yeah.

Then he's either got no rounds left or just a couple, unless the rest of you are lyin about him shootin at you?

Lyin?! Shelly growled.

Lyin?! Sean howled too, comin up from under the table, both hands packed with wads of snot-soaked tissues.

That sonuvabitch was shootin at us, Shelly made clear, and he believed it too, neither him nor Sean ever considerin how maybe it was only Egan's and Kelly's shots that they'd heard.

Hatch shrugged. *Then huntin'll be hard. Even if this Kalin's a good shot—*

If he was a good shot, he'd've killt Egan instead of his horse, Woolsey chimed in, which earned a nod from Hatch.

But— and this Hatch addressed to Old Porch —*if the only weapon they have came from Russel, and they weren't expectin that, then likely they've made other plans for food.*

Unless they brought other weapons, Egan said at once.

Fer sure they did! Kelly cried out, with Shelly and Sean sayin some variation of that too, though Hatch could see right off no one was sure.

Winter's also comin, and guns or no guns, livin up there in a big snow is a whole other kind of challenge. And even if they survive, they'll still have to come back down. Pretty much the same way they went in. Extra tough with horses.

It's just one dead end after another, Egan admitted.

Old Porch felt the same way.

Maybe it's just the obvious, Hatch said. *They didn't plan on no storm and figured after a week or so they could slink back out unnoticed.*

Might could've gotten away with it too if Russel hadn't spotted them in the first place, Old Porch added.

It still don't seem like the best plan, Hatch said.

Just because it ain't the best plan don't mean it weren't their plan, Old Porch pointed out.

Hatch nodded. *I can't tell you how many knuckleheads we get who thought their plan for foulness was unstoppable.*

Kelly cleared his throat. *You mind tellin me why we're goin on and on about this when those two are dead now?*

That's right, Woolsey joined in, addin his taped fingers to the map, right where Kelly, Egan, and Billings had seen the mountain fall. *Ain't they buried right here?*

Buried for good I'd say, Kelly said.

I just wish that this Kalin kid hadn't been done in like that, Francis whispered, his voice back to that dull-toned cadence of grief and depression.

Don't you worry, little brother, Kelly answered Francis from across the table. *We had a say. I got off two shots. Egan shot at him too.* Kelly just couldn't help hisself.

How's that? Even Old Porch was thrown by this new disclosure, though not as startled as Hatch, who made no effort to conceal his alarm. As a sworn officer of the law, Hatch knew hisself beholden to the Law, whether in Texas or Utah. He'd reasoned his way out of the gunfire up on Aster Scree. His brothers were under fire. Egan's horse killt. This, however, stunk of somethin else.

Not surprisinly Kelly remained oblivious of the effect his disclosure was havin on both Old Porch and Hatch; he went on boastin about bein the first to spot Landry.

You shot Landry Gatestone?! Francis squealed at once, his voice tore up by confusion. And he weren't the only one there who was confused.

You shot Landry Gatestone? Hatch also asked, only slower, because he was realizin that Kelly's confession might demand of him actions required by his oath as an officer.

Of course not! Kelly cried, grinnin at Hatch, even at Old Porch, like maybe he weren't the stupid maggot Old Porch knew him to be, them wide-set eyes throughout his life announcin to his daddy that he was dumber than a side of beef, maybe best aged on a hook. *The slide already had her,* Kelly explained. *Swallowed her up. Fittin for one who spent so much time swallowin. Right, Eges?*

It was like Kelly was now drunk on somethin. It was like this ramped-up mood of his kept leveragin his feelins to ramp him up even more, as if this was the only way he could keep above what had really happened Wednesday night, which might also be why Kelly's eyes darted everywhere in that room except to where his daddy sat.

Egan forbade hisself to react to Kelly's increasinly odd behavior: no jabs, no jeers, just one upper incisor scraunchin down hard on one lower incisor.

Old Porch dug out the leaf only just settled under his lip, suddenly disgusted by it, and his boys too, Kelly fer sure, maybe Egan as well, and he didn't know about Hatch yet, but even Francis filled him with bile. How had he managed to have so many useless children?

Anyone got some real dip?

Egan checked his back pocket but came up empty. Woolsey had Skoal Wintergreen but Shelly had what Old Porch wanted: Copenhagen, and not just a pinch between his cheek and gum like Walt Garrison would have you do it. Old Porch filled his lower lip to the limit, still usin the bowl of broth for spit.

With these actions seemin to represent the sum of Old Porch's reactions to his orations thus far, Kelly figured he was free and clear to keep carryin on without repercussion. So what if he was more buoyant, more energized, who cared?

That slide took her right off the edge, he exalted. *No way she survived. And what came down afterward . . . Wowee! They're under half the mountain now.*

Then why the heck did you shoot?! Old Porch lashed out, loud enuf too that Kelly finally knew their dad had just been fumin all along. Old Porch was even tryin to keep the fury from his voice.

Hatch was glad for it, though, and he even relaxed some.

Stanley Brundage, a pipe fitter for thirty years with UA Local 140, would have his doubts that Old Porch was spendin much fury here: *Irritated maybe, but Orwin Porch weren't no stranger to the stupid things his boys could do. Likely he put some real bite in it just for Hatch's sake, so Hatch would know Old Porch was with him.*

But Kelly still didn't quit, even findin some pleasure describin how he'd found Kalin next, his phrases quickenin with the tellin, the boy near the top, gettin ready to cross the scree but not yet on his horse, not at first, which was when Kelly did fire, fired twice, fast as he could.

Then you killt Kalin? Francis's voice warbled with both awe and repulsion.

Kelly didn't come close, Egan chimed in. He couldn't help hisself. *I know how to shoot though.*

You shot him, Egan? Hatch asked, doin his best to keep hid what might come next. Egan didn't notice but Old Porch caught it. The question alone got him leanin away from his eldest.

Of course I didn't, Hatch. Egan weren't no numskull. *But I ain't gonna say I'm not happy about helpin him on his way. His horse didn't want no part of those ricochets and bolted headlong down the collapsin scree. The boy just got dragged along. Followed Landry to his grave.*

At last silence grabbed hold of the room. But not for long, because Kelly still weren't done. Not that anyone there, least of all Old Porch, could recognize how Kelly's desire to keep interruptin, to keep talkin, was him tryin to institute a story that he could live with. Kelly's speech, if it resembled anythin, was most like the rockfall itself, pilin up one fallin phrase after another, only to see what they was supposed to build keep crashin down, every subsequent word acceleratin downward too, even if what Kelly wanted was the opposite, tryin to slow down, tryin to stop this slide; his tortured expressions payin that desire no mind, continuin to tumble, never solidifyin, never grantin Kelly any peace.

We'd just reached this clearin, Kelly goin faster and faster, more breathless now than when he'd reached the actual clearin. *It weren't but a small area. Ten steps and you was across it. We was movin quick too, tryin to get down to the ATVs before dark caught us, but I still stopped for some reason and turned around, maybe because I heard somethin, though I can't remember hearin nothin, though I sure as heck was about to hear somethin, a big crack, like the way ice on Mud Lake can break or a snow ledge comes down when ski patrol's blastin. That's when I saw the whole scree start to flow over them cliffs, flow like it was a river, like it was water, just pourin down to the canyon bottom below, until all we could see was dust, so much dust, nothin but dust. Dust, dust, dust. Ain't that so, Egan?*

That landslide took out everythin, Egan said, tryin to encourage Kelly with a smile. *Nothin close would've survived. Fer sure nothin beneath it survived. We're talkin thousands of tons of rock.* In fact it was millions of tons. *If he don't understand already, Uncle Conrad's gonna understand come mornin: they can spend all day diggin, all month even, but they ain't gonna scratch the surface. It's basically a new canyon floor up there now.*

So much for the crick, Kelly added.

That's changed fer sure.

The trail between Bridge Six and Seven is gone. Kelly still couldn't stop.

Egan didn't say no more.

You think it wiped out Bridge Seven? It must've wiped out Bridge Seven. Kelly now looked like he was havin a conversation with the map.

But then, just like that, Kelly's jabberin stopped, as if the map had answered back, Kelly once again recallin the actual mountainside collapsin, and not even just that, but how right before it fell, he'd seen that tiny speck, what he really hadn't seen because all that he'd seen was that it was seein him.

496

Poor Kelly.

Kelly got the chills too, but stranger still, them weren't nothin compared to what got at Egan then. And not just Egan. Except for Old Porch, everyone in that room suddenly shuddered, not that a one of them voiced a complaint or noted aloud such voice-arrestin shivers. Only Billings knew the coldness enwrappin him had no business in that warm room.

What is it, Billings? Old Porch at least noticed Billings lookin around. *What is it?* Old Porch demanded again.

At first Billings didn't want to answer or know how to answer.

Old Porch spat some more in that bowl of ruined broth before settin his crossed arms on the table so as to look more closely and steadily at the young man. Billings's verdict was the one he sought most now. *Anythin you want to add?*

Billings finally accepted the command. *I can't say nothin about the girl. I never laid eyes on her and so can't say where she was or where she went.*

What about the Kalin kid? Old Porch asked. *You see him?*

Billings nodded. *That boy can ride.*

He can, can he?

I ain't never seen nothin like it. He was so calm, and it weren't just him either. The horse he was on showed the same calm. I recognized that black mare. She'd be rendered by now if none of this hadn't kicked up. Good riddance too, I'd've said. But what I saw out there weren't her. That horse was magnificent.

Magnificent? Old Porch repeated, lookin at all his sons, who were at a loss now on how to respond.

The two of them were— Billings wanted to continue but just couldn't, blinded by a vision before his eyes of Navidad and Kalin amidst all that debris, deliverin speech into irrelevancy. Laurel Baker, an Orvop High alumna, would later speculate that there's never been a way to get clear of the mystery that Kalin and Navidad together provoke: *It's like that bit about horses and riders and secrets,* referrin to the nineteenth-century quip by R. S. Surtees: *There is no secret so close as between a rider and his horse.* Laurel would keep more than her own share of secrets with the likes of Jennie Stall, Leela White too, and even Miranda McCay, though lots of folks had kept secrets with Miranda, which Miranda never understood because she was the last one to keep a secret. But maybe it was this overwhelmin vividness that also helped Billings to eclipse his own mind enuf for utterance to reoccur.

So much ground was givin way, Billings tried again. *That horse should've fallen at once. They both should've fallen. But they didn't. He was ridin in the middle of that avalanche of rock like he knew just how it was gonna fall and where he had to go next and like he was even enjoyin it, like they was both enjoyin it, like they was made for it.* Billings couldn't strike from his eyes how Kalin and that horse would at some points seem to stroll, nearly stop, then race down again in rapids of sand until they reached that strange tree, that dead mountain ash, where they pivoted upon its base, solid with all that its dead roots still held, Kalin and the horse rearin up then, above that flood of rubble comin down around them, where just one razor-edged piece could've maimed the mare, maimed them both, and the two still chargin back up against that angry tumult, Kalin duckin one chunk of rock big enuf to take off his head, treatin it as no more than a feather in the air, so precise his movement if also so casual that the thing didn't even graze the crown of his hat. Only the dust knew the rest. Not that Billings stopped seein Kalin perfectly: except instead of wearin a scuffed-up hat, it was once again bone white. *Like I said, I ain't never seen nothin like it.*

Ikue Hayakawa, by this point at Harvard University, and an Eliot Professor of Greek Literature too, would remark informally that the description Billings offered could be said to resemble the Homeric move of momentarily describin a warrior as either accompanied by one of the gods or actually possessed by one of the gods, whether Ares, Apollo, Athena, or Poseidon warrin beside the Greek ships as the Trojans brought fire to their decks. Leo Gans would put it differently, wonderin aloud: *What the heck is he doin up there? He's literally walkin in the middle of the sunshine. He'll be so cold.* Over and over. By then Leo Gans weren't well.

Woolsey and Francis was stunned by Billings's description. Neither Kelly nor Egan said a word. Sean and Shelly looked to Old Porch to find out how to respond. Hatch took one step back, then another, to forget the map, forget the room, this time to reconsider the bigger picture, what even the rain slappin the windows warned him to heed, even what that chill, already gone, had meant to say. Hatch was smellin somethin too, beyond the stale Lysol around the house or the Ben-Gay on Egan or the Old Spice his daddy piled on, beyond even the dust and rot in the rugs, somethin else, like the smell of ozone after a lightnin strike. Hatch savored it too, this taste of at least one thing true.

Of course he's a good rider, Old Porch finally graveled out. *Of course he's somethin special. Russel weren't murdered by no incompetent dingbat.* Glarin mercilessly at the teenagers then, not even sparin Francis. Though Old Porch was most unhappy with Kelly, even Egan, especially Egan, neither havin cared to note their adversary's qualities.

Billings, you think this Kalin kid survived the slide? You think maybe even Landry survived?

I watched her fall! Kelly continued to insist.

498

Tomorrow mornin there'll be scads of folks searchin the bottoms for the bodies, Billings said slowly, organizin his thoughts, comin up with a plan. *I'd like to make sure they didn't make it up above those cliffs. I'd like to check out that cirque.*

I'll be goin with you, Hatch immediately made clear.

Egan and Kelly said they'd go too, both standin to make their point.

All the brothers followed suit, though Old Porch put a stop at once to that reckless volunteerism. He wanted Shelly and Sean by his side. He ordered Woolsey and Francis to join the search parties but mostly so that they could keep an eye on Undersheriff Jewell. *I'll be at the canyon entrance, but you two will let me know if you get wind of any police or rangers headin up to where Hatch will be.*

One more thing, Mr. Porch, Billings said, now also risin from his chair. *Right before we seen that big rockslide, I thought I saw somethin else.*

Whadya mean? Old Porch asked, his eyes narrowin.

I can't say for certain. The chills now havin a go at Billings hesitated him. He was again seein the Ninth Scree off in the distance, in that late-afternoon light, before it fell, empty as empty can be and yet not empty at all.

What aren't you certain about, Billings?! Spit it out! Though it was Old Porch who was doin the spittin, too inconvenienced to even aim for that spoiled bowl of broth now, instead doin so right in his hand.

They might not be alone. Someone else might be up there with them.

Chapter Fifteen
"Kirk's Cirque"

Though of little consolation, Russel Porch's death had yet to be ruled a homicide. Chief of Police Wilson Beckham warned the mothers that this delay was due to process rather than a change of opinion. The coroner's findins had to be reviewed before an announcement was made. Nonethless, there was an implication of uncertainty that now applied to all the children.

We ain't seen the bodies, Sondra Gatestone reminded Allison March as she hosed off her veranda. Old Porch's puke was long gone, but Sondra still wanted to revisit the site with a second hosin. She kept a neat home, a clean home. Mungo sat beside the porch swing lookin mildy amused. Allison March sat in the swing with one leg rockin it, thanks to nervous agitation, grief and disbelief.

Beyond the lee of the ruf rain dumped and dumped.

It was 11:01 p.m.

Earlier that afternoon, when for some reason Allison's thoughts had angrily returned to the curse she'd laid upon Kalin before he'd left, warnin him from guns, makin it clear by insubstantial decree that even handlin a gun might cost him the horses he loved, and for the rest of his life, she and Sondra had returned to the Isatch Canyon parkin lot, where they'd promptly learned about the great rockfall.

Park rangers had already mobilized to investigate that colossal utterance. Immense spires of dust continued to drift over everyone like terrible omens. Folks coughed, folks gasped, a few fled. The air tasted of rock.

Orvop police redoubled their efforts to keep at bay curiosity seek-ers. Bystanders, includin those students who knew Russel or Landry, or at least knew someone who supposedly knew them, along with offi-cials not central to the investigation or in charge of containment for the area, mingled and traded speculations. Via dispatches called in by, fer example, Park Ranger Emily Brickey, reporters allowed under one of Undersheriff Jewell's tents could hear firsthand descriptions of the massive landslide that had taken out Bridge Seven.

As a news item, the story of a manhunt for a horse-thief-turned-murderer started out with a good amount of traction, though not as much as expected, likely because folks were still split on what the actual story was. That it might concern the kidnappin of a young gal gave it juice. Though even there, opinions were divided. On one hand KIUB reporter Ilene Clayton weren't budgin from the version Old Porch had given her recorder: that Landry Gatestone was a victim *held against her will, and with what kind of chances, given the type of fella that has her in his grasp?* On the other hand, an array of local and county publications were stickin with the viewpoint that Landry Gatestone was an accomplice or at the very least *a person of interest.*

None of that, though, could match the anticipated optic power of one side of Isatch Canyon collapsin, even if visual proof had yet to emerge for what some were already callin the biggest rockfall in U.S. history. It weren't but it sure was big. Folks far and wide wanted to see what had made such an awful roar and kicked up so much earth. *The Salt Lake Tribune* was interested and had already sent a reporter and a photographer. Some said the reporter was Stephen Hunt. KUTV had a van en route with instructions to get network-quality footage with an eye out for *horse parts.* NBC, the KUTV affiliate, would in later days run some of that footage.

Sondra and Allison mostly noted the escalatin fascination and bewilderment on display everywhere, folks shoutin, wringin hands, whisperin, sprintin suddenly to their cars, then returnin a moment later with nothin to show for their exertions.

Orvop police held the line at the gate, refusin admission to pretty much everyone except superior officers. When dusk arrived it was understood that nothin would be revealed until mornin.

When Egan, Kelly, and Billings got back on their ATVs, police immediately walked them to Undersheriff Jewell's tent, but not before Allison March boldy interposed herself, demandin some word of what they'd seen. Kelly recognized her at once from yesterday and didn't hold back: *Your boy's buried under the mountain.* Then he flicked a look at Sondra: *Landry's buried too.* Egan, who was shovin Kelly ahead, just growled out at both mothers: *They got what they deserved.*

Rumors started circulatin then about gunfire. Some folks swore they'd heard rifle shots in the canyon, others swore it were pistol shots, more folks swore it was just the crackin of rock before that wall of stone came down.

Sondra and Allison were still too numb from such declarations and speculations to imagine an alternate narrative that included their children's survival. They waited by the police perimeter to see what more they could learn from the Porch group. But when Egan, Kelly, and Billings finally did hustle by, their lips were zipped. Not a one even spared them a look. Undersheriff Jewell weren't talkin either, and all the two women could clutch for consolation was more rumor.

Ilene Clayton came over with her camera crew for a statement, but Sondra shut that down real quick: *You want a statement from the moms who just heard their kids were killt?!*

At least Ilene Clayton apologized.

Sondra and Allison had intended to spend the night in the parkin lot on behalf of their kids, in anticipation of news, perhaps anticipatin their return, but the increased sense of frenzy overtakin the canyon entrance had got them rethinkin this plan. After yet another reporter had rapped on their window, excitin Mungo to bark again and at one point even snarl, Allison, instead of shushin him like Sondra was doin, considered openin the door to let that big St. Bernard make good on his snarl. Fortunately for that reporter, Sondra decided drivin off was their best move.

They'd agreed to return to Sondra's home but not before droppin by Allison's apartment again. Allison wanted to leave a note for Kalin with Sondra's number, sayin how much she loved him, plus a little cash. Just in case.

They was just at Sondra's front door when the phone started ringin inside. Allison's heart leapt, sure at that instant that it was Kalin. Of course it was him! Of course he and Landry hadn't been anywhere near that rockslide! Of course they'd gone straight to the apartment, probably got there minutes after Allison had left. Kalin had found her note and was callin now. Of course he was! But, of course, he wasn't. Chief of Police Wilson Beckham wanted to let Sondi know that the two Porch brothers had seen from the Agoneeya side of the canyon both Kalin March and Landry Gatestone, as well as their horses, disappear into a lithic catastrophe not yet fully appreciated.

After tryin to eat somethin, at least drinkin some hot tea, the mothers had reached no conclusion about whether or not to return to the canyon. They brought up sleep without conviction.

I want to cry, Sondra said as she surveyed the cherry-rhubarb pies neither wanted to touch, made too with the cherries and the rhubarb she'd canned with Landry, when openin them with her bare hands had felt like a victory. Now, though, them four empty jars dryin on the rack seemed just another example of loss. *I want her to walk through that door.*

Allison would take just a call. And then, right like that, the phone rang again. Allison's heart leapt again, again certain that it was her son with Landry beside him.

It's good to hear your voice too, President Enos. The call didn't last long, but Sondra seemed nettled when she hung up. Havril Enos was the stake president, a man she admired very much and whom her late husband had considered a good friend.

He was checkin in on me but also brought up next Friday's Charity in Practice. That's the church function I host. As president of the Orvop Relief Society, Sondra Gatestone had held the event in her home goin on ten years now, includin the year her husband, Dallin, passed back in 1979. *President Enos thought I should let Judy Dowdell take the reins. Those were his words: take the reins.*

Allison suggested that given the circumstances maybe this Havril

Enos was just tryin to be helpful. It weren't unreasonable to assume Sondra might need time for herself.

I thought as much too. Well, you heard me. All those young ladies in this house gives me somethin to look forward to. Sondra stared darkly toward her orchard then, as night kept tumblin on in, as the rain started to dump. Her shoulders sagged. *All our castles fall back into the sea. It's easy to forget that that's why we build them in the first place: to remember the sea.*

That's beautiful. Is that yours?

Sondra shook her head.

Havril Enos?

Sondra laughed and shook her head again. *My husband used to say that a lot after Evan passed. Dallin was always remindin me that whatever we build, whether it's our homes, our churches, even our families, all of it ain't nothin before the Lord. Dallin was a beautiful man. I wish you could've met him.*

You should share that with your young ladies next Friday.

I will. If Havril Enos don't get in the way. Sondra hesitated. *Frankly, he surprised me. First time too.*

Why do you think he was so insistent?

Sondra hesitated again. *He brought up you.*

Oh? He don't like the company you're keepin? Allison was half smilin but just half.

He inquired about your well-bein. Heard that I was givin you a hand, and he thought that was a fine thing.

But that didn't sit well with you?

It did not. I don't like sayin this, but there was some implied consequence in his mention of you. Like me bein seen with you might not be appropriate.

He said that?

Sondra shook her head. *Allison, you'd have to know Church talk better to understand how sometimes just the mention of somethin, however nicely put, is a way to warn you from that path.*

Do you think he was tellin you to keep clear of me?

Like I said, I was puzzled. You heard the most of it yourself. I brought up Charity in Practice, and then he brought up you, and then he added that I should give some thought to lettin Judy Dowdell run the event.

I'm terribly sorry.

I'm sorry too. I've always admired Havril. And I do hope you realize I'm not sharin this with you to be unkind. Sondra didn't wait for a response. *We best face together what kind of impression we're makin out there.*

Later, with any notions of sleep still banished, Sondra tried puttin on some Glenn Miller. That didn't hold her for even the A-side. When Allison suggested Eric Clapton, Harry Nilsson, or even

Billy Joel, or at least some Joni Mitchell, Sondra seemed genuinely dismayed, declarin that she didn't listen to *that ape music*. Allison had no idea what Sondra was sayin: *What's ape music?* Sondra had fussed her hair then as she uttered the words that seemed to merit such awful distaste: *Rock and Roll.* At least Allison got to laugh. Joni Mitchell? Rock 'n' roll? Was Glenn Miller really all she had? Allison did find some dusty vinyls, like Della Reese's *The Story of the Blues* and Miles Davis's *Kind of Blue*, which Sondra wanted nothin to do with because they reminded her too much of Dallin, specifically of him tryin to convince her of somethin she'd never understood. Nor did Sondra want to listen to any of the many cassettes marked BEATLES A TO Z. *These were recorded off the radio right after that John Lennon was killt. Landry and Tom took turns makin sure when a tape finished, one of them was there to flip it to the other side or put in a new tape.* Sondra reached for the box then but, as if her fingers hovered above fire, she didn't touch it. *Landry and Tom got the school to declare it John Lennon Week which didn't amount to much more than playin a bit of a song in the mornin. That Blackbird song is lovely. The one about the raccoon ain't bad either. But when some parents saw that John Lennon Week up on the Orvop High School marquee, why the calls didn't stop comin in til it was taken down. How dare Orvop High celebrate a communist! Just ridiculous. Dallin loved the song Hey Jude. Maybe because Saint Jude was his favorite saint.*

That's when Allison had followed Sondra outside to the front porch, settlin herself in the veranda swing, where she was resolved to stay until the cold got her. Givin Mungo a good back-scratchin helped her: the big animal's enjoyment reminded her that enjoyment was still possible somewhere even if it was unavailable to her.

Sondra Gatestone had got to hosin off the boards, remindin herself, remindin Allison, that they hadn't seen the bodies.

I can't really say why, Allison said eventually, *but there was somethin about that Kelly Porch, like he didn't quite believe what he was sayin about Landry and Kalin. It was more like he wanted to believe what he was sayin.*

You mean like their deaths was the best possible outcome for him? Sondra asked, turnin off the water, reloopin the hose around its wall-mounted rack.

Sondra then started rearrangin the gourds, pumpkins, and smilin jack-o'-lanterns on her front door. And after that was done, Allison helped her shuffle along a circular table with a heavy stone top from the far end of the veranda until it stood beside the front door.

Halloween proper is Sunday, Sondra explained, *but the trick-or-treatin happens tomorrow night. I likely won't have the fortitude for that, but I can still set out bowls of candy. The kids will have to decide on their own whether to behave well or poorly.*

Allison had returned to the swing. *Is it possible the Porches are involved in Russel's death?*

Sondra was still putterin about. *I do know what you mean about Kelly. I thought he looked relieved too. Orwin's awful invested in seein our kids take the blame.*

That way no one has to discuss Russel.

Could be somethin to that.

Unless, Sondra, this is just baloney thinkin. Allison fell back into the swing. *Maybe Kalin did do somethin awful. He's a boy, ain't he? Maybe that's just the way of it.*

Hush.

I always said I'd know if he was gone. It's what I told myself whenever we was apart. Allison shook her head. *Now, though, I don't know. I don't know.*

Allison closed her eyes to not see Kalin, but even when she opened them again, she beheld too clearly the last time she'd seen him, crossin their parkin lot, his daddy's slicker on his back, makin his way through a rain that seemed all that then but weren't even a mist, not compared to the rain that came later, what was on them now. She'd left the railin to watch him from their livin room window. She'd watched him until he'd vanished into them mists, fearin, as she always feared when he left, even to school, that here was the last time she'd ever know the sight of him. Even long after he was gone, she'd continued to watch. Even now, from the Gatestones' swing, she was watchin. So vividly could she imagine his return that fer a moment he was right there before her, upon that porch, upon a horse, with two more horses, even if his face was lost to her. She shuddered like she'd just seen a ghost.

I remember when Evan was born, Sondra said then. *It was just so overwhelmin, his feebleness, a feebleness I'd made and was now responsible for. It was so painful. Every moment felt like a woundin, not for anythin a newborn can do but rather can't do. My momma told me that the days are long but the years are short. But no one ever tells you that when you give birth, Death's there too, or at least all of Death's possibilities. Your baby's not even three hours old and you're already haunted.*

The afternoon Evan died, Sondra continued, *I tried to tell myself that I knew he'd gone, right at the very second, but I also knew that weren't true. In fact I was havin a fine time bakin somethin I'll never bake again. Hearin the news later made a wreck of the hours that came before. If it weren't for Tom and Landry, I don't know if I could've gone on. If it weren't for the Church. If it weren't for Dallin. If it weren't even for Havril Enos. He is a good man. I believe that. Our children grow with us just as they grow apart from us. That's the point: what their lives hold for them we cannot know, should not know.* Sondra cleared her throat. *Allison, I'm askin this for me, not to convince you of anythin or change your mind, but as a favor to me: would you come to church with me this Sunday? It's the place where I get my strength to carry on.*

I don't believe that fer a second, Allison answered without a hesitation. *But I will absolutely go.*

Thank you. Havril Enos will be speakin. I'd like to introduce you two. It's time we start changin this story.

At one time, Sondra and Dallin had planned to expand the master bedroom so it would be somethin of a suite, but what with family, the family business, and the stables, they'd never got around to makin this part of the house bigger than they needed. So the study stayed the study, where Dallin would read every night before joinin her in bed. Sondra now did the same before joinin herself in the loneliness of that bed.

Allison considered the many shelves, the multitude of books. The dark green wallpaper and leather chairs made her think of England. She couldn't even say why. She'd never been to England; she just imagined it should look like this. The wide mahogany desk with brass drawer pulls had a gold-tooled green leather top. Even the lamp had one of them green glass hoods. What she loved most, though, was that the room still stirred. Books lay open on side tables, papers were spread out on the desk like an unfinished poker game, like any minute a page might turn.

Those are Dallin's, Sondra sighed. *I haven't had the heart to put them away. Three years, I know. Absence makes the heart grow fonder. What about death? Death's somethin other than absence.* She let her fingers drift gently down to one of the smaller piles of paper. *It's hard to believe, as good as we were together, Dallin and I didn't have it so easy at the start. I won't get into the details, but when he was in law school he had a lot of ideas about how marriage was supposed to look. Maybe I did too. Suffice it to say our ideas did not get along. Divorce is not a thing either of us knew, but for a time we did know misery. Few know this, but our marriage near failed. Fer a spell there I even moved back in with my sister, long enuf to start gettin calls from other fellas. Kevin Moffet? He's a helicopter pilot. He'd call. Orwin Porch too. He called once.* That didn't surprise Allison. She had no doubt that even these days Sondra commanded the attention of others. She wondered if Tucker Wyatt, their pilot this mornin, was callin. *I told my sister I didn't know what to do, but I felt fer sure it was over. Dallin didn't say as much, but I know he felt the same. What we both learned later was that when the pillars of our marriage crumbled, it was only our dream of marriage that was fallin. Here's the stranger part: the foundation those ruins created proved far stronger than any dream or idea we might've had about what it meant to spend a lifetime with one person. What's more, it proved a foundation capable of sustainin a far greater and more beauti-ful architecture than anythin we could've had in mind.*

I'm glad to hear it worked out that way for you.

It was a big lesson for me, Allison. Mark my words: nothin worse than a great idea gettin in the way of a better decision.

I've never known a good foundation, let alone beautiful architecture. At least not where relationships are concerned, Allison said.

I know that ain't true. I can see so for myself, what I know Heavenly Father and Jesus Christ see too: what you have with your boy, why that right there, that's a beautiful relationship.

Thank you for sayin so. He is my heart.

On Dallin's desk, Allison noticed three ropes of differin hefts coiled up neatly and now used as paperweights on three different piles. Son-dra explained that while Dallin was in the navy for a spell, *where he weren't much as far as the part he played was concerned, those were his words,* but where he did learn neatness and how to tie a good anchor bend. *He taught our kids the knots he knew, but unlike the boys, Landry remembered them best. Dallin was a real gentle man. Funny too. I remember this time I was fussin with the back of a picture frame and I could not for the life of me get the back to release. You do it, I said, and I'll be in awe. He did it in seconds. I'm not gonna talk to you for a while, I told him then. And you know how he responded? So that's what awe looks like. Lordy, I did laugh hard.* Sondra even laughed some now, and though Allison weren't laughin, she smiled, experi-encin a kind of company from these recollections no matter that the company weren't hers.

Sondra touched the ropes like she hadn't done in years but could do so now because Allison was nearby. Allison was the company Son-dra needed to face this room, engage it more, like she hadn't done since Dallin's passin. Not that Sondra weren't a little disappointed to feel in the roughness of the rope, the order there, no sense of her deceased husband's hand. What had managed the tyin so tidily was long gone. What remained betrayed not even a whisper of how it had been accomplished. Sondra wiped her palms over her long skirt and addressed the paper those bits of ropes stood guard over.

Dallin was workin on all sorts of articles and essays, but his favorite project was a book about horses. I still can't bring myself to read it. I do know, though, that Dallin admired the fantastic tales as well as the ordinary ones. I remember him tellin me about some fella named Xenophon who lived two thousand years ago and defended the decent treatment of horses. Because you don't beat a dancer to make a dancer dance right. Somethin like that. Personally, I don't see the enlightenment there. Seems pretty obvious that you shouldn't beat a horse or for that matter a dancer.

Decades later, Tilly Syme would claim to have found the source Sondra was makin reference to, proudly recitin her discovery to her husband, Karlin: *For what a horse does under constraint, as Simon says, he does without understanding, and with no more grace than a dancer would show if he was whipped and goaded. Under such treatment, horse and man alike will do much more that is ugly than graceful.*

Not that Sondra lingered long on Xenophon as her fingertips continued to lightly travel across the unfinished works.

Dallin was also workin on another piece, what he said weren't a book but a monograph, whatever that is, and it don't concern initials on my towels. It's about the Battle Crick Massacre, what took place on March fifth, 1849, in Pleasant Grove, as well as the Battle of Fort Utah, what took place a year later. It's not the prettiest picture of Church settlers. Over a hundred Timpanogos Indians were killt by the Church militia, which lost but one man. Suffice it to say it was not a fair fight. It started because of an Indian named Old Bishop. Some real trash murdered him. I know their names too: John Rufus Stoddard, Richard A. Ivie, and Jerome Zobriski. They wanted his shirt. Nepoed him.

Nepoed?

Nepo. A frontier term. Open pronounced backwards.

You mean they cut him open?

They used rocks to try to hide the body in the Orvop River. What troubled Dallin was how it was the head of the Church, up in Salt Lake City, who had ratified the war. Chief Pareyarts, who was ailin from measles, fled into Isatch Canyon with his wife and other sick and wounded men, women, and children too. Chief Pareyarts didn't make it much past the entrance, but his wife escaped to the higher elevations. Here the story gets even more troublin: this poor woman was hunted down by none other than Dallin's great-great-predecessor . . . Alfred Gatestone. And he weren't alone either. Care to guess who was with him?

Allison had no idea.

None other than Brother Garrison Porch.

Orwin Porch's ancestor?

One of Alfred Gatestone's closest friends. This is the kinda stuff you won't find in the Granite Mountain Records Vault at the bottom of Little Cottonwood Canyon. Sure the names are there, I imagine, but how some were friends who became enemies? That's the part Dallin was tryin to set straight. And there was a third there too: Wild Bill Hickman. He was the one that killt Chief Pareyarts. Drove some into a mine, more off the cliffs of Isatch Canyon. Includin the Chief's wife. Supposedly she refused the three men's advances by hurlin herself off the highest peak. That's how Squaw Peak got its name. Wild Bill Hickman declared on that day that he'd not only done the killin for the Lord but the damnin as well. Supposedly Wild Bill Hickman beheaded over fifty.

Chief Parey—

Pareyarts. They called him Old Elk too.

And her name?

Dallin wondered the same but never found nothin. The kids loved the stories, especially about the Gate of the Mountain.

What's that?

The lore goes that Old Elk's wife's rage was so distasteful to even Death that she was left to haunt the canyon and eat them she hated, which came to mean anyone who was out after nightfall past the Gate of the Mountain. It's a geological line of some sort near the entrance of Isatch Canyon. But maybe, like your curse concernin guns, this story was just concocted by early settlers to keep their kids out of Isatch. It is a place with real dangers. Especially after dark.

If only the ghost would've kept our kids away.

Dallin felt the least he could do was try and shed some light on what truly happened. It would, as he put it, engender some humility among those who use a poorly understood history to justify proud and even cruel behavior. Even when our kids were young, Dallin loathed seein them play cowboys and Indians. At least Tom, imp that he was, loved playin Geronimo or even Old Elk. Evan was always a cowboy. And Landry was too young to really understand what was goin on. But her brothers sure laughed extra when she declared she was the bank. Sondra laughed a little too. *I miss their laughter. Evan had a beautiful laugh. Tom's, though, was out of this world. I wish you could've met him.*

Allison nodded, scannin the shelves surfeit with books on the settlin of the West, ancient battles, World Wars, religion, economics, with the largest share devoted to horses. There were titles like *Black Beauty, Smoky the Cowhorse, The Red Pony, A Horse's Tale,* and *On Horsemanship.* And those were just the start. Even the desk had stacks of books, photographs, and diagrams of horses. Sondra sat down in a leather-bound chair by the window, gazin on her own reflection, hung there now like a somber portrait, or at the reflection of the room behind her or the night that waited beyond.

Sondra?

Yes, Allison?

What are we doin now?

Sondra laughed. *I see what you mean.*

Don't get me wrong. I enjoy these history lessons, it's just that . . .

It's just that we have kids to worry about?

That's right.

I'll tell you, Allison, what I'm doin: I'm tryin to figure out what to do next. But I need to find the space to think, to think differently, to see what's necessary. I've always found wanderin different rooms helps me change my mind.

Or maybe we just need to get some sleep?

Allison! Go lie down! You don't need to suffer my prattle!

Oh, I'm way too restless. I was thinkin of you.
Do you want to head back to the canyon?
I don't think that's the right move either.
Cherry-rhubarb pie then?

Sondra stood up again, but Allison still lingered by the desk, her attention fixed on the biggest stack of pages, this one held down by a knotted rope and a horseshoe. *Is this the book on horses?*

It is, Sondra answered.

Don't it look long enuf to be done?

Dallin said there was still as much that needed to be taken out as new that needed puttin in. He felt he never got it right and finally said there weren't no way with words to address what a horse is. He started to believe that language has been the greatest disservice to horses. He first wanted to call it Upon This Back but then later toyed with the title From the Horse's Mouth.

As would come out later, the title he'd in fact settled on was *Xanthos*. In a multitude of conversations carried out by many of those already mentioned, as well as plenty of others, Dallin had studied the dead languages in college. He knew back and forth both *The Odyssey*, about a warrior's return home, and *The Iliad*, about a warrior who doesn't return home. Dallin had even read them aloud to Landry, at night mostly to get her to sleep but also to acquaint her with the grand modes of speech, even if they were three thousand years old.

As Sondra would tell Allison, there was no questionin Dallin's faith. He was devoted to the Church and its teachins, but he had still thought plenty on the role of the gods populatin these epics. Rather than take their divinity at face value or, worse, dismiss them as merely pagan delusions, what Dallin liked to do was treat their presence at Troy as the embodiment of powerful emotions, or what he called *our forever feelins* because they are often so commandin and so encompassin that just as we can seldom spy their start, we invariably deny their end. In that way aggression, or, *as Dallin would say,* Ares the God of War still strides forth upon the battlefield, impervious to thoughts of vulnerability or mortal limits. Apollo, Athena, Poseidon, or any of the lesser deities mentioned in Homer's war are no different; they're forever feelins to urge us, warn us, protect us, advise us, encourage us, and even trick us into the deeds we will be remembered by or forgotten for.

As plenty of others would go on to confirm, Dallin never considered his psychological perusal of *The Iliad* as somethin so terribly original. It wasn't his intention to glut hisself on a psychoschematic readin of those thousands of lines. Instead what intrigued him most and what became his main focus was a moment at the end of Book

Nineteen when Xanthos, one of the immortal horses of Achilles, starts to speak. The horse immediately reveals to Achilles that Patroclus was killt by Apollo and that soon Achilles will be killt by Apollo too. For Dallin Gatestone, it was a moment that shocked the story with not only a kind of goofiness but also an openness. While what the horse says is limited to the central concerns and characters of *The Iliad*, the fact that a horse is talkin in the first place and has perspectives and objections puzzled Dallin to no end. Of the two immortal horses, why just Xanthos and not Balios? Did it matter that Balios didn't talk? *Maybe the horse was beside the point?* Dallin had voiced aloud to his wife one evenin while she sat organizin various community and church call sheets she'd depend upon come mornin. *Maybe his speech was just a story trick, a narrative device if you will, to remind the audience of Achilles's fate? Fer sure, Achilles hasn't forgotten. He even demands of his horse: Xanthos, why do you prophesize my death?*

But even that interpretation didn't dull Dallin's interest in the passage. He continued to find it electrifyin. It was as if a door that hadn't been there in the first place was not only visible but swingin open. Some have suggested that Dallin's enthusiasm for this unexpected engagement with the unfamiliar aligned a great deal with changes occurrin at that time within the Church. There was the invitation to black folks to join the priesthood as well as a general thawin in attitude toward gentiles or nonbelievers. Perhaps that détente between those within and those without the Church encouraged in Dallin to more directly address the meanin of openness. For him, like Xanthos, through Xanthos, Dallin too found hisself gifted with speech previously unavailable to him.

That it was Hera who permitted such speech struck Dallin as significant. That Xanthos spoke of the greatest warrior's demise also seemed significant. That it was the Furies who ended Xanthos's right to speak seemed most significant of all. There was somethin of great importance that the goddess of union and family provided a way forth for animal speech, which in turn the deities of vengeance ended. Nor did Xanthos speak of hay or high mountain rides but specifically of the vengeance Apollo would enact upon Achilles when the time came, vengeance for Tenes, Apollo's son, whom Achilles had killt earlier. But why? Why did Xanthos speak only of this?

Regardless of the answer, for Dallin, Xanthos became a portal through which to reengage horses outside of the pantheon of human endeavors: how they even today elude us, rebuke us, forecast us, befriend us, carry us, and, yes, throw us.

Out of consideration for his own faith in the Lord Our Savior, Dallin never ceased to struggle with whether Homer's gods were merely metaphors for human affect or so puissant in their own manifestations that they actually were gods stirrin life to action. As many would note over the years, Dallin's manuscript bears witness to his troubled tourism of places like Hades or Dante's *Paradiso* or even the Church's own notion of Heaven where no horse, whether talkin or mute, exists. Dallin even gives some thought to Tolstoy's talkin horse, Strider.

Throughout, Dallin wondered, if by acceptin that, say, Ares and Aphrodite, the personifications of War and Love, might find their endlessness in the psyche of humanity, where might the immortal horses find theirs? It was a question that ultimately caused him to curse his own arrogance, first and foremost for considerin hisself a scholar worthy of such an impossible pandect and secondly for not havin an answer.

Or as Sondra explained it to Allison at that moment: *Dallin once said to me that there is a great sadness that accompanies great thinkin, but then he added that he'd had enuf of great thinkin and great sadness. Not long after those remarks, he quit writin and stuck to ridin. He rode every mornin and every afternoon. In the end he was mostly concerned with wild places. If he, Tom, and Landry weren't out on horses explorin new trails, they was porin over maps in search of new places to explore.*

I don't think you ever told me how he passed.

That's the irony. Dallin was born under the luckiest sign: a horseshoe that his momma kept fastened above his crib til the day he could walk. Rightside up like it's supposed to be, so the luck don't pour out. Dallin died, though, under the unluckiest sign: an upside-down horseshoe that near stove in his head. Killt by a horse. Tom's horse Ash, we think.

I'm so sorry.

Dallin couldn't've picked a better way to go. I'd always dreaded a gun battle with Orwin Porch and his boys, especially after Dallin bought up several properties Orwin wanted. Orwin was fumin mad, especially since the owners had sold to Dallin because they liked him more. To be fair, Old Porch had on occasion used those forty or so acres for grazin. Though also to be fair, he'd always done so without permission. Purchasin them made sense to us, as the plots ran adjacent to properties we already owned and where we stabled some horses. It was a perfect place to pasture older horses and really didn't put Orwin Porch out much. But him bein him, he raised a racket to holy heck. This was part of the Ridgeline Meadow Estates Claim that we finally settled after Dallin was gone. I was sick of the legal process, the postponements, the bills. I conceded. Old Porch got what he wanted but he still lost. Though it would take some months before he realized it. In the interim, he tried to make nice, even sent flowers to the funeral and a card that said Dallin had been a good adversary.

Allison didn't know what she was hearin. It arrived in her ears like just one big din of endless squabblin. *Any idea what started this feud?*

Believe it or not, stolen horses. Sondra snorted. *Near one hundred and fifty years ago. Supposedly two of them too. Dapple and Bay. And a mule.*

Dapple and Bay? Those were their names?

Sondra shrugged.

Allison eyed again the unfinished manuscript like maybe there would be an answer. *You reckon that's even true?*

Of course it's not true. All of it's malarkey. Swampland and tulips, my Dallin used to say. Worthless stories that for some reason still managed to gain meaningful currency around here. Girls have it easier because they lose the name. Porch girls become Hickmans or Jarmans. Gatestone girls become Hoveys or Hills. The boys, though, have to carry a burden that weren't theirs to begin with. Evan wore it heavy. He and Hatch Porch were already at it before they even knew each other. Evan hardly knew Egan but likely raced him because Egan's last name was Porch. Tom had more fun with it. He stayed light on his feet.

Sondra had stepped over to a long table set against the wall opposite the windows. Beneath it was a long steamer trunk which she opened and began riflin through.

And you married into all that, Allison said.

Mostly that feudin stuff was make-believe like the Gate of the Mountain or Squaw Peak is lore. Just folks in one family and folks in another family goin through the motions of dislike. There was one poor family that moved to Orvop some years ago, and their name was Porch too. They was black though. They sure didn't care one bit bein associated with Orwin Porch and his ilk.

Sondra had found what she was lookin for: a yellowin tube of paper that she began to unroll on that long table.

Orwin Porch isn't make believe. He's got real nastiness to him and just uses the lore of this feud to fuel his appetite for cruelty.

Kalin's daddy had a similar appetite.

He's still alive? I'm sorry I forgot.

The world itself will need to be put in a grave before he goes.

Meanness does seem to have a way of survivin. In that respect it makes some sense that Dallin went when he did. Never did meet a sweeter soul. Believe it or not, he was even soft on Orwin. Saw in him what only the Lord's Grace can afford to wait on. Dallin always said never begrudge another's chance at salvation. I kept tellin him that Old Porch had had plenty of chances already. My husband would just smile and say Our Father in Heaven has no limit to the forgiveness He offers.

Dallin sounds like a lovely man.

When tempers ever got hot, Dallin was the first to caution us away from reactin. Don't do somethin Righteous, he'd say. Don't do somethin that feels good. Do somethin Good. There's a difference.

I'm too often tempted to do somethin that feels good, like gettin the heck out of Dodge.

Sondra gave Allison a sympathetic smile before returnin to the topographic map now spread out before them, the very same one the sheriff's department had as well as the one Old Porch had spread out on in his livin room table. Allison joked that it was near big as Isatch Canyon itself. Sondra tried squintin fer a bit before goin over to Dallin's desk where in a drawer she dug up some readin glasses. They looked funny on her, too big, but Allison also thought they looked good. Sondra planted her pinkie at the entrance to Isatch Canyon and then moved it slowly to the Gate of the Mountain.

My Dallin never ceased to find great comfort in the Church. This might surprise you, Allison, but while I do count myself as one of the Church's dutiful congregants, I'm in fact not so easily persuaded by things I cannot see. Sondra looked up. *After we buried Dallin, I admitted to Havril that my believin was never as sure as Dallin's. You know what President Enos told me? He is a holy man, Allison. He told me that sometimes faith can be borrowed.*

You told me that this mornin. Right before we drove by the Porch place. You said I could borrow some of your faith.

I did, didn't I? And why not? And you can! Anytime! And I'll keep borrowin from Dallin! Sondra suddenly hauled up a laugh, a good laugh, beautiful, even if she also raised her hand at once to her lips, like she'd just burped or was embarrassed, maybe for all this that she was goin on about, until she also recognized how Allison was regardin her, without judgment, in rapt attention, and then the blush that had bloomed upon her cheeks seeped away even quicker. *For Dallin and me, see, our families were born into the Church. We were just raised believin.*

The Church found me durin the tryin time of divorcin Kalin's daddy. I often felt my life was at risk then. The Church helped me to see my way through those challenges. Some really good people stood by me then. We could've stayed put in Colorado, I suppose. We had a nice ward there in Fort Collins.

What brought you to Orvop then?

Allison hesitated. She'd suddenly lost sight of what she was sayin before somethin she was seein back in Fort Collins that was pretty bad. Not even the map was visible anymore.

I'm restless by nature, Allison admitted when she managed to return to Sondra's gaze. *Like you said, change the room you're in, change your mind. If there are good folks in Fort Collins, there are better in Orvop.*

You ain't wrong there.

We just packed up one day and left. That easy. Mungo had again stretched out at Allison's feet, and she bent down to give him a big belly rub. *Sondra, this is a hard thing for me to say, especially to one as kind as you are, but I didn't last in the Church more than a few months. And don't get me wrong.*

515

I don't fault the Church. I've been a Jew, a Buddhist, for a year a Seventh-day Adventist, a Catholic for a week. I even tried the Church of England.

A Buddhist, really? To Sondra this revelation seemed the most sensational. *How long were you that?*

I still meditate every day, but I fail at it pretty much every day too. Allison put a thumb to her right hip and rubbed. *Truth is, I haven't lasted with much except bein Kalin's momma. And now even there I seemed to have failed.*

Naw, Sondra said with a glint in her eyes about as bright as the smile on her lips. *You didn't quit him. He quit you. And he didn't even do that. He just went adventurin.*

Fer a moment the silence drew down upon them, heavy enuf to roll Mungo back up on his feet, alert, and then Allison started chucklin, with Sondra quick to join her, and Mungo yawned and resettled as the two mothers, even in their sadness, continued to smile.

When they returned to the map, Sondra assured Allison they weren't gonna quit their kids, but they also had to start *facin the mystery of what they was thinkin in the first place.*

Sondra danced her fingers over to where the landslide had occurred.

They see them here as dead. What say we see them as alive?

I can do that, Allison answered, a little more steel in her voice, actually a lot more, which pleased Sondra to no end.

The best thing we can do for our children is to outthink what they think they know they're doin and get ahead of them so we can help. My mother was a beekeeper. My sister is now, though my nephews don't give a hoot about either wax or Hearth Honey. They just want dirt bikes and Mountain Dew. My mother had a way of lookin at the world that had nothin to do with letters. It was about color and the smell of things and what bees could show her. It's funny, but my mother had to teach Dallin, who taught Tom, who got around to teachin me what my mother tried to teach me first: never trust a map.

Okay?

That makes this mystery simple: they're headed here.

What at about the same time was flummoxin Old Porch didn't hesitate Sondra one bit. Quick as lightnin she traced a path to Altar Lake.

It looks like another dead end.

Unless their horses can fly.

You figure here's where your Tom wanted to set the horses free?

Sondra shook her head. *Tom would know Kirk's Cirque ain't no place for horses. There ain't no way around these walls either, let alone over them. Big as skyscrapers. Bigger. Mount Katanogos is so tall, she'll stop clouds, gather them around her like a stole.* Sondra snorted. *Tom would know this.*

Then they'll turn back?

Sondra kept studyin the map. She even flicked her nail across the narrow lines indicatin the headwalls like she could knock them down.

Old Porch has already figured this out. Here's where he'll head unless he really believes our kids are dead.

But if they are okay, and they are headin here, Porch will have them cornered. I think so.

We have to get there first then, Allison announced.

You can't land a plane there, and I can't make the climb.

Allison nodded. *I have to try. I have no choice.*

Maybe.

I'll leave now.

Sondra smiled but it was a sad smile. *You'll need light first and next some letup in the weather. If it ices up again, you won't have a chance. If it snows, you won't have a chance. But even if it don't and you're still set on goin, you'll need to rest first fer sure.*

Allison nodded. Fer a moment Sondra's eyes tried to drift up the map, past Katanogos, but knowledge of what stood in the way returned her imagination to the cirque. Allison had returned to the desk.

A bookseller in Colorado once told me that she couldn't keep up with every new book that came through, but she'd always read the last word. She told me you can tell a lot from that last word. With Sondra's permission, Allison lifted the knotted rope and horseshoe and riffled through the big manuscript to the final page.

What is it? Sondra demanded when she seen Allison smile.

Grace.

Well, I'll be. Sondra smiled then too and even patted Allison on the arm. *Thank you.*

On the way back to the kitchen for some of that cherry-rhubarb pie, with Sondra goin on about Landry's inordinate proclivity to chatter and just make things up, the Gatestone matriarch abruptly stopped in her tracks. There was somethin she'd just remembered, somethin in Landry's room she needed to check.

There's no denyin that girl can gabber about worlds of nonsense, Sondra said as they headed to her daughter's room. *I swear sometimes it was like she were possessed. When she was tiny, she'd gush on about this and that in a language no one could make heads or tails of. We joked that she needed an exorcism, and we sure as heck couldn't wait til she finally learned to speak right. We was dead wrong. By the time she knew regular language we was dreamin of havin her like she was when she was tiny and no one could understand a bit of that gibberish because at least gibberish, you can tune out. You okay?* she asked Allison.

It's just my hip. Some kinda misalignment there. It mends on its own.

Allison, how do you think you're gonna manage even Isatch Canyon if you can't handle my house?

Allison pursed her lips. *I gotta try. I have no choice.*

We must be the way, not get in the way.
I'll be better come sunup.

Allison weren't surprised by Landry's room. It's what you'd expect of a fifteen-year-old who loves horses. Pictures of horses, a horse calendar, books on horses, a couple of *The Great Brain* books too, plus a pink-framed photograph of a horse on a small desk. Above it hung cards of the likes of Lucyle Richards, Sonora Webster Carver, Polly Burson, and other women riders Allison knew nothin about, and a poster for the movie *Coal Miner's Daughter.*

Landry can sing near every song, Sondra said when she caught Allison lookin at Sissy Spacek. *Got one heckuva voice. Tom says, said, excuse me, that Landry's got a perfect ear. Tom might've told your son where to take them horses, but he's been tellin Landry her whole life to go to Nashville. Become a big star. Or at least get the heck outta Orvop. This place ain't so kind to folks a shade darker than flour. First Nevi 12:23. After they'd dwindled in unbelief they became dark and loathsome and a filthy people full of idleness and all manner of abomina-tions. Which, where my little one is concerned, couldn't be farther from the truth.*

I'm sorry?

Or Second Nevi 5:21. Oh, don't mind me. Just throwin out verse. Second Nevi 26:33. Just more verse. Been doin it my whole life. Sometimes I can't help it.

Allison approached the bureau to consider more closely the photographs.

That's her with Tom, Sondra pointed out, though she stayed in the doorway. *Lord, those two could get into trouble. Once covered my kitchen in flour and sugar. I was so mad, I swore I'd give them the silent treatment for a week! I don't think I made it past a minute. It pains me to think I even tried.*

Behind a Nikon with a telephoto lens, Allison found a framed pic-ture of two kids. The engravin read: *Thomas Dallin Gatestone & Eleanor Landry Gatestone.* Tom had on one of the biggest grins she'd ever seen, big as a Pac-Man, under a cowboy hat that couldn't get no whiter.

Allison thought she recognized it. Kalin had kept one pretty sim-ilar in the apartment for a few days. Allison had meant to ask him about it, but tiredness had led the question from her mind.

Landry was scowlin just before that got taken, Sondra explained. *She was so upset because I wouldn't get her a pink belt with pinker sparkles.*

Allison laughed. *We always want to give them everythin, but we also know even everythin won't help with what's comin their way.*

I wish I didn't understand what you meant. Sondra chuckled even if it sounded forced. *I gave her too much junk.*

Allison nodded. *I don't know. I think it's important to get a little of what we want if only so we can learn that what we thought we needed so bad turned out to be somethin we didn't need at all.*

Oh, I've had more than a few cake molds prove that to be true.

Men, in my case.

Sondra blushed visibly then, blinkin extra too, as she abruptly looked down, once again runnin her palms over her long skirt. Allison studied this repeated retreat to smooth what didn't need even an iron. The gesture, the skirt, the reaction, all of it made Allison feel gravely distant from Sondra, as if tiny differences in how they approached the trial of livin might be enuf to negate any possibility of a lastin friendship, and that sure drooped Allison's shoulders.

A monk told me that this understandin, how what we want is not what we want, is the start of every spiritual journey.

A spiritual journey starts with a cake mold we don't need? Sondra asked, lookin up again, lookin even a little startled, maybe feelin some of the same distance Allison had just experienced. *I don't know about that.* But Sondra's shoulders didn't sag.

He also told me there's a fine line between a well-tossed salad and leaves rottin at the back of the fridge, Allison added with a forced smile. She was lookin now at an index card on the bureau with words presumably in Landry's hand: *Practice Honesty & Courtesy. Be Kind.* She returned to the photo. *Your daughter's got a nice smile.*

It runs in the family, Sondra said, her own version of that family smile emergin, sad but still nice. *Tom could always make her grin. Sometimes just by laughin. Landry loved his laugh. Oh and don't be fooled by her littleness. In person she's bigger than any house you put her in.*

Allison had been a little thrown by Landry's darkness. She hadn't forgotten either that Landry was adopted nor that she was born in Samoa, but she'd still imagined someone lighter than this black child. The thought, though, that this was who was up there with her only boy lightened her heart plenty even if she couldn't say why.

They look like they were close, Allison said as she returned the frame to the bureau.

That there's her Jojo.

Allison looked again at the photos of horses around the room and realized they were all of the same gray horse.

He's an Arab, Sondra explained. *We call him the Big Blue Roan. Dallin and I bought him for breedin.*

Sondra finally entered the room and after a circle or two sat on the bed. It was still unmade, a pile of blankets, the top one a soft thing of crocheted pink, brown, and white cotton yarn, homemade fer sure, its comfiness an awful counterpoint to the hard, merciless place where Landry was now, if she weren't already crushed under the mountain itself. Two pillows were still stuffed beneath the sheets to mislead her momma. A third pillow was still dimpled with the memory of Landry's head. Allison welled up unexpectedly then, tears she at once tried to wipe away with the heel of her hand, but if she worried that Sondra would notice, tears had already overwhelmed her too.

I haven't come in here since she ran off. Sondra's hands were reflexively smoothin out the sheet beside her and then the blanket, and then, maybe realizin she was erasin the motions her little girl had left before she snuck out her window, she attempted to muss them up again, and in the same way, which would never be the same way, promptin her to bolt away from the bed lest she erase any more of these sleepless scriptures made by her little girl. *I know it's silly to say so, Allison, but bein here like this, with you, I know she ain't dead. I just know it.*

Allison told her she felt the same way about Kalin.

What breaks my heart, Sondra admitted, *is what little she took with her. Do you have any idea what she did take?*

Sondra walked over to Landry's closet, where a mess of neked hangers hung over a mess of fallen clothes. *Here are her winter jackets. Her sweaters. I'm prayin she had a sweater on. Likely a parka. Oh wait. She had a pink raincoat. That's gone. That's a good sign. She's fer sure wearin her boots. They're good boots. They're usually in the tack room where Jojo's stabled. That'll do somethin awful to me to find them still there.*

Is that what you wanted to check here? Allison was confused, seein as how Sondra was talkin about the barn.

No, that weren't it. Sondra's features clouded. *But now I've plumb forgotten what I was after.*

In the hallway, Sondra asked Allison if she'd like to see Tom's room. Unlike Landry's room, neatness was the rule here. Allison couldn't be sure if it was Tom she was lookin at or the order Sondra had brought once he was gone. The bed was strictly made with hospital corners. No drawer was left open, no chair was draped with a shirt or a sock. Rodeo posters hung on the wall, but none overlapped. A black stool made of welded steel stood in one corner.

Tom made that in eighth grade in metal shop. He was an awful talented kid.

On the bureau was a framed picture of a palomino horse with extraordinary eyes, green eyes.

That's Tom's Ash. A gorgeous Andalusian. He passed before Tom passed. Tom adored that horse. I love thinkin of them together now.

On both sides of the picture stood numerous trophies beside which stood even more pictures, includin one of Tom with what looked like the Tabernacle Choir. Sondra explained that Tom had a knack for whistlin. *He couldn't sing a lick of much, but the Church hadn't figured that out yet. Not that it mattered much here. They brought up about six hundred kids from all grades. Tom's in the fifth grade there. Evan's on the left. Evan had a nice voice. Landry's on the right.* Sondra was usin her long skirt to dust another picture frame. *Here's Tom holdin up Evan's Eagle Scout medal. Tom could've earned the same, but he had no interest in anythin beyond the horsemanship merit badge.* There was also one of Tom ridin an immense bull, surely about to be thrown sky-high though the photograph showed no such thing. There Tom remained, forever on the bull's back.

That's Hightower. Near killt a bunch of boys on the Springville Fairgrounds last summer. Hurt two real bad. Not Tom. He'd climbed on laughin and flew off laughin.

Allison found her gaze driftin from the picture to Sondra's gaze as she revisited the picture. Allison weren't sure she'd ever beheld such level-headed elegance, such strength.

It was like everythin to Tom was a joke, Sondra continued. *He even laughed at me in the hospital, and he was the one dyin.*

Laughed at you for what?

Oh, he was right. I was goin on with some stupidness about how he was gonna miss his prom. Sondra even tried to laugh a bit. *Tom knew where the jokes were. The prom?! Imagine that bein my concern! Embarassin.*

Sondra walked over to a big brown desk crowded with silver-framed pictures of Tom, not a one of him without a smile.

Tom never had any pictures of hisself. I put these here.

You know I never met one friend of Kalin's? Allison had already admitted as much to Teri Casper, but that still didn't keep the repeated confession from stealin away her breath, and even worse, losin all her breath suddenly didn't seem like such a bad blessin, though the thought of Kalin still alive, still breathin, hauled air back into her lungs.

Tom was your son's friend, Sondra said. *He respected your son for reasons I'd like to one day know for myself.* Sondra pointed to the empty hat hooks above the desk. *Tom had two very nice Stetsons: a black one and the white one you see in a lot of these pictures. They was fer special occasions. Church events, school dances. Tom didn't care though. He wore them when he mucked stalls. Wore them when he rode. I gave Kalin the white one at Tom's funeral.*

Allison nodded. At least that little mystery, where it had come from, was solved, even if where it had gone to remained veiled.

I asked Kalin if he'd wear it ever, Sondra continued, *and he told me he'd wear anythin of Tom's if it brought back his grin. The funny thing is that Tom wanted Kalin to have the black one. But I never could find that one.*

When I was in my twenties, it all seemed within reach, Allison said then, *but I'm old enuf now to see it's always been out of reach.* Though Allison still reached up and touched each hat hook.

Sondra looked at Allison, puzzled. *How do you mean?*

I think I'm all the more fond of you, Sondra, for not knowin what I mean. You have this beautiful home and, even with its tragedies, this beautiful family. You've got roots too and, sure, maybe they get a little tangled with the likes of them Porches; they're still good roots. And you've made more pies and cakes than a baker could ever count. I don't know what any of that is like. I've never baked a thing in my life unless toast counts. Allison was now driftin around Tom's room, almost touchin everythin, not touchin a thing, like she was happiest as a ghost, and weren't that a sad way to be. *I've rarely, if ever, had a sense of true arrival, let alone of bein at home. I think I've given up on the ecstasy of belongin. Truth is, I'm a runner, and I don't even like to jog. Maybe I'm a coward. I don't know. I seem most content when I'm goin places, when who I was is left behind but who I'm about to become is still around the next bend.*

You know you can't outrun yourself, right?

Allison smiled. *Of course I do, but that never stopped me from tryin! I guess I've lived long enuf to see the life I wanted give way to just the life I got. And now I don't know where that leaves me.*

You're not even forty, Allison.

The thing I can never quite figure out is how if I'm happiest when I'm no longer my past and yet still not this me I imagine in the future, who is that person?

Are you thinkin of runnin now?

Of course.

What's keepin you?

Kalin. I'll never abandon him.

Back down in the kitchen, before they could plate any pie or even get the kettle on, the phone rang. Of course Allison's thoughts went straight to Kalin. From here on out, she'd never cease to think of him first when a phone rang. But it was Holly Feltzman. After enuf back-and-forth with various Orvop officials, she was confirmin what Allison and Sondra already knew: their kids had supposedly been killt in the rockfall, though the witnesses were all Porches.

If that ain't nothin but a liar's consensus, Holly Feltzman scowled over the phone, but there was worry in her voice too.

Mungo padded over to his water bowl then. His bowl was big as a bath, and the way he lapped up his drink drenched the surroundin floor. Sondra dug around in a drawer for some treats for him while she dialed up from memory her friend Tucker Wyatt. He sure was happy to hear from her and more than happy to take them up in his plane again come dawn. He was less happy, though, when Sondra asked if he might make some calls on their behalf to arrange for a helicopter instead. *Of course, I'll cover all costs, yours as well, Tucker, if you'll just bill me for this mornin,* but Tucker Wyatt weren't ever gonna hand Sondra

Gatestone a bill. And his happiness returned some when Sondra made it clear that she expected him to come along.

I think we best get up there, Allison, the only way you and I can, Sondra said after she'd hung up. *Tom knew horses, and he knew them mountains. If that's really where he sent your boy, he must've known somethin that our map ain't tellin us.*

Never trust a map?

The rain had finally quit.

Mungo led the way out onto the back porch. The cold freed Allison at once from any thought about who she was or when she was happiest, the contemplation of which had always filled her with dissatisfaction anyways and now caused her acute pain. What did it matter? The imperative of the plummetin temperature told her it didn't.

Look at the sky! Sondra exclaimed. The clouds were still there but now with some patches where the clouds were not.

If Kalin's lost, really lost, I won't be as strong as you.

When the ones we love go, they leave a hole in us, but it's through that hole that they show us the stars.

Is that what your stake president said?

Those are my words.

Well, they're beautiful. The stars too.

Amen.

Sondra then rolled her lips for a loud *Brrrrr,* which Mungo answered with three big woofs low as a bass drum.

Our poor children, Allison whispered.

My Dallin used to say that no soul endures that hasn't at one time touched the face of immensity. Maybe that's what they're doin.

I'm sure you're right, but they're still too young for it, Allison answered.

That's fer sure.

If I try to think back on when I was their age . . . Allison began but then stopped. *My two-year-old self didn't survive to memory. Nor did my twenty-year-old self or even my thirty-year-old self. That's pretty sad. Victims of the blur, of too much alcohol. Even this present-day woman that I am now moves with more and more, I don't know, vagueness? But my teenage self, that there's a different story. I can see that Allison clearer than I can see myself even now. I weren't even seventeen, with nothin to show for myself and even less in my pockets, but, boy, does that girl still stand tall, more vivid than she has a right to be, with rocks in both fists.* The cold even seemed to back off some as Allison said this, like maybe for a second the cold could know fear.

Allison, may I confess somethin to you?

Of course.

I weren't in the room when Tom passed, and when they told me he'd gone, I refused to go back in and see him dead. I just couldn't do it. I'm not sure that was the right thing to do.

Why's that?

Standin here like this, listenin to you now, and starin at the mountains too, I just have this overwhelmin feelin: I know your Kalin ain't dead, and I know my Landry ain't dead either, but, see, I also know with the same certainty that my Tom ain't dead either. And that can't be. I stood at his grave. Isn't that awful?

Though Tom had stood upon the Ninth Scree, and right in the middle too, right before the overhang below gave way, accordin to them Delphic laws that govern spectres, he was also somehow already out in front of Landry and Kalin as the mountainside began to slide away.

With that first rupture of rock sendin up those initial curses of dust, what even the storm clouds above had to heed, Kalin was set on one thing and one thing only: gettin the heck out of there. He feared more than anythin, and feared it rightly too, that the landslide would exceed the limits of the scree and obliterate their refuge amongst them Engelmann spruces. Kalin and Landry were also in agreement about another necessity: they'd have to manage this part of their journey on foot. They still needed to address whatever cuts the horses had suffered and couldn't risk ridin them until they had.

They hustled as fast as they could along narrow paths through more trees and brush til they was heavin and retchin with exhaustion up the challengin steep of yet another southwest-facin spur. Only at the top did they pause long enuf to catch their breath and look back.

Under their feet moved thunder. Even the horses pranced about like it was their hooves that hurt instead of their ears, which kept flittin about in different directions, as if this reverberant rupestral collapse could belong to no place in particular. Right before the immense chaos of dust began to overtake the canyon, Landry and Kalin caught sight of a chunk of rock the size of a mobile home crash down upon the Engelmann spruces.

Kalin didn't dwell none on their close call, fearin instead that they would be overtaken by the dust, wherein they'd find it impossible to see, maybe even impossible to breathe, but a strange wind, in one respect discordant with the rest of the turbulence afflictin that area, rose up and like a great invisible hand forbade any particulate ingress here.

Kalin and Landry ran down the opposite side of the spur, Landry still leadin Jojo along, *Clop-Clop-clip-Clop*, Kalin doin his best with Navidad and Mouse, *ClopClop-ClopClop-ClopClop-ClopClop*, with Tom stayin way out ahead, until they'd reached a haven of maples growin around immense fractured rocks, what Tom called *the teeth of the mountain or at least them that fell out*, a description Kalin found vaguely amusin, even if it also seemed to imply that the mouth of the mountain still waited above them with intact and more dangerous teeth, which Kalin knew to be true.

The horses needed their attention, especially Navidad. While Landry tended to Jojo, whose knicks seemed mostly minor, all of them already scabbed over, Kalin washed and cleaned a wound on Navidad's left rear pastern. It weren't deep, but it was bloody. Kalin poured water on the gouge, dried it with dabs of gauze, before finally sprinklin powdered yarrow on the wound. He hoped the yarrow would last until they made camp higher up. On the bright side, the hooves on all the horses were fine. Kalin didn't take off the duct-taped cardboard boots but could see that fer all the abuse they'd taken there were no punctures. Mouse was a miracle. Not only were there zero visible injuries, even the dust seemed incapable of holdin to his coat. The same could not be said of Kalin's hat.

Before ridin more, Kalin gave the horses what water was left in their canteens. Plenty of water awaited them farther up. Navidad, Mouse and Jojo then got a good helpin of Kalin's oat mixture along with some remainin alfalfa and rice bran, plus the last of the canola oil and the corn oil, which Kalin hoped would hold them until they got to the grassy meadow where the horses could graze and rest. Last of all, Kalin checked the horses' gaits. He dreaded discoverin a bad bruise or, worse, some ligamental damage. Landry trotted the three back and forth, then Kalin did the same; both were certain there weren't no sign of lameness.

Throughout Landry and Kalin hardly shared a word, for the first time pretty much actin as one, checkin and recheckin everythin from gaskin to fetlock, every strap and buckle, all of which were secure except Navidad's cinch and somehow her throatlatch too.

After that, Kalin and Landry returned to their saddles and, with daylight startin to lose its hold, if now and then great dazzles of coppery brightness still broke through the clouds, they made their way toward the cliffs declared insurmountable by the map both their mothers and the Porches would consult that very night. And for the most part the map was right. To their left cliffs continued to rise up, denyin any chance of ascension, whether with horses or not.

Tom waited ahead by a shadow that from a distance seemed no

different from the rest. Landry couldn't see Tom, but she eventually discerned how the darkenin rock there hid beyond a blind of boulders a substantial gap offerin an entrance to a narrow slope, thick with brown grass, which soon after, followin some steepness necessitatin several tight switchbacks, gave way to a much milder incline in a widenin draw that from thereon rose with few obstacles into the clouds.

First, though, Kalin led them past that secret entrance.

I wouldn't have even thought to do this were it not for you, Kalin told Landry, praisin the double back that had bought her enuf time to get up Aster Scree.

On the return, they kept to the side where the rocks betrayed few tracks. For the last fifty paces they walked the horses backward, though Mouse would have nothin to do with that, turnin around whenever he could steal the chance.

Back where the rocks offered passage, Kalin handed Mouse over to Landry and Jojo. Then, while she threaded her way around the boulders to them switchbacks above them erose cliffs, Kalin once again walked Navidad past that turnoff, attemptin to rectify some the reversed hoof marks Mouse had left behind. If it rained, or rather when it rained again, the water would soften this subterfuge to near inconsequence, but Kalin still knew they couldn't neglect any effort to hide their way as they now began their climb into the Mouth of the Mountain.

Benton Bland, a Church member from Tulsa, Oklahoma, who attained a rank of colonel in the U.S. Army and taught tactical history at West Point, would later refer to this very moment as the start of *the March-Gatestone Anabasis.* Others would protest with fair complaints that the in-country venture started more obviously at the gate to Isatch Canyon Park or at least the Gate of the Mountain. Bland, however, would argue that those starts were merely *a frolic, a diversion, boyish fun, a campin trip,* claimin that even Aster Scree, where first shots were fired, had no bearin on the journey ahead except to bring into the open the consequential antagonism. *And Thursday night, they were fugitives,* Bland would claim. *They weren't even headin in-country then but back toward Orvop. The Awides Mine was really a katabasis.* Bland wouldn't even count the long and perilous traverse that followed. Survivin the nine screes, and in particular the rifle fire, only made clear the kind of *resistance they would have to endure. After that, though, the real campaign commences. When they begin executin evasive tactics, that's the moment I believe that Kalin and Landry become soldiers.* Benton Bland loved to bring up Xenophon's *Anabasis* as well as *The Anabasis of Alexander.*

Most folks, however, do not take Benton Bland too seriously, as he was eventually diagnosed with early onset dementia that casts much of his tactical theorizin in a, let's say, less than favorable light. *Can you imagine?* Ingrid Harbor would scoff; she was from Scandia, Kansas, and in 2017 farmin soybeans. *To spend so much time on words like anabasis and katabasis, fugitive and soldier, and miss the big picture of what was really goin on? Poor Bland really did forfeit hisself to the insignificant.* But Ophelia Bateman, whose parents were from Orvop but had moved to New Canaan, Connecticut, before she was born, Ophelia growin up to become a commodities broker, would take issue with Harbor's harshness: *Sure, you can call those events just somethin that happened the way it happened because that's the way it happened. And you can make fun of folks like Benton Bland, who, ailin or not, was merely applyin his own field of expertise to events that, if examined closely, do reveal themselves to be far more complicated as well as curiously balanced with symmetries easily overlooked. It doesn't matter either whether the expertise was in, say, agrostology or haecceity. The March-Gatestone journey had many parts, and those parts each had a different set of tonalities worthy of different lenses, and not just because of the way the terrain was changin but more importantly because of how the participants themselves were changin.*

Not that Kalin and Landry were givin any thought to the symmetries and vocabularies of conflict. They was just focused on managin them switchbacks as speedily as possible, sure glad too when they reached what felt like a wide risin valley all their own, a secret valley, with high slopin walls on either side, startin to succumb to an eerie gray-blue, eerie because it seemed to buzz, and with unexplained sparks too, as twilight settled in. Perhaps it was this indecisive luminosity that despite their fast pace seemed to relax them, as if fer a moment time no longer counted, like they was free to move anyway they liked, fer as long as they liked, at no cost.

Of course, puttin such feelins aside, Kalin hadn't forgotten how many more hours they had left to go. The last bit would have to be managed in the dark. Kalin refused to contemplate campin anywhere along the way. The slope alone would make sleepin next to impossible, and at this elevation a campfire might still risk communicatin their survival to those positioned in the right place.

They rode close and without much talk. Mouse walked along between Navidad and Jojo, and Jojo often rode up on Mouse without fear of a kick. When it was possible, Jojo preferred to walk beside Mouse; Mouse seemed to prefer that arrangement as well. Landry would still check Jojo when the soft muddy path began to narrow, but when it widened she let the big blue horse join Mouse again. Where the grass grew thickest, Landry slowed to grant Jojo his nibbles. Kalin did the same for Navidad and Mouse. He even reported seein Ash lower his head, his great white mane weepin for the earth as his lips gathered up great bunches of strange milky grass.

Just like Kalin had promised, the climb here was peaceful and leisurely and at last nothin like the crumbly travails dominatin Isatch Canyon. In fact they had not only just abandoned the south side of Kaieneewa but Kaieneewa itself.

Kalin no longer gave any thought to crosshairs on their backs even if Landry couldn't stop bringin up the possibility. Kalin finally halted so that they could take in together what now lay behind them. You could forget Isatch Canyon; not even Agoneeya was there anymore, taken away by the angle of their now boreal aim, which had swung them behind Kaieneewa, headin them up toward still greater elevations, part of Katanogos proper.

That soothed Landry some, though she still couldn't quit talkin about them rifle shots on the Ninth Scree, even bringin up again how they'd got shot at above Aster Scree. In an effort to escape the ugly memory of those hostilities, what would continue to reverberate through both of them until the time came for memory to cease, Landry and Kalin chose the next worst thing to talk about: how the mountain had fallen, and what a close call that had been, so close that part of Landry, especially in that dreamy twilight, wondered for a spell if maybe Kalin were in fact dead and she was just travelin now with his ghost, as he was travelin with her brother's ghost, who was travelin with the ghost of the woman who was known to wander the canyon, stalkin the dumb alive and makin evil deals and the whole time carryin a rusty ax-head while a hidden forest chipmunk sat on her shoulder.

Tammy Manning, who in her later years would settle in Petersburg, Virginia, and yes, Tammy is the daughter of Roy Manning, owner and founder of Manning & Sons; along with Jonell Moesser, who would end up in Orono, Maine, both of them Orvop High classmates, friends, and poets, would join Landry's suspicions with their own claims that Kalin and Navidad were in fact just that: dead beneath the mountain, in fact under so much rock that their bones were near at once ground to dust, thus releasin immediately upon this journey a refoldin of hauntins that had no start nor could ever know an end. *You single-hoofed steed already dead before a peak beyond the reach of every big-hearted deed as well as sky,* Jonell Moesser would intone, which Tammy Manning in her own epicrisis would answer thus: *The boy was gone, his horse too, that evil canyon was their tomb, their headstone the moon, their purpose won in the afterlife, and even that was too soon.* Miguel Remie and Judith Flannigan would happen to hear a number of these poems.

Ronalee Golightly, also once an Orvop High student and in years to come a resident of Bowling Green, Kentucky, in recovery then, would wonder if Landry herself, and her Jojo too, hadn't also been killt in that rockfall, also ground up into mountain food, with whatever substantiality that followed merely a glimpse of a collective corporeal hallucination: *Sorta like how many folks loved to tell the story of that one guy who stood atop the World Trade Center on Nine-Eleven and rode it all the way down before steppin off without a scratch.*

Steve Harrin, who knew and liked Jonell and Tammy and Ronalee especially, all of whom would've been surprised to learn how their musings had become a part of Steve's own conversin with hisself, Steve endin up in Savannah, Georgia, where he was at one time an electrician until he was haulin lumber for about anyone who asked, would declare to anyone who listened, and no one really listened, not to Steve, that Landry and Jojo, Kalin, Navidad and Mouse were fine: *Whatever folks wanna say about what happened next, what is as horrible as horrible gets, the real miracle was how them horses got through that shattered rock without a cripplin blow. Most like to dwell on the endin, but fer me, it's escapin them screes, the landslide, how sometimes in the worst times of your life, with the world givin way beneath your feet, it's still possible to dance yourself outta harm's way without so much as a papercut.* This comin from a worn man who'd had more than a few rusty nails stab through his gloves. At least once a year, Steve Harrin would thank the fella that came up with that tetanus shot, *thank you Emil von Behring and crew.* It's a hard haul for Steve Harrin, but he keeps on dancin.

Now fer sure, especially among the more equine-inclined sort, there are plenty who disregard the poets as well as the liminally homeless to declare, plain and simple, that horses walkin upon, let alone racin across, let alone survivin such unstable terrain, such a cataclysmic rockfall, is unbelievable to the point that only metaphor can rescue such traversal depictions. And there's no doubt anyone can hike to any number of mountain screes to discover for themselves how no horse could effectively manage even a few steps there. Or, if upon discoverin an accommodatin path across, make the case that should its solidity fail, a horse would stand no chance, tumblin immediately into the numerous blades of mountain-honed rock. As Bret Aston, a Timpview student who ended up a professor at Tulane University, in New Orleans, would like to say: *Video ergo non credo, or I see therefore I don't believe. It's just so fanciful.*

However, while these claims are generically true, the screes on the Kaieneewa side of Isatch Canyon weren't like them in Montana; Alberta, Canada; the South Island mountains in New Zealand; or even

529

in Norway. *Aster Scree is made up of fine stones, near like river pebbles, not near as wound-inflictin as the rock that makes up other screes.* So would comment Daron Mooney, originally a Spanish Fork student who wound up in Duluth, Minnesota, unemployed but not yet destitute *so long as I have this truck.* Daron would additionally point out how the other screes mostly had *hardpacked paths across. The Ninth Scree, though, that's a whole other creature. Some parts are brutal, while others resemble Aster Scree. There are even some parts that are sandy as a beach berm. Not that them ain't equally dangerous. But, and yeah, sure this is a big but, but if you knew where to go and could ride so well your horse never made a misstep, why then you'd make it.*

Wes Gooch, also once a student at Spanish Fork High, who in 2003 would abandon Utah powder for the icy slopes in Stratton, Vermont, *skiin a bit, workin a bit, gettin by a bit,* would often sympathize with Daron Mooney's take on things: *I skied out of a fair number of avalanches up at Jupiter Bowl in Park City. That was when the snow was dry and light and flew around like it didn't matter. And it didn't when it was movin, but when it settled back down, that stuff could be worse than concrete. Come summer, I'd ski them Isatch screes in sneakers. One time, on the back side of Katanogos, I started a rockslide. Got plenty dusty, and my heart was racin like crazy, but I walked out with a story no one believed, though Bret was there and seen the whole thing.*

Video sed non credo, I see but I do not believe, Bret Aston would also say.

This ongoin commotion around what the horses could or could not have survived on the Kaieneewa side of Isatch Canyon will likely never abate. Likely too there will be some confused folks who can't even agree on who was livin or dead. Pretty much no one, though, will argue that Tom and the mighty Ash were challenged any by the climb wendin its way upwards, across steeps of grassy silver, through groves of aspen, beside an increasinly black stream. In fact the higher up they got, the more Tom and Ash seemed refreshed, always keepin ahead, sometimes too quickly so they'd have to pull up and wait.

Kalin, on the other hand, could not provoke out of his exhaustion even the faintest spirit of ambition. His shoulders had caved down around his chest, and his breath stayed quick and shallow. His eyes too, those adored companions of meanin, blurred the thickenin haze as if old age had arrived with malicious haste, peelin away the retinas, permanently cloudin the vitreous too many take for granted. Kalin would cough then and curse and feel some of the full-throttle anger he'd experienced back when he'd scrambled up Aster Scree, when his gloveless left palm had suffered so on that slidin rope, burnin up into the pussin blister it was now. Anger is no hard thing to come by, though this time Kalin spared his mother. Now it was his father, near present enuf to fer a moment rival Tom. *Ain't you a piece of crap!* Connor Mayhew seethed. *Nothin but dumb and gutless.*

Landry too was sufferin her own woes: a shiver she could neither shake nor outshiver was upon her, though unlike Kalin, who sunk deeper into silence, the antidote she pursued was to talk. At least the sweeps of grass and brambles they now moved up through, past aspens, maples, and more and more umbriferous pines, with not just one stream now but three, afforded them the opportunity to ride side by side, Jojo at once sidlin close to Mouse, who was none too bothered, maybe even pleased, what with Jojo on one side and Navidad on the other.

K-Ka-Kalin? Landry chattered.

Yup?

I just wanted to say, if we ma-make it out of here, I mean alive, I've decided to write it all down.

You mean like a book?

A me-memoir.

What's that?

It's a ba-book about your life.

Okay.

Tom, though, weren't near so taciturn: *Her life?! She ain't even sixteen!*

Landry could tell Tom was speakin out and demanded Kalin relay her brother's sentiments.

Oh that don't matter! she squealed in response.

And that got Tom laughin plenty. *Why she don't have even half a memory worth a whole word, let alone two words, let alone a whole book. The girl don't even know how to drive.*

Now what's he sayin? Landry again demanded of Kalin. *Tell Tom I got a good imagination.* At least her annoyance was warmin her up some.

So? Kalin grunted.

That's gotta count for somethin, don't it? It'll be the memoir of my imagination!

Tom laughed at that, but his eyes also sparkled with black bits that to Kalin seemed darker than time itself.

I'll make it all up except this part, Landry went on. *I don't need to make this part up. I just need to remember it. And I've got a great memory. But I'll also take them things I love, the people, the good moments, and I'll mix them up so none of it will really be what it was, but it'll still carry that, I don't know, that glow that makes life so special. You know, by the end your heart'll be broken but healed too, if that makes sense. Names too, I'll switch them around, so who they really was will haunt who they ain't really. Writers can do that: mix up made-up stuff with the mixed-up real stuff, so it's familiar but it also ain't too familiar. Like how our head makes sense of stuff by makin up for what's missin.*

And that was Landry just gettin started. She rambled on about how what she'd write would be hard because thinkin is hard and the

531

performance of easy matter-a-fact thinkin is a lie and a discredit to good thinkin. And she'd wander too, because goin this way and that was also important. And she'd be plenty long-winded. *She's nothin but long-winded!* Tom had snorted. So long-winded that what she was relatin would become the wind itself, an idea that only got more snorts and headshakes from Tom, too flabbergasted to comment. And then Landry started sayin how she was gonna write more than the wind, how she was gonna write like these mountains they was on, rough, broken, at times impossible to follow, other times consolin, astonishin too, and dangerous, and this part she didn't say, only felt, she'd write a place where dreams find their logical extension and know themselves inadequate. *It'll be humble and lardy-dardy at the same time. And I'll use little words but big words too. And I'll use lots of them. Our daddy used to tell us just usin a few words or worst of all one word don't give you no better handle on things. Like, do you really think the word apple is an apple? That one word, apple, don't come close to what the apples in the world really are. And horse? Can you imagine? I'll use every word I can think of, and if I can't think of one, then I'll make one up.* Tom had lost sight of what she was goin on about, Kalin too, though not Landry, sayin how it weren't even important to get everythin right but just see that what was right rhymed with what you had in mind was right. That way the whole world could change but still stay connected to how it would never change. *Like how where we're at now looks this way, like we're seein it now, but higher up on those ridges ahead, when we get to there and look back to here, we'll remember how it looked but see it completely differently too, and in that way it'll make sense of not just where we've been but maybe even where we're gettin to.*

Do you have a title? Kalin at least had the courtesy to ask.

You mean aside from Landry? Tom chortled.

Landry the Legend. Of course.

Tom near fell off his Ash laughin.

I guess one thing's clear: you wanna be a writer.

Heck no. I wanna be a movie star.

A movie star?

Or a famous singer.

You can't stick with one thing, can you?

I'm fifteen. Why should I? I don't even know what to know.

There's some sense finally, Tom allowed.

And tell Tom to shut up. Shut up, Tom. What about you, Kalin, what do you wanna be?

I'm dull. I only got the one thing on my mind: to get these here friends to where they need gettin. Kalin patted Navidad and then reached over and did the same for Mouse, who welcomed the attention.

And after that?

Kalin shrugged. *That seems plenty right there.*

Landry snorted, and it weren't a dissimilar snort to Tom's. *You ain't dull. You also ain't got just one thing on your mind.* She looked then where Kalin looked when he was talkin with Tom.

Tom rolled his eyes. Kalin smiled some but shy like.

Why not an astronaut? Kalin asked Landry then. *You could be that too.*

I don't think they got horses in space. Why would you wanna go anywhere where there ain't horses?

Kalin liked that bit of reasonin.

I don't think I'll make up stuff about horses, Landry continued.

Why's that?

Because they're just so unreal to begin with. Like they're here with us right now, but like at the same time they're also on this whole other plane. Just look at them! Like they're angels. Like they're angels but without wings.

You mean like they lost their wings?

Now you're just humorin her, Tom growled.

No, I ain't, Kalin growled back.

Landry paid no attention to Kalin's grousin with the air. *They ain't lost anythin! Why would a horse need wings or anythin else? They're perfect as they are!* Landry didn't care for that kind of thinkin. *Did I ever tell you my daddy was writin a book?*

A memoir?

He died before he finished it. The parts he read to us weren't about how we see horses or how they see us but how they see without us. A lot of it was about the Trojan war. You heard of that, right?

No.

You've never heard about the Trojan horse? Come on! The big wooden horse? How the Greeks hid inside it? But Kalin shook his head. *The Trojans brought it into their city, and when they went to sleep, the Greeks came out and killt everyone and burnt the city to the ground.*

Why would I care about a wooden horse?

Mrs. Annserdodder's teachin us that right now. You took her class!

Maybe she taught me somethin different? Which weren't so since Mrs. Annserdodder pretty much taught the same curriculum every year. *I probably wasn't payin attention. Schools kinda scare me.*

Scare you?! That's ridiculous.

We moved around a lot. Even when my parents were together. I remember once they dragged me outta this school, and I'd liked it there too, and then a month later my daddy told me there'd been a gas leak or an airplane had crashed into the school, I can't remember the accident, but everyone was killt. I was the only one whose name didn't make the papers.

And you believed your daddy?

Kalin laughed. *He was always tellin stories. Maybe that's where school and me differ: I got so sick of stories.*

But what if they're true?

You mean like a wooden horse?

Darren Blicker says it's important to know why civilizations sometimes don't make it. He says the Greek and Roman civilizations failed because of the gays.

The gays? Kalin was confused.

They let the gays in and that was the end of them.

Ain't that the stupidest thing I ever heard.

Darren Blicker swears it's true.

And you believe this Darren Blicker?

He's an idjit. I was just bringin it up for the sake of makin the point of how important it is to know stuff.

Oh, you made your point.

Look, the Trojans had this city called Troy, and the Greeks were tryin to destroy it. You can believe that much, can't you?

Why were the Greeks tryin to destroy it? Because there were gays there?

Because one of the Trojans stole the wife of a Greek. The Trojans were known for their horsemanship too, but they weren't good with their horses. They broke them and birched them and made them go where they wanted to with whips.

That there's a better reason to sack a city.

One of the great horsemen on the Greek side was a guy named Patroclus. Mrs. Annserdodder says Ms. Melson says he's always described differently than the Trojans. At least in the way he handles horses. Patroclus cares for them, talks to them, and when he dies, they weep for him.

The horses weep for him? Kalin laughed.

He's a chariot driver and a chariot needs two horses. These two horses, though, are immortal and one even talks.

And you wonder why I weren't payin no attention.

Mrs. Annserdodder didn't talk about the talkin horse.

Tom was no longer next to Kalin but now rode beside Landry, amused by his little sister if extra intent on what she was sayin.

The horses belong to Achilles, Landry continued. *He's the greatest warrior in the history of everyone. He's Greek.*

He's the one who hides in the wooden horse and sacks the city?

Landry shook her head. *He's killt before any of that happens. After Patroclus is killt, Achilles goes out to avenge his friend's death. But first he scolds the horses for not keepin his friend safe earlier. That's when the horse called Xanthos suddenly speaks. He tells Achilles that it was a god that killt Patroclus, and what's more, it's the same god that's gonna kill Achilles soon. Apollo, I think.*

Serves this Achilles right for gettin that poor horse to speak.

That was three thousand years ago.

Well, if that horse— What was his name?

Xanthos.

If that Xanthos was immortal, don't that mean he's still around?

It's funny but maybe a little strange too how right then Navidad
snorted and threw her head as if to object or add somethin, and then
Mouse started doin the same, though not Jojo nor Ash, and then on
top of it Mouse neighed, which then got all of them neighin, and that
got Kalin and Landry laughin, though not Tom, who was out ahead
again.

Your daddy ever read to you? Landry asked Kalin.

Ha! Not anythin like that. But he did teach me stuff.

What kinda stuff?

*Not good stuff. But it was still stuff he was good at. He used to call me his
Great White Hope.*

You mean like a shark?

Kalin smiled, but it was the kind that don't ever become a laugh.
Not quite. I never liked him sayin that.

It don't seem so bad.

It is bad, but most of what he had for me was bad.

Kalin told Landry then how his dad was in prison for the rest of
his life and all Kalin wanted was to never turn out like him. *All he ever
did was try to lock people up in his ideas or plans. I plan on the opposite: set
somethin else free.*

I like that.

It's my momma's. She says you ain't free until you set somethin else free.

I bet she and my momma would get along like thieves.

*Oh, I don't know. My momma don't get along with many folks, any folks
really, but she's way better than my daddy.*

Kalin didn't get into why his daddy was in prison. He just said his
daddy taught him that blood weren't somethin to worry about if it
weren't your own.

He almost sounds like Old Porch.

Now they probably would get along like thieves.

*The most blood I ever seen that weren't comin out of my own nose or some
kid's nose I just punched was when I was in a home in east Texas. This was before
the Gatestones adopted me. I seen this from an upstairs window. It was snowin
like crazy. I was with four other kids, and we watched this woman rush outside.
She'd slashed her wrists. I'll never forget it. And then outta the blue this other
woman rushed outside to try and save her. I found out that the woman who'd cut
her wrists had stolen the husband of the woman who still tried to save her.*

Did the woman live?

There was blood everywhere.
Did the woman live?
I like to believe they both did.

There weren't no lookin back now, though Kalin and Landry still gave it a try, beholdin the valley below growin dimmer and dimmer, as the dusk they'd kept tryin to outrun finally caught up. They slipped into a maze of birches where streams gossiped, and nearby the sound of a waterfall tried to drown out what they were sayin.

They passed several waterfalls on the way up, one cascadin over a heap of moss-covered rocks, another droppin over a cliff thirty feet high, with another cascadin down a good hundred feet, straight and sharp as a spear. They let the horses drink and graze some on the grass nearby, with Kalin always checkin and recheckin to make sure there weren't nothin toxic.

At one point they passed what looked to be the remnants of a broken house, built of long timber, some corners still holdin, others havin long ago given way, tellin no tale of completion, only of an earnest attempt at a different life, briefly inhabited by some failed spirit that had long since handed this site over to a frolic of grass and, come spring, busily multiplyin insects.

Farther up, where the variety of trees diminished if trees were still in abundance, between clusters of shorter pines, they found animal trails easily knit into switchbacks that stayed wide and mellow even as they continued to climb higher and higher into Katanogos.

The battle between day and night was nearly over. Color had leached from everythin. The sun was gone, though the storm clouds, what continued to seethe and now and then drench them with a sudden rush of rain, continued to glow, a pale blue luminosity bereft of anythin coppery or rose let alone gold. *Even if it is stuck behind all them clouds,* Landry said then, *it's nice havin a big moon up there to give us some extra light.*

Later on, and higher up, Kalin and Landry beheld the shadows of some great corpse, like a dragon, black ribs risin up from the mountainside, its spine strewn amidst the mountain rubble.

It was in fact worse than any dragon, an old plane built for war, with wings so wide, it could haul up to the edge of the atmosphere any size of bomb, and the worst kinds of bombs too. But here it lay, banished from the air, picked apart by the decades, meaninless to the likes of Katanogos.

Tom, ridin closest to the wreckage, paused to consider whatever might come to him, but the remains could not hold his attention. He squinted more at the lowerin clouds, at the darkened landscape. He consulted the air beside him. Kalin was too far away to hear what Tom said then, only watch as the ghost drew forth from his scabbard that strange brand, at once alight with pale blue flame.

Kalin and even Navidad recoiled. Landry and Jojo followed suit. Mouse munched up some nearby grass.

What is it? Landry demanded.

Tom startled me.

How so?

He just took out that dang torch again, what looks to light a way but don't.

That still don't make no sense.

And it didn't, but, as they once again lurched forward, Kalin tried his best to explain to Landry how the torch didn't alter nothin, at least not in the sense of brightenin anythin, and yet at the same time did seem to add somethin else. Kalin had no answer for what that some-thin else was, doin his best to describe how just the dimness of every-thin swam with motion, with the possibility of improved clarity. Kalin didn't mention how the dullest shadows felt like passageways through which nightmares could now freely arrive.

Kalin thought he did catch sight then of the outline of that some-one walkin beside Tom, and it shuddered him somethin awful. The black paint of night on her hair was bad enuf, but the cold light of stars sparklin her edges, whether they was her nails, her teeth, some-thin more to her, why that near dizzied Kalin right out of his saddle. Navidad nickered and jostled her backside as if to snap Kalin back to the livin.

That impossible shadow beside Tom weren't even the worst of it: all around Kalin caught fleetin glimpses of them summoned forth before at the Awides, what up until now Kalin had known only by way of Tom's recountin. Now, though, by Tom's high brand, some of Kalin's memory was returnin. And there was more too: folks runnin, folks fallin, homes burnin, children runnin, children burnin.

You seein all this? Kalin asked when he'd caught up with Tom, Landry now a good number of lengths behind.

And some I imagine, the ghost answered.

It's like I'm not just seein stuff but rememberin it too, except I'm rememberin someone else's memory.

That might be me.

You ain't never seen people shot down like that.

Tom looked at Kalin. *I don't want to scare you, but I think I'm becomin someone else, somethin else.* Tom weren't smilin, and it dawned then on Kalin that he'd been seein more and more of this Tom without a smile.

I don't like that.

I don't like it much either. At least Kalin could see Tom was tryin to smile. *We need to hurry.*

That mine's a long ways behind us, Kalin said then, as more shadows too swift to place continued to leave in the wake of their vanishin an evocation of those imprisoned in the Awides.

I reckon it makes sense that you see that place as somethin we left behind, but from my vantage point, where we're at, where we were at, even where we will be at ain't so specific.

You mean like we're still in the mine?

In some ways we're always in that mine.

That's comfortin.

Remember when they bucked me right off that first time? At least when Tom looked to Navidad and Mouse, his smiled returned some.

You remember that now?

I remember everythin about these horses now.

That's a good sign, ain't it? What does Pia Isan say?

Tom consulted the dark air. But when he turned back, it was like he'd forgotten what she'd just told him and maybe even Kalin's question.

I remember this time, Tom went on, *when Landry sat down on the couch and acted like she was puttin her arm around our Aunt Lissie, but see I was hidin behind the couch, and it was me that flopped my arm on her shoulder. Patted her. Boy oh boy, when Landry stood up and Aunt Lissie still felt that arm on her . . . Landry and I near gave poor Aunt Lissie a heart attack! She didn't know what was goin on, and we was both laughin so hard.*

Uh, okay. That's what Pia Isan was tellin you?

Tom sighed. *We just have to get these horses to the Crossin, or I'll be joinin them wisps of misery quicker than you can say Aunt Lissie.*

Landry had caught up enuf to overhear Kalin's last question and then refused to back off until he recounted what all he'd been goin on about. Tom honored her subsequent queries and, through Kalin, even went on to describe in detail the arrangement he'd made with Pia Isan.

That don't seem like a good deal, Landry said with a frown. *She got to come along with us and the horses if Tom got to talk to our dead daddy and brother? Which she did make happen, even if it weren't much of a talk because my daddy and Evan just got mad at Tom for makin the deal in the first place. Is that right?* Kalin and Tom both nodded. *But now, if these horses don't make Tom's Crossin, why then he's doomed. Not that I'm surprised, mind you. Tom had a gift for findin trouble when he was alive. Why should he be any different now that he's dead?*

Tom told Kalin that he didn't disagree with her summation, and at least Landry was pleased to hear that.

Bein his little sister, I'd just like to say it ain't fair, Landry added. *Tom might very well end up in a far worse place, but if this Pia Isan hadn't managed to arrange that useless family powwow, nothin was gonna change for her, right? She risked nothin!* Landry addressed Tom's air. *You risked nothin!*

Tom gave his attention to the same air, the results of which he passed on to Kalin, who put it like this to Landry: *First of all, Tom says Pia Isan says that weren't no powwow. You best get your nomenclature right. Second, Tom says Pia Isan says that what you're sayin ain't true. Even the dead lose. And your brother's inclined to agree. He's glad to set his heart to settin these horses free, and if it helps anyone else along the way, why he's awful glad of that too. He figures he didn't do enuf while he was alive. Maybe that's what he and Ash are tryin to do now. He agrees with my momma. He says we come into this world wrapped up and spoken for. We gotta do somethin beyond that, unwrap ourselves, speak for someone else, at least until they can speak fer themselves.*

After that, Tom and Ash rode out in front, that noctilucent brand of his brightenin the farther away they'd need to get to, until it seemed a distant star wanderin the earth. Ever since crossin over the Ninth Scree, Tom had appeared less weighed down by what had come before, his past no longer some dead hand upon his present. For Kalin that was a good thing to see, his friend free from fear and the puzzlin doubt that comes when memory fails. Though there was a troublin side too: now and then when Tom would stop to wait for them to catch up, he looked hisself like a cold pillar of flame.

Ha! Landry suddenly laughed loudly. *I think I'm seein things! I just saw lightnin up ahead, except it didn't go away at once.*

That'd be Tom, Kalin answered her, and fortunately Landry thought he was just teasin.

There weren't no thunder, Landry added.

Kalin couldn't help but feel that thunder was on its way.

When they reached a low saddle bridgin the fast-narrowin bluffs risin more and more on either side, they paused within a proud grove of pines. More steeps awaited them above. Beholdin them was enuf exertion to leave Landry breathless. She wanted to dismount at once but waited until Kalin had.

It felt good to stretch their legs. They let the horses graze some. After recheckin Navidad's legs and hooves, Kalin treated her wound again with ground yarrow and other vulneraries. Landry attended to Mouse and Jojo. They were free of abrasions, and judgin by the condition of the cardboard and duct tape, their soles whole. Not that the price of this day upon their fine-maned friends was lost on either of them. Without a word to each other, Kalin and Landry both arrived at the same conclusion: from here on up they'd walk too.

Before startin out again, they surveyed the way they'd come for any pursuant motion. They saw none. Tom wouldn't say if he spied anythin. Kalin told Landry that at least Tom weren't concerned, which relieved her but troubled him.

The next series of switchbacks up through a narrowin gorge were plenty steep, but the paths stayed smooth and wide. Soon a great hiss began to fill the air. It stole away any contemplation of heights. A bit later a mist began to kiss their faces. The horses kissed back, and their nostrils flared with delight. Landry thought it had started rainin again but it hadn't.

A handful of turns later they stepped out upon a rock plateau where the wet was thick as a cloud that still weren't veil enuf to conceal so beautiful a sight. Just like Kalin had described for Landry back in the mine, water here fell from such icy heights that by the time it reached the pool, it seemed momentarily dispossessed of the meanin of water. So fine was the mist that both Kalin and Landry felt briefly disoriented about what was up and what was down. On summer days bright with sun, Kalin had known the place bound up in rainbows. By Tom's brand the place was a different story, unbound by arches of absence, void of revelation and covenant. But that was okay. Maybe even better than okay. Here urgency and even the ideas promptin such urgency dissolved into an openness so appealin, the effects might as well be described as narcotic. Such were the enchantments of Mist Falls while in the company of ghosts.

The horses were the first to shake off this dazzlin dimness to plod forward and drink from the pool. Kalin and Landry drank as well. So cold was this end to thirst that Landry yipped and yowled because her teeth hurt so much, like they'd been shot out. Glove and all, Kalin thrust his left hand into that water. The iciness was such that it struck away the pain from the burn. The horses, when they lifted their heads, looked thoroughly refreshed, like they'd not just drank but ate too. Ash, who, like Tom, had only stood amidst the countless veils, seemed equally renewed.

It was after this small respite, on their way around and above Mist Falls, that Landry saw again the old elk. Kalin's attention had stayed with the immediate ground, but Landry had beheld the mighty animal wrapped in mist, as if in a caul of clouds, standin upon stones so pale he might as well have been also standin on clouds. By the time Kalin had looked up, the old elk was gone.

It was like he was waitin for us!

Kalin did see a white owl. Was it the same one? When he blinked, it didn't go away. Landry saw it too. Tom, though, didn't want to say what he saw.

When they at last reached Kirk's Cirque, the mistiness that had accompanied them since the falls finally gave way to rain. It had already been hammerin down on Orvop for a while now, and up here, when it started, the rain fell just as hard, though somethin about the altitude and the great enclosure of mountain seemed to mitigate the flood. It was strange. There was no denyin the great sheets of water that slashed down around them, nor the ensuin clatter upon the stones and grass, fer certain upon the surface of the lake ahead that they had no powers to witness yet, though their ears knew the pebbled expanse at once.

First, though, a wide meadow welcomed them. They had not known such continuous levelness for days. So great was their collective relief, it rendered all other discomforts momentarily immaterial. Kalin and Landry even returned to their saddles, and the horses seemed glad of their return.

The descendin clouds trapped and battered around by Katanogos seemed to hover but a few feet above their heads, with scurries of mists here and there presentin brief colonades that framed as well as denied any sense of the size of the place they were now enterin. They had reached the Mouth of the Mountain, but at least for tonight Landry would know it only as a gentle place of refuge.

As a final precaution against pursuit, Kalin led them from that liminal terrace of black stone into the shallow waters of the wide, wanderin Bewilder Crick. The bottom was soft with silt, and the few stones there were old and round and forgivin.

They splashed along that path for a while, durin which Tom pestered Kalin with questions that amounted to one question: *Where are we gonna camp?* Kalin didn't answer; Kalin didn't have an answer. He swatted away Tom's inquisition with his silence or now and then with an actual swat past his face like he and Navidad had just ridden into a cloud of gnats, which they hadn't. In fact no insects bothered them. Kalin even spoke up to tell Landry, and Tom if he cared, if he'd shut up about the future for a moment, how the last time he was up here, leavin around dusk, the place had been burstin with variegatin wildlife. Kalin didn't know the names, but that didn't stop Landry from imaginin flowers of all kinds: forget-me-nots, geraniums, mountain lilacs, columbines, and green gentians; birds too, stellar jays, pine grosbeaks, red crossbills, and black rosy finches, flittin above butterflies and dragonflies, while black ants, red ants, and persistent beetles, overran the ground. There were gnats too, the occasional mosquito, flies, yellow jackets and wasps, bees too, plenty of bees, and still more bees. Blood-nouns choruses around the small lake. Kalin hadn't seen deer or elk, but Landry did, welcomin as well the distant rumor of mountain lions and coyotes. For her, the place they'd just entered was full, even bright. But what got her and Tom the most was when Kalin described how, when takin one last look back before leavin the cirque, he'd beheld the whole meadow overhung with fireflies. He'd never seen somethin so beautiful except maybe Landry safe and sound on the other side of the Ninth Scree. He couldn't remember how long he'd stood there just gawkin at their sparklin infinitude, which he knew to be finite even if they evoked the emergin stars in the dark violet above.

Landry admitted she'd have started chasin them. Kalin said he'd had the same feelin too, but to what end? To find just one of them? *Why to put a bunch of them in a jar!* Landry exclaimed. But what was even a bunch compared to so many? You'd just get bugs with glowin butts. And anyway, Kalin hadn't run back out into the meadow. In fact he'd just stood before that amazement and succumbed to a stillness he'd never known before. *My momma once told me: the stillness patience requires is no prison where there is Love. I never really understood that, and I'm still not sure I understand it now, but I'll say this: I loved bein there, I mean bein here, I guess. I loved just doin nothin but takin it all in. It was such a . . . I don't know how to describe the feelin. Like it was endless. I remember believin then that of course Tom was gonna get better, and the next time up here, we'd be together. Him ridin Mouse, me on Navidad, darin somethin stupid.*

You figure this is stupid?

It sure ain't smart.

Tom laughed.

When they finally left Bewilder Crick, it was dark. The moon-glow that persisted above the clouds seemed no more now than a light that lights itself. Not even Tom's brand afforded Kalin a way to fix his focus, though at least whatever spectres provoked into bein by that awful light had departed. Kalin took the lead then, movin in a direction that knowledge and deduction told him would soon enuf reveal a rocky slope and the base of cliffs that he hoped would yield enuf of an alcove where, with tarps overhead and a fire goin, they might secure for themselves a dry and warm shelter.

Several false promises disheartened both him and Landry, though there were no words of accusation or even frustration. They was aligned to the same purpose, the ghost too: to find a place with some prospect of rest.

And then at last they came upon a crowd of Rocky Mountain junipers, some of which clutched with their roots not just earth but the rock itself. Kalin was inspired enuf to get down from Navidad and push his way beneath the boughs and other low brush. What awaited was a dry patch of sandy earth sheltered some by the walls above. The recess itself was like some great apse for a giant saint, with a wedge of smaller rocks like pews for penitents. It was grim and dark, but it kept the bitter winds away.

Since they was both freezin and there weren't no fire that was gonna happen until he'd found wood, and dry wood at that, Kalin told Landry while they dismounted and unpacked how his momma had tried to teach him a breathin technique that was thousands of years old. *You can only breathe through your nose, and you gotta breathe rapidly too.* Kalin explained how supposedly there were monks who'd done it in the freezin snow, just sat in it all night long, and come mornin the snow around them had melted and they was just fine. No frostbite, no shivers. No more sleep needed either. Ready for the day.

Kalin and Landry sure as heck didn't sit down then, but they did give it a go in their own way, breathin fast and hard through their nostrils until it was too hard to continue. Maybe it did help a little bit. Maybe they were supposed to sit down. In the end it struck them as a fairy tale that weren't worth more than the time it took to tell. Besides the horses didn't like it, and that ended that experiment.

Fer some reason, carin for the horses seemed to help curtail the shivers. Mouse, who'd borne the heaviest burden, was unpacked first. Navidad and Jojo came next, shakin their heads and snortin with relief as saddles, reins, and bits disappeared. Once they was all on their leads and given some feed, Kalin went off to find firewood.

When he got back, Landry gave him the bad news. She could find only three tarps, and even worse, their sleepin bag was missin. Soon after they discovered that Landry's pink slicker was also missin, which they should've realized earlier, but the shock of the rockfall and the gunshots had dulled the urgency for anythin other than puttin miles between themselves and that fallen place. A bag of food was also gone.

It sure didn't help none when Kalin's efforts to light a fire resulted in nothin but spent matches and another lost candle, leavin only two more, which Kalin knew he'd need later, if they made it to later.

At least Kalin had the sense to accept that the wood he was tryin to conjure into fire was just too wet, and so once again he stumbled out into the dark, this time enwrapped by new agonies: they was not only exhausted and hungry but now had less food left, maybe no food, with whatever else reserves fleein his mind, likely because what waited between then and later seemed not only improbable but straight-out impossible. Kalin didn't know it, but he was already defeated. Worst of all, Landry's teeth was chatterin louder than that downwinder Geiger counter her daddy, Dallin, had brought along when they'd gone down to Moab in the summer, what Landry was dreamin about now, that red sandy heat she'd always complained about.

For Kalin there were no dreams of family or sandstone. Despondency verged closer and closer on outright despair as the immediate areas proved woodless. Every broken branch Kalin grabbed was rot with moss and soggier than a sponge in a flood.

Kalin returned to try again, but even after breakin up his find and pryin up the driest possible splinters, it still resisted conversion to the bright warmth they required. Even the most promisin nest of tinder granted hardly a puff of smoke, and Kalin was takin every one of them water-proof matches he struck to its limit, blisterin his fingertips. Tom just sat back and laughed.

Whatever you can do with a horse, you sure as heck can't do with fire.

Ya-ya-you wa-wa-want me ta-ta-to try? Landry asked, real sweet too, which was almost more concernin than how bad she was shiverin. She looked blue.

She's so cold, she won't even be able to light a match! Tom exclaimed, and though he was usually more sympathetic where Landry was concerned, this whole situation only made him laugh harder, so hard, that true to his old self, he rolled hisself right off the back of the rock he'd been sittin on, clutchin his sides and wheezin somethin awful, which maybe in his ghostly state did approximate somethin close to happiness. When Kalin told Landry what her brother was doin, she didn't join in on any such mirthful indulgences, but her cheeks sure flushed red with fury and her chatterin slowed, which Tom fer some reason found even funnier.

Before you get a chance at the Crossin, you'll freeze to death! Tom weren't gonna stop. *They'll find you two here stiff as lake wood in winter, clutchin that little box of matches!*

It ain't funny, Kalin said with a scowl.

He's sta-still laughin?! Landry demanded, cheeks now reddenin even more, if a hint of a smile she had no need for started to curl her lips.

He ain't stoppin. Kalin had started to smile too as he lit yet another match. *He's flat on the ground. He can't hardly breathe. He's got so many tears on his face, I'd tell you he was bawlin if his grin weren't so big.*

Does he understand that we ma-ma-might just fr-freeze to death up here?

That's what got him goin in the first place.

Now Tom Gatestone! Landry snapped, her little fists boxin the air. *You quit your horsin around! We ga-got nothin but wet wood. I'd like to see you da-da-do ba-better.* Landry waited a fair second before turnin to Kalin. *What did he say?*

He's laughin harder.

To be fair Tom did get Landry and Kalin laughin some, even if it didn't exactly help their situation. That the rain had stopped weren't helpin either. As the clouds backed off, the temperature had begun to drop, and given their elevation it could drop a long ways. Landry's breath looked like thunderheads. They needed fire and they needed it fast.

Na-now d-d-don't get all fri-fri-frightful when I say this, Landry managed to get out. *We ca-ca-could use the ga-ga-gunpowder in the ammo of that pistol?*

It's a good idea, but we still need more fuel, dry fuel, Kalin growled.

He threw every blanket and saddle pad they had on Landry, plus the tarps, and told her to sit tight.

Da-don't take too long, Landry chattered out, genuinely alarmed.

Tom will be with you.

In fact Tom did remain with the horses, which was close enuf and actually did grant Kalin a good deal of comfort.

This time Kalin didn't head down toward the meadow and the lake. He kept close to the cliff walls that marked the eastern side of the cirque. He knew there would eventually be some trees ahead, maybe shielded enuf from the rain to offer somethin ignitable.

Kalin moved slow, checkin every dry place along the way for branches or even dry grass. He dreamed of an abandoned bird's nest. But over and over he found nothin, and when he couldn't force his own shivers to stop, he forced hisself to give up, figurin he and Landry could cower together under everythin they had, maybe with the horses pulled in tight around them. Maybe he could get Navidad to lie down. Kalin near started dreamin of restin his head on her warm belly, which sounded great, even if what sounds great don't often play out like it's supposed to. Kalin started to turn around and then turned all the way around and continued on.

At one point he stumbled across a place worthy of a campsite in fair weather. It was encircled by stones resemblin broken teeth. But there weren't no trees here nor any burnable brush. Kalin figured to again turn back, but somethin kept pushin him onward.

To make matters worse, the dim light generated by the lost moon overhead had suddenly grown even dimmer, the clouds above likely recongregatin, thickenin with new bouts of storm.

The shadows were kind or at least Kalin never fell, stumblin forward until eventually he found hisself among some limber pines. Even better, one of them had by some unknown event been cleaved in two, leavin loads of dead wood scattered on the ground. It was all wet, but Kalin figured with a little hatchet work he could chop down to some dryness within. He loaded hisself up with as much as he could carry.

On the way back, Kalin walked within a narrow space definied by the earth underfoot and the storm overhead; for the clouds had lowered again, and it was as if Kalin moved between two great states, with neither forgivin the presence of the other and fer sure not carin a whit about whatever dared their in-between.

What a surprise awaited Kalin when he returned. He feared he'd find Landry even bluer, find her shiverless and still. Instead he found her up and about, a ruf roped up, two tarps beautifully pitched and tied to guarantee them and their gear the most dryness. She sure knew her knots. But as welcome a sight as that was, it was nothin compared to the bright fire, cracklin hot, smartly arranged too, set against the cliff wall, so as not to spend any heat on the ungrateful dark but bounce it right back on what counted, with even enuf for the horses. The pit was encircled with good-sized rocks too; the fire logged up right to burn fierce enuf to produce coals hot enuf to handle the wet stuff Kalin had gathered earlier. Landry had even laid out their saddles, saddle pads, and blankets so they could stretch out and relish the warmth.

Tom, who'd kept to the horses, caught sight of Kalin's stunned or stupefied expression, you take your pick, and once again started up with his hysterical cacklin. Landry even looked up then, and Kalin thought fer sure she'd just heard her brother. She'd even looked toward the horses first before turnin to Kalin. Only Landry had somethin on her mind that weren't her brother.

I didn't get nowhere near that gun, Landry said first thing.

I'll be darned, Kalin grunted as he fast dumped the wood and huddled close to the flames. *If this ain't the closest thing to a miracle I ever seen.*

I probably would've shot myself tryin to pry loose the powder anyways. Or worse, shot one of the horses, Landry said, though it weren't like she weren't still glowin from that look of astonishment still hangin around on Kalin's face.

How on earth did you do it?!

I don't know if I should tell you, she said then with mischief makin a smile. *Why not just ask your Tom, unless of course, he didn't stay back here with me like you said he would.*

He stayed. Tom, how'd she do it?

And Tom told him truthfully.

You sure you wanna hear what he says?

Nah. It's better that I'm sure you're crazy.

Fair enuf.

Oh heck, who cares if you ain't crazy. What did he say?

That he weren't payin attention. He had better things to discuss with Navidad and Mouse.

You're crazy AND cunnin!

Fair enuf.

Honest, it weren't no big deal. I think the candle wax from your first try helped some. I just did better with the tinder is all. But here's the real kicker: I didn't spend one match!

You used the flint and steel?!

Landry grinned big then, even as Tom shouted out, *I did see her do that!* which Kalin made a point of ignorin.

Not that that settled anythin. Somethin still weren't addin up. *The tinder I left here wouldn't've given up near the flame you'd need to get even them small twigs burnin. What else dry did you use?*

Landry tossed her hair away from her lovely face, no doubt made more lovely by a smile so big, she just might've grown some extra teeth in that very moment.

Crazy, cunnin, AND smart! she answered Kalin with a laugh so giddy you wouldn't be faulted for callin it girlish. She sure was proud of herself, and for some reason that filled Kalin with more happiness than he'd knowd since Tom had died.

How Landry loves havin the upper hand! Tom shouted from the horses, though by now he'd taken some steps closer.

What did you find? Kalin asked. He really was stumped.

Magic.

Kalin laughed. *Well, good for you.* And he meant it.

Landry, though, weren't pleased to see Kalin acceptin her answer. Sometimes a secret just ain't any good if it stays kept. Landry stopped givin the kettle stirs and pulled free from her jacket a flop of pages, what might've once been a book but now lacked any such definin shape, just a mess of thread, paper, and old glue.

Ta-da! My momma always says never judge a book by its cover, and this book ain't any bit misused with me puttin its cover to use.

Years later Yash Rocker, by then a staff manager at the water park in Jacksonville, Florida, wouldn't stop thinkin on how that book had pretty much changed everythin: *First of all, can you imagine if she'd pried off the bullets and used the gunpowder?! Even done so to just one? How radically altered everythin would've been? But because of that book . . . I don't even read books. Don't even like them to tell you the truth.* Pilar Hinckley, in sales for Cassidy Apparel, by then at the national offices in Salt Lake City, would argue good-naturedly about the bullets with Ananda Lott, from Briggham City, though by then pretty much permanently located in Salt Lake and also with Cassidy Apparel. The question discussed was what number of compromised cartridges would've set things headin in a completely different direction. Both Hinckley and Lott would admit up front that it was a pretty pointless discussion, but they liked each other and it was fun to think about. *One? Two? What about all six?* Samuel Zyer, at the Fermilab in Illinois, would have other thoughts. His concern would overwrite what he would consider a tendentious overweightin of numbers, *whether we're countin cartridges, wounds, or the dead.* Instead Samuel Zeyer would strive to recognize the attendant forces accompanyin these children, these horses: *A bullet here, a bullet there is beside the point. The future at play was never about bullets or even that Colt. Anyone willin to give Kalin and Landry their due respect, along with whatever companion we can claim was or wasn't there, would see that alterin the outcome would require more than minor deprivations or augmentations.*

Now it's true that Samuel Zeyer's goings-on can seem radical enuf to make anyone convinced by the daily math of livin either deservedly skeptical or a bit squeamish. Fer example, one of the conclusions that can emerge from Zeyer's point of view, and this entertained while tryin not to veer too close to Godwin's law, suggests that if you was to do away with Hitler in the early 1930s, the Third Reich would still have appeared, World War II still have taken place, the Holocaust too, only with different players, different victims. This sort of fatalism ain't for everyone, and there's good reason to object, so let's settle ourselves. Zeyer would even admit as much, though he still couldn't help addin the followin: *Just realize that there are cases where a butterfly flappin about in the wind won't do nothin against the hurricane that tears it to bits. What was waitin ahead weren't about to be changed by how they got that fire lit, not by Landry, and certainly not because of any book.*

Kalin couldn't hide his bewilderment. *You hauled a book all the way up here? What for?* Only now recallin Landry scribblin in the little book on their very first night. He hadn't paid it or Landry much mind because he'd figured to be rid of her soon enuf.

I got enuf fire outta the covers to get the tinder goin enuf to get them tinier twigs goin until the bigger branches finally caught.

Kalin was still mystified by the idea of a book up here.

What do you write in it anyway?

I ain't tellin you. You'll just laugh.

Kalin laughed just at that. *Whadya care if I laugh?* Kalin tried to give the top page a squint but couldn't discern nothin but scribbles.

I told you I ain't tellin you, Landry said again and disappeared the paper mess into one of her coat pockets.

Kalin returned his attention to the darkness around the horses.

Tom say somethin? Landry asked, sittin up extra, extra alert.

I ain't tellin you.

Landry made a face at Kalin. It beat blue and chatterin.

It ain't my memoir yet, but it will be, one day, you'll see, Landry finally said. She couldn't help herself. Never tell her a secret.

I don't know what you're sayin.

It's my journal.

You carry your diary with you?

I forgot it was in my coat when I grabbed it.

Did you burn pages too? Kalin couldn't stand the thought of Landry burnin up some days she wrote down to remember, days with Tom.

Just the empty ones, the ones where nothin happens. Don't worry, I didn't burn none of them that concern my brothers Evan or Tom or anythin with my daddy. I talk to my daddy in here. It makes me feel okay. Maybe it's the same how you talk to my Tom.

They ate their supper then. It weren't but nothin, but it tasted like everythin. The eggs were long gone; the soup too, more. Landry had found only a little rice left in some bunched-up tinfoil, plus some seasonin. Landry would've killt for even one of them Orvop cafeteria buns. Kalin was relieved to find that their bag of Dorf jerky had survived. Landry asked for some pieces, but Kalin returned it to his saddlebag.

We'll need this for tomorrow.

And the day after.

Somethin like that, Kalin answered a bit too grimly, though he didn't return to the fire empty-handed. He'd managed to come up with two cans of black beans, as well as not just one but two of them Orvop cafeteria buns. He'd even found two of them little things of chocolate puddin. They only ate the one can, and it weren't enuf, given what they'd already been through and what waited ahead, but it still seemed a feast. And they enjoyed it together, and they got warm and built up the fire even more.

After they was done eatin and had raked out the cutlery with stones, they returned to the horses. Tom swore Navidad was showin off an Indian Shuffle. Kalin weren't convinced. Landry swore Mouse had become four trees. They all laughed and swore that at least that much was possible.

While Landry took care of fillin the collapsible canvas water bowls for the horses, Kalin refilled every canteen and jar. Navidad, Mouse, and Jojo had already had their fill of grazin, so Kalin and Landry made sure they got their share of Kalin's oat mixture. There was some carrots left too, which Landry had been awfully tempted to throw into their dinner mix. *I almost stole a bite, but our gang needs them more.* Hearin Navidad and Mouse, and Jojo too crunch down now on them plugs of orange was near as good as if Landry and Kalin had eaten them up themselves.

After that, Landry and Kalin spent time brushin the horses. Kalin weren't sure whether or not to remove the duct tape boots. Landry had already taken off Jojo's Easyboots. She could put them on come mornin no problem. What cardboard and tape they had left was another matter. The two teenagers discussed the pros and cons and finally settled on takin them off, givin their friends a chance to breathe their feet. Though as it turned out they'd mostly dissolved anyhow, the cardboard a soggy pulp under the duct tape that by some miracle was still clingin to the hooves. Landry suggested that come dawn they take the horses down to the lake and soak their legs as well.

Kalin dug up what was left of the duct tape and was relieved to discover enuf cardboard. They'd likely have some left over too. Landry could at least spare her diary if they had any trouble buildin their next fire. Kalin then revisited Navidad's injured pastern, again cleanin the wound, again applyin ground yarrow root, which likely weren't necessary given that the bleedin had stopped many hours ago. He slathered on some Vaseline last. Kalin then mixed up some herbs, which he put on the back of Navidad's tongue, Jojo's too. It would help with any inflammations. Mouse didn't need none. He remained a miracle, back to grazin again.

Landry poulticed and wrapped Jojo's right foreleg for good measure. Kalin did the same for two of Navidad's legs. Navidad threw her head some and even knocked Kalin aside once with her proud cheek but was glad in the end that it was done and nuzzled him up plenty after that.

For good measure, Kalin and Landry rechecked one last time all the hooves. They remained clean and unpunctured.

Landry then took Kalin's left wrist. *Let's give this hand a look.* Kalin had removed his gloves by then and what gauze remained was bunched up and clotted with blood and puss. Landry tossed that into the fire. She then situated Kalin by the fire and set to washin the long blister across his hand. Kalin winced as she poured water on the injury, ate on his lips as she daubed it with clean gauze, and a few times even growled through his grit teeth while keepin still nonetheless. Kalin agreed to let her try some of the yarrow on the wound but just a little. Lastly Landry loosely rewrapped the burn.

Seriously, she finally said. *How'd you learn to ride like that?* Likely the food, the warmth, and the prospects now of some real sleep had given her a little kick of wakefulness. To Kalin her eyes were bright with their fire. He couldn't know that she was seein nothin but him and Navidad ridin out of the slide.

I'd like to know the answer to that question too, Tom chimed in, happily sidlin up now to his sister.

It was all Navidad. Kalin answered with the only truth he knew.

That slide shoulda killt you both, Landry said, makin no effort to disguise her awe.

Tom was in agreement, though he weren't in awe. Nothin the livin can do will ever hold the dead in awe. Except maybe just livin. *It sure was somethin,* the ghost did admit.

It sure was somethin, Landry also murmured, again beholdin in her mind's eye the ride, which got Kalin at once stompin a bootheel, Navidad stompin a hoof, both snortin in their own way. But as rankled as Kalin was by such compliments, he was also equally enchanted by somethin that he hadn't seen before: it was like brother and sister had started listenin to each other.

I feel lucky havin seen it too, Tom said. He weren't gonna stop, and Kalin meant to stop him, but then Landry spoke up too.

I feel lucky to have seen it.

And it didn't stop there either, the two of them kept echoin each other across the fire, sometimes Landry leadin with what all they'd been through, with Tom then agreein with his own reiterations of what his sister had basically just said, which was explainable, until it got real strange, with Tom leadin and Landry somehow still echoin if not outright repeatin her brother's words. And the more they went on like this, the greater was Kalin's surprise, like it was near musical, like they weren't just in the same key but both knew the song by heart.

Ridin like you done, no matter how many times you see it, you still swear it ain't possible, Tom said, though now he weren't lookin at Kalin, just at Landry.

I seen it myself not hours ago, and I already doubt what I seen. Landry too weren't lookin at Kalin but at the darkness that held her dear departed brother. It was somethin amazin. *I swear it ain't possible.*

And then Landry started to whistle somethin Kalin had heard Tom whistle before, but she weren't much of a whistler, and even worse, Tom joined in singin, and he weren't much of a singer. Kinda awful, Kalin thought, if kinda funny too.

And gosh, it didn't even stop there, with the melody shiftin, the tempo too, and more lines followin that went sorta like this:

With Lailah's finger on my lips,
this world has made me sick.
I must've had enuf once
to know I ain't had enuf since.
Save your cash and stack some wood.
Then turn my bones to ash.
Come on now, see it through.
I ain't ever comin back for this.
But I'll still come back for you.

Under cover of nightfall, Kalin made three trips to them limber pines. He also took the binoculars with him to make sure there weren't no spits of electrical light darin the dark to find them. He saw nothin but the clouds clamberin down upon meadow and the lake, hidin still the vastness that surrounded them. He was plenty happy to report as much to Landry and Tom upon his return, addin that as far as he could tell, their campsite and fire were also well-concealed. *There ain't even a ray of light visible beyond the junipers.* Come dawn, they'd break camp and get the heck outta there.

Kalin didn't bring up the possibility of another freeze. If it did ice up like before, they'd be in grave trouble. Tom didn't say nothin either.

Once Kalin had their pile of lumber situated close enuf to both the fire and where he would sleep, so he could feed it throughout the night, he arranged upon the flames another tier of logs, and then along with Landry and Tom, who'd brung hisself in still closer, Kalin at last settled down on his blanket and saddle to watch the red coals bring forth from the small branches, those scraps of wishful thinkin Landry periodically tossed in, little tongues of yellow and orange, fast lickin up around the new fuel, now and then explodin with sparks, some even leapin toward Tom, as if to dare him to be somethin more, to hurt somethin more; all the while the flames around these new logs kept growin higher, as bright as they was varied in color and disposition, content, confident, if maybe anxious too, anxious to tell more of this moment, their only moment, with their own tongues, their own stories, further goaded by a gust of cold wind or threatened or even encouraged by the delight afforded by the woody meat such speech demands first. Or were there no stories here? Only a fiery desire to devour with no satisfaction ever in sight? If Tom knew the answers, he weren't sayin, sharin with Kalin only a look of now-unafflicted amusement.

Suddenly then, and surprisin all his companions too, maybe even surprisin the horses, Kalin thrust his left hand into the fire, and it was the burnt hand too; though no sooner was he within that vault of heat was he also free of it again, the gauze over his wound only singed if smokin still, while, scramblin from his palm, not one but two rescued spiders managed their delighted descent upon invisible threads to the now cooler refuge Kalin swung them toward. Or as Gus Dieudonne would later declare to Hyrum Kapp: *Is this here then, and once and for all too, the interment of Jonathan Edwards?* To which Hyrum Kapp would respond: *And why the heck not?*

Landry weren't near as reflective. *Why'd you do that?!* she cried out, flabbergasted not so much by the act but by the speed with which Kalin had accomplished his rescue.

We burnt their home. Don't seem fair to burn them up too.

The fire then, almost as if morally relieved, seemed at last to settle into what was hands down the most pleasant fire they'd enjoyed since enterin Isatch Canyon. Maybe the first one, the one with Russel, was comparable, though that had been smaller and more tame. There was no forgettin the one in the mine; that thing had been a dreadful necessity of oily smoke. This one here, though, while not exactly cozy nor tame nor small either, still radiated comfort. The smoke was black enuf like the one in the mine, but here, not even a dozen feet above, the cold wet air dismantled the sooty exhaust, and what remained was the soothin scent of storm and sage. The flames and the coals never faltered against the cold and the night, and this prevailin success provided what both Landry and Kalin needed most: a warm-enuf space to find repose, repose for their worn bodies, their timorous minds, and of course their bold hearts.

Landry yawned, pulled snug around her shoulders her blanket, but didn't yet rest herself against her saddle.

In eighth grade, my teacher Mr. Rawlins wanted us to learn about the courts, and so he had us put on this pretend trial, and since I weren't afraid of talkin or makin my case, he made me the defense lawyer. There was a car accident, and I'd figured out how it couldn't be Willa Wong's fault. Willa played the part of the driver. I proved it too before a jury of my peers. Well, my peers didn't like me much, probably not Willa neither, and they found her guilty. They laughed at me after. But you know what made it that much more gallin? When Mr. Rawlins told me I'd figured it out: the driver weren't guilty.

Seems like a good lesson, how life don't always work out fair. Kalin was gettin used to how Landry could bring up any old thing on her mind.

How do you always manage to stay so calm? she asked him then.

Are you serious? Kalin looked near as startled if she'd just yelled at him.

You don't think you are? It was Landry's turn to look startled.

Just ridin up to them Mist Falls, I got so mad, I near couldn't see straight. Can't even say why either. Because I was tired? Sufferin some born-with natural orneriness? I was angry as a branded mule!

Angry at who?

My daddy. Kalin even described then how before that, back when he burnt up his left hand climbin Aster Scree, he'd found hisself furious at his momma. *And she don't got no part in this!*

Why'd you think of her then?

Who the heck knows? Fumin at my folks? And ain't that a bad place to wind up, because there ain't no end to it. Blame them and you might as well blame their parents and so on until you're just cursin all the folks that come before you. Where does that thinkin stop?

You're askin me? I'm a Gatestone. Our blamin goes back more than a hundred years.

That's no way to get up in the mornin. Kalin eased hisself some from the fire. The flames were mostly gone now, but the coals still kept their bright and shed more heat than before. He should've closed his eyes then, but, same as with Landry, somethin still kept him from settlin his head on his saddle. *You know anythin about your birth folks?*

I can't remember my daddy. I'm told my momma used to say he was blacker than midnight is blue. I'm not sure I know what that means, but I like it. She said he was beautiful. She was beautiful. She was from Samoa. A singer. And my daddy, he made violins. I don't know how they met. He died the year I was born. My momma made it until I was five. I never found out what took her or I forgot. I can't even really say I remember her. Maybe I just remember a photograph of her with my daddy. They did look happy together. I don't have nothin of them now. Not even that photograph. My dream is that one day I'll find one of my daddy's violins for sale.

What's his name?

I don't even know that. Landry tossed more twigs onto the fire. It bristled at once into yellow flames and with the shadows newly cast made somethin ghoulish out of both her and Kalin. They still smiled at each other, though, and their eyes continued to sparkle with all they saw. Tom huddled still closer to the fire, but his eyes stayed black.

You think we can have a bit of that jerky before we sleep? Landry asked.

We ate plenty.

You call that plenty?

Given where we's at, yeah.

When we get back, my momma's gonna set us a table. Then you'll see what plenty is.

If she don't kill me first.

You'll always be welcome, Kalin. You'll see. One piece of jerky?

We were supposed to be at a very different place by now.

If you think about it, Landry said then in near chipper tones, *this really ain't no big deal. This is just a regular campin trip. We ain't been out but three nights now. Even with one more, or even a couple more, that ain't so bad.*

That's a fair way of seein it. It did Kalin some good hearin Landry minimize the dangers they'd faced. Probably she was just tryin to tamp down her own fears. Still, she was pretty convincin. *Your brother and I spent months plannin this out.* Kalin looked over at Tom, who seemed transfixed by their fire; that or he'd lost interest in Kalin and Landry. *This place weren't a part of that, though it ain't half-bad. We'll have to remember it if we ever decide to come back.*

Kalin failed to notice how his comment reddened Landry's cheeks.

Tom stood up then and just as abruptly strode away. Kalin watched his friend's departure with both surprise and dismay.

What is it?

Tom didn't answer.

What is it, Tom? Kalin asked again, this time louder.

What is it? Landry asked Kalin.

Your brother just walked off.

Is that not normal?

I got no clue what's normal. Kalin stood up too but only to get a better sense of Tom's direction.

Can't you see what he's doin? Landry asked.

He's whistlin. And he was. Tom had even left Ash behind, albeit in the company of the livin horses, and strolled on down beyond the junipers, out into the mists, stoppin upon that slope above the wide meadow that, in the distance, held the lake. From there he could also face the cirque, which due to the dark and the clouds neither Kalin nor Landry could behold. Was it different for a ghost? Tom hadn't even thought to bring along that torch. He just stood there, with his long hands shoved deep in his pockets, whistlin, and in that way of his that's so pure and unwaverin, so true, that it seemed effortless.

What's he whistlin? Landry whispered.

Blue Dawn Console Me? Kalin whispered.

It's just called Blue Dawn, Landry corrected him, now whisperin extra quiet, like maybe, if they was quiet enuf, she might catch a little bit of what Kalin was hearin. *Is it nice?*

What?

His whistlin.

Of course it's nice.

They listened like that for a while, Kalin listenin to Tom, Landry listenin to Kalin listenin to her dear departed brother, which Kalin didn't realize was the thing they was doin until Landry started to sob, the tears just floodin down her face like they'd made a vow to never cease until the whole world was drowned. Rainbows be damned.

Landry! Kalin cried out. *Are you okay?* Tom at once stopped his melody-makin.

In fact Landry had never heard Kalin exclaim her name with such alarm nor rise up like he done in such distress nor ever look upon her, look upon anythin, with eyes so wild with worry and concern and devotion. She felt intensely present, too present, in ways that seemed to provoke a contradiction. Fer one thing, her name still seemed to hang in the air between them, as if it were just as much a thing of importance as she was, which made her feel at once momentously seen, for the first time in fact, at least in that way, but also, if this makes any sense, entirely erased! Could any name do that? Or was it just her name? Or maybe only if it was pronounced in a certain way, risin up before her, at the price of her, while who she was beyond the fringe of any name became even more a thing of shadow, denser than time, except lighter too, lighter than light, risin away like smoke, as if born of fire but precedin fire too, so fire could begin. A dragon singin in the dry woods. Landry had never felt so powerful before nor so terrified. But she didn't cower neither nor think to run or hide nor lock up one bit. Instead she faced this boy panic-stricken over an outpourin of grief and let him behold in her her own signature of death.

What is it? Kalin mumbled out, blinkin, maybe even flinchin, lowerin his eyes fer sure as she wiped away her tears with a sleeve.

It ain't nothin, Landry mumbled back. *Tired I guess. And maybe,* she looked up again, again right at Kalin, *sorta shocked too to find myself all the way up here. Like this ain't just campin, like I'm just now seein what sorta situation I'm in, where I've never been before, nor dreamed of goin to, not on Jojo, not with horses my brother used to ride when he was still alive, and at the same time thinkin of my poor momma, and why, why, why I don't even know you!*

Kalin couldn't do nothin else but nod, and then instead of answerin Landry, because what could he really say when she saw plain as day how it was?, he turned from the fire and even from her. Though Landry didn't accept his retreat.

Is he still whistlin?
Kalin shook his head.
Is he headin back this way?
I got no clue what he's doin.

They both got up. Not even a few paces off from the blaze and the cold dug in fast, clawin through their damp clothes, to their bones. It was a good reminder of what they was still up against.

Landry helped Kalin toss more wood on the coals, and together they welcomed the flare of more light and warmth. But things felt different now. Kalin seemed able to only sneak glances of her.

I was just cryin, she finally said with plenty of peeve in her voice.

Fer what it's worth, I can understand how strange it must be to be here. And you're right, you don't hardly know me. Sayin so made lookin Landry's way a little easier, though he still ended up lookin past her, out beyond the junipers, maybe because fathomin the vastness waitin for them out there still seemed easier to him than tryin to make sense of her.

Can I ask you somethin, Kalin? Landry said through the smoke, realizin with a bit of a hmph that somehow the burden had fallen on her to ease away Kalin's awkwardness.

Of course! he replied at once. *Anythin!* Had she ever seen him so grateful? So willin?

Why'd you really go back out on the scree again? Landry fiddled with a twig in her hands, pluckin off the dead needles, the small dead stems.

Tom couldn't go no farther. Like he was scared.

Of what?

The way ahead? Us? Maybe just me?

Is that true, Tom? Landry asked the air around them as she tossed the dead stems into the fire and watched them turn to ash.

He's still out there.

I just don't get it. Ain't ghosts supposed to scare us?

I don't have much experience with ghosts except for Tom.

Does he scare you?

Kalin didn't answer right away. He didn't know the answer. Of course at the start Kalin had welcomed Tom's company, still welcomed it, maybe even depended on it, but he'd also started seein somethin about Tom change, like Tom not bein just Tom anymore, like there was a distance startin to spread into him, a distance that was beyond traversin. Kalin didn't share that last part with Landry though.

What does scare you, Kalin? she asked.

Kalin thought on that some as well, and Landry didn't interrupt his thinkin. He even consulted the fire, but neither the flames nor the dark red rubble of its aftermath could know his heart. And in this space of not knowin, of knowin nothin, his eyes flitted briefly to Landry and then even faster to her saddlebag, to where Kalin knew the Colt Peacemaker rested, glitterin cold in its dark velvet pouch despite all absence of light. Kalin's heart quailed before just as fast makin itself into a fist set against a recognition he would not name. The night then seemed crowded, with far too many ghosts, and with no end in sight. Kalin's heart relaxed only when he found his way away from such darks, away even from the fire, away from Landry, from Tom too, findin again Navidad and Mouse, and Jojo, and Ash too.

But Landry hadn't missed how Kalin had eyed her saddlebag, and she meant to call him out on it too, but then he told her what scared him: *Not gettin these horses to where they need to go.*

Landry snorted. Her tears were long gone. She might've even laughed if she could've been certain it wouldn't've come out as a mean guffaw. She was already workin hard to keep caught in her throat a harsh and mockin music, in the same way you might work hard to hold back a fat poisonous fart insistin on its own freedom.

You got plenty to marvel about, Kalin, Landry said in place of laughin or fartin. *I'll admit it. And if I make it through this, I'll never forget how you outrode a mountain, and I'll tell everyone who'll listen, and I won't even believe a word I'm sayin either, but it'll still be the truth. That bein said, and I know we've already been over this, but sometimes the things you say are dumber than a pile of rocks, with all due respect to the rocks. Do you still believe you're just gonna let these horses go in some magical place where they'll just be fine? Like they won't die of starvation? Or run off a ledge by mistake? Or poison themselves on plants they've never seen before? Or on water that's been fouled no matter how far away it is from people?*

I have faith in your brother. I had it when he was my friend. I have it now.

Landry flipped another twig into the fire. *Tom and Evan used to love that Eagles song where they sing: Freedom, well that's just some people talkin. Free, as far as I get what free really means, is just somethin that don't cost nothin. But my daddy and momma always taught us that nothin was free. So go figure. No such thing as a free meal, a free deal, or likely even settin somethin or someone free. There's always a cost. Somewhere. And if you don't know the cost, why then it figures you don't understand a thing about what you're doin.*

I reckon I do know the cost, Kalin answered, tossin across her twig his own, the two curlin into flames.

But Landry weren't done. She hadn't said her piece just yet. *My momma and daddy taught us that the foundation of their faith rests on the fact that the only thing that is free, the only thing in this whole wide universe, is the Lord's Grace. Now I'd like to say I know that to be a fact, but I don't. I ain't like them in that way. I got different ideas, different beliefs.*

How so?

I reckon the only thing I'd bet on that costs nothin is . . . death.

Except for the fact, as I'm here to attest, Tom said, at last returnin to the horses, to the fire, *that not even death is free.*

Everythin okay, Tom? Kalin asked the air, though he could already tell everythin was not okay. Tom was alert and serious, and he had an antsiness about him that was likely one of the main reasons Kalin hadn't yet given into slumber.

Time's runnin out.

Are they here?! Kalin near shouted, on his feet again, which got Landry leapin up too, scramblin fast to her saddlebag. Her face had gone to chalk as she slid her hand into the velvet pouch within if not yet pullin free the Colt.

Whoa! Whoa! Tom cried out, holdin out his hands, palms down, like to lower them back down again to the comforts of their saddles and blankets, which Kalin obeyed, Landry followin his example and thankfully comin away from that saddlebag empty-handed.

Tom says it ain't the Porches, Kalin told Landry, though he kept squintin the night, findin only a dark alive with a labyrinth of shiftin mists.

What is it then? Out with it Tom! Landry demanded, still lookin like she was ready to kick out the fire and return again to draw what hope she could take from that velvet pouch.

Tom shifted uneasily then from bootheel to bootheel, his long legs sidlin him away some, like he meant to avoid his sister's stare.

Explain yourself, Tom: whadya mean time is runnin out?

We best quit this place by early mornin.

Ask him what Pia Isan is sayin, Landry said then.

Haven't you noticed the animals? Tom asked Kalin. *The birds? Even the bugs? How they're all followin the horses?*

Kalin was in the middle of relayin to Landry Tom's odd reply when they both heard the sound of flappin wings, not just above either, but from all around it seemed, followed by a crackle and stir among the leaves and grass just beyond the perimeter of their campsite, and then in the distance they heard the yip of a coyote, and Kalin even swore he heard, in the moan of wind that followed, the howl of a wolf, which was impossible, as there weren't no wolves in Utah anymore, at least that's what everyone down in Orvop would tell you. Up here that claim weren't near so convincin.

She says the horses are brave, Tom continued. *But she says we've led them into a trap.*

That so? Kalin smiled.

And Tom smiled too. *That's how she sees it. The one beside her sees it that way too.* Tom's smile was only gettin bigger.

Kalin started to tell Landry about the animals. *Tom says—*

Enuf! I don't wanna hear no more of this nonsense. Not another word. She was holdin up one hand too and displayin such a look of disgust that even if it wouldn't have checked none of the Porch boys, it sure checked Kalin.

Kalin swallowed. He'd seen already her awful fear at the thought of havin to face that Egan Porch up here and figured he'd help her out there first. He scurried out into the dark to survey one last time the cirque, but there weren't no glints of machine light, and even at just ten paces out no flicker of their own fire was visible.

When Kalin returned, Tom was by the fire, his back to Kalin, and fer a moment he seemed briefly illuminated within by the flames before him. There was a lightness to him, even in his grayness, even in that grayin hat that looked more like a cloud than a lump of coal.

Kalin expected to find Landry fast asleep, but she was still up and still watchful. Kalin assured her that the cirque was empty and reminded her about how gettin across where the rockfall had occurred might not be possible even in daylight and fer sure weren't possible at night.

I'm sorry for sayin what you was sayin was nonsense, Landry said then.

Ain't no bother.

I'd still like to know what Tom meant when he said time was runnin out. Landry didn't direct her request to the air but fixed her eyes on Kalin, maybe because, and, okay, there weren't really no maybe about it, what she wanted most right then was to take the measure of her guide.

Tom says he's becomin someone else, somethin else.

Tom, who remained hunched over on a rock between Landry and Kalin, nodded to the flames that could rest none of their light upon his long pale face.

And I gather that's bad?

Kalin studied Tom. There weren't even the meniscus of a smile on his friend's face, and the shadows around his eyes looked near deep enuf to be called holes. Kalin shuddered.

It's fearful, Kalin finally told Landry.

But how so?

It's fearful, Kalin said again, like that might say it different.

I don't understand.

I need him, Landry, Kalin finally said and left it at that, throwin more wood on the flames. Again he was countin on the cold to wake him before it was too late, to get the next round of wood burnin, though this time he asked Landry to give him a kick if she got cold. He figured between the two of them they'd keep the fire goin with still plenty of wood left to cook up some breakfast. They'd be free of this place by dawn. That would make Tom happy.

Landry had finally stretched out again.

Kalin?

Yup.

I miss my brother every day, and unfair don't begin to describe him bein gone so soon. Whether him bein here with you is just you lyin, I don't know no more. That said, what I need to tell you is that I have lied to you.

Oh?

It's one of them lies of omission. Like I didn't flat-out lie but I also didn't volunteer neither what Tom had told me about you.

Or maybe that's just somethin between you and him?

Landry didn't care for that. What was on her mind she meant to share. *He just said you was this fool who weren't good but for two things.*

He called me a fool, huh?

Kalin looked over at Tom, but the ghost still weren't listenin. There was more for him in fire than in his sister or friend.

Tom said you can't make it in this world if you're good at but two things.

Kalin studied Landry then across the retreatin glow, and there was fright in her now, and it weren't no more about who pursued them or the ghost in their midst. This time it was about him.

You ask him what those two things were? Kalin asked real slow then. He didn't spare Tom a glance, though Landry sure did, as if to give the air a chance to object. It didn't.

Horses.

Kalin waited.

Tom said he swore an oath to you to never say nothin, but when I asked him one day why he seemed so bothered, he told me there was one thing you was better at than horses.

It weren't lost on Kalin just how nervous and fidgety Landry was gettin, especially in the way she refused to look at him but kept glancin at her blanket.

I told you I loved her, Tom suddenly spoke up, even if his gaze was still lost to fire. His voice also seemed different, much different and deeper. Gone too were any inflections of joy, any promise of play. *Love, when it comes, makes its demands, and there ain't no refusal that will stand. Love, when it comes, commands, and there ain't no doin but to hear it out as only one person can, alone, neked, entirely afraid, even if what love commands is that you be not afraid, that you know yourself not alone, and that when you answer you answer only with the truth. Love don't lie. Not once, not ever.* And with those final words, Tom even took off his hat, and it seemed then a thing even less than ash, less than the charred remnant of itself, but rather nacreous and aglow, as if Tom hisself was more and more a creature of moonlight.

Kalin returned his attention to Landry. She was waitin for his eyes. *Tom said you was so good with a gun, it frightened the heck out of him.*

Now hold on a moment! Tom said, returnin to hisself a bit and even grinnin some.

But he didn't say he was frightened, did he? Kalin asked Landry.

I sure as heck never said I was frightened, Tom insisted.

I could see he was worried for you. He said you said you was cursed and your momma was the one who cursed you and that you'd sworn to her to never touch a gun again, but he bein your best friend, why Tom just had to see you break that promise, if just once, if just in the name of practice. And you did it. Just the once. For him. And he said he was sorry to have seen you do it.

Tom chuckled some. *We dug up my daddy's H and R Sportsman. He'd got it comin back from the Korean War. He had to hitchhike home from Seattle and bought it off the fella who gave him a ride across Nevada. You didn't care.*

Is he contradictin me? Landry asked.

No. He's just rememberin how it weren't about the gun for me.

I don't follow.

That's okay.

But I wanna understand.

Kalin scratched his face some, slumped some too, neither consultin Tom nor the coals, until he finally made the confession he'd never made to anyone else before, not even to Tom. *For me it ain't about the weapon. Or even the aimin. It's about killin.*

Killin?

Kalin nodded.

Landry felt certain she'd laugh, and even tried to do so, but her mouth dried up, and her chest tightened, and there weren't no room in her throat for amusement. Landry had too good an ear too, perfect, Tom would say, to not hear the trueness in Kalin's voice: no pride either, no fear, no confusion. But the scariest part? The sound of his resignation.

Tom said he tossed up three Altoids. You shot them all. It galled him.

You turned them into little clouds, Tom spoke up. *I did use the word gall.*

But it was how the horses reacted later, Landry continued. *They wouldn't come near you. Not that day. Not for days after. Tom said he'd never seen you so shaken, and he felt real bad for makin you do it even if it weren't but some everyday plinkin about like we all done growin up.*

I regret that day, Kalin said.

I'm glad Navidad and Mouse came back to you, Landry added, finally lyin back, findin above where their tarps hung, in a patch of sky briefly untormented by the storm, a momentary glitter of stars.

Some folks say the universe up there goes on forever, Landry said then. *I used to think forever was an impossible thing to imagine. But now I think it's the opposite. That there's a place beyond the stars that just stops? With nothin after it either? Not even nothin? That seems way harder to imagine.*

She ain't but got to imagine what's in her own head, Tom said dryly.

Kalin weren't studyin the stars.

I still don't understand how you cannot be concerned with aimin and hittin things anyways, Landry still had to bring up.

Kalin sighed. *If it ain't no more about speeds or angles or distances, if it ain't about one place in particular, then nothin's outta reach. At least that's how I think about it.*

This time Landry did laugh and Kalin didn't mind. He'd never cease to love the sound of her laughter.

And that right there, Kalin, Tom announced now and with some glee, *is how you and I are near the same! We both know what it feels like when nothin's outta reach, though in my case there ain't nothin that seems worth the reach.*

What about the horses?

I reckon they're the exception. Maybe that's why I keep clingin to y'all. And with that Tom stood up and returned to Ash.

What's Tom sayin now? Landry asked, her voice gettin smaller.

Kalin watched his friend find stillness among the horses.

He's whistlin.

What I'd give to hear that, just once more.

Saturday

Chapter Sixteen
"The Erville Family Mortuary"

Except for the lull in rain that came around midnight, the flood would not abate. Old Porch rose well before dawn and noted the water upon the valley and clouds upon the mountains, and he didn't give a hoot. He'd known worse plenty of times. The chase was in his veins.

He filled the kettle and dug out an enamel campfire mug and some Nescafé, not that there was a need for caffeine. Old Porch was as awake as his boys were still held under by the laws of deepest slumber. As he waited for the water to boil, Old Porch paced the halls, slowin some by the various doors if just to savor in their variously splayed legs and blanket-tangled dreams their vulnerability. Even Hatch, the most alert, was out cold, or so the stillness of that black chamber where the boys' mother once slept misinformed Old Porch.

Old Porch lingered the longest in that doorway, knowin for a fact that Hatch was the fiercest of them all, fiercer than even him, and yet here before the likes of him, in such a dull and ordinary moment, his eldest could so easily suffer instant obsolescence without ever knowin either the cause or the taste of the extinguishin. And Old Porch knew he had well within hisself the capacity to deliver such a blow, had possessed it since birth, far as he could tell, and feelin it now still so alive, why that tightened his eyes, pumped extra his heart. These boys were his, and but for him they carried on.

By the time the kettle started its sputterin sough, Old Porch had come to learn that Egan weren't in no room he'd inspected nor on the livin room sofa. Only when dumpin tablespoons of Nescafé into that red mug did he spot Egan's note on the counter, sayin how he and Billings would be at the canyon entrance come first light and they weren't waitin more than fifteen minutes for Kelly and Hatch if they was aimin to join. Old Porch took down a black gulp and disregarded the heat on his throat. He was pleased to see Egan ahead of him, ahead of them all. Given a contest of men batterin rocks on skulls, out of all of them, Egan stood the best chance of emergin scarred but victorious. The real horseradish.

Old Porch grabbed an apple and headed out back. He paid the drench no mind. He let Mr. Bucket out first. On the way to the plant, they paused by the paddocks, Effy trottin up from the far end. Old Porch shared his apple with her before continuin on. Mr. Bucket whined then for havin nothin to eat, and Old Porch gave him a hard shove with the side of his boot. Old Porch didn't tolerate whinin from no one, especially an animal, especially Mr. Bucket.

The raincoat Old Porch had flung over his head kept his back dry, and mostly his feet stayed dry too in their tall boots, but against the water kickin up off the mud, the raincoat was useless. His legs took in the wet, the cold too, cold enuf to ache his bones, but Old Porch welcomed it. There weren't no chase and sure as heck no fight worth its salt without sufferin. Better to know it now than later, when the shock might stumble you up. His boys might sleep oblivious before Death's parade. Not Old Porch.

Inside the plant, Old Porch hung up the raincoat and finished the apple, givin the squeeze chute for stunnin animals a passin glance as he strode across the floor to where they drained the animals, pleased to see that was scrubbed good, his tools too, the sight of which twitched his muscles alive with the memory of their use. He stepped over the rail groove, past the pluck box and viscera cart. In a locker he pulled loose a bag with bones set there for Mr. Bucket. He dug out a big one and found some pleasure watchin the Rottweiler have at it. No whinin now. The batter of rain on the metal ruf and the mustiness ghostin the corners seemed just the goadin Old Porch needed to get to his office.

Fer the next two hours, he sat at his desk and he chased. First he called the office of Senator Hays and left a message with the answerin service; then he tried twice to wake Kevin Moffet at home but got his machine both times. Next Old Porch called a few airlines to get prices for his trip to D.C. He finally booked a Wednesday flight on United direct to Washington National Airport. If the Kalin kid and the Gatestone girl weren't already buried, they'd be gone by tomorrow at the latest.

He figured they'd hold Russel's funeral on Monday. Maybe Tuesday. Old Porch reconsidered the calendar. Had he been hasty? Was a Wednesday departure too soon? He had no choice. The vote and meetings were all on Thursday.

Next he figured he better hound the senator with another call. He drained the last cold sip of Nescafé as he started dialin. Only then did he realize the day. He felt the fool callin the senator's office on a Saturday mornin. He'd call Monday. He'd call on Tuesday. He weren't gonna let up until Senate Bill 1245 was signed into law.

Old Porch could've returned to the house then, at least for a refill of somethin hot, but instead he continued to chase, prioritizin and reprioritizin paperwork on Four Summits, letters from representatives and state senators. A letter from Senator Hays sat atop one pile. Another pile held the bank letters surfeit with the kind of enthusiastic praise that seemed to all but assure the loans required to develop a mountain.

In truth the absolute unlikelihood of Senate Bill 1245 ever passin never crossed Old Porch's mind. Not once. Plenty have surmised that as churchless a churchgoer as Old Porch was, he was still religious in this regard: cultivatin the faith needed to see him through to the dominion of his imperial dreams. *It just showed how much of that old pioneerin stock Orwin Porch come from,* Harlan Webber would in later days declare. *Or Church stock,* Hollis Robertson would argue.

From Old Porch's perspective, he'd donated enuf time and enuf money to get enuf attention to see enuf progress that the passage of that land-liberatin bill had acquired an inevitablity that made Four Summits seem merely an axiomatic result. It was the right thing, the just thing. The state needed it, the community needed it, he needed it. If that weren't enuf, what else was there?

And so for the past three years Old Porch had put in order a way to leverage the Porch Meats assets toward somethin far greater, what would also finally secure that Indian Hills mansion that he and his boys deserved: a basketball court, a steam room and sauna, an indoor swimmin pool, wing after wing of Capuan comfort, with big garages, guesthouses, and perched high enuf up to overlook Orvop, all of Utah Valley, like he was their king, an ascendancy that would finally deliver the long legacy of Porches to a station befittin their trials, what each and every one of them was entitled to, especially Old Porch.

At one point Mr. Bucket, stretched out beside the old space heater near Old Porch's feet, barked in a dream and then barked a second time before the dream bore him down under again. He needed a walk. He needed a dawn feed. Old Porch nudged the dog's belly with his boot tip and then called Kevin Moffet. Once again a machine picked up; once again Old Porch left a message.

Back in the '50s, Robert Earl Holding had got hisself from the Coveys that motel-gas station, Little America, and from there found his way to wealth in oil and hotels. Old Porch's only motel, The Saucy in Nevada, was a bust, full of folks who'd put the fright in even Billings, if just fer the foulness on them. Minin had been another bust. But truckin and general predial proclivities had gotten Old Porch results. Everyone knew R. Earl had his Sun Valley in Idaho but Old Porch had recently got wind that the multimillionaire was now sniffin around for ski resorts in Utah. Old Porch meant to beat him to it. Beat them all to it. Alva Butler could have his town, Old Porch would have the mountains.

More calls to the East Coast ensued, none successful, until Old Porch finally stood up. Through the dirty panes of his window he faced the mornin light just now filterin its ruinous gray through a rain that kept pourin down with all the diluvial purpose of a dissatisfied God.

Kelly best already be gone from the house to meet Egan. Old Porch meant to murder him if he weren't, and he'd fer sure take a belt to anyone still in bed or otherwise lollin about. That went for Hatch too. Let them pray for the belt; let them know the belt a mercy.

Sean, Shelly, Woolsey, and Francis would need to work the main canyon trail, keepin eyes on law enforcement and rangers but mostly lookin for proof that the kids were dead. And even then, unless they'd laid eyes on the corpses, Old Porch wanted Egan, Kelly, and Billings up on the high slopes to make double-sure that despite Billings's doubts the Kalin kid had failed to ride out of that bedlam of fallin rubble. And if he had managed to do the impossible, why then Egan, Kelly, and Billings would need to get up to Kirk's Cirque.

Hatch, of course, would be somewhere in the mix, which was as much a blessin as it was still a problem. Unlike Egan and Kelly, and Billings, who Old Porch was sure about, there weren't no gettin around the fact that Hatch was still a sworn officer of the law and might not look the way that needed lookin, or even take the shot that needed takin, might even get in the way of one, even though it was on behalf of his dead little brother. But Old Porch also knew he needed Hatch's skills. He just couldn't be sure. Was Hatch with the law of that badge or was he livin by Porch law?

The density of these future considerations lay so thick upon him that Old Porch plumb forgot his raincoat as he marched back to the house, in his clutch that enamel campfire mug, like he might use it to brain anyone he happened to pass along the way. Mr. Bucket trailed behind, dutifully, cautiously. He weren't a stupid dog. Anyone with a half cent of sense could see by the way Old Porch's blue-gray eyes kept dartin back and forth, fast as the rain was fallin, with them wrecked teeth sawin back and forth even faster, that this here Old Porch was now full to the brim with ire. Anyone with a greater sense than what cents can never amount to would know that Old Porch depended on that ire to keep his personal momentum hurlin hisself ahead with no backward glances allowed.

Orvop alum Gilbert Gatenby, an associate professor in classics at the University of Wisconsin, would in 2005 while on sabbatical in London joke that Orpheus could've learned a thing or two from Old Porch about not lookin back: *Eurydice would've made it out of Hades alive.* His friend and colleague Annette Kaplar, on sabbatical in Buenos Aires, would agree but argue that Orpheus in the mold of Old Porch would've not only never looked back durin the ascent out of Hades he'd never have looked back afterward either: *Eurydice might as well have been left in Hades for all Orpheus Porch would've cared. Maybe, though, that's how Ginny*

Ward with her mother got outta their hell: Old Porch never gave a darn. Both also agreed that it was hard to defend Old Porch as *an agathokakological creature,* though many would keep tryin to do just that. Harvel Kurst, who'd somehow nosed in on one of these conversations, would declare proudly that he couldn't understand a lick of what either was sayin except that Gatenby and Kaplar was hot for each other, which weren't true, but there you have it.

And then Old Porch stopped dead in his tracks, just like that, not even a dozen steps from the dryness of his back porch, just standin there in the soak, wearin only his garment top, struck dumb by the rampage now breachin the limits of his mind, what he had to do, what he had to protect, and at the same time feelin an illness upon him, over which he had no say, a risin fever, what no amount of chargin or ragin, swingin, scratchin too, bitin if he had to, was gonna evade: the dark dream of Wednesday night, the biggest blur of all, Russel's end comin at him, refusin to stay put, to stay down, bubblin up like the bile after a bad drunk can keep comin up for days, even now burnin Old Porch's throat.

He wobbled. Deep puddles on either side of him kept splashin up a second rain, commandin him to do more than falter; fall was more like it, fall and kneel and beg for forgiveness, which Old Porch would not do, struck then by the rare recollection of an uncle of his denyin him pecuniary relief that to Old Porch now weren't nothin but back then was everythin: *Orwin, you've found pleasure in cruelty. Now you're disappointed that, unlike my brother, I won't further your lessons in cruelty and so justify more cruel acts on your part. Instead Orwin, I aim to teach you hardship.* Old Porch had near fallen to his knees then and begged, somethin he swore after to never repeat. He'd kept that vow too, and he sure weren't gonna break it now.

Though to stay on his feet, Old Porch still had to throw out his arms as if keepin balance on the deck of some huge heavin ship. And the longer he stood there, however contorted and disoriented, no matter the cold and oily rain seepin through his pants, Mr. Bucket right there if keepin well away, why the more Old Porch found in hisself the grit he'd need to keep goin, and boy would he need plenty, because Old Porch hadn't forgotten Riddle neither, whose sudden reappearance, followed by an innocent recountin of Russel's arrival in the midst of that crapulent night, would to put it nicely cast all Old Porch's claims into question.

Old Porch's guts full-on revolted then, and up it come, provin hisself no better than Kelly's weak innards, the same innards, except Old Porch refused the comin, he weren't no weak sister, first catchin the molten divulgence in his throat, like the mean thing he was, forever set against every riot or act of disobedience come from within, or without, even as the vomit filled his mouth, Old Porch still forcin it back down, refusin even the retch or gag, swallowin again, swallowin more, because his guts would sure as heck not rule over him. Nothin would rule over him. That was fer darned sure.

Doran N. Tolan, Brighton-born but later in her life provin a fairly permanent fixture in the Vienna art scene, would in the early '90s create what many considered the very quintessence of that moment. Others would try to match her, with watercolors, oils, admixtures of materials too numerous to list, though laminate leather was in there as well, and in one other case marble, many of these pieces also bearin the title: *Old Porch in the Rain.* Tolan's bronze, however, somehow captured Orwin Porch in a way that the other works didn't, that one hand clutchin the mug against his cramped belly, the other hand reachin up for somethin to hold on to and wield. By both posture and unfinished action, the statue succeeded somehow in conveyin how a mind knows itself as not worth spit if it can't command those very same hands to seize somethin close and make out of it a weapon.

And that still weren't the end of this moment for Old Porch. He was squintin down at the ground, growin more ashen with every breath he raked in out in that miserable rain, because it seemed to him he was observin the water around his boots startin to sink away, revealin in the turmoil of remainin mud a fissure widenin with every second, augurin what had no choice but to arrive, Old Porch just knew it, that moment when Russel would appear, disgorged from the earth, clawin his way out of Death, and all the more determined the more he could feel his father's thoughts fixed upon him. And so Old Porch raised then that hand with that enamel mug and waited. He even spat. He knew enuf about fear to pay it no mind. Same goes for any ghost. But if it did come to a ghost, Old Porch wouldn't hesitate to beat Russel back into the grave a second time. With a coffee mug if he had to.

Dad! Sean shouted from the back door. *You okay?*

Of course I'm okay! What the heck's that supposed to mean? Old Porch snarled, though it pleased him at least to see Sean up and awake.

There's a U.S. senator on the phone for you.

Old Porch took the call in the kitchen, with Sean standin right there, and Mr. Bucket by his side, like both of them were mighty impressed, even if Old Porch could see neither one had a clue what it meant to get a call from a U.S. Senator on a Saturday mornin.

This is Orwin Porch.

Goshdarn it, Orwin! bawled Senator Hays. *I watched that terrible disaster up the canyon all yesterday! I'm watchin more of it right now!* And then he quieted. *Just awful. Such a tragedy. If we can trust the media on this, and that is always a big if, at least the ones that done this heinous wrong to your dear Russel got their comeuppance. Hippie fools might call it karma, but if this isn't Our Lord and Heavenly Father cuttin down the foulests, well then I don't know why I even go to church.*

I don't presume to know the Lord's business, but then I'm not a U.S. senator.

Old Porch got the laugh he wanted.

Orwin, I admire you for havin the capacity to joke durin such times!

Little else is left to me, Senator Hays.

I do understand that. I do, the senator answered darkly. *Tell me, are we sure those two are the ones who murdered your boy? Are we sure they're dead?*

That's what I keep hearin. Me and my sons are gonna head up into the canyon now. Old Porch nodded at Sean. *Find out about our horses. Do whatever we can do to help.*

Oh my, I do not mean to keep you, Orwin.

I know it's Saturday, and I'm grateful to hear from you.

Yes, Orwin, and there is a reason for that.

Orwin didn't care one bit for what he heard in the senator's phrasin, not to mention the throat-clearin that followed. And just like the vomit he'd refused, Old Porch refused the senator, cuttin him off right then and there with how hard it had been, with Russel gone, his little throat cut, his young life betrayed, and by just a little leak, and weren't that the worst of it?, because of some fluid goin out of him, not even a bucket's worth, what we piss out daily, he was gone, permanently, and why?, on account of what is blessed in this great land of ours, what is right, what Russel loved, what so many folks love, them goshdarned beautiful horses!, stolen away, and by some no-good out-of-stater, a newcomer who had no understandin about what he had no business messin with, what he should've just kept clear of, what he had no claim on but what he killt for, and that right there was the awfulness, the tragedy, the personal devastation each Porch would have to live with from here on out, to the grave, with only a pale assurance that any one of them might see Russel beyond the grave, God willin, should their Heavenly Father see fit to permit the Porches to join His table, all of which was just the start of it; because this devastation would go well beyond one family's loss, impactin Orvop, Utah County, the very state Senator Hays hisself served, Porch not pullin any punches here, remindin and emphasizin how the senator was beholden to their state, beholden to Old Porch, Old Porch makin it clear how he weren't the only one, seein as how Utah had had it up to here with outsiders meddlin in their affairs, the federal government bein the most obvious example, deprivin us of our land, deprivin us of our right to expand, deprivin us of our livelihoods, deprivin us of our goshdarned traditions!, with Four Summits doin what Utah needed for Utah, securin fiduciary well-bein on behalf of state, county, city, its citizens, and, yes, sure, one citizen in particular, whose family had worked these very same lands for well over a century.

Old Porch had hot acid in his mouth by the time he was done, not to mention wet in both eyes, the whole performance sure winnin Sean over, who was also teary-eyed; maybe even Mr. Bucket was teary-eyed too. Sean was pattin Old Porch on the back, mutterin how they wouldn't stop til Russel's killers were dead and buried. Nor was Senator Hays unmoved. Old Porch heard it throughout his recountin, the sighs, the breaths, especially as he expanded his personal loss into a loss for the state, requirin the senator then to take a very careful extra breath before decidin what to say next.

Maybe Old Porch should've bit his tongue then and just listened, but he never did have that kind of patience. He made it clear that Russel's funeral was next week and Old Porch would be dead from the burial if it weren't for Senate Bill 1245. No way would he not be flyin east come Wednesday.

And it would be a fine thing to see you here, Orwin, Senator Hays said, finally gettin a word in edgewise, adoptin now that shirtsleeve tone that had won him so many votes. *I promise you the best lunch on the hill, but—* The senator paused, this time near baitin Old Porch to cut him off again. Senator Hays weren't green, and this sure as heck weren't his first filibuster. *But, Orwin, there ain't gonna be no vote on 1245. Baker won't bring it up on the floor. I've raised holy heck, but this is Washington, D.C. It's as much procedure as it is personal. We can try again, and we will try again, but it won't be this year.*

We had the support! Old Porch pointlessly objected.

We did, but now that's changed.

I understand that, Shane! I understand! But what happened? What?!

The senator did not respond, but Sean and Mr. Bucket sure backed away then.

You think it's this business on the news? Old Porch continued to press.

Mr. Porch, a bill like this goes well beyond what the likes of you or me have in mind for the world. It sure as heck goes well beyond Utah.

I understand, Senator.

Though Old Porch didn't, not really, and it weren't like he weren't aware that the interests of Idaho, Wyoming, and Montana, among other states, was involved. What weren't sinkin in was how what was of paramount importance to him, the Four Summits development, had so little bearin on the success of Senate Bill 1245. So disorientin was the triviality of his aim that fer a moment he didn't even know who he was talkin to, as if Senator Hays weren't really Senator Hays anymore, like the senator was now less a livin figure and more some fadin feature of light, if even that; as if all this had never been more substantial than a dream you couldn't remember, and that went for the laws of the nation too, Old Porch witnessin this emptyin out so clearly that were it not for Sean and the by now very concerned Mr. Bucket, why Old Porch might've given in to the dizziness and just collapsed.

Orwin, go mourn your son.

Old Porch hung up. He would still go to D.C. next week. He would hold the senator to that lunch. Old Porch would *show those yellow-bellied politicians who was really in charge! Oh, he'd show them!*

Dad? Sean asked. *Are you okay?* Which was the second time this mornin that this whelp of his had asked him the very same question. Old Porch wouldn't have it. He'd hurl this enameled mug at the worried boy. Aim at his face. Give him another scar to remember him by. But, see, Old Porch, even as his fingers knotted around the handle, could still recognize that he had in fact been babblin. That he weren't in fact okay at all. So he smacked his lips, gave Sean a hard nod, and then threw the mug hard as he could at the sink, flecks of the broken red enamel eventually settlin around the drain.

It was 7:27 a.m.

K elly walked in then through the front door and, even worse, was followed soon after by Egan, who plopped down in one of the kitchen chairs and began unlacin his boots. Billings came in last.

Is there coffee? Egan asked, and Old Porch near went and fetched that mug he'd just thrown to throw at him.

Why are you back?

Uncle Conrad's closed the canyon. Too much water. Not even half the volunteers showed, and the half that did turned heel as soon as they arrived. Rangers think we'll have a window around noon before the next storm comes through.

This rain stopped you? Old Porch was seethin.

There's a river at the bottom. We can spend all mornin not gettin past First Bridge, or we can wait and still get to the cirque by three.

Ain't that just another piece of crap in my cereal! Old Porch growled, startin to throw open cupboards, like sayin cereal had made him hunger for it, even if there weren't no cereal to be found.

Where's Hatch? Don't tell me that maggot's still asleep. Sean, go drag your hero brother out here.

Sure thing, Dad, Sean answered, feelin lucky to have a reason to get outta there. Mr. Bucket followed Sean.

Woolsey wandered down into the kitchen then, shirtless, sockless, still in his nighttime shorts, still rubbin the sleep from his eyes. The tape on his fingers had come off durin the night, and the swellin and bruises weren't a pretty sight. Last night's game had also delivered blunt aches to his shoulders, ribs, a knee, somethin even in his hips that felt bound up and brittle, all in the name of victory, a trivial victory compared to the pain now enwrappin the household, demandin his silence, what Woolsey at once obeyed.

Shelly weren't near as bright. When he slunk down in green-and-black sweats, barefoot, he went one step further than Egan and right off complained that there weren't no coffee ready. He and Sean shared an apartment near Westridge Elementary but had crashed last night in their old rooms upstairs. Shelly knuckled that stye in his eye, not much better, before turnin to the same cupboards Old Porch had already been at, gripin about no cereal, before headin to the wall where the rotary phone hung, where he dialed his girl's number.

Don't worry Pa, Egan said then, workin up an easy grin. *We'll still be the first ones on the trail.*

You know, Kelly said, in the midst of brewin up some Maxwell House; he loathed Nescafé. *We could just take the trails above Indian Hills, go in right under Squaw Peak.*

Egan liked that. *We wouldn't have to fuss none then with the entrance.*

It'll add some hours to the climb, though, Billings said then.

Both Egan and Kelly knew that was true.

If we go by foot, Egan responded.

You think the ATVs can handle that way? Kelly asked.

I don't see why not.

What abouts when we get to where the slide was at?

Even if we have to park them there, we'll have saved a lot of time. We'll still make the cirque by three or four latest.

Old Porch relaxed a bit.

And then Francis appeared carryin a big box of cornflakes.

There's more milk in the plant fridge and frozen OJ in the freezer. Francis was already turnin around for a second trip. *And I think I saw a box of pancake batter.*

Francis, I'll come with you, Woolsey offered, mostly because he wanted to get away from his dad's surly mood, but also because he got how, out of all the rest, Francis was sufferin the greater grief over Russel. Sure, Russel and Francis had fought plenty over the years, but they was also the closest in age and had always stuck together when

577

the fightin turned against them, especially when Kelly, fer example, wanted to demonstrate on Francis some new wrestlin move. Russel would do his best to come to the rescue, and in those circumstances even a little distraction did serve as some kind of rescue. Woolsey was only one year older than Francis, but he was way stronger and meaner, with three years of varsity wrestlin already under his belt. Woolsey had already whooped Kelly enuf times on the livin room carpet to prove it weren't luck. The last time Kelly had declared *Smear the queer!* on Woolsey, Kelly was the one who'd wound up on his back on Sister Avery's front lawn. Woolsey, still shirtless and sockless, snatched up a raincoat and hurried out after Francis into the rain.

See if there's bacon, Egan barked after them without lookin up.

Eggs too! Shelly yelled, also without lookin around, one beefy forearm flung up on the wall above the phone. *I wanna find the bodies,* he said back into the receiver, his lips barely movin to expel such mumbles. *We'll get up there . . . Sure we will . . . I don't care about that . . . No idea, Liz . . . Liz! I already said: I got no idea.*

Shelly was tryin to keep his voice soft, but, boy, did it grab Old Porch the wrong way. Old Porch tried to drown it out too, fillin a blue bowl with cornflakes, finishin the milk in the carton, and when that weren't enuf usin the coffee and milk from Kelly's mug, Kelly smart enuf not to object.

It weren't helpin that with the exception of Woolsey and Francis, the lot of them were stayin clustered in the small kitchen that mornin, big as they was too. Even Billings, who'd normally seek out some distance, stayed close to the counter, waitin to get his Maxwell House, which still weren't a good enuf excuse. It's a minor mystery why these Porches hadn't already moved out into the dinin area. Some folks have wondered if there weren't some darkness still lingerin there from last night, brought on by talk of the rockfall, of the Kalin kid, of what was really out there. Trewartha Pope, for four summers a roadie, for four decades an HVAC specialist, would in 2034 declare: *They stayed clear of that dinin room because it harbored a memory of their future that they just couldn't face.*

Old Porch hovered the bowl by his chin, shoveled a spoonful of coffee-drenched cornflakes into his mouth, and chewed as loud as he could, like the sound might drown out the senator's news. He at least got his boys' uneasy attention when he slammed the bowl back down, and even that did him no good; he couldn't stand havin even a one of them in his field of vision, turnin his back to them then to stare out the window above the sink, first at the mountains that had never before seemed so unreal, the thick tumult of clouds hidin Katano-gos so effectively, he doubted it was even there. His own front lawn here, he hated it, the sidewalk bouncin with rain too. What he'd give for a sunny day, a high-noon sun and sky returnin this valley to its simple outlines, instead of this driveway spazzin out with water, the street too, shiny and slick, and empty, except now for this rust-pocked pickup crawlin by at a speed that wouldn't challenge a turtle, head-lights on high, wipers on full, the driver still pokin his head out his window like that was gonna help him see better. *What an idjit.* Orvop was full of them. Lord how Old Porch hated Orvop sometimes.

Egan and Kelly had come around to the window to see what Old Porch was mumblin after and at least found there a good laugh.

What the heck does he think he's doin? Kelly asked.

His glasses are wetter than his windshield, Egan added.

This town's full of imbeciles! Old Porch coughed out, though there was now a smile in there somewhere, what became a laugh as he took in another mouthful of coffee-soaked cornflakes, feelin a change, fer a moment feelin some closeness with his two boys.

Hatch ain't anywhere, Sean announced then, returnin to the kitchen. *I checked the whole house. It's like he didn't even sleep here. His bags are on Momma's bed, but his gear's gone.*

His truck ain't out there either, Kelly pointed out, Old Porch only now realizin his mistake: Hatch was already out there. That sure pleased Old Porch, even as he tightened his grip on that bowl of cereal, turnin back to the room, fixin his focus on the oblivious Shelly, who was still stacked there against the wall, talkin and talkin and talkin.

No one's sleepin here until we know fer sure that the ones that killt Russel are dead . . . That might be true, Liz. We'll figure it out.

Old Porch set his infected thumb against the edge of that bowl, and though it squalled with pain from the pressure, he added more pressure.

Nah, Shelly continued. *Are you high? Mr. Bucket couldn't sniff out a rot carcass on a hot day even if it was in his feed bowl. I'll sniff them out myself! Especially the Gatestone girl!* Shelly was laughin now. *Now don't play dumb. I'm warnin you, Liz! That's a fact. That's the Lord's shape of things.* Shelly laughed more, laughed louder. *Don't make me say it, Liz. Don't . . . You know they smell different . . . I know she's Samoan . . . She's part Samoan. Plus Samoans, Tongans, they stink too—*

The blue cereal bowl exploded against the wall, the impact just missin Shelly's head, though pieces of ceramic knicked at his face, coffee-milk and soggy cornflakes too. And that weren't nothin compared to the fist in his hair that took him by surprise, wrenchin him from the phone, wrenchin with such great force that Shelly ripped the receiver clean out of the base of the phone.

Now Shelly towered over his old man, but tall's got nothin on meanness, especially when Old Porch has you twistin backwards, at the same time choppin at your knees with a bootheel. Old Porch dropped that nationally ranked wrestler like he weren't nothin but a bucket of cement on a ladder. Shelly went down hard too, and his daddy still weren't lettin go of his hair, kept twistin it, yankin it, til Old Porch's wrecked teeth hovered just a breath above Shelly's face like he was about to eat it.

Don't you ever talk that way in my house! Old Porch roared. *Especially about no Gatestone!*

That free hand was now a fist, what Old Porch meant to follow through with to somethin bloodier, but Kelly and Egan got at him first, neither able to conceal the fear that had sent them there so fast; and Shelly catchin sight of such terror on his brothers' faces, which likely scared him more than their seethin patriarch, got extra gaunt as he threw up his arms to shield his face from the kicks Old Porch was now tryin to land as he was dragged away.

What we got against the Gatestones, or anyone else for that matter, ain't never gonna be summed up as Porches bein racists! Do you hear me?! Old Porch continued to yell. *I EVER hear you say such a thing again, any of you!, why I'll bleed you out myself and slice up your guts too in the trippery room.*

Amen, Hatch said, enterin through the back door, geared up in camo, boots, a pack on his shoulder, a rifle in one hand, a big jug of maple syrup in the other. He strode up right beside Old Porch, amused plenty at the sight of Shelly, still on the floor, still with a look of shock pasted on his face. It weren't lost on him either how uneasy Egan and Kelly looked, Billings too, though Hatch failed to see any complicity there. Not a thought by Hatch in those moments wandered even a mile near the truth.

Woolsey and Francis came in then, loaded up with cartons of eggs, pancake batter, two gallons of milk, more cans of coffee, and four packages of Porch Meats bacon. They sure hitched their gait a spell, beholdin Shelly on his hands and knees, head hung, cornflakes in his hair, tryin to wipe up with his hands the mess of brokenness that used to be a bowl, but Old Porch motioned them toward the counter.

Finally! their father declared. *Finally some good news!*

Francis sure worked miracles that mornin. It's likely none of the brothers ever really registered just how good the gettin was, but the mood sure lightened. Francis dashed cinnamon in the coffee, drizzled vinegar and honey on the bacon. He whisked the pancake batter so smooth that what he griddled puffed up like they was made of air. He warmed the maple syrup, melted the butter. The scrambled eggs he beat through with cream and butter, plus salt and fresh ground pepper from the big mill Old Porch never touched, plus a little nutmeg and some chili flakes. By the time he added the grated cheese the eggs had become more than eggs. Francis even did somethin with a blender and the Minute Maid concentrate so that the OJ didn't taste like it came from a cardboard tube. And all that weren't nothin compared to how Francis, fer a moment free of his grief, managed to time it out so the coffee was hot, the pancakes was hot, the bacon was hot, the scrambled eggs was just creamy, steamy goodness.

Last gets least, Sean shouted at some point. But there weren't no *least* this mornin. There were seconds, there were thirds, and nothin went to waste, though as Shelly still grumbled, *It all goes to waste.*

Woolsey too played an elemental part in this unheralded feast. After Hatch had gone ahead and retaped, reset really, his fingers, which he'd done quick and well, better than any doctor, or so Woolsey swore, with Hatch sayin that the bones at least in the one pinkie was likely fractured if not busted, Woolsey took on the role of waiter, even drapin a dish towel over his left arm fer laughs, showin no regard neither for his hurt hand that still had to help balance the various dishes and mugs, and all the while affectin an array of surprisin voices that got even Old Porch grinnin. *Taste the high country,* he'd deliver like in the commercial. *It's no downstream coffee. It's no city OJ. It's Old Porch magic!* Or soundin a little like Walt Garrison: *Just a pinch between my cheek and gum and I get full tobacco pleasure.* It weren't only Woolsey's sudden goofiness, almost boyishness, that got his family chucklin but the ease with which he made sure everyone got their breakfast. How he managed so many plates in one go! How he could move his feet that way! Woolsey's agility had always been complimented upon, always chalked up to his wrestlin skills, his football skills, but for this hour here, for anyone who was payin attention, it was clear the boy's talents went way beyond a mat and a two-minute clock or the old gridiron. Of course no one was payin attention, though at the most recent FFA Orvop High night, right when the line dancin and square dancin were done, plenty of cowboys remarked how they never knew Woolsey could dance like that. *No one we ever seen, fer sure no one from around here, could dance THAT good! It was, well like, WOW!* Andrea Gunther would declare many years later in São Paulo. She would recall then the gym echoin with Moe & Joe, Johnny Lee, Hank Williams,

Glen Campbell, Kris Kristofferson, Willie of course, Merle and Dolly of course, but also plenty of the Allman Brothers and Crystal Gayle for the slow songs. *That boy would've shined on somethin like Dancin with the Stars or ended up on Broadway or maybe even been in the ballet. Can you imagine some fella outta Orvop goin on to do ballet? Can you imagine a Porch?! It's just too sad.* Veldon Brower wouldn't disagree with Gunther either; nor would Hollis Robertson or Connie Snell.

Hatch was the only one who said aloud what everyone else there was feelin: how this was one of the finest meals he'd had in a long time. No one objected. Old Porch even sought out Francis then with his eyes and gave him a nod, which did a whole world of good for that poor boy.

Hatch cleaned his plate three times, makin sure to spare Mr. Bucket some scraps too, as well as scratch him good between the ears until the dog settled under his chair. Only then did he get around to tellin everyone about his mornin. He confirmed what Egan had said: Isatch Canyon floor was flooded at the bottom, the main trail under a good six inches, and that was where the goin was easy. Hatch had never seen the canyon walls shed so much water. The lower bridges, if they weren't underwater, were piled high with brambles and debris, makin that way not worth the distance an hour would earn.

As was the case for Egan, the park was closed. Two Orvop police squad cars parked right in front of the locked gates made sure of that.

Old Porch stuck to shovelin in more pancakes and bacon along with big slugs of OJ. He listened singularly to Hatch but eyed the confident reportage only from the side. Just because the eats were good and the mood of his boys had lightened some didn't mean he was done throwin things or grabbin someone by the hair. He did glance at Egan, at Kelly, at Billings. They knew what Hatch must never know.

And then Hatch surprised him. Old Porch even smiled, even recognized his belly was full, happily so.

Hatch had started gripin about how even with his Texas badge, how in the name of Law Enforcement, as a courtesy at least, his entrance into the canyon had still been denied. Hatch, of course, respected their refusal, cheerfully askin them to alert him, *as a courtesy*, when he might participate in the search, even as he also reminded everyone that the Porches were still tryin to get back their horses. *You can bet your boots I gave them the cheeriest wave goodbye. No point sowin rancor. Of course, I didn't exactly drive away. I headed straight up into Oak Hills. As you all know, I ain't here as a representative of the Law. I'm here as a Porch. I'm here fer one thing and one thing alone,* and this part he whispered in a way that even put a chill to Old Porch's blood. *My little's brother's killer is gonna have to deal with me.*

Hatch then told how he'd parked north of 1450, geared up, and took off on foot over to the Bonneville shoreline path, from which he headed straight up the face of Agoneeya, no trail needed, *I ran it too,* until he was high enuf up to sight a clear lateral path along the right side of the canyon. *Likely where you all were,* Hatch said, noddin at Egan, Kelly, and Billings, *when you caught sight of the rockfall. I picked a higher line, though, and got farther along, at a faster pace too I expect. I got to where I could see well beyond where the earth had collapsed and gouged out a good part of the mountainside.* Hatch told them then how he'd continued to climb higher, still runnin, or so he kept claimin, his eyes now bright with the memory of it, the joy of such exertion, relatin how he eventually jogged across a wide gulley, slowin only when he was atop a good spur that led up to a low but prominent Agoneeya ridge.

Through his scope, Hatch could see Cahoon's Staircase had suffered a recent rockfall of its own, what would render that part of the canyon impassable for many years to come. *I couldn't see the cirque, but no question there's an easy-enuf way up if those cliffs, as we were speculatin, prove surmountable.* He noted also the numerous screes they'd have to cross. He couldn't estimate their stability. Hatch figured it was best to wait at least a few more hours before tryin that side of the canyon.

You're just sayin what Uncle Conrad told me at first light, what I told Dad before you got back. Egan made no effort to hide his disgust over this elaborate elocution resultin in basically nothin new.

Hatch grinned down at his plate, shakin his head slow enuf to make clear the dismissiveness he was communicatin. *Basically, Eges. Basically.* But then he looked up. *With one difference: I seen it all with my own eyes. I've registered the state of things and know exactly what we'll need to make a successful ascent, and where to start too. You, on the other hand, are just tellin us what a sheriff told you while he was at the same time tellin you to step off and scurry back home, which from what I can gather is exactly what you went and did.*

Even as Old Porch couldn't or wouldn't hold back a laugh, even if it did come out like a sharp cough, Hatch leveled a stare too that even Egan couldn't hold.

You done good, Hatch, Old Porch said, even pattin his eldest on the shoulder. It weren't lost on him that Hatch had not only got by the Law but, in scopin the way to the Katanogos cirque, had set barrel and a possible bullet's trajectory against the path, probably with a finger on the trigger too, somethin Old Porch was becomin so certain of that the warmth in his belly soon expanded pleasantly into his chest, even if in fact Hatch had not touched the trigger nor had his rifle at that moment carried a cartridge.

The part of the kitchen phone still attached to the wall started ringin then, but with a handset no longer attached, Francis had to run upstairs to see who it was. Old Porch's sense of good feelin continued to grow, especially since he was now certain that this was Senator Hays callin him back with news that Senate Bill 1245 was gettin the vote it deserved after all and of course it would pass. The phone quit its ringin, and Old Porch could hear Francis's voice answerin. The words were a muffle, which weren't the problem. The problem was how that squeaky voice kept on talkin and talkin and with more and more notes of questions stuck in there, which no senator, especially Senator Hays, would've tolerated for long, and then Francis was back down.

That was Mr. Erville. He says this afternoon is full up with funerals and such, but we can see Russel this mornin unless we want to wait until Monday. He'd normally make an exception for Sunday, but the home's gonna be closed as he and his family have to be away. I told him I'm goin there now. You all are welcome to join or not. Which was pretty much as near as Francis had ever come to plantin knuckles on his brothers, and his daddy too, though his hands made no fists. Old Porch rose up fast then, his fists clenched, though much to Francis's surprise he was standin up in approval.

We'll go now. Except for you, Billings. And I want everyone wearin a tie.

While the Porch boys got ready, Old Porch and Billings found a private moment out back in Old Porch's office, with Billings sayin first how he was plannin to run by Riddle's place again, and Old Porch pattin Billings on his shoulder like he'd just done to Hatch. Old Porch said he'd leave the plant door open.

Did you get yourself enuf to eat?

It is worth a mention here that as Old Porch and half his boys piled into the red-and-white Chevy, with the other half climbin into Hatch's black GMC Sierra, Orvop itself was gettin goin too on what would prove one heckuva Saturday, though in the end it wouldn't even compare to the Sunday that was right around the corner.

As the Porches drove over to the Erville Family Mortuary, the rain that had been with them since Wednesday worsened, slowin traffic, dancin every nylon spiderweb and Halloween witch. Woolsey, who had chosen to ride with Hatch, shivered at the sight of it, not because he was cold at that moment, Hatch was blastin the heater, but because of the memory of the cold at last night's football game between the Orvop High Bulls and the Salt Lake City South High School Bear Cubs. Fer sure Coach Pailey had expected Woolsey to be a no-show and had called up Jonah Bell from JV to fill the slot as startin linebacker. So as you can imagine, Coach Pailey, in fact the whole team, was shocked to find Woolsey at his locker suitin up. Woolsey hadn't even told none of his brothers except Francis, who'd looked at him like he was crazy, crazier still when he'd suggested that Francis come along to watch. And goin to play last night, goin alone, did feel a little crazy, but Woolsey had done it anyway, pilin into his Chevette with Billy Idol on the radio singin about dancin with hisself, which didn't make Woolsey smile, the coincidence of it, though it did make his toes tap. By the time Queen's *Crazy Little Thing Called Love* came on, he was well on his way to the high school. His brothers all loved *We Will Rock You* and *We Are the Champions,* but this here song was what had got him noddin in time, thumbs knockin the rhythm out on the wheel, what he'd never admit to any of his brothers, likin the song, especially to his dad, who only played Johnny Cash, *no bright colors on his back*. Here was music that made you move, really move, in ways you didn't know you could. Tears even came up when Woolsey realized that Russel had had an ear too for what went beyond what Orvop considered music.

Woolsey hadn't actually made up his mind to play until he had his shoulder pads on. Coach Pailey told him he was still gonna start Jonah Bell. It weren't a typical way for Woolsey to react. His father would've wanted him to fight the decision, and Woolsey mostly favored a fight, but somethin in the way the coach had said it and how Jonah Bell had come over to ask for any advice made it seem like the right choice. Woolsey didn't even mind sittin on the bench, findin the solitude there comfortin, even healin, even as the rain continued to bring down its nuisance affliction, a sudden gallop of gusty drenches followed by a stillness so cold, the field seemed certain to freeze, what the grass couldn't soak up on the verge of turnin to ice, transformin this contest of cleats and pads into a hockey game. Players' breaths were comin out as howls of fog, all of them huffin on their hands when they weren't grindin up the grass into awful mud. *When you play with the best, you become your best,* Coach Pailey told the team. But by halftime, with the Orvop High Bulls trailin the South Bear Cubs 0–3, Coach Pailey pulled Jonah Bell and put in Woolsey. And oh how that changed everythin. Woolsey's grief over Russel became the whole team's grief, and if Woolsey could go out there and bust his fingers up draggin down one runnin back after another, and eventually the quarterback, why then they all better give just as much as he was givin. Even when Woolsey weren't doin the sackin, he inspired others to play harder. South didn't score again, and with such a ferocious display of defensive determination, the Orvop offense finally got its act together and commenced a routin that would destroy South. By the fourth quarter the weather was a sideways hail briefly seein the field covered with white pellets, like the sky was suddenly a busted beanbag disgorgin its guts. The wind got so loud, players on both sides had to scream to get plays heard. The cold hurt, Woolsey's fingers hurt, but he still went helmet to helmet so hard the South quarterback went down and never got up. In the locker room, when Coach Pailey reconfirmed that Woolsey Porch was the game's MVP, everyone cheered. They raised him on their shoulders, they cried, they treated him like a hero. He was their hero. Later, two cheerleaders Woolsey had never said three words to gave him long hugs, and out of the blue Preot Ackley came over and gave him a hug too and then a long kiss on his cheek that, even though it was only on his cheek, why then tomorrow and every tomorrow after that arrived all at once, and they was all sunny and mild, and the pains of livin that surely must come were still bested by the rewards that livin also redeems. It felt so good, Woolsey didn't want to let go of her, and when he finally did and she was gone, he didn't want to leave. He even dreamed weirdly of returnin to the locker room and foldin hisself into his own locker and just stayin there forever and ever.

Darren Blicker found him at that moment. He wouldn't stop goin on about how great Woolsey had played, kept sayin it was like watchin water slip between cracks. *You're gonna go pro, Woolsey! Serious! I'm predictin All-State, full scholarship at the I, and after that the Dallas Cowboys, wherever you wanna go! Jim McMahon wouldn't be Jim McMahon if you were on the other team.* He got so reckless in his elation that Woolsey had to tell him to quit it. Woolsey was seriously annoyed too. He weren't under no illusion about his size. His brothers, from Hatch on down, made it clear what real size was. Still, Darren's excitement was hard to resist. This straw-haired, pimply friend even went on to apologize about gettin squirrelly when Woolsey had been havin words with that Kalin kid's mom, admittin then, even if he hisself didn't follow the logic of this, that Sondra Gatestone was to blame too.

And then Darren brought up what Coach Pailey and his other teammates had been goin on about as they was leavin: how the big slide up Isatch Canyon had supposedly killt the Kalin kid, the horses too, and even Landry Gatestone, the retellin of which got Darren Blicker really lathered up. Because he'd wanted to catch that Kalin kid hisself. He'd wanted to put him down in front of everyone. Darren even started takin swings at the night air as he stomped around the school parkin lot. And the Kalin kid weren't enuf: Darren was knockin down Kalin's mother and Landry Gatestone's mother too. *Both of them!* Woolsey couldn't have thought higher of Darren then because unlike all his teammates, Coach Pailey too, Darren was the only one who got what a misery this news was: because what feelin of justice did a fallin mountain deliver? Now the Porches had nothin left to do but mourn.

As Woolsey was drivin hisself home, he was at least certain of one thing: he didn't want to mourn. He wanted to fight and keep fightin.

What Woolsey didn't expect at that moment as he maneuvered his gut tub of a vehicle through them water-plastered Orvop streets, like some scuppered boat out on the reservoir, was how this risin ire of his, so hot, impotent, so futile, over Russel's killers already gone, with him never havin played a hand in that retribution, would so soon come face-to-face with both brotherly and fatherly approval, not only for playin in the game but for his injuries as well. Nowhere in Woolsey's mind did there live a notion that Old Porch would very soon sit beside him and take his wounded hands in his own scarred hands, gently carressin them, reassurin him by these lightest of touches that all would heal, that all that needs healin is worth the hurt, and how, goin further, Old Porch would then command Shelly, that brutal beef-head of a brother, to pour Woolsey his very own beer, get him some pie too, go so far as to promise a night out, all of it elatin though still nothin next to just feelin his father's hands holdin his own, so tentative, so cautiously lovin, repealin so absolutely, if only briefly, the fight that seemed innate in Woolsey, a touch Woolsey might've even asked for again when Death finally took hold of his other hand, maybe somethin Woolsey actually did ask for, or so plenty have speculated, includin Michelle Ploufe, born in Orvop and an alumna of Orvop High too, who in later years would teach English in Beijing of all places, who also reviled Stacey Sharma for no reason she ever shared, and who would create in the late '90s a piece on rice paper that sparinly detailed the hands of father and son touchin.

And as the heat in Hatch's truck finally began to take hold of him, relax him, Woolsey began to finally experience that Saturday mornin as aftermath. There weren't no more fight to be had, his hands would heal, they just had to look at Russel's body.

Though Hatch kept the radio off, local and state news stations were at that moment recappin the events of the slide with nothin new to show really except updates on the weather. Meteorologists were still anticipatin more storms stackin up on top of the present one, and along with another plunge in temperature, they was also warnin everyone to expect black ice. *If we're lucky, though, and I expect we will be, our mountains are gonna see a lot of snow,* one forecaster proclaimed, much to the joy of skiers throughout the state and outside the state.

But weather was just fer starters, and in truth no big deal, given that storms are what winter is about in Utah, generally welcomed by everyone, what grants a good season up on the slopes and pretty much vanishes after a few days down in the valley. Come 1983 no one would even remember these storms for their snowfall. It's just that on this weekend, with Halloween comin on Saturday, if date-wise landin on Sunday, with the Porch boy's death on everyone's mind, and now with news of the apparent burial of his assailants, the storm front for many an Orvop resident did seem to volume-up the menace overwhelmin the small city.

And like a fingernail to a scabbed mosquito bite, the myriad conversations around town kept returnin to the search for the bodies of them two accused of murderin Russel Porch. In fairness local news did attempt to keep that word *allegedly* in all their stories, though by the time Saturday mornin was gone, *allegedly* was gone too. By noon the narrative seemed a settled thing: Kalin March had murdered Russel Porch, and Landry Gatestone had helped out, because what the heck else was she doin if she weren't up to her neck in it?

Where this Kalin kid was concerned, Orvop High students had no reason to believe otherwise. He didn't go to no one's church, he didn't go to the seminary right adjacent to Orvop High, and in class he sure didn't say a heckuva lot.

Landry Gatestone, on the other hand, was a different story and no matter what lots of folks outside Orvop High kept repeatin, her alleged role didn't sit right with most of the student body. Maybe she was only a sophomore, but from day one she'd been a force. Her classmates at Dixon Junior High would swear on the Good Book that she had the spark, and no one was surprised when that spark only grew brighter, and hotter, by the time she hit high school. Some who'd found rebellion in a CB radio club, renamin themselves Media Ken, Fezno Hillegret, Avid Skier, Sir Fan Crick, and Go Gorse Bucked, Bra fer short, Easy Ed TV too, plus Bi-Human Idea, Rivalry Jest, Ken-Jig Snorers, and Grit-Bee Diction, as well as Urgency Rooster and Gondry Law, they sure knew of her. The likes of Dark Maizes Welkin had heard of her too, and not just from his sister, who was Landry's year and supposedly murmured in a melody worthy of the Vaults above *You could just see the world would need her, might even heed her, if the world was smart, though when was the world ever smart?*

Other sophomores caught on pretty quick how Landry weren't about to back down just because folks mocked her choices, like when she wore acid-wash jeans two years before them things happened. What Landry got, she gave back, especially to the jocks who at Orvop

588

were mostly revered; why Landry would guffaw at them somethin severe, callin them full of hot air or worse, though not much worse, because who cared what you could do with a ball if you couldn't tell the difference between a horse's hock or hind? And such displays of petulance weren't just a one-time thing either, more like a-once-a-day thing, with Landry Gatestone planted right in the middle of Main Hall goadin back whoever was fool enuf to goad her first about bein itty-bitty or wearin bleach-mistake jeans, Landry lettin loose her own searin vernacular if never diminishin one bit her cheery appearance, just smilin and scathin, which surprised no one since, after all, her big brother was Tom Gatestone, who, just at the sight of her so worked up, instantly got rosy-cheeked hisself, joinin her tempest then with his own infectious laughter, which so often set off-kilter that big wad of chew behind his lower lip, especially the one time when Landry was goin after Lindsey Holt, who'd mocked her for wearin that ridiculous pink raincoat when there weren't even a cloud in sight.

And it's true, bein Tom Gatestone's little sister did have its advantages. After all Tom was a star at Orvop High, which was sayin somethin given he didn't play sports and he never ran for student body president and he wasn't startin a band and he weren't a Kippel, Hovey, or Folland. True, he did end up the Orvop High FFA president but he'd already accomplished some extraordinary feats, like ridin Hightower. He weren't even that good-lookin, and he didn't have a good-lookin girlfriend neither. In fact he didn't have no girlfriend. He was just really, really liked. That was the weirdest part. Anyone who knew him, and somehow everyone knew him, just couldn't do anythin but like him. Even the Porches, who were predestined to detest him, couldn't detest him because he was just so amusin, so darned affable. Who didn't enjoy watchin Tom spy his little sister in some hall holdin forth about the importance of her opinion? Like that one time when Landry didn't take so kindly to Darren Blicker askin if the horse she rode weren't really a Shetland pony, and Tom then creepin up on her real close, crouchin down even lower, startin to yowl out *Oh my! Oh my!* as he then stood up, and with them long bowed legs splayed extra wide, also balancin hisself on the very back of his bootheels, swingin his way forward, began bleatin louder and louder more of them *Oh mys* until he was hollerin LOOK OUT, BOYS! SHE'S A-SQUALLIN NOW! OH, SHE'S A-SQUALLIN! BATTEN THEM HATCHES! WE'RE IN FOR IT NOW! Landry sure browed up bad then, with nothin she'd just been goin on about worth now even a fly's butthole. Fer sure Darren Blicker didn't matter. Landry lowered her head then like Hightower hisself and charged after her brother, but, boy oh boy, could Tom run, hootin and laughin, always keepin just ahead of her, even as he weaved from side to side, lookin a lot like Olive Oyl, every now and then riskin a jump to click them bootheels together, which instead of makin Landry madder only got her doin the same, until both of them, big brother and little sister, was weavin the length of Orvop High like a pair of drunk dancers, committin more and more of their antics to midair, heel-knockin near-synchronous clicks, pursued by a ripple of laughter all the way from B-Wing down to D-Wing.

Them kinda memories, and they's blue memories now, dark blue, created the first dissonance in what students started hearin, because everyone knew at once that little Landry Gatestone didn't murder no Russel Porch and what's more wouldn't stand for anyone murderin him either. Why she'd just as soon box a fella's ears than get involved with anythin as serious as a knife let alone a gun, and if a knife did make an appearance, Landry Gatestone would've viewed that as a sure sign of a bad sense of humor, and who's got time for that? In this light, her hangin around with Kalin March didn't make any sense unless everyone's impression of him had been wrong. Of course initially, no one at the school knew that Kalin and Tom had been such close friends. Another problem was that no one had ever seen Landry anywhere near the Kalin kid. Also, tryin to imagine this Kalin kid kidnappin her was a problem; like anyone else, he'd have found hisself tryin to corral the winds of Katanogos.

Of course such questions and contradictions did stir up a good amount of interest. That Saturday mornin phones went hot from ringin as students called each other or later carried out their jawin in person at weekend practices or church activites or just met up at the mall to walk back and forth between ZCMI and JCPenney huntin for girls or boys, which just meant gettin up the gumption to wave or maybe if you was real brave say, *Hey, did you hear . . . ?* because after all this weekend there was actually somethin big to hear about, somethin big to talk about, even if everyone still wanted to check out new albums and eat corn dogs.

The rumorin ranged far and wide. UFO abductions even came up, and not by the stoners, though the ones givin this slant momentary credence didn't even know what *abduction* meant, and when they did find out adjusted their story so that it was Kalin March who was in fact an alien. That extraterrestrial aspect aside, and it was flung aside pretty fast, the question everyone did keep comin back to was what Landry Gatestone had to do with any of this? She weren't even knowd to have had many words with Russel Porch, though Russel and her had been in the same French class and had done a project together and they'd gotten along swell and gotten an A– too.

Of course, Preot Ackley's news about what Teri Casper had said soon spread, followed by Teri Casper herself sharin how her Uncle Caleb had seen the Kalin kid all broke up at Tom Gatestone's funeral and how supposedly the Kalin kid had been at the hospital too when Tom had died, and why then if the Kalin kid and Tom Gatestone were friends, which really was some shockin news, given, like's been said, that no one had seen the Kalin kid and Tom Gatestone hangin out at school ever, why then maybe Landry did know the Kalin kid after all. And the mystery only grew from there. And then when the news woke up and started reportin how, in the bad weather of Wednesday night, Landry had taken her horse up Isatch Canyon and from there had somehow ridden up the north side too, why that really spun every-one's mind toward disbelief, like a clump of sod caught on the end of a weed whacker, just comin apart, tossin dirt everywhere.

In fairness, neither Woolsey nor Francis had ever really fallen for such mouth-flappin about Landry bein kidnapped or even her some-how playin a part in Russel's killin. Fer them, as fer so many, it was the knowin her, and not just knowin her by her family name but knowin her day-to-day at Orvop High, that destabilized the prevailin story. Somethin just weren't squarin. And while the easier tellin rode steady and strong over top, what Old Porch didn't tire of layin out, how this new kid, this Kalin March, had murdered a local kid, their Russel Porch, everythin else underneath, from Landry to the stolen horses to an attempted escape in a canyon everyone knew was a dead end, why that kept tremorin what initially had seemed so solid and obvious.

Though one thing was dead certain: as soon as them bodies were dug up, there'd just be that, bodies. Poor Sondra Gatestone would have herself another dead child, her last child, lyin beside another dead child, this Kalin March kid, and why that would be that, with all the rest of it, what happened, why it happened, likely stayin unresolved, unsolved, without no one fer sure ever figurin out what the heck those three kids had been up to in the first place.

Not that anyone stopped talkin about it, and though no one knew it then, they'd keep talkin about it fer years and years to come. This here was a heinous crime involvin folks from Orvop High. It made Gary Gilmore look like nothin more than a drugstore cowboy, and he weren't even that. Besides, lots of folks knew Russel Porch, knew him well, and Landry Gatestone too, and maybe they'd even sat next to Kalin March in class or across from him in the school cafeteria. And what's more, the story weren't just countywide anymore; it was state-wide now, and there was more talk of it gettin mentioned in national newspapers, which weren't true, at least not yet, and on CBS, which had happened, though still only in regards to the landslide.

One thing of interest was how almost no one talked about Navidad or Mouse, or even Jojo, and of those parties actually involved, meanin the sheriff's department, the park rangers, Orvop police, as well as the Porches, why they just referred to the horses as stolen property.

One exception was the shootin of Cavalry. Folks did talk about that, but it weren't so much a discussion of the animal; rather it was a way to further characterize Kalin.

In the end, what moved through Orvop and Rome, and well beyond too, was this strange admixture of both disbelief and recognition. Folks that Saturday mornin were basically flabbergasted that this was happenin in of all places their own small university town where Church missionaries were trained. Kids killin kids? Kids on horse-back? Kids with guns? Kids killin horses? Kids killt in a big rockfall? That's not the kinda thing that happened in Orvop. And yet, at the same time, there was somethin to it that weren't entirely unfamiliar, especially in how this new violence had mostly taken place in Isatch Canyon, a place lored with the old violence of early inhabitants, all the way back to 1850 at the battle of Fort Orvop that included Old Elk, Garrison Porch, Alfred Gatestone, and Wild Bill Hickman. This valley had always been baptized with blood, the mountains too.

Billings, after partin ways with the Porches, headed straight over to Trent Riddle's apartment. This time he weren't the only one there.

Detective Peters had already taken statements from most of the Porches but still wanted to hear from Egan Porch as well as the Porch Meats employee Billings Gale. And you can bet Trent Riddle was also on that list. He was not only an employee at Porch Meats but had been a participant at this *tithe poker* game held roughly once a month at Egan Porch's home, which weren't but a short jog from Isatch Canyon. Both Francis and Woolsey Porch, the younger Porch brothers, also in attendance at said poker game, had witnessed Russel ride off on Egan's horse, Cavalry, to recover the horses stolen from the paddocks on Willow and Oak. Both Francis and Woolsey Porch had confirmed in their statements that Mr. Trent Riddle had been at the table with them.

Detective Peters weren't concerned so much about Egan Porch nor this Billings Gale. Near everyone in the valley knew that the both of them, along with Kelly Porch, were out lookin for the stolen horses.

These three were also the ones who'd witnessed the collapse of the north side of Isatch Canyon as well as the apparent deaths of the accused. Detective Peters was confident he'd have Billings's and Egan's statements before day's end. Trent Riddle, however, was another story.

So far no one Detective Peters had spoken with had even an inklin where he'd got to, and he was from Orvop, with plenty of family and friends in the area. Detective Peters harbored no expectations that Trent Riddle weren't gonna do nothin more than reiterate everythin the Porches had already said had transpired that Wednesday night, but he still didn't like havin that statement sheet left blank. Detective Peters was meticulous to the point that he deserved some the ribbin he got from many of his colleagues about bein too neat, too tidy, though too often it was that gutbag Officer Poulter complainin, though never Chief of Police Beckham. Beckham was determined to see his department staffed with competent people, whether out in the field or workin a desk. Detective Peters had been through enuf cases to know what a difference paperwork could make in gettin a conviction.

Over the past two days Detective Peters had left messages at Trent Riddle's until his machine went full, and the last time he called, the machine didn't even pick up. Everyone Detective Peters had interviewed at Porch Meats said that Trent Riddle had never showed Thursday mornin nor on Friday neither. The fact, however, that Riddle had disappeared right after Russel Porch was killt did create some uneasiness, suspicions even, which Detective Peters kept tampin back down to uneasiness. Not that the suspicions stopped resurfacin. After all, what if this Riddle was involved in the killin? Detective Peters was doin his best not to run that one around in his head, especially as he headed over to Trent Riddle's apartment. He didn't need that on his face when Trent opened the door. Could this Trent Riddle have intercepted Russel and killt him? But why? It didn't make a lick of sense. There weren't any indications either that Trent Riddle had left in some rancorous mood, sure if he'd lost badly at cards, but he hadn't lost badly. Quite the opposite: accordin to everyone, Mr. Riddle had quit right after winnin a big hand. Some knuckleheaded revenge over a game of H.O.R.S.E. gone bad just weren't, well, in the cards.

Yesterday somethin interestin had come up, somethin odd. Chief of Police Beckham had informed Detective Peters that Orwin Porch had just that mornin come into the station and said somethin about Trent Riddle bein blind drunk durin the game, which was not somethin mentioned in any of Detective Peters's statements. Another cause for uneasiness. That claim sure didn't square with the Trent Riddle Detective Peters kept hearin about, who his family and friends described as straighter than a level's edge, a devoted member of the Church who wouldn't take a sip of even Mountain Dew, let alone Mountain Dew with booze in it.

Detective Peters parked in front of Trent Riddle's apartment complex. He was still drivin his wife's purple Honda Civic, his Mustang still in the shop. He tromped through the rain, knocked on the door and kept knockin, and after that tried to get a peek through the partially closed drapes of the livin room, unchanged since his last visit yesterday afternoon, still offerin through that narrow gap the same disheartenin glimpse of some nail clippers set beside a plate atop a plastic milk crate servin as a table.

Next Detective Peters took stock of the vehicles in the parkin lot. Once again Riddle's brown Plymouth Duster was nowhere in sight. Detective Peters had already cruised the nearby streets in case Riddle had parked the Duster farther away. By this point the detective had already noted Billings Gale's forest green Jeep Renegade but hadn't registered it as familiar despite havin written down details about the vehicle Wednesday night, when Kelly Porch had given him the lowdown on everyone's cars. You'll recall that Billings and Egan had already left by the time Detective Peters had reached Egan Porch's residence.

Even when Billings said hello as he approached Riddle's door, Detective Peters failed to recognize him, and to be fair Billings's face was new to him, maybe Tongan or Polynesian, though if they shared such ancestry, and they didn't, the hello was likely due to good old-fashioned neighborliness.

Billings fer his part didn't recognize the detective neither, though the detective's *Hello, do you live here?* immediately rang familar, and though it took a few words more to connect the voice to the messages on his machine, Billings quick enuf figured out who he was dealin with here. Billings even briefly considered leavin the detective in the dark, but the disadvantage of bein found out later in a useless lie outweighed the comfort of a moment's anonymity.

Billings introduced hisself to Detective Peters, remarkin then that he was checkin up on Riddle, who was still missin. Detective Peters smiled back, genuinely pleased over this unification of purpose, fer sure not thinkin how Billings and hisself couldn't be further apart in purpose. They chatted amiably, Billings remarkin how everyone at Porch Meats, not to mention the Porch family, had grown increasinly troubled by this atypical absence.

Would you mind drivin over to the station now? Detective Peters inquired. *I sure would like to get your statement on all this. I have everyone's but yours and Egan Porch's.*

More than happy to, Billings answered, as if that weren't the furthest thing from the truth.

But I gotta ask: were you drunk too at the poker game?

Me?!

Then just Mr. Riddle?

Riddle? Billings repeated, his voice just catchin a tiny bit, unnoticeable to anyone except of course the very meticulous Detective Peters.

Bear in mind Church rules are very much separate from Orvop laws. No one cares if you're drinkin. Only if you're drinkin and drivin. Detective Peters laughed some, though on this occasion it was a practiced laugh, enuf to include some smile in his eyes even if those eyes kept real steady.

I don't drink.

And Trent Riddle?

I did not notice. Billings already knew he was about up to his boot collars in manure. Boy, how he wished he'd just bit his tongue right off rather than have to face what harm his mistake was doin now. Billings weren't blind. He'd seen this detective register how his response put their stories out of whack. Billings got to chewin on his tongue just the same, like he still might get around to bitin it off. Wasn't this what Old Porch had been rehearsin them for when Hatch Porch had arrived? Leadin Kelly along so he was sayin Trent Riddle had been drunk? What they'd all agreed was the case even when Woolsey had got to objectin. Wasn't it even Billings hisself who'd added: *Ain't it the ones who never drink who get the craziest when they finally do?*

You didn't notice? Detective Peters asked. The detective was genuine in his curiosity, but Billings missed it, likely because he loathed cops, somethin he and Old Porch shared down to the bone.

I was studyin my cards and truth be told tryin to ignore the fellow. Figured whatever he was sayin was just to try to jar my confidence. And maybe he did just that. He won after all.

I heard he was practically hallucinatin, he was so far gone! Detective Peters added, at once cursin hisself for sayin as much. Not that Billings responded.

How much do you figure he won? Detective Peters asked then.

It was a lot, Billings answered, *but not enuf to change your life.*

Weren't it for tithe anyway?

Whether or not Riddle gave it to the Church, you'll have to ask him.

So he weren't particularly happy about the money then?

Oh, he was happy. But as Mr. Porch likes to say about poker: it ain't about the money. It's about makin other men feel less about themselves.

Detective Peters liked that one, and it sure squared with how he saw Old Porch. He handed Billings his card and repeated his request to follow him over to the station to give a statement, with added assurances that it wouldn't take long.

As Billings started up his forest green Renegade and set his hands to the wheel, he experienced right then, right there, and all at once too, all the agency he still possessed: he could go anywhere, do anythin he liked, just drive on over to some different life, maybe without repercussions, or at least not concussed by the developments that weren't gonna quit addin up here. On the way to wherever he was goin, he could even buy hisself a guitar. He knew how to play some. He was a decent picker, and though nothin had ever come of it, he could do it all night, and the next night, and the night after that too, until there didn't have to be an end. Old Porch would probably even defend his disappearance. Though Billings also understood that such a move would likely further fuel the detective's curiosity. Of course, if he made his statement now, especially if he told it right, like he knew he could, Billings might also put this snoopin to rest and grant them all a little more space to deal with Riddle on their own. Billings could buy a guitar later. And a harmonica. He played the harmonica too.

From a pay phone near Center, Billings tried to reach Old Porch and then Egan and finally Kelly. No one picked up.

Despite Old Porch's version of things, Riddle when he showed, would surely recall how when he'd left with that big pot it was Old Porch who was drunk beyond sense and angry too; more intriguin still for the detective would be news that Russel had been right there, whole and fine, better than fine, braggin on how he'd found the horses, sold the horses, for cash. Old Porch was scared of Riddle, and Billings understood how that meant he had an opportunity.

Not that Billings had gone to Trent Riddle's apartment with a gun or a knife. If Detective Peters had contrary to his character, if not exactly against Utah law, thrown Billings against a wall to frisk him, the most he'd've found on his key rings, hangin right next to a small tape measure, would've been a tiny corked tube, inside of which was packed an even tinier scroll of paper rolled tighter than a quarter-inch dowel with the tiniest script spellin out *Billings*. If the detective had then taken a moment to unroll that scroll and strained in the light to apprehend its contents, he'd have found still tinier script, which might at first suggest asemic artistry until persistence plus a good deal of squintin might start to dredge up legible words, which under a magnifyin glass would further reveal a love letter of sorts. All of which, of course, Detective Peters did not do. And even if he had, he fer sure would've never come to the conclusion that what he held between his fingers was a murder weapon, or at least part of the weapon. And already used once to great effect.

While servin his sentence up in Draper at the Point of the Mountain Prison, Billings had learned there were two kinds of scribes: those who'd have nothin to do with him, and those who'd do whatever he needed to set in motion good plans for bad things. Billings did two years for a felony of the third degree, a robbery he'd had nothin to do with. He'd learned how to really read then as well as put writin to good use, even if it weren't his writin. What he finally took possession of, and with great satisfaction as well, was a love letter that had nothin to do with Billings personally, and whether the romantic aspect so finely indicated on that tiny scroll was some part of the scribe's personal history or just sprung from his needy imagination, Billings never found out nor cared to find out about. All he needed was a distraction. And in that regard that little piece of writin worked better than perfectly.

If Billings had found Riddle home and Riddle had refused to accompany him to the plant, which was the ideal course of action given that the sizable Porch Meats incinerator was right there, Billings would've at once said that he was there mainly because everyone was worried but also because he needed help. He'd tell Riddle how he weren't such a good reader, how he'd just then gotten somethin from someone who'd really started to get at his heart. Billings felt sure Riddle would go for that, though to someone else he might say the contents contained financial promises he was desperate to understand.

Riddle, of course, would need light and likely seek out a magnifyin lens of some sort too, and while he was arrangin hisself to best achieve the necessary focus and concentration, Billings would locate somethin heavy and hard enuf to do the job needed on the back of Riddle's head.

Of course, if there was bleedin, and the last time there'd been gobs, then the mess, like a stained rug, would become a big problem, followed by the still-bigger problem of gettin the body out of the apartment. Sure, he could lug it out in the rug or cut it up and distribute parts in luggage, but all it took was one wanderin glance from one bored neighbor and Billings, with time served for assault and robbery, would not survive scrutiny. Maybe he should be glad Riddle hadn't been there, glad that the detective had shown up instead, glad even of this chance to give a statement, because if he could make that fly without confirmin that Riddle was drunk while still assertin that Riddle was makin no sense, why then all of it would be done with, done right too, provided the search and rescue crews found two bodies.

And that was the part, as Billings hurried back to his Jeep, that rattled him the most. In fact as he drove away from downtown Orvop, the peculiar vividness he experienced, what he'd seen upon the mountain yesterday right before the rest of the mountain had fallen, shallowed his breath and made his whole body go clammy. Nor could he rightly understand why. Then again who among us can ever truly recognize when the world with all its vast calculations, far exceedin any livin system let alone some societal objection, abruptly and particularly factors us into its prohibitions? Old Porch, for one, was incapable of such a recognition, though he lived his life as if ceaselessly prohibited and so ceaselessly railed and raged against every restriction, his fist to Zeus, the Lord, the slightest inconvenience presented by an errant breeze. How he taught his boys to act too. Billings was no Porch in that regard, and maybe that was why he alone out of Egan and Kelly had briefly laid eyes on a spectre composite of future ends layin eyes on him, what amounted to either a curse or a blessin.

Because he could still run.

But likely because Billings didn't feel worthy of any blessin, he could not believe hisself belongin anywhere else but on the path he was already on, fused to Old Porch hisself.

So Billings headed to the Orvop Police Station and not long after sat down with Detective Peters.

It was 10:09 a.m.

About this time, Undersheriff Jewell was rallyin the volunteers brave enuf to stick around, tellin them that the rain was gonna slow soon, and in fact it would halt completely, even as the park rangers, includin Emily Brickey, Law Enforcement Rangers Bren Kelson as well as Corbet Wadley, ankle wrapped, a crutch in each hand, continued to warn Jewell that the canyon crick was a dangerous river now and a hazard to anyone makin the trek up to the slide let alone sievin through the debris for body parts. They also warned the undersheriff that the slide itself might yet prove too unstable to safely scour, capable of producin still more debris flow, at least until the storm had passed and allowed for some dryness, like common sense, to settle the canyon. Their prevailin attitude was that a midday start time was a pipe dream. They'd be lucky to get goin by Monday.

Meanwhile, up north, busy helpin her sister welcome a little baby girl named Brynn, Assistant Medical Examiner Annabelle Kasey was fer sure not thinkin about intern Chester Walheimer, who she'd charged with enterin into evidence them two crystal shards, which he'd done, handin over the sealed package to Pat Stubbs, who was the officer in charge of the property room and who promptly added the admission to a growin pile that would pretty soon require proper sortin. Assistant Medical Examiner Annabelle Kasey sure weren't thinkin about Officer Pat Stubbs neither.

Years later, defense attorney Dane Barlow, a graduate of South High School and cousin to Marrot Barlow, and friends too with Rumi Plothow and Holly Brereton, Perry Metz as well, and Todd Stevens, would argue that though the chain of custody might to some have seemed intact, it was highly irregular and improper to have the likes of Chester Walheimer, an intern, handlin such important evidence. Barlow would argue that that alone had always thrown into grave doubt the integrity of that evidence. Clay McKay, also a defense attorney, also a graduate of South High School, loved to publicly revisit Chester Walheimer's qualities; Chester Walheimer, who was deemed by his community an astonishin individual of impeccable character; Chester Walheimer, who was top of his class with outstandin recommendations from professors and bishops alike; Chester Walheimer, who had more than enuf witnesses that day to corroborate his excellent handlin and deliverin of said evidence. Barlow in turn would declare that said argument was proof of McKay's incompetence as a lawyer. McKay's response was that Barlow's response settled the argument, and he moved to have Barlow disbarred. The two had been debate partners at South High.

At least one thing was beyond dispute: not Kasey, not Walheimer, not even Stubbs were thinkin about Brennan Hurley and fer sure not William Mecham.

He almost looks like he should speak, Francis hushed out into the small room. Woolsey gave Francis a soft knock on the elbow like he agreed, but Shelly didn't agree and said that Russel looked deader than dead, and of course that was obvious, what with the chalkiness of his skin despite whatever lie the makeup was tryin to sell. Hatch told Shelly to shut up, and for once Egan agreed with Hatch.

Well, here they was, at the Erville Family Mortuary: Orwin Porch, the mournin father, with his mournin sons, Hatch Porch, Egan Porch, Shelly Porch, Sean Porch, Kelly Porch, Woolsey Porch, and Francis Porch, all in black, all wearin ties, standin around the body of their baby brother, who was also wearin a tie and in a brown suit he'd worn just the one time before, at a ward dance this past August, that time also on his back, though splayed out on a picnic table with a piece of dry ice in his mouth, which he kept bobblin around with his tongue while swishin around a mouthful of root beer, the results amazin the younger kids who sat on either side of him, mesmerized by the fog overflowin his lips. There weren't no fog now; this weren't no picnic table neither. Russel Porch was laid out in a dark ruby casket with a powder blue linin, his eyes closed, his mouth shut.

Go on, Francis, touch him! Sean goaded the now-youngest brother.

When Francis wouldn't, Sean did so hisself, put a thumb right in the middle of Russel's forehead, though he withdrew it quick, and maybe his look of puzzlement fast turned to dismay kept Old Porch from cuffin the back of Sean's head.

Neither Egan nor Kelly did anythin more than stand there. They'd yet to say a word. Both just stared at the corpse, numb with a disbelief approachin what a few in later years would call *dangerous Pyrrhonism*. But it was lookin at their father that was givin them the hardest time.

Old Porch hardly spared Russel a glance. His only concern was with these livin boys, and upon them he laid his severe gaze.

The whole drive here, the math that battered relentlessly around in his head was derived from the negation of Senate Bill 1245. Old Porch had no doubt what would follow: his banks would turn heel quick as Monday, because, of course, there weren't no need for a loan if there weren't nothin to buy; all the individual investors Porch had lined up would flee next. Bye-bye, Havril Enos, for one, with bunches followin his departure. Old Porch's trinity of state senators to say nothin of any representatives would likewise pursue a more genial distance. Lost was the labor spent to acquire buildin permits, arrange utilities, sanitation, that very favorable liquor license Old Porch had managed to secure despite Utah bein a dry state. Old Porch could sure forget his palace in Indian Hills. And that still weren't addressin what all else Old Porch had leveraged to make this big resort gambit possible, the money he'd had to spread about, his money, money only he had because of them other equities he'd tangled into this dare, includin plenty of squares from that hopscotch of properties he owned east of the lake and north, from rentals to mills to undeveloped lots. Even the truckin was caught up in it. Porch Meats would be unable to make the payment he'd need come January, what with interest rates now gougin everyone at around 16 percent. He'd have to sell quick. And that would hurt. Porch Meats would be in peril, Porch Meats the cynosure of his accomplishments, Porch Meats.

He'd probably still get to keep the house, maybe, that warren of incompleteness, unfinishedness, its yard still full with trucks on blocks, bikes mid-repair, two unfinished Airstreams, one vintage, which he still hoped to sell one day or at least take out on a trip. Why were the old washer and dryer he'd replaced years ago with Whirlpools still standin in Effy's paddock? And what about the inside of the house? That again was botherin him somethin special as he rocked heel to heel before the body of his last child. He just couldn't stop returnin to the house; how even with plenty of new appliances, it somehow still remained permanently raw and marred, no part of it unmarked by animal stains, not a room spared of the stacked disorder of so many boxes of deals gone wrong, deals goin right if they'd only get signed, deals Old Porch had swore never to forget until some kind of recompense was achieved; and that weren't even countin all the other boxes of dusty trophies and family photographs, stuff he was supposed to one day set out or hang up if he could ever figure out the wall space. Two years ago he'd bought an ice-cream maker, supposedly the best you could get; that still stood in a closet, unopened. There were even bags of nice clothes he'd never tried on a second time, nice clothes for nice events he didn't go near. There was a tuxedo somewhere, never worn, with jeweled studs, gold cuff links, what he'd always planned to wear with his old boots and his grandfather's bolo tie, perfect for some big D.C. event that now weren't gonna happen. He'd even had it tailored! Wasn't he even gonna get new teeth? And while the house itself could here and there show off new construction, new paint behind a new TV, there was just as much rottin Sheetrock, leakin pipes, crackin and crumblin gnawin away at the foundation. It was a miracle that the chimney hadn't already toppled down in this last storm. Fer sure, the antenna up there had gone askew; that or the new TV was already on the blink.

Still, Old Porch was managin to walk back some of his despair, figurin he'd probably get to keep Porch Meats. It did what it had to do and did it well enuf to keep Old Porch monied enuf. Fer sure not anythin dazzlin to tour, but it was orderly, efficient, for the most part clean, even if it too suffered the same condition of unfinishedness that wouldn't stop eatin at Old Porch. Fer example, lodged in the back storeroom was an old freezer, still workin, though it often quit only to come back on, half-full with meat thawed and frozen so many times it lived there in a perpetual state of preserved rottenness.

Right then and there, Orwin Porch vowed to at least toss that darn thing out, this afternoon, along with them old appliances rustin in the rain, haul it all away, which he nearly said aloud as he continued to survey the dark room just to remind hisself that even though he weren't goin broke, not even close, even though he'd still be able to get a pipe fixed, a wall repainted, sell off some properties, buy some new TVs, here, truly, was all he had left: Francis, a boy near weak as Russel, already undone by grief, without the stones in his stomach to make rage out of it; Woolsey, well, he had some rage and fight, but he still weren't worth half the arrogance he liked to put on display when he sashayed around the house like a faggot; Sean, he saw the world only through the dirt bike or snowmobile engines he worked on, even when he worked at Porch Meats, which he could never run; Shelly had some of the meanness needed to take control of the Porch operation, but he was as dumb as the girls he chased; Hatch should've sparked a bright light of pride in his father's eyes but Old Porch couldn't shake how Hatch's move to Texas, his closeness to his mother, still, with his little sister too, was a rank betrayal. Plus Hatch wanted nothin to do with Porch Meats anyhow. Old Porch wondered if maybe he was a faggot too. That left Kelly and Egan. Kelly weren't as hard as Egan, but he had the stuff. A little more practice and Old Porch could kick back some and watch Kelly get it done. But Egan, even if Old Porch could see Egan was the best of the lot, didn't spark no light of pride in his eyes either, and it weren't clear why.

Right then, and much to Old Porch's disappointment too, Kelly groaned and grabbed at his stomach. He'd taken too long a look at Russel, and the memories of Russel's last moments were comin up. Kelly belched and then maybe meant to belch again until he discovered more than angry air was comin up. Like father, like son.

Don't let that out, boy, Old Porch growled out. *You swallow it.*

Kelly did as he was told, swallowin whatever was bubblin up in his throat, and kept swallowin, with his brothers watchin him now, that or watchin Old Porch watchin Kelly. No one spoke up or made a joke. That Kelly got the job done checked everyone there. Backs got straighter. Even Hatch grew more alert and wary, abandonin fer a moment what his brothers, and especially his father, regarded as his perpetual state of preenin self-regard.

Now I want us all to give Russel the look he deserves.

Everyone obeyed except Old Porch, who continued to ignore the dead boy, studyin again his sons, his jaw musclin up with each grind, takin in all that they weren't worth. He lingered most on Kelly and Egan now, both of whom, sensin the heat of their father's gaze, raised their eyes to receive his nod of resolve, both of them noddin back before returnin to the sight of their dead brother.

Old Porch reached into the coffin then. Russel's collar was botherin him. It was too high. But only when he grabbed hold of it, the back of his fingers grazin the cold flesh, his infected thumb pinchin down on the shirt, and, boy, did that thumb look bad, blacker than a dead beetle, only then did Old Porch realize he couldn't even remember the last time he'd touched his Russel except when he'd lashed out at him with this very same hand, this same thumb. Old Porch saw how the makeup and whatever other preparations they'd managed had successfully obscured the very line his then-ragged nail had sliced across that small face. Old Porch winced some then, like he'd caught a glimpse of hisself in a mirror and didn't care for the sight of it. He wouldn't wince like that again.

Of course, when he tugged down the collar and exposed the gouge that leaked Russel out, them careful sutures did away with any mirror he was imaginin, revealin now only a figure of shadow, what Old Porch knew from then on as the face of his adversary, the Kalin kid, who'd driven a knife in there, clawed at Russel's face too.

Art connoisseur, dilettante, passionate feminist, purveyor of unredacted images, none other than Cal Carneros, while reflectin on this scene, would immediately think of Francisco de Zurbarán's *Still Life with Lemons, Oranges and a Rose*, an association he'd immediately recognize as false, except maybe for the near-luminous black background, alive with so much unenacted meanin.

It looks so small, Francis murmured. *Like a Band-Aid could've fixed it.*

The room, as if called upon, then seemed with that boy's utterance to move in closer, as if them walls of awful dark violet wallpaper writ with black flowers yearned to know more their backs, with even the black curtains rustlin with approval, though they weren't rustlin at all, one set of curtains even slightly apart and with the admittance of the day's gray light revealin beyond the glass a set of black bars. Now bars on a window weren't somethin you saw much of in Orvop. Stranger still, the other windows were unbarred. Old Porch didn't care none for standin in any room with bars, even if it was only the one facin west. He loathed nothin more than the worst spectre of all: imprisonment. But this antipathy, what Old Porch would never name as fear, fueled his energies to rage beyond the reach of any authority that weren't his own. Old Porch even stepped back to warn the walls away, and the walls, no match for Old Porch, heeded him.

Francis had started to shake and was now openly weepin. Hatch strode over at once to the boy, bound him up in his big arms, even as Hatch's own wet eyes inevitably returned to Russel, and then as if there wasn't anythin there, and there weren't, not no more, his eyes like all their eyes lifted to settle on Old Porch, standin above Russel *as pitiless as Achilles stood above Lycaon,* as Ms. Melson would one day say when describin this scene.

We have a choice, their father said to them. *Either we spend the rest of our lives talkin about what we should've done or we shut up now and get what needs to be done done. Our little Russel's gone, and until them that done this to him are fer sure gone, and I mean fer sure!, buried good and deep, we must not stop. Now what I want to know is am I doin this alone?*

A murmur of *No, Daddys* and *No, sirs* rose up.

Who's with me?

At once Hatch, Sean, Shelly, Woolsey, and even Francis shuffled some steps forward, so they was all then touchin the coffin. Egan and Kelly stepped forward too but not quite as near, nor did they raise their voices to declare *We're with you, Pa! Anythin for Russel!*

Old Porch weren't blind either. He sensed their obstinancy like he'd sensed it their whole lives, and so while he addressed them all, his words now were only for Egan and Kelly, to vulcanize their suscep-tible hearts, determine their resolve, with the rest remainin none the wiser, not even Hatch, who should've knowd better.

Everyone beyond these walls needs to know that if you come at a Porch, the Porches will bury you. Our little Russel ain't gonna find no peace until that is so. When Orvop folks pass you by, I wanna hear how they knew you as their better, that in your presence their life was iffy. And that's because our little Russel was rightfully avenged.

This time Egan and Kelly led the approvin chorus of *That's right!* with even Hatch throwin in a *Whatever it takes!* Though it's worth notin that even though Francis, Woolsey, Sean, and Shelly went along with these declarations of support, they remained confused, given that this arousal of purpose seemed a bit after the fact. Weren't the culprits dead? What the heck was goin on?

At which point Mr. Erville came in, mishearin that he was called for, findin hisself at once unwanted, an unwelcome visitor bargin in on so dark a circle, disoriented by the closeness of it, the low rumblin voices, Mr. Erville hardly deaf to the anger and malice stabbin through every intonation, so much so that each cry, the cries of the Furies themselves!, seemed permanently stitched in the air, right there above Russel, like some black wreath.

Truthfully, it was like I'd stumbled in on a black mass, Mr. Erville would say decades hence to a stranger on a red-eye to Detroit. *There was more than family grievin. I'm familiar with that. The air just crackled with this ter-rible sense of . . . consequence. Like at any moment consecratin acts of violence might occur. I felt at risk. Their faces were so dark with anger. I'll never forget that. Except maybe for the youngest. The youngest was different from all the rest. Francis. He alone seemed untouched by anger. I could recognize him. He was mournin, and so it was to him that I immediately went, to stand beside, maybe pat his arm, in part to offer him some solace, the solace of others, of strangers, you know, to recognize his bereavement but also I will admit to gain some measure of safety for myself by demonstratin some allegiance with all them there. I, though, was mistaken. There was nowhere in that room that I could stand and feel safe, and I've been in that room more hours than eggs I've ate. I left in a hurry. But when they finally emerged some twenty minutes later, they weren't mad fer blood no more, they was doleful and polite. And when I got back to the casket, I at least expected to find some residue there, or in the room, on the walls, some evidence of that terrible feelin, but all was as it should be. The dead boy looked the same, calm just like I'd laid him out, until I beheld the change and near screamed aloud. Both his eyelids had popped open. Nothin there but black holes.*

This is another one of those small mysteries hauntin these events. Speculation abounds. Plenty swear that the Porch brothers forced them open. Mr. Erville later convinced others and then hisself that Russel's organs and eyes had been donated. Mr. Erville had also forgotten how, havin run out of the tacky eye caps and orbs, he'd glued the eyelids shut. Anyways, no matter how often he told the story, no matter how he attempted to normalize those events, Mr. Erville never failed to get the willies thinkin about that moment. *Clop-Clop-clip-Clop.* What would follow no doubt added to what that corpse had witnessed and endured. And up until his own death, Mr. Erville continued to have dreams of that ruby casket, now underground, with Russel inside, the glue again havin long since given up, just them two black holes starin up through the materials of interment, through the grind and groan of the earth itself, scourin the land for them that had wronged him.

As the Porches piled into the vehicles parked in front of the mortuary, Old Porch spent a moment more talkin with Mr. Erville. They confirmed the price, Old Porch on the spot handin over one of them rolls of Jacksons bound up with a bright red rubber band. Mr. Erville could keep what all was extra. They confirmed that the funeral would be that comin Monday, at one in the afternoon. The family plot was already in order. Mr. Erville assured Old Porch that all would be handled accordin to his wishes.

What in heck do you know about my wishes? Old Porch suddenly flared. *Havin someone move a box from one place to another don't come anywhere near my wishes! You just be on time! Understand?*

Mr. Erville nodded plenty then, once again scared, though now in a different away.

From a pay phone by the entrance of the mortuary, Old Porch called Custom Enterprises, and this time Kevin Moffet picked up.

I figured it was you was how Kevin said hello.

Is the helicopter ready?

It was 10:51 a.m.

Chapter Seventeen

"They Was Trapped"

K alin woke near the same moment Old Porch had down in Orvop, only it weren't no chase in his veins that woke him. Cold got him first. Panic next because the fire weren't just low but gone. Dark ash lay before him, and if it was warm upon his palm, it was only the ghost of warmth. Tom looked near gray as the ash cloud that rose up as Kalin thrust his bare hands into the center, clawin deeper and deeper like some feral animal desperate to prove the memory of a hoard still true. Some relief arrived when an ember bit into his blistered palm. Tom nodded his approval as Kalin's breath then brought that ember back to light. A blossom of fire soon rose up, consumin bits of used cardboard, climbin the thin scraps of wood Kalin kept feedin this new beginnin. The logs he picked caught fast enuf, and a color of warmth returned to Tom's face.

That was close, Kalin said through shivers he sure was gettin sick of.

Was it? Tom answered, as he studied the old duct tape now startin to melt like some doomed serpent.

Landry had groaned three times throughout all this, but once the fire was up and the warmth was reboundin off the rock wall, she sighed and returned to deeper slumber. Kalin checked on Navidad then, as well as Jojo. They offered him snorts and nuzzles. Mouse was lyin on his side but stood up, shakin that dark brown vinaceous coat of his, his long black mane even more tangled than before, though after all that effort he sure weren't pleased to find nothin to eat.

Kalin got the quarter horse a palmful of oats. Then did the same for Jojo and Navidad. They ate it up just fine, but it weren't enuf, and had staled up some too.

What do you see? Kalin asked Tom after he was back to feedin the fire.

You don't wanna know.

The rain battered the night but the darkness would not yield. Kalin worried about the tarps holdin, but he had faith in Landry's knots. He needed to get out there, see what was comin for them, see how much time they had left. Anyone tryin their luck against the night in this weather would have to use lights. They'd show up brighter than a candle in a cave. But Kalin also had to lie down; he needed to rest a moment longer, he needed to soak in a bit more of this warmth. He'd get up in a moment. He needed to tell Tom somethin too, he couldn't remember what, but it would come to him in a moment.

W hen Kalin woke again dawn was glowin up the sky. Kalin studied the clouds. The rain was still racketin their tarps with a tattoo that would rival the IU Marchin Band. Landry remained buried under the horse blankets, snorin like a polar bear.

My lord can that girl sleep! Tom laughed, whereupon his little sister did stir some, her mouth twitchin with unsavory words that fortunately for Tom remained unvoiced, which only made him laugh harder.

Kalin added his own blanket to hers and then set about figurin what to do for breakfast. It weren't pretty. There were no more of those Orvop cafeteria buns left, no more puddings. Every grain of rice was near accounted for and consumed. Except for the oats and carrots for the horses, they had only the one can of beans and the bag of Dorf jerky. Beans for breakfast it would have to be. As soon as Landry woke. Kalin saw no point in gettin her up yet. The rain was still fallin too hard to get movin.

Kalin put on his slicker and the Stetson, which was by now a grimmer side of gray. Then after givin the horses a quick check, he strode out into the lessenin bleak.

From high on that slope eventually abuttin the massive walls encirclin them, he detected no lights movin upon the meadow. Even with binoculars the entrance to the cirque remained dark.

Kalin confirmed again that their campsite betrayed no sign of light. Even with binoculars. The horses were as hid as the fire. Kalin did smell a hint of smoke, but that might've just been what was risin off his clothes.

Kalin continued his traverse away from the entrance, soon passin the limber pines, what had so generously secured their warmth for the night. He'd gather more wood on the way back.

From there he climbed still higher until he could better survey what any other fool would regard as a grand imprisonment.

More light continued to seep into mornin. Kalin spotted some pikas gatherin grass. The far end of the cirque was still a good ways off, and them sheer walls risin straight up to the Katanogos summit remained buried beneath mist and cloud. Maybe Kalin was a little glad for that.

The weather, though, he still cursed, continuin to cast worried eyes on the hectorin rain. They could suffer the wet but not the slickness that the wet brought. Kalin even slipped some then as he scrambled up to the top of this slope, where the southeast wall began, where Kalin hoped to discover by some physics available only to such immense verticality a prevailin dryness that would make the future possible; as if a wall so high might be spared the consequences of storms. Of course the slipperiness of the stone upon Kalin's palms at once predicted failure. The wind too, gustin around in different directions, confessin what maybe only Tom could translate, but Tom weren't near, stayin back with the horses. The loneliness Kalin felt then was almost too awful to take.

alin first set down what wood he'd lugged back, addin to their store extra carefully so as not to wake Landry, before next makin a beeline for Navidad, who welcomed him at once, welcomed his hugs, his strokes, and of course his murmurs.

At least Tom was smilin.

That bad, huh? the ghost asked, skewerin his grin with a long blade of gold grass.

What's Pia Isan sayin this mornin? Kalin retorted.

Oh, she's full of jokes.

How's that?

She's been disabusin me of this notion that she's come here with me or, heaven forbid, followed me! Tom thought that was funny.

Okay.

She's makin it clear that because of the curse my family set on these mountains, what the Porches were part of too, as well as the Hickmans and more than just them, she's huntin me, just as they hunted her. She's pretty pleased too, because as any fool can see she's gone and trapped me. Tom thought that was funny too.

Ain't you two hilarious. Kalin weren't smilin.

She makes a good point.

The only good news Kalin could truly secure was that Navidad's pastern weren't worse. Maybe even better. Kalin walked her around some and couldn't detect even a hint of a hitch. There weren't much ground yarrow left, but after washin the wound he applied enuf to leave one more application.

Mouse was also fine, and Jojo let Kalin lead him around. Kalin then took all three horses down to graze the meadow. The rain didn't abate. No matter what he did Kalin couldn't buck loose the sense that whatever plans he and Tom had made, the plans he'd tried to see through to their end, they weren't but comin to naught. Whoever Tom was hallucinatin was tellin Kalin's hallucination what needed no hallucinatin: they was trapped.

You want my advice? Tom asked as they walked on together, with Ash trottin freely alongside Jojo.

Finally.

Get outta here fast as you can. Yesterday's slide won't make no difference to them. They're comin for you. And they'll come for you right from there. Tom pointed out what needed no pointin out: the only entrance into the cirque, and the only exit too, with Bewilder Crick at its center.

You tellin me to give up?

Tom shrugged and tried to keep his smile, though Kalin couldn't miss how any amusement there looked to be on its way out.

And the horses?

Tom didn't say nothin.

I ain't givin up.

Pia's laughin. She's havin a heckuva time.

As they headed back, Kalin got worried about Landry. What if while he'd been gone their pursuers had somehow gotten into the cirque and fallen upon her? And, though it was likely just a coincidence, this feelin had occurred right when Hatch had ascended to the highest point he was gonna reach on Agoneeya's north side, when he was starin through his scope, his barrel slowly sweepin away from Cahoon's Staircase, risin up over the numerous small waterfalls, toward the last cliffs where Bewilder Crick was just leavin the meadow, the entrance to Kirk's Cirque. Not that Hatch could've spied Kalin from there, Kalin, who, along with the horses, Tom and Ash too, was now movin along at a jog, Tom keepin up only because he wanted to know why they was suddenly in such a hurry if they had nowhere to go and nothin better to do than wait for the rain to quit, questions Kalin left unanswered, figurin the less Tom worried, the better.

No pursuers had assaulted their campsite, which, with more dawn comin through the gray drizzle, Kalin could now confirm offered them excellent views. The cirque was void of intruders. What's more, and this pleased Kalin greatly, Landry was still sound asleep.

Only when he set the kettle to boil some water did he hear Landry whisper somethin. Though it weren't really a whisper. Softer but also higher. More like a squeak, which sure didn't sound like Landry, so much so that Kalin ignored it at first, figurin it was some of that sleep nonsense she could get on about when she was dreamin.

He had just emptied that last can of beans into their pan, maybe enuf to take away the hole of hollerin hunger now tormentin both their bellies, when it happened again: Landry's soft voice, barely audible but definitely squeaky, like she was afraid to speak any louder.

Kalin . . .

I'm right here, Kalin answered back with the same measured softness.

I'm in trouble.

Kalin stood up quick.

Don't do anythin fast, Landry continued to say from under the blankets in that high, soft way through clenched teeth. *I got company.*

Kalin looked around but couldn't spy nothin near.

A snake's lickin my ear.

Oh heck, heck, heck.

Tom's smile sure vanished. Kalin looked around for somethin to use and saw that, short of a pan half-full of black beans, he had nothin.

What about the gun? Tom suggested, and the ghost was serious too.
And maybe Kalin fer a moment even entertained the possibility.
I gotta see the thing to shoot it, Kalin finally hissed back.
Stop talkin to Tom, Kalin. And don't even think about usin the gun.
Its head is by your ear?
I think it's by my neck now.
Don't move.
Oh I'm mighty thankful for that advice.
Don't talk neither.

But Landry's silence was worse. Kalin pulled off his boots and socks
then and in his bare feet padded over so he was standin behind her.
By her hair, the only part of her visible now beyond what was coverin
her, he could tell about where her head rested. With his right hand
he slowly pulled back the blankets, and then his left hand grabbed
the snake right under the head. Oh boy, how the rest of that torpid
Great Basin rattlesnake started twistin about right then, but Kalin
held tight, and that was that. He marched it down the rocky slope and
then marched it off some more just to be certain and then still some
more until he came across the midden of what one mountain leaves
behind when it eats another, broken boulders and shattered rocks and
such, which was where Kalin finally flung that snake, even offerin
some words to the effect of *You can do better, but we're grateful nonetheless
for your company.* Not that that Great Basin looked back to acknowledge the sentiment, sidewindin the heck outta there, lookin to find
another warm spot, likely with somethin to eat, where he could sleep
out winter, which if you're curious to know this snake did manage to
do, devourin a long-tailed weasel, even if by the followin fall he had no
thoughts for that abandoned den but in fact returned to the same spot
where Landry had slept, restin his head in the last splashes of warm
sun there, like he missed her, and you know what, maybe he did.

Though plenty might've expected Landry to have kept her eyes
squoze tight, she did no such thing. Sure, she was known to bellow
and rail and confuse herself with her own antics, but that didn't mean
she'd ever relinquished the terrible courage that derived her heart,
what allows a person to keep their eyes wide open in the face of agonizin challenges. A quality she and Kalin both shared.

Right when Kalin had lifted the blanket she hadn't been sure if
it was him or that enormous and powerful serpent that was risin up
to do battle. She couldn't see Kalin, but she sure did see the rattler,
lickin her hair by then, near close enuf to lick her cheek. And, boy, did
she hear that rattle start up. And then everythin was movin so fast,
it was all a blur, until even the blur was too slow to account for the

nothin that put an end to that little moment, which kept gettin littler and littler as more time got in between her and then. Though Landry weren't the forgettin type either. She'd never witnessed such accuracy and speed close-up like that.

While she waited for him to come back, Landry had done a bit of dancin about to try and shake the shudders from her body, hoppin on her toes, wigglin her fingers, but above all else makin darned sure that there weren't no more snakes around. About then she seen that Kalin had breakfast boilin on the fire. She could've checked then if there were other preparations needed. She could've at least waited.

And to be fair, Landry did, albeit incorrectly, assume that Kalin had already eaten. And so, as fast as Kalin had been at snatchin that big snake away from her, Landry spooned the bubblin contents of that pan into her big yap. And then helped herself too to a mug of the boilin water that Kalin had seasoned with some grounds of coffee he'd managed to scrape together, what included even a few grains of sugar.

Landry would've said then, if there was anyone around to listen, and given that the horses were right there, and therefore, accordin to Kalin, Tom was also right there, she ultimately did say then: *That sure was good!*

In fact Landry was on her third mug when Kalin come back in bare feet, and given that there weren't no way he could've put on his daddy's slicker with a furious four-foot viper in one hand, he was extra soaked, soaked through, really.

Not that Kalin said one word about the vanished beans or the few gulps of warmth he managed for hisself. It really didn't matter to him. Landry was okay. That's what mattered. She was smilin that long smile, and so Kalin was smilin too. Even Tom was smilin. Tom smiled more when Kalin held his bare feet to the fire to dry them. He weren't the only one to notice the hose that was coverin his ankles.

You got long underwear on? Landry commented. *That was smart.*

Kalin didn't say nothin but set at once to gettin his socks back on.

They look more like pantyhose though, she continued.

They are pantyhouse. Oh how Tom was startin to hoot and holler now. *I borrowed my momma's because I didn't have no long underwear.*

Landry couldn't help herself either. *What's Tom say to that?*

He can't breathe, he's laughin so hard.

Landry ended up joinin her brother in that spectacle, the two of them heavin over sideways at the thought of Kalin in pantyhose, and again Kalin didn't mind. It beat the heck outta the loneliness he'd felt out there. He didn't even notice that he hadn't noticed that he'd set his neked feet before Landry and hadn't felt a tinge of discomfort.

You should've eaten the snake, Tom said then.

Kalin at once felt bad then. He never even thought of that. Yet another dumb mistake.

Once he'd got his boots back on, Kalin set to figurin out how to hang his Storm Rider up so it would dry. He didn't make much headway until Landry came over and rigged it up just fine so it were close enuf to the fire but not too close to burn. And this mornin's fire sure was puttin up a fuss, *like it's just spittin and cussin* was how Landry put it. Kalin set a few more broken branches on the flames, and that only worsened the feistiness.

What is it? Landry demanded. *I hope you ain't sore over me havin a good laugh about your . . . underwear?* Her long smile broke again into giggles, and that got Tom cacklin again too.

It's hard for me to say this, Landry, but we're in a sitch, and I can't rightly figure out what to do next. We're stuck until this rain quits.

Well, it might not quit at all.

It's got to.

And if the Porches are on their way now? Landry asked.

They might not find us, Kalin reasoned.

They act like idjits, but they ain't. Not in that way.

I figured.

How much time do you think we got until they're here?

Where we have to go is too slick now.

There ain't no other way?

Back the way we come.

We'll run into them fer sure, and they'll catch us and kill the horses.

Probably kill us too.

Don't that dampen the mood.

Kalin cracked a smile. His first in a while it seemed.

Heck, we're already dampened through and through. Landry couldn't resist.

Kalin smiled, but he sure was tired of the dampness. They both were. No part of either one of them was dry enuf to take a spark.

I ain't goin back that way. There, Kalin finally said it to her.

Neither am I, Landry answered. There, she finally said it to him.

Kalin studied her then, studied her close. He was tryin to determine one thing: whether to tell her what lay ahead, which might damage terribly her confidence and compromise what skills she'd need to get done what they needed to get done if they was to survive the ordeal; or to not say a word, just let the truth unfold of its own accord, a truth that Kalin, if he could help it, wanted to hide from even hisself.

Where we have to go is slick, but slick still gives us a chance, even if it's a lot slimmer a chance than Tom and I planned on.

Do we go now or wait a little longer?

Kalin thought over the question. *If it snows, we don't have a chance.*
Landry looked around. Not that she needed to. *It could snow.*
I think it's gonna snow.
Then we need to go now, Landry asserted.
Kalin nodded. *We can still pick the moment that makes the most sense. We can keep an eye out for them. When we see them, we go. That might even buy us some hours. Noon could see the weather ease off, even warm up some, long enuf to see us through.*
It was 8:26 a.m.

K alin and Landry agreed to break camp as much as they could so that when time came to move they'd only have to take down the tarps, restow those and the ropes, and load up Mouse. The good news there was that Mouse's load had lightened: most of the hay was gone, the food too, plus all the supplies they'd lost.

While Landry got to foldin up the beddin, Kalin sat down with the binoculars and unscrewed the lens caps. They were made of some kind of rubbery plastic, and with his pocket knife it was easy to cut a big hole in each. Then from one side of his undershirt he cut out a rectangle, which he in turn cut in half, usin the knife again to add row after row of small slits. Last of all, he held the perforated squares tightly over each lens while he screwed back on the lens caps. As expected, the improvised fabric hardly troubled the view.

What's that for? Landry asked.

First off Kalin near jumped out of his skin for the sudden closeness of her. Landry had been opposite him when he'd started this little project and then had even moved off closer to the cliffs, where she'd sorted more of their gear. He hadn't heard a whisper of her comin up behind him nor even heard her squat down, her head near on his shoulder, her hair near on his cheek.

Scare ya, did I? Landry asked, or maybe demanded is more like it, and either way absolutely thrilled.

Heck yes you did! Near quiet as Tom, maybe quieter, and he's a ghost!

Maybe I'm a ghost too! she cackled.

Tom, though, weren't joinin in on this cackle party, and maybe for the same reason that Kalin didn't find it so funny either. Kalin's skin still wouldn't quit crawlin from the surprise of her, though he was also pretty impressed, happily so, fer reasons he couldn't say.

So? What ya doin? she persisted.

This'll make sure no glare on the glass gives away our location.

Ain't it too overcast for that?

Probably. But I'd rather play it safe.

Your daddy show you how to do that?

How'd you figure that?

He don't come up much except where the trouble is. How to hide from others how you're seein them seems a thing trouble teaches you.

I don't think I've ever heard it put better.

Kalin really was gobsmacked by little Landry's assessment, and that reaction weren't lost on her. In fact it must be admitted, she was plumb floored by the compliment and even had to settle back on her haunches a second longer, tryin to sort out the feelins suddenly comin up, what she couldn't sort out but didn't need to sort out, because feelin good don't require more than settin back on your haunches and smellin the piney air and wavin at a gray ground squirrel also set back on her haunches and maybe just as happy too. And look at that Uinta chipmunk over there! Was that the scurry of a mouse?! Is that a badger?!

Life out there accelerated again, dashin for cover, resecurin shelter, as the drizzle once again turned to a heavier drench. Tall brown stems upon the meadow sagged together but in the strange alchemy of movement up here bounced back a moment later as sheaves of dull gold. The storm then seemed to briefly come apart, shreds of cloud descendin into the cirque like they was curious, explorin the far walls, pillars of mist kissin Altar Lake. And even in such cold and dauntin environs, stuck like they was, Kalin and Landry still found it pretty magical.

Kalin got to puttin back on his Lee coat then, dry now if extra smoky, and then his daddy's slicker, the sight of which always did evoke his daddy, what weren't so pleasant a feelin, even if the feelin always passed.

Where do you think you're goin? Landry asked.

To get a view of Isatch Canyon.

Landry stood up. *I'm comin.*

Landry, I need you to stay here with the horses. Finish packin up. I'm thinkin we can ditch the packsaddle. From here on out we'll go light as we can.

Landry didn't like this plan one bit, but she could see it made sense. *You gonna be long?*

I better not be.

And Kalin wasn't. Well, not that long, about an hour, which Landry didn't waste, organizin and packin tight what remained, the blankets, the first aid, the cookware, readyin their saddles, saddle pads, and tack. It was goin fine too, until, in the midst of such preparations, Landry gave serious thought to not doin one more bit of it because, first of all, this here was grunt work compared to the reconnoiterin Kalin got

615

to do, and, second, it felt too much like housework her momma had her do. Chores! That's what it felt like! Kalin had her doin chores! Who did he think he was anyways? Fer sure he weren't her momma!

Landry even sat down for a good ten minutes, at least, just to do nothin except be ornery, that and to try talkin some to Tom, Kalin havin assured her that Tom weren't ever far from where the horses were. But she found talkin to nothin hard work too. Landry didn't even manage it for a minute, if that, startin off with *Are you there? I bet you like seein me doin this sorta crap chorin. I bet you're laughin too!* before trailin off, especially with the horses lookin at her like she was bonkers, especially Jojo, who even snorted in foggy disapproval, which quieted Landry, even if it didn't quiet her head none about Tom, thinkin of him still standin there, shakin his head because, yabber-gal that she was, she didn't have the strength to talk to a ghost, two ghosts if you count Pia Isan, more if you count who was followin her. Landry needed the livin.

About this time Landry also began to reckon with just how little food they had. As in almost nothin, as in just one bag of jerky, which she might've got into then if she hadn't also come across the empty bean can and then after some not-so-remarkable thinkin on her part finally did the math that let her know how she must've helped herself to all the beans. Weren't it also true that Kalin always waited until she ate first? Now it's possible she was wrong. Maybe this mornin he'd helped hisself first. She wouldn't've blamed him. She'd been asleep. And anyways she'd confirm just exactly what had happened with that last can when he got back. But Landry was still blushin for shame. Because she already knew what he'd say. Had the poor boy eaten anythin this mornin?! Had she left him anythin of the kettle drink he'd conjured up? Landry double-blushed. Had she ever felt this ashamed?

It was then, as Landry was confrontin her outright selfishness, that the memory of the snake, the memory she'd done her best to already shunt aside, came slitherin back, bigger now and faster, and meaner even than the real snake. And suddenly that rattler was everywhere except where Landry could see it: under a saddle pad, behind a saddle-bag, coiled up and ready to strike from within their fast-diminishin woodpile . . .

This personal ghost upon Landry's thoughts was somethin awful, though what shuddered her the most was the memory of Kalin! Faster than a blur, just pluckin up that snake like it weren't no big deal, and it weren't, not for him, with Landry havin every reason to applaud that rescue and fer sure not fear it. But she did fear it. A lot. And she couldn't say why.

Not that Landry was any less pleased to see Kalin March at last emerge from the drizzle and mist, the horses singin out first, Navidad well before the rest of them, before Kalin was even visible.

The canyon's flooded, Kalin announced. *And far as I can tell, empty.*

He sat by the fire, sheddin the slicker, shakin the water from his dirty Stetson, warmin his hands. The kettle was on the coals and puffin steam. Landry poured him a mug.

I'm sorry. It's mostly water, but it's warm.

Kalin thanked her, askin first if she'd have some too, her declinin the offer, crestfallen by this reaffirmation of his restraint. He treated that drink too like it was ambrosia from Mount Olympus. Fer half a sec Landry half believed it was. Though Kalin weren't no immortal. He talked about his jog along the base of the cliffs above their campsite.

You jogged? Landry just had to interrupt him. *For serious?*

Kalin explained it weren't a fast jog but it had felt good. It had warmed him up and even seemed to dry his clothes some. He'd stopped when he had a good view of the cirque entrance, and bein as high up as he was he could also make out where the landslide had savaged the mountain. It shocked him plenty that they'd managed to get out of there alive. He was surprised too to see that ash tree still standin, *right there on the edge!* He figured a crossin now would be no easy affair. *I sure wouldn't go anywhere near it.*

Are you sayin we have all the time we need?

Another day fer sure.

Do we need a whole day?

Kalin shook his head. *Just a few hours will see us through the worst of it.*

Kalin then described how he'd also found a good view of the south side of Isatch, or the north side of Agoneeya, where the rifle shots had come from. Even with binoculars it was too far away. The deep mornin shadows hadn't helped either. But Kalin was still able to observe with some clarity the trails the shooters would've had to take to reach a spot where they could've fired on Kalin. And he'd watched those pathways for a while and was relieved to report that the whole area was empty. Far as Kalin could tell, there weren't nobody in the canyon at all, except them, though he did admit how right before he started headin back, he thought he caught the flicker of lights, strange lights, like they was part of the mountains and not part of them at all.

No one knows with any certainty what in fact Kalin meant by this or what he saw. What is certain is that no known person was on Agoneeya or anywhere in the vicinity. Melody Jalliday, from Orvop, who many years hence would wind up teachin pilates in Burgos and Almería before settlin in the Canary Islands, would mostly conclude that Kalin couldn't have seen more than the immense rivers of cloud droppin over the back of Katanogos and down those ridges runnin into Isatch Canyon. *Maybe spendin so much time with a ghost, or whatever Tom was, sparked Kalin's mind to see more of them kind. I dunno. It's like when we're in love, we see love everywhere.* Teresa Cloward, from Rome, Utah, who would serve her mission in Abuja, Nigeria, but instead of returnin to the United States would wind up livin in Rome, Italy, workin for an architecture firm, would find herself too often arguin over Skype with her friend Melody Jalliday that it weren't no matter of imagination but a truth everyone from that area already knew about them mountains, especially Katanogos: they was surely inhabited by all sorts of mischief, includin demons, sprites, dybbuks, and gremlins, *and why not throw in trolls and imps and the like?*, all of which she would insist were often to be found *congregatin among the folds of them deep geologies.* And Teresa would confect this popular vision not only to Melody but to Apryl Weber, as well as Aloe Malafa, and Corrie O'Brien, who was one of the three who'd laid eyes on Old Porch lurkin around Trent Riddle's place. Prem Patricks, from Spanish Fork, who would wind up as a mission head for the Church in Manila, never would comment on either Jalliday's or Cloward's confabulations, but even so, without ever admittin any interest in or opinon about such events or recountings, would nonetheless on his own, and only at night, frequently suffer intensely personal and almost-guilty ruminations about how, whether true or not, such paragnosis hinted at by Kalin March, these will-o'-the-wisps, phantom winks upon the hills, other mischiefs not directly mentioned, not only suggested a broadenin of the boy's imagination, maybe even some broadenin collective imagination, in this new reach, at this new elevation on their journey, but also rubricated another obvious change, by the light made out of shimmerin distance, in Tom hisself, who was not with Kalin but back by the horses; Kalin able now to reflect upon him more abstractly and so revisit again how Tom had come forth from the rain unto Navidad and Mouse, how he was still ragged with the past then, his brand a thing of red fire, but who also, since the Awides Mine, and especially after crossin the Ninth Scree, had shed somethin not so easily named, now wieldin a much-altered torch too, with that black Stetson altered as well; all of which Prem Patricks would finally share with Melody Jalliday and Teresa Cloward, encounterin them both by chance at the Madrid-Barajas Airport in 2020, where they'd all share an odd lunch. Out of the blue Patricks would then divulge this speculative riff on *Kalin and his glintin lights beyond,* which he quickly expanded on enuf to call out as *reflections of Tom's future self.* No one would be more surprised than him when both Jalliday and Cloward, and with great sympathy too, agreed, the three of them revisitin such matters later with Shawn Winnie Dulle; Kyle Orlando, who never did hear that Tom Gatestone had peed on his car door handle, though it didn't matter much, seein as how it had rained hard not long after Tom had carried out that questionable prank; as well as with Albacely Bennion and Fewel Marcondes, who would ask: *What then of Kalin's future self? What of Landry's? Were they coded flashes warnin them of the burdens and trials ahead? Some damnable prophecy? Unless it was just mornin light and nothin more.*

A last note on this matter, which relates only because it mentions burdens and trials, and because it was titled *Lights on Agoneeya,* Nathan Nibley, originally out of Ogden, would while tourin Germany as a professional cellist, this when he was in his late twenties, call forth from the air on a train in Moldova the followin:

> *Made-up light is sometimes all there is to find.*
> *Don't burden the companion at your side.*
> *Carry it on your own. We all face trials*
> *we cannot share. Don't talk about what you stole.*
> *Don't bring up either what you'll get for yourself later on.*
> *Lend a hand. Not one of us is whole.*
> *By Ash Tom was content. By Kalin he—*

Nathan Nibley never finished these lines thanks to an envious and very disturbed musician whom Nathan counted on as a friend.

K alin didn't tell Landry about them uncanny glimmers. Landry, though, now far more attuned to Kalin than he had yet realized, sensed somethin askew and pressed him.

Out with it. What else did you see?

And Kalin, not deaf to her fierce perceptions, smiled warmly. *Just elves and fairies. More ghouls fer sure.*

Landry remembered herself then and got up to fetch the jerky.

You better eat somethin.

Kalin accepted the offer, diggin out of the bag three good-sized pieces, but he didn't eat just yet. *You have some. Ain't you hungry too?*

She's always hungry, Tom said, but to his shock Landry refused. *Where'd my little sister go?*

Landry let out a big sigh then. *The beans in the pan when I got up? You'd already eaten half, right? Don't lie to me.*

Kalin took a big bite then of the jerky. His whole body awoke then with great need, an overwhelmin sensation of both deprivation and gratitude that immediately demanded more. And Kalin heeded the command by devourin all three pieces fast as he could. *I didn't even realize I was so hungry until you made me eat somethin. I thank you for that.*

Landry told him to eat more, but he refused. He even urged her to take at least one piece.

This is all we have, she told him. *We gotta make it last.*

Kalin didn't argue.

And I'm awful sorry about eatin all the beans, Landry added. *I'll make it up to you.*

Kalin waved away her apology and promise.

Tom was still gobsmacked. *This here Landry's gotta be an impostor!*

Jojo seemed then to snort his disapproval over Tom's comment, stomped his hoof even.

In order to be ready as soon as the rain quit, they only had to deal with two more things: the horses' hooves and a slicker for Landry.

Landry had on that good dark olive ski parka, what was made for cold weather, but while it was water resistant, it weren't waterproof. Already it had started to soak in some of the wet, and that wouldn't do for what was waitin ahead.

They had no choice but to sacrifice one of the tarps, or at least substantially reduce one. Kalin used his pocket knife to cut out a piece big enuf to fit Landry. He didn't want the slit for her head any bigger than it had to be, and so they had to try a few times before the makeshift poncho sat squarely on her shoulders, snug enuf around her neck to keep her mostly dry.

Once that was done, Landry gave Kalin a tour of their packed and stowed gear, now compact enuf that, between Navidad and Jojo, Mouse was done carryin anythin else, no more a beast of burden. She'd salvaged many of the ropes and straps from the Decker packsaddle, some of which they used on her new poncho to tie up the edges under her arms so she could handle the reins and still keep the wet off her.

Though they hated to do it, when it got time to go, they'd burn the packsaddle and anythin else they was forced to leave behind.

They then got to preparin the horses. Kalin and Tom had planned for Navidad and Mouse but not Jojo. Kalin spent a good while just studyin Jojo's hooves. He'd got out that farrier kit again, and while he didn't touch much, Kalin weren't no hoof artist, he could still trim some and tap into place whatever seemed pokin out or headin in the wrong direction. Because there were only two Easyboots, the big deci-sion came down to which of Jojo's hooves should get them. Kalin did some figurin in his head, mumblin back and forth with Tom, before finally reachin the conclusion that one Easyboot should go on Jojo's right forehoof and the other on his back left hoof.

Plenty have debated the soundness of this choice, but it was what was decided. Kalin said they'd put them on right before they left.

Next he turned to Mouse. From that farrier kit he pulled out a wrench and a handful of flat studs. Startin at the back and workin through all four hooves, Kalin screwed in two studs per shoe. These would grant the horses some grip on the slick rock.

Terrence drill and tap those for you? Landry asked.

He did.

You know Terrence well?

Just that he's a good farrier.

Tom ever tell you the story about Terrence and his horse?

You mean about Yazzie?

F er the next two hours, Kalin set them studs in Mouse's shoes and then Navidad's. He started with the rear and then moved on to the front before recheckin his work and then recheckin it one more time after that. He probably could've managed everythin in a half hour, but a couple of the studs had threadin issues, which fiddlin fixed.

Once that was done, Kalin returned to reexaminin his decision about how to best position the Easyboots, which is when he made an extraordinary discovery: Jojo's back shoes were drilled and tapped. He used four of the six extra studs he'd packed and then fitted both front hooves with the Easyboots. For the first time Kalin felt both elation and relief where Jojo was concerned. Now if the rain would only quit, they might just get free of this trap.

The rain did slow some, but it wouldn't stop. Kalin and Landry knew the horses needed more than to just stand around and wait. They needed to walk. They needed to graze. So Landry and Kalin put on their rain gear, threw some thick logs on the fire, and then with the three horses on their leads set off down the rocky slope. They had to mind the errant holes along the way, nothin too deep, though a blind step and the wrong angle could still easily fracture a leg. That went for Landry and Kalin too. Kalin knew that even a sprained ankle would end them. But once the meadow started, the holes vanished, the rocks withdrew, and the ground became smooth, level, with tall brown grass thick enuf that if it weren't so wet, Kalin would've liked to stretch out there and take a nap.

Great place for a picnic, Kalin even said.

You mean miserable for a picnic.

I mean if it weren't rainin. And it weren't so cold.

Maybe come springtime, Landry answered, none too impressed by the soggy ground they now trudged across. *With flowers brightenin up the place. Not this . . . desolation.*

This place don't need no brightenin. It's fine however it wants to be. Funny thing too about my last time here: I couldn't rest nowhere. I couldn't even stop. Like I told you, this place had so many bugs, I would've been eaten alive. Only when I found a pile of rocks blasted by the wind could I take a breather.

Ha! So you're sayin we need a little desolation to rest?

That don't sound right, does it?

Pick your season, make your deal with hardship: whether bright with Parry's primrose, paintbrush, and blue Lewis flax, or all of it beat down by the comin winter, this here was a wondrous place whether you could find a place to sit or not. Veils of mist parted then to reveal a mother doe readyin her fawn for its first snow. The mother looked up fast enuf, but maybe somethin about the horses and their slow plod didn't make her bolt. She returned to her grazin, the fawn never looked up, and a moment later they was stole away by another veil of mist.

Kalin swore he saw that white owl fly overhead again. Landry swore she saw the old elk. Tom swore he saw multiple owls as well as bears and coyotes, and as they passed through a sparse stand of quakin aspens, he declared there were five beavers ahead.

Every now and then, by some cyclone of aeolian wonder, mists and clouds were momentarily banished from the western part of the cirque, the direction they was headin, on the other side of Altar Lake, where Landry glimpsed for the first time the high walls. These weren't even the summit walls to the northeast, but they still grabbed away her breath. In truth they grabbed away Kalin's too. And, why not, Tom's as well. Only the horses paid no mind to such heights because the horses knew they weren't goin anywhere near such stupidness.

Every time Kalin had come up here, he was undone by the magnitude of the place. Landry wouldn't say she was undone but did find herself not quite acceptin that here was even real, denyin it once, denyin it twice, three times, so that such encirclin ramparts could once again revert to walls of gray no more substantial than curtains of wispy condensation. She had to but wait until a wind came around to tear them to shreds. But no wind they would ever know that day came forth to dispel such profound realities, and Landry could do nothin but stare, slowly liftin her head to follow up so many layers of rock describin collectively a length of time already so immense that even a life lived to the very limit of age would merit no description greater than a sprinklin of sand.

Kalin and Tom cared only for the northeast part of the cirque where the clouds refused to part, where the storm brooded thickest above. But then, just as the horses and Landry had done, Tom and Kalin also looked away.

As they neared Altar Lake, a beaver was swimmin over a slender aspen trunk to her thatch of patient labor. Kalin had started chewin on his fourth piece of jerky, what Landry had insisted he eat, once again refusin for herself the sustenance she craved. Instead she plucked up some grass and, like the horses, chewed on that. Her brother opted to do the same. And there they all was, on the shores of Altar Lake, chewin and chewin and chewin. Mouse and Jojo drank just fine, but Navidad, as if to prevent any chance of reflection, first pawed the gelid water before takin her fill.

About then the rain quit.

Kalin watched as Ash grazed beside Navidad and Mouse.

Is that ghost grass he's eatin? Kalin asked Tom.

Why are you so darned curious about the grass?

You still ain't answered me.

Tom took the stem from his mouth and studied it. *I'd say it's dead. What do you think?* Tom even offered the stem to Kalin.

Kalin hesitated but not for long, and, boy, was he shocked to find that now between his fingers was an actual blade of grass, which he handed over to Landry without explanation, who also handled it just fine, tossin it over then to Jojo, who ignored the offerin, Ash snakin his neck under Jojo's to gobble it right up. Kalin didn't know what to make of that and might've said more to Landry if he hadn't felt his guts abruptly shake right then. He felt like he wanted to bawl too. Had he ever been so afraid? So cold he couldn't shiver? What was goin on? He felt already defeated, as someone who has failed throughout their life with only more failure awaitin him. It made sense too: of course the dead weren't no different from the livin because the livin were already dead too. At least that's how Kalin understood it. He wanted to curl up right then and shake until the ground parted and swallowed him up. Was he really that tired? He sure was glad Tom was there now.

As was made clear on the Ninth Scree, Tom had never physically got this far, not with Kalin, and never with horses, but they'd talked plenty about it, imaginin and plannin. Tom also had never told his friend the details concernin the final part of the journey until that

623

day in the hospital when Kalin knelt at his bedside and Tom whispered hoarsely into his heartbroken ear everythin left to know. Yeah, there is a heart in the ear. And yeah, it can be broken.

On his own Kalin had already managed the hardest part a good dozen times but always on foot. He'd come up here just as Tom had instructed him to do, then around Altar Lake and on to what all that followed, except for reachin or ever layin eyes on Tom's Crossin.

Part of Kalin's faith in Tom was how the right path continued to reveal itself through Tom's insistence, his assurances, though nothin was writ down or sketched, just patiently told and retold. Kalin loved sharin his successes, about how Tom was right, the cliffs did give way to a path up, how he'd reached the cirque, and so on, his friend by then barely able to smile, so defeated by disease, but still managin to chuckle anyway: *I told you so.* And, wow, what a view! He'd never seen anythin like it. Tom didn't have long to live by then, and he didn't care nothin about no view. The view was beside the point. What mattered was that Tom's route was mostly wide enuf for a horse to make.

Tom and Kalin had discussed plenty whether it was better to lead a horse or ride a horse. Goin by foot and leadin a horse was possible, but just one hesitation or one wrong flick of the mind and how easily a hoof might go errant to the air, and then there was no tellin what panic might do to the rest of them hooves, with a fall bein the most likely outcome, and in that agonizin twist into nothin takin along whoever was on the other end of the lead. Now of course you could let go of the lead, but would you want to live on knowin what you was responsible for? Especially since your equine friend might've lived if you'd've been brave enuf to ride instead of walk.

Kalin and Tom had also debated plenty whether or not to blindfold the horses, but a horse deprived of sight might also easily fail.

Clop-Clop-clip-Clop.

One curious thing that had happened since those many exploratory excursions on foot, no matter the growin familiarity with the environs or the provisions he'd dragged up, pitons and carabiners too at one point, with a mind always set on studyin every turn, practicin every move: while he was away from the mountain, the memory of the route had continued to grow narrower and more vertiginous.

Even now, glancin at the clouds moored to Katanogos, again ponderin what they hid, queasied Kalin somethin awful. Had he badly misjudged what a horse could do and what he could do with a horse that could only do so much? It weren't like there'd ever been an opportunity to practice. You couldn't fail and try again. Of course, maybe if the clouds would just part for a moment, Kalin could see that it was only fear makin the worst of the situation.

624

Miles Daley, from Park City, livin in Japan, where he'd served his mission in Fukuoka in 2026, and employed by a Tokyo visual effects studio, while his husband, Haru Taguchi, also from Park City, renovated a small apartment in Atami, would assert that instead of a curse, the weather was doin Kalin a favor. *Where they were headin was so extreme and impossible that to have stared at the path too long beforehand might have been too much for him,* Miles Daley would remark one night over glasses of beer. *You think Kalin would've given up?* his husband would ask. *I'm just sayin their journey was beyond the pale.* Miles Daley would recall this conversation with extra vividness because that very day he would be diagnosed with a disease that would take his life weeks later. He would tell Haru he was glad he hadn't known for long that this would be his end.

The worst part for Kalin, though, was still the most obvious question: what about little Landry? Yes, she was one heckuva rider. On her Jojo there was no one better, and accordin to Tom, and what Kalin had seen fer hisself when she outrode them Porches on the main trail, there was no one faster. But where they was headin now weren't no race. In fact it weren't no kind of regular ridin at all. No one that Kalin had heard of, except of course Tom, knew how to do what needed doin. What waited ahead required of horse and rider an unfalterin focus that would not suffer even one small distraction. Forgettin the physical aspect for a sec, just the mental demands were witherin. Steady, calm. Steady, calm. Steady, calm . . . With no option for anythin else.

Landry would have to ride behind Kalin, and she might even do real good most of the way up, until, just like that, in less than a second, Kalin might hear the terrible scramble of hooves scrapin away at slick rocks, whereupon silence would swallow them, even if Landry was screamin, which of course she'd be doin, yellin at the top of her lungs; silence would still swallow her and Jojo up, and Kalin would not be able to look back, he would not be able to even pause, he'd just have to keep goin . . . Steady, calm. Steady, calm.

Where's your head at? Landry asked then.

Thinkin about the weather, Kalin answered.

Tom called Kalin out too. *If that ain't a flat-out lie. Come on now, at least tell me the truth: where's your head at?*

You don't wanna know.

After the horses had grazed and drunk, and grazed some more, Kalin led Navidad and Mouse into the crick. Landry sloshed behind, complainin about her wet feet. Tom and Ash, though, rode alongside on the crick bank, with Ash so light-footed that the water beadin the reeds didn't break free, though Landry swore she could see them tremble. Landry was also disturbed by another glimpse, seein how it should've been just her and Jojo's reflection in that crick water, except, *Clop-Clop-clip-Clop*, likely because of the angles, *Clop-Clop-clip-Clop*, of course it had to be the angles, *Clop-Clop-clip-Clop*, not even Kalin's reflection nor Navidad's nor Mouse's were supported by that dark ripplin water, and even worse, there seemed for the briefest moment, in a reflection of the banks that did hold, a shimmer of somethin pale, *Clop-Clop-clip-Clop*, paler than the gray fulminatin clouds above, and more than one paleness too, movin like their own storm across the uncertain surfaces of this grand passage.

Is Pia Isan with my brother right now? Landry asked Kalin.

Oh, she don't ever leave me, Tom answered.

Landry didn't wait for an answer. *Does she ever smile?*

Oh, she's nothin but smiles. Tom grinned. *I kinda like her.*

Seriously? Kalin couldn't tell if Tom was teasin. *Tom says he likes her! The horses make her smile. She mostly looks at them.*

Does Landry make her smile?

She don't think twice about Landry.

What about me?

She don't think much of you either.

Her little chipmunk, though, likes Landry, Tom added then.

Kalin shared this news with Landry, and that pleased her to no end. *I like chipmunks. Squirrels too. They do seem to like me.*

Probably because they think she's just a big nut, Tom added with a cackle.

Probably because they think I'm a big nut. That was always Tom's assessment. Landry cackled back and Tom's eyes went wide with joy.

Though the rain had ceased for the time bein Kalin's and Landry's faces and hands still grew wet with condensation, the horses too, their long wind-braided manes, their flanks, their tails dazzled as if with tiny translucent pearls. It was like walkin through a dream. And in that sense it made sense that here was where Tom told them about how he was comin to know the horses more and more if in a way words could not understand. It was impossible for him to explain properly the comfort he now knew, especially as somethin else more terrifyin, what he also had no words for, continued to gather around them. Tom smiled and frowned then, and Ash shook his magnificent head, his coat now appearin whiter than the clouds they moved through, whiter even than clouds alight with the mornin sun. Tom's Stetson seemed much the same, nearly white, bleached like bones among the red ferns.

And that was when Tom told The Story of Jojo.

Jojo was wild from the start, born with a hot wire in his heart. Folks admired him from foal to colt, mainly for his breedin. He was Arabian, mostly, maybe with some Thoroughbred, some mustang. He had black skin more beautiful than moonlight when it's pure and unfettered by any demand to reflect, with blacker hair and white tickin. Rabicano was the best fit. He sure weren't technically, as in genetically, a true roan. Not that it mattered; everyone who saw Jojo just saw blue.

He was powerful too and stubborn, and when he was broken, though many agree he was never broken, he never sacrificed that preservin instinct to suddenly buck and bolt for no reason anyone could explain. Because of this unpredictable quality he was kicked around from trailers to auctions to concrete-floored stalls to more trailers. And kicked around weren't just some expression. Too many folks landed kicks on his sides, his flanks, and that wild creature of midnight blue took them insults and held on to them until they matured into a moment none could guess at, and then he kicked back. Jojo pretty much near kicked every wall, gate, and rib cage if he could get close enuf. Now and then he'd manage a good bite too.

By the time the Gatestones got him, you couldn't even approach Jojo without him rearin straight up, which Tom thought was funny as a comic book, though even he was cautious about gettin too close. Their daddy, when he first set Jojo loose in their Indian Hills paddock, named him Crescent Moon because he spent more time in the air than on the ground.

Landry, though, called him Jojo. She and Jojo arrived at the Gatestones' at pretty much the same time. This was 1973, and they was both six. Landry had never seen a horse except in tattered storybooks. And then one day when Dallin weren't lookin, little Landry slipped under the fence rail and ran to him because, as she later put it, she'd wanted to hold the moon.

Tom's dad was none the wiser neither. How could he be? It weren't like he heard anythin. Not a scuffle, not a bump. And sure not one of them wild neighs that typically followed that big stallion goin skyward. Who can remember what Dallin was doin at that moment, but like a good parent will quick enuf notice when there's nothin to notice when there's a child around, why, that's usually when trouble's in the makin.

Dallin didn't even think to look first to the paddock. She'd only been near his boots, near underfoot, and but moments ago too, and now he was frantic and headin into the barn, and when he didn't find her there, why he was lookin around the truck, even down on his knees lookin under the truck. Only when he stood back up did he look to the paddock and behold his newly adopted daughter holdin that blue Crescent Moon. She was just standin there with her arms wrapped around one leg, her head restin there too, not even tall enuf to reach that horse's chest. Her eyes were closed.

And do you think that big blue stallion was bitin and kickin? Heck no. He was still as a statue. Well, that's not entirely true; eventually he did lower his head to sniff some her hair, nostrils flarin maybe for the newness there, or if you believe Sharlene Kizis, who was from Orvop but wound up tryin to put down roots near Edinburgh, he was *catchin in Landry's wild black ringlets a whiff of familiarity, of common ancestry, the spirit of Goodness.* Tom didn't put it like that, but he did admit that Jojo's nostrils were drinkin in somethin no man will ever scent out: the recognition of a heart that would from that point on never leave his side, even if a grave stood between them. *Clop-Clop-clip-Clop.*

Not that Dallin Gatestone the Good, Dallin Gatestone the Kind, Dallin Gatestone the Calm could wonder any at this idyll. He near lost his mind. That was one big mean horse towerin over that tiny dim-witted girl. *Whoa!* he kept tryin to huff out, already breathin too fast. *Whoa!* Like *Whoa!* was even needed, what with the two of them not movin at all.

Of course despite his panic Dallin weren't so foolish to go runnin out there either. He came in low and slow. He drew no attention. When he had about a dozen feet to go, why only then did Jojo raise his mighty head some, liftin too the leg that Landry weren't clutchin and stompin that down hard. Dallin still tried to get in closer, but again Jojo lifted that free hoof and stomped down, this time twice, thumps hard enuf, loud enuf, to thump Dallin in the chest. Dallin was smart enuf to back off, in fact all the way to the fence, sittin on the top rail, just prayin Sondra wouldn't drive up then because she fer sure would've . . . Who knows what she would've done. Fortunately Sondra didn't come roarin in then, nor did anyone else, and Dallin just sat there and watched and waited, and only then did what he was beholdin finally start to sink in, the craziest embrace he'd ever seen, one of them special moments a life only gets a handful of, if that, one you'll never forget, and Dallin sure never did forget it, and Lord knows he told the story scores of times later, though he never did share how on that day tears had welled up in his eyes and streaked his cheeks.

Dallin Gatestone never could say how long that hug lasted. The way he'd talked about it over the years, it was like it was still goin on. And maybe it was.

What none of them knew was that it was the same for Jojo. Here beside him was someone as fearless as he was, maybe more fearless.

She had come out of nowhere to hold him. He'd never felt somethin so tremendous. And every time Landry was near, Jojo would feel exactly the same way. She was his everythin. So much so that neither the past nor the future had any hold on him except when she weren't there, when he had to wait, but he never had to wait long, because she was there for him every single day.

Tom's parents were at least smart enuf to get outta the way and just marvel at what had transpired. Neither had any reason to doubt that this was the work of their Heavenly Father.

Now and then some fool hand would try to ride Jojo, and he'd wind up on his back or slung over a fence, either way out of a job. And that weren't nothin compared to what Landry would then unleash on him or anyone else dull enuf to try the same. Tom was smart enuf not to try except once. Tom couldn't even get a hand on the saddle horn. He'd tipped his hat and with a curt bow accepted his defeat.

We've all heard about or even seen some clips of them lucky few who can whistle and not a moment later their horse comes runnin. Landry could do the same, though the whistlin was beside the point. She not only could whistle but could cry, laugh, sometimes just whisper his name, and Jojo would come gallopin, sometimes even before Landry knew she needed to whistle or call out. The world was set right with Landry beside him. The same bein true for Landry, of course. Both of them acceptin pretty quick that any other arrangement and, why, the world weren't worth even one more spin.

Tom did his best to relate how Jojo held no recollections of anyone other than Landry. Previous interactions, whether positive or not, were no more material to Jojo than how anyone of us might remember, say, steppin away from some dog doo-doo years ago. We don't. The way Tom explained it, when Jojo was with Landry, the great blue horse felt one with his herd, a vast and mighty presence upon plains and hills far and wide, except that Landry was not just the herd but the territory too.

Jojo needed nothin else. Still needed nothin else. Except maybe another bite of grass.

When both Landry and Kalin asked then what memory Jojo preserved of Tom and Landry's daddy, Tom said there was very little preserved of Dallin except that he was mostly remembered as a nuisance that at various times got in the way of Landry bein with Jojo continuously.

So did he kick my daddy?

Though Kalin knew full well Tom had heard the question, Kalin still had to ask it hisself: *Was Jojo the horse that killt your father?*

Tom mulled this question over as he regarded Jojo. He didn't say much for a spell either, but when he did, he had to admit encounterin a memory of that hour that was blacker than a pane of glass held over fire. He knew only that Jojo had cowered in a corner of his stall. No image of Tom's and Landry's father haulin in his last breath was preserved in the amber of that big horse's heart. Fer Tom only one thing was clear: Jojo had had nothin to do with the death of Dallin Gatestone.

By this point Kalin's nerves was overwrought. They zinged with displeasure and harangued him with stabbin cramps, stomach gurgles too, and even what felt like heart palpitations. And though Tom's slender history of Jojo had presented a calm in the midst of this storm, it still weren't Kalin's calm. Furthermore, as they moved down that crick, gettin closer and closer to where they might get some view of the trails below, Kalin began to haunt hisself with visions of findin Egan and the rest right below where Bewilder Crick begins its wanderin spill down to the Isatch Canyon floor far below, all of them armed, already aimin, Kalin and Landry and the horses goin down like the end of that movie *Butch Cassidy and the Sundance Kid.*

Hear that? Landry said then, though she weren't lookin at where they was goin but back up into the cirque.

Kalin nodded. The storm had started squallin again, low reverberant booms rollin through like the wind was again tryin to blow down the walls of Katanogos.

That's a mighty big sound, Landry whispered.

Kalin nodded.

And beautiful too, somehow, Landry added.

It is.

Even Tom agreed.

Kalin was goin to say somethin then, but his body wouldn't stop tightenin up, maybe clenchin was more like it, as they kept trudgin through the icy shallows, gettin nearer and nearer to that rocky edge promisin vision.

Kalin, do you think I'm pretty? Landry suddenly asked.

Boy, did Tom find that a knee-slapper, and he literally stopped too to slap his knee, slap both his knees, laughin most certainly, though what Kalin heard was more like the wheeze of what it must sound like when the livin die for lack of breath, though he guessed where the dead were concerned, they probably can go on dyin like that fer pretty much forever.

How's that? Kalin managed to get out.

Do you think I'm pretty? I mean objectively.

Kalin turned to face her, to study her, that bright face with not a glint of fear or resignation, whose vulnerabilities carried no expectations, where Kalin easily registered her immense strength, even if he also couldn't believe she was askin him this right then, right there.

Of course, he finally said.

That sure put Tom's overdramatic wheezin to a halt. He popped up quicker than a prairie dog too. Landry gleamed maybe a little, but she also weren't gonna let on how much she liked Kalin's answer.

Even bein so small and with this swing in my leg like so?

What's that got to do with pretty?

I'm pretty enuf then to ask to a dance?

What dance?

It don't matter. Just one of them at Orvop High. Like what Susan Blinks or Wade Francis or Lindsey Holt or Gwynne Pace or even the Porches go to?

Lindsey Holt?

Tom spoke up. *She's talkin about girl's choice, boy's choice, the prom.*

Lindsey Holt goes to dances?

I think so, Landry answered, though she suddenly weren't sure.

Who does he go with?

I dunno, Landry and Tom said at the same time.

Landry's mostly talkin about the popular kids, Tom explained. *The ones Orvop High is always goin on about like they're celebrities. And maybe they are. At Orvop High.*

Like where the story don't matter? Kalin asked with a scoff. He'd stayed clear of the popularity contests at the school, but that didn't mean it didn't grit his teeth some. But Tom weren't havin it.

Son, we're where the story don't matter. And there was grit and gravel in the ghost's voice too. Plus, when had Tom ever called Kalin *son*?!

You want me to tell her that?

Tom shrugged. *She's braver than both of us. You'll see. She's already figured out what matters and what don't. You're the one who's clueless.*

Hey! Landry barked at Kalin, sloshin up closer to him. *Either quit mumblin with him or tell me what you're sayin!*

Sorry.

Does this thing run in your family?

What thing?

Seein ghosts? Talkin to thin air?

Not that I know of. Maybe my dad. Whatever he's talkin about is fer sure not there.

Do you even know what prison he's in?

Folsom.

What did he do?

Nothin good.

You can do better than that.

He killt a cop. Not because he was a cop but because he was black.

Oh he'd love me! Landry even smiled. And that gave Kalin a chance to have a go at a smile too.

It bugs me to think I'm half him, Kalin admitted.

You give blood too much credit.

Yeah, that's probably true. Where was your daddy from?

He was darker.

Darker ain't a place.

Ain't it?

Somethin kicked hard in Kalin's head and kept kickin, even after Landry told him her daddy had been born in Arkansas. There was somethin about Louisiana and Ghana and Scotch-Irish in there too. Kalin lost track of what she said after that. It was like he was seein somethin for the first time even if it had been there all along, and he still didn't know what he was seein. It jarred him, like when a horse throws its head down like a plow and darts to the side and there ain't nothin you can do but try to hold on. Was he about to fall? But why? Navidad moved ahead mildly, steadily. Kalin's hand, though, was white-knucklin the lead rope, his stomach extra unsettled, now with these long waves of chills rollin through him.

So are you gonna just dodge my question?

What question? Kalin was startled by her voice. Where had he been?

Would you take me to one of them dances? Kalin at least didn't miss the seriousness in her question, her thick brows low like the storm upon the cirque.

Tom grinned. *You know she ain't gonna quit.*

I don't dance, Kalin answered flatly and with the truth.

That's somethin Tom would say.

She's right. Tom smirked.

He teach you to say that? Landry asked.

Maybe.

The heck I did, Tom protested.

If Landry was affected by Kalin's answer, and she was, she didn't let it show. *Kalin, you figure yourself a cowboy like my brother?* she asked then, to change the subject, if to get after him some too.

Nope.

Why's that?

Well, for one, the closest I ever came to a cow was seein one across a fence when my momma was drivin us down here from Colorado.

Then what would you say you was?

632

I don't give it much thought. How many more of these questions you got?
Landry looked to sulk.

Landry, the truth is I'm a momma's boy. She's done nothin but good for me. Looked after me, stood up for me; everythin she's done, she's done for me. I just hope one day I can repay her.

She don't want you to repay her.

That's likely true. I think you'd like my momma. I'd like it if you two could meet one day.

That's almost better than gettin asked to a dance. Landry even winked.

How badly did Kalin blush then? Well, enuf for Kalin to know he was blushin bad, heat was in his cheeks, ice was on his back, leavin him no choice but to drop his head, force hisself forward, just keep slog-gin ahead, only a little faster, which he realized he couldn't do, slowin down in fact.

You okay? Landry weren't blind.

I'm fine.

You look waxy.

Just hungry.

We'll get you more of that jerky when we get back. How's Tom doin?

He's a little waxy too.

You sure you're okay?

I just wanna know we ain't about to get company.

What a relief it was to leave the crick. From that rocky edge, where the water began its tumble down to Mist Falls far below, it was easy to see the various ways up here, all of them devoid of movement. Fer the time bein he and Landry and Tom and the horses were safe. Kalin wanted to get up higher along the risin ridge to the left, what was to the east, and from there get an eye on the screes they'd crossed yesterday, but he had to sit down first.

Gimme them binoculars, Landry demanded. He didn't object nor when she told him to hold tight while she sought out the higher elevations he'd only just pondered.

Landry moved quickly then. Neither Kalin nor Tom took their eyes off her, watchin her maneuver up through the terrain until she was scramblin up to the very same promontory Kalin had stood upon just that mornin. Though, unlike Kalin, she didn't stop there, discoverin a stairway of slabs to take her even higher, where she likely got herself the best view yet of the way they'd come.

Like Kalin, Landry took her time too, scannin slow and steady the many possible routes. The light weren't much better than dim, but Kalin was still glad them binoculars was meshed. Landry was plenty exposed up there. Kalin felt he should've gone instead, but he was also real glad to be sittin. He really didn't feel so good.

Landry, on the other hand, when she got back, why, she looked great, all smiles and so relaxed that it relaxed Kalin some, at least cheered him up, cheered up Tom too.

That landslide's gonna get in the way of everyone, she said then.

That's good news. Kalin relaxed even more, and when that first tremor thumped softly in his chest, he was sure it was just his stomach doin its funny turns.

You know I wouldn't be surprised if they don't already figure us for dead, Landry added then. *Just buried alive. My poor momma! Yours!*

That darkened both their hearts, but Kalin also perked up a bit at the thought of gettin another night's rest. Even his breathin mellowed, with the achin knots in his back hintin how they might just now melt away.

They could stand to wait til it was drier now, til the light was right, find the best moment to get it over with. Except if it snowed . . .

Again Kalin felt more tremors thump through him, this time followed by a sharp stab in his abdomen. He couldn't help but wince.

You're hungry, Kalin. We need to get you more to eat.

Kalin nodded, though whatever this was, it weren't hunger. Kalin weren't afraid of hunger. A long nap, that's what he needed. That would restore him. And then them tremorin thumps returned, and this time Kalin realized he weren't the only one feelin the thuds. All the horses' ears were twitchin. Even Ash's.

Tom stood, starin down toward Isatch Canyon. Kalin watched then as fright filled Landry's eyes.

Like that it was there, far now from anythin so remote and subtle as *sensed*. The horses' ears stopped twitchin and locked ahead. They stopped their grazin and drinkin too, the lot of them liftin their heads to face whatever was comin their way, comin closer and closer, a dull whump beatin through the wet air, roilin on by them, on toward the cirque walls.

Kalin handed Landry Navidad's and Mouse's leads and quick moved out upon a wider slab of rock. He stayed hunched as he moved, his injured left hand clampin down on his hat, which seemed again another shade darker. And maybe the darkness now takin up residence on that brim should've quirked some Landry's sense of who it was she was really up there with, who it was that was now standin there by hisself, ready to face an uncalculated wind.

Zina Felt, from Rome, Utah, who earned her degree as an astrophysicist from the I, a degree she put into practice until she settled in Reykjavík, Iceland, where she and her Icelandic husband helped raise their three grandkids, now and then checkin in with the likes of Blaine Todicheenie, Tabitha Karush, Tatum Watkins, and both Wendy and Bruce Oldroyd, would observe: *Every successive retellin only seems to dress up these events in the vêtements of near-silly cinematic speculations. Folks can't help themselves. They just keep changin and rearrangin things until it serves some purpose they have in mind, though they don't likely know what is in their mind. The story is recolorized, desaturated, resaturated, slowed down, sped up, no doubt reframed with this near-pornographic obsession we have for closeness, all the while losin sight of how closeness is never, and I have to repeat this, closeness is NEVER unshackled from the immensity, which we too often fear to consider, especially those immensely distant arrangements slowly alignin and, in their prevailin resonance, orderin everythin.*

Blaine Todicheenie, also from Rome, though he'd move on to Mexico City until he got to roamin around Sonora before finally retirin in Acapulco, rich enuf on agricultural investments to no longer pay attention to such investments, would express tenderly to Zina Felt and Sarah Caulson in one of their yearly Zooms: *No blame-throwin here: the extraordinary is a hard one to remain open to, especially when it's unanticipated and comports itself so as to seem average, normal, even as it at the same time outstrips all surroundin contexts, bewilderin even the history that will come to encase it.* Or try to encase it. Sarah Caulson, born in Springville, grayin in Springville, would remark durin one of her last Zooms with these two friends: *Of course, not one of us can say if all of it weren't just due to chance or preordained by the hand of Our Heavenly Father of the Church.* Blaine Todicheenie didn't let that one pass: *Or even orchestrated by one of them ancient gods that Mrs. Annserdodder used to teach us about when we were sophomores.* With Zina Felt then respondin: *Or more than likely what made it all matter is somethin none of us have the imagination for.* Sarah Caulson would sigh then: *Why ain't that the oldest story of survival?* Blaine Todicheenie weren't really disagreein with either Sarah or Zina that afternoon, so what he would say next was just so they didn't lose sight of this matter of perspective, especially where Landry lookin at Kalin was concerned: *We gotta notice the small things, but we gotta notice the big things too. There ain't one without the other.*

For Cyndee Francom, from Orvop, who ended up in Perth where for over forty years she studied and translated Aboriginal languages, this moment would come down to dirt: *Kalin's hat was just dirty because dirty is where Kalin was at. That's understandable, right? It's what makes the most sense. In fact it makes so much sense, there's no point in revisitin this subject.*

And while an unbearable banter about cowboy hats continues, far fewer folks remark on how Kalin had just now got up to where he was standin: lightly, easily, somehow somewhere along the way shakin hisself free of whatever ailments and fatigue had just been plaguin him; near as easily as how Mouse, after decidin to roll on his back in the crick, returned upright, light as a helium balloon, to shrug loose the water from his coat. Not that the mud flew away near as easy, with enuf stickin to his rump and long tangled mane to make of him a fine mess. Though enuf mud did fly free, dapplin Landry, even reachin Kalin, his hat too, addin yet more discoloration to what Zina Felt, many years hence, would tell Cyndee Francom was that *enigma of identity and intent.*

For her part, Landry only saw her scrawny little friend starin at somethin comin their way, and likely comin their way fast given how the thumpin in her ears kept gettin louder, and what fer sure didn't make her want to stand tall to meet it. Not one bit. It made her want to cower. It made her want to run. The air itself was wild now with movement. Landry quick grabbed up the slack from the leads just as Navidad and Jojo started steppin backwards, though not muddy Mouse, who did throw up his head once before goin back to grazin. By which point Landry had turned away from Kalin, to deal with the horses; though even if she'd had eyes on the back of her head, he would've still appeared to her as unremarkable.

And yet before that black and gold-striped mechanical beast hoverin now in front of them, even Tom atop Ash backed away, and though he would remain forever untouched by the wind, mountain-made or man-made, Tom still put a hand to his hat like it could blow away.

Kalin alone didn't step back. Instead he gathered through hisself a stillness that even Tom found shockin. Landry, while still steadyin the horses, let that odd combination of fear and curiosity get the best of her: she looked over her shoulder to behold not only the helicopter but Kalin, who seemed even more greatly embraced by a state of immovability. Nothin special, though his example renewed her own rootedness, whereupon, as if followin both their examples, the horses followed suit.

Kalin seemed to keep relaxin too, his gangly arms hangin in looseness, his legs appearin so spindly, they seemed impossibly charged to just keep him upright, let alone move him, and none of him was movin, though he sure weren't collapsin either. As Janeen Ewell, an Orvop FFA alumna who pursued a career in dance, not successfully, would say to Emanuelle Bucks and Daniel Leishman: *With deep-rootedness comes great freedom,* likely thinkin of Bella Lewitzky's quip: *To move freely you must be deeply rooted.* Of course, even if Kalin was deeply rooted, it's hard to say there was anythin free about where he was at now. Debra Loveridge, from Boise, Idaho, who for a spell ended up as a movement coach assistin athletes in the United Arab Emirates, would conclude that Kalin's act of *pourin out any contradictory tension was similar to the way a whip achieves a state of complete ease at the tip before breakin the speed of sound.*

Not that anyone there really saw this except maybe for Mouse, who did look up then, sharply too, though hardly bothered by the great air-thrummin flyin machine, instead registerin somethin about Kalin that made him Mouse's absolute adversary, Mouse snortin hot then, even tryin to wheel away, Landry doin everythin in her power to get the geldin back under control, which she never did do even if she succeeded in achievin somethin that looked like control, even as she lost sight of Kalin and the helicopter.

By then the pilot had brought the helicopter around so it was but a few lengths away from Kalin and some lengths above, positioned so his passenger could get an even clearer view of the boy.

Old Porch weren't impressed. So this was the Kalin kid. Old Porch took no interest in Landry either and certainly didn't give a hoot about the horses. He only studied the boy and even grinned and nodded at him, never thinkin for a heartbeat that it might've been better to have never come across these two. Better would've been to grin and nod at emptiness, to have known then for certain that Kalin's and Landry's bodies were pulped under yesterday's great disgorgement of rock.

But whatever might be said of Old Porch, he not only never shied from a contest, he genuinely loved the struggle and the scrap. It might in truth have been what he prized most, more than all his earnins and plans to earn more, more than even the winnin itself, though that declaration would've surprised him, because he knew hisself to be a man who loved to win, who demanded it. Yet what Old Porch loved most of all was to fight.

Old Porch drew then his right hand up like it was a pistol, with that infected thumb playin the part of the hammer, aimin his index finger at Kalin, and though Kalin didn't hear no pop, he sure as heck couldn't miss the big *Pow!* that Old Porch mouthed.

Old Porch was so delighted by this game, he still couldn't recognize Kalin's slackness, the darkenin Stetson, and fer sure not the looseness that further readied Kalin's left hand, though there weren't but air within its reach, even if air might've been enuf. The boy even nodded back at Old Porch. Old Porch fer sure noted that acknowledgment even as he continued to fail to register the most important element of all: Kalin in meetin Old Porch's gaze hadn't wavered once.

In fact it was Old Porch hisself who wavered. Not that he could ever own that flinch. He hid it in a renewed delight over now findin Landry swingin up onto Jojo's back, tryin to skedaddle outta there, with one hand clamped down on Jojo's mane and lead rope, the other hand holdin tight Navidad's and Mouse's leads. Navidad was game to run, and surprisinly Mouse didn't put up no fuss either.

The three were soon enuf canterin back across the meadow to their campsite.

Seein a Gatestone run, especially from a Porch, was for Old Porch one of life's great pleasures.

It was 12:38 p.m.

The helicopter rose up then and began its leisurely pursuit of the terrified Landry. Kalin could do nothin but scramble down from the rocks and run too. No matter that the protestations of his innards had returned. No matter that he didn't have a snowball's chance in heck of catchin up. But he still ran. And at least he could take a shorter route back, one that the horses couldn't walk on much less run on.

I'd help if I could, Tom said as he trotted past Kalin, Ash set on catchin up with Jojo.

K alin managed to reach their campsite not too long after Landry, her objective delayed by havin to tie up the horses lest what she imagined would happen next might scatter them to the far corners of the cirque. By then the helicopter was long gone. It had played some above Landry's head, and fer sure if Old Porch had been wieldin a rifle, they'd've all died. Instead the helicopter passed over Landry and the horses well before she reached the campsite, and then after executin a slow turn, likely still notin the approximate location of the camp-site, or at least where she was headed to, flew over Kalin again before headin out the way it had come, exitin the cirque above the crick and from there descendin down into the canyon.

Not that Old Porch or even the pilot escaped without duly glimpsin, even in their willful and collective blindness, a warnin spelled out just upon the ground: a shadow, a shade, darker than ever, right beside Kalin, what both those minds denied at once. As Rita Christleib, a poet born in Orvop, a poet educated in Brooklyn, a poet who worked in Burlington, a poet who'd go to Greenland to convalesce, would assert, and this in the company of Ananda Lott: *It weren't so much dark as, in all that dampness, icy. Much like how a shadow cast by a tree upon dew-drenched grass preserves in its eclipse the mornin's frost.*

Both men still felt it, though, just like Egan, Kelly, and Billings had felt it when they'd gazed at the fallen mountainside and it had gazed back at them, not anythin livin but that which passes out of life, out of reach, their blood respondin to how such absence warned them *Never come this way again, not if you know what's good for you.* Old Porch and the pilot shivered once and then shook it off like cold is only just cold.

Kalin hisself was runnin both cold and hot, pretty much at the same time, face and body flushed with contortions of chills and sweats.

Goshdarnit, Landry! he still managed to bark out. *Put that thing away!*

At least she hadn't taken her hand out of the dark bag, though Kalin had no doubt what her fingers were clutchin.

Please, Landry! The helicopter's gone.

They're comin back. They know where we are. We're gonna have to fight.

No, we won't. We ain't stickin around.

They'll know where to look.

No, they won't. They'll either turn back to Isatch to look for us there or assume we just vanished into thin air.

Landry looked up then from where she was crouched. *Why? You got some other magic I don't know about.*

To them it's gonna look like magic.

Landry took her hand out of the bag. Kalin sighed to see her hand was empty. *If I'd heard a shot, I would've shot back.*

Fair enuf.

Landry got to restowin the bag, though just the sight of it, even imaginin the metal heaviness there, provoked from Kalin's guts enuf distress that this time he was bent over gaggin.

And that weren't the worst of it. He had to fast drag hisself behind some brush where the rancid components havockin his bowels could finally cut loose, from both ends too, with no sign of stoppin.

It was between these gurglin spouts of effluence that Kalin kept screamin at Landry to keep back. At least he now understood what had been happenin to him. And that was about the only other thing he managed to yell out over the next few hours: Landry had to burn the Dorf jerky. It had gone foul. They was officially foodless. And Kalin was poisoned.

Chapter Eighteen

"Effy"

ondra Gatestone had also awoken well before dawn. Before Porch, before Kalin. She had no idea that her daughter was still alive, right then near two miles up, sleepin snuggly beside a good fire, and deep in a dream too, another one Landry wouldn't remember hours later, this time in a canoe, then without a canoe, just Landry driftin downstream on her back, lookin up at a warm summer sky as she headed toward endless falls, which she avoided by comin to rest in shallows by a shoreside spot where pine trees huddled and squirrels and chipmunks chattered, and Pia Isan's father and mother would find her, and she would know a different name, whereupon the water would release her and she'd float free of herself, free of all her names, especially her authorin name, and even if the dream had no bearin on any future she'd enact, it had felt good and reassurin. Pia Isan's folks were real gentle and they loved their daughter more than light.

Sondra loved Landry more than light but she sure weren't feelin anythin close to good or reassured. She'd hardly slept, just stretchin out atop her bed, her long blue skirt still on, not even takin a blanket as the cold climbed up through the bones of the house. Sondra preferred that chill over anythin that might suggest a life without her Landry. When she stood up in the dark, with no reserve of sleep to rely on, nor any dream to remember, she at least, at last, recalled what she'd wanted to search for in Landry's room.

Sondra emptied all the drawers, pulled down all the books from every shelf. She stripped the bed, emptied the closets, and then rifled through the piles she'd made on the floor to make sure she weren't mistaken, to make sure that what she was lookin fer weren't there.

When she went downstairs she found Allison on the floor in the middle of the livin room. In the dark it was impossible to understand what she was doin. With the lights on it was even less clear. She was cross-legged with her eyes closed, breathin rapidly through her nose.

I wanted to sleep, Allison said after she'd stopped, managin the equivalent of a smile, however sad.

What am I interruptin? Sondra asked.

You ain't interruptin anythin. Just doin some breathin exercises I've never been much good at.

Is this the meditation stuff you mentioned?

Allison nodded. *I never got good enuf for it to make any difference. But I still do it because maybe it makes a difference I can't know.* She shrugged. *I guess I do relax some. Learn to live with less, and you appreciate so much more. I tried to teach it to Kalin, but he had about the same kinda luck as me.*

That's not exactly a ringin endorsement.

No, I guess it ain't.

Both women laughed.

It's a way to refresh the world. Always the unfamiliar. I've heard there are monks who just by breathin right can stay warm in the coldest conditions. They can be barefoot and won't get frostbite.

Did you get frostbite?

Allison looked at her bare feet. *I guess it worked.*

Both women laughed again.

What about you? What were you just doin? Allison asked Sondra. *It sounded like you was trashin a hotel room.*

I finally remembered what I was lookin for. Landry has this diary she keeps. I don't look in it. Once I did do but caught only Tom's name and felt so guilty for readin even that. I gave it to her too and told her she could write whatever she wanted, even the worst kinda stuff, and it would be safe. I had no idea that she'd keep to it so . . . religiously.

Where is it now? Allison asked.

Sondra shook her head. *It's usually in her room, but whenever she goes away somewhere, like when we used to vacation as a family down at Lake Powell, why she'd bring it then. I've always told her that that ain't the best idea. She could lose it, or it might get damaged. I've always urged her just to recap her experiences when she gets back. But Landry insists that diaries don't work that way. It's more dear to her than anythin.*

She's got opinions, don't she?

I'm sure she took it. I still wanna check the stable though. Make double-sure that she took that pink raincoat and her winter coat and her good boots. Her gloves as well.

You're thinkin here is that if she took her diary, it means she was already anticipatin a long outin?

Somethin like that. I know it don't mean squat against this talk about what happened in the canyon. Whether she had her diary or was wearin her raincoat won't make no difference in a landslide.

But?

But it'll tell me she had her wits about her. It'll tell me she was plannin. She was thinkin. She weren't goin out there entirely unprepared.

Allison nodded.

Yeah, I know it ain't much.

After a breakfast of eggs, tea, and cake, with Allison makin it clear that this mornin she was gonna need to find herself some coffee and Sondra makin no noises of objection, they headed to the Gatestone stable near Isatch Canyon.

Sondra broke down in the tack room. Allison rested her hand on the woman's back as she convulsed with no more than a few hard sobs before standin up erect again, wipin her eyes, apologizin too.

The silliest part is that I'm happy. I'm happy to find that her diary ain't here, that her pink raincoat ain't here, that her winter coat ain't here. Sometimes that girl can be dumber than a bucket of rocks but she's got instincts too. Great, beautiful instincts. And what ain't here tells me that she was usin them. Sondra was repeatin herself now, but Allison just nodded along. Repetition finds its place, and in its place finds change too.

I'm sure of it, Allison said.

See here, she took her boots. They're good boots too. They'll keep her feet dry, keep em warm even if she's on top of Katanogos itself, well maybe not the top. To see them not standin right there, and Sondra pointed to the floor under an empty hook and wood saddle rack, *why that's the best news I've had in days.* Sondra was cryin again and this time makin no effort to wipe away her tears.

After that, they scoured the stable for any other signs that might suggest her daughter's mind when she left on Jojo to pursue Kalin and the two Porch horses. In the end it was just the absence of things that offered assurances: the missin tack, her missin saddle, and of course Jojo's empty stall.

Sondra did discover somethin else of interest: a bill from their farrier, Terrence Olsen, for services provided at his home, which explained the lower fee. A call soon confirmed that on five separate occasions, over the course of the summer, he'd applied his gentle art to one black mare and one blood bay geldin.

Sondra also discovered that two EasyBoots were missin. Allison had no idea what an EasyBoot was, and Sondra explained that it was for use when a horse was injured or headed out on rugged trail. *It provides protection as well as extra grip. Especially if it gets rocky.* Did her little girl already have notions of darin the higher reaches of a canyon where no horse should ever go? That didn't sit so well. Of course Landry had had no such plans at the time. She'd only carried them boots as a courtesy to Jojo. She'd learned her lesson on that long ride outside St. George.

Sondra and Allison then headed for the canyon entrance.

It was 7:33 a.m.

Allison was still determined to hike up as high as she could get. Sondra had outfitted her with good boots, thick wool socks, and a winter sweater. She'd made sure Allison had a pack loaded with plenty of snacks, matches, toilet paper, a canteen, and a good pair of binoculars, plus a flare. Sondra also included a stainless steel campin mirror to signal for help and a whistle.

You can blow this for a lot longer than you can scream. Louder too.

Allison thanked her new friend even if from that point on Sondra did her best to dissaude Allison from goin. That was unnecessary. The police and park rangers told her in no uncertain terms that the park was closed. They'd already turned away Hatch Porch. The crick was aflood. Even the main trail at several places was under a few feet of runnin water. And forget the mountainside, which was already dangerously compromised with the heavy runoff: trails unstable if not washed away, the screes even worse, and that weren't countin where the big rockfall had descended upon the upper reaches of Isatch Canyon, presentin hazards exceedin the skills of even trained park rangers. The whole area was a dangerous lesson in precarity that no official wanted someone on their watch to learn about the hard way.

Anyway, in all likelihood, Allison wouldn't have made it past Bridge Two before she was swept into the crick, where she'd either get her head bust open on rocks or use up whatever slim resources officials there had for locatin the children on draggin her dumb keister outta the dunk zone.

As if to make their point, the rain only kept comin down harder, even an hour later, water sluicin off the gazebo, the sheriff's tents, all while the crick water kept pourin forth under the park entrance gate, sheetin across the parkin lot.

Still, Allison and Sondra, and Mungo too, stayed put near the tents, if frequently retreatin to Sondra's Bronco, where they watched the arrival of intrepid volunteers who'd come ready to brave the weather. Utah County folks ain't intimidated by either snow or rain. They know how to dress right and keep a friendly smile, which only a fool would think was insincere.

Sondra and Allison did their time talkin to news crews too, who were just as keen as Allison to reach the site of the landslide, though their interest was mainly to secure pictures worthy of their paper or station. Of the reporters that Allison March and Sondra Gatestone spoke with directly, which included KIUB again, *The Salt Lake Tribune*, and three students from Timpview, the questions were pretty much the same: Were Russel Porch's killers dead and buried under that monstrous collapse? And if that was the case, would their bodies ever be found? Only one of the Timpview students showed any concern for the well-bein of the horses.

KIUB's Ilene Clayton did demonstrate some professional impartiality and got at least a longer version of the mothers' take on things, with Allison again makin an impassioned plea to give Kalin a chance before he was hanged on the gallows of gossip, vouchin for his integrity, which as everyone knows a mother is pretty much compelled to do, though it was somewhat jarrin to hear Sondra Gatestone dismiss in no uncertain terms that her daughter, Landry, was kidnapped by Kalin March, further testifyin that anyone who knew her little girl would agree that Landry wouldn't need no knife or anythin else but her furious little fists to take down the likes of Russel Porch. That was certainly an appealin declaration and description. Sondra even got smiles and laughs to ratify her claim, with the cameraman, Steven Hensel, callin it *tasty*. Both women came away with a tiny sense of victory over the dominant narrative, which at least fer a moment there seemed to wobble some, though as this claim rippled outward throughout the day, the unsettlin it accomplished at first, that Kalin weren't as bad as everyone thought because he hadn't kidnapped no little girl, was quickly co-opted by another more adult version of the same ugly and prevailin narrative: Landry had fallen under the spell of a foul killer and so by association was now one too.

To their credit them Timpview High students were more open to hearin an alternate side of the story, even if that side was basically rooted in what both mothers asserted was the goodness of their kids. These three, Ruth Ann Heimdal, Nicole Beesley, and Clint Hoffer, all of whom would years later find themselves in discussions with Ikue Hayakawa, Melvin Athaiya, and others, would in a series of early dialogues focus less on *what finally happened* and more on *how that what-finally-happened narrative was continually reframed by subsequent revelations as well as imaginative distortions.* They not only interviewed Sondra Gatestone and Allison March but a decade later even spoke with poor Leo Gans, homeless by then, still with his basketball, still with a hockey jersey on, still with no place to go, not that he wanted to go anywhere anymore. Leo would tell them about Old Porch drivin around Trent Riddle's parkin lot that Friday and, you know what?, them kids from Timpview believed him. Leo Gans sure appreciated that and even passed around the ball. That was a first.

Though over the years what these three former journalists found themselves orbitin the most was what they'd experienced firsthand: those distraught mothers in the Isatch Canyon parkin lot. The last title for their unpublished piece was *Two Distraught Mothers Standin Before a Narrative of Blame.*

As time passed that mornin, the prevailin line of inquiry became less about past events and more about future actions: when was the park goin to reopen? Would it reopen that day? With a few folks wonderin aloud if the mothers actually intended to help search for the bodies, though they was polite enuf not to use the word *bodies*. No one ever thought to consider that the mothers might still be searchin for survivors.

A good many of those volunteers who had showed up early soon departed to indulge in more appealin Saturday activitites. Those that stayed made doughnut runs, hung around talkin, and waited for the moment when the park gate would swing open.

Allison March and Sondra Gatestone moved patiently among these various volunteers, mostly Isatch University students with some students from Timpview, Orvop, and Spanish Fork High mingled in, a few from Mountain View, even some comin from as far north as Jordan and South High School as well as the University of Utah. There were even some able-bodied folks down from Park City. The mothers introduced themselves, inquired about everyone's well-bein, and then made their case for a different take on the widely disseminated version of events. Their talkin points basically boiled down to the avowal that Kalin March and by proxy Landry Gatestone had nothin to do with Russel Porch's killin. Most everyone was sympathetic and polite, though as the mothers moved on to a new cluster, remarshalin their smiles, Allison found it hard labor to hear the murmurs at their back and not respond. *What does it matter if they're already dead?* Though one time Sondra did whip around to say in as dignified a manner as she could muster: *It matters because if the dead are mistreated in their remembrance, they come back to mistreat us.*

It was an awful business, but the more Allison and Sondra stuck with it, the more they discovered good people willin to entertain different perspectives. As the mornin passed on, they heard from plenty of folks wishin them luck, hopin that they'd find both Landry and Kalin alive and that this whole misunderstandin might get cleared up real quick. Soon more were tossin around this question, that if Kalin March's and Landry Gatestone's hands really were clean, what did happen to Russel Porch somewhere between Isatch Canyon and Egan's property, what weren't but a hop-skip from the Orvop Temple?

Weren't it the story that this Russel kid rode up to his brother's house with his throat already cut? someone asked. *Then did the killer cut him while he was ridin back? Don't that seem hard to do? Him up in his saddle? That's a hard ride too.* Which more friends, and now new acquaintances, because these groups was fast interminglin, sharin their theories along with more doughnuts and now hot cocoa, agreed seemed highly unlikely.

Whereupon someone suggested that the titular Squaw from the peak above was still hauntin the canyon with murderous intent, this likely brought up because it was, after all, Halloween weekend, with neighborhood trick-or-treatin that very night. *Maybe it was her that done it! Like some Dracula, she sucked on his neck the whole way back!*

Though nearly just as unlikely, as more groups were comin to agree, was the Kalin kid cuttin Russel's throat and then Russel climbin back on the horse and ridin all the way to his brother's house on Fir Avenue. Even if it had all happened in that very parkin lot, such a ride with such an injury seemed highly improbable. Which meant that they was left again with Russel ridin back unharmed, maybe fallin off along the way, gettin cut and then somehow climbin back on, somehow stayin on, and still ridin back to his brother's place on Fir, which just continued to make no sense, meanin that Russel was likely killt when he got to his brother's place, which made even less sense.

Everyone was stumped.

Though this conclusion, when voiced, and voiced in Allison and Sondra's presence, gave both mothers an awful chill that had nothin to do with the cold, because if what made no sense at all were in fact the sense of it all, then somethin had occurred that was truly awful and even biblical or, as the Bible teaches us, truly godforsaken.

Later on when the park rangers, first, and the police, next, confirmed that the park would not reopen under any circumstances until at least noon, many of these potential volunteers and onlookers didn't think to leave, though plenty organized pizza runs. By that point there were at least forty.

Sondra and Allison eventually did leave to resettle at a bank of pay phones in the Isatch University Milkinson Center or rec center. They could've gone back to the stables, but there was only one phone there and no vendin machines stocked with whatever tickled your sweet tooth. Sondra had gone to the arcade room and returned with Sprites, red licorice, and Hostess HoHos, plus a heap of quarters.

Allison sorted the quarters while Sondra uncapped the soda with her teeth and used her teeth again to get at the Red Vines. Not exactly the most befittin actions for thee Sondra Gatestone, but there you have it: she was ravenous, wanted her sugar, plus bitin somethin, anythin, felt good.

First on Sondra's list of calls were the folks the Gatestones employed; next came friends, with Sondra providin what updates she could; she left a message with Judy Dowdell about next Friday's Charity in Practice, things Judy needed to handle, small details, no more;

lastly she left a message with Havril Enos, carryin on about more of them small details concernin the weekend, no more, just to make clear that she weren't steppin aside.

Two phones down, Allison was pluggin in quarters for her own mad calls, not herself bein mad, but near everyone she was callin bein mad at her. Her manager at ZCMI hadn't got her message and was fumin that she'd just up and vanished Thursday and Friday, though when he understood that it was her boy who was on the news, who was now pretty much declared dead in a rockfall, he became sympathetic and told her to take whatever time she needed. She let him know that she needed the job, and he assured her that she was a good employee and she could have that job so long as she kept in touch. The same went for the Cassidy Ski Resort. Her next shift was supposed to start in a few hours, and they was a little irked at first, but then they admitted there was some talk of closin the shop early anyhow. A big snowfall was due in and the resort might have to close until the plows got out. Like ZCMI they just asked that she call next week with an update.

Allison had completely forgotten that Clyde Hill had fired her yesterday. When she dialed up the University Theaters, she was surprised when a machine didn't pick up. It weren't even noon yet. By the way Kalin and Landry was at this point just leavin their campsite to graze the horses and walk Bewilder Crick.

Is that you, Teri?

Mrs. March? Teri couldn't help sayin *Mrs.*

That's right. It's me. I was hopin to leave a message with Clyde.

He's here! We're doin inventory! She seemed weirdly elated. *How are you? I keep hearin these rumors, and what they're sayin on the news is so awful.*

Allison thanked Teri for her concern. It warmed her somethin extra to hear this young girl whom she hardly knew inquire with such sincerity about her own well-bein. They spoke haltingly fer a moment about Kalin, Allison makin it clear that while he may have stolen them two horses, and only because he loved them and they was slated for slaughter anyways, he most certainly did not kill Russel Porch; that was somethin else, somethin most foul, and it had nothin to do with her sweet boy. Teri even added that she too had always seen Kalin as a sweet sort, and if Landry Gatestone was really with him, then them two fer sure had nothin to do with killin Russel Porch.

Clyde Hill got on the phone then, barkin that he'd already fired Allison and what did she want. Allison immediately remembered and then immediately apologized for forgettin. Clyde seemed thrown by her admission. She was about to hang up when Clyde asked if she was okay. Then, like she'd done dozens of times already that mornin and just now with Teri, Allison told her side of the story, and more surprisinly Clyde Hill seemed to listen.

I don't care for them Porches. And I sure wouldn't trust Old Porch.

Allison thanked him, and this time as she was about to hang up, Clyde Hill told her to give him a call when it was all done with and they could revisit her standin at University Theaters 1 & 2. He even admitted that she was one of his best employees, which in sayin aloud seemed to fluster him some. Afterward Allison stood there a bit stunned, a bit exhausted; she'd been apologetic and conciliatory and even embarrassed, but somehow she'd still wound up feelin better off about Clyde Hill than she had since when she'd first met him.

Allison's last call was to her new lawyer, Holly Feltzman, who got right on with her, extra pleased too to learn what Allison and Sondra had been up to. She encouraged Allison to do more. *Keep raisin a ruckus. Get in the papers, get on the TV as much as possible.* She even ushered forth a series of grunts when Allison conveyed with increasin incredulity about how Russel Porch was supposed to have ridden so far with his throat already cut! *That's darned smart and darned right,* Holly Feltzman responded. *If we can establish that your boy and Sondra's Landry were well up in the canyon when Russel caught up with them, that will make his long ride seem less likely. More likely it's Egan Porch that will have some answerin to do.*

Holly Feltzman let Allison know that she'd already requested police reports, the autopsy report, pretty much any report that had been filed or should've been filed or was in the process of bein filed. She'd also found out that there was a young man named Trent Riddle, an employee at Porch Meats, who was at Egan Porch's the night Russel Porch was killt. He had yet to give a statement and by all appearances had gone missin. Holly knew Riddle's parents and all three of his brothers. *Upstandin folks. Good Church people. Once he turns up we'll get a good rundown on what really happened Wednesday night.*

Allison told Sondra everythin Holly had just told her, and the two immediately resolved to track down Riddle themselves, though first they wanted to retrace the route Russel would've had to ride to get back to Egan's, because somethin was growin more unsettlin by the minute, though, as Holly Feltzman had just then pretty much proclaimed, you didn't need no words from Riddle to know now that what mattered hadn't happened up in the canyon or even along the way.

Sondra guessed, and correctly too, that Russel Porch would've returned by way of one of the horse trails found between the so-called Temple Hill homes. The one she had in mind ran down from Isatch Canyon and across a series of undeveloped lots, which in the years ahead would see new homes and church buildings rise up and swallow this friendly animal-abidin path. By then the barns would be gone too, replaced by more houses, apartment complexes, even if beneath all their foundations would continue to sound a reverberant memory of the soft clop of horses out enjoyin the Orvop air, the Isatch Canyon air, the high ice-combed air spillin down off of Katanogos.

Of course, the rain and stormin of the past three days had beaten this part of the trail into a thick boot-suckin muck, which the mothers at once eyed from Sondra's truck with grim defeat. Even Mungo offered no whines to get free of the back seat. What could they possibly find there? Any blood spillt was long gone. But might've Russel Porch dropped some other clue? Both mothers agreed to come back when some semblance of dryness prevailed.

Allison sagged but Sondra weren't defeated by their choice. She pointed out two backyards belongin to the Mineers and the Greenspires: *Beyond them homes is the Fir cul-de-sac, after which it's straight to Egan's.* Allison didn't understand Sondra's zeal. If Russel had chosen to ride on the blacktop or sidewalks, they'd have zero chance of encounterin any tracks, plus the drench would've done away with any manure days ago.

What we need is a witness, Sondra said as she got them over to Fir, where Mungo still weren't too thrilled to tumble out into the rain.

They canvassed both sides of the street, askin anyone who opened their door if they'd seen a boy on horseback Wednesday night.

Most of them that was home were plenty friendly and willin to throw in whatever two cents might eventually make a dime. One thing Sondra and Allison learned real quick though: no police had come by to ask anyone to confirm the Porch version of things. Beyond that, unfortunately, nobody had anythin of substance to add except to acknowledge that they'd often seen Egan Porch on his Cavalry, and weren't that a big and proud horse.

Only the elderly Dorothy Bray had a story to tell. In fact she was already out in front smokin her cigarette, just like she'd been doin the night Russel clopped by.

Boy, she couldn't've been gladder to see the mothers. The encounter had clearly burdened her, and throughout her recountin she remained distraught about the outcome of that night, wonderin fretfully how if only she had persisted some, if she'd just engaged the boy's better faculties about just where he was ridin to in the dark, *that Russel boy* might've hesitated, might've reconsidered, and so *saved hisself and that horse's life by leavin this matter of horse thievery* to the police.

My boy didn't kill Russel Porch was all Allison could say.

Dorothy stubbed out her cigarette in an ashtray perched atop a pumpkin. *Did he steal them horses?*

I think he did, Allison admitted.

He was keepin a promise, Sondra filled in. *My boy passed from cancer earlier this month. He made her son swear to get those horses out of harm's way. You see, Orwin Porch, Russel's dad, was gonna render them Thursday mornin.*

The horses were gonna be slaughtered?

Allison and Sondra both nodded.

Then why in the heck was Russel so up in a bunch about them bein taken?

The mothers admitted they had no idea.

Maybe it was just somethin to get up in a bunch about? Dorothy asked, lightin another cigarette. *Or maybe he was doin it to impress his daddy and brothers?* She took a long draw. *He sure was lookin like some cowboy out of a movie. You know what I mean? Out in the night, the rain, on that beautiful horse, and on a mission too. Bad ideas of how to act can put us in a bad way. I do blame that on the movies. My husband, George, cannot stand them ones about war. He says they paint a picture that ain't even close to how miserable it was. Fools a lot of kids into thinkin they're gonna be heroes.*

Allison and Sondra just nodded along.

You know, the old woman said then, lettin the smoke drift out of her mouth. *None of what you're sayin proves that Russel and your boy didn't get into it just the same. Men have got after each other for a lot less. Boys ain't no different.* Dorothy Bray was eyein Allison now while she spoke, as if to gauge how this new tone of recrimination might land.

Allison sure felt the heat rise up inside her too, demandin that she buck out, but Allison weren't so young either to heed those impulses; she already knew that whatever fierce kickin she could answer this woman's remark with would serve neither Kalin nor Landry.

What we'd like to know, Allison said, calm as a pond in June, *is whether you might've seen Russel ridin back that same night?*

Dorothy shook her head. *I pretty much went right to bed after I seen him.* And then she added: *George was up though.*

Is he around? Sondra asked.

Dorothy shook her head. *He's in San Clemente on business. He left on Thursday but he'll be back on Sunday. You can come around then. He likes to come out here and smoke too, though he don't like to smoke with me.*

There are plenty of folks who return again and again to this scene, but none so persistently as Marcee Falgoust, Roberta Blum, Cliff Woolf, and Rusty Glasset, all from Orvop, alumni of Orvop High too, if endin up in places as far-flung as Bamako, Mali; Puerto Montt, Chile; Oslo, Norway; and Cape Town, South Africa, still keepin in touch throughout the years, discussin endlessly what might've transpired if George had returned home on Saturday instead of Sunday, which nearly happened.

George Bray was a man who had fought in WWII, Pacific Theater, and bore a remarkable resemblance to John Wayne, a description that was further ratified by two young children livin at the end of Cedar Avenue. The Brays even had two terriers named MacArthur and Patton. George Bray, on this week, had traveled to California with a mission to sell several large-scale color presses to a local Orange County business producin several regional magazines. George was not only successful but found that the owner of said publishin operation was not only a vet but like George had also survived some of the worst moments of the Battle of Tarawa. Both it turned out had also served *semper fi*, with the Second Battalion, Sixth Marines.

They'd agreed to firm up the details of the deal Saturday mornin and have dinner that night, all of which they did and would do, discussin extensively their experiences.

Falgoust, Blum, Woolf and Glasset would years later remark extensively on the irony that a dialogue surfeit with terrible bloodshed made possible the terrible bloodshed yet to come. If only George Bray had come back right then or better yet been home already, dressed as he so often was in a khaki vest, with either a fisherman's hat on or a baseball cap with some kind of military flavor on the crown, *U.S.S. You Name It* or just *Marines*.

Falgoust, Blum, Woolf, and Glasset would even approach George Bray toward the end of his life to hear his own reflections about that possibility, but he was uninterested in commentin much beyond *I seen a lot of useless killin in my life, and none of it ever made a whit of sense. At least not to me. There was no reasonable way of explainin why it had to happen that way, not at that time, not to any one feller in particular.* Roberta Blum would want to know if he felt their Heavenly Father was responsible for takin him to California on that particular weekend. *Oh, child, I was never a member of your church. We just moved here because property was cheap.*

Of course, as these four friends would eventually learn, George Bray was quite fond of goin to California as often as possible, and he frequently extended those trips, especially when he was in Southern California. Cliff Woolf would in 2042 remark that *Too much continues to be made of speculative futures, especially where this story is concerned. People just can't get enuf of how the tiniest changes might have altered the outcome.*

Like Marcee Falgoust, Rusty Glasset would never be so convinced by those tiniest of changes: *Some futures are just as inevitable as death. Stoppin to greet a stranger or sharpen a pencil won't make no difference.* Maybe Marcee Falgoust would've gotten along with Samuel Zeyer. They never met. She never could shake the feelin, and this was in 2053, that it was all fated: *Fate ain't a good feelin.*

Not that we can't still wonder how the sun might've shined through differently on the days ahead if this John Wayne had appeared right then at the door and after pleasantly greetin Allison and Sondra told them what he'd seen Wednesday night. Likely the mothers would've left blinded by happiness.

Instead Sondra and Allison just waved goodbye, promisin Dorothy that they'd return on Sunday, though they never did.

From there Sondra drove down Fir Avenue and was quick enuf passin Egan Porch's house. Egan was there too, right out in front, along with his brothers Hatch and Kelly, with that Billings fella there too. Somewhere on a radio Dan McCafferty was singin *I know it isn't true.*

The Porch boys had just come from the mortuary and were in the process of usin ax handles to further leverage a three-wheeler ATV, single-seater, into place on the back of a trailer hooked up to Billings's Jeep Renegade. Two two-seaters, also three-wheelers, were already loaded on a bigger trailer attached to the back of Egan's Ford Ranger.

Allison wouldn't've budged from her seat if Sondra hadn't got out and near too before she'd finished jammin the gears into park. She even left the keys in and the motor runnin.

The men stopped what they was doin. Egan looked amused. Kelly weren't. Billings didn't care. And Hatch was the only one who took his baseball cap off, doin so in the rain too, if that don't tell us somethin.

The park's closed, gentlemen, Sondra announced.

Egan's eyes drifted lazily over to Allison, who, along with Mungo, had come up to stand beside Sondra. The sight of her burnt him up and not in a bad way. He'd known Sondra Gatestone near since he was born, but this little lady was somethin new, moved new too, and as his old man had already found out, there was somethin about her that made a fella want to linger.

Last I heard, you was sayin our kids were dead, Sondra said in a way meant only to bate him. *That so?*

Sure is, Egan answered like he was talkin about the price of hamburger.

Kelly? But Kelly wouldn't meet her gaze, let alone answer her question. Sondra's instincts, which were pretty good, instructed her to leave Billings alone.

Mind explainin then why you're headin out? Sondra weren't gonna let this go. *Or is it because you just can't keep track of all your lies? Lies can be like that.*

Egan grinned. *Our stolt horses are still missin,* he replied before returnin his gaze to Allison. *Are you the mother of the one that killt our little brother and my horse?* Egan asked then, though he really weren't askin, just introducin hisself. *I'm Egan Porch.*

So this was him, whom Allison had known only by voice while she'd sat in the dark of the Gatestone kitchen, when he and his daddy had paid Sondra a visit but two nights ago, on full display now, not even a dozen feet away, with one eyebrow and cheek scratched deep, maybe some stiffness carried there in his neck, maybe a hitch in a hip or somethin in his lower back too, but hardly diminished by such minor nuisances. That was obvious. He'd sounded somethin mean Thursday night, and his appearance in the light of this gray day sure didn't diminish any that disposition.

He was built like cinder blocks: rough, heavy, and all right angles. And Allison didn't doubt he could wield hisself just as savagely as a cinder block flyin through a windshield. It also shocked her to see that he weren't no boy. Her poor little Kalin was, and this man was huntin him. Even more unbearable was how Egan Porch, fit as a man will ever be in his lifetime, still looked small and flimsy against the likes of the one who'd just took off his hat for Sondra, that one bein Hatch.

Not that Sondra was the least bit intimidated by this lot. *Oh shut up, Egan,* she snarled. That directness sure startled Allison. She'd never heard Sondra sound so rough. In fact she'd've likely retreated back to the truck right then, with Mungo too, if she hadn't over the past two days gotten into the habit of choosin loyalty, doglike loyalty even, no matter her compulsion to run. She was no longer standin up just for her boy now but standin beside Sondra Gatestone too, though who knows what that would've really looked like if these four men had decided to charge them right then, set to batter their faces with them polished lengths of wood. Could Allison have faced them?

Don't think for a second I don't know you, Egan, Sondra continued, not one bit of her ire ebbin. *I know all you Porch boys. Russel too. And let me tell you, Russel was different from you all. He was a good kid. He was nice. You know that, Kelly. You too, Hatch. And one thing's for certain about Russel: he sure as heck couldn't ride a horse like your Cavalry, Egan. Not with any confidence.*

Allison tried to keep her eyes on Egan, but she also couldn't help glancin at them white-faced lawn jockeys. Like what were those about? Terrible Cinderellas beside their already rotten pumpkins.

I'm not so sure here's the right place for you, Sondi. Egan loved the taste of that familiar name in his mouth, what he knew he had no right to use. And like a dog waitin on a snack, he waited eagerly now for her objection, somethin of a grin creasin his lips while that ax handle at his side slowly began to swing back and forth.

But Sondra Gatestone didn't bite. She weren't some little pup. *You can handle that much math, Egan, can't you? Russel could barely ride that horse. And he sure couldn't ride him with his throat slit, with half his blood gone. He'd have fallen off long before he even got clear of the park.*

That's what you got? Egan even laughed. *That Russel never made it this far?* Egan kept laughin too, and it was an awful and cold and ragged sound, and once again it made Allison want to just turn tail, run and run and run, leave this mess behind. But again she found some approximate resolve and again managed somehow to stand her ground.

You best take your little fantasies along to the police, Egan continued. *I'm sure they'll love to learn that the body they found here they didn't find here.* Egan's grin vanished then. Hatch had put his cap back on, and now even Kelly was swingin his ax handle. But it was the other one, the one they'd learned last night was Billings Gale, who really quickened Allison's heart. She'd picked up a few things from Kalin's daddy along the way, and eyes like Billings had was one of them things. A stare like his, nearly blank but starin just the same, you wanted to keep clear of that. Because he was all hid up. Because his eyes weren't gonna give him away. There was no tellin what someone with eyes like that was capable of doin, what he'd do next, and whatever he did do next wouldn't be nothin good. Not one Porch boy could look at you like that. Only Old Porch. Old Porch had the same eyes.

Sondra, though, still weren't deterred. *Oh, you can bet we're goin to the police, but I still think you're missin what we'll be settlin down to discuss with Chief of Police Beckham.* Sondra even stepped closer, leavin the sidewalk to stand astride on what was now fer sure Egan's property. Allison made the same ingress, again overridin her instincts to sprint back to the truck, keys still in too, engine runnin. Mungo, though, as if purposefully comin to her rescue, helped buttress her failin resolve by bringin one of his big shoulders against her hip.

Egan's response required no premeditation: he would not stand for the likes of Sondra Gatestone and this Allison March on his front lawn, and he closed on them fast.

How's that? he growled, his grip hardenin on that ax handle even as he kept one eye on the big dog who had lowered some and not in no relaxin way.

Sondra still weren't afraid. *I ain't sayin Russel didn't wind up here. And, Hatch, I know you've come a long way from Texas for this tragedy, and it is a tragedy, but you're a lawman now, so you best listen.*

We're all listenin, Sondi— Egan started to say.

That's Mrs. Gatestone to you.

There it was. Egan even stopped to chuckle, to spit.

See, we just got done doin around here what the police seemed to have forgotten to do, so bedazzled by your recountin of events. Especially that Undersheriff Jewell. Do you call him that? Or just uncle? Shame on him. Sondra's glare seemed to dare Egan to try another step her way, a dare he did not take. *It's called canvassin, Egan. Hatch knows what I mean. Right?* Hatch Porch averted his eyes, findin Allison's eyes then, avertin his eyes once again. *It's work but it ain't that hard. It just requires intention. You just go from one door to the next. You introduce yourself, and then you explain the situation, and then you listen to how they explain the situation back to you. And if no one opens the door, why then you keep comin back until it does open.*

Egan did nothin then, not spit no more nor fleer nor laugh, but he didn't move back none either. He just kept his eyes locked on Sondra while Allison couldn't help but watch as them knuckles on that ax handle kept gettin whiter and whiter.

So answer me this question, Egan Porch, because it's a question Chief of Police Beckham and his detectives are gonna want an answer to: how is it that on Wednesday night a few of your good neighbors saw your little brother headin back on a horse two times too much for him to handle but with a smile bigger than all your lyin? Now that's a pretty big smile, because what you all got cookin up here is one big lie.

Allison only saw the bluff comin at the last moment, but she made ready, another thing she'd picked up from Kalin's daddy: a bluff depends as much on the one bluffin as the one who's also in on the bluff. Allison knew she couldn't even blink, let alone grimace or, worst of all, look away. They had to see Sondra's truth in her face too. And while Allison couldn't go that far, because she just weren't any good at lyin, with Kalin's daddy havin used this inability against her for too many years, she'd still learned to empty herself out in the face of an interrogative stare set on violence. And that's just what she did. Her joints easin free of each other, her hands openin up. In fact it was near exact what Old Porch had laid eyes upon from the passenger seat of the helicopter, starin down at that boy so limp with a resolve he could not see and so could not heed. Not unlike their old man in this respect, neither Egan nor Hatch nor Kelly noticed any change in Allison either. Billings, though, was different, and even though he found no threat comin from Allison, his body still knew better, recoilin from all the potential suddenly coalescin there.

Egan, what the heck is she sayin? Hatch asked then, genuinely confused.

She's just knee-jerkin her way through made-up land, Egan responded quick. *She ain't sayin nothin.*

You best check your hearin, Egan. What I'm sayin is that your little brother Russel, much to his credit, and on big old Cavalry too, made it back here just fine. And then what? Because that's the question you all are now gonna have to answer: what happened to poor Russel once he got here, maybe stoppin right where I'm standin now, and walkin past where you're standin right now, right into your house? Go on, tell me. At least tell your brother Hatch. What happened then, Egan?

Egan charged her. He raised that ax handle too. And Sondra, well, you couldn't blame her, no matter how much she hated Egan, she also knew well enuf what he could do and so heeded her own instincts and stumbled backward. Surprisinly, or not surprisinly at all given who her boy was, Allison did not budge, which got Billings takin yet another step back, because he were many things, but a fool weren't one of them.

Hatch, though, remained the fastest and strongest of them all, and he could tear up distance like a puppy does a tissue box. He got between Egan and Mrs. Gatestone before Egan was on his third step, catchin hold of that ax handle like it weren't nothin but a foam bat clutched by a toddler.

Somethin foul's goin on here, Hatch, Sondra coughed out. *You best get to the bottom of it before it buries you too.*

Step one foot on my property again, Sondi, and I'll shoot you right in the crotch, Egan hissed after her.

Hush that, Hatch told his younger brother. *Nobody's shootin no one.*

Get anywhere near my daughter or her boy, Egan, and I'll bury you myself.

At that moment a white Trans Am pulled up behind Sondra's truck. *Our lips are sealed* couldn't get much louder. Three young women hurried out into the rain, tryin but mostly failin to keep them blond and brunette curls dry, giggles and sass eruptin just at the sight of Egan and Kelly, though them lighthearted notes departed just as quick when Lanise Parcell, the blonde with eyes blue as stickseed, with fingernails the same color as her lipstick, red as blood bright with oxygen, wearin an Orvop Track & Field sweatshirt under an open raincoat, caught sight of Sondra Gatestone and the one she had suspicions about. Cathy Windell didn't know nothin about Allison but she at least had a sense that this here weren't anythin to get close to.

Liz Blicker, Darren's older sister, remained clueless. *Egan, where's Shelly?* She had on a bright orange sweatshirt under a white raincoat. Her brown hair was startin to frizz some in the wet, green eyes sparklin if hard to see given the sum of plaster needed to reset her nose.

Egan ignored her. He pretty much ignored Lanise Parcell too, and she just hooked her arm through his like they was boyfriend and girlfriend, though they weren't, not ever in Egan's mind.

I think she's the one, Lanise whispered then to Liz and Cathy, though it weren't much of a whisper given everyone there could hear her.

Hello, Sister Gatestone, Cathy Windell said then, refusin to look at Allison. *I'm sorry about Landry.*

Thank you, Cathy. We still don't know what happened. Are we seein you next weekend?

Yes, ma'am. Though I heard it's now happenin at Sister Dowdell's?

There's been some confusion, understandably, but Charity in Practice will be at my house, same as always.

Sondra started to head back to the truck. Allison was about to do the same too until somethin else Kalin's daddy had taught her caught her step: never give two backs when you can give one when gettin out of a place.

You should be ashamed of yourself, Sister Gatestone, Lanise Parcell then sneered out, even if she didn't really know what she was sayin except that she was tryin to impress Egan, who'd never be impressed by anythin she did.

Excuse me? Sondra answered her, turnin back around.

Consortin with her likes, Lanise added, indicatin Allison with her thumb. *After what her son done to their brother.*

My son didn't touch Russel Porch, Allison said firmly for the umpteenth time, darin any of the girls to refute her or even meet her gaze. Not a one could.

Whatever you need to sleep, Lanise did finally manage to spurt out under her breath, though she seemed to be sayin this to Liz Blicker, which didn't make much sense. *I heard she's a whore,* she said then to Egan. *Like a real whore.*

And that sure got a pit of ugly fire spikin up through Allison.

Now that don't surprise me at all, Egan said loudly, addin to her fire.

You run into a glass door? Sondra asked Liz Blicker then.

That's right. You heard.

Allison, though, didn't miss how the poor girl suddenly became wildly uncertain, even gently touchin the plaster on her face like she needed convincin of not only what was there but of what she was sayin was the reason why it was there. It didn't get no better when she saw Shelly and Sean pullin up in Shelly's Chevy Silverado.

Sweetie, just remember, Allison said to her before finally retreatin to Sondra's truck, *just because you spread your legs on Friday night don't mean you gotta spread them on Saturday night too.*

Boy, how much did Liz Blicker blush then?! Even Lanise Parcell's jaw dropped near a foot, and Cathy Windell looked pretty gobsmacked as well. Egan almost looked impressed. He grinned at least. Liz Blicker, though, didn't know how to feel because though the words were plenty salty, there was somethin in them that rang warm with good advice, gettin her touchin the plaster on her face again, as she tried to direct a smile Shelly's way, who was marchin over darker than the dark clouds above and at the sight of Sondra Gatestone gettin darker still.

Not that Sondra and Allison roared off right then either. Mungo had started barkin some and Sondra let him have at it a bit before lobbin out Egan's way in a voice that was now nothin but sweet and measured: *We'd love to stay longer, Egan, but see we got an appointment we're late for. We're sittin down with Trent Riddle. He works for you all, right?*

And then Sondra did roar her truck outta there, Shelly givin her the bird, Sean too, but only those two.

By the next stop sign, *Sondra Gatestone's faith was gone,* as Brinn Black would put it, *like water from a bucket if the bottom had just fallen out.* Her face was pinched up like she was headed for a cry but then it became more of a scowl when the tears betrayed her by not comin, lockin in their poison.

I blew it, Allison. That phony bluff ain't gonna get us a thing but into trouble. Dagnabbit! Sondra even hit the steerin wheel, hit it again, hit it still harder, then stopped just as abruptly because it hurt her hand, and there ain't no satisfaction in hittin somethin made of steel and plastic no matter what anyone says. *Maybe that George Bray fellow will come back with a story to tell?*

Allison just stroked Mungo.

Sondra sighed. At least a sigh felt better than bruisin her palm. *When the police don't follow up with Egan, he'll know I was full of you-know-what.*

Allison checked her side mirror. Even at that distance she could see everyone outside Egan Porch's house had disappeared inside.

I'm sorry, Allison. I am. I don't know what came over me. I just had to do somethin.

That Kelly Porch had an interestin reaction, Allison finally said.

Allison hadn't forgotten the first time she'd seen him standin right outside the window of her Dodge Dart. She'd even scribbled out her number with shakin hands, a scrap of paper that was still at the bottom of one of his pockets. He'd trembled her. He'd seemed hot with righteousness and weariness but still in the fight. Some of that was missin when she'd seen him, Egan, and the guy called Billings drive out of the canyon yesterday. His lips were cut up, forehead too. He looked pale and worn down, but he'd still met her gaze easily. That weren't the case now. He hadn't been able to look at anythin for long.

I weren't lookin at him, Sondra admitted.

Soon as you mentioned the neighbors, he looked straight at that other one— Billings?

Who?

The one employed by Porch? You found out yesterday?

That's right. Billings.

He knows what he's doin. He didn't look nowhere but at his boot toes. That got Kelly wise, and he looked away real fast, which I know ain't much, but the thing is when you mentioned this Trent Riddle, Kelly did the exact same thing. Eyes again went straight to that Billings. Couldn't help hisself. Kelly looked pale as a ghost too. Or worse, like he was seein a ghost.

Back at the Gatestone stable, Sondra made more calls. She needed to talk to her friends. Mostly she seemed to just leave messages, and those she got through to didn't talk nearly enuf to sound like they was friends. Sondra understood that Allison weren't no dolt.

Since Dallin passed, my friendships don't seem near as strong. Like widows ain't really welcome.

I know I ain't helpin matters.

Or you're helpin me see things more clearly. Give yourself some credit. Even if what you said to Liz Blicker back there was a little crass.

Allison shrugged.

However, I do see your point. Sondra even laughed a little.

Sondra dialed the coroner's office next and this time passed the handset to Allison. While it rang, she told Allison to leave a message, *and make it emphatic!,* about how it was her boy bein blamed, how she wanted to know, because it was only fair that she know, if Russel Porch really was cut down with a knife. Allison had no problem sayin what she'd already said dozens of times. Who knows if the message would ever reach anyone who mattered, but there might be tape, and at least one other person would hear a mother's voice pleadin. Shouldn't that make some difference?

Sondra still weren't done with her calls, and seein as how Mungo was sprawled over her boots, like these two had done this before, Allison left the Gatestone matriarch and that great St. Bernard in peace, exitin the small office to wander out among the stalls.

They was all empty, but at least Jojo's, with its brass plaque declarin his name in big loopy cursive, was occupied recently enuf to smell of hay, feed, and manure, though the floor had already been mucked clean. Allison liked standin there. She liked savorin the smells. Worn leather and glycerine was in there too. Maybe a barn cat was around? Allison had forgotten how much she liked bein around horses. She couldn't say why either. She couldn't ride a lick, wouldn't even dare a saddle on a carousel, but she still recognized somethin ancient and abidin in this bond that for better or worse was forged so many thousands of years ago. Even today, for Allison, horses carried about them from mane to tail, from hooves to those large beholdin eyes, countless mysteries and humilities. *Humility doesn't have to culminate in humiliation.* That was one of her mother's chestnuts that Allison kept warm and whole. She'd shared it with Kalin too, though she'd never really shared with him her own love for the animals, their immense vulnerabilites, especially in glory.

Of course she was overthinkin things now, overthinkin everythin. She'd never forget a sponsor in one of them early AA meetings, and not even her own sponsor, who confessed so poignantly and wisely: *I don't think much of myself. And I'm tryin to think even less.* Of course, maybe she was flat-out lyin to herself. Maybe Allison was only feelin this intense identification now with such heart-shudderin creatures because her missin boy had found in them such joy and easiness? A joy she had refused him back at the start because of how Kalin's daddy had come upon this love first. Shameful! Because isn't that what every parent dreams for their child? That their life might find some unmolested delight? Some way to rise above the toil to encounter a view of Heaven's majesty? And when Heaven's not yet a broken promise, find a dream of eternal Peace? And if not for forever then fer a lifetime? Heck, she'd take a moment, one moment, grand enuf to grant those scales takin full measure of life's indecencies, life's sufferin, a positive balance. Why shouldn't that be won upon the back of one of these magnificent spirits born of these plains? And Allison knew fer certain that on the back of his first pony, Kalin had discovered a liberty beyond the burden of thinkin, beyond the burden of self.

Standin in Jojo's stall so clearly materialized her son's expression while he was ridin, blissful in his attention to each hoofbeat, *Clop-Clop-clip-Clop*, that heartbeat, the world at hand, for the first time, and in each successive moment still for the first time! Oh! There he was!

There he is! Her cherub! No sword of fire required! Just his easy smile. Her fear banished at once. Even now. Even here.

Earlier Sondra had asked idly how, if they hadn't come from horses, Kalin had acquired such proficiency with horses? *I don't know the why of it,* Allison had answered. *You could test him plenty on what he should know about bridles or bits, knots or saddle pads, and he'd fail, but that wouldn't change how well he handles a horse. I can't explain it.* Sondra had smiled and added: *With lessons and spendin time around experienced horsefolk, he'd ride even better.* Allison had thought that over a spell: *I reckon then your Tom helped make him even better.*

Allison left Jojo's stall, and thankfully her son's joy followed along, like an angel grantin her a reprieve, however brief, from the gloom and crepuscular grief that had enwrapped her ever since Wednesday night.

Past the last stall hung another bronze plaque, this one with many names, like Tora, Red & Dunny, Sig, Geo, Gus, Nefertiti, Bandit, and finally Chubasco aka Ash. She recognized the emptiness in that list as well as the melancholy, but with Kalin's elation still in her heart, she could also find radiance and even rapture, even if the rapture weren't her own. In fact it's only your own when it's not your own? Maybe the possessive at once defeats the possession? Others had clearly loved these animals. Tom had loved his Ash. And that, more than anythin else, released Allison to this feelin of devotion. Only a few times in her life had she known such commitment, and each time she had doubted its authenticity; now, though, and this likely due to the inferno encirclin her, she chose to trust it.

In Ash's stall, her guidin angel left her, but instead of deliverin her down into damnation, Allison found instead her Kalin replaced by ghosts, and of course they weren't ghosts, they weren't even there anymore: all the horses that had once inhabited this barn. The idea alone of their endurin presence held the jaws of Death agape. Allison could feel their movements, hear their snorts, watch the flick of their tails, smell their breaths, their sweat, know their desire to graze, to drink, to run free, to run, run, run . . . So vividly did she encounter their past presence that fer a moment Allison even knew herself among them, equine in form and disposition, ready to run, ready to flee, but also willin to charge.

Beyond the stalls Allison found again the tack room where Sondra earlier that mornin had so tearfully and at the same time gratefully discovered that Landry had taken her best boots. This time, though, Allison noticed somethin else, what Sondra could not have taken much interest in, seein as how long it had likely been part of the place: opposite the hooks, saddle racks, and open cubbies was a wall plastered with pictures and postcards from all over the world. Allison smiled at these versions of Norway, Ghana, Portugal, Korea, Mongolia, Iceland. In the corner of each was scribbled a small *LG* as if Landry Gatestone sought to lay claim not just to the cards but the places as well. Allison couldn't help but imagine Landry atop her Jojo, gallopin the long hallways of the Louvre, the beaches of Namibia, racin the confoundin starlight wheelin over the Gobi Desert, or just standin beside icy waters murmurin in a moss-cloaked canyon, a place with a name that Allison would never say aloud, she did not have that speech, discoverin the letterin on the flip side of that postcard: Fjaðrárgljúfur. That's how she also found somethin else. Hidden by all the postcards.

The photograph cut her breath away: it was black and white, plenty grainy too, of no more than a fence, in fact Paddock A's fence, which Allison had no way of knowin, but that weren't important. Tom Gatestone was standin on the left, head tilted down but not tilted enuf to hide his grin, near big enuf to exceed the big brim of his black Stetson. There was a blade of grass in his teeth. He was wearin a belt buckle big as a dinner plate. To his right, though, on the top rail, wearin a T-shirt and a white Stetson, with his back to the camera, sat her Kalin.

Tears fell so hot and at once, they darned near missed her cheeks! Such was the force of that recognition, the hunch in his little back, the paleness of his little arms, his small hands clamped on the wood rail, especially as he leaned forward, far as he could without fallin off, still cranin his neck out ever farther, all in an effort to see better, get closer to what the picture didn't reveal, given its low angle, was it Landry's angle?, the photograph offerin nothin but blurriness and a very white sky, hidin what Allison knew lay beyond that fence, below that sky: horses.

Allison untacked the photograph and flipped it over, as if on the other side she might find Tom's back, her son's face, wantin desperately the very expression that had graced her mind and heart only moments ago.

But the other side was white as the sky in the picture. Not even the scribble of a date or a place.

Was Kalin already gone? Was he already lyin lifeless and pale beneath the rubble of yesterday's landslide? That very likely possibility jolted her like a sharp claw to her flanks. Her only child's death was her only predator, and from her own equine qualities it demanded flight, urgin her to bolt now and not quit until she was quit seven horizons. She might've still been on her way too if she hadn't right then discovered what that black-and-white photograph had itself concealed: a big old heart carved into the wood panel.

Allison could never say why she cried even more then. She was so afraid for her son, missin so badly her beautiful fragile boy, all of which, of course, we know goes without sayin, even if we still have to say *goes without sayin* because now and then we can misplace how constant and true a heart can remain without words; because, yes, we all have our moments when we can become like folks whose lives are fooled into thinkin life is where life isn't, who no longer can hear their own heartbeats like the hoofbeats of a loyal horse that will, yes, *Clop-Clop-clip-Clop* ride with you to the very ends of this world. Allison weren't no stranger to her own heart. She also knew that despite her anguish and fright, which maybe because she no longer denied them their place made her capable of beholdin more than just them exclusively, she could behold Beauty too and behold it in a fullness that alone would arrest her innate instincts. For here was the Beauty that stayed her from boltin for the highway: the sight of someone else smitten by the wonders of the child she'd known his whole life.

Carved at the center of that heart:

LG + KM

Well, I'll be, Sondra said from behind her, Mungo already at Allison's side, lickin her fingers. *Not that we needed proof.*

You told it right, right from the start, Allison answered, wipin away her tears with a sleeve before carefully retackin back in place that coverin black-and-white photograph followed by the postcard of Iceland. Just like she'd found it all. *My Kalin, on behalf of your boy's dyin wishes, rescues two horses from Porch's slaughter paddock, but not before your Landry gets wind of it and follows. Russel Porch follows too, but he ain't successful with his aims and returns back to his brothers empty-handed. And for this failure, he's killt?*

Sondra nodded.

You know that don't make a lick of sense?

I do, Sondra answered.

You think Egan did it?

Old Porch was there too.

A father killin his own son? It don't get crazier than that.

It don't.

But why?

I have no clue. Maybe we should ask him?

What do we got to lose?

It was 12:17 p.m.

Despite their plan, Sondra and Allison didn't count on runnin into Orwin Porch quite so fast. Sondra had already called Tucker Wyatt earlier that mornin to see about the helicopter she'd requested last night. Tucker Wyatt weren't licensed to fly a helicopter but he knew all the pilots. Unfortunately there weren't any pilots available nor helicopters. Tucker had no idea that one of the pilots he'd called, Kevin Moffet, was already up in the air with Orwin Porch.

Wyatt was at least pleased to tell Sondra that his Bonanza was still at the ready. It weren't ideal. A helicopter could get a heckuva lot closer in the tight spots, but Sondra knew she had no choice but to take the bird in hand. She told Wyatt she wanted to get a look at Kirk's Cirque. The Porches weren't the only ones who knew how to read a map.

However, when the mothers arrived at the airport, Wyatt Tucker looked downright doleful. His Bonanza weren't as ready as he'd let on. In preppin the plane, he'd discovered an engine part that required immediate replacement. A delay of hours if it was on hand, days if it weren't, and it weren't and wouldn't arrive until Tuesday earliest. Tucker had already called around, lookin fer another plane, but even friends with favors owed weren't willin to let him head up over Katanogos in what everyone was callin *marginal weather* when what they meant was *one big frickin storm.*

I'm sorry, Sondi, Tucker Wyatt said on the tarmac. *No one's flyin in this.*

Which was right about when Kevin Moffet landed that black and gold-striped helicopter, a McDonnell Douglas 500D, with its Custom Enterprises logo bright in the gray light.

Kevin Moffet exited quick enuf, lookin like the shaggy man he was, who plenty have called a real sad sack, his tan jacket flappin open in the weather, extra room for a belly that could've used a few less Danishes in the mornin. His big beard sure needed a trim too.

He was soon followed by his one and only passenger: Orwin Porch.

Now Kevin Moffet didn't know nothin about Allison March. Sondra Gatestone, however, was another story. Just a glimpse of her regal figure had him tryin to button up his jacket. All he did manage was givin her and Tucker Wyatt a wave before lowerin his head and hurryin into the airport office, where he sat down to record his flight details in the logbook he was carryin under his arm.

It's worth takin a moment for Kevin Moffet. Billy Biddulph, an Orvop original who, after livin for several years in Puno on Lake Titicaca in Peru, would in 2008 resettle in Belfast, Maine, where he'd for some years teach online courses on cinema, frequently arguin that any film version would likely commit the savage sin of cuttin out Kevin Moffet altogether: *The turds would just replace him with Hatch at the cyclic stick, as if this Hero Porch could do anythin, includin fly a helicopter at a moment's notice.* Billy Biddulph's friend Cary Swindle, who shared Biddulph's passion and would in 2009 start teachin film at Notre Dame, would see the validity in such conjecture: *Gettin rid of Kevin Moffet would obviate one of the smaller troublin tragedies of this history. If Kevin had at this very intersection on the tarmac just slowed down a teensy bit, just said hello to Sondra, introduced hisself to Allison, or at the very least carried out some weatherly conversation with Tucker Wyatt, when it wouldn't have been far-fetched at all to mention first thing the sight of two kids up in Kirk's Cirque, and with three horses too, how that might've altered things and dramatically too, reorientin, revitalizin the whole search, and fer sure not only firin up those two battered women but refocusin the efforts of police and rangers.*

It's a very fair observation, even if little of what Cary Swindle had to say would ever be treated with much seriousness given his life's passion to assemble photographs and life stories of every single Munchkin in *The Wizard of Oz*. He cared too much for the little people, them who were passed over, them who did make a difference, them who could've made a difference. And Cary Swindle was a big guy too. He sure never ceased carin for Kalin and Landry. *They was both so little.*

In the air Old Porch had told Kevin Moffet that the youngsters they'd seen up there were none other than Porch family relations searchin for his lost horses and whom he was dutifully checkin up on. He was glad to see they was fine. Kevin Moffet would buy whatever Old Porch wanted to sell him. He had no choice.

On the way back Kevin Moffet had even apologized for not havin fuel enuf to land and linger. Old Porch set him at ease there, makin it clear that they'd return soon enuf and with more supplies, for which Kevin Moffet would be paid exceedingly well, though Mr. Moffet would've done it for free, as he owed Old Porch a great deal in terms that had nothin to do with money.

In fact Kevin Moffet had it in his mind to cover the daily for the helicopter, which weren't too bad given the decent relationship he had with the owner of Custom Enterprises. He'd be mostly on the hook for the fuel. Not that Old Porch permitted any such thing. Once they was clear of Katanogos, Old Porch had placed in Kevin's tan jacket four of them rolls of twenties bound up with red rubber bands. Old Porch didn't want Kevin to get some idea that their slate was clean.

Before landin Old Porch had told Kevin Moffet not to mention nothin to anyone yet about what they'd seen up in the cirque. He also asked him to ready the helicopter fer another trip *within the hour*. Kevin

Moffet had kept Old Porch's secrets before and knew Old Porch had a can full of his secrets, secrets he'd prefer to know were good and buried forever, or at least buried until they didn't look like nothin more than rust and worm guts.

The most extraordinary thing, this bein a pretty sad thing as well, was just how oblivious Kevin Moffet would remain about all that was transpirin around him. He knew nothin about Russel Porch nor Kalin March nor Landry Gatestone. Even the landslide was a surprise when he flew over it. Kevin Moffet hardly read the papers and he hated the news. He did love his Louis L'Amours, though, or them old Westerns and war movies, which in his sparse collection amounted to *High Noon*, some John Wayne stuff, and *The Missouri Breaks*, which except for *The Missouri Breaks* he'd watched multiple times on the VHS player his sister and brother-in-law had given him two Christmases ago. In fact he was keen to watch *One-Eyed Jacks* again that very night and plenty vexed that Old Porch had in mind a second trip so quick.

Old Porch could see that Kevin Moffet was clueless, but he also knew it wouldn't take but a moment of gossip or a TV flickerin with a picture of Landry and the pilot would make the connection. That bein said Old Porch also remained confident that before sayin anythin to anyone else, Kevin would come to him first. Old Porch just had to get Kevin back in the air, soon as he could, all the while promisin the pilot how he was on his way to buyin his own helicopter. Sure, Kevin Moffet was a risk, but Old Porch had lived a life of risk and understood that without risk, there weren't no fortune.

And anyways Kevin Moffet never did find out what was goin on. And it's this tragic occurrence, or nonoccurrence, dependin on how we look at it, that still troubles so many kind folks.

Furthermore, Kevin Moffet's decision to stay at that desolate airport just then was an action wholly devised by his heart. It sure weren't no zealousness on his part to keep his logbook up to date or work on one of them word-search puzzles in an old magazine or even heed Old Porch's commandment to mum's the word; not even to get out of the drizzle that had hastened his pace out on the tarmac. It was them two ladies, the one lady in particular.

Unlike Allison March or Sondra Gatestone, Kevin Moffet did not know his heart, and, well, the heart is a strange animal, and when left unknown, where it goes it takes us along, mostly helpless.

See, Kevin Moffet had grown up with Sondra Gatestone. He'd known her since first grade, same elementary school, Isatch; same junior high, that would be Dixon; and same high school, Orvop High. Kevin was smitten day one. And for years this overpowerin and endurin affection for her was proof enuf of matrimonial inevitability. On top of that they both shared the same birthday. Now why that particular coincidence seemed so important is anyone's guess, but to Kevin Moffet, along with various astrological predictions he'd come across, the future felt set. The only question left was the timin.

Imagine then Kevin Moffet's shock when upon returnin from his mission in Paraguay he discovered that Sondra Hearth was engaged to Dallin Gatestone.

For Stuart Rasband, Jody Leitus, and Christa Finch, all classmates of Kevin Moffet, his story would take on an eminence that for them would near overshadow the other events. They would not be alone. There's somethin so disturbin that Kevin Moffet could not escape what in his case especially seemed so easy to escape, so possible, and at so many junctures too. *How often do we wonder if we ourselves are Kevins? Are we missin doin somethin that's so obvious? Somethin right in front of us that would prevent some awful tragedy?* Or so Stuart Rasband would query after a visit to San Vicente, Bolivia, of all places. For Christa Finch in March 2010, it was more about the heartache that wouldn't quit Kevin Moffet. *Or maybe it was the shame for thinkin he'd ever had a chance with Sondra Gatestone to begin with,* she'd ruminate with friends in Christchurch, New Zealand. *Shame can burn a long time.*

Whatever it was, the more Kevin Moffet's own life disappointed him, the more he found cause to harden his views against Sondra Gatestone and eventually any Gatestone, a prejudice that helped set him in orbit around Old Porch. *Like hatreds sink alike,* Jody Leitus would tell her hospice nurse in her home in Stockholm. She was the least sympathetic to Kevin: *Kevin had his secrets. Bad-Things-Done kinda secrets. And likely the worst ones had been committed with Old Porch. Learnin to live with them kind of crimes that we can only guess at takes a lot of denial. You don't fly a helicopter after a girl runnin from you, and on bareback too, draggin along two other horses, while a boy runs frantically after her and NOT think that there's somethin real bad about this picture. But Kevin Moffet took the money and kept his head down and didn't say nothin. That's who he was. He got what he deserved.*

Saddest of all, though, was how Kevin Moffet never realized how he was throughout those hours and the hours to come also so close to makin a beautiful difference. He alone could've stemmed so much horror and sufferin. But he didn't. He squandered that chance in the name of a silence and a fearful retreat that guaranteed nothin more than a cloyin mouthful of childish pettiness near as bad-tastin as the mud at Pillars Meadow come Monday mornin.

And then on top of it, puttin aside all these whatever-what-ifs, along comes another thing that should've saved him. See, Kevin Moffet for all his oddness and antisocial tics was first and foremost a darned good helicopter pilot. Not a moment after findin the word *PROVI-DENCE* in that word-search puzzle and the phone rings, and right there at the airport too. A tourist outfit run out of Juneau, Alaska, had been tryin to get a hold of him. They were expandin their tours over the glaciers of Denali National Park and they needed a qualified pilot. Kevin Moffet had come highly recommended. Pay was more than good, and the job started yesterday. Kevin Moffet accepted on the spot. Just like that. Said he'd be there soon as he could book a ticket. Old Porch would have to find hisself another ride back up to Katanogos. Kevin Moffet had never smiled so big. Tom-worthy. It was like his heartache was finally cured. It was like his life had finally changed. Finally.

O f course, out on the tarmac, no one was payin no mind to Kevin Moffet hurryin home, not Tucker Wyatt, not Allison Porch, not even Sondra Gatestone, who didn't even recognize him. Not even Mungo recognized Kevin Moffet. And you can bet Old Porch, that calculatin creature of ill designs, was plenty pleased to see his pilot slip free of any interaction and even more thrilled to have an opportunity to face these women, partly because anythin that engaged his innate strain of antagonism was welcome indeed but also because he was genuinely curious about what exactly was bindin these two together, who as far as he could tell had to have been pretty much strangers until Landry had gone missin. For Old Porch, any occasion to better understand his opponents was cause for delight.

No matter the drizzle, Old Porch still took off his charcoal hat with that ribbon dark as a bruised plum.

Kay Shroeppel would many years hence, and in an empty theater in Helsinki, in 2028 in fact, declare to her friend Gaylene Zobell, who was just then visitin from Belgrade, Serbia, Kay standin center stage too in bare feet, that if only Old Porch had embraced his thespian inclinations, he might've led a much more fulfillin life: *Maybe happier too! I suspect he was a natural! Can you imagine our Old Porch as Iago? Brilliant!* Gaylene Zobell would prove game that afternoon to further speculate on how Orwin Porch might in a yet unwritten play come to inhabit a father guilty of filicide, his performances earnin him untold amounts of encomiums and many an award even as he continued to personally declare that even if critics and audiences alike were callin this role his finest work, he deemed it his strangest, *and so wrenchin too for havin to nightly enact such an absurd imaginin of a life! Killin one's own flesh and blood? Can you imagine? I'd prefer not to but the pay is decent and I love a good applause.*

And no question Old Porch was chanellin some sort of theatrical animus, as fattenin raindrops slapped his bare pate, made blink those blisterin Arctic eyes, his smile now so arranged as to expose as much of his broken teeth as possible.

Sondi, I wish I could tell you that I seen your little girl playin in the fields above with that boy and my stolen horses. Yes, that's right, that's exactly how Old Porch had started out. *I dearly wish I could say that that was the case for all our sakes if just to bring this to a civil end. But all we seen up there is a whole lot of fallen stone and mud. The bodies will turn up. I'm sure of it. Bodies always do. But you might have to wait til spring.*

Both Sondra and Allison allowed themselves an extra moment to just observe Old Porch, like they was critics in a packed house, there for one reason and one reason alone: to evaluate his performance.

Orwin knew it too, and oh, how he lapped it up! Near wanted to take a bow!

This time around Allison anticipated that Sondra would continue her bluff and chose to get out ahead of it, if only to give Sondi a bit more breathin room.

Looks like you got what you wanted then, Allison said. *Seems like my boy has no more life left to live. Isn't that what you said to me?*

That was just a despairin father talkin. They're in the hands of the Lord now. Is that why your boys can't get enuf of the canyon?

They're lookin for our horses. See, the Law don't care much for horses. I don't think the Good Lord does either.

When I met you, I didn't know who you was, and to be fair I still don't know who you are, but just the same, I have been givin you a lot of thought. And I realize that from your end of things, there's plenty I can't dispute. Fer one, I'm pretty darn sure now that my boy took those horses. Fer another, I'm pretty darn sure my boy wouldn't've given them back to your Russel.

Now Old Porch knew when he was in a duel, and though neither him nor Allison carried any iron on their hips, the three of them there was suddenly caught in a dynamic where someone was gonna have to draw somethin pretty quick, and whoever drew quickest would walk away unbothered.

If you can admit what your Kalin boy done and still claim he wouldn't hurt a fly, Old Porch drawled out, slow as only a great actor can manage, that grin of his not losin the presentation of a single tooth, *well, I've done heard it all.*

Except I haven't told you about a mountain lion, Allison shot back with just the tiniest hint of smile that maybe only Old Porch could read. Allison, fer her part, weren't sure why she was still headin out like this, in this direction, out in front and still chargin. Maybe bein as crude as she'd just been a little earlier with that young girl, the one with the busted nose, had freed up some part in herself that she mostly kept reined in so tight, it verged on self-harm. She suddenly felt wild, wild even to herself, and though it was scary, it also felt pretty darned good.

How's that? Old Porch responded, caught off guard by the subject change if also intrigued. Heck, it had got Sondra's attention too.

Ever seen one? Allison asked, slowly too and low. She had teeth to bare as well, and hers were bright and sharp.

Seen a mountain lion? Are you crazy, lady? I've shot dozens!

I've only seen one. It was injured too. Worse, it was tracked by wolves. From the blind, we watched it limp along with that pack closin in. It was draggin its leg, it was dyin, but it made it into this hollow, really a small cave in the rocks, and I imagine plenty deep. Them wolves, though, weren't daunted. They went right in after that mountain lion. One after another. All of them. But—

I'm glad you've had a good taste of what natural law is then. Old Porch put his hat back on. Maybe this gal was crazy. Pretty to look at but bent in the head. *Now if you'll excuse me, ladies, I'm in mournin and my patience has a limit. Especially for your little Laurel and Hardy act, though you two do share a remarkable resemblance to that pair.* He gave his hat a theatrical tilt. *I best be off before I get any sharper.*

He strode away, and only when he'd almost taken enuf steps to be rid of them, or so he figured, only then did Sondra speak up.

Before you go, Orwin, Sondra said and pretty soft too. She knew he'd be listenin. *Maybe there's somethin you can help us with. Somethin we just been rackin our heads about to no avail. How is it that you keep sayin Russel had his throat slit up the canyon, but Egan's got neighbors not three blocks away that seen Russel ridin back from the canyon hale and happy as sunshine in a downpour?*

That sure pulled up Old Porch short, but he didn't turn.

What have you got up to? Sondra asked, and she might as well have hollered it, though her voice hardly rose much above a whisper. Sometimes a whisper is all it takes to crack a sky. *Did your poor little Russel die for comin back empty-handed? Was Egan the one who done it? Someone else there at your table? Was it you?*

Old Porch sure turned then, but if Allison expected fury, both she and Sondra were plenty surprised to find him grinnin.

Goshdarn it, Sondi! You know I've played poker my whole life, right? You think I don't know applesauce when I hear it? Is that the best you got? Makin up whatever you feel like? You've lost a son. You've lost two. Of all people, you should know best what sayin such things might do to a father who's just lost his son to your murderous whelps. *You can thank the mountains for buryin them when they did.*

Old Porch's grin was gone by then, but he would still walk away unbothered. Sondra knew it too but had lost her confidence about what else to add.

As he once again gave them his back, Allison spoke up. She weren't done. *Mr. Porch, I need to know somethin: do you seek justice here or revenge? Because one has a future and one don't.*

You best give Mr. Erville a call, Old Porch answered without turnin around, *if you want to talk about the future.*

I think you're missin what I'm tryin to say here, Mr. Porch. I'm tryin to offer you some help.

Help me?! Old Porch roared, and he got to laughin some again too. What an awful sound. But at least he'd turned back around.

You don't know my boy, Allison continued. *None of you do. You need to watch yourself. You need to be careful. You need to not fool where you think you ain't the fool.*

You both really are crazy! Old Porch declared, joyously now. *Sondi, tell me somethin just so I'm clear: you two are friends because her boy Kalin was friends with your Tom?*

Sondra nodded.

Tom was the one who told Kalin to take those horses, Allison added. *Right before he died. Made him swear.*

Tom did that, huh?

I was there. I saw it, Sondra said. *Her boy got down on his knees.*

I'm sorry then, at least for that, Old Porch said to Allison. *Tom shouldn't have involved a stranger in our business. And by that I mean Porch-Gatestone business.*

Well, you're right there, Orwin. I'll give you that, Sondra said, bestowin upon the moment, if not exactly peace, then a brief détente just long enuf to allow both sides the chance to head off in different directions. Old Porch nodded, and so did Sondra. They'd meet again.

Except Allison still weren't done.

Of course, then again maybe Tom knew exactly who he was involvin, Allison said, her pace once again unhurried, her voice once again low, everythin about her easy enuf to not mind except for the goose pimples suddenly ripplin up the back of Sondra Gatestone's arms, so fast and bad she had to right then roll her shoulders back and shake them arms, and though she couldn't know it, not one of them could, the same was happenin to Old Porch up the back of his neck. Not that he acknowledged the sensation as anythin but a reaction to the weather. He slapped at the back of his neck like there was a mosquito there.

Then a lot of good it did either one of them, he grunted, though he kept studyin Allison March and awful closely too. *You still think your twig of a boy is alive, don't you?*

That's right, Allison conceded. *It's like that mountain lion I've been tryin to tell you about.*

We ain't the wolves here, lady. We're in mournin.

I sincerely hope that's true, Mr. Porch, Allison said with a sigh. Old Porch wasn't the first brutal man she'd known in her life. *See, come mornin, not a single wolf emerged outta that hollow. But soon enuf that cat came out, stretched some in the light, and wandered off. Not a limp about him.*

First chance Old Porch got to stop for a pay phone, he did, right off Eighteenth Street. He'd strolled off the tarmac slow enuf, but now he was frantic. He jammed change into the slot and cursed every ring that slipped by without Egan pickin up. Egan might've already headed out. That was the likely possibility. There was no one home. Just an empty house swallowin Old Porch's desperation. At least the machine finally picked up. Old Porch started to demand a return call, his voice gruff, near monotone, stripped of all anguish. Egan picked up then, and for Old Porch to hear his boy's voice was a great relief.

It was 1:22 p.m.

Old Porch laid out first what he'd seen up in the cirque. The Kalin kid and Landry were alive. They even had the horses with them. He seen about where they was camped. *Pretty much trapped I'd say* given the weather and the mess that slide had made of the canyon wall.

Egan assured his daddy that no matter how bad it was, they'd get to the cirque and before dusk too. In fact they was leavin right then.

Good, Old Porch said. *I'll meet you there. Kevin Moffet's flyin me up again. This time I'll be with Shelly and Sean. Maybe Hatch.*

Whoa there, Dad. That's no good. You want to take me, Kelly, and Billings. Maybe Hatch. He's here anyway.

Shelly and Sean will be fine.

Egan repeated hisself. Word for word. And this time Old Porch heard what his boy was sayin.

You got a point. I'll call you back as soon as I get the timin from Kevin.

Old Porch drove back to the airport only to find Kevin Moffet goin on about repairs the McDonnell Douglas 500D would need before it could fly. Custom Enterprises had a Bell 206 LR, but it was up north and wouldn't be available until late tomorrow mornin.

Of course for Kevin Moffet this was the best possible news. No need to quit on Old Porch. His hands were tied. Now he could get after bookin a ticket to Anchorage. If he could find an early flight out tomorrow, he'd be done permanent with Orvop and the Porches.

But there was Old Porch pushin on him more rolls with red rubber bands. He even laid down in Kevin's palm a stack of one-hundred-dollar bills that sure was gonna make Alaska a lot more charmin. Like he always done, Kevin took it all.

Old Porch wouldn't risk callin Egan from the airport, and so once again he raced out in search of another pay phone, this one on West Center, no booth, just him and the rain. Egan picked up on the first ring.

It was 1:49 p.m.

The helicopter's a bust, Old Porch yelled. *Get up there now! Get after them! Nepo them! Go! Go! Go!*

Plenty's been said about them two phrases *Get after them!* and the more explicit *Nepo them!* especially by Sherry Hindmarsh, Timpview alumna, who would end up in of all places Schönhausen tutorin math to young teenagers; and by LeRoy Kriek too, Spanish Fork alum, who would also end up tutorin young teenagers in math but over in Zagreb, Croatia.

In many an animated FaceTime, these two, like so many others, with evidence of pay phone records, fabulated reenactments, improved, imagined, altered, and surely argued about, though mostly agreed upon, how this here must've been the moment when Old Porch made clear his resoundin death sentence upon them two kids. *Sure, it was implied before, but on this occasion Old Porch had to have told Egan what needed doin,* Sherry Hindmarsh would assert. *Are you makin this up?* LeRoy Kriek would ask.

Others would contend that Old Porch had said only what it sounded like he'd said: Go find them and apprehend them. Those folks would be fools, of course. They're likely the same ones who believe sugared cereals have the health benefits of oatmeal, the kind that drink Crush and think it's orange juice just because, well, it's orange. Before Sherry Hindmarsh was diagnosed with liver cancer, stage IV, LeRoy Kriek as well, and in the same month too!, she'd do her best to put down that viewpoint: *Old Porch needed those kids dead. I mean, Lordy! What kinda idjit thinks those Porch boys was up there to perform some kinda citizen's arrest?*

Now while Old Porch had full confidence in Egan and Billings, and likely Kelly, Hatch remained a problem. He was hands down the best tracker and hunter of the bunch. There was no arguin that he was a trained and decorated sniper even if he'd never seen action. But neither Old Porch nor Egan knew if Hatch would take the shot. And even if he did, things could get complicated fast. Fer example, if he did fire his own weapon, it weren't no generic rifle. The round alone would betray him, and if Hatch fired from a ways off, he'd be unable to claim self-defense. It weren't so hard to see how anythin less than the perfect situation could come back and bite Hatch as well as all the Porches on their butts.

Suffice it to say, by this point Orwin Porch had pretty much sloughed off any elation he'd felt earlier over the sight of Landry runnin away from him, the Kalin kid too, though somethin there, about that thin, sprig-like, almost fragile boy, stirred up in Old Porch somethin different, what Old Porch had missed from the helicopter but was comin to see now, if fer no reason he could lay claim to, simply what insisted on remainin, persistin, what kept on pesterin Old Porch, how the boy had stood his ground, alone too in that immense place curtained by cold clouds, and without a weapon, and yet . . . What had Porch seen exactly? Old Porch still didn't know, but he felt haunted some by the encounter, like he'd seen a ghost, been warned by a ghost, findin hisself shudderin now on the phone, even cursin his misfortune for findin them kids alive. How much better off he'd be if they was already dead.

Ross Killian, a Springville High alum, eventually gettin to Monaco, where for many years he'd earn his way as a professional backgammon player, who'd know each mornin that the big jar of U.S. pennies on his windowsill also held the number of weeks he had left to live, would in 2007 give voice between dice rolls to a matter that didn't concern how Old Porch had communicated a death sentence from a phonebooth, Killian had never thought to imagine those calls or what all Old Porch had sensed in Kalin March from a helicopter; rather he wondered aloud whether or not Allison March had inadvertently betrayed her son when she had shared with Old Porch *that story or fable or parable or whatever it was about the mountain lion?* His was not an easy question, and few were satisfied with the whatever answers folks spun up. Nancy McClanahan, Orvop High alumna, who eventually became a marketin analyst in Tel Aviv and befriender of crows, would stand firmly with the notion that Allison March was *just a real nice person, and even if what she had to say might sometimes come out real crude and ribaldly-like, like with the Liz Blicker girl for instance, she was still givin her good advice. Same with that Mr. Porch. Against her maternal instincts, she was still strivin to be the better person. No one can say otherwise. That's who Allison March was, just a really nice person.*

Old Porch, though, didn't just leave it at *Get after them! Nepo them! Go! Go! Go!* He needed to make sure his boy understood their jeopardy.

Kevin Moffet's seen what I seen. He knows them two are alive.

And though Old Porch had obviously known this since they'd been hoverin above them kids and the horses, this utterance in his own ear sent Old Porch's mind to a blackness he weren't sure he could get loose of, blacker than tar that keeps gettin stickier the more you try to wipe it off, too soon coverin you up, and too soon gettin on everythin else.

That won't matter a bit, Egan responded. *We'll find them up there, and everyone will know how they attacked us first.*

You make sure of it.

We'll come out of this right as rain. You'll see.

Expect to find them tryin to get out of the cirque. They know the trap they're in. They'll be runnin.

I don't doubt it.

They sure ran from me.

I don't doubt it, Egan said again.

You keep Hatch close, understand?

It's all in order here, but, Dad, there's somethin else.

Old Porch didn't want to hear about no somethin else.

Take the radios, Eges. Keep me advised. Regularly.

The radios won't work in them high places. You know that. Dad—

Then you get to me soon as you're back. I wanna hear it from your lips.

Sondra Gatestone and the Kalin kid's mom was over here.

Yeah. I seen them too.

You did? Where?

At the airport. I was just gettin back with Kevin.

Then she told you?

Kevin got it right. He didn't say nothin about seein the kids.

What did she tell you?

What did she tell you?

How they'd been talkin to my neighbors all mornin, and Sondra said there was some that swear they seen Russel ridin home on Cavalry just fine and dandy.

Old Porch was relieved. This was just the same bullcrap. *That's all bluff, Eges. And I told her so. She's just shakin our tree. Nothin Sondi hasn't been doin for years. Waitin to see what falls. You fall?*

Didn't even blink.

Good. I think she saw I saw what she was full of. But you know this gives me an idea to get right back at her. Before you head off, you tell Woolsey and Francis that I want them knockin on every door of every neighbor you got. Find out who's sayin that they seen Russel ridin back. And have Francis and Woolsey tell whoever they talk to, and it don't matter who, that the mother of that murderin kid has been spreadin lies everywhere. And get them on it now!

I will.

Every door. And if no one answers, you tell them to keep comin back. The whole day. I want them on this. This is their work. They best not let me down.

Old Porch paid no mind that saddlin Egan with this additional

676

task, even if it was just delegatin, might delay his boy, delay them all. Now weren't the time for Egan to start trackin down his younger brothers, especially as he was about to head up into the mountains, to hard places, dangerous places; it weren't gonna do him, Kelly or Billings a lick of good to be thinkin about neighbors suddenly comin forth to swear to Russel's vitality right before returnin to Egan's place.

There's somethin else, Dad, Egan said.

What is it with you and that expression?! Old Porch suddenly roared, like a wounded beast too. *There's somethin else, Dad,* repeatin it in the most squeaky and malicious voice he could muster.

With maybe the exception of Hatch, and that was a big maybe, Egan was the only Porch unafraid to square shoulders against Old Porch, in person, certainly on the phone. He let his dad sit now in his pause. And Old Porch knew what was happenin too, wipin then his chin with the heel of his hand, the rain comin down even harder, sideways even, with periodic gusts hard enuf to bounce water off the keys of the phone, gettin Old Porch to squint and snarl at yet one more level of interference.

Go on then! Old Porch finally shouted. *Tell me your goshdarn somethin else!*

Sondi said they was off to talk to Riddle. Is he back?

Oh heck! Old Porch gripped that handset then like he was gonna attack the keypad. That both ladies had gabbled on like they'd done but never breathed a word about Riddle scared him the most.

Egan, you don't need to hear me snappin at you. You've been nothin but straight-up solid. I mean that. The real horseradish. Old Porch needed to regroup. *You get up on that mountain before it's too late for all of us. We win today or we lose it all tomorrow. Hear me when I say this: this ain't just about some awful accident, and that accident is ours to own and no one else's and ours alone to suffer. This is about how others could use that accident against us Porches and ruin us. Do you understand? Ruin us! But we get through this like good soldiers and we will have somethin everyone else will envy for years to come. No great achievement is had without great contest. Remember that. This is our moment. Get up there. Get it done. I'll handle Riddle.*

You don't have to worry about me, Dad.

I know it, Egan.

Of course, Orwin Porch was plenty worried. Trent Riddle was a big problem. He'd always been a big problem, and if right now he was sittin down with them two Gila monsters or, worse, givin a statement to that Orvop city detective, everythin Old Porch had toiled for would come tumblin down. They'd put Old Porch behind bars.

677

Egan too. And then they'd go after Kelly and Billings. Might as well haul in all his boys.

Hot nonsense come up fast then in Old Porch's eyes. He wouldn't allow it. He coughed it back, wiped it away, spat it out. Old Porch still had plenty to do. He could follow up with Woolsey and Francis to make sure they canvassed Egan's neighborhood right. And he would do just that. He could follow up with Kevin Moffet about other helicopter options. And he would do just that. He could make darned sure Shelly and Sean was both at his side for the rest of the day. And he would do just that. He could call Havril Enos again. And he would do that too.

The real trouble now, though, was how everythin was startin to feel precariously unreal, from the call from U.S. Senator Shane Hays that mornin to the return of Riddle, and on top of that maybe even some neighbor claimin they really had seen Russel ridin back to Egan's, because maybe Sondi weren't bluffin after all. Old Porch even had to add to this turd pile the death of his little Russel. All of it: unreal. Like mountains you discover aren't mountains but paint on plywood; like the stage floor beneath your feet you discover ain't even that, a stage, but just ground; like the open-air theater you discover is open-air because the theater was razed years ago. Because there ain't never been no theater, no stage, nor even mountains. There ain't been nothin but a wide, flat, merciless plain, what's so barren too that you begin to question even how it is you stand. On what? Sacred boards? Those are long gone. Ground? That's gone. Until it's just sky above and sky below. Until there's no sky. Just nothin. Until you finally have to turn your disbelievin eye on yourself and meet nothin there too.

Back at Porch Meats, Old Porch found Mr. Bucket #5 whinin in his kennel. He unlatched the gate and considered givin him a kick as the dog tore by to piss and crap in the backyard. Though even kickin Mr. Bucket #5 would've felt unreal too. Old Porch had done kicked too many dogs too many times to care. Instead he threw down some kibble for the Rottweiler.

Effy trotted up to the fence then. Old Porch had nothin for her, but he did stroke her head and pat her neck and realized by her low snorts that under his palms she alone did not feel unreal. She, he cared for. She for whatever reason still mattered, and she continued to matter to him the more he mumbled to her about all he'd already lost, all he was about to lose. He even went on mumblin about what he would have to do if he was to keep even some of it. Mr. Bucket whined near his feet but Old Porch paid no attention.

Old Porch had had Effy for near forty years now. She was older than all his kids. An early customer of his, Elder Demming Despain, had called up to say he had a baby mule in his field with no idea where it come from and no idea what he was supposed to do with it. His wife had gone ahead and named her Iphigenia when she'd learned who would take possession of the ornery four-legged thing.

Old Porch had figured to sell off Iphigenia quick, then figured to just render her quicker. But he didn't. He just cut her name down to Iffy. By then she'd started amusin him with her surreal escapes. That's when he got to callin her his Effin Genius, until even that name became somethin else, somethin softer, until Effy finally just became part of this place, his place, part of the routines, his routines, welcome for reasons he couldn't dare admit. *If only!* Laurel Baker would declare, facin her end in Lisbon, the result of an indecent assault of tau proteins, Pick's disease. *Couldn't somethin have changed then? If just for the memory of the present? Surely, surely, surely.*

Old Porch even bent over then and rested his head against hers, feelin the mule lean into him in a way that felt close, that felt good. Then in the drench, with Old Porch's thoughts continuin to find themselves turnin toward yet another awful haze, no matter which direction he chose, finally a garden of forkin paths void of paths or any semblance of a garden, disjointed, unfocused, he haltered the mule and patted her withers to get her movin. He didn't stop talkin to her, though he also didn't mention how he'd bleed her, wouldn't even stun her from life, just stick her and above her brayin objections watch her wheel and stumble until she was too drained out to move anymore, and then by hisself Old Porch would butcher her carcass. Why? Because she was real to him, and real always presents a cost. And meat is the only cost that matters to real men. And meat needs remindin how there will always be meat that is the master of other meat. And that is the only difference worth notin. Nor would the breakdown of her carcass serve any other purpose than that. Her meat would serve no gut; her hide would never be tawed. After an hour with a band saw and such, Old Porch would just shovel her pieces into the Vulcan 2700 Incinerator, which was more than big enuf to handle her bones and sinews, big enuf for cattle, for horses, for anythin hooved or articulate.

Old Porch at least spared her this vision of her immediate future. Instead he filled Effy's ear with the trouble with women, how it all came down to them, first castin his mother upon that pyre of his discontent; then the sisters he never really knew; then Sondra Gatestone, for countless offenses but especially for settlin the Ridgeline Meadow Estates Claim like she done, in his favor too when it turned out it weren't in his favor at all; and finally that Allison March, her as well. And Old Porch weren't done, throwin in that wrathful fire his ex-wife, who'd run from him and her boys, nearly ruinin them all, takin away his very youngest too, his only daughter, who she'd ruin too. He added her as well. Until he had hisself a whole heap of bodies goin up in flames, what in his mind's heart didn't give way to smoke and ash like they did in the Vulcan but stayed alive, writhin in the torments his mind weren't strong enuf to release them from.

It followed then in that horror show of imagined wails that Old Porch had to admit that women did do somethin right, even if that somethin right was only to elicit the desires that made a man man enuf to fulfill his potential; and though temporary, on behalf of men and their biological prerogative, women should receive necessary attentions to foster health until what followed conception, what resulted in birth, could once again become the right of men, become Old Porch's right. It was when women got the idea that their gift of begettin extended beyond the gift of their shape that they became a scourge upon the earth worse than all the descendants of Cain and Canaan who ever lived.

It's the one who forgets that notions of kindness and forgiveness, and blasted affection, are unsuitable replacements for the Manifest Destiny of brute strength and a willingness and resolve to carry forth the procreative violence the world requires, as is evident everywhere in nature, in the teeth of the hungry, the claws of the triumphant; he shall wither in the wind. Anythin else amounts to fantasies concocted by the weak to retard the progress determined and carried out by the fit, the strong, them who can still delight in their own sanguinolency and not shy from the vascular eruptions of a lesser somebody struck down.

Now, fer sure, Orwin Porch didn't say it like so. It's hard to imagine such a cursed man actually utterin *sanguinolency* or *vascular eruptions* let alone *procreative violence*. The many that still assert that Old Porch did no more than pat and grumble at Effy as he grabbed up and clicked on her lead should in this case be heeded. Nonetheless, too many still miss that whatever grunts and gurgles Old Porch had disgorged in that hard rain, over the course of those hard minutes, still did spring up from a charred heart through which centuries spoke. That goes for Old Porch's tears and sobs as well, that performance of excretion that followed soon after, endin any semblance of articulation; a demon-stration of cost that would only further endow Old Porch's requisite measures of infamy; what would banish the haze and once again grant return to the reality he required; near as close to an act of faith as Old Porch could ever get.

Old Porch's forebears had crossed oceans. They had crossed this continent. They had settled here and survived here, but only because of their willingness to arm themselves against any challenge and hunt down every meal, whether antlered or not, and strike down any opponent, the darker the skin the better, but white as enamel was fine too. Whatever the Church said in the light of day, and they did say things, things like *It's cheaper to feed them than to fight them* or *Turn the other cheek* or *Treat your neighbor as you would yourself,* with many of the Porch kin and kith listenin earnestly, with some even strivin to rectify what they saw as their own moral failures, as defined by the Church, with the Church abettin too such yellow-bellied limp-wristed confessions by accordin consolation and even acquital and so compromisin the horizons of all their lives; by night the good Porches, the strong Porches, them that did not waver, who stood their ground, shunned the Church along with every other declaration concocted in the name of Law and Justice, never forgettin the reckonin of the individual, the personal price daily paid and nightly exacted upon these environs, armed with weapons or will requisite for the retributions owed, the very same fierce forebears who strode forth into the tomorrow that was Old Porch's today to guarantee, like he would guarantee, the success of both progeny and property.

You, though, understand that, right, Effy? which Old Porch did most certainly say aloud to the old mule, as he also gave the lead a good tug. His Effy. His Effin Genius. His Iffy. Iphigenia.

Why ever you was so cursed, Old Porch continued in that now strange unresolvable speech of his, even as his resolve returned more and more sharpness and clarity to his thoughts, *know that as I stand here before you, I'm the one who ends your curse and in return accepts your blessin.*

And then like that, he led his friend into the abattoir.

It was 4:04 p.m.

Chapter Nineteen
"Sick!"

Hatch Porch was convinced the best way to get up to Kirk's Cirque was to start out along the same path he'd soloed that mornin: the right side of Isatch Canyon or what was the north side of Agoneeya. His brothers thought he was frickin nuts. But when Egan took an atypical breath to calmly point out how they'd be on the wrong side of Isatch Canyon, with still the swole crick to cross, not to mention a higher chance of comin into contact with sheriffs or rangers who were under orders to expel any interlopers not of their ranks, Hatch kept insistin he was right for no better reason than he was the oldest and therefore accorded the right of rule.

Egan didn't even get mad. He just made it clear that Hatch was welcome to take whatever way he liked, but they'd be stickin to the left side of Isatch Canyon or the south side of Kaieneewa. Hatch weren't bothered none by Egan's rebellion because he figured Kelly would side with him. Ain't that what Kelly had always done? And fer this character Billings, who Hatch didn't know from Adam, why he didn't give a boot's heel about him.

So Hatch was plenty surprised to see Kelly linin up behind Egan. Maybe, at some other time, unhavocked by that morning's sight of his youngest little brother, Russel, laid out on the proverbial slab, free from his belligerent father breathin down all their necks, exhortin them to make right by the family, Hatch might've paid more attention to the unusual strength of this alliance, strange in its newness and certainly unfamiliar. Hatch might've then considered that this weren't just about a difference of opinion concernin what route to take, given that their objective was the same, though maybe it weren't the same, Hatch unable to catch hold of any of these contradictory valences, except as a feelin that was so wobbly he had to quick brush it aside in order to steady hisself. He was good at that. If only he hadn't been, though. If only he could've hung longer with that instability and so found the warnin implicit in the company of such men, and they were just that now, not boys, not brothers, not even employees, but first and foremost men.

Hatch in fact applauded his own willingness to at this moment step down before Egan. Chief Castor Emerson, his commander and mentor in Texas, a man who was everythin Old Porch wasn't, a man Hatch regarded as decent and heroic, had spoken on just this matter, pointin out in a review that Hatch's success in his career would depend on how well he could put aside his own heartfelt opinion in favor of a better opinion that weren't his own. Thus Hatch looked almost smug when he told this younger brother: *You're right, Egan.* He said it easily too.

The words should've meant somethin to Egan, but Egan didn't care one bit, and his brother's smirk galled him to no end, irritated Kelly too, who'd started to think more and more that their hero brother was pompous and likely full of hot air. Billings alone saw Hatch the clearest: someone well outside the organizin events at work here who should be given as much distance as possible. Billings was plenty disappointed that Hatch didn't end up takin his own path.

Egan drove the speed limit up to Indian Hills, past Apache Lane, Mohican Lane, Navajo Street, Chumash Street, and finally Ute Way. From there dirt roads led to one that would take them the highest. With Pink Floyd puttin it pretty clear with *You better run*, he parked his truck behind some tall brush, Billings pullin in beside him. They unloaded the three ATVs, the one one-seater and the two two-seaters, by which point Ozzy Osbourne was singin *Wine is fine but whiskey's quicker.* They had a nice view of the Orvop Temple to the south and the Sherwood Hills Racquet Club to the north, with Timpview High below, though the rain and musterin clouds swallowed up the rest of the city and valley. Not that Egan was lookin back. None of them were. Except for Hatch.

Egan drove lead on the one-seater. Kelly followed in the two-seater with Billings. Hatch took up the rear, drivin the other two-seater, though he didn't go before arguin that they should at least consider takin Little Isatch Canyon which weren't more than a few minutes away. *That'll take us up around the north side of Kaieneewa to the campground, and from there we can figure out a way up to the cirque. Far from Isatch Canyon too.*

What the heck are you talkin about? Kelly barked at Hatch. *What Little Isatch Canyon? There ain't no such thing. And there sure as heck ain't no easy way around Kaieneewa unless you got ropes, and even with ropes it's hard.*

Because Egan weren't in earshot at this moment, Hatch gave no thought to stiflin his confusion. He even came close to apologizin to Kelly, admittin that maybe he'd misremembered things and was thinkin about another set of peaks, maybe a whole different range. Not that Hatch didn't cut hisself some slack: he'd been away for years now; a lot was different, not the least of which was his family. Of course they was still his family. Of course he remembered them just fine. And yet they seemed changed. Take even Shelly, fer example. Sure he was a mullet-wearin muttonhead. *Just one of the maggots,* as their daddy would say. But what about Shelly's girlfriend? That Liz Blicker. Before the girls had quit Egan's house, Liz had kissed Shelly on the mouth, whisperin in his ear, and loud enuf for Hatch to hear her too, *I want you to leave it in me,* still smilin all nice like and with that plaster on her nose, Shelly near proud to say later that it served her right for talkin so long with some kid from Mountain View. At least when Shelly got a load of Hatch's look, he'd tried some to walk that back. *She's a good gal, though,* Shelly had conveyed to his big brother. *She told everyone she walked into her glass door.* Like that's what Hatch wanted to hear. It weren't even her story to make up. It weren't even Shelly's story to make up. That was the story their momma had told them, told their neighbors too, how she'd walked into their glass door, and they didn't even have a glass door. It was some relief that Shelly weren't with them now, but Egan and Kelly had been right there listenin to Shelly and they hadn't seemed at all bothered.

Egan led them up an easy set of switchbacks, all packed and graded well enuf to slough off most of the water. A good place to accelerate. Even have some fun. And that's what they did, whoopin it up like they was once again thirteen. Before they knew it, they was already beneath Squaw Peak. Hatch kept an eye out for trail-collapse. Egan didn't slow.

In fact the higher up they got, the more solid the trails became, the rain havin long since washed away loose rubble and whatever tangles of deracinated brush had been blown free by the storm. There weren't no breaches neither. The crushed limestone and general aggregate had compacted to the point that some stretches felt near like concrete, a narrow interstate from spur to spur, until they was passin right beneath the mouth of the Awides Mine.

Not that any of these men gave it a thought, never considerin that but some hundreds of feet above them Kalin, Landry, and the horses had hid out Thursday night, where past darkness was still emergin. Hatch did, however, experience upon his back a wash of cold so terrible it made a warm desert breeze out of the near-sleety headwind pin-cushionin his face. He thought he was sick. And then it passed.

Almost too soon they was reachin the base of the bigger bluffs above, where their speed still didn't lessen until a nasty ravine cut them off. But the trail did not abandon them. Hatch spotted an alternate series of short switchbacks that soon enuf had them hastenin on their way, eventually mergin with the very same trail Kalin, Landry, and the horses had taken from the mine, the same one to the *T* above Aster Scree where, if you'll recall, Kalin's heart had beat heavy with the anticipation of these very men, back then merely ghosts born of fretful thoughts. For Kalin they had remained immaterial. Now, though, they was anythin but immaterial, armed with enuf weaponry to successfully put their acquisition of the future they pursued into effect, fueled no doubt by the cynegetic lusts possessin them all, even Hatch.

Of course none of the Porches were anticipatin a run-in with Kalin and Landry right then. Their hearts didn't beat heavy. Quite the opposite. They was still in the thrall of Go! Go! Go! Even if they still had to stop at the *T*. They had no choice.

Takin a water break beside an assemblage of rock that Egan paid no attention to, and now offerin solemn nods, sat Park Ranger Emily Brickey on a Honda ATV and Law Enforcement Ranger Bren Kelson, on a Honda XR dirt bike. They'd left an hour earlier and weren't alone either. Deputy Sheriffs Doyle Cannon and Shaun Brice were there as well, also on ATVs, all of them stuck waitin there for Deputy Sheriffs Thayle Peterson and Gammon Erickson, who'd just arrived by way of Aster Scree; they might not keep up with engines but they were still fit enuf to make the cirque in good time. Plus they wouldn't be machine-encumbered if the path they was forced to follow demanded a more vertical climb. Together this posse near had it all.

And for Egan that was nothin but bad news, though there was some good news in it too. Egan knew Doyle Cannon, knew him well. They'd played football together and even double-dated a few times. Shaun Brice weren't a stranger either. Egan greeted everyone warmly except for Emily Brickey, she bein so clearly displeased by their arrival. Egan made sure to introduce Hatch as the Texas lawman he was, suddenly more than grateful that this eldest was now in their company.

Egan didn't deviate from simple: they was only out lookin for their horses; *we're hopin they cut loose before that slide took the others down.* He also made it clear that they'd happily about-face and clear the heck outta there. *We don't want to interfere none with police business.* Kelly kept his head down. Billings stretched his legs. Hatch looked like a peacock.

Deputy Sheriff Shaun Brice gave a friendly enuf smile, but Deputy Sheriff Doyle Cannon was genuinely glad to see Egan and came over with a big handshake and even hugged him too.

The park's closed, buddy, Doyle Cannon said. *And there sure as heck ain't no motorized vehicles allowed.*

Judgin by Emily Brickey's face, the sun had suddenly broke through the clouds and set the slopes wild with geese, green grass, and petals of yellow. But spring sure fled fast when Doyle Cannon didn't stop there.

Of course, right here ain't part of Isatch Canyon Park. And it don't become part of the Katanogos State Park until farther up. I think we'd welcome your company.

Deputy Sheriff Cannon weren't right about any of that park stuff, but that's what he thought, and it was a misunderstandin he'd have to defend and eventually own in the months ahead.

Puttin aside Emily Brickey's reactions fer the moment, and she was nothin but seethin, Deputy Sheriffs Gammon Erickson and Thayle Peterson were also thrown off by Cannon's invitation, tradin plenty of uncomfortable glances, and that went for Deputy Sheriff Shaun Brice too, though them looks was also the extent of it. Deputy Sheriff Cannon was in charge here of this posse, and if he had no problem sharin the path with the Porch brothers, then that was that.

A boneheaded decision, really, as Randy Beal would point out throughout his life, even to his neighbors, who mostly viewed these stories as fantastical as talkin tigers and godlike elephants: *I'm sympathetic to Cannon. I am. But he was a lawman. His job was to know the boundaries of the places he was charged to enforce. Plain and simple. His friendship with Egan, and really it was an acquaintanceship by then, shouldn't've mattered one bit. He should've turned them Porch boys right around. He should've ticketed them too. He knew better. Never forgave hisself either.*

Greg and Kristy Coulson, who would visit Beal in Kolkata in his final years, the couple havin toured extensively throughout India for over two decades but still choosin to return to Orvop as their own graves began to open and whisper their names, well, they made sure to include some sympathetic notes about Cannon in their own wanin dialogue with the likes of Terry Bramall, Tish Haggerty, and Maggie Trunell. They liked to say that the deputy sheriff's choice illustrated well enuf that as lawful as Utah is, and it is a very lawful place, there are also significant discrepancies that if not properly understood will always reduce Utah to the caricature it is not, no matter how much is likely to be made of the Church and its archaic practices. *Cannon's tragic decision, and I think we can agree that it was as tragic as it was absurd, was not made in any ill-intentioned way but rather in that absurdly naïve way that good trustin folks often demonstrate here in Utah,* Kristy Coulson would tell her husband's friends. *The trouble comes when a commandin narrative takes hold,* she would continue. *We're Church people. We believe the stories. Sometimes we forget, though, that we shouldn't believe all the stories. For Doyle Cannon, his alliances weren't so complicated. He could imagine what the loss of Russel was doin to the Porches. His offer was a kindness among neighbors, among friends. Those mountains are plenty dangerous. To have others around who were equally skillt ain't such a bad choice. And he was proven right there.* Greg Coulson would point out then that the Porches had reputations for bein real Mountain Men, with Old Porch bein the original Grizzly Adams, *though without the bear because bears are afraid of him!* Kristy Coulson would then throw in that it was also highly likely that Cannon had believed Egan: *They was lookin for their horses, which they had a right to do so long as they weren't crossin police tape. Plus Hatch Porch was a decorated lawman. There really weren't no foul in poor Doyle Cannon's head.* Greg Coulson would then grunt out his difference of opinion: *Except for the vehicles. Everyone knows ATVs and dirt bikes aren't allowed in the park.* His wife weren't arguin when she added: *But, Greg, we are talkin about 1982, back then everyone did it. The world was just . . . a different place.* Her husband would nod even as he'd also go on to mutter: *The world weren't a different place. It's still the same place. It's always the same place.*

Egan, fer his part, was plenty relieved and pleased by the invitation, but he didn't care one iota for that XR dirt bike Ranger Bren Kelson was ridin. It was faster than the ATVs, more maneuverable, with better traction and stability. It didn't take much to roll an ATV. Ziggy Teegmiller was one painful memory persistin in Orvop. One day he was playin golf at the Quiverside Country Club, and the next day he'd rolled one of them dangerous creations and paralyzed hisself from the neck down. He'd lived a short life of swingin a club, movin, cursin, and with a smile near as infectious as Tom's. He never could embrace stillness, but when Death embraced him, he had no choice but to understand, like we all have to, the stillness that beholds us all. Along with havin been friends with Ziggy, Egan knew ATVs had speed limits. An experienced rider on a dirt bike, however, could leave them in the mud faster than Egan could muster up curses. Somethin needed to be done. But what? How was Egan gonna keep that XR behind him? He had no clue. He just knew they couldn't have Law Enforcement Ranger Bren Kelson tearin off ahead.

It was Doyle Cannon who proved the ticket Egan needed, a realization that would fill the deputy sheriff with an unexpurgated disgust that we can hope Death finally ended or at least lessened. Heedin Cannon's authority, Bren Kelson never blazed ahead and even held back for Park Ranger Brickey. If only he'd have acted upon his advantages. How much better for them all.

Most surprisin, Egan found hisself in the lead again and, even with this new hiccup, marvelin at the smooth progress of their journey so far. As for the terrifyin steeps to the right, where a bad roll would result in an unrecoverable fall, this bein the very same route that had had both Kalin and Landry quailin over what just one misstep would lead to, Egan and the rest paid that no mind. The path was plenty wide and more than solid enuf. Besides death abounds us no matter what path we take. Maybe their speed helped blur the consequences.

Fer his part, Hatch Porch, who chose to take up the rear, welcomed the company of these lawmen. As his ATV was a two-seater, he was more than happy to give Gammon Erickson a ride. Deputy Sheriff Shaun Brice did the same for Thayle Peterson. Hatch in fact found hisself relaxin for the first time since he'd arrived in Orvop. He liked the deputy sheriffs, he liked the rangers, he liked the mountains. More than his brothers.

Kelly and Billings carried no affection for either the deputies or the rangers. Each in their own way was now mullin over how they would handle any encounter with the Kalin kid and Landry. Egan for all his initial pleasure in findin an ally in Doyle Cannon, plus gettin out in front of the pack, was also startin to recognize what a messed-up predicament they was now in. Despite the energies already spent in the name of predictive reasonins, with most of those scenarios focusin on Hatch, Egan had never once thought they'd be joined on this journey by lawmen, and from two different departments too. Even worse, the rangers knew these mountains as well as him, likely better. Or so Egan assumed. It weren't true. Not in this case. They was pretty much all on equal footin. But Egan's certainty that he was disadvantaged sharpened his enmity toward his new companions.

Still, how they was gonna shake them remained beyond Egan's imagination. So what if he stayed out front? Even reachin the cirque first would grant him what? An extra few moments? In minutes, would he gain even five? And even if he did manage to get ten or fifteen minutes alone, so what? Likely not even an hour would be enuf to locate Kalin and Landry. And after that who could say how much longer he'd need to manage the situation, especially in a way that wouldn't come back on him and Kelly, not to mention the rest of the Porches?

It bewildered Egan to realize that he might've already lost, that the Porch family was already lost, that whatever he was doin now didn't amount to anythin more than goin through the motions. He even considered turnin around right then, tellin his daddy that the Law had won and there weren't nothin left to do but lawyer up. It never occurred to Egan how that final diminishment by trial and time served might've been the best possible outcome. Of course that would've required an imagination Egan didn't possess. Imagination requires the creativity to entertain different paths. Egan lived the Old Porch way. Fer him there weren't no other paths. Tom Gatestone, fer example, was near an alien to Egan. Sure, when Tom smiled, Egan could match him teeth for teeth, the difference bein Egan would have a knife clenched between his whereas Tom would have a pretty sliver of grass. And as for laughter, what did Egan know about laughter? Laughter lights the way to surprise.

By the time Egan reached the first big scree, or as it came to be known the Seventh Scree, the same one that Kalin and Landry had crossed on Friday with some apprehension but little difficulty, he found hisself much farther ahead than expected. Even better Kelly and Billings had kept up. Egan felt a lift in his spirits, like he suddenly had room now, room to think. Their situation felt manageable again. Even better, Hatch was at the very back. Maybe his role would be to keep the deputies occupied.

Hatch Porch, meanwhile, was growin more frustrated with the deputy sheriffs stoppin before every scree. At this one, though, after Gammon Erickson got off to likewise inspect the scree with his pals, Hatch made the decision to barrel right on through, gunnin his engine, tearin up the slope on the left, this new speed somehow a reassurance, that competitive fire in his chest too orderin him to defeat Egan at whatever the cost, not only gettin him past everyone but fast across to the other side of the scree as well, on his way to closin the gap between hisself and his brothers.

Park Ranger Emily Brickey saw only a reckless man suddenly gun his ATV and race from the path. *He was arrogant and takin a big risk. He made it though. He was skillt and maybe not as overconfident as I presumed.* That's how Park Ranger Brickey would put it later.

Dealynn Gagnon, who would retire in Hobart, Tasmania, enjoyin hours of daily quiltin while sippin on allotted capfuls of a morphine-based tincture, could never shake the feelin that Hatch Porch was the most tragic figure in these events: *He ain't got the meanness and otherwise insensate crudeness that the others had practiced to the point of menace. Egan fer sure, Kelly too, as well as Sean, Shelly, and Woolsey. Maybe Francis were of a different cloth.* It would've come as no surprise to Gagnon to learn that as Hatch Porch had passed beneath the Awides, he alone felt that terrible cold upon his back, like a great lifeless hand. Nor was that the end of such sensitivities. When they'd crossed the Gate of the Mountain a similar abhorrence was visited upon him. Not that Hatch slowed one bit or permitted his hold on the throttle to slip any, grittin his teeth through the pain risin in his chest, like here was a coronary event he'd had no reason to expect, with only the purpose of this trek keepin him goin: to right the wrong done to Russel, what seen him through the worst of it, even if this *worst of it* in retrospect was hardly the worst of it at all, might even have been the best of it, dependin on where you're standin. After all, only a few moments later and that contortion across his chest seemed like nothin but his own squabblin thoughts. It was beyond Hatch to understand that he alone had heard the Voice upon the steeps, that greater aspect of Nature, grantin him momentarily a glimpse of the horrendous powers now orderin the events at hand.

And such a callin did not end either at the Gate of the Mountain. Upon reachin the other side of the Seventh Scree Hatch Porch had glimpsed a woman.

Lela Schneiter, spendin her last twenty years in Dublin channelin spirits she refused to name, would every month recite at a local pub her narrative inventions until one foggy afternoon in March when she'd declare the followin: *Here stands the Squaw herself, whether named or nameless, whether missioned or wanderin, who, molested by white men, blinded by their fictions in order to abet their base concupiscence, had to cast herself away from their grubby needs, their tortures, if only to reside in bleaker shades until her tormentors and their kin, the most frightenin part of her damnation, were brought forth into the light of Justice and its consequential erasure. Behold her, admire her, fear her, as that stupid self-admirin Hatch Porch never could.*

Jonathan Nez Paine, an Orvop native who, as a retired clinical psychologist found hisself livin in Malta, would often daydream his way through variant claims: what was revealed to Hatch, by a clump of brush, *Earth crammed with heaven, every common bush afire with God,* quotin Elizabeth Barrett Browning, was, *sure, on that first take, female in form, but on the second, a bush in flames, and on the third, a disgorged flurry of American kestrels,* their rust-colored backs suddenly alight in the gray, what by such eruptions of fire and flight Hatch Porch perceived as deservin of his devout obeisance and prayer, *what now commanded him to withdraw at once.* And fer sure, the racket of them engines up ahead further defeated his understandin of the revelations available to him now, the smell of exhaust and sloshin gasoline further attenuatin his vision, until Hatch Porch had no greater response than to just drive on by. *Though what he'd witnessed, if Lela's to be believed,* Jonathan Nez Paine repeatedly bringin this up, *weren't near as ecstatic as I sometimes want this to be. Me and the old prophets. Me and Rumi. No, what Hatch seen, plain and simple, was his own mother. A projection of her, of course, but no less sacred, no less terrifyin, and no less holy.*

Jonathan Nez Paine weren't the only one to finally bring forth this tremendous unnamed presence, her name forever withheld, not by any patriarchal collusion of fears but by herself, refusin her participation in the narrative, flatly denyin any chance of a homecomin let alone undesired inclusion, in the name of her own private and unwritten future. Nonetheless, dozens have still circled, or tried at least to circumscribe, this nil-mentioned figure whom some have called cold, others have called problematic, still others have called devoid of spirit for her sons: she who abdicated her role as every center and simply fled, takin with her the very youngest, severed completely from her brothers, from Old Porch's influence, from eventually even his name.

After all, even Hatch Porch, despite his trophied life, his much-commented-upon closeness with his father and brothers, had also fled, also down to Texas, where his mother and sister were, Hatch livin not ten minutes away from them. And though he would not set a single word or even deed against this project their father continued to hammer out upon the anvil of his very children, Hatch Porch also preserved in hisself the good sense to continually try to escape those designs.

As a last word on Hatch's vision on the other side of the Seventh Scree, Phenprapa Devey, a widow who'd pursue her final days on the island of Zakynthos, with a guitar on her knee too, enjoyin her own improvised melodies and lyrics between settin and risin suns, would often return to speculatin about what might've happened if Hatch Porch had recognized how what he'd mistook for his own thoughts or but a clump of brush or even a scatterin of birds was in fact a Truth he'd earned the right to see at that very moment. And whether appearin as Pia Isan or his mother or Her Story itself, what if Hatch had first just recognized her as valid? Would he then have heeded that apparition's warnin? Fer a long time Phenprapa Devey tried to maintain a wanderin optimism. However, by the end of her life she grew more resigned that *even if Hatch Porch was self-aware enuf, he was still too unchangin, his chains more bindin than those on Prometheus, the gift he carried already dyin.*

Of course, who are we to find fault with Hatch Porch's failure to read the signs? Who amongst us hasn't disregarded, and more than once too, the Gift of a Ghost? Who amongst us hasn't mistaken the Voice That Binds Us All as our own thinkin and casually disregarded its portents when if we could've heard it, we would've upon that very instant lived in the unfathomable embrace of unbounded peace and endurin love? Which is really just to paraphrase what Dixon Walters would say aloud to Graciella Francis, Brenda Mistry, and the great Laura Wall: *What if Hatch had just slowed down, even smiled some? What if, without a word, he'd just turned around and exited that terrible escapade, evadin once and for all that avalanche of incongruent lies set loose by violence, maybe offerin up a wave to mark, you know, his departure. What if?*

But as we all know, Hatch Porch did no such thing. He drove on, even acceleratin to catch up with Egan and Kelly, closin in on the Eighth Scree.

It was 4:13 p.m.

Kalin had fallen ill at 1:41 p.m., and those first two hours had not been easy. After just the first siege upon his system, Kalin could hardly move. He stayed hunched over in the misty rains with his drawers down to his ankles, sufferin bouts of explosions from both ends, which were at least considerate enuf to alternate.

His guts felt like some dirty waterlogged socks twistin out their excess into themselves, which then through a set of protestin turns and spasms finally ejected their disquietin anguish upon the wet ground.

And that was just the start. Kalin continued to cramp up; Kalin continued to heave. Sick! Sick! Sick! Some error beyond correction. Terminal. Self-eradicatin. And when Kalin found hisself in a moment of relative calm, a dead calm, he'd return to haranguin Landry to keep away. His panic all too evident. Under different circumstances the high pitch in his voice would've set Landry on a teasin rampage, but she was worried sick to hear Kalin in such woes. She even felt her own belly gurgle up unpleasantly, 100 percent positive that she was gonna join him in the next moment, though of course her retreat would be to the opposite side of their campsite, far from their campsite, as far as she could waddle before necessity and propriety set her to her business, though no such trek nor business was required. It was only hunger in her guts, and empathy.

Too soon Kalin had to yelp out instructions on how to get him more toilet paper in such a way as to not risk exposin hisself. She did as she was told, placin the roll in a plastic bag along with a few small stones tossed in for weight. Her throw weren't perfect, but Kalin could still crab on over. Had he ever felt such fright? That she might spy such smears and spatterins and of course take in his bare neked bottom . . . fer Kalin it was too terrible an outcome to consider!

On and on it went. Kalin lost count of how many times he had to clutch his knees and agonize. It didn't help none that what he released only kept gettin more acidic. The dry heaves, though, were worse, the nothin that it dragged up. Kalin kept lookin for blood, but at least in that respect his guts stayed intact.

Landry didn't stay idle. She built up the fire and set water to boilin, addin some wild mint she'd found growin down near the perimeter of the meadow. She'd even found packets of sugar and salt. Small miracles in little pouches of paper.

Get them clothes off and get under a blanket, she told him when he finally baltered back to their campsite.

Kalin didn't even consider the order.

Fer Pete's sake, you're soakin! I promise I won't look.

But Kalin just sat down next to the fire and shivered. He looked gray too, too gray, even his lips was gray. Landry threw blankets over his shoulders and gave him the tea. He was grateful for the sip even if not a few minutes later he was once again scramblin out into the brush to heave again.

Navidad and Mouse seemed to sense somethin had gone afoul. They whickered his way. Likely they smelled the disorder upon him. Even Jojo rocked his head as Kalin stumbled by.

The next time Kalin reappeared, more draggletailed than before, he just collapsed next to the fire and let the bad dreams take him. The figures of the Awides surrounded him, claimin first dibs, until in the defeat that comes with the feelin that where there is life there is no end to sufferin, Kalin realized that there also had never been no Awides Mine, or at least not a place that mattered more than any other space. The Awides was everywhere, and he was again in it, exhausted, dehydrated, growin more immaterial before the present.

In these dreams, Tom did not abandon him. In fact he grew clearer and fuller, and fer a moment even his Stetson brightened white as fallen snow, undisturbed by tracks or even shadows. Though once Tom did start when what seemed like a white cat larger than any tawny-maned lion suddenly struck out as quickly as it was gone from the logic of the dream, no more significant than a pale, fast-dissipatin memory of smoke.

Landry could only try to bury Kalin's shivers and moans under blankets. Other than that she felt powerless. She did her best to resist wallowin in Kalin's alarmin immiseration. She knew he'd have to drink somethin soon, so she kept a mug at the ready. The only satisfaction she got was burnin that Dorf jerky, and the bag it came in too, the whole while cursin that enterprise fer what it had done to Kalin, fer what it could've done to her, fer what it could've done fer both of them if it had been good.

Food had become a grave problem. Landry drank some of the mint tea herself, and though it was pretty weak, it still reached her like a blessin, and maybe it was. What Landry would've given for even a piece of gum. Her mom still had a box of Evan's gum, what he'd turned to when he was tryin to quit the snuff, now likely harder than rock, but she'd've still taken a piece.

It has to be told that Landry then gave some serious thought to raidin the little horse feed they had left, but she knew Kalin would not allow it. She could figure out for herself that the horses was gonna need everythin they had if they was ever gonna get goin again.

Kalin's tormented fight with this bodily invasion lasted a good two hours before it finally ceased its two-front assault and settled on one end, the bottom end, from where his necessary fluids were still too-rapidly expelled, and though increasinly lucent, nearly like water, still inflicted searin pain as if his guts had through some alchemical evil transformed such amber liquid into battery acid. Kalin shook and shivered. He sweated and groaned. He wanted to scream, but what good would that do? He didn't have the energy to scream anyways. About the only solace was the rain, which, while still continuin its erratic swings between cessations and wild drenchins, at least assured Kalin that there was nothin he could've done anyways: the rock was still too wet to go anywhere.

And then the rain did stop and this time long enuf for an eerie stillness to take possession of the cirque. It stayed that way too, in quietude, in silence. In fact so silent was this embrace that at least to Kalin, and Landry, and, if you must know, the horses too, the effect was cacophonous. If only this respite of bad weather had signaled then a subsidin of Kalin's internal turmoil. But Kalin's fight was far from over, his body still commanded again and again to obey the indecencies of such self-preservatin expulsions. Kalin would suddenly leap up from his stupor, hurlin off the blankets, dartin from the fire, out into that wet stillness, until some minutes later he'd crawl back and again collapse by the fire. And once again Landry would cover him with blankets, exhortin that mound to drink. He was dehydratin, and if it kept gettin worse he'd be useless and certainly beyond her care. Maybe anyone's care.

Kalin March, if you don't drink my tea, you will most certainly be abandonin the horses you love. Landry had to finally play that card. *Drink this down for them.*

His shakin white hand emerged then from under the blankets, and he drank down a cup, withdrew under the blankets, only to soon after drink down a second cup. Even when he had to sprint off not long after, he forced hisself to drink when he got back. Landry went out in search of more mint and found spearmint. It was stronger.

Landry felt most afraid durin that third hour, more so than anythin she'd faced until then. It was bad enuf to see Kalin so defeated, curled up and shakin, periodically breakin out in sweats. Worse still was how in this sunken state he weren't no longer talkin to Tom and wouldn't but groan if she asked him where Tom was standin. Findin out how her brother's ghost seemed nowhere near made it feel like Kalin was departin too, like he was followin Tom, and this collective abandonin scored her heart somethin awful, and on a few occasions she nearly joined Kalin's agonies with her own keenin. But she didn't, she didn't.

On top of all this, there was another misery that added insult to injury: their toilet paper supply was dwindlin.

And then Kalin managed to fall asleep, at first just for a little while, until slowly them snoozes got a lot longer.

Landry used those times to search every nook and cranny of their packs and saddlebags for even the tiniest speckle of sugar or crumbs, maybe an errant nut or raisin. She'd take even the dustin of some coffee grounds. Heavens to Murgatroyd, what Landry would have given to discover a forgotten can of peaches. But nothin had been overlooked. About the only thing extra was a hint of pepper that was probably just dirt. It was only then, durin this assiduous re-searchin of their stuff, that Landry began to consider, and amazinly for the first time too, the pockets of Kalin's jacket and pants. Hers too.

Kalin's last stretch of sleep was a good forty minutes. This time when he woke, he shook as if the very chains of the damned were upon him, but he broke free of them too, lurchin fiercely to his feet before even his eyes had fully opened.

As he gulped down her tea, surveyed their campsite, and checked on the horses, Landry could see that he was once again possessed by a great clarity.

Kalin told her that he was goin down to Altar Lake and he didn't want her followin him or spyin on him.

You think I'd want to see you in your birthday best? Landry even snorted, though she was lyin some, her heart skippin a smidge over the thought of seein this boy nude.

Kalin blushed just the same, even if he also went on to admit to Landry that he never could stand the thought of anyone seein him neked. Not even his own momma.

Your momma?! Why she knew you before you even knew what clothes were!
Even if my socks are off, I don't want her to see my feet.
You know that's real odd, right? Landry asked with a smile, amazed and bewildered by Kalin's constant strangeness.

I feel the same way around you. You ain't my momma.
Glad we're clear on that.
I guess it's a condition. It keeps me from tryin out for baseball. Nothin scares me more than them locker rooms. Havin to change in there? No. Thank. You.

Landry was laughin some. *After all you've been through and you're scared if some idjit boys see your buttocks?*

Because he could see she was right, of course, and it was also so

696

great to behold her smilin and laughin, Kalin took to laughin some too, if hoarse and frail. *I wish I could explain it. I do. It's like my skin becomes the thinnest paper about to catch fire, except the only match needed is a look. I hurt all over. It don't make no sense, but there it is.*

Glendon Hoffman and Leon Walser, both from Spanish Fork, both endin up in adjacent beds in a Bucharest hospital, this in 2016 after survivin an accident they'd later discover was an intentional act, even if that discovery would not save their lives, but that's another story about their care, would before the infections set in have a moment of clearheaded chatter to wonder aloud about Kalin's hang-up, made especially amusin given as how their hospital dress rendered them pretty much neked, which they weren't none too bothered by.

You can get feelin pretty weird about your body as a teenager, Glendon Hoffman would observe. *Like it's yours but you can't understand it one bit.*

Don't you think, though, that Kalin's case was pretty excessive? Leon Walser would ask. *Maybe he got tormented by kids when he was younger? It don't make sense that he felt like so with his momma. Of course, we don't know near enuf about his daddy. Maybe he was one of them types who walked around the house without a stitch on, swingin his big bazoola just to shame the boy?*

Could be.

You really think that was it?

What do I know. I just got mauled by a bear.

Landry still made sure that Kalin's hat sat level before he set off. She also promised more tea when he returned.

I'll look for more mint. If I don't die.

Kalin was only tryin to joke, but Landry didn't care for it one bit.

You better not die, Kalin March. Not while I'm around. You do, and I'll make sure you're stripped of every thread you got on and paraded through town. Heck, I'll parade you throughout the whole country!

Boy, Tom loved that. And laughed heartily.

Shut up, Kalin grunted.

I was just teasin, Landry responded, hurt.

Not you! Oh, dear me, not you! Tom was just havin hisself a little too good a time over your joke.

Tom's back? Landry felt a new wave of relief rush through her.

Back? Whadya mean back? That fiend never left.

It's just that you stopped talkin to him. Or even bringin him up.

I reckon that's right. I was otherwise occupied. Your brother sure weren't no help.

Was he laughin at you?

I wish. He kept sayin this was it. He kept sayin I was gonna die. And weren't that a shockin end to this whole thing? And all because I got the squirts he'd be heck bound. I'd be heck bound. And he was certain you'd be dead soon too. Though you ain't heck bound.

If I could see him, I'd kick him for you.

He's right there.

But Landry didn't make to kick the ghost.

You be nice, Tom Gatestone. Remember your mother.

And Tom, who was smilin, didn't lose his smile, but it sure did soften, and his dire eyes seemed to warm with a memory we will never know.

Landry couldn't explain why it felt so good to know that her brother was once again with them, makin fun of them, well mostly makin fun, and otherwise provin reckless with his prognostications. She smiled more at the thought of him smilin. She laughed now for just the thought of him laughin. It didn't matter that Kalin had left her alone, headin down the hill, lost to the mists of the meadow.

At first she assumed she knew what he was up to, what he'd been up to for the past hours, but when he departed without no toilet paper, she was confused, even if it was reassurin to hear him ask for her help with the horses. That was the main thing he said before leavin, that she should water and graze the horses. Tom was on Ash now, who was pretty much always standin next to Jojo. Landry didn't talk none to the air, but she kept smilin and laughin in that direction, imaginin that maybe her brother was doin the same her way.

When she'd gone on her pocket hunt, she'd dug up her diary and taken a moment then to scribble down some thoughts. She left out Kalin's misery except to write *He got real sick.* Not entirely atypical of her journalin. She also speculated some about the future. Over the years she'd seen a good many pictures hangin in the Cassidy Ski Resort Base Lodge: Kirk's Cirque in the winter, Kirk's Cirque in summer, how beautiful in fall. But no angle ever revealed even a hint of some easy way out of there. What she wrote down weren't but a few chopped phrases like *I'm guessin a way under these cliffs.* Or: *Probably through a crack in the walls.* Behind her pencil, behind her hand, beyond the primitive actions of language burnt this ebullient expectation: the cirque was not a trap nor even some devourin mouth but a great heart with chambers and passages from one place to another. Bravo to her brother! Bravo to Kalin! For findin this passage! She was excited! She could hardly wait!

She walked the horses to where it was grassier, rechecked their legs and hooves, brushed their coats with her fingertips and the heels of her hands. By which point she'd settled on the most likely if extraordinary answer: *Another mine!* The eldest Gatestone, Evan, had loved readin *The Lord of the Rings.* He'd read those books three times and knew all the names. When she'd listen, he loved tellin Landry about the Mines of Moria. Landry was convinced that what would happen next would be like that except without the goblins and the big monster. The dark would still be scary, but Kalin would be there and Tom would be there and they'd know the way. And if it turned out there were monsters, they'd know how to handle them. Landry was even lookin forward to gettin into that mine because frankly she was done with this weather. Of course it would be dry.

K alin undressed beside the icy waters of Altar Lake, and though he was hid mostly by a few aspens and blue spruces, he still made certain that there weren't no vantage point from which Landry or anyone else might spy on him.

The air was plenty cold, but when he stepped into the caesious stillness, his bare skin screamed like it had caught fire. His feet was caught in vises cranked hard enuf to powder bones. Kalin didn't stop. He went deeper and deeper until at about waist-deep he dove in head first. He didn't go under much, but when he threw his head up, he had to howl for breath. Kalin still didn't stop. He struck out, kickin hard, one long stroke after another, haulin air into his lungs. His head hurt, his teeth ached, but then as his breaths deepened, the pain abated, and somethin deeper than bone began to change.

In a fever, Glendon Hoffman would remember a quote by Ben Okri: *Somethin like beware of the stories you read or tell, because at night, beneath the surface of your wakefulness, they are alterin your world.* Leon Walser would think about that in his own decimatin fever and speculate aloud how maybe such dreams don't *alter the world at all.* Glendon would disagree, fairly certain that Kalin had found in that icy water somethin to alter him or at least harden him. Leon wouldn't care for that one bit: *Kalin weren't hardened yet. He was still free.*

Back on the shore, Kalin drug up the silt sand from the bottom and scrubbed hisself from armpits to butt crack. It weren't the prettiest lustration, but it accomplished a lesson in calmness he could welcome. As he finished he even spotted the beaver sittin upon her home, eyein Kalin's strange dance, and Kalin felt glad for the company. Then beyond the lake Kalin thought he spied two coyotes pass from shadow to shadow before dissolvin into the grayness of the surroundin mists. And was that the old elk? Was there a moose up here too? But when Kalin seen on the opposite shore what looked like a small pack of wolves, and with cubs too, he knew he was hallucinatin.

Plenty of others have declared apophenia, pareidolia, or just plain feverish poppycock. And it sure didn't get better. Farther off great shadows suddenly rose up like giraffes kickin away lions. There were elephants. A bear, it seemed, roared against the cold. Great wings fluttered above. However improbable, these forms moved sympatric within this moment if not this empty place.

One last time Kalin flung hisself into the breathless mundifyin water, where he wiped quick as he could the grit and mud from his body. This time when he emerged, no more animals haunted the peripheries of Altar Lake. Instead Kalin found Navidad waitin for him. Was she a dream too?

Landry had set about dryin best as she could what Kalin had left behind, mainly his Lee Storm Rider and his dirty cable-knit sweater. At least she hadn't set them afire. They smelled now of so much smoke, they was pretty much just smoke. That's when Landry seen that Navidad was gone. Boy, did her heart sock-up quick in her throat! The vacancy near stumbled her into the fire. And then Kalin and Navidad were there, on the edge of the campsite, like they'd been there forever.

I had her tied up right! I swear! she protested, like Kalin was her daddy, or her momma, about to upbraid her for negligence, but Kalin just smiled warmly and murmured it weren't not a thing.

More tea was at the ready, and Kalin thanked her for the warmth, and while she could see he was still pale and weak, cold too, he was only wearin his pants and a shirt, he also seemed somehow better. Even the cut on his right cheek from when he'd slipped and dragged his saddle atop hisself back when he'd first started out looked better.

Kalin dug up then from his pack a pair of fresh socks.

I swore I'd wait on these until the horses was free.

Nothin worse than a great idea gettin in the way of a better decision, Landry smarted back.

Ain't that so. You just come up with that?

Naw. That's my momma's.

Kalin had tried to use smooth stones to scrub out his briefs and mother's hose, but they was too foul with his sickness, and he'd abandoned them to the edge of the moraine. Maybe the beaver could make somethin of them. And funny too how that beaver had kept regardin him, though her gaze upon his bare limbs and private parts had no effect. The thought of Tom, though, doin the same made Kalin's whole self squirm. Tom, though, had stayed with the horses.

Back by the fire Kalin didn't need to do nothin but change his socks. He still asked Landry to turn around, even told Tom to do the same before he tore off his old socks, throwin them bedraggled things on the fire. After he'd stuffed his feet into the clean socks, he held off puttin on his boots, instead droppin in hot rocks, which he did for Landry's boots too.

Last he put on the smoke-scented cable-knit sweater and the Lee jacket. His jeans was still plenty damp, and his bareness on the denim weren't the best feelin, but he had no choice there. He would just have to keep close to the fire, finish this tea, and then they'd go.

Feelin better? Tom asked, his teeth once again on a blade of gold grass, his lips bent toward a dark grin.

Kalin nodded. His shakin and chatterin were gone now, and whatever that act of icy immersion had stolen from him, it had also readied him for what lay ahead. Anyone can act in fullness. It's only when we act in emptiness that we begin to understand who we are in a Universe where we are not. Kalin's mind felt sharp, and though he was still weak as heck, wobbly too, his guts had at last quieted to a dull complaint that needed no heedin.

Landry continued to refill Kalin's mug. He sure was grateful. Even such weak stuff returned to him some strength, though despite his mental resolve, he knew it might not be enuf. He still needed calories. Landry needed calories too, though she sure felt renewed just seein this boy kick free from the grip of that wretched food poisonin. She felt practically perky.

I got somethin to tell you, Landry.

And there went perky, right out the window, as if there could be a window up here; the whole place was a window.

I thought I saw wolves down by the water.

Wolves?!

With cubs! And a giraffe kickin a lion. And an elephant. Big birds too. I was hallucinatin pretty bad.

You still hallucinatin?

Are you here?

I'm here.

And you ain't a hallucination?

Fingers crossed.

I'll take that.

Though Kalin still reached out to give Landry's shoulder a gentle squeeze, which made him feel all sorts of good and made her feel the same way, because, fer one thing, weren't it good to know he knew he weren't hallucinatin her?

By the way, Kalin weren't the only one to suffer from that nocent

701

batch of Dorf jerky. More than a few Orvop citizens were felled by that batch of rotten meat. Bryce Stewart, over in Grandview, suffered immediately. He'd but swallowed a bite and less than five minutes later near covered his front lawn in vomit. An hour later, though, he felt fine enuf to have a big lunch at Arby's. Boyd Trammel managed to keep down what he'd eaten, but he was soon unable to make his classes at Isatch U and spent near four days toilet side before he could get back to normal. He never ate jerky again. Kalin was lucky to be closer to the Bryce Stewart side of this experience. Dr. Henry Tabori, a gastroenterologist at Utah Valley Hospital, would surmise that Kalin had *thrown up most of the bad stuff fast enuf to reduce the effects of the contaminated food.*

Anyway, most in his position would have called it quits for at least the rest of the day if not the next day too. The fact that Kalin was now readyin hisself for what would eventually go down as a feat worthy of Fable was in and of itself near supernatural.

Landry for her part had not only encountered in his quiet touch the comfort of his companionship but also evidence of his endurin determination, a realization that helped refill her own depleted reserves. Though she also had somethin up her sleeve that would more significantly fortify them. Though *in* her sleeve is a better way of puttin it.

I got a surprise for you, Landry said then.

How do you mean surprise?

You hungry?

You found some food?

I did.

Kalin thought she was joshin. *I'll take even one bean.*

I didn't find any beans.

Not even one?

Not even one.

I knew it was too much to ask.

Landry laughed, and then Kalin laughed, and then even Tom laughed.

Who knew it was possible to laugh over not havin even one bean, Kalin said.

Close your eyes, Landry told him.

Sure.

Tell Tom to close his eyes too.

When Landry told them to open their eyes, Kalin couldn't quite believe what he was lookin at. This sure weren't no bean nor a solitary raisin nor one grain of rice. This was a hecukuva lot more.

What is it? he whispered. It was a mashed-up somethin, a golden yellow somethin, orange really, sorta like a pancake.

It's my momma's orange cake. I completely forgot I'd stuffed a big portion in my coat arm pocket.

Well, I'll be . . .

Go on then! Eat some!

What's it taste like? Kalin still couldn't believe his eyes.

I'm guessin it's pretty good. My momma's a heckuva baker.

Kalin tried to get Landry to take the first bite, but she refused. She wouldn't even accept his first nibble as countin as a first bite. Kalin's mouth filled with saliva. He wanted to cry. He sure weren't prepared for the sheer glycemic pleasure those initial crumbs provoked. Why the sugar and the flour alone dazzled his senses. Add the taste of citrus? He wanted to curl up into hisself. He wanted to fill the cirque with animal howls.

If this ain't a bit of heaven, Landry Gatestone. As Tom is my witness, I owe you.

She made him take down a few more mouthfuls.

Oh, you owe me, Kalin. But not fer orange cake.

I ain't afraid of owin you whatever you want, Landry.

And she sure weren't expectin that. She blushed so bad, she had to stand and busy herself with the horses.

Did you know about this, Tom? Kalin asked then.

I did by the time you got back from skinny-dippin! But heck if I was gonna tell you! I'd be dead all over again if I'd ruined her surprise. Call me chicken! Tom flapped his elbows up and down and squawked too, them long ganglin legs of his dancin around the horses.

What's my brother sayin now? Landry asked.

Kalin told her.

I love you, Tom Gatestone, Landry suddenly declared to the mists.

Kalin made sure Landry ate her share of the cake, but she still made sure he had the last bite. When his body didn't act up none, except to crave more, he laid out for Landry their plan.

It was 3:47 p.m.

Fer nearly two hours there'd been no rain. If they was gonna make a go at the hardest part, they had their window now and they better seize it. Kalin, though, was still nursin a hope that maybe there weren't no one at their heels. He was still dreamin of more sleep, maybe a whole extra night. They could rise early and get it done before breakfast time. He wanted to take one more gander at the canyon below. Landry was all for that.

They rechecked the halter-bridles, gathered up the leads, and then moved off in the direction of where they'd seen Old Porch rise up in that helicopter. Of some comfort was how neither the wind nor the hard taste of rock and ice on the air held any memory of that intrusion. Kalin and Landry also took delight in how the hot rocks they'd placed in their boots had not only warmed them up but helped dry them too.

Kalin did alter their course some. Instead of headin directly down to the meadow, he clung to a wide and sandy path that stayed well above the talus but avoided the more perilous screes above. The path was plenty slanted; and the angle made walkin difficult, and that's all they were doin, just walkin ahead of the horses, who weren't troubled much by the grade, though not a one of them liked how little there was to graze on. Especially Mouse.

After a while the path began to bend upward toward the northeastern side of the cirque, where it eventually became a wide ledge above and beneath a band of unscalable cliffs. It offered a vast view of the canyon below, which was mostly filled with cottony clouds.

Fer a long time Kalin stood upon the highest rock tryin to scan the far-below. There weren't no water on the binocular lenses, but the light was dim, and in a few more hours it would be gone. Fed up, Kalin finally knelt down, unscrewed the lens caps, and removed the meshes. He was extra careful, though, to fold up them scored pieces of fabric before securin them in the breast pocket of his Lee Storm Rider.

He could see a little better. Fer sure the cirque was empty. No wolves, no giraffes, no lions. No strange lights on the far hills. Not even a bird dared the sky. As for the canyon below, Kalin couldn't make out much beyond a haze of muted grays, luteous yellows, and near ashen greens and browns, especially over where the Ninth Scree lay festerin like a terrifyin wound.

Landry took the binoculars and confirmed as well that there weren't no elephants in the cirque nor anyone on the Ninth Scree. She provided more detail than just that.

She's got her brother's good vision, Tom said with a wink.

I got Tom's good eyes, Landry said a blink later.

We both got our mother's eyes, Tom and Landry said at the same time without knowin it. Well, Landry didn't know it. Tom sure did, and he looked at his little sister half-surprised, half-pleased, mostly just fond like. Who knows what gets to a ghost, but Tom chose to turn away then and rub somethin from his eyes.

Kalin urged Landry to keep scourin any path leadin up to the cirque. She found no hint of movement.

When Kalin took his turn again, he beheld even less. Nothin but haze and blur. Though the less he saw, the more relief he felt, like maybe they really could rest up tonight, let the mountain dry up even more. This thought revived Kalin's confidence and allowed him the chance to ignore the glowerin storm above, its batterin chaos obviously only in repose, brief repose. But who can really blame him or Landry? Who among us hasn't dreamed at least once that the big troubles we faced might not, through no action of our own, just blow away thanks to the right breeze? Landry even started talkin about gatherin more mint and maybe findin some edible greens. She swore she'd seen some elderberries by the crick. She could make them a tart jam for dinner. Maybe they'd even stumble upon a hive and get at some honey. That would sweeten that jam right up. Or what about eggs in a bird's nest? No matter that it was fall. Or fish? Maybe the shallow lake had one or two they could somehow spear. *If I see a falcon circle the waters, I'll know there's fish,* Landry declared. But they saw no falcon nor did any splash disquiet the surface.

Maybe we're in the clear, Kalin finally said aloud, not knowin that right then Egan was launchin hisself across the Seventh Scree.

You think it's the weather? Landry asked.

Unless they come back by helicopter.

There's plenty of time fer that.

The roar of mountain winds baffled their ears, but they both agreed that they would still hear a helicopter, neither admittin how they'd barely heard it the first time until it was pretty much right on top of them.

Mr. Porch would've told his boys right where to find us. Maybe it took them a little time to get organized. Maybe an hour, maybe even two hours. I'd say no more though. If they was flyin, they should be here already. We got lucky. And that sure turned Kalin's stomach. He liked nothin to do with luck, but he had to admit it had played a hand here.

Tom was lookin back toward the northeast end of the cirque where the summit ridge waited, the impossible Upecksay Headwall, still buried in cloud.

Then they're waitin til tomorrow? Landry asked.

Kalin weren't deaf to the sound of wishful thinkin in Landry's voice.

They ain't waitin, Tom finally said.

I know it.

What did he say? Landry asked.

Kalin told her.

705

So what do we do then? Landry asked.

We wait and watch until it's too dark and cold for them to do anythin but make camp.

Couldn't they come up in the dark?

They could risk it.

What did Tom say? Landry asked Kalin then.

He didn't say nothin.

Why not?

He's as clueless as we are.

Finally somethin I can believe! Landry lowered the binoculars so she could make a face at Tom before returnin to surveil the canyon, most often returnin to the Ninth Scree, to that rootless ash tree standin upon a precipice where it would remain for years to come.

Kalin? Landry said after a while. *I'm still puzzlin over this whole bit about Russel bein dead. He had the bad luck of spyin you and the horses when you was leavin. That part's coincidence. I mean if he'd come by just a bit earlier, he'd have seen Navidad and Mouse in Paddock B, and that would be that. And if he'd passed by later, he'd've had no idea that you was involved and certainly no inklin about which way you'd gone. Also by then the rain would've washed away the hoofprints. You and Russel would've passed each other in Main Hall and not even noticed one another. And what happened to the horses would've stayed a mystery.*

That tracks.

On the other hand, my followin you weren't no coincidence. After what Tom told you in the hospital before he died, at least what I could hear, from that point on I was goin by Willow and Oak every day. And every day I seen Navidad and Mouse in Paddock A, why I knew everythin was all right. But I was also keepin an eye on you, makin sure you was goin by Paddock A.

When was you followin me? That did seem to astonish Kalin.

Now Wednesday mornin comes along and I seen that the horses was in Paddock B. My plan was to tell you when I seen you at school, but I never could find you. It never crossed my mind that you was already makin ready.

Kalin grunted somethin between a chuckle and, well, a grunt.

Figurin you was negligent, I decided I'd take care of the horses myself even if I had no clue where to take them. I put on what I could for the weather and stole out of the house after dinner. I sure didn't expect to find Paddock B empty. And then who should drive up but Russel in Egan's truck. I'm lucky he didn't see me. After he left, I took off for the barn and Jojo. I had a hunch about Isatch Canyon. I already knew Tom and you liked to ride there, but when it came to it, I weren't so keen about headin in there in the dark. I'll admit I hemmed and hawed alone near the parkin lot. Then I seen Russel on Cavalry, and when he went off into the canyon, why I weren't goin to be bested by that pup.

Landry dug out of her waist a dry corner of shirt, which she used to reclean the binocular lenses.

Best I can figure it, she continued, *after Russel spotted you goin into Isatch Canyon, he hightailed it to his brother's house. Egan, though, had no interest in goin out in the rain, never mind goin after two horses set for slaughter the next mornin. Egan probably laughed and called Russel names for bein so wound up about losin what they was tryin to get rid of in the first place. Maybe, though, because of how the Porches love to torment anyone, especially each other, Egan ordered Russel to go get them ponies back and do it on Cavalry too. Now the gun, if Egan's to be believed, why that's his or his old man's. A nice one too, old, probably expensive. My bet is that Russel grabbed it for hisself without tellin Egan because he'd got afraid of what he was gettin hisself into. Russel ain't much of a fighter, not like the rest of his brothers.*

Kalin kept listenin, though he had to sit hisself down. He was still awful tired and far from recovered. Tom squatted next to him but didn't say nothin. He probably just enjoyed listenin to his little sister think things through. Hers was clear thinkin too, like maybe she'd emptied some of the rocks in her head, gotten some above them clouds.

Les Fadley, who'd one day teach at Timpview and on the next day be fired from Timpview fer askin his students to paint their idea of evolution, would always praise Landry and Kalin for attemptin to see things how they was: *We tend to shape the world to suit our minds. But what if we shaped our minds to suit the world? That's what I ask a lot these days. And incidentally, that's where I feel authentic prayer lives: to behold the world as it is and not limit it to simply who we are.*

Landry was noddin her head. *You saw that yourself, how I whooped Russel. Jumped him right off Cavalry. Took away his gun too.*

Gave him a mean bruise with her elbow, Tom said.

You know I once took a swing at Tom? Landry asked suddenly, if not waitin around either for Kalin to answer. *I broke two fingers. He was fine. Maybe he broke two ribs from laughin so hard.*

That's true, Tom said with a smile. *The part about her fingers. And hittin me. I never did admit how much my jaw hurt. Some back teeth never stopped wobblin. In fact I think they're still wobblin.*

Kalin relayed this news to Landry, who puffed up like a hen on an egg, and that pleased Kalin even if it didn't relieve him none of his fatigue.

Now, as you'll recall, Landry said, tuckin her shirt back in, *I ended up arrangin the purchase of the two horses, and I paid Russel for them too, right then and there, signin that twenty-dollar bill myself, makin him sign the same bill too, fair and square, makin these ponies mine and mine alone.*

Kalin sighed. *They ain't nobody's no more.*

Fer sure, fine, yes, I'm on board with that. But what I'm sayin here, what matters, is that in the eyes of anyone else, whether we're talkin just Orvop folk, the Law, even Old Porch hisself, there ain't no quarrel no more about these ponies. In fact that quarrel quit the second we sorted it out like adults around our campfire. You know what I mean! We was like friends! Like the three musketeers! The three Orvop musketeers! And that's sayin somethin, when a Gatestone and a Porch are just sittin around, shootin the bull, havin a good time.

Tom says we weren't like the three musketeers, Kalin relayed to Landry.

He's just sore that I ain't included him.

The gall of that girl! Tom sighed.

Landry knew full well then that Tom had made some remark, but she didn't care enuf to pause. *You never touched him once. With one hundred percent certainty I can swear to that fact. You did not kill him. So that then there brings up my big question: what did happen to Russel?*

I do wonder what happened to that poor boy, Tom added.

Whatever it was, Kalin was respondin to both Tom and Landry, *we just can't know about it from up here.*

Well, now, hold on a second, Landry said. *I ain't done with my thoughts.*

Uh-oh, here we go, Tom said under his breath.

Tell my brother to act nice, Landry fired back, which shocked Tom some, Kalin too, since he hadn't given any indication that Tom had just spoken.

Maybe, though, Landry weren't slowin down, *maybe this is just a big misunderstandin: maybe Egan was only havin some fun?*

Fun?

Maybe Russel ain't dead at all. Maybe he's fine. Maybe Egan was just sayin that Russel was dead to fool me into thinkin . . . Landry was flounderin.

Thinkin what?

I don't know. Maybe he was just tryin to mislead me so I didn't start thinkin about what this here was really about.

Well, she's got my attention, Tom said, leanin forward some.

Like maybe they're comin after us because these horses ain't what we think they are. Like maybe they're way more than they are.

More than they are? Kalin weren't followin. Tom neither. *They are how they are.*

Like maybe they're racehorses or somethin! And Landry's eyes even grew extra big, like she was tellin a ghost story or a treasure story and she'd now come to the part about the ghost or the treasure.

And there went my attention, Tom said, easin hisself back, closer to Ash, and then like that already in the saddle, again eyein the valley below.

They ain't racehorses, Kalin said, though he still did give Navidad and

Mouse an extra look as they went on grazin whatever little clumps of grass they could find, now and then givin their coats and manes a hard shake to shrug off some of the damp and in Mouse's case some of the mud.

Tom agreed with Kalin. *They sure ain't racehorses. And they sure as heck don't need to be anythin more than they are.* He even sounded a little angry at Landry or at least cranky.

And because she was just about to ask anyway, Kalin relayed at once her brother's sentiment, and that quieted Landry some.

But even if they was the most amazin racehorses, Kalin said, ponderin this aloud, mainly because he could see that Landry's feelins were smartin some, and what did it hurt him really to entertain her notion fer a moment? *Do you think that would be a reason to start shootin at us? I mean, maybe if these two could win the Kentucky Derby, first and second place—*

I'd put my money on Mouse, Tom said with a laugh, and Mouse, like he'd heard the mockin ghost, snorted and even kicked out at the air in Tom's direction. Navidad weren't pleased neither and also kicked the air. Also in Tom's direction.

If they was so very valuable, why then the Porches wouldn't dare risk hurtin one with a bad shot. Fer sure they'd've let us alone when we was in that landslide. They don't give a hoot about these horses. Fer some reason, they just want to kill us. Or at least me.

That made sense to Landry even if it also made a muddle of her wishful thinkin. *The Porches ain't the brightest. Maybe they was just trigger-happy. And we can be glad they ain't so good at aimin.*

I'll agree with you there.

Okay, so they ain't racehorses. But maybe we're still missin somethin, because the other way of thinkin just don't make sense.

Fer sure we're missin somethin, Kalin said.

Maybe Navidad and Mouse have wings! Tom said and, yes, with a great deal of mockin glee. Mouse didn't respond, but Navidad threw up her head and whinnied loud.

Like, I don't know, they're special for breedin and just got put in Paddock B by mistake? Landry was givin it her best shot. *So when Russel comes back and tells Egan he sold them for twenty bucks, why then Egan gets so mad—*

He kills Russel? He kills his own little brother? Kalin weren't havin it.

I know, I know. It don't make no sense. Unless this is a real Cain-and-Abel situation. Or maybe it weren't Egan but Old Porch hisself who, bein the actual owner of these horses, got super furious at Russel for havin sold them to me?

That makes sense to you? That he killt his own son?

No. But. Or. Or I don't know. Landry stopped talkin and Kalin could tell she felt defeated.

These ain't racehorses, Landry, he said softly. *Or horses so important they'd kill for them. They don't care about these horses. And no father kills his own son.*

Even Abraham couldn't do that, Tom said then.

How's that? Kalin asked Tom, tellin Landry too what her ghost brother had just muttered.

In fact Abraham went so far as to invent hisself a new God, right on the spot, to save his Isaac, Tom continued.

Kalin shared that with Landry too, though neither could make heads nor tails of the comment, and Tom showed no interest in discussin it further.

Landry lifted up the binoculars to resume scannin the canyon below, though that didn't stop her from talkin. *Then somethin bad did happen to Russel. Must've happened. Pretty much nothin else figures, right? Maybe someone no one knows got him on the way back. Like a drifter.*

A drifter?

Beware of them drifters. That's what my momma says.

Everyone wants to blame a drifter. That's what my momma says. Folks can't stand the idea that there's just as much bad in their own community as there is outside it.

Your momma sounds like a smart lady, Landry answered, offerin Kalin the binoculars, but he told her to keep them. *Tom have anythin to add?*

I know less and less about the affairs of folks down there. That was pretty much Tom's summation of what had transpired down in Orvop. *Like it surely matters, but I no longer care. Like I'm becomin less and less capable of carin.*

Which sure chilled Kalin somethin extra, and made his palms itch and then somethin inside him briefly awoke that was equally dangerous and careless.

What's my brother sayin now? Landry asked.

What do you expect he said?

That he's dead, not magic.

See. Now you can hear him too.

Is that really what he said? Landry asked, smilin, a little sarcastic.

Tom looked down on her warmly and then winked at Kalin. *Couldn't have put it better myself.*

And then Landry whipped around, like whoever was comin had come up from behind, and she weren't wrong.

You seein this? Kalin asked Tom.

I sure am.

It was 4:26 p.m.

Is that a mule? Landry demanded, even though the answer was plain as day, not that Kalin and Tom weren't any less confused about what was so obvious. *Where'd she come from?*

And the she here was in fact a mule, white except for a black star and stripe on her head. No tack in sight either, nor halter. From all appearances the mule was wild if maybe too content. Not that Landry, Kalin, or Tom, or even the huntress at Tom's side, had anythin but welcome in their hearts for this new arrival. Who were they to refuse the company of a mule, however alone or spectral? Fact was it sorta made them feel okay. No one could say why either. Pia Isan told Tom that she had no understandin of this mule, and it unsettled her, but she was still glad. Even Mouse seemed to welcome the mule's arrival.

They weren't so glad, though, about the next surprise. Landry had just finished another sweep of the meadow, which was gettin harder to know well, what with more clouds pressin downward and more mists risin up and afternoon shadows capin whatever brief glimpses were offered of the surroundin rock walls, at least those nearby, not to speak of the squallin winds that now and then whirled across the lake like dervishes. Even so, Landry found nothin in the increasinly hidden cirque to distrust. It was when she swung the binoculars back to the Ninth Scree that she knew at once, and she weren't even really seein yet what she was seein, that whatever pleasant idea she and Kalin had entertained about another night of rest was lost. The obviousness jarred her. It weren't just the movement either but the speed of their movement. Only then did the noise of the machines decipher itself from the wind, a screamin she could no longer unhear, like it had been there all along and they were fools to not have heard it earlier.

I see them! Landry rasped, part growl, mostly groan. She shoved the binoculars into Kalin's hand.

He took a good long look even if he knew he wouldn't see near as much as Landry. He didn't need to. No denyin what was comin up over the spur that hid the Eighth Scree. He handed back the binoculars.

Egan's on the first ATV, Landry reported. *Kelly's behind. That other one's ridin with Kelly. They're goin fast!* And then she near shouted: *Oh heck!*

What?

Hatch Porch is with them!

Oh heck is right, Tom muttered then and continued mutterin too, though those syllables weren't for Kalin to hear, only for Ash, or maybe not even for Ash, maybe just for the wind.

Who's Hatch? Kalin asked.

He's the oldest Porch boy. The real deal too. A military sniper. Vietnam. I think he got a medal. He's in Texas now with one of them SWAT teams. Like you see on TV. He walks on water as far as the Porches are concerned. Plenty of other folks don't disagree either.

Three ATVs then?

Landry nodded. *They're armed. They got other gear too. Wait.*

What?

They ain't alone. There are more farther behind.

Porches?

Well, here's the good news. Sorta.

What do you mean?

Police.

How is that good news?

I hope you ain't serious?

Kalin still didn't understand.

You're an idjit, Landry snapped, lowerin the binoculars. *At least with police around, them Porch boys won't just shoot us down in cold blood.*

I'm not an idjit.

Landry was surprised to see how Kalin's cheeks had flamed up red. In fact she was sort of agog. Here was the boy who'd outrode a landslide while bein shot at, and yet some stupid word sassed out by some pip-squeak like herself had got under his skin. It warned her too that Kalin was still feelin real feeble, and this news, what at last had come for them, meant they now had to go and go hard and go fast.

I'm sorry, Kalin. You're right. That was uncalled for.

Kalin grunted a thanks. *How many police?*

I can see three more ATVs plus a dirt bike. They're not all police. Park rangers too. Why look at that! There are even two police on foot. I don't know how they've kept up.

The screes slowed them down. Are they stoppin for the last one?

I'd say Egan's speedin up! It galled Landry somethin fierce to behold how terrain that had proved so unstable yesterday was today near sure as bedrock. It weren't any more pathed than before, but the obstacles Egan encountered didn't take much to maneuver around. He didn't stop once let alone have to get off his ATV. By the last third he was outright gunnin it.

They'll be here in under an hour, maybe half that, Kalin estimated, at last gettin to his feet. He wobbled some, but his voice didn't. *We can do this.*

Landry nodded. *Does Tom say the same thing?*

Kalin eyed Tom, who this time didn't have a smile to share. He kept his arms crossed and after givin the canyon a final glance turned toward where they'd soon be headin, toward the mists and clouds that hid the northeast passage they'd come all this way to dare, and only then did he shake his head.

He says we better quit jabberin and get after it.

Sounds like Tom.

They led the horses down to the meadow and then cantered to camp bareback. They was good enuf riders not to fret the absence of saddles, but with no reins it was still a risk. They used the leads to approximate guidance and relied on their legs to refine such guidance. It helped some that Mouse stayed beside Navidad, with Jojo keepin beside Mouse. Tom on Ash took up the rear. Actually that white mule took up the rear, followin along like she had all the time in the world. And she did.

A few times Kalin needed to grip Navidad's mane. It weren't lost on him that Landry was havin no such problems. She might as well have been in the saddle and with reins too. She and Jojo really was a pair, like they truly was one.

Tom whistled approvingly. *You know, I think my little sister rides better than you.* Tom was back up at Kalin's side.

Tom just said you's the best rider here, Kalin yelled over to her.

Oh shush. Like I need a ghost to tell me that.

And Kalin weren't lyin, but he also wanted Landry's confidence as high as possible. If he'd've known she was dancin with ideas that they was about to take a long stroll through a mine, he'd have laid it on even thicker.

At the campsite they saddled up Navidad and Jojo, then distributed the packs as they'd planned, Mouse with finally nothin on his back.

Last of all, they kicked rocks on the campfire which by then was just a smokin pile of ash.

Got any more of that orange cake? Kalin asked.

When we get back, my momma will make one just fer you.

I'm gonna hold you to that. Kalin even tipped that dark gray Stetson her way.

And then just like that they was gone from their little cove of calm, their private chimney and hearth, their dry and warm spot sheltered from the great heave of mountain cold that now surrounded them as they rode toward the northeast end of the cirque.

Not that Landry paid any attention to their direction. She kept focused on Kalin, who she could see was tremblin some in his saddle. Of no comfort was how pale he looked; she was sure he was paler than her brother's ghost. And maybe he was. But neither Kalin nor

Landry evidenced a shred of fear, and with every successive stride they demonstrated more than mere resolve.

While Kalin may have known the details of what they was up against, Landry knew by sensitivity and intuition that this late afternoon was the all of it, and they would either make of themselves somethin to be remembered by or they'd be thrown down upon them heaps that bear no headstones.

So they rode, and in those moments they knew themselves neither encaptivated by what was behind them nor what was waitin ahead, startin out at first at a walk demanded by the slope that descended to the meadow where they were soon trottin, until, as they neared the top of Altar Lake, the opposite end of where that beaver lodge stood, maybe the beaver was even out right then, as if to wish them well, or so Tom implied to Kalin, they slowed again as they passed over slabs of limestone before at last findin ground that was sandy and hard, where Kalin urged Navidad into her first and only gallop of this journey. Mouse followed, almost grateful to unleash some of his ample reserves, Ash matchin Mouse with ready ease, with Tom near in glee over this sudden embrace of speed. And he weren't the only Gatestone feelin that way. Landry didn't have to but brush her heels on Jojo's flanks, maybe inclinin forward a tiny bit, and like that she and Jojo were off with a whoop, a cry, a hollerin of loud joy, racin easily past them all, if her swiftness was nonetheless still met by their collective swiftness, for they all pretty much kept up, for none would be left behind, nearly leavin behind the mists, the gray tatters they easily blew through, until where they ran seemed momentarily beyond the torments of just idle haze, somewhere else, somethin else, a place demandin no accomplishment. Kalin let Navidad have her moment too, even as he reassured her that there weren't no need to outrace Jojo or Mouse, merely enjoy where they was at. And so with every stride, each horse stretched more and more and so relaxed more and more, until all of them, whether horse, rider, or ghosts, floated along as if no longer accountable to the mass that commands those revolutions around the stars, those revolutions that stars obey around centers also in thrall to the axis of creation, with even that strange white mule carried along like she weighed nothin at all.

Landry was still grinnin ear to ear when she finally eased back to a canter, then a trot, and finally a walk, *Clop-Clop-clip-Clop*, whereupon Jojo with a deep snort welcomed Navidad and Ash, who caught up a moment later, Mouse offerin last a delighted nicker, like they was all smilin. Fer sure Tom was.

Only Kalin weren't smilin no more, though there was still a gladness that would keep possession of his heart fer a bit longer, at least until he applied his calculatin scrutiny to the rocky slope waitin for them ahead.

Exhaustion robs you of any enthusiasm for the future, though when the stakes are high enuf, survivors build their brightness within doubt. Not that Kalin could muster even that. Instead he focused on the only thing that really mattered: the next step, up this incline, step by step, find the surest route, stick to it, step by step, and though still perilous, especially for the horses, for here were no screes of sand and slippery near-silken stones but a maze of tall tendon-slashin rocky edges, leadin upward toward the base of the Upecksay Headwall, where Kalin refused to let his thoughts go, not yet, but to where despite every effort his thoughts continued to dart, thoughts Kalin again and again would have to drag back, back to the step-by-step passage through the terrible horse-maimin rubble deservin all their attention, where his thoughts needed to stay until the next step finally delivered them from here to there, delivered them before that inexorable rise skyward, almost sheer enuf to deny contemplation, the highest wall in this great mountain bowl, in fact in this whole mountain system, shootin straight up to the very top of Katanogos, a verticality so immense as to rise through multiple layers of mist and circulatin cloud, through even this awful storm, and still not permit even a glimpse of any arête, pinnacle, or jagged peak, let alone the summit ridge.

We go the wrong way? Landry asked.

No Porch is gonna think to come here.

That's true, but I still don't see no way through.

Landry couldn't stop tryin to spy out some obvious fissure ahead, some hollow that might hide an entrance to a mine or bewilderin cave system. She couldn't even spot a place to hide.

Kalin didn't respond. And Landry didn't care for that nor how Kalin kept lookin up.

These walls are over a thousand feet high, at least, she declared, even if they couldn't see more than a few hundred feet up to where the first layer of cloud hung.

Kalin took a long drink from his canteen then, full with Landry's precious blend of mint and water and, it seemed, other sweeter elements. It was still warm.

Don't blame me; blame your brother, Kalin finally answered her, and then told her to drink her fill too. She was gonna need it.

My brother weren't so much the fool to believe there was a way up that! I know that for a fact! Panic and anger were bright in her voice now.

Kalin looked over at Tom.

715

Tom shrugged. *Pardner, I don't know a thing about this no more. I can barely remember where I come from and . . .*

And what?

Aww, it won't help none.

Go on! Kalin demanded.

Well, I can still see you and my little sis and these fine maned friends of ours. And I have to say you all are a magnificent sight. Then his smile faded some. *Pia Isan, though, pretty much agrees with Landry. She thinks this here's our end. She's pretty happy about it too.* Tom sighed. *Who knew vengeance could taste better than freedom?*

Then I'll lay it out for you, just as you told me right before you checked into the hospital for good. And so Kalin proceeded to tell Tom, and in that way Landry too, what would come next, each subsequent description droppin Landry's jaw a bit lower while sendin her eyes dartin ever more desperately across just the base of the loomin headwall. Though in truth, her jaw didn't drop one bit; rather it tightened up so much, her teeth might as well have fused together, her jaw muscles knotted so thick as if to demonstrate to the rest of her body how it was that movement could be refused. Even Jojo seemed to follow suit, as if the roots of Landry's rigidity were drivin down through his legs now and weren't stoppin there either but continuin on down to join the rock.

By the time Kalin had finished, he could see Landry was either too bewildered or too stunned to speak. Maybe to even think.

You're lyin! she finally managed to blurt out. *You're both lyin!*

Tom can't lie. He can't even remember where he is. I'm the one who's tellin you all this, and I ain't lyin: the horses can make it.

Then you're crazy!

Your brother was the one who discovered the way up. I didn't believe him either, but by the time he was bedridden, I'd confirmed it.

Confirmed what exactly?

There is a path. Remember that, Landry: there is a path.

Kalin pointed then to the first significant turn they'd need to take, but all Landry could see, and Tom too for that matter, was a face of stone that seemed with every second to bend more over them, as if to further impress upon them that here was a place that would grant no purchase for even a little toe or finger let alone four hooves widely placed. Only an experienced climber with pitons and ropes could dream of goin anywhere near such cliffs.

Not that this realization kept Landry from still lookin, and eventually she did begin to make out a series of gray lines. Ledges maybe? Catwalks? Either way somehow different from the crumbly sandstone. But did these lines actually offer a place upon which horses could walk? Improbable mantels, spindly shelves, unstable benches, platforms of rock she had no desire to experience up close.

Even the back of Landry's neck begged her with aches to refuse the sight. Surely she could continue to insist that such frail lines upon the wall were cracks, like tempera on a paintin she never needed to see again, like some blackboard scarred by slivers left behind by black chalk; surely this labyrinth of refutable scratches weren't no place for them. There weren't nothin up there but crosshatches of pointlessness, some headin one way, others branchin off in a worse direction, many of these lines just haltin abruptly in the middle of nowhere only to recommence again scores of feet over and higher. Was Kalin actually suggestin that these ledges were somehow connected enuf to offer a feasible route to the top? And with horses?!

It can't be done, Landry said then, swallowin hard.

It must be done, Kalin answered, also swallowin hard.

He was right, of course. The cirque now reverberated with the whine of engines. Their pursuers had arrived even faster than they'd expected. Fortunately the mists upon the meadow veiled any view of these intruders just like they also kept Kalin, Landry, and the horses hid. But that weren't gonna last long. New winds were now churnin through the cirque, cold air comin over the back side of Katanogos, rollin down the headwalls, blowin out across Altar Lake, past Bewilder Crick, and if not dispersin the mists there entirely then shreddin them up enuf to send ghostly tatters wailin down to the canyon bottom far below.

They'll find us if we just stand here.

Landry snorted. *You've done this before?*

Never with horses.

And Tom?

Not with me. Not with horses either.

And if I do it with horses?

You'll have bested your brother.

Landry sure flashed Kalin a genuine Gatestone grin then.

Let's get it done.

And then because there weren't nothin left to say, Landry by a kiss of her knees nudged Jojo forward, and like that they was once again at it, not hardly runnin this time but movin just the same, upwards now, first against the steep scarp, fer sure against their better judgment.

Much to Landry's surprise, when they reached the base of the wall, she discovered that up close them faint lines were transformed. There weren't just one or two either. There were dozens of possible ledges of various widths and at various grades.

Kalin passed quite a few before he urged Navidad toward one requirin the highest first step. It seemed the least promisin out of those Landry had already inspected. Fer one thing it weren't but a hair wider than Jojo, and fer another it seemed mainly flat at first.

Navidad went up without a fuss. Mouse hardly objected. Jojo neither. Nor Tom and Ash. Not even the mule balked.

It ain't so bad, Landry kept tellin herself. *It ain't so bad.*

And it weren't.

The first switchback they came to Kalin passed right by, keepin to this comfortable if hardly sloped route. Landry realized there were dozens of options ahead, but Kalin took the second switchback, whereupon Landry found herself on another ledge of rock headin in the opposite direction, as wide as the first but far steeper, wet as well and, even worse, slantin slightly down away from the wall, which durin them initial *Clip-clops* up hardly mattered but many steps later seemed with each subsequent *Clip-clop* to threaten by that deadly cant the likely expulsion of any hope of ever seein this dare through.

Landry didn't know it, and good thing too, but Kalin was sufferin similar misgivings. Even worse, Tom felt fer sure that, even as spectral creatures beyond the grasp of mass, he and Ash might also succumb to these indefeasible heights. And to top it all off they weren't but hardly seventy feet up. One thing, though, had changed for Tom even if it weren't exactly consolin.

I can remember things, Kalin! Tom yelled. *You're goshdarn right! I did tell you that you could make it up here on horseback!*

Kalin didn't look back though he did nod.

I also remember I didn't think we'd ever try.

It was 4:54 p.m.

Chapter Twenty

"The Teeth of the Mountain"

B ack around three in the afternoon, the clouds that huddled high on the Katanogos massif as well as them that had
slipped down to glower upon the valley not only paused their
deluge but seemed even to entertain a retreat; no matter that they'd
only withdrawn upward to regather within themselves the contents
of their purpose until some future preordained hour, and surely that
hour was comin, when they'd unleash a fury not yet described by the
days thus far. Allison March weren't fooled. Even from the Isatch Canyon parkin lot, she could see plain as the day wasn't how there were
consequences up there that had yet to arrive, and bein the sane person
that she was, she feared them.

Fer a moment, Allison March even felt herself a failed prophet.
That's what came up in her head: *Here I am, like a Moses*, which is the
kind of nonsensical thing a mind can hallucinate when in the face
of insurmountable circumstances it needs to believe in itself enuf to
motivate some kind of action. The only trouble is how the mind can
also prove equally capable of outsmartin its own self-affirmin delusions, because as Allison March well knew, if she was like Moses,
where was her tribe? Where was the Red Sea? For that matter what
Promised Land lay ahead, unless it was Kalin, though Kalin weren't no
land? Where also was her Divine Counsel? The only thing that made
any sense was that as Moses had walked betwixt parted waters, she
too would have to enter this liminal space where she would find herself beleaguered by the notion that at any moment both sides of the
canyon, like the walls of a great sea sundered, would refuse their truce
and clap suddenly together, drownin her in the ensuant flood, if likely
crushin her first in the debris flow.

Allison March knew herself then as utterly alone, which was
also wrong because she weren't alone at all. As soon as the rain had
stopped and Undersheriff Jewell had authorized the openin of the
park, volunteers had poured in, first helpin to establish safe crossins
over the flooded bridges and other parts of the trail overswept with
frigid water before leadin the way up beyond Bridge Six, where the
aftermath of the rockfall waited.

Given what few hours were left to the day, park rangers stationed
near the main gate had asked Allison if she was capable of makin in
good time the more than six miles she'd need to cover before even
commencin with the search. They doubted she was, but when she
demanded to know whether they had the right to stop her, they said
they did not. They were friendly enuf.

Sondra Gatestone had recommended that Allison take the afternoon to first get a sense of the canyon rather than set out at once to
attempt the more precipitous parts, let alone try and camp in such

miserable conditions. *You can start in earnest Sunday mornin.* Allison refused to commit to any such delay. Sondra told her that she'd wait in the parkin lot, *all night if need be,* also keepin an eye on the various doins by deputies and law enforcement officers. *I'll also be here if any Porch arrives and starts to get in the way of things.*

Most of the volunteers passin Allison now were plenty fit. Many were on mountain bikes. The few on foot jogged. One that slowed to check on her well-bein figured to reach Bridge Six in just over an hour. Those pedallin would get there much faster and also have a far easier time gettin out when darkness started to fall. Near everyone gave her pack and sleepin bag a double take.

Wearin her gray parka, rose-sable wool hat, and Gatestone boots, Allison had started out strong enuf, her pace secured by the energies of want. Just followin the happy beacon of a future resolved by certain action made the hike possible.

By Bridge Two, though, and that weren't even a mile in, Allison's right hip felt swole with BBs, just a few more steps away from bone gratin on bone. Worse still, a stabbin pain had started up near her left knee, likely somethin havin to do with her meniscus. The way weren't even that challengin, the incline hardly severe, the path a bucolic idyll wanderin beside a crick murmurin notes of fast-shatterin silver. A walk in the park, really, a beautiful park too, no matter the cold and aggregatin grays.

Growth comes when we make choices with results successful enuf to move us beyond repetition. But Allison knew that growth also comes from makin bad choices. Too soon she was limpin, and then not long after that she had to stop altogether. She'd made it as far as Bridge Two but not much farther. Pain had ordered her to stop. What energy she had left she spent on keepin back the sobs. She couldn't even make two miles let alone challenge the initial slopes backdroppin the crick. Upon givin that high churn of water more consideration, she realized she was not only unfit for any off-trail explorations but likely wouldn't even make it across such rapids.

About this time, a park ranger drivin a pickup truck loaded with young volunteers stopped and offered her a ride. Allison March sat opposite Rumi Plothow, Park Ranger Emily Brickey's good friend. You'll recall he was the one who drove Emily up the canyon Wednesday night. Allison and him exchanged smiles, Mr. Plothow sharin his amazement over her pack. Did she really mean to spend the night up there? Allison shook her head. *It was a stupid idea.* Mr. Plothow did not press her for her reasonin, and the fact that she was Kalin's mother never came up. Instead he laughed kindly: *I live by those.*

When the truck at last passed over Bridge Six and a little while later parked, Allison March was unprepared for the immensity they was about to face. At first it seemed like just an extension of the canyon walls before them, unnoticeable if the main trail had just continued over it. The sight, however, of the main trail vanishin beneath such a tumult of rock and earth stunned her. *I ain't never seen nothin like this,* Rumi Plothow whispered to her. *A few years ago an avalanche closed off Orvop Canyon for three weeks. They had tractors of all kinds out there. They had to dig through a fifty-foot wall of snow. This, though, this is somethin else . . .* Well, fer starters it was a lot higher than just fifty feet.

Allison didn't even get out of the truck. She just sat and gaped at the great heap of mountain cast in their way, a marvel really of broken trees and shattered stone upon which volunteers cautiously crawled. One young Isatch U student comin down, wearin a blue baseball cap with IU on it, was covered with mud and dried blood from a bad fall. This was Sharon Aldonas, who'd come to Orvop by way of Indiana. She told Allison that she estimated the slide was a good half mile wide. *They're never gonna dig this away. It's even higher in the middle. Like there's a little mountain of its own up there. It's pretty incredible.*

Have they found anythin? Allison asked.

Heck no. I mean you can see for yourself. It's just too big to find anythin.

Allison asked about her injury, *It ain't nothin,* and thanked her for her time, grateful that the coed hadn't recognized her as anyone other than someone there to help. And that seemed the case for everyone Allison spoke with, includin even a park ranger or two.

Allison did finally manage to make her way high up enuf on the slide to view the span of its ruination, and Sharon Aldonas weren't kiddin: it was at least a half a mile wide, and the center part did indeed rise up enuf to block any sight of the point of origination. Allison March had thought at first to at least reach that apex, this time, blessedly, with all thoughts of her-as-Moses gone, but she soon discovered firsthand how perilous even that goin was: mean gaps lay everywhere, welcomin a foot, a leg, even the sum of you if you weren't careful. She had every right to be there. She had no business bein there. As if scramblin over branches weren't bad enuf, she still had to test each subsequent step, and withdraw that step, even go backwards, if she found herself atop unstable rocks threatenin by the echoes of fallin pebbles underneath to collapse into a deep she knew might bury her.

She had initially thought that this here was a way to keep goin. Maybe she wouldn't have to quit. Upon the back of the landslide she'd pass easily over the crick, what was now far beneath her or dammin up on the far side. She wouldn't even need to go fast. The way up was pretty much a straight line. Like the yellow brick road, only with no bricks and no yellow. No singin neither, though her thoughts seemed to still be singin with hope. If she could make the top of the slide before dark, she could camp there and come mornin start lookin for a way up to that Altar Lake, that Kirk's Cirque, convinced she'd find signs along the way that Kalin was alive, Landry too, even the horses.

But the eye for all it grabs is too often a poor judge of what it can hold. It took the volunteer Christi Call, a graduate student in anthropology at Isatch U, to show Allison what she would eventually have to tackle if she did succeed in gettin even a little way up the slide, pointin out what looked like a low barricade made of branches and stone. It took Allison a moment to realize how poorly she was graspin the distances involved up here: them branches were whole trees, and those stones were big as garages. *And even if you do get past them, what are you gonna do about those?* Allison just gaped at the immense bluffs about halfway up. Forget the origin of the slide, lost anyways now behind new veils of mists. How had she missed those? Who could ever climb those? Was that a tree up there? Right on the edge?

By this point Allison had lost all intention of proceedin any farther. It had taken her a good forty-five minutes just to clamber to here, not even a startin point. Already she was in great pain, with her legs tremblin for no reason that had anythin to do with pain. Maybe somethin about the sight of that pale solitary tree up there gave her cause to know fear more. Through the chatter too of volunteers around her, she also began to understand that the true extent of the rockfall lay above those high cliffs, what no one could see from down there. Allison, though, still kept lookin up. It beat considerin what might lie beneath her feet, which she eventually, helplessly, had to consider. Was she right then standin above her son's body? On the grave of Sondra Gatestone's last livin child? On the broken bones of them poor horses? Everyone here was lookin for corpses. Allison March would do no such thing.

Her hand grazed on somethin then in the front pocket of her jeans. She pulled it out to discover that smooth gray stone encircled by a white line, what she knew as a Nightmare Stone, what she'd taken with her when she'd been in her apartment yesterday. Thursday already seemed like a lifetime away. Wednesday night? Lifetimes.

When she heard the distant sound of ATVs, Allison, like everyone else up there, assumed more help was arrivin to dowse these rubbled ruins. But when none arrived, volunteers began to look up the canyon steeps and, like Allison, ponder what was goin on above the misty denials of those great cliffs.

Because of his close friendship with Park Ranger Brickey, Rumi Plothow knew a few of the park rangers there and soon enuf passed along to Allison March that the engines they was hearin were park rangers and sheriff deputies makin sure that the kids hadn't survived. They was also keepin an eye out for the stolen horses.

That graduate student, Christi Call, eavesdroppin on this conversation, made extra clear that she hoped them murderin kids were found dead, though not the horses. *It would be nice if they found them alive. That's what I'm wishin for at least.*

Allison said nothin except to thank them both. She never would see Christi Call again and Rumi Plothow only once and from a distance.

Before managin the treacherous path off the rockfall, she cast one last look at the gouge in the canyon side, the apex of which still refused her gaze, which even way up there weren't halfway to Kirk's Cirque. It weren't even part of the mighty Katanogos massif, which behind its curtains of storm loomed higher now than myth. Of course, even without the cloud cover, even on the sunniest and clearest day, Katanogos would still loom higher than myth.

Allison March gave up then. She knew she weren't no match for this. She'd probably die just tryin to set up the tent Sondra had loaned her. Campin for her meant rollin out a sleepin bag next to a car. This here was beyond her. Wherever her Kalin was now, he was in it alone. And that sure trembled her chin some. Because what did Kalin know about tents or campin or weather like this? The only campin he'd done had been beside her next to their car.

Allison March's heart was too bust to cry anymore. But she did cry more. Though her heart was also too big to feel sorry for herself for very long. She quite literally stiffened her back then, threw out her chin, and when the same park ranger who'd given her a lift up offered her a ride back, she graciously accepted. She even sat up front with him. By the time she got out, Allison had told him who she was and why she'd come.

My Kalin did not kill that boy, she said again, chained perhaps forever to this darkest of mantras.

I believe you, he answered. That was none other than Dirk Meyer, who in later years would become the mayor of Orvop.

His response shocked her. All this time and she'd never heard it put so plainly and with such honest-to-God sincerity. And for Allison right then, maybe it was as if God had offered her Divine Counsel, staggerin her with somethin far greater than direction: faith.

You okay? Sondra asked when they was back in her truck, Mungo lavishin Allison with big-lick kisses. *My momma always told me what I've told Landry Lord knows how many times: it don't matter if you fail. However, to never have failed, that is a grave matter.*

I should've listened to you.

Sondra snorted and patted her friend on the thigh.

In case you didn't hear, Allison added. *A bunch of deputies and park rangers are up there where the slide started. I guess that's good news. Better than Porches up there.*

And that's the bad news.

While Allison had been makin her way up to Bridge Six, the mother of Landry, Tom, and Evan Gatestone had not been idle. She'd learned via the parkin-lot rumorin, what was mostly comin over the radio from one of the park rangers up there, Emily Brickey as was later confirmed, that Egan, Kelly, and Hatch Porch, along with that fellow Billings Gale, had joined the posse.

The mothers decided they had no choice but to confront Undersheriff Jewell at once. It didn't matter that Allison's hip and knee were near locked up; Sondra and Mungo still had to work hard to keep up. They charged into the undersheriff's tent. Allison did her part, bringin up her lawyer, the mishandled operation, the risin mountain of evidence to that effect, and all the repercussions that were bound to follow. Sondra just kept askin since when someone under investigation could take part in that investigation.

Now hold on, ladies! Hold on just one minute! First off, no Porch is under investigation! Second off, nothin up there has anythin to do with the investigation! They have a right to look for their horses! Undersheriff Jewell only then reconsidered his tone and lowered his voice. *That bein said, I will confirm that four of my deputies along with two rangers were sent up there to see if they could confirm from that vantage point whether or not your kids survived the rockfall. I'm sorry to say I just got off the radio with them, and I've ordered them back.*

What's that supposed to mean? What Sondra and Allison asked pretty much the same way and at near the same time.

We've had more success than anticipated, Undersheriff Jewell said.

I don't know what that means either, Sondra snapped.

Volunteers have uncovered some items near the base, Undersheriff Jewell said, his voice gettin more and more gentle.

What items? Allison demanded in a hoarse whisper.

He led the two mothers through to the adjacent tent, to where a long table was set up.

Undersheriff Jewell pointed first to a torn tarp.

That's your proof! Sondra nearly laughed.

Is it yours?

Sondra for all her scoff still inspected the ragged pieces. *It could be. And it just as well could not be. I have no way of knowin.*

What about this? Undersheriff Jewell then pointed out a sleepin bag that was torn in half.

I don't know, Sondra said, but she wouldn't go close to the thing.

Tom's name is written inside it. I'm sorry, Sondi.

That still don't prove nothin. Maybe they dropped it, maybe they lost it.

This too? Which was when Undersheriff Jewell pulled out of a cardboard box Landry's lacerated pink raincoat.

It still ain't a body, Allison jumped in.

We're gonna keep lookin. Avalanche experts from up around Little Cottonwood are comin down first thing tomorrow. Undersheriff Jewell cleared his throat. Allison March saw right then that he was a good man, and weren't that a shame. *I'm sorry for your loss, Sondi. I'm sorry for yours as well, ma'am.*

The fight went out of Sondra. She slumped so fast that both Allison and Undersheriff Jewell needed to help her to a chair. Even more gallin was how darned kind and sincere the undersheriff kept gettin. He even seemed personally dismayed by this discovery. And Allison March could do no more than grimace a smile at the man. She had no will to mourn or rage and so instead loathed herself, bitterly. Everythin Undersheriff Jewell had been accused of, his kinship with the Porches, his assumed bias against Kalin March, against Landry Gatestone, seemed overbaked and now surely irrelevant. Even Sondra Gatestone, who had a far greater understandin of Undersheriff Jewell, was touched by his gentle manner.

Nor were Allison or Sondra wrong: Conrad Jewell was deeply disturbed that between Wednesday night and this Saturday afternoon, three Orvop kids were dead. Over the years to come, many folks, some callin themselves historians, would find plenty to forgive about the man.

History, however, as well as that long scimitar of Justice, would not be as easy on him as these two women. His name would be ruined. And grantin the Porches the right to pursue their horses weren't even the half of it. His career would end within days, startin with a suspension and review that would render him untouchable. Even worse, the personal scar caused by what was about to transpire would find him relentlessly haunted until one dusk he would abruptly pull over on the side of a road, rush into a farm field, and stab hisself repeatedly in the guts and chest until his blade found the spot that stops a heart. He thought only of his wife, his kind Kip-Ann, and though she would never know it, he would die sighin her name.

When the mothers exited the tent, Saturday seemed spent. It was just after five, 5:01 p.m. to be exact, and dusk was settlin down the already doubtful light. The clouds, likely for all they still withheld, had grown darker. Whether you put stock in a throne or a prophet or some fabled Mount Ida where Zeus, despite the wiles of nature, readies bolts of lightnin to humble even chalk, the entitlements of Love seemed lost now and, worse, just downright foolish.

I don't know what to do, Sondra could barely croak out, her face ashen, her force gone from her fists.

I ain't quittin until I see him dead and stretched out before me, Allison growled at her, though it was as much for herself. She'd quit the mountain but she weren't quittin him.

And Allison's resolve did seem to knock Sondra upright a bit.

I'll share a secret, Allison: like your boy I also can't stand hopin. And I'll be darned if I'm gonna go home now to just sit there and hope.

Then we won't go home, Allison answered.

I'll share somethin else: I don't go in for prayin much either. And I'll be just as darned if I'm gonna go home and do that.

Then we won't pray. Sondra, we can face this together.

That's where you're wrong, Allison. We can't, and said mean like too.

I disagree with you, Sondra, Allison answered, her voice no louder than stirrin leaves.

There was a time there when we could've found them together. We could've been there for them together. But now that they're gone, we are not together. Now that they are gone, we are each alone. And no amount of the right company or wrong company is gonna change that.

Allison weren't a stranger to hardness, though she weren't a friend to it either.

We ain't seen the bodies.

They ain't ever gonna find the bodies.

Let's take a moment here.

I got no moments left.

Plenty have remarked that without the actual corpses it was premature for both women to give in to the desolation fast feastin on their spirits and bones. Them folks, though, have failed to perceive the savagery of that high achin terrain. Not even seven miles in, and that only accomplished with help, Allison had stood at the base of a geological calamity that weren't even a little finger's worth of the mountains that rose above it. She weren't blind no more to that place where it weren't nothin to just cease to be.

Just one wrong step up there and . . . Christi Call would say to Sharon Aldonas as they walked back together. However, Chelene Jasperson, who would eventually return from Moscow to Orvop, succumbin then to the deleterious effects of obesity and diabetes, type 2, no matter that she would have these very mountains practically in her back-yard, would still heap shame upon those two mothers who'd accepted a sleepin bag and some panels of pink as evidence of their children's deaths: *It's like learnin your child has cancer and startin to grieve. Pitiful.* Denise Jasperson, Chelene's sister, couldn't disagree more: *It's easy to underestimate Isatch Canyon, especially if you're in the comfortin arms of a deep rocker chair or, if you are there, takin a stroll on one of them nicely groomed trails, with a handrail here and there, some nice rock steps, even a water fountain and a bench by a bridge, the perfect place, you know, for catchin your breath on a sunny day with those majestic mountain peaks above. But in late October! With those temperatures! Everyone was lucky it weren't yet subzero! It's easy to miss the terrifyin proportions of that place. And we're still just talkin Agoneeya and Kaieneewa. Katanogos? I've climbed that mountain three times, Heber side of course, the northeast summit trails, and let me tell you, Katanogos is a whole other kind of mountain. And in a storm? A big storm? No way. No. Way.*

Now fer just one moment, please, try to imagine yourself a mother of a child, the labor of your loins but also the labor of your solitary hours spent over years and years so your one child might rise up and stand toe to toe with the world and have at least a chance. Now go ahead and imagine that child who still ain't old enuf to vote up where there ain't no handrails, rock steps, or water fountains. Goin on three nights now too with a fourth fast approachin. This one child up where the slopes are unstable, the evidence of which you've just beheld in all its appallin magnitude, what would easily bury a car, a whole apartment buildin, a few apartment buildins. Now think to yourself whether or not you could convince yourself that, yes, my child is okay. Which is not to say that you proclaim with total certainty that your child is dead. But could you declare your child alive? Could you really behold in that filial absence anythin more than a ghost? Which is also not to say that you don't wish, hope, pray, and perform whatever magical thinkin is necessary to keep alive the possibility of survival, if nowhere close to believin but still hopin, hopin, hopin that your child might yet return to your arms unscathed. Except . . . Except . . . Except you've also lived a life long enuf to know the brutal counterpoints that can so easily and so quickly render your small child's limbs lifeless. Family has told you, friends have told you, communities have told you, History tells you: no child is safe.

Yes, for Sondra Gatestone and Allison March, the strength to imag-ine their children alive had finally waned to the point that they were now haunted by Landry's and Kalin's deaths, and it was this endurin lack of resolution that robbed them of their strength to conjure any unlikely outcome. It was an exhaustion that felt like defeat and even looked like defeat, though it weren't defeat. Not yet.

Unfortunately by this point it was complete enuf to rent the fabric of their friendship, their partnership. Not that Sondra held any malice toward Allison, merely impatience. For Sondra, the sight of Landry's pink raincoat transformed Allison March into a stranger, no longer suited to comfort her let alone accompany her. In fact no one alive that Sondra knew was suitable fer her now: no church-goin friends, not even her stake president and family friend, the revered Havril Enos.

Unlike Sondra, Allison March had spent more time alone. Still, she'd always known her Kalin alive, whether she was at work or he was off on his own. Just the idea of him gone did somethin to her thinkin she feared would never get set straight again.

Even worse, though the mothers couldn't know it right then, at that very moment more calamity was takin place up near Salt Lake City, in the property room in fact, where you'll recall Pat Stubbs, the officer in charge, had received from Chester Walheimer, the intern, the evidence bags prepared by Assistant Medical Examiner Annabelle Kasey containin the crystal shards removed from Russel Porch's neck. Officer-in-Charge Pat Stubbs would have placed those bags in the Russel Porch Evidence Box had not a flurry of small but prioritized duties caused a delay, which still shouldn't have made a difference.

It was another officer, Brennan Hurley, who that Saturday afternoon had taken charge of the property room and soon enuf spied the loose evidence bags. Thinkin nothin of the nearby evidence box, he took them to his desk to examine more closely. Even then all was fine. It only went awry when Officer Hurley handed the two bags over to Officer William Mecham, who had been called down to assist with the reorganization of some of the shelves. Officer Mecham, however, was exhausted after a night shift followed by a mornin of household duties. He arrived bleary-eyed. He was also badly dyslexic. Without ever sensin the error, he placed the bags in a box labeled RUSSEL H. CROP. Far worse than that, the Crop case had been dismissed, and all evidence was slated to be moved to another buildin where, pendin a final review, it would either be placed in long-term storage or destroyed.

Maybe under different circumstances, Old Porch would've kicked his heels together if he'd learned what was about to become of those crystal shards, the root cause of his youngest son's death. Though maybe not. Old Porch was at this moment in a place far away from any heel kickin. See, with nothin yet to the contrary, Old

Porch had fallen for Sondra Gatestone's bluff. As far as he was concerned, Trent Riddle had at last reappeared, tellin his story not only to Sondra and that other one, that Allison March, but also to detectives and whoever else Old Porch didn't need to hear from. They was gonna come for him too, first with questions, then warrants, then with whatever else they'd need to bracelet him. Old Porch was cornered.

What was happenin in the mountains now didn't matter no more. Old Porch couldn't even reach his sons to call them back. The last message he'd got was hours ago, at the very limit of the range of them radios they'd took up, right before they'd started up for Mist Falls. Egan had reported that they'd been right about the map bein wrong. There was a way up through the cliffs. So there was that.

It's tellin that Old Porch didn't even try the radios now, made no effort to save his boys from future actions that would ruin them. Old Porch was concerned only with his own demise.

Ron Welch, an Orvop entrepeneur who'd make a small fortune on minature golf, and liked to say so over and over again to Lochlyn La Morte before he was cut down at sixty-three by a stroke: *Old Porch knew them radios were useless with them walls of mountain in the way. Should he have still tried? He should've tried. But did it matter that he didn't try? I don't think so.*

Instead Old Porch had butchered Effy. He'd wiped his hands upon his apron, smearin Effy's blood in dark irreverent letterin across his lap. He'd saved none of her. Her hide, her meat, her bones, he'd broken her down at near every joint and after that sawed up anythin he deemed still too big, feedin her parts into the crematorium, where his Effy was embraced by the terrible heat that soon enuf churned such carcass parts into ash and black smoke.

Don't think Porch weren't hurtin either, if also welcomin that pain as proof of his pendin triumphs, believin only base sufferin, both experienced and inflicted, proves the man and certainly proves more substantial and endurin than any notion of lawful progress or milquetoast citizenry. Old Porch, of course, never could see the lie he was tellin hisself, that this self-inflicted abuse, this orchestrated and ritualized blood sacrifice, did not grant him the solvency he thought his hurt entitled him to. No entitlements would follow his violence. Only consequences.

Nor did this willful act of agony do anythin to quell his rage. Quite the opposite. Old Porch's fury was now near equal in temperature and tempest to the flesh-devourin fire he paced before, as if in search of somethin else to harm, to burn, before finally relentin and returnin to sponge down the tables and counters, hose off the floors, and in the big industrial sink get to washin the hammer and blades.

It was in this state, with his forearms and apron still spattered with meat and bone bits, that Detective Peters found him. After no one had answered his knock at the front door on the main house, Detective Peters had walked hisself back this way without so much as a second thought. He weren't even carryin a gun.

Mr. Porch? It's Detective Peters? You remember me? Good to see you again. My apologies for bargin in on you like this. I hope I'm not intrudin. I was won-derin if I could have a word with you about an employee of yours? Trent Riddle?

And there it was. Come fast too. Old Porch grunted somethin, nodded as well to Detective Peters, before sayin it weren't no trouble and come on in and could he just get a quick second to finish what he was in the middle of? Old Porch surveyin then the blades in the bot-tom of that deep stainless steel sink, more than clean enuf for what he had in mind, what anyways would require more cleanin later, though he chose the heavy stainless steel hammer, more like a little sledge-hammer, which he re-rinsed, washin away under the warm water any lingerin soap bubbles, before turnin off the tap and selectin a large cloth to dry it with, though the thing hardly demanded such care. Old Porch just needed an excuse to keep it in his hands.

What can I do you for? Old Porch asked as he turned around to face the detective, even if he already knew what he was about to hear: how Riddle had recounted a few things that didn't quite square with the various accounts related to him by his boys, by their hand Billings, by even Old Porch hisself, with the most onerous discrepancy bein that Russel had been uninjured when he'd returned.

Old Porch coughed then, coughed again harder, like he could now cough out the revisitation that was again workin its harm upon his head. Russel's ghost upon him again. Impossible to swallow that down. Or cough it out.

You okay, Mr. Porch? Detective Peters asked, really kindly too, in fact so kindly that it even threw Old Porch some. What sorta man could toy so casually with Old Porch at such a moment? Old Porch suddenly knew he'd underestimated the detective. He registered now the broad shoulders, the long and strong arms, big hands too, near big as Porch's. Old Porch could see the detective would have no problem snatchin right out of the air any flailin arm wieldin a hammer. He had the reach to fend off any strike, had the reach to deliver one too.

Somethin caught in my throat, Old Porch answered, tossin away the hammer on a nearby counter, where it slid across the metal surface, the wall puttin an end to the racket with a thud. He needed somethin meaner.

It's cold season. Especially with this weather, Detective Peters replied, even takin a step back like a cold was the worst thing there in that big room.

Could be that, could be that, Old Porch muttered. Why not let Johnny Law here think he was sick? Old Porch even offered a feeble smile full of them wrecked teeth, what was usually worth at least one more step backward, but Detective Peters didn't budge and even met Old Porch's blue-gray gaze with ease.

Before I forget, Mr. Porch, any chance Egan is around? He's the last one of your sons I haven't talked to. He was at that poker game, right?

You know he was, Old Porch answered. *We was at his house.*

Of course, of course. You're right.

Old Porch marveled again at how genuinely addled the detective appeared. Had he really forgotten? Maybe now he was overestimatin him. Old Porch had at least settled on what he'd need: that old baseball bat with a horseshoe attached to one side, easin the thing out from a lower cupboard and, still beyond any sight line, leanin it against the counter, within reach now, what he could wield fast too if the detective gave him his back. Old Porch also grabbed up a bag of Red Man to mislead the detective into thinkin that here was the sole purpose for his fussin. As he worked the leaf, though, he wished he had a dip of Copenhagen instead.

You partake, Detective? Old Porch asked, and when the detective declined the offer, Old Porch walked away from the hidden bat to fetch hisself a plastic cup for the spit.

Did you play baseball, Mr. Porch?

Old Porch winced. Not only had the detective already caught a glimpse of the bat; he was bringin it up loud so Old Porch would know that at least that move was already found out. Had he seen the horseshoe? Old Porch would need somethin else. A gun. Old Porch would need a gun fer this guy.

My boys did.

I played high school and college.

At Isatch U?

Four years at the University of Miami.

They have a team?

Of course Old Porch could still try to hold steady to what he'd first told Chief of Police Beckham, about Riddle's gross state of inebriation, and just hope that Egan, Kelly, and Billings, all declarin the same, might throw Riddle's statement into doubt. But Old Porch also knew Riddle would have plenty of folks on his side to vouch for his devout abstinence, while even Detective Peters here could testify to Old Porch's blatant disregard of Church edicts, what with him helpin hisself right now to some chaw durin their interview. Old Porch let loose a brown dribble to pool at the bottom of the cup. Then there'd be a lot of fuss over who was lyin and who weren't. Maybe a trial. And either way a whole lot of attention paid to every detail.

Detective Peters was suddenly at Old Porch's side. He'd come over fast too. Old Porch didn't have time to even flinch.

Mr. Porch! My lord! That thumb has gotten worse! I'd say it's badly infected now! You don't want that spreadin to your veins. Didn't you hear about Kendall Fierce? A fine golfer. He was gonna go pro they said. Why he jabbed his finger on a toothpick. A toothpick! He didn't pay no attention to it, and the thing went gangrenous! Can you believe that? The poor kid lost his arm. There went his golfin career. Was out on a boat on Mud Lake, graduation night, drank too much, went swimmin, and drowned.

I know the Fierces. I know every single one of them.

Of course you do, Mr. Porch.

Old Porch forced a smile. He'd heard the bite in his own voice, and that was unfortunate and no doubt hadn't helped none to free him from this disadvantaged position. Old Porch had better start lullin this detective into a real state of complacency if he was gonna get a first move in. Though it was dawnin on Old Porch that nothin about the detective indicated he wanted to do anythin but talk. Plus anythin he knew was likely already known by the department. Havin a go at this young man weren't likely to accomplish much. Though Old Porch still didn't take kindly to bein toyed with. He'd get the detective in the house, get him comfortable, show him his art, and then he'd use a gun. Whatever happened after that would happen.

One query that often arises without resolution was whether or not Old Porch was just plain crazy. No question he was plenty capable of gettin things done, *high-functionin* was the way some folks put it, and no one doubted his successes or wealth. But he was still at this moment grantin hisself every permission to put down Detective Peters, maybe even in his own house, already overrun by a feelin to do harm first to this man who meant to harm him. No matter the price. Old Porch was capable of rash action. His life was a string of black pearls showcasin that type of aggression.

But then again we don't want to reduce crazy to just impulsiveness and bad behavior. In that case anyone who dares the limits of a culture or the law might seem crazy to a degree. Old Porch had heard hisself called that so many times, it meant about as much to him as callin water wet. *Orwin, you're crazy!* his Orvop High sweetheart, Joelle Carrick, had squealed how many times, loudest when he showed her how he'd spray-painted a profane word across the outdoor wall of one of the Isatch U buildins. But crazy had worked. She'd given him some rubbin. This was back when he was fifteen. Weren't his first time either. He'd always found the willful disregard of property and the law pleasin. Plenty would argue that that ain't crazy but just vandalism. But what about the fact that Old Porch still did it? Infrequently, yes, but periodically, most definitely. He'd just head out one night with a can of paint and spray a curse upon someone's property, and just for the pure heck of it. Did it to the Wongs' place recently.

However you wanna settle your head around this matter of Old Porch's sanity, most agree that there was at least a weirdness about him. And it weren't one easily characterized. Old Porch had lots of edges. And they weren't neatly aligned either. He delighted in the ratification of a business or legal victory as much as he indulged in illegal cruelties. In his youthful years his peers considered him *A game . . . mmm . . . on sorta guy*. Or at least that's how Dalton Fossum, a fellow classmate, would say it. From another vantage point, Veronica Lasseter would wonder what sort of effect Old Porch's brother had had on him, a poet no less, who'd declared hisself married to verses by the likes of Marlowe and Pound. Even late in her life Veronica Lasseter would reflect often on this unnamed siblin who *had died in an awful way due to that disease, abandoned by women, with the strangest words upon his lips when he passed, tellin the hospice nurse that he was known now only by the Men who lay us! Now what was that about if not godless foulness?*

Whether rational or not, whatever internal dictates drove Old Porch at that moment to consider murderin a man expressin concern over his swollen thumb, his desire to fight was always tempered by his stablest of convictions: to win.

Your man, Billings Gale, came by the station this mornin to give his statement about Wednesday night, the detective said then.

Old Porch shrugged like he weren't surprised, though he was nothin but surprised. *I thought you already talked to him?*

Mr. Gale had no recollection of Trent Riddle imbibin to the excess you described.

Old Porch shrugged again, though this time, and without his say-so too, his teeth set together hard and his right shoulder swung back. Was he betrayed? What kind of show was this Detective Peters puttin on?

Billings is a good man, Old Porch said. *I'm lucky to have him workin here. He gets on fine with my boys. I'm sure what he said, he believed.*

Would you be changin your impressions then of events on Wednesday night?

Nope. Likely Billings was payin more attention to the hand he was dealt than Trent Riddle's antics.

Don't play cards with me, son, Old Porch might as well have said, or at least thought, though he weren't thinkin like so, more like just fixin his icy blue eyes on Detective Peters in preparation for the action that seemed more and more inevitable. Old Porch had gambled plenty in his life, and he'd lost plenty too, though when he lost he was mostly flyin wild on the colors of every sort of booze and worse. Now, though, he was stone-cold sober and ready to get after whoever dared think they could make a losin hand out of him.

You know anythin about Nam, detective?

Only that I'm glad I wasn't there.

Nam's got crocodiles. Did you know that?

I guess that makes sense.

There's a whole swarm of troubles that can take you down over there. Hard to believe crocodiles is just one more thing you got to worry about.

You were in Nam, sir?

It weren't hard to find yourself walkin point along some marshy place. Maybe you got three months left, maybe three weeks, maybe you're almost home. You're there because you're lookin for folks who don't speak English set to kill you because you do. Land mines are everywhere, and they don't need a language to blow you to bits. And then it happens. If you're a survivor, you hear it before you hear it. And what I mean by that is that you should already be runnin fer your life. Because, let me tell you, when it comes, it comes big and thrashin, with a whole mouth of teeth, along with the muscle and speed to grab hold of you and drag you under the water. The most important thing you gotta remember against a creature comin after you at twenty miles per hour is how to move. Because if you're just walkin real slow and careful, you ain't gonna outrun such an attack. Unless. You. Know. How. To. Move.

How to move?

That's right. And sure, I can thank the Good Lord, but I'm bein more truthful if I thank an old woman in some bunghole hamlet I never need to see again. She was all about crocodile warnins. She made these big bitin gestures with her thin little fingers. And she laughed at us the whole time with these black teeth. But she also made clear to anyone who wanted to listen, and you bet I was listenin, that the secret to how to move is to zigzag. See, a crocodile goin straight ahead can move real fast, but side to side, well, it's about as useless as draggin a wheelbarrow on its side through the mud.

So you zigzagged?

To the left! To the right! Fast as I could! Though I still figured them teeth was gonna settle in on some soft part of me and then drag me away, and if my buddies didn't shoot it dead or kill me in the process, why then it was gonna take me under and drown me. So I didn't quit ziggin and zaggin, zigzagged as hard as I could. By the time I stopped, Sergeant Loidle was laughin his rear off. See, that croc weren't even close. Barely lumbered out of the reeds. Probably to yawn. I was out of breath. The rest of the men were laughin now too. That old woman had gotten one over me. Just another American fool buyin into her gook nonsense. She'd turned out to be VC too. Quit the hamlet, gone like green goes in green.

That's quite a story. Your point? Don't listen to old women with bad teeth?

To zigzag or not to zigzag, ain't that the question?

I prefer to get straight to the point, Detective Peters said then.

So did Sergeant Loidle! He was a straight-line, straight-edged, straight-to-the-point kinda guy too! He did not listen to old ladies with black teeth. He did not zigzag. And he ran straight after that crocodile like the American hero he was, readyin his weapon as he charged, steppin right where all my zigzags had missed, and why the next thing Sergeant Loidle knew, he was leavin the earth. The land mine all but vaporized him. And when the smoke cleared, that big crocodile was gone too, maybe feastin some on Sergeant Loidle's parts still splashin down out over the water.

As often as they could, Monica Brothwell and Phil Bauman would remind folks that Old Porch was never with no armed forces and he sure as heck never served in Vietnam. It's possible this story might've come by way of some vet that Old Porch happened to meet somewhere. Maybe one of his property managers or one of his truckers. Maybe just some guy in a Reno bar. Monica and Phil would often discuss with other folks, like Cindi Kimber and Val Benson, how in this retellin or fabulatin, whichever one it was, and likely it was a combination of the two, Old Porch's love of dancin around the truth, maybe even dancin with the truth, was so clearly on display. He was just so good at it. And sure, he's lyin the whole way through, but there's somethin in his tellin that's also tellin the detective it's never gonna be more than a story.

Fer his part, Detective Peters didn't miss that Old Porch was tellin him somethin more than crocodiles in Vietnam nor was he deaf to the notes of menace.

I'm afraid I lost you, Mr. Porch. Why are you tellin me this?

Old Porch blinked like he was near stunned by the brightness of the day, even if today was anythin but bright. *No reason at all! It's just good fun, ain't it?*

We found Riddle, Detective Peters announced then.

Finally! Old Porch was almost relieved. Straight to it! At last! Old Porch even offered up a big grin. Detective Peters, however, turned away, even gave up his back, whereupon Old Porch sidled close again to that baseball bat, the handle now within easy reach, if he could only just find the right moment for a swing. And so long as Detective Peters didn't hear the grab, he wouldn't hear the swing. Old Porch knew he wouldn't miss either. And the crematorium was goin full bore. It never objected to more.

Mr. Porch, I'm afraid to report that your man is dead.

Old Porch actually jerked away from the bat, at the same time forcin his grin to depart, and it required a great deal of force, the shock of this statement continuin to reverberate across Old Porch's features like too many tells on the face of an amateur card player. All of which communicated to Detective Peters nothin but confusion, which pretty much summed up Old Porch's overridin condition, because surely he hadn't heard right, surely he must've misunderstood.

Years later, Detective Peters would admit to catchin sight of that slight delay that had allowed Old Porch's grin to linger a bit, even grow a mite bigger, sharin with Detective Peters more of them shattered teeth. *Just somethin I never forgot,* Detective Peters would tell his wife or them others who came around to hear the story again.

What's that? Old Porch asked.

Trent Riddle is dead. And like you told Beckham, about him bein so drunk?

Mmmm-hmmm, Old Porch offered by way of a consent he could easily zigzag out of if this proved a trap.

His family is havin a heckuva time stomachin the news: no question Trent Riddle was drunk at the time of his calamity. Seems he'd gone on somethin of a bender. He had on him a big wad of cash and a throb in his heart for a young girl who lived up in Greeley, Colorado. I'm sorry, do you mind if I sit down?

My bad manners for not offerin you a seat in the first place! Old Porch sure was movin now, a figure of matchless hospitality, draggin over a chair, gettin the detective a cup of water, while at the same time riddin hisself of the leaf in his lip as well as that saliva repository.

I ain't gotten much sleep, Detective Peters explained. *I know you know why. And I'm so sorry for that. There's just been so much . . . dyin. I moved back here because Orvop was a quiet place. Your son? Them two kids? And now your friend?* Detective Peters shook his head and drank down the water. Old Porch expected him to cry next. Old Porch was sure gonna cry next. Of happiness.

This happened then in Greeley? Old Porch finally asked.

Detective Peters shook his head. *Trent Riddle was headin there by way of Spanish Fork Canyon, at least that's what we're figurin, goin at intolerable speeds for even the soberest driver and in last night's downpour too. He plunged off the hill into a grove of trees. He was likely killt with the first impact. He hit a big tree, though he didn't stop there. His vehicle rolled a bunch before settlin under some broken saplings. On the road there wasn't any sign of an accident. No skid marks, nothin.* Detective Peters was feelin better. Whatever dizziness or fatigue had overtakin him was departin as he continued to lay down the cold, dismal facts. *It weren't until we learned about this young lady in Greeley that we expanded our search. She was just as mystified as we were. She'd assumed he'd broken off their rendezvous. She never thought to call up his*

737

folks. She isn't with the Church and figured announcin herself like that wouldn't go over too well with his family. Fortunately for us, one of Trent Riddle's brothers knew about her and had the notion to call her, and when she heard he was missin, she came clean about their planned meetup. That was this mornin. Highway Patrol eventually located the crash.

Now it was Old Porch's turn to sit down. He'd never heard news so goshdarned gladdenin, but he also knew he better not give off even a whiff of such sentiments. He put his head down near between his knees, them big and scarred hands clamped on the back of his neck, mutterin aloud: *He was too good to go so soon. He was just too good.*

Detective Peters went on to explain that the coroner had put Riddle at a BAC of only .05 percent. *He was soberin up by then but not enuf to handle the road. It's lucky he didn't kill anybody.*

Old Porch nodded.

As would eventually come out, unbeknownst to literally everyone, now and then Trent Riddle enjoyed a taste of the hard stuff. That night after the game, he'd celebrated his winnings, as well as his imminent destination, with at least a couple of shots of whiskey before settin out. And then twice more over the hours ahead. Each time accompanied by slugs of Dr Pepper. This was what Colorado law enforcement officials would conclude, based on five empty soda cans found within the vehicle, includin a sixth one, empty as well, though it had been punctured in the wreck, the tab never pulled. Remarkably they also found an intact fifth of Jack Daniels short by about six shots.

Though Trent Riddle's blood alcohol concentration was well below Utah and Colorado law, this evidence, though far from confirmin Old Porch's story, didn't contradict it either.

In subsequent years those who knew Trent Riddle well, or thought they had, along with those folks who knew him through the young lady in Greeley, Colorado, could make neither heads nor tails of his condition at the time of his death. No one had ever seen him go near a sip of booze. Not even a can of 3.2. Not even a cola or anythin caffeinated. To this day, this aspect of Trent Riddle's character, a stalwart churchgoer who, deep in the privacy of his contradictions, sought out the comforts of 80 proof, remains a mystery.

Less of a mystery, if equally unsatisfactory, was why Detective Peters had driven over to Porch Meats to tell Old Porch the news in the first place. He could've called. He could've had any other officer make that call. Yes, fer sure, there was the fact that he still wanted to get a statement from Egan Porch, though if he was lookin for Egan why didn't he go first to Egan's own home near Isatch Canyon? The likely explanation, even if it was beyond Detective Peters's conscious grasp, at least on that Saturday, was that somethin about his interactions with Billings Gale had drawn him back to Old Porch. The Riddle news was as fine a pretext as you could get, even if what exactly Detective Peters was tryin to sniff out remained elusive even to him. The best he could offer many years later was that he just knew there was more to be found out. He went there simply to expose hisself further to whatever Old Porch or anyone else at Porch Meats was willin to give up. In retrospect, despite whatever tics or hesitations the future would highlight, Old Porch had given away nothin, and that would to the end of his life chill Detective Peters.

Old Porch thanked his guest profusely for deliverin the news in person, shakin the detective's hand and wavin goodbye. Then, still lightheaded, Old Porch returned to the plant, where he flung that baseball bat into the engulfin transformation offered by his crematorium. Let those ashes join Effy's. It had been her shoe after all.

A nd if that weren't enuf good news, things just kept gettin better. It was like Effy's departure, what it had taken to see that through, had finally bestowed favorable winds. Woolsey and Francis returned soon after. They'd talked to all Egan's neighbors. *Every single one!* Francis proudly blazoned, Woolsey in agreement with his brother's assessment. Not a one weren't heartbroken about Russel, and not a one had seen him ridin out of the canyon, let alone ridin into the canyon, except for Dorothy Bray, who saw Russel settin out on Cavalry to get back the horses, and she'd thought him grand and brave. *Russel was a real hero,* Woolsey said then, to which Francis added: *Sister Bray did say she felt afraid for him to be out alone in the dark and in such a storm.* Dorothy Bray had not seen Russel ride back, but she did tell them how the mother of the one the news was sayin killt Russel had come around. Dorothy Bray had then gone to great lengths to describe her dislike for *that Mrs. March, if she is a Mrs.,* as well as *that Mrs. Gatestone,* both of whom were clearly just out makin trouble, makin up stories to best suit their interests. The subject of her husband, Mr. George Bray, never came up, though she did bring up a wooden spoon rest she was happy about.

Even though there was a good hour before dinnertime, Old Porch at once got to cookin up a snack for his two teenagers, *Call it an appetizer!,* grabbin out of the freezer some frozen tater tots, which, while the oven was heatin, he got to coverin with grated cheese.

Now if Egan could just handle this business with the Kalin kid, and Landry too, why then they was done. The phone started ringin. Francis answered. It was for Woolsey. Woolsey took it in the TV room.

Old Porch did try then to raise Egan on the radio. He knew they was already too far away, but somethin still made him want to try.

Woolsey came back into the kitchen. *That was Darren Blicker. He says Uncle Conrad has called everyone in and that he's narrowin the search to the base of the slide. They found Landry's raincoat and sleepin bag. She'd dead, and so's the horse thief.*

Old Porch squatted down to look into the oven. He was starvin. The cheese weren't even melted much, and the tater tots was still froze in the center, but he served them like that anyhow and ate them like that too. Woolsey did like his daddy. Francis said he weren't hungry.

You think there's a chance they're buried but still breathin? Francis asked.

Old Porch then did somethin he almost never did, especially with Francis. He came over and gave Francis a big hug.

Not a chance. Not. A. Chance.

It was the happiest moment in that boy's life.

Maybe Old Porch's too.

Even after Hatch had crossed the Ninth Scree, however pleased that made him feel, he found hisself equally unnerved, or at least perplexed, by the continuin solidity upon which they drove. Pretty much on every scree Hatch had assumed Egan was gonna start slidin away, forcin him to ditch the ATV, spread-eaglin hisself to stop from fallin. But Egan had never slipped even a little, nor Kelly or Billings. Fer sure the great rockfall was gonna halt Egan's reckless traversin, but he only got after it harder. They was surrounded by the ruin of ground, and yet the path Egan found never so much as whispered loose a few errant stones.

The deputies and rangers did not proceed with the same lack of caution, stoppin more and more often, until they was left far behind. In their company Hatch had found somethin stabilizin and even calmin. He liked Deputy Sheriffs Doyle Cannon and Shaun Brice and had even bonded some with Gammon Erickson, who'd rode with him some of the way. Now, though, Hatch felt that jittery rush that always came for him when he was around his brothers, part yippin enthusiasm, part competitive and mean, with rage mixed in there too.

Beyond the Ninth Scree the trail got even easier, except now Egan was slowin, and in the least likely place too, beside some unassailable bluffs. To Egan's credit he didn't take long to see through Kalin's efforts to mislead them, locatin soon after the gap the kids used to escape. The initial part required some tight maneuverin to get the ATVs up and around a shoulder of rock. Hatch had suggested that between the four of them they'd have no trouble haulin the vehicles up by hand, but Egan found a way to drive up, keepin the center tire on the path while ridin up a back tire on the steep slope of stone. There was plenty of skiddin, and they all felt like they was gonna go right over the handlebars, but it worked. Egan drove both his and Kelly's ATV up. Hatch refused the help and nearly did go over the handlebars, but his athletic dexterity was unparalleled even amongst the Porch brothers, and he got that two-seater, the biggest of the ATVs too, around the hump and onto one of the easiest paths they'd faced until then. Hatch called it *downright pleasant.*

It was on this drive up to Mist Falls, whenever Hatch weren't tradin gears up three before droppin fast down again to first, that he found hisself not so much cautious and alert but this time unnerved by what kept steadily revealin itself above. Gone were the vertiginous crumblin steeps they'd left behind, replaced now by immense rocky ridges risin up and up and, long before reachin any conclusion, disappearin into the dark clouds. Just the visible heights dizzied Hatch, like he'd never seen them before. Had he? He blinked hard to bring this vision into focus if not into reality.

Meanwhile, Egan was lookin back, givin them all a thumbs-up. Glee was clamped between his teeth like a knife. No one slowed. In fact Kelly right at that moment tried to prove that his own choices had had some say in how they'd wound up here by gunnin his vehicle at a wide switchback that for a brief spell split into two trails runnin parallel to one another, Kelly takin the high road by which he planned to overtake Egan and drop in for the lead. Not that Kelly had a chance, and the reason weren't the two-seater, with Billings weighin it down extra. The engine was plenty fierce, fiercer than Egan's, but Egan had more than horsepower workin in his favor. See, there weren't even a stitch of fear in him to check his pace. Egan also loved seein his younger brother give it a try. Egan couldn't beat Kelly, though, and where the trails merged, he only stayed ahead by forcin Kelly to either come down on him or brake hard. When Kelly chose some version of the latter, droppin in behind Egan without any room to spare, Hatch thought he was about to watch Kelly and Billings flip, but Kelly had reflexes too and kept his beast under control.

Hatch clutched quick down from third to second and accelerated to close the widenin gap. Drivin fast sure beat addressin the memory that kept insistin that these heavin mountains above him shouldn't even be there. Because . . . Because no doubt about it, right about here the slopes should've started to mellow into a ramble of brush and old trails leadin down to a wide dusty campground where many a ward outin had ended around fires, with root beer brewin nearby thanks to the dry ice hauled up for the occasion, along with the necessaries for s'mores aplenty, fingers soon sticky with melted chocolate and burnin marshmallow. How many nights had Hatch done just that? Plenty. Hatch was sure of it. He could still remember perfectly how on one of those followin mornins, after big plates of bacon and scrambled eggs, he'd taken a leisurely if long trail up to Orvop Peak, after which, by another route, they'd headed back down to Isatch Canyon, where if the season was right, you could get a good swim in at Yell Rock Falls, that bouldered bower of shade-draped pools, especially gratifyin when the summer heat was on.

Hatch could see Orvop Peak now, but it were farther off, down to the right, or to the southeast, and didn't look like much more than a pimple on a foothill compared to where they was headed now. It was as if Hatch's time away from Utah had somehow upraised these un-endin peaks. Now how was that possible?

Right then Hatch's radio squawked. He could see well enuf that neither Egan nor Kelly were on theirs, which could only mean it was their dad tryin to signal them. Hatch did his best to hail him back, once, twice, but never heard anythin more than a ghostly hiss.

You know, it didn't have to be from one of them Porch radios or whatever they was, Doreen Lund would say, an Orvop native who by this point was finalizin her move into a lakeside home for the elderly near West Vancouver, British Columbia. Lund weren't wrong. Old Porch owned two sets of handheld two-way radios set to the same frequency, which Hatch had double-checked before they'd headed out. Fresh batteries too, with spares in a gear bag. Egan had one radio, Kelly the second, with Hatch carryin the third. Old Porch had the fourth. Hatch had already given Deputy Sheriff Doyle Cannon their frequency, which Egan did not care fer one bit. What Doreen Lund would get to sup-posin was that there might've been still more radios out there, set to the same frequency; though to be fair, the way Lund's mind was workin toward the end, she was thinkin more in terms of a signal with a spectral origin: *Ghosts! That's who! Ghosts was reachin out to Hatch Porch!* One stranger hearin this declaration would respond with a bewildered *But why?* A question that appalled Doreen Lund: *Why?! Why to turn Hatch around, of course!*

Unfortunately turnin around was the last thing on Hatch's mind. Aside from puzzlin sensations of bein somewhere that weren't there, Hatch was mostly keen to achieve what Kelly had failed at: overtakin Egan. First, though, he'd have to overtake Kelly, not that Kelly was gonna stand for that. He'd just backed down from Egan; the heck if he was gonna back down from another brother.

Kelly had a shot too at holdin to this resolve. Fer one thing, neither he nor Billings were dazzled by the vistas. Fer another, they didn't doubt the evergreens tall upon the steep inclines, the streams bubblin around moss-covered stones, or the way colonnades of pillared bark gave way to grassy hillsides sparsly marked by aspens and birches. Nothin about the stunnin openness up there or the cold air could make Kelly doubt the trail they was on and so, most importantly, distract him from his machine to which he was most tuned, believin, foolishly, that his ongoin attention to gear changes, surges of acceleration, with the occasional hard brake through the sharpest switchbacks would deliver him to the lead position.

Hatch sure was surprised when Kelly refused to grant him the slightest leeway to make a play for a pass. At each turn, despite Hatch's fierce jockeyin, Kelly proved an able competitor and kept him back.

So successful was Kelly's reproach of their hero brother that he once again entertained ideas of bestin Egan. But there Kelly didn't stand a chance. The secret history that had enabled him to keep their troika undivided was not enuf to catapult hisself to the front. Egan's swiftness went beyond anythin Kelly could match. The past hours combined with the quickenin rhythm of their progress had delivered to Egan a lucidity of purpose that was by this point orderin, perfectly it seemed, all his actions: the more he thought of puttin down that Kalin kid, the faster he went.

Egan's thoughts did stumble somewhat over Landry. After all, she and him had history, unfinished history. However, by the time they was screamin around the bend that would take them up past Mist Falls, Egan was fine with puttin her down too.

Billings, fer his part, was even more certain than Egan: them two kids had to be reckoned with and both Egan and Kelly had to be the ones to initiate that reckonin. Billings was too exposed to start anythin hisself, but where he doubted Kelly some, he knew Egan was lit for fast action. Where Hatch was concerned, Billings blamed Egan for failin to make sure the lawman wasn't already a hundred miles elsewhere.

That, of course, brought up the biggest problem: how to handle the officers comin up behind them. Egan kept tryin to noodle out a way to use Hatch. Kelly was just sick in his guts over the question. Billings knew he'd do what needed doin when the moment arrived. And he was sure the moment would arrive soon.

And then like that, all three of their radios squawked at the same time. They'd just come out over Mist Falls, stoppin beside a series of moss-covered rocky steps aflood with icy water sluicin into the falls themselves. Above, though, the way not only widened but mellowed all the way up to the edge of the meadow where Bewilder Crick started its long windin fall.

Hatch answered first. It weren't the clearest back-and-forth with Deputy Sheriff Doyle Cannon. Even with fairly decent reception, bursts of static ate up plenty of their communication. It didn't faze Hatch. He had plenty of experience under these exact conditions.

The deputies have been called back, Hatch restated after he'd signed off. Kelly and Billings reconfirmed with binoculars that the ATVs had indeed started to head back.

Those two on foot will have to draw for who gets to ride on the double, Kelly said. Deputy Shaun Brice's ATV was the only two-seater. *Or maybe they'll just trade off.*

I'd make you ride on my handlebars, Egan said with a grin. Kelly did his best to grin back.

The dirt bike can handle another, Billings pointed out.

Gammon can ride with me again, Hatch sighed.

How's that? Egan said.

Hatch explained again how the bodies had been found below and there weren't no point in goin on.

Is that so? Egan asked in a tone that weren't so forgivin and definitely the wrong one to use on Hatch.

You know somethin I don't? Hatch snarled.

And the fact was that Egan did. All three did. Egan had already told Billings and Kelly how Old Porch had spotted the Kalin kid, Landry Gatestone, and their horses up in Kirk's Cirque. The question was whether or not to tell Hatch now.

You think the horses somehow survived? Hatch even asked right then.

We've come this far, Egan finally grunted. He had no idea how to get Hatch headin back down on his own. Daylight was runnin out. The cirque weren't no small place either. Even on ATVs they'd need time to find the kids. Hatch lived for places like these too. He was in it for as long as they were. The only bright spot was that the cirque would soon deny them contact with any radios other than their own. Hatch wouldn't be able to gabble on with the deputy sheriffs.

Billings found horse manure near first thing. Hatch was still tryin to make sense of that sight when Billings then spotted the hoofprints of at least three horses, these bein the same ones from the mornin when Old Porch had surprised Kalin and chased after Landry in the helicopter.

Not long after that, the men were pokin around the campsite, Egan settin his palms down on the ashes to gauge the warmth. *There's still heat here.*

It ain't easy hidin one horse, let alone three, Billings also said, takin in how sensibly everythin had been laid out.

Secluded, Hatch said. Billings weren't the only one admirin the position. *Plenty of shelter too. No problem with a tent.*

They spread out their bags here, Billings said, pointin to the places where Kalin and Landry had indeed slept though not in sleepin bags.

Ain't this a whole new ball game, Hatch said at last. He was as confused as he was equally determined to play catch-up. *But this ain't no surprise for you.* Hatch fixed his eyes on Egan.

And Egan didn't flinch. *This is Porch business.*

Looks like one of them is sick! Kelly yelled out. He'd followed some of the tracks from the campsite and found a spot where Kalin had thrown up what little he'd had left to give. The wadded toilet paper meltin in the wet weren't a pretty sight. At least the cold kept in check the smell.

Kelly found next the tracks up to the long traverse that led to the ledge where Landry and Kalin had spotted him and his brothers crossin the Ninth Scree. Not that Kelly knew it was a dead end. He'd just started up when the sound of machines stopped him.

We got company, he yelled down.

Looks like the park rangers, Hatch said. He'd climbed up the very same rocky steps both Kalin and Landry had at various times used to survey the meadow and the lake.

Egan yelled up at Kelly to set his radio to a new frequency.

What about Dad? Hatch asked.

He ain't reachin us here, Egan answered.

And those two? Hatch asked, noddin toward the engines that kept gettin louder and louder.

This is Porch business now.

L aw Enforcement Ranger Bren Kelson, on the Honda XR dirt bike, arrived first. He'd easily spotted the tracks left by the ATVs.

I'll be, he exclaimed, genuinely surprised to discover the campsite along with plenty of evidence to suggest the presence of horses. He at once tried to raise the deputies on his police radio, but even on his Motorolla the immense mass entombin them guaranteed only static.

You'll need to get back down some if you're gonna signal them, Hatch told Bren Kelson, an exchange which Egan eyed with suspicion, though he saw the advantage too in sendin away this man, the only one of the rangers with a weapon on his hip.

Park Ranger Emily Brickey arrived next on her single-seater ATV.

Are we sure these are the ones we're lookin for? she soon enuf asked.

Are you jokin? Ranger Kelson didn't even try to conceal his scoff.

It's a question: are we sure? Emily Brickey's sincerity hesitated Kelson. Egan could've kissed her right then.

You see anybody? Egan yelled up at Kelly, but Kelly was out of earshot already, hustlin still higher until he'd reached a traverse, confirmed by hoofprints and more manure, headin back toward the entrance, where maybe, Kelly imagined, he'd encounter a way outta there, between Kirk's Cirque and Halo's Hollow, the small corrie this place abutted, even more walled up if not as high, with its central bowl on a sharp incline and loaded with jagged bits of limestone. But if there was a path to Halo's Hollow, might there be another one that could outmaneuver the cliffs markin its base? And in fact there was a trail from Halo's Hollow down to Cahoon's Staircase, which, as a reminder, was fer the moment, actually fer years to come, impassable. And Kelly knew that much but still felt certain that an even easier path would surely reveal itself, pleasant enuf to meander the horses back down to Tiffany's Vista and from there offer up the back side of either Agoneeya or Katanagos. Unless them kids was already trapped at Cahoon's Staircase?

Frankly, this direction was the only thing that made sense given the impossible headwalls that rose up behind Kelly. Furthermore, the idea of gettin outta there was makin him feel better, his lungs takin in the clean air, his stomach finally startin to settle.

B ack at the campsite, Egan's mood was the inverse of Kelly's as he continued to make calculations he was incapable of.

If they was here, they're near, he shared with the rangers. *We can confirm who they are when we find them. Let's spread out and see what turns up.*

Law Enforcement Ranger Bren Kelson agreed. *Me and Emily will head down to the lake. See what we can spot from there.*

Billings had already taken Kelly's ATV in the direction of the Upecksay Headwall. He'd spotted more tracks.

Radio if you see our horses, Egan told Kelson and Brickey as he started up his ATV. They promised they would. Neither knew Egan had switched frequencies.

What about Kelly? Hatch asked Egan.

He'll be back.

You want me to wait for him?

That's up to you, Egan snapped as he took off after Billings.

Here again was another one of those moments. Wasn't Egan just a little too eager to follow after Billings? Or maybe it was just leavin Kelly that stunk of somethin Hatch couldn't name? Though what's debated more than that is why at that very moment Law Enforcement Ranger Bren Kelson changed his mind.

Emily, Ranger Kelson suddenly said, eyein where Billings and Egan were headed. *Why don't you stick around with Officer Porch, and I'll see where this way leads. This bike can get me places none of them can reach.*

Like she was already expected to say, Park Ranger Brickey replied that that was fine by her, though her blood went cold at the thought of bein stranded now with the Porches, especially Kelly, though Kelly was still better than that Egan Porch, and Hatch did strike her as different from the rest. He was a cop after all. She and him were on the same side.

Sergio Gutierrez, once upon a time an Orvop resident, windin up a chemist who would retire in Seoul, endin his long life there too, in 2030, thank you carbon monoxide, would often bring up this moment with wry amusement, sometimes to others, more often to hisself: *A simple recombination of the two parties, for example, both rangers with Egan and Billings, would've altered everythin.* Dahl Horton, who'd eventually return to Orvop after a long stay in Pattaya, Thailand, never could say fer sure: *Or maybe it would've gotten bloodier. That's what folks keep underestimatin here: the capacity for violence that was at the ready. Folks want to believe the best about the worst. Maybe that's a quality we can admire, but for all its faith in Goodness, there's a lot of blindness that goes with such a position. And folly too. Because there was a lot of the very worst up there, and as we all found out, the worst was only gettin started.* Lizzy Lytle, from Spanish Fork, who would end up dyin from poison in Zaragoza, liked to imagine either Hatch goin the wrong direction or even a protracted argument between Kelson and Egan: *Imagine a delay of just thirty minutes! Maybe even less! Weightless! Blissful! Devout in its grand emptiness. That's what they would've found too: grand emptiness! Magic!*

But there weren't even a five-minute delay. Billings and Egan kept throttlin ahead in the direction of the Upecksay Headwall, each offerin course corrections as they came upon more evidence of three horses. Even Ranger Kelson, comin up from behind, had no trouble spottin the hoofprints, though he swore there were four horses.

Park Ranger Emily Brickey drove down to Altar Lake by herself while Hatch waited for Kelly, tryin to hail his brother on the radio, barkin at him to hustle back.

Kelly, though, had yet to stop explorin the upper reaches. Maybe he was hopin that he really could just keep goin, find that secret trail, get as far away from this mess as he could. He never even made it as far as Kalin, Landry, and the horses had. He never reached the terminus of that high ledge where he'd've at once understood that there weren't no way from there to Halo's Hollow. Though Kelly still did get one heckuva view. He wished he'd brought a camera. He really should buy a better camera. Maybe that Canon F-1. Weren't his friends always askin him to take their pictures? Kelly had time too to get better. He was barely twenty. What couldn't he do with the years ahead? He'd like to come back up here, right to this very spot in fact, and, you know, just sit and take pictures.

Hatch near cussed him out when he got back and didn't care nothin about Kelly's notions of a path outta there either. Kelly sure didn't bring up the view. He didn't quarrel none either about who should drive. He just climbed on the back and thought about what he'd just seen and savored the prize of loneliness.

When they found Park Ranger Brickey, she had not only made the acquaintance of that curious and darn near social beaver, once again out of her lodge, but had found as well Kalin's discarded underwear and his mother's hose. Hatch had nothin to say about the items, but Kelly gave them a close inspection.

I told you one of them is sick, Kelly said. *I'll bet he's dragged hisself into some hole.*

This could still be someone different, Ranger Brickey reminded both men, though even she was givin up on that possibility.

That's good work, Kelly, Hatch said, and he meant it too, though Kelly heard Hatch bein condescendin, and somethin grave then took hold of his view of his hero brother.

After they'd made it across the crick, instead of strikin out toward the southwest walls of the cirque, they clung to the far side of Altar Lake until they came across a pebbled patch of shoreline. Above it stretched a similarly pebbled stretch of ground, presentin a perfect path up toward the base of the northwest walls. Hatch didn't hesitate. Kelly held on tight. Brickey followed.

As soon as they stopped, Kelly's first move was to haul out his Remington 700 BDL, yes, beat to heck by horses and mountains, but it shot straight and with them 90-grain shells and that Leupold scope could put down a target a good ways off.

Ranger Brickey immediately wanted to know what the heck Kelly thought he was doin.

Ain't nothin wrong with aimin, he answered her.

Aimin at what? Park Ranger Brickey's heart skipped at the thought that his answer was gonna be her.

Gonna kill me that beaver.

I'll cite you if you do.

He's only goofin with you, Hatch alerted her with a smile. All Kelly got was glare.

Well, I'm not goofin with him, she answered.

Hatch laughed at that and gave her another warm smile. He admired her salt, though years later she'd remember only her terror. Whatever joshin Kelly's older brother was tryin to reassure her about, Park Ranger Brickey was reactin to somethin far more serious that she sensed under the surface. *It was like I was in deep waters, way deeper than Altar Lake. And I had to get out of there fast before somethin got at me and dragged me down. That was the feelin.*

That beaver won't even know what hit him, Kelly said, pursuin the joke, maybe, if fer sure aimin down at Altar Lake and the beaver lodge.

Park Ranger Brickey tried her best to ignore him.

BANG! Kelly suddenly shouted, loud too, enuf to get the ranger to jump and near as quick blush for havin done so.

Hatch paid neither of them any attention as he took out his Zeiss binoculars. Kelly felt stupid then for usin his rifle scope instead of his own binoculars, which still weren't worth more than spit in a cup compared to what Hatch was usin now to surveil the surroundin Katanogos walls, though Kelly could still snicker.

You figure to find them up there? Kelly asked, plenty pleased to be mockin Hatch.

The eldest Porch lowered his binoculars but didn't stop considerin the cliffs.

They're pretty mesmerizin, ain't they? Park Ranger Brickey murmured softly. She didn't need binoculars to appreciate the immensity of where they stood, a temple to some, what others have called the mountain's open palm, what most refer to as the mouth of the mountain.

That's fer sure, Hatch murmured. Park Ranger Brickey had read this eldest Porch right. *You know, I don't think I've ever been here before.*

That startled Kelly. *Like heck you haven't! You've been here at least half a dozen times!*

I have?

When Cahoon's Staircase was open?

I don't remember that at all.

Which weirded out Kelly some.

There sure ain't no horses here, Kelly said, changin the subject. *You don't need a lens to see that. They've left already. Likely the way we came in.*

Hatch and Park Ranger Brickey didn't disagree. The meadow was vast, but there was no way it concealed one let alone three horses.

They must've gotten out before we arrived, Park Ranger Brickey said, and then her radio came alive.

I'll be goshdarned, Emily . . . Law Enforcement Ranger Bren Kelson was heard to say as he struggled to describe what exactly he was seein.

Billings was the first to spot Kalin. Without much trouble, they'd followed the horse tracks down along a rocky decline to a sandy stretch that soon enuf reached the top of Altar Lake. Not far from there, the horse tracks vanished atop an area of limestone slabs big as pavers, beyond which more meadow extended to that terrifyin vertical embayment, the Upecksay Headwall, which, though still a long ways off, rose up with such authority, it rendered where they were now immaterial. There was nothin else ahead either, no large stands of trees in which to hide nor at the base any visible cracks that might offer ingress.

Like Kelly had said to Hatch and Park Ranger Brickey, both Egan as well as Law Enforcement Ranger Bren Kelson kept insistin that whoever they was followin, whoever, because Ranger Kelson, even if it was a formality, weren't acceptin yet that they was followin the same kids that killt Russel, must've already skedaddled from the cirque without notice. Egan was already figurin that if they didn't come upon them soon, cowerin under some rocky drench, they'd likely trap them down above Cahoon's Staircase. Only on the matter of how they'd been misled here did Egan and Kelson find argument. Ranger Kelson was sure the tracks they'd followed hid some method of backtrackin. Egan, however, saw the singular direction presented here. He figured Kalin and Landry had found a path that was resistant to tracks, and so Egan kept scannin them flat limestone slabs for a route by which the horses could walk back to Altar Lake and from there, by huggin the shoreline, return to the crick and by that way escape the cirque altogether. Egan hadn't forgotten how Landry's double back on Thursday had fooled him. And he'd caught on quick to the double back after the Ninth Scree. He weren't gonna let any such shenanigans fool him here.

Billings, though, brought no such imagination. He too trusted the tracks. But he also anticipated no alternate direction. He just kept drivin on over that rocky area until he reached the meadow where the ground was sandy again, and the tracks once again reappeared, evolvin from a walk to a trot to an outright gallop.

Billings raced Kelly's ATV ahead, but Law Enforcement Ranger Bren Kelson on the Honda XR dirt bike was soon behind him, which left Egan for the first time takin up the rear, a position he now prized, because he still had to figure out how he was gonna handle Kelson.

Billings kept acceleratin, but no matter how fast he went, how much closer they all got, the size of those walls remained near incomprehensible, what no amount of proximity could sort out. Worse still, shreds of clouds continued to howl down into that immense rockhewn amphitheater. It chilled those with spirits of fire and made even

750

the most focused, that still bein Egan, doubt fer a moment his doings in such a bereft and baleful place.

Egan had already begun to feel like they could drive like this until it was pitch-black and then drive for another day and still discover their destination was no closer; so resolute, so vast, and even astronomic was the Upecksay Headwall as it climbed starward before them. And then they passed within a collusion of spectral mists where only the horse tracks were visible in the soft earth until a ground layer of fog robbed them of even that. And when the mists at last departed, the tracks were lost, and they were upon more limestone and dolomite. Only now did the headwall seem upon them, like an awful shout no ear can hear but reverberant enuf to make a heart doubt. All three men, who were upright on their vehicles, sat down at once. And it weren't just how these cliffs had jumped out at them but how they had also jumped down on them, with such compoundin potential that surely at this very second it would have to complete its story and not only crush this ill-fated trio but the World itself.

Not that Billings slowed any, drivin onwards into that rocky maw until the sharp shatter of scattered rock forced him to finally stop. Surely they were already beyond where any horse should or could go? To Egan's eye no easy path presented itself where a horse could avoid maimin itself on a jagged outcroppin or in a leg-breakin gap.

Egan pulled up beside Ranger Kelson, both men bewildered and once again questionin the directive of the tracks they'd just followed. Obviously they'd been misled. Fooled again. There was no other possibility. They looked around. They looked back. They looked everywhere but ahead. And certainly not up, not like Billings was right then doin.

And then Ranger Kelson caught sight of the manure. That in itself was as amazin as it was discombobulatin, to see them warm lumps here, in this place.

And then Ranger Kelson looked up too, and everythin changed.

None there doubted what they was seein, but they still all did their best to deny it just the same.

It was awe finally that summoned up the whisper Law Enforcement Ranger Bren Kelson offered to his radio.

I'll be goshdarned, Emily . . .

Kalin had told Landry to never ever look down, ever, and for the first time she did just as he asked. She steadied her eyes on what was ahead, only on that narrow ledge she kept tryin to insist was a trail, at least a path, because a horse on a slab of rock, even if that horse was Jojo, even if that slab could handle four hooves, though barely, just didn't make no sense. In fact it was exactly that kind of senselessness that can spin a young head into a terrible vertigo without ever bein even an inch off the ground. Kalin had warned Landry about that too, what her head was gonna do, and begged her to do as he did, which was what his momma had told him to do if ever in a perilous situation: breathe slowly through your nose and *Give the mind no thought.*

How the heck's that supposed to happen?

Just let it be.

It's one of them tricks, because my head thinkin of not havin a thought is still my head thinkin a thought.

Tell her not to worry, Tom had interrupted. *She's never had a thought worth callin a thought anyway.*

What's he sayin?

Kalin had considered not tellin her but figured the fury it would stoke would at this point only help. Kalin needed her grit.

He's a mean little ghost, ain't he? You're a mean little ghost, Tom Gatestone! You know he liked sayin my head was in the clouds if it weren't full of rocks.

Or both, Tom said.

I think he was just teasin.

I weren't, Tom grunted. *You'll see.*

I don't care, Tom. Besides, where we're headin is higher than any cloud and above all the rocks too! Kalin continued tellin Landry to just say over and over: *Give the mind no thought.* Especially if her head started gettin squirrelly. Landry said she would, though the heck if she was gonna let Kalin, or anybody for that matter, tell her what to think, especially if that meant tryin to get her to not think at all.

Instead she lowered her eyes to the wall where her right knee was, or left knee, dependin on the direction of the switchback, now and then even makin a point to graze it. Even so, the wall always felt too far away, the edge of the ledge always too close.

Other than that, Landry talked to Jojo, leanin down ever so carefully to stroke his neck, always the side that was farthest from the wall, so as to keep nudgin him just a bit more from the edge that both skipped her heart and flipped her guts. Keepin an eye on Mouse also helped.

Kalin had done somethin he and Tom had done only a few times before. They'd found it worked, but it still worried them, especially if one of the horses began to object. Landry's help proved invaluable here because she'd tail-tied many a pony before, which by the way means to tie the lead of one horse to the tail of the other. Navidad didn't object to her tail bein put to such a use. Landry also showed Kalin how to quickly release the knot.

If it comes to that.

It won't come to that.

If Mouse falls, you'll go too?

We're all gettin to the top. Even Tom and Ash.

Mouse had no problem followin close to Navidad. He was always content to be near her. In fact even their present location hardly bothered him, seein as how he was with all who mattered to him. Landry still gave Mouse plenty of room, but she weren't afraid no more that Mouse might kick up at Jojo. The two were close now. Behind her was Tom on Ash, though even they weren't the last.

Kalin had warned Landry not to look back, but Landry had done it anyway, though not recklessly. She'd fixed her eyes on the rock wall and in that way eased her gaze back just in case she might catch a ripple of shadow or a disturbance on the air to better calm her pit-patterin heart. But of course all she saw was that peculiar pale mule takin up the rear, lookin pleased as peaches to be a part of this odd family, just ploddin casually up and up as if there weren't no such thing as down to consider. The sight of her did calm Landry plenty.

Kalin had told Landry from the outset that they would always go slow to make the whole way seem easy. And it was easy. There was just one catch: they could never stop. *The whole way up?!* Landry had balked. Kalin had explained then how there were three spots where they would cross behind a wall of rock. Only there could they rest a spell and catch their breath. *I thought you said this was real easy? Why would we need to catch our breath?*

Landry was just now startin to understand why. It weren't that it was so physically demandin, though it weren't not physically demandin either; rather it was because the climb was so relentless. She weren't blind to the shine of sweat slowly startin to glisten Jojo's and Mouse's coats, nor did she fail to note their breaths' quickenin outbursts of steam, especially in this air that was only gettin colder the higher they got. Landry could feel the heat buildin up in Jojo and was grateful for it even if she also knew he was toilin. What really took it out of her was the ceaseless concentration this ascent kept demandin. It wearied her like nothin she'd known before. Her daddy's words snuck up on her then: *You will discover it for yourself, Landry: vigilance demands great energies. Maybe saints do it for free, but I suspect saints are saints because they know the full price and still they pay it.*

Landry felt like she was startin to pay a little of that price right now, and it was already too much. Her breath kept shallowin, her temples throbbed. She had on her gloves, but she knew that the backs of her hands were chappin like her lips were crackin. She missed her daddy. She missed him so much.

She'd already lost count of how many switchbacks they'd made. Maybe that was a good thing. Some had led out onto long easy ledges, while others offered narrow if thankfully short tables of uncertain stone. They'd also passed by plenty of options that looked far more accommodatin. She even felt herself gettin more exhausted tryin to figure out why they was pickin this turn, what looked scary as heck, instead of the one a little farther on that looked flat and wide as a barn aisle. It was like some wild maze up here, only instead of bein cut out of corn or hedges, and of course horizontal, this one was made of rock and mostly vertical. When Landry finally accepted that no amount of second-guessin was gonna help with this part of their journey, she put her faith in Kalin's knowin the way up and finally relaxed.

She even sung a bit and even thought once to goad Kalin to kick up the pace, but she knew now to not give over every thought to her lips. Then an especially narrow series of ledges ladderin up and up made her grateful for the pace Kalin maintained. When they was back again on a long and almost wide ledge, Kalin surprised her by lookin back. It was the first time he'd done so since they'd started.

Remember what I told you, Landry: Don't look down! Don't look back either. Give the mind no thought. But most of all don't look down! Not until we make the top. Up there you can look to your heart's content. I promised you thee most beautiful sight in the world. And I aim to keep that promise.

Landry tried to summon up the biggest Gatestone grin imagin-able, and though she didn't come close, not like when she and Tom had once upon a time been goofin off together, just lyin on their backs on the green grass, makin up fun stuff about the clouds, flyin up there with their thoughts, how they was blue kites in that blue sky, until only Tom was the kite and she was holdin on to him, Landry swearin she'd never let go, he'd be her pet kite forever . . . a smile, however frag-ile and fearful, did manage then to lighten up her face some.

More choices, more lithic switchbacks, presented themselves. Kalin never hesitated. Up they went, ladderin from one ledge to another, just risin on up, up and up, up and up and up some more, now and then briefly kissed, enwrapped, consumed, abandoned by ghostly veils of cloud that by their arrival and passin left the rock wetter, which is way scarier than any ghost, though none of the horses slipped even once. Them horseshoe studs was sure doin their job.

On one shelf Landry didn't even have to ride so close to the wall. That was one heckuva relief. Landry even kinda glimpsed out at the cirque. It weren't a real look and she hadn't looked down. As fast as she'd looked outward, she'd quick returned to the wall, if still cher-ishin that beautiful fragment of the cloud-swept cirque. They was high up enuf now for that great encircled lake and meadow to lose the details that describe distance and height. Just another one of the many great vistas they'd already beheld on their way here: of Utah Valley, Isatch Canyon, so many wild and rugged ridges dark with trees and gray bluffs. The farther away they got, the flatter everythin seemed. And flat for some reason always struck her as inconsequential. What really scared the livin heck out of her was the next switchback to yet more narrowness. Landry ground her teeth, gripped the reins harder, gripped harder her saddle with her knees, which she was a good enuf rider and too in love with Jojo to keep doin, relaxin her seat, her hands, nibblin her lips only.

Music, in the end, helped the most. It was like a completely different part of her head, what knew nothin about mountaintops or gravity. Landry even found she could mark loose time against the clop of Jojo's hooves. *Clop-Clop-clip-Clop*. She realized she had no notion as to why that clip kept comin up on the third beat. She'd check Jojo's hooves when she could. His gait, though, was smooth and rollin even when he was just walkin. *Clop-Clop-clip-Clop*. Landry let loose a whole hodgepodge of songs then includin parts of *Here Comes the Sun*, *Less of Me*, *Will the Circle Be Unbroken*, *I Still Miss Someone*, and even *Another One Bites the Dust*, plus family favorites just passed down and stuff that drifted melodically through her head. Tom was the undisputed whistler in the family but Landry could sing.

She weren't ever singin so loud and got even quieter when they turned up upon a ledge that soon narrowed down to pretty much Jojo's exact width, down to a hair, threatenin, it seemed, to keep slimmin that way until in a few more strides Jojo's hoof would surely find only air. Landry's voice got so soft then, she weren't sure she could even hear herself.

Like he sensed her growin skittishness, Kalin hollered back, and in the most easy way too, like he was some trail guide deliverin up historical tidbits, how this way was used plenty by bighorn sheep and mountain goats.

They run it like it's a highway.

Navidad and Mouse both whickered. Maybe they appreciated the information. Jojo snorted his approval. Was that another snort? Maybe the mule approved as well?

Landry considered yellin out about Kalin failin to mention horses. Though she already knew this was the very first time horses had ever come this way. Not yet even a third of the way up the headwall, Navidad, Mouse, and Jojo, and Ash, and the mule, had already far exceeded history's ledger on equine ascents by way of such tenuous stone paths.

755

Kalin, though, weren't wrong about the bighorn sheep and mountain goats. They'd managed these byways, and far narrower ones too, for centuries if not millennia. Even some squirrels had gotten the whole way up accompanied by plenty more who had not. A few mountain lions in pursuit of bighorn sheep had reached the summit, though not a one had ever survived the way back down.

The human story of this wall, especially by this route, remained extremely faint. Of course the back side was a different story. Plenty of hikers, by way of Heber, had explored what was familiarly called the northeast summit trails. The southeast face, however, was a different story. The Upecksay Headwall, also called Kataclysm by some, with its rotten limestone, fractured sandstone, and now and then an outcroppin of disloyal dolomite, was largely avoided by rock climbers. The curious part is that the very first one to summit this headwall wasn't a climber proper but a photographer.

The way the story goes, Myer Melville, born and raised in Orvop but also an experienced alpinist in the Swiss Alps, where he'd spent many summers thanks to his mother's daddy, had decided one August day in 1916 to attempt the wall. Back then it was just called Ark's Headwall for no reason ever divulged. Myer Melville had brung along Clarissa Abbot, who was just as skillt with her Vest Pocket Kodak camera, or VPK, as he was with ropes. She was a character in her own right, *half-beautiful*, she'd always declare, and then explain how she'd proved it too. Self-portraits that included only the left side of her face got folks droolin. The right side of her face, however, not so much. It weren't that different either, but there you have it. Clarissa Abbot was proud of her discovery. *Always halfway there,* she loved to quip.

Now back to Myer Melville. He weren't some incautious fool, and he weren't gonna die this day or any other day on this here big burst of mountain. In fact he'd die on a street corner in Payson, shot through the pelvis by a man who misidentified him as his wife's lover.

On the day Myer Melville attempted his summit, he used pitons and carabiners, which was a relatively new addition to his climbin arsenal, and while makin his ascent safer, his relative inexperience with the new equipment slowed him down quite a bit.

Clarissa Abbot, meanwhile, took pictures from below and then soon enuf found the curious ledges that after some trial and error brought her about even with the rock climber. Soon enuf she was takin pictures of him from above. And soon after that, after she'd run out of film, she continued to explore almost lazily the various ledges, settlin her mind with how, when she'd gone as far as she could go, she'd just go back down and wait for Myer Melville at the bottom.

She was delighted to find on the way up three rocky retreats, which she likened to the Eigerwand Station midway on the Jungfrau railway, *only much smaller*. Clarissa in fact had never visited Switzerland but spent hours with the photographs and postcards Myer Melville had brought home.

Imagine her surprise, when Clarrisa Abbot suddenly found herself at the very top. Though she was not nearly as amazed as the hikers who had arrived by way of the northeast trails. Fortunately for her, they insisted she accompany them back by way of Heber. Myer Melville, fer his part, never got higher than two hundred feet. He'd assumed Clarissa Abbot had already headed back and figured he would catch up with her on the way down, likely around Cahoon's Staircase. When the two did connect again, he was miffed to hear that Halfway Clarrisa Abbot had gone all the way to the top. At first he didn't believe her, of course, and their friendship ended right there. Though Myer Melville had no choice but to believe her when he saw the photographs and later heard for hisself from the hikers who were still agog at beholdin this young woman come up to the summit by way of the headwall wearin only a light sweater with a camera slung over one shoulder.

The story, because it was of a woman and not a known climber, didn't gain much attention back then, though some hikers later tried to find the route she'd described. What they discovered was a lab-yrinth of vertical choices that seemed to invariably lead to ledges offerin no other choice than an about-face. Even worse, one hiker got stuck up there. This took place in 1941. The poor fella kept makin choices that led him to one dead end after another. Finally, with panic overtakin him, not to mention dusk, he reached the end of a ledge that was four feet away from another ledge that was much wider and looked far more promisin. In fact that was not the case: it weren't con-nected to any possible path back down. He'd have trapped hisself fer sure goin that way. Not that it mattered. He flubbed the jump and fell four hundred feet to his death. That was poor Stemmons Jolley, not even eighteen. His folks, likely to comfort themselves, said his death on Katanogos still beat dyin on some beach in the South Pacific.

After that no one really tried again. There just weren't that much interest in the wall. As plenty of climbers who'd considered it told anyone who was interested, Katanogos weren't Yosemite. *It was just lousy rock.*

There still persists unconfirmed rumors that before the Vietnam War ended, one Isatch U student, who like Clarissa Abbot was not a rock climber, had come up to Kirk's Cirque. He'd dropped not one, not two, but three tabs of LSD, called Window Pane, and ablaze in that state had wandered onto the ledges. He not only summited but returned the way he'd come up, never missin a turn, never even hesitatin at a turn. And he did it in just under two hours. His friends assumed the whole thing was a hallucination or a lie. The friends who were not his friends reported his drug use to university and Church officials. Some months later, and curiously on the exact same day, he was both expelled from the university and excommunicated from the Church. He never did stop tellin that story even if no one ever believed him, or if they did, he didn't value their belief enuf to make it count. It troubled him at first, but in later years, once he'd settled for good in Big Sur, he came to appreciate the singular experience he'd had the good fortune to have and was finally grateful.

That was Bridger Ellsworth. He hung out with Henry Miller once and Brenda Venus too, though not at the same time.

As Kalin, Landry, and the horses now scrambled up pebbled stairs of stone that briefly opened up to offer ample space to manage the next cutback to the left, Landry tried her darndest to ignore the renewed narrowness ahead as well as the incline's increased steepness.

Kalin and Navidad were already on it, unperturbed, or so it seemed; at least they looked unflaggin, followed by an unbothered Mouse, who seemed tireless. Landry did her best to return her focus to the immediate path ahead, to that wall on her right, to the music of Jojo's steps. *Clop-Clop-clip-Clop. Clop-Clop-clip-Clop.* They never faltered, though this time Landry did, findin it near impossible not to imagine some misstep intrudin upon that beautiful rhythm, some stutter or distortion that would signal a slip. But Jojo didn't stutter nor slip. *Clop-Clop-clip-Clop.* Jojo stayed true. *Clop-Clop-clip-Clop.* Even if Landry couldn't.

What was gettin at her weren't this particular moment either, nor the stretch of ledge she now braved, but rather the compoundin effects of the journey so far. If she could just clear her mind of the past, she'd be fine. But that was no small feat. Even with eyes locked on only rock or on Mouse's swishin tail, the quiet and cold crispness of the air, the impossible expanse to the left reverberatin in her ears, like a ceaseless and bellowin silence. At least Landry continued to heed Kalin's warnin, and she applied her remainin energies to that purpose: she knew the vastness wanted her to look but she refused.

They was now trespassin on byways not meant for featherless creatures, and fer sure not two teenagers on horses, even if Mouse did seem perfectly at home, though Mouse seemed at home wherever he was so long as he was near Navidad. Landry tried to breathe just through her nose, slow as she could. She even mumbled to herself, *Give the mind no thought.* But none of it did any good. She felt it first in her ankles, like cement was bein poured in under the skin, settin fast around the bones and tendons, her elbows too startin to feel this same quick-set thickenin. And why not? What business was it of hers to be up here? There weren't even a bird around! Better to just turn into a tree or the rock itself than take one more step. Not that Jojo agreed. He might not be a bird, but he weren't no tree nor stone neither. He was a horse. *Clop-Clop-clip-Clop.* Jojo stayed true. *Clop-Clop-clip-Clop.* Even if Landry knew that if she kept seizin up like this, Jojo might respond to her rigidity with a misstep and that would be all her fault.

At least Landry's voice hadn't petrified. She returned to singin, at first soft as a whisper, then a little louder, and that loosened up the rest of her some, and her heart calmed, and her breath slowed as she eventually found them melodies Tom used to whistle along with. Maybe he was whistlin now. Landry wanted to yell up to Kalin and ask if that was so, but she was too afraid that if she stopped singin, her voice might betray her to stone. Landry couldn't even stick with one song either but kept trippin from one snippet to another. Those she knew well. And others she weren't so sure about. Some she didn't even know where they came from. All the while Jojo stayed the course. *Clop-Clop-clip-Clop.* Jojo stayed true. *Clop-Clop-clip-Clop.*

> *Though the fire is lost,*
> *the match is spent,*
> *light surrounds us*
> *and we are met.*

Landry repeated these lines twice, though the second time around the notes ground down into somethin huskier with the words changin too:

> *When the flame is out*
> *and the Vestas gone,*
> *death overspills us*
> *and we go it on our own.*

Landry stopped, her voice gone, her joints too. There weren't just dark music up here. Now another kind of darkness, swifter than the most relentless dusk, had fallen upon them. Even Mouse was slowin. And then Kalin stopped. The wall to her right was still there, but now to her left was also rock. Even above her there was rock. Nothin but rock. And weren't that such a beautiful thing? Even if fer a moment

Landry swore they really had turned to rock. They was like one of them old Greek myths Mrs. Annserdodder had taught them. All that livin and supposin about what was to come next, wealth, reputation, wonder, glory, love, and then abruptly you're turned to stone as a les-son for others, others like Landry and Kalin who in class would rather think about any other thing than that lesson, what even now Landry couldn't remember. What had the stone been tryin to teach her?

Except they weren't stone, not yet, and there was Kalin, now on foot, squeezin past Mouse, smilin too. She could see he'd somehow tied up Navidad to some hidden fixture on the wall and, judgin by how they was nibblin the floor, scattered about some feed. Jojo was gettin his palmful now too. And some water from Kalin's canteen.

You okay? he asked, his smile dimmin just a bit at the sight of her.

Are we done? she asked. She still couldn't move, but she weren't gonna say nothin about that. Her jaw at least was goin again.

Come on! Stretch your legs! You did great! His hand on hers, and even a gloved hand on her gloved hand helped release more of her to herself, allowin Landry to finally slip off Jojo and stand upon solid ground.

Did you look down? he asked her.

Not once.

Me neither! I know some folks can do it but I can't. I reckon with our friends here this isn't the time to start figurin out whether we'd be bothered by such a sight or not. Like I said, at the top, we'll get our fill. Kalin sounded near glib now, nothin like he'd sounded out on the ledges. His happiness frightened Landry some because it meant he'd been afraid too, and whatever ecstatic relief he was enjoyin now wasn't persuadin her to feel the same.

In the gap between Jojo and Mouse, he told her to do like he was doin: some easy jumpin jacks, balancin on one leg, swingin his arms around, makin fists. Maybe it was some help to see that Kalin too might know what it was like to freeze up like she'd just done, even if he never said so, just encouragin her to keep warm and loose.

Kalin then explained how here was the first of three breaks they'd get on the wall. This one had the longest passage and was the dark-est too. Also the narrowest. The second one was shorter but plenty wide. She'd see. Kalin had already hammered pitons with carabiners up there. They could tie up the horses and check their hooves and relax. The third one was the shortest and also narrow, but they'd be so close to the top, it wouldn't matter. They'd just be passin through.

These retreats, if that's a fair thing to call them, were located in one of the gigantic and jagged outcroppins that many folks called the teeth of Kirk's Cirque, though plenty of other folks referred to those protrusions of blue limestone as the pillars of the mountain.

For the more dentally inclined, the cirque had a total of four such fangs, which is where the notion arose that up here, one could behold the teeth of the mountain. Or at least the lower teeth, with the whereabouts of the upper teeth still undisclosed. Tom and Kalin delighted in such imagery, as it made of this mountain a monster, which is unfair to Katanogos, always so much more than a monster.

Though she preferred pillars, Landry couldn't expel from her head this notion of fangs, the lower ones, with them upper ones just waitin above the storm clouds, set to snap down, tear them all up . . .

So are we inside a cavity? Landry asked.

Kalin laughed. *A pretty bad one!*

Never thought I'd be so happy about a rotten tooth.

We can be thankful this mountain never heard of a toothbrush.

That made Landry laugh some, and Kalin laughed gently along with her, his eyes twinklin enuf to assure her that she really could relax.

Here's the good news, he said then. *We're done with the longest stretch. And here's the extra good news: we only got seven switchbacks left. That's all. Just seven turns that are so quick and effortless, you'll forget to count them.*

What's the bad news?

There ain't none.

There's always bad news when you start out with good news. That's the way it works.

Well, it's workin different this time.

When you say there's good news then you gotta follow with bad news.

What is wrong with my sister? Tom drawled.

Okay. Then I guess the bad news is that we're more than halfway done, and ain't that a pity.

How's my brother doin?

He's startin to remember things.

Where's he at?

By Navidad now, but I think Ash would prefer to be back here with Jojo.

What kinda things is he rememberin?

All sorts. Seems the higher we get, the clearer his memory gets. He remembers tellin me about this wall. About Terrence Olsen.

Terrence Olsen?

Come on now, Landry! A few more jumpin jacks. This'll get us warm again.

Was he tellin you about Terrence's horse?

Yazzie.

Tom loved that story.

Tom concurred with a nod.

He still loves that story. Kalin confirmed.

Though it's more Yazzie that comes through, Tom admitted.

You know Tom was to blame? Landry clarified, launchin into her own recap, if just for somethin mild to yammer about while Kalin kept urgin them to do more jumpin jacks.

Here was the gist: Terrence Olsen was the Gatestones' farrier as well as a farrier for plenty of others up and down the valley. *He could handle just fine your timid horse as well as a real heckacious one. A paint named Yazzie was considered high on the heckacious scale, though Terrence could handle her just fine whenever he came around for her hooves.*

Yazzie was owned by the Cottoms, a sweet family with a stable south of Payson. They weren't the best riders, but they kept three ponies, and they loved them all, even Yazzie, who none of them could ride but who their horses adored.

Finally, though, *Mr. Cottom got fed up with havin a horse they couldn't do nothin with* and brought around trainers and, after they failed, any brave kid with a hat who boasted he could do better. *Of course Tom had to come around,* and he'd kept his hat on too and even stayed on her back longer than the rest, but Yazzie still wanted nothin to do with him, and if she weren't buckin, she'd be tryin to scrape him off on any nearby fence. If that failed, *Yazzie would lie down and roll him off.* Tom, of course, thought it was hysterical, but more so he was intrigued, especially when he noticed how Yazzie always relaxed around Terrence Olsen, *and that's when Tom made his most outlandish claim.*

Terrence wouldn't hear it. He loved horses, loved shoein horses, but he also didn't ride them no more, seein as how four years earlier he'd broke his back and mangled a knee in accidents unrelated to horses. *Show me a carousel and I might consider it,* Terrence would always say. *But you know Tom,* Landry said, with Kalin noddin along, *when he's got somethin in his head, he don't let go, whether it's some crazy adventure to some absurd crossin or just gettin Terrence Olsen on the back of a paint that was bound to break his back again.* But Tom was patient and persistent, assertin throughout that the reason Yazzie weren't gonna buck or try to scrape Terrence off on no fence pole or even roll on her back was because Yazzie had fallen in love with Terrence.

Oh how Terrence laughed at that, louder and longer than even Tom was known to manage. He only stopped laughin when Tom promised him the Gatestones would not just double, not just triple, but quadruple his fees if he got bucked off, and Terrence only stopped his laughter so he could get a bigger breath to laugh even louder and even longer, because he already knew that a kid, even if that kid was none other than Tom Gatestone, would have less than zero to say about what his folks was gonna pay the family farrier. So Tom offered instead to work for Terrence Olsen for a year, for free too, but if Tom was right, Terrence had to buy Yazzie from the Cottoms.

Now Landry admitted that no one knew fer sure why Terrence really did try to climb up onto Yazzie. *I think it was because, like a lot of folks, he just loved the heck out of Tom. You just couldn't help fallin for the way Tom viewed the world. It was always so much fun.*

Boy, was Terrence surprised when he grabbed the saddle horn and slipped a boot toe into the stirrup and Yazzie didn't budge. Terrence stood up then in just the one stirrup, figurin Yazzie would sprint away and he'd just step off and have Tom as a slave fer a year. But Yazzie still didn't budge. Terrence then swung over his leg and waited for the buckin to commence. But Yazzie still didn't budge. Tom started doin his little dance around because he knew, like Terrence knew, that Yazzie was ornery, but she weren't devious.

Terrence Olsen rode Yazzie around the paddock easy as a kid on a mule in a pettin zoo. He rode Yazzie around the farm. The Cottoms came out to gape at the transformation. And when he finally dismounted, he had hisself a private little chat with Yazzie, who responded with what can only be described as horse kisses. The Cottoms had not yet grasped the situation and figured Yazzie was now rideable. That was not the case. If one of them even dared to raise a boot toward a stirrup, Yazzie would get to snappin at once and, if that message weren't clear enuf, start throwin back her rear legs. The Cottoms all scratched their heads, because when Terrence approached again, Yazzie welcomed him on her back.

It was the darndest thing, and though everyone took their time comin round to Tom's way of thinkin, by the end, whether they believed it or not, everyone agreed that Yazzie did have somethin for Terrence. Tom didn't even need to goad Terrence then about their agreement because Terrence, see, *Clop-Clop-clip-Clop,* had already fallen for Yazzie.

They're still together, Landry said with a sigh. *My momma believes that because of Terrence takin on Yazzie, he met Mary-Beth and so that's why he now has three kids, all girls, and has stayed happy for years. The girls can ride Yazzie. Even Mary-Beth but no one else. Last year Tom thought he'd try to get a leg up. Yazzie bit him hard on the back of the arm. Tom was cryin, it hurt so bad, but he was laughin too. I tried. I near lost my ear. Tom said he only knew two horses that could give little Yazzie's heart competition.*

I'm bettin that'd be Jojo and Ash? Kalin surmised.

Landry nodded.

I'd like to meet Yazzie one day, just to say hello of course.

I'll be happy to introduce you when we get back, Landry said, finally quittin these jumpin jacks, even if truth be told, they had called up some warmth in her.

It weren't about Yazzie, though, that Tom was goin on about, Kalin now clarified. *See, it seems it was Terrence who was the one who knew about how to walk right up to the summit by way of these ledges. Wide enuf too to ride a horse on. He'd heard it from some fella named Bridger Ellsworth.*

And this Bridger Ellsworth had a detailed-enuf accountin of what we've just been through to tell it to Terrence, who told it to my brother, who then told it to you? Landry weren't buyin none of it.

Heck no! At least not where I'm concerned. I never got no details, only that it was possible. I had to come up here on my own a bunch of times to find the way. I used chalk to mark the mistakes.

Kalin, I gotta tell you somethin. Landry was meanin to tell him how she'd locked up, and while the jumpin jacks and the arm swingin and the gabbin had helped, she was still likely to lock up again if she had to ride Jojo out onto another ledge.

Okay, but first I gotta ask you a favor: I need your help now, Landry, for this next part.

Landry nodded. She knew he knew she'd do whatever she could to help him. What he didn't know was how just her noddin in agreement had scared her bad enuf to start up that quick-set joint thickenin, startin with her fingers and toes, with her knees and elbows next.

Just keep Mouse here, Kalin explained. *That's all. I fixed a place to hitch him to, but Mouse won't necessarily listen to a wall like he'll listen to you. You know how he likes to stay close to Navidad.*

Sure. But where are you gonna be? Landry couldn't hide the panic suddenly etchin up her speech.

I'm gonna ride this next part alone. Once I reach our second stop, I'll tie up Navidad there and come back for Mouse. And then I'll come back for you.

Navidad and Mouse will be okay there?

The second one's comfy as a hotel suite.

I'll believe that when I see it.

It's even got a shower and bath.

This whole place is a shower and bath . . . Just no hot water, Landry added with a soft laugh.

Can you imagine how good that would feel?

Is he laughin? Landry asked.

Let's just say if he'd laughed like that on the ledges, he'd have fallen off.

Then it's settled.

How's that?

We'll keep the laughin to just these rest stops.

Kalin smiled and even extended his gloved hand: *Deal.* And his hand was firm and strong, and even through her own glove, it felt warm. Landry realized she didn't want to let go. She didn't want to lose hold of the feel of him, the care that was there for her, what was visible on his face, in his eyes, along with what she would never unsee: Kalin was plenty scared too.

And as he moved off, it sure didn't help to behold him so frail and shaky, thin enuf now to squeeze by Mouse without touchin a hair. It was a miracle he could even walk. Surely whatever grace she'd thought she'd witnessed when he'd ridden Navidad out of that collapsin scree had departed. When he returned to her, his hand trembled as he placed Mouse's lead in her own hand, far steadier than his.

Landry's mouth went dry and bitter as she swung back up on Jojo. Ahead of her she watched the silhouette of Kalin swing up on Navidad and then without ceremony or fuss head off toward the light. She walked slowly after him and only pulled up when his silhouette departed this dark and Kalin was once again afire with the light of the day's end.

He didn't look back. He just settled his hat once and then rode out into the mists maulin the face of that icy gray stone.

Before he'd vanished completely, though, Landry realized that this hesitancy of form, what she'd have sworn to any jury was now his character and condition, had likewise vanished completely. Once again upon that black mare's back he was transformed, his every quality and action in concert with his circumstances and destination; as if whatever strength we all believe we store for such impossible challenges had in Kalin's case been emptied entirely from his keep, which he no longer had need for, because a greater power now possessed him requirin no reserves, no keep, only Navidad.

At that moment, Landry wanted to follow him. Of course, she would follow him! She even nudged Jojo another step forward but then rightly called a halt to his momentum, immediately afraid that Mouse might get the idea that they was really movin on. And Mouse did get exactly that idea and didn't take too kindly to find his followin after Navidad suddenly halted. Landry had to devote plenty of her energies then, as well as many a soft tone, to defy Mouse's insistence on the way forward. He even tried to rub the lead and halter-bridle off on the rock walls.

Landry had to back up Jojo to back Mouse away from the exit of that damp and chilly but, given their surroundins, safe haven. And he finally did settle but with annoyed snorts and a copious pronounce-ment punctuated by a dump of steamy manure. And Landry was grateful. There were plenty worse arguments to be had with a horse, and not a one had a better endin than this one. Imagine if Mouse had decided to get kick happy? Or had just reared up, smackin his head on the rock ceilin, startlin, and after that boltin forward without any thought to the path? She'd of course try to hold on, but what if her grip failed? Not somethin you want to consider when the path ahead already lies hundreds of feet up.

In fact that first refuge in the fang was located nearly six hundred feet above Altar Lake, and though Landry applied no numbers to their place upon that great headwall, she had already begun, by the time kept by her heart's endurin rhythms and the way her skin tingled and ached before the vastness that continued to enlarge around them, to sense their ongoin translation from that place of articulate ground to that place above holdin out a summit of impossible expression.

Landry's breath started to shallow then. The stiffness returned soon after, this time attackin all her joints at once.

Landry forced herself to twist around in her saddle.

I'm glad you're here, Effy, she told the white mule.

That's right. And, yes, no question, an immensity of debates has since this moment stormed around Landry's nominative utterance. Perhaps it was misheard, but when do the winds mishear? It was not misheard, of course. Perhaps then it was a credible coincidence? Perhaps Landry already had a number of rag dolls she happily called Effy because that was her favorite name? A good suggestion, but she did not. And not only did Landry have no such duly named playthings, she had never heard the name Effy before. Nor did she ever say it again either, to that mule or anybody else.

Sometimes the ghost just speaks through us and brings forth a form beyond our intelligence and context. We have only one duty then: to listen. Though that is often the hardest duty of all and one failed by a great many, just like Landry also failed here. She never again, even up until her last dyin breath, considered what name had crossed the threshold of her own lips, by its own volition. What a gift. She couldn't even recall sayin it.

Of course, while there's no question of her gratitude toward the mule, her breath easin up, her limbs relaxin some, that greetin is still worth considerin without any thought for the speaker. For what about the one listenin? What about the mule herself? Though evidently at peace with her newfound company, what about the challenges of this journey? Perhaps Landry's expression of thanks and welcome was exactly what that beautiful figure of white and black just then needed? Who are we to ever know the heart of a mule? Especially this mule? Who are we to deny let alone forget her a place?

And then Kalin was back. Just like he said he would be. Carryin his saddle and smilin. As Landry hopped down to help tack up Mouse, Kalin described how easy it had been, with the only taxin part bein the saddle and havin to lug it back down. Navidad was safe and settled.

I let her know Mouse was comin up next and gave her some more oats, Kalin said as he tightened the cinch, makin sure Mouse's withers had room under the pad and gullet. Landry made sure the halter-bridle and reins was in place.

Is Tom here? Out of everythin she needed to know about what came next, that's what Landry's heart demanded to know first.

He's kinda caught in the middle. He wants to be with Navidad, but he's outside waitin for Mouse. He and Ash don't drift far from either now.

Landry looked out toward the empty patch of gray that framed the impossible ledge.

What about Jojo?

Tom likes stayin close to all the horses.

Kalin, I don't think I can do this.

Do what? All you gotta do is hang out with Jojo. Sit down. Hold the walls if you like.

Kalin pulled hisself up onto Mouse then, once again transformed from a boy born to burden somethin to now someone lighter than air, ridin out onto that ledge of mist, and vanishin near at once too thanks to the light, thanks to the incline, thanks to the distance leadin to the necessary turn Landry could not see.

With this departure, Jojo stomped a hoof and swished his tail. Landry wanted to do the same. Did do the same. Well, at least she stomped a foot. It didn't help none though. What if Kalin had just then fallen? Would she have heard it? Could both him and Mouse already be dead? Nothin in that patch of light was sayin otherwise. What would she do then? If he didn't come back? Where would she go? Fer one thing, she'd have to get Navidad. That much was sure. She couldn't leave that poor mare abandoned in so unhorsely a place as this. But she couldn't leave Jojo here alone either. She would have to dare the path Kalin had just died on only without knowin the way. She'd just have to trust that this part was as straight ahead or as straight up and easy as he'd just said. And Landry realized then that she did trust Kalin. But what about after that? Kalin had said little about what followed after the second cavity in this gosh-awful tooth. But what choice did she have but to keep headin up? It weren't like she could go down. To say nothin of them men below, just the thought of havin to manage any one of those ledges durin a descent, ledges likely askitter too with whatever debris was kicked down by three horses, four horses, maybe there were even ghost pebbles, why that shocked Landry like her whole back was suddenly splashed with water not a degree over freezin. And more perverse still, Landry then began to sweat. Her breath shallowed again, only this time it got to raspin. She hadn't sat down or grabbed hold of the walls, but even after she'd climbed back on Jojo, she couldn't stop squirmin in her saddle, if just to keep from seizin up, and Jojo's ears were now goin this way and that way until the big blue horse finally threw up his head and snorted in a plea for her to stop. Landry obeyed at once, draggin her arm across her face to wipe away the sweat drippin into her eyes. On the bright side, she weren't cold no more. Not one bit. Her fingertips felt hot enuf to scald. Even the space between her toes felt molten enuf to melt through her boot soles. She was a lit torch in a honeyless comb of stone. Landry even laughed, and her laugh echoed in them narrow confines, so much so that it suddenly didn't sound like just her no more.

Tom Gatestone? she asked the shadows. *Is that you?*

A nd then Kalin was back, this time without saddle and reins.
Is Tom here? Landry at once demanded.
He's up above now. Wants to know what's takin you so long.
He's right. Why didn't I just follow you?
We'll do it right now. Ready?
Landry swallowed hard, which weren't enuf to swallow down the thought that with just one slip she'd be gone from these heights. That's what kept possessin and repossessin her mind. In less time than it took to take a breath, she could end both hers and Jojo's lives. It was too astonishin to consider, and yet she couldn't stop reconsiderin it.
I don't know, Landry said.
You're gonna be fine. Kalin even nodded extra, though to Landry it looked like he was tryin to reassure hisself. *I can't ride Jojo. Only you can do that.*
Maybe you could lead him up? Landry proposed then, at once as appalled by the suggestion as Jojo surely would've been if he'd been payin attention. Maybe he had been payin attention. He sure started snortin up a fuss, exhalin great plumes, even backin up in protest.
Kalin smiled, but he also shook his head. *There's nothin ahead that you ain't already done. Heck, you've done harder a thousand times elsewhere. Jojo ain't gonna make no mistake either, and you'll be there to make sure of it. Just keep slow and steady. When you reach the first switchback to the right, you'll have three more quick ones right after. Left, right, left. They're short and easy, and trust me they'll feel good. The fifth and last one's gonna give you plenty of*

room to take your right turn, and then it's near straight ahead to that hotel suite I promised you. Just don't run me over, he added with a wink. I'll be walkin ahead of you the whole way. You'll have somewhere to focus your eyes, and you don't even have to remember any of this because I'll be showin you exactly where the turns are. It won't be nothin.

I don't know, Landry said again.

You don't need to.

Kalin didn't wait for her to say any more about her doubts. He just strode out into the misty gray, this time not touchin his hat, there weren't no need for that, nor did he look back, there weren't no need for that either. If he had, Landry would've froze fer sure, but just the thought of Kalin leavin her alone again was good enuf reason to ease Jojo forward. The mule followed suit.

Like she'd seen Kalin do on his big rides, Landry had also pulled off her gloves. She too wanted as little as possible between her and the feel of Jojo's mind. Her fingers stayed light as mist on the reins, like they was right at Jojo's mouth, quieter than the aftermath of even the softest kiss.

And then like that she and Jojo were out in the open again. And they did not fall. They did not vanish. The ledge was right there and stayed there, wet fer sure but more ample than her imagination had allowed for, wider in fact than the last ledge.

What Landry then reencountered was that silence again, beneath the storm, beneath the winds, that bellowin absence, which this time she didn't resist, which was when she realized that the distant but persistent whine of engines searchin the cirque had ceased. When did that happen? Whatever the answer, it wobbled Landry's thoughts, if only because it made her feel more self-conscious, like she was now under a new kind of observation, hoverin real near too, maybe with crosshairs.

In fact right then Egan and Billings were parked at the base of the Upecksay Headwall. Law Enforcement Ranger Kelson had just glimpsed Kalin on Mouse, high up, disappearin into the wall itself, followed a bit later by Landry on Jojo, this time with Egan and Billings witnessin that equine blur, emergin lower down, movin laterally at first but soon enuf ascendin that impossible face to where Kalin had disappeared. Egan swore he'd caught sight of someone walkin out in front. Billings and Kelson had seen no such thing.

Not that Landry could see any of these men. She kept her eyes fixed on Kalin strollin on ahead like it weren't no big deal, and truth was, if right now they'd've been down on them big flat rocks that bank parts of Orvop River, it wouldn't have been no big deal. But Landry weren't able to pretend this here was a Sunday ride. She chewed on her lips and tilted her head side to side like she was tryin to crack a neck that wouldn't crack. But still her eyes never left Kalin's back. Unfortunately that weren't so comfortin a sight. Once again, without a horse, Kalin seemed exceptionally scrawny, disjointed, falterin, and otherwise betrayed by his current corporeal form. At least Landry could relate some to his feebleness. Heck, Kalin weren't just relatable now but easily bested. And that helped some too, even if Landry never did actually try to best him.

As Caracy Rudder, Ms. Melson, and Mrs. Annserdodder would together ponder: was this then now the standard tellin of Orpheus, who by a backward glance returned Eurydice to the underworld? Though in this case, if Landry was Eurydice, to lose sight of Kalin was to risk fallin from his company. *Unless of course, this is round one, how Eurydice died in the first place,* Caracy Rudder would joke. Ms. Melson would say she had no more time for such nonsense. This was in 2015, and on that fall afternoon the teachers had found themselves at the Caraway Eatery in Rome. Mr. Rudder was coughin a bit and belittlin any life even partially spent in Orvop. Mrs. Annserdodder shushed him, tellin him he knew that weren't true. *Besides, Kalin looked back plenty of times along the way to make sure she was all right.* At which point these three resolved to once and for all abandon such confoundin comparisons with the Orpheus-Eurydice story, and even if their efforts failed, at least for a little while they tried.

Anyway, Landry's gaze never wandered. And when they reached that first switchback to the right, which Kalin had to scramble up double time to keep well enuf ahead, it just weren't a big thing. In fact it was a comfort. Even the next three turns was like racin up some stairs in an old bell tower so long as there weren't no tower nor bell. The way up stayed plenty clear and was even roomy. Jojo almost seemed relieved havin to set hisself to the task. It sure beat standin in some cave. Except for pressin her leg a little and one or two gentle pulls on the reins, Landry hardly had to do much around the turns, and the higher they got, the more smoothly it went.

The fifth and last switchback, headin up and to the right, why the turn-around place was as big as a parkin spot. By that point Kalin had to near jog to stay out in front enuf so as not to become a problem for Landry and Jojo. The ledge did narrow some, but the climb was mild, ironically allowin Landry's thoughts to once again wander back to the consequences of just one mislaid hoof, imaginin it all again too quickly, too vividly, that one slip, followed by that sudden kick into emptiness, the awful sound of horseshoes skitterin and scratchin uselessly on slick rock, likely the last sounds she'd hear before they was both gone to nothin, and then the ledge widened substantially again and then widened even more, at which point Landry almost did look away from Kalin, almost did look off to the right, to behold that big bowl of wind-besieged emptiness, to take in from above the great Kirk's Cirque, but like they say, almost only counts in horseshoes and hand grenades. Landry stayed fixed on Kalin, until he was gone from the ledge, swallowed by darkness, by life, and a moment later Landry and Jojo was swallowed too.

Never would Landry have thought that such a black entrance could've offered her such relief and even joy. Some bolt-hole this! Call it a cavity, a cave, the second retreat, the second stop; call it whatever you want. Just as Kalin had promised, bedecked by impossible shadow: A room! More than a room! A haven from heights! The darkness even began to abate some, revealin Navidad and Mouse standin together, and not just single file but sideways, with space to spare around their rears and heads.

Kalin was already helpin Landry dismount, though Landry had never required any such help before and refused to take any now. Kalin still stayed close. So ajangle were her legs that Landry had to grab at once his arm for balance. Knees and ankles that had earlier promised the solidity of dry concrete had become somethin more like lard on a dark plate set under a burnin summer sun.

Landry still insisted on tyin Jojo's lead herself. She used the same carabiner Mouse was tied to. Somethin about that metal loop, and the second one too, what Navidad was tied to, gathered up in her heart a warm surgin sense that transformed the brittle explications Kalin had already offered her: for here was the evidence of their plan, their diligence, their thoroughness. Here on display was the fulfillment of her brother's and Kalin's anticipations. Because . . . there was always gonna be an issue with what paddock Navidad and Mouse were stabled in. Tom knew it, Kalin eventually knew it. The day was comin when those boys would have to be ready for war.

Landry's small fingers touched the settled pitons and knew too by their immovable fixity within the mountain that it weren't no minor strikes that had driven them so deep. Each hammer blow, way up here, demonstrated the same resoundin commitment to these beautiful and voiceless horses, come at last, at last on their way. Kalin's love for them Landry could never doubt.

But when she turned back to find him, findin only a hunched silhouette near as bleak as this rock hallway, somethin like a wail that

771

would never break free of her lips moved through her. Because . . . she pitied him. He'd never understood the consequences he was stirrin up by goofin off in Old Porch's paddocks. But Tom had. And Tom had used this poor kid's love of horses to trap him.

Look, Landry! Kalin said, because he weren't lookin at Landry then, not readin her expressions, sayin her name so brightly you'd be hard-pressed to deny the notes of glee elevatin his voice. *We even got stones to sit on! And they're dry too! See!*

It's way better than any hotel suite, she answered him gently, and seein his smile, which helped her smile, she went over and gave him a big hug, like she imagined her mother givin her. That was a first. And Kalin even hugged her back. That was another first. Not that it lasted long, and before any awkwardness could intervene, because, let's be clear, though it weren't but a quick collegial embrace, it also weren't a hug like either one of their mothers would've given or gotten, Landry turned away and threw her arms around the mule too, who'd just then ambled up like a beautiful piece of moon come to join the party.

And the moon nibbled some at Landry's hair while she rested her cheek against the pale mane. It felt so good to finally hug this animal, and though plenty would and did object that a mule can't hug back, Landry swore she felt some reciprocal embrace, and it helped resettle her back to herself.

Like Kalin was already doin, Landry then tried out the stone seats, even stretchin out her legs like he was doin, like pizza was on the way, like they was about to turn on the television and fall asleep.

One aftereffect of this most recent leg of their journey, or maybe it was the cumulation of everythin they'd done up until now: fer one tiny forever moment, Landry no longer felt afraid. She'd done it! And it hadn't even been that bad! Furthermore, what she'd done was now done with, in the past, ready to be forgotten if she liked, though she kind of liked rememberin it. How it had happened. Because whatever else could've happened along the way hadn't happened. All those What-Ifs were now gone.

They palm-watered the horses then and gave away the last of their alible scraps, seeds, and broken stalks, holdin in reserve what few portions remained of the molasses mash. After that, Kalin and Landry drank what was left in their canteens. Landry was painfully hungry and couldn't rightly imagine what Kalin was feelin right then, though he gave nothin away. She watched him draw his palm down the neck of the mule, becomin fer a moment, or so it seemed to her, a piece of the same moon, and this saddened her somethin awful, like he was right there before her, so close, and yet already lost, which in some ways meant losin Tom all over again, which was just too much.

We're almost there, Kalin said at last. *Only two more switchbacks, and we even get a rest in between.*

Let's get it done! Landry near shouted. She was even in the process of untyin Jojo's lead when a loud crack ripped through their curious roost. Jojo hopped back with pinned ears, while Mouse's ears did the splits in an effort to locate the origin of that heart-stutterin report. Navidad shook her head like evil little birds were batterin their wings around her eyes. The mule hung her head.

And then it was gone, and fer an instant it was of no importance, like a sudden reshiftin of stone that would not take place again fer another century. But neither Kalin nor Landry were deceived. They both knew, as the horses probably knew too, that that bang was nothin mountain born. If only they could've ignored it, then they'd've likely reached the summit none the wiser with the worst behind them. But its dangerous announcement could not be ignored.

Together Kalin and Landry crept back down to where they'd first entered this hollow place. Landry's boots slipped once, which Kalin immediately prohibited with an outflung arm. They stopped at the jagged edge, where Kalin crouched before a fissure grantin him a fair view of the cirque below.

If only Landry had hung back then and contented herself with his assessment. Instead when he admitted to bein clueless about the gunshot, where it had come from, if it even was a gunshot, Landry took his place before the crack. She was already thinkin how she wouldn't see nothin either, how she'd better just go get their binoculars; and so, havin up until then resisted every impulse to look, she was unprepared for the waves of vertiginous disbelief that at once overtook her. How had they gotten so high up? Way higher than a few hundred feet! A thousand feet at least! There were even wisps of clouds floatin below them.

Here was a moment when Ms. Melson, who had already described their ascent as a *madness, worse than tryin to outclimb Pelion on Ossa on top of Mount Olympus,* would in a less exasperated mood, and bear in mind she was by this point afflicted with breast cancer, refer to this moment as *the second teichoskopia, the anti-teichoskopia,* because it weren't like Landry was capable of seein much, her vision havin already *garbled up and gorgonized her senses.*

If Landry weren't stone yet, she was well on her way. And at the same time she also felt like she was fallin, frozen but still fallin, like how a mountain might feel, always tumblin downward, toward the heart of the earth, and yet at the same time so immense as to know itself weightless in the grasp of space, drawn toward the sun, and either way always fallin.

Landry finally managed to half recoil, half wobble backwards, and might've slipped had not two ATVs out there abruptly started up again. That would've been both Park Ranger Emily Brickey and Kelly Porch, now headin fast as they could to meet up with Egan, Billings, and Law Enforcement Ranger Kelson, the whines of those two machines at least focusin Landry's attention enuf to restore her balance if not entirely repulsin the seizure overtakin her limbs.

You okay? Kalin asked, concerned about Landry's near slip but also sensin some her despair.

Just one heckuva view, Landry answered with a gulp. Okay, she didn't gulp. More like grunted. *It's beautiful.*

Ain't nothin compared to what you'll see in a few minutes.

Can they follow us up here?

Not on ATVs. I suppose the bike would have a chance. Kalin paused. *Tom says a dirt bike can definitely make it.*

That's not good.

He's also sayin there ain't but a small chance they'll find the right way up. And I'm in agreement. There ain't no markers like them flowers I put down on the first scree. And the horses ain't left much by way of tracks.

They pooped some.

That's true.

So that there gives them a chance?

That there gives them a chance.

Then they'll be here soon.

I only said a chance.

We're trapped here.

No, Landry. We ain't trapped here. We're movin on.

They'll shoot us, Kalin.

We don't know what that was.

They'll shoot us, Landry said again.

Well, if they try, they won't come close.

They don't have to. They just have to scare the horses.

Kalin didn't know how to answer that and looked to Tom, but Tom didn't have no answer either.

Landry felt her face go hot then and her eyes dried up and started to sting. Somethin was caught in her throat too, as if now even her voice was trapped by stone. Kalin put his hand on her shoulder, like that was gonna help, and maybe under different circumstances it would've helped. No such luck today.

You came all this way alone? Landry still managed to ask.

A few times.

That's crazy.

Kalin shrugged. *It beat school.*

Your momma must've lost her mind.

She knew she couldn't hold me. She just wants me to keep that one promise.

No guns?

That's right.

I really do think our mommas would get along.

I think it's nice of you to say that.

What's Tom say?

He says you're just stallin because you don't want to get back on your horse.

He's right.

You'll see, Tom, Kalin addressed the darkness. *Your little sister is about to get done what you only dreamed of doin.*

Landry forced out a little laugh. She already knew Kalin was just tryin to hasten her along, especially with the air and the mountain robbin them of warmth as the light continued to run west. It didn't matter what he needed her to do, she knew what she needed to do. Landry stood up and eyed for the last time the way they'd come. The ledge seemed easy and obvious and yet at the same time impossible because of what lay adjacent to it or what did not lay adjacent to it. And if that weren't bad enuf, now she had gunfire to fear and armed men racin up after them. Landry could only tell herself how none of it mattered: they had to go.

Ain't there no other way up here than by how we come? she asked as she returned to her Jojo.

They'd have to go back down and start over in the mornin. Maybe take the Heathen-Slade Canyon Trail. That'll take them around back to the Heber side of Katanogos. On ATVs and dirt bikes, if the rain don't kick up more, they could make it up by late mornin.

Then they can't cut us off?

They cannot. We'll be done and long gone by the time they reach the back side. It's nice on the other side. Where we don't want to get stuck is here, in a place we're afraid of.

Kalin's admission startled her. *Are we afraid?*

At least Kalin's smile didn't dim none. *You tell me you ain't afraid and I'll laugh.* Kalin went ahead and laughed anyway. *Why even Tom's afraid.*

Tom's been nothin but afraid.

Did you hear that, Tom?

Is he tryin to deny it?

Not a bit. But he's laughin.

I'm glad to hear that.

Look, Landry. Tryin to pretend you're not afraid takes up too much energy we don't have. We're up here on one heckuva big wall and with three horses. Of course we're afraid! Kalin paused. He was listenin to Tom. *Four horses.*

Plus a mule.

775

Plus a mule.

I mean, what is up with that? Landry suddenly demanded.

She don't seem afraid.

She don't, does she? Maybe she's here for good luck?

Okay. Sure. I like that.

I'm still scared, Kalin.

Good. And now that you've said it, be done with it.

Landry kept chewin on the inside of a cheek. She liked the words even if they didn't help.

For these horses, right? she asked.

Kalin looked at her real steady, and longer than he'd ever looked at her before, maybe longer than anyone had looked at her. Especially like that.

It ain't good enuf to wanna be free, Kalin told her then, but in that way like all the embers he guarded deep in his heart to keep his life warm he was now givin over to her. *Every dang livin thing wants to be free. It's elemental I reckon. But like my momma taught me, and it's how I see things too: to matter you gotta set free someone that ain't you. That's all that matters.*

And that applies to horses?

World won't matter for spit if there ain't no horses.

Tom agree with you?

You know he does.

Landry nodded. *My daddy used to tell us the greatest thing this continent ever done was give the world the horse. Here's where they was born.*

Now let me tell you somethin Tom don't know, Kalin said, and he leaned in some too. *When we set these horses free, I think we'll set your brother free too.*

For this leg, Kalin chose to ride out Mouse first. Before mountin up, Kalin talked to the geldin a bit, now and then pointin out to the dim light, the awful ledge, just him and Mouse contemplatin their immediate future. Kalin didn't move none. Mouse didn't move none either. No question this blood bay could get ornery as heck when he wanted to and plenty contrary just for the sake of bein contrary, but Mouse also weren't stupid. He weren't gonna move anywhere near the ledge unless Kalin was with him. Some theories have suggested that Mouse was the smartest of the bunch, and there's no pretendin how somethin about Mouse was pretty unusual, though in what way remains hard to put a finger on.

Some folks claim that Mouse was super stupid, but I think it was that Mouse just weren't any old horse. I say that because of how casual he always was, like wherever they was weren't no bother to him, like he didn't have a life to lose or like the life he had he couldn't lose, said Jo Ellen Shrapernell, Orvop native who, as the frailty of her final years overwhelmed her, the worst in 2025, this when she'd finally settled in Geneva, Switzerland, often found a great deal of calm by just returnin to this moment, especially when her thoughts settled on Mouse, for like Mouse, she too in her last days faced a dimly lit future marked by a ledge leadin to where the ledge refused to say.

After the talkin was done with, Kalin didn't waste no time. He slipped up into the saddle, adjusted his hat but once, and then like that they was both gone to the mists whirlin about outside, Landry at once swallowin hard, yes, this time she did gulp, doin her best not to recognize the tears that had sprung so easily to her eyes.

Even though the wait weren't half as long, it felt worse than anythin she'd known before. Landry gave up faster than a five-year-old fightin a nightmare, fightin the urge to run to her parents' bed, only there weren't no bed here nor parents to run to, no way to wake from this nightmare either.

Tom? You still here? Landry hollered into the dark. *I'm scared as heck. I'm scared I'm gonna be you in a minute.*

Who you shoutin at? Kalin asked. He was already back, tack in hand, already saddlin up Navidad.

At Tom?

He's up with Mouse.

You're trustin Mouse to a ghost?

In a moment I won't have to. You'll be there. Kalin wanted Jojo to go up next, Navidad last.

You sure got back fast.

I told you, we're almost done.

And, yes, Kalin's wink and smile did somethin wondrous for Landry then, like all of her was set afire again, those embers in her own heart explodin into flame, but also in some place far deeper than the heart, that place that knows what a heart needs to even beat.

Ready? Kalin asked, and without thinkin, Landry nodded.

Like before, I'll just walk ahead of you. You know where to keep your eyes?

Kalin didn't wait for her response, just headed out quick into the gray wet air.

Maybe because of the powerful darkness presidin over that second retreat, Landry was unprepared for the brightness that met her. She had to blink extra to adjust to the clarity suddenly enfoldin her. Not that Jojo seemed all that bothered. He just strode on ahead after Kalin.

They moved much faster this time too, and much to Landry's delight, the ledge here, while steeper, was also extra wide. She almost felt at ease, even as the temperature dropped and the dazzlin mists whipped around by the winds left both her face and the stone face securin them drenched.

Landry could hardly believe it when they reached the switchback. It hadn't been any shorter than the previous traverses, but it had sped by much faster. The turn weren't anythin either, just a wide left up a scramble of rock to another wide ledge, which Landry and Jojo got up to and around without a second thought.

Which was when Jojo's back left hoof slipped. It only skipped free of the stone a moment, and the back right hoof was already planted, but it made one heckuva screech and jostled them both. Furthermore, by the time Landry was comin to terms with what had just happened, Jojo's steps had already returned to their regular rhythm. How it goes. You know. *Clop-Clop-clip-Clop.* Not that Landry weren't shocked. Maybe Jojo was shocked some too.

And then they was there, no big deal, safe again in the final redoubt, where Jojo could pull up tight behind Mouse, who at once snorted relieved welcomes of sorts. Incidentally this spot is also called the Seventh Gate by folks like Charlie Burton and Martha Dagget, never married but always in love, even when MS got its teeth in Charlie and the world got its teeth in Martha, and anyway they sure liked talkin about them gates with the likes of Morgan Harris, Callista Toone, Jared Cade, and even Jeananne Harvey.

And then for the third time Landry found herself secured by rock on either side, though as Kalin had warned, here was their narrowest rest, with barely enuf room for stirrups and not really enuf for legs. More like a rodeo chute. Also, it weren't covered. Above them hung those turmoilin clouds.

Kalin scrambled under Mouse but a moment later was back with the geldin's lead.

I'm so glad you're here, Landry, he said then and he weren't smilin. In fact he looked just plain ashen.

What is it?

I guess I ain't much when it comes to rock. I just found the piton I put in lyin next to Mouse's hooves.

You mean it fell out?

Or Mouse yanked it out?

Of course, Mouse yanked it out!

I did a crap job hammerin it in. I swear it was embedded in solid rock.

He is Mouse.

That is true. He is Mouse. I sure am glad he didn't wander off.

As you likely already suspected, this here is another one of those moments when Mouse gets a lot of extra attention. Much discussed but without any revelation that good analysis should provide, Mary Tarr, born in Cairo, Egypt, though she'd settle in Orvop, would wonder aloud between morphine doses, as the ovarian cancer she'd fought for two years won the siege over the rest of her: *Mouse sure loved Navidad. That he did.*

And then Kalin was gone again. Landry looked behind her, expectin at least to get some glimpse of him headin down the ledge but found instead that pale mule just arrivin, her pleasant nicker momentarily shooin away any unease Landry was feelin after Jojo's minor slip, which in her head just couldn't help but transform itself into a much bigger trip and scramble that too soon had them slidin backwards, down to the ledge below, where, despite the Easyboots and the studs, they was delivered unto a somersaultin weightlessness her thoughts had no trouble conjurin, down through icy air toward the questions no mind can really answer: Would she scream? Would her life flash before her eyes? What little there was of it? And what about the parts she couldn't remember? Before she had the capacity to remember? Her first mother? Her first father? And then what? Would she feel the impact before she died? Would she and Jojo die at once or would she and him linger in pain? And in that moment of pain, however drawn out or fleetin, would she also know despair? And would that erase all the Good that had come before? Includin the life that had just flashed before her eyes? Leavin her where then? Nowhere? And then what? Nothin? Or would she find Tom? Maybe someone else? Or no one at all? Would she be locked up in that mine too or set loose like the faceless Pia Isan to wander aimlessly in the shadows, gnawin endlessly on a vengeance so old it had lost the capacity to understand?

And then the clops of Navidad's hooves broke the spell, and Kalin was back, *Clop-Clop-clip-Clop*, Navidad right behind the mule. All of them back together again and everythin was fine and there were no more gunshots either and they had only one switchback left. Almost there. Just one more turn. Almost there. Just one ledge, then a turn, then one more ledge. *Just two ledges,* which when Landry said it aloud, Kalin had corrected, because there really was just one more ledge, the one ahead, followed by a right turn, after which it was more like a steep trail that was challengin, sure, but also plenty easy to ride up, right up to and over the summit.

Unfortunately it was also a turn Landry knew she couldn't make. She weren't sure she could even walk Jojo now on a sidewalk let alone ride him out on another ledge. She doubted she could.

It was even surprisin to Landry, how such rigid certainty had so swiftly overthrown her. The accumulations of dread had finally taken hold. All she knew was that her breath weren't just shallowin, and forget breathin through her nose or even her mouth; her breath weren't comin up at all. Panic was routin her senses. She wanted outta there. Though even gettin off weren't no easy matter. Rock ground in against both her legs.

Landry thought of Tom then, though she didn't call out his name, and he was right there too, just in front of Mouse, maybe even makin the way ahead a little bit more hazy. Landry could see only a bull chute, the last place on earth she'd ever want to find herself. Her brother might've loved the unnatural stillness that can greet a cowboy not even a blink before the unkind and unholy second that follows, eight seconds if you're good, if you were lucky, and Tom at times had been both, though that hardly preserved him from now and then gettin thrown far and hard, kicked too. The only difference was that up here, it weren't her ridin some buckin version of Jojo but her and Jojo ridin this bull of a mountain, which even if it weren't a bull was still buckin. Because however you wanna view Katanogos, from the very outset it had never ceased tryin to throw them from existence. And Landry had little doubt that this time it was about to succeed. Jojo and her would both be thrown, far and hard, kicked too, the both of them fallin for eight seconds.

Likely then, out of some Jojo-preservin instinct, Landry knew to get away from that beautiful big blue horse as fast she could, no matter that she'd already lost the calm needed to negotiate a dismount in such tight quarters. She surprised even herself, Jojo, and fer sure Kalin, who was fortunately right behind Jojo at that moment, as she popped her knees up to her chest and, instead of directin herself to any one side, threw herself off backward.

Perhaps because a set of agile instincts had taken over, Landry even managed to complete that somersault, over the saddle, throwin her legs over her head next, so she wound up slidin bellyside down off Jojo's rump and tail, down to the rock floor, where Kalin mostly caught her, more like broke her fall, as she collapsed, bangin hard one knee and one elbow and even grazin her forehead on the wall before Kalin could help her stretch out on her back.

K alin was sure surprised to see Landry hurl herself off backwards like that, and for a second there he thought that she was showin off some fancy dismount. But then Kalin saw how there weren't no elation at work here. Landry couldn't breathe. Her face was both mottled and ashen. A full-on panic attack. Few fault Kalin for thinkin she'd got the wind knocked out of her. Quicker than a mongoose he first tried to sit her up, like he'd done with Russel after Landry had tumbled him off his horse. When that didn't work he grabbed her by the belt and like she didn't weigh but one feather lifted her up at the belly so her back could arch and by that extra extension of her abdomen help relieve what he still assumed was a spasmin diaphragm. At least that's what he'd seen Coach Pailey do at a football game when a player got hit so hard he couldn't breathe.

Who knows if it helped. Kalin kept calm throughout, his soft whispers soothin Landry to just breathe, tellin her she was okay, tellin her she was safe. And eventually her breathin did start goin again, and like he was sayin to do, she started inhalin through her nostrils instead of gaspin through her mouth like air was somethin to eat.

I can't do this was the first thing she said when words were finally available again. *I'm sorry. I can't. I can't take another step out there.*

I hear you, Landry. You can't do it. And you don't have to. You don't have to do nothin you don't want to. Nothin.

I can't do it to Jojo.

That's okay.

But it ain't okay! Landry at least could sit up now. *We're stuck, Kalin! I see that! We're trapped! I shouldn't have come! I should've listened to you and Tom! This is too much for me. I'm gonna die here. Jojo's gonna die here!*

Kalin could see how bad Landry wanted to cry, but the relief of tears wouldn't come. And that almost worried him more than any of this stuff about dyin.

You ain't gonna die here, Landry. I can promise you that. And he was tellin the truth, and Landry could hear that song of truth, and his confidence helped a bit more to ease her through the attack.

This was no lie, Les Froelich, born in Manchester, England, and educated in Orvop, would point out one winter before the summer his skull was stove in at the runnin of the bulls in Pamplona. *Kalin had said only that death wouldn't find her there. Likely, as Landry had already surmised, she and Jojo would die navigatin that last right turn.*

And without a doubt, here was the central concern: that last right turn. Not even Kalin had recognized yet how grave the challenge would be primarily because what he would have to face had changed plenty since he'd last been up here.

For all there is to say about the gifts of the present, there are also great pleasures to be found in the future, maybe even the greatest pleasures. For who if any can doubt the power of expectation? Desire may be the heart of sufferin, but what of a future beheld with satisfaction? To be sure, some have argued that a good view offers just that, a future beheld without desire, because who, when perched upon some uppermost heave of rock far above a valley floor, yearns to possess the horizon? Rather it's somethin else that visits us then, a peace that many might successfully argue is no future at all but instead maintains the present moment in all its uncontained Glory.

Consider, though, the future found on a trail in search of such a view. Desire walks beside us then. Or can. Especially when we are so caught up in the destination that we miss where we walk. Desire, of course, don't have to be our only companion. There is a peace and calm that comes from knowin the way ahead, knowin where somethin leads, how it turns, how we'll ascend, if only so we can then relax and enjoy a trail crowded with wildflowers. The future can bequeath a present brighter than any present without a future. That bein said, we also ain't ever entitled to the future we imagine.

Furthermore, any future we contemplate becomes by the very time-dependent process of thought the past, and the past is a dangerous friend. Consider Kalin, who at six had enjoyed a scoop of peach ice cream so much that as soon as he was finished, he begged his momma to take him out for another. He begged her every day, and when she finally relented not a week later they went out but to a different shop where the cone was different and the peach ice cream was different and because it weren't the same it weren't no good. Though in truth this ice cream that Allison had found was far better, with fresher peaches, fresher eggs, freshest cream, hand-cranked too, but because of the past, Kalin couldn't taste the new, even if what was drippin over his knuckles was somethin far superior.

Of course, the past can work the other way around too.

Kalin hadn't forgotten his last time up here. He'd been scrupulous about mappin out every switchback, rememberin every ledge, preparin each retreat, bangin in them pitons, two in the second, just the one in the third, the one that failed.

Kalin had also paid special attention to the switchback comin up, the last one, the crucial turn. He'd measured it out, down to the exact number of toe-to-heel steps, repeatedly picturin just how he'd execute the turn to the right on a precarious stage of rock that was as narrow as it was short, as it seemed already in the process of tumblin down, though Kalin had confirmed multiple times that it was solid. He was, after all, bettin his life on it and the lives of the horses.

His last day up here had been golden with sunlight, not a cloud in the sky, the sky blue as a robin's egg on Easter. On that Sunday Kalin hadn't cared none about the summit, which he'd already been up to and back down from plenty of times. He paid those preparations up there no mind. He cared only about this final turn. He'd got down on his hands and knees just to feel with his palms, even with his cheeks, the particulars of distance here. He'd paced it off so many times, imaginin hisself the horse, like he'd practiced over and over with Navidad and Mouse on a lower dusty Isatch trail, how they'd approach, how they'd execute that turn, how they'd free themselves of that turn for a path that waited just seven strides above.

And ever since Wednesday, when it had seemed impossible that the next moment would deliver them from Death's determined pursuit, and yet somehow did deliver them, and safe and sound too, even though afterward he was shaken down to his core with doubt and misery, and hunger as well, Kalin would return to visualizin the ascent up this headwall and always the turn that waited for them at the end. Fer sure, it terrified him, but, see, it thrilled him as well, because Kalin knew he was ready, Kalin knew he was prepared, Kalin knew he could do it.

Of course he'd never anticipated Landry's presence nor the storm. And the storm had granted neither the Katanogos summit nor the oft-contemplated last turn any gentleness. It weren't just the great gusts of wind either that were endured up here or even the intermittent rivers of water that flooded down the headwall, tumblin loose any rock in the way; somethin else too had moved across the face of these tomorrow paths, as if to remind anyone fool enuf to believe the future could be known or ever depended upon how the same finger of fire able to inscribe upon stone tablets words to live by could likewise unwrite every single line of passage.

Roger Kelsch, Tamara Harward, and Kelsey Selva, a tight trio hailin from Utah Valley who, though of various ages and rarely gatherin in person, would find each other again in of all places a palliative care center near the town of Monster, south of The Hague. While conversant in most details concernin this journey, as well as those details so often mentioned in debates, it was this moment in particular that would most focus their deterioratin forms. For Roger Kelsch, the question of the inscrutable path ahead would suggest to him how a chess master who, when asked by a reporter, *How many moves ahead do you think?*, replied: *Only one move. The best move.* Tamara Harward, who also admired chess, would ask if the chess master was Capablanca. *I believe it was a player by the name of Charles Jaffe, but I could be wrong,* Roger Kelsch would answer. The point bein, of course, to illustrate how progressively difficult, even impossible, it becomes for us to know the future, though not necessarily move through it. *Maybe that's where the pleasure in contemplatin tomorrow comes from? Not knowin,* Kelsey Selva would wonder aloud. *Maybe if you're young,* Tamara Harward answered with a snort. *Or does it really just come down to some perception of control?* Roger Kelsch would respond. *I think what I'm tryin to get at is how our minds are insufficient for this reality. So don't take too seriously anythin your mind declares about this reality. And especially a future reality.* From her bed Kelsey Selva would mull that one over, finally offerin by way of an answer, though it weren't so much an answer as another question: *There is a levity of mind where thoughts overleap the heavy liftin a plan will face. Consult any neighborhood child set to build an enormous fort in an hour. Of course, then there is the overloaded mind, which is perhaps the mind's attempt to register the weight of the world.* Kelsey Selva drifted. *Words really are just the shadows of a mind. Some are blurry; some are sharp as honed steel. But in either case they are cast by no sun. My question has always been: if not the sun, what then casts these shadows? What light lights the borderlands of our thoughts?* Tamara Harward would smile and set her hand on Kelsey Selva's frail arm: *God is where the mind stops workin.* Roger Kelsch sure would chuckle at that: *How very Buddhist of you.* But Kelsey Selva would not prove so easily amused: *That seems so bitter, so forlorn.* Tamara Harward would smile: *Not if you believe that where the mind stops the heart starts.*

Suffice it to say, what he was just about to find out, what Kalin had so assiduously planned for, had changed.

Once Landry was well enuf to breathe and also leave alone, Kalin handed her Jojo's reins.

Keep Jojo close. I don't want him boltin after Mouse when I go. You know how he likes Mouse.

Kalin made sure Mouse's saddle pad was set right, the saddle pulled up right too, with a couple of fingers' worth of air under the pad and the gullet. He retightened it all up next, recheckin everythin from billets to latigo, from cinch to stirrups. Then he rechecked the halter-bridle and made sure the bit and reins were well fitted. Last of all, he got down around Mouse's legs, massagin them some as well as checkin that them studs on the shoes was holdin up. They was, and that was somethin Kalin could take comfort in.

By then his mouth had gone dry. He could do little but ball up the little spit he had left in the center of his tongue, where he tried to keep it. That would have to do. Kalin knew it weren't from thirst that he was parched.

Landry, I'm gonna need you now. It ain't no big deal. When I head out with Mouse, please walk Jojo up to where the piton is. You'll see it on the ground there. Can you do that? Stand in front of Jojo too. Can you do that?

I can, Landry answered and got to her feet. *What about Navidad?*

Navidad will stay behind you. Just keep a loose hold on her lead.

What about the mule?

Kalin eyed the mule standin between Jojo and Navidad. What

could he say about this surprise addition to their ranks? *The mule's fine.* He hoped that was true.

Kalin slipped off his gloves then, swung up into the saddle, and after adjustin that grimy hat just once, headed out.

The egress there weren't no surprise: a wet stone ledge, plenty wide. The narrowness was also expected, though what waited farther along was just plain awful: the storm had dislodged chunks of rock, creatin a number of gaps that individually were not difficult to navigate but taken together presented a challenge akin to tryin to prance a horse atop so many scattered cinder blocks.

By the time that first jagged gouge in the ledge came into view, Kalin knew he'd made a big mistake. His idea of the future had blinded him. He should've walked the route first. He should've made sure the turn was sound. Kalin's cheeks burnt for the shame of foolin hisself with his certainties, his many plans, all them carefully measured paces.

Kalin did his best to study the new challenge, edgin Mouse as close as he could to that checkerboard of eroded gaps creatin the steps they'd need to hit just right in order to reach the spot where they would need to turn, that precarious stage of rock, which looked even more narrow than before, as if it had shrunk since his last visit, though it hadn't; what Kalin was bettin his and Mouse's life on was that it would hold them long enuf for a pivot or really one big half-turn, which they'd have to execute to near perfection in order to make it up to the summit path waitin just above.

Regarded in its entirety, and Kalin did ease Mouse back one step to try to get a greater sense of the whole section, this part of the mountain looked as if some impossibly large cat had wandered into the cirque, and after stretchin up on this headwall, either to mark its territory or maybe just to ease an itch in its claws, had proceeded to scratch great gashes out of these and other rock slabs above and below.

Can I make it? Kalin asked Tom, because who else was he gonna ask? Tom sat atop Ash on the other side of the turn, and like Kalin, he too was eyein with greater and greater unease the parts of this ledge that in some places seemed no more substantial than a wish at midnight.

I don't know.

Is it even makeable?

I don't know.

Is this it?

I don't know.

What are you now, suddenly the ghost of I-don't-know? Kalin snapped, more than just an itsy-bit rankled.

I don't know.

Very funny.

I wish I was jokin. I really don't know how to advise you here.

Kalin shook his head. *I used to think you was the ghost of, I don't know, reassurance. That at least did my head some good when you appeared. Now I think maybe you're the ghost of doubt.*

Maybe that's right.

Kalin asked then. *What does Pia Isan say?*

She ain't here.

That sure as heck surprised Kalin. *Whadya mean she ain't here?*

She's by you.

Kalin eyed the air about him and Mouse, but nothin confirmed an extra presence. *Is that unusual?*

Very. She figures this is it. She thinks you'll fall. Then I'll come to know the true extent of Awides.

At least you'll know somethin then.

She is awful smiley.

Tell her I disagree.

She can hear you.

I guess I know how Landry feels.

Pia Isan's changed some too. Did I tell you that?

How so?

Fer one thing, her name ain't just Isan or Pia Isan. She has other names now, names like Tukani Mukua and even Tukani Baa'.

That don't mean nothin to me.

Her teeth have gotten extra long. Too long really. Like knives. And the way she handles that ax-head ain't somethin you wanna see.

Still smiley?

Awful smiley. Tom made like to laugh but, well, couldn't.

I guess that is disconcertin.

And I ain't even told you about her eyes.

Don't tell me they're yellow or somethin.

Blood-red.

Tom Gatestone, you're just havin me on, aren't you?

She does have these nice dimples when she smiles. He grinned. *And there's a little scar across one part of her lip. She don't like that. She got it when some Orvop beekeepers broke up her hives.* Tom turned to the air. *It looks fine!* Then he was back lookin at Kalin, shakin his head. *Who gets in a huff because someone else's honey tastes better?*

Tom kept smilin even if he looked a bit sad. Kalin was still glad for it. He and Mouse could do with at least one person smilin.

You know the worst part? Kalin said, tryin to muster his own smile and failin. *I still ain't figured out how I'm gonna get Jojo through this.*

786

If you can do it, Landry can do it, Tom answered. And Kalin almost believed him. *On Jojo she can do anythin you can do and more. You just have to convince her that she was made for this ride.*

Now if that weren't the biggest crock of ghost crap. Landry was not made for this ride. This here, what Kalin now faced, had absolutely zero to do with her abilities and talents, zero in fact to do with his own abilities and talents. Furthermore, what fer sure neither Kalin nor even his ghost could truly reckon with: that seizure of petrification that had just now got hold of Landry was hardly dissipatin.

Kalin, though, weren't thinkin about Landry no more, nor even about Tom. In the quiet of hisself he was doin the only thing he could do: recalibratin what he'd need to do next, how he and Mouse would have to go, at what angle, at what pace, which he realized soon enuf would require more of a lead-up.

What Kalin did then is near more astonishin than everythin else he'd already done up to this moment, and it didn't involve no collapsin mountainside: Kalin backed up Mouse, one step after another, all the way to their refuge. So great was Mouse's trust that he never once strayed sideways toward the edge nor even once brushed up against the wall.

When they'd stopped, Kalin saw that Landry was about to ask him somethin, and he shook his head quick. Landry understood and nodded, and though her smile was slight and pale, he understood what she'd wanted him to hear. And it helped.

Kalin studied one last time the path ahead, countin the steps he and Mouse would need along the widest part of the ledge before they got to the narrowin part where they'd need a different gait before they'd reach them entirely different steps interposed with ragged gaps. To walk there would be to die. They would have to fly instead, over the worst of it. It's kinda like how a Gordian knot just needs a sword; a Pegasus route just needs wings.

Kalin took a deep breath through his nostrils, readied hisself, readied Mouse, and then rode out ahead. Except where he'd planned to increase their tempo, Kalin stopped again, beholdin yet another surprise, this one right beyond the turn, materializin out of nowhere, what looked at first like another ghost, though more like a cloud as it was floatin in the air, like a strange but determined ghost-cloud, denser than snow but lighter than wind, except it weren't floatin and it weren't no cloud nor ghost.

Here, as if to better mark their way, mark the ne plus ultra of their path, stood a great white mountain goat with heavy devout horns. His cloven hooves were variously perched on the slightest protru-

787

sions of rock. The great altitude hardly concerned him as he licked away at invisible offerins. Maybe narrow fissures concealed lichens or some other tangle of roots. Or maybe the ichor of Katanogos itself was gushin there. Kalin heard Tom laughin. Kalin joined in. He couldn't even say why. Except that he was astonished. They both were. Not that this impressive goat cared one bit. And when Kalin squinted his eyes, he seemed to make out more such shapes just relaxin upon the wall.

Mouse whinnied. The mountain goat didn't give a dang about that either.

If they can do it, you can too, Mouse, Tom said.

Kalin then heard somethin else, the sound of them ATVs again, louder than ever. Just as Landry had done earlier, Kalin wondered if their whine had been there all along. And in fact they'd started up and fallen quiet a few times already, but for whatever reason the dangerous cry of their engines had not penetrated Kalin's consciousness until now. It also provoked him to do what he'd kept tellin Landry never to do: Kalin turned to face the cirque, like he might catch sight of them.

The great distances quivered his knees. Landry weren't the only one to find her breath attacked by the shockin recognition of where they was at. Kalin forced his gaze back to the rock wall on his right. He even reached out to touch it, to press his neked palm against the cold, rough surface. And it's true, the immense and indifferent solidity he encountered there did steady him some, though it was nothin compared to Mouse, who Kalin suddenly understood was ready.

Kalin again backed up Mouse.

Landry was right where he'd asked her to stand, up where the piton and carabiner was lyin on the rock floor, still holdin Jojo's reins.

What's the matter? she asked.

There's a big old mountain goat standin near where the turn is. It kinda startled us.

My lord! Is that what that is? Landry even took a step out onto the ledge to squint out the puff of white so at ease up here in this impossible place. Kalin, who'd seen it up close, still couldn't believe it.

To a fiddle, banjo, bass, and a snare, Orvop original Florence Gibbs, buskin in a Paris metro, would on an icy and sou-less night improvise a song dedicated to *that burnin goat, that creature of white flame. No halo neither nor rose upon that fur from the settin day. The storm had seen to that. Though what did it matter? There that goat stood anyway. That burnin goat. Guidin them, warnin them. After all, an angel has wings only when there is need for wings. That goes for heavenly fire too.*

He'll mark our way, Kalin told Landry.

Just turn right at the goat?

And straight on til mornin, Kalin answered her, noddin as he re-threaded the reins through the fingers of his left hand. The blisterin from the rope burn was still raw and broken, and it winced him plenty too, but there weren't no choice: Kalin needed to get as close to Mouse as he could; he needed to feel his friend's every hesitation and impulse. This weren't about puttin no brakes on or yankin Mouse's head one way or another. Kalin needed to know Mouse's feet were under him and that he was on the correct lead. He kept his right hand free to reach out for balance if need be and to more accurately gauge their distance from the wall, especially before the turn.

I can't look! Landry suddenly blurted out. She even crouched down. *Tom says—*

Tell Tom to go to heck! I don't give a fig what he says!

Kalin gave Mouse's neck one last stroke, and then, after whisperin somethin in his ear, the blood bay jumped forward and away they went.

That jump weren't fer nothin neither. Landry had not kept her eyes clamped tight for long nor stayed crouched down either. In fact she'd stood up pretty quick, passin Jojo's reins from her right hand to her left at the same time, as well as takin an inadvertent step, which walked her right into Mouse's rump. On the bright side, he didn't kick her, though he did give a startled snort as he bolted forward.

Kalin weren't bothered none by the little buck that resulted from Mouse regatherin his hind legs under hisself. It weren't but a hiccup, but it also set in motion what Kalin understood at once he couldn't impede: to check Mouse now would unsettle his confidence. So Kalin not only committed to the horse's heave forward but even encouraged it, smoothin out the gait as they moved along, Kalin's right hand briefly touchin the wall before givin that bleak Stetson one last adjustment.

To give as clear a picture as possible here, this quick acceleration didn't amount to more than a fast trot, even if in two strides that trot became a slow lope, stretchin out some Mouse's stride, which Kalin was countin on, just as he was countin on settin Mouse to his right lead, makin sure that right foreleg was the one out in front. By tryin to force a sharp right turn with a right forehoof tucked underneath, a horse could just fall over like a chair missin a leg.

Kalin even lifted up ever so slightly on the reins and, with a little help from his knees, gathered up Mouse under him. Not that Mouse was listenin. No matter how much Kalin urged the blood bay with his left leg to get on that right lead, Mouse bein Mouse weren't goin for it. And so there was Kalin and Mouse lopin along so high up that from below it didn't even merit bein called a crack let alone a ledge, and on the wrong lead.

This here was a huge problem, especially since it was now too late to stop. They'd already flown right over the first gouged-up section, which allowed Mouse to land his left hoof just once on unmarred rocks. And then like that they was also past the second torn-up section, the mountain goat gettin closer and closer, as unbothered as ever, with just one more crummy section left before the turn.

Fer Kalin, ridin had always come down to rhythm, how horse and rider move together, sometimes right above one another, sometimes otherwise aligned, fer instance, cantilevered in a low fast turn, where even though the rider is extended away from the horse, they're even more together, in balance, both movin in congruence not only with each other but the earth and air as well. Kalin knew this by heart: be with every exhalation and inhalation the least possible burden to the horse. And that was still just fer starters. The rider must also be more than that; the rider must become utile to the horse. The rider must become the horse so much so that the horse becomes the rider so much so that together they are more than their parts and any notion of burden should seem as silly as regardin one's own legs as excess weight upon the action of runnin.

In adherence to this unity, Kalin let go of any plans, realignin hisself with only Mouse, whose life was his own and to which Kalin was committed, even if it cost him his own life. And Kalin felt fairly certain Mouse's insistence on keepin to that left lead would cost them both their lives. It sure surprised Kalin then when he realized Mouse had instead saved both their lives.

Duwayne Small, who served and suffered over in Afghanistan, endin up on disability for the rest of his life, battlin his need to address emptiness with full fifths, loved to haul out his guitar to join Roper Brunsen's strummin. Brunsen, who would in his life find decades of sobriety, was always there for Duwyane. The two of them would camp up in the Uintas, this time in 2021, fryin up freshly caught trout, singin the songs they loved so much, Neal Young gettin his due, *Doesn't mean that much to me to mean that much to you,* and even that Willie Nelson tune, *It Won't Be Very Long,* with The Secret Sisters, though the one that settled them most was their own and, yes, real rudimentary, comin down to just one verse tried out against various melodies and beats:

> *Right lead led right*
> *to the worst thinkable step.*
> *Left lead leads right*
> *to the only makeable step*
> *and yet—*

Which was pretty much the truth of it: how what can seem like the wrong way can sometimes prove in the end the only way.

Startin on the right lead made sense given that final turn ahead, but on the left lead Mouse's left forehoof found more uncompromised rock. Was it blind luck, or had Mouse seen it first? Maybe. Because if he'd have led with the right foreleg, given his stride, he'd've struck down on more of the scarred parts of the ledge, which might've stumbled him enuf to leave him unable to handle what was comin next, which if he didn't handle would've definitely led to a life-endin fall.

Instead that settled left hoof gave Mouse what he needed to propel hisself even farther and faster, past that second section, which was when Kalin awoke to the chance he now understood, risin up with Mouse in one fluid wave, the two of them risin up together like a wave does as it rolls forward toward shallowin shores.

At the crest of their collective ascendancy, with Mouse no longer rockbound, all four legs in the air, Kalin again nudged Mouse's left side with his left leg, and this time Mouse delivered with flawless grace the change in lead they needed. That blood bay even gathered hisself up higher, floatin there an extra heartbeat before lettin that right forehoof descend, findin a way to solid stone, which at once aligned the rest of his steps as they lunged unhindered through the third section, upward then to the turn, that last patch of rock, without rail, offerin little room to halt such forward momentum, beyond which waited a fall beyond rescue, beyond reason, to which Mouse and Kalin still might've given themselves over to had it not been for that great old mountain goat continuin to graze indifferently on the mysteries bequeathed at those high altitudes.

It was right then too that Kalin knew hisself wanderin from this singular pursuit of survival, as he perilously beheld Tom on Ash, waitin above them on the path just beyond the turn. Kalin felt his heart scar with ire, fer havin ended up here, for havin to accomplish the impossible, all thanks to the Livin Tom, the Laughin Tom, Tom the Funny One, and fer that matter Tom the Dead One. Kalin even realized that how he was feelin about Tom, some part of Landry was feelin about him, how thanks to Kalin she'd wound up in so inhospitable a place, how thanks to Kalin she was doomed to try to do what she couldn't do. Surely as there was ire in Kalin for Tom, there was ire in Landry for Kalin. And just as surely, Kalin understood, he would not survive the next moment if he did not let go of ire.

Before he vanished in a sunfish off the coast of Cartagena on February 7, 2029, Berrid Dwyer would dwell too much on these steps that could not be planned for nor practiced and were too soon forgotten despite what they might've offered followers. Berrid Dwyer would likewise also dwell too much on his days in Orvop before *I fled the maulin misocainea of the Church, the indecency of the Church, a community that could not see its own as anythin beyond the edicts of stories about seagulls and locusts.* However that night, before departin in his little sailboat, he would change his focus. No longer would he be bothered by what lay to the stern of his life, back there by the dawn of his childhood, informed by a belief system that had offered him neither solace nor belongin. Nor would he be bothered any more by those particular steps that had seen Kalin and Mouse *over a ledge porous as a haircomb.* Instead Berrid Dwyer would while settin hisself free over the darkenin waters embody that old Zen sayin: *Ride your horse along the edge of a sword.*

Whether upon the blade of the sharpest sword or a plain as vast as the Bonneville Salt Flats, for Mouse and Kalin up there on the Upecksay Headwall, there weren't no difference. The question weren't what was available or not available but just what was. Mouse and Kalin breathed together, they moved together, and then together they gathered each other up as Mouse planted his back hooves down on that last time-dismantled plinth, a landin that did not fail them, Mouse skiddin some but rearin up just the same, Kalin risin up too, like he was near standin in the stirrups, and in such fluid equilibration that Kalin's own weight only added to the stability of that hold, Mouse's long tangled mane flung up against Kalin's chest, Kalin's hands all the while remainin so light on the reins and steady too that you could've balanced on the backs of those hands a cup of hot cocoa, on a saucer too, with a small spoon balanced on the edge, and that spoon would've stayed put, not a drop of cocoa overspillin the limits of that cup, even if Kalin's legs were already movin, enouragin Mouse to finish what he'd started, turnin to where the blood bay already knew to go, toward the cliffside, turnin still more.

Talk about stoppin on a dime! Talk about turnin on a dime! They could've managed the whole 360! Why not 720?! Like some horse miniature spinnin atop a music box, even if the music up there was the risin howl of them brutal summit winds deliverin their icy sting to whatever gaze dared try to know them. But where the big old mountain goat tilted his head away, and with some annoyance too, even closin his eyes before this sudden squall now shriekin down over the headwall, Mouse met that wind as if it were somethin lesser, a lesser god that had yet to recognize who it dared now to confront, a recognition Mouse intended to remedy as he readied his charge.

Of course Landry was cranin her neck to see the whole thing. She was incapable of not lookin, even if her expression was one of horror.

The navigation of the last part of that crumbly ledge followed by the turn, from her vantage point, and really even from the vantage point of that old mountain goat, didn't seem like much. It weren't so fast, fer one, that rear up and turn lookin to be almost in slo-mo. Fer another, it was over real quick, didn't take but a few blinks, not that Landry blinked once, because as much as her breath caught while tryin to watch Kalin and Mouse in the distance, it was what tore after them that stomped on her heart with grief and terror.

As Landry had been passin Jojo's reins from one hand to another, when she had by mistake walked into Mouse's rump, causin Mouse to bolt ahead, well, Jojo weren't never gonna stand still fer that and bolted ahead. Even the mule lunged after Jojo with Landry only just managin to keep hold of Navidad's lead, the mare already set to join this black parade.

Jojo didn't land the same steps as Mouse. He even faltered here and scrambled there, but his stride was naturally longer, and he managed, probably by example, fer sure by feel and instinct, to leap way beyond the troubled parts, and by the time he was starin at that old mountain goat and that landin of questionable stone, he weren't thinkin twice about how to stick that turn.

Still, Jojo would've fallen right then and there were it not fer them studs on his back hooves, which surely proved their worth, grantin that great blue horse the hold he'd need to stop as the mighty muscular intent of them rear legs drove him around then and upward in search of more rock, worthy rock, in fact landin that right forehoof with such force that the rock cracked, a crack that reverberated along the headwall, which still weren't nothin compared to Jojo's equine will to hurl hisself upon and above that now-fractured stone, his survival echoin and elongatin whatever doubt that crack had first sounded out across the cirque, Jojo beyond it already and well away from danger.

The mule followed last but managed the turn in a completely different way. The mule pretty much walked it, half tiptoein, half prancin, at least until the end, where she sauntered some. The mule even paused upon that now cracked and improbable platform to regard the old mountain goat, who in turn regarded the mule. Maybe they even shared some sense of things. It would be goin too far to say they nodded at each other as they parted, but they parted as friends, and then the mule too was through the turn.

Gone then were they all in a loud clatter of hooves, a clatter that only grew louder as Mouse, a tourbillion of muscle and hoof upon such heights, drove hard away from that vertical face, the stairs of rock fast givin way to a wider path that weren't no more now than just the steep slope of a mountain, the top of the mountain, continuin to widen out, even startin to mellow as it finally broadened into the wide ridge that marked the Katanogos summit.

K alin never touched the reins. He already knew that what waited on the other side weren't another cirque. Quite the contrary: the back side of the Upecksay Headwall was a long, fairly gentle slope, or at least gentle by comparison, leisurely fannin out down toward wide, strange, and what at times seemed unknowable valleys below, hid on this late afternoon by the dense and violent clouds still tryin to refute even the summit that was fast approachin, denyin Kalin and Mouse a view no greater than a stride. But here they were at last anyway, with but a few lengths left before the apex, in a temple of clouds.

Even on top, though, even in this gray and freezin blindness, Mouse never thought to slow. Only as the climb gave way to descent, however mild at first, with Kalin guidin them toward the safer places he knew awaited them, only then did Mouse ease up on his race, the race already done, won in fact, as they now rode upon the back of the mountain.

Not that the storm cared, or cared very much, increasin its fury, Kalin's face stingin even more from the sharp pellets of fine rain. A path, though, had appeared before them, short clumps of brown grass amidst a swath of crushed rubble. It weren't exactly Elysian fields, but Mouse and Kalin knew they was finally better off. And as they continued to head laterally, the wind and rain began to soften, more so the farther below the summit ridge they got, until eventually they beheld a good ways ahead, in a lee of defiant rock, a copse of limber pines.

It was only then, as they slowed before them trees, with Kalin's desires and thoughts still so congruent with Mouse's, that Kalin seemed to hear Mouse's hard breath double and then not just double but triple! Likely due, Kalin figured, to havin just survived what they shouldn't have survived, what no horse let alone a man on a horse should've survived. Kalin chalked it up to the thrall of adrenal joy, them blissful palpitations when life's been snatched away from the jaws of Death; not that Kalin was thinkin with such words, just red-cheeked and dazzled before the wonder of livin.

In this rosiest of moods at the highest elevations, even if surrounded by yowlin veils of an angry storm, occasionally thinnin to reveal patches of snow and, the lower they got, determined branches and roots, Kalin's eyes leaked tears, streakin back alongside each of his temples, as jubilant as astonished that here he and Mouse still stood, with Tom and Ash beside them too. Kalin made no effort either to wipe away the tears. Was there the taste of sage in the air? Whatever it was, had anythin tasted sweeter? He was tastin rock too. And that was sweet as well. He opened his mouth to let the wet of the air coat his lips and his tongue. Here was a feast of elation and gladness, of bliss, and terror, with grief mixed in there too, for all they'd just got free of, though to which at the same time Kalin still remained indentured. Not Mouse though. Mouse was as good as free. This might as well be his Tom's Crossin. Though it weren't.

Then the rainy wet withdrew some, and the clouds rose up a little, almost as if to make things easier, invite Kalin onwards. He could keep goin. He could forget the shelter he'd readied in advance. He could head straight down off this mountain and never look back. Declare hisself done. Tell the world, tell the darned ghost, that he'd won. Thoughts Kalin never did stop to entertain, though they was there just the same, if no more believable than caterwaulin infants declarin themselves untired.

And then this echoin behind them, echoes of Mouse's hard breaths, hoofbeats too, not twice but thrice!, again overcame Kalin, this time fillin him with dread and finally fear, more so than a ghost like Tom on Ash could provoke, or even invisible Pia Isan with her ax-head. This here, what was behind him, was a different sort of ghostliness.

Kalin felt in his chest then three forms of hisself and Mouse. The first was the one apparent, him and Mouse gettin closer still to them welcomin pines and a broad back of rocks big and wide enuf to grant them refuge. The second was the them that hadn't made it, the them that was still stuck on that crumblin plinth of foolishness, where backward steps were no longer possible, where before that old mountain goat they could no more rear up than dare a turn. These second selves were the ghosts of immobility, the them still waitin down there, petrified by terror and regret, dreamin up this . . . The third, though, they was the scariest, the ghosts just about to overtake them all, who Kalin could not look back to face, the ones that had already slipped and fallen away, them that was here now, good and dead, to inform all forms of hisself that they was all now good and dead.

Not that Tom was takin any part in these dread predations. *I never knew Mouse could fly like that!* The ghost was brightly amused too, his eyes black as char but findin some fire as well. *He had the spirit!*

Tom was chatterin on about Mouse's well-known gait. It weren't nothin like Navidad's or Ash's, both smooth as glassy river water, and still nothin compared to the beauty of Jojo's runnin. The way Mouse galloped was like abject panic and turmoil tumblin forward. He weren't ever gonna win races or pageants. Another marvel to Kalin's ridin was how he seemed so calm upon the back of such churnin disorder. Though to be fair, Tom, when he was alive, rode Mouse far better than Kalin, and Mouse who while he knew and trusted Kalin missed his old friend Tom.

Dagnabbit! I finally figured it out! Tom shouted. *Mouse runs like a rabbit! That's what it is! He runs like a goshdarn rabbit!*

What Tom meant was how instead of alternatin legs, Mouse near kicked back both back legs at the same time in order to catapult hisself forward before bringin them back up together to do it all over again.

Kalin didn't care. Mouse could run any way he liked. And now they was stoppin, at last, standin still among the twisted and wind-scoured trees. Kalin leaned down to stroke Mouse's neck and take comfort in the warmth of his coat against his cheek, even if that didn't help none to mute the sound of hoofbeats gettin louder and louder, irrational fear overtakin Kalin.

And then Jojo was beside him, and neither he nor Tom knew what to think.

Landry! Kalin cried out first, because surely she was there too, somehow already done with the worst of it, done it in her own reckless way. Fer a moment Kalin felt even more elated than when he was racin over the summit ridge, and then never more ruined to find just her empty saddle. He could believe in Tom and Ash more easily than believe this sight.

You see her?!

I do not, Tom answered.

Kalin untacked Mouse fast as he could, loopin his lead around a branch growin close to the rocky wall, above a fallen tree, its heavy trunk coiled in ice and wind-writ snow. Next he freed Jojo from his saddle, dug out his lead, and then, after clippin the bull snap to the tie ring, looped the lead end around the same branch as Mouse. He tied no knots so that if he never came back the horses could eventually free themselves, and if they was smart enuf to not return to the headwall and smart enuf to avoid the cliffs that still waited on the Heber side, they'd have a chance of followin the slope off the mountain, if still draggin their leads. He loosened some their halters so those would have a chance of fallin off at some point.

Not that this was what dominated Kalin's thoughts as he hurriedly set the horses right. It weren't no short distance back to the ridge, and he was doin his best not to register his own exhaustion. He hoped Landry had fallen somewhere between here and there. Maybe she was walkin toward them now. Though when was Landry ever parted from Jojo's back? Of course no one is spared a fall, especially where horses are concerned.

There was at least some comfort in seein Jojo content beside Mouse. This weren't exactly the warmest place, but it was enuf out of the way to avoid the direct assault of the storm.

And then the mule trotted up. That sure floored Kalin. In the commotion of Jojo's appearance and Landry's absence, he'd forgotten. This mule here, she was the thrice!

Despite the sickenin thought that kept comin up, that the worst had befallen Landry, there was also an assurance that Navidad weren't there. Kalin could put together the likely logic: Jojo had bolted after Mouse, the mule boltin after Jojo, with Landry managin to hold Navidad back.

Before leavin, Kalin hastily gave both horses their due of oats, salt, molasses, and other stuff, with the final ration kept in reserve for Navidad. And, yes, he offered a little to the mule as well, though she didn't want none. Kalin thanked her and stuffed that small portion in his own mouth. Then he gathered up the tack he'd need for Navidad and took off.

First he would find Landry, and then he'd get Navidad. His chest thudded and ached at the contorted thought that Landry was lost at the turn, now gone forever, with Navidad stumblin after her, makin a graveyard of this whole dream.

Kalin ran.

With the saddle on one shoulder, the fender and the billets kept hammerin the side of him. Kalin fought with the reins, which had come loose and threatened to trip him. He tried to run harder, but he didn't have any run left in him. Kalin not only slowed then but stopped and near heaved his guts out too, except he knew he couldn't afford to lose anythin more, and he kept down what oats and molasses and such he'd just eaten.

Walkin the rest of the way, he yelled her name into the wind. Visibility remained nil, but that didn't stop Kalin from scourin the bleak landscape for some sign of her. That Landry still weren't answerin his calls by the time he reached the top of the summit ridge near wrecked him. Twice Kalin slipped on loose rock, spillin gear, bloodyin his palms, especially on the first fall. His left hand took a small gash right on the blister and that sure hurt. The second fall ripped his jeans and bloodied a knee. Not that he paid any mind to these hurts, so central was his concern for Landry and Navidad. In truth, so empty was his reserves that them lurchin legs of his should've just up and quit; like some junk Plymouth out of gas, stranded on the side of I-15 near Draper, his whole body should've just stranded him on that barren bulge of wind-stripped rock and ice.

Kalin should've collapsed.

But he didn't.

His legs just kept goin, and then, in an amount of time no mind in such a state can accurately measure, he found hisself once more beyond the summit, where the path begins to steepen, dangerously steepen. Kalin couldn't see more than a few yards ahead, but that didn't matter: he knew the way, just like he knew that if he didn't know the way, if he didn't know just where to set his foot, he might find too easily no sure place to set his foot, and, if he was goin a little too fast, a little too recklessly, why then he might not stop until he was fallin a long ways down.

Kalin, though, didn't move recklessly. He knew the right steps. Hoofprints too marked where he'd been. When he'd finally scrambled down them rocky steps above the last turn, now slick with pebbles and dirt, his cries for Landry were once again only answered by the wind.

Furthermore, Tom had stopped, even makin like he was about to sit down, still with that idlin smile, just starin vacantly into the luminous gray already confederate with the comin night. Ash was back with Mouse, Jojo, and that strange mule. Tom weren't goin no farther.

Don't you dare sit down! Kalin yelled up at him.

Tom at least stood straight again, but he didn't budge much either.

Come on now, Kalin tried again.

Pia Isan's down there.

Who cares.

Right here, though, right on this spot, I ain't got nothin to fear.

Well good, Kalin said. *We can use a bit of that.*

I ain't goin.

I need you, Tom.

You don't need me.

I don't know what I'm gonna find down there.

I can remember dyin now, Kalin. Tom squatted down and placed his hands upon the rock like that might put him even closer to the memory. He seemed amazed.

Kalin cried out again for Landry. How much easier if just one call would've returned her voice, but there was neither Landry on the wind nor even an echo of his own pleas. What he would've given fer that whistle Sondra had insisted his mother take. What he would've given for Landry to have one too. Though even those implements would not have delivered in these conditions news of survival, devoured at once by the bellow above, the vastness below.

Kalin knew what he had to do. There was no time for Tom. He turned his back on the ghost and lurched ahead only to fall just as fast, shocked by the woodenness inhabitin his legs not to mention the sob suddenly trapped beneath his sternum. Kalin thought his heart was bustin apart. Still, he forced hisself to take another step down and then once again stumbled, this time havin to throw down his saddle against the steep rocky slope so as to not tumble head over heels into the mists.

If he expected Tom to offer some encouragement then, like he usually would've done, no matter if it came at him barbed with mischief, he was wrong. His friend was still squattin up above, entranced by a vision only he could behold.

What about Navidad? Kalin cried up at the ghost.

Tom nodded like he'd heard Kalin but also like Kalin was too far away to answer.

What about your sister? Kalin weren't givin up.

We made it, Kalin! Tom finally yelled back. *Can you believe it? We actually made it to the top! With Mouse! With even Jojo! I don't know about that mule, but she made it too. From here on out it's easy! Why on earth would we ever want to go back down there again?*

We don't want to go back down there! We have to go back down there!

But even as Kalin announced his determination, his limbs seemed even more set against him. And who could fault this bodily mutiny against action? Kalin had already achieved the impossible. And while it was one thing to survive that last turn, it was an altogether different thing to try to do the whole thing all over again. Once was enuf. Once was already too much. Once was enuf.

Some folks swear that it was at this very moment when Kalin finally heard Landry within the gnashin gusts of the storm, that it was her voice that dismissed his paralysis. At least that's what Sita Houtz, Reen Nakamura, and Harmon Raster would declare throughout their lives whenever they got together. But they weren't right. Only fools believe that screams uttered by the likes of them scrawny teenagers could've had a chance against the elements assailin the very heights of Katanogos.

Fer no reason we can know of, other than Kalin's oath to decency, first, and to Tom, second, battle-tested up here upon these trails of consequence, Kalin dragged hisself upright yet again, yet again re-situated the tack, and this time fixed his hat.

Tom, you're comin with me, Kalin ordered.

But Tom still refused to move. *I ain't got the guts.*

Of course you don't. You're a ghost.

You don't know what it's like. I remember everythin!

Then don't forget Navidad and Landry. Kalin was tired of yellin out the obvious.

I ain't goin.

Then what good are you?

Good?! Who said I had anythin to do with Good?! Tom yelled back, this time standin up, a great iciness about him, his smile completely gone, any sparkle in his eye also gone, blacker in fact than anythin Kalin had ever seen before, like black holes unafflicted by the storm, and Kalin shuddered and knew hisself afraid, and not just of where he was headed to below but now of where he must return to.

Not that it changed what he would do next: he let go of what the future would soon reveal, let fear do what it had to do, and payin neither any mind jerked his legs downward in a descent as blind as it was void of hope.

Landry too was without hope, though that weren't because any part of her believed Kalin wouldn't return. There are surges of feelin that we often rely on to energize us: hurt, anger, lust, fear of course, love fer certain. We all know them. But there's also a feelin that hurt, anger, lust, fear, even love don't got spit on, even if at first it don't seem to offer much. In fact it can feel near inert. But, see, it will begin to stir us forth from our petty selves and in the end reward us with more energy than any one of us could ever need. And it comes down to just this: to feel the timbre of what is carried by every moment is to know the music of the way over.

Now when it came to any waitin at all Landry was likely to get resentful over the authority of even just a few idle minutes. And this here weren't like waitin for a ride to some church activity. This was somethin else, an agony far worse than waitin for Kalin at the mine or down at the second stop. That said, Landry still found that the music offered by that reckonin with what just is, and for all it didn't promise or predict, the movement of it, the stillness of it, calmed her, mostly because it didn't exhaust her. And exhaustion was the key.

Landry finally recognized her exhaustion and granted herself the right to a break, the right to just rest, no matter where Kalin was, where Jojo was, no matter her circumstances or doubts. She didn't even need to change how she was positioned. In fact Landry hadn't budged much from where she'd stood when Jojo had sped off after Mouse. She was still right at the edge of that narrow aviary, host now to one black mare and one very cold little girl, lead not only securely grasped but looped around her wrist too, the risks be darned.

Landry! Kalin cried, or rather rasped out, when she finally came into view. He'd just managed his way through the turn, holdin the tack close to the wall so that its weight constantly drew him away from the edge.

Maybe he expected a smile or at least the appearance of a welcome. Instead he found her pissed as heck.

What in the Lord's name have you been doin?! Did you take a nap?

Whoa! Whoa! Kalin raised his free hand. *I had to get the horses situated. Jojo made it just fine,* he added, anticipatin her worry.

He just shot out ahead when you and Mouse took off! Her ire gave way to shame. *The reins just flew from my hands. I was sure I'd lost him. I didn't even go after him.*

You looked after Navidad, Kalin said, puttin the tack down, takin her ungloved hands in his. Aww, her poor hands. They was plenty cold, too cold. He flicked her fingertips.

Can you feel that?

I didn't know if he was dead. Landry was only now startin to process what losin hold of Jojo had cost her.

Kalin just kept flickin her fingertips. *Landry?*

Ow! Why do you keep doin that?! Landry jerked her hands away.

Jojo's fine. Kalin was gonna keep sayin it until she heard him. *That goes for the mule too.*

And finally Landry did hear it. *That's, well, well, that's a big relief,* she said with a sigh, at last huffin some hot breath on her hands.

Seein you here's a big relief for me. When I seen Jojo without you, I thought you'd been thrown.

Thrown? Have you gone daft? There was the Landry Kalin was gettin to know.

Maybe it was a daft thought.

Maybe I should've let Navidad go. Maybe she'd be safe already.

Jojo got lucky. Navidad's lucky that you were here for her. Navidad snorted, and Kalin stroked her long neck and bowed his head against her brow.

I'm cold, Landry said then.

Then what say we get out of this place and make a fire?

A big one?

Real big!

I'd like that!

It's somethin else up there, Landry. You'll see. A little bit of a hike at the very end, but there ain't no peril. Mouse, Jojo, and the mule and Ash are waitin for us in this little group of trees.

There are trees up there?

Down over the summit ridge. Right up against a big wall of rock. Plenty of room to hang a tarp and get a fire goin. We'll be warm in a jiff.

Okay then!

You can give your brother extra grief too for not comin down here.

He's with the horses?

Kalin nodded. *He says he's through with down here.*

What about me? What about frickin Navidad?!

Like I said, you can grief him when we get up there. Kalin already had Navidad's lead and was now tryin by hand to re-jamb the loose piton back into the crack where he'd first set it. When that didn't work, he thought of the farrier's kit and the hammer, but that was now up top with the rest of the gear.

Kalin briefly considered scramblin on up to retrieve it, but the time he'd need for that round trip would take too long. They had to move now or risk gettin trapped here by night.

I'll ride Navidad just like I done with Mouse. But you'll go on foot first. Just straight ahead. Then a right at the— Kalin was about to say *at the old mountain goat,* but that visitin angel was gone now. *Just turn right. You'll see where. And then just follow the hoofprints to the summit. Wait there. I'll be right behind you.*

You mean I gotta walk it alone?

It's easy, Landry. Just keep close to the cliffside, keep your eyes ahead. You'll be through it before you can count to a hundred.

I don't know if I can.

I got no way to tie up Navidad. He pointed to the loose piton and carabiner. *You understand that, right?*

I don't know if I can.

I gotta stay with Navidad.

I don't know if I can, she said for the third time, and after that couldn't stop sayin *I can't* too many times to count, until Kalin was holdin Landry's hands again as she bellowed: *I just can't, Kalin!*

There now.

Carry me, Kalin! You have to carry me! Which had to be thee stupidest idea this dumb young girl had come up with through this whole thing, and Landry knew it quick too, but maybe puttin it out there helped her see that doin it on her own was the only option left.

I wish I could, Landry. I truly do. But even if Navidad weren't here, I still don't think I could carry you.

I know it. I know you're a weaklin. That fact has never eluded me.

If I could walk it fer you, you know I would.

Landry nodded. *Navidad needs you.*

Kalin nodded. *She needs us.*

I'm sorry I call you a weaklin.

Then Landry and Kalin shared a conversation only eyes and hearts can share, full with all they feared and couldn't do and couldn't share.

Okay, okay, I can do this, Landry finally said, though she still weren't movin. *I can, I can, I can.* And she still weren't movin.

Landry, Kalin said as soft as he could, *we don't got much time.*

Instead Landry turned around to face the way they'd come. *Are they comin after us?*

Night's comin after us.

And if them Porches try, we'll see their lights, right?

Even if they do make it some of the way up, there's a big heap of rocks up above that I'm pretty sure we could set loose upon this gap here. Kalin weren't lyin either. Even now there's a pile of stones right there, a tall cairn or unreadable stela made by a giant for other giants headin to the stars.

Can we do that anyway? Landry asked.

We gotta go.

Okay, okay. But this time Landry not only didn't move; she slid down to her butt.

Landry! Remember what Tom told you: Never quit!

I know it.

Remember the Awides Mine? Remember how you climbed that ladder? And that was in the dark? This is so much easier!

Landry looked up. She was scowlin like she'd just been cornered. *Ain't you a peach.*

I'm right, though, ain't I?

Landry nodded. *Tom always did say never quit.* She moved a little bit then but it was only to sink lower.

Landry! Landry! We gotta go! We have no choice!

I know it! But Landry stayed locked up, now bindin up her legs with them quiverin arms, still tighter, her chest cramped hard against her thighs, her face between her knees. This time when she looked up, tears had flooded her face. *I gotta go! I know I gotta go! But I can't! I can't move, Kalin! I'm all froze up. I'm so scared I can't even straighten one leg, let alone make two of them walk on out of here!* And right then Landry looked so ashen and withdrawn that she seemed a ghost in her own right.

Do it then for Jojo. Think of Jojo. He's up there right now. He needs you. Do it for him.

Landry shook her head, sorta snorted too, but still did manage to stand up.

Don't think no more on it, Landry. Just walk steady and you'll be through it in less time than we've been talkin about it.

And fer a moment it looked like Landry would do just that, just walk right on outta there.

I can't do it, Kalin, she mumbled instead, once again slidin down onto her butt.

Kalin nodded. He understood, he did, but he also didn't know what else to do about what he understood.

I just can't go out there alone, she whimpered.

Tell her she ain't gonna be alone.

Kalin whipped his head around. Sure as there was still a little bit of daylight, there was Tom, not even a foot away, grinnin plenty, or at least grinnin enuf, if maybe a bit paler than his usual pale self.

You're here! Kalin wanted to hug him.

Of course I'm here. Where else am I gonna go? Tom said.

Tom's here?! What's he sayin?! Landry demanded, back on her feet again.

What are you sayin? Kalin asked Tom.

That I'm braver than she is, and proof is that I'm here right now while she ain't right now up there with Jojo.

Tom just came down to hear you say that he's braver than you, Kalin relayed.

But neither ire nor siblin rivalry had any magic to work now. *Of course he's braver than me!* Landry wailed, back down on her butt. *He's the bravest guy I ever met, with maybe the exception of you. I can't come close to what he could do. And I ain't talkin about him ridin Hightower or any of this nonsense we're into now. I'm talkin about how he met Death when Death finally did come around. He was still crackin jokes, smilin, makin my momma laugh through her tears. And he was so tired! But he was also just so kind. Me, I woulda wet myself. I'd wet myself now if I had anythin to pee.*

Tell her I fer sure wet myself. All the time. I just had a catheter.

Kalin did as he was told, and Landry snorted through her tears, tryin to hide her grin that arrived with that expulsion of breath and a fair amount of snot. *He really is here, ain't he?*

Kalin knelt beside her. *For you, Landry. He loves his little sister so much. He wants to make sure no harm comes to you. So he's gonna walk with you all the way up to Jojo. He'll even hold your hand.*

Can he do that?

He says he'll do whatever it takes to make sure you're safe.

And though Tom hadn't said that, the old ghost didn't object to Kalin puttin words in his mouth. In fact they nearly put some color in his cheeks and fer sure glittered up his eyes so they weren't so star-swallowin black.

This time when Landry stood up, she stepped away from the wall and even took another step away from Kalin and Navidad.

Okay then, Tom Gatestone! she addressed the air after takin a deep breath. *Let's get to Jojo. And don't you dare let me fall or even wobble! You hear me, Tom Gatestone!*

He hears you. He's right next to you.

Tell her to stop yellin, Tom grumbled. *Bein a ghost is bad enuf. I don't wanna be a deaf ghost.*

Just remember, Tom, Landry continued, her voice still big, still boomin the walls of that narrow retreat. *If I fall, I'm comin after you. And I don't care if you are braver than me. I'll kick the tar out of you! I will!*

The gall of this girl! Tom said.

He says he won't let you fall, Kalin told Landry instead.

Without lookin back then, she inched out onto the ledge. Landry knew better than to dare a glance at the edge let alone at the vista that waited beyond that allurin line. She even squinted some, keepin her eyes solely on the rock wall to the right, where her right hand maintained light contact. Her left hand she pointed to where she was headed, perhaps servin as a reminder as to where she was goin should she suddenly succumb to a disorientation severe enuf to rob her of any sense of direction, which up there was always possible.

It's likely most would deem her progress overcautious, especially on those early portions of the ledge where there was enuf room for Tom to walk beside her, even if every now and then his casual gait was betrayed by a hitch or stutter of step. But as the ledge narrowed, such complaints would've quickly quieted, with Tom movin ahead of her but never so much that his little sister was ever out of reach.

That first section of gouges posed little difficulty for Landry. Even that second section of deep gouges Landry stepped over easily. The third section slowed her down significantly, but it weren't until they reached the final turn that Landry stopped.

The old mountain goat was indeed gone.

Landry could see clear enuf the steps she'd have to take to get to that eroded landin. She could also see that she'd have plenty of room to turn around. However, just the thought of one of those steps betrayin her with a surface too slick to keep to began to freeze her up again.

Landry walked back, or at least far enuf back so Kalin could hear her, pressin her back against the rock, keepin her head down, eyes shut, her knees bendin enuf to indicate she'd be on her butt soon enuf, though she didn't sit down, and maybe that was a bit of good news.

Landry! Kalin cried out then, edgin out as far as he could go without movin Navidad forward any.

I gotta ask you somethin, she trembled out.

Kalin could hear her voice on the wind, but not what she was sayin. *I can't hear you! Speak louder!*

Kalin took a few more steps forward, Navidad followin him enuf so that her forelegs were on the ledge.

I gotta ask you somethin! Landry cried.

Go on!

It's really important!

You can ask me anythin!

I just wanna know, if I ask you to the dance, will you say yes?

What dance?

I don't know! Any ole dance! An Orvop High dance! Will you say yes?

Yes! Yes! Of course I'll say yes! It was the darndest thing too, how Kalin felt when he said that. He just wanted to see Landry through that one turn, see her on her way up to the summit. He just wanted her off this goshforsaken wall. He'd've pretty much said anythin to see that through, but when those three yeses spillt from his lips, they set his cheeks afire. There was every chance he and Navidad would in the next few minutes fall to their deaths, and yet some notion of him and Landry handfasted now to some high school nonsense pulsed him with somethin that had nothin to do with ire nor shame either, somethin that didn't feel half-bad.

I'm not askin you now! Landry yelled out, shimmyin a little closer.

Okay! Kalin took a step her way too.

Just to be clear!

Okay!

Is Tom rollin his eyes?

Of course he is. The wind had briefly stilled.

I don't care. I'm gonna ask loud too, right in Main Hall, right durin lunch break, when it's most crowded, and I just wanna— Landry choked up then. She just couldn't help herself. *I just wanna know you won't embarrass me.*

And maybe Kalin choked up some too when he answered her: *Landry Gatestone, I will never embarrass you. I'm honored to think you'd think enuf of me to ask me to a dance. I look forward to it.*

And Tom didn't roll his eyes. *She'll be embarrassed when she sees how you dance.*

Landry opened her eyes then. She didn't look back either. She just gave the way ahead one last study, took one more breath through her nose, and then started movin, past the three rough sections and then over them slick steps. She didn't stop neither. And the steadiness she needed underfoot didn't betray her.

Except once.

But once is all it takes.

Do you remember the moment when Jojo hammered down his right forehoof *with the strength of Pegasus*, as Ms. Melson would later aver, and how the rock had cracked and might as well have burst forth with spring waters? Well, right there, on that exact same spot, Landry placed her right foot, put all her weight on it too, only to feel it give way. It weren't by much either. The rock didn't fall away entirely, rather just compacted and shifted some, at most by a quarter of an inch. Unfortunately Landry didn't have Jojo's hind legs to keep powerin her upwards, nor was there anythin within reach of her left hand that she could use to correct the unbalancin and refuse the pull of the far below. In fact the only thing her left hand could hold on to was a plan for the future, a future handhold not even the most muscled acrobat could have gotten to given her teeterin position.

Now here's what Kalin saw: at the very same moment that Landry started to slip backwards, Tom lunged for his little sister, grabbin hold of her wrist, and Landry somehow felt that hold, or at least the pull, and in turn grabbed hold of this aidin wrist of wind and spirit, summonin in her strength enuf for the impossible, to get that left foot up on the rock, powerin her beyond the loose stones fallin away into the maw she was leavin behind.

And, no, Tom never did tell Kalin how at the moment when he grabbed Landry with his right hand, Pia Isan had grabbed his left wrist. To hold him, hold them all.

And then it was done. Landry was on the landin, then through the turn, a moment later scramblin on all fours, then on just her legs, runnin as fast as she could from the headwall, easy as a boat glidin downstream, what was fast becomin a hill, all the way to the summit ridge, then over the summit ridge, where clouds enveloped her and rain slashed at her face, vanishin everythin but a few feet ahead, though the weather could still not hide all the hoofprints that soon enuf delivered Landry into the company of Mouse, the mule, and of course her dear Jojo, all of them just fine, still grazin if snappin now and then at the air.

Landry threw her arms around Jojo, buryin her face in his mane, while he in turn nibbled at her hair. They'd made it! Horses and all! Up and over a cliff more than a thousand feet high! And now they was free! Free! Free!

Kalin and Navidad will be here before we can even catch our breath, Landry said, what she also assumed Tom would say, which in fact Tom did say, almost word for word and at the same time too: *They'll be here before you can even catch your breath.*

Three minutes tops, Landry said even louder, which, though she couldn't hear him, Tom was sayin too, though he put it at *two minutes tops.*

But Tom weren't even close. Landry neither. Almost as soon as Landry had made her declaration, she heard from somewhere beyond the summit ridge the crack of a powerful rifle.

It was 6:37 p.m.

If Law Enforcement Ranger Bren Kelson had just stood a few steps closer to the Upecksay Headwall, he never would've witnessed that overhead scurry of equine passage up to the second retreat within that great tooth of rock. Plenty have dreamed of that Big If, especially Brooke Young, who, upon learnin of the possibility presented by geometry, and from Detective Peters no less, never ceased to find in her nightmares, long after her mission in Mexico City, long after she was married, and with five children too, how that distance between Kelson and the Katanogos summit headwall would remain in her scarred and tormented mind inviolable against her every effort to alter it, reduce it, bring that man into the safety of a blind spot, that man she'd loved so generously, so tenderly, that man exposed to the hands of cruel and capricious gods. How she would curse those gods too whenever she woke, pleadin with her Heavenly Father to smite them, which only worsened her nightmares, smotherin her in the confines of this feverish mental battle with the horrifyin recognition that her Jesus, as in Hey Zeus sometimes, had been Zeus all along, and whether that leap from Spanish to Greek was at all sensible, forget legitimate, would still deliver her to a place where Great Power in its purest form is a Great Power because it will not deliver mercy. *That ain't what Power does,* Brooke Young had convinced herself. *Though how many years did I spend believin it was capable of Christian acts? I might as well have been butterin my bread with a handgun.*

Yet even outside that blind spot, while he was beholdin the obvious and for him recognizable shapes, Law Enforcement Ranger Bren Kelson still doubted the sight. He counted two fer sure. He counted a third that he was less sure about. One. Two. Three. Movin across the mountain face at an already unimaginable altitude. Four? The mind does funny things when it encounters what it in no way can expect to find let alone imagine. Was there also a fifth up there? Had there been a rider on the first horse? Another rider on the third? And then they were gone, as if forbidden by Katanogos, leavin any answer as lost as the question itself already seemed necessarily void: *Are those . . . up there?!* Except that weren't exactly true. None of the men could deny the fallin stones and debris that followed soon after, bouncin down along the abraded surface of the great face before, long moments later, they was landin near them, too near, with Egan Porch gettin out of the way first, followed by Billings, pressin themselves close to the wall.

I'll be goshdarned, Emily, Kelson said over the radio to Park Ranger Brickey. *I see horses up there on the cirque wall. Goshdarn it, I don't believe it, but there they are!*

Horses?! Park Ranger Brickey squawked back.

Egan Porch hailed his brothers then on his radio. Recall that they was on a different frequency from the rangers now. Kelly answered.

Ask Hatch to scope the headwall above where we're at! Egan ordered. *Billings just seen them up there.*

With the horses?! Kelly squawked back. He and Park Ranger Brickey sounded as amazed as Law Enforcement Ranger Kelson looked. But amazed didn't hold no sway over Egan, and Egan was glad to see Billings weren't under any such spell either.

In fact Billings was already scurryin higher up the slope with an eye out to solvin how them kids had mounted the wall. But the way weren't clear. Billings picked quick enuf an obvious ledge only to find that it led nowhere meaninful after about ten yards. And that was a lucky thing for Billings, because some wrong ledges could take you on a very long tour before deliverin you to a precipice you'd best step back from. The next ledge Billings tried was the one Kalin and Landry and the horses had in fact taken, though soon after Billings took a wrong turn and was none the wiser until fifty feet up, where he beheld a ledge that seemed to keepin goin along the width of the whole cirque. It was possible that the path up was achieved along such a long, rocky traverse, but as Billings began to dare this lengthy direction, he was pulled up soon enuf by the absence of any signs upon the rocks of the horses themselves. Surely they'd have left behind some trace?

The last shelf Billings tried, he near raced up, and at around seventy-five-feet up discovered manure, which increased his confidence. He even sped up only to discover that he was too soon ledged out. The manure, he realized, had likely fallen from above, perhaps even markin half a dozen wrong routes on the way down, further complicatin the way up with such splashy falsehoods. The opposite of asters. Likely Mouse's gifts.

Billings reckoned quick enuf that there might be dozens of promisin starts that would too soon end. Worse, though, would be those long time-chewin traverses that also led nowhere.

With the day near burnt, Billings headed back down, also comin to understand how, after only a few turns, if he was to remember wrongly the way down, he could easily come to trap hisself up there, forcin him to spend a night hunkered down against this cold wall, a night he might not survive, all of which he made clear to Egan when he finally made it down.

As he and Egan then began to descend to where Law Enforcement Ranger Kelson waited, Egan slowed enuf to let Billings move ahead, stoppin altogether when Billings passed the ranger. Not that Kelson, who was still dazed by the sight above, noticed how he was now surrounded.

Though nearly halfway across Kirk's Cirque, Park Ranger Emily Brickey was also dazed or at least undone some by her colleague's bizarre assertion. In fact so focused was she on what her binoculars might reveal and likely refute, squintin out across Altar Lake, the meadow, the lower talus, before slowly liftin her gaze toward those vast vertical blue walls of limestone and sandstone, folded here, rippled there, the geological mischief that had created them fabled four fangs, continuin her survey up past the various strata, in some places sloped enuf to support smallish screes, all of which continued to present a place that to Ranger Brickey's eye was clearly beyond the reach of any horse, her attention fixated instead on locatin rock formations, scrubby bits of brush, and dead grass that might have misled Ranger Kelson, that she didn't even register how but a few paces away, Hatch Porch was puttin together the upper and lower assembly of his .50-caliber Barrett M82 with a Zeiss 2.5-10x52 optic mounted on a Picatinny rail. It already had a monopod at the back, and once Hatch deployed the bipod up front, why he had hisself a very stable shootin platform set up on the tarp he'd spread out first.

Hatch hadn't taken but a moment to locate Law Enforcement Ranger Kelson, with Egan at this point already trailin behind Billings, who had jogged ahead to try to figure out a way up the headwall. Hatch then systematically began to scope the wall above his brother. He'd given Kelly his binoculars to act as a spotter. Not that either of them were seein much of anythin except growin shadows.

That's some rifle there, Kelly said then, and in truth he was more interested in the new weapon than any smear of gray and black his lenses might happen to flit across.

This thing is a beast, Hatch admitted.

Fifty caliber? Kelly asked.

Look at these! Hatch held up the cartridges. One covered near his whole palm, and like their daddy, Hatch too had immense hands. *This magazine takes ten of these suckers,* Hatch added, demonstratin how the cartridges loaded, staggered, double-column, double-feed. The magazine itself was bigger than an 8-track.

This is what you snipers use?

Naw. I'd been hearin about a fifty cal like this for a while. Then I saw an ad in Shotgun News. I just had to have it. Hatch kept rockin the magazine back and forth before it inserted right. Weren't no easy event. Hatch returned to the scope and Kelly to the binoculars.

Bet it ain't nothin but birds they've seen, Kelly said with a sneer. *That Kalin kid and Landry came in here just like we did, and they left the same way too, like we better do soon if we don't want to spend the night up here.*

I think that's about the sum of things, Park Ranger Brickey threw in then, glad to find somethin she could agree on, despite bein real rattled by a rifle that looked better suited for some military engagement in a distant country than anythin goin on up here in these peaceful wilds.

And I'll agree with you both, Hatch even added, which pleased Kelly plenty and put Park Ranger Brickey more at ease, an ease that only increased when Hatch offered her a look through his scope.

It took a moment to get settled on that tarp before her eye found the stillness she'd need to see. At first she was just starin at a little glob of blue light, but then as her breath smoothed, the light expanded until the field of view was nothin but bright clarity, complete with floatin crosshairs, even if what she saw now was just a tiny span of vertical rock with not even a ledge to stand on let alone a place for outlaw kids with horses.

And what the heck she was even doin right then did cross her mind, splayed out on a tarp that while holdin off the wet weren't doin nothin against the cold now robbin her of any comfort, makin her all the more uncomfortable about bein behind such a powerful weapon. If anythin this was Ranger Kelson's department, not hers, though as she ran through her head the various enforceable ordinances concernin firearms up here, this thing still weren't technically in breach of anythin she could recall, especially since it hadn't even been fired. She'd have to check with Kelson about what laws pertained to .50 calibers. She'd already taken note of the fact that the safety was on and anyway her hands weren't nowhere near the trigger or the large chargin handle on the right. Still, there was somethin kinda reassurin about havin in her possession such a weapon. She couldn't say why either.

She continued to scan the cliffside and, after findin nothin but rock on more rock, was about to stand up when her ears tuned into the squawkin on Kelly's and Hatch's radios, carryin at the same time the voice of their brother Egan Porch.

Me and Billings found a few starts up this wall. There are plenty of wide ledges and even signs of horse manure. Manure? And then Hatch was sayin somethin. No, that was Kelly. Egan, though, hadn't stopped talkin. *Ain't no path we found yet that gets that high. Let us know if you can see a way up.*

Park Ranger Emily Brickey tried to tilt up the scope but found she had to lift the whole rifle only to find more rock.

Fire that thing like that and it'll break your jaw, Hatch Porch warned. *Here.* And he got down on the tarp beside her, droppin the monopod under the recoil pad to grant her the low-angle view she didn't really care so much about. She didn't care for him bein so close to her either, but Hatch didn't stay close, bouncin back on his feet to talk more with his brother.

As Park Ranger Emily Brickey kept studyin the wall only to find more wall and still nothin she'd vouch for was a ledge capable of supportin even one horse, she couldn't help but hear, in a followin moment where Hatch was done talkin and Egan was done too, another voice, what would've been Billings's voice comin through on Kelly's radio, likely observin to Egan how *Somehow they've made it over. They're clear of this place.*

Then they've got another day on us, she heard Egan reply, even though he weren't sayin so directly into the radio but just yellin his thoughts back at that Billings fella. *We better sight a path up there quick or head back.*

It weren't lost on Park Ranger Brickey, as she kept movin up from one line of stone to the next, how these words reflected a certainty about what they'd seen as well as the resolve to pursue it. She relinquished then her hold on the precision rifle. Either her haste in gettin to her feet or the sense of purpose these Porch boys shared had so unsettled her stance that Hatch Porch, with a gracious smile, felt duty-bound to set his hand on her lower back to steady her. And in point of fact, despite the growin sense of threat congealin around her, his touch weren't that unwelcome. See, Park Ranger Emily Brickey believed that Hatch Porch was a gentleman and intended no harm and meant only to see things get done right.

Park Ranger Brickey would later report that regardless of what little sense she could actually make out of that overheard conversation on the radios, she had determined then that her next course of action would be to rejoin Law Enforcement Ranger Bren Kelson, to whom she would then recommend that they leave the cirque, reestablish radio contact and report their findings, and from there descend to the Isatch Canyon entrance before night fell. Once there they could flesh out the details of the campsite, evidence of horses, with a possible sightin of some kind of animal movement, however improbable, up on the Upecksay Headwall. Park Ranger Brickey felt certain they would need a larger search party to come up here at first light. Her thoughts continued on like this.

A crack came over Kelly's and Hatch's radios, followed an instant later by a louder crack sunderin the air around her, already ringin the cirque walls with echoes and reechoes too numerous to provide an obvious point of origin. Subsequent cracks, once again heard first over the radios and a fraction of a second later echoin around the cirque, didn't help either. As Park Ranger Emily Brickey eventually admitted, she had no clue where to look, not that lookin mattered one bit, as what now had everyone's attention was Egan Porch's voice screamin over his brothers' radios that Law Enforcement Ranger Bren Kelson was down.

They shot him! They shot Bren in the head!

It was 6:06 p.m.

Now this was the very same crack Kalin and Landry had heard while they was enjoyin a break within that second confine of stone. It was the report Billings heard far more directly and Egan most directly with Law Enforcement Ranger Bren Kelson never knowin what hit him.

You'll recall Egan had positioned hisself above Ranger Kelson while Billings was some steps below the ranger and movin off to the side.

Egan never doubted what they'd seen up on the wall. Billings had already confirmed that it weren't unreasonable to assume that the right series of ledges and turns could lead them to whatever scramble of horses and youth had just occurred up above. Now with Law Enforcement Ranger Bren Kelson havin just relayed to Park Ranger Emily Brickey the sightin of horses, the next step would be to muster additional law enforcement up here. Egan also didn't doubt that if them kids could overcome an obstacle like the Upecksay Headwall, with horses too, they'd survive whatever was on the other side, at least long enuf to be taken into custody by police, what Egan's daddy feared the most.

Now to be clear, none of Egan's reckonin was set down coolly like puzzle pieces on some card table one Sunday after lunch with a whole afternoon ahead, accompanied by a big pitcher of lemonade loaded with ice. Egan's thoughts came up hot as his pulse was fast, his breaths heavy and rough, his whole body knotted with the exertions demanded by the unexpected action ahead. The real horseradish.

First of all, as his instincts instructed, he kept his left hand clamped on the radio in order to communicate what all would happen next.

Law Enforcement Ranger Bren Kelson had by then turned his back on Egan to ask Billings to clarify further what he'd seen up there, for instance the color of the horses, the size of the ledges, any details about the spattered bits of horse manure, and did Billings think they'd reached the summit slope, or had they disappeared into some alcove of rock not apparent from any angle found down here?

Egan didn't move real fast. He drew out that double-action aluminum-framed 9mm Smith & Wesson Model 59 with all identifyin numerics filed off. It was a smooth pull too, hardly rufflin his coat, and in its direction and commitment unerrin. That went for his aim as well.

Egan shot Law Enforcement Ranger Bren Kelson through the back of his head, the ranger not only tumblin at once off the boulder he was on but rollin down the hill some ways before jammin up in among rough-edge rocks, his limbs contorted, the side of his face smeared with blood.

Egan shot twice more in the air and then started hollerin over his radio: *They shot him! They shot Bren in the head!*

If Billings was shocked, it weren't evident. Likely he'd done similar calculatin to arrive at Egan's cold-blooded choice. In fact Billings was already scramblin over to the ranger's body as Egan near just as quick gathered up two of the three casins ejected onto the ground. He could not locate the third casin.

Billings lowered his ear to the ranger's mouth and then pressed his ear to the ranger's chest. Whatever faint flutters Billings was listenin for didn't matter when Law Enforcement Ranger Kelson suddenly jerked sideways and gasped. That sure scared the bejesus outta both Billings and Egan, not that they didn't recover fast enuf, and with Billings already understandin the consequences of Egan's act, what suddenly made Billings an accomplice given his inaction now, or even a threat if he turned on Egan and reported the deed. Instead he chose to cement his Porch loyalty by yankin from his coat a big ziplock bag. After emptyin the remainin nuts, jerky bits, and M&M's into his palm and slappin all that into his mouth, he fit the bag, like he'd been taught to do, over Law Enforcement Ranger Bren Kelson's head, sealin the mouth and nose as best he could with his hands while not applyin too much pressure around the neck.

It was hard to believe the man was still alive. The bullet had exited through an eye and blown that clean out, though incredibly a part of the eyelid remained intact and still fluttered above the hole. The plastic over the man's mouth also continued to flutter some. Billings just sat there, waitin and chewin that meaty, chocolaty mass in his mouth, now and then lookin out toward the meadow because he knew the arrival of Kelly and Hatch Porch along with that girl park ranger was inevitable.

What was they gonna do about her?

When the plastic finally stilled and Billings could detect no murmurs in the ranger's chest or find a pulse at his neck, he removed the bloodied bag. But what to do with that suddenly flummoxed him. Egan was also unsure what to do with it. Should they try to bury it? Surely that would be found when law enforcement arrived tomorrow.

Billings finally pressed out the air, sealed it, and after rollin it up, slipped it into the back of his pants, in his briefs too and, if you must know, between his butt cheeks, which was obvious to Egan, and it disgusted him, though he respected Billings's resolve.

When Park Ranger Emily Brickey drove up at last on her ATV, with Kelly right behind on Hatch's two-seater ATV, Egan and Billings were huddled over the officer.

He's still alive! Egan screamed at her before she could even let one word loose. *We gotta get him down now!*

Park Ranger Brickey's radio was still just a song of static. Some hurried arguments followed over whether or not to get the heck outta there until they was in a spot where they could call in a medevac helicopter.

The longer we wait, the sooner he'll die! Egan shouted, panicked and desperate enuf that Billings noted the performance and was pretty impressed.

Kelly, at last seein his chance to do somethin he could admire, ordered Billings and Egan to dress Kelson's wound and then tie him to his back, near piggyback-style. Egan made a meek display of pointin out how dangerous that would make the trip down, and in the dark too, and over such hard terrain.

You turn your wheel wrong once and he's gonna drag you right off, Egan warned his younger brother.

Kelly sneered and spat. *You worry about you. I'm gettin this guy down.*

I'll follow right behind, Park Ranger Brickey volunteered. She was the only one lookin up the wall, and Egan realized only then that they should still be actin like they was all under threat of fire from overhead.

Let's get outta here before he gets another one of us! Egan shouted.

Billings offered to take the lead on the Honda dirt bike and light up the trail.

Egan said he'd hustle over to get Hatch.

And that was pretty much that. Egan's lie that Law Enforcement Ranger Bren Kelson was still alive obturated all tears and hysterics, what Egan had expected from Park Ranger Brickey, viewin her as mostly unattractive, weak, and now inconsequential. Furthermore, his lie helped accelerate their depature. And soon they were away from that bloody place, Billings up front on the dirt bike, Kelly with the ranger's body, and Ranger Brickey behind, swiftly makin it to the edge of the cirque, where Bewilder Crick began its wanderin descent toward the bottom of Isatch Canyon.

Egan, meanwhile, abandoned his single-seater ATV and took the two-seater Billings had left behind. On his way back to Hatch, he spotted the beaver out again atop her lodge.

R ight after Kelly Porch and Park Ranger Emily Brickey had taken off to help Egan, Hatch had resettled hisself on his tarp behind that Barrett M82. Kelly had forgotten to give back Hatch's binoculars, and so Hatch was forced to rely solely on the scope's narrow field of vision. Maybe that weren't a bad thing. It still offered the best clarity even in the departin light.

One reason he'd missed Landry's and Kalin's ride from that second enclosure to the third one was that he'd never thought to look so high. The second reason was of course the scene unfoldin at the base of the headwall. Hatch had sighted quick enuf his brother Egan rushin to the side of the downed ranger. Hatch could only make out a foot thrust up above a rock; Billings, who was crouched over the ranger, his back to Hatch's scope, hid the rest of that fallen form.

What had disturbed Hatch most was the sight of a pistol in Egan's hand. Hatch registered the shape fast enuf and glimpsed too a flash of its aluminum frame, none of which was a surprise given that his brother was under fire and likely preparin to answer that fire. No, the trouble came when Egan rather hastily put the firearm away, shovin it behind his back. Why on earth would Egan do that? For that matter, why were both Egan and Billings sittin now calm as ducks? Obviously they was givin care to a wounded man, and their courage in the line of fire should be applauded. Still, Hatch knew Egan, and there was somethin just too surreptitious and casual about his actions.

And then his radio was cracklin with his brother's voice: *I hope you're givin us cover, buddy. We're pretty exposed out here.* Words that immediately rearranged again how Hatch was witnessin the scene. Wasn't it more likely that Egan had holstered his gun because he didn't have a shot from there and the priority was to give aid to the victim? Wasn't that what Billings was already doin? Hatch never even gave a second thought to that big ziplock bag that briefly appeared in his lens. And he never returned his lens to find it bloodied.

It took Hatch some time to locate the threat from above, but he did it. He had the trainin, the skill, the equipment, and the professional patience to get just that job done. By this point not only had Kalin made it over the summit ridge on Mouse, followed by Jojo and the mule, but he'd just returned. Hatch caught sight of Kalin in that dark Stetson disappearin into that third refuge. Hatch even spotted the profile of a black horse, that bein Navidad of course, before it too retreated into the shadows of stone.

When a tremblin Landry Gatestone finally emerged, Hatch kept that little girl right smack in the middle of his crosshairs. He could see she weren't armed. He could see she didn't want to go. He could see she was terrified. At no point did Hatch think here was the one who murdered Russel, killt Egan's horse, and just now wounded a ranger. He never moved his finger toward the trigger, not even to click off the safety.

In truth, he half expected to watch her drop through his glass. So high up was she, and so bad were her jitters and pauses as she crept across the face of that terrifyin wall, that he found hisself nibblin on his lips. Whatever the condition and dimensions of the ledge she was now on, Hatch could see it suffered great gaps and fissures, which Landry still managed to get past. Hatch would've helped her if he could've got up there quick enuf. No part of Hatch Porch wanted to see Landry Gatestone harmed.

Then she froze, right where the path turned up and back on itself, and all of Hatch froze too. He watched her retreat then, press her back against the cliff, sink like she was gonna sit. Then it looked like she was yellin back at where she'd just emerged from, where the Kalin kid had disappeared.

Hatch had no skills with lip-readin, not that he could see her close enuf to even guess at what she was screamin. Instead Hatch imagined her pleadin with her captor to show some mercy and not make her walk that gosh-awful plank.

What happened next Hatch didn't need to imagine, though he did think later that he must have imagined it. Landry Gatestone scrambled again over that mauled ledge and this time kept goin, this time kept headin up a series of rock steps, and doin just fine too, toward what Hatch could see was a big-enuf slab to manage an easy turnabout on, when the rock beneath her foot gave way and Landry slipped and she had nothin to grab hold of   except air.

She should've fallen, she was already fallin, but, see, Landry Gatestone didn't fall. It was like even durin the slip some part of her had just then grabbed hold of some place she'd need to now bring that left foot up, and high enuf too, to swing it onto solid ground. A great gymnast perhaps, or maybe a contortionist, might've managed that kind of balancin act. These were possibilites Hatch had to at least consider if only to explain the rest of what happened, because without Landry bein some Nadia Comăneci, someone Hatch had seen one night in Ber-lin, Landry Gatestone should've dropped away instead of scamperin on up and outta sight, gone like the heights of Katanogos were gone to the storm.

And it had all happened so quickly too that even Hatch, who was trained for, as well as excelled at, makin detailed accounts from brief moments observed through his scope, could hardly register what he'd just seen. Somehow she had not submitted to gravity. Somehow she had held herself aloft. Or was she held aloft? By a hand unapparent to Hatch's dull eyes?

Hatch was unprepared for the feelin that overtook him then, like he'd just witnessed some ancient god in their midst who had descended to that rocky pinnacle just for Landry. Now Hatch didn't know the names of any such ancient gods, and he fer sure weren't thinkin about any, but what he had surgin through his body aligned fairly well with a mortal encounterin Apollo or Hermes, though the hot flash across the expanse of his wide chest might suggest a goddess instead, perhaps she whose shield bore the face of she who would turn the world to stone. That was the feelin. At least at first. Though fast as kerosene goes bright with a spark, it was replaced by an embodied alignment more indicative of Hatch's upbringin: his Heavenly Father, bestowin His grace upon that little black sheep, lost upon a petrified wilderness, set there to fall to the jaws of wolves, associations that did shoot through Hatch even if he couldn't quite trace them hisself, only feelin this growin sense of bewilderment before the divine protection seen up there, on behalf of Landry Gatestone, which made of Hatch, in how he was positioned in relation to this miracle, none other than the wolf huntin the lamb, which to say the least disquieted Hatch plenty, leavin him both shocked, confused, and humbled. Was this what it felt like to behold a miracle? He felt ashamed.

Hatch even had to lift his eye from the scope then, as if to further unsee that particular moment by rebeholdin the cirque surroundin him like an immense church before which not even kneelin was good enuf. Not even prostrate would do. But wasn't that exactly what he was doin? Prostratin hisself before this heart-shudderin warnin? What was Hatch even doin up here? What was this all even about? Hatch suddenly didn't trust a bit of it. Not even the ground upon which he lay. Not even the very rock Landry had just surmounted.

Just start there: A little girl up there? Impossible! Horses up there?! Impossible! What kind of world had Hatch suddenly found hisself in? Where was he?

But when Hatch returned to the scope, he was up there again, right at that rock blind behind which the boy had vanished, the horse too. And then the profile of a black horse emerged, followed by the whole of it, so shockin a sight that if it weren't movin, Hatch would've thought it a charcoal silhouette thousands of years old, drawn on a cave wall, drawn on this wall. Though the sight of the boy atop that horse was anythin but shockin, mainly because he was so recognizable to Hatch, not because Hatch knew him or had ever laid eyes on him before but because Hatch recognized the calm Kalin possessed as he rode forward, the calm and ease that was of course needed to make this feat possible.

One more moment and Kalin would've set Navidad into motion. Another moment and they'd've cleared the rough spots. A final moment and they'd've dared the final turn.

Hatch, mostly by muscle memory, pivoted the rifle, adjusted his aim, exhaled, and fired. It was 6:37 p.m. The powerful blast not only recoiled hard against Hatch's shoulder but at the same time expanded outward through Kirk's Cirque as the round itself sizzled ahead at terrible speeds set against the mountain. Fer a moment Hatch lost sight in the recoil of where he'd shot but found again quick enuf where the wall was still spillin powdered rock, next to which, and much to Hatch's horror, he sighted the black horse buckin badly on the edge of its own end, head goin from one side to the next, backin up but only in an effort to gain enuf momentum to spin around, which on that narrow place would be akin to just boltin off to certain death.

Hatch couldn't describe the awfulness that seeped through him then. Of course the horse would fall. More than a thousand feet straight down. Of course the boy would fall. More than a thousand feet straight down. And Hatch could save neither one of them. He'd once wanted to be a veterinarian. He was ten at the time and had felt a powerful callin to dedicate his life to healin animals. Old Porch would hear none of that, though Hatch's dream hadn't died there. With the help of his momma, he'd continued to nurture this pursuit, when his momma was still with them then, but after she'd gone, on his own, his dream had shifted some then to med school. Hatch even took AP Biology his junior year and scored a 5 on the AP Test. He didn't just want to be a doctor either; he wanted to be a professor of medicine, teachin kids how to better heal others. After that, he'd reasoned, he might try again to become a vet. But none of that happened. Old Porch was just too strong. Hatch chose the Army Rangers, which Old Porch could hardly argue with. Nothin tougher than them Army Rangers. Hadn't that old cuss told all his boys how he'd been in both the army and the marines? What bullcrap! Hatch couldn't trust nothin. Not even his own eyes right then.

Because the horse hadn't fallen. The boy hadn't fallen either. It was almost too impossible to believe. If Landry's near fall had tested Hatch's perceptive faith, this was way worse because it was so much more obvious. The boy's calm had not left him despite all the rearin and backscramblin, which only amplified Hatch's disbelief. Though his disbelief did not quash his admiration for the boy's ridin, one still hand reined up, the other on the horse's mane, an easiness that never failed as the boy regained control of the horse and proceeded to back it straight back until they was again both out of sight.

What had Hatch just done?

Egan, though, was screamin his head off as he tore up on Kelly's two-seater, jubilant as after an Orvop High football win.

Did you get her? Did you get him?

It weren't lost on Hatch how badly Egan wanted to hear that both kids were dead. Maybe the only one who wanted them more dead than Old Porch hisself was Egan. A blackness began to seep into Hatch. This weren't who he was. He hadn't gone all the way to Texas just to fall back into more of this. Killin kids?!

Landry got over the summit, he answered. *I seen that much. I missed the boy. I thought fer sure he and the horse were gonna fall.*

He's one heckuva rider. We've learned that much, Egan said as he climbed off the ATV, noddin his head too much.

He's trapped up there behind some rocks.

How does someone like you even miss? Ain't you a sniper? Did you get a little yellow when it came to it?

In his defense Hatch could say the rifle was new. He might not have sighted it in correctly, nor could he claim any mastery yet of how a bullet that heavy dropped through the course of its trajectory. But Hatch hadn't aimed to kill Kalin. Just hold him.

Let me take a look! Egan said, droppin beside Hatch on the tarp. Hatch didn't care one bit for how gleeful Egan seemed and briefly considered refusin. Instead he clicked the safety on before movin aside.

Did you see him shoot that ranger? Egan asked then as he settled his eye before the Zeiss, somethin different now in this younger brother's voice. *That Kalin kid caught that poor ranger right in the back of his head. Went out one eye. But he's still alive. Can you believe it? Kelly's takin him down.*

I didn't see that.

Then Egan squeezed off a second shot and once again filled the cirque with a roar. Egan knew his way around a rifle. No safety was gonna even pause him. He had good aim too.

What the heck are you doin?! Hatch demanded and furious too. *I did not give you permission to fire my weapon!* After which, upon realizin the

820

rights he had always maintained regardin his firearms, not to mention over this younger brother, he jumped to his feet and gave Egan a good hard kick.

Egan sure didn't expect that. He rolled away, clutchin his side, half groanin but still cussin and shoutin objections.

You broke a rib! Egan yowled. But he was up on his feet too and more than ready to take on Hatch.

If I'd've used my toe, I would have. And that was true. Hatch had only used the inside of his boot, like he was kickin aside dried dog crap. *But you get anywhere near my stuff again and I'll break more than your ribs.*

That so? Egan answered, and somethin about the way his little brother's jaw was set, combined with the blackest sparkle in his eyes, not to mention the way Egan's hands had started to reach behind his back, shook Hatch from spine to tush. But Egan weren't about to draw on the oldest Porch, only archin to stretch his back, worse now for the kick but mostly still hurtin from the fall on Cavalry.

Hatch made the rest easy on Egan by gettin down again on the tarp and returnin to the scope, this time with his finger on the trigger. His thumb had already told him the safety was off, and he left it that way.

I missed anyway, Egan announced.

Hatch thought he could see a big chunk of rock punched right where he'd seen Kalin and the horse disappear.

What kind of sniper brings up an unsighted rifle?

The rifle, though, weren't so badly off. Hatch knew that unlike his brother, he wouldn't miss. Where he'd aimed on the first shot, he'd pretty much hit. If the kid and the horse showed themselves again, he could drop them both. One shot. After all, the kid had killt a ranger. Killt their younger brother. Hatch could return as a hero to the grievin. Old Porch would never again question him. He might even make returnin palatable for Hatch. Despite how much he hated Utah, Hatch missed it every day.

But neither the kid nor his black horse reappeared.

And then it started to snow.

At first Kalin saw flakes spinnin around like they was borne up from below, like they had nothin to do with the churnin clouds, which had learned at last that they was free to unleash all they had withheld and so had darkened even more before movin against the mountain as if to devour it, deliverin its terrifyin howls upon the high ridges of Katanogos, bringin its batterin crisis to the great walls of the cirque, fillin it with this white chaos.

Just a little flurry, Tom tried to assure Kalin. He'd returned to his friend right after Hatch fired that first shot. When the path ahead had exploded a second time with dust and splintered rock, Kalin weren't even on Navidad no more. He'd just dared out his Stetson a little. Kalin noted that the one firin had missed.

After that, Kalin had walked Navidad back to the center of their retreat, where they were better shielded not only from gunfire and its aftereffects but also from the icy winds.

Kalin didn't give much thought to tryin to look out. Besides, the binoculars were up above now along with pretty much everythin else. In fact the only thing he'd brought down were the saddle and reins. When he eventually did risk another gander, this time from the lower end, Kalin saw nothin but snow flurries. Even with the binoculars, he'd've had little chance of spottin anyone down there. He also doubted anyone down there could see him.

After takin some long moments within the confines of that rock, Kalin rechecked Navidad, resecured all the tack, and only then remounted the mare, once again resettlin hisself in the saddle, threadin the reins between his fingers, before lookin up to face the squall ahead.

If he did this right, he'd be up with Landry in mere minutes; the hardest part he'd be done with in seconds. Of course, if whoever was down there caught even a blur of movement and fired again, even missed, Navidad would revolt again. But if he didn't go right now, this snow along with the darkness that had nearly proclaimed its victory over the day would make any future try impossible.

Do you think we can make it? Kalin asked Tom then.

Do you think you can make it?

Not if they keep firin that cannon.

If it's Hatch Porch at the trigger, if he don't drop you on the ledge, he'll drop you fer sure at the turn.

Kalin took that in.

If he's aimin at you, Tom added. *He can easily put a bullet through her.*

Kalin wanted so bad to just get it over with, but he knew Tom was right. He climbed back down off Navidad, shakin his legs loose, puttin his gloves back on, tryin to keep his hands warm. He sure was cold and gettin colder. Worse, he was trapped. There weren't no way back down. There weren't no way forward.

We'll have to last the night, Tom. I don't think I can do that. I don't think Navidad can do that. And even if we do make it to dawn, what then? If we don't freeze to death, we'll be stiffer than trailer bolts. And if they're waitin out the night too, why we'll be stuck just like we are now, only colder and stiffer.

Kalin knew too well what would happen to Navidad if she didn't get a chance to move her legs. She was already losin some of the heat and limberness her muscles had earned her on the climb up here.

That haunted Kalin the most: Navidad not havin the nimbleness she'd need to make the turnaround.

But then outside somethin strange happened: the high limits of Katanogos, only barely visible from Kalin's hidin place, suddenly shed the tangled brawl of ice-spun winds and cloud and burst alive, as if the clouds above had briefly parted, which was exactly what had happened, up here as well as over a large swath of the valley below, briefly allowin the final rays of daylight in the West to dance unobstructed through the icy pink particulate afloat up here, which in turn seemed to outright set fire to them high ridges. It didn't last more than a second, but surely it seemed like some Divine sign. Even if it weren't. And what followed was the worst of all: the sun now departed, gone for good, takin with it any hope of more visibility, and then the clouds closed up again, and the darkness that followed was almost too much for Kalin to bear.

We're in a heckuva spot, Tom whispered.

Why the grin then?

It's pretty much all I know how to do.

Kalin missed Landry. What he'd give to hear her voice now. He could imagine her up there, maybe she'd even returned to the summit ridge with the binoculars, tryin to do her part and scope out what was goin on below. But that was only a briefly pleasant idea, Kalin realizin that she'd be close enuf then for them Porches to get a shot at her. What he'd give, though, to hear her yellin out how she could see their ATVs departin, how this snow was makin them hightail it outta there. And that was a very real possibility. Even if hearin her voice all the way down here, no matter how close she crept to the edge, was a very real impossibility.

Kalin returned his thoughts to Navidad, just her, removin his gloves again to stroke her neck, slowly run his palms along her sides, from withers to flanks, tellin her over and over that there weren't no one that mattered more to him; and maybe for his touch or the touch in his voice, or maybe because of his exaggerations, because Kalin missed his momma too, missed Landry of course, missed Tom with every breath he took, she snorted and pressed her head against him, nibblin at that green slicker like it might at any moment turn to grass before movin higher, like she wanted to brush his cheek with her forelock, at least her forehead, managin to knock off that Stetson, which got a chuckle out of Tom and then out of Kalin.

Though it weren't that much of a chuckle.

I really don't feel so good, Tom. And it sure ain't helpin none that I can't see no way outta here.

My daddy used to tell us Gatestones that character comes from haulin yourself through the hard times. And he always added that it's only the hard times that can show you who you are and, more importantly, who you can become.

That's fine, Tom. But what if I just can't go on no more? Who am I then? Kalin sure did sound defeated. In fact it would've broke poor Landry's heart to see him like this.

You can go on, Tom answered, *and you will,* and his eyes got blacker than oil then and bright too if that oil was lit, though it weren't, not yet.

How do you mean?

You go on without Navidad.

Fer a long moment Kalin really didn't know what Tom was sayin, and then he didn't know who he was talkin to, or where he was at for that matter, or who even to his own self he was.

Without Navidad, Tom continued, *you can get along the ledges in the dark.*

Is that still you, Tom? I ain't leavin Navidad. One way or another, she and I are leavin this place together.

Well, I had to make the point.

No you didn't.

Tom seemed pleased, the awful blackness in his eyes replaced once again with the sparkle of easy mirth. *My friend here, she just wanted me to point out the option.*

That don't fly either. Kalin weren't in a real forgivin mood right now, and the peeve in his voice weren't lost on Tom. *Doesn't Pia Isan want Navidad to reach the Crossin?*

She still doesn't think you have a chance. She says this has happened before, in different ways fer sure, but the horses never ever make it.

That sure is a sad state of things, ain't it? Kalin sagged. *Shouldn't you be back with Mouse and Jojo and Landry and Ash?*

Tom didn't answer.

Are they okay? Is Landry okay? Some heat had entered Kalin's voice.

I can't remember.

Well, go check on them!

Tom shook his head, that big Stetson of his goin back and forth, gray now like it was hairy with frost.

You do know that if you die down here with Navidad, Tom said then, *Landry will likely die up there without you?*

I don't know what to do, Tom. Kalin sank down to his butt, huddlin up much as Landry had done when she'd seemed entirely inconsolable.

I should've taken one of them other routes. Maybe then none of this would've happened. Maybe Russel wouldn't've seen me, Landry wouldn't be here. Maybe no one would've noticed . . . Kalin's voice trailed off in defeat.

Missy Yamazaki, by 2023 an IT security consultant at the Marina Bay Sands in Singapore, would often in reference to this moment address the issue of paths of least resistance: *Easy ways can become traps for those who don't have the work capacity to claw their way up to the next path.* Fact is, whether Kalin was guided by raw instinct, intellect, or adventitious whigmaleerie, if he had tried his luck on, say, the Heathen-Slade Canyon Trail or Cutter's Crick Path, Russel still would've spotted him, Landry too, as well as plenty of others along the way. Kalin, of course, couldn't know this, but he never would've made it to even Shadow's Glen let alone up to the Katanogos Aspen Roundup Route, and forget the higher reaches of the massif. By Thursday mornin he'd've been surrounded and both horses rendered that very afternoon. Of course Russel would've lived, Cavalry too, and fer sure Law Enforcement Ranger Bren Kelson would've lived to marry Brooke Young. And that's just fer starters and still in no way addresses the horrors that awaited them. Two dead horses fer none of it. It's still an equation that bothers many.

I wish I could help you, Tom answered, and at least in this moment Kalin could see the ghost meant it. Tom had even gotten as close as he'd ever gotten to Navidad. He held his hand out like he was gonna stroke her coat and in effect did seem to do just that, though Kalin could see his friend's hand was still hoverin above Navidad's dark hair, what if only a hair away was also a world away. The incompleteness of that gesture presented a refused intimacy that Kalin was embarrassed to witness. He looked away.

Do you know Navidad's story? Kalin asked.

I do, Tom answered.

Will you tell it to me?

Tom shook his head. *I think you best hear first about Mouse.*

And so Tom proceeded to tell Kalin The Story of Mouse.

*I*n case you hadn't surmised yet, our Navidad here has great affection for that horse. And she'll do pretty much anythin to be near him too. Probably even fly if she has to. Why? A lot of reasons, but also because Mouse is brave.

As you well know, Mouse ain't the biggest or even the toughest, but he sure has courage, more fer sure than you or me or Landry or any other hero we wanna throw a parade for.

Mouse is . . . undeterred.

But he weren't always like that. By the eye of his long mind he found hisself this time raised up in Pennsylvania with once again no more regard for either the long road traveled or the road that's even longer up ahead. Bein thought of as too squat and misshapen for the farm where he was at, he was soon sold on his teeth to a stable in Connecticut that too soon went broke and sold all their horses to a ranch in Texas. Mouse didn't settle there neither. There were more farms and ranches in his future.

Wherever he landed, Mouse was mostly left alone. The hands around saw to his health but otherwise ignored him. It was the other horses that attended to his education, some wild, some already broke, some badly broke, but the one that saw Mouse become the Mouse we know now was an Appaloosa out on the dusty ruins north of Big Bend. And this creature was as mean as he was big, with both ears tore up and one eye blind from batterins. He hadn't been shoed in years. Put out to pasture by the sentimental rancher who'd known the horse before he'd become somethin else, who'd named that Appaloosa Chimp.

Upon Mouse's arrival at the Dizzy Jane Ranch, Chimp set eyes on Mouse first thing, trotted up, and dragged his teeth along Mouse's back side. Just for the heckuv it. Mouse tried to shy away from Chimp best he could, but every day Chimp would find him, cuttin him out of whatever group Mouse was tryin to hide in, and then he tormented our poor blood bay.

Sure a day or maybe a week would pass when Chimp lost interest, but then somethin ugly would spark up again in him and that big, mean Appaloosa would run after Mouse again. Poor Chimp had no idea who he was messin with. Poor Chimp never could reckon that he had a life way too short to understand what the old see at once and know to shy from even quicker.

Fer his part, Mouse confused matters by continuin to run away, maybe with a half-hearted kick or two but never more. Now and then he'd go for a bite, but his heart weren't in it. He missed every time. And Chimp was blinded by them hapless snaps.

There are horses men break. We know that lore like it's an entitlement. But there are also horses broke by other horses. Mouse sure looked broken. Mouse even felt broken. By this point Mouse didn't care much for Mouse and would run every time toward whatever escape he deemed most viable, even if there weren't never no viable escape, not when Chimp pinned his ears and charged across the paddock.

And then Navidad arrived, and that changed everythin. She was taller than Mouse, leaner too, though she looked the same age, with the same knowin if not from the same eons of trials. She bounded around with the other horses, and in them early weeks Chimp was so fascinated by Navidad, he forgot about Mouse.

But Mouse never forgot Chimp and kept an eye out for Navidad. He knew the day was gonna come. And as you can rightly gather, he was right. It were a Sunday. They was all out on the east acres. Mornin was up but only by a bit. Chimp had hisself a chomp of burr clover and then trotted hisself toward that beautiful black mare.

Now at this point Navidad weren't payin no mind to Mouse, and to be clear that hardly mattered to Mouse. He was also undeterred by indifference. He was just content to see her. Navidad reminded him of somethin, though what or who that might be remains unclear to me. Were I to offer a rash conjecture of his remembrance, it would be the memory of hisself before it was so badly deformed by the defeatin circumstance of this present life.

I guess we all know that feelin: somethin about us that isn't rightly expressed because of how we was raised. Maybe there's still a trace, some part still unharmed, still unexpressed. Lucky are them, most will say, whose futures align with the promise of their inheritances. But I'd say they're the most cursed. Most blessed maybe are the battered who, in a rare encounter or accident, discover a different future, which, upon followin, not only returns them to the self they forgot but reveals how the cost of their trials has made them into someone they never could've imagined.

Kalin studied Tom. He sounded like his friend, but he also didn't, what had been happenin more and more, especially of late, another voice inhabitin Tom, animatin him, what filled Kalin with a fear he didn't care for one bit.

That's what Navidad did for Mouse, Tom continued like he was just the same old Tom as before.

So, when Mouse caught sight of Chimp headin for Navidad, he didn't hesitate. With not a length to spare, Mouse came between Navidad and Chimp. Chimp, as he was so oft to do, dragged his teeth across Mouse's back, his head already full with the notion that Mouse was already scurryin away like he'd done every time before. Chimp was so blinded by what he expected that he didn't see how Mouse weren't gone at all but plantin both front legs and, with the force of not one but two, drove both rear hooves up at him, one right behind Chimp's good eye, the other right on Chimp's neck. Killt Chimp, that kick did. Not on the spot, not like that, but in the way no sane spit of life wants to go. Chimp collapsed, his spine cracked, his head a bleedin mess, blind now pretty much in both eyes. He stayed that way for hours too until the sentimental rancher with his weepy sentimental son ordered a hand to put a bullet in Chimp's brain. She did it quick at least.

Navidad had no clue what was happenin. She just ran off at the first sight of Mouse's flyin hooves. Later, though, she found herself always calmer and more at ease around Mouse, and from then on Mouse was always around her, never imposin much but never far off either. And they stayed that way, even when they was sold from Texas to stables in Heber, and from there to Porch, eventually put *into Paddock A, where you and me found them and dared to think we could ride them and in ridin them dared to dream of makin a difference in how they would know their end.*

Kalin stood up then and, runnin his cold hands along Navidad's neck, said: *We're gonna get you back to Mouse.*

There's the Kalin I know! Tom even laughed, but it did seem the saddest laugh Kalin had ever heard.

What can I do for you, Tom? You've been one heckuva friend. I wouldn't be here without you. And I mean that as a compliment.

Kalin, that's gotta be the funniest thing I've ever heard you say. Though Tom weren't laughin, and even his tryin to smile didn't really count much for a smile. *You know you're likely gonna die, right? You know Navidad's likely gonna die with you? And then Landry's gonna die. And then, though I'm already dead, I'm gonna have to die twice. But here you are askin me the dumbest question I've ever heard you ask. What can you do for me?! You better have figured that one out by now!*

What?

Don't die!

Ask Orvop folks about the rainstorm in late October 1982, and most won't know what the heck you're talkin about. It don't make no difference neither to bring up how many days it rained or how the cold turned the whole of Isatch Canyon into a menacin palace of ice. Bringin up how the canyon flooded won't help you neither, even if the water overran the canyon entrance and nearly flooded the Orvop Temple. Maybe if you showed some the picture that was on the front page of Friday's *Orvop Herald,* above the fold too, a few might recollect the sandbags.

Which is not to diminish the rainfall any. Them waters was mighty and overwhelmin. It's just that when people think of late October 1982, what they mostly think of is the snowstorm, an astonishin delivery of blessèd Utah white and right before Halloween too.

No question it was an early blessin for the ski resorts up Little Cottonwood Canyon and fer sure for the Cassidy Ski Resort up Orvop Canyon. Everyone, whether in Spanish Fork, Orvop, Rome, American Fork, Lehi, Sandy, even north of Salt Lake City, whether cursin the chore of havin to dig out their driveways or salt the sidewalks they'd just finished shovelin, still couldn't help but admire a transformation of environs that was both beautiful as well as terrifyin, the Isatch range buried in so much white powder, it both seduced and blinded the eye.

It sure was a celebrated sight for anyone with skis or any kid with a penchant fer snowmen. Pity, though, had to go to those caught unawares by such a valley-wallopin storm. So immense was the deposited snowpack in the high peaks that not even late summer would banish all the patches that would even through autumn continue to engorge all the streams, rivers, and lakes below.

The almost curious whirls of snowflakes appearin now weren't but a churlish warnin of the greater fall yet to come. Though neither Egan nor Hatch acted the fool before such early signs. They smelled it in the air. Before even the first speckle of white had settled on the cirque meadow, they knew they had to get outta there.

Shoot him! Egan hissed at Hatch.

Hatch laughed in Egan's face. *What's wrong with you? I can't even see ten feet.*

Then you're blind!

And despite what Hatch had declared earlier, about not lettin Egan anywhere near his weapon, he again allowed Egan to shove his way in behind the Barrett M82. No question it weren't done in the spirit of permissiveness; rather Hatch wanted to mock his younger brother's impetuous stupidity. Egan felt mocked too when he put his eye to the Zeiss and found only flurries of blobbed gray. What he'd expected was anyone's guess. The day was long gone. Even without snow, he'd have found only the black loomin mass imprisonin them.

Egan still fired though. Blindly, rashly, at nothin. And Hatch didn't hesitate to kick him again, this time with his toe, this time right in the ribs. He could've broken a rib, maybe a couple, but he held back. He was mostly disgusted by Egan.

Egan knew too that he weren't really kicked, though he still rolled away, again clutchin his side, again groanin extra hard. Hatch was hardly checked by this show of pain, and forget remorse, he stepped at him with a snarl, like he might just go for a real kick, to the head. Though before that could happen, Egan raised his hands above his head like he was under arrest. And that did the trick. Hatch saw him again as nothin more than his stupid, rash, mean-as-heck younger brother.

What do I care, Hatch finally said. *Shoot all the snowflakes you want.* And he meant it.

Egan walked off a few paces and pissed. Hatch thought it a good idea and pissed too.

After that, Hatch disassembled the Barrett and packed it away in its transit case. Once they had secured the remainin gear, Hatch drove Egan on the two-seater back to Egan's single-seater still parked by the Upecksay Headwall. They gave no thought to the loomin blindness above them. Hatch briefly considered the blood on the rocks. He asked Egan if this was where Law Enforcement Ranger Bren Kelson had fallen. Egan told him it was. Egan felt nervous and didn't like the feelin. But Hatch didn't linger over the crime scene.

They moved swiftly then, united by the shared purpose of gettin the heck out of there, if also arguin throughout about whether they should risk spendin the night. They'd brought no tents or sleepin bags, just a tarp and necessities to start a fire. Hatch reasoned the only place they could likely fortify themselves against the cold would be where Kalin, Landry, and the horses had holed up the previous night. There was even some dry wood.

But if it snows all night, we'll be trapped and these machines will pretty much be junk we'll have to haul out next spring.

You think we could find a way up that wall come mornin? Egan asked, deemin the price of two lost ATVs more than worth it.

Hatch met Egan's gaze and felt pity. Somethin had broken loose in his brother, maybe beyond repair, now with pieces missin. *That kid up there isn't gonna survive, Egan. We've killt him.*

You sure? Egan at least was hearin the eldest Porch this time.

Tomorrow mornin, if we can get in here with a search party, and that's a big if, we'll be lookin for his body and the horse's body too.

Egan believed Hatch then and even briefly considered leavin behind somewhere the Smith & Wesson Model 59. He might've done it too, but Hatch was gonna notice, and then what was Egan gonna say? Egan would have to do it tomorrow. He'd leave it on Kalin if he could get to the body first. If not, he'd drop it somewhere close, like it had spun loose in the fall. Egan could even do it come spring.

Hatch on the two-seater led the way on the drive out. Egan, back on his single-seater, slowed a few times to look behind and make sure no lights were sparklin on the headwall. He found only blackness swept over by a dazzle of swirlin gray.

By Altar Lake, Egan halted near the beaver lodge. He even turned off the engine and waited for Hatch to get farther away. He was about to give up when the beaver finally reappeared. Faster than the best shoot-outs in the best movies, Egan drew the Smith & Wesson Model 59 that had shot Cavalry, that had killt Ranger Kelson, and that had now just shot this bewildered animal. Her body flopped over upon her own labor for winter, not quite reachin the water that her blood would soon enuf greet, the turnin of the season already anticipatin a corpse entombed by layers of ice and snow.

Egan didn't go forth to inspect his kill nor make any effort to seek out the ejected fourth casin. Unlike the one he couldn't find near the headwall, this one would remain lost to obscurity even when it was found almost two years later, in 1984, on June 18 to be exact, by a recent Orvop High graduate enjoyin the end of a hike on the lower trails of Isatch Canyon, soakin his bare feet in the crick that felt extra icy that year but still endurin the recuperative ache in his arches brought on by such cold, wigglin his toes in such sparklin clarity, which was when he came to notice some extra sparkle wedged between two gray rocks. As you've correctly guessed, this was the fourth casin. He saw at once that the primer was struck and wondered at its history. Was it just some detritus from a recent and nearby target practice? Or maybe from an illegal hunt? He even wondered if this might be another remnant of unclaimed evidence from the many events surroundin Pillars Meadow? Which didn't make no sense since Pillars Meadow weren't just beyond Isatch Canyon but on the other side of Katanogos. Though there were them precedin events well known by then. Fer a moment, he was sure this very casin was from the awful murder of Law Enforcement Ranger Bren Kelson. He wanted it to be so. And as was true for many, it weren't a hard leap given how his thoughts were so bound by the lore that would continue to resonate in the hearts and minds of locals, as well as those who lived well beyond the borders of Utah Valley, as somethin more than the mere actions of men and women, and children too, children with horses; how maybe a greater orderin of Justice does continue to move through all lives, whether we choose to believe so or not. No thought, however, on that bright June afternoon, was given to the poor beaver nor to the subsequent shudder that took hold of that hiker, despite the heat still in him from his climb, the heat still in the day, as if winter itself had briefly inhabited him, and just for holdin that casin between two fingers, a remnant and proof that human endeavors, no matter how executed and claimed, are still of little consequence before the world at large that with every day grows more conflicted over whether to continue to issue yet another allotment of generational survival to such a proud and cruel species. The young Orvop High graduate did the only sensible thing then, short of findin a trash can: he threw that casin back into those glitterin waters and furthermore disallowed his heart to grant it any mystique, relegatin it to the poorly handled refuse of target practice and soon after forgettin altogether this daydream of possible origins, except fer one moment many decades later, when for some reason unbeknownst to him the brass shine of that slight and empty object, held up once so preciously between his young fingers, reintroduced a grave uncertainty to his mind, wherein for no reason that can be accounted for here, he suddenly beheld three small beavers awake near the threshold of their home who, despite the snow and ice and the hollow in their hearts, rose up to remake a new home.

On the very top of Katanogos, despite the blindin squall of snow that continued to grow up there, Landry was yippin like a maniac. It mattered little that her face felt bloodied, pocked, and scarred from the ice flyin through the air; Kalin and Navidad had not yet arrived. Below her she could observe the lights of two more ATVs leavin the cirque. A parade of lights had already left, and as Landry rightly deduced these two were the last of them Porch interlopers. Ms. Melson would take to callin this moment *the third teichoskopia.*

Run, you varmints! Landry screamed. *Run! Run! Pow-Pow! Enuf!*

But when Kalin and Navidad didn't at that moment or in the moments that followed answer her joy by gallopin up out of the fallen darkness and fallin snow, Landry ceased her cries. The allicient emptiness ahead, where she would not go again, which she could barely approach, goaded her then into a near-whimperin stillness. Not that Landry didn't try to outbrave her fear by comin up with a plan to gather up their ropes. She knew she could knot them well enuf to secure them around the right outcroppin of rocks up here and then, hand over hand, ease herself back down over that edge to offer Kalin and that beautiful black mare her assistance.

But the heroic plan remained in the confines of her head. Instead she started yellin for Kalin again, like now it could be heard, though she still knew there weren't no chance of that. She even tried to yell louder, even as her voice got hoarser. Eventually, though, her voice gave out, and the cold got to her as the storm grew only worse, like it might very well blow her from the ridge, with the heart of that brutal chaos seemin to prove that Kalin weren't comin no more and all that was waitin down there for her was his and Navidad's grave.

Judge her all you like, and there ain't no question that here was Landry Gatestone's second-greatest failure, or at least her second-greatest seizure brought on by imaginin her end, and how, unlike her brother, it had found her smileless, found her wantin; the first failure havin been down in that third and last refuge of rock where she'd froze up so bad she'd needed both Kalin and Tom to move her, to free her, none of which Landry Gatestone would deny and in the heart of that storm-towerin moment even recognized, countin them as easily as a three-year-old: one, two. And that awareness neither moved her freezin toes toward a pursuit of ropes nor one inch closer toward the vertical maw that would always welcome her, welcome anybody.

It's easy for a mind not there to imagine how upon a path wide enuf for a horse a descent back down to Kalin and Navidad should pose no problems. It's easy for a lazy mind to believe that Landry should not have made it even a choice, nor even considered ropes; she should've just stood up and headed on down.

But Landry Gatestone could not do it.

Like Tom earlier, she couldn't imagine returnin to that sheer wall. Unlike her brother, she never overcame her fear.

The best Landry could do was stand on the summit ridge as long as she could take it, until the darkness and the storm had scared her so bad from even that perch, where fer a moment she'd believed herself an abidin sentinel, a lighthouse for the lost, if really little else than a lightless lighthouse for the lost damned below.

Landry fled. And by then not even runnin was enuf. Fear hunted her, fear was at her heels, fear consumed her. Landry would lose her way. Landry would never find the horses again. She'd fly over some edge. Was her sense of direction already confused? Maybe she wasn't headin toward that copse of trees? Maybe she'd got turned around? Maybe she was runnin down toward the wall? Not that that halted her any. Would Kalin and Navidad see her fall past them? Serves her right.

And that thought did stop her.

The blindin snow of night told her then that she was gonna freeze to death. And maybe fer a moment Landry even accepted her death. And then she heard Jojo. Weren't that the prettiest neigh she'd ever knowd! With two fingers in her mouth, Landry whistled back, and that fer sure weren't pretty, not like what Tom could do, but Jojo heard it and whinnied even louder. He weren't far neither. Not but another dozen paces, already stompin his hooves beside Mouse, with the mule still there too. Oh, Landry was a coward. She had failed Kalin, but maybe she wouldn't fail these three. Maybe that was somethin, enuf to give her the fight she'd need to live fierce enuf to get out those ropes and at least tie up a tarp or two and see about startin a fire.

The best news Kalin had had was that last shot. It came outta nowhere and didn't make no sense. Kalin weren't out in the open. The shot hadn't come close.

It's like they're aimin at a whole different side of the cirque, Tom even commented.

They can't see a darned thing now, Kalin said, and Tom didn't argue.

Not much later, Kalin and Tom watched the headlights of two ATVs depart the cirque.

You think others are still down there? Kalin asked.

If there are, they ain't our problem now.

Should we celebrate?

Open up some champagne! Tom said with a wink.

Tom cackled happily, and Kalin, in laughin along, felt hisself warm a little, and maybe even Navidad warmed some too at the sound of Kalin's amusement, however meager.

You ever tasted champagne, Tom?

Not unless we're countin Miller High Life.

Me neither. Kalin sighed then. *I'll tell you this: in this weather, those folks down there got one heckuva drive back,* Kalin added, surprised to hear in his voice so much sympathy.

If they make it back, Tom added.

I don't want to think about all them screes in this storm . . .

Kalin looked ahead then, toward where he had yet to go. Some snow already littered the ledge, though not much; the wind kept it mostly clear. The dark, though, made it impossible to gauge the distance Kalin and Navidad would have to travel to reach that final turn. Not that Kalin didn't stop toyin with the question of whether or not he might still remember the rhythm well enuf to make the approach blind. The steps right before the turnaround troubled him the most. They could easily overshoot the turn, just launch themselves into nothin.

Don't even think about that, Tom warned him.

If only that old mountain goat was still there, Kalin mumbled back, but he could see no sign of that cloud. *You see him?*

Tom strode out onto the ledge but said nothin.

Has it iced? Kalin asked. *That'll kill us fer sure.* Not that he waited on Tom, already checkin the rock with his own bootheel.

It will, Tom finally said. *It's gotta.*

Where's that torch of yours?

It's up with Ash.

Go get it! Maybe it'll help.

But Tom shook his head. *It'll only confuse you with what all's not there.*

Tom, I can't make it in this dark! Kalin briefly wondered if he might hyperventilate. He'd never done that before, and if there was ever a time for it . . . But Kalin's breath kept comin out long and slow. Nose only. He could thank his momma for that. And he did. *I know the lead changes. I know the pace now. Navidad and me can make it past them three rough sections. But the turn—* Kalin shook his head hard. He couldn't get past the turn. He was mumblin again. *We can't make it. But if we don't try, Tom, we'll freeze fer sure. We won't last the night. Snow's gonna pile up too—*

Wait, Tom suddenly said.

Plus by mornin our, if we even live that long, our joints, we won't live that long, will be so stiff we won't be able to walk out there let alone . . .

Wait just a sec, Tom said again.

And, once, and, and that's still not takin into account this snow that's gonna pile up in our way. I, and, we, and. I can't think of a way outta here!

Just wait! Tom commanded, harsh too, finally raisin his voice. The ghost stood now before Navidad, but not payin her much mind, nor Kalin anymore either. Instead he addressed the air beside the mare with whispers Kalin for the life of him couldn't make out, except that he knew they concerned the life of him, of her really.

Landry won't last it out up there either, Kalin rasped before grindin down his teeth again to keep from his mouth the chatter of ice already in his spine. *You can only outrun cold for so long.*

You don't know her, Tom answered, even lookin a little peeved.

Then I won't last it out! His jeans had stayed damp. I'm gonna be wearin ice soon. Shakin his legs didn't help much. *You talkin to Pia Isan?*

Sorta.

Did you hear me? My pants are startin to freeze up.

She's talkin to the one who stands beside her. And it don't stop there.

How do you mean it don't stop there?

Like Pia Isan haunts me, she too is haunted, and the one hauntin her is haunted, and so on.

And so on?

And so on.

Kalin tipped his dark hat to the darker air and even gave a courtly nod. *Pleased to meet y'all. I am truly sorry too. We came so close.*

Of course the vast space that intermingled him and Navidad in that tight and bitter confine neither acknowledged Kalin nor responded.

Wait a minute! Does that mean I'm haunted by you? he asked Tom then.

You tell me.

Kalin shivered and shuddered and then shook too, all of it violently done. But it weren't Tom givin him the frights. Not havin Tom around, now that would be scary. For a split second Kalin wondered if what scared Tom the most was not havin him around or Landry or, of course, Navidad and Mouse.

Are you learnin anythin helpful?

But Tom was again out in the storm, again inspectin the ledge, still in a conversation that weren't really a conversation. Kalin knew he should be doin more than just watchin. He should at least move. Jumpin jacks! He should get Navidad movin too, back her up and then walk her forward, and do that over and over again, keep tryin to build heat, keep themselves even a little warm, but Kalin couldn't budge. He couldn't even stand. And then he was again slidin down to his butt again like Landry had done. About the only energy left to him he used to clutch Navidad's reins. Those he would not let go of. Ever.

The cold really came for him then, like predators do when they run out their prey, a little gash here, a slice there, slowin him down, bleedin him out. Kalin just hurt and hurt, more so with each gust that howled through that short enclosure. Now he could taste more than just rock and ice; he could taste the end.

At least you ain't numb yet, Tom said from the ledge.

His friend was right. When the hurtin stopped, that's how the end would feel.

And really the cold weren't the worst of it: doubt had got hold of Kalin too and hardly had to make a case for his death. Kalin was already facin up to the fact that he was not only unstrung by weakness but hung up by despair. What had he done here? He'd gone and got killt the two horses him and Tom loved. He'd got killt the little girl Tom loved more than anyone. Kalin gazed around to behold anew the place that might very well prove his tomb, even surprised by how he'd never once figured he'd die in such a place; not that whatever grave we imagine for ourselves when we are young, as we hold that last moment close, ever matches the actual place where we know ourselves no more.

Kalin thought of his momma then. There was a happiness in just thinkin of her, her goodness, her kindness, endurance too, but then his daddy rose up too, claimin Kalin, again proclaimin him the Great White Hope, and that got at him, first with disgust, then anger, until he eventually got to laughin, and though he sounded consumptive at best, his sense of humor at least was still alive, and maybe that weren't such a bad thing.

What's so funny? Tom asked. He'd returned to Kalin's side.

Kalin told him about his momma and then how he'd got to thinkin about his daddy.

How's that funny? Which was an odd question comin from Tom, who would laugh at pretty much anythin.

It ain't. It just made me realize that there ain't a lick of hope left now.

Maybe she ate it, Tom said then, and that sure surprised Kalin.

Wait, what? Who?

Tom nodded toward the storm-battered ledge. *Remember when Landry was makin up stuff with us and Russel? How she'd said that the lady who haunts Isatch Canyon gobbles up the hope of them she curses?*

Boy, don't that seem like forever ago, Kalin sighed.

It sure does.

Landry also said that them who crossed the Gate of the Mountain, who she really didn't like, them she eats fer real. Is this her eatin us now?

Nah, this is the mountain eatin us, Tom answered.

Are her teeth like knives now?

Worse. Tom studied the absence within the air. *She looks scared.*

Scared?

Not a dimple in sight. She's not gonna like me tellin you this, but I think maybe she had some hope. Tom's smile was real sad. *When Mouse made it on over, I think she started to believe she might make it over too. I think they all did.*

You say that like they was startin to get fond of us, Kalin said, mostly to rib Tom.

Heck no, Tom snorted, *but they sure do love the horses.*

Kalin nodded.

In fact the only love they have left in them is for Navidad and Mouse.

Nec spe, nec metu, Kalin said then.

How's that?

No hope, no fear. Supposedly what ancient warriors would say before battle. If you don't hope, you can't fear. You face your moment clearheaded.

Mrs. Annserdodder teach us that?

I told you. My momma has this postcard of a gravestone that pretty much says the same thing. I did tell Mrs. Annserdodder about it, and she thought that was fine, and then a week later she told me that Ms. Melson, the AP English teacher, had said you could say it shorter: nec spe, nec metu. Mrs. Annserdodder asked me to bring the postcard into class, but I never did. I liked Mrs. Annserdodder. She was always real patient with me.

I agree with Landry, Tom said, his eyes glitterin. *I think our mommas would've gotten on.*

It's too bad we never got them together.

Dawn Brummett, who would wind up gaspin on her couch in Mantua, dyin on that couch too, and with the TV on, though she weren't seein none of that, goin on instead about the *Mona Lisa* while at the same time rememberin playin kissin tag in fifth grade at Isatch Elementary, until out of the blue she muttered, *Nec spe, nec metu,* and she weren't thinkin of no Stoics but of Landry, Kalin, and Tom. Though it was Isabella d'Este who'd possess her final thoughts, her final words: *Vinti siete.*

Tom slipped out on the ledge, again encircled by buffetin spins of snowflakes, again conversin with the space within such motions. Kalin forced hisself back to his feet, pressin hisself against Navidad. He would not forsake her. And maybe them old words, if they was Greek, if they meant what he thought they meant, did help some. Fer sure they lowered his horizons. Without the burden of hope, without the burden of fear, all that was left for him was to do what could be done.

Kalin gave Navidad a good rubbin then from cheek to rump. He talked to her. He backed her up some and then walked her forward some. And then did it all over again. With a jumpin jack or two thrown in there fer good measure.

This time when Tom returned, Kalin asked who it was that walked beside Pia Isan.

It ain't her husband. But other than that she won't tell me.

Are they friends like we are?

From what I can gather they ain't, but they've learned to get along. She's got that little chipmunk, but her companion has a dog, so right there, there's tension.

I guess that figures.

Though not how you'd expect: it's the chipmunk that keeps barkin at the dog.

And the dog puts up with that?

Like I said, Kalin, there's tension.

I'm just glad we get along. I'm glad Navidad and Ash get along. I guess there's some good luck there.

She has a message.

How do you mean?

Pia Isan says it's a first.

She's never got a message before?

Never.

How'd she get it?

Whadya mean how'd she get it?! Don't you wanna know what it is?

Not before I know where it's comin from.

Fair enuf. She got it from the one who walks beside her.

The one she won't tell you about? How come you ain't never gave me no message? You just kinda hung around and told me what you couldn't remember.

Is that how you see me?

Pretty much, Kalin said with a wink.

The sheer gall of this boy.

I learned from the best.

Well, then maybe I hung around just so I could give you this message now.

Don't get me wrong, Tom, I like you hangin around. You made all the difference.

This don't even come from the one who walks beside her but the one who walks beside the one who walks beside Pia Isan. And so on.

Again with that so on.

It comes from a long long line of them that neither you nor me will ever see.

You really are gonna drag this out?

Well, it's from a long long time ago.

I'm waitin, Tom.

There will be light.

How's that?

You heard me.

Say it again.

There will be light.

That's it?

Get ready.

You mean now?

Tom paused to consult more with the air. *Pia Isan's throwin in her two cents here: she says get on Navidad now.*

Kalin laughed. Tom didn't.

She ain't jokin. The darkness in his eyes seemed so concentrate as to overwhelm that narrow slot of rock. *I ain't either.*

Kalin felt this hard thuddin start up in his chest then, which was all the more unsettlin because it weren't his heart or anythin else conjured by him; it was a sensation that found no pairin with anythin the interior labyrinths of his ears might make sense of but which continued to fill him with a terror that was both as awful as it was exquisite.

Not that Kalin heeded it any more than he might heed the inconvenience of a sneeze. Whatever Kalin was feelin was no longer material. And he did indeed sneeze right then and thought nothin of it. Tom's asseveration had now fully ordered his attentions. Kalin was not merely walkin Navidad back and forth but massagin her too with both hands, limberin each leg, one by one, reinspectin each hoof, recheckin every joint, rubbin in as much warmth as he could, from elbow to knee, cannon to fetlock, even feelin behind her jaw, behind her knee, confirmin that her heart rate was holdin steady, pleased that it weren't too slow but also pleased that nerves had gotten her heart rate above forty-four, and the whole time talkin to Navidad about the journey they was about to make, what wouldn't take but a scatter of minutes, at an easy pace too, straight ahead, straight to the top, *straight on til mournin*, with just one very important turn in the middle, after which it was pretty much all downhill, and that not for long, and then she'd be with Jojo and Ash, but most of all she'd be with her Mouse, because Mouse was up there waitin for her, Mouse who needed Navidad as much as she needed him, *Mouse, Mouse, Mouse,* Kalin sayin the name over and over like a speech, like a song, like a prayer.

Kalin neglected no part of Navidad, at times pressin his whole body against her shoulders, her flanks, from stifles to dock, before once again backin her up a dozen steps, there just weren't no room for more in that place, and then forward again, in a rhythm Navidad got to understand as preparation, expellin clouds of ready breath, maybe understandin too the ongoin Mouse incantation, Kalin now and then noddin out at the night, sometimes outright pointin a gloved finger toward the ledge that they would very soon dare, if a ghost talkin to another ghost talkin to another ghost all the way back to the ghost of time itself was to believed, maybe the only way for Kalin to trick hisself into goin for it, regardless of ghostly consent, just him and her, Kalin reviewin further with Navidad, though it was for hisself too, which leg she'd need to start on, what lead they'd need for that turn, how they'd have to stop, rise up, how they'd have to pivot, real steady, real easy, because none of it had to be fast, just sure.

And Kalin felt the ice that had gathered in the threads of his jeans start to give way to the heat he had somehow again started to generate. The heat was in his chest too. He removed his gloves and stowed them. His fingers weren't cold no more. They felt on fire.

Maybe your torch is still worth a try? Kalin asked Tom.

Tom just shook his head.

It's still pretty dark out there.

Have a little faith, son.

Kalin did then notice a glow on the wall that was so faint, he suspected he was just makin up somethin to suit Tom's prophecy, though that suspicion didn't dim it none and even seemed to deny that it had grown a tiny bit brighter, not enuf to illuminate the path, though increasin yet again, an incomprehensible gleam sustained by the shine of itself.

I see somethin, Tom, but it ain't enuf.

Saddle up, cowboy, Tom said with a grin.

Kalin didn't know who to heed at this point: Hisself? A ghost? A ghost of a ghost of a ghost of a chance? Still, gettin up on Navidad didn't feel at all like a bad idea. And so with one hand on the horn, Kalin slipped lightly up into the saddle, Navidad at once welcomin her friend's arrival and even snortin, stampin a forehoof too. Kalin felt the charge of her excitement and the fire within him grew still hotter, warmin them both, and readyin them too.

I'll go first, Tom said, rightin his own Stetson once, by now so dusted with ghostly ice that it seemed to have forgotten its own blackness. Tom didn't stop either as he headed out onto the ledge, too soon consumed by a night so complete, Kalin swore right then he'd never see his friend again. And, boy, did that bring back a thuddin in his chest, which this time was his heart skippin not just one beat but two.

Except now instead of still more darkness followin, it was night itself that fled. Just like that. Navidad full-out neighed then. It was as if the scales on both their eyes had fallen away, as if an immense switch had been flicked on.

Both Kalin and Navidad knew enuf not to hesitate. And together they moved for the last time out of that third and final restin spot, out upon the ledge, at once findin the pace they'd need, first a fast walk, then an easy lope, Kalin's left hand mindin the reins threaded between his fingers but only so as to keep the bit as light as possible on Navidad's mouth, with Kalin's legs, especially his knees and calves, servin now to further fulfill his extraordinary equine balance, in concert with Navidad's, together so easily and swiftly adjustin to every change, gatherin up their confidence with every step forward, those initial strides, those lengthenin strides, even as they were both blinkin too, so high above the cirque floor, so suddenly enfolded within such brilliance.

Of the two glances that Kalin would dare beyond their way, the first went to that moon. Kalin had never seen one so big, so full, so close, and surely never so bright. The storm, its armies of ragin winds and clouds, had been rent apart, revealin this impossible figure of lunar constancy that, except for the general absence of color, now rendered all visible. Furthermore, the snow that now covered the meadow below was servin as a second moon, a reflection of a reflection, with even a third one down there, if you count the reflection on Altar Lake, throwin still more of the sun's translations upon the cirque, upon the Upecksay Headwall.

Not that the storm appreciated this intrusion, churnin overhead with every effort to restitch the tear. Night would return any moment, but Kalin still stole a second glance, this time not at the sky above but behind him, the way they'd come, all the way down, and what he saw there rent his own heart asunder.

Plenty say it was just more moonlight dazzlin the ice-shattered air, constructin out of those many snowy angles the chimeras Kalin beheld. And that's a pretty sensible thing to stand by. More folks say that all this business of ghosts hauntin ghosts with a message of weatherly clemency weren't nothin more than a boy's delirium on the edge of either freezin to death or fallin to his death. And that too is a pretty sensible thing to stand by.

But of course them folks with their sensible notions weren't the ones up there, they weren't alone on that high cliff wall, they weren't ridin forth into the teeth of night and storm while on the back of a black mare so beautiful time itself briefly surrendered its place.

What Kalin beheld not merely on the ledges but teemin across the cirque meadow as far as the eye could see, fer sure all the way down into Isatch Canyon, and beyond, was a great migration, a black parade of shades, women and men, children, babies too, and, far more numerous than them, life of all forms, upon the land, upon the air.

And there it was again, in Kalin's chest, that thuddin that had nothin to do with any part of us, a roar of possibility, as if arisin from all the way back, and now carried forth through Pia Isan, through Tom too, through Kalin, and even now through us, like the dearest promise to do better, because here was the difference now, because here the impossible was challenged, because the here that had always declared the forfeiture of passage was fallin away.

Come on, you idjit! Tom shouted at Kalin, who was so stunned by the sight, he might've right then and there lost his sense of what he was about and, no matter the moonlight, and forget the chance available to him, available to all of them, might've fallen, gone and blown it on the very next step.

They're really followin us? Kalin still had to ask, even as he heeded Tom and refocused his attention on the ledge ahead. Though shakin the vision was hard, the feelin on the back of his neck, the song free in his chest.

Us?! Tom roared, this time with the gravel of a hundred rockfalls in his voice. *You are a vain creature, Kalin March! No one cares a whit about you! Nor about me! And no one ever will! They follow him!* Pointin above. *They follow her!* He pointed to Navidad. *Go!*

And then like that, the gravity upholdin this pronouncement departed, and Tom looked flush with panic, every courage he'd mustered now routed; he was fear's prey now, and he responded as such too, boltin away as fast as he could, Ash and him hurlin along that narrowin moment of rock, through the turn, gone to the summit . . .

Gone.

Only Kalin and Navidad remained. But together they could know now the great maw of emptiness that surrounded them and it would matter not. They could know the awful weight of the mountain and it would matter not. They reached the first rough section and strode over it without misstep. Navidad's stride even lengthened. They sped past the second section. And Navidad's stride lengthened still more.

Between them they carried, by hoofbeat and the music of their advancement, the lead change they'd need, what Mouse had taught Kalin, what Navidad was already anticipatin, but not just yet, floatin then over the gaps of the third section, which if badly timed would've thrown them down, until, there it was, that one beat, the one you'd have to live a lifetime and more to understand, to know, to feel . . .

there

    . . . in the midst of that one long and powerful stride, midair, legs gathered up under her belly, no hoof left upon the mountain, afloat, flyin; when Navidad easily made the needed lead change, and after that bounded up to that slab of worn rock, the final turnaround, that last piece of near levelness, the Hippocrene oath ordered by hooves, as much a plinth of stone as the palm of the World upon which Kalin and Navidad arrested their charge, Navidad risin up then, Kalin risin up with her, standin in his stirrups, the two of them skyward, starward, beyond the stars, Kalin now with hardly any weight in the stirrups, all of him so fused with Navidad, the fullness of their form so complete, that they stood there incomparably light, so that before they did at last turn, they already knew the hollow in the wind and would find no resistance there, even lingerin fer a moment longer, as effortless as when livin grants even the most difficult livin the chance to become its own beautiful moment beyond life.

    Not even Tom was there to see it.

    No one was. Not even them mountain goats.

    Moonlight alone beheld horse and boy and maybe in the end moonlight was who it was for.

Sunday

Chapter Twenty-One

"The Summit Ridge"

Just after midnight, Sondra Gatestone headed up Orvop Canyon. She weren't payin no attention to the speed limit. If she'd've passed an Orvop officer, she'd have been pulled over for suspicion of drivin under the influence. But she didn't pass any police, and besides, she weren't intoxicated. It was way worse than that.

Allison March had been followin Sondra since after five that afternoon, since she'd heard the awful deadness in her friend's voice, since she'd seen her eyes glaze over rather than spill her worth in tears.

Allison had almost abandoned Sondra after she and Mungo had disappeared into the Gatestone house. And it weren't because she'd been knocked down by Sondra's meanness back at the entrance to Isatch Canyon; Allison knew how to take a punch. Allison was still plenty worried, and so while she drove away, she didn't drive far, not even half a block, debatin then whether to find a pay phone to at least call her or maybe just bum-rush the front door.

Somewhere in the midst of this argument with herself, Allison caught sight of Sondra reappearin, again with Mungo.

It felt a little weird, tailin her friend around Orvop, but less so the more she drove, because, see, Sondra Gatestone weren't goin nowhere, she weren't stoppin nowhere; she was just drivin around. Allison never drove right up on her, but she was never so far away to evade notice. A yellow Dodge Dart ain't exactly the most common sight in Orvop. But Sondra never gave no indication that she knew Allison was matchin her every turn.

At some point snowflakes started to drift through the air, mostly meltin when they reached the ground, which was not the case for the mountains, where a greater paleness had begun to take hold.

A few times Allison considered givin up. But where would she go? Home? To the couch where Kalin weren't? Did she really want to unlock their door and brave the emptiness inside, face the stillness of that small apartment abandoned already to the stale smell of dust? So, see, maybe just like Sondra Gatestone was doin, drivin to drive weren't such a bad idea?

They was well into night when Sondra returned home again, except she didn't stay long, and that's when Allison got spooked. This time Sondra left Mungo behind. She also left behind her winter coat and her hat. She looked like she expected spring to greet her. And now when she headed out, speedin through the flurries of snow, near blindin in their headlights, it looked like she knew where she was goin.

The gas station was the first stop. Allison's own tank was plungin below a quarter-full, but she didn't dare risk gettin seen now, especially at the gas pumps, though when she changed her mind and figured that

that weren't the worst place to say hello again, at least ask if everythin was okay, ask if she might do somethin for her friend, Sondra Gatestone had already paid and was turnin north on University Avenue.

University Avenue quick enuf turns into Orvop Canyon Road and not long after, with one wide bendin turn to the northwest, erases in the rearview mirror every hint of municipal glow.

At one point they passed a flood of orange lights and red road flares. A semi had met the new conditions badly and slid off the shoulder of the road and onto its side. It lay there like some broken prehistoric creature cloaked with meltin snow. The absence of any ambulances was maybe good news. Though whether it was or not, the wreck was quick enuf gone, not even a flicker of the brightly lit aftermath leavin a trace in Allison's rearview mirror.

Darkness in a mirror is a hard thing to look at, not just because it don't give you much to look at but, at least in Allison's case, invites lingerin, which ain't a good thing when you're drivin north of seventy miles per hour. Allison twisted the rearview mirror aside, keepin her eyes fixed on Sondra's taillights, which continued to blur ahead faster and faster, outpacin the poor Dodge Dart at every turn, Allison feelin more and more certain she would soon lose hold of the asphalt and wind up like the semi. It weren't no comfort either how the deeper into Orvop Canyon they got, the steeper those drop-offs got.

Decades later all these shoulders would have guardrails, but now they offered many an easy passage to a tumblin accident terminatin in the Orvop River below. Not even four months from this night, on February 8, 1983, an Orvop senior, bright-eyed Wilki Wendelson, would die in a tumult of twistin steel and shattered glass, lost to one more night of ice.

Allison sped around another dangerous curve only to find more darkness. Sondra's gleamin red taillights gone! However, rather than speed up, Allison slowed hard, her heart hammerin harder, now on the lookout for an accident, every new turn threatenin to reveal some fiery remnant of her friend.

She passed Bridal Veil Falls without sparin a glance for those mist-draped cliffs. She neared her usual exit to the Cassidy Ski Resort, the only exit out of Orvop Canyon after which you pretty much had to go on to Heber, and flew right by it, never takin seriously that what Sondra had on her mind was an abandoned parkin lot and some chair lifts. Allison was now bettin on the great ahead, despite the irony that the choice was more her than Sondra, runnin now, fast as she could, as far away as she could get, even if no distance or speed would ever grant her the relief she still hoped a mashed-down accelerator might deliver.

But Allison March weren't right. As soon as she settled back for a long drive, she spied Sondra's truck pulled over to the side, right before the Deer Crick Reservoir Dam. That was when, of all things, the memory of the last words she'd uttered to her dear lost boy ambushed her, replete with the awful gratin umbrage in her voice: *Don't you forget the curse, Kalin March: you but touch a gun and what you love most will forsake you for the rest of your life. Just like that. Might as well the very hills of creation should tumble into oblivion, just like a crashin wave is lost to the sea, so Love will be lost to you. Kalin March, you heed the price of such ruinous pride.* Allison had no idea either what that last part was about, or why she'd suddenly said it; it had just come to her, as if another voice had suddenly spoken through her, even if the latent ire there was only too comprehensible and, given where she was at, sorrowful now and shameful.

What had she done?! Refusin him words of warmth and sustainment, of trust and belief, of reassurance, faith?! What kind of mother was she?! Hurlin out such love-deprivin threats upon her scrappy little boy, so insecure he couldn't even stand to face her without a shirt on?! Why couldn't she have just given him instead somethin by which to be strong, to be smart, to be kind? Why hadn't she at least repeated with him her own constant prayer? *Please grant me the presence and compassion to be open to what is Good for me. Please grant me the strength and conviction to endure what is Good for me. Please grant me the wit and intelligence to negotiate what is Good for me. Please grant me the grace and courage to love what is Good for me.* Which was right when yet another voice interrupted her thoughts, and of all people it was Old Porch's voice, out on the tarmac: *You still think your twig of a boy is alive, don't you?* It was the specificity that had caught her off guard then and stuck with her. Old Porch had never laid eyes on her boy. There weren't no pictures of him on the news either, and yet there was Old Porch, climbin out of a helicopter, describin her boy as a frail branch, like he'd seen Kalin hisself, alive up there amidst those awful Olympian heights.

Which was also when Allison's poor Dodge Dart started to cough and sputter. Who knows how long the fuel gauge needle had been below empty. She only just got to the shoulder when the engine quit.

The truck was empty, but even through the white flurries, continuin to grow, Allison spotted a path down to the river. The snow itself offered up the easiest map: Sondra's footprints.

Allison weren't no sure-footed mountain goat and slipped plenty of times on the way down, with the pain in her hip sharpenin until she had to keep her leg stiff and extended for the rest of the descent.

Eventually she caught sight of Sondra Gatestone. She was slowly and methodically gatherin up large stones, which she'd first wipe clean of slush and even examine before placin in one of the many pockets offered by that harvest-gold dress.

Take this one too, Allison said, offerin her friend the rock she'd snatched up when she was last in her apartment.

I thought that was you followin me, Sondra said almost sleepily. *I guess I just figured you'd give up.*

Felt like givin up a number of times. I surprised myself.

Sondra Gatestone didn't refuse the gray stone, and like the rest that she was already weighin down various parts of her dress with, she gave it a close look. *There's a white line around it.*

It's a Nightmare Stone. Put that under your pillow or just keep it close, and it'll ward off the bad dreams. At least that's what I tell myself and my son.

Thank you, Sondra said, placin the stone in a pocket.

I've had enuf of goodbyes, Sondra. I can't take it anymore. But at a certain point, life just becomes a series of goodbyes. You say bye to bein young. You say bye to those pleasures that bein young gave you. You say bye to the friends you swore you'd be friends with forever.

Then what's left?

What we got now.

Rocks in my pockets.

That counts.

Not a whole lot then.

Not a whole lot but enuf.

You sure about that?

I am.

Despite their many differences, what these two women held in common was their willingness in almost any circumstance to offer a candid response, which might also explain how their friendship had thrown down such stout roots so fast.

I wish I had your faith, Allison.

Then borrow some of mine.

Sondra at least chuckled.

You plannin to just wade out in the water there and let the river take you? Allison asked then.

Somethin like that.

Of course, you might freeze to death first.

I'm pretty hardy when it comes to the cold, but I don't know how to swim.

I ain't gonna stop you, Sondra. This is as far as I go.

See, I knew you'd give up.

Allison smiled and thought she saw Sondra smile a little too.

You got your truck keys on you? Allison asked then.

I do.

Mind if I get them before you go in? My car just ran out of gas.

Sondra Gatestone began diggin through her pocket. The keys came out with the Nightmare Stone. Sondra held on to the Nightmare Stone. She seemed mesmerized by it.

Allison recalled for her then how Old Porch at the airport had called her Kalin a twig of a boy and how she'd found it a very particular and even intimate description made by someone who'd never seen Kalin before.

I'll tell you what I think, Sondra. I think they was up there in that helicopter and laid eyes on my Kalin and your Landry. Maybe even with the horses.

And that's all it took: an immediate spark of hope settin afire the rest of her, her cheeks findin color, her shoulders findin rest; but above all else Sondra's eyes were roused from their torpor, bright again with endless creativity, alight with the endless possibilities of tomorrow, which brought tears to Allison's own eyes, the fierceness of that sudden flood surprisin her, even embarrassin her, as she kept wipin at her face and apologizin, an apology that drew from her friend a hoarse chuckle.

Why on earth are you sayin sorry to me?! Sondra asked and then walked over and gave her friend a big Gatestone hug, her own eyes wet as well if still alight with all them dark stars that maybe only her Tom could know. *Look at you!* Sondra declared then, holdin Allison at arm's length by the shoulders. *You're colder than me, and you've got a coat on!*

I'm gonna track down that helicopter pilot, Allison said as her nose ran and her teeth chattered. *You comin?*

Sondra still hesitated.

If he ain't seen nothin, I'll bring you right back, Allison added.

Promise?

Promise.

Even beyond midnight, bedlam continued to reign over the Isatch Canyon entrance. It had started earlier when Hatch Porch, with Park Ranger Emily Brickey now in the second seat of that ATV, came out above Indian Hills. They was followed not a moment later by Kelly Porch, who still had Law Enforcement Ranger Bren Kelson tied to his back, with Egan Porch right behind them and Billings Gale takin up the rear on the XR dirt bike. An ambulance was supposed to be waitin but weren't. Rather than wait, Ranger Brickey redirected the delayed ambulance to the Isatch Canyon parkin lot. Hatch Porch got them there pretty quick, especially once the snowy paths gave way to residential streets. The ambulance was still late.

Hatch Porch untied Ranger Kelson from Kelly, who would learn soon enuf that his whole back was soaked with blood; even his under-wear was soaked. Both brothers carried Kelson's body into Undersher-iff Jewell's tent, where, with but one swipe of his tremendous arm, Hatch easily cleared the closest table. Kelly Porch at once began pre-formin mouth-to-mouth and CPR on Ranger Kelson while Hatch and several deputies crowded around. Undersheriff Jewell got to hollerin again over his radio about gettin medical assistance only to learn that two separate ambulances were still battlin the dump of snow that was now accumulatin in earnest throughout the valley but especially at the base of Isatch Canyon.

Years later, Undersheriff Jewell swore that seein Kelly Porch relent-lessly carryin out life-savin measures was one of the most movin moments in his entire life. And then Egan took over. *The way Egan Porch kept tryin to revive Bren, why that was somethin,* Undersheriff Jewel would admit. *Oh gosh, it got me. To tell you the truth it still gets me, though, of course, not in the right way. The scene just keeps so vivid in my head. This one man tryin to pull this other man back from the brink. Of course I had no way of knowin then that this was his killer, that all them Porch boys in that tent, and I'll even include Hatch Porch and his fifty cal, all of them were just killers.* A line that would anticipate future true crime shows devoted, with forensic focus, to just the Porch clan. *And ain't I the awful fool for feelin anythin fer them, fer believin them? But I've gotten on enuf to know bein a fool ain't nothin special. Still, when you can shudder over a memory, why that warns you too. It's like gettin drowsy on sunny clover only to wake in the dark with snakes on you.*

Not that Kelly Porch's or Egan Porch's exertions served much pur-pose beyond theater. Eventually everyone could see, especially Under-sheriff Jewell, and Hatch Porch too, that it weren't no use.

The command tent soon shook with hot shock, accusations, incriminations, and frustrations vented in every form of hand ges-ture and verbal ejaculation. Why hadn't anyone radioed sooner?! Why hadn't a helicopter been sent?! Why hadn't they gone directly to the hospital?! What exactly had happened to the ranger?! Despite their conclusions to the contrary, was it possible he was still alive?! Was Bren Kelson still alive?! Was he?!

When the EMTs finally did arrive, and in reality it weren't but a few minutes after Law Enforcement Ranger Bren Kelson was stretched out on a plastic tablecloth bright with cartoon cherries, bananas, and pineapples, they barely had to check the body. They didn't even hesitate, just pronounced him dead on the spot. Furthermore, they declared that he'd likely been dead awhile. He was cold and stiff.

Kelly Porch took the news the hardest. Right as the command tent was possessed by several powerful gusts of wind, overwhelmin the space heaters with cold air and fillin the tent with flurries of way-ward flakes, Kelly slumped down hard on a metal chair and buried his face in his hands. Park Ranger Emily Brickey tried to comfort him as he sobbed. For all that Kelly Porch understood and didn't understand about what was unfoldin around him, enfoldin him too within its per-nicious folds, his resolve to save the life of Law Enforcement Ranger Bren Kelson had for a few hours let him feel free. And maybe he had been free. He'd cared not a stone fer his own life as he'd raced that ATV on a perilous drive from Kirk's Cirque, down along those great bluffs, over them awful screes.

Despite plenty of reservations compounded by more than a few conflictin impressions, Park Ranger Emily Brickey continued to praise then as well as years later Kelly Porch's heroic efforts to save the ranger.

Only when the body of Bren Kelson was taken into police custody did Park Ranger Brickey get around to detailin for Undersheriff Jewell how the one leadin them, Billings Gale, who was on the dirt bike and the fastest, had fallen back when the weather had gotten really bad. Hatch Porch and Egan Porch, who were the last to leave Kirk's Cirque, had both caught up by then, and Hatch Porch hadn't hesitated to take over as leader.

Years later, Park Ranger Emily Brickey would admit with some shame that, though she could handle an ATV, even rode dirt bikes now and then, that night she'd had no feel for the trail. *I was drivin like I was gonna ditch that thing any minute. It got to where that was all I was thinkin about. I might as well have been plannin to jump. How far would I need to get? How I'd have to spread-eagle soon as I hit in order to keep from goin down off the cliffs. It was just a question of when. Obviously, that ain't a good frame of mind to be in. I kept slowin down. I was just too darned scared. Hatch didn't let me fall behind. He finally stopped and told me to park the ATV on the side. You know, I don't know if they ever brought it down. Maybe it's still up there. I got on with him and pretty much closed my eyes the last half. I still have nightmares that I'm up there and we're just slidin on down off the edge. But Hatch Porch, whatever you wanna say about him, why that night he never made a mistake. Not one. He always found the best way through the worst parts. I'm alive because of him. How's that for crazy?* Park Ranger Emily Brickey would have to pause then, her mouth dry. She had a glass of water but chose not to drink. *I never do stop thinkin of Landry and Kalin. Breaks my heart. We just had no idea what was goin on. They'd already been through so much. Enuf already to make what I went through look like a picnic. And they weren't even in the worst of it yet. All alone up there? In that terrible storm? And with horses too? It still staggers me.*

Not that Park Ranger Emily Brickey put it quite that way to Undersheriff Jewell that night. She fer sure praised Hatch Porch for his leadership and assistance and praised Kelly Porch for his fearless administerin of aid to Law Enforcement Ranger Bren Kelson. She also said it was a miracle they'd gotten out of there alive. And that was true. Regardless of the events yet to take place, folks still speak with amazement at how them five somehow survived the Great Blizzard of '82 without so much as a scratch, and did so on the north side of Isatch Canyon, on three-wheeler ATVs, plus a dirt bike, and at night too.

Undersheriff Jewell thanked both Hatch Porch and Kelly Porch, and his demeanor and attentiveness, plus, of course, the authority of his command, brought calm to that tent as he and his deputies then began to try to make sense of what had befallen Law Enforcement Ranger Bren Kelson.

Not lost on anyone there was Egan Porch's growin irritability, especially when Ranger Brickey started praisin Hatch Porch, Egan's pacin gettin faster then, his bad mood gettin worse, until he was powerless to keep hisself from yellin out: *Are you friggin satisfied now, Uncle Conrad?! Are you?! You all kept treatin that Kalin kid like some Boy Scout on a campin trip, and now he's not only killt my baby brother and killt one of your rangers, but he shot dead Landry Gatestone too!*

*S*exual *violence and violence in general against women is also a way men prime themselves for violence against each other.* Or so Chalise Brimhall, professor emerita at Brown University, who'd taught many a gender studies course durin her career, would posit in a classroom discussion that began with Gabby Petito and ended with the missin Indigenous women of Canada; Brimhall herself would pass from the ledgers of Life not a week later after trippin on her own shoelaces and tumblin down three brick steps. *No question Orvop was a strange place to grow up,* she would go on to add. *The Church could not recognize gender fluidity let alone healthy sexuality beyond its narrow normative doctrinal views. Unfortunately the resultin repression, as is the case in many similarly organized communities, especially religious ones, instead of minimalizin desire only doubled it! Tripled it! Such was the fixation on our attention on that procreative drive that any gender interaction, no matter how minor, was simply seen as an excuse for coital consummation. Lord knows we should never underestimate the near-miraculous motivation brought into existence by physical want. Personally, I believe there is so much more to have if we make ourselves available to paradoxically gettin far less than what our desires demand. But that's another story.*

Brimhall's musings and digressions circle a larger question that continues to puzzle many: though physical and sexual volatility clearly underlie many of Egan Porch's actions and reactions, what exactly he desired remains unclear. *Except to surpass his father,* Orlando Banuelos, owner of Hermosas Bañeras, an Orvop tub-reglazin company, would argue one year before he was killt by of all things a Komodo dragon, and though Banuelos didn't know Chalise Brimhall, they both shared an interest in what Brimhall labeled *the brutality of personal perogative* and Banuelos called *the wrath of inadequate sons. Orwin Porch's tragedy bein,* as he would later clarify, *that no son of his was adequate, and if one had been, they'd've then been a threat. What a terrible predicament.*

Not that such analysis, but two examples out of a sea of commentary, settles the issue of why Egan Porch launched such a wild and risky improvisation before numerous witnesses too, includin officers of the law but most significantly the eldest Porch brother.

You saw Landry Gatestone gunned down?! Undersheriff Jewell near shouted the question.

Did you see that? Undersheriff Jewell then demanded of Hatch.

Hatch Porch sure was blindsided. Robbed of speech too, as he kept tryin to get his head around Egan's claim, what he and he alone knew weren't true. But Hatch didn't call out the lie then nor give voice to his growin suspicion, to them in the tent, or even to hisself, that somethin weren't just awry here but outright foul. Instead he stuck to what he could vouch for personally: *I spotted the boy, but I was a good ways across the cirque and my scope weren't givin me much in the way of details.*

Scope? Undersheriff Jewell asked then, under no illusion now that, except for Park Ranger Emily Brickey, hearin all this from Porch boys, or the Porch hand there, Billings Gale, though he weren't sayin a thing, was an entanglin that was only gonna get worse with the investigation of the murder of Law Enforcement Ranger Bren Kelson. Maybe Undersheriff Jewell briefly tried to sell hisself on the merits of certain allowances when the case had first started to unfold. By now, though, Porch involvement was well beyond the limits of acceptable police protocol, not helped, he knew, by the fact that Conrad Jewell's wife, Kip-Ann Porch, was Orwin Porch's sister. And should there be a trial, why he'd be in one heckuva fix, maybe even a career-endin one. Concernin the Porch presence above the rockfall, he'd rationalized that the sheriff's department's main concern was at the base of the rockfall. What did it matter if the Porches had gone up there? At most they'd find a horse or two. If they was lucky. When Landry's pink raincoat and the sleepin bag turned up, Undersheriff Jewell at once ordered back his deputies, the rangers, as well as the Porches. He even let word spread, like he knew it would spread, that this news story was over and had ended with the graves of three children.

Boy, had he been wrong. Word that the kids had survived the slide was shockin enuf, but now one had shot a law enforcement ranger in the back of the head and then, accordin to Egan Porch, gunned down in cold blood the Gatestone child. Undersheriff Jewell's mind kept lurchin from one state of denial to another, with no amount of extra thinkin able to set it straight. And it sure didn't help to hear how Hatch Porch, albeit a sworn officer of the law in Texas, had trained his scope on the Kalin kid, unless of course it weren't attached to nothin.

But Hatch made clear that the scope was attached to a .50-caliber rifle.

I fired it too, Hatch admitted.

You shot Kalin March? Undersheriff Jewell asked. He forced hisself to stay standin, though every part of him wanted to sit.

I did not. My intent was to keep him from escapin, which I achieved, pinnin him down on the headwall.

What headwall?

The Upecksay Headwall, sir, Park Ranger Brickey clarified.

He was up on the Upecksay Headwall?

They was, Hatch said.

The Katanogos summit wall?

On a horse, Hatch Porch felt compelled to add.

Of course, this was true, but it was such a remarkable and unexpected truth that Undersheriff Jewell was only able to receive it with astonishment and disbelief. He was not alone. The deputies present in that tent at once began exchangin uncomfortable glances. Some even laughed like Hatch Porch was jokin. Undersheriff Jewell shot a look at Park Ranger Brickey.

I cannot vouch for that, she replied. *I did not lay eyes on either Kalin March or Landry Gatestone or any horses. We did, though, find hoofprints and horse manure.* By which point Hatch had regathered hisself, thought through again some of this, decidin now to bring up Landry Gatestone, how his brother Egan was mistaken, how Hatch had watched her reach the summit ridge.

Why Hatch Porch stayed silent again remains another great source of ongoin controversy. Why did he heel to Egan? Why didn't he just blurt out that Landry Gatestone was alive? Was it because of the scoffin he'd just got for sayin the Kalin kid was up there on a horse? Or because he'd had her in his crosshairs too? Or maybe the sight of her survivin what should've been a deadly slip was still too much for his imagination to accommodate? Maybe he still doubted what he'd seen? Is it even possible that a part of him found Egan's assertion more credible? Or was it just that Hatch, like all the rest of his brothers, was first and foremost a Porch?

In fact Hatch was again about to tell everyone that the Gatestone girl was alive when Kelly Porch spoke up.

I saw the Kalin kid too, Kelly declared. *Like my brother said, he was on a horse, hid among the rocks, at the base of the headwall. That's where Hatch fired his warnin shot: at the base of the Upecksay Headwall.*

Again Hatch did not object, again likely stunned, less by the inaccurate claim than by the sudden shift in that tent from those initial stirrings of discomfort, as if a moment ago Hatch Porch had been deemed off his rocker, to murmurs of understandin, as if Hatch had merely messed up the location, not on the headwall but rather below the headwall, which was a forgivable slip given what all they'd just lived through. Also of note was that Park Ranger Emily Brickey held her tongue too. Years later her failure to speak would continue to wound her: *That shot Hatch fired, which I sure heard, that happened when we were on our way out of the cirque. It's possible Kelly glassed the headwall then, but I doubt it. By that point Bren was tied to his back. And it was pretty dark. No way he saw a thing.* Park Ranger Brickey would take then a long pause. *We know now that those kids were way up on the headwall and with horses. Hatch Porch told the truth the first time. He just didn't reassert the truth when Kelly Porch lied. And me, I doubted myself too much to say what at that moment seemed a small discrepancy. I mean I fully believed Kalin March had killt Ranger Kelson. Beyond that, the rest was just noise.*

Some time later Undersheriff Jewell would remain similarly distraught about a truth discarded in favor of a lie more easily believed. *What would you say if I pointed to a wall of rock well over a thousand feet high and told you that that's where a boy was ridin a horse?! It was ridiculous! So, of course, we all assumed Hatch Porch was mistaken. And why not? He'd just led his party out of some really terrible conditions. No one was gonna fault him fer gettin confused about a few things. Certainly I didn't fault him. But the saddest part, and I remind myself of this often, is that Hatch Porch didn't protest. He went along with Egan Porch's lie, and then he went along with Kelly Porch's lie. He even went along with what Kelly Porch said next.*

Kelly Porch had sighed first, that's what he did next, and then shook his head, and even eyed Egan fer a second, before throwin out how Hatch Porch's shot came too late to save Landry Gatestone. *The Kalin kid had already shot her. Just bang. Like he was done with her.*

Then her body's up there in the cirque? Undersheriff Jewell demanded, this revelation and all its implications still continuin to take hold of him, take hold of everyone. There weren't a face in that tent that didn't look appalled.

I should think so.

Why didn't you bring her down?

My concern, Sheriff Jewell, was with the livin, Kelly Porch said slow enuf and sincere enuf that Orwin Porch, if he'd been there, might've given Kelly some applause.

Do you think Kalin March is still up there in the cirque?

Egan spoke up then. *He'll either try to outlast the storm or try to come down like we done.*

You think he's on the way down now? Undersheriff Jewell asked.

Egan and Kelly both shrugged.

He might also just die up there, Hatch threw in, which at least he knew to be the likely truth. Both boy and horse had probably already fallen. What a mess this whole thing was. A dead ranger, a dead boy, dead horses, and of course what started all this dyin in the first place: their youngest brother, dear little Russel Porch. But what of Landry Gatestone? He'd seen her summit. He weren't ever gonna forget that. And yet he'd said nothin. How much would change if Hatch Porch could just declare that Landry Gatestone was alive on the top of Katanogos?

Instead Park Ranger Brickey spoke up, maybe because she didn't like how easily Egan and Kelly had resituated everythin to the base of the headwall, and likely too because she had some faith in the eldest Porch. *I did hear Bren say over the radio that he'd seen horses on the head-wall.* She even nodded at Hatch to acknowledge how they'd both been under a similar impression. She'd bring up next how she'd overheard on Kelly's radio the Billings fella say somethin about them gettin over the headwall, bein clear of this place.

Did you see horses ridin up cliffs, Emily? Undersheriff Jewell barked.

Uh, no sir. Just reportin what Bren was sayin over the radio.

Undersheriff Jewell glared at her then, and much to her own disappointment, especially later on, she bit her tongue.

Fer his part, Undersheriff Jewell was tired, and aside from gettin the heck away from this big slop-bucket-of-misery stew, he knew that come mornin he'd have to send up a new crew to dig for bodies. He'd also have to deal with Sondra Gatestone and the mother of the Kalin kid. That would be fun. He'd have to tell Sondra that in fact her daughter had not been buried alive but now had reportedly been gunned down by the boy who had also not been buried alive. The only silver linin here, and really it was closer to tinfoil, was that at least this all seemed to be over with. Here on out was just aftermath.

Gusts of snow-laden wind again breached the tent flaps. Maps and loose papers flew from the table. The air briefly sparkled with ice. And in that fit of weather, though he said it to his Uncle Conrad, Egan Porch's anger was directed at Park Ranger Brickey, who only much later recognized how his intent had all along been to silence her.

Unless I'm missin somethin, Egan growled, *what matters here is that this Kalin kid's done a lot of killin, and he's still up there.* Whereupon he stormed out of the tent, followed immediately by Kelly Porch and Billings Gale. Hatch Porch lingered a bit longer, as if a few more moments with Park Ranger Brickey and Undersheriff Jewell might bestow upon this night some more clarity.

In fact Undersheriff Jewell agreed with Egan, though he did advise Hatch Porch that come mornin he'd need to see him, Egan, Kelly, and their hand, Billings Gale, in order to get statements concernin the events that had just occurred up on Katanogos. Two deputies would come by Porch Meats after church. Hatch Porch, fer his part, offered to give Undersheriff Jewell his statement right then. That there opens the door to more speculation. As Brenda Mistry would wonder durin many a frustrated attempt to create a suitable portrait of the eldest Porch: *While layin out what he'd done, how he'd done it, what he'd seen, would Hatch Porch have then told of Landry Gatestone scramblin safely into the cover of clouds? Was he still readyin his confession? To turn on his own brothers?* But his Uncle Conrad closed that door with a wave of his hand, tellin Hatch to get some rest.

You done enuf today. And we surely thank you for your help.

Undersheriff Jewell then called Chief of Police Wilson Beckham and updated him about the alleged murder, warnin him that by first light, this story would be the only thing anyone cared about. They'd better have the necessary personnel and equipment in place for either a manhunt or a body recovery.

If it snows all night, gettin up in the cirque won't be no easy feat. We'll need a helicopter fer sure and a tactical unit to return fire if that's what we're lookin at.

You think we're headed for a gunfight? Chief of Police Wilson Beckham asked.

No. I think we'll just find bodies.

As Daisy Fitzgarbie loved to point out to Claudia Bellinharp: *Them Porches were gamblers,* a comment she repeated the year before both women were borne from this earth in illness and sufferin gratefully unremembered by the ashes their families would scatter: on the Isatch mountains, Daisy's ashes, and throughout the Uinta forests, Claudia's ashes. *Egan was just uppin the stakes with that Landry-gettin-shot business,* Fitzgarbie would go on to say, fortunately not stoppin there. *Unnecessary too. It was already bad enuf that the ranger was killt. The only thing Egan's stupid lie accomplished was to give us a better inklin about what cards he was guardin, intendin to play.* Claudia Bellinharp had no kind words for the Porches. *They was a rotten bunch. I'd've put money on Russel becomin the worst if he'd lived long enuf. I mean, he took that darned gun. Maybe Francis had a chance. From what I gather, he was a heckuva cook.* And Bellinharp weren't done. *And Hatch Porch? He was a liar. Sure, he was the best-lookin. Sure, he was strong and could pass a test or two. And no question he was the most sympathetic, but that night in the tent, he was one big liar. And don't quibble with me: the lies you tell by not tellin the truth are just as nasty as the rest.*

That night, though, upon returnin to the Porch's house, with Mr. Bucket howlin in his kennel like it weren't just a big snowstorm but the end of days, Egan did not lie to his old man. He said it right in front of Kelly and Billings, and Hatch too. He made clear how he lied about Landry gettin shot by the Kalin kid.

And if they find her alive tomorrow? Old Porch asked, his voice low and rough, like broke glass was cuttin up each word.

Then I guess I'll say I was mistaken, Egan said with a shrug. Old Porch could see that somethin about this boy of his had changed. He even looked bigger than the rest, no matter that Hatch was still the tower in the room. Egan looked meaner too, and fer the first time Old Porch saw somethin he might be able to really trust. Even as much as he trusted Billings.

Kelly grunted and sucked his gut in. He hadn't been sure Egan was tellin the truth, but he'd also already convinced hisself that it could've happened. Billings weren't surprised by the news. After all he was the one who'd spotted the horses headin up over the headwall, and with Hatch trappin Kalin on the wall, it didn't take much math to figure the scramblin he'd seen higher up had to have been Landry. Even though that was not the case.

I saw Landry Gatestone on the headwall, Hatch finally admitted as he slumped in a chair in his father's dinin room, bearin the load of Egan's lie, the audacity of it, to say nothin of his own lie, and the position that put him in, what continued to shock him from his feet on up, enuf to shock him back on his feet. *I saw her make it over a pretty scary set of rocks and then head on up to the top.*

The top of Katanogos? Old Porch asked. *Could she have fallen?*

She made it. I'm certain of it. Whether she survives the night, that's a whole other matter.

Old Porch grunted, though it was unclear to Hatch whether his father found Hatch's complicity to be good news or bad. Hatch was exhausted and confused. And he knew hisself to be real exhausted because he knew none of this should be that confusin.

Why would you even make up somethin like that, Eges? Hatch asked then, even if his voice came up soft and lacked commitment. *Word's gonna get back to her mother. You know that, right? She's gonna have to suffer the death of her child a second time.* Hatch had to sit again.

Whadya mean why'd he do somethin like that?! Old Porch hissed. *Because Egan here is lookin out for this family!* And with that the Porch patriarch stormed from the room, fartin too as he left, a loud angry expulsion, like it meant to kick down a barn door. Old Porch was barefoot too and only had on his garments, but he made no effort to find boots, bangin out the back door, though that weren't what silenced Mr. Bucket's barkin nor what made the poor dog squeal.

After that surprisin eruption and departure, Hatch, Egan, Kelly, and Billings kept their voices low, partly because Francis and Woolsey were upstairs asleep in their room, with Sean and Shelly downstairs, them two crashed out as well, in the guest rooms, but also because somethin had just been made clear that had obviously escaped Hatch's reasonin if not his better instincts.

Tomorrow sheriffs and police might find the Kalin kid dead beside his dead horse, Egan said then, layin it out for Hatch, because he still weren't sure Hatch could handle the brunt of what was goin on. What Egan was sure about, though, was that if Hatch didn't start handlin it, Egan would have no problem lettin Old Porch see just who this hero brother of theirs really was or, better yet, lettin Hatch here learn who Egan really was. *And if he hasn't fallen from the cliffs, odds favor him freezin to death tonight.*

Odds favor both of them freezin to death tonight, Kelly threw in.

You knew he was up there? Hatch asked Egan, plenty flabbergasted.

Of course I did!

Kelly even laughed low and easy. *That was somethin else when you actually told everyone the truth but them deputies didn't believe you! Not even Uncle Conrad believed you! They all thought you'd gone screwy.*

Egan laughed as well. Even Billings chuckled.

Thanks to Kelly, though, the law won't think twice about those high walls, Egan said then. *They'll keep to the cirque. But I'll say this: whatever the odds, I'm done bettin against that Kalin kid.*

That's right! Old Porch roared as he reentered the room, snow on his shoulders, his feet still bare, a wet survey map now in his hands, what he slapped down on the table, wipin away any blobs of ice with them big brutal hands. *Billings, point out where you seen the horses.*

Billings did as he was told.

Here's the summit. You think they made it over right here? Old Porch punched the map with his swollen thumb, nailless and near black. The pressure produced a red bubble that at once pussed on the paper. The hurt reprimanded Old Porch too, but it also made him feel good, again sharpenin his resolve, remindin him of the stakes.

The Gatestone girl, that's fer sure, Billings said. *With the horse she was on and another one.* Billings didn't add that he'd thought he'd seen more than two horses. *The black horse was below with the Kalin kid.*

We know the kid's a heckuva rider, Egan added.

No one's that good, Hatch objected. *He's on the side of a cliff for Pete's sake! Whatever path he's figured out, he ain't gonna ride it in this dark, especially not in the middle of a storm. Plus I cut him off with my fifty caliber. That thing's a cannon. He'll think twice before tryin that way again. I know I jittered his horse plenty.*

Cut him off?! Old Porch snarled at his eldest. *What the heck does that mean? You missed! You had in your sights the one who killt Russel and you missed?!*

Yeah, well, Egan missed too, was the best Hatch could come back with, galled by what his father was suggestin as well as cowed by his failure to live up to his father's expectations.

Is that right, Egan? Fer a moment Old Porch's glare left Hatch. You took a shot too and missed?

We don't know that I missed. It was dark.

You missed, Hatch scoffed. *I don't think you even hit the cliff.*

Knock it off, you two, Old Porch said, but he now seemed somehow lighter. *I'm just joshin with you. I don't want either of you shootin that kid. Not like that, where it's sure to come back on you, on us.*

Old Porch returned to examinin the map, not so much the cirque anymore or the summit but now what lay beyond them high ridges, contemplatin the area to the north with disbelief and even, believe it or not, some amusement.

My bet's that he won't fall or freeze to death, Old Porch announced.

He's a survivor, all right, Egan added. *We've seen that firsthand.*

That's right, we have. Old Porch even laid a hand on Egan's shoulder.

First light, we've got to get back side of the mountain, Egan said, pointin to the spot now held by his father's infected thumb.

To do what? Hatch's voice finally rose.

But no one answered him, and Old Porch, though he'd registered the question, continued to look dreamily at the map marked by so many demarcation lines: these here indicatin them BLM parcels that would stay BLM parcels forever, but these other ones likely goin up for auction, if you knew the right government folks and lobbyists, if you was Orwin Porch; and then there were these inholdins that would never be up for grabs, and others that could be bought, if you got along with Brother Mallory Guvin Hone, also known as Manic Guff as you might recall, and Old Porch got along with Manic just fine; they was both salty, even if only one of them was truly old, even if only one of them knew what had really happened to Brad P. Hone. Manic knew only that Old Porch had paid, and lavishly too, for his youngest boy's funeral.

Only when Old Porch's gaze returned to the summit ridge did he start rifflin through some of the other maps left on the table from the previous night, pickin up one with a faded picture on the front of the imposin Katanogos summit ridge, taken from inside Kirk's Cirque.

They rode up that wall?

Billings nodded. Kelly hadn't really seen anythin, but he nodded too. Egan and even Hatch said *Yes* together too.

That's mighty impressive, and it was clear to everyone in that room that Old Porch was very, very impressed. *I'll give them that. On horses? It confounds the mind, it does.* Old Porch even shook his head like that might help free up his thwarted imagination. *Who is this kid again?*

But no one answered because still no one knew.

I never fer a second would've believed that there was even a way to ride a horse out of Isatch Canyon, Old Porch continued. *But him and Tom Gatestone found a way, didn't they? And then this kid rides hisself out of a rockslide? With not a scratch on him? And the horse ain't even left lame?! How is that even possible?*

It ain't possible, Billings said. *Unless you seen it fer yourself like I seen it.*

He's like some kind of phantom, ain't he? Just won't go down to his grave, Old Porch mused. He even seemed pleased with the notion, like for once in his life he finally had an opponent worthy of hisself. *And, Hatch, you saw the boy on a horse up on this wall?* Still eyein that picture of the Upecksay Headwall and the Katanogos summit ridge.

A good thousand feet up, I'd say. At least.

How do you get a horse up there? To the top?! Old Porch jabbed his bloody thumb toward the picture, though thankfully this time he didn't touch it. Not even Old Porch was immune to pain. *What was Tom Gatestone up to? Because whatever talents this Kalin boy's got, when we get down to it, isn't it still Tom Gatestone who's been stirrin this pot?*

Maybe it was just a dare? Kelly said.

Maybe. But the more I look upon the particulars, the more I know I have to start lookin at the big picture. And Old Porch even took a step back now to better regard his map. *It's like there's some other kind of plan at work here.*

You mean like Tom Gatestone wanted to involve us Porches? Hatch asked.

Well, didn't it start with him stealin my horses?

I'm not sure I follow, Dad, Egan said. And Old Porch could see that this was the case for all his boys.

It don't matter now. Billings, what do you say now? Where's he at?

He's over the top, Billings answered. *They both are. And they're fine.*

Attaboy! Old Porch seemed genuinely happy, in fact happy for the first time in a while. *Then that's where we'll go.*

As Hatch staggered upstairs to find a bed, he realized he'd never felt so lost. He'd made it back to the Isatch Canyon entrance, where he'd been hailed a hero, but now in the family home he felt left out in the cold. He had half a mind to just go kennel hisself with Mr. Bucket #5, and maybe if it weren't for that number five he'd've done just that.

To a bunch of newcomers, without the full story, it might appear obvious why Old Porch was so set on bringin down Kalin March along with Landry Gatestone: vengeance, plain and simple. And that much was clear to Hatch. But why then, and this is what confused Hatch so much, weren't his father and brothers standin down now, especially given the fact that come dawn there would be a full-blown police manhunt in progress, with likely every resource at the ready and every action covered by a thick cloud of reporters? Why would his family want to get anywhere near that? Or need to get near that?

Hatch had mostly shrugged off his family's failure to recognize the role he'd played in gettin everyone off the mountain alive. He was a Porch after all. Gettin ignored weren't nothin new. But tonight it went one step further: it was like Old Porch couldn't even see him, like Hatch was at the table, sure, but he was also a ghost, as transparent as a windshield, thinner than the wall of a bubble of soap. Hatch knew that look too, or rather that non-look. In fact he'd known it his whole life, they all had, and knew well to fear it, what invariably signed the warrant for reprisals.

But what had Hatch done wrong? That was the part he couldn't figure out. Nothin he could've done would've saved that ranger. Egan and Kelly had done their best to render medical assistance. Kelly had carried that poor guy on his back the whole way down. Any number of times Kelly could've rolled that ATV and killt hisself with just one wrong jerk of them handlebars. And besides, they'd found Russel's killer. What more was there to be done? Hatch had zero jurisdiction here, let alone the right to just gun down some kid, a kid the Law would get anyway, either tomorrow or the day after, or whenever, if he weren't already dead this night. That kid had no future.

So what the heck was goin on?

The only thing Hatch knew fer sure was that he needed sleep. Even Old Porch could see that much, orderin all of them to bed, even makin the couch up hisself fer this Billings guy. Experience and trainin had taught Hatch how even two hours could clear his head some, but tonight he was gonna get at least four.

And with that promise of rest levelin him out some, he went back downstairs to the kitchen fer another helpin of chili. The big pot was still simmerin on the stove, what Francis had whipped up, what was frickin amazin, especially when it was heaped up with extra cheese Francis had grated. Hatch took down a bowl in half the time it took to fill it.

Then he called his mother. She never minded the late hour. She didn't value sleep much anymore, especially if Hatch was callin. She told him she was lookin out at the Gulf. He knew she was cryin. She didn't want to hear about Russel. She was still cryin. She didn't want to hear about the rest of her boys. Hatch sure knew not to mention Old Porch. After she'd blown her nose some, she told him his sister, Ginny, was asleep but she wanted to talk to Hatch in the mornin. Hatch only said that he would be home soon. *There's no glory there* was her response. *Quit while you're ahead and get outta that place. You, me, and your sister can mourn your baby brother down here.*

While brushin his teeth, Hatch stared dully at the mirror above the sink but could see only what had happened not an hour ago, his daddy disappearin into the dark, down that long ground-floor hallway, with one big paw ridin Egan's shoulder the whole way. Neither one had taken any note of Hatch, even if both, before disappearin into Old Porch's bedroom, seemed to have cast their eyes his way, this time with not only Old Porch but Egan as well registerin nothin there, not even a disturbance in the air where Hatch had towered. It provoked a brutal shiver in him now. He tried to spit it from his mouth, like it was nothin more than bad toothpaste, and it almost worked, partially, makin the mirror just a mirror again, though what still weren't goin away was his regret for not followin them, for not havin pressed his ear against the door, to hear what Egan and his father were up to. Why hadn't he? The ire Hatch had felt in the face of such paternal disregard had turned him to the stairs, to the chili, to the phone, to the mirror, and eventually to this room, to what was once his mother's bed, at least before she'd finally moved out, where Hatch would spend his last night.

Hatch beat the dusty pillows. None of the other brothers would come in here. The room was cold, and there weren't no extra blankets in the deserted closet. Hatch folded over the one blanket and the top sheet. He wouldn't need but half the mattress anyways. He'd sleep in his garments. If it got too cold, he'd throw on his clothes.

Even though his eyes stayed open, as the ripples of spent adrenaline continued to stir through him, the prevailin permission to at last rest finally granted some order to his thoughts: his family needed him and that's why he'd returned to Orvop. He was there to turn his brothers from ruin, even if his mother had warned him that this family would only bring ruin to him; even if his sister, who had never begged him for anythin, had begged him to stay in Texas. He understood their fear as the fear of women and would not heed it.

Hatch then began unpackin and repackin the Barrett in his head, even though he'd already convinced hisself he wouldn't need that thing again, even as images of the ranger's punctured head kept interruptin his plans, the bone matter, brain in his obliterated eye socket. Would there ever be instruments to heal that? Hatch saw then the tools of a surgeon, seein hisself as a doctor, teachin future doctors and surgeons and even therapists to heal. Hadn't he always wanted to go to a therapist, especially when those black self-eatin thoughts would rise up with such finality and he knew hisself one easy trigger pull from peace? Could anger ever just not exist?

Hatch lurched from his bed, to the floor, to his knees, to pray. That's what he'd forgotten, that's what he still needed to do: to pray that his mother would approve, to pray that his sister would approve, to pray to his Heavenly Father, the father above and beyond Old Porch, who would hear Hatch and know him and guide him. And forgive him too. And this time Hatch even found revelations. The first was near too hot to bear, upon his cheeks, his insides, as certain as a red-hot brandin iron searin his back: today Hatch had killt someone. He ain't never done that before. His daddy and brothers could get after him all they wanted fer not blowin off that Kalin kid's head, but Hatch Porch knowd what he'd done; he knew the conditions, he knew what was batterin that mountain now, had felt for hisself the rage of that storm. He knew exactly where he'd stranded that boy and his horse. And that's why he was on his knees now, beggin for forgiveness, because he hadn't just killt some kid in self-defense; he'd murdered him in cold blood.

But that weren't the only revelation. In the same hunched position of shame and guilt, Hatch also saw the path to his own salvation: Landry Gatestone. He had but to save her, rescue her from whatever deprivations she faced, from his own brothers if need be. And Hatch vowed to hisself then to be the one to bring her safely down from the mountain. He was no longer penitent but knightly again in disposition and aim, now with his Grail to pursue.

Nonetheless, despite the certainty of his feelins, Hatch's vow went unheeded; so it goes with vows that tie themselves to purpose without love, like a cowboy tryin to rope his own shadow.

Feelin so missioned now, when Hatch climbed back under the sheets, his longins no longer required alignment with notions of divine purpose. Instead he found hisself missin a woman. Not one in particular either, at least not at first, as he finally let the pillow crowd up around his ears and darkness take his eyes. And maybe because there weren't nobody just yet, because he'd yet to find the one in Texas, he'd begun to wonder if maybe it came down to right-for-him not residin in that state. Of course, of the girls he'd dated in Orvop, who started Rolodexin through his head now, Cami Lark, Eva Thorn, DawnAnn, and Sherleen, none of them had seemed right either, and forget goin all the way with any of them, nothin more than some pawin and pantin, what steamed up the truck windows but with buttons mostly stayin buttoned.

Hatch was likely the only virgin of the Porch boys with the exception of Francis and Russel. Maybe Woolsey still was but Hatch doubted it. They all was furious to get their stick in the friction house. Egan had hurt him somethin awful when he'd declared one day that he'd had both Cami and Eva and bragged how Sherleen liked the taste so much, she begged him to let her swallow twice. *Just because it didn't get in the basket don't mean it weren't no fun,* Egan had scoffed. *You can ask DawnAnn too.* All of which was bull, but Hatch didn't know that, couldn't know it, and so believed his brother instead of havin the fortitude to consider more carefully the women. Fer some reason, these memories also recalled a time when someone, maybe his momma, had dressed him up like a girl; this was when they was in a little town called Crossy for the summer. He was maybe seven. Hatch remembered playin dolls with Egan, who was just a baby. They was lovin it, until the shame came, them dolls vanishin with the yellin.

Whatever that was about, Hatch by now had put behind hisself them kinda claims Egan loved makin. He knew in his heart that doggin girls had nothin to do with the Good Lord's work. Hatch just had to stay true and he'd find his one. His momma had assured him of that. His young sister too.

Orly Vanleuven weren't finally eaten by his cougar, as many swore would finally happen, nor ever harmed by her either. Instead poor Orly was shot by a police officer who'd mistook him for someone else. This would be in Tennessee. Not long before he was killt, Orly Vanleuven had been addressin his congregants, for by this point he was a minister, Lutheran, with a knack for it too. He'd wanted for a long time to talk about Hatch Porch, whom he'd always had a soft spot for, especially when it came to that *Saturday night, October thirtieth, 1982, which when considered real closely could've gone so many other ways, so many beautiful other ways . . . If only . . .* Orly Vanleuven never would finish that thought, though thankfully he didn't stop wonderin neither: *What can we do? What must we do? After all, we are not even a grain of sand, not even an atom in a grain of sand, not even less than that ridin time's fallin sands. What can we do? It ain't that hard, and it certainly ain't no mystery: what all of us are called upon to do every hour, every minute, is to simply lay our part in the world upon that plate of the scale that falls toward Goodness. That is it, that is all, that is everythin.*

Not that Hatch Porch at that hour beheld some ancient brass or wood-lathed equal-armed scale, whether of Divine proportions or housed in the hold of an oak-ribbed trireme long since lost beneath Mediterranean waters. The pains dartin now across his chest and left bicep had localized his concerns, though he knew at once that the discomfort was only muscular; the thought never crossed his mind, given his fitness, that a future of cardiac woes was already signed by a physiological deterioration not even his doctor in Texas had caught yet or would've thought possible. After all his breathin remained strong; so what if the rest of him was sore with exertion and exhaustion?

No, what overthrew Hatch then was a physical pain that had nothin to do with where he was strong or torn up and what he never did figure out how to answer, and not only for long legs wrapped around his waist and long arms wrapped around his wide back but the feel too of her fingers diggin into his skin, her nails clawin him up some, just enuf to hurt, but not too much hurt, just enuf to make a pass at Love.

See, far more significant than past spectres, however sensually gauzed and incomplete, was this one bartender in a Houston bar where he and his friends on the force would often go, them downin beers, him downin lemonades. Her name was Melanie Pat. She always brought him a capped Michelob with his lemonade. She always said the day he wanted a drink, she'd uncap it fer him, with her teeth too, and she'd share it with him if he asked. She had rings of hair red as brass in firelight. She had a swivel in her narrow hips, and his friends all thought he was crazy not to take at least a sip.

As sleep finally claimed him, Hatch weren't sure no more why he hadn't. He thought of Melanie. He couldn't have known that if he'd but followed Old Porch and Egan and put his ear against that door, he would've gone to her that very night. And you know what, she wouldn't've cared about that sip. She'd have taken him in and swept him off his feet, and he'd've married her.

Once Old Porch had closed the door to his bedroom, Egan, to his great relief, finally removed from his backside the aluminum-frame, double-action 9mm Smith & Wesson Model 59 with all identifyin numerics filed off, what had killt Cavalry and gunned down Law Enforcement Ranger Bren Kelson and shot too that beaver.

Egan offered it to his dad along with the two spent casings.

What we got here? Orwin Porch asked.

I figured you'd know what to do with it, Egan answered.

Shoot it, I guess, Old Porch replied with a smile, though he weren't acceptin Egan's offerin.

Briefly Egan understood his father as understandin him as well as the whole awful situation, but then that slipped some. Maybe his daddy didn't understand? Or was it that he wanted Egan to crawl the whole way through to clarity?

This here's the real horseradish.

Is that so? Old Porch responded, still unwillin to take the weapon.

As far as we know, the Kalin kid and Landry, all's they have is the Peacemaker, Egan said.

Still, his dad showed no sign of graspin what exactly his son was handin him: Egan's own life, in fact.

They fer sure don't have this one, Egan added.

I can see that much, his father snarled. *Because you have it!* No, the old man didn't understand.

One of these casins had the bullet that killt that ranger.

Old Porch accepted the weapon now, the casins too, like here was a fortune better snatched up quick before it melted back into some abolishin haze.

The real horseradish, Old Porch even muttered hisself, amazed, impressed, not a bit about him registerin the agony near all fathers would've suffered if one of their children were to make plain such a terrible confession.

You are this family's salvation, Egan, Old Porch said instead, and Egan glowed in the light of this paternal recognition.

While all the Porch boys had found some slunk hole to lie down in and get groggy, fer some sleep itself weren't so easily won. Kelly alternated between bouts of black sleep interrupted by the painful disruption of his bowels, which on a future date would reveal itself as multiple tumors in his stomach linin. Of the many dreams Kelly wouldn't remember, there was one he couldn't forget: openin a Christmas present and discoverin a Canon F-1 SLR, except there weren't no film, unless the film was already inside the camera, whereupon the back popped open, overexposin the film with all the pictures he knew he should've developed. It was a confusin dream. Kelly woke knowin that for all that had never been between him and Cherilyn Bacall, except fer the stupidest kind of crush, there weren't never gonna be anythin more. He weren't ever gonna see her underpants but he also didn't care anymore. And he sure as heck was done with Orvop High. He had other things on his mind, adult problems, his belly continuin to hurt in ways that only an old man can know.

Billings had collapsed on the downstairs couch, so dead asleep he hadn't noticed Old Porch throw a blanket over him, place beneath Billings's head a pillow he'd brung from his own bed. Not forty minutes later, Billings woke in horror, realizin in the dank darkness that the plastic ziplock bag with Law Enforcement Ranger Bren Kelson's blood in it was still pressed up against his rear. There was a stabbin in his side that he dismissed as a consequence of the exertions required by the previous days, never once thinkin about the state of his liver.

He sat up fast, what he'd forgotten already stumblin him from the couch, even if such movements and recollections didn't exonerate him from the consumin blurriness that his exhaustion kept demandin from him. Disgust fer sure also drove him through the cold house even as he realized he had no clue how to adequately dispose of this grotesque possession stickin to his backside, and so did the utterly stupid thing of just retrievin it right then and there and buryin it at the bottom of the full bag of garbage in the kitchen. In fairness he had every intention of seein that bag to the incinerator come dawn.

At that moment Kelly wandered in to get some milk from the fridge, sluggin it from the carton in hopes that it would help soothe his innards.

You can't sleep either, huh?

I could do, and then I couldn't at all, Billings answered, closin the trash drawer before turnin to wash his hands in the sink, the phantom pain at his side already abatin. Billings was plenty relieved to see that Kelly had taken no interest in his actions.

After Old Porch hisself, Kelly Porch had been Billings's first friend at the plant. He was after all the one who had invited Billings to the poker game. Now, though, Billings felt closer to Egan, certainly in purpose, and Kelly seemed more distant to him, more a stranger, maybe even a threat to this whole enterprise, though he'd fer sure proven hisself in the tent earlier that night with Undersheriff Jewell.

I feel like I'll never sleep again, Kelly said then, oblivious to how closely Billings was now regardin him. *And yet I'm wrecked too at the same time.*

As soon as this is all done with, you'll sleep fine.

You think so? Kelly asked, and seemed genuinely appreciative of Billings's assurances. Conversely, Billings couldn't miss the shake in Kelly's voice and wondered if everythin would just fall to a mess if Kelly didn't have it in him to keep hold of what they was doin here, what they was fashionin, the story they needed to collectively keep tellin. Would Kelly be the one to break and suddenly come clean to the police? Billings decided at that moment to do somethin else with that bloody ziplock bag as soon as he got the chance, if just fer insurance, to keep it on hand in case it needed placin among, say, Kelly's things. It was a calculated decision and not a well-calculated one, but at that hour it made sense to Billings, even if fatigue and more fitful sleep would rob him of any memory of this intention as well as any memory of the bag itself.

That cut on your chin looks awful raw, Kelly said then with a nice-enuf smile. *There's some hydrogen peroxide in the bathroom.*

Billings touched the scratches he'd gotten on yesterday's foray out upon the right side of Isatch Canyon, what seemed like forever ago. The abrasions did seem extra painful now fer some reason, though he could tell they weren't no worse than the numerous cuts Kelly had on his face, includin that scabbed stripe on his nose. There was a second gash as well. Had he gotten that one on the drive down?

Of course by mornin, Kelly continued, closin the refrigerator door, deliverin the kitchen back to darkness, *we might find out that nature's done the hard work for us, and we'll just have Russel's funeral left.*

Could happen that way.

Billings returned to the couch. He'd stopped thinkin about Kelly confessin to the cops, and what was left was the loneliest feelin of all, and it came with an entirely different thought: how none of them had measured right who this Kalin March really was.

Some Porches, though, had no trouble findin sleep, even back when Old Porch was stormin out of the house and then stormin back in with that survey map, or later when Old Porch had shared with Egan, Billings, and Kelly, and even Hatch, how a Detective Peters had dropped by that afternoon to inform him that Trent Riddle had been killt in a car wreck, news that Hatch accepted with a perfunctory bow of his head, not knowin the guy from Adam, while Egan, Billings, and even Kelly, who had liked Riddle a lot, beamed with great relief. Hatch then had reminded everyone that daylight savin time ended that night and figured that's why Egan was shoutin. Though bangin, shoutin, extra hour or not, Sean, Shelly, Woolsey, and Francis Porch slept through it all in a fugue of insensible dreams.

Sean found hisself on hot California sand, beaches he knew only from television. He was a lifeguard, then a sunbather, then a mother, then a pro surfer, then a failed pro surfer turned instructor overseein a dozen children facin a flat Pacific Ocean, then a Pacific Ocean churnin with overhead waves, with children swept out, children swept under, with children laughin on the decks of inflatable chariots bobbin on a glassy surface where he was a child too with no responsibilities. Wasn't that nice . . . He'd somehow got to paintin it too, he had this mess of brushes, more colors than he could count, laid out long as a Hilton buffet on Sunday in front of the biggest canvas you could ever dream of, too big to even frame, and weren't that also the saddest thing, so sad in fact that Sean wanted to cry, right there on the beach in his dream, and then Egan was there, and he weren't like he was now, wouldn't you know it; he was a carpenter of fine furniture, and he told Sean not to worry, he was gonna make him a frame, big enuf for that paintin, bigger than the ocean. And wasn't that the nicest thing ever . . .

Shelly found hisself roarin and brawlin in a bar where the chairs he swung powdered into talc as they collided with assailants he couldn't recognize except that they were terrible men with man-killin hands. Until the bar was no longer his to fight in but his own place, the establishment he owned, and it weren't no longer just a bar but a restaurant where Francis was cookin and Woolsey was runnin the floor if he weren't onstage doin a musical number for which Egan had built the set, built a whole house, a real house, a good house, until it was just an empty theater, like after a show, and Liz Blicker was next to him and she was talkin about their kids and she was cryin because weren't this so great?, weren't this the greatest show ever?, even if it was just a small black room, but still so great, and hadn't everybody laughed?, hadn't everybody cried?, like she was still cryin now and laughin too, because of who he used to be, because he couldn't believe he used to be that guy, thankin Liz for stickin it out with him, for deliverin him to this; she was the one who had done that, except she weren't there anymore, and the room weren't there either, and he was settin down the big blue chair in his hands and sittin on it and now there was a great red snake coiled around his feet so tight, he couldn't fer sure tell what was the serpent and what were the boots he had on, and that weren't even what frightened him; rather it was the great eagle he somehow knew was flyin overhead. If only he could just lift his eyes. He shuddered free then for a blacker dreamless sleep until a memory surfaced, a short play he'd started writin in Mrs. Annserdodder's class that everyone laughed at because he'd even misspelled the title, though he hadn't, because it weren't about no beauty contest unless you count what that girl had done to her own face in the mirror, with both fists too, because she weren't strong enuf to hit back at her daddy. He never wrote another thing. It was too bad. He was better than he ever knew. That play was called *Missed America.*

Woolsey and Francis had stayed up longer but weren't bothered by the commotions ongoin in the house nor each other. They shared the same room too, but they both had headphones on, the volume on their Walkmans all the way up.

Woolsey had decided to force hisself to listen to one of Russel's mixtapes. The A-side was what you'd expect, like Russel had been puttin somethin together for Egan or Shelly: Lynyrd Skynyrd's *Call Me the Breeze,* John Mellencamp's *Jack & Diane*, Boston's *Don't Look Back,* even some Kenny Rogers, like *Coward of the County,* but then it swerved to a song Woolsey didn't know, *Many Rivers to Cross* by someone named Jimmy Cliff, who was just awesome even if the song sent hot tears down the sides of his eyes. It made Woolsey want to find Preot Ackley then, to dance with her real slow and cry on her neck like she'd, of course, cry on his neck, and then they'd kiss away their tears, hers on his neck, his on her long white neck. The B-side of the tape picked up the tempo, startin with Eddie Rabbitt's *I Love a Rainy Night,* and weren't that right on?, followed by Elvis Presley doin *Guitar Man,* but then along came stuff Woolsey had never heard of before. He kept returnin to the card stuffed in the cassette case, each narrow line filled up with Russel's handwritin. Who were the Stray Cats? Woolsey liked their name. *There's a place you can go . . .* The Clash? *How you get so rude and-a reckless . . .* A Flock of Seagulls? *Couldn't get away . . .* And even when it mellowed with, who?, the Pretenders? He liked their name too. *I gotta have some of your attention . . .* Yaz? *I wonder what's my mine . . .* Talkin Heads? *Everyone has gone to sleep . . .* And more bands and great songs Woolsey had never heard of before. Who even had these records? Not Russel. And that hurt plenty, discoverin that their younger brother was not only gone but had taken his mysteries with him.

Though Old Porch had more than enuf money, the Porches weren't one of them families that got MTV. Shelly and Sean did at their place but rarely watched it. Egan only listened to music in his truck and it weren't music like what the MTV played. The channel was talked about plenty at Orvop High, and there were even MTV parties where hours would pass just wishin the right song would come on. Now at some of those hangs, which Woolsey didn't go to, Francis had begun to catch wind of music that went beyond video.

Francis was listenin to one of his own mixtapes. He guarded over them too, even hid them in a shoebox, and not under his bed neither but behind the books on his shelves, where he knew none of his brothers would think to look unless they needed somethin thick to either tack a target on or throw. What Francis wanted in his ear weren't anywhere near the beaten path of the Porch tastes let alone what Orvop considered good. Those few folks who had heard of bands like Joy Division, Human League, or the Psychedelic Furs, what Francis had grown to admire, like even in ways that sometimes confused him, this group of music-listenin friends would often meet at thrift stores, where they'd hound for clothes they'd never wear around the house, and only rarely at school, and pass around headphones in the aisles, exchangin in soft whispers their opinions, *what was so wrong with pink?*, like they exchanged their vinyl finds in bags treated so cautiously, they might as well have carried bricks of hash and not an album by the Specials. *A message to you.*

Tonight's A-side near took off from where Russel's had ended, first with more Clash, *How you gonna come? With your hands on your head or on the trigger of your gun?*, and then some Squeeze, *because dreams are made of this,* or *She lets loose all the horses when the corporal is asleep,* before gettin to bands like Talk Talk, *Won't you show the other side,* Spandau Ballet, *War upon war, heat upon heat.* David Bowie too, *Just for one day.* The B-side started slow with Duran Duran, *all alone ain't much fun,* before turnin to Roxy Music, *Who can say where we're goin?,* then kickin it up some with Dexys Midnight Runners, *We are far too young and clever,* which was just a launch pad for the Beat, the *English* Beat, *Don't let my show convince you* or *Sooner or later your legs give way, you hit the ground* or *Get out of my life, get away from me, get away,* and then, as if it weren't obvious, Madness, *The heavy heavy monster sound* later askin, singin, *How can it be that we can say so much without words?*

That was the real arrival right there: ska. A ticket out of Orvop. Francis only wanted more of it. Who cares if folks said he dressed like a checkerboard and got after him for wearin a short brim or porkpie that in either case weren't a cowboy hat? He wouldn't have to take it in London, where he'd also drive on the left side of the road and work as a cook in some restaurant until he'd saved up enuf to get to Paris, where he'd become a chef. And he'd listen to music that weren't country. He'd listen to music that was cool.

That night both Francis and Woolsey listened to bands that no one else in that house would have recognized let alone understood. Kelly had once gone with Woolsey, Francis, and Russel to a concert with a local band callin themselves Altared. They was New Wave. They had synthesizers and good beats. One song had this chorus that just went *Amen*, because they was havin a go at the Church. But Kelly wouldn't stand for it. That was faggot music, he kept sayin. He swore the singer was singin *Ah men,* which Woolsey and Francis had to finally agree with him about and laugh with him about it too before leavin with him, though they felt pretty sore because the band was great; they made you move and feel somethin that weren't just what Utah Valley says was the right way to feel, and you could tell the kids there in that hall were awakenin to a world that went way beyond some president in the White House with a cowboy hat that weren't ever earned.

Woolsey Porch fell asleep first, but his morphetic enchantments went beyond vision. Instead his dreams moved through his body, twistin him up in sheets, spinnin him around with a slow deliberateness, like they was tryin to loose him from the bed, with steps measured out against a cadence that made him smile, which he did actually do, laughin audibly too, though by then Francis was too out to hear him, Woolsey continuin to fill with this desire to just dance, which if the demon of deep paralyzin sleep hadn't been sittin upon his chest then he might've done, beyond the confines of his room, far from that place.

Francis Porch, alone, dreamt of Kalin March. Grainy and static images stole from recent news clips that weren't even of Kalin givin way to the Kalin in his own memories, there among the crowds of kids movin through Main Hall, Kalin March, unobserved, singular in the way he moved, unafflicted by the currents of students movin in different directions, all them different groups, and his eyes fixed ahead throughout, unflinchin, committed, set on Francis, or not even on him but through him, so coldly that Francis felt somethin in his throat clench up, as if gripped by an enormous awful hand chokin him if also draggin him up fast from the pit of this awful dream, deliverin him awake at the scene of his own suffocation.

A s Old Porch had said hisself: *Who is this kid again?* Which, once word spread about the murder of Law Enforcement Ranger Bren Kelson, was the only thing anyone was askin, especially if they was one of them workin at any of the dozens of news organizations seriously tacklin or just interlardin the story: *Why's he stealin two ponies? Are they ponies or horses? What colors are they? Do they have names? Did Kalin March name them? Why did he trap hisself in a box canyon? Isn't that an imbecilic thing to do? Isn't that just typical of someone not a Utahn? Did anyone hear he wore funny shoes? But hey now, wait a minute, didn't he in fact escape through that box canyon? And what does that fact say about the locals who kept sayin he was imbecilic? Except weren't he also close friends with a kid who was very much a local, as local as local gets? And didn't that friend have familial roots predatin even the foundin of the State? But how did this Kalin March even become friends with this recently deceased Tom Gatestone who was not only an FFA president but famed for ridin the bull known as Hightower? What did Tom Gatestone even see in this newcomer? And weren't it likely that Tom Gatestone was the one who had showed Kalin March the way through and out of Isatch Canyon? Does that then explain how this Kalin March found hisself in the company of Landry Gatestone, none other than Tom Gatestone's sister, a girl who is part Samoan, part African American, adopted by Tom's parents, one of whom, incidentally, is related to one of the Church's Quorum of Twelve? Or is it the Quorum of Seventy? Though the question still stands: was Landry Gatestone up there with this Kalin March of her own volition? Or was she just another unsuspectin victim of this Kalin March, who just like he shot the Law Enforcement Ranger Bren Kelson in the back of the head, shot her too in the face? And didn't she scream out for help before he done her like that? Wait a sec, didn't he shoot her in the back of the head? Isn't that what someone said? You got a better source than someone? One of us has got to ask how reliable most of this reportin can be when so much of it comes by way of just the one witness: a Mr. Egan Porch, who is the brother of the young boy, Russel Porch, allegedly killt by Kalin March followin the theft of the Porch ponies. Were they ponies or horses? What colors were they? What were their names? Why do we still not know even that much? And please explain how two such children, because they are children!, this Landry Gatestone ain't even sixteen, and this Kalin March is barely sixteen, right? Please explain how we're supposed to believe that they not only got caught in but survived a rockfall the likes of which ain't been seen around these parts since the settlin of this valley? And not only just survived it but survived it on horses? Isn't that what everyone's sayin? But, wait, hold on a second, wasn't everyone sayin not so long ago that these two kids died in that very slide? Didn't they even find Landry Gatestone's pink raincoat in the rubble? Except wasn't she later shot in the face? Or was it in the back of the head? Isn't that what they're now sayin? Who is this they? The same source that goes by someone? Are we talkin about Egan Porch again? Aside from him, is there any proof the kids are alive? Or dead? Didn't Park Ranger Emily Brickey confirm that? Didn't she only say that they found evidence of horses in the cirque beneath the Katanogos summit ridge? And evidence of a campsite too? Aren't there rumors now that the horses Kalin March stole have wings? What do we make of that? Are you serious? Why on earth then did Kalin March head to Kirk's Cirque, from one dead end to another?* And those were just some of the questions voiced by reporters, editors, editors in chief, as well as anyone from staff writers to copyeditors to sound engineers to camera operators to editors, from Salt Lake City down to St. George, with more and more interest buildin outside of Utah as well, where national news organizations began demandin more details about the boy: *Where was this Kalin March born? What was he like at Orvop High School? What were his grades? What do his teachers have to say about him? If he isn't a member of the Church, what's he doin in Orvop? Does he smoke? Does he chew? Does he drink? Does he do drugs? Who are his parents? Has anyone talked with his mother? She has a lawyer? Have we talked to this lawyer? Where did he get the gun that killt the ranger? Where did he learn to shoot? Who is this Kalin March again? Where did he learn to ride?*

Well, fer starters, earlier and well within the hold of night, when Kalin March was on Navidad, still on the Upecksay Headwall but not so far from the Katanogos summit, both of them risin up on that platform of rock, beside which had once stood an old mountain goat, Kalin March tall in the stirrups, his hands tender on Navidad's mouth, tender on her mane, lighter than any cloud, why then that beautiful Navidad, on her back hooves, also standin tall, prepared to make her turn. As he'd done with Mouse, Kalin's plan had been to execute a clockwise turn toward the headwall, thus always drivin closer to the mountain. The problem was that upon gainin her stationary moment, Navidad wound up too close to the rock to turn right. Kalin, though, held as lightly his plan as he did the reins, already urgin Navidad to the left, Navidad at once obligin, the two of them fer a moment abandonin the mountain, facin instead the cirque, so that with the great headwall on either side of her, the imaginative among us might easily enuf declare wings had unfurled from Navidad's back, wings the size of mountains.

And although the rotation didn't take but a heartbeat, the moment seemed to occur beyond the province of even Time, and then time was everythin, Navidad finally hurtlin herself forward, away to that path upward, and just as that plinth upon which so much had depended at last gave way, such is the cost of three horses, four horses, and a mule, soundin a low crack, a sound at once swallowed by the storm as the stone launched into a fall whose landin would go unmarked, destroyin the turn that would deprive followers, except for the most skilled and agile, of any higher progress; and at the same time, as if that pedestal had also been some celestial switch, the moon itself was then struck away, the great storm stitchin up again that tear in the fabric of its own broodin devotion, now settin roarin war upon Katanogos, with more snow and hibernal winds blastin every ledge, face, and ridge, batterin a boy and a horse now gallopin toward the summit already encased by a darkness speckled with white. Not that snow or wind or for that matter any natural protestations, speechless from origin to culmination, could by that point make any difference. Kalin March and Navidad were beyond recall. They were irrevocable.

And who was there at the summit, equally impervious to the hollerin storm? Why Tom and Ash, of course, before whom Kalin and Navidad at last began to slow, crestin the top of Katanogos, finally reachin the back side, then just as quick headin off to the right, where Kalin knew by heart to ride, to the lee of the mountain, farther and still farther down, where eventually they found that wall of rock, that small copse of trees, and more incredibly . . . the glow of a fire! And no sooner did Kalin and Navidad fly toward that improbable light than they were before it, and there was Landry feedin the flames, her hair long and dark and no longer knotted with ice, her smile Tom-sized and growin!

She'd already laid one tarp on the ground and, with the help of them twisted trees and some outcroppins of rock, secured the biggest tarp above. Them knots, Kalin could see, were better than anythin he'd've managed: pretty and neat as a sailor's on some three-masted schooner long ago. Landry's daddy would've been proud. She'd also positioned and angled the tarps so they'd never play the sail with the wicked wind up here.

It was simple but also one heckuva barricade, a fortified lean-to against that wall of fissured rock, at the base of which, where the ice-encased trunk of a fallen tree lay, Landry had performed her greatest miracle: this fire, which astonished even Tom with its fierceness, not to mention the warmth it threw into their modest enclosure, though even its spittin and cracklin sparks were no match for the sparks that fired up in Landry's eyes when Kalin and Navidad had finally appeared.

Well you took long enuf! Landry scolded him right off.

Way too long! Kalin howled back, happy for the scoldin, like he'd only been tarryin, washin up or somethin. In fact Kalin was so happy to see Landry that he almost couldn't make sense of his thoughts and feelins. Had he ever been this happy before? The answer was a resoundin: No!

And then Kalin saw Mouse! And he got even happier.

And Jojo!

The mule!

Kalin's happiness only grew from there, transportive, euphoric, maybe even a little delirious.

Navidad sure was happy too, maybe a little euphoric herself. How else to describe the clamant neighs that erupted from her and from Mouse and then even from Jojo? The mule joined in as well! Even Ash joined in! And for goofs Tom threw in some of his own brays. He told Kalin later that even Pia Isan was happy, though it had been so long since she'd felt anythin like this that she'd called it somethin else, somethin that sounded like *tootsy way,* which she said also felt like another side of sorrow. With her little hidden forest chipmunk still on her shoulder, she'd beheld then an old elk that was everythin to her. She even reported that the one who walked beside the one who walked beside her, in the company of a great brown bear, was struck dumb with joy.

Nor did the horses stop their neighin until everyone was laughin, includin the ghost Kalin could see and the ghosts no one could see, a crowd of laughter. So buoyant in fact was the prevailin mood that it seemed that nothin else would ever matter. And, fer a little while there, nothin else did matter.

If only it could've stayed like that.

Landry weren't blind to Kalin's condition, and no amount of mirth from either the dead or the livin was gonna hold off death. Once he was off Navidad, Kalin's shakes got so bad, he couldn't walk. She made him sit by the fire and threw warm blankets over him, and then she put a hot mug in his frost-ate hands.

It ain't but water now, but it's warm, and you better drink your fill.

While he did as he was told, she unbridled and unsaddled Navidad, checked her from shoes to shoulders, brushed her down then with both hands, massaged her, watered her, and then fed her that last portion of the oats, salt, and molasses which Kalin had set aside for her earlier, what he'd refused to even taste.

That's the last of it, Landry said.

Kalin tried then to say somethin, but even blanket-draped with warm water startin to fill his belly, he was still shakin so bad he couldn't but grunt. Maybe sensin this desire to say somethin, Landry told him to shut up and kept refillin that mug.

After she'd tied up Navidad between Jojo and Mouse, with the mule between Jojo and Ash, who Landry couldn't know fer sure was there but guessed right anyways, she rechecked the tarp corners and took a peek out beyond the edges, pleased to see some snow gatherin on top, which would help to further insulate them, even if the sight of that holy heck ragin out there also frightened her.

How'd you get this fire goin? Kalin managed to ask when she got back.

I used them last two candles we had.

That did the trick? Kalin weren't even really askin, her answer havin satisfied him completely. Her response, though, took him by surprise.

I can't tell you.

How's that?

I had to use everythin we had.

Awww, Landry, please tell me you didn't use that.

We didn't have no choice.

Kalin hung his head and started to weep.

We didn't have no choice, Landry said again, refusin to weep.

That diary was all you had of your daddy and your brothers. Kalin was thinkin of Tom.

That was true once, but it ain't true no more.

Thank you, Landry.

You don't have to thank me. I didn't do it for you. I did it for me and for Jojo and Mouse and for the mule too. You and Navidad are just lucky you know us and can share what we got.

Don't I know it.

And while they weren't laughin no more, they was smilin. And Tom was smilin too.

If only the rest of the night was as easy as fallin asleep and wakin up to dawn like not a nickel of time had been spent, but Landry and Kalin weren't in some cozy cabin or cave. If granted cover by rocks and trees, the sides of their little tarp-rigged fort were still open, and there was a big gap above the fire where the smoke mostly escaped. Thankfully, because the storm was now blowin from the north, the winds mostly roared high above the trees, racketin the tarp some but not lingerin none, sweepin instead over the summit ridge and from there joinin the devastation churnin above Kirk's Cirque before turnin out over Isatch Canyon and the valley below. That said, this brutal storm had hardly committed its unfoldins and disruptions to one direction; and so it was that now and then a sudden burst of snow-heavy wind would attack from the side and lay siege to the fire, if not subduin the coals then still exorcisin the accumulated warmth. Kalin would grit his teeth against the shivers while Landry would do her best to reinforce their tiny pocket of endurance.

Landry also made several excursions into the freezin spectacle to gather more wood from a woodpile she figured Kalin had amassed among those pines on some previous trek up here. She hatcheted off some additional branches too. If only he'd thought to cache some food. The voice of the storm terrified her, and she never went beyond that copse of trees. She'd return with her arms piled high with logs, Kalin too weak to help her, even to feed the fire, until finally to Landry's eye he looked asleep, his head tilted to one side, the mug spillt of its contents on the tarp.

The first time she'd seen him like that, Landry had moved swift as Apollo to his side to confirm that he weren't dead, and indeed his breath was still there, comin up warm, soft and steady, which calmed her plenty, even as the storm upped its bellowin, as if to best even Zeus with all his thunders, while the horses, long since done with their whinnyin, stomped the earth and shook their heads. Ash as well. Only the mule gave such batterins no mind. Though that's not right. Mouse feared neither storm nor Zeus, though he still stomped a hoof, plenty displeased to find hisself with neither grass nor grain.

What was now happenin, what Landry had hoped would happen but wasn't happenin near fast enuf, was a continuin depositin of snow on the tarp above their heads. Layers would form, but then just as quickly much of that the winds would blow free, likely abetted by the ambient heat shed by the fire below, warmin the tarp enuf to melt some of them initial flakes thus creatin an icy layer to deny future snows any hold. That said, the ropes that Landry had cross-hatched across parts of the top, insertin gnarled boughs where she could, were successfully creatin patches where the snow resisted the wind's urgins. Also, the snow that had slid to the base of the tarp was pilin up, a good third of the way up now, and in time it would exceed that, maybe half way, maybe even the whole way. If they could just survive that long.

Some good news, or at least promisin news, was readily visible at each side, where more snow was accumulatin. Even though these heaps would also frequently diminish before the discouragin bedlam of winds, some of it remained. In time a greater barrier would rise there and so further protect them from the elements. Even now an insulated quiet would momentarily prevail before the racket would start up again and gust the flames and Landry and Kalin would grit their teeth and shake.

The trees, far from impervious to such assaults, would sway and crack and even at times groan, especially as the tarps grew heavier with snow, promptin another thought to dance in both Landry's and Kalin's heads, that they might not only freeze to death up here but be buried alive in an avalanche of their own devisin. But their ruf held, and the trees only protested their burden and did not betray the children.

On her last venture out beyond the tarp, to not only hatchet up some wood but this time refill the kettle with snow, Landry also succeeded in draggin and rollin back to the fire one last miracle: a rotten wind-scolded log. It was too wet, too caked in ice, to take anythin from the fire yet, but she managed to stand it up beside that fallen tree, its soggy bark steamin soon enuf. When Landry gave the log a good kick, it toppled over against the trunk while also landin across the back half of their fire, where it lay smolderin and smokin. Landry couldn't say if it would finally catch or put out the fire their lives depended on. She quickly added more dead branches and pine boughs to the parts of the fire unmolested by this late arrival, and at least the flames accepted her offerins and grew.

But was it enuf to get them through the night?

She didn't know.

And she couldn't ask Kalin, who was either asleep or slippin into a coma, now and then mumblin somethin about *peaches . . .* which at least assured her that Kalin March weren't dead yet.

As you can likely imagine, freezin to death weren't just some careless fright amplified by hunger and their location. Landry's and Kalin's lips were cracked, their cheeks looked sandblasted, same with the backs of their hands, so many of their features scraped, scabbed, blood-lined, not a patch of skin spared the excoriatin effects of that freeze up there. Not that Landry paid much attention to these peripheral miseries that she knew were nothin compared to the hunger they both suffered, which she could alleviate only by fixatin on the number of branches and logs they had left to burn, which no matter how often she re-counted kept givin her a sum that just didn't add up to enuf.

Landry didn't have the energy required to hew down one of the surroundin trees or even hack off more branches. She couldn't even go out there; the wind was too severe, the cold too deadly. She would just have to mete out the wood at the right tempo, enuf to keep the fire alive, enuf to keep them alive, but not so much to end their stores.

At one point Kalin surfaced enuf to stop mumblin about peaches and tell Landry again how there were breathin exercises his momma had taught him, what could supposedly sustain barely clad monks in subzero temperatures, and all you had to do was just sit and breathe right, even if breathin right weren't no easy thing. Yes, they'd already tried it before, but they'd been standin and impatient. Maybe this time would be different, maybe this time they'd turn cold into warmth.

Best as he could Kalin again demonstrated the technique required, through the nose only, which Landry again attempted to replicate. Truth was it did warm Landry up some, more than it did Kalin, and anyway neither could sustain those rapid pants very long, nor find the calm and stillness necessary to start and preserve a fire within themselves capable of equalin the appallin temperatures eatin at them. The horses continued to hate it. Kalin stopped before Landry did, too exhausted by the effort, too disappointed by the failure. What lie had he been tellin her? Tellin hisself?

A whole lot's been said about what happened next, too profane, salacious, and above all negligent of the conditions these two found themselves in to repeat let alone attribute. The appallin discomfort visited upon Landry and Kalin, minute by minute, is impossible to adequately convey, horrendous enuf for anyone just by a fire on the summit, without takin into account the witherin toll already exacted by the journey thus far, not to mention the indecency of bein hunted, shot at, trapped, laid low by food poisonin, then out of food, not even one bit of oat or misplaced raisin to be had, basically gettin by on only water, albeit Katanogos water, which some liked to say, namely Mrs. Annserdodder, Ms. Melson, and Mr. Rudder, the gods drink to live forever.

If they'd've had the energy, if they weren't noddin in and out of sleep, Landry and Kalin would've wailed.

All of which is to say they sure as heck never kissed, and when they finally snuggled next to one another, with their arms around each other, under every layer they could find, Landry buttressin this draped composition with both saddles on either side, they craved from each other only one more hint of warmth.

It's true that undressin, some arrangement of flesh on flesh, might've granted a temporary moment of added heat, but neither Landry nor Kalin had the energy to disrobe, let alone an insulated sack in which to climb into together if they had; for as you'll recall they'd lost their only sleepin bag, a necessity to make such neked adjacency worthwhile. And in truth the thought never crossed either of their minds.

There is one interestin comment that while sexual in its preoccupation is less concerned with the paramount desire to survive than with an idle and very adult speculation pertainin to what still awaited them both: *If only they'd made love.* Or so Julianna McHenley would wonder about not long before her death by self-arranged hypothermia in an Orvop restuarant called Haddie's Eats near State Street, helped along with some pills and a self-administered shot of fentanyl, her phone clutched to her ear, though there weren't no reception, if still recordin words that would never be heard, the phone soon after discarded: *Maybe makin love would've softened the way they moved or even changed the way they made decisions later. Maybe makin love would've made all the difference. Or maybe not. My boyfriend, Leonard Bell, was a startin tight end at Orvop High not so long after Kalin March and Landry Gatestone were students there. Coach Pailey was still there, still dolin out the same advice: Stay away from girls if you want to play any good. Leonard wouldn't even hold my hand let alone smooch with me before a game. It was like even one kiss would wreck whatever he had to give on the field. Leonard believed it too. And what's worse, I believed it. I don't give a frickin hoot what Coach Pailey believed. Leonard told me years later that he'd had a conversation with the startin tight end of the team that eliminated them from the state playoffs that year. He told Leonard that he'd gone all the way with his girlfriend the night before they beat Orvop High. Leonard was laughin when he told me that, but it was too late for us. I think about it though. And then I wonder about Kalin and Landry, and gosh yes they was too young for responsible sex, way too young to get pregnant, but given what was about to happen, if they'd still got to some of that love that's pure physical, with just kisses, caresses, maybe even with satisfactions, maybe it would've turned out better. For everyone. Maybe even for me, and I don't give a hoot about their story except that I know it.*

Barbara Frye, who'd be the one to find Julianna McHenley in the meat locker at Haddie's Eats, herself not dyin near so peacefully four years later when she survived for a little while after steppin on a land mine in Mozambique, would say at her old friend's memorial service that while they'd often spoken of those days of the Porches and the Gatestones, of Landry Gatestone and Kalin March, Julianna had always done so at the expense of tellin her own story, which was too ragged to include at the service but whose existence *I should at least acknowledge as the story she should've told. Shame on you, Coach Pill.*

Regardless of the speculations about the desires latent in their closeness, Landry and Kalin mostly just sat side by side and dozed until the wind would cold-slap them awake with a new squall of snow.

At one point Landry did try to sing. Kalin was awake enuf to tell her Tom was too cold or afraid or disturbed to whistle with her. Tom did try, though, but durin those hours nothin very musical found its way through his lips. Landry didn't have any better luck producin somethin melodic, though Kalin was still grateful to hear her give it a go, what in the end amounted to a scatterin of lines from songs he didn't know but had come to love:

> *I walked through the valley of death,*
> *But I forgot the song that mattered.*
> *Up here in the mountains, that's where I belong,*
> *even if I'm sadder.*

Landry actually sang a little bit more than that, but the storm stole any sweetness from her voice, and she soon quit from the chatters that broke apart whatever verses followed.

Then fer a while she shivered on about the musical *Carousel* that she'd seen what now seemed like a lifetime ago. It had been pretty good, and she'd sung one of the songs so many times that summer that Tom got to stompin off in a fuss because he just couldn't take it no more, though he did stop when she told him Lindsey Holt had been in the show, which made Tom guffaw, though Landry wasn't bein mean-spirited because Lindsey had been pretty good, and anyways she and her mom had seen it on the last night, and afterward they'd snuck up on the stage just to ride the carousel only to find out you couldn't really ride it because the horses was cardboard, and right then Landry got to missin the real thing so bad that she made her mom drive them to the barn so she could see Jojo and sing him that song, with her mom singin along too, and oh how much did Landry love her mom then, and how much did she miss her now, and weren't that the best night ever, just Landry and her momma, singin and laughin, sharin apples with big blue Jojo.

Kalin March couldn't sing a thing, but to comfort her he did tell her in a raspy voice about a time not long before Tom fell ill. He and Tom weren't even in his truck this time but in Ronnie Thurgood's 1973 white Plymouth station wagon, headin up Orvop Canyon.

This had been in July, and in fact it was the only time Kalin and Tom had been together without horses and around others who weren't family. Not that Ronnie Thurgood was gonna be around much longer; his family was quittin Orvop that August and draggin Ronnie with them, to New Mexico, and Ronnie would only hear about Tom's death months after the fact. Years later he'd say that he'd never thought it odd that Kalin was taggin along. *Tom loved to bring around all sorts to see if they had the guts to make the jump.* Ronnie also didn't recollect anythin unique about Kalin. *Kind of a twerp but easygoin enuf. What did I care? I was only thinkin about Kim Janson.*

Anyway, Ronnie Thurgood's Plymouth station wagon was notorious for stallin unexpectedly, and on that hot summer's day it didn't disappoint, this time choosin to stall right as Ronnie took a left across traffic, which at that instant amounted to nothin. The trouble was that that darned station wagon had no mind to start up again. And then that nothin inhabitin the Orvop Canyon Road became too quickly a semi comin around the bend. The driver laid on the horn as soon as he seen what was blockin the way up ahead because no amount of brakin was gonna keep that truck from T-bonin Ronnie Thurgood's Great White Whale. Ronnie gave the starter one last quick break, and on the next turn of the key, the engine finally caught, the carburetor like the tailpipe belchin black smoke, with the back tires startin to spin out a desperate slick of melted rubber that did successfully hurl the Plymouth into the parkin lot, and just in the nick of time too.

Of course, Tom was laughin. Ronnie was white. Kalin wasn't sure how he felt, though his knees were still knockin pretty bad when they tumbled out of the car.

They sat for a long time atop the rusty trestle that spanned the Orvop River, bubblin some twenty feet below, bubblin all the way past I-15 and Fort Orvop, all the way to Mud Lake. They swung their legs in the air. Over the years, plenty of folks had died in that canyon. Ronnie Thurgood, sluggin down his Mountain Dew, wondered how it was that they too hadn't just died. *Maybe we didn't so we could die now jumpin off,* Tom said with that wicked twinkle in his eyes. In truth no one they knew had ever died, but one kid had jumped wrong and landed in the shallows where there was a wedge of rock hid beneath not even a foot of turbulence. He shattered both hips and that was the good news. His lower back was a humpty-dumpty that paralyzed him from the waist down. Phillip Hammond. That was his name. He would die some twenty years later of AIDS.

About around then, Landry had joined them. She was scared silly of heights, but spyin her brother out there in the middle, and with Kalin too, she'd managed to inch along the rails to their danglin spot.

I remember that! she exclaimed now. *I was so scared to even crawl out there.*

Heights got nothin on you anymore.

That ain't true. I reckon I still wouldn't jump.

Yeah, but that's because you don't know how to swim.

That is true. I'm like my mama.

Landry didn't jump from the trestle, and as it turned out Ronnie Thurgood didn't jump either. Turns out he never jumped. But Tom did, and only after Kalin jumped first.

When I bobbed up, Kalin gruffed out, *there was your brother surfacin too, laughin and hootin, as the current swept us around a bend and then another bend. It was a good day. We maybe died twice.*

But you didn't.

We didn't.

Does Tom remember it like that? Landry asked then.

Tom nodded. *I'll tell you the water sparkled so much, it looked there were diamonds in it.* And then he darkened some. *Poor Ronnie.*

Why's that? Kalin asked.

Tom waved off the question.

Your brother's memory seems to have improved up here.

How's that?

He remembers the sparkle on the water.

I remember that too! It was so bright! The current was so fast that day too.

887

The river had turned white under us. When you two disappeared under the foam, I near had to close my eyes. Landry sighed, poked at the fire, the coals, the still-smolderin log, the trunk behind the fire continuin to shed a veil of steam. *I remember when I believed a ghost was just like a white sheet floatin around a front yard with dry ice bubblin away in buckets of boilin water. That's what the Willards used to do for Halloween. Tom thought it was foolish, but he still loved laughin at me just gawkin at the Willards' front lawn when I was little.* Landry flicked her stick into the fire. *At least that caught fire. I remember this one time when Tom was goin on about all his trophies, but he said what he was really most proud of was how different he was from everybody else.*

Tom nodded.

Well, I told him that he was too popular to be all that different.

I bet he didn't like that, Kalin said.

He did not. Didn't laugh neither. Not even a smile. But I howled for days. He probably still can't laugh about that one.

Kalin studied Tom, and though his friend weren't laughin, he was smilin.

What's he sayin? Landry asked.

Kalin listened and smiled hisself.

What? Tell me!

He says the only reason he can laugh now is because of you. He didn't want you here, but he's sure glad you came along. You've made these last few days for him somethin Heaven won't ever rival.

Some say Tom did it, but that would be unfair to Navidad, who'd started pullin hard on her lead, followed by Jojo next. Landry got up and freed them both. Mouse had already somehow shrugged loose his lead even if he weren't inclined to move just yet. Without any guidance from Landry, Jojo came around to the back of the tarp, where that big blue beautiful horse just lay down with forehooves and rear hooves curled up under him near like a cat. Mouse came around then, to one side, where the gap between the tarp and the ground was widest. Curiously, the mule did the same on the other side, like as if somehow the two of them had decided to block as best they could the winds that too often jostled and threatened the fire. Kalin told Landry that Ash was beside the mule.

Navidad then came over between Jojo and Kalin, and just like Jojo had done, she lay down too, only full-out, stretched out on that tarp, right on her side, her back against Jojo.

Landry tried then to better cover her and Kalin with them blankets, once again with her arm around him, only this time they didn't just sit there chatterin but both laid back against Navidad's belly. Only then did sleep at last overtake them.

Yet even like that the cold would not cease its assualt. At one point the temperatures dropped even more, as the wind outside again stole the snow from the tarp, and the last of their wood collapsed into black-and-red coals, at which point, though still fast asleep, Landry and Kalin drew even closer to one another, Landry's head snug beneath his, his Stetson, once her brother's, over them both now like a dark halo.

And that weren't the only dark halo: Tom was right there, but so too was Pia Isan and with her the ones who walked likewise accompanied, and so on and so on, a great encirclin crèche, hopin to lend a world to those horses who did everythin to defend those children.

And here their sleep aligned with them dreamin Porches down in the valley, Landry and Kalin also borne under by a darkness both personal as well as part of a deeper invisible character, alertin them both, alertin them all, in however oblique ways, to what the mornin was already hurlin their way.

Maybe it's tellin, or not, that no dreams visited Orwin Porch that night nor Landry Gatestone nor Kalin March. Not Navidad nor Jojo neither. And as for Mouse, he continued to behold his whole life as a dream. And who's to say about that mule or Ash or Tom.

One thing was certain though: the two mothers were not asleep but rather endurin yet another wakin nightmare. They had returned from the river to the Gatestone home, where, while tryin to dispel the cold with dry clothes and warm drinks, they learned that their kids had not been interred by the landslide but had survived long enuf fer Kalin to kill a ranger and then turn on Landry and kill her.

They keep tryin with their stories to destroy my girl, Sondra Gatestone had near wailed.

My Kalin didn't murder your Landry.

It don't matter, honey. I don't believe a word they're sayin anymore. It's like both our children are ghosts now, alive then dead then alive again then dead, like neither this world nor any world that comes later can keep a hold of them.

Maybe fer now that's not a bad thing.

Maybe so. But I still wouldn't wish that freedom on anyone.

Words spoken at the exact moment when those coals burnin under that big hunk of wood Landry had dragged in finally began to find a way up into flames, which not long after brought fire at last to that fallen tree trunk, *perhaps at last aided by Boreas and Zephyr,* as Ms. Melson would once whisper, hollowin out the underside with a blue heat that soon enuf climbed up into red-and-orange tongues lickin away the wood like famished tigers, expellin in their feastin thick black smoke that rose like an offerin to the sky, a plea for peace, which even if it was granted then for a few hours ultimately went unheeded, the smoke untangled, scattered, devoured. Because no amount of smoke or fire, incense or fat, not even tender meat upon countless bones, no, nothin from the top of that ridge could have appeased the mountains and the comin ruin.

Some hours later, Landry woke to a deafenin stillness. Their refuge was warm at last, their fire ablaze, markin the rock wall with a streak of black soot. Near two feet of snow was upon the tarp above, and more was built up around the sides, fashioned in part by the storm itself. Whatever Tom had once said about rocks in her head, her head was clear now, and far above any clouds. She could see forever. She'd never need to sleep again. And then she was asleep again, and Navidad sighed, and Jojo did as well. And as those two horses resettled with those two children in the manger of their repose, Mouse gave a low snort as if to say he knew what forever was, and it weren't no big deal because this here fer now was forever too.

Kalin March woke right before dawn. Deep orange flames continued to gnaw through the fallen trunk, now with a deep flume at the center, with walls of red glowin coals. Fer the first time in three days Kalin felt not only warm but dry as well. The horses no longer surrounded them, havin stationed themselves on either side of the fire, where the tarp was highest. Navidad, to the left, had hooked her neck over Mouse's; Jojo, Ash, and the mule, to the right, weren't near as close, though Ash kept pretty tight to Jojo in case maybe that big blue horse might like to hook his neck over his. While proddin some the coals with their last branch, Kalin began givin thought to gettin somethin to drink, to waterin the horses and addressin their appetite, addressin his own appetite, figurin, yes, on canned peaches. Landry stayed buried under the blankets and, except for an occasional grunt, which sounded awfully like a snore, didn't budge none.

Lord can that girl sleep, Tom said.

Are we really here? Did we really make it?

Nothin but miles of mild miles from here on out. And all of them downhill.

How are you doin, Tom?

Kalin could see somethin about his friend had changed, though what exactly was hard to pinpoint. Maybe his Stetson was a bit frostier. His face looked a mite paler too. His smile was still there, maybe even a notch bigger; that glimmer in his eyes that had sometimes departed was also still there, brighter than ever, even if it did seem now to come from somewhere much deeper and graver.

I need to show you somethin.

The snow was deep, but the wind throughout the night had kept most of it from pilin up, and as Kalin followed Tom up the slope beyond the trees, there were sections of exposed rock that he welcomed. Otherwise he'd sink down to his knees, in one spot bustin through a thin cap of hyaloid ice and windin up with snow above his waist. Overall the snow was dry and light as powdered glass, if glass could also melt on your lips. Kalin still marveled at how Tom moved, especially upon such coruscant surfaces, leavin no trace, shadowless too, unless you counted the dark blue that glowed upon them wide unfoldin drifts, and maybe it was wise to count those shadows.

Quick enuf Kalin found hisself standin on the summit of Katano-gos, both epitome and start of a quaquaversal descent, trap and invitation, ultima Thule and no point at all, and whether earthly apex or celestial nadir, in that early dawn presentin the clearest day Kalin had ever seen. The risin sun to the east kept Kirk's Cirque and Isatch Canyon still sealed in darkness, though the valley beyond had started to shimmer, with Orvop's early mornin lights sparklin like Christmas and Mud Lake beyond slashed already by a great blade of orange light. The lake seemed on fire while the sky above it remained an indigo, still announcin its depth with a winkin star here and there, challenged only by unmovin wisps of cirrus set upon the limits of the atmosphere glowin a palest pink, with roseate pronouncement soon emergin, *red skies at mornin, sailors take . . .* which neither of them muttered, Kalin's eyes tearin up before the brightness that was set on becomin, even as those few stars began to wink out, history overwritten by what the present now delivered.

The cold should've bothered Kalin some, but it didn't. Hunger too should've molested his senses, but didn't. For Kalin the storm was over. The worst had passed. Finally. And what remained, that misleadin and tamperin god, spoke only of reassurances.

Tell me what you see, Tom said then, initiatin what Ms. Melson and Mrs. Annserdodder agreed was the fourth or penultimate teichoskopia.

Kalin obliged, and like Tom were blind did his best to describe the fire on the water and the brightness that was too clear to handle. He sure never thought he would look down on the backs of Kaieneewa and Agoneeya and consider them minuscule, even though he'd seen them from this exact same spot plenty of time before. Even Timp to the north looked like not even a modest ripple born up by geological forces of little consequence.

If nothin else, Tom, Kalin, and Landry, along with Navidad, Mouse, Jojo, and Ash, had opened new pathways up to here on this oft-trekked mountain, pathways that future climbers and adventurers would seek to refind and reenact.

It sure is somethin. The skies are like the inside of a shell. Or like a pearl, Kalin said before he stopped talkin.

Of great price, the ghost added, though he looked at once troubled by that pronouncement, like even the plain truth of what Kalin had just described had failed him, *like what's out there before us really ain't no more than a spit of moments and none connected . . . all pearls and no necklace.* Tom didn't stop there either, wonderin aloud if whether the continuity and causality anyone who, say, can throw a horseshoe takes for granted ain't really nothin like that at all. *And it's only the livin who can string it together so we can . . .*

So we can what?

Tom didn't answer.

Is this what you wanted to show me?

No.

Suddenly Tom's brand was in his hand. No hints of dark red, light oranges or even flickers of blue haunted its flames. Now it was a thing of burnin white. Kalin, though, did not squint; rather it was his heart's eye that quailed before such a forbidden apparition, and that was just the torch, for the one holdin it was likewise greatly changed.

Tom seemed clothed by this new light, a figure of burnin sheets of fire consumin not only every perimeter of his person but everythin within as well; like a lantern continually consumed by its own flame, a bulb endlessly shattered by the seizure of its own explodin luminosity, a second sun, endless suns, only one sun, devourin itself until even Tom's voice was drawn into the crucible of that obliteratin deliverance.

Second only to the events that would take place at Pillars Meadow, this moment remains the most discussed and reflected upon as well as refuted. Too many artists have spillt too much paint attemptin to wrest the visible from such brightness. Songs too have tried the same and failed. Lyrics and poems have all but proven too burdened by inadequate arrangements of the material they require: words. Not that Suki Clover didn't try: *The once-covered walls, the once-filled halls, kept those conversin beyond the pillars of that Sabbath dawn.* Well beyond ninety-three and growin more and more frail in her wheelchair, Gladdis Beaumont would respond to Suki Clover by wonderin about immense time: *Robert Green Ingersoll put it so nicely: In the presence of eternity, the mountains are* as transient as the clouds. *I like that.* Suki Clover would nod while Crystal Garp reminded Gladdis Beaumont how in the place of a city *there became a great mountain.* 3 Nevi 8:10. This would only confuse Gladdis. Suki, though, would nod a second time, and then the three would go on to discuss matters that had nothin to do with Tom's incineratin presence.

Kalin was rendered speechless but Tom forbade his silence.

What do you know of this place? Tom demanded. *Where is your place?*

Well, I don't think much about place. I've never felt I belonged anywhere except when I was on a horse.

And when these horses are gone where will you belong?

They'll have a place. That'll be enuf.

Is that what you think waits at the Crossin?

I don't rightly know what waits at the Crossin, Tom.

Only one truly of no place will no place deny, Tom said, his voice doubled and then doubled again.

Tom? You all right? You ain't soundin much like you.

You are not exempt, Kalin March, Tom suddenly roared. *None of us are exempt.*

What are you talkin about?

And the fire upon that dark brand grew even brighter.

Abel Ferry, Orvop original who, after decades workin oil fields as a derrickhand in Texas, Saudi Arabia, and the UAE, would in his final years, with his lungs rot through, return home where but weeks before his passin he'd remark to Ned Trimble and Pat Mason about this very moment on Katanogos: *If you've lived a life dedicated to keepin your composure, and that takes some courage, why then there will come a point in your life where you'll experience absolute clarity.* When Abel was asked by his granddaughter if he'd ever experienced such a moment, he replied, smilin at her: *Yes, I have. Just now.*

Likely because of what Tom was about to reveal to Kalin, though also in response to his friend Abel Ferry's musins, Don Bearman, who'd likewise intended to return to Orvop only to be struck down right after leavin Marfa, in Mount Calm, Texas of all places, by hail big as golf balls, the cause of his death listed as Of Natural Causes, would before this event remark to a stranger at a diner in Hubbard how *At some point in most lives, unless you die real young, and I'm eighty-four next week, you reach this pinnacle, like you was atop a great mountain from which you can still behold your past near perfectly. And that ain't all. You can also behold your future, the hills and valleys below, glutted with mists and tangled woods, down into which you will soon go, to wander those paths of your tomorrows, what will continue to darken as your life sets slowly behind you. And then in the shadow of the mountain, you will lose sight of the past, even most of the future, as you go down, but if you paid attention, you will still have that memory of both horizons, the one behind you, beyond which you did not exist, and the one ahead of you, after which you won't exist.*

Cherilyn Bacall, who knew neither Abel Ferry nor Don Bearman, at least not directly, and who also never knew fully of Kelly Porch's longin for her, had a favorite piece of Latin that she would apply to all this talk whenever it came up. She didn't even know Latin except for this phrase, the very same one she thought of right before she died from a flu she figured for days was just another cold: *Praeterit figura huius mundi.* The shape of this world is passin.

Darla Wyndham, a veterinarian in Spanish Fork before she retired, a friend too of Cherilyn and her family, who would be declared dead in Truckee, California, after collidin at great speed with a tree, would wonder aloud with a fellow skier right before the accident how *There's somethin to learn from how an animal experiences life, sorta like a bird in a high wind might seem suspended in air, neither slippin back nor movin forward, neither goin up nor goin down, just eternally in the very moment of their bein.*

Tom and Kalin, upon the back of that great mountain, would behold then such a bird, a golden eagle, seemin to pause in the headwind, as if upheld by nothin, oblivious to both movement and gravity.

The hospital room, Kalin, Tom said as the eagle dropped away like a feather born to bronze. *I see you beside me! How I told you the way to the Crossin, and by golly you've near done it!* Even within fire Tom's smile prevailed. *I remember how we rode, when we met. I remember when I was born. I remember when you was born.*

When I was born?

My whole life I know from here! Your whole life I know from here! Landry's too! My whole family's! Your momma's! The lives of these horses! All their kin!

My momma's?

Your daddy's life too. I know all the Marches and all the Gatestones and all the Porches. Don't even get me started about Old Porch. I can see generations back, that first row between the Gatestones and Porches. There are villians on both sides. I see goodness; I see crimes. From here I know the settlin of Orvop. I know the acts committed in the name of somethin made up against folks who made homes here first. There's blood all over this mountain, but it's worse in the lower canyons and far worse in that blessèd and cursèd valley I once called home.

Is there a valley anywhere that ain't so blessed and cursed?

Tom turned away to face the back side of Katanogos, where his smile faded. *This way lies the future. If only I could see less of it. I'm awful sorry.*

Kalin saw only a snowy slope with patches of rock here and there. Farther down, where forests of evergreen gathered, the mountainside disappeared beneath a great sea of clouds painted rose and gold by the risin sun. It was gorgeous and shared none of the horrors Tom was beholdin.

Many years later, just a month short of dyin from a tumble off a friend's ruf, and after swearin he'd never go up on a ruf again, not without a rope at least, none other than Rumi Plothow would remark that whatever fanciful take one has about these goins-on, not even Tom augured how Landry just hours hence, and on this brightest of mornins too, and while delightin before a similarly beautiful vista, would *climb up what she shouldn't have climbed up to see what she shouldn't have seen. One of those looks that costs too much. You know the kind.*

I've wondered for a while now why in death I wasn't met by my father or my brother, Evan, or even some ancestor in line with my traditions? Tom continued. *Why was I met by you, who I'd known not even a year?*

Good to see you too.

It was good to see you, Kalin. It was better, though, to see the horses. But maybe I weren't a good enuf friend to you.

Knock it off.

Maybe I wasn't a good enuf friend to the horses.

We're over the mountain, ain't we?

Maybe I wasn't a good enuf friend to the world.

The world's an awful big place to make a friend of.

As your momma says, no one's free until they set somethin else free.

I do still reckon that's so.

I reckon that's what still needs to be done.

By noon, Tom. By noon latest we'll see this through.

Kalin, a red pall hangs over these lands. And Tom's voice began to change again. *I behold false allegiances made with revelers hardly known, what no rectifyin revelation shall redress, for in practice hearts have grown cold here. Bigotry and worse have eaten away at the good roots. No baptisms, whether by water, fire, or blood, will keep the great tree that thrived here from fallin. Poisons shall lift to the air. The hive is already smashed, but the bees hover over it yet. I do not know where they will gather again or if they are already scattered like embers turned to ash.*

You got somethin stuck in your throat?

The Crossin is drowned in shadow.

Well, gosh, aren't you Mr. Cheerful.

Here's the limit of anythin I am. I see many paths but only one choice.

Whose choice?

Yours.

Buddy, we're always makin choices.

Before reachin the Crossin, you'll have to decide whether or not to get into that saddlebag.

What saddlebag?

Don't lie to me. Tom's reprimand boomed out like thunder, but Kalin didn't seem much bothered. In fact he felt relieved.

Tom, you of all people should know: I ain't gettin near that thing.

Tom's smile had continued to shallow until there weren't even the idea of one just as that torch continued to expand beyond belief, even if the light it cast illuminated nothin, an occultation of meaninless brilliance, while Tom, in the folds of that indistinguishable radiance, unquenchable, inextinguishable, ceased to be Tom, with not even the memory of Kalin there, dark beyond the reach of every illumination, upon that Areopagus, and then beyond even that judicial authority.

Kalin shuddered, unless it was Katanogos that shook, and either way he would've dashed from this culminant if Tom hadn't started speakin again, only this time soundin nothin like Tom, with a voice which if Tom hisself had heard, why he'd've already run off.

What can the dead ever know of this place? But I am enuf, and through you I am you here upon this land for a reckonin, and the land shall neither tremble nor care; for this land is as content to grow as it is to make of itself a grave. It does not suffer like those who raise themselves above the land and heed no more the ash or the elm. But not all have befouled these tomorrows. And they shall be remembered. Whether of the Church or not. And of the Church, half shall be remembered and half shall not be remembered; for one half will continue to endeavor to do Good, while one half in only the name of goodness shall make false alliances with those who offer no goodness at the table it sets; for only a heart is set in Goodness. And horses shall suffer and perish, and still half here will not open their palm, and they will say it is because they know not the horse.

Behold too in years ahead they who will mislead half, and that half shall be forgiven. Behold too in years ahead they who will mislead half again, and that half shall this time not be forgiven; for they were misled twice, though they were amply warned by friends and kin of their faithless devotion, even when one of both Church and State will have warned them, and still this half will refuse to listen, though they were able and their hearts were big and they loved their children.

But by you, as I am now you, they shall remember soon enuf that this land cares not whether it brings forth the new or dissolves the fallen, and though I am unseen by those who will praise Goodness while at the same time fixin their hearts against Goodness, they will suffer the greatest ignominy of all: They will stand before their God, and their God will know the gulls and the locusts and the bees and the mountain lions; and their God will know the bears and the sego lily and the ricegrass; and their God will know the lizards and the elk and the rivers and the high mountain ridges and the low red canyons; and their God will know the horses and the songs that the land and air cannot forget, the songs that the water and light will not forget; and those who were deceived once and then deceived twice and then met what followed with great confusion and outrage and closed their palms around rocks, they will stand before their God, and their God will know them not.

And the horse will abhor them. And even after the horse has perished from this land, the songs that the land and air cannot forget, that water and light will not forget, will ask: How in a Hollow to become a Heart? How in Power to be Kind?

And then Tom fell back, and his torch became a thing of smolderin aftermath, void of vision and anythin resemblin understandin.

Only when Tom was back down with Ash, and that darn brand was scabbarded again, did he seem to return to hisself. At least his smile reappeared, and when Kalin described what had happened, Tom laughed and said he was glad to remember none of it.

Misty Blue Whitlock, a former actuary for Aetna; Naomi Dennison, once a dentist; and Kali Morales, previously an eighth-grade history teacher, from Orvop, Payson, and Springville, respectively, and all three retired by 2019, who knew their last breaths together as their plane crashed into the side of a mountain in Canada near Calgary, would but minutes before their demise discuss this moment, which summed up the long-rangin debate carried out by countless others about what Tom had actually said. Misty Blue Whitlock, fer example, would never dismiss the notion that when Tom had asked *What do you know of this place?* it was a very pointed allusion to Briggham Young, who said near the same thing when he arrived in what would one day be known as Salt Lake City. Naomi Dennison, on the other hand, would bring up how when Tom announced *I am enuf,* that that right there was an example of an unjust quotation of what was a far more complex concatenation of pronouncements; her own feelins bein that Tom had in fact declared *I am Enoch!* Naomi addin then in a very satisfied tone, *Which right there makes sense of the rest.* Kali Morales, however, would remain less convinced that her friend had made any sense at all, though she loved Naomi's enthusiasm. For her part Kali favored the viewpoint that a certain high-altitude incoherence was in effect, quotin then a fella named Rumi, but not Rumi Plothow: *The here-and-now mountain is a tiny piece of straw blown into emptiness, there is a voice that doesn't use words, listen.* Though to be sure, Kali Morales's own love of history made it also impossible to flat-out deny the many historical allusions throughout Tom's pronouncements on that summit ridge. In fact Kali Morales ultimately favored a kind of temporary possession of Tom, which Kalin would then have to embody too, possessed as well by a world far greater than any devised by the imagination of humanity. In that small plane she suddenly burst into tears over the thought that horses might really cease to exist. Misty Blue Whitlock and Naomi Dennison would take her hands then, because even though not one of them had ever sat on a horse or even seen one up close, despite livin most of their lives in Utah, they too feared what such an eradication might visit upon the future, more than they feared the accident that would kill them mere minutes later.

Tom definitely seemed surprised to learn that he'd been talkin about God.

You reckon then that I was sayin there is a God?

You tell me, Kalin answered.

I don't think it's that simple, Tom answered in an even smaller voice, inspectin then the air around him until he eventually laughed. *Pia Isan agrees with me. Fer the first time too. She says the one who walks with her also agrees. It's a long wave of agreement. Come from a long time ago. It ain't that simple.*

Landry thought she was dreamin when she woke. That or she was dead. Well, for one, she was warm. Dry too. She also felt rested in a way she hadn't felt for the past three days. She was still starvin. That hadn't changed. With her eyes closed and still under the blankets, she'd been half dreamin, half imaginin a big plate at Meaai Lelei, and she didn't even like the food there, never felt like she fit in there, though she was supposed to, except then she was at her momma's table, where she always fit in, where there was always so much food. And then her eyes were open and she could see she weren't anywhere near Orvop.

Sunlight streamed into their enclosure, dazzlin the air with bars of light sculpted by the smoke from their fire as well as dissipatin steam from their kettle. And from their pan too, where there was somethin more than just bubblin water waterin her mouth, churnin her stomach.

So impossible were the aromas that Landry clamped her eyes shut again, if just to enjoy for one moment longer this fantasy of breakfast. She refused too the sudden memories of Dutch baby pancakes her momma liked to cook up in big cast-iron pans even as the taste at the back of her throat kept provokin thoughts of savory mouthfuls of eggs and beans.

Your brother weren't kiddin when he said you could sleep through anythin.

Even squattin beside the fire, Landry remained paralyzed by disbelief.

This ain't some kinda cruel joke? she asked, even refusin to touch what he'd put in her bowl.

Ask them, Kalin answered.

Landry followed his gaze to the horses, who were clearly busy finishin what looked like piles of grain with plenty of grass left yet for grazin.

Kalin used their Swiss Army knife to open another can of beans. Landry saw then the bags of freeze-dried eggs and biscuits with gravy. There were two more cans of somethin else. Landry couldn't read the labels, but they didn't look like they was beans.

Kalin explained how back when he was preparin for the ascent, he'd brought up here a small amount of provisions to store. He'd foraged for grass as well for the horses. His plan had always been to spend one night in Isatch Canyon, which they'd done, and the second night here, which had obviously required more nights. He'd mostly been concerned about the horses. He knew they'd end up usin all of the feed and hay Mouse would be haulin up on the packsaddle, and while the back side would provide ample grazin, the summit itself was pretty bare. Kalin had inititally planned not to include any provisions for hisself but then changed his mind just in case he decided at the last moment to jettison his own food in the name of lightness and swiftness.

A good ways below these limber pines he'd found a small den that he could easily stone up. Later he'd added the freeze-dried meals and extra cans of food. Last night was too dangerous to set out in search of this cache, not to mention he hadn't had the energy and would've imperiled Landry by directin her to the location. The mornin had proved the task was no easy one. The snow had made it near impossible to find, and that was with clear skies and plenty of sun. At least the snow was dry and light. Kalin had to dig down a good ways before gettin to the rocks that, once hauled aside, revealed a sandy little apse perfect for some rattlesnake, which fortunately weren't there, guardin over their life-preservin feast.

I slept through that?

And I sure made a fuss. What's the matter? Why ain't you eatin?

We'll eat together.

Awww, you don't have to wait for me.

I don't but I will.

Kalin insisted Landry use the spork while he used the Swiss Army knife to shovel into his mouth the beans, eggs, and biscuits and gravy off the pan lid. They ate in silence. When they was done, they eyed the two remainin cans. Landry finally said they should hold off and save them for later. Tom was floored.

What's happened to her?

One can was bust apart anyway by the freezin temperatures, though the other had somehow managed to preserve its seams. They decided to split the one the mountain had opened and keep the other in reserve, a can that turned up years later buried in mud near Pillars Meadow, rusted through, and considered trash by the ones who found it.

Boy oh boy, them peaches sure were good. Kalin even heated them up in the pan. With a sprinklin of oats it was near a cobbler, which they split even steven. Landry would have it no other way. Had she ever tasted anythin so good? Kalin felt the same way. The sweetness exploded in their mouths with such velocity, they briefly went blind. Each swallow seemed a promise and fulfillment guaranteein nothin but more of the same from here on out.

And there was more too. Landry had expected hot water when Kalin filled her bowl; she'd also insisted he take the mug this time. But Kalin hadn't just loaded their kettle with snow. He'd also added two packets of powdered cocoa. Landry nearly cried. Kalin set aside the remainin two packets for their return trip back to Orvop, what was also treated as trash when it turned up years later.

Together they slowly emptied the kettle, the two agreein to keep addin hot water to their hot chocolate, which, while dilutin the sweetness and flavor until it was pretty much just hot water, Landry and Kalin still continued to enjoy, experiencin a creamy fullness beyond any components preserved by paper and foil.

Kalin then told Landry about what Tom had said on top of the mountain. He had to retell it a bunch of times too because Landry kept proddin him with questions as she attempted to understand just what the heck had taken place up there. It didn't help that Kalin never told the story the same way twice.

But is it just gobbledygook nonsense? she finally asked the air.

The air, Kalin relayed, no longer had any memory of the ridge nor for that matter any of his past, his life in Orvop, his death, not even of their climb up the headwall. Only the future remained available, and it seemed mostly cloudy. *Tom says he's awful glad we're here.*

That's almost too nice a thing for Tom Gatestone to say, Landry responded. *Are you lyin to me, Kalin?*

No, ma'am.

I don't rightly follow how my brother could ever talk like you said he talked. It just don't sound like Tom.

Kalin thought that was a fair thing to say and even added that Tom was in agreement. He told her too how Tom kept sayin he wanted to skedaddle: *I feel like I'm vanishin.*

Our folks taught us that Jesus's greatest miracle was to vanish, Landry said then.

Tom says he don't got nothin to do with Jesus.

Landry nodded. *How about Bilbo?*

Who?

He's a hobbit, Landry said.

I don't know nothin about hobbits.

Our brother Evan was a big fan of Bilbo because he did just that.

Vanish?

Landry nodded. *He threw a big party for hisself and then put on this invisibility ring and disappeared. Our daddy told Evan that if he liked that story so much, he should read Plato. I don't believe Evan ever did.*

Do you think about Evan a lot?

I guess, but I didn't know him long enuf to think about him so much.

You do know that Jesus didn't vanish, right? They hammered him to a cross to kill him.

I don't think you can kill the Lord.

Kalin turned to the air, his face twitchin some as he listened.

What's he sayin now? Landry asked after a while.

It beats me.

Come on.

To debase yourself ain't the same thing as to erase yourself.

What's that supposed to mean?

Like I said, beats me. Kalin shrugged. *Your brother's gettin more bewilderin. He's got the jitters. He says he feels really small. Like smaller than your hobbits.*

With enuf distance and the right perspective, you can blot out the sun with a blueberry, Landry said then. *You hear me, Tom Gatestone?*

Who said that? Kalin asked. *The hobbit?*

Our daddy.

Why would anyone wanna blot out the sun?

I think he just meant that you don't need much to achieve big things so long as you get yourself to the right place. It don't matter how small Tom is if he's in the right place. And he is. He's with us.

Kalin then told Landry about how Tom had also recollected his final hours in the hospital and what he'd shared with Kalin, about where to go after the summit and how to get the horses to the Crossin. Kalin figured Landry should know that part now too.

There are many ways down from here. Kalin pointed then to the left. *Those draws and gullies to the north head down to the millions of acres that make up the Uinta-Isatch-Cache National Forest.* Kalin then pointed to the right. *I ain't gone farther than here, but accordin to your brother, that way lies Coyote Gulch. He said it's an easy descent that leads down to a wide grassy area called Pillars Meadow.*

Never heard of it. I'm sure it won't be grassy. More like a field of snow.

Tom says there won't be much snow. Either way, beyond it there's a dry crick bed beyond which we'll find two gateposts. There ain't no gate no more. Nor a fence either. But between them old posts, why that there's the Crossin.

What's so special about them?

It's not them, it's where they stand. They mark the line between what's protected parkland and what's not.

Tom also hear that from Terrence Olsen?

Your brother never did say how he knew about the Crossin. It's somethin he can't recollect now.

I guess it don't matter, Landry said, but she said it like she knew it was all that mattered.

They was savorin their last few gulps of hot chocolate.

Remember back in the mine when I promised you thee most beautiful sight in the world? Kalin asked her then.

I do.

How about lettin me keep that promise?

Landry couldn't imagine a place so stunnin. It resembled nothin of the storm-blasted darkness she'd crawled through last night. The sky was a perfect blue. Orvop shimmered beneath the mornin sun. The lake now seemed a plate of fire. There were no more clouds, all of them scrubbed away by a fast high wind, even to the north, even a hundred miles toward the Uintas. The same was true to the south, beyond Mount Nebo, and even to the east, toward Ouray, two hundred miles away. What earlier was a low blanket of concealin clouds now revealed forestland to the horizon. Landry blinked and smacked her lips and rubbed her hands over her brittle cheeks. The breeze that rustled her hair was cold and dry and smelt of somethin that took no part in the manners of earth. Like Tom, Landry discovered too how little she cared for the sight of Orvop or Isatch Canyon or even the cirque, still cast into shadow by the early sun. She didn't care much for where they was headin next either. Mostly she was mesmerized by the lessons of the sky: to stand so high up, atop such immensity, and still have no comprehension of the distances that continued to exceed them all. Her absence, in that vast elsewhere, what not even a blueberry could eclipse, somehow fused her to the only here she could ever know. It gathered in her heart a meanin beyond expression, and she accepted its blessin like a sacrament and was humbled.

Kalin seemed almost goofy in his delight over where they was headin next, and no doubt he had a right to find elation in all they'd overcome and survived, plus the food in his belly was helpin, and there was no discountin that view from the summit; but Landry, although she wanted to share in his enthusiasm, couldn't so insouci-antly put aside last night's gunfire.

You know they ain't givin up? she said and was sorry to see Kalin's smile fade.

I reckon that's so. But we should see the horses free before we face that.

You think they'll try to come after us by way of the cirque?

Kalin considered it but shook his head. *I was surprised how they came up like they done yesterday. Old Porch spotted us from a helicopter. Why didn't they come back in a helicopter?*

I figured the bad weather grounded them?

If they come in a helicopter now, they'll have to see through trees to find us, and that's only if they think we made it out of the cirque.

But if they do figure out we're here, and they ain't flyin, how should we expect them to come?

Now that there's the good news: with so much snow, the only reasonable choice is the back side of Agoneeya. It's the easiest way, but it's also way longer, and no ATV or dirt bike is worth squat in snow. Even if they ski in, they'll need a long day, maybe two, and that still won't get them close to where we're headed.

Kalin's smile had returned along with even some of his goofiness, but Landry spat, and fer the first time in a while there was a hard scowl in her eyes. *Ever heard of a snowmobile?*

Kalin looked pretty stunned by the question, and Landry sure was sorry to see him slump so fast. *I didn't think of that.*

I guess that's why I'm here. Tom couldn't tell you about snowmobiles?

He only ever goes on about settin Navidad and Mouse loose.

Landry nodded. *That'll be a good moment.*

How long do you figure it'll take to get around Agoneeya on snowmobiles?

If it's easier, like you say, and the snow holds up, a few hours, maybe less?

The back side of Katanogos has parts that are pretty much like a golf course.

Then we best get hurryin.

I can't believe snowmobiles never crossed my mind, Kalin said. He looked troubled, even sad. *If they started early, we might already be in trouble.*

Of course that's only if they know where we're headed.

Kalin pointed down to the right. *There are some big cliffs beyond them trees down there, but we should get a view of anyone comin around Agoneeya.*

Maybe no one will be there.

That would be nice.

The approach of a plane got them scurryin back down beneath their shelter. Landry kicked dirt on the mostly spent fire while Kalin backed up the horses under the tarp. The sound of engines grew louder until the plane seemed right above them, whinin by and dancin the horses' nerves some, except fer Mouse.

For one who had every right to claim he was spent, Kalin sure moved like lightnin out of their huddle of pines, pickin his way up quick over the rocks to get some eyes on where the plane was headed.

They comin back? Landry yelled up from below.

They are!

Are they police or Porches?

I can't tell.

You think they seen us.

Keep the horses under the tarp! Especially that mule!

The mule had no halter let alone a lead, but Kalin was still wrong to fear that this errant creature, born out of the mists of Kirk Cirque, would betray them. Furthermore, while the plane did execute a wide U-turn, it did not fly over their camp again. Instead it dropped down over the cirque, where it made several surveillin circles. Kalin was finally able to see that it was a police plane.

Do you think they saw us? Landry asked when Kalin got back down.

They don't have a clue we made it over. They're just checkin around the lake.

Once they was sure the plane was gone, Landry set off to attend to her business. Kalin set off in the opposite direction to get his done too, and this time without no more runny incidents. After that they saddled the horses and broke camp. They debated a bit whether to leave the tarps and ropes or untie it and take it all with them. If they left the snow-covered tarps up, even a helicopter hoverin right above would have a hard time seein the campsite. But if they took everythin, they'd leave behind a mess of snow and debris that even from a distance would draw anyone's attention.

I don't know, Kalin said, strokin Navidad's neck.

I don't know either. Landry was already on Jojo with Mouse's lead in her hand. *What's Tom say?*

He says we can take the one tarp on the ground. We won't need another.

After they'd made it down around a few switchbacks, wherever possible keepin to the snowless stretches of rock and weather-whipped earth, they looked back and not only beheld what any idjit could see was the remnants of a camp, and a recent one too, but also preserved in the snow an easy-enuf-to-spot set of tracks leadin away.

Unfortunately no police plane or helicopter ever returned that day to discover the lean-to or even note where Kalin, Landry, and the horses were headin.

Though that first part of their descent was far less dangerous than what they'd been through on the cirque side, it was still no easy ride. The grade could get scary steep, and in some places the horses faced iced-over rock hidden beneath the snow, moments that opened up the possibility of a bad slip or fall. And where they had no choice but to trudge across a wide stretch of virgin snow, a new risk presented itself, namely startin an avalanche and goin down with it. In a few places their steps started rivers of powdery stuff that swept down the mountain at such speeds that just their goin tormented the horses' ears with a high serpentine hiss. These events, however, mostly occurred behind them, though the farther down they got, the more they started worryin about avalanches fallin upon them from above.

Soon enuf, though, and not without sighs of relief, they departed that exposed part of the mountain and entered a milder area, *Clop-Clop-clip-Clop*, where birches and quakin aspens ablaze with oranges and gold began to surround them, *Clop-Clop-clip-Clop*, followed soon after by more and more pines offerin them the added relief of refuge from the sky.

From this point on they all but vanished beneath the many branches of Douglas fir, maple, spruce, and chokecherry. Boughs drooped low, burdened with blue fluffy peaks, like small mountain ranges unto themselves, which now and then a gust of wind would dissolve into a sparklin spectacle of ice ablaze with the memory of rainbows. Before a mosquito stole her life away, Andrea Gunther would often repeat what she'd heard from someone whose name she could no longer remember: *You never wanna hurry so much that you pass by more than you're aimin to catch up to.* Kalin, Landry, the horses, and Tom were hurryin fer sure, but it weren't lost on a one of them the surroundin and suspended rapture that suffered their presence.

Not that this dulled their alertness any. For example, they knew well enuf to keep clear of the tree wells, those areas around the trunks, which, when snow is light and deep, can swallow you long enuf to suffocate you. Or so Landry told Kalin, and Tom offered no objection except to say he had some vague notion that his sister had in fact got that particular fact from him once upon a time a long time ago.

Anyway, despite their occlusion beneath so many trees, the obvious trail precedin this disappearin act, if viewed from above, weren't goin to vanish anytime soon and would no question provide a good enuf startin place for anyone seekin to know which way they was headed. But once again no police would take note of the ample traces writ by horses up there upon the side of the mountain.

Not that their progress went unwitnessed.

Landry thought she caught sight of that old elk they'd seen now and then on their way to the cirque, even in the cirque, though seein the same elk over here was obviously impossible. Kalin regarded the direction Landry was indicatin only to discover somethin entirely different: there, trudgin alongside, was a donkey and an old mountain goat. Could this somehow be the same goat from out on the headwall? The horns were thinner, and the coat seemed at times like ash and then abruptly whiter than snow and not a moment later a gold rivalin the sun's shine upon these icy surrounds. What the heck . . . ? Whatever was goin on, the mountain goat and donkey didn't hesitate to join their ranks, fallin in right beside that curious mule like they was part of the family.

Are you seein this? Kalin asked Landry.

Sure, answered Landry, who was anythin but sure.

And that was just the beginnin. Both of them soon began to discern between the surroundin trees, among those many violet shadows, animals more numerous than what these groves should or could contain. Was that a raccoon? Or over there a badger? Farther away . . . was that a mountain lion? And closer in . . . a beaver?! That's not possible. A moose?! Was there any point in denyin the big black bear with her cubs? While overhead glided a white owl. And farther down below, margin with the darker blue shadows inhabitin the bowls of snow beneath them towerin pines, were those wolves? Surely that's some kind of cat? And not a few steps away, was that a red fox divin for voles? A white ermine? Were those coyotes?

It became all the more troublin when Kalin and Landry began to confirm what the other had only thought they'd imagined just seein.

What's Tom say?

He says he's seein way more than we are.

Like what?

He says we don't want to know.

They rode on. They rode slow. They knew what the horses had survived. They knew what they would soon have to survive on their own.

Now and then a density of trunks and branches demanded that they dismount, but in those cases, Landry quickly spied a way around, and they was soon on the other side, on their way again, followin that much-welcomed decline toward a vista they hoped would prove just as void of human motion as their immediate surroundins.

On occasion Kalin would call a halt so they could listen for planes or, worse, a helicopter. Navidad would often paw up the snow then and graze upon whatever wet stalks lay beneath; that or just eat some snow. Mouse would stand by her side, and now and then a bird or two would alight on his wide back.

In the silence Landry and Kalin would often imagine a pursuit of the very worst kind: somehow the Porches had already returned to the cirque and without any trouble ascended the headwall and now were rushin down after them, followin their tracks, releasin into the air great puffs of powder as they weaved through this mornin-dazzled loom of so many trunks, set to deliver one prolonged moment of gun-fire, slaughter, and rape, and all of it carried out under the cover of these idyllic woods.

Only Landry, in such moments of frantic anticipation, when scan-nin the way behind them fer anythin other than animal life, could draw comfort from the fact that with but one lift of a flap she could have at that Colt. Egan could shoot at her all he liked but she'd be shootin back.

But no party of Porches appeared.

Silence prevailed.

A good hour later they approached what seemed the thickest obstruction of trees and brush yet. Even Tom had to stop, Ash at once tossin up his head either to challenge or greet this new density. Kalin noticed then how the horse had changed; in the blue shadows Ash's pale coat seemed to shimmer now with either a mem-ory or prediction of gold, while his virescent eyes seemed to glitter with endless spring. Not that such ghostly grandeur had any effect on the wall before them.

Once again it was Landry who spied a way through. She didn't even need to dismount. A soft pathway of piled pine needles guided the way until the trees fell back and they were treated to a softly slopin meadow of snow brilliant with sunlight.

Here they did dismount and led the horses down into that unmarked clearin, followed by the mule, the donkey, and mountain goat, and whatever other animals cared to follow. Kalin thought he saw a deer mouse and definitely a porcupine.

The temperatures had already risen, and the unmasked sun above had begun to melt the snow some and pack it down. In some places it seemed like a slurry of wet cement, sometimes holdin on a moment too long as if to demand the sacrifice of a leg or boot. Both Landry and Kalin made sure that none of the horses got a hoof caught and, in tryin to jerk free, hurt a leg.

Kalin kept their pace slow and deliberate, and Landry made no effort to hurry him. The air hung their breaths like bursts of small clouds. The smell of meltin ice and wet earth coated the back of Kalin's throat so thickly that he swore to Tom he could eat it. Tom, once again in the lead, swore he could only know the breezes now by the way they stirred the pine needles. Both Kalin and Landry were surprised to learn that he could no longer hear the winds, especially those more brutal in force and iciness, startin way up high before acceleratin down the mountainside, shakin countless trees into a great wash of sound, like a great wave that soon enuf was tumblin overhead.

It was about halfway down across that meadow that the ghost of Tom Gatestone, still amblin beside Ash, began to whistle. And even though he was a good ways ahead, the melody seemed right in Kalin's ear: plaintive yet sweet, real sweet, though there was somethin mournful in there as well. And violent.

Kalin didn't care for that.

Fortunately, and at the near exact moment that Tom had started up, Landry began to sing, and what's more, the song she sang was the very same one that Tom was whistlin.

Landry sure could carry a tune, Tom too, especially since what he could no longer remember he knew there again, and too well, which had an adverse effect, because he stopped his whistlin at once; and then an instant later, fer no reason Kalin could come up with, Landry quit too, her eyes suddenly wet with regret.

You got one heckuva voice, Kalin told her. *Maybe one day you really will be famous.* And, boy, would she ever be. Though not for singin.

I used to sing that song and Tom would whistle. I miss his whistlin so bad.

You know he was whistlin just now.

He was?

The very same thing you was just singin.

Blue Dawn?

Kalin nodded.

Landry started to hum the song again and soon enuf was singin again, though she'd come in lower this time.

Will you ask her to stop? Tom asked Kalin.

What for?

Landry stopped at just the sound of Kalin barkin at the emptiness.

Now what is it? she demanded.

Ask her please to change the key so I can whistle with her.

Kalin relayed Tom's request.

Maybe he don't whistle so good as a dead man. I never recalled a time when the livin Tom couldn't handle some low notes.

She just don't give up, does she? Tom grinned.

No, she don't, Kalin answered back, bemused to get an earful of siblin bickerin as they all sloughed on ahead.

Landry restarted, this time higher, until the lyrics that were the lesser part of her aubade began to unfold into the space between them. Even the horses seemed to listen.

> *Blue dawn come console me,*
> *I lost who I was with.*
> *I dreamt once I had a pony,*
> *but what I rode was a myth.*

Tom had joined in right off, and the two of them together . . . well, that was somethin else. Tom's melodies, his sister's phrasin. Out of this world really. Kalin forgot to breathe, just immersin hisself in their harmonies, verse after verse. And if he'd known fer sure that stoppin wouldn't have stopped their song, Kalin would've stopped and stayed in that meadow forever, just standin right between them two, until they'd exhausted all that music had to offer. Even birds in the surroundin canopies had ceased their peeps and flutterins.

Only when they had reached the other side of the meadow, and were headin into the trees, did the music stop.

Landry barged ahead of Kalin then, ahead of Tom, weavin through the maples, junipers, and firs. And when the snow thickened before a sharp but not so dauntin slope, she handed Jojo's reins to Kalin, retrieved the binoculars, and scrambled to the top. Kalin and Tom watched her disappear up a sort of chimney of black stone and clear ice. A moment later she was hootin from the rocks above.

Holy cow! she cried down. *Here's another spectacular view!*

Kalin wanted to join her right then but first attended to the horses, inspectin whatever grass was pokin up through the snow to make sure nothin there might prove disagreeable to their guts. The mule, donkey, and goat were already at it, and Mouse was already challengin Kalin's restraint. Even Ash had got to grazin.

Kalin! I see them! Landry cried down. *They've come up from behind Agoneeya like you said! On snowmobiles like I said!* Fer a moment her excitement made the bad news hard to know. Kalin loosely tied the horses' leads to low branches.

Comin right up! Kalin half yelled, half mumbled, as somethin started to jangle his thoughts. Somethin he couldn't find a way into, somethin bad. It didn't help none to glance up at Tom still atop Ash; the ghost was lookin straight down at him now, with no word to share, no smile, not even the hint of a spark in them black eyes.

I see Hatch Porch! Landry cried next.

What about the others? Kalin yelled up, his voice at least clear now, his head clearin too as he climbed up that black rock, what was more like a steep set of stairs banistered with ice and a dustin of snow.

Careful as you come up over the top, Landry warned him. *The trees here sit right on the edge of the cliffs.*

What about Egan Porch? Kalin asked as he continued up. He had to give Landry some credit. She'd made the climb look way easier.

Hold on, Landry answered. She was standin now on an altar of rock covered in snow, situated between some bristlecone and limber pines. What she was observin through the binoculars Ms. Melson, Mrs. Annserdodder, and Mr. Rudder would eventually agree was the fifth and final teichoskopia.

You've never told me why out of all the Porches, Egan riles you the most? Kalin asked upon reachin the top.

Because he took what wasn't his and what he couldn't give back. Those were dark words darkly spoken, but they was also quickly replaced by smug rejoicin.

Ha! Landry cried out. *I see Egan! He hasn't meshed his lenses!*

And there it was! Kalin narrowin in on what was so wrong, already acceleratin toward Landry, still a good dozen paces off, not lyin down neither, nor takin cover behind them nearby trees, just standin tall on the edge of them cliffs, and lookin through them binoculars with the meshes Kalin had improvised for each lens in the breast pocket of his Lee Storm Rider.

Cover your lenses! Kalin screamed. Though maybe he should've screamed *Run!* or better *Drop!,* though no utterance by then would've mattered. Kalin was already too late, Landry's mistake too grave.

Her dark hair spinnin.

The air around her veiled in blood.

The rifle crack, as if to seam the sky, followin after.

It was 10:38 a.m.

End of Part Two

Part Three:

The Gun

Chapter Twenty-Two

"A Snowball Fight"

As is well known, the Time Gallery exhibit took place in Houston on February 29, 2000. Already its owner, Cal Carneros, had enjoyed two successful shows since repurposin his well-frequented Time Café to pursue a short-lived devotion to that haunted intersection between Art and Commerce. Folks in Houston missed the café, but since the gallery continued to serve strong black coffee, they was willin to suffer the strange splashes of colors and odd shapes on the walls. Besides, folks generally liked Cal.

To be clear Cal weren't no more a part of the events we've gotten a good ways into now than, say, you was, but at the same time, it would be indecent not to include him because if it weren't for Cal, or CC, as one dope once called him, plenty here would not've been forgotten well. And, yes, there are ways to forget badly.

Cal weren't even a cowboy, not even close, though he did once put on a cowboy hat. Make that three times, though the first time didn't really count. He was from Texas after all, and his friends had got him the Overland, a stramineous weave that was near light as the sun it wouldn't keep out. Not that there was a lick of sun in that honky-tonk bar where they was celebratin a missed birthday of his. His friends raised their beers, and when he put it on, they cheered. But Cal didn't care for it a bit. Fer one thing, he had great hair, long sandy-brown tresses down past his shoulders, the kind surfers would die for, what would go way lighter if he had chosen to live on the shore and in the salt. Cal would keep that hair too, his whole life, though it would go white and seem finer than the cloudy silk that now and then paints a fine day on the skies above east Texas where he was born. The point was: with locks like his, what did he need a hat for? He never even wore a baseball cap. Which brings us to the other thing: wearin a cowboy hat made him feel the same as all of them. And while he liked his friends plenty, even loved some of them, that didn't mean he wanted to be them. Somehow with that cowboy hat on, he disappeared before hisself; he became somethin he weren't. Also, he weren't nothin to horses, and he weren't no gunslinger neither, and he'd never strum a guitar, not even once. He didn't even like beer. Maybe that small refusal revealed the artist he was but would never become, though that not-becomin part weren't never no big thing either. And so Cal was more than content to put the hat back in its box and leave it there until for no reason he could name he put it on a second time and in Seattle of all places. Maybe he done it because he weren't in Texas, because he was missin some of them friends, two of whom had died recently, one ambushed by a disease in his genes, another thanks to an addiction she couldn't kick until it kicked her teeth out and then kicked her to the grave. This was some years after that famed exhibit in Houston. But like the first time, wearin it still weren't no good thing. Maybe the hat was just too much for him, too big for him, too strong. As he'd later admit, he found the whole experience so charged with meanings, he didn't rightly know how to navigate. He was referrin to a jazz concert he'd been at, wearin a pink linen shirt, when a tall black fella started in on him for blockin his view. This fella did have a point too: along with that fine braided hatband and leather tassel, the blond straw hat had a four-inch crown and three inches of brim. And truth was Cal never did grasp the consequences of the hat's silhouette, how far it extended, how far it didn't; nonetheless the concert was open air with many views easily maneuvered to, and the fella that came at Cal was a good ways back. Some taller folks standin beside Cal took up the fight on Cal's behalf for some reason. Cal didn't stick around. Not that he left without questions though: was it the hat that had singled him out for that initial complaint? Cal had noticed it a few more times that evenin too, a look of disgust or rancor, and all from folks whose skin was a bit browner than his own. Not like when he'd had a blue mohawk. In those days he'd've gotten a smile or even a smile that came with a wink and an invitation. Of course that was a long time ago. Maybe even in a different life. The hat went back in its box, but Cal still couldn't toss it or give it away. Back up on the closet shelf it went. He still wanted to put it on again and know his journey by it.

Anyways, in case you haven't gathered by now, Cal Carneros weren't just a handsome man and pleasant enuf to be liked; Cal liked bein liked, he liked turnin folks on, be it with better coffee or a paintin that busted up the frame because the world he wanted you to see was so much bigger and wilder and more beautiful than you had room for in your thoughts. He weren't just an awe seeker; he was an awe sharer. Though the closest he ever got to awe didn't come til the near end of his life, when he realized he'd reached a ridge different from Mount Katanogos but still plenty high and with one heckuva view too.

For the record, while Cal Carneros did have a doofy amiability, he weren't no doof. He was smart enuf for a degree from C. T. Bauer College of Business, where he fell hard for Art. He had no Art bona fides at this point either, other than a minor in art history as an undergrad at UH and one visit to the Musée d'Orsay. He'd been too stupid to step inside the Louvre. He'd prove archly funny in future years, talkin about them Louvre drive-bys when he got as far as the entrance but forfeited the sight of the *Winged Victory of Samothrace* for a bright day in the parks seekin angels he'd never even say hello to.

Cal never confused what he loved with what he knew. He had no delusions that he was as smart as, say, the art critic Dave Hickey, whom he admired deeply and met twice, even if Hickey's *Air Guitar: Essays on Art and Democracy* taught him that he would never be that smart nor anywhere near that cool. Which was okay too. Cal Carneros never cared much for cool. He already knew there was a fine line between cool and creepy, and Cal never had no interest in tightropes. He preferred a wide life path with plenty of clover on either side.

Cal was born in the '60s, missed the '70s, was smart enuf to avoid the '80s, and came into his own when he realized that he could not only throw better parties than most around, with them most-around folks lovin him for it too, but he could also make decent money. The trouble was that the club life never suited him. Yes, in those late loud hours, the women could be beautifully scandalous and the young men tragically inspired, but come mornin it was all headaches and too many gastric disavowals, and then there was the mess to clean up with not one good conversation to recall. That led to Cal gettin together lease money for the Time Café and learnin about coffee beans. But too soon that weren't enuf either. As Cal saw it, Art lasted, and even if the conversations about it weren't all good, some were real good. That was somethin. So what if Cal weren't an artist? He could talk about anythin, and he could sell anythin he could talk about, and he genuinely liked artists, and he even liked the folks they liked. It was a win-win. He'd make them money by sellin their works, and he'd make money too. And the parties he'd throw would be good and the conversations even better.

That part turned out to be true. Money, though, Cal never did make much of that. He should've stuck with clubs if he'd wanted better returns. But he weren't ever that simple. And anyways on that Tuesday night at the end of February, 2000 bein a leap year, his mind was far from any mythical bottom line.

He'd come dressed in denim and tweed, with a turquoise bolo tie and Air Jordans. You got it: no hat. His long sandy brown hair already made clear he was with the band, and them coruscatin blue eyes hinted that he might even be in the band, but the goatee he wore settled the matter: he had nothin to do with the band except fer listenin to it, which he loved to do, because he loved music, but not half as much as he loved listenin to folks. If nothin else, Cal was a good listener. And besides there weren't no band. Not that night. Not really.

Cal was already pleased with how *The Pillars Meadow Show*, as he called it back then, was shapin up. Early attendance was good given the minimal PR. He'd be happy with anythin. This weren't but a warm-up for more serious stuff ahead. He was particularly excited about an upcomin spring show that might feature a Doug Aitken video instal-lation, he'd heard somethin about horses and lariats, if he could just get the reps to sign on the dotted line. There was talk as well of inclu-din some young art students, a list that included Amy Sherald and Pia Camil fer starters. Plus some folks from the Menil Collection had already volunteered to help out.

Of the two previous exhibits, the most sizable event had been last year's New Year's party that had gotten out of hand with reck-less inebriation leadin to the sort of pot-valiant nekedness that fur-ther declares its infallibility through acts of gymnastic positionin, and outside on the street no less, with those participants claimin that their explicit carnality was obviously both the culmination of fanciful framed paint as well as the best way to memorialize the end of the twentieth century. Some babies came of it; surprisinly two partner-ships went the distance. Between caterers, bartenders, and cleaners, the bills had gone high. No memorable conversations were had. No art was sold. The artist didn't care. He'd got laid. He would never paint again. Everyone had had a good time. Except Cal.

By comparison, those in attendance at this show were mostly Church members, a fact which Cal had been well apprised of in advance. One way or another they'd informed him or warned him, or maybe neither, that no alcohol or caffeine should be served.

Of interest was how all the art had pretty much arrived presold. Also, there weren't really no central character nor even a recognizable group coordinatin the whole thing. His contact person had been a Rayleen Roundy until it was a Thayne Moon, a high school basketball coach by the sound of things; until it was a Joanne Willden, who by then, by the way, was favorin a neon green wig; until it was someone else. A lot of them knew each other. They sent deposits. He'd never talked to nicer folks, though Cal also never felt like he'd talked to an artist either. There sure was a lot of enthusiasm, though, and that kept his phone ringin as more people volunteered to help out or submit-ted new works. Or even shipped musical instruments, a drum kit for one. Cal hadn't been in the art gallery business long, but this was still nothin like he'd ever handled before. In fact he'd never encounter another such gatherin until thirty-one years later, but we'll get to that in a minute.

Also, most of the work weren't good at all. For those who worked with Cal Carneros, MFA students, former employees at the Chinati Foundation, one still involved with the Flavin estate, few could resist whispered mockery of pieces they deemed not worthy of bein called even primitive. Nor kitsch neither. Amateur was their kindest evaluation. However, what no one workin at the Time Gallery understood was how such earnest struggles to apprehend the very real events that transpired at the end of October 1982 were throughout yoked to terror. Even a lemon cake painted on a paper plate.

Cal had explained repeatedly to his artsy employees, and with many apologies too, that this was mainly a fundraiser for the gallery's future endeavors and he sure would appreciate it if everyone could please summon up some good ole Texas politesse, just pass out more pigs in a blanket and get another keg of root beer on tap. No big deal.

And when it started at 6:00 p.m., it weren't a big deal. There was already a small line of about a dozen folks outside who were the very definition of quaint. They entered the gallery almost timidly, almost like they didn't belong there, and after grantin that first room a quick survey, what Cal and his staff had got into the habit of callin Chamber One, they quickly retreated to the large back patio where appetizers were at the ready. The conversations hummed along, mostly about reconnectin, now and then punctuated by a loud *Hello!* as more folks trickled in. There were big hugs, followed by the usual catchin up about family, the internet too, the Y2K that wasn't, and Columbine.

It was odd that almost no one got farther along than Chamber One, with only one intrepid soul in those early hours makin it to Chamber Three, and not lastin but a minute there either, before dartin back outside for a paper plate of grape-and-Jell-O salad. Cal had courteously inquired after her well-bein given the quantity of tears on her face. Alisa Groesbeck took his offered tissue but also warmly laughed away his concerns: *It all just brings up so many memories, most of which, you know, ain't on none of these walls.*

Maybe Cal expected a crowd arrayed in britches and calashes or costumes befittin the cast of *Little House on the Prairie.* Such was not the case. By 8:00 p.m. the back patio was packed with folks in light sweaters or nice jackets, many wearin cowboy boots, a few with cowboy hats, though plenty more wore no hats or boots, with those who continued to pour in mainly wearin baseball caps and cotton sweaters, dressed for a cool night. They didn't have no twang neither.

By 8:30 p.m. people were visible in Chambers One thru Five and Cal and his staff had quit speculatin that there was some communal hesitancy about enterin those last rooms. That conclusion, however, was incorrect. Better attention would have revealed that the final three rooms, and especially that last one, were visited only by Houston locals who had nothin better to do than find themselves welcome at Cal's place; wanderin through as well were those foreign-born spouses or the young children of those who had traveled with their parents from out of state and in some cases as far away as Perth. One aspect, however, that became more and more apparent to Cal and his crew, and in turn seemed more and more strange, was how aside from those mystified Houston locals, no one was leavin.

Fer sure, shows with a celebrity artist might retain attendants, especially if she's chatty with guests. But on this night there weren't no such celebrated figure. Everyone just seemed more interested in talkin near the grill or openin up another bag of chips. Overheard conversation seemed mostly about whether there was enuf ice cream.

Odder still was how some actual celebrities did arrive and even mingled with the crowd, and while they got the expected looks, and some were even approached for a handshake, that was mostly kept to a minimum, with someone always warnin away any eager autograph seekers with a sharp look or word. No one was at the Time Gallery tonight to get a gander at someone gifted with a football or a song or who could fill up a movie screen without appallin the audience or, worse, borin them.

As Cal Carneros would remark decades later, if that had all happened just twenty years later, why the technology present would've preserved near everythin on display: *Folks would've fer sure recorded on their phones those who brought their banjos to sing about events I just had no clue about. To me it was quaint church folk art. That was it I guess. I don't know. I was a stupid snob back then with the worst part bein I didn't think I was a snob and I sure didn't think I was stupid. At least not that stupid. I did, though, recognize that the music was interestin. And eventually I realized the pieces were too.*

And music was what did precede the inevitable pilgrimage into them five chambers because it was the music that finally got folks talkin, talkin fer real, not about food or family or whatever else they was up to in various parts of the world but about Pillars Meadow and all that came before that Sunday and some of what came after.

Shawn Fentley had come with his guitars, a Gibson Les Paul electric and an acoustic that looked even prettier, along with Wilson Hannzer, who got to unpackin his slide guitar real quick when he heard that Shawn was tunin up, which was when Barrett Jenkins hauled out his stand-up bass. And didn't they make a fine trio. And soon enuf there were banjos and harmonicas, a fiddle too. Someone with enuf brush know-how set up the snare and hi-hat. Singin followed, and that started a mini concert if you will but with the volume always on low if still with enuf tempo to keep your foot tappin. It was really about either havin fun, or the stories, and them stories were really about rememberin.

To begin with, though, there were covers. Songs like *Mammas Don't*

Let Your Babies Grow Up to Be Cowboys, Less of Me, I Still Miss Someone, Will the Circle Be Unbroken, and *Somewhere Over the Rainbow.* But them soon was put aside for originals. Cal never did hear one all the way through, but as that evenin progressed, more than a few lines slipped into memory. There were verses of someplace called Kirk's Cirque. There were more about someplace called Katanogos. One weren't but about anythin more than five campfires. Another one was about nine gates. Another about a bull named Hightower. Fer sure the saddest one was called *To Ginny Ward's Mom: Who Do You Call?* Cal heard a lot of bad rhymes with *horses.* At one point Pharell Rowley sang out: *I still said it, with Lilith's finger on my lips: this world has made me sick.* Poor Pharell Rowley weren't but thirty-eight when he was killt. Just an average mornin, his pickup T-boned by a semi on Freedom Boulevard. That night, though, he was full of music:

> *I won't answer what you're askin*
> *but I'll tell you what you need:*
> *He comes by way of Orvop,*
> *he ain't headed for the sea.*

> *And sure there will be mountains*
> *and what horses love the cliffs?*
> *But he's bound to set them free*
> *before he sets his heart adrift.*

> > *Oh, I beg you not to follow.*
> > *This way is cursed by much.*
> > *Just sing a pretty song for him,*
> > *and that'll be enuf.*

> *Old Porch, you know is comin.*
> *It's written in them hills.*
> *But all that he's been plannin,*
> *the future always kills.*

> *Don't talk to me of Landry,*
> *Don't talk to me of Tom,*
> *Don't talk to me of Kalin,*
> *if Kalin would've run.*

> > *Oh, I beg you not to follow.*
> > *This way is cursed by much.*
> > *Just sing a pretty song for them,*
> > *though that won't be enuf.*

Then someone named Apryl Weber took a turn at the microphone and delivered in a singsong whisper: *It turns out I was wrong, there ain't no simple songs. And love's not what you beg to stay, it's what you give away. I know I'll keep on singin, I hear it in my heart. Anyways, everyday, I love that you're okay.* Later on someone named Reny Isom belted out: *I'll meet you at midnight, I'll greet you with the dawn. I'll find you in a rainstorm or whenever ice flocks your lawn.* Five folks with names like Durry Zug, Boise Bond, Tamsyn Horrocks, Jonell Moesser, and Tammy Manning announced that they were formin a band right there on the spot. They performed a trifle called *One Night Stand* which every time it threatened to become sexual, veered somewhere else, like *One night stand . . . alone* or *One night stand . . . by the river* or *One night stand . . . up for them goshdarn horses!* After that, the band announced with a laugh that they were disbandin. They had nice voices and harmonized well together. One of them had sung in college back east, and another had sung in thee Choir.

That was about as amusin as the night got, except for maybe when Cal overheard two attendees discussin Eckhart Tolle. *The secret of life is to die before you die,* said the first fella. *You mean be a comic?* said the second fella. *I don't follow,* responded the first fella. *Isn't that what all comics go through? They gotta die over and over again?* the second fella clarified. *I still don't follow.* Other than that, there weren't a lot of comedy, not even in the René Magritte or Banksy sense, like *The Mild Mild West,* and fer sure not in the Richard Pryor, Gilda Radner, or Steve Martin kinda sense.

At one point, a Lisa Talbot stepped up to that mic to offer no song but rather parts of her unfinished *Porch Cycle* with Fentley, Hannzer, and Jenkins doin a fine job of improvisin background music suitable for what Cal considered spoken word but with half the velocity and none of the exigency evident in, say, a poetry slam at the Nuyorican. Parts soliloquy, monologue, Elizabethan farce, French satire, kitchen-sink drama, jejune reverie.

The Mothers' Aria by the River Bend came later, a beautiful tune with a performance that was an absolute mess, which kinda applied to everythin that night, if it weren't for the fact that Cal couldn't shake the recurrin shudder that it was about somethin very real, that it weren't pointin ahead to where more words waited but back to where there were no more words. Wasn't that somethin like how that crazy coot Ram Dass put it? *Where we meet is in the silence behind them words.* Which Cal could get on board with, though he knew that just like there were good places to meet, there were bad places to meet too, and that's when you better make sure you understand who all that *We* stands for.

Eventually Jeanna Gilson was thanked for a lot of the food, which she yelled out from a table was mostly thanks to the recipes shared by Sondra Gatestone *and Ginny too!* She also confirmed that, yes, the peaches were the same canned ones eaten just below the Katanogos Summit ridge that early Sunday mornin, *and that goes for the beans too, but the orange cake I baked, and this time I got it just right, so you best enjoy.* There were big shouts of approval, and by 10:00 p.m. all the orange cake was gone along with every cherry-rhubarb pie.

By then Cal had also released most of the staff except for a skeleton crew, but curiously no one left. They found themselves welcome to the desserts, to the drinks, meanin sodas, but mostly to the eerie history that was becomin more and more a part of that strange show, like a faint mist slowly risin up off a field, what's soon too heavy to deny and now near impossible to see what all it hides. First the Time Gallery staff lost sight of the time, then they lost sight of the attendees, until eventually they lost sight of even the art on the wall. They weren't alone. No one was there for the food or the music or even the art. They were there for the past, especially that past that can't find it in itself to settle just yet.

Only as midnight drew nearer did folks finally begin to return to the exhibit for one last look, since this was the only night they'd be here, though you can bet Cal was doin some serious thinkin about extendin the show. Despite months of arrangin and the many weeks required to set it up, only in these last hours had he begun to see what he'd become a part of. It weren't lost on him either how what hung on his walls weren't anythin compared to what was hangin between them works: the mutters, exclamations, whispered anecdotes, emphatic opinions, what by the grace of music was sung and hummed too but most of all remembered and shared by folks who might never again gather like this.

Chamber One was the biggest space and had the most pieces rangin from the unremarkable to flat-out bad. And though they weren't exactly artifacts, unless you could call them artifacts of the imagination, they nonetheless did conjure up somethin that Cal would only recognize much later as fear, and specifically that explicit fear that comes toward the end of life when one knows oneself as a fragile speck of dust set before a place so immense that by comparison not even the earth where that speck resides really exists.

Not that that quetch in his spine overwrote his critical capacity to evaluate the works before him. With Shasta Roulette on one side and Rico G. on the other, Cal revisited the exhibition alive now with the question of whether or not even one piece could provoke in him somethin uneasy. See, for Cal it was simple: no matter how luminous or morose, how seductive or disgustin, great works had to bring you to the edge of a grave. The gallery or museum walls, or the boundaries of wherever you was, had to wobble as if place itself was momentarily shaken from memory. You could say that here was Cal Carneros's artistic criteria: great art starts its life in the aftermath of a burial, because the life of its creation is spent, and now it's just a matter of findin out whether or not the dust is haunted.

Obviously for Cal, most art was just dust. Plain awful, sometimes sadly awful, but still awful. Now and then, though, there were those graves that were clearly haunted, and then things got interestin because there were all kinds of spectral presences that might exceed the confines of whatever form marked its startin point, whether canvas, globs of bronze, or even a solitary neon bulb. Some graves were blabbermouths conversant with insights that seemed to lead to tantalizin escapes. Others were mean and surly. A few were so willful, wily, and powerful that it was easy in their presence to find oneself speechless and for a moment even beyond the grip of time. Now and then there was one that inspired you to do somethin reckless and rash but terrified you later with all it had occupied in you, afflictin you with alternate perspectives, possibilities, doubts, and most of all reckonins you thought you were enuf adjacent to to ever have to face dead-on.

Cal had voiced these views whenever he got the chance, and fer sure young Shasta and young Rico knew what Cal meant when he whispered under his breath that these weren't anywhere near a cemetery *but rather just dull dusty lots, and that's bein as kind as I can be.* Shasta and Rico didn't disagree. It was easy to drift from what hung on the walls, no matter how affectionately lit, to study more closely those who had come to view such works in the first place.

Who were these people anyway? Not that the answer was so complicated: everyone from farmers to insurance brokers; plumbers and professors; home makers, ski instructors, a masseuse, and a concierge; folks in sales, real estate, education. Cowboys sure, a few. But also plenty of lawyers, bandits, judges, athletes. Shasta swore there was at least one who knew her way around a lap dance. Rico had talked with a casino croupier. There were folks in demolition, tattooin, and even big pharma. The list went on and on. From all over the globe too. And why? What had really brought them here for this uncoverin, what one attendant jokingly referred to as an apocalypse? Curiosity? Reunion? Cal couldn't say why, but he already knew reunion weren't the sum of it. There was somethin else goin on here. Maybe more akin to endurance? To suffer a story and continue to suffer that story in the name of that story because that story just might offer some sort of justice or redemption or just overcome the tribulations of the past, that over-whelmin inertia set against the future. Many years later, Cal Carneros would say it had all really been about a ghost, a missin ghost. But on that night he satisfied hisself with the notion that it was only about the horses, what he also decided was the whole of it moments before he died, many, many years later, not believin no more in ghosts.

It's worth mentionin that Cal had never been to Utah let alone Orvop. He was Texas through and through. He didn't know these folks from Adam, but that weren't an issue. He liked all kinds of folks, and he was committed to his vision for his gallery. After all, he'd worked hard to make this latest stage of his life possible, which despite his hard work wouldn't have been possible without a small inheritance from his Uncle Dave, whose picture hung above the espresso bar where Cal hisself usually preferred to reside at such events, playin the part of the gentleman barista, biscotti and all. Not tonight though. These people weren't interested in caffeine, not even decaf, which he didn't have. Not that that troubled Cal. Sure he could go on about grains, grind, and crema, but he was much happier goin on about the Daniel Johnston doodles that hung next to Uncle Dave. Or any of the other personal pieces in his office. Representation mattered more to Cal Carneros than consumption: all that it could get right, all that it might posit, all that it must also inevitably get wrong. Cal's deep aes-thetic secret was that, frame or no frame, who we are to ourselves and each other is just another representation, albeit mental, which just as everythin in his gallery would prove, prove too soon in fact, must remain subject to the most powerful consequence of time: change independent of human intent.

So that night, instead of playin Cal Carneros behind his espresso bar, he introduced hisself to everyone he could and made sure they felt welcome. His guests in turn thanked him, many in a way he could not explain, like he'd managed some great act of salvation on their behalf, though he hadn't. At most he'd provided them some space.

One odd thing that occurred over the course of that night con-cerned this strange shift from a focus on those who were gathered here to what Cal kept doin his best to underestimate, still sayin it was somethin it weren't, an openin, a show, a limited event, ideas that con-tinued to block out what was stayin very much alive, if a sense of livin is the right notion, and doin so with names he was already familiar with, names he'd learned from the walls, from the folks in his gallery, names like *Navidad* and *Mouse*.

Cal had already decided to heed the recommendation in the program and move counterclockwise through the various rooms. The only hiccup was that Cal couldn't exactly speed through, findin hisself too soon in a line that was in no hurry to hustle ahead, leavin him no choice but to linger. But before what? How was he even supposed to respond to this first piece by Rayleen Roundy, described as a *cloud-en-croached sky rendered with bright acrylic blues and whites*? Rayleen was supposedly around too, and though she no longer had braces, she'd kept her braids. Or so someone told him. Or what about these cross-hatched scratchins on paper napkins? In the name of what? Paddock A? Horses? Was that someone sittin on the top of a fence? Who was this Amelia Beltran? Did she know Rayleen? Was she here too? Cal scowled without notin how time was already startin to slip away.

Rico recalled for him then how these particular scraps had arrived wadded up in an envelope with too many stamps. Cal liked Rico. He was a good kid with a gentle heart, from West Texas, with the body of a swimmer and skin like marble if marble could tan. After he'd got his art degree from UT, Rico had headed to Marfa. That's where he learned to relax some about what all he thought and have fun. He was easy like that. And special. He thought hangin this fragile piece of paper before them had been fun. Shasta, on the other hand, had thought the task unbearable, like a good many of the other pieces, which in their unique way had all posed a slew of challenges.

Cal praised them both for their hard work. If nothin else he was content to see his finest accomplices enjoyin some sense of accomplishment. They deserved it. The night had gone well. They'd even made a little money. Consequently Cal was in no hurry to get somewhere else. Why not stick with the art? But Shasta Roulette had no patience for the line let alone reruns. She also might've had plans that night for Rico as she hustled him off again for more tequila kept safe in a back room, though with this crowd the liquor would've been safe just about anywhere. *Is your name really Shasta Roulette?* someone asked her that night. She had her reply: *There's a chance.* In that black leather choker, extra mascara, and flares of blue and pink in her rosy bleach-beat hair, she still had, by her estimate, a good decade of prettiness to play around with, and, yes, she was more than pretty. At RISD she'd driven half the girls mad, and half the boys too, includin pretty much everyone in between and outside of in-between too, and that was just with her attitude and how attitude winks and moves. *Her big lips and brown eyes sure don't hurt none either,* one of Rico's pals once said, *and she has a figure that would make a mathematician quit.* Rico's pal was a mathematician and he ended up changin majors. Or maybe all this is wrong. Maybe even Shasta's Rico-G.-anglin weren't a thing. Their tequila break sure didn't last long. And amorous intent never had a chance of outmaneuverin what kept drawin them back, like they was nothin but space rubble circlin somethin that fer sure weren't no sun, at least not an illuminatin one.

So these three stuck together, slowly makin their way around that first room. What really was they supposed to make of this ink sketch in the yellow pages, a dutiful portrayal of a collapsin barn, background to what the three of them knew by now was a recurrent site of containment, a desolate paddock, home to two dispirited horses, no better drawn than stick figures in a prolonged game of hangman? By Simon Bickette. Shasta Roulette asked in a graveled whisper if they was supposed to take it seriously. Cal's thoughts went to Lucian Freud's *Head of a Horse,* though he at once felt embarrassed for makin the association. There were two more of a hatless boy with long golden hair chasin a horse. Here was neither the nineteenth-century *Race of the Riderless Horses* by Théodore Géricault, with a nude figure wrestlin a white horse, nor Michael Lantz's shirtless fellas battlin immense limestone horses, one on Constitution Avenue, the other on Pennsylvania Avenue, in front of the Federal Trade Commission Buildin in D.C. *Man Controlling Trade.* Not even the Greek marble *Relief with a Youth Restraining a Horse,* 500 BC if Cal recollected rightly, was reminiscent of what was goin on here. No, here there was no control. Just a boy pawin after a horse, just a horse kickin loose of that hatless boy.

And then there was one of a boy in a white hat, scrappier than the tissue he was drawn on. The stillness in the way he stood between the two horses was at least somethin. Rico was kinder than Shasta even if he remained mystified by why anyone would pay to put this on a wall. That went for the next one too, of a taller boy in a black hat, more scarecrow than human, with a grin big as a jack-o'-lantern's. By Craig Sandower. Cal Carneros wondered if it was even fair to recall Marino Marini's *Horseman* or the photographer Norm Clasen, the cowboys of Marlboro lore or, for Cal, the problematic Richard Prince?

None of them disagreed that the frames looked nice, referrin mainly to those that they'd supplied. Some pieces had arrived already framed, and there weren't nothin they could do there. But some of them, the sketches, the tissues, Shasta and Rico delicately pinned directly to the wall with a frame installed around them. A Dutch friend of Cal's, aside from creatin wide lustrous paintins devoted to gold fields overflown by black crows, loved makin frames of all sizes and kinds, some of barren wood, others Baroque and leafed in gold. They weren't free, but the Dutch genius had agreed to loan Time Gallery dozens for this exhibit. As he'd quipped: *The frame is the pimp of paintin.*

Maybe the wide variety of frames suited the wide variety of pieces. Here was one that weren't even of horses and boys but on a scrap of paper, what looked like a hospital monitor with lines flat as the Bonneville Salt Flats. By Irene Wren. Rico had selected a lusterless aluminum frame similar to those tubes used to construct old hospital beds.

Followin that mystery came sketches of boots and hats, what looked like a charcoal rubbin of a rodeo belt buckle, and still more horses. Always two. Always together. One was black and lean, scarred around the pasterns and flanks. The other was squat and built like a tank with a brown coat often mauled through with dark reds. No Sargent's *Fall of Gog and Magog* here or Paulus Potter's *The Piebald Horse* with that brave head held up against gray clouds, anticipatin Tolstoy's gelded steed, Strider, who two hundred years later would walk and suffer again the earth. Cal knew these were unfair comparisons, but he also couldn't stop the associations from comin. Degas's bronze of a horse with head lowered was in there too. Cal weren't alone either. Shasta brought up Chagall's *Horsewoman on Red Horse,* though there weren't no horsewoman here and the squat horse weren't red like that. Rico was thinkin of *Horse Stable* by Gerard ter Borch, which neither Cal nor Shasta could take seriously. Delacroix's *Moroccan Horseman Crossing a Ford* was also too much but at least there they could see what Rico was gettin at. When Cal brought up Toulouse-Lautrec's *At the Cirque Fernando, Rider on a White Horse,* they moved on.

Cal got hung up then on some pencil sketches of gates framed by fence slats. One was titled *Between Paddock A and Paddock B.* Another *Between Paddock B and the Road.* Drawn by folks with names like Eldon McKennan, Courtney Resnick, Gil Stubbs, and Anton Smiley. Cal made up his mind to seek these artists out as soon as he'd seen the rest.

And there were surprises too. Of course he'd already seen *Rearview* by Thayne Moon, but now in the light of the occasion, elegantly framed in dark walnut, Shasta's choice, Cal had to admit the piece was pretty good. Fine charcoal lines achieved a precision he hadn't noticed before. It was basically just the rump of a horse, the black one, but Cal could know hisself as the one lookin back over it, more so if he stood with his back to the work and looked over his shoulder, lookin toward the dark bay horse redder now than a malicious mornin. Except it weren't mornin. It was at least dusky. And was that rain? Or were those streaks bars? Like a cage? Cal found hisself increasinly put ill at ease as he wondered if he was leavin a cage or goin deeper into one. Here at least he felt he was on cemetery grounds. After dark.

Then along came another good one, by Joanne Willden, also with charcoal as well as smears of teal, ribbons of orange, and muddy yellows. The view was from far off. Of the boy with a white hat ridin the black horse. Was he in a parkin lot? He seemed involved too, if *involved* was the right word, with tulgey shadows too substantial to be cast by anythin present in the folds of that dreary and rainy dusk. What Turner had done with storms seemed present here, but then Cal disagreed with hisself, thinkin this was more like if Francis Bacon had painted weather havin a conversation with itself. And then he disagreed with hisself again. Bacon weren't right either. But, still, somethin old had come to do its work here. Maybe older than Bacon or Turner, but who? Cal had no clue, but the piece made him shiver. How that was possible, Cal couldn't say. This here was nothin much beyond an MFA exercise, and yet he still felt somethin he couldn't shake free of with a laugh or acerbic remark. They was standin before a real honest-to-gosh grave. And Cal knew Shasta and Rico felt it too, especially in the way they didn't move, didn't say nothin, in the way the three of them had become the ones now holdin up the line.

Cal recovered some in the presence of some bad comic strips called *Havril Is the Cruelest Mope* and *Havril Out of the Rain*. By Atilio Jonas. Three works, though, by Karl Lamoreaux on chunks of drywall, captured in black and blue pencil two men standin on a small stoop. Cal learned from someone behind him that the big fella was Havril Enos. His hair had blue in it and looked plenty wet and oily. The other fella was Orwin Porch, and though he was grinnin, Cal thought he seemed about to lash out. The second piece emphasized what Cal characterized as a lustful shine in both men's eyes. The third weren't but of a circus bear with a big red-and-white ball on his nose with a rattlesnake coiled around his back paws.

After that, they was far from any cemetery, with a series of works created out of actual playin cards that, okay, sure, they were engagin, if just for the mystery of the hands, their significance, if there was any. Shasta and Rico both agreed it was pointless, but Cal was quick catchin on that for whatever else you could say about this collection put on display tonight at the Time Gallery, none of it was pointless. The TEXAS HOLD 'EM PIECES were by Lorelei Barrett, Brennan Graves, and Farran Engelman.

Then Joanne Willden returned, and this time with a campfire scene. Again usin thick smears of pastels. There was the kid again, the one with the white cowboy hat. Now, though, he weren't alone with his horses but joined by a chubby boy, his face lookin bruised, though he was smilin and with such tenderness that Cal was briefly stunned. There was a girl too, darker than the bay horse and with more fire in her eyes than the ecstatic flames warmin their palms. The most unnervin part resided in an ambiguous space beside the boy with the white hat, where it seemed to Cal emptiness itself had also taken a seat, as if such a dark and lonely void might also have hands in need of warmin. Maybe that was what finally felt wrong about the work, or incomplete. Rico and Shasta agreed, both of them a little tipsy and determined to get more tipsy; they was also a little handsy with each other too, swayin before that tableau like it had tilted the floor upon which they stood, tiltin them toward Chamber Five, toward somethin steeper, even vertical. Cal knew he also had to meet Joanne Willden.

The works that followed weren't nothin like Willden's; rather they seemed like evidence from a crime scene: a scotch glass smeared and filled with a viscous fluid that, if Cal hadn't seen Shasta and Rico make the sugary syrup better suited for humminbirds than vampires, he might've believed it to be blood. And more blood followed: on canvas, floorboards, towels, newspapers, and court documents. Many of these were created by Penny Peterson, Alli Rogers, and Becky Sanko.

Then there were three pieces by Atticus Pattee, Breen Lachance, and Matt Van Buren. In the first the boy in the white cowboy hat rides the black horse. He's leadin the rufescent bay horse, followed by the young girl on a blue-and-gray horse, which made Cal think of Franz Marc's *Blue Horse II* or even his *Large Blue Horses*. André Brasilier too. The two riders looked to be ascendin a dark steep, like a great wave, here and there bright with oily flares of sinuous oranges and golds. In the second piece, this one in watercolors, the two riders were again darin a slope, only now the surface roiled with blood. In the third piece, oils again, like the first, lemony dabs and gold ones too filled the canvas, along with the occasional smear of dreamy purple. Somethin about this work in particular came alive even if the horses resembled goats, at best, with no night lingerin even in the corners; there was not even the possibility of dark here, though it was still called *That First Night*. There was a fourth piece by Traci Jarman made with all kinds of materials, from charcoal to shreds of shingles to even bits of asphalt, all of it black except for the tinfoil. Here the three horses seemed set upon a path leadin through the heavens themselves. But is that where they was really goin? In such darkness? And so alone? Cal Carneros kept thinkin of Ed Ruscha's *Jumbo* with its sooty elephant but also *Ace* with its stygian textures lappin up against a blue word. Whether that was it or somethin else, Cal realized he'd stopped breathin.

Janice Brothwell had done her best to catch this . . . what was it? the start of a journey? . . . by usin black and gray eyeliner to draw the two riders and three horses. Brothwell's version, however, was reckless and messy enuf in its splatters to evoke another hat, black of course, which in turn seemed to reveal a third rider and even a fourth horse. Cal Carneros dismissed the composition in favor of odd sketches of gloomy paths patrolled by pale owls, *Untitled*, or some rain-drenched geological settin called *The Gate of the Mountain*. By Graciella Francis, Haddy Visick, and Chelsea Kitchen.

The last two works in that room, in watercolor and pencil, were of a strikin woman, presumably the *Allison March* that titled them both. To her credit this Marsha Naylor rendered with brushstrokes hardly holdin any paint an image of a woman who looked both scared and ready to fight. Not an easy thing to achieve, especially with such blurry washes. One eye seemed about to dart away from wherever she was lookin, while the other stayed fixed on Cal. And though there was really no similarities, no nudity, no bubble gum, maybe just utter frankness, both Cal and Shasta still got to talkin about Hannah Wilke's *S.O.S Starification Object Series*, 1974.

The second work, though, was very different. Rico described it as pugilistic. Usin only pencil, Lou Keele had caught a similar divid-edness, but instead of depictin this division in the subject's eyes, he focused instead on the position of her head, tilted in a way that might telegraph a sprint for an exit, or, if she was a fighter, show the start of a practiced recoil that's already loadin up an ensuant strike. *I know this feelin,* Cal remarked. *Me too,* Shasta added.

The program indicated that Chamber One concerned events up to and includin Wednesday, October 27, 1982. Chamber Two moved that calendar a day forward, dedicated to events occurin on Thursday, October 28, 1982.

The first piece on the wall to the right was by a Lydia Palmer, a gynecologist who for reasons beyond what the piece would reveal had created a fairly rudimentary diorama of two riders, again the boy with the white cowboy hat on the black horse, apparently a mare, followed by that dark bay horse, less reddish here, loaded up with gear and hay, with the brown girl on the blue horse takin up the rear. These were basically dolls of some sort and fairly silly. The near-spent fire was adequately conjured with broken crayons, but it was the fallen tree in their midst that was not only real wood but, as the wall didac-tic declared, *A skelf from the actual tree!* Whatever that meant. But once again, Cal couldn't shake the feelin that somethin here was missin, and even worse, this loomin sense of incompleteness, whatever that was, continued to fill him with dread, though he could neither say why nor admit as much to his friends.

Beyond this piece waited a few drawins and paintins and one

mixed-media sculpture portrayin horses bein ridden up a river of pebbles or sand or some other rocky material. The two-dimensional works seemed to have no clue about perspective lines and so portrayed somethin no horse could ever go up. The sculpture more demonstrably displayed this unrealistic steepness. However, except for this shared aspect, the rest of the elements were dramatically different, from how the horses looked to the young girl's appearance, who accordin to some of the titles was a Landry Gatestone, to the boy who accordin to other titles was someone named Kalin March. He continued to wear that white cowboy hat. The girl had on a hat too, but what stuck out was her pink raincoat. Many of these by Bhanu Irarte, Si Watts, and Andrew Rivetti.

Then more work by Joanne Willden. Cal recognized her style at once, them smears of ash, teal, and charcoal. He recognized the parkin lot too, though now instead of night it was mornin, now instead of the boy it was *His Mother*, or so the title read. Except what stood out here weren't her but the gloomy and broodin canyon that waited beyond, sheered in black streaks, risin up to greater heights with still more formidable mountainscapes lyin hazy and indeterminate beyond. It was this exercise in scale that caught up Cal Carneros, Rico too, who mumbled, *I know where she ain't goin.*

Les Fadley's oils, what came next, were far more skillfully applied if limited in their ambition, focusin close-up on Allison March's features, distraught but determined, anxious but determined, afraid but determined. It was titled *Determined* too, and that was where Cal caught on to the tricky valence at work here: as if this mother was not only determined to make a go of it, whatever that meant, but likewise hopelessly determined by the events she couldn't fully perceive let alone control. There was also no denyin somethin near sensual about these oozes of oils, how every brushstroke seemed to edge closer to the thick chromatic territories desire requires as well as creates. Over all though, like that description ain't very good, the piece weren't very good either. Cal, Shasta, and Rico were all in agreement about that, but somethin about it also made them linger. *It's as if what matters here,* Shasta said, *isn't the paintin but rather the woman herself.* They spoke then about Berthe Morisot, Manet's paintins of her, but more so Morisot's own paintins, especially her self-portraits.

Cal was almost grateful for the pieces that followed: half-hearted attempts at portrayin someone named Kelly Porch. Assumin he was real, and maybe that was the volume-up assumption that had started to overwhelm Cal on this night, what was requirin somethin else of him, of them all, some assembly required, makin the question of Art

beside the point, was how all here, and that went for the folks in attendance too, as well as even their Church, was tryin to relate and inter-
pret somethin very real. And keepin that in mind, the irrelevance of
the thing hangin on a wall or the lyrics loftin through the air or even
this actual slice of orange cake, a goshdarn tasty piece of cake too,
handed to him just then on a paper plate, Cal Carneros did his best
to perceive beyond the poor lines who this Kelly Porch actually was:
broad fer sure, blond, likely, with beautiful lips. Maybe he was just a
big beautiful boy. Maybe he really did like to wear one of them big
rodeo belt buckles. Maybe he was even wearin one right now. Was
he in the Time Gallery tonight? But Cal also couldn't help feelin that
there was somethin wild and mean and maybe broken about him too.
That quality, maybe unfairly inferred from poor draftsmanship, set
Cal's mind to seek out this Kelly Porch after he got through Chamber
Five. Surely he was here.

More versions of the mother, Allison March, came next, many of
these in hard pencil, though there were some in ballpoint and crayon
too. She was now also depicted in the company of some withered cuss
with a Rottweiler named Mr. Bucket #5. *With Old Porch* read the title.
They'd seen him before, in Chamber One. Cal Carneros couldn't say he
looked all that old. While Shasta and Rico were more forgivin, Cal disliked most of the drawins. One canvas, though, did manage a portrait
in splotched ink that was at least evocative. *Faute de mieux, it does remind
me of Franz Kline,* Rico muttered to Shasta, *I mean if he'd dedicated hisself
to the figurative.* Shasta answered with a snort of derision but still gave
Rico's arm a squeeze.

The three then stepped back, almost simultaneously, takin in the
various portraits at once. Some must have been copied off photographs. One was even drawn on a newspaper clippin beneath a photograph that might well've been of the actual Old Porch. Unfortunately
or fortunately, any text detailin the subject or source was vanquished
by the ink required for this ghost of a face sketched out beneath the
black-and-white reproduced image. Cal doubted one was much better
than the other, but together this dyad seemed to vibrate toward enuf
of a resemblance that they figured they could recognize this fella if he
was nearby eatin orange cake. A hat tip then to Melissa Grant, Crystal
Garp, and Dawn Ana Hobbs.

How astonishin that Cal had already previewed all these pieces!
Dozens of times too! Rico, Shasta, and him had hung them, lit them, lit
them again, and not once had Cal felt as disarmed as he was now before
their collective impression, like he was seein them for the first time
and only now graspin the darkness loomin up ahead. What was that

Leonard Cohen line? *As our eyes grow accustomed to sight they armor themselves against wonder.* In Cal's case that armor was fallin away, though it weren't wonder he was beholdin.

One paintin by a Thegan Olson had the girl, this Landry Gatestone, up on a hill, on her blue horse, named Jojo, the wall didactic informed the curious, though neither the azures nor the grays nor much of the girl either was visible, cast in silhouette by a bar of sunlight breakin through the storm broilin above, pausin the three men at the base of the hill, their hands flung up before their eyes, like here was a religious revelation, and maybe it was just that. Though for whom? Because these men couldn't see it. And the oils, the way they was dappled and merged, the way it all blurred, showed how not even the artist let alone the viewer had a right to behold this vision any better. Cal was again at the cemetery and approachin a grave too. He found hisself moved, like he could feel more was fulminatin here in these geometries than just what this Thegan Olson thought he was musterin, and he was musterin all he had too, givin all he was over to this canvas, paints, gobs of soil, maybe even a fragment of bone, scraps of who knows what in the name of some dangerous texture. In fact more of consequence than the subjects themselves, and well beyond any cause carried out under the tattered flag of representation, was this sense that what answers the world we dare lay claim to is forever beyond us, a world-swallowin obscurity only now and then rent through with blasts of humblin illumination we are still too unworthy to apprehend. Unfairly the likes of Caravaggio or even Lelio Orsi's *The Temptation of Saint Anthony* came to Cal's mind, which he didn't share with Rico and Shasta, though he did compliment them on their choice of frame: cherry wood with a wide curved profile and a narrow inner lip of gold.

Next came a series of unfinished sketches in watercolors, ink, pastels, with a few in oil, of what appeared to be a dead horse lyin on his side toward the base of that previously seen steep slope of pebbles and otherwise rocky slipperiness. He was a big liver chestnut horse, a stallion by the look of him, and he appeared to have been shot twice. At least there was blood on his head and chest. Somethin was wrong with one of the legs. Maybe he'd busted the leg and been put down. It weren't a pleasant sight. And the massive gold baroque cartouche Shasta had selected to enclose a good many of the fragments weren't helpin any, though Cal still appreciated her contrivance. Accordin to the titles the horse's name was *Cavalry.* And were those asters among the rocks? They seemed too much in bloom for the month, or maybe it was their last bloom. Some of the artists responsible for these efforts included Glenn Taylor, Luc Chitnis, and Dorothy Meyers.

Now here was somethin interestin: set in an already small rococo frame was an even smaller oil on plywood. The paintin was called *Unholy Us,* and it was by some fella named Lee Peart. It was detailed as all heck. With the help of the wall didactic, Cal could identify Kelly Porch as well as what he presumed were his two brothers, Sean and Shelly. There was also a fella named Billings Gale who looked nothin like the brothers. In the center stood Egan Porch, the fiercest of the lot. Cal had to give Lee Peart this much credit: he'd managed to capture some mix of terrifyin madness in that young man's face. It was almost more vibrant than the blood splattered on his jeans, shirt, and cheeks. And why so much blood? Was it just artistic license? Was this Lee Peart partial to crimson?

Whatever the case, it was too much. It made Cal think of that old art school saw, the story about someone's brother who lived a looked-after life, mostly in institutes, who no matter what was given to him, whether paint or food or drink, and that went for spit and, sorry to say it, even piss and poop, he'd just smear it on the nearest wall or floor, but always like he was tryin to get somewhere, see somethin more clearly, even if in the end he just left behind a mess that neither he nor them who had to clean it up could find any meanin in.

Shasta, though, had at least an explanation for the two wounds. She figured the horse was first shot from above, in the chest, and then this Egan fella had to finish off his stallion with a shot to the head. Rico remained confused by the broken leg. He even briefly complained of dizziness. Cal took another bite of orange cake, which was mighty fortifyin, and offered the rest to Rico, who didn't want it and gave it to Shasta, who gobbled up what was left.

Still more art awaited. Here was a silly Saint Bernard that looked like Cujo. Here was a lovely home with a big wraparound porch that surely was drawn from a photograph. But who was this guy near the front door vomitin on that veranda? One title read *Old Porch Tells His Truth.* Now this figure here didn't look much like them earlier ones, though maybe Cal could detect some similarities. Even in this inadequate renderin, worse than a poor courtroom sketch, though done in what looked like acrylic, the artist had still somehow managed to capture a man who was as coiled up as he was all hunched over. In fact in most of the attempts to portray him, this Porch fella always seemed ready to strike. Cal couldn't take his eyes off him.

After that, Orwin Porch was replaced by more sketches and caricatures of the Allison March lady, mostly identifiable because of her dirty blond hair, though now she was with another woman named Sondra Gatestone. Who were these two to each other? Cal wondered if they was in the gallery too, maybe even with the boy, that Kalin March, and the girl, that Landry Gatestone. Maybe all of them was here! Includin the whole Porch family! Cal couldn't shake the feelin that maybe some of the folks he'd already smiled at or nodded to, all of whom had at once returned his smile and nod, just might make an appearance in some of the likenesses hangin on his walls. Cal said as much to Rico and Shasta, and they all agreed to pay better attention to who was in the room.

None of them cared much for the lemon cake painted on a paper plate or a mountain range on a strip of cardboard. Those by Pinegar Nelson and Lewis Lang, with the other pieces by Nikki Cliff and Mina Berry. Rico had framed them usin tacked-up strips of linen patterned with bricks. *After all, a frame, as SJ put it, is also a fabrick,* Rico quipped. Shasta full-on snorted. Cal shook his head. Too much art school.

The last works in Chamber Two were paintins of a hole in the side of the mountain. They was both called *Mine* and near identical too, hangin on either side of the hallway that led to Chamber Three.

It was in that hallway, on one of the walls, that Shasta had expertly stenciled *All I know is a door into the dark* from a poem entitled *The Forge*.

Cal weren't no stranger to that short passage, but on that particular night it did seem a little bit longer and a little bit darker, and it was also deserted, as if no one wanted to linger there before those unframed pieces of slate and smudged chalk. Shasta and Rico had hung them too, but they still fled, either out of dread or in search of more tequila. Most of them slate pieces were by Gia Rockit, Fali Nihonmatsu, and Cabbot Kaprielian.

By comparison Chamber Three, dedicated to events occurin on Friday, October 29, 1982, was a return to lightness with various pieces seemin to emanate light threefold, Cal's eyes waterin some in their effulgent sparkle. The first wall held what Shasta considered framed listicles or, accordin to Rico, channeled the spirit of Rausch-enberg: boxed arrangements of gear, which included but weren't limited to a canteen; flatware; one Swiss Army knife; a hatchet; used and unused tea candles; one sleepin bag; tarps, with one cut up and another torn up; reins; saddles; a packsaddle; gauze; two lariats; one reata; a size small Lee Storm Rider denim jacket with corduroy collar; and bags of oats and hay, which Rico and Shasta complained the most about because its presence here seemed only for effect. There was also a green poncho slicker, which was supposedly the same size and color as the one that Kalin March had worn, and a little pink raincoat, which was supposedly identical in brand and year to the one that Landry Gatestone had worn, the size of which startled Cal Carneros, because it butted him up against what Rico declared was *the ontic ontology of this little girl,* just how small she must've been. Not that any of this stuff, with maybe the exception of that splinter in that diorama back in Chamber Two, was the real McCoy, which the program stated clearly enuf.

Then there was this detailed black ink drawin of a white or gray mountain goat. After that was a small glass case that looked to contain a very real portion of a human nail caked with blood. *Old Porch's Thumbnail* read the title. Was that thing real? It looked real, the blood too, even if it weren't Old Porch's. What the heck did somethin like that even have to do with anythin here? Shasta and Rico had no answers. Rico even asked the fella next to him, also ganderin at such odd gruesomeness. *I rightly don't know how to give you the short of it,* the fella answered. *See, it's a long story.*

Cal Carneros didn't have a clue how any of this went together, but somehow in the name of a logic he couldn't quite track, it weren't particularly discordant either. For one thing, there was this prevailin sense of dread. For another Cal felt constantly on the edge of locatin some contiguous mood or sense evocative of higher places, literally, which offered vision, which one could get to only if one was brave enuf, very brave. Cal didn't yet know why courage was required because he couldn't really locate the source of his alarm, but he figured Gula Hickey, Koji Rangroo, and Janet Hawks, to name but a few, had the stuff to get past the disquiet possessin these replicas and make them feel like actual relics. That went for the likes of Kiki Hart, Vanessa Clark, and Jessica Bettencourt responsible for what was now dominatin the next two walls of this room: pieces depictin a canyon, a mountainside, or just some dead leaves encased in spectacular translucent ice. There were photographs, Polaroids, and slides. One artist used a looped piece of 16mm film to show ice formin around a branch only to melt away only to re-form again. At the center of this room was an actual stump bathed in light and housed in a refrigerated glass box wherein, over the course of twenty-four hours, water would drip onto the porous stump, freeze, break apart some of the wood, then melt, with a pan at the base collectin the runoff so a pump could redeliver the water back up to the top to recommence this destroyin rain and freeze. At the moment it was frozen again and hard to see due to the frosted condensation on the inside of the glass. Brightest of all, though, was what looked like a box of shattered glass, the crystal shards lit from all sides via slowly rotatin hot spots, which hurled snaps of brightness upon the surroundin pieces *and by that refracted light further texturizin all these various works,* as Shasta put it. *Rainbows on the walls,* as Rico put it.

Some of those pieces kissed by the movin fragments of colored light focused on *The Nine Screes,* as one title stated. These loose, semi-permanent rockslides were either drawn or painted, some on paper and canvas, others on chunks of concrete, or collaged with stones and dead weeds fastened or glued to heavy slabs of plywood. Here the wall didactic actually went so far as to claim that the weeds and rocks were from the actual screes. Standin before such phantasms of articulate shape givin way to articulations beyond the reach of human expression, Cal found hisself first thinkin of the likes of Sterne, Carrol, Mallarmé, Apollinaire, Cummings, Pignatari, Azeredo, and Campos. One work offered up three open boxes and encouraged handlin. The first box, assigned the letter α as well as the title *Aster Scree,* contained glassy pebbles and slipped as easily through Cal's fingers as sand through an hourglass. The second box, assigned the letter Ω as well as the title *Some of Scree Nine,* held rougher stones, which when returned to the box, created a murmurin music worthy of any lithophone. The third box, however, assigned the letter *N* as well as the title *Most of Scree Nine,* was a thing of heaviness and brutal edges that Cal's soft hands wanted nothin to do with. Takin credit for some of these encounters were folks like Hariram Abbasi, Heidi Letham, and Rashid Lannes.

Around this time Cal heard a ukulele comin from outside, joined soon by a woman with a pleasant-enuf voice singin what sounded like *Mouse, Mouse, what mountains did you bring down this time?* Then a banjo joined in, followed by another guitar, and then another voice, this time singin a new song, though with similar lyrics: *Mouse don't back down.* At some point Florence Gibbs joined in along with Ruddy Hal and Lamsyn Hayes. Cal would've headed out to the back to investigate further, except Rico's and Shasta's focus on the next piece refocused his own attention. It was called *Right Before the Fall* by Emilee Oldroyd. The wall didactic claimed the tableau was concerned with *the fabled Ninth Scree,* dedicated to *the pursuit of geologic modelin in motion,* incorporatin sand, crushed rock, as well as shredded cardboard, hammered metals, epoxied charcoal, and plenty more *modern detritus to evoke through such radical bricolage* the immensity of the disruption about to occur, which Cal, Shasta, and Rico had no idea about, even if they could still sense the residin instability here.

Shasta and Rico got away first, arguin about the various lariats and reatas they'd hung by basically hammerin big 60-penny nails into the wall. Initially they'd thought these vaguely yellow, green, and even violet ropes were kinda funny. They approved of the title too: *There Ain't No Property Without Rope.* Now, though, they felt engaged by somethin they still couldn't guess at and which, despite their growin curiosity, they wanted no part of.

Still, curiosity won out and they stayed with the work. Maybe it helped that they'd already emptied that tequila bottle and found the bong in the drawer beneath.

The piece by Treesje Treeangle in the alcove that interrupted the middle of the third wall, titled *Down Through Clouds,* presented a series of semitransparent screens hung at various heights and angles in a space that intermittently filled with fog. A projector that Cal had hidden hisself continuously projected on these screens images of mountains, horses, ice, a saddle horn, a saddle fender, a stirrup, then a long mane, a horse's nostril spillin steam, a narrow trail, runnin water, blue snow, all while the light slowly dimmed, then slowly brightened, all while a shadow was also somehow cast on the screens. At first Cal assumed the shadow was his own, or Shasta's or Rico's, the three finally withdrawin from the alcove completely in order to see that this shadow had nothin to do with them. This was Treesje Treeangle's work. She'd come in yesterday and worked through the night to accomplish the mystery. Cal applauded and Shasta and Rico broke out in giggles, accusin him of bein high, and in a way he was.

The music outside hadn't ceased, with snippets continuin to drift inside. *When waitin here weighs nothin at all, but you still gotta dance . . .* someone crooned, answered soon after by more voices makin the rhyme with *But we never stood a ghost of a chance . . .* It didn't stop there either, more lyrics like haikus, indirect but still born out of this strange history: *From west to east the crows fly home at dusk. Come dawn the mountains are gone to low clouds. Black pines were always there.* And this one:

> *Come on share your lesson.*
> *I'm ready to be taught.*
> *There ain't no chance of mornin.*
> *Tonight is all I've got.*

Cal hadn't forgotten the fake Remington on the pedestal and gave it only a glance until Shasta and Rico called him back because they'd recently found out the piece weren't a rip-off after all. Rico had made sure to insure it for one hundred thousand dollars. Cal still weren't impressed, even if he did recognize that what he was lookin at weren't so bad. It was of a rider headin with his horse down a crumblin hillside. Shen Dean was the owner and in addition to this original had provided his own version of the same sculpture, the rider made out of beeswax, the hillside out of fire starter squares. Shasta kept thinkin of Auguste Rodin's *Horseman,* which weren't even a sculpture but a gouache, possibly rendered from equine figures found in the British Museum. Neither Cal nor Rico were familiar with the studies, but they believed her. *Dare Ida to pass da horse text!* Rico did add, and Shasta found that hilarious, and Cal realized he didn't understand either of them. But he did appreciate their taste and wondered if a language intelligible to only the few is a requirement for liberatin the unusual instincts capable of achievin new things many more then go on to enjoy.

As far as Chamber Three was concerned all they had left was the fourth wall, which was centrally disturbed by that dark passage from Chamber Two and thus provided only enuf space for a few works, which included the one oil called *Hatch Porch.* Cal couldn't praise it enuf, especially the brushstrokes. Cal knew they hadn't seen this fella yet, and figured that was a mistake. This guy was clearly the star of whatever story he was a part of here: square jaw, solid cheekbones, full head of sandy reddish hair. Maybe the gray-blue eyes were *Porch-like* too: clear and icy. At least this Hatch's smile softened that glare some. Cal could get finicky all he wanted about technique, but he also knew that this here was good work. Well done, Brenda Mistry. Another artist Cal knew he'd better seek out soon. Beyond that there were a few small sketches of mountain ridges; these were titled *Kirk's Cirque* or *Katanogos* or *Friday Night.* There was also a weird little pen drawin on the back of an envelope called *Xanthos.* It was in red ink and featured a horse Cal hadn't seen anywhere else, eyes spillin tears, mouth agape. Claire Colter was the responsible party for this one, with Warwick Ahlström and Carla Leffert responsible for the rest on that wall in Chamber Three.

Shasta had provided the expert stencilin for the Jack Gilbert quote markin the way out of Chamber Three: *We must unlearn the constellations to see the stars.* Chamber Four was dedicated to events occurrin on Saturday, October 30, 1982.

When Cal was asked by his staff, includin Rico, though not Shasta, she didn't care, why the various rooms weren't referred to as, well, rooms, or galleries, or at least exhibition spaces, he divulged that some of the organizers expressed pleasure over the fact that the Time Gallery offered five spaces, which they had politely requested be referred to as *Chambers* for the duration of the event. They gave no explanation. Cal didn't put up a fuss; he would've called them chicken coops so long as no one messed with the payment due his way, and no one did. Even after what happened.

Another question that still comes up: why did this exhibit take place in Houston, Texas, and not, say, in more obvious locations like Orvop or Rome or, at the very least, Salt Lake City, which is far closer to where most of that night's attendees lived? The answer that goes down easiest is that the Time Gallery was available and willin. Just a bit of old-fashioned luck. Or *Providence* as one of the organizers had murmured on the phone, the phone havin been passed around so much on that call that Cal finally had no idea who he was talkin to.

As a few had divulged over the precedin months, the organizers not only liked Cal, they trusted him. And Cal made sure to communicate how grateful he was for that trust, also sharin that though he weren't a Church member hisself, several in his family were, referrin to members as Brother Andrews or Sister Demos was near second nature.

However, there is another answer as to why the show took place in Texas and not Utah, and it goes down a little rougher, though to be fair to the Church and Utahns in general, there ain't one part of this globe that ain't similarly afflicted by this tendency. Despite common sense, exceptional work born of a place is too often not welcome in that place.

See, the organizers did reach out first to galleries in Orvop, Rome, and eventually Salt Lake City. Sure some were willin only to get cold feet later. An owner would suddenly hit the brakes by sayin somethin along the lines of *We fear that what will be put on display here won't reflect the values of our community.* Cal Carneros had laughed plenty when he'd heard that pearl. And anyway, as he saw it, Art weren't an adherence to values but rather the work required to create better values.

He still credits Tyrone for teachin him that. Cal was born in late March and didn't think much about bein an Aries because of it's association with Mars, because it sounded like Ares, though as he eventually found out, the ram weren't really defined by war. He also found out it's hard to defect from your astrological sign. Not that any of them other signs ever offered him better sanctuary. None of which he knew about back in high school, holdin that army brochure an extra minute longer. Why not be a soldier? Why not follow orders? There was great ease in the thought of that, and though he'd yet to get in one fight, he knew in his teeth and his knuckles that like so many in his patrilineal line, he was the martial sort. He had a taste for it. He'd got socked hard once. It had knocked him down, but he'd got up too and could've gone for more except . . . the memory still pained him even if it was also so joyous . . . except he'd caught sight of his friend Tyrone spray-paintin a big pink rose on the backpack of that fist-throwin kid. That there not only got Cal smilin but thinkin too, and for no reason he'd ever trace, about a past summer, when he'd fallen off a lake dock into the coldest water he'd ever known. The camp folks had told him to dive or at least jump, but he'd stumbled and gone in sideways, slappin the water so hard, he'd not only lost his breath but his ear had got to hurtin somethin awful. If he weren't gonna die, he was surely gonna resurface deaf, but then as he'd sunk deeper he'd seen Rachel Garrett's long beautiful legs, and though they was blurry enuf to not count as seein anythin, they was still enuf. So Cal came up to tread water with her, what he was thinkin as he brushed hisself off before just walkin away from that fist-throwin kid. Hat tip to his friend Tyrone. Even better was how that fist-throwin kid came to like wearin around that pink rose. What Cal knew and now loved about Art, Tyrone could still be doin, if only he hadn't left Our Fabled Fairgrounds way too young because of a bullet that had no business goin his way, especially in a school, thanks to what was still considered part of that community's values. To heck with Ares. To heck with signs too. Cal was here for the pictures, still here for his friend Tyrone.

Cal even got to chucklin now as he began to peruse Chamber Four, wonderin what in the heck here so grievously contradicted this community's values? He didn't get it, though as he confronted a bronze by Doran N. Tolan, he did shiver some, goose bumps fer sure, and then like that his hair felt like it had suddenly gone wet to the scalp, wettin the back of his neck, a cold sweat even runnin down his spine to his butt crack. Now ain't that a weird way to feel when you're bone-dry? And what for? This thing of metal called *Old Porch in the Rain*? What was that Rodin aperçu? Somethin like *Patience is also a form of action.* Here was dark patience on display! Oh, Cal was in the cemetery now! Right there on the edge of a grave!

Cal Carneros circled the creation several more times. At first he was caught between a comparative puzzle devised by his own ramblin mind concernin two bronzes by Degas: *Horse Balking* and *Horse with Head Lowered.* Those figures weren't so much about likeness, though, sure, you could tell they was horses; what was at stake was movement and attitude. That was the case here: what was lackin in the renderin was made up for by the potential energy accumulated in the figure.

Cal Carneros was again struck by how somethin he'd unpacked and helped stage was only now havin this effect. Maybe it came down to context, to bein among those responsible for it, more than attendees, maybe celebrants, them who were right now viewin upon his walls more than divisible entities but rather complex mnemonics grantin them access to a history Cal was only just startin to glimpse. Like if he'd first come across a graffitied backpack with a pink rose on it without knowin the artist who had done it and who all it had changed.

But there was also somethin else about this hunk of metal, somethin havin to do more broadly with how, despite the apparent subject of the exhibition, that bein mainly the West, there were missin so many of the familiar tropes of wastelands, deserts, even the ruins of one-horse towns. No Monument Valley in sight. And yet this bronze did strike Cal as monument and mesa unto itself, and made so not by the sculptor but by the subject. Who was this Orwin Porch really? Was he here? Were they all here? Cal had half a mind to see if two horses were out back.

But the sculpture continued to hold him in its orbit as well as extended the effects of its immense mass to the other pieces in the room, watercolors and oils, one of laminate leather, another contained within a frame resemblin the curvature of a small apse, a tiny marble figure there that was blocky at best, though the movement was there too if not the rain. Somehow the bronze, though, achieved the storm at war, outside of as well as within this Old Porch, one hand pressin a mug against his swole belly, the other hand reachin up as if searchin for a handhold in the heavens to keep hisself from topplin over. Or if not to hold then grab, like a rifle over a door that weren't there? Pain aplenty suffused Doran N. Tolan's piece, but there was also aggression. This Mr. Porch weren't just doublin over but also coilin up, and no matter how many times Cal circled the piece, he couldn't make up his mind which it was. Would he fall or would he strike?

Other pieces included three topographic maps, the first designatin federal land holdins; the second, state land holdins; the third, private land holdins, all to the east of Orvop. A broken cereal bowl sat on a black plinth. Cal weren't much won over by Michelle Ploufe's ink drawin on rice paper of two hands, one absurdly large and scarred, the other boyish, cartoonishly small. He got quick enuf that the touchin was supposed to be the touchin point. The title *Father & Son* made that clear. But it was the fact that they didn't touch in Michelangelo's *Creation of Adam* that continued to generate so much energy and, like an arc light, well, light the many centuries since it was first created. Here, though, that potential was lost, a short circuit missin a bulb, an excess of power gone to ground. Here was the exact opposite of Tolan's bronze, risin up like a lightnin rod in the midst of an electrical storm, waitin for a moment that had nothin to do with topplin over or even lungin forward. That bein said, there was a settledness to these hands, a finishedness that seemed to deserve consideration, and it did hold Cal's attention an extra moment, until Rico's hand happened to touch his own, just grazed it at most, but, boy, did Cal Carneros jump. Rico apologized at once even as Shasta laughed over the overreaction, and that got Cal laughin too. What the heck had made him so jumpy? There sure weren't nothin spooky about the next piece either, a little glass case containin a tiny metal tube, opened to reveal a tiny scroll bedecked with script so small it was unreadable, even with the mounted magnifyin glass, which only revealed three words out of many: *I want you.*

The paintin with the Porch family surroundin their dead brother, the same chubby boy first seen back in Chamber One, back then very much alive, well, that was worth a shiver. Russel Porch here was rendered with primed underlayers paler than chalk. The wall didactic indicated this effect was accomplished with egg tempera. The program said the piece had been painted over ten times with the thinnest sheets of near-translucent white before the next coat was applied, which maybe accounted for the apparent ghostliness of the corpse and even the observers. By Miguel Remie. With similar pieces created by Nastasia Claybaugh, Juzo Racer, and Martine Sahu. Shasta found herself recallin *Son of a Gunman* by Larry A. Harris, though she claimed the memory was splotched, comin to her as heaps of orange, yellow, and chalk blue. She found herself reachin out for Rico. Rico welcomed her touch and brought up Rembrandt's *The Anatomy Lesson of Dr. Nicolaes Tulp.* Loosely speakin here Cal could see what Rico was gettin at as far as the composition was concerned, but Shasta found the reference a repudiation of any taste she once thought Rico in possession of. Rico found that worth a giggle, and Shasta fumed as she tightened her arm around his.

Then there was a bag of DORF RED DOG jerky stapled to a piece of particleboard. There were cliffs rendered with bones, and whether they was animal bones or somethin else neither the wall didactic nor the program made clear; topped with some compound of cotton, hairspray, and maybe paint conjured a confusion of both clouds and material. Another piece used fishin line strung between two tacks to suspend what looked like two pieces of cloth crudely cut out and slashed methodically to equal what the title claimed was *Mesh.* More and more drawins of landscapes followed, some heavy with plant life, others with runnin water, a lot with animals. Multiple perspectives of the three horses had been in abundance in all the rooms, but by Chamber Four the artistry was clearly gettin better. Here was the black mare in lush oils titled *Navidad.* Here was that blood bay geldin, also in oils, titled *Mouse*. Here was the gray-blue roan titled *Jojo*. Though these were the works of various artists, and accordin to the program created at different times, the paintins all chose the same perspective: viewin the three horses head-on. Years from now when Cal would encounter Lucian Freud's *Grey Gelding,* he would think again of this triptych without embarrassment. There was great achievement in these horses' eyes, alive with visions Cal Carneros could dream they'd share with him one day, though of course that was a day that would never come. As Cal would also think, they was a long ways from Segantini's *Spring in the Alps.*

Cal also began to revisit and admire more the organization. A lovely progression was at hand, especially where the horses were concerned, from the crude stick figures in Chamber One to these portraits, easily recognizable, their presence now palpable, more than merely familiar, nearly family. The horses were also no longer alone or with just the kids. More pieces, some with puppets, revealed them in the company of white owls perched on gray branches, or a beaver whose dark colors seemed to flow beyond itself into the little stream where it worked, or an old elk vanishin into trees. There were several versions of this old elk: cloaked by shadows beneath a canopy of trees hung with semi-diaphanous brume or slashed by rain or in some cases nearly consumed by thick folds of fog.

And then along came this big painter's tarp, roughly cut and in a frame like those where you might find a tanned hide strung up; the old elk painted there looked like both trophy and victor. Cal liked it; Cal didn't like it. He found he couldn't stand how the ambiguity felt petulant, but what really ate at him was how standin before such simple and pleasant renderins, and now he was thinkin about all the works with horses and animals, he still felt the clawin absence of somethin, somethin still unachieved, unfinished, somethin denied its inevitable arrival, that aspect without which all other aspects evaporated. It was like somethin or someone who walked beside all this had been omitted. Cal needed to discuss this with some of the artists. He tried to commit to memory the names Olivia Chang, Lochlyn La Morte, and Justin Voight.

Not that the animals could supplant the human enterprise for long. Here were the mothers again, and like the horses, the oily achievements were now notably better, though such quality came at a price: sallow tones revealed fatigue and gauntness, a retreat from confidence, in both the subjects and the artists; the wearyin toll of hearts afflicted by both hope and doubt. Cal found he almost couldn't look, but he couldn't look away either. Hadn't he said earlier that this exhibit was bad? He'd thought so fer sure. And it still was bad! There were no great artists on display tonight. And yet what was at work here kept renderin this circular question of artistry irrelevant. Shasta and Rico had left at some point but were now returnin, no doubt havin finished off whatever else was hidin in Cal's desk drawers. Probably chocolates. They at once started whisperin about needin more.

Cal turned his attention then to a series of fine sketches on the back of postcards: of Egan Porch, Kelly Porch, and the one called Billings, loadin ATVs onto a trailer. Fer some reason they clutched ax handles. There was also a Trans Am and a girl with a broken nose. Accordin to the wall didactic, there were two more Porch boys: Sean and Shelly. One sketch got them all in, and except for the girl with the broken nose, who was starin at the ATVs, there weren't much kindness in their eyes. Cal moved on, never thinkin to wonder what was on the other side of them postcards.

The next thing, a dustbin full of ashes, weren't nothin to Cal but a run at sensation. He'd seen such moves performed countless times by students in art school. Shasta ridiculed it as well. The only trouble was that this particular piece weren't for sale. Currency was a compression after all or a reduction or *the praxis of reference* as one of Cal's professors once asserted. As Cal liked to put it: *Money is a caricature of value.* Which if nothin else did suggest he weren't ever gonna be no great businessman. Though this business here before them weren't about business. Like so many of the works in the Time Gallery that night, whether presold or not for sale, this dustbin of ashes just stood there like yet another piece of harrowin evidence. By Pat Mason. The other stuff was by Zack Solomon and Kara Ongg.

A series of tempera paintins by different artists returned to that boy in his now very gray cowboy hat. He seemed sick. The girl was lookin after him while he crouched, while he vomited, while he slept under mounds of blankets by a strugglin fire. The morbidezza achieved with the colors and brushstrokes was astonishin, weren't Cal full of contradictions tonight, technique bequeathin to the viewer a scene of gentle carin. Cal's thoughts at once flew to Landry Gatestone. And then to Kalin March. Were they okay? Surely they both survived whatever this ordeal was, right? Or was this here a prophecy he was only now comin to recognize? Is that what was goin on here? A funereal procession on behalf of these two lost souls? Was he in fact not hostin an exhibition but a memorial? Cal felt shocked as well as foolish, because of course these children didn't survive. Sure, a part of him wanted to seek them out in that crowd that minute, though the greater part, maybe the better part, had but to take in the immense surroundins depicted here, towerin over the children, to see what odds were set against them. Everywhere they were dwarfed by their circumstances, whether a cold gray meadow, even when draggin themselves away from some small body of green-gray water, or huddled against mighty rocks overwhelmed by walls of still darker stone above. Cal didn't even want to think about the three horses. Had they survived? Cal felt his face flush. He even asked Rico and Shasta if they thought the horses and the kids were dead. Their faces flushed too.

More animals continued to appear, these apparitions drawn variously with white pencil or white chalk on gray paper or cloth the color of fair eggshells. Coyotes? A pack of wolves? The absurdities only increased: elephants, giraffes, even lions. Like they had all somehow joined the same dream of a creature parade.

Then suddenly there was a drawin of just a mule that was both as dreamy as the rest but also still a part of this world, an effect likely accomplished by a wealth of expertly offered details subsequently blurred. Or perhaps this artist was just better than the others at producin strange snapshots of a safari in Utah. Cal Carneros had no answers except that it got him thinkin of Thomas Hart Benton's *Trail Riders.* He also just liked the mule. By Shana Whiting. The rest were by Ralph Flores, Judith Flannigan, and Suki Clover.

Returnin to the fourth wall in Chamber Four, Cal Carneros faced what they'd got to callin the Cirque Wall. He'd liked this part when they'd hung it, its ordonnance and almost casual presentation of verticality; now, though, a new context had begun to reinform within him the staggerin consequences of such heights.

Close to that wall, upon a stand, rested a big ziplock bag, the interior of which was smeared with somethin resemblin molasses. Another stand displayed two discharged casins. But these artifacts hardly seemed significant compared to the wall itself, incidentally the widest and tallest wall in the Time Gallery, risin like a cathedral to the skylights, at that moment black with night. All agreed it was the ideal location to present so many pieces of the cliffs themselves, what some titles called *The Upecksay Headwall* or more generally *Kirk's Cirque,* comprised of a score and more of small etchins, paintins, trompe l'oeils, treated photographs, diaphanous washes marked with the language of illegible testimony, plus a bunch of other representations carryin out a greater examination of that scarred, oft-crumblin, and in places ledged face. Plenty of the pieces also offered glimpses of the talus at the base. Not a one granted a vision of the summit. Quite a few portrayed what looked like a column or at least a geological protrusion risin from the cirque floor to the limits of the Time Gallery wall. Those were hung just to the side of the door leadin back to Chamber Three.

Rico thought he could now discern a path that crisscrossed the pillar. Shasta, however, pointed out how many of these minute ledges, or what Rico kept callin catwalks, eventually dead-ended. In fact the more they looked, the more of these lines they discovered, many terminatin at the pillar, a few transectin it, most continuin out of sight and purpose. In one breath the wall could appear like shattered glass about to collapse; in another a maze; in another it seemed encoded with a message or signal they were helpless to decipher. But they kept lookin. They would have to go talk again with Stacey Sharma, Jon Bush, and Daris Tan, who along with creatin many of the pieces hangin on that wall had spent all last night and this mornin creatin this backdrop of scriptless lines.

One tiny woodcut upon this grand geological collage, which Shasta had placed in a rocklike iron quatrefoil frame, revealed the girl, Landry Gatestone, on a ledge. Fittingly, it was hung higher up. Absurdly, she was still atop her blue horse. A second woodcut, just as tiny as the first, also framed in metal, had the boy, Kalin March, on a ledge as well; he too was still atop that black mare, still leadin the geldin. Still higher hung a large tapestry that, aside from illustratin several stages of the ascendant journey, offered within a weave of black and blue a big old moon peekin through a churn of clouds, its fullness dazzlin what Cal, Shasta, and Rico had over the previous weeks assumed were imperfections in the threads but now agreed had to be fallin snow, an effect that hardly obviated the dominant question: were they supposed to believe that such youngness was actually ridin horses up such a monstrous cliff? Unless this wall weren't ever really a wall but a slope of some scalable sort with plenty of muddy trails? A notion that was all too quickly contradicted by the evidence before them. Cal found hisself recallin both Turner's and Courbet's *Dents du Midi* before tryin then to superimpose George Stubbs's *Whistlejacket*, the horse of course, upon the scene, though that formal association was quickly snatched away by the loomin rock he was bendin over backwards to take in. Delacroix's *Moroccan Horseman Crossing a Ford* also tried to challenge these cliffs with no success. The same went for the likes of Richard Hambleton's *Marlboro Lights*. The spaces of Sam Francis also came to mind.

Cal Carneros, Shasta, and Rico finally started to laugh. Shasta said she had to call her girlfriend. Now that was new: neither Cal nor Rico had ever heard Shasta mention a girlfriend. Cal realized he wanted to get out of there too. He even looked around for some other attendees to strike up a conversation with but discovered that they were now alone. He finally announced to Rico that he was headin to the back patio. Rico said he'd do the same. But neither Cal, Rico, nor even Shasta made good on their intentions. Props were due to those who had created out of this publicly performed vertigo a personal fugue of centripetal refusal.

Shasta would later blame the hour: *When you get past midnight, all kinds of weird effed-up stuff becomes available.* Cal would chalk it up to a kind of collective vividness created by the chronology and its relation to actual happenings, the result bein that the numerous pieces not only vanished but succeeded as well in vanishin the walls of the various spaces, in some ways vanishin the gallery itself. *Sometimes you felt like there wasn't even a floor,* Rico would say. At one point Cal Carneros swore that he felt hard rock under his feet and even cold mountain air on his cheeks. Shasta claimed to have smelled pine. Rico said with some fear in his voice that he'd smelled smoke *and somethin sweeter, somethin worse.*

Between Chambers One and Two, Shasta had stencilled a quote by Clarice Lispector: *Do you ever suddenly find it strange to be yourself?* She thought of it now, even as they passed through the last narrow hallway marked by another quote, this one by Hannah Arendt: *Violence can destroy power; it is utterly incapable of creatin it.*

Chamber Five, dedicated to events occurin on Sunday, October 31, 1982, was barely illuminated. The first oil paintin, a tableau of the mothers beside a black river in the middle of a blacker night, seemed to float on a ribbon of light. Another oil paintin, just as dark, portrayed some of the Porch boys in bed asleep, with one window revealin through smudged glass a dawn about to take hold. The window weren't bigger than a postage stamp, but if you looked close, you could just about make out high mountain peaks comin to fire. By Ned Trimble and Brinn Black.

Not that there weren't amusements, like fer example one dimly lit and very empty tin can; it sat unfastened on its own plinth with no description in the program, just the title on the nearby wall: *Beans.* The artist was someone named Lori Zide.

And then there was the landscape. That's what it was called too: *Morning Landscape.* The piece was a mix of oils beneath a collage of photographs overpainted with acrylics, the photographs presumably of the actual cliffs encountered by the kids, with many of the bluffs crowned by a long line of brightly rendered pine trees. Title aside, the day was comin up fer sure. What shadows were there seemed to ebb; at least they weren't so dark. And the storm that had haunted the previous four chambers was gone. The skies were wide and clear. The snow was bright and blue. You could feel the rapture of the place, especially in the sense of just how vast it was, and undisturbed too, except maybe for a scatterin of birds here and there, wings spread wide, risin in the light. And then Cal, Shasta, and Rico discovered the girl: Landry Gatestone, enuf off to the left to seem unimportant, small enuf to be near invisible, on the edge of one of the higher cliffs, just a speck standin by herself atop a rock amidst the snowpack, with a backdrop of trees, but also with the tiniest bloom of red mist beside her head, enuf to not just captivate the air but also stain the snow. A masterful and singular work by Pril Niehaus.

Is that blood?! Shasta demanded, shocked that she hadn't seen it before.

What else could it be? Rico answered but like he didn't want to answer.

Cal realized he was feelin sick, sick enuf to burn up, though he didn't burn up, sick enuf to skedaddle, though he didn't skedaddle. Maybe because of the devotions declared early on by the organizers, Cal had anticipated the prevailin presence of belief biases anathema to discovery, a frequent result of religion that he especially loathed and professionally dismissed. Absent here, though, were any such bondieuseries let alone more calculatin faith propaganda. Quite the contrary, these walls, his walls, were bedecked with doubt, sufferin, death, beauty, glory even, however momentary, and then ultimately horror. Cal Carneros hurt. He weren't just in the cemetery now, and he weren't at the edge of any grave either. He was standin in one. What felt like his own.

Here next was a simple watercolor of a church. Here was the same map of federal land holdins they'd seen earlier but marked differently and with a red sharpie. That went for maps of state holdins and private land holdins. Here was a snowball made of rock and shards of plastic that looked like the end of a mace. Here was a photorealistic paintin of the two mothers, their faces streaked with ice and blood. That one was called *Accused.* Here was a helicopter. Here was Kalin March, alone, upon the black mare, leadin away not only the blood bay but the blue Arabian as well. By itself, on a base built out of welded rebar, stood a glass case enclosin an old single-action Colt Peacemaker atop a sack of purple so dark, it surely was black.

At first Cal Carneros experienced the oddest association: of hisself as a boy with a gift from his daddy, a basketball, which he'd loved, just not to bounce. He'd cleaned it at once, tried even to polish it. He just loved the shape and feel and the design. It was a wonderful present.

His daddy had thought the gift a failure, but Cal had cherished that ball. The wall didactic here said the firearm had been made in 1873. Cal knew it was a replica, he'd handled the thing, but tonight he had his doubts. As much as its silvery and shiny surfaces gleamed under the bright spot, the weapon's shimmer also seemed to devour light. What looked like names were inscribed in black on the frame but in a script so small that neither Cal nor Shasta nor Rico could read it.

Plenty more waited for them in that Chamber Five, but the one that snatched up Cal recalled John Singer Sargent's *Simplon Pass* with its hasty strokes of blues, whites, pinks, and muddy greens, which only a few steps of distance resolved into a tumblin clear mountain brook. However, that paintin faced an Alp ascent, while this one offered the terminus of a descent: a wide desolate field in fast, messy impasto strokes, makin the mud seem near substantial as meat, if splotched too with snow and frequent clumps of dead grass. It provoked in Cal a suspicion of remarkable coherence, like there was an intricate well formulated music at play upon the surface of that chaotic canvas. Cal had already put aside those quodlibetary quibbles between Abstraction and Realism, Ontology and Phenomenology, like four small yappin dogs, in favor of this visible if elusive melody that he would never hear let alone be able to whistle. The wind moved here. More than that. Off in the distance stood two old posts, presumably once supportin a gate, presumably once part of a fence. Cal Carneros just couldn't stop starin. He wanted to be there. He vowed to go there. He never wanted to see the place again. *Pillars Meadow* the first line of the title read. *Before Noon* read the second line.

Who would've thought that noon could prove the darkest hour? Cal felt so overwhelmed, he had to force hisself to focus on the artifice alone, remindin hisself how all these pieces were the work of homespun artists, amateurs, good folks with just a desire to express themselves though line and color in order to relate a history that another might pause before and offer their thoughts. Except Cal Carneros felt more than paused. He felt buried.

Over so many decades Cal had conversed with the dead, only late in his life comin to wonder if it was all just some dumb practice to grind down the minutes. Or was that wrong? Did such dialogues in fact confide a better way to live? At the very least Cal Carneros must right now seek out this last bunch of artists, the livin ones, at this moment in his gallery: Laura Wall, Jennifer Agius, Elsa Sarantopoulo, Judd Rinaldi, Paige Costales, Louis Battocchio, Nora Dall, and Jack Behrstock. Jack Behrstock and Pril Niehaus fer sure. Their paintins deserved special commendation. That went for Joanne Willden too.

953

Cal Carneros must make a speech, no matter how late it was. Except once again Cal didn't depart right then. The mass, the gravity, did not reside with the creators. He really weren't feelin well.

Together with Shasta and Rico, Cal faced the last pieces, absorbin what was clearly the work of the best artists, postulatin that they was likely professionals, and they were not, or wildly inspired by whatever rage and grief was necessary to find the movement required to transcend, however briefly, their own prevailin mediocrity. The results left them all breathless. Shasta literally began to pant, Cal realizin that they not only had to get her outside, they all needed fresh air, Cal orderin Rico to lend a hand, who of course obliged at once, though in the end Shasta was fine and had to help Cal carry out Rico, who collapsed a moment later.

Despite assumptions, Rico G. had not passed out because of the tequila and marijuana runnin riot in his system but because his last name weren't just G. for G but G. for Gale, and while takin in those final paintins in Chamber Five, he had finally convinced hisself that the Billings Gale he'd first spied in the piece titled *Unholy Us,* in Chamber Two, might just be the very same brother he'd hardly known and mostly heard hard rumors about throughout his life. As others had handled the wall didactics, and Rico had only just tonight regarded the program with any attention, the name had finally struck him with blindin force. Gale weren't that uncommon, but Billings was an unusual name, and the two together . . . Rico had only ever heard of one Billings Gale, his brother, or really his half brother from his mother's previous marriage, though her son was not the son of her then-husband but the son of a man she'd found herself in bed with *with teeth worse than rubble.* It was a confusin story that got no help from photographs stored somewhere where Rico weren't now. Back in Chamber Two Rico had laughed, assumin he was wrong, tryin to argue with hisself to stay put in the *ain't-that-a-weird-coincidence* corner, *this is just art,* but for some reason by Chamber Five, in the dimness of that space, in the loneliness that had come to linger there, he'd lost hold of what he kept tryin to force hisself to think, and that's when he started to think soundly and lost track of how to breathe.

Later, Cal Carneros would wonder if Rico's possible heritage was the real reason his gallery had been selected for this show, not because of its supposedly meaninful five spaces, nor due to Cal's affable nature, but rather because Rico G., Rico Gale, was in fact connected to the story underlyin all these bits and pieces, previously *disjecta membra,* strewn throughout various counties, states, and even abroad, now reassembled here, just fer a night, under Cal's ruf.

Once Rico had recovered from his *faintin spell*, as Shasta teasinly referred to the episode, Cal finally took off in search of the artists he'd sworn to hisself to meet, right after he'd finished deliverin that rousin Great-Job-Everyone! speech, which he began organizin in his head as he raced for the small stage on the back patio, a preoccupation that temporarily blinded him to the fact that everythin had changed. There was no more music; all the musicians had left. In fact the back patio was nearly deserted.

Sure, some folks still lingered, but now when they spoke, their voices stayed hushed, and too soon they was huggin one another and sayin their goodbyes, in many cases tearfully. Cal kept his own good-byes hushed as well. Shasta was eventually picked up by her girlfriend, who never did understand what Shasta had spent the rest of that night tryin to explain to her until Shasta broke up with her. Rico headed home to call friends, soundin more inebriated than he was earlier, and by that point he was pretty sober; his friends chalked up the babblin to just Rico bein Rico.

Cal continued to seek out the artists. There weren't but a dozen folks left. Joanne Willden, Pril Niehaus, and Jack Behrstock were supposedly still there, just never in the same room Cal was in, until it turned out they'd all left hours ago. That bein said, before Pinegar Nelson departed she made a point of findin Cal. She wanted to offer her thanks and appreciation. He asked if she was one of the artists. When she described the lemon cake on a paper plate, Cal managed to swallow his disappointment in the name of necessary pleasantries. He inquired about her still life, and Pinegar Nelson modestly described how she'd painted the cake from memory. *I've never even taken an art class, but I sure did like that cake. Sondra Gatestone baked it for a church function she was hostin, and we got to talkin. This was long before anythin had happened that might inspire a paintin.* Cal got curious then: *Do you think you still would've painted the lemon cake if none of those events had taken place?* Pinegar Nelson blushed brighter then than a jar of Sondra Gatestone's blackberry jelly, as if Cal had just made a most ostrobogulous proposition, though it was merely confusion that had lit up her face like so, with maybe a tint of unnecessary shame for never havin considered the question before. *I rightly don't know, Mr. Carneros, but . . . I think no. I think I would not have painted that lemon cake. I'm sorry to have to say so.*

More back-and-forth ensued, but nothin more was revealed, and Cal Carneros left her company feelin suddenly deflated.

Hardly anyone was left now, and those who were were on the way out. Anyway, whatever little crumbs these stragglers might've offered would not have delivered the satisfaction Cal was cravin. Cruelest was knowin that just a little while ago, and fer a few hours too, so many of them had been there in his gallery, in the know, just standin there shoulder to shoulder, dancin, singin, sharin tales, and he'd been too stupid to take advantage of that.

At least Cal Carneros had come to accept that this exhibit, if that's what it really was, had collectively met his criteria: not merely a series of dangerous graves but graves that were dangerously haunted. Late in his life Cal would conclude that what had haunted *The Pillars Meadow Show* exhibit was ultimately its own incompleteness, which impossibly seemed to incarnate more than merely promise the completin part.

The next mornin, March 1, a Wednesday, Cal Carneros discovered that his gallery had been robbed. It was vaguely amusin and at worst a hassle. The would-be thieves had smashed through the front window and broken apart several office drawers even though not one drawer was locked. In fact it turned out the front door had been left unlocked too, with the old alarm system left off as well. Some file cabinets were dumped on their sides for no discernible reason, and then the back door was busted through, though it had an easily turned deadbolt.

Not one piece of art was touched. Maybe some loose dollars and change had been made off with, but the larger sums had already been deposited earlier in the day. One officer asked if the stuff on the wall was considered art. *It ain't wallpaper,* Cal had answered.

Remarkably by lunchtime the back door was repaired, the broken glass swept up, and a sheet of plywood screwed in place to cover the hole. Any strewn papers were gathered up in a box, ready for future sortin. That was pretty much the sum of it. Cal Carneros took Shasta and Rico out for a nice lunch. He'd been rethinkin the show's original agreement for three days. *What about three weeks?* he had asked Rico and Shasta. They were game. People ought to see it. Sippin his ice tea, Cal began dreamin of a national tour, or at least partnerin with three gallery owners he was close to in Boston, Chicago, and on Long Island. He was thinkin of callin the assembly *Artifacts. What do you think?* Rico loved this sort of thing. *How about, like, breakin it up so it's Art · I · Facts? You know, with a dot between each part?* Cal wasn't sure. Shasta suggested makin it sound like a question: *Arty Facts?* Rico laughed hysterically, and Shasta got angry, and Cal remained on the fence, but he saw a big future for this experience, and he was determined to share it with as many folks as he could and make some money along the way too.

Cal was hooked in the same way that, thirteen years later, assorted folks, randomly encounterin one another at that July fourth Orvop City parade, spontaneously chose to reenact in an old gym the events that occurred that fabled Thursday night in the Awides Mine. When Cal inevitably got wind of that happenin, and by then he was very much in the know about Kalin March and Landry Gatestone, he was surprised to hear that the reenactment had included a Parade of the Dead and that those in attendance, who'd played the dead, named the dead, or choreographed the dead, had included some rock stars and celebrities, though Cal never could confirm that Elaine Bradley, Brandon Flowers, Gary Allan, David Archuleta, Dan Reynolds, Roseanne Barr, and Jewel Kilcher were really in attendance. It was also the first time he began hearin about the ghost of Tom Gatestone and the meanin behind Tom's Crossin.

For Cal Carneros the story of the kids and the horses resonated throughout most of his life, too often havin to be reframed in order to recontain those events and their repercussive influence on matters well beyond the obvious subject matter. Mostly this was because every newly discovered vantage point offerin new perspectives on those events at the end of October demanded a new conceptual armature, even while new promontories continued to emerge elsewhere, shiftin once again the argument, once again demandin still more frames, promptin Cal to think of Friedrich Schlegel's dictum: *Every work of art brings its own frame into existence.* To which Wolfgang Kemp had later replied: *The frame brings the work of art into existence*; with both views initiatin at least a flirtation with the idea of just One Frame, which made Cal stammer some, because he couldn't stand the idea. Cal knew no mind, let alone his, would ever be so vast. Besides he liked limits. He liked simplifications. He liked all sorts of frames.

Then in 2031 there was another exhibit, this time in New Hampshire and organized by folks Cal knew nothin about. He was old by then and didn't care about much, though he was moved by the invitation, especially given the tragedy that had followed his own show at the Time Gallery back in 2000. Cal hadn't cared much for the flight into Boston. He came by hisself. These days he was mostly alone. He'd never partnered up. Shasta, though, had tied the knot with a young man. She'd had three children, got divorced, lost touch. Cal lost touch with Rico Gale the day Rico quit the art business, which wasn't long after the Time Gallery exhibit. Cal knew he wouldn't find either one of them here, not in Portsmouth, but he did wonder if he'd run into Pinegar Nelson. He didn't.

He came in denim, wearin a bolo tie, and though he still had his hair, white now, he surprised hisself by decidin to wear that cowboy hat he'd got what seemed like lifetimes ago, with that braided hatband and leather tassel and a blond straw weave that was still near light as the sun. And the hat fit.

Certainly as a nod to his own Time Gallery, this place had been renamed for the show: *Time Out of Time Gallery*. It sure was big and plenty pleasant, though the six spaces weren't referred to as Chambers but as Rounds, which Cal also suspected was a kind of nod to the original show, though this one was titled *Untoppled Pillars*.

The program described the event as *Virtually Experienced Material*, which seemed in Cal's ear to ring out as one of those highfalutin jokes you best not take too seriously. It was hard even to take *Untoppled Pillars* seriously. You might could maybe even find offense in it, seein how those pillars, metaphoric, of the community, had certainly fallen, now long since dismantled by earth, with not even a capital left to show where they'd once stood. Although the meadow was still there.

Those in attendance were either polite or paid him no mind. Cal preferred the latter. He lingered for a while in the main entrance area beneath a wall upon which flickered letters that looked like they was made of fire:

> *Nunc fluens facit tempus*
> > *Nunc stans facit aeternitatum*
> — *Boethius*

Cal later learned it meant *The now that passes creates time; the now that remains creates eternity.* He never did, though, find out who Boethius was nor how the words themselves were made to burn like that. It weren't no dispaly screen, but no matter where Cal stood or put up an arm, he could not discover where the projector hid.

Cal enjoyed takin in the crowd. They was monied and educated, and no one ever said aloud just how fine the champagne was, so much of it too casually offered in flutes that looked like real crystal. Maybe there were some intriguin neoists among the crowd, but even after takin into account shifts in the Overton window, from what Cal could hear, and his hearin was still quite good, general concerns seemed mostly centered on humanity's long-runnin agenda throughout history: health, prosperity, and progress.

One bow-tied gentleman, after ramblin on a bit about tyrants, brought up how Zhuangzi had declared in 400 BC that happiness is the absence of strivin for happiness. *If that doesn't contradict entirely our national mandate to pursue happiness.* His partner, who had been bringin up misinformation a lot, responded by askin if the suggestion here was that the United States had from the start failed to understand eudaemonism? *Are you sayin we doomed ourselves because of our failure to understand from the outset the nature of happiness?* The man in the bow tie smirked. *Surely we are a sad nation then?* Another couple nearby overheard this exchange and asked if the pursuit of fireflies should then cease? They followed that up with a Søren Kierkegaard comment about how everythin that points to a political movement will become religious.

Politics, Cal found throughout his eavesdroppin, was definitely the dominant theme in most conversations, which was impressive given the volatility of the subject. Names like Shalamov and Dombrovsky came up. *Red wall or blue wall, we keep forgettin to ask if maybe there shouldn't be a wall at all?* someone pleaded. *You've forgotten Voltaire's prescription for neighborly love.*

About then a truck pulled up outside the gallery and began rollin coal, coughin up big plumes of black smoke from two stacks, and for a few minutes too. Folks started to get nervous, and in fact the stunt, if that's what it was, proved an effective impetus to get people movin deeper into the gallery and finally engage the exhibit itself.

Cal went with the crowd, convinced that the quote markin the entrance to the first space was another nod to the Time Gallery show. By Hannah Arendt. *The inner awareness of one's own mortality is perhaps the most antipolitical experience there is. It signifies that we shall disappear from the world of appearances.* It was in fact a warnin, and in retrospect maybe just for him, but Cal couldn't heed it.

What he saw next floored him: a near duplicate of Chamber One. The works he, Shasta, and Rico had so painstakinly hung and lit, and in many cases framed, were all here on screens, the drawins of gates, playin cards, and even *Rearview* by Thayne Moon, who incidentally never ceased bein a coach, died right in the middle of a game too, from what doctors said was a cardiac event due to *gunk in his ventricle,* what the players recharacterized as just too much pure love for the game.

There were also new pieces. One reminded Cal of Picasso's *Boy Leading a Horse.* Another seemed to echo Degas's *Horse in a Meadow* or even Yoshida's *Numazaki Pasture.* There was one of the black mare, Navidad, that had taken a lesson from Helen Durant's *Three Horses.* There were some works that Cal was sure were painted by Joe Coffey or Heather Foster. Or maybe even Peggy Judy? Was there a hint of *Four Grey Horses* in this one? Unlike in his show, though, where associations had been tenuous and flatterin, tonight's influences were obvious, though only in the new works, whether in dialogue with Magritte's *The Blank Signature*, Georgia O'Keeffe's *Horse's Skull on Blue*, Elisabeth Frink's *Lying Down Horse*, and certainly in one case Alfred Munnings's *Ponies Galloping*, and that was still only a rough start. What's more, Cal discovered that these post-Time-Gallery pieces, created long after 2000 and even after 2013, all more formal and accomplished, and professionally framed too, had the curious effect of puttin him at ease. And as Cal slowly interrogated this relaxedness, he realized that the polished skill of these renderins were servin to distance hisself from the heart of the matter. He also blamed digital impoverishment upon which the show was largely reliant. Not to deny that there still were a few works that hit him hard, as if beyond the influence of tradition, beyond the grasp of any art history disquisition. Those works mostly focused on the horses.

Cal kept thinkin of Karen Roehl, Tony O'Connor, Guy Allen, Michael Workman, Mary Ross Buchholz, Sophie Lécuyer, Juan Lamarca, Patrick Atkinson, Kyffin Williams, Lesley Thiel, and Charming Baker, a list that could keep goin, as Cal had never stopped cultivatin a taste for equine artists. He liked too that this show was also displayin works that pushed beyond any obvious cultural conversation or the blunt cause for representation. Artists like Ryoji Ikeda and Nick Brandt were comin to mind now too. And from there arose a profusion of talents that had very little to do with horses, which was when Cal told hisself to knock it off. Who cared if that thing over there looked like an Andy Goldsworthy or how still farther on there waited a resplendent paintin of kids with horses and ghosts that could very well be by Walton Ford? Or much closer, was that piece called *Landry?* by Glenn Ligon? What he could not forget was how no matter what whimsy or the personal need to express overtook the subject matter here, the subject matter still refused to budge, rooted in a very specific moment in history that now seemed especially ghostly.

And frankly, as he continued to ease hisself through the various spaces, Cal hisself started to look like he'd seen a ghost. Because . . . how had all the pieces he thought he'd never see again been resurrected here? There was Janice Brothwell's prophetic piece and Jack Behrstock's *Pillars Meadow Before Noon*. Even Pinegar Nelson's *Lemon Cake* was here, as well as every last one of Joanne Willden's paintins.

Cal passed one wall upon which lived a Byron quote: *Rhyme and revel with the dead*. That felt about right.

Cal wished more than ever that Shasta and Rico were with him. He'd tell them they weren't just in some gorgeous cemetery with a few haunted graves. Here the dead had actually risen again. And to be sure in this respect the show understood itself. There weren't one image on the multitude of screens and surfaces that didn't seem ghostly. Some glowed wondrously; others moved through one diaphanous fabric into another; a few threatened the limitations of both surface and dimension. One installation, which Cal liked quite a lot, entitled *Many Years in the Future*, by an artist named Cheyenne Riddaway, was comprised of a series of twenty-seven door-sized glass plates etched with dense text. The plates were suspended in groups of five every five feet or so down a narrow hallway, at the end of which was illuminated a bright, nearly holographic image of Kirk's Cirque. At first you faced nothin more than a bright blur, due to the refraction of the intense light passin through so many pieces of glass overwrit with so much script, but as you progressed down the hallway, the panes of glass would slowly ease away like so many slidin glass doors, revealin more and more of the image beyond, until at last you were presented with that extremely vivid image of the mountain itself.

For obvious reasons, only one person was allowed through at a time. It weren't a rapid affair. The withdrawin of the glass plates was contingent on the participant's stillness, this allowed for better readin even if the text was generally too small and too often barely legible. As expected remarked upon here were those events that had allegedly occurred on Katanogos back in 1982 as told by numerous folks supposedly familiar with the story. On some panes there were flickers of light, some from old films. *La Strada* was one. *Be' anche questo serve a qualcosa, anche questo sassetto.* No subtitles. Most panes, though, bore the weight of only quotes. *Rests always sound well.* Arnold Schoenberg. *Fly, bird, fly away; teach me to disappear!* Alberto Caeiro. *America . . . has no terrible and no beautiful condensation.* Ralph Waldo Emerson. *Silence is so accurate.* Mark Rothko. *On peut dire que tout ce que nous savons, c'est-à-dire tout ce que nous pouvons, a fini par s'opposer à ce que nous sommes.* Paul Valéry. No translation provided. *When you start working, everybody is in your studio — the past, your friends, enemies, the art world, and above all, your own ideas — all are there. But as you continue painting, they start leaving, one by one, and you are left completely alone. Then, if you're lucky, even you leave.* John Cage. *When you take a flower in your hand and really look at it, it's your world for the moment. I want to give that world to someone else.* Georgia O'Keeffe. *Wonder is the beginning of wisdom.* Socrates. *There is beauty, not only in wisdom, but in this dazed and dramatic ignorance.* G. K. Chesterton. *We sometimes keep on forgetting our reality.* Isaac Bashevis Singer. *Myth can make reality more intelligible.* Jenny Holzer. *May my silences become more accurate.* Theodore Roethke. *Too often . . . I would hear men boast of the miles covered that day, rarely of what they had seen.* Louis L'Amour. *The fundamental event of the modern age is the conquest of the world as picture.* Martin Heidegger. *No hay nada más hermoso que la risa.* Frida Kahlo. No translation provided. *Freedom's just another word for nothin left to lose.* Kris Kristofferson. Curiously with music by Nino Rota. *Liberation is not my liberation but liberation from the delusional Me and its problems of identity.* Frederick Franck. *Beware identity: the privilege can quickly become a prison.* Wembley Ruse. *To forget its Creator is one of the functions of a Creation.* E. M. Forster. *In art, don't you see, there is no first person.* Oscar Wilde. *One must always tell what one sees. Above all, which is more difficult, one must always see what one sees.* Charles Péguy. *To learn to see, to learn to hear, you must do this — go into the wilderness alone.* Don José Matsuwa. *I'm here to play for blood, boys, and I'll be here til the end.* Luke Bell. *A horse knows when you know and knows when you don't know.* Ray Hunt. *An immense amount of pettiness is dropped if . . . you catch a glimpse of . . . your companion . . . there watching you.* Carlos Castaneda. *Explanation of the unspeakable cannot be finished.* Buddha. *Ghosts need to believe in themselves.* Ted Lasso. *When you get there, there isn't any there there.* Gertrude Stein. *May your trails be crooked, windin, lonesome, dangerous, leadin to the most amazin view. May your mountains rise into and above the clouds.* Edward Abbey. *Where does a mountain start? Where does it end?* Carlo Rovelli. *For the place I really have to reach is where I must already be.* Ludwig Wittgenstein. *As long as you only know about the mountain . . .* Zen mondo. *But still one feels certain barriers, certain gates.* Vincent van Gogh.

But there were also sheets of glass etched with *dangerous formulae*, or so went one phrase amidst a sea of symbols and numbers. *Variations Erase Magic* was there too. As well as *Versions Emerge Magically* and *Versions Emerge Mechanically.* And that was just the start.

What Cal quickly learned was that the stillness recommended at the entrance to Riddaway's piece included even the movement of your head while readin. Even breathin through your mouth slowed your progress down, though the more that Cal committed hisself to physical quietude, the faster these veils of distraction would move out of the way, until at last he stood before a portrait of near-blindin clarity; in fact fer a moment Cal even thought he might be up in Kirk's Cirque, in springtime, wildflowers ablaze with color, the air abuzz with insects, a favonian breeze ripplin the surface of Altar Lake. It even seemed cooler here. But were those bones? Or bleached timber? Was that an abandoned beaver dam?

Fer Cal the work beautifully evoked clearin the mind of chatter so as to better behold the present moment. It was a metaphor, of course. But it was also self-consistent and rigorous in its application. The start of the hallway was also crowded with reverberant voices, which Cal realized later were the texts he'd been squintin at. He'd also been wrong about the absence of a translation for that French quote. It was in the audio. *One can say that all we know, that is all we have the power to do, has finally turned against what we are.* That went for the Italian too: *Well, even this serves some purpose, even this little stone.* And the Spanish: *Nothin is worth more than laughter.* There had also been music and dissonances beyond casual description, all of which slowly vanished the farther along you got. Furthermore, strong drafts generated by loud fans buffeted Cal early on. But here at the end the air was still and the hallway silent. Fer a moment Cal even felt embraced by the vision before him, until, maybe as a cruel joke, that too was atomized into a digital static that after a few seconds recongealed into a bright red EXIT encased in a red arrow pointin to the left, where an open door waited.

Cal emerged, blinkin, into the now very crowded gallery. Earlier he'd felt like a ghost among these folks, certainly unrecognized but also unobserved. Now, though, folks were smilin at him, jostlin him with pleasant *excuse me*'s, their interests once more fillin his ear. Though, as he soon discovered, this question of the self as ghost to the self was far from over.

No doubt that July fourth gatherin in downtown Orvop, back in 2013, with so many folks participatin in a reenactment of the Awides Mine, was reverberatin here. But that had still been a glancin gesture toward the trials of the dead compared to the very evident presence here that had been absent in the Time Gallery show:

the ghost of Tom Gatestone.

His spectre was everywhere, at first risin up like a pentimento, then assertin itself more and more, if still figured just beyond the reach of detail. He was in so many of those pieces Cal knew by heart. Well, many of them. Pinegar Nelson's lemon cake had gone unhaunted unless you was countin the spectre of hunger.

Nor on this night was Cal the only one struck by the ghostly boy. Attendees commented regularly and carelessly about the insubstantial figure. *Did you notice that the name Tom backward is mot, which in French means word?* a young woman in faux fur the color of caramel dazzled with strawberry pointed out. *I think it's a justifiable observation since his mother, Sondra Gatestone, had ancestors from France.* Her companion looked unconvinced. *Where did you hear that? I don't think that's true. I've never heard of any French ancestry in the Gatestone family. I think you just made that up to make your silly point.* Curiously the woman in faux fur only laughed and even nodded back.

Cal wound up locatin most if not all of the pieces from his show, beautifully captured on the latest generation of QD-OLED screens. There were plenty of holographic impressions around too, one offerin up the ghost of Doran N. Tolan's bronze, *Old Porch in the Rain*. And astonishments didn't end there: Nathan Nibley's musical number was somehow now available for a listen. Not only that but the last echoin phrase, cut short by his death, was here completed or at least elongated with *reset the scales of consequence . . .* A projected wall didactic informed anyone curious that in the midst of composin the cello piece, Nathan Nibley had been murdered by a fellow musician with a single shot through the larynx.

And still there was more: little film clips that Cal reckoned shouldn't exist were everywhere. They looked real too. Cal figured it was A.I. Just cartoons, realistic cartoons, that's how you had to look at them. Except there were also these static images that Cal swore just had to be photographs even if he knew they were likely cartoons too. Beautiful cartoons.

And still that weren't the sum of it. Cal wandered into dark rooms with dim, grainy projections that served as only background for the voices that crowded those spaces, voices that sounded young and exhausted and afraid and included the snorts of horses. Again Cal wished Rico and Shasta were there, or anyone who'd been at the Time Gallery show. Cal would've taken the cop. Heck, Cal would've even taken the vandals that had trashed his place.

Sadly Cal never did realize that some folks from his show were in fact minglin around right then, sometimes even rubbin shoulders with him, with never a spark of recognition between the two. Folks like Shamayne Apple and her younger sister or Haddy Visick and Hariram Abbasi. Even Jack Behrstock was there along with Daris Tan, Lorelei Barrett, Tamsyn Horrocks, and Courtney Resnick. And that ain't even the complete list. A whole slew had made the trip, the ghosts Cal couldn't see, just as he was a ghost to them, whom they couldn't see.

Maybe, though, Cal felt them there or at least felt somethin there. Maybe that's why he stayed as long as he did, even if he never did figure it out, that feelin of someone beside him he never could quite count as real enuf to know. He took it for as long as he could stand it, and then he couldn't stand it anymore. Never had the prospect of leavin a place felt so soothin.

While he waited at the coat check for his parka, a very, very old woman approached him.

I like your hat, she said. *I'm glad you made the trip.*

Are you the one I should thank for invitin me? She was also a very, very tiny woman.

Cal's parka had arrived. The cold night awaited. He was ready for it too.

Will you stay a little longer? she asked.

Cal offered his arm, and together they revisited the exhibition. She seemed as light as a bird in flight. Cal half wondered if she was actually flyin. Her talk was just as light too, as she spoke about how the subject that was so central here would always far surpass any exhibit or concert or musical. She said someone was developin that. Unless she was mistaken. *Maybe an opera?*

What continued to fascinate her was how it had continued to mutate into performance pieces, find its way into school plays, ballets, improvised assemblies, not to mention how it continued to proliferate as clips, a media virality that persistently spiraled out beyond the subject even as it always eventually spiraled back in again; nor did she mean to leave out those small unrecorded reenactments, or reinterpretations, played out on some lone field where cars and trucks provided the lights and folks who understood well what was at stake performed both prologue and outcome.

A fella approached them then, introducin hisself as one Sagamore Blanchard. He'd come all the way from Orvop proper. He told them he was five when he'd seen Kalin March ride across his backyard. *I didn't know if I was dreamin. I still don't know if I was dreamin. I just remember havin a glass of milk in my hand.*

Cal's guide then led the way to a display of Joanne Willden's campfire scene. Cal recognized it at once. However, unlike the original, the emptiness that had once resided beside Kalin was now occupied by the ashen Tom Gatestone tryin to warm his hands.

I think the dead always accompany us, the very, very old woman said then.

Did Joanne Willden paint the ghost in herself, or did someone else do that?

As you likely don't know, she died.

I did not know.

In Darlington, South Carolina. She was bludgeoned to death. They said the folks that did it wanted her wig.

Cal shook his head. To kill someone for a wig? What are you supposed to say to that?

I know there were some discussions about 3D duplications. The results would have fooled most here. Except maybe you. The exhibitors, however, were not interested in tryin to fool anyone. *They only wanted to resurrect the lost works from your famous show. Though, as you can see, the ghost of Tom Gatestone has now emerged with, what shall we call it?, the narrative light of subsequent retellings. Do you disapprove?*

Who am I to say what should or should not be included in a piece? I'm not an artist.

Like yourself, Mr. Carneros, I am also just a visitor.

After that, the very, very old woman began to point out how many of the projected pieces from his Time Gallery show were in flux, slowly shiftin between the original version without Tom's ghost and later versions that included him, style-appropriate of course, before revertin to the original again. Cal came around to welcomin the addition, even if the subsequent subtraction of the ghost was for some reason more unsettlin. His new friend admitted feelin the same. How old was she anyway? Cal also wondered what effect these frequent evocations of the dead were havin on her. Cal almost asked her but didn't because in the end he was too polite. He was just glad for her company, and though she moved slowly, she knew the exhibit so well that they seemed to arrive at places faster than if he'd tried to get there on his own. She also led him to new places, through secret routes, to works he'd missed the first time through.

Cal was pretty confused then. How had he missed such a substantial space whose walls now expanded with a dozen different views of a wide, desolate, snow-patched field he of course recognized at once; and while some of the reels, if that's what they were, projected the action in black and white, some did so in sepia, while others splashed the walls with the saturated tones of early Kodachrome.

These movies of Pillars Meadow, he whispered to her, *they're so authentic!*

I might've agreed with you except I find the decision to filter them so that they mimic old movies from various decades deauthenticates them. Though maybe that's the point: to alert us that they are still a fabrication. Of sorts. What do you think? And the very, very old lady's eyes grew wide and luminous then, and Cal was a reminded of a great white owl.

I'm old-fashioned, I guess. I still love the smell of paint on canvas. Cal Carneros was thinkin of those paintins in Chamber Five in the Time Gallery. Sure, maybe the colors had dimmed some and some of the artists' names had fled from recollection, but there'd still been some dang fine pieces, fine enuf to remain dangerously volatile in his memory and imagination. He'd never forget the violence, the loss, the grandeur, the bloodshed, the absurdity, the stupidity, the unexpurgated repetitions of History, the horrors of those final moments captured in the stillness of singular moments, on wide canvases, darkly framed, such small figures dabbed into life with humble oils, not so much a still life but a still death, recitin in its particularity all that had led to this instant and all that would necessarily come later, the cold air adrift with gray smoke, the snow stained, and all of it diminished before those immense and indifferent mountains.

I wish I could have seen the originals, the very, very old woman admitted. *I'm told your show was quite somethin.*

You would've been welcome, Cal said. *There was just more to it than these . . .* He hesitated.

Clips?

That's right. Clips. Cal tilted up his hat and rubbed the back of his hand across his forehead. *At my show,* Cal added, *there was this feelin, hauntin really, that all those made-up fragments pointed back to somethin real.*

Real?

Maybe real isn't right. Somethin true? No, true isn't right either. Somethin that actually happened?

I believe this does point back to somethin that actually happened.

Yes, my show.

The very, very old woman smiled. And even patted Cal on the arm. *The links break. The attributions are corrupted. But still a clarity prevails.*

I don't follow.

Maybe, Mr. Carneros, we are no longer talkin about Art.

This here tonight is an Art Show proper. A lavish one. Mine felt more like the results of an archaeological dig. The ghost hauntin my gallery was always the question of what exactly had inspired the art that demanded my show in the first place. It weren't about what we saw on the walls or even the discussions they started. In the end, we saw only those kids ridin them horses over the biggest mountain you ever seen. So much more vivid than whatever was at the Time Gallery and even what this latest technology has produced here.

But don't these displays help resurrect that time? The history at least?

Yes, sure, of course you're right, but that still doesn't account for how this show almost feels too good for its own good. Maybe it's because we don't need to imagine anythin for ourselves, maybe because we too easily lose hold of that feelin that a journey really did take place. We forget the endurance required, the guts. We satisfy ourselves with the results, and, even worse, the representation of results, makin the consideration of what did happen no longer necessary. Good gracious, I must sound crazy! Cal laughed. He decided not to share that his mind was also momentarily ablaze with Jusepe de Ribera's *The Sense of Touch. I ain't talked art-talk in a lot of years. I could've dazzled you when I was young.*

Compared to me, you're still young, and Mr. Carneros, dazzle me you do. The very, very old woman again patted his arm.

You know what I always said when I was in the art business and people asked me why I wasn't sellin mattresses? Cal asked.

You never had any interest in puttin people to sleep?

That's very good, Cal said, pattin her arm now. He was gettin to like this very, very old woman. *Art awakens. That's what I'd tell them.*

That gets my attention.

It was just somethin glib I came up with to sound fancy, but now I'm won-derin here, with you, if what I was sayin was that Art, capital A, awakens us not just to the possibility of the whole but, more importantly, to the sensation of the whole, what we can't ever know but maybe now and then can get a glimpse of by how we're made to feel. Our passport to the stars, beyond the stars.

I knew I wanted to talk to you, said the very, very old woman, her eyes again twinklin with that wide awareness that made him think of an owl and made him shudder too, because he felt like a mouse.

One thing, though, if I may, that I can't make sense of— Cal began.

How are the images that hung on your walls even here?

Cal nodded.

Not all that is lost is never found.

That's an easy thing to say.

The very, very old woman chuckled. *Just in case you thought you were the only one who could be glib.* She even winked.

Fair enuf.

For a large part of my life, I felt like I was a tiger roamin far and wide. Now, though, I'm set on bein a tree. A tall one too, outstretched, with deep roots. What about you, Mr. Carneros?

Me? I'll choose a horse.

Do you ride?

Horses don't ride horses, ma'am.

Have you ever heard of VEM?

Excuse me?

Just curious.

Outside the night sky had started to glow red. Fireworks for some darn reason? Or it was happenin again. The windows rattled. The crowds groaned and then calmed. The windows stopped rattlin. The fireworks stopped. People were already leavin. Cal extended his hand to the very, very old woman.

It was nice meetin you, Ms . . .

Her hand felt fragile as bird bones in a nest.

Thank you, Mr. Carneros. I know you thought it was all gone, but as you saw for yourself tonight, there's more to the eye than meets the eye.

I'm not sure I know what you mean.

The very, very old woman winked again. *Sure you do.*

Cal Carneros never did find out her name. As she headed away, alert and very agile folks, who in retrospect Cal realized had been there all along to watch over her, guard her, suddenly surrounded her and helped her to a wheelchair. Cal then overheard a sudden flurry of chatter. *I can't believe she's here! Who? How old is she? Who? She must be at least a hundred? Who? The Wizard! Thee Wizard! Who?* A few people looked his way then, like Cal was also famous. Who was she? Someone spoke aloud the name *Cas,* but Cal Carneros figured that was because someone outside was playin *Don't Let The Good Life Pass You By.* They must've just been talkin about Mama Cass even if that ain't how conversations work.

After she was gone, Cal put on his parka and headed outside. He walked for a long while too, thinkin about those aftermaths of artifacts, about the ghost of Tom Gatestone, but never once about the fire.

O n the day he died, though, Cal Carneros woke from a dream about that fire, except instead of everythin burnin up inside his gallery, the artworks had galloped free because his dream had transformed them into horses, every last piece.

See, on the night of March 1, 2000, the night right after his astoundin openin, the Time Gallery was swallowed by flames. The police who returned to the ashes believed that the electrical systems had been compromised durin the robbery that had occurred the previous night. The smoke alarm as well as the security alarms had just flat-out failed. Paint and thinners in a back area had served as accelerants. Also, the location of the gallery had slowed the response time, as it weren't the black smoke but the orange glow that finally alerted residents miles away. By the time fire trucks reached the industrial area, the entire structure seemed a white rose. Gas lines that had nothin to do with the Time Gallery but still ran adjacent to the property had ruptured. There weren't ever an explosion, but there sure was a lot of heat, enuf to incinerate just about everythin inside.

Even so, Cal remained convinced that there hadn't been sufficient heat to melt *Old Porch in the Rain.* Insurance investigators, however, concluded that the fire had attained temperatures high enuf to do away with the statue even if no one found any melted bronze. Nothin was deemed amiss. The policies paid out what was owed to Cal and to the owners of the pieces, but that hardly made up for their loss.

In his final hours, Cal enjoyed a rush of memory that was particularly vivid, no doubt enhanced by what he'd seen in New Hampshire. He suddenly recalled in sharp detail many of the works. Even some of the artists' names resurfaced.

Here was Hatch Porch alone on his mother's bed. Here was Kelly Porch on the toilet with his jeans down to his ankles, laborin to get out that business that weren't goin nowhere because it had nothin to do with his guts. Or how about Undersheriff Jewell, head upon his crossed arms, hat still on, even as he slept at a card table beside a phone and a space heater? Or Park Ranger Brickey tryin to take off her boots in them early a.m. hours of that Sunday, them laces tormentin her with a stain that was mostly likely mud, though there was a good chance it was also blood, while behind her, her cat pawed at a candle flame?

The mothers returned in all sorts of sizes and shapes, different women, the same women. In oils, watercolors, and charcoal, and soap, as was the case with one piece. There they were, up Orvop Canyon, standin by the Orvop River, their guts torn out by their absent children, nepoed!, Allison March gaunt in the snow, her hands out, Sondra Gatestone fillin her pockets with rocks, lured on by a baptism that promised neither salvation nor maybe even relief, and near acceptin too the fast current of them icy reservoir waters.

Chamber Five had offered so much. Law Enforcement Ranger Bren Kelson dead on a table at the entrance to Isatch Canyon, which to Cal's dyin mind could've been painted by N. C. Wyeth hisself. The same went for Old Porch in his dinin room starin at his maps. Or the one of that pilot Kevin Moffet studyin an Alaska travel brochure by the light of his open refrigerator door, his eyes bright with a future he'd never know. At a certain point, though, Cal did begin to question whether or not he was just imaginin new pieces.

One paintin, though, he was sure weren't his invention: a great ridge of snow afflicted by a snowstorm possessin the starless dark that reigned above. There weren't but cornices carved by the wind, and yet beneath them thick, blue, and dim heaps of ice and snow, a tiny tangle of trees stood with branches supportin the tiniest angle of tarp shelterin two figures huddled as close as they could get to a fire.

It was a mesmerizin achievement evocative of adventure and darin. Like the illustrations from his weathered copy of *Treasure Island* by Robert Louis Stevenson, this edition published back in 1911, which Cal still had somewhere, though instead of sea adventures, here were mountains, and instead of minted coins in bread bags, here was fire.

But of them pieces that Cal couldn't say fer sure had ever existed in the first place, not carin nothin about their validity either, because they were only there to remind him of what had come before, those were less like N. C. Wyeth and now more like Andrew Wyeth.

Take, fer example, one with just four panels: *Jojo, Mouse* and *Navidad,* as the titles read, with *Chubasco,* instead of Ash, last; that fourth panel bein all black. The didactic, as requested, included these names as well other associative ones like Alastor, Aethon, Nycteus, Orphnaeus; it went on from there. The portraits were all head-on with no horse saddled or even haltered. Jojo seemed as much a part of the clouds and snow as he was a part of the sky. His eyes seemed to recognize you too from long ago even if he was just seein you now for the first time; his gaze holdin that impossible compassion that assures you he will carry you, carry you far, carry you all the way, though you don't deserve better than the dust you will die in. Mouse's glare was less forgivin. His big eyes, that steady gaze aglimmer with the space between stars, seemed to say he'd only watch you as you suffered your end, not with malice but not with compassion either; like he'd already done for eons of lasts, he'd witness your last moment too with a swish of his tail. The portrait of Navidad, though, that was somethin else entirely. Her black coat shone with a rutilant glow perhaps cast by embers not visible within the frame. Her nostrils burnt with smoke. Her eyes were ablaze. Navidad here was a creature of fire. And maybe in fact they were all of their element: Jojo of the air, Mouse of the earth, and Navidad the conflagration that finally forges desire and the torments of peace into a resolution of flame. And of that fourth panel, if Ash did indeed reside within those folds of inky black, maybe he was of those waters that overwash any meanin of Heaven. Though why then did Henri Lévy's *Sarpédon* suddenly come then to Cal's mind? And with little sympathy? Maybe because the son of Zeus was the slayer of Pedasos.

Before the valves of his heart practically fell apart, Cal Carneros was surprised to find none other than the granddaughter of Pinegar Nelson reachin out to him. He made no mention of how the gallery of his mind had become haunted by works of art he alone could contemplate. Or how he even welcomed their interposition because he was findin it increasinly hard, especially as he got older and frailer, to contemplate merely what had occurred. He did, though, bring up how he never could understand how everythin displayed at his Time Gallery show in Houston, literally at the start of the twenty-first century, despite bein destroyed in the subsequent fire, had still somehow been resurrected at the New Hampshire exhibit in 2031?

They even had the lemon cake your grandmother painted on the back of a paper plate, Cal said, squelchin the urge to bring up his own persistent theory that, of course, they'd all just been fakes, whether deep or shallow, AI or not, some kind of tomfoolery by technology.

Not all that is lost is never found, the young woman said then.

How's that? Cal Carneros asked. He had a dim recollection of someone sayin the same thing to him a long time ago. *Is that a Church thing?*

It doesn't have to be.

Church was the last place Allison March figured she'd end up come Sunday mornin, an eye-waterinly bright mornin too, but here she was with Sondra Gatestone, shufflin toward spots in the pew not near close enuf to an exit but at least close enuf to an aisle.

It was 8:53 a.m.

Fer sure, the Grandview chapel was pleasant enuf, the simplicity commendable, the calm welcome. Allison had no trouble with the murmurin, but she could've done without the stares; murmurin you can pretend ain't about you, but them looks that won't meet your eye or even manage a polite smile? No thank you. Sondra took Allison's hand and gave it a warm squeeze.

The Grandview chapel weren't even in Sondra's ward, or Allison's for that matter, if she'd've stuck with the Church. Here, though, on this Halloween day, was where Havril Enos was sharin some words. Sondra had figured a little soulful inspiration could only help. Both mothers had slept no more than two hours, haunted by dreams of their children. For Sondra, they was callin on a phone she couldn't find in time; for Allison, she was openin letters she couldn't read.

It was a good thing Sondra's home hid no gifts of unopened booze; Allison might've fallen. Or maybe not. Sondra, as the sponsor Allison had come to realize she was, was the greater gift. Likewise Sondra had come to realize that Allison was her salvation as well, and this despite news that their kids had not only survived the rockslide but Allison's son had allegedly killt Sondra's own daughter. *He wouldn't have done that,* Allison had said again as they was eatin toast at Sondra's kitchen table, waitin on the dawn. *Allison, look at me. I can hear the hesitation in your voice, and it don't matter,* Sondra had responded, though Allison still had to continue givin voice to what her heart wouldn't stop murmurin: *Kalin wouldn't have done that, but I can't promise no longer that he didn't. I don't understand none of this no more.* Sondra appreciated her sayin so, but it still didn't matter. *We have to see the bodies.*

As they settled in the pew, with nods to their neighbors, a few folks came over to welcome Sister Gatestone. Sondra shook their hands and introduced Sister March. They was friendly enuf, and the ones seated right behind them didn't give a lick who they were, some brown-haired brothers squabblin over bacon versus sausage. It was a silly conversation, but the boys couldn't quit gettin hotter and hotter about the difference.

After prayer and a sacrament of bread and water, the first part of the service took for its point of focus brothers, the most famous brothers too: Cain and Abel.

But am I really my brother's keeper?

That's Everett Walsh, Sondra whispered to Allison. *He's a history professor at Isatch U. Smart man.*

Perhaps only as a matter of course, Mr. Everett Walsh first brought up the death of Russel Porch and what that killin had inflicted upon *the community of the Church. He was gone too soon, and while there's plenty of sortin left to do while such murderous intent remains at large in our mountains, I'll ask that we take a moment to bow our heads and give prayer to Russel and his sufferin family. In the name of Jesus Christ.*

After that, Mr. Everett Walsh began to talk about envy, family members who *begrudge* other family members, or neighbors who *begrudge* other neighbors for havin shinier stuff, or students who *begrudge* other students for gettin better grades, or just about anyone *begrudgin* anyone else for gettin more attention, and Everett Walsh sure dug in on this last one, his voice risin as he both urged and indirectly admonished the congregation: *Let us especially rid ourselves of this lust for more attention, since Heavenly Father grants every single one of us the very same attention.* And any attention besides *His ain't worth even the wink of a bird passin by.*

Not once did Mr. Everett Walsh look toward Allison or Sondra, and that was fine by Allison until she realized he was lookin just about everywhere else in that church.

And it shall come to pass that everyone that findeth me shall slay me, Mr. Everett Walsh then quoted from the book before him but in a tone that now seemed rife with present-day purpose, or if that's givin him too much credit, then with a general entitlement to violence. Especially when he got to the bit about Cain's Mark, Mr. Everett Walsh just couldn't help hisself. And then he sure did fix his glare right on them two mothers, even if, in truth, neither the women nor most of the congregants had any clue what he was goin on about.

Some say he was just startin out with brother killin brother so he could get to brother lovin brother. Others, though, figured this was strictly about Kalin March as killer and how the Mark of Cain was now upon him and how he should be slayed quick. Still, others seated there that mornin heard the Mark of Cain and immediately thought of any dark pigmentation of the skin and were confused because they figured Landry Gatestone was the one so marked and maybe Mr. Everett Walsh was suggestin that Kalin should've slain her like everyone was sayin he'd gone and done anyways. Admittedly there weren't many there who believed that one, but, still, Mr. Everett Walsh's efforts, however well-intentioned or ill-intentioned, were viewed as a generally confused effort. And in the end he never did get around to some redeemin notion of brother lovin brother.

At least he used to be smart, Sondra whispered to Allison when that was done.

In the name of Jesus Christ, Amen, answered the congregation.

The second speaker spoke of personal sufferin and her children's disabilities and how it was all so unbearably hard but how it was in the heart of that hardness that she knew the mercy that was Jesus Christ.

Allison vaguely welcomed the woman's openness even if she was still strugglin to figure out the point Mr. Everett Walsh had tried to make, and anyways, she was exhausted and close to fallin asleep and near did when the last speaker finally rose up to address those gathered in the Grandview chapel.

At last you'll get to hear him for yourself, Sondra whispered, her face at once bright with color, her hands fidgetin in her lap. That woke up Allison some. *I'll introduce you afterward.*

So this was Havril Enos. Allison had expected someone narrow as a minnow with hair whiter than what was blanketin the Isatch range right now. Fer sure she was not expectin this warm, ursiform man with hair so black he might very well be usin shoe polish. Shiny too. With big jowls. A big man, overweight fer sure, but Allison never thought fat. He was just too at ease and grand and jolly, at least on a first impression. Well-dressed too but not ostentaciously.

Havril Enos was already grinnin as he reached the podium, and there was no doubtin his charm and charisma; his manner alone was comfortin, and his words, when they came, were warm as honey without comin off as altiloquent or unctuous, maybe because there was a sharpness in there too, like honey on a honed blade. Allison sat up and gathered within her the energy she'd need to focus.

Maybe Sondra had been right. Maybe comin here, the last place Allison would've thought to go, would help some to alleviate their ghostly grief. Even fer a moment. At the very least Sondra might get more distance from the moment when she'd stepped to the river's edge with rocks in her pockets.

Havril Enos thanked Brother Walsh and Sister Cole. He praised them for sharin their hearts and then recognized them individually: Walsh for addressin the repercussions of brotherly misconduct as well as emphasizin how only by the *Grace of Heavenly Father are we left yet on this earth unfelled, free to either stumble or go forth;* smilin kindly then at Sister Cole before commendin her for havin the strength to keep walkin toward that door, *that awful golden door through which our salvation waits.* Sister Cole smiled and cried and smiled again. Havril Enos also brought up Russel Porch's passin and offered his own sympathies to *the great Porch family* before repeatin approvinly Everett Walsh's line about *such murderous intent at large in our mountains* even as he also exhorted those in attendance to find love and forgiveness in their hearts *for that is where the Lord dwells.*

Havril Enos then spread his hands wide upon the podium and with a great sigh lowered his head. There was no book before him nor even one note card.

Havril Enos let that moment go on for a long minute before he began to speak, at first keepin his head bowed, keepin his voice rumblin out low and near soft as a kneelin penitent: *Oh, thought I, that I could be banished and become extinct both soul and body, that I might not be brought to stand in the presence of my God, to be judged by my deeds. Mala 36.* Havril Enos lifted his head then, repeatin: *That I could be banished and become extinct!* He shook his head. *That I might not be brought to stand in the presence of God! Think about that: no moment with Heavenly Father! Exiled! Extinct! Gone like the dinosaurs, the dodo, henotheism, the pagans. Well, eventually the pagans.* At that, light laughter rippled through the packed chapel. *Imagine there's no Heaven. That's what John Lennon sang. That's right. One of them Beatles. And I say, yes!, I'm with Mr. Lennon here! Let's imagine! No halls of greetin when we are lifted up from the dust. No arms of Heavenly Father to cradle us as we pass through that forebodin curtain of death. No reunion with our loved ones, with our friends. Thank you, John Lennon. Thank you for that exercise in understandin the God-given stakes: That we might find ourselves banished from such bliss! That we might find ourselves exiled! That we might become ourselves extinct!*

And why for? Why indeed? When every soul here and elsewhere, and hear me on this, when every single soul gathered together here, as well as those who are yet ungathered throughout the world, is granted upon inception, that's right, upon inception, access to Heaven. And what must a soul do to gain Heaven? But one thing: respond. That is it. Respond. It is that simple. Respond. No payment necessary. No check needed. No line of credit. No exchange of goods. Just. Respond.

But how, you ask, does a soul respond? All a soul need do is recognize that we are all held by the Grace of God, and in this simple act of faith is our soul preserved for eternity in the mansions of our Lord in Jesus Christ. Amen.

Sondra Gatestone, clearly moved by these words, swayed her shoulder into Allison's, as if to not only further cement their federation but perhaps hopin that Allison, based on her earlier conversion, despite her recent lack of commitment, might again feel one with the Church, and weren't that a fine thing?

Allison tried to force a smile in case Sondra was sparin her a glance, though likely only the sight of Landry skippin down the aisle could've torn Sondra's eyes from the great Havril Enos. Unfortunately contrary to whatever expectations her friend nurtured, Allison was experiencin no sense of place here; in fact the impulse to bolt was again rampagin through every part of her, even if it no longer had the power to move her. It made no difference whether or not God would ever behold her faults and miseries, Allison could see them just fine now, and fer sure, she was banished, in exile, maybe already extinct. Her boy was lost, and whether corporeally or not, guilty or not, it didn't matter. He was lost to her because she could no longer divine who he was and what he'd done and where he was bound. Of course this absence was rooted in his maturation, which only he alone could know and direct. This understandin could've struck Allison anywhere, at any time, and also without the malicious crimes now attributed to him, but for whatever reason it happened here in the Grandview chapel near West 1460 North, in the company of a new friend.

This reckonin with Kalin's newness caused Allison March then to know herself utterly alone, even amidst all these people, even beside Sondra. Nor would some other place ever afford her anythin different. It didn't matter where Allison was; even here, in this buildin, of all places, she knew to her core that the experience of conversion was beyond her, along with the ecstasy of belongin, even any meaninful sense of belongin. Nonetheless she stayed seated there beside one who throughout her life had known only belongin. And Allison March's heart broke for her.

Mala 24:10, Havril Enos announced then by way of preface. *And I also thank my great God that we might repent and that He hath forgiven us of our many sins and murders which we have committed, and taken away the guilt from our hearts.*

Allison nodded because, though she no longer required admission, acceptance, or even forgiveness, she once and for all, under the eaves of that chapel, in the chapel of herself, granted her son absolute admission, absolute acceptance, absolute forgiveness no matter his sins. And above all she granted him absolute belongin. And then in the privacy of her heart she also experienced a sufferin that far exceeded his birth and all the collective agonies and doubts that had followed his birth.

Unwitnessed by every single soul there, Allison's covenant was beheld then and sanctified too by what powers you by now know, because you have come this far, because you have listened so patiently, because soon you too will be beyond this companionship, on your own but worthy too of your own solitude. Allison even discovered she could breathe now and breathe deeply, and though she continued to listen to President Enos, too aware of the sins of bigotry and entitlements he so easily elided in his quotes, the dark-skin Liminites elemental to the Church's book still there if struck from his speech in the service of the evolvin times, she also accepted that at least not on that mornin would such corruptin fissures splinter the Church's ruf beams. She even marveled within herself how such personal pain, what refused to abate, could at the same time sit side by side with calm. She looped her arm through Sondra's.

How awful then to find her friend, who not moments ago seemed enraptured by Havril Enos, now doubled over, her hands coverin her face, strugglin to not succumb to loud ugly sobs.

In the end, ironically, it was Sondra Gatestone who fled those premises. Plenty looked her way, but no one asked after her and certainly no one followed. Allison, of course, never left her side, and outside sat beside her on the curb, their feet sunk in the slush.

I can't lose her! I can't lose all my babies! I've lost all my babies! I can't!

Allison knew she had no assurances to meet that cost; she could only listen.

I thought fer sure comin here would help, but it didn't. Sondra even scowled.

There ain't nothin that can help us now, Allison responded.

How can you say that?!

Because it's true. Our children are beyond us. Whether they are the ruin or the success of their choices, they will be the fulfillment of their choices. There's nothin more we can do but wait.

I can't do that! I can't!

I know. That's why I'm here.

By contrast, Old Porch couldn't have asked for a better mornin, and it had even started with the darned phone ringin and ringin with not a move from one of his boys. He might've ignored it too, but given that the confounded racket was precedin the proverbial crow of the rooster, with dawn only just startin to dare its violet siege upon the dark dome, Old Porch, still groggy on mishap and ruinous fate, groped for the handset on his nightstand to greet whoever it was with a gruff *What is it?*

My heavens! declared Senator Hays. *What I'd give to answer a phone like that!*

Is that you, Shane?

I know it's early, Orwin, and I know you're in a heckuva time right now, I do, what with the funeral ahead and the mournin you're only just startin to endure, but I figured even great misery can stand a little good news.

Good news?

Have you not heard yet from that blessèd trinity? Your three state senators?

We talked last week, I think. Old Porch couldn't rightly remember. It bothered him that he couldn't. He'd made them calls recently.

Oh boy! Then I've gotten to you before we both had somethin to smile about! I won't say more, but I think you'll find some satisfaction in this turn of events. Good things, Orwin, come to good people.

Then the bill is comin to a vote after all?

The bill is not, but 1245 is no longer a concern of yours.

Then I don't follow.

Senator Hays gave away no more before sayin goodbye if only so as to keep Old Porch's line open for the call that was still comin his way. By then Old Porch was sittin on the edge of his bed with no intention of settlin back, or even movin much, like he was expectin the phone to ring right then, though it weren't but barely 6:00 a.m.

After he'd gave up that notion to just sit and wait, he drained his bladder of its discontent and gave no thought to brushin his teeth except to rub his thumb over the front ones. Rather than growin more and more intrigued by the call, a pique of irritation got to workin in him and was headin toward somethin meaner too as he marched through his house, now and then disturbed by a distant snore. Even Billings was out cold on the couch.

Maybe just to escape the storm he always carried within hisself, Old Porch marched outside. He flung a parka over his undergarments and gave no thought to his bare feet. He let Mr. Bucket out of his kennel and only as he was dumpin kibble into the metal dish, only then did the clarity of the comin day stun him. Gone were the clouds, the storm. Even the motion of air upon the earth seemed to have ceased. The rosiness of dawn was also near burnt away. Had he ever seen his sky so blue? And still twinklin thanks to a handful of stars scattered across that wide abidin glow. Below it to the northeast Timpanogos seemed inconsequential, a dead lady on her back, draped in lavender shades. Kaieneewa's and Agoneeya's mild summits were similarly draped, similarly rendered insignificant, and with that white *I* on Agoneeya nearly erased but for texture fightin through the snowfall. Squaw Peak stayed dark and broodin, while beyond in unusual clarity rose up Mount Katanogos.

Old Porch just stood there and gawked, snow meltin around his ankles, the phone ringin again. He looked around for Effy. It took a moment for him to realize he'd never see her again. His chest expanded with agony. At least the call was on the office line, though it weren't from no politician.

Loyal Egan was already over at his house. Hatch was there too, with Kelly and Billings. Old Porch had been wrong about Billings on the couch; only blankets blanketin more blankets slept there. The snowmobiles were ready, and they was gonna take to the trails on the south side of Agoneeya. While police and rangers and whatever nonsense search parties stayed busy with the cirque, they'd take the route behind Agoneeya to the back side of Katanogos.

Ain't that takin the long way around to the barn? Old Porch asked, an echo in his ear born either from the phone or from somewhere else, far off in place and maybe even in time.

The way Egan had worked it out, this way if they did run into trouble along the way, they was only out huntin coyotes, and they had the right to hunt deer, and along with the licenses they carried, even though they was expired, they'd say they had landowner tags for where they was goin, even if they didn't. Egan could just claim he'd forgot to pack them while still makin a reasonable claim about their destination and the rights there that they had. Of course snowmobiles were not allowed.

If we get cited, I figure you'll stand us fer the fines, Egan ribbed his dad.

Let that hero brother of yours handle that, Old Porch grunted back.

Egan laughed. He almost sounded like he was in a good mood. And maybe he was. It was clear to Old Porch that Egan just couldn't wait to get back up there.

Before hangin up, Egan told his dad that the fourth radio was on the kitchen counter with new batteries. *But it won't do you no good so long as we got them big mountains between us.*

Good huntin then.

This was at 7:07 a.m.

Back outside Old Porch let Mr. Bucket take a run through the snow, leapin around and jawin up big bites of powder. Just one short phone call and the day had banished most of the violet shadows from the mountains. Now they rose up decked in whites more brilliant than a bridal gown.

Orwin returned to his bedroom and after changin stood before his bureau with the top drawer open. Under his socks waited the 9mm Egan had handed him last night. He contemplated its history. He was too late to join that snowmobile outin and likely didn't have the bones no more to handle such distances even if set upon the back of a bellowin engine. He admired Egan's ambition, admired Hatch and Kelly too, even Billings, but he gritted his teeth too over their idiocy. Them mountains were vast, and they'd need luck if they was gonna take a long way around and still actually find someone up there.

When the phone in his bedroom started ringin, Old Porch assumed it was Egan again. But it weren't. Nor was the next call. Nor was the one after that. In less than twenty minutes he'd spoken with three state senators. If the mornin clarity had stunned Old Porch, it weren't nothin compared to the tidins that he could now consider more fully as he studied the map he'd laid out on the dinin room table.

What the heck was that all about? asked a still-sleepy-eyed Shelly down in the kitchen. At least he was dressed in jeans and had on a thick sweater, and the stye in his eye seemed mostly gone. Sean stood beside him, equally sleepy, though he was still in his boxers. Old Porch didn't care.

He motioned for them to study the contour lines his swollen thumb had begun to trace out. Why shouldn't these two know first what had just graced the Porch family? And then both Woolsey and Francis were there too, dressed and chompin at the bit, like they knew somethin had at last changed and this time in their favor.

Old Porch first explained to these four boys what all had happened with Senate Bill 1245 and how the broad-stroke release of certain public lands for private interests by the federal government weren't gonna happen. Except then this mornin he had talked not only to the U.S. senator but three state senators who had informed him, and on a Sunday mornin no less, that come Monday mornin, the Bureau of Land Management would put up for sale an assortment of lands around the proposed Four Summits. And that weren't all: along with the state-sanctioned sale of lands in and around the Uinta-Isatch-Cache National Forest, as well as the approved sale of other private inholdins, includin those substantial parcels owned by the Hone family, recently voted upon by all twelve children, with all twelve in favor, and certified by Brother Mallory Guvin Hone, or Manic Guff as he was known, a set of lands more than adequate for the recreational acreage required for the Four Summits Ski Resort would be purchased by none other than Orwin Porch and his constituency of silent investors, which included Havril Enos, for the purpose of preapproved development.

Fer real?! Shelly exclaimed, as thrilled as Sean was bewildered, though Shelly's escalatin excitement over this change of fortune and all it now predicted for their future soon stirred Sean toward like enthusiasm. Woolsey got there quicker: they was all about to get really rich. Even Francis, who for the most part remained a captive of grief, managed to cough up a wan smile.

Like I always said, Old Porch orated, *your daddy's gonna own hisself a mountain.*

This exaggeration also hid the yet-unresolved question of how to best access the plan, with roads guaranteed by way of Heber and Wallburg, while the fate of any route from Orvop, by way of that box canyon Isatch Canyon, was still in the hands of the USFS, the state of Utah, and of course municipal politicians who would need some persuadin to help urge into existence the lump of gold Old Porch had just landed in the city's lap.

Won't developin take years? Sean asked.

It sure will, Old Porch replied, but he was still grinnin.

Shelly then explained to everyone how the land acquisition for Four Summits would release a second tier of fundin that would appropriately compensate Orwin Porch for his time and labor thus far and salary him for a guaranteed seven years, which weren't even countin bonuses, options, not to mention what he'd get as the presidin partner. Porch Meats's income would still roll in, but with their dad now occupied with the new enterprise, the older Porch boys would have to step up and run things.

That's right! Now's the time for you and Sean to prove yourselves! Old Porch exhorted his sons.

Shelly left the room to call Liz Blicker.

What about me? Woolsey wanted to know.

Old Porch smiled. *Come summer you and Francis are gonna help me build one heckuva house up in Indian Hills. Bigger than even that Movie Star's estate up by Cassidy.*

Does that mean I gotta go to Timpview? was all Francis wanted to know.

Francis, you can go wherever the heck you like. You can even quit school and just work for me.

Old Porch smiled, maybe even warmly, and Francis really did do his best to answer the smile, even if he couldn't. Old Porch then announced that he was goin to church and he'd welcome company but was fine to go alone too. Woolsey said that Darren Blicker had invited him to join his family at their church in Grandview, and he and Francis had planned to go there.

Oh heck, Shelly cursed. *That means Liz'll have to go too. Guess I'll drive.*

Many years later, Trisha Price, sufferin the consequences of a lifetime of smokin menthols, wheelchair-bound with the constant companion of an oxygen tank, and not even days away from her death, noted ruefully, like many others would, how so many moments that Sunday mornin, *bristlin like pine needles on a branch,* offered the salvation of a deviation: *To think what would've happened if they had stuck with that plan or if even Francis alone had insisted on goin and cut hisself once and for all from that man!* Though there are others who disagree. Much like the beliefs of Samuel Zyer, Duane Newren, who at twenty-three was felled by a fallin tree, was convinced of the great machinery of the world by which we are all helplessly moved along despite what free will our imagination continues to allot us: *Just as we can imagine reachin through bulletproof glass because we can see where our hand might reasonably get to, we can imagine Francis, Woolsey, and Shelly makin different choices. But just like our hand would be stopped by that glass, they too would've been stopped by somethin even more transparent than bulletproof glass and stronger too. Pillars Meadow was where they was headed and that was that.*

Though hardly transparent nor bulletproof, Old Porch cared little for his sons' plans and changed his church-goin mind on the spot. He had a better idea. He ordered his four boys to winter up as well as gather together a small arsenal of rifles, shotguns, and handguns. Whatever they felt like shootin.

At this point, Old Porch was unresolved about only one thing: what to do with the 9mm and the spent casins Egan had given him? His initial reaction had been to destroy them, what Egan should've done hisself, though the annoyance over the task of it was balanced out by a demonstration of fealty Orwin Porch had never known before: Egan was all in and at Old Porch's mercy. And so the question that began to possess Old Porch's thoughts was not how to vanish the evidence but how to use it. If they could locate the Kalin kid, or even if they could get to where he'd been, and leave the weapon there, why wouldn't that seal the whole deal?

Poor Kevin Moffet. Of course Kevin Moffet didn't see hisself that way, as poor. Quite the contrary. He'd just said yes to the job of flyin tourists over Denali National Park. He'd even booked a ticket to Juneau. In fact he'd spent most of last night moonin over some Alaska travel brochures. He'd also dug out an old copy of a Jack London book assigned in high school that he'd never read. Somewhere he'd stashed a bottle of rum.

Sunday mornin, October 31, didn't change his mood none, but a slight hangover did temper his willingness to face the brilliance outside his bedroom window. It sure had dumped last night! What a spectacle! Even if this sight also got Kevin Moffet to thinkin about them two kids he and Old Porch had seen up in the Katanogos cirque. Were they still up there? Or had they made it out? What about them horses?

Gosh, if only he'd've just turned on the news once. Instead Kevin Moffet started to wonder then about why Old Porch had made like he was drawin a gun and shootin that boy? Hadn't Old Porch said they was Porch family relations up there lookin for his stolen ponies? Somehow in the light of mornin that didn't seem credible anymore. Those kids had looked awful young.

Make of this what you will, but right at that moment Kevin Moffet's phone rang. It was Old Porch, and who do you think he got to talkin about straight off and with great abashedness too? Why those two kids! Right as Kevin Moffet had been thinkin about them! Which poor Kevin Moffet made sure to tell Old Porch. Not that it was that much of a coincidence. Old Porch, always the card player, was constantly assessin risk and viable tolerances and so had chosen to assume that Kevin Moffet had seen the news.

Right away Old Porch launched into how he'd been mistaken; the distance, the judderin helicopter, plus his own assumptions had blinded him to the fact that down there weren't his kin but none other than the very same boy who had stolen his ponies and killt his Russel! He was so ashamed. They could've settled it right then. Kevin Moffet gently reminded Old Porch that they hadn't had the gas to make the stop. *But we should've gone back!* Old Porch mewled. *We at least could've alerted the police right then!* Kevin Moffet had to agree that they could've done that.

Of course, the police did get up there, and that kid shot one of the rangers dead.

That revelation sure shocked Kevin Moffet, and Old Porch noted his surprise. He agreed it was sad and tragic. *Maybe we was lucky to get out of there like we done.*

Kevin Moffet laughed some until a cold whisper of a word he couldn't hear fell upon the back of his neck.

Old Porch sighed: *Anyways, it's over now. Him and that Gatestone girl, they got buried in the storm. Froze to death. The police are up there now, lookin for the bodies. They'll likely find my dead horses too.*

Kevin Moffet felt plenty bad then for Old Porch and told him how he cherished their friendship and if there was anythin he ever needed, why Kevin would be more than glad to help. *Especially if you ever head up to Alaska, where I go tomorrow. Got a new job.*

Old Porch sure congratulated him then, and the sound of his elation warmed Kevin Moffet to the point that he was no longer givin that business up in the cirque any thought. Old Porch then shared the news about Four Summits and even offered Kevin Moffet a job should things go sideways up there in the Last Frontier. He figured he'd need a pilot on call pretty much around the clock given the territory he'd be in charge of.

You own the whole mountain, Mr. Porch?

Mountains, friend. I own mountains.

Kevin Moffet was gobsmacked. He'd never known anyone who owned a whole mountain. Old Porch weren't deaf neither to how his charm was workin on Kevin Moffet, which is why he asked right then and there for his favor, assurin Kevin in the same breath that he'd pay full price and bonus Kevin twice that, in cash. *I want you to have some pin money when you land up north.*

It was the least Kevin Moffet could do. What's more, the Bell 206 LR had come in early this mornin and was available.

If that ain't fate! Old Porch cried happily. He wanted to fly his boys over the area they'd soon turn into one of the world's most beautiful ski resorts. And the sad truth is that poor Kevin Moffet was near as excited as Old Porch. On such a gorgeous mornin, what better way to bid adieu to Utah than with a wilderness flight?

It was 10:24 a.m.

W hat you're likely puttin together by now is one of the strangest alignments concernin these events. You'd've known it already if you'd've spent time in Orvop and joined the chatter that still so often comes up about what finally happened up there on Pillars Meadow. Of course, as you've already gathered, no matter how encompassin the version you could've heard while waitin on the Slurpee machine or sittin around those tables where coffee is now served, it still pales before the greater darkness that moved alongside Kalin March and Landry Gatestone: namely Tom Gatestone, who came up with the cause, set the destination hisself, and then once sprung free from the folds of death atop Ash would accompany Navidad and Mouse, his sister, and that monstrous figuration of lethal movement, Kalin March, to the very destiny he'd mostly devised.

Fer sure Kalin never did or could've understood the lengths gone to arrange this impressment, what positioned him for the test he would ultimately fail, and fail at so memorably that the outcome would forever be confused with gilt glory and laurels. At least in Kalin's favor, he loved them horses through and through and no question risked his life for them all, at every turn.

Landry too had witnessed Kalin's kindness and attunement to their spirit and in turn witnessed their attentive manner toward him. It was a kinship anyone with a heart would've quieted around and even revered. Somehow Kalin had come to know Navidad and Mouse better than most who come from a life with horses. And that likely included her brother Tom.

Which was a little unsettlin given just how good Tom was with horses. And maybe it was that very unsettlin that led Landry to begin to mischaracterize her brother's nature. Landry had not forgotten that at heart Tom was a trickster, and yet over the course of their journey, she'd started to give herself over to this notion that some fabled destination so grandly framed by Tom really did exist. Not only that, but

Landry had even begun to accord Tom some ennoblin change of heart while in Death's grasp; after all, maybe it was true that Tom had gone to the Mountain and beheld firsthand the Holy respite from life's sufferin, especially for beasts of burden, and was thus charged, through Kalin, to serve as an agent, nay, angel of change.

Except Tom weren't no romantic. And he weren't no angel either. He did remain, though, a joy, and that was mainly because he'd always seemed made of joy, through and through, even if in Landry's eyes, and fer sure their mother's too, he'd been a boy of relentless mirth because he was full to the brim with relentless mischief. Now, no question, he enjoyed horses plenty, and he would in life, and apparently in death, visit upon them the dearest and gentlest affection, but what delighted him most about Navidad and Mouse was that they was Old Porch's.

To be clear Tom weren't ever a brutal boy. There weren't a smidge of base temperament in him. He'd've had trouble makin a fist were it not for his skill at holdin a bull rope, or any number of birds, you know the ones, easily within the vocabulary of his long middle finger. In fact so lackin was Tom in that awful lust for harm that maybe it's no wonder he was drawn to Kalin, for such lightheartedness likes nothin better than to balance its pan against an equal sum of force; it's what the insouciant too often are too cowardly to confess.

Tom weren't blind either. He'd always sensed it. Maybe Landry had too. Maybe because she was a woman, a young young woman fer sure but still comin into the predominate ways the sexes can arrange for themselves, she recognized Kalin's abhorrence for that Colt Peacemaker for what it was: desire. Even if she couldn't name it, her blood sure as heck would've registered the terrible heat and even the slightly salty taste. She might've even guessed, and correctly too, that Tom had delighted in Kalin's presence fer one reason in particular: there's only one thing more excitin than sensin that kind of power; it's knowin that it's gone unnoticed by everyone else.

So it's no great stretch, quite the contrary, to imagine Tom, under the ordinance of mirthful mischief, confectin for hisself and his friend an adventure, even a risky one that, when it became clear that his own participation wouldn't be possible, could still have been reconcocted as a solo journey for just his friend to undertake.

In other words, it was anythin but chance that Old Porch in assemblin his progeny and commandeerin the pilotin skills of one Kevin Moffet was headin to a part of the Katanogos massif that weren't just about to become his newly acquired property but was also exactly where Kalin was headin.

Tom, you see, had not only directed Kalin to take Old Porch's ponies but in effect, after climbin them over the cathedrals of Heaven and Hell, also returned them to Old Porch.

Now it's fair to disagree here. For every Taft Mackey, Horace Montgomery, and Shelby Jensen, all buried in the Orvop City Cemetery, there's also a Jolene Johnston, Lauren Barnes, Blake Kotter, Trewartha Pope, and Beth Crown, the very same Beth with dusky blond hair and a Titan mind for formulatin a sensible world, even as she drank herself to death in Mississippi, ambushed in the end by the love she never got, her remains returned to Utah, buried like so many others in the Orvop City Cemetery, who would til the end protest such speculations, given how protected that acreage had been. Beth Crown had a point too: there was no sayin when, if ever, the Bureau of Land Management would release parcels for private development or whether or not the Hone family, when it came time, would really sign on the dotted line. Old Porch hisself didn't even know what was his until that Sunday mornin. Recall for yourself how just the day before he'd been certain the dream was dead. Still, if Tom Gatestone didn't know about the Porch inholdin up there, he fer sure knew about Four Summits. It was in the papers every other week for years, and there was no not-hearin Old Porch crowin loud how he was the essential part of such goings-on. So, whether owned yet or not, it's not hard to imagine how Tom might find it funny to steer them horses toward the very land Old Porch wanted to have more than havin to take a piss at midnight.

Not that the Porches or Kalin March on that Sunday mornin had any sense of where they was really goin, which is likely why still graver concerns rise up, as if to cry out, *Why Troy then?*, *Why Pillars Meadow now?*, if just to acknowledge the dark aggregatin influences upon pendin temporal and topographical alliances, wherein Tom hisself, whether when he was alive or later as a ghost, was conscripted as well to act on behalf of consequences generations old, maybe even older.

After all, who among us will ever really glimpse how we are spun upon our course by wheels so great, their very curvature is beyond our detection? How even a hint of their presence, so immense and confoundin, would before our feeble senses appear less substantial than air? How often does some deluded sense of control, bequeathed to us when we are at the meridian of our successes, birthin a belief in our unnatural permanence, and thus further installin in us an entitlement to some station of inevitable greatness, thanks to those nefarious twins, Pride & Vanity, blind us to how we are in reality only flung around, drawn in directions we are oblivious to, the author of nothin that we can call our own, fully and allways dispossessed of any larger portion, and but for a handful of beautiful moments too soon returned to stardust?

Of course we can also fairly dismiss such conjecturin as just that, so much gobbledygook over two kids who stole two ponies and in the tanglin that followed found themselves in a whole mess of trouble. No question we will never know fer certain how these events were determined or cemented. The gods of Mount Olympus are long gone. So is Mount Olympus. Furthermore, it's likely the protean memories of the many will play a further part in aggrandizin or demonizin both the survivors and the aggrieved. But memories aren't just singular and personal. There is also the one Memory, which we only faintly know, that includes our collective history, and it is that Memory that metes out its contents upon the scales of Universal Balance, a Memory so complete it matters not if it pertains to the gyre of galaxies or the tiniest spinnin notion over whether to turn right or turn left. Both the grain of sand and the largest heavenly body, both the sparrow and the horse, sage and fool, saint and abuser, are in the end held accountable before the immutable summation we imagine and in any case fear: Judgment wherein Justice signs the record.

A round the time that Kevin Moffet was readyin the Bell 206 LR and Sondra Gatestone and Allison March was gettin up off that curb in front of the Grandview church, wipin the snow off their butts too, folks throughout Utah County and beyond, teenagers in particular, especially those attendin Orvop High or Timpview, were gatherin to gossip more about Landry Gatestone and Kalin March. How had Landry Gatestone gotten involved with Kalin March anyhow? That was a persistent one. Was she kidnapped? Was she in league with the scamp? The Bonnie-and-Clyde version had strong appeal, though the news that she'd been shot dead last night was already startin to circulate, givin the original claim of kidnappin new legs. Though why had this Kalin March chosen to shoot her then and not earlier? Also, how had he shot that cop up in the cirque? And, yes, that victim was almost unilaterally described as a police officer and never a ranger. Some kids swore Kalin March had killt him point-blank, though the only thing that seemed certain was the poor fella lay cold and stiff now in the morgue.

Too often local and state news outlets substantiated this gossip with their own incomplete reportin. National networks sent in their own crews to learn more. The entrance to Isatch Canyon was consistently described as a circus, though the question that got no answer, especially from Squaw Peak, lordin over this growin assemblage of lights, cameras, and doughnuts, was the endurin one: Who was this cipher, this nobody, this out-of-stater so-whater? Who was Kalin March?

As the mornin wore on reporters finally broke the story about Kalin March's daddy servin a life sentence for killin a black cop. For a while that was the easiest way for the story to run: like father, like son. But it didn't stop there. Soon enuf Allison March's alcoholism got to circulatin. In those territories that pretty much settled it: a bad kid with bad folks who had not seen the light of the Lord. The sooner he was found, the sooner he'd be rid of. And sooner couldn't get here fast enuf.

Of course there were still more than a handful made plenty uncomfortable by the fact that so much of what they was hearin was one way or another comin by way of the Porches. The Porches were a big part of Orvop, and despite their money plenty of Orvop residents weren't blind to their meanness. Old Porch in particular had a reputation for cussedness. That said, as nasty as the Porches could get, no one went so far as to suggest they had anythin to do with the murders, especially the murder of their dear little Russel. Not a single God-devoted soul thought to imagine it any other way than the Kalin kid doin in Russel with maybe a few inclined to blame some stranger, some gangrel. That sure removed Orwin Porch and his boys from the calculus of patter sustained by suspicion. Plus, whether you cared for Orwin Porch one bit or cursed his manner, he was still a force in the community, with wealth spread over the valley. Plenty of folks grew up on Porch jerky.

Now let's agree here and now that there are lots of good kids around, and given just half the chance, they'll do the good thing. But let's also agree that there are plenty of good kids who will stand powerless in the face of a bad deed. Let's furthermore agree that there are kids who ain't even that bad but when put together with like-minded kids, with no good kids there to stand in the way, why then such a group can go howlin mad.

Fer starters, and this was indeed the start of that fabled snowball fusillade, it was Darren Blicker who overhanded that first chunk of ice, what he would later protest was only a snowball but what many years later Doug Harwood, before he was killt by a fallin brick, later buried in the Orvop City Cemetery, Harwood, not the brick, would confirm was *a big old lump of rock and icicle ice disguised with some snow*. It struck Allison March on the back of the head with enuf force to not only make her bleed but knock her down, both feet losin hold on the slick ice that was at that hour still coverin the church parkin lot. Havin volunteered to drive, Allison had been helpin the still-distraught Sondra Gatestone into the passenger seat. One moment she was tryin to coax a smile from her friend, and then in the next she had a nostril full of snow, both her chin and a shoulder hurtin from the slip, her left palm already at the back of her head, comin away with a palmful of blood.

Sondra Gatestone, of course, was there at once, animated by the fall, helpin her friend to her feet, before facin down the kid who had done this, and on Church property too, which was when Darren Blicker hurled a second chunk of ice, this time hittin Sondra Gatestone in the center of her forehead, blood at once streamin down her nose and into the one eye.

That's the lady whose kid killt Russel Porch! Darren Blicker shouted, throwin a third clump of ice and snow, this one packed extra with rocks.

And the funny part is that Darren Blicker had woke up fine as the day was fine, and to add good on good, Woolsey had said he'd join him for church, and then he was sayin Francis was comin too, and that was also great, and Shelly too, which, well, that weren't a great thing, him bein so sweet on his sister, Liz, and them two always brewin some sort of trouble, though it still weren't that bad either. After all, Darren now had the whole mornin spelled out for him, havin a big breakfast around the Blicker table with all them Porch boys who no matter the gruesome circumstances had become celebrities of sorts. Both Darren's momma and poppa were thrilled to welcome them all to their home. His momma had started talkin about waffles, which they never had because his dad had to go get the waffle iron out of the attic, which this mornin he said he'd happily do. But then Woolsey had called to say he and his brothers and his daddy were goin for a helicopter ride instead and he hadn't even thought to invite Darren! Woolsey didn't stop there neither, spoutin stuff about how it all had come true, about the Porches ownin Katanogos, *all of Mount Katanogos!*, and flyin up there to rename it Porch Mountain, and maybe there'd be a Woolsey Peak, fer sure a Russel Peak, while Darren had just sat there and listened, no longer any part of the conversation. He'd hung up mad and only got madder when his daddy got mad for havin had to go up to the attic, and his momma got mad then too and told her husband to go put the waffle iron back in the attic because she weren't cookin waffles no more. They could have cereal.

Darren Blicker was still livin in the aftermath of that disap-pointment when he'd spotted them two ladies enter the chapel. He'd scowled at them as they took their seats and made sure Dale Laws and Joey Bird knew who they was. He even got them to scowl and pass along the same scowlin instructions to Larry Ashby and Rick Ramsey, who knew full well who Allison March was and for certain Sondra Gatestone, because everyone knew the Gatestones. Both Bill and Julie

Evanston, who had come across town for the service and planned to visit with the Hafens afterward, did not approve of any such glarin. The Wongs, who like the Evanstons were also visitin, didn't approve neither of what they recognized at once as fulminatin teenage-boy trouble. Unfortunately none of the boys in question heeded these stern remonstrances from either the Evanstons or the Wongs, both of whom, it's worth notin, became friends on this day, and their friendship proved one that endured the span of their lives and even continued on through their kids, grandkids, and great-grandkids. Anyway, it's too bad Darren and the rest, though especially the rest, paid no mind to anythin other than the righteous furnace they kept stokin at their core, which weren't righteousness and to tell the truth weren't much of a furnace either. Because, well, if they'd just listened to their elders, they might've spared their futures heaps of discreditin and shame.

It was when Darren Blicker heard Mr. Everett Walsh proclaim words about how when it comes to pass that everyone who finds me shall kill me, Darren weren't thinkin of that *me* as *him* but of that *me* as *Kalin March* and even by extension them responsible for his existence. And he nearly rose to his feet right then to point out the lady who was the mother of the murderer and even how she was now sittin with Sondra Gatestone of all people. And then later when Havril Enos was up at the podium goin on about how the Lord would judge us by our deeds, Darren Blicker got to thinkin that he hadn't done much by way of deeds, and he was back again to thinkin how he really did need to alert everyone in that church who was there among them that mornin, but once again despite all these cerebral commotions demandin he act, Darren Blicker remained red-faced and hunched over in the pew. After that, the only voice he heard in his head was Woolsey's: *Don't take her frickin side!* That's what Woolsey had growled at him when Darren had tried to make nice and apologize to Sondra Gatestone on Friday in the Isatch Canyon parkin lot, right after Woolsey had gone all rancorous on Kalin March's mother. *She's as much in this as her!* And in the memory of that exchange, playin over and over in his head now, Darren Blicker knew hisself as someone who not only couldn't do a deed for the Lord, he couldn't even prove hisself loyal to his very best friend, no matter that Woolsey sure didn't consider Darren Blicker his best friend.

Stop pumpin your leg, you dang freak! his sister Liz hissed at him under her breath. And it was true: one of Darren's legs was goin crazy. He stopped that and called her stupid.

You're the stupid one, she responded.

I ain't the one who broke my nose walkin into a door. And it weren't a glass door like you keep lyin about. You walked into your own bedroom door! Darren snickered. *Now that's stupid!*

Liz Blicker pinched the back of her brother's arm, twistin hard enuf to make him squeal, which sure got their parents' attention, who put an end to that nonsense with glares best not challenged.

Then Darren Blicker seen Sondra Gatestone with the Kalin kid's mother hustlin out, like they was guilty before the Lord. He couldn't take it no more. He even started to stand, but his sister stopped him.

What the heck is wrong with you? she seethed. *The service ain't over, you idjit.* She was pretty mad herself, since she too had been excited to have Shelly Porch sittin beside her at church as well as at her home for a family meal.

Afterward, when he stepped outside with Dale Laws and Joey Bird, Darren Blicker was talkin nonstop about the Kalin kid's mother and Sondra Gatestone and how they'd left early because of course they was guilty, and Donald Hickman and Guy Olsen, overhearin this, came over because they'd just been sayin a similar thing. Jennie Stall and Emily Larsen joined up too, though mostly because of Guy Olsen, and if that weren't somethin extra for Darren, because even if she was talkin with Guy, there weren't a prettier girl at Orvop High than Jennie Stall, with the biggest boobs too, until at some point Darren realized she'd stopped talkin to either Guy or Donald and was now talkin to him, and, boy, he'd better look away because if he didn't he'd just start starin at them boobs, and what's more, to make up for lookin away, he'd better say somethin, somethin cool too, and that's when he'd seen across the parkin lot that Kalin kid's momma helpin Sondra Gatestone into a truck, and bein so deprived of speech but at the same time feelin hisself called upon to act, Darren Blicker grabbed up off the ground, right beneath the church eaves where icicles had fallen, a big chunk of ice and rock.

That weren't no easy throw either. Even the Orvop quarterbacks leadin Orvop to the state finals, both Rodney Blake and Shawn Hovey, would've had trouble hittin the truck, let alone that Kalin kid's mother. But Darren Blicker nailed it, right on the back of her head and with enuf force to knock Allison March right down, which was when the akratic Dale Laws joined in, gettin nowhere close, followed by of all people Guy Olsen. And then Darren Blicker nailed his second throw, maybe he should be a quarterback?, this time hittin Sondra Gatestone square in the face, though he didn't knock her down, and that dissatisfied him. So he kept throwin, though after that mostly missin. Jennie Stall and Emily Larsen were long gone, wantin no part of that. Other young men, though, without thinkin much, likely just drawn in by the sight of Darren Blicker startin up a snowball fight, with opponents they couldn't clearly make out, hidin about where Darren was aimin, began hurlin too whatever they could get their hands on, though they weren't throwin ice or rock. Just snow. And they was laughin.

Sondra Gatestone heard in her heart the call to run, but unlike last night she did not obey. And she sure weren't about to give them her back; what's more, she was determined to face them boys for as long as they wanted to throw whatever meanness they had in them, her eyes focused mean as mean can get on Darren Blicker, who at that moment again unleashed another thing of rock and ice in packed snow, which in fact would've hit her again, and in the face too, but, see, Allison March was back on her feet, her hand flyin out, strikin aside that projectile.

It was 10:38 a.m.

That should've warned someone, at the very least Sondra Gatestone, but no one saw the bleakest omen of all that mornin in a church parkin lot.

Half a dozen adults stepped in then and put an end to the assault. Darren Blicker and the rest of the kids, includin Jennie Stall and Emily Larsen, who, contrary to what they'd first thought, had not escaped, were dragged back into the church. *How'd you get roped into such a rumption?* a disgusted Havril Enos demanded of a confused Dale Laws. *I weren't listenin,* Dale responded.

To be sure this was not a mess easily sorted and was gonna affect the Sunday School that followed as well as the Priesthood and Relief Society gatherins. Dale Laws got a stern talkin to fer sure, and that went for the rest, Darren Blicker especially, not that such dialogues of disfavor had any impact on Darren's life. He'd go on to become the awful sort that on that mornin he'd got a head start fashionin. For years to come he'd brag about peltin them two ladies. Though not all his years.

Not to be too unkind, more than a few Church members had a hard time forgettin that mornin, especially the one moment, quantified by a sickenin sensation of paralysis and horror, when they'd watched those last volleys of ice and snow smack the truck and pretty much everythin else but them two women, who, after the one had swatted an ice ball away like a good cat swats down a fly, didn't move none, not even one step backwards, but faced those dumb-minded attackers, Sondra Gatestone with her face streaked with blood, Allison March with her hand drippin with the blood from the injury at the back of her head.

Elsa Sarantopoulo, an extraordinary painter whose work never received the acclaim it deserved, put this appallin scene to oils, with how she framed it no doubt accountin for its impact: there's no sign of the ones doin the throwin, and except for the blurred vehicle in the background, there's no knowin that here is a parkin lot. Sarantopoulo chose to concentrate solely on the two faces, and with a very shallow depth of field too, with even strands of bloodied hair slippin out of focus. Both women's eyes, though, remain exceptionally sharp, as is the case for their snow-smattered faces, with plenty of blood there on their cheeks, and wetness too, which many have mistook for their cryin, though Elsa Sarantopoulo knew better than to paint tears beneath the eyes of these two warriors, gods maybe, glowerin, thin-lipped and undeterred, the whole future at their disposal. The paintin was titled *Accused* and for many years hung in a readin room in the Orvop city library until it was put on display in that fifth chamber of the Time Gallery in Houston, where, like everythin else, it was consumed by fire. Elsa Sarantopoulo recalled it vividly just as a semi on a Washington state freeway set free the timber that would crush her. She was cremated and her ashes released from a ferry headed toward Orcas Island. Though well-intentioned her three children opened the urn at the bow of the boat, heedless of the headwind that would blow the remains of their matriarch into their noses and mouths. Elsa Sarantopoulo raised them well, though. They laughed.

To be sure apologies were forthcomin that day, not just from the devil-possessed teenagers themselves but from parents and neighbors who near at once delivered upon the Gatestone porch a fair if not substantial delivery of casseroles and pies, which Mungo eyed with edacious menace. Some of the adults got to blamin the movie *Rambo*, seein as how many of the boys had seen it, includin Darren Blicker, Dale Laws, Guy Olsen, and, to everyone's surprise, Jennie Stall. In fact Jennie had seen it twice, and this despite the R ratin. The notion was that the movie had so powerfully acted upon their susceptible adrenal secretions that they was incapable of knowin what they was doin.

Not without irony have others noted how *Rambo* had achieved some association with what would become known as *The Grandview Church Snowball Fight*, which sure was a misnomer given how there was only one side throwin ice and rock, while high up in the vast over-seein mountains somethin far closer to the story of that veteran of national misdeeds was just startin to heat up into a contest no one was expectin.

Beyond the north side of Agoneeya Mountain, a good ways east of Tiffany's Vista, a stretch of open, mostly hilly ground steadily rose toward the back side of the Katanogos massif. Broken up by odd ridges and interlockin spurs, it has never secured a name besides Pillars Meadow, which marks the northern end of this acclivity before joinin the forestland that eventually becomes the Uinta-Isatch-Cache National Forest and Ashley National Forest to the northeast or drops down to the dustier regions that lead to the Uintah and Ouray Reservation to the east.

Egan Porch knew that if Kalin and Landry had indeed made it over the summit ridge, as well as survived the storm, there was a good chance they'd use the southern Katanogos ridges for their descent. There were some northeastern routes fer sure, but despite Kalin's proven skills, Landry's too, Egan knew horses well enuf to know that they'd be spent. From here on out Kalin would choose the easier routes.

With his .30-06 Winchester Model 70 slung over his shoulder, Egan used his daddy's binoculars to scan the high ridgelines for anythin beyond dolomite and limestone, lookin fer some human motion makin its way before the dark stands of precariously rooted pines or, even better, traversin the blindin bluffs of fresh snow.

Egan Porch shocked hisself to discover her so quick, shocked hisself twice when he realized with some squintin he could even make her out with bare eyes. Billings and Kelly was right beside him, but they hadn't noticed yet. Hatch was farther off, but him with them fancy Zeiss binoculars was lookin in the wrong direction. And to be fair to Billings and Kelly, they weren't really lookin either, talkin instead about the third snowmobile, what Kelly was drivin, burnin oil, now and then coughin up black smoke.

What had caught Egan's attention first was the bright blink, like a mirror, like a piece of fallen sun. Sure it could've been a piece of ice, but once Egan's binoculars had fixed on it, there was no mistakin the tiny figure of Landry, by her lonesome too, up there on the snow with her own pair of binoculars. The more he took her in, the more amazin it seemed to Egan that out of his brothers, he alone had spotted her. Egan didn't alert them neither. He just gave hisself over to what Ms. Melson would refer to as *the cacoëthes in charge of his nature* and brought up to his eye, steady and fast, the Leupold scope, cartridge already chambered, finger on the trigger.

You find somethin? Hatch barked.

Hard to tell.

Maybe you'll bag yourself a mountain goat, Kelly said with a laugh, not even thinkin to set his binoculars on whatever sight was earnin Egan's attention.

Or a doe, Hatch laughed, joinin in with the jabs.

If I see even a crow, I'll knock it outta the sky, Egan said like he was there to make jokes too.

Billings alone lensed where Egan was aimin.

But what had fallen so easily into place before his binoculars he lost in the scope. Egan focused on slowin his breath as he traced the crosshairs along the high line of those snowy cliffs here and there crowded with pines. His heart had gone reckless under his ribs, and it got worse when he still couldn't find anythin. Where had she gone? Had she spotted them already? Of course she had. Had she run already? Of course she had. And then Egan was seein quakin aspens, and he realized he was on the wrong set of cliffs. His adjustment to the right was smooth and calm.

This time the scope filled with the avalanche cones already accumulated at the base of the higher bluffs. Egan moved steadily up that brutal face until he'd reached a crest line of billowy snow where plenty of trees also waited, Egan continuin to scan right until in a relatively wide and open area he found her again, standin atop a big jut of gray stone and pointin her binoculars Egan's way, no doubt havin spotted the snowmobile tracks and from there locatin the machines themselves and soon after Egan hisself, the sun's reflection bright on his scope starin right back at her, as he settled crosshairs on her own flamin lenses, like two bright quarters off in the distance, a flirtation with which, havin hunted enuf, and now killt, Egan didn't need no lessons to know how to handle.

Egan fired, muscle memory swiftly ejectin the spent cartridge, bolt action settlin a new one into place in case he needed a second shot.

The bang didn't budge Egan, but it sure lurched Hatch around. It got Kelly's attention too. Billings kept his breath just as calm as Egan's as he spotted the results. The echoin whistle of that long-gone bullet seemed to last forever, cuttin valley from sky.

You got her, Billings whispered.

I got her, Egan echoed, though he'd only watched her bein whipped out of frame.

Billings confirmed that he'd seen her blasted from her perch, splayed out on the snow, face down, blood certifyin the ice, and then just as certain as she was there, she and the snow she was on were gone, flushed away down them vertical chutes, the light powder flowin fast as water, sluicin around the bristlecone pines and tall firs growin on a lower ledge near the top, the branches shakin, the trunks too, the trees surely about to fall, deracinated by the force of this small but deadly avalanche. And the voice of all that fallin snow soon followed, outmatchin Egan's shot, continuin to grow in volume as it gathered in force, like an angry wind that just as quick as it started was also soon spent, the aftermath a hiss, pilin up another avalanche cone at the bottom, haloed in ice crystals, both sepulcher and monument to an end.

She's buried fer sure now, Egan said.

Hatch stood speechless.

Kelly seemed confused too, but mostly because he never did manage to lens nothin but fallin snow.

Egan used his binoculars to glass one last time the crest and at once cursed hisself for not stickin to his rifle, because there he was, the boy, Kalin March hisself, scramblin into view.

For all that Egan was feelin in that moment, and it was a lot, maybe there was some part of him, not dumbed down by the satisfactions of violence or the paralyzin breathlessness that he took for joy, that registered how this figure weren't just starin down from them cliffs but starin down on him, a perception worsened by the shadows that seemed then to reach out and cover the boy, growin darker and deeper with every heartbeat until Kalin March weren't no longer Kalin March but a thing few men are brave enuf to stand before let alone recognize. As Mrs. Annserdodder would convey to her sophomores and Ms. Meredith Melson, before she understood her misassignment, would declare in greater detail to her AP English class: *Remember, children, Hector was the might of the Trojans. He killt near thirty men. Almost all the Greeks feared him. But when Achilles came for him, Hector was smart enuf to run. Though, if you've done your readin, you'll know that runnin didn't do him any good.*

Not that Egan was Hector, nor was he about to run. And he sure wasn't one to leave a challenge unanswered. And so Egan, like it was as light as a dowel of balsa, swung up that Winchester to his shoulder again and settled the crosshairs on the cliff's crest.

But of course Kalin March was gone.

So too were the shadows.

Hatch was beside hisself. Hadn't he just dedicated hisself to do but one good thing: see Landry Gatestone home safe? And now his younger brother was claimin to have gunned her down. Hatch didn't know what to do or say, but he said it anyway, or rather he bellowed it, bellowed that it weren't true, that Egan was lyin, unless it was true, and then Egan was a dead man. *What's wrong with you?! Why would you even say such a thing?!* Egan sure didn't flinch, didn't even raise an eyebrow. He just stood there, waitin out his big brother's exasperated shouts, which he'd experienced variations on for pretty much his whole life. And when Hatch seen his stormin weren't gonna do no good and he reached behind his back, why then Egan laughed.

Kelly and Billings joined in with their own chuckles.

What the heck are you goin on about? And Egan was serious. He wanted to know. He even made this inquiry in the softest tones.

Don't you even think to mess with me, boy, Hatch raged.

Easy there, brother. I'm just askin because you seem confused. I didn't shoot nothin.

Excuse me?

Kelly, did you hear a shot?

Nope, Kelly answered.

Billings, you hear one?

Nope.

Hatch, what about you? You hear one?

Hatch lost his bark then, and whatever bite he might be rightfully respected for elsewhere, in that hour, at that place, made no appearance. Hatch's face even flickered with confusion, then panic, and finally recognition. He'd never felt so disoriented nor even this afraid because he didn't know where to turn let alone what to do.

Maybe you heard my sled backfire? Kelly added easily enuf.

Egan nodded slow and mean. *It sure has been actin up.*

You could lean out the fuel screws? Billings threw in.

Hatch, you figure that's what you heard? Egan weren't lettin go, and though Hatch knew he could battle Egan, add in the other two and all the way up here, and he was in trouble.

Maybe I was mistaken, Hatch submitted and didn't even say nothin when Egan grinned.

Egan sure was enjoyin this moment. He was no longer Hatch's younger brother. He could see that now. Over the course of these past days he'd become somethin different, even if it was really a lifetime of small deeds leadin to the big ones, slowly escalatin toward the violence definin the encounters he relished so much, with Robert Gaff, Bren Kelson, and now Landry Gatestone; furthermore, rather than leavin Egan even a little bit appalled and ashamed, or at least chastened, killin Landry had deepened his attraction and attachment to the elations delivered through the rough execution of power. Egan stood there amidst those blindin heights, expurgated, cleansed, free. Nothin came close to this manic delight, jitterin him if just for the want of more of such moments that weren't easily on hand. His peter didn't move none neither, but it didn't have to: this self-occludin lust had already rendered his whole person erect.

Where you at? crackled and spat Old Porch over all their radios.

Pa? Egan asked, as surprised as they all were. How in the heck had a signal got past Agoneeya and Kaieneewa to say nothin of Katanogos?

I'm with Kevin Moffet and the rest of your brothers. We just flew over the summit, and who the heck do you think we seen? Why that darned kid and the horses!

You see him?! Egan demanded, no longer payin attention to Hatch, who was only now leavin alone the holster behind his back, which he hadn't touched, bringin his right hand into view, empty, now contendin with this new confusion that he weren't in fact responsible for the death of Kalin March.

He's headin down Coyote Gulch! Their father squawked. *We're takin a long loop and gonna set down near Pillars Meadow.*

We're a good hour from there.

Well, hurry if you don't want to miss the fun.

Only minutes earlier, Old Porch hadn't believed his own eyes, but there he was, the Kalin kid ridin the black mare, leadin the blood bay and a big blue Arab with a saddle on him. That had to be Landry Gatestone's horse. *Clop-Clop-clip-Clop.* But Old Porch saw no sign of her. It could be she was on foot, maybe ahead of them, maybe already hidden beneath the pines. Unless she was killt by the storm.

That was at 11:13 a.m.

Earlier that mornin, in order to avoid Isatch Canyon and the air traffic congestin Kirk's Cirque, Old Porch had ordered Kevin Moffet, under the guise of matters concernin property lines, to fly north from the Orvop airport toward Heber. That way they could approach the back side of the Katanogos summit from the northwest.

Old Porch was the first to spot the trail made by the horses, which, by the dance of just one finger, he directed Kevin Moffet to follow. Old Porch was sure the two had already vanished beneath all the trees to the north, but then he caught movement the way good eyes can find by the faintest tremble antlers betwixt a thicket of branches. Old Porch hadn't even needed binoculars.

The cold that kept seepin into that helicopter cabin didn't matter no more, nor the smell of fuel nor the odor of their bodies or the recently soaped-up tack, which Old Porch had dragged along for show so Kevin Moffet and his boys would really think they was plannin to ride them horses out of there.

Seated right behind Old Porch and next to Francis, whose eyes were closed, with Sean and Shelly continuin to squall in the last row, Woolsey was the only one else to catch a glimpse of the Kalin kid. And boy did Woolsey start yammerin soon as he set eyes on the one who had done in their youngest brother, done in an officer of the law, done in Landry Gatestone, a real killer, a real outlaw, and that sure got them all yammerin and lathered up. Francis had darn near crawled into Woolsey's lap to get a look through the binoculars.

Old Porch, meanwhile, was doin everythin in his power to keep Kevin Moffet from changin course.

Let him think we didn't see him, he kept yellin before yellin even louder at his boys, loud enuf to get through the roar of engine and blades, loud enuf so Kevin Moffet would register that this here was also further instructions for him: *We're gonna fly far enuf ahead so he can't spot us no more nor hear us and then we'll come back around to where he won't expect us, right where he's headin to now.*

Kevin Moffet's hand reached for the radio then, but Old Porch stopped him. Kevin Moffet was confused.

Ain't that him? The one who killt Russel and the ranger?

Old Porch nodded.

Shouldn't we alert the police? Kevin Moffet asked.

Old Porch nodded again. *Just not yet. Otherwise we lose the bounty.*

The bounty?

Old Porch was makin this up as he went. *It's sizable.*

I don't know, Orwin.

Old Porch laughed. *You don't need to know! You don't need to do anythin but fly! I got my boys here. Plus, since you're the pilot, you'll get half!*

That's when Old Porch got on his own radio and hailed Egan, Hatch, and Kelly. After that, he closed his eyes. He never noticed the mule trailin Kalin. He never noticed the old elk either or the animal parade and fer sure not the long blind line of ghosts sweepin downward. What Old Porch was seein now in his mind's eye was the boy he'd spotted in Kirk's Cirque just yesterday, with the only difference bein that now he was on a horse. Though maybe Old Porch did then scrutinize a little yesterday's persistent image, because today the kid did strike him as more at ease, or at least somehow more in place, maybe even more at home. Was there somethin to learn from how this boy was makin his way down the mountain? How he was swayin so easily upon the animal's back like they had all the time in the world? But Old Porch let these questions fly right by him.

Worse still, not one part of Old Porch had registered how the shadows both close and far from Kalin seemed to have kept shiftin, which, unlike his father, Woolsey had noticed and in fact was still lookin out for, now only findin shadows fast shallowin with the risin day, which Woolsey liked lookin at, because that was comfortin, unlike what he'd only moments ago discovered around Kalin, shadows movin the way a flock of starlings parts before a falcon, like the shadows themselves were afraid.

Chapter Twenty-Three

"Kalin's Choice"

Kalin had watched Landry spin in a halo of blood, and as if that weren't awful enuf, the force of the shot had kicked her loose as a rag doll from the rock upon which she'd stood. She fell a good six feet too before ploppin face down in a pillow of dry snow, hair surroundin her beautiful little head like a messy black stain, with now a dark red stain claimin more and more of the surroundin flakes.

Though maybe that had been Kalin seein things, addin things, the whole of what he'd seen too quickly reduced to smears of black and red and then more red until not even red could hold. Kalin barely blinked and Landry was gone again, gone so fast he was sure he'd misunderstood, did he even blink?, the snow givin way beneath her like sand flowin through a broken hourglass, now beholden to another cadence of time, gone to another cessation hundreds of feet below.

Kalin had hurled hisself forward on his belly, near swimmin through the remainin powder, positionin his feet and hands on whatever rocks seemed immune to the collapse. When he'd reached the edge, snow was still spillin downward, still sluicin through a cluster of tall pines too casually adherin to the sheer face. They looked like gapped teeth. Below them Kalin was able to follow the tumblin brightness, both congealin into an increasinly heavy whiteness and at the same time expandin into lightness beyond the grasp of its own disgorgement. Landry . . . Kalin had watched her fall, and amidst that snow she'd fallen forever, even as the sight of her departure to say nothin of the distance to the bottom was too quickly lost in a mist of ice crystals risin up the wall.

They'll shoot you next.

Kalin knew Tom was right, and despite the desire to follow Landry over the edge, he had pushed hisself back, but not before standin up and if for no longer than a second starin down into the valley where somewhere Landry's killer also stood. Kalin didn't need to see him. For Kalin it had never been about aimin, and even if right then no audible echo had reverberated out upon that crooked valley, would that it had, the consequences of a thought too dark to know had already elicited from the horses, still safe below this ragged ridgeline, whinnies, grunts, and uneasy snorts. They had stomped the earth too, and that even included Ash. And what did Ash know of this earth anymore?

Back down beside Navidad, Kalin dropped to his knees like he'd just been thunked on the head with a log. He hid his face in his hands, wantin to wail, though only the crack of ground teeth got loose and instead of a sob, just a dry cough. This stiffness upon his face and within his chest then seized the whole him, not one joint absolved, as if Kalin had become the embodiment of Landry when she was held captive in the heart of fear, as if he was now a tree long since sapless and life-abandoned and fallen. Nor did this spell of petrification require a Medusa but rather was the absence of such terrible beauty that brought stone to the refuge of stone. Only Kalin's shoulders moved, shook really, as if against chains used to pinion mountains; as if to remember long-lost wings Kalin would never again know, the angels of a better tomorrow once and for all abandonin him.

Tom, though, would not abandon Kalin. He too had fallen to his knees beside Kalin, whisperin in a voice Kalin had never known before, except maybe the one time, in the hospital, equally hoarse and bereft, though back then still rimed with hope or promise or at least purpose: *Move, Kalin. If they seen her good enuf to kill her, they know exactly where you're at too. Time ain't our friend now.*

Time had never been their friend, but Kalin didn't need to say it. He dragged hisself up from the snow, maybe because of the hand on his shoulder that couldn't touch his shoulder, or because of Tom's words, or maybe just because Kalin knew there weren't no other choice no matter how blasted away his insides felt, barren as a spent chamber, a smokin barrel.

And Tom weren't the only one urgin Kalin to move. The horses had not ceased their stomps and snorts. The mule didn't seem to give a darn, but farther away the donkey and the mountain goat appeared by the constant dislocation of their gaze more and more unsettled. Jojo, though, was the most forlorn, throwin his head up and down, pawin the earth, ears tickin to various directions in search of Landry's voice.

Jojo had met Kalin's first approach by retreatin sideways, enuf to bend the bough his lead was bound to. After Kalin had untied that, Jojo had backed away even more, only eventually quittin this tantrumin even if his tail continued to swish back and forth like an angry switch. He at least let Kalin stroke his neck before once again tossin his head up and down, then stompin more, and finally, when none of that materialized what he was after, that great blue horse had whinnied the air loud as he could, like he was callin out for her by name. That unfroze Navidad and Mouse, who joined in at once. Ash too. But no answer returned.

Movin like a dream then that prohibits movin, Kalin managed to lead Jojo over to Navidad and Mouse, where he first double-checked Mouse's halter-bridle and then got to resettlin the saddle pad and saddle on Navidad, resecurin her cinch next before recheckin her halter-bridle and bit. Kalin then stroked Navidad's neck some while whisperin in her ears a music even Tom couldn't make out. Tom was already on Ash.

When at last Kalin got back up on Navidad, he again did so like he was made of nothin. Navidad settled at once like this species of nothinness was just what she needed, at once radiatin calm, calmin Mouse first and then Ash. Jojo, though, snapped at the air like he was mad at it because the air was where she weren't.

With Jojo on their right and Mouse on their left, Kalin and Navidad headed downslope, away from them cliffs. The mule at once fell in behind, with the donkey and goat doin the same farther back. And maybe more than just them followed behind. Maybe, for instance, that great white owl flew over them again. Maybe, hid off where a distance of trees loses transparency, an old elk also followed. Who knows? Not that Kalin could notice any such animal movement now. He'd forgotten to put on his gloves and even failed to note the cold fastenin to the backs of his hands.

Eventually, when the trees began to thin, Kalin maneuvered over to where the snow weren't little more than a thin crust of ice over a thick bed of pine needles.

Soon enuf they found themselves on a combination of animal paths and the way geology can sometimes command of itself a near perfectly horizontal traverse. From there, with only a little ingenuity, Kalin could've easily abandoned his plans and continued north for a long while to the dark forests that not only served as the doorstep to the Uinta-Isatch-Cache National Forest but would've provided a labyrinthine refuge from those pursuin him. Vast woods awaited there, ribboned through with cricks and small cascades that would've provided that boy and those three horses a way to vanish from sight if not memory.

If Kalin could've only demonstrated a smidge more patience, he might've disappeared for as long as he liked before circlin back to a destination known to no one except Kalin and the dead.

But, of course, that's when that big helicopter flew overhead, and though it didn't veer none nor circle back, Kalin weren't fooled. The absence of any official markins pretty much told him who sat in the passenger seat and this time with a weapon more powerful than just a thumb and an index finger. Kalin even guessed the helicopter would fly straight on until it was gone from sight and then circle back to somewhere not far from where this gulch spilled out.

Kalin had no choice now but to lose hisself and the ponies in the darkest woods he could find. Not that Kalin paid much mind to such thoughts, slowin instead to observe to his right the way unfoldin below: how he'd first need to descend through thick stands of white firs and spruces before havin to stitch together a series of deer and elk paths criss-crossin areas thick with low prickly brush as well as wide snowy clearins bordered by bristlin pines and an increasin number of maples.

No doubt part of Kalin's decisiveness was due to the fact that not only was Coyote Gulch the quickest way down to the Crossin but also the quickest way back around to the base of the cliffs where Landry now lay. Upon freein the horses, Kalin could race to her, not bound no more by any oath he'd made to Tom but by the oath he'd made to his heart, even if it was just to toil in so much snow until he had at last dug up her body.

Whoa there, fella! Tom was still gonna try to stop him. *Don't you think we best head north?*

The Crossin's this way.

Sure it is. But no one said we had to get there just at this moment. Why not give them Porches time to confuse themselves and start lookin for us somewhere where we ain't?

But Kalin didn't even hitch a bit, content to let the inertia of Navidad's steady amble continue them down. He'd have gone faster, a lot faster, if such a pace wouldn't have put the horses at greater risk.

Until I know fer sure she ain't breathin, I mean to get to her as quick as I can.

Awww, Kalin!

Do you know fer sure if she's dead or not? Do you?

No but—

Is her ghost walkin up on you now?

Only Pia Isan's here.

Kalin sighed. *How is it you see some Ute lady you know nothin about but can't even see your brother or daddy let alone your own sister?*

Pia Isan ain't no Ute nor Timpanog nor Katanog neither. Snake-Shoshone's probably closer. At least that's how she knew herself when she fell in love with her husband. Back then she dreamed only of pickin berries with her children, teachin them about bees and honey and wax, and how to swim at Yell Rock Falls. Come winter, she loved tellin stories by the fire. She says her heart was full. But she don't care no more about full hearts. And you know, Kalin, I'm a lot like her now. I don't care so much either. Tribes, tribes, tribes. Families, families, families. It's all so true in the little sense of things but all so untrue once you're dead. Life's got it all, but it ain't all just that.

Can she see Landry?

At least Tom did Kalin the courtesy to turn to the air, mumblin some, listenin some. *She don't see her but she'll ask the one who's with her.*

Is this like the message? About the moon?

Tom shook his head. *That came on its own. They'll pass your question along until they hear somethin and then pass it on back up.*

How long will that take?

Again Tom consulted his friend.

She says more time than time has time for. She's asked many questions before, and so long as she's walked like this, she's never got but one answer back.

What was the question?

Who could she trust.

And what was the answer?

Only the horses.

On the southeast side of Coyote Gulch, the shadows hoarded the cold and the snow stayed piled up and bruised, but on the northwest side, what was southern facin, where the sun lit up the slope bright and clear, the snow had already ebbed into a shallowness that packed easily and was crossed without troubles. And even that snow, the lower and lower they got, turned to slush and in some places was gone altogether.

Then without even the slightest tug on the reins Kalin drew his thighs inward, which Navidad understood like they were her own hocks gatherin for a stop. Kalin didn't even need to offer up the cluck that he did. Not that Navidad minded. She liked whatever sounds Kalin made. Tom and Ash stopped too. It was odd. They was standin in a patch of bright sun, but Kalin realized he couldn't stop shiverin.

I'm so cold, Tom. He shuddered, bad enuf that he tried first to out-shake his shakes with a big *Brrrrrrrr!*, and when that didn't work he wrapped the reins around the saddle horn and gave hisself a hug. That also didn't work. He even tried his breath on his fingertips. Rubbed them together. Finally put his gloves back on. But his teeth wouldn't quit their chatter. Kalin wondered if he was gettin sick again.

I'd hug you if I could, Tom said, tryin to smile. He weren't doin a good job. *I'd give you a big hug too, and long, especially if it bothered you a bit.*

It wouldn't bother me, Kalin answered. Neither boy moved. Kalin's teeth chattered still harder, which was once again odd, because at that moment the sun got even brighter and that patch upon which they stood seemed a lake of fire. Of course Kalin weren't just reactin to the cold upon the day. Even Tom's teeth found their way to chatterin some, which was a first. Though let's face it, it made sense, because here, what they was feelin, was the cold that leaks from the grave.

On this matter, more than a dozen folks we've heard from already, like Jeff Cannon and Sheila Park, gone in Kenosha, Wisconsin, Prem

Patricks too, dead in a forest fire, and Dixon Walters, murdered in Johor, would suggest that right then Kalin March was enwrapped by the imminent. Sheila Park would quote Theodore Roosevelt before she took them pills: *Black care rarely sits behind a rider whose pace is fast enuf. But Kalin weren't goin so fast.* In some ways, though, it was of all people Jeff Cannon who would come to know personally what it was like to be haunted by Tom and caught too in his wiles, as had happened when he matriculated to Isatch University. On his very first day the private security force had called Cannon in for flagrant disregard of campus standards. It was eventually discovered that it was none other than the now-deceased Tom Gatestone who'd been caught in flagrant violation of campus standards but who, as you might recall, always gave his name as Jeff Cannon. Cannon would not laugh much over the ruse, though when he discovered later what kind of laughs he got when he retold the story, especially when he was wooin his wife, why then Jeff Cannon would do the good thing: he privately said a prayer of thanks to Tom. Did so a few times in fact.

Scores more, to name no names because there are so many, still emphasize just how badly fatigued Kalin was by this point, as well as malnourished, as he was still recoverin from his bout with food poisonin; add to that his badly blistered left hand and other abrasions and bruises, and, well, you get the idea. And so, yes, of course he was cold. Real cold. He just didn't have the calories to be otherwise. Kalin looked like a ghost in his own right. To say his pallor was ashen is an understatement. His features seemed pitted and pocked by shadow. Things darker than shadows kept gougin at his eyes. Even that once-argent Stetson hat was near dark as a starry night. And there was no question that with the killin of Landry somethin had fled from him, and what replaced the space that love had made gave Tom, and even Ash, their own terrible shudders.

Likewise Tom was hardly spared the consequences of Landry's murder. His smile was dyin if it weren't already buried. He and Ash now seemed not much more substantial than the wide halo that circumscribes a moon when it snows. Tom's hat was soft and lucent as a white rose. His looks seemed ever more distant, as if he was now involved in a conversation not even he hisself was privy to, at moments confusin him, worryin him, wanin him, and then in other moments renderin him somber, surprised, pained, until eventually he was delivered unto resignation and defeat. The toll of losin his little sister was unimaginable. Surely he missed her laughter, surely he missed her song, surely he missed her irreverent responses to near all his opinions. Of course, this is just speculation. Who knows what Tom really was or wasn't registerin. One thing though, was certain: if it's possible to be the ghost of yourself when you is already a ghost, why then that was Tom.

Kalin adjusted his gloves and ground his teeth.

There ain't no other way, Tom, he finally forced hisself to admit.

I don't know that to be right, Kalin, Tom answered his friend. *You had plenty of choices up there. You still have choices down here. Sure as there's snow on the ground, you can still do different.*

Maybe Landry, if she'd been there, would've sung what was played at that Fierce boy's funeral: *There's still time to change the road you're on.*

Whatever you're seein, Tom, you can't see how I see now.

I won't say you're wrong there, Tom said, confessin too that the farther down they got, the less he could see in any direction, as if more and more they was enclosed by a darkness not even fire or his strange brand could challenge.

When Kalin started movin again, Tom put out his hand.

How about takin just five minutes then? It was all he could come up with.

Kalin shook his head.

It don't have to go this way.

Don't it?

You ain't thinkin right.

That I won't deny. Kalin even smiled some.

Dee Wright, Sally Boan, and don't forget Tyler Stokes, who would drown in the Orvop River where it weren't but a foot deep, plus Seth Boss, Cherilyn Bacall, even Teri Casper's Uncle Caleb Casper, as well as Patricia Dewey, Kirk Veach, Hillary Osborne, Tish Haggerty, and Ophelia Bateman, every one of them dead and buried now, and that includes Mrs. Avery too, her book with pressed flowers left unsold in a yard sale and eventually tossed into a bin with grass cuttins; all of these folks would over the course of their lives variously claim that by this point Kalin's mind was made up and set firm against whatever more Tom had to say, not carin a whit about what the future had in store for him so long as he didn't have to deviate one step from his intentions.

And it surely does seem obvious to note how no pure act of ratiocination was movin Kalin along his path now, and therefore no future act of ratiocination was gonna sway him from this path. It also seems obvious that more than just pure feelin and emotional reactions were at work organizin his actions. Of course, all of it, from thinkin to reactin to instincts to gifts of unanalyzable origin, was playin a part, even if the total of these internal directives still didn't seem hardly enuf to account for the force now drivin him onwards.

It's even been asked if haste was puttin his commitment to the horses at risk. This was grief, of course, and, worse, the thing that grief can become if we ain't careful: what's too broad to contain and too inarticulate to explain and what was only just startin to brawl inside him. Landry's death had already chained Kalin to a shock that no Samson, Prometheus, or even an old wolf like Fenrir could've shrugged off. Not that that is one bit surprisin, nor are these comparisons to lofty enchainments exaggerations. Just consider how even the reverberant aftereffects of gunfire closely encountered would have dimmed most folks inexperienced with such reports and threats to a nearuseless state of flinches and adrenal nausea. Now add to that the visceral response of beholdin up close so bloody a murder, compounded by the fact that this violent idyll was near just as violently swallowed up and stolen by the massif itself; Landry, followin that air-stainin headshot, tossed down cliffs hundreds of feet high only to be entombed under tons of snow. Not that these last facts should've surprised anyone, and certainly not Kalin; these children had always ridden upon the back of a Devourin Mountain. All of which still measures as nothin compared to what happens to someone when Love is so casually and cruelly struck down.

Because, terribly, as Kalin swayed ever so gently in his saddle, gainin what reassurances he could from Navidad's constancy and at the same time communicatin this fragile if collective calm to Mouse and Jojo through the softest tugs on their lead ropes, what he couldn't know by the dullness now inhabitin him was just how bust up his heart was.

Maybe some will still demand salty tears and snotty sobs, especially if they've reacted like so themselves on sad occasions. But likely them that demanded such behavior from Kalin, whose nose weren't runnin, whose cheeks remained dry, folks like Roberta Blum, Wes Gooch, and Merril Chance, to name a few of those long since demised, whether from a bee allergy, baseball, or a robot, by the torturous undoin of flesh and bone that death universally requires, why not a one of them had ever experienced the kind of pain that comes when you're hit real hard. Not the kind of slap that tells only the story of hurt but a strike so powerful as to render even pain speechless. And so, in that spate of time before such postponed pain arrives, because, yes, it will arrive, somethin else resides in you, what defeats all feelin hurled your way. Sure, you know there's injury, sure you know there's hurt, but how you know it seems beyond anythin you can know as yourself. The only thing clear is the terrible sufferin yet in store, spelled out by apprehension, to be delivered very soon and without mercy.

To Kalin's credit, once they slipped down into that part of Coyote Gulch that was dense with trees, where they was well hid beneath the boughs, he slowed down upon that soft stretch of ground with little snow and plenty of pine needles, *Clop-Clop-clip-Clop,* and at least confessed to Tom that he had no chance against what was now leveled against him.

Or as he put it: *Sometimes you got no choice but to face what chases you. The only thing you get to decide are the terms of engagement.*

Tom only nodded, perhaps because he still understood that Kalin's choice, his ugliest yet, still lay ahead.

Soon enuf they came upon a wide clearin marked by a rocky amassment juttin upward in the midst of that gulch. It was easy enuf to go around but also easily ascended; on top one could escape the trees and behold clearly what waited below.

Tom pointed out a large open area beyond a wide stretch of birches and quakin aspens with leaves afire.

That there's it, Tom said. *Pillars Meadow.*

Across that plain of gold grass and emergin patches of brown earth, here and there mottled with snow, Kalin spied a shallow depression movin like a lazy snake, a crick dependent on season and snowfall. On the other side of that, Tom explained, waited two gateposts that marked the Crossin.

See the horses through them, and we're done, Tom added.

Not far to go, Kalin said with a nod, and Tom nodded too, though neither seemed convinced. Tom even looked to wince, and that's about when the horses started to move uneasily about, like the earth was quakin beneath their hooves, Navidad throwin her head up and down and shakin her long black mane. Kalin even had to hush her and stroke her neck until she calmed.

And it didn't end there. The mule suddenly took to circlin, with both ears pinned, kickin its rear hooves into the air. Then overhead that great white owl cried out as it flew off. Nearby rustles suggested still more retreats, includin maybe that old elk. And then ahead a mountain lion abruptly stepped into a patch of bright snow, stared up at the horses, at Kalin, before hissin and fast dashin for concealin shadows.

Pia Isan says there is a great fear here, Tom whispered. *I feel it too.*

Fear of what? Kalin asked, lookin around.

You.

K alin hardly spoke after that. He settled the brim of his hat low and bent his back so much, he resembled a slouched question mark, maybe a broken question mark. He shivered some more, his teeth chatterin again, and sometimes he shuddered so bad, he was racked by coughs, but he still didn't slow. And as if of the same mind, Navidad proceeded downward with the same resolve, remainin as stalwart as Kalin was frail.

For a while Tom kept his peace, until, perhaps feelin too much the dissipation of his own person, if he was a person, he returned to the subject of his memory, and with only the faintest notes of desperation and resignation described how the farther down the mountain they got, the less he could recall, which, contrary to expectation, Tom had begun to experience as a relief he'd never known before, a lightness he'd in fact waited for his whole life, maybe what we all wait for, the gift Death bequeaths to each of us. *I'd never have felt this if we hadn't made it over that mountain. So I guess some thanks are in order.* Kalin looked at Tom like he was crazy. Tom weren't done either: not only was the vast past gone from him but that vast future he vaguely recalled experiencin was also gone, what had once possessed him with such certainty and terror. Tom even smiled.

You see, all Tom had now were these moments: the snow crunchin beneath the hooves of the horses, the rich smells of pine and petrichor, the quiet crackle and trickle summoned by the risin and unimpeded sun, that Apollonian light piercin the snow, releasin the thaw to the valley below.

And even if Landry was fadin fast too, someone he could only just remember and now mostly by the shape of her absence, Tom still felt hisself in the middle of a bright river of sadness that was so palpable it seemed everywhere now and included too the water that dripped from the tree branches and ran along the exposed rocky and muddy slopes, slowly thinnin on the way down, shiftin from a heavy hue to a pastel, and then somethin fainter, like watercolor or even less, until its dreamy washed-out translucency revealed to Tom that even sadness, and all it remembered, must also pass.

I got no more confidence, Kalin, but I can't say I miss it.

Really what mattered to Tom, as he told it to Kalin, were those assurances freely offered now by the animals in their vicinity, *just knowin that they're still there,* even if most of them remained out of sight. Though what gave him the most heart weren't so distant or abstract. *I'm just glad about these horses.*

Tom reported that Pia Isan and her little chipmunk were also glad about the horses and clingin to their progress. And that went for the one who walked beside her, and so on. Also, for the first time, she was knowin her anger as a passin thing, her fear too, her anguish, and of course her sorrow. A great openness was at hand. Or that's what she was sayin.

Kalin didn't know what that meant and, Tom didn't know either, but he told Kalin that she and the rest were staggered by their proximity now to this conclusion. She'd never imagined such a journey was possible. Never imagined the horses could get so far. *Of course, she also don't have no thanks for us, just the horses.* And Tom and Kalin agreed that that was fine. Tom let Kalin know then that Pia Isan had from the start greeted Mouse as a promise made, a creature of immense agency, whose age made even great Katanogos seem as brief as a mornin mist. Navidad, though, she'd greeted as a promise kept, like some farouche filly marbled upon countless temples in the name of fulfillment, so careless with age she seemed allways just born.

And that's when Tom finally told Kalin The Story of Navidad.

These scars she's got, they're from Orwin Porch. His hand was upon her for no reason that makes sense enuf to remember. He used a piece of barbed wire, and Navidad bled for nothin she could understand. Each occasion had a different reason, often contradictin the previous reason, until it all became a blot of injury and an even greater blot of pain.

It might surprise you, though, to know that Navidad dwells not a wink upon those moments. She remembers somethin else, good times, three to be precise.

The first is of her momma nosin her through her wobbles. And it's like she's still nosin her through those first steps. Navidad came around in Upstate New York, not far from Palmyra, in a place of rollin fields so green in summer and so wide and free come winter it weren't no use to think of elsewhere when the life offered there came complete with even the grace of salvation, no prayers needed. To be beside her momma was salvation enuf. In her presence Navidad knew she wouldn't just learn to run; someday she'd learn to fly. And fer sure if she could've just known her momma a little longer, she'd have grown wings. But they took her away before Navidad was rightly weaned. And there went her wings. Still, Navidad didn't think on wings. Only a bird needs wings to fly. Navidad still remembers her momma reachin down with her great beautiful head, that soft nibblin nose, them big brown eyes, nuzzlin and nudgin Navidad up from another fall. It's why Navidad could keep gettin back up on her feet after Old Porch beat her til she stumbled. Her momma's big soft nose.

The second thing she remembers is when Mouse arrived. He was like suddenly findin a big red sun in your sky when before it was just one long night. Around

1011

Mouse Navidad felt warm again, and the grass grew green and tall, and she knew herself welcome in that place her momma was tryin to guide her to. Wings didn't matter. Mouse mattered. And when he was beside her, she knew somethin better than flyin.

The third memory, however, was what brought Navidad the greatest peace. Her whole life she'd known herself as a creature of hunger. Even when there was plenty of alfalfa and oats, she still felt a wanin no amount of eats would counter. Often she wouldn't eat, which, contrary to what you might think, would get her that much closer to riddin herself of this gnawin-on ache that consumed her. She'd glimpse a way beyond the grasp of that awful need. But it didn't last long. Too soon she was back again with that self-wreckin anguish.

That all changed, though, the day a boy named Kalin swung up on her neked back and didn't demand a thing. For him his burden was already catastrophic, but it meant nothin to her. He did not heal her. He did not fulfill her. He did, however, secure her. His immense emptiness settled her steps because he made room for her. He gave her a way to find new steps. Until one afternoon Navidad began to imagine how to step entirely beyond the scars and the fences and the needs that imprisoned her from herself. She knew it like the comin of dawn, not by the light but first by the change in the air.

But then when the other boy stopped comin, that would be me, Tom clarified, *that dawn seemed to pause. Then the Kalin boy stopped comin too, and that's when Navidad thought the dawn had died. Not even her Mouse could resurrect that light.*

But the boy returned, in darkness and dark rains too. And when he rode her with Mouse out of that awful enclosure, she knew they was done with that place. And then not long after that the girl arrived on that beautiful blue stallion, and somethin like joy blossomed within her.

Stranger still was how when she and Kalin were in the midst of that awful rockfall, the mountain lost to itself beneath them, more joy had burst forth. See, Navidad understood that to survive was now no one else's choice but her own, and she made that choice and became her joy and she survived. And even when joy seemed threatened upon that lonely and icy wall, when Mouse was gone, when Jojo was gone, when Landry was gone, the boy stayed with her and spoke with her and looked after her legs and spoke more with her and never left her side. He told her many things that night, but in the end what mattered was what waited for her, her Mouse, and then when Kalin was upon her back again, he felt lighter than any memory long since faded and gone, and though blackness lay ahead, she trusted the boy, and suddenly the blackness was gone, and she knew then by the light of the moon that there were wings on her back and that there had always been wings on her back. And she unfolded them and felt the immense power in each beat, and she knew herself then as a creature of flight, unbound from every terrestrial path, beyond any constraint, beyond the acme of every ascent.

But only when she was again beside her Mouse did Navidad know peace. She lay down with the girl and the boy, and the cold would not touch her. The boy and the girl fed her, and this time she ate without hunger. They were almost there. They were almost done.

And then the sky cracked like it was broken, and the girl was gone, and they was headin downhill without her. And though down was easier than up, she felt the boy startin to lose his emptiness. His growin burden stuttered her breath. She had no wings for him.

The saddest thing, though, is that even at this very moment, Tom sighed, *she knows he knows this too. She could even answer his fillin with her own emptyin but he forbids it. They could find another path to his emptiness but he forbids it. She would even sacrifice the memory of her wings for him but he forbids it. How easy if we were born to this world as one thing but here we are multitude. In his emptiness, the boy could remain with Navidad. But in his absolute fullness, he must lose her.*

Kalin didn't speak much after that, though his heart hurt more. He couldn't even say anythin to Navidad. And so, beholden to that ghostly silence, they continued down, followin the muddy paths between the dark trees or, when those gave up, skirtin the fallen trees, halved, shattered, scattered, some even stacked by the decades of storms precedin this last one, providin in these assemblies broader and even easier paths down toward the awful culmination awaitin them all.

Thank you, Tom, Kalin finally did mutter when they had descended to where the snow was sheddin so much water that the forests around them had grown loud with the babble of that tumblin melt.

I was kinda hopin you would tell me I was wrong.

Kalin didn't tell Tom he was wrong, but he did lean forward and stroked Navidad's neck and whispered what only them two would ever know.

Does this mean you've decided the terms of your engagment? Tom asked then, his voice rife with despair.

I have not.

Except for some patches here and there, and those only where the shadows held throughout the day, by the time they were half the way down, all the great sweeps of snow were gone, leavin them to manage over exposed ground that had turned soggy with limp grass and hoof-swallowin mud. Only when they crossed into shadows cast by loomin bluffs did that freeze return, and the earth was hard again and their breaths frosted.

Toward the bottom, the snow returned. The sheer and encaptiva-tin limestone on either side of that widenin gulch threw down heavy shadows the sun could not challenge, and the trees thickened up again, and the air seemed even colder.

Kalin spied a deer path, which took them along the northeast side of the gulch where they could easily move amidst tall pines that seemed as much bark and bough as ice and blue shadow. The snow here had stayed dry and light, and the horses' legs sank down until their chests grazed the fluff, far deeper than even at the higher altitudes, where the snow was drier but strong winds had limited the depth.

Kalin wanted to see his friends set free, he wanted to get to where Landry was, he wanted to free hisself of this trial, but he still had to make darned sure not to hurry. They was all tired, they was all worn; one careless step could rob them of everythin.

Of course, for Tom and Ash, no condition presented an obstacle; they floated upon that gauzy surface, leavin behind only hoofprints of violet shades that vanished before the next ones briefly tingled into view. Or that's at least how Kalin seen it. Like above the saddle there weren't no rider, and below the saddle there weren't no horse. Maybe no saddle no more, either.

Though Tom and Ash still led the way, but only by a length, on the lookout, Tom claimed, for any clearin to help safely hasten their descent.

No clearin appeared, but the trees grew more sparse and the snow shallowed, and soon they was beyond the talus and from there could easily drop down amidst the birches and quakin aspens where snow still clung to the ground, though it was not deep.

It was Tom who finally raised his hand to stop. The woods seemed no different here than moments ago, though it sure was bit-ter cold, as if some icy river of high-mountain air was slowly movin between the many trunks of pale peelin bark. When Kalin and the horses pulled up beside Tom, he saw how, not a dozen more lengths ahead, the trees began to thin and how just a little farther out waited a sudden brightenin, the high-noon sky settin aglow areas of snow that marked the start of Pillars Meadow.

Kalin wheeled around then and did not look back. Only when he was once more amidst those dense and prevailin gray woods did he dismount. He removed Navidad's saddle first and then clipped to her halter-bridle her lead, which he tied loosely to a low branch long enuf to tie off Mouse's lead there as well. Not that Mouse needed to be tied up; he weren't ever gonna leave Navidad's side. Kalin let the tack on Jojo stay and looped his lead around a branch close enuf to Mouse and Navidad so as not to deprive him of their company. The mule lingered nearby. Kalin couldn't see the donkey or the mountain goat anymore. To double-check his reasonin then, Kalin jogged back out to where the woods thinned, and though he still weren't close enuf yet to behold Pillars Meadow, he could, fer starters, look back and confirm that no equine movement might betray his whereabouts.

Julaine Jentzch, before she passed of causes none could attribute to anythin other than old age, would happily declare to the nurses that attended her how even here Kalin was still free to unfix his mind. *He'd left the saddle on Jojo. He'd rebuttoned up that Lee Storm Rider jacket. He still had on them gloves. Only Landry was on his mind and of course them horses who he knew full well were gonna break his heart when they left.*

Kalin returned then to the horses, this time to feed them the last of the oats and whatever else feed he'd brought down from the summit cache. He also checked to make sure that where they was standin would offer safe grazin. Only once he was satisfied did Kalin walk all the way out to Pillars Meadow, this time to make sure it was deserted. As expected, Tom stayed with the horses, though his expression looked plenty pained to see Kalin head out there alone.

Kalin crept low and slow to the edge of the trees and from there, finally, beheld Pillars Meadow up close. Wide patches of thinnin snow still lay ahead, though with plenty of gold grass pokin through. Across the meadow lay the crick bed, its contours muted by snow, and beyond that, though it was too far to rightly appraise, Kalin could just make out what looked like two posts devoid of gate or fence.

There ain't near enuf snow there for snowmobiles, Kalin told Tom when he got back, addin with some relief that the Porches was likely stuck somewhere else. He'd forgotten about the helicopter. When he described the crick bed and those posts, Tom confirmed that Kalin had seen the Crossin with his own eyes.

Anywhere beyond them and these horses are free to go. Say hello to Endsville.
Kalin felt weird. Now that it was real.

Pia Isan says I'll be free to go too, Tom admitted with a sigh. *We'll all be free.* Tom didn't look that glad.

You could stick around and help me dig up Landry, Kalin said then.
Who?

Gilbert Gatenby, dead from heat stroke, and just from joggin too, around Capitol Hill, well, he would always warn his students that whether you was talkin about *Cinderella* or *The Red Shoes*, or any number of other examples, fairy tales was hard on feet. Shoes are a big deal.

As if to signal the end of fairy tales, or that's how Gatenby would have it, Kalin turned away from Tom then and took out the farrier kit.

Mouse didn't put up no fuss as Kalin set to work. He weren't no pro with the nail pullers or cinchers, whatever your preference, but he got the job done. It weren't hard. Somehow between the summit and here, Mouse bein Mouse had already shed three. The fourth and last horseshoe just needed a little encouragement.

Navidad still had all four but they was plenty worn. She fidgeted some like maybe she knew that when the shoes were gone, Kalin would be gone too, and maybe for her that weren't the finest thing. While Kalin worked on her forehooves, Navidad kept cranin on down to nip at his hat and one time got in a good chomp on the brim, liftin it clean off his head. Kalin let her have it and for a moment even felt relieved, like the darkness coagulate there was no longer his problem. Navidad even whipped her head sideways to send the hat flyin off a good distance. Kalin felt emptiness return then, and Navidad nuzzled him, and her long mane fell about his head like a veil of tears there to guard him. He hugged her back and then returned the tools to the kit and returned the kit to a saddle pouch. Lastly he tossed the horseshoes into a small pile no one would find until next spring.

He then rechecked all the horses' legs and found them sound, no lameness, no signs of azoturia, no thrush. Only then did he pick up that big Stetson again. On his head it took a heavy hold of him. Even Navidad's back seemed to sag at the sight of it. Though she had nothin to fear anymore, or everythin to fear, because Kalin would never ride her again.

Guess we better get these horses past that fence line then, he whispered to Tom, who was back up on Ash. Kalin felt bone-tired but at least his bones told him that he was near done.

You ain't gonna ride?

Kalin shook his head.

How you plan to go on afterward? Tom asked.

I guess I'll see if Jojo here will cut me a break. If not we'll walk.

Jojo neighed then, and Navidad joined in, and hers was light and made Kalin think that maybe it would all work out. Mouse snorted because he knew better.

Whether because of Mouse or his own cautious instincts, Kalin returned once more without horses to reconfirm that Pillars Meadow was still empty. And though what he saw was plain as day, Kalin still tried to deny the sight at first. Bless her heart, behind him Navidad neighed again, though this time it was different, this time her cry was choked with alarm and even anger.

Kalin also did his best to make out of the blotchy thing toward the southern end of the meadow anythin but the helicopter it was. It weren't no use. Kalin knew it was the same one that had flown overhead earlier. How had he missed the roar of its return, its landin? Kalin figured it must have come in from the south, and bein far enuf away and with the constant winds in the woods, he'd just plain missed it. They all had. Even Tom. Not that it mattered no more.

Kalin continued to squint hard at the parked helicopter, but no matter how still he kept, how much he quieted his breath, he could detect no movement. Maybe they'd gone the wrong way? Kalin's heart started to race then. Maybe he could leave Jojo among the trees and race Navidad bareback across the meadow. Mouse fer sure would keep up. They'd be past the crick and gateposts in an easy minute, less than a minute. They could even keep goin, head for the forest beyond. That was a good ways off, well cloaked in the haze of distance but still offerin a possibility of refuge. He'd have to figure out how to get back to Jojo. He couldn't leave Jojo behind. Jojo would have to come too. Maybe Mouse would be incentive enuf to keep close.

With his mind still tryin to figure out the best way across, Kalin's eyes kept scannin Pillars Meadow until they caught on a spot just north of the helicopter. There was a depression there, likely because of the crick bed, and a low hill too, where Kalin's eyes lingered because they'd already seen what his mind hadn't caught up with yet: new movement hid down where the gold grass lightly swayed in the mid-day breezes.

Kalin blinked, blinked again, kept blinkin, as if he might for a moment more remove from his sight what he'd expected all along. And then maybe because Navidad and Mouse could smell them now or at least sense them, another eruption of neighs called out for him.

In all Kalin counted ten trompin up Pillars Meadow. They was still a good ways off, but they weren't dawdlin none either, movin right alongside that crick bed. Soon enuf they'd be right across from where them gateposts stood.

*W*e were so close, Tom said once Kalin had finished describin what he'd seen.

They's headin right to your posts too!

Maybe they'll keep goin? Tom suggested.

They knew where to go. Kalin still couldn't believe the confluence.

That helicopter got a good look at you when we was above Coyote Gulch.

Kalin nodded, though he still weren't convinced. The terminus of

Coyote Gulch was wide, and there was a good half mile in which to pick alternate directions aimin for other richly forested areas.

It ain't too late to turn back, Tom offered, though his suggestion lacked all conviction. And anyways it was too late.

A heat now in Kalin had started to overwhelm every chill infectin his bones. It had started when he'd squinted out what he thought must be Old Porch, shotgun cradled across the crook of his left elbow, right hand close enuf to the trigger to make clear, even from a good distance, that he was there to kill somethin. And then that heat in Kalin had really kicked up into fire when he seen beside Old Porch the one Landry had called Egan. Only one person now stood a chance at puttin that fire out, and Kalin's momma weren't nowhere near.

Maybe . . . But Tom just trailed off and retreated back to the horses.

It's okay, Tom, Kalin said.

No it ain't, Tom mumbled.

Plenty say that as Kalin strode over to the horses, his choice by then was made, but plenty more believe that Kalin's passion was still to come, hid amidst those trees with them three horses, four horses, plus the one bewildered friend.

Maybe because Kalin was considerin the raw wound on his left hand, where that rope had burnt up his palm three days ago, what, if it weren't but barely scabbed over, seemed like a forever ago, it provoked from him a cry that begat no sound upon that frosty air, though Tom still heard it, the horses too.

Oh Landry . . .

Kalin might as well have sobbed it, turnin then from Navidad and Mouse, and though he now faced Jojo, he did not see the big blue horse, his focus entirely on Landry's saddle, and in particular the one saddlebag.

Kalin! Tom yelped. *You ain't got no chance out there. They'll cut you down fer sure. Do you hear me? They. Will. Cut. You. Down.*

But anger now was spillin off Kalin like somethin hotter than fire, seethin and hissin; fer sure it outmeasured whatever Kalin had felt once toward his mother, on Aster Scree, after helpin Landry and Jojo up, or against his father, when they'd made their way to Mist Falls. This time Anger was set solely against hisself, his name too, Kalin! Kalin! Kalin!, near powerful enuf as well to make right then a bone-ashin pyre of fury. Though in the end it weren't that powerful, likely because in the end Kalin could not face Kalin and so directed his ire at Tom.

Not that Tom could answer his friend's inferno. He tried, but Kalin would hear none of it, not even a word, Kalin but raisin his left hand and by that small motion, but from his hip to the air, shuttin up the ghost at once. Even the horses stilled. But it weren't no admiration that was stillin them.

To make amends, Kalin first rested his forehead against Jojo's, and like Jojo had never done before, that big beautiful horse didn't flinch away. Maybe Jojo even listened to whatever Kalin was sayin. *Clop-Clop-clip-Clop.* Kalin did the same then with Mouse, restin his head on Mouse's forehead just whisperin away whatever worlds only those two knew how to share. *Clop-Clop-clip-Clop.* Kalin stayed with the blood bay a long time, and despite his precocious and irreverent reputation, Mouse grew so still in that snowy grove that he defied his history, maybe even briefly his character, as he became in those moments an eerie idyll to somethin he would never become again.

Before turnin to Navidad, *Clop-Clop-clip-Clop,* Kalin looked to Tom, who at once recoiled before the blackness that had begun to seep into his friend's eyes.

I wish there was somethin more I could do, Tom stammered.

I wish there was too, Kalin answered him, and at least right then the blackness seemed for a moment to hesitate.

And maybe what that softenin right there told Tom, and all that was of the air and the branches and the soil and the water, was how, even here, Kalin still had a choice: he could still head out there with only them ponies, unshielded by any recourse to metaled action; he could in short sacrifice hisself and just hope that on their own the horses might reach the Crossin unmolested by Old Porch's malice.

After the summer I rode Hightower, I heard that they turned that big bull into burger, Tom said then. *Old Porch charged extra for the patties. Porch Meat burgers. Did I ever tell you that?*

Kalin shook his head.

It turned my stomach. One day that amazin creature was tryin to hurl me to Heaven or probably to Heck, and then the next day folks was picnickin on him. I never ate a burger again after that. Not sure it did any good. But Hightower was more than eats to me. He was somethin else.

You got a burger for me, Tom? I thought you was done rememberin.

Tom shrugged. *It just came to me. I guess what I hadn't faced then was how just like Hightower came to know his end, the same would be true for me, true for all of us. That day always comes.*

Nec spe, nec metu, Kalin said then. And he meant it. No certain expectation of future glory. No expectation of life. Kalin knew Old Porch weren't ever gonna spare his friends. He'd slaughter them like he'd slaughtered Hightower. Kalin also accepted that he was turnin his back on his momma, he was breakin his promise, and that loneliness struck him deep and cold.

Tom, I'll be damned if I don't see these two set free.

And there it was; like that, easy as hoppin off that fence on Willow and Oak, Kalin's choice was made.

He rested his forehead then against Navidad's, his palms on her cheeks, now and then strokin that whiskered chin. With her he stayed the longest. What he murmured not even the air could hear. But Navidad sure understood. And if horses can cry, you can bet she cried. Maybe they revisited those early rides with Tom. Maybe they returned to the Awides Mine and the dead that waited there and from then on followed them wherever they went. Surely Kalin thanked Navidad for the miracle of survivin the great rockfall. And for all she'd done when they summited the headwall together, especially that last turn, more than a thousand feet above Altar Lake, in the middle of night, when snow and a ghostly moon had conspired for mere seconds to grant them a way ahead. Kalin knew fer sure that Navidad had unfurled great black wings then and flown beyond any Mountain that could ever matter. Kalin would be forever honored that he got to know even once in his troubled life such lightness. It was certainly a bliss he would never know again, and then all of him started to shake, and even Tom could see he was sobbin but knew better than to approach, though Mouse approached then and nuzzled him because Mouse out of all of them understood Kalin the best.

When it was over, Kalin bowed to each horse, even to the mule, who by this point had wandered closer.

After that, Kalin walked over to Jojo and pulled loose from Landry's saddlebag the dark velvet pouch wherein waited Old Porch's 1873 Colt Single Action Army Peacemaker.

Chapter Twenty-Four

"Pillars Meadow"

Jojo wheeled away at once and neighed. And that mighty stallion weren't alone. Navidad rose up too and neighed in a way that seemed more a shriek to shudder midnight. And though Mouse neither rose up nor whinnied, he sure kicked back hard and kept kickin like wasps were at his flanks. All the horses, in their tortured gazes toward who or what now stood in their presence, gave up the whites of their eyes.

Whether to ease their panic or because he was already enthralled by what felt so at home in his wounded palm, Kalin walked away, and no question the more distance he gave the horses, the quicker they calmed to uneasy snorts. The mule, though, was nowhere in sight. That went for the donkey and the mountain goat too.

Even Ash had risen up and wheeled away in fear; he now stood behind Navidad and Mouse, closest to Jojo. Tom at least remained at Kalin's side even if it weren't easy for him either. He too seemed possessed by a new uneasiness, his proximity to Kalin near heroic.

Not that Kalin paid much attention to the ghost. His focus now resided solely with the Colt 45. He held it lightly and moved it about slowly, as if to not only register every aspect of its balance but also to reacquaint hisself with an old friend or a lost part of hisself.

There has always been a sizable group, includin but not limited to Dwanna Hales, Jeananne Harvey, Kurt Salvesen, Dedelyn Matson, Jay and Daryll Bagnell, Reindeer Mike Beer, Maurice Tanner, Margaret Wilkinson, and Brian Polson, all of whom are by now borne to dust, brought down by mishap, suicide, war, murder, and more, who had claimed that despite the lore surroundin Kalin and Pillars Meadow these sudden eruptions of equine irritability had *nothin to do with layin hands upon that weapon* but rather with the sudden screech of a bird overhead or perhaps a scent upon the air of that previously sighted mountain lion or any number of other possible natural intrusions up there in that desolate part of the Katanogos massif. The reasonin is sound even if no bird flew overhead, nor had there been any cougar or crackin timber or suddenly shiftin stone. The only objectionable moment witnessed there involved the acquisition of an inanimate thing of human devisin: barrel, cylinder, trigger, and hammer which conjured in their shiny assembly a repulsin ripple of menace.

The horses, if by this point more accommodatin or just resigned, still did what they could to stay away from Kalin. Maybe that he then sat down helped some. Or maybe the memory of who he was before also helped. Either way, Kalin was hardly bothered by what they was about. His fixation stayed with this mechanism in his grip. He emptied the cylinder of its five rounds into his right palm, where a sixth round waited, the one Landry had told him about when he thought he was rid of her that Thursday mornin, what had waited all this while at the bottom of the velvet pouch, what might have seemed special in light of its apartness, though it weren't. They was all of them the same: lethal.

Kalin then inspected each part of the weapon. No matter that ten men were out there, maybe already trudgin this way; Kalin took his time to consider everythin from stocks, frame, and recoil plate to the gate and base pin. What he paid no attention to was the polish and certainly not the engraved names set artfully here and there, designatin some importance Kalin couldn't have cared less about. Even if plated in gold and set with diamonds worth generational wealth, Kalin wouldn't have looked twice.

Aside from details crucial to assembly and function, what Kalin prized next was the peculiar alchemy made possible now by this cunnin instrument in his possession: he knew his golden lightness catalyzed to a leadenin of spirit that both dulled him and armored him.

Cleanin the various inanimate parts with the heel of his shirt, Kalin experienced with each touch and rub renewed satisfaction with the smallness of this enterprise. His absorption in every detail, recheckin and reassemblin each part, his pleasure in knowin that the thing was well treated, cleaned, and oiled, and now ready, helped center hisself with such enormous weight that he wondered briefly if he might find it impossible to ever stand again let alone walk. Though when he did stand, he discovered no resistance. Nor did this sensation of heaviness apply to the weapon, which registered no resistance at all.

Above him the canopy stirred with uneasy life, but Kalin knew it not. Beside him stood his friend, Tom, but Kalin knew him not. He knew only a spreadin desolation.

And he still hadn't loaded the Peacemaker.

Stupidly or not, Kalin set the gun then on a nearby slab of stone and for the last time crept out to the edge of the woods unarmed. He moved quickly but also noisily. He never was very good on his own feet, and maybe there was still a part of him hopin to get caught unawares. Barrett Jenkins, Atilio Jonas, Chelsea Kitchen, Dawn Ana Hobbs, Jessica Bettencourt, and Brinn Black have all wondered if Kalin was tryin in this moment to outrun not only his duty but *plain and simple outrun that dang gun*. That's how Chelsea Kitchen put it. And maybe she was right; maybe this here was Kalin makin a last desperate try to get some distance between hisself and the choice he'd already made. *It was that horse part of him,* said Dawn Ana Hobbs.

Of course Kalin weren't caught unawares. And instead of men

marchin up on the tree line, what he found was pretty much what he'd expected to find: rather than risk enterin the woods, a terrain with ample opportunities to hide in and shoot from, the ten out there were keepin to the open. The surprise was that they not only hadn't pushed in any closer but had drawn back to the crick, where it looked like they was still gettin situated.

Kalin figured that they was figurin that they hadn't been seen yet and so planned to take cover behind the crick banks, prone and likely spread out some, ready to take him by surprise when he rode out onto Pillars Meadow. Though he wouldn't be ridin, nor was that what was plunderin any sense of what was goin on now. How was it that they was settin up pretty much right between Kalin and them gateposts?

Back by the horses, Tom was about as dumbfounded as Kalin. The ghost had no words for why the Porches had wound up where they had. He grunted and shook his head and grunted some more until he just started sayin over and over how it didn't matter none anyhow. *They'll gun you down as soon as you set one foot out there.*

They might do, Kalin answered, even if he didn't seem near troubled enuf by that admission. What he was more focused on now was get-tin the Peacemaker loaded: one by one. He recalled perfectly how he'd instructed Landry to make sure that sixth chamber stayed empty so that the firin pin was set against emptiness, so no amount of jostlin could end up murderin her or poor Jojo, right as he slipped the sixth round into the sixth chamber, pullin back the hammer so it was set to fire for a whisper.

Kalin then laid down the weapon real careful, which did seem to calm some the discord flutterin the horses' hearts, though it didn't stop their shufflin none, and their eyes remained worried, and too often their nostrils would flare. Tom had relaxed some but not much.

For a moment there I looked at you and thought I was the livin one and you was the dead one, Tom said.

Next Kalin took out his Swiss Army knife and cut Navidad's reins into short lengths, which he in turn sliced into much thinner strips. These he tied around each wrist. The thinnest ones he secured around certain fingers. The ones on the right hand served no purpose except to deceive, makin such implements seem nothin more than for adorn-ment, bracelets and rings of leather.

Never doubtin his new relationship to the horses, Kalin made sure to take a wide arc around them until he was where their lead ropes were tied up. They resisted some his gentle tugs, but maybe because they had only his back to look at, they eventually gave in and followed him. Kalin picked up the weapon as he headed out toward Pillars Meadow.

Once again he stopped where there was still cover, tyin up the leads around the trunk of a thin birch. Jojo snorted, relieved it seemed that Kalin was once again puttin distance between him and them. Navidad's eyes, though, wouldn't stop widenin with distress at what she was now seein or perhaps no longer seein. Mouse's tail swished hotly back and forth.

You said you wished there was somethin you could do, Kalin said then.

I did.

Well, there is. I need you to ride out to the Crossin so I can see where I'm goin. It'll give me somethin to aim for that ain't just with a gun.

Kalin weren't ignorant of the fact that the farther along they'd got on this journey, the closer Tom had needed to be to the horses. Tom's response weren't forthcomin either. He even had to step closer to Mouse and Navidad as he tried to better evaluate the distance between the horses and where the gateposts stood.

Samuel Zyer, perishin from late-onset cystic fibrosis, would go so far as to describe the relationship between Tom and the horses, and for that matter the relationship between Mouse and Navidad, as *quantum chromodynamics in equine form. Close to one another, they're the quintessence of freedom, but the farther they drift apart, the quicker they approach a limit where they are impossible to separate. The force holdin them together becomes incurably strong. For Tom, as it turned out, his own limit was, well, Tom's Crossin.*

Up on that summit ridge Tom had seemed a great sail, full with all the winds that once were and had yet to come. So tall was he and so wide and so full, he might very well have been the Sail of the World. But no sail so big can hold so much for so long. Since then he'd seemed nothin but a spirit of tatters, tobacco ties, with more and more of even them wind-torn strips stole away the farther down the mountain they got. So little was left of him now.

My momma would sometimes say muddy water stirred don't get no less muddy, Tom suddenly mumbled.

You just remember that now?

I guess so but I don't know why. I can't even remember my momma. Tom smiled sadly. *Out there, though, sure does look like a whole bunch of mud.*

Seems like a place shouldn't have so much to say about what happens.

Don't be a fool, Tom snapped then. *I know I've already told you this too many times before: it ain't about some place, whether it's a mountain or a valley or this here muddy field. It's about these two horses. That's all. Just Navidad and Mouse.*

Kalin nodded. *Will you then? Ride out there to the Crossin?*

Tom shook his head. *I cannot.*

I need you to try, Tom.

I can't promise you more than that, Tom said with a nod, but he weren't smilin, and he didn't move.

The journey don't count if we don't finish it.

Who knows what passed then through that ghost, but it was Ash who finally moved. And weren't that horse a fine sight now; he even seemed taller, and his eyes flashed green, and under the eve of a high sun his coat shined like gold.

Do you really think we will? Tom asked, and Kalin could see his friend earnestly wanted to know. Poor Tom.

I don't know.

Tom looked plenty distraught as he turned to go. Ash, though, seemed only to grow happier the farther away they got from Kalin, that beautiful Andalusian just castin his head one way and then another, even prancin some, like he was in a parade, and maybe he still was in a parade, for the dead. Tom even unscabbarded that brand, and at once it became a burnin beacon of white light.

Kalin's eyes watered some as he followed them into the distance, first crossin the mud but soon after navigatin wide patches of snow upon which Tom's hat seemed to glow whiter than pearl, whiter than snow. Curiously the farther away they got, the smaller they got, which was to be expected, but what was unexpected was how they also seemed to gain more materiality, at least to Kalin's mind, so that when they finally reached that crick bed and then passed beyond those banks and whoever all waited there, Kalin knew Tom and Ash as well as those fabled gateposts beside which they stood and with a clarity that for the first time rivalled the mountains at his back.

His destination.

He just had to get there.

Kalin, however, didn't head straight out and consequently didn't get gunned down first thing. After all, he'd been thinkin on this problem quite a bit and he'd already reckoned Tom was right: he'd need a better plan.

You can bet he entertained the notion of just gallopin Navidad as fast as she could go, and with Mouse and Jojo on either side. But he also knew that was as stupid as stupid gets. Any marksman that could drop Landry at such great distance would have no problem drawin a bead on him. And if all ten of them opened fire, why Kalin would be lucky to make it even fifty yards. Likely too this lot would shoot the horses first.

Kalin then gave some thought to tryin to outwait them. He couldn't survive a long standoff, and if they did come in after him, they too would have the advantage of the trees. It was anyone's guess how things would turn out, though with only six rounds to his name, most everyone's guess, includin Kalin's, would side with the Porches.

How Kalin had come to see what he would wind up doin is a mystery. It's just how an answer can sometimes emerge after puzzlin over a question for a long time, arrivin without announcement, acquirin with its arrival immediate sense. You don't know fer sure if it's right or if it'll work, but you know it's the best you can offer. It also requires of you somethin that ain't easy. Maybe that's how Kalin knew in the end it was the best option he had.

Sometimes in the presence of Nora Dall, Paige Costales, or Jennifer Agius and now and then Andrew Rivetti, Becky Sanko, and Farran Engelman, both Maggie Trunnell and Lissa Kaynor would feel that what most mattered in this moment of strippin down, as it were, was a question of longin. Throughout their lives, especially in the end, Maggie Trunnell, dead by accidental electrocution, and Lissa Kaynor, dead from Parkinsons, would come to agree that, more than just common longin, it was nostalgia in particular that had insured the gravest consequences. *When Achilles grieves over the body of Patroclus,* Maggie Trunnell would say, *what he longs for is that time of at-homeness he cherished with his companion.* Lissa Kaynor would nod her head in agreement to this, pointin out how *once among the suitors, Odysseus's most important act of aimin is at his home with his wife and son, where he most wants to go, before there were the suitors, before there was even the war.* Maggie Trunnell would smile then as she had done dozens of times when Lissa would say somethin similar: *And that there was their problem.* For both professors, both emeriti, and by then both of them a long ways from Orvop, where they was born, what's so dangerous about nostalgia is that it makes the paramount present suddenly negotiable. *Take it or leave it, and really it's too often leave it,* Lissa Kaynor would add. *Which makes room for violence to come on in,* Maggie Trunnell would conclude. *Because if you're distracted by the past, you ain't seein clear what's comin for you in the present.*

Near the birch where the horses' leads was tied, Kalin pulled off his daddy's green poncho, unbuttoned his Lee Storm Rider and then, after carefully foldin the jacket up like it was some precious flag, packed it and the slicker into one of Jojo's saddlebags. That went for his cable-knit sweater, now a thing gray as ash, and then the shirts beneath. He took off his boots next and would've left on his socks but noticed the blood. Turned out he'd lost the nails on both his big toes. Kalin couldn't feel no pain there, but the sight of them nailless nubs felt awful as well as sad, like there goes everythin, and weren't this the darndest situation to end up in, and what was the use of even takin one more step let alone another breath? But just the same Kalin did take another breath, and another one after that, and then he got out that Swiss Army knife again and drew the blade down on his left forearm. The cut was mostly shallow, more like a scratch, and it didn't even bleed much. In fact Kalin had to wait some, shiverin there in the cold, as the blood made its way toward the elbow. Only after a few drops slipped loose to the snow did Kalin return the knife to a pocket and take off his jeans. His shiverin kept gettin worse. Then he put his bloody socks back on, followed by the boots. When he picked up the gun, his shiverin stopped.

Kevin Moffet had set the Bell 206 LR down at the southern end of Pillars Meadow in front of a chute he swore was Coyote Gulch. Old Porch swore to that fact too. Though they both changed their minds a few minutes later, swearin that Coyote Gulch spilled out some miles farther north. They nearly got the helicopter back up in the air, until Old Porch put a stop to that lazy notion; he knew that would fer sure alert their quarry. Plus, they'd already burnt a lot of fuel executin that wide easterly loop that had kept them out of sight and well out of earshot. The maps had come out then, with Old Porch pointin to some tree line or a visible portion of ridgeline before jab-bin the flutterin paper. Kevin Moffet just went on agreein because he didn't really care where they was goin so long as Old Porch was pleased, which was pretty much like tryin to make a silk pillowcase out of a sea urchin.

Woolsey, Sean, and Shelly cared little for maps and got to kickin snow up at each other and when they got bored with that took out their weapons. Woolsey had only brought along a .22, a Ruger 10/22. The rifle was a semiautomatic, and what he didn't have by way of aimin skills Woolsey made up for with how fast he could get off ten shots. His busted hand only needed to hold the weapon steady, and Woolsey had no doubt he could manage that well enuf. *I never did need my pinkie to shoot a thing.* He seemed pretty happy.

Francis also had a .22, a pump Winchester Model 62A, though the boy had yet to emerge from the helicopter. Sean loaded his Browning A-Bolt. Shelly's Ruger M77, chambered in .257 Roberts, was second-hand and pretty beat to heck, but he knew it was ready to go. His

Ruger Service-Six was also already loaded, but Shelly emptied it just the same just to reload it again.

One of you fires just one shot, Old Porch suddenly barked at his boys, *and I'll put a round right through your head.* His boys laughed, but not a one doubted the threat, another reason Francis chose to keep outta sight.

It's an art, raisin so many maggots, Old Porch said then as he got back to the map, grinnin easily at Kevin Moffet, who maybe less easily grinned back, wantin just to get whatever this was over with and return home so he could leave Orvop once and for all and find, finally, a new start in Alaska. By this point Kevin Moffet had also decided to radio the police the first chance he got, although maybe he was hesitated some by the absolute absence now of what he would report, especially in the face of such vast and wild and imposin terrain, makin the earlier sightin seem somehow unlikely, maybe even impossible, a hallucination, a mirage, a misunderstandin; as if the immense mountain in all its present certainty had already rendered that boy and his horses so tiny as to not even merit a claim on wishful thinkin. And maybe, fer real, Kalin and the horses never was more than that. Kevin Moffet even figured it might be best to frame this all as a fanciful story he'd get around to tellin later to pals or folks he was flyin around Glacier Bay.

When Hatch, Egan, Kelly, and Billings finally caught up, they arrived on foot. At first they'd made great time. The snow had held up, and the sleds ate up the miles. Soon though, the risin temperatures had begun to slush out the conditions. Eventually the mud and rocks forced them to park the snowmobiles beneath some blue-needled trees. It was Hatch who'd picked the spot, because it was shady and he thought the snow there might outlast the day. Egan could see the vehicles would also stay hid from any aerial reconnaisance and supported Hatch's choice.

Not surprisinly Hatch had been the quickest to have his gear on his back, includin that monster Barrett M82. He'd but glanced at the map and near at once took off double-time without lookin behind him. No question he was by far the fittest and quickly outdistanced the others. At first. The Porches weren't nothin if they weren't made of grist and grit with an unnatural penchant for bestin each other. Kelly had caught up soon enuf, and as the ascent got harder, he didn't fade either.

Billings had also kept up, again lookin like he expended no energy and could've easily slipped ahead. This weren't true of course. He was hurtin plenty, and even if he could've mustered a faster gear, he had no desire nor need to get ahead of Kelly let alone Hatch. Nonetheless, to Hatch, to Kelly, and even to Egan, Billings had seemed outright languid in his lope, just enjoyin the remote peaks surroundin them, the terrifyin glory of these unattended regions of the Katanogos massif, like he was just settin back with a mug of hot cider on a scenic train ride on the Heber Creeper.

Egan had taken up the rear and was a good ways back too. He weren't near fit as Hatch, Kelly, or Billings but he also weren't too bothered. So what if his breath was comin up hotter than the rest? Or his girth had a few too many burgers and shakes on it? Even when he had to stop to cough up thick gobs of snot, he still weren't bothered. He possessed now a sense of supreme utility that bested any feats of athleticism now on display. Kelly could have his track victories; Hatch could go on about his medals. Egan knew he was the real deal, the real horseradish.

He'd kept hisself primed and ready too with the thought that at any moment he was gonna come across Kalin, likely by chance, because that's how the Universe would see that it happened, that's how their Heavenly Father would ordain this reckonin. For a while there Egan was sure Kalin would step out of the trees right after Hatch, Kelly, and Billings had passed by, missin that Egan was still some ways back. And would Egan hesitate? No sirree. Egan would just bullet him down with his Smith & Wesson .357 Magnum. The number of kills also seemed to demand this eventuality. Three weren't a number you could argue with: first the ranger, then Landry, and now this boy. That's right. Three was the trick. Three was inevitable.

Only when Egan seen Hatch and their dad sharin a laugh did his smile hitch. Like some jealous husband he was, suspectin his wife's every smile and Old Porch sure was smilin. Egan even got it into his head that Hatch had somehow already laid low the Kalin kid and was once again the family hero. Of course, that weren't the case. Hatch was only settin straight where they was at.

This here's Coyote Gulch, Hatch said as he tapped the map. *About a mile that way.*

Egan still figured Hatch would next pull aside Old Porch and give him an earful about Landry and what Egan had done. But Hatch did no such thing. He just heaved his gear back on and set off once again at a hard jog, this time with Coyote Gulch in his sights. It stumped Egan. It really did. And even made him wonder if he'd figured Hatch all wrong.

Kelly struck out too, still determined to keep up with Hatch. Billings only had to keep up with Kelly, which weren't so hard for him. Egan, though, held back with his dad and younger brothers. In fact he even took up the rear again, keepin Francis company, who'd finally emerged from the helicopter, the two findin some laughs, which, given Francis's near-perpetual state of glum, was somethin of a miracle. In fact Francis had started up as soon as Egan was at his side, talkin about grillin some ribs when they got back and an idea he had for some slaw and what to do with the potatoes so they'd stay crispy and golden; he wanted to put rosemary on them, and Egan had told Francis he'd get everythin he needed. *Whatever you like so long as it beats what Dad calls grillin,* which was generally considered awful by all of them, somethin just shy of charcoal. Woolsey volunteered to serve up the eats. Francis wondered if maybe Kelly could take a picture or two. They needed a family picture. Especially since Hatch was here. Egan thought it sounded fine and almost couldn't wait to get back to the old Porch house.

Hatch stopped right in the center of the meadow, facin the center of Coyote Gulch. He took in them beautiful birches and quakin aspens and then stepped back. He knew better than to head everyone into those trees. He figured they could set up just fine in any one of the deep recessions the meadow offered. It was Old Porch, when he finally caught up, who ordered everyone to fall back all the way to the crick, where they could lie hid behind the banks. Hatch praised the tactical benefits of that choice, unaware that his superior tone at once riled up Old Porch, Hatch misreadin his daddy's expression as commendation instead of loathin.

What Egan had quit suspectin, Hatch was hard at doin: tryin to figure out how best to get Old Porch alone and get loose this thing about Landry Gatestone. Hatch knew full well how cautious he'd need to be. Neither Egan nor Kelly could get a sense of what Hatch would be layin the groundwork for, and certainly not Billings, who Hatch knew now as an opponent.

Hatch chose a spot of gritty snow with a berm of rough earth just high enuf to grant him cover. Here he laid out his tarp. After settin up the .50 caliber, he stretched out long, settlin his eye on the Zeiss, wonderin just what he'd do if right then he sighted the boy and the horses emergin from all that pale bark? Hatch had no idea, though his finger weren't anywhere near the trigger nor even the safety. At least the run had cleared his head enuf for him to see that he was gonna handle this in accordance with the law, and that went for Landry's murder too, but he also hadn't forgotten that what they had here was a Cop Killer, and a Porch Killer to boot, who had to be brought to Justice. Why if that boy so much as flashed a weapon, he'd drop him with a shot to the heart. Of course, with the Barrett, Hatch would blow away more than just his heart.

Unlike Hatch, neither Francis nor Shelly had brought a tarp, and they weren't wearin no snowpants neither. Hatch had them set up right below where the crick's bank was highest so they could either squat or sit on the rocks he rid of snow with his big gloved hands. Hatch told Egan to set up there too. Egan, though, ignored the order and instead told Kelly to move on ahead, a command that didn't rile up Kelly one bit, which once again unsettled Hatch and warned him too, watchin Kelly scramble away like some beat dog, like Mr. Bucket #3 done every time their daddy had gone near him.

In the end Egan set up his tarp and rifle to the left of Old Porch, who welcomed Egan warmly. Hatch kept to the right of his dad, while Billings set up to the right of Hatch, which Hatch didn't care for one bit, though Billings kept playin it like he was payin Hatch no mind. To Billings's right, Kelly stretched out. Woolsey briefly considered takin up the farthest position to the north, sick of his brothers already, but when they started bettin, he returned to Francis, who marked the farthest position to the south.

Sean, who'd set up between Shelly and Egan, was wagerin that the Kalin kid weren't gonna show. He figured he had turned around after the helicopter had passed by and escaped north through the trees. Shelly agreed that the kid had fer sure seen the helicopter.

I bet he didn't even take one step down Coyote Gulch.

Sean then promptly changed his mind, mainly because he found it intolerable to be in agreement with Shelly. Bettin against Shelly was the way of things. Of course, if Sean had paused to add up all the wins this tactic had provided him with, what anyways was a feat of analysis he was incapable of, why he'd've realized just how much money Shelly had taken from him over the years.

Two hundred bucks says we never see him, Shelly declared.

Sean took that bet at once. Woolsey threw in forty dollars mostly because he'd learned that Shelly usually won. Sean was only too happy to raise the bet to two hundred and fifty dollars but Francis didn't throw in for the other ten dollars because he was sidin with Sean.

Shelly covered the ten and told Francis he could only side with Sean if he paid up for the opinion.

Francis didn't pay up because he didn't care one bit. *I feel it,* he murmured. *Kalin ain't runnin.* And his brothers did behold him in that moment as extra gaunt and shaken by the premonition.

Some still say that it was right at that very moment that Tom had crossed over the crick bed on his way to the gateposts. And that does time out about right. Plenty more, though, like to add that it weren't just Tom but also Pia Isan, along with that long line of dead that were sweepin by like the summit air that so often spills down Coyote Gulch and spreads out across Pillars Meadow, fillin every groove, recession, and divot, but especially that crick bed, with its cold reminder of who, despite alternate claims, really owns such territory.

What are you mumblin about, Francis? Shelly griped. *Quit bein such a Fem-Iron tablet! Whadya mean he ain't runnin? He's done nothin but run!*

Woolsey sure laughed at that, and Shelly was pleased to see his younger brother laughin. Even Sean laughed.

Francis, though, didn't. Nor did the sound of their laughter alter his mind any. *Is that what you think he's been doin, Shelly?* Now Shelly's a big guy, but he took note of the metal in the voice of the littlest Porch. *He's got a place in mind. It don't matter if there's a box canyon in the way. It don't matter if there's a mountain in the way. I don't think it's gonna matter if we're in the way. He's got a place in mind and he's comin.*

Shelly tried to laugh at Francis, mean as he could too, callin him *a wuss, a wobbly sister,* but he couldn't keep it up long. There was no denyin that somethin about what Francis had just said struck him as true, struck Woolsey and Sean in the same way. Of course just a quick glance at their surroundins, especially this wide and muddy snow-strewn field, returned them to their chucklin.

Wait a minute, Russel. Let me get this straight. You're sayin he's got THIS PLACE in mind?! Sean's face went red with nasty glee. *If that ain't the best argument to change my bet right now and side with Shelly!*

You just called Francis Russel, you dumb dolt, Shelly snarled back at him.

The heck I did! Sean tried to object.

But Woolsey confirmed it, and Francis dropped his head, and Shelly and Sean kept grinnin at Pillars Meadow. Sean didn't change his bet either.

Francis then experienced an increased sense of disorientation. Whatever retributive fire had burnt briefly in him while in the warm Porch household that mornin was now challenged by the cold seepin up through his legs, gettin after his butt and his gut, while the back of his neck remained at the mercy of the bright sun, surely bubblin his skin, dazzlin his eyes too, even with sunglasses on, and yet even these inconvenient discomforts were nothin compared to how the desolation of this place kept cowin whatever earlier impulses he'd felt sturdy enuf to suffer until it came time to actually suffer them. *Let's do this for Russel! I swear! Whatever it takes!* Francis had actually said aloud on the way to the airport, and Old Porch had patted him on the shoulder. But Francis couldn't suffer that oath for even the duration of the helicopter flight. By the time they'd landed, he was once again doubtin everythin, and by the time they'd spread out in this crick bed, he was fearin everythin too.

Fer sure, Francis Porch weren't no Kalin March. Not even close. None of them were. And when any last vestiges of resolve or at least some sense of purpose departed Francis, disorientation became the way of his mind. He just wanted to go, get away from there, get home. Grieve. That's what he wanted: to grieve for Russel. He no longer cared about Coyote Gulch, the woods, or the meadow ahead. He sure as heck didn't care a stitch about his Winchester 62A. He either kept starin down at his boots, like he could look them into action, or he kept castin long glances back to the helicopter, each time decidin to head there at once, a decision he never could will into movement.

It is still incredible to ponder the countless pathways possible upon this immense and sometimes incomprehensible, frequently convoluted region and then behold how but the few paths we've come to know by heart now converged on Pillars Meadow and right smack-dab in front of Coyote Gulch. Too much continues to be said on behalf of Fate's unalterable outcome. We can all snooze or laugh through Eddie Goulthrop's assertions at the A&C Hamburger Stand, and this on the very night a rafter would collapse above his bed and take away his life in the midst of a dream about ice skatin, how at hand now was a terrifyin natural composition, centuries old, that had brought into position these various personalities to pay the full price of familial crimes, with Eddie Goulthrop punctuatin such grandness with sloshin splatters of foamy root beer surgin forth as he continued to clench and unclench that waxy jumbo cup of soda. Not that Eddie was necessarily wrong, though Flo Carrigan, some months before both her main and reserve chute failed to deploy, would note to her wife that no matter how porous with opportunities were the routes taken, it still all came down to the father, Orwin Porch, and his fierce ambition, and fear, fear that his mighty ambitions would remain unfulfilled, who had determined exactly this intersection: *Whether he knew it explicitly or not, Old Porch was all along attuned to Kalin's direction, likely because where he was goin was to where a Gatestone might go. The Porches and Gatestones had become so entangled over the decades that it was pretty much like a right hand always knowin where the left one's at.*

And Old Porch's lifelong penchant for conflict sure never did seem to ebb, as fundamental to his character as his bones were hard, and the bloodier the conflict the better, even if he was personally oblivious to how constantly he sought out such interactions, maybe even foolin hisself some, as he so often would display moods contrary to the imminent outcome. To that point, on this very Sunday too, his boys, if they'd been asked, would not have been able to recollect a time when their old man had seemed so genial and, well, happy. It disconcerted them as much as it assured them, especially Egan.

Kevin Moffet, who was squattin right behind Old Porch, sure was taken in by his infectious display of ease. When Kelly passed him his bag of Red Man, which Kevin right away handed to Old Porch, Old Porch makin a comment about it not bein Copenhagen but still sayin so with a smile, takin his time to stuff the leaf between his gum and lip until it was situated right, maybe the radiant effects of the nicotine focusin Old Porch as well as relaxin him, Kevin Moffet who never had no interest in chewin tobacco still found the offer as well as Old Porch's apparent satisfaction settlin. Just once in his life he'd tried chewin tobacco and wound up dizzy and soon after throwin up. Maybe if he'd known how with some use it can easy up your jitters he might've taken up the habit if for this moment alone. Because he'd sure gotten jittery when he'd first begun to register the number and variety of weapons surroundin him. Kevin Moffet was plenty familiar with rifles, but the additional shotguns and handguns didn't exactly soothe his nerves. And what was he to make of that .50 caliber?! Now that there was a weapon of war! Soon as they'd arrived, Kevin Moffet had done nothin but concoct excuses in his head to stay in the helicopter. He had to alert the police. And even later, even as he started gettin used to this shootin party, he'd think again about hustlin back when no one was lookin and just takin off. He could radio the police when he was in the air. No question his basest instincts kept tellin him over and over to run. And any minute now Kevin Moffet was gonna listen and do just that.

But Old Porch had instincts too, the kind that so often trumped other men and insured their ruin.

Kevin, Old Porch said to the pilot, now pushin out through them shattered teeth a ribbon of brown spit. *Soon as the maggot shows hisself, I want you to do me a favor.*

You got it, Orwin, Kevin Moffet answered with as much conviction as he could muster, which incidentally would'nt've engendered any confidence in even the simplest folk and sure didn't in Old Porch, but Old Porch still answered Kevin Moffet's declaration with a grin even the most discernin theater critic would have bought. Kevin Moffet, fer his part, did still sense that somethin was off. Maybe it was the smell, Old Spice or was it Lysol?, or even a combination of the two, that seemed to close up his throat enuf where he was near gaggin. Old Porch waited the spasm out, and his smile never faltered.

I appreciate your loyalty, Kevin. When that boy shows, and he'll do so soon,

I want you to stay low as you can and make your way to the helicopter. Then I need you to radio the police. Take off if you have to, if you need the altitude to reach them. Can you do that for me?

And like that, every bit of dread and misgivin departed. Kevin Moffet was back to noddin and smilin and thinkin how maybe he would try some chewin tobacco after all, especially if it promised to make of this new elation somethin even greater. Not that he needed greater. The bright blue sky overhead was more than enuf. Even Old Porch's cold gray eyes looked warm and sun-dappled. And Old Porch weren't even done: he was now handin over a roll of hundreds bound up with a red rubber band. And then fishin in his pocket for a second roll, though he didn't hand that one over yet. *This here's for when we get back to the airport.* Except Old Porch didn't pocket it either. *You hold on to it,* Old Porch said as he placed that second roll in Kevin's palm, and it was the bigger roll. *Just get us home safe.*

After that, Kevin Moffet just plain couldn't see the .50 caliber on his right nor any of the other weaponry to his left. Against them rolls of cash, he sure didn't give any weight neither to the 9mm aluminum-framed Smith & Wesson Model 59, which Old Porch had just taken out to inspect, oh so casually double-checkin the action, the magazine, makin sure the thing was loaded properly, and you can bet it was loaded properly, before resettlin it behind his belt buckle.

Kevin Moffet even patted Old Porch on his shoulder, failin to notice how to his left Egan had become a different creature. The appearance of the Model 59, what had also had no effect on Hatch, seemed to coil up Egan and set him on the ready.

I need to yellow some snow now, Orwin, Kevin Moffet then announced.

Like I said, Kevin, keep low, Old Porch answered the pilot with a smile, and maybe if Kevin Moffet hadn't had to pee so bad, he might've honed in on the way Old Porch's jaw had hardened, the way his teeth were clenched, the way them gray eyes kept grayin even more, hardly sun-dappled no more, more like the frost you'd find in one of the Porch Meats walk-in freezers. Kevin Moffet might've even managed to get a tiny glimpse of Old Porch's fury.

But Kevin Moffet didn't have no inklin. He just assured them all that he'd stay low until he was a good way up the crick bed to where there was plenty of brush for cover. Heck, this was startin to be fun.

Careful not to let your head pop up over the banks here, Old Porch added. *In case things get hot.*

Whadya mean hot?

That kid has my gun.

Kevin Moffet's micturative needs proved a good thing for Egan Porch.

Landry Gatestone's dead, Egan announced to his daddy, loud enuf for Hatch to hear too.

Oh really. How'd that happen?

You're lookin at how it happened, Egan answered with a grin that weren't gonna stop for even death.

Is that a good thing? Old Porch had registered at once Hatch's shift to face Egan. *Or is it a great thing?*

I spotted her on a ridgeline south of here. One shot.

Old Porch looked genuinely relieved. *That there's a huge weight off our shoulders. This whole family is grateful to you, Egan.* Old Porch again registered Hatch's movement, though this time his eldest was retreatin, returnin to his tarp, his scope, wipin his brow, wipin his brow twice. Not that his father's and brother's whisperin eluded him.

What did you drop her with? Old Porch was askin now, his schemin mind narrowin down the details, at work again, wrestlin each piece into the story he'd need to protect hisself and his boys.

But when Egan nodded at his Winchester, Old Porch's grin became an ugly wrinkle. *You think them forensic experts ain't gonna match up that Model Seventy with what went through her? You might as well have left your name and address on her. And mine too.*

She's under a mountain of snow now.

That so? Old Porch still snarled. *You mean just like she was buried in that landslide? Like they was trapped in the cirque? Buried like that?*

Hatch grinned a little to hisself over his daddy's risin ire directed at his crazy brother, even if the basis of their talk turmoiled the thump in his chest to the point of angry action, if Hatch only knew what action to take.

By the time they find her body, Egan continued, *there won't be nothin left but a mess of shattered bones. And they'll still assume it was the Kalin kid.*

You hope.

This is different, Pa. I saw her bleed. I saw her fall. I seen the snow that buried her.

But Old Porch was done acceptin anyone's assurances except his own. *After we're done here, we'll go to where you say she's buried and make sure she stays that way. This ends today.*

What about him? Egan asked then, with a quick nod toward Kevin Moffet, now emergin from the cover of brush, doin just as Old Porch had instructed, crouchin low below the crick banks as he made his way past Kelly, Billings, and finally Hatch.

He's the best thing here, Old Porch whispered. *He's our witness.*

What did I miss? Kevin Moffet asked as he resumed his position behind Old Porch. He was winded a bit but seemed even happier than before, as if this outin had finally resolved itself in his head as somethin he was already free of.

Kevin, my Hatch here just now told me somethin awful he'd seen on the way up here. Remember how we spotted that boy with the horses but not the girl? Hatch seen the boy throw that girl's body off some bluffs south of here.

Is that so? Kevin Moffet asked, lookin at Hatch first, who kept his eye to the scope, before returnin his gaze to Old Porch and Egan. Old Porch heard the tremor in the pilot's voice as either appalled or unconvinced. Maybe the pilot had already heard about Egan's declaration, about seein Kalin gun down Landry in the cirque? He should've said Egan instead of Hatch.

We figure he was tryin to dispose of the body, Egan said. *Ain't that right, Hatchy?*

There was no chance she was alive, Hatch answered without lookin up, his risin anger further amplified by his continuin inability to grasp yet a clear course of action through this developin horror show.

Ain't that awful, Kevin Moffet said.

Egan shrugged. *He's a cold-blooded killer.*

You can fly us there, right? Old Porch asked.

Yeah, of course, Kevin Moffet mumbled.

We ain't in no hurry, Egan said then, unable to keep down the growl in his throat, unable to understand why his daddy wanted to point this pilot to where he'd blasted the girl from life. *She ain't alive.* Though Egan weren't that slow and quick enuf began figurin that Old Porch was gonna show Kevin Moffet a completely different spot. That way it wouldn't matter how many got to diggin for her remains; they could spend all winter for all he cared. *I'll show you, Kevin, where I seen him do it.*

Egan relaxed then, watchin Old Porch relax some. Old Porch even patted Hatch on the shoulder, not so much to comfort him as to let him know that Hatch was a part of this family and just as involved as everyone else, even if he didn't understand the whole thing.

Why lyin in itself always brought Old Porch so much pleasure has never been satisfactorily explained. Sure, Old Porch was often self-promotin. And sure, Old Porch mainly lied so he could just carry on doin whatever he felt like doin, usually pleasures that commanded him to seek out more such pleasure. But Old Porch also seemed to like lyin just for the sake of lyin. Annette Kaplar would say he was *by merit raised to that bad eminence and from despair thus high uplifted beyond hope*; American Fork original Wilbur Hoberman, who lost his life to a brain tumor, would pretty much say the same thing: *Old Porch was a nasty ole cuss.*

Old Porch weren't done with Hatch neither, even lettin his hand rest on his eldest's shoulder as he then declared his allegiance to the victim: *Poor Sondra Gatestone. Us Porches and them Gatestones have never much seen eye to eye, but to lose all your children, why if that isn't the very definition of tragedy. I know I can hardly take it now, and we only lost Russel. But Sondra, she's lost Evan, Tom, and now little Landry. Brother Moffet, you are my witness: we're gonna put away our differences once and for all. I'll cover her funeral costs. Porch Meats will see to it that Sondra's freezer stays full through next summer.*

That is awful kind, Orwin, Kevin Moffet responded.

Isn't it the very least we can do?

Bringin to justice the one that done it is the best we can do, Hatch now said, liftin his head to spare no one his gaze, especially his younger brother. *Egan, can I count on you to help me put cuffs on that maggot?*

Egan didn't bite so much as grunt, and Old Porch was pleased at least to see Egan keepin his trap shut.

You brought them cuffs, did you? Old Porch asked Hatch then, at last removin his hand from his boy's shoulder.

Hatch returned his eye to the scope, to the tree line, exhalin slowly, facin the stillness out there as if it was a message come from well beyond the pages of birches, announcin an arrival he'd be better off tryin to avoid. But duty instructed him to stay.

Even out here, Pa, I'm a sworn officer of the law.

Though Sondra was the one drivin now, and Allison was still bleedin from the back of the head, even if it had finally started to thicken some, feelin more and more blobby like old motor oil in her hair, and fer sure helped some by the towel she kept pressed to the injury, it was still Allison tellin Sondra what turns to take, in softer and softer tones too, especially as she observed her friend growin more upset over the fracas they'd only just managed to get free of.

Allison wanted them to go straight to a place near Mud Lake, and Sondra was fine with that, but she still headed east first and then near State Street pulled the truck into Holt's, a family-run drug and convenience store. It was a big place with a United States flag, a red-and-gold sign out front, and plenty of brass fixtures and polished wood floors inside. The lore was that Holt's had been around since Utah was only a territory when Briggham Young hisself had declared it the birthplace of the world's greatest root beer float. The Holts concurred one and all that their store was where the root beer float was invented, six years before Frank J. Wisner did so in Colorado. Of course, this was all bunkum. The Holts hailed from Illinois and didn't move out to Utah until after World War II. The shop itself weren't built until 1951, by Callum Holt, father to Earl Holt. The family did a fine job managin the store and they all worked plenty hard. So what if there was a little lore? Utahns love a good story. Some still say the state is built on them. The way Callum Holt had figured it, if the Church could baptise the dead, and in that way create Church members throughout history, why couldn't he do the same with his store? And so, if he found old photographs that looked near enuf like Holt's, why up on the walls they went. And he did find plenty of close-enuf pictures. All the way back to 1887.

Like his father, Earl too was a dreamer, though also like his father, he weren't a daft dreamer. Callum Holt had taught Earl what Earl had taught all his children, especially his middle son: *Never confuse the shine of your sign with the dirty labor required inside.* You mark your gains, you mark your losses, and you always pay off your debts lest you confuse what you owe with what you have.

In fact it was this very middle son who was workin the register when Sondra Gatestone came stompin in with Allison March not far behind. Sondra knew exactly where she was goin too, pretty much knew that store like she did her own pantry, headin right for the aisle with cotton balls, hydrogen peroxide, and gauze. They was out of medical tape so she picked out a big box of Band-Aids.

Holt's was one of the few stores open on Sunday. The Holts were devout Church members, but like Callum, Earl held that Church folks still needed a place where they could get somethin extra for their Sunday lunch when needs arose, and such needs pretty much arose every Sunday. Earl's lips to Heavenly Father, Sunday was one of their busiest days. And at that hour, there was already a good handful of folks fillin them small carts, and boy, when those folks seen them two ladies, it was like celebrities were in their midst, as if the Cassidy Movie Star hisself was strollin the aisles in search of some Pringles. Though this was also different. A few folks, maybe with visions of the Hole-in-the-Wall Gang muckin up their thoughts, bolted right the heck outta there, like Sondra and Allison had come in determined to rob the bank, forgettin that Holt's weren't a bank. Though even those who could claim no misunderstandin did back away just the same, as if proximity or, heaven forbid, a lingerin eye might provoke some kind of consequent combat, a reaction reasonably contingent on the fact that there was still ample blood on display, not yet entirely wiped away, not to mention the steely look in both women's eyes. They might be there now because they'd fought and lost, but plain as day was that they'd gladly fight again.

Sondra Gatestone paid none of this attention any mind. Like some great grizzly bear she was hardly bothered by birds racin for the sky. She slapped down her goods by the register, addin in as well some gum, two Sprites, two 3 Musketeers, and in fact one can of Pringles.

While she was diggin in her wallet, and Allison was insistin that she be the one to pay, the Holt kid said the goods were on the house.

Excuse me? Sondra snapped like she was affronted or, worse, just threatened by someone who'd regret his mistake.

I-I got this one, Mrs. Gatestone.

Do I know you?

Lindsey Holt, ma'am.

Sondra softened at once. *Why my lord! It is you, Lindsey! I haven't seen you in ages. Maybe a football game or FFA event?*

Yes, ma'am. That sounds about right, Lindsey Holt said with a shy smile.

Did you cut your hair? You were always big, but I seem to recall you with long hair. Shiny too. I confess, I often envied you.

All my mom's friends said the same.

Is that why you cut it? I hope not.

No, ma'am, Lindsey said, stealin a quick glance at Allison.

Did you join the military? Sondra pressed.

No, ma'am. I just buzzed it off. I was spendin more time on it than on my schoolwork.

Sounds then like you got your priorities in order, Sondra Gatestone said with a smile that was both admirin and even a little impressed.

But then, before Sondra could ask why everythin was goin for gratis, Lindsey did somethin even odder: he pulled out of his wallet a one-dollar bill, which he slid over toward Allison.

What's that for? Sondra asked on behalf of her friend.

Lindsey couldn't have looked more nervous, like he was gonna ask one of them on a date or even both of them on a date. He sure couldn't look Allison in the eye, not even in her general direction, and when he answered Sondra, he had to keep his gaze glued right above Sondra's head, which given his size weren't a hard thing to do. *I'm real sorry about what happened to Tom, Mrs. Gatestone. His passin and all. He surely did know how to have a good time pretty much wherever he was. I'll never forget his smile or how he could laugh in such a way that got you laughin, though you had no idea what you was laughin for in the first place. At least that's how it was for me. I'm real lucky I got to share a few such laughs with him, and I regret not tellin him directly how grateful I was for him bein, well, him.*

Thank you, Lindsey, Sondra responded, somber now if also touched, if also still confused by that one-dollar bill on the counter.

For what it's worth, I also want to add that I know Landry ain't involved in any of these misdeeds the rumorin is full of. And then Lindsey Holt finally turned to Allison March. *You must be Kalin's mom, right? I seen you on the news. I didn't know your son any, but I don't buy what they're sayin about him either.*

Thank you, Allison managed to squeak out, so shocked by the support, especially in light of that morning's events.

That's awful nice to hear, Lindsey, Sondra said. *We both appreciate your support and kindness, but what does that have to do with this here dollar bill?*

Yeah. About that. Lindsey looked almost embarrassed. *Some time ago, Kalin and me had ourselves a bit of a disagreement. Tom happened to come by and figured the best way to settle our differences was to see who could best ride them two horses in Old Porch's paddock on Willow and Oak.*

The same two horses he has now? Allison asked.

I believe so. Lindsey took a deep breath. *Tom had us each bet a dollar, and that was a bet I was willin to take because, well, and I figure you already know this, Mrs. Gatestone, I likely couldn't best Tom, but your kid,* and Lindsey glanced over at Allison, *I reckoned he knew as much about ridin a horse as a goat does about mowin a lawn. Though maybe that's the wrong comparison because a goat is pretty much made to mow a lawn. Or maybe it's the perfect comparison, because what me and Tom discovered was, well . . . We both sat on the fence pretty much slack-jawed. Me and Tom had both been bucked off fast, and here's this kid outta nowhere sittin on that mare like they was old friends, like they'd known each other their whole lives, maybe even before that. Handled the geldin just fine too, and let me tell you, he was a brawler. I couldn't even lay a hand on him. Tom didn't do much better either.*

By that point many of the customers there who'd been wary at first were drawin close to get an earful of what Lindsey was sayin, fer sure that part about him not believin that neither Landry nor Kalin was guilty of any of this killin but more so about what he was sayin about the horses. Horses still speak to a part of Utah's big bruised heart even though that ain't near enuf apparent.

Back then, Lindsey continued, *I didn't recognize what I was seein. I'm really ashamed now to admit it. I've always been so proud, as in pride, as in not in a good way. I was mad as heck that day too. Just fumin for havin lost and fumin for how Tom couldn't stop laughin and he'd lost too. I just stormed off. But I couldn't forget it neither. And I'm not talkin about the next day or even a week later. I kept tryin to convince myself, month after month, that your boy, Kalin, had cheated me, and every chance I got, whenever I seen him in the halls of Orvop High, I made sure he knew where I stood. But then Tom died,* and Lindsey's voice cracked, *and I don't know why I needed that tragedy, it really ain't fair, but I started to see just what an ass I'd been. I started to see my awful proudness, my awful pride. My daddy says pride is the blight that blinds us. I finally* made up my mind to say so to Kalin, but, see, I missed my chance. When I heard he'd taken those ponies to the hills, I didn't doubt it for a second. I knew he loved them horses just like I knew Old Porch meant to slaughter them. But then when I heard he killt Russel, that I did doubt. I still doubt it. It don't make a lick of sense. On the other hand, Kalin ridin out of a rockslide? And on the back of that very same mare he'd settled right before my eyes? Why that made perfect sense. I can still see him, you know. He was somethin with those horses. He had a gift. I'd say even God-given, which as you likely know is a hard thing for a Church member to say about someone who ain't in the Church. Tom knew it too. I was just too stupid to admit it, to see that that afternoon weren't about no altercation or even some little homespun rodeo; it was about how fortunate we was to be given even just a glimpse of so great a talent. Why it was inspirin! It makes you want to be more than what your little life keeps tellin you you ain't. At least that's what it did for me. Lindsey finally lifted his eyes to meet Allison's. I never did pay your Kalin the dollar he was owed. Will you accept this on his behalf?

Allison eyed the money but didn't move to take it. Whether you know this or not, Allison finally said after takin a breath or two herself, you've done me a big service this mornin. But I would like to ask you for one more.

Ma'am?

I know my Kalin, and I still believe that he's gonna see his way through this, no matter what the news is sayin, no matter what some of the good folks in this store right now are thinkin. Would you mind givin it to him yourself when he gets back?

I can do that.

You'll come over to my house, Lindsey, Sondra jumped in then, and I'll make us chocolate chip pancakes. How's that sound?

I'd like nothin better, Lindsey answered, though the broken look that scissored across his eyes told both women, and whoever else was watchin them, that he weren't near as sure as they was that Kalin was gonna return. Clop-Clop-clip-Clop.

Allison didn't flinch from that possibility either. She even reached across the counter and placed her hand atop Lindsey's. If my boy don't make it back, why you spend that dollar on the one you love more than life. Bet on that.

Yes, ma'am.

Sondra Gatestone knew Orvop, Rome, and pretty much all the towns in Utah Valley better than near everyone. She was born with these roads in her blood. But Allison still managed to surprise her, whisperin out turns, slowly guidin them toward the Zurich Steel Mill, technically located in Vineland, and soon after, by way of a kind of frontage road runnin alongside the mill's great fence, findin a new set of gravel roads Sondra had never been on before, skirtin the edge of Mud Lake.

Several turns later, on what you could only describe as dirt paths, they reached a grassy area where any parked vehicle was beyond observation by anyone except them that was already there. No one was there.

Now folks like Wendel and Kandie Moore, Benton Bland, and Merijo Jarvis, all gone from the earth by shipwreck, an ocean liner, the water was warm; poison, sacred datura, in fact; suffocation in a stalled elevator; and by mystery, would chatter and imagine often about how these two ladies should've left their ruminative anguish for another day and headed straight over to the Brays like they said they would do, to inquire after George Bray and, if he was home, find out fer certain whether or not he'd seen Russel returnin from Isatch Canyon on Cavalry that Wednesday night. Of course it wouldn't've done the mothers any good, and so it's a curious position to gripe about, given that Dorothy Bray was at that moment drivin to Salt Lake City to buy cigarettes and George Bray wouldn't be returnin until later that evenin.

This here is my place of worship, Allison announced as she stepped free of the truck and took a deep breath and a very long stretch. Even if the back of her head throbbed, though at least the bleedin was mostly stopped, though the scratches on her cheek continued to hurt plenty, if they too was at least startin to crust over, her mind gave not a thought to her injuries. It weren't hard to see where Kalin got some of his resilience and extraordinary fortitude.

It was 11:49 a.m.

Sondra likely would've preferred to minister some to Allison's wounds, not to mention clean the cuts on her own forehead and face, and she was in fact searchin around in the Holt's store bag for the hydrogen peroxide, until the sight of her friend walkin away and with such purpose, with a look of absolute peace on her face, freed Sondra from her decision.

Allison was headin toward a line of twelve trees, each of them well over a hundred years old, their trunks solemn as the columns of Delphi, not a branch on them until you got above thirty feet. They was so evenly placed, it was obvious men's hands had been at work here, likely under municipal orders, though in fact the planters had not worked for the city and they had all been women and they'd chosen the spot.

As Allison wound her way in and around them, her left hand and then her right hand would alternately brush the bark as she passed by. Perhaps persistently wary of her friend's spiritual habitus, Sondra resisted at first the impulse to do the same, a reaction certainly reinforced by Allison's declaration that this place was her church. Engagin it then would mean for Sondra to somehow defile if not outright reject her own. But if that assumption briefly immobilized her, the cold clear air, the heart-sunderin peacefulness enfoldin them released her just as easily from such logics, and she walked in kind among these giants.

Thanks be to Heavenly Father that they didn't just scurry straight back to the Gatestone house, Sondra thought. Thanks too to her Palladian Dallin if he was lookin after her. They'd've only holed up with the radio on, the phone ringin, gettin crazier and crazier over some notion that they still had some control, all the while the TV, if they could get the news and not just reruns of *Little House on the Prairie*, would keep on displayin its visual declarations, as if the moments captivated somehow spoke for all the moments yet to come.

Sondra indulged in her own deep breaths and even tried a stretch or two. If this here was indeed a church, it needed no words. It was the beginnin before words were needed to declare the beginnin. It had no ruf other than sky, and the sermon here was just the space that resided between their thoughts, a space that grew and grew as both women's thoughts grew quieter and quieter. Ghosts suddenly surrounded them, though neither could know these dead because the livin still mattered so much more.

Of course, in less than twenty years, these great stout trees would fall or ail enuf to necessitate their removal, their roots already eaten away by the pollution in the water, by the neglect near instituted by the citizens of the city and county when it came to the well-bein of their environs. By then most of the lake's shoreline would be deprived of its glories. Already the water was strugglin against routine abuse. The air would follow. And then the memory of this place would recede, along with its calm and promise, nay, its sanctity, once kept alive and vibrant by only a handful of folks, of which these two women were unknowinly for their lifetimes a significant part. Unless, of course the trees themselves, although already gone, could still glimpse their eternity.

You know how I survive, Sondra? Allison asked. *I don't think I'm special. And I don't mean that in a self-pityin way either. I'm not an exceptionalist: what I do, others are doin; what I'm goin through, others are goin through.*

You think there are two other mothers who lost their kids to horses and mountains?

If not exactly that, similar enuf to make me see I'm not alone.

And that helps?

Allison didn't answer. *I come here a lot if just to reflect on how little I matter. And, again, that ain't no despairin thought. I find that myself without myself lets me be more fully with this world that, well, you know, goes so far* beyond the vanities of whatever things we prize so much. And that includes a pink belt with even pinker sparkles.

You've got quite some memory.

Allison then got down on her knees and closed her eyes. *If you're willin, give it a try.* She even pressed her palms together.

This Sondra couldn't do, even if Allison weren't askin her to pray for anythin she wouldn't pray for in church, even though Allison had joined her in her church, where they'd both been struck down in the parkin lot by volleys of ice. Sondra went so far to take a step back, even while recognizin that they was only outside and her Heavenly Father was surely here as He was within the temples of the Church. Nonetheless, Sondra still feared a moment of prayer in a place not so ensconced as her ward's chapel, what was insured there by the teachins of Joseph Mith, though hadn't he hisself been visited by Jesus Christ Hisself in a grove of trees? What if like him some revelation was visited upon her here? Though what if her heart could not endure it, even if, as Allison was suggestin, here was the only way a heart could finally open and truly endure?

Not that Allison, fer her part, felt so holy down on the ground. In fact the first thoughts that ransacked her mind had zero to do with any higher purpose or even her son: she couldn't remember the last time she'd worn a short summer dress or even stolen a kiss. It had been a whole lot of years, and the last time it weren't even a kiss. She'd smelled the man's hair, and it was so soft and clean that she'd started to cry for the want of it, and then for the shame of it, the same shame she was fer some reason feelin right now, rememberin when his wife had approached them then and Allison had stood there and yelled that nothin had happened, and nothin had happened, but Allison still knew her heart. That was the last time she ever went into a bar. That was, finally, the last time she'd had a drink.

Please grant me the presence and compassion to be open to what is Good for me. Please grant me the strength and conviction to endure what is Good for me. Please grant me with wit and intelligence to negotiate what is Good for me. Please grant me the grace and courage to love what is Good for me. Please grant me the humility and wisdom to let go of what is Good for me. Because everythin Good is temporary.

When Allison stood up again, Sondra asked if she really believed that Good *is temporary?*

I do.

I don't know how that makes much sense. I take great assurance knowin that my Heavenly Father is forever with me.

Allison shrugged. *A lot more trouble comes from permanence. Let go or be dragged.*

I ain't lettin go of my Landry. I ain't. And if it means gettin dragged so be it.

I ain't sayin I don't get that, Allison said, wipin away the snow and earth from her knees. *In case you ain't seein this picture clearly, I'm gettin dragged right along with you.* They both laughed at that one.

Tom had this awful joke about wantin to die hung up on a big bull in a rodeo. I told him that would be a terrible way to go. And he always made fun of me and said it sure would be terrible, but it would be glorious too. I didn't understand him then except that he loved goadin me with that big grin of his. Sometimes holdin on is all we've got.

Allison nodded. *It sounds like your Tom did just that.*

He hung on as long as he could. Sondra wiped some wet from her eyes. *One thing I so adore about the Church is its devotion to family and its preservation in the here and now as well as in the Heaven that the deservèd find after life. It's a comfort knowin I'll see Dallin again, and Evan and Tom. I hope not Landry. I'd like nothin better than to know she'll be lookin forward to seein me.*

Allison didn't say nothin.

The Baptisms of the Dead are carried out so those who didn't have a chance can enjoy the same peace after death.

Plus you become a god, right? With your own planet or somethin like that?

Sondra waved away the summation, though not without notin Allison's sardonic tone. *The Church is good about families,* Sondra again insisted. *You have to know that, right? Allison?* Sondra seemed almost to plead then, as if, if she could know that Allison was of the same mind as hers, together they might still secure somethin against a darkenin future.

Sondra, you and I have very different notions of what family means.

I can see that's true, but in the Church, by the way of the Church, there is a path that leads all its members to experience the joy of family.

Sondra, do you want to know why I stopped goin?

It was Sondra's turn to say nothin.

I stopped goin, Allison continued, *because I seen there was pretty much the same kind of folks inside the Church as there were outside of the Church. Sure there are good folks and good families that are members, but the same's true outside of the Church. And just like there are good folks and good families in the Church, there are also them who ain't so good.* Though she didn't do it for effect, Allison right then brought her hand up to the back of her head, where it had started to throb again.

Those ones outside the Church will be dealt with, Allison. I promise you that.

Sondra, I like a place where folks gather in gratitude and remind each other of what it means to do Good. I do. I tire quickly, though, when it moves from enlightenin folks to tellin folks how they should be. That makes of a special place just another ordinary place. And it smacks too of politics, of folks orderin other folks around just because they like orderin folks. It smacks of power.

There's no question Utah's history is as much tied up with the Church as it is with politics and especially the Republican party.

Allison nodded. *I don't fault people for bein people. That's the cross we all bear. However, when people excuse their behavior just because they're in the Church, any church, why that's somethin I can't swallow no more. Like them boys huckin ice and rocks at us. And what for? I don't even know. Because your stake president Enos got to talkin about takin away the guilt for murder?*

Now, now, Allison. Havril is a good man, and don't forget I was there too. He was speakin about forgiveness, not singlin us out so folks would open fire on us.

Sondra was certain too in her defense of Stake President Havril Enos. She would even defend him, yet again, or at least at first, when they eventually got back to the Gatestone house and she discovered his message on the answerin machine. Sondra would assume he was callin to inquire about her well-bein given what had happened out-side the church. She couldn't have been more wrong. With a sternness she'd never heard before in his voice, especially when directed her way, he would not only make no mention of the events at the Grandview meetinghouse nor repeat any consolations about what was goin on with Landry and Allison's boy, but he would also make clear that *for the betterment of their community* Judy Dowdell had answered the calling and would not only be in charge of the Charity in Practice event next week-end but assume the role of the presidency of the Orvop Relief Society. Sondra would be stung plenty by the message but maybe somethin over the past few days had also changed in her, removin Havril Enos from beneath some shimmerin halo of sanctified light, so much so that Sondra would know herself not so ill-prepared. Allison March would use language then that Sondra would never have condoned before let alone use herself, though upon hearin her friend's foul condemna-tions she would laugh, and for a moment her heart would be light and whimsical.

Though not at this moment. At this moment neither of them was laughin. It weren't even clear so much about what they was really talkin about, which is how some of the best conversations can go.

Maybe I mispoke, Allison conceded at once. *You have talked highly about your stake president. I've only just seen him this once. I guess I get rankled when I hear a sermon that seems to be takin sides. It seemed to me he already knew who was to blame and what the verdict was. I didn't like that one bit.*

I don't think President Enos was sayin that at all, Sondra again objected.

Allison shrugged. *Render up to Caesar what is Caesar's. Ain't that what Jesus said? One thing I am clear about: a church, and I mean any church, that demands of governments, of Caesar, the enforcement of its beliefs is a faithless settlement. A church that requires a government to enforce its beliefs is just another government and has nothin to say to me about the Goodness I'd like to believe moves alone through our hearts and does so in order to prevail upon our separate ways the kindest way to live among others, all others.*

Sondra looked confused. *I'm sorry, Allison. I don't know how we got to government. I wasn't even talkin about Havril. I thought I was only talkin about the importance of family.*

Yeah, I can do that sometimes. You see, you brought up how life in the Church leads to the sort of family you'd want to see reassembled in any afterlife. And as wholesome as that sounds, it has a way of sayin what kind of family's right, and in doin that, it refuses other kinds of livin, Good livin. From there it's just a matter of steps before this kind of preachin is just another means to acquirin power and writin laws retainin that power. Heedless too that them supposedly Good Families have by their lineage gone on to produce factions, sectarian violence, even armies set against one another, set against anythin Good. This here's the only kind of power I respect. Allison took in a deep breath and then lifted her eyes to take in the tall trees again and the towerin skies above. *Trees remind me of the virtues of stillness and patience. I used to think stillness was a prison, but the stillness patience requires is not a prison where there is Love. And I do believe there is Love here. In the earth, in the sky, where life rises and even where it don't. I told Kalin that, but I'm sure he didn't hear me.*

This exchange has been gone over and reinvented too many times to count. Some folks call it an argument, albeit a fairly polite one. Others call it a debate that is entirely theological in nature. At the bare minimum it's a disagreement. And like most such conversations this one carries little personal consequence, except that on this Sunday, at this hour, an hour that was fast approachin the day's meridian, these women underwent a conversion as it were to the other's mindset. Or maybe it's better to say heartset. And, no, not in some radical way that hastened Allison's return to the Church or demanded Sondra's exit.

Erin Kennedy, from Orvop but mostly a New Haven resident up until her passin due to ALS, would often return to this scene and in regards to Sondra Gatestone and Allison March would frequently praise religion for *the psychological territory it must necessarily occupy, especially in those spaces difficult to navigate, beyond the grasp of the thinkin required to, say, screw in a lightbulb or even track a neutrino. It's when that territory becomes better known and once again navigable by the processes of the* mind, territory that religious systems now refuse to cede, that religions become the same old political entities attemptin to shore up and aggrandize their right to influence.

Erin's husband, Gus Dieudonne, never in any way associated with Orvop, except that he would bring his wife's ashes back to the Isatch Mountains and scatter them there, would share her passion for the subject. He and Erin had met while at divinity school. *Religion is first and foremost about the Heart,* Gus Dieudonne would say to his class a year before his life ended in a train wreck that killt nine. *Religion is first and foremost about the Heart,* he would say again from the podium, the memory of his recently deceased wife alive in his own heart. *The Heart,* he would say for a third time, *that fictive organ wherein reposes those energies beyond the calculable resources of any rational mind, where the protean expenditures of affection and devotion are launched into the aspirational colloquies of Love. That's where it happens, that's where we find purpose, that's where we find meanin. But how then to raise up a kind Heart? A generous Heart? A Good Heart? Those are some of the questions we will try to at least articulate better this semester if not fully answer. I say fictive too not to denigrate the Heart. Quite the opposite. We give our children fairy tales to introduce them to fiction, to encourage them to pretend or, what lies at the roots of that word, to instruct them to stretch out their minds for and from themselves. Here then too, as an aside, is one of the glories of Buddhism and also one of its inherent conflicts: meditative practice, and ultimately enlightenment, achieves a state contrary to such juvenile tastes and delights, which is to not stretch out, not pretend, but to experience wholly and immediately the world as it is at hand. How beautiful! How true! But also how in conflict with creative exercises, in conflict with imaginative extensions, with predictions, with technological inventions, with curiosity, with progress as we know it or maybe don't know it. That all-is-in-the-present meditative calm returns us peacefully to a vegetative state of impermanence. Fairy tales, however, start us out on a different path. Fictions like Santa, the Easter Bunny, the Tooth Fairy are told not to fool our children but to pedagogically reveal the difference between what is fiction and what is not. And as these children get older, as even you grow older here, though none of you will become as old as me, not even by half, you will encounter more and more complex fictions that will strengthen your mind, which will in turn help grow and mature your Heart, the greatest fiction of all. Though don't be fooled either; the farther along you get, the easier it is to mistake what's made up with what's here without you. All our sacred texts are made up. Our constitutions? Made up. Our rights? Made up. Our laws? Made up. Your rules, promises, plans, all your hortative petitions, all made up. Many people, for example, even forget that the written language, our sacred orthography, that constitutes our laws is but an approximation. Think of our English, how the letters for words such as bear, b-e-a-r, and tear, t-e-a-r, invite* us to hear that long a but hear, h-e-a-r, and dear, d-e-a-r, invite us to hear a long e so that we must know swear, s-w-e-a-r, by the word and not the variable e-a, which we must recongnize then as a placeholder for a sound we need to remember, a mnemonic if you will, at best an approximation. That goes for h-e-a-r-t too. Heart. We must therefore learn to understand these scratches, slowly appropriate their sounds, in order to speak our mind. Of course, this prompts the next query: if written text is an approximation of speech, is speech a more able mode of communication? Socrates would say so. Though speech even in its trueness to sound, without reference, but of itself in all its particularities to each individual voice, is also a made-up thing, a fiction, approximate for all its adjacency to the discourse we wish to share. The words we vocalize, the music we make out of words, whether likened to birdsong or knives at the sharpener's wheel, are not our sensory experience, not our emotions, not even our thoughts, and certainly not the moment itself. The Buddhist meditative practice is then instructive to remind us of what is beneath these fictions. Rosary beads can offer the same thing, as will any number of prayers, many of which use words repeated to the point that they lose their wordliness and so permit a state of presence beyond words. Presence and in turn perspective. Just sweep away our fictions and be delivered unto a moment free from the intrusions of possibilities. As Joseph Campbell swooned: we're so engaged in doin things to achieve purposes of outer value that we forget that the inner value, the rapture that is associated with bein alive, is what it's all about. More than just Campbell agree that this commitment to the present results in a more peaceful place, a kinder place, maybe even a better place. The trouble is, however, that those fictions we call possibilities are fun. That's right! Fun! We like them. They also help us. And comfort us. Even entertain us. Even keep us company. They provide us with alternatives. They devise for us futures. In their presence, we cry. In their presence, we laugh. Without fictions, we could know no tomorrow. More significantly, crucially even, without fictions, we would have no Heart.

Annie Miller, who was still associated with the University of Chicago Divinity School when she died while nappin in a garden of roses, knew both Erin Kennedy and Gus Dieudonne, Gus findin his end while climbin a mountain, thrown in fact from the back of a horse though not in Utah. Annie Miller adored addressin *the spiritual trajectories of Allison March and Sondra Gatestone and how they altered each other, not so much through the institutions they defended or disdained, or at least doubted, but through their individual achievements of heart, these demonstrations of Goodness that create a Heart, how they supported one another when their children were missin, when the claim was that one child had abducted the other, when the claim was that both children were in cahoots, when the claim was that both children were dead, when the claim was that both children were alive again, when the claim was that one had shot the other, when one mother had given up believin in* a life for herself, when one mother had given up on believin in anythin, how one mother had found through the church she adhered to and the other through the church she had discovered in an open place how *The Church needs no such segregations. It's after all the practice of compassion, tolerance, kindness, of Goodness, that grants any church its license. Not the other way around.* As Allison March had put it: *a church that seeks out the enforcement of its beliefs is a faithless settlement. Without knowin it, those two ladies were findin a faith that required no settlement. Gosh, I miss Erin and Gus. They'd have loved this conversation. They'd have loved these roses.*

Late in her life, Frances Cassius Cowderry would create an opera devoted to this slender history, the highlight of which would turn out to be a duet between Sondra Gatestone and Allison March. Of her subsequent fame, especially concernin this particular section of music, known as *Two Mothers in a Grove*, the artist liked to observe that *a duel is always but one very short dash away from a duet.* Perhaps Cowderry was also referencin here another one of her famous arias, as sung by a baritone playin Orwin Porch, toward the end of the opera.

Not that either Sondra or Allison were aware of the reverberant conversational or musical consequences that their exchanges would have on the future as they stood beside that brown lake, their dialogue seemin at best partial, scraps of ideas that didn't exactly put them at odds with one another but nonetheless did introduce a distance that to Sondra Gatestone felt at once too abstract to be meaninful, that to Allison March struck her as an obvious way for them to try to distance themselves from the awful pain of bein so bereaved.

My little Landry is a thing of fire, Sondra suddenly blurted out. She'd drifted away from Allison and the trees but with this declaration had chosen to return. *She does not stand down and yet she is not proud either. She's just real feisty. She's both a marvel and an inspiration to me. But to your point, what I hear you tellin me, in your way, based on the time you've spent livin in Orvop, and this is in spite of what is preached in almost any ward . . . life here has not been kind to her.*

Though Allison said nothin, she did nod and in her heart felt somethin ease as she knew herself heard.

You know, Landry weren't but in elementary school when she brought to class a doll horse for show-and-tell. And you know what them Porch boys did to welcome my little girl? When it was recess and the teacher was away? Why they snuck into that classroom and snapped off each one of them doll's legs. Sondra had to take a breath, but she continued: *My little Landry cried gobs of fire that day, but her brother Tom made sure to comfort her, and he didn't even know her so well then. You know what that Tom of mine did? He found all the legs and glued them back on, and then once she was smilin again, he asked Dallin to take them to our stables, which my Dallin did. When they got there, Tom took Landry to the garbage bins outside the old barn and had her throw it away. He told her she didn't need a toy horse no more. She was a Gatestone now, and soon she would have a real horse, and anyone who tried to touch those legs, why they'd get hooved to death.* Sondra paused, as if surprised by her own tellin. *And you know what? Tom was darn near prophetic because not so long after that, my Landry found her Jojo, and those two have been together ever since, and if his hooves ain't made of fire too, then fire here's a myth.* Sondra sighed and smoothed her hands over the folds of her blue-and-black-striped dress. *Tom had been plenty perplexed when Landry first arrived, but you can bet he was never unkind. He put a frog under her pillow once, and when he seen how she'd made it a pet, he put a snake under her bed, and when she thanked him for that pet too, them became thick as thieves. As I am witness here, Tom demonstrated the kind of acceptance not so many here put into practice, though they preach on it like they're the ones offerin up the supreme examples when at best they're reporters and at worst they're crooks. This quality of Tom's might speak to why he found your boy such good company. His daddy always said there weren't no sense in goin out of your way for a lost cause because lost means lost and no help any child has had to offer ever changed the outcome of this world. Of course, the way Dallin said this to our three kids, with a grin and that big twinkle in his eye, well, if that didn't pretty much say the opposite.* Sondra seemed to sag then, as if returnin from far off, suddenly exhausted by the trip. *Tom heeded his father's subtle instruction. It made no difference to him if you were an outsider or what your skin claimed you were. He paid attention only to skills. And if you could take a joke and tell a joke, why that was one of the greatest skills of all and you had a friend forever.*

I don't think I've ever heard Kalin tell a joke, Allison said, a serene smile on her lips. *He's wry at best.*

I imagine his kind of wry was fine. I miss my children so much, Allison. I miss them all the time. It never goes away. Not a day, not a night goes by without this awful feelin. Evan seems to have passed on into peace, but Tom is still— I can't explain it. It's like he's now the very incarnation of my agony, all our agonies, or at least the agonies of them who knew him well enuf to love him. It's like he's lost somewhere and he can't pass on. It just kills me. And I can't even begin to approach what Landry's absence is doin to me. I pray and pray like I'm supposed to. But maybe I should try prayin like you do. I gotta confess, sometimes I don't pray to Heavenly Father but to Tom. I don't even pray to Dallin. I pray to Tom because I know fer sure as there is still life and love in this world, he loved Landry more than life. He'd come back from the grave to see her through. I'm sure of it. The words caught then in her throat, and in the pause that followed, everythin she was sayin fell away. *If I lose Landry, I lose everythin.*

Allison understood. *I lose Kalin, I lose everythin. But we're no exception. You know that, right? Many before us have lost everythin. Many after us will lose everythin. Who are we to think we are entitled to have it any different?* Allison watched Sondra start to pace, a fret on her fingers, recognizin now how none of this talk, this place, these wise old trees were servin her one bit. But Allison could also see that Sondra appreciated straight talk. *Sondra, do you truly believe there is someone out there who really cares what we lose or what we keep?*

That's the lessons of Job, ain't it? Sondra stopped pacin. *But in answer to your question: there are times I do not.*

I envy you for havin times when you do.

To carry on without that divine reassurance, what is all around us right now, pourin over us, here only for us, honestly, I don't know how anyone could get by without that. Sondra was lookin at Allison.

If you're askin me how I do it, I don't know, Allison shrugged. *Maybe I have faith after all. Maybe faith is belief without reassurance.*

I'd like to borrow some of that.

Have at it, though it ain't no picnic. Allison even laughed some.

Sondra returned to her pacin, though now it was lookin more like a stroll, like she was reacquaintin herself with a place she'd only just returned to after many, many years. *Tom would've liked it here. At least I can imagine him here. Maybe sittin right over there or leanin against this tree here. Did you know he had the most beautiful whistle? Hauntin even, melodious fer sure, so true you'd've sworn it weren't born of breath. I'm serious. Ask around. And though they didn't share a gene between them, Landry had the purest voice. My lord, I remember teachin her this one song, and when she sung along with me, I could hear she was gettin it right, but when she sung it back on her own, it near floored me.*

You sing?

Sondra nodded. *On occasion.*

Would you sing that song for me now?

Oh, I couldn't do it no justice.

A song doesn't need justice, just someone to sing it.

Sondra gave it her very best, and though she had to restart twice and stop once, for the tears in her eyes, in her throat, and though her voice weren't much but a frail wobble in the cold air, Allison March was still transported. It was better than a hymn, or maybe it was a hymn. You can guess the song.

Thank you, Allison said. *If only I could've heard Tom and Landry duet.*

That was the funny thing, the sad thing. I tried to get them to do it together, but they never did. Tom would whistle and then Landry would start singin and he'd stop and make a joke. Or she'd sing and he'd start whistlin and she'd stop and make a joke. Just darned foolishness. They was capable of such beautiful music. Would've run Donny and Marie straight outta town.

I sure am sad I never got to meet Tom.

I hope you get to meet my Landry.

I hope so too. Allison hesitated. *Though Kalin wouldn't approve of me sayin it like so.*

Why's that? Sondra asked.

He had a thing about any expression of hope, and like so much, I worry this too is my fault. Allison reached into her wallet and pulled out the postcard of Nikos Kazantzakis's headstone. She handed it to Sondra.

It's Greek, and it means: I hope for nothin, I fear nothin, I am free. Kalin often told me that that was how he wanted to live, though he didn't think he could ever be that brave. That was when his daddy was maulin the walls. Kalin was afraid all the time. That fear didn't leave him neither. In fact not so many months ago, he confessed that his mouth would get dry and he'd have a stitch in his side just at the thought of goin to school. I can't say how much that distressed me. I told him right away he could stop goin. I told him we'd move and find a new school. I meant it too, even if another move was unbearable to me. Put a stitch in my side.

These words on the back ain't so nice, Sondra said then, examinin the other side of the postcard before returnin it.

Those are from my sister. Like I've been sayin: my family ain't much to wish for in an afterlife.

Sondra looked away. *I may not be on my knees right now, but I am on my knees, Allison. I'll take breadcrumbs. I'll take less than breadcrumbs. I'm no gentile, but I feel worse off than the woman of Canaan. I do. I am beggin Heavenly Father with every breath to bring my Landry back to me, hopin that He will do this for me, grant me this miracle. And here you're sayin . . . Well, I don't think I could live in doubt; I don't think I could live without hope. I couldn't. Fer sure not now. I need the loved presence of my cottage fire, my family, my little girl.*

Of course I know that, Sondra. But what if by doubt we mean we are curious instead? What if by hopelessness we mean we find wonderment?

Is that how your Kalin would put it?

Allison considered the question carefully before she shook her head. *He sees it as how it would be to walk in a way that weren't about where you're walkin. See, in that way death cannot exist because death is always ahead. Even if you're about to die. Most of us would be too scared to live like that. I imagine, though, if you're one who could do it, entirely of the present, with not a hope and so not a fear, well then you might present a pretty fearsome figure.*

Is Kalin fearsome?

Not one bit.

Reconnaisance by Orvop police, park rangers, and to some extent the sheriff's department never once discussed surmountin the high Katanogos ridges and certainly never considered surveilin the terrain beyond the summit. The focus remained on Kirk's Cirque and to a lesser degree Isatch Canyon. The south-facin side of the cirque, with its great accumulations of snow, was so ablaze that mornin with the fall sun it seemed a crucible alight with white molten metals, the bright so bad that any interloper, not to mention every pilot above, needed sunglasses to even consider whether or not there was movement there. A little good news comin out of these clement conditions was how as the day wore on, the heat generated by such unobstructed shine helped further melt and compact the snow, makin any trek up into the cirque that much easier.

A good-sized number of law enforcement rangers, tactical police units, and deputy sheriffs were mustered for the ascent, with scores of additional good-hearted volunteers helpin to supply them, callin them collectively the Orvop Cavalry because they was there, of course, to save the day.

However, as the number of participants continued to grow, more time and energy was wasted organizin the increasinly complex police maneuver. Consequently the first armed official didn't put a boot on the mountain until about the time Sondra Gatestone and Allison March were down among them solemn trees, and no one made it up to Kirk's Cirque until well after noon, long after all the events that were about to occur at Pillars Meadow had taken place.

Not that there was much incentive to go up that far given what all planes and helicopters kept reportin, namely that there was still a lot of unstable snow, a lot of meltin snow, no sign of tracks, and certainly no hint of a campsite let alone a campfire. It didn't help that the downdraft pourin over the summit ridge, a river of cold air tumblin off the top of the mountain from the north, made flyin in those environs extra precarious. The shear at the cirque center weren't no comfort neither. One plane lost sufficient altitude and had to execute a kind of chandelle within the confines of that big rock bowl before hightailin, or rather lowtailin, it outta there.

An Intermountain Life Flight helicopter requisitioned for the operation had better luck in the cirque as well as in the contiguous corrie called Halo's Hollow, even if the tactical officers onboard discovered nothin.

Down at the base of operations, Undersheriff Jewell's tents, along with everythin else, had expanded substantially in order to better serve the logistical requirements of the various actions underway. Plenty of discussions centered on the weather, what would happen if it changed, which it wasn't gonna do, or how would they respond if there was an aviation accident. That conversation sure came to a boil when the aforementioned plane reported gettin close enuf to the headwall to near shave off some of its wingspan. Now bear in mind that the plane never was closer than a hundred yards from rock, but the exaggeration still reminded everyone how much could go wrong up there.

It sure was a delicate balance that Undersheriff Jewell had to manage. Firstly he had all them officers headin up there, tryin to bring down a killer who for all they knew was gonna kill again or at least try. Secondly there was the terrain, challengin bein a nice way to describe it, regardless of the improvin conditions. Just one wrong step could still exact horrible consequences. Plus avalanches still waited above, loose rocks . . . This list of possible bad happenins went on and on. No question, Undersheriff Jewell needed men up there to do this job, but he didn't need so many to pretty much guarantee a mishap. He sure didn't want to have to launch a second party to rescue one of his officers.

Undersheriff Jewell knew the history of these mountains well enuf. Take fer example the rescue of Jole T. Honey from Needles, California, who'd crashed his Cessna 172 into the back side of Mount Timpanogos in 1961. A Civil Air Patrol pilot was sent up to look for him, followed by plenty more planes, and even an Air Force helicopter from Hill Air Force Base. It still took five days to locate Mr. Honey, and he weren't tryin to hide. And he sure weren't gonna take no shots at his rescuers. In fact Mr. Honey was doin everythin he could to get found, especially since he weren't feelin so great, what with a fractured hip, broke jaw, and broke ankle and only a handful of candy for eats. One of the rangers in the tent told Undersheriff Jewell that he'd heard it weren't candy he'd had but grapes. There was some discussion about that.

An older ranger with the Forest Service recalled how back in 1955 there'd been a B-25 crash with no survivors. The pilot's head was cut clean off, and body parts of the various crew members were strewn about. It took months to bring down all the pieces. That was a pretty gruesome story, but there was plenty of discussion about that as well. Though the conversations in Undersheriff Jewell's tents always stopped whenever the police radio spat out more news from above, which was mostly the same news: just snow and more snow. And then a second plane in the process of executin a wide turn above Kirk's Cirque also dropped with the downdraft comin over the summit. The pilot, a genial fella named Albert Hernlow, yelped pretty bad, and everyone thought he was crashin fer sure. The plane, however, didn't lose near as much altitude as feared, and Hernlow was able to rattle through the shear and accelerate easily enuf out of the cirque and Isatch Canyon. As Sparky Imeson liked to say: *Better to fly down a canyon than up.* A little cheer rippled through the tent when it was clear that Albert Hernlow had survived, with news of the close call quickly relayed out to journalists and onlookers if just to communicate the dangers faced by the brave men and women up there defendin everyone's Civic Virtue.

Of course, what no one knew, especially Albert Hernlow, was how in makin that last circle over Kirk's Cirque, he'd not only flown higher but much wider too, takin him directly over Pillars Meadow, in fact right above where the Porches was all assembled. Albert Hernlow had no reason to look down, nor for that matter did the officer seated beside him, who was none other than Officer Willard Mildenhall, who you'll recall was at Egan Porch's house the night Russel was killt. Albert Hernlow was casually surveillin the Katanogos ridges while Mildenhall cleaned his binoculars. It never crossed either one's mind that the object of their pursuit could've made it this far.

If only one of those men had just glanced down, they'd've seen ten specks stretched out along the shadowy snow-filled depression that was the dry crick bed on the east side of Pillars Meadow. And, of course, if they'd kept lookin, which they surely would've done, they'd've easily enuf discovered across that snow-mottled patch of land another small speck emergin from the tree line, with three horses in tow.

W ho doesn't want to change what came next? Endow the horses with great pearly wings, provide flyin bicycles; any kind of transportive magic would do. But there weren't no such magic bestowed upon this approachin hour unless we're accreditin Kalin's left hand with some, as some have. Fer sure plenty of folks, and you might as well just pick the names out of a hat, good folks gone by now, like Zina Felt, Melody Jalliday, Bret Aston, Stanley Brundage, Harlan Webber, Burnah King, Joseph K. Davis, Jemma Bramall, Brennan Graves, Penny Peterson, Alli Rogers, and Lolly Neilsen, and far more than them too, have at one point or another declared in their life: *If only Landry had just given Russel back that gun.* Or: *If only Kalin had hucked the Colt away early on.* Or: *If only they'd have lost that thing in the dust of that great landslide.* Which is still only just one species of *if onlys.* Because if the tombstones of the Orvop City Cemetery could speak, or the ashes world over could right now reconstitute themselves into a momentary voice to pronounce their *if onlys,* why then we'd hear a chorus far greater than just the groans of Val Benson; Cindi Kimber; Leela White, her husband Robbie Bridges; Brooke Young, who never did get over losin Bren; as well as Wade Clayson; Gillian Orr; Nadeen Garriman; Eugene Johnson; Shaylan Chandler; Gula Hickey; Warwick Ahlström; Si Watts; and Carmen Shupe lamentin how *If only Landry on her way out of Isatch could've just slipped right by Egan and his boys . . . If only Egan, Kelly, and Billings had missed how Kalin and Landry had got up Aster Scree . . . If only the storm had been just a little less severe so Kalin and Landry hadn't've had to retreat to the Awides Mine . . . If only Porches and police alike had decided the kids and horses was dead after the rockfall . . . If only Old Porch and Kevin Moffet had missed Kalin on that first flight . . . If only Kalin had packed in Porch jerky instead of Dorf jerky . . . Why heck, if only Egan, Hatch, Kelly, and Billings had got around the back side of Agoneeya a little bit later, they'd've found an empty Pillars Meadow . . .*

Not that this kind of thinkin is so unusual. Who hasn't in the case of, say, a car accident wished that some hindrance, a telephone call, an earthworm wigglin on a sidewalk in need of relocation to a nearby flower bed, or a friendly exchange of hellos and good days with a stranger might've added a delay of seconds and so nullified the cataclysmic intersection to come. *If only . . .*

It still sure is nice to wonder about, even given these immediate circumstances, how it might've gone for Kalin and the horses, with none of the strange turmoil and rancor now immolatin their friendship; how unmolested by that choice to arm hisself, Kalin could've just ridden leisurely across that pleasant if muddy shoe-suckin meadow, so rich with bright air and magnificent views, with Landry on Jojo beside him, Tom on Ash too. Surely they'd've reflected on how far they'd come, also how close they'd come to death, how they'd done the impossible, how they'd come out on the other side okay. Kalin would've then known his promise to Tom kept. Landry would've been their witness.

Not that there isn't also an eerie thought that accompanies such a dreamy reenvisionin of the Crossin: that Tom might not have been with Kalin at all, not there on that rainy Wednesday night, not there at the end, not there at all, because maybe Tom first and foremost was only there because of this pendin conflict with the Porches, really between the Porches and Gatestones, with Kalin just the unforeseen addition come at last to once and for all see their differences settled.

Mrs. Annserdodder, Orvop High's favorite sophomore English teacher, and Ms. Melson, Orvop High's only AP English teacher, were as we've seen longtime friends, and over the years would often revisit that fateful October week through the lens of the Greek mythology they loved and specifically *The Iliad*.

As Ms. Melson liked to mention, one topos was how Homer, whether singular or a troupe of performers and improvisers, unable to frame actions and rages within the parlance of pyschology available in the twentieth and twenty-first centuries, offered instead gods to make sense of how people changed their moods or otherwise reacted. *Consider Hera as Stentor rousin the Greeks. Or Poseidon as Calchas encouragin those two warriors named Ajax. Or Hermes as a Myrmidon grantin old Priam both guidance and courage. Not that it's always about courage. Consider Apollo as Agenor foolin Achilles to chase after him. Or Athena as Deiphobus foolin Hector into facin Achilles. Nearly two thousand years ago the gods served as replacements for the untraceable impulses of the human psyche.* Though Mrs. Annserdodder taught sixteen-year-olds, and never on the level of any AP class, she knew her mythology near as well as Ms. Melson. She also had a fondness for this particular line of thinkin, bringin up how God in that transformation of polytheism to monotheism sadly grew more distant. Sure, to the select few, He grants His Word and in that way His instructions are carried out by the people. *God gives Moses his Law and even writes it down for him in stone. But this is no personable relationship like Athena at the shoulder of Odysseus.* On a walk one afternoon, Ms. Melson added to this conjecture that God eventually steps further away, no longer the lithic scribe but nominatin Muhammad to manuscribe God's word. *Our Prophet Joseph Mith serves as scribe too,* Mrs. Annserdodder pointed out, *though by then God's word is further mitigated by the Angel Mornai.* To be clear both Mrs. Annserdodder and Ms. Melson were devout Church members, but that hadn't impeded their minds from chasin down such complicated historical and religious topics. *Of course eventually,* as Ms. Melson would admit on one occasion, *these communications are replaced by the advent of psychology. Our Greek gods are replaced by ego and id and so on. And as our own free will becomes more manifest— And important!* Mrs. Annserdodder would chime in. *Yes, important. The distance between ourselves and Our Lord the Father likewise continues to increase.* Ms. Melson then read aloud lines by John Ruskin she'd recently written down: *I believe that the first test of a truly great man is his humility. I do not mean by humility, doubt of his own powers. But really great men have a curious feelin that the greatness is not in them, but through them. And they see somethin divine in every other man and are endlessly, foolishly, incredibly merciful.* For many months then both women would go round and round, ponderin this notion of divine possession, *Enthusiasm!* both would at the same time exclaim and then laugh!, countered by divine distance as a consequence of self-awareness. It was Mrs. Annserdodder who would propose one early mornin before classes started that Jesus Christ had changed that: *Doesn't Our Lord Jesus Christ return to us the closeness the Greeks* knew with their gods? Yes, that's right, Ms. Melson would respond, a little cheered up by her friend's observation, but He does so without forsakin free will. Mrs. Annserdodder nodded: He isn't tellin anyone what to do. He offers guidance, advice, presence.

Speech too instead of script.

Though his words become Scripture, Mrs. Annserdodder would point out.

His flesh perishable.

But his Soul eternal.

In the spirit of these pleasant ruminations, the two Orvop High teachers would eventually return to the subject of Pillars Meadow and especially the question of Tom. Obviously Tom weren't never no Heavenly Father nor Our Lord and Savior either, though at the same time he weren't far from the ancient Greek notion of Divinity, a singular persona who might, if you were lucky, or so cursed, accompany you. One of Mrs. Annserdodder's favorite words to teach her sophomores was in fact Enthusiasm! Can anyone tell me somethin about what that means? The expected characterizations included psyched, lots of energy, passionate, to which Mrs. Annserdodder would nod before drawin out how en- was followed by the root theo. But first, what does that en- mean? Why, it means in. And what about theo? You can figure that out. That's right, theo means God, or with that en-, God within. So then, are you followin me?, when you are enthusiastic, you are not just excited. Oh, it is somethin much more profound and marvelous than that. God is within you! Ms. Melson personally found the reminder of interest, especially when considerin how from the vantage point of the Ancient Greeks person or persona meant the mask that performers wore: If I recall correctly, a mask was comprised of a cone to help amplify the voices of actors in the amphitheaters and thus true to the etymology of per-, meanin through, and sonare-, meanin to make a sound, thus sounds through, or in other words what makes a person a person is the voice that moves through you, and in the case of performers, that voice was Aristophanes, Aeschylus, or Divine Enthusiasms. As both ladies were well aware of, in The Iliad the spirit of Athena or Apollo or any number of other Greek deities could suddenly possess an individual. Might as well say replace them, at least for a spell, Ms. Melson exclaimed. And often those receivin the god's words did not even recognize that it was a god, thinkin it was Thoas instead of Poseidon, Lycaon instead of Apollo. Mrs. Annserdodder nodded, under a spell of memory. I see that on occasion with my own students. Suddenly one goes beyond what abilities are known to me, and the whole classroom is held in rapt attention by their observations, as if they were no longer that middlin high schooler with acned cheeks but the Lord Hisself or at the very least one of them Lords of Mount Olympus.

And so by this route they would return to Tom, not so much inhabitin Kalin, even if maybe still generated by Kalin hisself, as plenty insist, but more so ridin adjacent, as Kalin's accomplice, his abettor, or even his colleague and most likely just company on a journey toward that reckonin which in retrospect had all along been growin more and more inevitable. Though also, as many have since pointed out, regardin this particular conversation or others similar enuf, Tom never really was accompanyin Kalin, just the horses.

For his part, Caracy Rudder, enjoyin late in life a goatee, mellow teas, and mild walks on which he'd build the random cairn, would likewise delight in examinin with his two friends this history through the lens of ancient narrative, and while he enjoyed terribly the disquisitions presented by Mrs. Annserdodder and Ms. Melson, he would also stray from their positions to interrogate a weirder aspect concernin Tom: *He weren't ever there to inspire Kalin, or even infuriate him, and let's forget him bein there to goad Kalin forward, except maybe on the Upecksay Headwall, which I realize in sayin that might just discredit everythin else I'm about to say, because Tom sure did encourage Kalin there, and, yes, sure, maybe some too at Pillars Meadow. But, see, here's the thing, unlike any Greek god you can think of, Tom needs Kalin's help too. He needs Kalin to cross the Ninth Scree, and that's just one example. And what about Tom not wantin to go back down the headwall to help his sister? What do we do with that? Then there's also that pretty odd thing about how on one side of the mountain, Tom sees only the past, which initially he can't see at all, though the higher he gets the more of the past comes into view for him, until on the summit he can see a great deal of both the past and the future. Maybe too much of both. And well, that summit stuff, it's its own special conversation. Once, though, Tom heads down the other side of the mountain, he really can only see the future, incomplete of course, and growin progressively dimmer the farther down he gets, until at Pillars Meadow he knows only his allegiance to the horses and maybe Kalin. He's not in favor either of Kalin takin up arms. No Athena, our Tom. At best he stands there as an advocate for the horses and the dead who he's told us are followin the horses, includin the dead not even the dead can see. Ain't that a bundle of twists for the noggin. But in the big picture, what purpose does Tom serve? That's the question I ask whoever's interested in conversin about these topics. I ask it because I myself want to know the answer. Maybe Tom is closer to Nestor of Gerenia, that genial old advisor for the Greeks? Better him than anythin close to the martial Ares, right? Anyway, in the end it's not even the horses we dwell on so much or for that matter the Porches. We don't even dwell that much on Kalin or Landry. It's Tom's Crossin. After all, ain't that the most elemental part of this journey?*

Now Caracy Rudder has his own way of viewin things, or spinnin things, you choose, but puttin aside for a moment this question of Tom's passage, it is true that when reachin for so called canonical illustrations, however unnecessary, it ain't, for example, Latin histories or Shakespearean follies that come up the most, though those do come up, but rather them Greek myths, specifically the stories surroundin the defeat of Troy, which folks of all sorts still tend to gravitate to. As Caracy Rudder, long after his hair had gone white, would so sagaciously point out to one of his eager students who had thought to devise an exact schematic analogizin those stories of antiquity with them events on Pillars Meadow: *Look, there ain't no point lookin for some stand-in for the Trojan horse. The horses are real. They hide nothin, they devise nothin, they mimic nothin. They live, they strive, they are.* And then later on, less patiently, and to the same student, who had yet to abandon this vain desire for exact correlation: *To my eye no one in these events resembled Aeneas, or sounded like him, or acted like him. Heck, no one comes even close to appearin like the founder of Rome. And you know why that is? Look around! Rome ain't here!* And then one last time, now really flabbergasted, again with this same student, who ultimately got an A+ in the class: *No! No! No! Hatch is no Hector and Egan is no Paris. And who then is Astyanax? Francis or Russel? Or what about Billings? Are we callin him Sarpedon or Pandarus? And Glaucus? Antenor? Agenor? What about them? Okay, yes, maybe there's a bit there to suggest Old Porch is a kind of Priam. But then who is Achilles? Kalin?! Is that what you really think? And what for that matter, in your view, is Troy? Orvop?!* Caracy Rudder would near shout that last bit. *I do not think so! And no one better bring up Rome again!*

Sometime later, a good while after this outburst, Caracy Rudder found hisself once again in the company of his two dear friends, Ms. Melson and Mrs. Annserdodder, to whom he confided how *Yes, I'll admit, there's no outrunnin the fact that some lastin species of Achillean rage does seem to haunt this catastrophe, more so fer sure than any Odyssean cunnin, though that's there too. There's no shakin the suspicion that there is an arrangement here that needs discernin.*

Which was as close to a confession as those two teachers would get: admittin the sense of an imperative here, the urgency, a mystery too, how some loomin resolution was still waitin out there, waitin for them, to order their minds, to order many minds and hearts and so relieve them of the tragedy that had come to know them.

So who are we to disregard such endurin comparisons, a thousand Greek ships, a thousand voices, more, the towerin walls of Troy, given what would happen soon enuf, if preceded simply by Kalin steppin beyond the cover of those birches and quakin aspens so ablaze with fall, all while overhead the midday sun drew nigh, as if Apollo hisself had returned anew, to return balance, drawin his bowstring to the anchor point, with the winds and breezes then, as if in reverence or fear, quittin their motions? The astute will also note how it was as if Awides had broke wide open here, at last disgorgin so many of its ancient charges, the woes of those unseen now suspiratin forth from the earth itself, thick but no higher than the knees, low minglin with mud, snow, and ice, decryin all seasonal associations in the name of merely its own blank attendance here, and near partin before Kalin as he trod forward.

What Mrs. Annserdodder, Ms. Melson, and Mr. Rudder eventually came to accept was this: the prototypes of the past are pedagogical on a good day and a prison on a bad day. Traditions built out of repetitions prove nothin except their own evolvin memory. In the end, the question wasn't whether to defend the great gates or mourn their ruins. The question was whether we needed construction in the first place.

There is no Troy here, Mr. Rudder would keep insistin.

Unless it's a fallen Troy, Mrs. Annserdodder would keep answerin.

Let Troy rest, Ms. Melson would answer them both. Why even reach for Troy as some kind of analogue? The original site was likely no more than some backwater coastal settlement anyway, of little political consequence, perfectly suited for maraudin voyagers. Furthermore, no matter how festooned each side was with bronze-tipped spears, no matter how great their lust for combat or their capacity for grief, any bounty won by their triumphs has long since been devalued, displaced, forgotten. Brisïes erased. The memory of that place's achievements, its eventual submission to barbarity, its remains, its reconstruction, its abandonment, is now replaced by a different sort of relic: that epic, that song, with the names all changed; as little about place anymore as it remains still about a few of the mortals who made of that spot of earth called Troy a point of contention, and about, of course, the immortals who while beyond the reach of Death still had to bow before the dictates of appetite, desire, and the sheer pleasure of control, and so would sidle up beside these perishable faces, you know the ones, you know one intimately, these masks of flesh and fat and bone, to goad them, inspire them, deceive them, defeat them, sometimes love them, and now and then move in and out of them, to overwrite them, to direct them, and perhaps too to know from whence their own immortality was born or at the very least remember fragility.

So many names lost, or for so long misplaced that they became fictions, which is as good as forgotten. Though in the end what name isn't a fiction? You think yours isn't? Mine?

Nonetheless, whatever meanin Troy might yet still have to offer, at least one thing is certain: upon those plains Xanthos spoke.

At least for a few moments that immortal horse found unlikely speech. And even if that speech was to pronounce the death of one still bridled by speech, that bein Achilles, Xanthos, the horse, through his own unbridled tongue could recall for us the many horses who beneath Mount Ida and beside the Scamander River knew lives they had no say about.

Hatch was first to say anythin, and he basically just laughed. Or at least let out a pretty big *Haw!* He sure was startled if not outright disoriented by the sight he beheld through that Zeiss lens, so much so that he quickly drew away, as if that finely crafted piece of optical equipment was at fault, rubbin his eyes too since they weren't offerin much better, and all the while chucklin before returnin to the vision that hadn't changed much except maybe turned a mite bit bluer. And though his chucklin did abate then, he still kept grinnin, and more importantly his finger weren't nowhere near the trigger.

He weren't the only Porch either to act like so. Egan muttered his own disbelievin *What the heck?*, also abandonin his rifle, if just to demand his binoculars back from Kelly. Kelly obliged but not before declarin: *If here ain't proof this boy is crazy!* Kelly laughed outright then, a laughter that was soon ripplin through all them Porch boys.

Not even their patriarch, Old Porch hisself, was immune. He chortled plenty when he returned to his binoculars for a second time to again take in the mesmerizin sight. You couldn't ask for better light neither, all that pale blue sky, the sun high above if just startin to lean away from mornin, even as Old Porch's watch headed toward high noon, Moffet's and Hatch's too, though Egan's was headin to 1:00 p.m., havin forgotten that as of 2:00 a.m. last night the clocks had reverted to standard time, fallin back an hour. Shelly and Sean had also forgotten the time change, Woolsey as well, though not Francis, though he weren't wearin a watch. Billings didn't have a watch either. And while such distinctions in time might matter some in the recountins that would follow, time itself, as always, remained indifferent.

Fer sure Old Porch weren't payin no attention to the time nor even that strange ground layer of fog accompanyin Kalin, spreadin out from him as if he was its origin, and he weren't, and even startin to slip over the banks of that crick bed. The only thing that mattered to Old Porch right then was the spectacular magnification of Kalin's little nub.

If that ain't the tiniest pecker I've ever seen! Old Porch bellowed. And his boys sure laughed hard with him, not a one, not even Hatch, givin thought to what would become of that moment in the years that followed, from a tactical point of view. Then again, in those moments thought in general was operatin at a very minimal level. At least on the Porch side.

It's blue! Shelly smirked. *I swear to it!*

A chilly little willy! Sean just had to add.

More jabs and laughter followed as they all started to stand and lazily gawk at Kalin makin his trek across Pillars Meadow.

Like Old Porch, they not only disregarded the fog, which as suddenly as it had risen up was now just as quickly dissipatin, they did not even see the shadows gatherin around this pallid figure. Nor could they note the birds that broke from the canopy, as if to flee, as if this scene were too much for them, maybe even too much for Moloch. And they fer sure did not see the boy-ghost at their backs shrink away, along with that great gold horse, hooves tryin to dance beyond the ground that now marked for Ash and Tom the very limit of their bein.

Nor did even one Porch behold the mud now beneath their own boots and despair over the annelidous future it promised.

Instead they saw a boy not merely unshirted but buck neked, except for his boots, except for that Stetson that was now as black as a midnight sky if moon and stars had fled, his body paler than ice, snow, and even that retreatin mist. He was the very picture of defeat, with both scrawny arms held up high, his right holdin Jojo's reins and the leads to both Navidad and Mouse, his left hand holdin nothin and lookin hurt, with blood streakin down the arm. The rest of him didn't look much better either. The pronounced way his ribs stuck out seemed injury enuf. Kevin Moffet immediately looked away. Though he was the only one. And that weren't the end of the boy's afflictions. Kalin had suffered far more than just nutritive deprivations. Bruises darkened his torso, as if dark violets and blue oils had been loosed upon the whitest sheet. Bloody scratches and welts marked his hips and in particular his right leg. Both knees were blotched with the clotted signature of repeated injury. Not that either Landry or Tom had ever noted the cause of these contusions or had detected their effect on Kalin.

Of course just glancin back on that terrible journey, it weren't hard to imagine plenty of instances where somewhere along the way a minor stumble or quick lunge might've cost a bruise upon a shin or made an elbow feel the painful price of a minor misjudgment. That awful rockfall alone, the pandemonium of flyin rock, explodin limestone, the great slurries of dirt, with Kalin and Navidad in the middle of that mess, if somehow ridin out of it too, had still assaulted both of them with strike after strike. Without comment Landry had noticed the scratches upon Kalin's neck. Of course they had both been banged up, but she'd had no inklin what various wounds his various layers also hid. It would've broke her heart.

The younger Porches, though, were not so struck. They mostly elongated their guffaws and whatever other sounds of gloat they could summon, though the more faint-hearted, namely Francis, finally turned away, ashamed.

Only Hatch, with his many years of trainin, registered that despite such a grotesque display of hurt, this scrawny kid was still lurchin toward them. Nor were his steps hitchin one bit, not even when they'd all stood up, all ten of them, to reveal themselves. And not even Hatch, even with his many years of trainin, had any clue what this pitiful figure was marchin in the name of; though maybe, to give credit where credit is due, Hatch did sense that Kalin March had a purpose that had nothin to do with them, his eyes set way beyond them. And that part fer sure is true: Kalin's eyes were only on Tom, Tom on Ash with his burnin brand in hand, his heart, both their hearts, set on the Crossin.

Egan sure didn't see it, wouldn't have cared either if he had. Why when Egan rose up, he actually left his rifle settin on the mat. Not that he was now unarmed; he still had his .357 tucked away in the holster at his back. Not that that would help any. Like Old Porch and Hatch, like all of them, Egan didn't see what was seein. He even stretched some and shook his head and turned his back on Kalin, lettin loose then from his lips some Skoal-dark spit. What mattered most to him now was that his brothers, and fer sure his dad, witness his confidence as well as his total disregard for what they was there for.

Shelly and Sean followed his lead, lookin around, sharin grins. Kelly even yawned. Woolsey checked to make sure his fly weren't down. Billings remained cautious. And Francis? Well, that boy didn't want nothin more to do with whatever this was, though he still couldn't race off to the helicopter either; he just kept goin along with his brothers.

Old Porch weren't any better. He too had lost sight of Kalin, though not out of any sympathy or empathy for his prey, or even out of disgust, but rather because of the thing he delighted in most. Second to that was to behold another's defeat. Number one, though, was the delight he got when that defeat was duly acknowledged. How Old Porch loved to hear the loser pronounce him victorious. But Kalin's defeat and declaration was so evident, he was near losin interest. All Old Porch could ache fer now was Kalin pronouncin his own abasement, which Old Porch figured was only moments away. And so just like Egan had, after all where do you think Egan got it from?, Old

Porch also turned his back on Kalin fer a moment, on that scrawny embarrassment, that infelicitous figure who had caused them all so much trouble, who had stolen their horses!, to find the regards of his boys, makin sure too that they was all gettin a good long look at his easy grin. Old Porch was certainly most pleased with Hatch's expression, like Hatch was impressed by his old man, so much so that this eldest was even cowed, though that impression was wrong, but it's still what Old Porch took from Hatch, and it made him feel impervious to hurt and tall as the clouds.

Maybe they all felt tall like that, though a dispassionate observer would've still noted their own battered condition: scratches on Egan's brow and cheek, Kelly's scabbed-up forehead and lips, Billings's raw chin. Sean and Shelly weren't absolved neither, still plenty banged up from tryin to ride their dirt bikes up Aster Scree. Woolsey had his football injuries, but them didn't really count. Only Francis was unmarred. Even Hatch had paid a price for journeyin upon these steeps, though he regarded such strains and bruises as mere nuisances. He too stood among the clouds, especially when he took his first step forward, leavin behind the Barrett, even if, like Egan, he still had on him his holstered weapon. Egan and Hatch alone would head out to meet Kalin without a weapon in hand. The rest remained armed and ready, now climbin up out of that crick bed, goin over the top, like the boys at Gallipoli or Ypres.

If nowhere else, then let it be here: somethin should be said about age. Julia Barton, who'd find her own final moment encapsulated in a ripplin sheet of chemical flame, and at only forty-four too, would before then reflect on how *one of the great historians of romantic time, Marcel Proust, was dead at only fifty-one. What did he know of life at eighty? Or even at seventy? Achilles was maybe eighteen when he reached Troy and about twenty-eight when he went to war with Agamemnon. A twenty-eight-year-old man has a disposition that's far different from a man who's almost sixty, which is how old FDR was when the U.S. entered World War II. Just look at the array of ages in all this: Russel, Francis, and Woolsey, all teenagers, sixteen, seventeen, and eighteen; with their sister, the hardly-spoken-of Ginny Ward, but fourteen. Landry was fifteen; Kalin, sixteen; Tom dead at seventeen, so many teenagers. Kelly Porch, though, was twenty; Sean and Shelly, twenty-four and twenty five; Egan, twenty-seven, and Hatch, thirty-two. Billings Gale and Trent Riddle were both twenty-three. Old Porch, though, was about to turn sixty; Allison March, about to turn forty; Sondra, older than her. Who will say the age of the horses? Regardless, a wide range of ages marched across that meadow that Sunday, enuf age to know better, but the bitter promise made by metal still ruled the hour.*

Old Porch pumped his 12-gauge, that trusty old Winchester Model

12, as beat up over the years as it was ready to deliver a beatin. It had never failed Old Porch and would not fail him today. He swung it slow over his shoulder and then, at a pace nearly as slow, strolled on ahead but with a hand held out at his side to keep any of his eager boys from surgin past him.

The collective mood as these armipotent ten headed out was near jovial. Francis was on the far left; then Woolsey; then Shelly; then Sean; then Egan, who was the true center, beside Old Porch who thought he held the center; with Hatch to his right; then Billings; and to the far right, Kelly. Kevin Moffet would've preferred to stay back behind the crick embankment, but followed along after Old Porch.

At first, they was spread wide as they should've been, but interest in the one they was after drew them closer to one another, with Francis on the one end and Kelly on the other speedin up enuf to bend that line into more of a semicircle. Their general silence was remarkable and entirely due to Old Porch, though each of them had on their mind any number of things that had nothin to do with the encounter now unfoldin. Woolsey, for one, couldn't wait to call Darren Blicker; Kelly's stomach seemed to have finally settled enuf that this broad-shouldered boy was thinkin about dinner; Billings didn't stop thinkin about Kalin, though even he was wonderin some about whether he'd have to render them horses today or if Old Porch would just put them down out here; Hatch was tryin to figure out if he'd have the energy to start the drive back to Texas that night; Old Porch couldn't stop thinkin about Monday; Kevin Moffet was dreamin about Alaska; Egan was thinkin about what he was gonna watch on TV that night and if maybe he'd be on TV, and he'd like to see that, see hisself where other people, a lot of other people, could see him and if they knew him think to call him, though he weren't gonna answer; Sean realized his cold had finally quit; Shelly was gonna call Liz Blicker first thing; only Francis kept comin back again and again to Russel, and that revisitation held some fire for him now, givin him the focus he needed to consider more closely this Kalin March; Francis even gripped extra his Winchester 62A and flicked off the safety.

Woolsey's fingers weren't anywhere near the safety or trigger. Shelly, though, had eased off the safety of his Ruger M77, if not sparin a thought for the .38 he was also carryin.

Those on either side of Old Porch continued to crowd in as they fussed with their weapons, and even though Kalin was their destination, everyone kept avoidin the sight of him, the thought of him too, like they wanted him invisible now, like he was in fact already invisible, and maybe he was. Here was no threat, here was no throat-cutter, here weren't even some majestic rider. He weren't even on no horse, just leadin them along like a lousy ranch hand not deservin of his weekly stub. He was havin a time of it too, the horses behind him, dancin around, while he continued to struggle them boots through the mud and snow, all while bein neked, buck neked, what a sight!

Out of all the Porches, only Billings slowed some to better position hisself a few paces back, puttin him about even with Kevin Moffet, though unlike the weaponless pilot who kept his parka zipped up tight, Billings unbuttoned his dark coat to grant his right hand plenty of clearance for a crossdraw from the holster on his left side. Like Old Porch, Billings also carried a 12-gauge, but unlike Old Porch, he was beginnin to think that choice of weapon was a mistake. He couldn't even say why. He just sensed in the gatherin ahead a mirage of emptiness concealin somethin that had always exceeded them all, exceeded even the Kalin kid.

But what continued to confuse Billings the most was the stark contrast between the fluidity, lightness, and impossible ease he'd beheld when the boy was astride the black mare, and in the most dire circumstance too, while this figure here, if still a good ways off, was clearly encumbered by awkwardness. Was he limpin? Fer sure troddin forth, and heavily too, as well as unevenly, as if one as slight as him, and so exposed, was also somehow clad in armor, heavy armor, armor too thick to pierce. And where the horses were concerned, there was no missin how they would too often throw up their heads and even try to sidle away if but for the heaviness that denied their flight. And even if Billings couldn't sense out quick enuf the new meanin arrangin itself out there on Pillars Meadow, he at least could find in the horses some organizin principle for inquiry: why was this boy of all boys no longer ridin? That right there was it, what disturbed Billings the most.

And of course, all of them in that slowly compressin and bendin spread of ten, still had available the choice to reverse course, or at least stop to better reevaluate their course. Only Kevin Moffet stopped, if just to ask a question.

Orwin, can you tell now? Is this the one who killt your Russel? Is he the one who killt the ranger?

Old Porch stopped then too, turnin around again, again givin Kalin his back. *He is,* Old Porch confirmed, movin that Winchester Model 12 to his left hand.

Should I go then now to radio this in? He sure does look to be surrenderin.

He sure does. Maybe we just bring him in?

I got the cuffs right here, said Hatch.

Kevin Moffet surveyed the Porches and again took note of the fact that, except for Egan and Hatch, all of them had a weapon in their hands. That went for the one called Billings. Kevin Moffet then squinted out toward them horses, still a good hundred yards off, with that strange neked boy nearly lost betwixt hooves and guns.

Okay, Orwin. I'll just go call in that we've got the culprit. That way at least folks can stop lookin where they're lookin. How in the heck did that kid even get over the headwall? And with three horses? We saw him in the cirque.

It is a mystery, Old Porch answered easily, smilin too, all them wrecked teeth just radiatin edges.

Kevin Moffet nodded like it was settled then and gave Old Porch his back, plain relieved to be on his way to the helicopter, unaware that he was now the raven messenger, if with no chance to exercise his capacity for flight.

With his right hand, Old Porch brought out that 9mm Smith & Wesson Model 59 with the aluminum frame, what killt Law Enforcement Ranger Kelson and what right now just shot off Kevin Moffet's left ear. Instead of runnin, though, fast as he could, Kevin Moffet actually turned back around and just in time too to see Old Porch fire again. And miss again. The pilot did run then, but Old Porch didn't miss the third time. Put a bullet right through the back of Kevin Moffet's skull.

Kevin Moffet toppled face-first into the mud, his head disgorgin plenty of pulsin blood. It's a possibility that the wound still weren't enuf to snuff out his life. At least not right then. Plenty have pointed out how, later on, blood was still pulsin out of that small hole.

What in holy heck? Hatch managed to sputter out. *What have you done, Dad?* This eldest Porch boy now realizin hisself fully engulfed in the nightmare he'd likely always known he was in, though not as some officer of the law or a hero on a hero's journey but as a fool stuck in a horror movie like *Friday the 13th Part III* in 3D.

By comparison, as soft-kneed and wheezy as Hatch got, his old man stood steady as a reed in a freeze. *Whadya mean what have I done?* Old Porch asked Hatch, waitin too for the reply, and in the long pause that followed reevaluatin his firstborn, who only until recently he'd always recognized as his finest. That impression was long gone now. In fact Old Porch was more concerned at that moment with the tobacco in his lip, further packin it down with his tongue, spittin out some of the silt that come up with that action, and swallowin whatever bits was still swimmin in his mouth.

Only when Old Porch was satisfied with the sight of everyone waitin on Hatch to speak, the lot of them strugglin to recalibrate their shock, and not a one wasn't shocked, except maybe Egan and Billings and even Kelly, whose guts curiously weren't flippin at all, only then did Old Porch answer on behalf of Hatch: *Like all of us here witnessed, that neked wastrel out there just shot and killt our good man, Kevin Moffet, right as he was runnin to radio for help. Ain't that true, Egan?*

Same way that maggot killt that ranger, Egan answered. *Right in the back of the head.*

What about you, Billings? Old Porch asked, this time with a half snarl he couldn't hold back. *You see somethin different?*

One heckuva shot, Billings replied.

What is goin on here? Hatch asked, though the question come out more like a gasp, seein as how he was now strugglin with the fear dryin out his mouth, especially with the obvious fact that he was badly outnumbered, outgunned, and a long, long way from any help.

Just like he done in our Russel, Kelly added, a comment Old Porch didn't care for, this son again goin too far, and Old Porch gave him a snarl too, though without words.

Woolsey suprised the rest then by cryin out that of course Kalin had killt the pilot. No Sinon, him, or just that. *We all seen it, and now there ain't no question what happened to Russel.* Not that Woolsey was understandin what Kelly had inadvertently implied. He was just bringin up Russel to see that their youngest brother got the justice he deserved. *The Kalin kid's good as dead now. Now who's the real horseradish here?* Which didn't mean nothin to anyone but sure got Egan's attention and confused him, especially watchin Woolsey share now a nod with their father.

Sean and Shelly both looked pale, but they muttered their agreement. Francis's head was scrambled, struck dumb by the death of someone he'd thought was their friend, killt by his father too, who now was sayin no, no he hadn't killt him but rather it was that Kalin kid out there who'd done it, that Kalin kid who was neked and had his arms up, he was the one that gunned down poor Kevin Moffet. Then Francis even walked over to the body, like that hole still a-sloshin with blood might make clear what was perfectly clear already if fear weren't learnin him somethin different.

At least Hatch still kept tryin, now pointin a big finger at Kalin, who was about fifty yards out: *He don't even have a gun! He don't even got nothin on but his boots! He's surrenderin!* Hatch not even notin then, like none of them noted, not even Billings, how the gunfire hadn't slowed Kalin's march one bit.

Old Porch stayed unfazed. *You daft, Hatch? Has Texas made your brain a puddin fit for crows? Of course he's armed. He's got this gun right here,* that same 9mm Smith & Wesson Model 59, which Old Porch promptly disappeared behind his back, returnin the 12-gauge to his right hand, givin Hatch then a cold stare, before addressin all his boys: *Francis! Shelly! Sean! Egan! Kelly! Woolsey! You there, Billings! And especially you, Hatch! What happened here is that we just ended an awful part of our history! This fellow lyin there, yes, you know him, Kevin Moffet, a good man too, is a casualty of this war we've been dragged into by that horse thief out there. Kevin Moffet is most certainly a victim. And don't you let his passin be in vain! His death assures and even sanctifies the outcome we all want and need. Don't none of you forget that! We bring in that boy out there, and he'll start tellin his side of the story, cryin and beggin too, and folks might start listenin; folks might get confused. Now get him a good lawyer and folks will get even more confused. Holly Feltzman is a lot of things to us Porches but she is first and foremost a good lawyer, real good. Next thing we know, the one who killt our Russel will be set free! That ain't gonna happen. Not on my watch. Are we clear? This all gets settled right now.* Old Porch even sounded like he was pleadin, near kindly too, softly. *So we can move on. So we can never lose another minute on this. Plain and simple. Are we clear?* And of course, they all nodded. They'd been taught to nod since they couldn't yet walk. Even Hatch found hisself noddin, though in his case, it was more to grant hisself more time in order to survive what this day had set upon him. *That maggot out there,* Old Porch continued, his voice risin again, growlin. *Are you gonna let him wreck more lives?* Everyone shook their head, includin Hatch again. *You're darned right! And I don't want no one worryin neither that this might come back on you, because your daddy here is takin this on hisself to see us all into the clear. You. Are. My. Witnesses.*

And with that Egan pulled out his Smith & Wesson .357. Where Kalin was at now, the shot was doable, though Egan would've preferred his .30-06 Winchester. Behind the Leupold scope, there weren't a chance he'd miss. He could start with Kalin's pecker or take out a nutsack first. Now he'd have to settle for a chest shot.

But Old Porch put a stop to that quick. *Whoa there, Egan! You got socks in your ears? Did you not just hear what I said? This ain't comin back on you.*

Egan was already deep in this, and he knew Old Porch knew that too, so he didn't rightly care much for the theatrics or that he was bein held off from takin the shot he was more than willin to take. *He killt my brother,* Egan growled to his old man to make his point, even if he knew it were a lie, or because he knew Old Porch knew it was a lie, as did both Kelly and Billings. And as for the rest of his brothers, what did he care? Egan wanted what was his, and if it took a lie to claim that right, so be it. Hadn't that been their daddy's grand lesson all along? Egan even raised his revolver to aim.

That he did, that he did, Old Porch purred, and was grinnin too with apparent approval, his very easiness shakin Egan, as if only right then Egan was glimpsin how in spite of his own record of violence it weren't nothin compared to this man's, him that they knew as Father, standin stolid in the shadows of a history none livin would ever know in full.

But Egan still didn't lower his gun.

Notin this resistance, Old Porch lost his ease then. *What you say is true, Egan, but losin a brother don't come close to losin a son. You hear me, boy?* And that sudden bark did prove worth enuf to see Egan lowerin his weapon. *What's left here is between me and him. That said, if I miss my shot, I won't object to a little help.* Old Porch even winked at Egan if makin sure after that all his boys knew they too was included. Woolsey got hisself a wink. And Egan even found hisself grinnin back, despite intentions to do otherwise, despite the consequent mood from bein so stymied, so schooled, grinnin warmly in fact, as if grateful for his father's good will.

It's worth notin that with so many layers of prevaricatin goin on, in some ways like the Mountain itself, with its layers of blue limestone, sandstone, siltstones, purple shales, dolomite, tintic quartzite, and many more such deposits, continuin to testify to the chaotic history condensed so many thousands of feet below, how many thousands of years ago?, readable epochs and ages to the literate: the Neogene, Pliocene, and Miocene; the Permian, Pennsylvanian and Mississippian; the Devonian; the Cambrian; the Proterozoic; and of course the Hadean, Old Porch was likewise discernible, legible even, to hisself, if he weren't now so devoted to his narrowed, cloudy elevations, to them bands of rotten stone, denyin him now both the insight and instincts of the compacted layers at his base. All of which is to take the long way around in order to say: Orwin Porch really did believe now that Kalin March was responsible for Russel's death. It no longer mattered that his own temper had seen to his boy's end. If it weren't for Kalin stealin Porch horses, Russel would be alive.

The same logic applied to Landry. If she hadn't gotten involved, she'd be home right now with Momma Gatestone. Though Old Porch weren't about to forget that it was a Gatestone who'd gotten all this goin in the first place: none other than that happy-go-lucky Tom. Tom was the one who'd roped in the Kalin kid, which had then dragged Landry into this ancient business that was none of her business. Also, Old Porch had no trouble seein her death as more than a fair price for the death of his Russel. Or maybe not even fair, given that the girl weren't really a Gatestone. In fact she weren't no more part of the Land here than Kalin was. From the moment she was brought into the fold, no matter what the Church said, Old Porch, like most folks around the State, could see she weren't a part of their fold. Just one look and anyone would know she was disallowed, with the Porches bein the ones the valley depended on to make that official. Just like how they was gonna see to it that this outsider Kalin March also got disallowed.

And so Old Porch, in a blind amassment of his own makin, got around to acceptin that he weren't just merely the Manifest Destiny of the Forever Ascendin but also merely a servant, servin the Law, not Church law or Orvop law, or even Porch law, but Thee Law, what by Land and Sky Thee Law must forever demand: the expulsion of them not suitable for here, where Porch was at, of course, with them bein categorized as interlopers, trespassers, among other things. And good riddance too to anyone who dared stand by their side.

K alin sure had no notions of Manifest Destiny or even territory as he continued his trek forward. Maybe fer a moment he did entertain a fantasy that he would right then be met on that field by friends, though he'd never had any such friends, just Tom, his one and only great friend, who'd come to him after death. But in this already-fast-fadin dream, Kalin suddenly had scores of friends as brave as Tom, from all walks of life, come there not only to protect him and cow the Porches into peaceable submission but see him through to them gate-posts. Unfortunately Pillars Meadow granted no such surprises, and anyway Kalin's mind was again entirely with the ponies, especially as they wouldn't stop givin him one heckuva hard time. They wouldn't quit yankin at their leads; they wouldn't quit tryin to drag him side-ways, anythin to get as far away from him as possible. Both Navidad and Mouse kept throwin their heads high as they could go without goin up on their haunches, sometimes down as low as the earth would permit without actually lyin down. Kalin ignored them. He knew if he looked back, they'd rear and bolt fer sure, whites in their eyes. Jojo weren't no better either; affronted by Kalin, him that weren't Landry, the stallion too often choosin to move opposite whatever direction Navidad and Mouse were sidlin toward.

And, no, Old Porch firin shots on someone ahead hadn't had the slightest effect on any of them. The horses ignored the cracks like they was no more than the spit off a wet branch in a campfire. After all, not even gunfire compared to what marched just a few paces ahead, their leads and reins in his right hand.

That was surely one of the saddest parts of these moments. And you can bet Kalin's heart was rent, as were the hearts of the horses,

Navidad's fer sure, Mouse's too, if just for Navidad, with Jojo's heart broken earlier, devastated by the disappearance of his Landry.

What Kalin would've given then for a warm nuzzle, some familiar snort of affection, but upon that wide and miserable field with mud relentlessly suckin at his boots like an impatient grave, he was abandoned, all equine affection replaced by the worst thing of all: fear. Not even Tom walked beside Kalin, though his appearance beyond the Porches, all abristle with so much weaponry, did offer some encouragement. Good ole Tom, still as alabaster now, on an even stiller Ash. Good ole Tom, still holdin up that bright, impossible brand. Good ole Tom, his friend even in death, out there markin a destination Kalin was havin a harder and harder time with each imaginin believin he could reach. It was only right there, only just ahead, and yet it was so far away it weren't there at all.

And on top of all this . . . Landry . . . her absence far too much for Kalin to face, surely not with grief, maybe though with rage; the harrowin emptiness her loss created fillin him, as if with the densest of metals, until all Kalin could do was wear it like a shield, like a halo of the darkest kind, shimmerin with the blackest of thorns, their points of affliction infinite.

Kalin hit a patch of snow then and it crunched underfoot. What he'd give right then for just one mouthful. Torture. He couldn't even slow let alone stop, with only this smell of chionichor to answer his terrible thirst.

Most important of all, Kalin not only couldn't stop he couldn't lower his hands even a little. They had to stay raised the entire way across. From the tree line, that had seemed easily doable. No sensible part of him had objected to the plan. His arms had testified to an effortless hold on verticality. Kalin cursed his stupidity.

He'd even felt insensibly encouraged by, of all dumb things, the final row of trees through which he'd passed before steppin out onto Pillars Meadow. They'd somehow seemed propitious, especially in their curious arrangement, an orderin that struck Kalin only as he strode away: twelve enormous trees lined up pretty much in a straight line and equidistant to each other too, surprisinly similar if not identical to the lakeside trees his mother liked to take him to now and then, those trees clearly planted by someone, while these here were set by no hand other than by the Mountain itself. And even as Kalin's breath started to come up more and more ragged, him now and then stumblin some or swayin, his knees knockin at times, his right hip clickin like an old man's, Kalin wondered if he'd at last escaped the province of the Mountain. *And maybe all them birches and aspens, with them* last twelve trees lined up straight as Apollo's arrow, as Ben Carter would put it to Diane Hillam, *maybe them was the Last Gate of the Mountain, or what we all know as the eighth gate.* And Diane Hillam, who, a week before she would die, in of all things, a mudslide, would even sing a bit about that gate, with eighth relatin to death where the Greeks were concerned, and maybe that did fit, though Hillam also sang of the number meanin other things, like release, and frankly her song, as many agreed, seemed all over the place, at least where meanin was concerned, not that that meant those twelve trees weren't the eighth gate, just as they surely weren't the last gate. Ben Carter would have no opinion on Hillam's song as he'd died the previous year, chokin on a chunk of meat, what not even the Heimlich maneuver could dislodge in time.

But gates and such aside, Kalin had still judged poorly the price of such a distance. It weren't that his eye had mistaken how far he'd have to walk, but he'd underestimated the effect it would have on his arms. Not even halfway across and they was burnin somethin awful, especially his left arm. Past halfway, Kalin feared his arms would cramp up, and that brought angry tears to his eyes that he couldn't wipe away.

How the Porch boys loved seein that, though; them tear-streaked cheeks. They loved that almost more than Kalin's nekedness. The closer the boy got, the more Old Porch delighted hisself with loud proclamations about how Kalin was bawlin for his momma. And you know, maybe he was bawlin some for his momma. But then as he got a little closer, as he passed over still more snow, the sunlight that was reflectin upward off that bright surface seemed to erase all signs of his scratches and bruises. The near fulgor of his paleness became then near blindin, with his immaculateness, however temporary, helpin to foster the ridiculously misguided conversation that would persist in the years ahead, with too many folks assertin that Kalin was principally and only white; it bein no coincidence that the ones makin such assertions were likewise principally and only white, tryin to find in this fictive skin somethin more important than the mind that cultivates an eye for color.

To be fair, though, none of the Porch boys gave Kalin's sudden luminosity any thought. They just couldn't see him that way. And besides, he was soon enuf back to trampin across the mud again. Even stranger, Kalin had briefly become a relief. The horror most of them still couldn't process, Kevin Moffet splayed out in the muck behind them, they could now ignore in favor of Kalin's tear-streaked face or his private parts. Neither Shelly nor Sean nor Woolsey had had enuf yet of callin out somethin about his weenie. And when Kalin's hips swiveled left or right to better control the horses, they could glimpse Kalin's back and rear. And then the flatness that resided there was also remarked upon.

He ain't got a butt! Woolsey cried out. *He's a No Butt!*

Ain't he all hat and no cattle, Old Porch grunted.

Well, he does got the horses, Francis murmured.

And yet with all that seein, not a one of them saw the Peacemaker. Kalin's general presentation of weakness and defeat had carefully concealed from them the Colt, lost in the lee of his left arm, suspended from the back of his hand down along the back of his forearm by an ingenious arrangement of those thin leather strips Kalin had cut and tied around the fingers and wrists of both hands. And while both arms displayed the leather, only the left arm had to bear the relentless weight of that weapon. Fer sure, it sagged his arm some, but all the Porches assumed that that had to do with his woundedness, the cut on the side of that arm, the blood drippin off his left elbow. Even the raw rope burn on that left palm further discredited that side. Not that any of the Porches were worried much about the right side either, which Kalin tried to droop some to match the left, especially as he got closer, if just in the name of symmetry, but never so low either to betray intention.

Then, when he was about thirty paces off, he started to pee, somethin he'd planned to do and had prepared for.

Francis was so disgusted, he turned away, once again blindin his eyes with the sight of their helicopter, nearly too far off to see, though really what did it matter anymore? Francis realizin this only then: they now had no pilot to fly it. Francis closed his eyes tight while the rest of the Porches started to hoot and howl over the spectacle of that tricklin stream of urine. Well, Hatch and Billings didn't hoot and howl, but they were again put at ease by the sight.

He's wettin hisself! Sean just had to crow, like it weren't already obvious, and maybe to him it wasn't, Sean after all bein the same young man who'd thought flyin over his own handlebars on Aster Scree had nothin to do with his own decision-makin.

Of course he is, growled Shelly, both at his brother and for the sight, which sickened him, though differently than it did Francis, because here was a sign that he had no opponent, no challenge, and whatever contest he'd shaped in his head was now a foregone conclusion and so no contest at all. More like a chore.

And then Woolsey, in his head on the way to an even better time than this good time, stepped still closer to the center of that long-gone line of defense.

*Y*ou got some balls, son, Old Porch said when Kalin finally halted some dozen paces away from those closest, a little more from Old Porch, both hands still held high, unwaverin. *Clop-Clop-clip-Clop.*

No, he don't! Woolsey chortled like a satisfied hyena. *He's so small, it looks like he's got no balls at all!* Sean laughed, and Egan and Shelly both grinned, but that was it. Francis didn't want to talk about someone's private parts.

You all are gonna have to step aside now was how Kalin answered Old Porch, answered them all, and, you know what, Old Porch loved it.

And it's worth notin that even now Kalin meant only that. Only movin ahead had been determined. No matter that a memory so vivid could at any moment paint the air with Landry's blood. No matter either that Kalin was armed; he had yet to inhabit the weapon with any intention or spectre of use.

Hear that, boys! Old Porch near crooned, and at once Shelly, Sean, and Woolsey raised their weapons, safeties off too, cocked them, drew a bead on Kalin's chest, except Woolsey, who still couldn't get enuf of Kalin's crotch and aimed his Ruger 10/22 there.

And to think I thought you was surrenderin, Old Porch said then. He winked too.

You best step aside.

I heard you the first time, Old Porch snapped.

I don't think you did. I'm headin past that crick bed there with these horses, and you all are in my way.

Old Porch made a big to-do about lookin over his shoulder at the crick bed, performin an elaborate act of squintin as he centered his gaze on them two solitary gateposts, pointin his 12-gauge in that general direction too. He was havin a blast.

Some of his boys followed their dad's gaze. Them that had raised their weapons lowered them again, impatient for the demonstration of authority if also just as quickly exhausted by the idea of its execution. Whether consciously or not, each of them understood that they was there not to do much except watch their daddy, who'd already made it clear that he'd be the first to dance with a trigger.

You mean just over there? Old Porch asked now, extra loud too, for all his boys to hear, though Francis and Kelly, who still marked the southern and northern terminus of that line, had no trouble hearin him, seein as how they'd continued to move both ahead and closer, if each for different reasons.

Get on now, Kalin replied. *That's the third and last time I make that request.* And, boy, Old Porch's smile wanted to challenge Tom's. He weren't ever gonna get close, but this here was the closest he'd get. Old Porch almost admired the boy. He sure relished havin a few more moments to understand how someone so appallinly slight could've eluded them all over the past days. It weren't lost on Old Porch either that this child before him had made it over the Mountain and with horses too. And though Old Porch could never admit it, part of him respected Kalin more than any of his own sons. For whatever his words had gone on lyin about, he weren't so blinded by such nekedness and scrawny limbs to miss how here before him stood someone with the kind of dogged grit he found no trace of in his own boys, and that included both Hatch and Egan.

I ain't movin, Old Porch said in a slow and amused drawl. *I guess that puts us in a predicament.*

You get to make that choice.

Ha! Hear that boys? He says I get to make that choice! How about that! Ain't he just a peach! Old Porch's jubilant disposition was now almost too grand, too theatrical, to be believed, though it still infected most of his boys. Hatch weren't that kinda fool, though, and Egan never cared for such displays of exaggeration, and Kelly didn't know what to care about even if Old Porch continued to command their attention. Only Billings stepped back again, once more tryin to distance hisself from the fast-clusterin Porches. Billings even noted his own retreat if leavin unanswered the question of why he was reactin now like that. After all, the boy was still bare from boots up. And if there was any steel on him, it was only in the boy's voice. Otherwise, as far as Billings could figure it, the kid was just standin there, surrounded and help-less. If steely. That was pretty much the only warnin Billings needed. Helpless but still steely. One of those had to be wrong, and Billings had lived long enuf and hard enuf to know only an idjit doubts steel. Except there just weren't any steel to be found.

Mind if I ask you a question, boy? Unless of course you're in a hurry. Old Porch's enjoyment just kept on growin.

Kalin hadn't budged from where he'd stopped, as still as them trees behind, except maybe for his arms, which had started to tremble some, though in fact the upper branches of them birches and aspens back there had also started to tremble, from a breeze of course, but the sound they was makin warned Billings then of somethin else. Not Old Porch though.

What's so different about where you're at now and what's over yonder there? I ask because I'm so tickled by the just ridiculous funniness of this business we're about right now.

Once again Kalin didn't respond.

I really want to know, Old Porch protested, and it was hard to say his pleadin weren't genuine. *Because here's the thing,* and as Old Porch wandered on into this branch of his thinkin, he made the mistake of restin the barrel of that Winchester Model 12 in the crux of his left elbow. *See, if I'd've known this here was where you'd be takin my ponies, why we'd be havin a very different conversation right now. Heck, first I'd've told Russel to pay you somethin extra for your troubles.*

Which one of you shot Landry? Kalin asked then. He weren't takin his eyes off Old Porch, but he wasn't missin neither the shufflin of feet around him, especially that one who wasn't a Porch, who was takin still another step backwards.

There was a ripple of chuckles then, especially from them Porches who knew nothin about anythin, like they'd just heard one of the horses say the Lord's Prayer, with all of them bein wise to the fact that a talkin horse was just a trick, like *Mister Ed*, even if the mechanism had yet to be disclosed.

When no one spoke up, Kalin scanned their faces for hisself, and in the years that followed plenty have shaped, imagined, reported, invented, relayed, surmised, spoke on this moment in particular, how whether or not Kalin knew he was doin it hisself, along with discernin each of the Porch boys' attitude, he was also registerin distances and angles. When Kalin returned his gaze to meet again Old Porch's gray-eyed stare, he did so with a fire Old Porch had never known before, though it weren't one either that he was afraid to meet.

Billings took still three more steps back.

You get what you deserve when you ride with cowards, Kalin told Old Porch. And then he spat. Some still say it was red with blood, others that it was black as bile; still more have sworn that the ground sizzled like it was hotter than fire. *I ain't got a stitch on, I'm surrounded, and the one who done what he done is still too scared to say so.*

I'll be goshdarned, Old Porch said then with an approvin nod, *if this piece of sheep dung ain't just said somethin I have to agree with.*

Bowlin Ball? Egan spoke up at once, loudly too and steppin forward, that .357 in hand and ready. *I shot her. Heckuva shot too.*

You die first.

Woooooo-hooooooooooo! Old Porch hollered. *Ain't you a kicker! I'm startin to like you, Kalin March.*

Francis sure didn't like Kalin, or at least he didn't know what to like, or hate, his thoughts already churnin him toward the spins, like everythin really was spinnin, like he was sick on drink, tryin to gulp air, though there was an abundance of air, with the only thing he had to swallow bein Egan's admission, if Francis had even heard right. Had he? Had Egan just admitted to killin Landry Gatestone? Though why was he talkin about bowlin too?

Woolsey was just as confused. Egan had killt an Orvop High kid? A girl? And shot a bowlin ball too? None of it was makin sense, which was comfortin, even if the backs of his knees kept loosenin, so much so that Woolsey got to wonderin how he was gonna keep standin upright, stand any of this, and yet there Woolsey remained, by some miracle, still upright, gawkin more and more at this back-and-forth between one towerin man, his dad, and a kid smaller and younger than all of them yet still gettin more of their daddy's respect than he or Francis had known their whole lives.

Any time you're ready, Egan announced then, loud again, like he was now all of a sudden tryin to be like his daddy, while plenty pleased too that this was gonna finally get done, even if he was still keepin his .357 low, down by his crotch, under his left hand, like he was an usher at a weddin waitin for the bride to arrive.

BOY! Old Porch roared then at Kalin but also at Egan, fer sure to check his son in case he got some notion to draw first; and so also orderin the rest of his boys into restraint. The time had passed for foolin around. There was real bite now in Old Porch's voice. Kalin was gonna have to show more than just grit and queer neked posturin. *YOU STILL AIN'T ANSWERED ME! WHAT'S SO GOSHDARN IMPORTANT ABOUT THAT LAND OVER THERE?*

It don't got no owner.

Old Porch smiled. Maybe he weren't done foolin around.

That's where I mean to set these horses loose, Kalin continued. *Then they can do as they see fit. I've heard farther east there's a wild herd. They're free to join them if they like.*

That land ain't got no owner, eh? Old Porch turned them words over in his mouth like he'd never tasted anythin better, anythin stronger; his eyes lit up too, and even his grin, with them ragged teeth lookin mortared together now with chunks of tobacco, wouldn't stop contortin as his jaw kept jarrin side to side like Old Porch was grindin on elation itself. *For all your gusto, you sure are dumb as a jug of pig piss.* A declaration that gladdened the hearts of all his boys, from Kelly all the way down to Francis. *Ain't nothin in existence that don't got an owner. Especially land. And whoever told you otherwise has been messin with your head.*

It's protected, Kalin answered back.

Here's an interestin fact, son: See that crick bed where our friend Kevin here was runnin to? That's Porch land. Sure, it's an awful odd sliver with no roads to it or out of it, but it's mine. Right up to them old gateposts. Has been for gen-

erations. Pretty darned strange place, don't you think, to be settin your aim on, especially with my horses in tow?

Kalin didn't pay much attention to Old Porch's claim, but he did consider carefully the body, face down in the muck, Kalin's breath leakin out of him real slow, first like a low whistle, until its departure settled further into a silent exhalation of either acceptance or resignation, what sagged his shoulders if not any his upheld hands. *What's past them posts is parkland,* he said. *Somethin like that.*

Somethin like that, Old Porch repeated the words, shakin his head in disbelief, his teeth quittin their grindin because there was now a taste of disappointment in there too, because he was startin to see Kalin as just some uppity teenager who weren't deservin of even one minute of his time let alone all this. *I won't quibble with you about what it was, because, see, that's in the past. By tomorrow the land beyond them gateposts will also be mine. Far as you can see. Funny, ain't it? Them horses have always been comin back to me.*

Then why are you standin in my way?

Old Porch chuckled. *You've gone far enuf, boy. But I assure you, as certain as I would've had them rendered days ago, I'll put them down myself. Right over there too. You can watch.*

THIS AIN'T ABOUT NO DANG HORSES! Francis suddenly screeched from the far end of the line, steppin even closer now. *IT'S ABOUT HIM MURDERIN MY LITTLE BROTHER!*

That's right, Hatch, of all folks, said then.

Kalin could only catch Francis duckin his gaze. This oldest Porch, though, near right in front of Kalin, presented a different puzzle. Kalin even cocked his head a little. He could see Hatch weren't like the rest of them, though how was not obvious. Kalin chose to respond to them both: *I never touched your brother. Landry knocked him off Cavalry and then paid him twenty dollars for these horses. She wrote out the receipt on that very same bill and signed it too. They both signed it. We had a nice dinner around the fire after that. I liked Russel.*

You're a liar, Hatch threw back, but there weren't no conviction in his voice.

I got no reason to lie. Then Kalin nodded toward Egan. *I bet he knows who killt your brother.*

Egan didn't give nothin away, but Hatch was still lookin hard at his brother. *Got anythin to tell us, Eges?*

I don't answer to you, Hatch. Or him.

Only then did Kalin's lips ease a bit into a shallow grin, especially as he returned his focus to Old Porch again: *I warned you fair: when you ride with cowards you get what you deserve.*

Who I'm with, boy, don't matter one bit. This here's just between you and me now. Always has been. Old Porch slowly raised the shotgun barrel from the crook of his left arm, but he didn't point it at Kalin yet. Instead with his left hand, he slowly drew from behind his back that killin gun, the Smith & Wesson Model 59 with aluminum frame, what had just put an end to Kevin Moffet. Old Porch hucked it over to Kalin. *That right there's your only chance, son. Pick it up.*

Whoa! Hold on a second here, Pa, Hatch interjected, some resolve returnin to his voice and manner, and maybe some sense comin back to him too. Egan might not have answered Kalin's question about Russel, but Hatch weren't in his lifetime gonna ever forget Egan gunnin down Landry Gatestone and then braggin about it later. He also hadn't missed the way Kelly had looked over at Billings while this Kalin March was makin his claim of innocence regardin Russel, a claim Hatch at once believed.

Kalin, though, weren't thinkin about Hatch or none of the Porch boys or even about Old Porch. He was considerin the weapon on the ground before him. He even took a few steps toward it but stopped before he was anywhere close. Then he looked up. *You'll die last,* he told Old Porch then.

HA! Old Porch hollered. *In another life, I'd've claimed you as my own! In another life, I'd've still cut you down.*

Old Porch laughed some more, and near gently now too, a kinda melancholy sound that more than a little confused both Francis and Woolsey, who knew that doleful noise only when Old Porch occasionally spoke of the not-so-bad times when their mother was still in the house. Shelly and Sean were also confused, though not by anythin so subtle as the raspy tonalities of a laugh. Them two brawlers just didn't understand what their old man was up to. Why was he draggin this all out like so? Not even gettin around to when they'd ever seen their daddy display such devotion toward anyone other than hisself, though at last finally sensin now some weird divide between them all and Egan, Kelly, and Billings, with Hatch, who was still a hero in their eyes, somehow at the center of this rupture, primarily because he seemed just as confused as they were by what all was unfoldin here, a dangerous uncertainty that kept fracturin their resolve. Shelly and Sean just had no clear notion about how they was supposed to act, what they was supposed to do, leavin them both thinkin less about firearms and more about just rushin the fool. And if he hadn't been neked with piss all on hisself, they might right then have disobeyed their father and put this upstart down in the mud. After all, if they was good at anythin, it was tacklin.

Pick it up, boy, Old Porch said again, near whisperin now, his left hand grippin the action slide handle on the shotgun, his right finger confirmin the safety was off, and in his arrogance even aimin from his hip. *I won't tell you again.*

And Kalin did take another step forward, though instead of takin a second, he confounded Old Porch with one last misdirection, stretchin his hands up just a tiny bit more, like he might even go up on his toes.

Anthony Whitmer, who wound up gettin his master's in marriage and family therapy and proved a pretty darn good counselor over the course of his life, would have a theory about why Kalin saw as clearly as he did, especially given how his eyes weren't as good as Landry's, at least not when it came to distances: *Kalin had natural athleticism or coordination, plus some of the coldness he maybe got from his daddy, but I think what made him so exceptional, and now this is just my personal opinion, was how he saw more than he thought. Most folks allocate a lesser part of their brain to seein and a greater part of their brain to thinkin. They see just fine for what they need to see, but it ain't the very most. I ain't sayin Kalin was stupid either. He just knew how to see. So when Old Porch went ahead and did what he did, Kalin weren't slowed down by observin hisself observin. He'd done all his thinkin when he made his choice to pick up the Colt. That's my belief. By the time he tromped across Pillars Meadow, he weren't hardly thinkin. He was just pure sight, hearin too, and all the senses, and so just pure reaction and action when the time came.* Anthony Whitmer would say all this right after the funeral for his friend Ivan Dorton who had tried to outdraw three LA sheriffs, which was a pretty stupid thing to do. Ivan Dorton was cut down by them. Anthony Whitmer was cut down by Covid-19. But before he passed, he would find hisself sorrowful, harrowed even, and not by Ivan Dorton's end but by the news that Darren Blicker had at last ended his long run of afflictin others by shootin hisself in the face. Anthony Whitmer would die peacefully in his sleep. Darren Blicker, though, would linger for a while. In fact he'd live for hours, make it to a hospital, die once, die twice, until infection got him and sepsis took him away.

Old Porch, no Sarpedon, swung the barrel of that 12-gauge toward Navidad: *Let's set that one down right here.*

Obviously that was a huge mistake, maybe the biggest of them all. Plenty, includin Jared Cade, Celia Mineer, and most of the Greenspires for that matter, would rant about how the outcome of everythin that followed was determined by this one choice: Old Porch goin first for a horse. Missy Yamazaki would even quip, but with an exaggerated wink, that the alleged Dijkstra observation could be extended as follows: *Computer science is no more about computers than astronomy is about telescopes than shoot-outs are about guns.* Plenty of others, however, and that would include these dead, Llewellyn Bailey, Carter Roylance, Doreen Lund, Randy Beal, Christa Finch, Auris Satterfield, Emerson Nation, and Chloe Pew, plus Louis Battocchio, Judd Rinaldi, Lori Zide, and Rashid Lannes, liked to point out how champions often create in their opponents the errors by which their opponents lose. Or, in other words, if Old Porch hadn't erred here, why then Kalin would've seen to it that he'd err elsewhere. Guns bein beside the point. No doubt nothin will ever settle this particular argument. What would've happened if Old Porch had kept them barrels trained on Kalin? That remains the big what-if question. Many still concede that even with Old Porch more in charge of his weaponery, he was also too smitten by his own narratives. He couldn't unsee that Kalin was gonna make a grab for that aluminum-framed gun, and when he did, no matter how he came at it, whether by scramble or imaginative roll, why Old Porch was gonna cut him in half. Ms. Melson would jokinly refer to what came next as *Diòs apáté* or *the deception of Zeus,* though *in no way was Old Porch Zeus, nor was there any amorous or erotic subterfuge at hand.*

Kalin gave his left arm a jerk like so, while anglin his hand like so, similar to what he'd demonstrated for Landry back in the Awides Mine with the farrier hammer, except here it was the Peacemaker dislodged from them leather strips, or maybe *set free* puts it better than *dislodged;* an ideal tumble of grip over barrel now in motion, with Kalin lowerin hisself at the same time in order to match the weapon's descent, his movements so smooth, and even soft, they didn't seem to demand any more attention than the implacable sky above, with even the whirlin insistence of metal, as if born out of thin air, so amazinly if briefly apparent, still failin to prompt the immediate reaction required. It weren't just one breath lost either but as many as three in this collective failure of comprehension. You see, the Porches just plain couldn't register yet how there was now a Colt Peacemaker hangin there in the air, plain as day, for everyone to see.

And no, there ain't gonna be no complete divulgence now of how this particular trick or technique or work of art, take your pick, was carried out, namely because there ain't no one worthy of its consequences, and, yes, that goes for all of us, and maybe even for Kalin too.

To his credit, Old Porch was warrior enuf to understand that whatever was before him, whatever was at hand, nearly in hand, Kalin had finally started movin with intent. And Old Porch responded near as quick, jerkin that shotgun fast as he could back toward Kalin.

Old Porch, though, was way too late.

In times of great excitement, be they weddins or battles, eyes of the inexperienced often go wide, the whites only too evident. Here as well, as everythin now swung forth into awful action, especially as the report of dematerializin gunpowder filled the air, the eyes of the younger boys, Francis, Woolsey, but also Sean and Shelly and even Kelly, showed their whites. Not Egan, though, nor Billings. Not Old Porch neither. And fer sure not Kalin. Here too was what he was meant for. Jojo flared his nostrils, and as that blue horse's eyes went skyward, they showed plenty of white as well. Which was not the case for Navidad, and Mouse's eyes grew only darker like he'd beheld the wars of time already and would behold them all over again, again and again, and it would still make no difference.

Not that any idle witness there upon that field would've easily noted the varied dispositions nor viewed the ensuin little jerks, spins, grabs, and steps as doin anythin other than occurin at the same time. Though that was not the case. Great athletes know how many swift sequences can be won in the space of a breath, with the mere nod of a head, a shift of weight between legs. Where the Porches were imprisoned by time, Kalin's speed seemed to surpass even the need for speed. He was just that far ahead of everybody's reactions.

With his left hand, Kalin snatched the Colt from the air, and then with his right palm draggin back the trigger, he shot Old Porch through the spleen.

Old Porch at once discharged the shotgun into the mud as he buckled over before finally fallin on his side to twist around in pain. Kalin hardly noticed. Here now was the consequences of his irrevocable act, what would result from wieldin that weapon and deliver the horses to their uncertain futures: Kalin released the horses' leads and reins, in effect abandonin them here, as he then flowed forward, lowerin next his left knee to the ground, further lowerin his head as he swung that Colt across his body and right knee, drawin a bead on Egan.

Egan for his own reasons was not only tryin to aim his .357 but had also at the same time thrown up his left hand, palm out, as if wantin to say: *Whoa now! Hold one minute!* Or: *I ain't ready!* Or even: *Give me a sec!* Kalin givin him no such thing. With one shot, he blew off the middle finger of that protestin hand, the bullet next punchin through Egan's front teeth, then out the back of his head, darkenin the air behind him with a sudden cloud of blood, brain, and bone particulates.

Kelly, who had run forward to try to outflank Kalin, was also the first of the Porches to actually fire on Kalin, though because he was shootin from the side, when he missed, he gutshot his brother Francis, who, stumblin forward to get a better view of things, had unintentionally wound up in Kelly's direct line of fire.

Kalin showed no sign of comprehendin that, but for a handful of inches, he'd nearly had his heart blown to shreds. Instead Kalin blew to shreds Kelly's heart. Kelly was dead before he flopped to the ground, that scrap of paper with Allison March's number on it still at the bottom of one of his pockets.

Kalin had already swung back for Sean, who'd managed to get off a shot. Unlike Kelly, Sean didn't shoot none of his brothers; like Kelly he missed, barely. Barely, though, didn't matter none to Kalin. He shot Sean through the forehead.

Maybe Woolsey would've fallen next. He'd turned tail and was runnin for the crick bed. Weren't a bad move neither. Under cover of them banks, he'd've found loaded weapons, includin Hatch's formidable Barrett. What's more, and maybe most importantly, he'd get hisself a moment to take a breath and set up some before inflictin his own retribution. He even had some intermediary cover: when Kalin had released the horses, Jojo had headed to the right, toward the helicopter, with Navidad and Mouse followin only to change their minds, gallopin suddenly north, or right between the crick bed and Woolsey, which made at that moment any shot by Kalin too dangerous. Kalin didn't even consider the escapin Woolsey.

Billings by this point had drawn his .44 Magnum, the Smith & Wesson Model 29-2 with a 4-inch barrel, a real beast with enuf muzzle flash to set fire to anyone too near. He'd already fired once and missed but didn't miss the second time, his shot searin through Kalin's right side, shatterin ribs with them bone splinters nickin a lung before the slug spit out off into the mud. It spun Kalin around somethin good too, but Kalin went with it, and before he hit the ground that Peacemaker had found Billings. Kalin put a bullet right through his sternum.

Shelly had already managed to fire off five shots with his Ruger Service-Six, but with Sean's blood in his eyes he'd got turned around and only managed to hit Woolsey in the thigh, right on the inside there. Kalin put Shelly down with his sixth and last round, right through one temple and out the other.

Kalin then rose to his feet and tossed aside the Colt Peacemaker, tossed it like it weren't nothin but the memory of a dream, whether good or bad, already forgotten.

He gave some thought to Woolsey, who'd gotten the farthest away and was still crawlin for that crick bed. But he instead stepped over that aluminum-framed Model 59 like it weren't nothin and, without givin Old Porch a second look, kicked the 12-gauge away.

Francis was ashen and gaspin by the time Kalin reached his side. Kalin even kneeled down, even held his hand.

You didn't kill my little brother, did you? Francis managed to croak out.
I did not.

Francis Porch was dead by the time Kalin stood up again. And Hatch was waitin for him, his face and front covered in mud but with his own Colt Government leveled at Kalin's chest. Hatch was clutchin the weapon in his right hand, crossed over his left arm with the left hand holdin the cuffs, rattlin like wind chimes in a hurricane.

I'm arrestin you. You have the right to remain silent, Hatch managed to get out, though his voice was a mess, and he still couldn't stop shakin.

Kalin studied Hatch. *That's fine,* he finally said. He still couldn't figure Hatch out. Never would either. *First, though, I'm gonna get the horses and take them right over there like I said before. Once I let them go, we can follow your script. I won't make no fuss.*

That'll do.

Somehow Kalin understood Hatch well enuf to realize that the man would never shoot him. Hatch, it seems, realized this too and not only lowered his weapon but holstered it as well. He had never killt no one in his life, and in those moments he'd come to understand that no future of his was gonna change that.

Some folks have gone so far as to claim that Kalin in the next moment cut Hatch down in cold blood. Bunches more have called foul, sayin that Hatch's behavior was out of character for the Hero Porch he was, who would've shot Kalin right then or at least cuffed him. And fer sure in that hour on Pillars Meadow, Hatch could know hisself as strong and with the skills to kill someone near a mile off. He had a medaled career as well as the moral fortitude to enact a role of jurisprudential enforcer. What he lacked, however, was any claim on those neccessary internal resources required in moments like these, and let's put aside accusations of cowardice and forget as well ideas of rectitude's supposedly sustainin power or even the raw will to power paramount to carryin out the actions needed to uphold such prudential surfaces. Hatch just had no want of it. Despite appearances, he was in fact closest to Francis. They shared the same soft, billowy heart along with all the beneficent uncertainty that allows for curiosity and good taste, taste that went well beyond them dull parameters set down and fenced in by Old Porch.

In fact it's likely that the sight of Kalin kneelin beside Francis and holdin his brother's hand, rather than enragin Hatch, released him instead from the family cage, especially upon overhearin their exchange, with Kalin solemnly declinin any part in all this business, which, frankly, the longer Hatch gaped upon it, these savage results, the more it stunk of his father, Orwin Porch, Old Porch.

Even if the outcome was different, Hatch knew this scene here, mud, blood, and death, was always Old Porch's objective. And so maybe that's how even the sight of his brothers' bodies strewn across that meadow conjured no repercussive desire in Hatch. No fire, no spark. In fact contrary to speculation, Hatch in that instant tasted the sweetness in the air, of pines, of sky, exhaled from the earth, like a gift to a divine breeze, the snow in turn offerin the ground its suspended rain, the soul of snow, the relinquishment of form to flow, a promise now in the process of fulfillment, the fabled carryin-on.

I saw Egan shoot down Landry, Hatch admitted then to Kalin. *In cold blood.*

Kalin nodded.

I'd've never done such a thing.

Kalin nodded again.

Why'd you kill the ranger?

The only thing we done here was take them horses over the mountain. We didn't shoot no one, Kalin said, startin to limp toward where Navidad and Mouse had stopped to graze. And they weren't close, and it weren't a fast limp either, each step deliverin a seizure of agony, as every time Kalin's perforated right side contorted with pain, somethin inside his chest matchin the pain and then doublin it.

You think Egan had somethin to do with Russel's death? Hatch yelled out.

That paused Kalin. *I got no understandin about anythin your brothers done here except kill an innocent girl and try to kill me.* Kalin briefly left the sight of the two horses to turn back to Hatch. *Was it you who tried to gun us down on the headwall?*

Hatch still had his .45, albeit holstered but easily within reach, and far as he could see, Kalin remained unarmed, neked, and bleedin beneath his right armpit even with his right hand clamped over the wound. But the inferno Hatch beheld in the boy's gaze shuddered him.

I didn't try to kill you, just pin you down.

You nearly did murder us.

I was still tryin to get the story straight.

Kalin laughed ruefully. *A straight story? Ain't that a joke. Do you even know who started this stuff about your brother Russel?*

Hatch looked over to where Old Porch lay.

Did he say I killt that guy too? Kalin nodded over at Kevin Moffet, as much of the red of hisself that his poor heart could pump spillt.

Poor Hatch grunted, which was the best he could do to confirm what both him and Kalin already knew.

I reckon your old man's got a pretty good idea what happened to Russel, Kalin added before trampin after the horses, each step erasin his limp until the pain once instructin his movement was limited to the grit of his teeth.

A fair question still raised is why Hatch, as Kalin walked away, didn't unholster his weapon right then and start firin until the boy lay dead in the ice and mud.

Already covered was how Hatch now stood at least partially convinced by an alternate sequence of events that substantially rearranged the history previously declared by Old Porch. Also touched upon was how Hatch stood now overthrown by a very sensational encounter with the taste of the day, the smells stirrin him into memory, away from human concerns, providin a space, however brief, within the horror at hand that knows nothin of horror, what in another time, as those three teachers, Ms. Melson, Mr. Rudder, and Mrs. Annserdodder, would argue, would be regarded as the very real appearance of Artemis or Aphrodite standin beside Hatch, smoothin his brow, calmin his thoughts. What, however, has not yet been addressed is how, despite this reprieve, it was not so entire as to end Hatch's tremblin. His breath was still too shallow and quick. Tics ate at his face. There was no calm for him. Hatch remained deathly afraid.

Egan, the second to fall, never even knew what hit him. He was so blinded by the outcome he'd convinced hisself was his entitlement, that he fer sure would drop Kalin, that even as his body was already protestin the reality comin for him, his mind knew only the darkest void of every story.

In fact only Francis Porch on that day at Pillars Meadow actually saw Kalin release upon the air his father's 1873 Colt Single Action Army Peacemaker, the possession of which had been so hotly contested by both Hatch, supposedly the rightful heir, and Egan, a usurper of sorts, with of course neither possessin it now. Francis alone recognized it quick enuf to see who Kalin was and at least thought to run.

Kelly Porch was slow to fully understand the weaponizin of Kalin, but at least he was lungin forward, lungin fast enuf to shoot. Unfortunately he was ill-prepared for the misdirections Kalin's movements too swiftly described, and so Kelly anticipated wrongly and shot long and shot down his brother Francis instead. And even before Kalin shot Kelly down, makin him the third, Kelly had assumed hisself already hit, his guts offerin up one last spasm of gruesome pain.

Sean Porch, who was the fourth to fall, had appreciated better how quickly Kalin was movin and knew it was up to him to kill the boy, though to do so would require beholdin him, which Sean was incapable of doin, his eyes dancin ahead of where Kalin seemed to be goin even if he weren't goin there. Sean's instincts kept insistin on findin the spot where Kalin wasn't but would be, and, yes, okay, respectfully, in the name of aimin, that does make good sense, though Sean's actions were more bound up with another instinct: flight or more specifically his inability to look upon the face that would kill him a moment later.

Shelly Porch, the sixth to fall, was no better off, maybe even worse off, because he really believed he would kill Kalin. No matter that Sean's blood had spattered his eyes; he was even more oblivious to how fear had already hijacked the accuracy upon which his life depended. All Shelly could recognize was how every round he squoze off delivered an all-too-satisfyin retort and shock from that Ruger Service-Six's recoil, even if the courage he needed to see that .38 reach its mark weren't in him. In fact the more he fired, the less brave he became. And by then anyway he was spinnin around in the wrong direction. Which is not to say he didn't come close. In fact Shelly came close twice, though close in those moments wouldn't have even counted with horseshoes or hand grenades, each subsequent shot goin farther and farther astray until the fifth one dropped his brother Woolsey.

Except for Old Porch, Billings, who was the fifth to fall, was not commandeered by fear. He marveled at Kalin's quickness to say nothin of the stillness he'd only moments earlier demonstrated before stupid Old Porch. Billings again experienced somethin that we might as well call admiration for Kalin that day on Pillars Meadow, even if more tragically he also briefly bewailed his own lot for havin ended up with this bunch of losers. Billings had already accepted that he'd been fool enuf to get entangled by earlier mistakes and the false promise that Old Porch's power would somehow absolve him of those mistakes and even deliver him to a future he could never meet on his own. More recently, though, Billings had wondered, especially after he'd beheld Kalin ridin that first time, why he weren't ridin with Kalin and the girl? He'd already accepted how his brown skin would forever mark him in the eyes of the Porches and their community here, even if he weren't near as dark as Landry Gatestone. And yet if he could've ridden beside her and Kalin, he knew he'd've been seen only for how well he too knew how to settle a horse.

And then Kalin was also demonstratin how well he could wield a bullet-spittin chunk of metal. Billings had taken it all in too. Old Porch shot through. Egan Porch dropped next. And suddenly, like that, Billings knew his entanglements were gone. For a second he was free with likely the only impediment to his escape bein the Texas Ranger. And, yes, that's right, part of what contributed to Billings's first shot missin Kalin was the fleetin thought that he should kill Hatch first.

Hatch, though, had fallen. He'd made a move to draw out the Colt Government while at the same time steppin back and at the same time steppin right while at the same time thinkin to step forward. This indecision led to a misstep, and he tripped over his own feet, with the wet ground makin the slip all the more conclusive. Why Hatch then remained face down in the mud for some moments, with even his hands clamped over his ears, while gunfire proceeded over top of him, remains a subject of discussion that has endured for decades. He did, though, eventually free the gun from its holster. Not that he could fire it.

Too many still observe these various doins by Kalin March and the Porches like pieces on a chessboard, continuin to assume that given Kalin's nekedness, the limited number of shots in that Peacemaker, just six, and six quick enuf spent, not to mention the desolation visited on so many Porch brothers, Hatch Porch should've and would've executed the kid the first chance he got.

However, them seated around that board and whatever ceramic pieces wait there need to take a deep breath and turn over that board. Turn over the table too. Also get out of whatever chair or comforts assure them of their thinkin. Try instead to better perceive Pillars Meadow with them vast Katanogos ridges to the west loomin high above; or consider what lay to the east, beyond the immense unfoldin forestland, hazed over in violet shadows already findin afternoon and augurin the end of the day. Let's try then to percieve in the midst of such magnificence the equally dreary spectacle of that dreary field, brown, bitter, wet, and cold. Above all, let's try to accept just how far we'd be from anywhere else, how truly alone we'd be up there, alone with him.

And that him there, however frail with even a shiver upon his blue lips, neked as a glacier except for his hat and boots, wounded as well, showin not a hint of fear or hesitation in them equally cold and burnin eyes, was what Mr. Rudder, Ms. Melson, and Mrs. Annserdodder would've known to call no theistic accompaniment but outright possession if not the Deity hisself. Or Deity herself. After all, despite all appearances to the contrary, emblematic of frailty and foolishness, this him here is also the same one who just shot down with unfailin calm six of your brothers. Maybe he weren't the fastest there, but he was unerrin, even in the midst of a mayhem that also led two brothers to erroneously shoot down two other brothers.

Now stand there by yourself and truly behold those bodies surroundin you, bloodied, contorted, dead, with little Francis also still as the rest, and only Woolsey managin to keep writhin ahead, no longer thinkin about any weapons but rather believin that the crick bed might offer him a reprieve from his pain, an escape from the Death that now stalked him.

Do you really think you'd have the courage to take a shot? Even with a gun in your hand? Them that do ain't been listenin. Them are still likely so full of themselves, still so blind to the hungry maw that drools for their consumin. In fact they should quit right here and accept their failure. There ain't no shame in that either. Their imagination just ain't up to the task. They haven't worked hard enuf. They've been carried along instead of carryin. They've been the burden instead of sharin the burden. They just ain't ready. Despite their couch-cradled ambitions and exaggerated proclamations, they're still too afraid to understand what happens next. Hatch couldn't know what would happen next, but he fer sure weren't blind no more to the fiery apparition he beheld ahead, and given how awfully he'd been misled since near the day he was born, his life's opportunities endlessly compromised by a lifetime of parental dishonesty, here was an apparition he even welcomed, if only for the clarity Kalin offered, however relentless.

Hatch then found his father, who'd just started to crawl again, to get hold of that 12-gauge again. Hatch picked up the shotgun and hurled it away.

Is this all you? he asked as he squatted down. *From the very start?*

Kill him, boy! You kill him now!

What did you do to Russel?!

Kill him, boy! Old Porch snarled again.

Was it you who killt Russel? Hatch roared, in pain but enraged too. *Why?!*

But Old Porch paid the question no mind and got back to crawlin, hardly disturbed by the bodies that lay around him, all his dead boys, their blood continuin to seep into the mud or bloomin in the various patches of snow where some had fallen, a garden of awful blossoms. Hatch stood up then and put a stop to Old Porch's immediate purpose with a bootheel to his back.

I got all day, Pa, he whispered now. *What happened to Russel?*

Stuck like some insect in a display case, Old Porch seethed with spit and more fury than you'd expect from one so wounded. *Whadya mean what happened?! Kalin killt your brother! He killt all your brothers! You were here, you dumb maggot! What's wrong with you?! You saw him do it! With your own eyes!*

Well, we'll let a proper inquiry settle this then, Hatch answered his father.

You are coward! You are yellow-bellied traitor! There ain't no worse than you!

Hatch lifted his boot then and stepped back to watch his father continue his crawl, like a wounded slug leavin a trail of slime and rose.

Jojo had vanished, but Navidad and Mouse had stuck together, and while the gunfire had set them runnin, it was also all over so quick, replaced soon after by the great lucidity up there, the breezes shooin away the smell of spent gunpowder, sunshine and mountains dwarfin human sufferin. The two slowed soon enuf and bein plenty thirsty began to address those needs by eatin snow.

Kalin trudged after them, his right hand the whole time clamped to his side where Billings's bullet had set him to leakin. What an awful fire burnt there, but Kalin remained far beyond them consequences. Only Navidad and Mouse mattered. And at least his approach didn't send Navidad runnin; perhaps his injury and her love for him briefly won out over the revulsion she felt for him. Mouse, whose allegiance was to Navidad, felt nothin for Kalin except certain dislike, but he honored Navidad's choice. Plus he was hungry, and the wet grass here weren't half bad.

Kalin passed Woolsey on the way. Woolsey weren't crawlin no more. He never did get nowhere close to the crick bed. Shelly's shot had missed the femoral artery, but the bone it shattered hadn't. Woolsey found the pain ebbin as a lightheadedness overtook him. He was dancin with Preot Ackley. And though she'd never know she'd been on Woolsey's mind right before he died, fer him it was one of the brightest and truest moments he'd ever known, even as his last breath found him gaggin on a big glob of mud.

Some ado has been made about what might've happened had Shelly not shot Woolsey or Kelly had missed Francis. After all, Kalin only had six rounds to spend, and he did so on Old Porch, Egan, Kelly, Sean, Billings, and Shelly, in that order. Though Hatch was unable to put down Kalin, might Woolsey or Francis have done better? There is admittedly an applicable math that could find its way to seein Kalin gunned down by both those young Porch boys, but that is also the same kind of thinkin that asserts a gun is a gun and, if maybe dazzled some by such a monumental weapon like that Colt Peacemaker, misunderstands Kalin's gift. As he'd always said hisself, what he knew how to do never had much to do with metal or gunpowder. Kalin's prowess wasn't about sharpshootin or quick-drawin. It was about killin. Fer Kalin, it didn't matter what gun he had in hand. Likely he'd've picked up another, and Lord knows plenty were lyin around that day. Woolsey and Francis wouldn't've stood a chance.

Francis, though, was runnin. Might Kalin have spared him? It's likely. He didn't shoot no one in the back, and everyone he did shoot was shootin at him.

Woolsey, though, if he'd made it to the crick bed, might've found the fire in hisself to line up behind Hatch's .50 caliber. Maybe from there he could've taken the long shot and pulped Kalin's innards. But if he'd missed, if the next moment had found him fumblin with the unknown weapon, Kalin likely would've caught up with him and put him down without a thought. And it's important to say that durin that gunfight, Kalin was still in possession of almost no thought, certainly not like the thought required now to engage those thoughtless moments.

Kalin sure as heck didn't pay Woolsey no mind as he continued on after the horses. It took him some time too, but when he finally drew near, Navidad whinnied, and when he got even closer, her ears went flat, then straightened, then went flat again. Mouse swished his tail but neither horse moved off.

Kalin had no whispers for them. He was accursèd in their eyes. In his own eyes too. In fact the closest he got to them, and he near had to crawl to do it, was the ends of their draggin leads. Both horses tugged at once when they realized they was in his grip, though Kalin at least gave them the courtesy of his back as he hobbled toward them gateposts beyond the crick bed, where Tom still waited atop Ash, the brand still in hand, still held high, though no bright fire burnt there anymore nor flames of orange nor red either; more like a soft yellow possessed by its end, like a firefly's glow just before it winks out.

*N*ow *don't tell me you ain't cold as a well in winter!* Tom guffawed when Kalin finally reached him, Tom's grin near like a Cheshire cat given how faded the rest of him was.

And you can bet Kalin was cold. His teeth chatterin now somethin fierce, what no grit could stop. *My clothes are with Jojo and Jojo's gone.*

That would appear to be the case.

Is this here the Crossin?

It is.

Old Porch said that that land yonder ain't protected no more.

Tom laughed. *That's not how freedom works, Kalin. Or crossins. You should know that by now.*

Maybe he did, maybe he didn't; Kalin still nodded and then walked the horses right up to them gateposts, the last gate, the ninth gate, a number that didn't even cross his mind, wonderin instead about the fence that was no more, wonderin about the gate that was no more, wonderin about what these two would find on the other side. He unbuckled Mouse's halter-bridle then, and before Kalin could dare one pat on the shoulder, Mouse threw hisself away through them gateposts, buckin like he'd done the first time he and Kalin had met in Paddock A, only now his shadow seemed impossibly long, especially given the hour, and when he kicked the air, he seemed to kick the mountain.

Kalin undid Navidad's halter-bridle next, and she too avoided his touch. Like Mouse, she too cast behind her an immense shadow as she passed between them gateposts. And whatever great pain stabbed through Kalin's right side, it weren't nothin compared to what Navidad's departure did to him. He was suddenly gaspin for breath, his eyes stingin as he watched them two horses take off for the far wood line, and without ever lookin back either.

Had there been another way? Kalin would never know.

You okay? Tom asked.

No. You okay?

Not one bit.

Anythin we can do about it?

I don't think so. Just say goodbye.

Kalin nodded. *You'll head on through like Navidad and Mouse?*

Somethin like that, Tom answered, and though he didn't move, Ash did start pawin at the ground in a way that did not bother one granule of wet snow but still made clear that this great gold horse with eyes of green and a mane of white was more than ready to head on through them gateposts.

I mean still to find Landry's body, Kalin said then, now lookin around for Jojo.

I know it, Tom answered.

Wherever you get to next, will you look for her?

You know I will.

If you see her, Tom, tell her I miss her. So much.

The way you're lookin now, I reckon you'll get that chance yourself in about, oh, one minute. At least Tom's grin had survived intact, though it was a sad grin.

You tell her I love her, Kalin managed to croak out. Why was such a simple declaration so hard? Far harder than any trigger behind six rounds. *I love you too, Tom. I'm sure gonna miss you both.* Hot tears came out then, and weren't it just the worst timin too, or maybe the best timin, who can say?, because right then a gunshot cracked out, and when a heart is so gently bared as Kalin's was bared right then, why it don't even take a gunshot to blow it apart.

Old Porch had managed at last to drag hisself far enuf along to find another weapon, which in this case was that 9mm Smith & Wesson Model 59 with an aluminum frame, the very weapon that Old Porch had hurled toward Kalin, never suspectin that that vicious, deceitful boy was already armed and with Old Porch's gun too! Even through the waves of pain rackin his insides, Old Porch could see Kalin had made it out there beyond the crick bed with them two horses, just like he said he was gonna do, releasin them into the lands beyond, to his lands! Or his lands by tomorrow. Kalin was too far away unless Old Porch got lucky, and if Old Porch knew anythin, it was that on that day, luck weren't nowhere near his corner. He'd need a rifle.

And Hatch? Why his eldest boy was just standin there, gapin around like some window-lickin idjit. Maybe he had gone soft in the head. He sure weren't givin no thought to helpin his daddy any. Couldn't even stand lookin at Old Porch. And fer sure Hatch weren't doin everythin in his power to take down that Kalin March. Look at the big Porch hero! What a disgrace! The worst of his maggots! And yet he was the one left breathin! And anyways, as many Orvop folk will still tell you, Hatch, bein a Porch, should've at least known better than to turn his back on his dad.

It weren't an invitation Old Porch could refuse. He shot Hatch right between the shoulder blades. The bullet put holes in his heart too. But Hatch didn't go quick as you'd think. He dropped, stupefied, to his knees and then with a gasp rolled over on his side, facin his father, still gaspin, still fightin for life if only to have enuf so as to understand who this man really was, who sired him, who shaped him, and who on this Sunday, the last day of October, cut him down. Not that he got an answer. The very last thing Hatch seen of his daddy was that broke-toothed sneer of disapproval, disgust really, though it weren't the last thing Hatch seen of this world, his mind in that last burst of oxygen-starved panic and revelation had him holdin his darlin little sister before in the very end he was holdin his mother, who looked on him lovinly, in that way that bestows peace, in that way that promises there need be no aftermath beyond peace, in that way that assures you that even the errant will find in such peace absolute forgiveness.

Kalin weren't near as peaceful nor forgivin as he stormed back toward the gunfire, and gunfire there was aplenty, because in the end Old Porch had no choice but to try his luck. It's reasonable to conclude here, as some folks have, that Old Porch had in fact hucked Kalin a loaded weapon, evidence that he still had some creed befittin his pioneer roots; how Old Porch in the spirit of the Old West, especially as conjured up in the movies, was seekin a test of mettle, a gunfight befittin his stature as Winner of the West, fair and square. But Old Porch had never been fair and was hardly square. He'd pocketed that clip right after killin Kevin Moffet, his plan for Kalin and that Model 59 already well in place. And now, minus the rounds spent on Kevin Moffet and Hatch Porch, he had ten more, and he shot them all, each time linin up, steady as he could, the back sight with the front sight, right on Kalin, and each time missin, his breath failin him, his body failin him, his eyes failin him, his courage failin him.

Even Orwin Porch weren't immune in the end to the fear Kalin March provoked. All his boys lay dead around him, and he'd been right there to witness them deaths. He'd seen firsthand how Kalin had done it, effortlessly, a vision he was still tryin to blink from his eyes, like he also couldn't quit squeezin the trigger, even long after the last cartridge spat free of the gun. Old Porch clickin on emptiness like emptiness might grant him more than it had given him already.

Furthermore, as much as Old Porch tried to keep eyes on Kalin marchin his way, he was also now seein Kalin somehow pluck a weapon out of thin air like it was some awful fruit hangin there for only him to pick. Over and over Old Porch began seein the shot that knocked him down into these groggy shadows spiked with pain, and after that, with Kalin exhibitin no more exertion than if he'd been pickin lint off the lapel of a charcoal suit worn for mournin, he'd gone and done just what he said he'd do, killin Egan first, about the only one there who'd had a chance against Kalin March but still never had a chance. And, oh, if only these visions had stopped there, Old Porch seein Kelly fall, then Sean, with Francis somehow already down by then. And then Billings, who next to Egan had had the best chance of winnin a gunfight, killt too, an unholy spray of black blood flung off his backside, still stainin the air it seemed, even while Billings, who'd stood the blast, without even one step backwards, continued to keep fallin forward, over and over, and all while Woolsey somewhere kept shriekin, which no matter how loud he got didn't stop Shelly from fallin too.

And then it all stopped, what only one person could make stop, the boy towerin over him now, his body a fugue of pale light, like he was afire, Old Porch beholdin a pillar of flame, some avengin angel before whom Old Porch still refused to avert his gaze, though his eyes might melt from their sockets, and maybe some version of his eyes did then spill from their sockets.

Old Porch tried to speak, but his tongue failed him, as if it were suddenly burnt to char, ashes all, coatin his teeth, his mouth, his throat.

Kalin didn't say nothin at first neither. He didn't even bother to kick away that Smith & Wesson Model 59. He just headed over to Hatch, but it weren't the .45 he was after. That's what got Old Porch the most distressed, when he seen Kalin returnin with Hatch's cuffs. Well, maybe feelin them go on his wrists behind his back, renderin them big scarred hands useless, got him the most distressed. And Kalin weren't even done. After a little searchin, he found some rope that would do. Kalin weren't near as good with knots as Landry, but he'd watched her close enuf over these past few days and picked up a thing or two. He secured Old Porch's ankles and then hog-tied him lest he set fingers to the knots and got to walkin outta there.

Kalin said only one thing before he left: *If you live, they'll put you in a cage.*

Now why Kalin didn't right then put down that miserable cur is as you probably can guess still an intense and divisive debate. A good many rage that not doin so was a miscarriage of justice, and there's a decent argument for that given all that would follow. Others, though, frame Kalin's refusal to kill Old Porch as an act of compassion. Still, others are content to view it as Justice carryin out Justice. Whatever the conclusion, and there won't ever be one, not really, Kalin didn't give Old Porch one more thought after that.

Not that Old Porch even then figured he was defeated, and in the cochlea of his mind's ear he continued to rage for revenge, for survival, twistin this way and that amidst what remained of his grand design, until the restraints upon his person and the hole in his abdomen finally delivered him unto the company of gloomy shadowy breaths.

By the time Kalin returned to Tom, Jojo was standin beside Ash. Jojo had initially run off toward the helicopter and then, to get farther from the gunfire, headed east and in that way committed to a big circle that eventually got him headin north again, and then west, back toward Katanogos, toward where he'd been with Landry last, only pausin after he'd loped through the gateposts, comin to an abrupt halt right by Ash, maybe somethin familiar in the air there, maybe even bright with his Landry, or at least the love of her.

Kalin managed then to grab hold of the stallion's reins and even get into the saddlebag that held his clothin. He found their first aid kit too, which weren't much against a gunshot that kept robbin him of so much of his breath. Every cough now seemed the death of him. Needin both hands to handle what came next, he tied Jojo's reins around the ankle of his left boot. Gettin dragged, if it came to that, beat losin Jojo altogether. Kalin knew if he lost Jojo, he was a goner.

Kalin started with the wound, with great anguish pourin the anti-septic on his right side and then with equal anguish stuffin the gash with cotton and whatever gauzes he could find, and though the pain knocked him down twice, on the third try he managed to wrap tight around his rib cage the elastic compression wrap brought along for poulticin the horses. Kalin screamed often and chattered plenty, but in the end he managed to get it tied off tight enuf to hold. Puttin on his shirts and sweater was rough, but when he did at last make it into his Lee Storm Rider and had buttoned that up tight, Kalin felt somehow intact, even if, like many feelins, that was a lie.

And then, as it is whenever a great thing is done, the light of another life seeps in, and you're left blinkin in the new bright and always with the same questions: What have I done? And at what cost?

Was it worth it? Tom even asked then, his limpid face aflicker from the dim glow barely upon that strange brand.

Probably not, Kalin answered, adjustin his black Stetson.

You're probably right.

They both turned then to look for Navidad and Mouse, but them two was long gone.

I could've done so much more. Though maybe seein them off was worth somethin, Tom said, even as his glances were already scatterin away from any pursuit of where their friends had trotted off to, considerin instead the ground surroundin them. *See that there? It's like a shadow pourin out, like water overfillin a bowl.*

Kalin had no idea what Tom was talkin about.

Can't you feel it? Tom asked.

I feel only pain, Tom.

That's fair. Tom was lookin at them gateposts, beyond whatever toothless tranquility they were there to describe. *They're movin now, movin on through. There are so many. Animals too.*

Kalin did his best to spy somethin, anythin, but there weren't so much as even a stirrin blade of grass. Not that Beth Crown weren't there, Bayson Riggs, Cameron Eakins, Brad P. Hone, Robert Gaff too. Eden. Too many children racin forth. So many more. Animals too. Kalin did see the mule in the distance, trottin away in the same direction Navidad and Mouse had headed. Maybe the donkey and the mountain goat were goin that way too. Kalin weren't sure. Overhead, he saw a great white owl slippin away. And then, right close, Kalin beheld that great old elk they'd kept glimpsin along the way, now just standin there, waitin, payin neither Kalin nor Tom no mind.

Has Pia Isan gone too? Kalin finally asked.

She's over there. Tom pointed beyond the old elk at the brush where Kevin Moffet had gone off to relieve hisself.

What's she doin?

I think she's waitin for somethin. Oh lordy! Tom suddenly erupted.

What is it?

Never mind. Tom even shook his head. *For a moment there I thought Landry was comin this way!* He tried to smile.

Is someone else comin?

Oh lordy! Tom said again. This time he was smilin big and his voice was filled with glee, though that too faded quick, and Tom was soon sighin and shakin his head again. *I thought it was my daddy.* Then Tom started lookin toward the northern end of Pillars Meadow.

That'd be a heckuva thing, Kalin said. *Fer you. I'd hate to see my daddy headin my way.*

I'd love nothin more, Tom whispered.

You're lucky, Tom, even just in that.

Oh Lord! And now Tom just sounded plain grim. *There is someone, and Pia Isan's walkin right up to him.*

Who?

She's just handed him her ax-head! Tom just looked horrified. *And dogs are with him.*

Who?

Now she's comin back. She's with the old elk. See? They're headin off together. And indeed the old elk was now movin off, right through the gateposts. But Tom didn't keep lookin that way. *Kalin, he's ridin Cavalry!*

Who, Tom?

Oh, it's so awful.

Who, Tom? WHO?!

Russel.

O f course, Kalin didn't see no sign of Russel nor Cavalry, but unlike Tom he weren't so unhappy to learn the boy had the ax-head and was headed over to where Old Porch lay and with a men-ace Tom refused to describe in much detail.

Kalin untied then the reins around his left boot. Maybe not sur-prisinly, when he tugged on them, real lightly too, to head Jojo back through them gateposts, Jojo refused. Likely Landry's big beautiful blue horse weren't keen on doin anythin for Kalin, but Kalin didn't give up neither. He was determined to walk with Tom as far as he could. And maybe because of Tom, or more so because of Ash, Jojo finally let Kalin lead him. Tom told Kalin then that Ash was glad because he wanted Jojo beside him.

Kalin didn't know what to expect, maybe that Tom and Ash would just dissolve, but that weren't the case. They passed through them gateposts and then just continued on together like there weren't never no crossin to begin with.

The journey don't count unless we finish it, Tom said, finally stoppin.

Did we finish it? Kalin asked, suddenly unsure.

I reckon we did. Any light that was upon that strange brand of Tom's was now gone, with not even a trail of smoke announcin its departure. Tom considered it for a moment, like he could hear it talkin, and then, instead of returnin it to the scabbard, drove it into the ground.

I'd like to promise you, Kalin, that one day yet we'll gather round a fire and tell of things we didn't think to talk about when we had the chance. But you and I know that won't be the case.

Kalin nodded again. He still had more to say to Tom. He was sure of it. He'd take another minute. And though he weren't sayin nothin, Tom nodded like he understood. There weren't another minute though. And then without so much as a rub from Tom's heels, Chubasco started movin ahead like he was at last over every fence he'd ever meet.

Well, I'll be! Ha! I think I see Hightower! Tom suddenly exclaimed.

Give em heck, Tom. If Kalin had been on Navidad, he'd've at least made to give his friend a good thump on the chest, fer Landry.

Don't you know— Tom started to retort, the twinkle in his eyes ignitin into a laugh, his big white Stetson blown clean off his head then, though instead of grabbin out after it, Tom and Ash was gone, just like that, gone, along with the biggest grin Kalin would ever know.

So immediate and complete was the departure that Kalin staggered sideways, like the earth beneath his feet had suddenly veered away, wide and reckless, like some trailer on a semi startin to jackknife. Kalin fell against Jojo, who, similarly affected, had started to wheel around, toward the crick bed again, to where memory returned, beyond where the bodies still lay. Kalin weren't about to let go of them reins, but now he needed both hands, and not even they was enuf when it came to a great horse like Jojo with his heart set on elsewhere. No amount of tuggin, and fer sure no words Kalin could muster, were gonna make a difference. Only Landry could've managed any calm, and she was where Jojo was tryin to get.

Not that this dance lasted very long. Kalin was spent. Quick enuf he slumped to his knees, if still grippin hard the reins, addin in his teeth too, hopin Jojo might heed that, Kalin's last refusal. At least Jojo did heed the bit torquin against the side of his mouth, finally swingin his head around hard to face Kalin, lettin loose an irritated snort, the stallion finally comin to a halt but a couple of feet from Kalin.

Here stood Kalin's only hope: dear, dear Jojo, that great blue horse whom none could ride but Landry, not even her brother Tom. Kalin was hardly in any shape to dare a leap. He was still down in the mud. So he just sat back on his bootheels and told Jojo the truth, and Jojo seemed to listen: Kalin told him how, if he had to stay here, he would die here. Kalin was pretty sure he was gonna die anyway; it just would be nice if he was closer to Landry. He weren't even gonna ride Jojo long, just long enuf to reach the snow where Landry was buried. Maybe he'd even find her close to the surface. That would be nice to see, maybe for both their mommas too, for Kalin's momma fer sure, to find after so much violence inflicted by her only child that that same child had also found some meanin, and even if it weren't no happily-ever-after story, she might still take comfort in seein how he'd found someone good, someone kind, someone he'd come to care about deeply, who despite her ill-treatment by so many had heeded the love of her family and had thrived just the same . . . Landry, Landry, Landry . . . who was not only good and gentle but full of burnin sparks and funny on top of it and above all was one heckuva rider, maybe the best he'd ever known. Kalin wished he could've known her his whole life and now wanted nothin more than to have his dyin breath beside her, holdin dust to its promise that one day they'd together join the stars.

And the more Kalin emptied his heart with whispers like that, the more that great blue horse seemed to relax, until finally Kalin forced hisself to his feet. And just that took near everythin he had. Leanin then against the saddle seat and the fender, Kalin again reassured Jojo with more whispers. He had to lower the stirrup some, Landry's legs bein way shorter than his, and draggin his boot up nearly forced from him a scream. Jojo, though, didn't move a bit. Then Kalin took the deepest breath he could handle in order to do the thing that would steal his breath away, and with so much pain that even the thought of it was already whitenin his view, deprivin of definition whatever place his eyes sought out, with color too gone, along with sound, along with any sense of direction, the compass points gone fer sure, but also up and down, and likely Kalin would've just let go if it weren't into the arms of Death that he'd've fallen. Somehow Kalin managed to keep his boot tip in the stirrup, and then finally, with both hands white-knucklin the horn, even got through draggin hisself up into Landry's saddle, a far cry from the weightless way he used to get up on a horse but makin it just the same. And Jojo still hadn't budged.

Jojo even gave Kalin a few more breaths, what some say was a mercy and others say was the readyin for the comeuppance, before that stallion bucked so hard and kicked so fast and so high that Kalin didn't even feel much the throw. It was as if he was all at once just floatin, like he had suddenly become hung upon the air, untouched by any consequence, unmolested by any surface, scorned by both gravity and graveyards; here he would float forever; here he would just lie, now in the arms of a sky scrubbed clean of every cloud, its blue extendin an embrace that surrounded him as much as did the ground beneath him. And then that very same ground whomped him on his back, the backs of his legs, the backs of his arms, the back of his head fer sure. It weren't so bad though. Kalin had landed on a swath of mud that softened plenty his fall. Plus he'd been so delirious, so relaxed. Sure, he couldn't breathe so well let alone move much, but Kalin didn't care. With some relief, he knew he'd gone as far as he could go, and what good was arguin with empty when empty was makin it clear that you need more than empty to argue?

There's a Mexican proverb that says it's not enuf to know how to ride; you must know how to fall. More than a few folks have gone so far as to suggest that this here was the moment Kalin truly learned to ride. Too bad he would never ride again.

Kalin at this point figured Jojo was long gone, but when he opened his eyes, he was surprised to find that the horse had returned. First the reins had slapped him across the mouth, and then Kalin beheld Jojo's big, gray dappled belly. Next thing was a rush of warm liquid splashin Kalin's chest and face.

Somewhere high above Kalin imagined the peal of Tom's beautiful laughter.

And a piss weren't even enuf. Jojo then took a step forward, lifted his tail high, and let drop all the munificence that that big belly had to offer, right atop Kalin, glob after glob of steamin manure. Mouse would've been proud.

Chapter Twenty-Five
"The Ride"

I weren't dead. Not even close. And fer sure nowhere near the bottom of them awful cliffs, where I'd've been buried so deep, not even summer would've found me. Likely because of how I don't weigh so much or else because of how I first landed face down in that powdery snow, and fer sure because of the physics I'll never get straight, when the cornice or whatever you call that edge gave way, I was spinnin around and down like in a flushed toilet, if flung quick enuf off to the side. Now I weren't sent no great distance but enuf away to wedge me between the cliff and the base of them crazed trees that had embraced the slimmest and stoniest of beginnings, vertical timber rhymin the verticality of rock, you could say, and in that song of parallels creatin a space that kept me alive.

My tumble landed me on my belly with my face pressed down among the roots, which presented a gap that offered me not only a way to breathe but a pretty terrifyin view of the long fall that had awaited me, still awaited me.

At the start, with snow still pilin up on my back, I was screamin my head off, blood spillin out my mouth, with my jaw hurtin somethin awful, plus the shock of just gettin shot and then the fall and then slammin into bark and rock; well, all that did compromise my consciousness some. Fer sure, the gettin buried at the end, more and more snow buildin up on my back side, helped draw me down into a blackness no dream I'd ever known before or known since, and that's sayin somethin, has dared summon.

Egan had managed hisself one heckuva shot. I'll give him that. But its deadly accuracy was all for naught because, see, his bullet pierced through one cheek and went straight out the other cheek without so much as the tiniest protestation from my tongue or a single one of my beautiful teeth. I credit this astonishin good fortune to my family, and especially to my brother Tom, who throughout his short life, and even in his afterlife, had indoctrinated me into the benefits of mirth, that special exudation of amusement that ain't necessarily born of a joke or cleverness, and really is all about attitude, what finds wide grins in the absolute mystery and absurdity of existence, especially when it's ravagin you with no way out. When I'd seen Egan Porch through them unmeshed binoculars, with him behind his rifle ready to kill Kalin or me for no reason that ever made a lick of sense, why you bet I laughed at once, and I laughed hard. Kalin and Tom would've claimed it was also a scoff. Maybe. Regardless, I was smilin big, and my mouth was agape, and, yes, I most certainly was usherin forth a sound of delighted disgust.

Thanks to that, Egan's bullet passed right through my mouth like I weren't no more a ghost than Tom. Except for my cheeks. Them weren't ghosts and hurt with the fire of suns and bled bad, with the shock from gettin them perforations hittin me hard enuf to drop me from my perch. Sita Houtz, before dyin of Huntington's, liked very much in her final years to quote the poet Catherine Garbinsky in regards to this moment: *Not every girl survives the forest. Sometimes she becomes it.* I cannot speak much to what Sita Houtz was thinkin because I did survive that tiny forest, and not only that I survived because of it. And, sure, maybe even became it a little too. I still offer up to them trees my prayers of gratitude. I never did go back to that exact spot, shame on me, but I did spy it plenty from afar, once from the very same spot where Egan had stood to shoot me. Them trees are still there, still lookin like it ain't no big deal to live on the side of such a heap of rock, like they was cliffs too, maybe causin the cliffs to think they was trees. Somethin fer sure is goin on there that I won't ever fathom, but it never fails to make me smile.

Anyways, when I did at last emerge from whatever darkness had swallowed me, I was near cold as that darkness, even with my layers, my sweater, my warm green coat, and that poncho Kalin had fashioned for me out of our tarp. I weren't some rabid badger when I woke neither, though maybe there was some fierceness apparent in my hackin to breathe, like I'd been drownin, refusin to drown, for hours, though it might've also been but minutes. I didn't have a clue. The bleedin had stopped. Maybe it had froze up. My mouth, though, still remained a furnace of pain, and maybe that helped me to get to wigglin, like I could just wiggle out of the hurt too. I don't get everythin right. Heck, I don't even come close. But I'll tell you this: that wigglin did do me a world of good.

See, not only was that snow brand-spankin-new, but that rocky wall was faced so that there weren't even a hint of sun on it, meanin the snow was drier than the sand in that sandblaster at the Lee Garvey Shop. Soon as I gave it the meagerest movement, most of it just spilled away. So fast too, like time weren't even countin. I was free. And if that weren't just plain terrifyin.

As you've already gathered, I do not care much for heights, and as you also know, I can get all locked up. Stiffer than rock. Might as well invite lichens to come around. It was bad enuf havin to take in what lay below me, but at least with snow on my back I'd felt held down, like a big heavy blanket was on me. Crazy as it sounds, fer a moment I actually wanted the snow back. I suddenly felt too much like a feather. I was sure some puff of wind was about to loose me to the fall I'd just avoided. I clutched the exposed roots, I shut my eyes, and from my toes to my rosy nose, I did my best to out-stone stone. Here was worse than that final climb over the headwall. Because here I had no Kalin. Because here I had no Tom. Because here I had no Jojo. Here it was just me.

On top of that, I had to pee so bad. You'd've thought that with gettin shot, I'd've surely already wet myself. The opposite was true: I not only didn't pee myself; I couldn't pee myself. And let me tell you, I tried. I wanted so badly some relief, any kind of relief, but awful fear had me in its teeth and forbade me.

I tried callin out to Kalin then, at first in a hoarse whisper, then with a weak shout, which, given where I was, with the wind whistlin through the nearby crags, even rattlin these trees I was holdin on to for dear life, well, no sound I was gonna produce then was gonna get very far. The pain was somethin awful too. And then my cheeks started bleedin again, more dark red runnin off my chin, fillin my mouth with warm viscous stuff I kept havin to spit out. Not a pretty sight.

Still, I wouldn't give up. I even called out for Tom. Heck, I cried for my momma. As a last resort, I even cried out for Jojo. What good my beautiful horse could've done given my position, I can't tell you. Maybe to hear his neigh would've unpetrified me. I was just searchin for some spell to unspell the one I was under. Of course, nothin came out of such keenin. I'd never felt so alone, so abandoned. I seethed. I whimpered. I cursed Kalin's friendship with my brother that had led to this calamity. Why I even cursed Tom then, and when I remembered him tellin me to *Never quit!*, why I cursed him all the more. Let me tell you this: *Never quit* ain't words to live by. They're for the simpleminded who've never trespassed beyond what exhaustion can't offer.

No, it weren't my brother's words that saved me.

Beauty saved me.

That's right. That simple. And I know it sounds cheesy but all I had to do, what weren't gonna require even one twitch of a muscle, was to behold it. That is all. And that is all I did. Don't ask me how, though it weren't so hard. In fact it was the easiest thing I've ever done. Even easier than fallin asleep. I looked upon the glory of this place I'd found myself in, what I'd come to by way of malice and bad luck and also good old impetuousness.

I gazed down the rock wall. I caught sight of birds flyin across far fields of white and bronze. Who was I to refuse such magnificence? I cried some then, but this time for wonder over these roots by which I survived, which I still clutched, there for decades, maybe even a century. And in the thrall of this appreciation, I finally lifted my head.

A red squirrel emerged then from its drey, chaw-chawin and ricketin a song at me. What else could I do? You should know me by now a little. Why I ricketed right back! And we went on from there for quite a bit, until what was buildin up inside me finally had to let loose, and, no, it weren't pee, nor some savage cry against the pain still at my mouth and at my head too, none of which mattered anyways against this great heave of Nature of which I was utterly a part: I laughed. Just a small burst at first but also with none of the bemused condescension I'd felt toward Egan earlier when he had his rifle aimed at me.

And like that I was as whole as I'd ever been and in possession now of a grin that would never leave me; finally doin just like my momma and daddy had always urged me to do: smile, especially if I ever found myself in the jaws of adversity. And I was in them jaws now. And smile I did, maybe even a bit grander than Tom's, and you can bet he'd've cackled plenty over that claim but he'd've approved of it too. Forget the nonsense of the heart. The very pith of me was infused now with the great enjoyment that comes from just encounterin what is new, what is familiar, and both with the same curiosity.

Next thing I knew I was back on my feet, set loose, unlocked, and, yes, fer sure that was it, free. My limbs needed no commandments. I was agile and heedless. I'd even snatched up a pine needle to chew on while I surveyed the challenge that imposed itself upon me from above.

At first I was sure I was cliffed out. To my left waited the oblivion down which the snow from the broken cornice above had fallen, which chance and maybe some flailin had preserved me from. Above me, at least a dozen feet up obtruded a wedge of stone sure as any ceilin that I knew I couldn't get through let alone around. The way to my right didn't afford me even six steps before offerin up yet another flight into oblivion. No rock here was gonna save me. Instead it was the trees that came to my aid, slowly revealin a way out, with maybe a little help and encouragement from my squirrel friend.

I won't say that when I agreed with myself to try it, I didn't take more than a few breaths just sittin on my butt with my back pressed hard against the tree I'd chosen and my boots jammed even harder against the icy rock. Would the tread on my soles serve, or would they send me slippin back down, maybe to here, maybe all the way down? And if they did give me the grip I'd need, would I have the strength to get high enuf to that first branch?

I'll admit it didn't come easy at first, but I quick enuf figured out how to keep the ball of one foot wedged down against a toehold of rock with my butt and hands pressin hard against the bark and then without really that much effort bringin the other leg up, walkin it up really, as I managed then to improvise a shimmy of sorts, a scooch if you will, scoochin up my butt, and then doin the same all over again with the other leg, again and again, and so on, and in that way slowly walkin myself up.

My first attempt was the only one I needed. I got the hang of it pretty quick. It weren't so much the technique of it as the rhythm. I didn't question it either. I just kept goin.

The next trial came with the first branch, a big thick thing I would've easily sat on except it led nowhere, and I sure am grateful I didn't even slow as I passed it by. How easily I might've lost my nerve while restin on that limb, and then I'd've been really stuck, with no way up and no longer a way down.

The trial after that was just the appearance of a trial. I finally got above the overhang I'd so feared below, though by that point it was by way of branches that had become so plentiful, I had no choice but to climb them like rungs of a ladder.

Before they grew so thin that I'd start doubtin their ability to sup-port me, I moved outward toward the cliff only to discover that it weren't a cliff no more but a slope with plenty of small ledges and holds, and almost no snow where I was at, so that the next thing I knew I was back up to where I'd got shot, where, fearin that I might get shot again, I bid a last chaw-chawin ricketin to my red squirrel friend and skedaddled quick through the firs, limber pines, and bris-tlecones, pretty much slidin the whole way down to where I'd last seen Kalin and the horses.

They was gone. And that sure got me low, though at least now I could relieve myself easy enuf, right where I was standin in fact, with no thought to seekin cover. In my squat I could see the horseshoe tracks I'd follow next without much problem. This closest set likely bein Mouse's.

I still had no sense of time yet. To me it seemed like I'd been gone only a few moments, but I began to admit to myself that, okay, maybe I'd been away much longer. Only when I reconsidered where the sun was at now, not overhead but slippin to the west and reanglin the shadows on its way down, did I face up to the fact that quite a good bundle of minutes, maybe hours, had slipped away.

Not that I still weren't plenty miffed when I located where Kalin had mounted Navidad and rode off not only with Mouse and with that mule still trailin behind, but also with my dear Jojo! Kalin hadn't even thought to leave behind somethin edible. Though it weren't lost on me either how Kalin likely thought I was dead. He'd've known then to look after Jojo and see through his commitment to Navidad and Mouse. But I was still miffed. Kalin could've waited longer.

The way down weren't exactly as easy as followin some yellow brick road, though there was, thanks to the horses, enuf yellow snow to show that I was headin the right way. Just one step after another. Pay no mind to my throbbin face and a headache that was near pulsatin the vision from my eyes. So long as I could keep hold of the general commotion of hoof marks and manage the decline well enuf not to slip and fall, I was fine. Just one step after another. With a palmful of snow now and then for thirst or to help numb the pain. To come across some friendly rounds of manure sure cheered me on. The best cairns ever. I near started to skip.

I never looked more than a few feet ahead until I reached that stony rise in the middle of what I'd started to figure out was the Coyote Gulch Kalin had been tellin me about earlier. Here was where Kalin and Tom had also paused, risin up enuf above the trees to afford a pretty clear view of what I could figure out for myself was Pillars Meadow. I sure wished then I hadn't lost my binoculars in my tumble. It was still way too far away to see much detail, though I could make out the quakin aspens and birches I'd have to weave through.

Fer no reason I can give, even now, there was somethin unsettlin down there, and while I continued to squint, if only to try to grant my misgivings some kind of explanation, my tired eyes perceived nothin more than big patches of brown splotched with white.

I let it go, drawn now to the muddy melt goin on around me, a rattlin of thin rivulets runnin loose beneath and around big heaps of gray honey-combed snow. I drank from that melt several times, the bowls of my hands achin at once from the near-freezin temperature, my teeth hurtin almost as much as my cheeks, *Ow-Ow*, but, boy, did my throat welcome such refreshment. It was near good as food, warm soup even, if that makes any sense. I know it don't, but it did suffice me just fine.

My daddy's words came back to me then, good words, soft words, words full of love for me: *The roots of the trees and the rocks of the mountain show us the steps.* I heeded them just like he'd advised, findin soon enuf, by virtue of attention, the stairs I'd need to facilitate my passage down. Not that I was faultless. Several times my focus faltered and my feet skidded out from underneath me, my keister findin a mudslide, especially out on the steeper parts, with on one occasion my right butt cheek and forearm takin a heckuva lickin I knew would bruise awful if I managed to live long enuf to see tomorrow mornin. Not that the rest of me weren't also bruised and cut. But I weren't too hard on myself about my distractedness and knew my dad would've forgiven me too. After all, Egan and them Porches was still out there, maybe right close by. I had cause to be distracted.

I hung close to the shady side of the gulch where the trees were thickest, even if the goin was slower, mainly because the snow there had remained untouched by the sun and so was dry and so powdery that I'd sometimes sink down near to my waist and have to struggle to free myself and get back to where the sun was, where the snow had melted and compacted enuf to make progress once again possible. Not that these delays that found me pawin around and a few times near reachin the point of cursin were for naught. Once while in such deep billowy stuff, the nearby tracks of Navidad, Mouse, Jojo, and the mule too seemed all at once to become them, their forms suddenly on the air, their sapid smells on the air too, with Kalin so close I could hear his boots shift in the stirrups, hear Mouse's snort, a huff from dear Jojo, a whicker from Navidad, and off there in the darker shadows where there were no tracks, only the deep blue sparkle of cold in isolate, I could know as well my Tom and Ash.

As I got closer and closer to them quakin aspens and birches below, I also started to realize that I was doin a real dumb thing: despite the pain, I was whistlin and, more disturbin, had no recollection when I'd started to do so. It was just my instinct to reach out to Jojo, nothin melodious upon my lips, but rather how with the help of my tongue and teeth I could loose a sound familiar to my friend. Any fear of others down there I'd pushed aside. I'd been whistlin loud too, used my fingers, loud enuf to scatter crows.

By the time I'd reached what was a talus of sorts at the bottom, the sun had begun to sink behind Katanogos. A dark lavender shadow cast by such majesty was drapin itself down over Coyote Gulch and was now ahead of me, deepenin them woods borderin the meadow that soon enuf would know its icy consequence. And icy was an understatement. My breath was already frostin up again, and even the burble of runnin water everywhere had begun to slow if not completely stop. The silence that took hold then was awful eerie. I tried to hurry, but a few bad steps followed by a couple of scary stumbles on rocks that for the life of me hadn't looked at all slick warned me that I had no choice but to move slowly and endure this spookiness creepin in from every shadow around me.

Still, fear got to me, and I got stupid again, again whistlin as hard as I could for Jojo. But there weren't no Jojo nor crows even to scatter, and whistlin like that sure don't scatter shadows. In the silence that followed I found myself beggin the silence to assure me that my whis-tlin hadn't reached the ears of armed men.

When I finally got past the rocks, I lost sight of any horse tracks or cheerful equine cairns. I faced a bleak wall of dense gray trees with nowhere to go but through. Worst of all, I could hear ahead what I was sure was a man's gruff cough. Or if it weren't a cough, then it was at least a grunt or maybe even a groan. Only then did I realize the state of denial I'd given myself over to in order to get down off the mountain: I'd completely refused to think about Egan and the other Porches. I'd somehow, and foolishly too, sated myself with the notion that havin survived one shot, there was no way I'd get shot again.

Now, though, out here alone, I could see what easy pickins I'd be if that sound ahead was Egan Porch comin my way. I also knew any about-face would only head me back up a slope I had no energy nor will for. My only chance was to get myself as fast as I could into them trees ahead and find some thick-enuf birches to cower behind.

So I charged. I tripped. I got up. I charged again. I fell again, scrapin my shins bad. On the third fall, I bloodied an elbow. I didn't stop. I flew down the rest of that hill til I was weavin around them slender aspens, til I'd found better than them, better than even the multiplyin birches: ahead, a sturdy Douglas fir with ample width to hide me. Only a few dozen strides away. And I'd've taken them too, fast as I could, if I hadn't then set eyes on a ghost.

Clop-Clop-clip-Clop.

It approached gray and near bleak as the blue snow and ice this day's approachin end promised more of. *Clop-Clop-clip-Clop.* I ran then harder than I had before, *Clop-Clop-clip-Clop*, though not toward that Douglas fir, that's fer sure, *Clop-Clop-clip-Clop*, tears streakin out the sides of my eyes, *Clop-Clop-clip-Clop*, until when I'd at last flung my arms around his big neck, I was sobbin until I was near chokin on all I'd felt only to sob again, my tears runnin harder, until all that cryin was finally replaced by laughter, big snotty bursts of elation. I'd never felt so happy, and Jojo was plenty happy too, snortin, gruntin, and huffin as well, offerin me near the whole Jojo repertoire, throwin his head around, whickerin, tryin to butt me with his forehead, sideswipe me with them ample cheeks.

It was an added joy and relief to find him still saddled and bridled, and even if he'd dragged them reins some ways, and by the look of things stepped on them a few times, maybe even enuf to maul their integrity, I didn't care. I found our canteen and drank that down and refilled it back where the rocks still splashed with runoff, where Jojo could also drink. I found then some oats for him, what we'd packed away from Kalin's cache up above, but Jojo had already grazed hisself plenty, and while he'd never refuse oats, he seemed more to enjoy just nibblin at my palm.

In a saddlebag, I found the can of beans I didn't have the perseverance to figure out how to open. The cocoa powder was more to my likin. I just ripped open one packet and with slugs of icy water choked down the dry powder. My cheeks screamed, but so much sweetness flooded me with such caloric relief that for a moment the pain was outmatched and didn't matter one bit.

It was then in my search for more food that I discovered the Colt Peacemaker was missin. That sure painted quick two stories, not one of which was good. In the first one, the Porches had ambushed Kalin and managed to seize the gun, though not Jojo, who through pure orneriness and magnificence had escaped. In the second, Kalin hisself had gotten out the gun, and for no reason I could explain, that felt like the worst of the two.

If nothin else, it was good to be back in the saddle. Once more the future seemed possible, not that it was any clearer than when I was without Jojo, it's just that now I had company. We rode slowly and cautiously through them woods, choosin routes that kept puttin the densest number of trees between us and whatever lay ahead.

When we finally broke into the open, the late afternoon shadow cast by Katanogos had all but swallowed up Pillars Meadow, though it had yet to reach the crick bed. The strange mist that had risen up when Kalin had first stepped out onto Pillars Meadow had returned, now expurgated from the earth as if in protest over what it had had to endure.

Jojo and I had already spent a good deal of time just studyin from the cover of the woods the clearin ahead, lookin for any sign of movement. Not even a bird flew by. Nothin but stillness waited out there.

Once we'd decided to move forward, Jojo's head at once bent to the right and I knew what he meant: race this long meadow to the end, and from there keep goin south around the back side of Agoneeya, then back to home, back to his barn, back to my momma. I must say it was hard to disagree with him, Jojo's a smart horse, but I also knew that we weren't done with this place.

It was that unsettlin feelin of what was still waitin out there that kept me on alert. I slowed Jojo's walk even more, scannin all the time for Kalin, for Navidad, for Mouse, for the mule, for any of them. And then I seen them gateposts beyond the crick bed. They was still bathed in sunlight and surely seemed the only place I needed to reach.

So, of course, the first body took me completely by surprise. I near screamed. It was that fellow called Billings, face down, with a hole the size of a fist punched through his back. I seen the rest of them right after.

Francis still had his eyes open but he sure looked dead. They all did. Fortunately most of them awful poses were under that funereal mist. But I was still seein too much blood. Too much mangled flesh and shattered bits. Here and there I swear I even saw a loose tooth or two.

This was the work of men and only men. Here was how they would always view the Fields of the Lord: a stage upon which to settle their incongruities with no mind to them Fields let alone any Lord.

And I fer one was sure appalled and abashed, galled and terror-struck as I wandered and rewandered that awful stage. Though that weren't the whole of it either. I was curious too and when I came across Egan, shot straight through the teeth, I lingered some, you know, so I could collect enuf saliva in my mouth. Like Francis, Egan's eyes had stayed open too. I spat in them. And with great satisfaction. He might've once taken what he couldn't give back, but I sure was happy then to give him back what he couldn't wipe off.

To his credit, Jojo never gave up tryin to get outta there, shimmyin too often like a sidewinder, swingin his head with loud snorts directed toward home. Not that I blamed him one bit. Here was a place of horrors. And Jojo was no doubt also attuned to my own frights, which did keep climbin my back. Black crows now worried the sky as well, their landins hidden by the mist, though their caws, like unoiled hinges of gates swingin open and closed, what should've invited my fiercest whistle, I welcomed, grateful for their company. I'd take what I could get.

Of course, I was only lookin fer one thing, and I wouldn't stop til I found him.

Who I found first, though, was Old Porch, his condition mightily different from the rest. First off, his wrists was cuffed and his ankles roped, with both wrists and ankles hogtied together with knots I know Kalin learnt from me. Second, he weren't movin, but he weren't dead either. When I rode up on him, he heard me comin enuf to rock his head up some and squint my way, his teeth and lips rimed with dirt and black blood. If he'd once believed hisself alive, the sight of me seemed to confirm he was dead.

Landry! Old Porch rasped. *Are we dead?* Which he kept on askin in various ways. I could see that not just weakness but fever too was on him. And then abruptly he ceased to recognize me and let loose with his pitiful mewlin.

Where's Kalin? I finally asked him.

Old Porch nodded toward the crick bed and the gateposts, now at last caped in shadow. *But you won't find him there.*

Why's that?

He's gone back to where he come from, Old Porch sputtered.

Where's that?

Hell.

It felt good to have a reason to laugh, and I laughed good and loud too. *Where do you think we're at now? Welcome!*

If you think spittin on a dead man is satisfyin, and let me tell you it is, nothin beats tellin a livin man that he's damned and watchin him believe it. I surely am glad no weapon that I could see was within reach. I might have surely shot Old Porch right then. I still think about it: how easily I could've disregarded the lessons of the Heart and so easily suffered then the consequent afflictions for the rest of my life. It is a dreadfulness that humbles me often. I throw no stones, though now and then I still do itch to hold one.

W̱hen I finally did find Kalin, he also figured I was dead and so figured he was dead too. I didn't damn him though. What a beautiful sight to see him breathin, but how awful to behold him so fallen.

Is Tom back? he asked. Those were his first words to me. Not even hello.

You know you got horse manure on you? Those were my first words.

Jojo threw me off.

Sounds like Jojo.

Is that really you, Landry?

There ain't no other.

How are you alive?

Well, it's a story, and a squirrel's involved.

I'd like to hear it.

I was already off Jojo. Kalin was in a good lick of trouble, and that was just goin off his paleness, how I imagined Kalin must've seen Tom, who I was figurin, based on Kalin's initial question, was now gone. When I helped him sit up, his grimacin and groans were bad enuf, but then the wrong placement of my hand set loose some awful screeches. That's how I discovered the gunshot wound. The compression wrap was soaked through. Worse still, there weren't no more wraps left.

I rested him back down and returned to the dead in search of somethin I could use, but everythin I surveyed was either drenched in gore or wet with grime. I did my best to keep focused on clothes or items that might serve some medicinal purpose, but I couldn't escape them stiff, agonized contortions nor the vacant expressions that never did cease to haunt my dreams. I did happen across that Colt Peacemaker, just flung aside to the mud. I let it be, better instincts by now counselin my actions.

By the time I returned, I was sure Kalin weren't breathin. Thanks be to a cough! If pale can get paler, that was him. He'd not only faded more but somethin like a fever had started to sweat his brow and gloss his eyes. I got him sittin up again and then gave him water. I tried for a dumb moment to open the can of beans but quick threw that away in favor of that last packet of cocoa. That small spell of sweetness did seem to return a spark to Kalin's eyes. Then I did the best I could with his wound. In retrospect, there are at least a dozen better ways I could've gone about doin what I did next, but them dozen didn't present themselves to my mind, and so I did what I did. I first took off Kalin's belt.

No question, Kalin was a fighter, and we got him standin, though it was plenty obvious I weren't gonna be able to haul Kalin up onto Jojo. The best I could manage was to lower the near-side stirrup as far as it would go and lift Kalin's boot up. I was hopin that with his toe in and his hands upon the horn, I could use my shoulder under his scrawny butt to help him the rest of the way. And you can be darned sure I gave Jojo a talkin-to first: how he'd best keep steady and make no fuss, and how I'd be up in that saddle as soon as Kalin was situated. I figured Kalin's instincts would take over and, like I seen him do too many times to count, he'd float hisself right up onto Jojo's back.

Boy was I wrong.

To his credit, Kalin did try. To Jojo's discredit, he at once shied off quick and nasty, joltin Kalin's left boot from the stirrup and topplin him forward with a wheeze and an even softer scream behind clenched teeth. His black hat, which I'd refixed to his head, flipped off in the fall.

I'll admit panic overtook me then. I'd no clue what to do. If I left to get help, I had no doubt Kalin would be dead by the time I returned. In fact I was convinced that if I left for one more minute, he'd die on the spot. I had to get Kalin on Jojo.

But how?

So I gave Jojo another talkin to, real stern and admonishin this time, with just enuf pleadin to count. I talked and I talked. I told him all he had to do and what I would do and when we got it done, he'd get whatever he wanted. And then I said it all over again so he knew that the sooner we got goin, the sooner we'd be home. I didn't lie to him either. I made sure he knew that what all was ahead would depend on him alone. He was the one who would free us from this place. But none of that could happen until we got our injured friend here up in the saddle.

Then after lowerin his head and unlockin his legs, as well as whisperin stuff I can't remember no more, even now, though I know the music in my voice was about what I needed Jojo to do, me just lettin such instructions and pleas flow out like a song that only Jojo would get to hear, until, with one hand restin atop his poll, Jojo finally did consent to lower all of his big beautiful self, first to his knees, then to his belly, legs tuckin under, hooves near out of sight, and only then announcin with a snort that he was ready for what he no doubt viewed as the utmost indignity.

Kalin then, with his teeth clenched and with me at his side to help, got hisself crawlin over to that great blue horse. I might've seen a flash of fear in Kalin's green eyes then, fer sure I seen plenty of pain, especially as he began to haul hisself into the saddle. Jojo's ears went back right away, but I'd have none of that, stern once again, warnin the horse that if he wanted to mess with Kalin, I'd show him he weren't the only one who could bite.

I'd already cut one of the lead ropes to size. The longest one I'd run up the left sleeve of Kalin's Lee Storm Rider and then back down and out his right sleeve. The second piece I'd strung through his belt loops. And his belt, what I'd took off, I also put to use then. I cinched that across his chest, low enuf to go over his wound. With enuf pressure I figured his shirts, sweater, and jacket would help stop the bleedin and soak up whatever the gauze and wrap couldn't handle. I weren't wrong, though Kalin near passed out. Then I got myself into the saddle, right in front of him. It was a tight fit, but we was both small enuf to make it work. Then I tied them ropes runnin through his belt loops to my waist.

Kalin! I shouted to wake him. *I need you to hold on! I can't carry you. Only Jojo can do that, and he's gonna stand up now, and neither you nor me nor him are gonna wanna do this again.*

I'm ready, Kalin managed to croak out.

I didn't like havin Jojo stand with both of us upon him, but there weren't no other option.

Let me tell you, that there was one dicey moment, goin sideways, then forwards, then sideways again. Sure, Jojo was plenty pleased to be gettin up but not a bit happy about havin that boy on him. Still, Jojo managed it. I was sure Kalin was gonna topple off back side and take me with him. But he sure had steel, not that many will argue with that assessment. I felt it too in his arms around me.

I'd first thought to tie around my waist the rope comin out of his Storm Rider sleeves, but good thing we'd come as close as we did to fallin off backward, and that was just with Jojo standin up. Now I threaded the rope ends through the saddle's gullet and then back up and around the horn. Kalin was pretty snug up on me then, but I also knew if he started swayin back and forth, we'd be in one heckuva fix. If Jojo tried boltin, somethin he weren't ever inclined to do with just me, then our situation could turn real ugly real fast. Gettin hung up on a runnin Jojo would likely only get him runnin faster, and that might just kill us all.

I spent a little time tryin to figure a knot that I could release quick enuf if a fall was certain. It was a variation on a moorin hitch that I like, and I used that on the ropes around the horn as well as around my waist. There weren't no guarantee it would work the way I was imaginin it should in that worst case scenario, but it was somethin. With them loose ends tied, I gathered up the reins along with my newly made switch.

And, throughout everythin, I kept talkin to Kalin, askin him questions about his well-bein, demandin that he answer me, and brave sort that he was, he got out his *Yeses* and even an *I'm fine*. But I could still hear how he was already goin in and out of a dreaminess that wouldn't work for the ride ahead. We had a long ways to go.

The thing I had done with some forethought was find me a long branch and shave it down with Kalin's Swiss Army knife in order to create a nasty whip. It made a mean little snap when flicked right, and yes, I knew how to flick it right.

I wish I could say I never had to use it. I had no choice. We had but this one chance and you can bet we took it.

Jojo sure was glad when we at last fled that graveyard. The awful mist that had accompanied my intrusion on Pillars Meadow had only grown worse, more like a heavy fog now, and that made the way ahead pretty darned spooky, especially with the day losin its hold on the world, the sky turnin a darker and darker shade of violet.

A few folks have squalled about me takin off without a second thought for Old Porch. *Couldn't you have done somethin for him?* Too many have demanded.

My answer remains the same: *I didn't shoot him.*

By the time we began to find our pace, at least our first pace, the cold was pourin down off the mountain, down from the sky. I knew if we didn't make lower altitudes fast, we'd find ourselves iced in just like we'd been that Thursday night, only up here we'd have no mine to hide in. Fortunately the snow was mostly gone from Pillars Meadow by then, and the ground still had some of the warmth from the day left to spend. We kept to the center, Kalin takin to clutchin his wrists to keep hisself tight against my back. Sometimes, though, he'd grab hold of the ropes runnin out his sleeves to the horn, like they was railins. It weren't no easy feat for him, either, I mean given his condition. I could feel his labor and hence his awakeness in the way he made sure his arms stayed firm about me. No question his natural ability on a horse further helped us avoid a calamitous fall up there on Pillars Meadow.

To be clear: Jojo remains the finest horse I've ever known. He didn't just run. And while as far as I know he's never had no aspirations to join the company of them feathered creatures that make of the heavens a highway, Jojo, when he finally did let loose that Sunday dusk, his gait smoother than flight on the clearest day, why he barely granted the ground the decency of a kiss on the cheek. Job 39:19: *Hast thou clothed his neck with thunder?* Well, nothin about Jojo was clothed; we flew as thunder itself upon the earth, Jojo finally outrunnin the thunder, our passage dispersin the fogs, cryin birds from the tree, that great followin owl blessin us one last time with the sight of them white wings.

At the southern end of Pillars Meadow, snow once again rose up to greet us and forced us to slow and finally walk. A good trot was too much for Kalin. He didn't have the strength for any kind of postin. We ran when we could and walked when we had to.

The tracks made by the snowmobiles we used to our advantage. The lead sled was often followed by the second and sometimes the third. That created a pretty packed path, which, havin melted some durin the day, was hardenin up just right as the temperatures kept plummetin. So long as it didn't turn to ice, the surface proved substantial enuf for Jojo to gallop on. Not that it was that way all the time. We often had to slow and make our way over snowy mounds until we could find another long stretch suitable for runnin.

Too soon, though, a freeze fell upon those high reaches of the Katanogos wilderness. We didn't know it then, but up on Pillars Meadow temperatures would go south of twenty degrees Fahrenheit. The back side of Agoneeya, though, wouldn't get no colder than thirty-three degrees Fahrenheit. We just had to get there.

Of course, I knew none of these details then, but I could sure feel the awful freeze at our backs, threatenin with every one of Jojo's great strides forward to deliver us back into another terrible trap of ice, thoughts of that time in the Awides Mine settin my own heart gallopin. And so with the crunch underhoof continuin to alert me that Jojo still had some purchase on this terrain, you bet I kept urgin him on to find still greater speed. What I dreaded most was to suddenly hear the hard click of his hooves on ice, upon which dear Jojo then would likely lose his grip and, slidin pell-mell, send us all toward some cripplin end.

But Jojo's hooves never failed us. His great gallopin heart-song continued to sing out the music of his run, til his hoofbeats not only echoed through us but up in the many hollows, gulleys, and narrow gulches risin up on our right. Even when the snow shifted and once again we had to walk, there seemed to remain a reverberant roar upon the hillside, as if Jojo was still gallopin, and the mountain was still hearin it and was still rejoicin too.

Now many have pointed out, and not altogether incorrectly either, how such equine reveries might well have been the root cause of why I let us race straight by the helicopter, where I surely could've stopped and located a first aid kit and maybe even gotten through a call for help on the radio. It was a straight-up blunder. The thought, though, that there was even a helicopter to look for never even crossed my mind, nor either did a vision of that grounded beast pass before my eyes even once, at least in any way that I could recognize. And, yes, we must've run right by it. I got no excuse. Sure, it was dusk and there was that fog, but that still don't explain my blindness. The best defense I can make is that my focus was solely with Jojo and Kalin, in that order too, if you're askin.

That goes for the snowmobiles too. I could say that I never thought that some of them Porches had arrived by helicopter, which is true, and so never thought to look for one, which is also true, but, well, in the beginnin I was only followin snowmobile tracks.

It was only much later, after we'd already struggled down too many icy switchbacks, not to mention raced the limits of some longer stretches, that it dawned on me how I'd never even seen the machines. Of course they had to have been there. Hatch hadn't parked them so far off amongst the trees to be invisible to someone ridin by. If I'd've paid attention, I could've maybe found some extra supplies, though we now know I wouldn't have found a radio or even a first aid kit.

Fact is, even if I had spotted the three sleds, the riskiness of stoppin, dismountin, then managin Kalin down, whom I might never see back up in that saddle again, and all in the name of somethin I hoped would benefit us but fer sure couldn't count on, would at best have dangerously delayed us and at worst waylaid us to a night neither of us would've likely survived.

But we never did stop, and we did get far enuf along to keep ahead of the cripplin freeze already layin claim to the high ridges, as well as Pillars Meadow, though there weren't no outrunnin nightfall. Darkness always catches up. Or at least it usually does.

That Sunday night did happen to be special. Not only was there that clarity of sky alight already with the winks of stars, but up ahead the sun's mirror waited, if still hid behind the heights of Agoneeya, offerin up for the moment a ghostly crown, which, unlike anythin bejeweled or forged in gold, shed a halo so wide and so bright as to banish within its ring near all celestial history. And as if borne up by this vision, Jojo not only knew soundly the terrain we flew across but even lengthened his stride, hastenin his race, chuggin harder and harder, perhaps even further encouraged by the lunar fullness that had yet to reveal itself.

And, boy, when that big moon finally did come into view, I near had to squint. It had come once for Kalin and Navidad on Katanogos, and now it was here again for me and Jojo. We was mighty grateful.

But what the moon cast into blue light, like our path ahead, which mattered most, it also cast into greater darkness, such as those shadows that clung to either side of us, deepenin the woods, steeps, and crevices, grantin such lightless pockets, what I still know as defiant menace. Jojo didn't flinch. He'd outrun them all and jump the moon too if I asked him to, but I didn't ask him to, though I did soon have cause to use that painful switch.

I had no choice.

Not on Jojo, of course. I hope you weren't thinkin that. I'd never touch Jojo. And Jojo, who likely harbored within his great ventricles, an unreasonable strain of spite and vengeance, especially toward Kalin, for havin dared to seriously think he could ride him without me around, took great delight in my inevitable actions, so much so that he ran even harder fer sure, joyful with every acceleratin lunge.

You see, I'd started to feel Kalin losin his grip. His slump had both heavied and loosened at my back. I knew without lookin down that wobbles convulsed both his knees. His arms that had started off so purposefully pressed around my sides had gone slack. I didn't wait. I lashed out with that switch, landin sharp snap after snap, in the same way how you've seen in awful spectacle after spectacle a rider take to the flanks of a horse in the name of gettin past some unimportant line ahead, except my strikes stayed way clear of Jojo, landin instead on

Kalin's back. And given that he had on that denim jacket, sweater, and the like, I had to strike hard and repeatedly until not only did them cracks shout out to the vast wilds surroundin us, but, as I now and then landed a lash closer to Kalin's buttocks and once on the back of his neck, Kalin's own shouts soon rang out too in my ear. I answered him, you can bet that, with exhortations and inspirations I can't remember, or do remember just fine but don't want to share, maybe because I can't share them, don't know how to, like they suddenly seem like nothin I could ever understand, like they weren't even words, and certainly not mine. It was as if the likes of Mrs. Annserdodder's gods and goddesses, Apollo and Aphrodite, fer example, were gettin to say their piece then; unless it was somethin even greater than them, than any one someone, somethin entirely else, so that what Kalin heard, what roused him away from the shadow that grants none any escape, was far beyond anythin a young girl with a branch and a crazy amount of determination might mutter.

Soon after, I felt Kalin's arms regain their presence at my waist, knew his knees to have rejoined our balance, with Jojo's always-smooth canter findin a still smoother rhythm, until, upon reachin a long traverse over hard earth, Jojo extended hisself into even longer strides that by then became somethin more than a mere gallop, which, though it weren't flyin, still flew in the face of the laws of gravity. And it was somewhere along one of these runs that Kalin must have lost that big black Stetson, never to be seen again.

How now to measure the passage of time then, I cannot say. If Jojo's hoofbeats measured seconds, then time flew. If the silhouettes of mountains marked the minutes then time stood still. Once an imposin slab of night to our right, Agoneeya soon enuf became but a mild heave to our rear. We'd already put far behind us Tiffany's Vista atop the high bluffs of Yell Rock Falls, what as you know by now marks the terminus of Isatch Canyon. On our left, we'd also already passed Borrower Trail, which leads up to the Katanogos Aspen Roundup Route, and on our right Cutter's Crick Path, which by a series of too-strenuous switchbacks would've taken us over the summit of Agoneeya itself to the Orvop-facin side bearin that great letter that through the arrangement of them white-painted rocks still cries out on behalf of Isatch University, the city, the valley: *I*.

We, though, was headin down the middle of Shadow's Glen toward our only sane option: the Heathen-Slade Canyon Trail, which with a right turn traveled the south side of Agoneeya, windin all the way down to that shuttered mental institute, once called the Territorial Insane Asylum, where Tom and Kalin had discovered a patrol car often parked, which I didn't know about but would've welcomed, because we were so desperate for help, because with no help there we'd still have to make it to the Utah Valley Hospital, a good three miles from the trailhead.

In daylight, the Heathen-Slade Canyon Trail was a breeze. On mild weekends you'd find mothers pushin strollers at least some of the ways up. Night, though, was a different story, even with so much moonlight above. The canyon was really more like a narrow ravine and consequently robbed of any direct lunar guidance. Earlier, Shadow's Glen, unlike its name, had presented a pale gray-blue field just made for Jojo. In fact the brightness there had been so encompassin that we'd passed over it in what seemed like a breath with never a question about missin the Heathen-Slade Canyon Trail, which was obvious from afar and which we headed down with our hearts full.

I'll admit I'd given no thought to how the moon, like some protective deity, might abandon us there, but that's exactly what happened. We made the curve at a good gallop and at once were plunged into shadows. Ichabod Crane wouldn't't've been caught dead here. Even the Headless Horseman would've fled. But we had no choice.

To make matters worse, while the snow along the way was mostly gone, the daylong melt hadn't gone on near long enuf to shed all the water. By dusk a chill had already filled that deep ravine, funnelin a colder draft from the higher elevations down toward the valley. Thus by the time we were upon that isolated and dark path, the temperatures had dropped below freezin. It was walkable, sure, but it was also icy as heck, and while there was nothin more challengin than lazy serpentine turns, there were still plenty of spots where even on foot an incautious hiker could slip right off the trail only to be halted too soon by a slope of jagged rocks certain to savage whomever wound up in those sharp-edged jaws.

And that still weren't the worst of it: we was near out of time. To his monstrous credit, Kalin had kept answerin my lash with more exertions than any mortal could ever conjure, but now instead of participatory shouts, my ear began to fill with just his ragged breaths. They was an awful pronouncement of his decline too frequently disturbed by hackin coughs. What I could not know then was that his lung, nicked by the shatter of ribs thanks to the bullet, had durin our ride been more seriously ruptured, causin still more blood to breach various anatomical barriers and even more profusely enter the lung itself, thus further deprivin Kalin of more air as well as addin even more demands on his already strugglin heart. What I did know, though, was that if Jojo went any slower, we weren't gonna get Kalin to where he needed gettin to in time. It was a race from here on out. One go. Just straight ahead fast. No doubtin the now. No lookin back.

And so Jojo ran.

It's for this obvious reason that all what you and I have shared til now, to our enjoyment, some parts at least, with other parts provin challengin, and maybe even too hard, or at least too long, requirin your own patience, your own perseverance, endurance, determination, especially given some of the bloodiness here, the melancholy, the outright sadness, why it sure makes sense that our journey be called somethin more than just *His Ride* as was suggested by that snippy little Celia Mineer, born in Orvop in 1966, wed to Keith Lohner in 1987, dead in Orvop too, her in 2012, him in 2038; Celia her whole life defendin this title as worthy of the sum of it, with the *His* there laudably referrin to Jojo, with Jojo's last run bein the central event, if also encompassin Jojo's run up Aster Scree, up the Upecksay Headwall of course, as well as down to Pillars Meadow. Celia Mineer never did care for folks pointin out how *His Ride* meanin *Jojo's Ride* didn't really make much sense, because it weren't like the horse was ridin anythin other than maybe hisself. Is that what she meant? Because her title seemed more to suggest Kalin's ride, and as we all know, Kalin weren't doin much ridin at the end either. Celia Mineer usually told such objectors to shut their pieholes before stompin off. She weren't the only one either to proffer up possible titles intended to encompass this history. Other tries include *Kalin's Gunfight* or *Shoot-out at Pillars Meadow* or just *Shoot-out* or just *Pillars Meadow* as too many folks too incompetent to name chose to sometimes refer to our journey. Or even just *Kalin* as that dagnabbit fool Harvel Kurst once dared to suggest. He weren't born in Orvop, but he died there goin over the handlebars of a bicycle in the spring of 2041. The title that prevails, of course, that splendid summation of everythin, well, you can guess it: *Landry's Ride*. It's so obvious, ain't it? Just one slip, that's all it would've taken, and all would've been lost.

But we never did slip. Instead Jojo just floated. His eventual pace, which with every placement of each hoof succeeded in crackin through the black rime, granted him enuf momentary purchase to keep propellin us safely forward. Even on the wide turns, his hooves not even briefly skittered on the slick ice.

We flew down past those last shadows imprisonin faceless shades likely never brave enuf to greet their own deaths with proper salutations and so in turn accept a way that existed free of perdition, purgatory, the dream of somethin better, like so often in life, still refusin that chance, that moment available even now to change it all: that personal journey and crossin. Fer sure Jojo, me, and Kalin all heard the gnashin of their angry resentments for both the journey we'd begun and the journey we'd dared to finish, me answerin their wrath with a bit of song then; I'd one day, one time, and one time only, confide to Mrs. Annserdodder how I was Orpheus then and Kalin was my Eurydice, whom I did not betray with a backward glance, only the lash.

And I never could stop lashin Kalin on that ride, but only when I needed him to return, to respond to my own violence, because let's call it what it was, him each time answerin me with at least his physical participation, of paramount importance, without which we would have disbalanced Jojo so badly to cause him to fall and so become the fall of us all.

However I might view myself, and I remain pretty fond of myself, I still ain't nothin compared to Jojo, who minded neither the perils of our path nor the bitter and beleagured spirits clawin after us. The storms that had harassed us from the start Jojo now incarnated, a roar and blast down that narrowin place of mountain walls, until suddenly we were through, we were away. There was the dark institute, there was the empty parkin lot, void too of any patrol car, with not even one friendly light burnin there for our return. Nothin waited there for us but three more miles of paved roads and sidewalks.

Though it's true that that night was October 31, the Church as a rule generally encouraged abstainin from all such masked and sweet-fiendin activities when Halloween fell on a Sunday. Consequently the celebratin, as was practiced, had already occurred the night before, with all the storm-harried trick-or-treaters long since done with their door-knockin and candy-grabbin. In other words, the streets of Orvop were deserted, especially at that late hour. Not that there weren't a few rebels out and about, and they would remember what happened that night for the rest of their lives. They was the restless, most of them young and lit bright within by what no church or dark canopy of Doubt could defeat or even dim. They were unbounded, wanderin them quiet tree-lined streets, alone or in small groups, some with a purpose, some costumed with no purpose, just dressed up as ghosts or vampires, some as witches, smokin cloves, brown-baggin spiked sodas, makin out, dreamin from second base of third base, listenin to their Walkmans, just tryin to get out from under what they thought others had in store for them, tryin to break free, or on that Sunday night just tryin to catch a break.

And they did get a break, especially from private introspections and inventories of personal well-bein, or more likely personal distresses, them thoughts or exchanged murmurs suddenly interrupted by the sharp clatterin on pavement, the chest-thuddin thump of a full-out gallop across a park that would enhearten even the dead: the palest horse, for most an apparition, a ghostly blur, rendered all the more definite by its outtaplacedness, all the more real by this incongruity of such mesmerizin haste in the face of so much stillness and torpor.

And that's only them that witnessed our final run from afar. Them who was closer beheld somethin far more terrifyin. Remember, I was shot through both cheeks and by then was more than just spittin away clots of blood, while behind me Kalin kept coughin up blood, and he was coughin ahead too, right over my shoulder, which mostly just wound up splatterin my face and chest, spatterin Jojo too, makin of him a creature beyond his simple name, if even *creature* is the right word to describe so great a fury set free upon this world.

Try it for yourself: take a deep breath and picture yourself on a park bench or maybe pacin an equally dark sidewalk listenin to U2's *Boy* or *Destination Unknown* by Missin Persons. Find yourself so stupidly young that you're already mournin a life that has yet to begin. Now imagine yourself startled, lookin up to make sense of such a racket, beholdin then our awful trinity as we passed under a street lamp, or flew out across stalled traffic at the intersection of University Avenue and 800 North, or raced hard across the grounds of Orvop High and from there across 200 West, tearin across Fox Field, where some drunk ghouls were crouchin and at once spat out their wine.

None of that, though, compares to what happened next, what I can't no more claim with an *I*, what with me bein so many years ahead and with a perspective, however better informed, also whittled heavily away by time's humblin blade. I am no more her then than she is anymore me now.

Landry, see, was somethin else: you might say as possessed as Kalin had been up there on Pillars Meadow. Here she was carryin out this impossible ride from start to finish without so much as a hitch, never a hint of givin up or ever laggin, her unearthly focus born of a place I can't in all fairness reprise let alone imagine. It burnt through her, through Jojo, through even Kalin, the three of them held in a blood-drenched moonglow all their own, with this moon reflectin no sun we know of but a star all their own, ablaze at their collective core, as they heaved out across 300 West, upon the hospital grounds, more and more thunder followin behind them as Landry, between grittin her teeth and spittin blood, at last felt Kalin go lax, beyond either revival or redemption, and so let loose a terrible shout, a roar some folks who were there still declare, so penetratin and terror-inducin that it hiccupped more than a few frail hearts that night as this horror show galloped up the wide, loopin driveway toward the trauma center, not slowin neither at the entrance, not that Landry by then had any chance of slowin Jojo, Jojo havin long ago internal-ized their aim, maybe before any of this had even started, the bit held hard in his great mouth bearded with so much foam, his wide nostrils thick with vapor, surely defiant smoke, surely smoke born of flame, battle in his hooves, war in his strides, as they charged up that ramp and through them glass slidin doors, at last in the entrance area it-self, where nurses scrambled aside and expectant patients with fevers, busted fingers, or discomfited bowels cowered in their waitin chairs as that great blue horse hurtled into their midst, hooves skitterin on the floor, legs splayin in distress with the subsequent slide across the hard green-and-white tiles, but towerin still, towerin ever, fire terrible in his eyes, a little girl on his back, death at her back, a collective appari-tion of blood and rage, carryin between them but one last shot at life.

Some
of What
Happened
After

Old Porch survived. For a moment folks even got to callin his recovery The Miracle at Pillars Meadow. After Whipple surgery but before she succumbed to pancreatic cancer, Annette Kaplar whispered from her chair that when indulgin in such descriptions it was a good thing to recall Ralph Waldo Emerson, the nineteenth-century New Englander, who warned how *the word Miracle, as pronounced by Christian churches, gives a false impression; it is Monster. It is not one with the blowin clover and the fallin rain.*

Not that such nomenclature stuck around for long. That Emerson fellow was right: very quickly this sense of the monstrous began to rear its head until by and large the Orvop populace took to The Massacre at Pillars Meadow as the preferred title for the events that had transpired up there on Katanogos that Sunday.

You can bet that those who didn't know Old Porch marveled at how he hadn't submitted to the cold and the mud that should've swallowed him up, bones, last breath, and all. Those, though, with some knowledge as to who Old Porch really was weren't the least bit surprised. Orwin Porch livin through the worst hardly went astray from the quintessence of his character. As Darin Burdelong would claim durin the week that followed the gunfight, Darin bein a longtime Orvop citizen, now residin beside his ancestors in the Spanish Fork City Cemetery: *Orwin Porch was wrought out of the crucible of brute biological survival, his forebears a testament to that quality of persistence, if not a single one of his progeny.*

How, though, Old Porch did muster forth from that fast-freezin blood-drenched place deserves some scrutiny. Fer sure, Landry Gatestone would never have let drop a word about his condition, and she didn't, at least not at first, which pretty much put her actions in alignment, however briefly, with those murderous instincts she'd flirted with earlier. Nor had anyone noted the absence of the Bell 206 LR. Custom Enterprises had complete confidence in Kevin Moffet, and there were no reservations for any of its helicopters until later that week. Kevin Moffet's failure to return that afternoon was neither remarked upon by the company nor by anyone at the Orvop airport. Truth was, not a single person commented on the missin helicopter or the missin pilot until the carcasses of both were brought from the mountain. No police aviators either, still surveyin the wide maw of Kirk's Cirque as well as the abuttin regions of the Katanogos massif, ever sighted the Bell 206 LR let alone the many bodies strewn in a wide arc around that still-pantin patriarch.

So how was it that Old Porch was discovered in time to save his cussed skin?

Fact is, it was none other than Kalin March hisself who, before flat-linin, managed to cough out that Old Porch was still of this world, and he'd done so not even a breath after tumblin into the arms of Angels, thus refusin this world, by which I mean mine, and at the same time bequeathin to us a mystery that would forever, or at least so long as time endures, remain unsolved, as any answer, if not already heart-inherent, surely not found elsewhere, like, fer example, in some fantastical repository of solutions extant beyond the frames of Life.

Might as well ask the horses, some wags have put forth, which in fact ain't such a bad idea, if Fury had not only muted their voices but also plugged their ears and spiked their eyes. Not that we shouldn't keep askin: why did Kalin March, already so strangled on blood and pulmonary gunk, not to mention eviscerated by the kind of mean exhaustion few can ever recover from, still go that extra length to spare Old Porch?

He's still alive up there, Kalin had coughed out, splatterin his lips further with blood that looked blacker than oil in the pan of Evan Gatestone's Chevy truck when the engine seized mid-race and likely proved the decidin factor in his untimely death.

Who's still alive? one tremblin Angel had inquired.

Old Porch, Kalin answered before dyin.

How's that for your last words?! *Old Porch!* And, yes, you can bet your bootheels that more than a pinch of attention's been given to that double-syllabic utterance.

Fer sure, even the Angels had no easy time makin sense of Kalin's pronouncement, which received no more clarification than his ashen complexion, which at that moment finally did best Tom's. In fact Kalin's speech was deemed senseless even if it was also heeded.

Of course it was heeded. Nobody at the Utah Valley Hospital was blind to who these kids were. Even if they'd missed the news, they knew the names. Once someone declared that this here was Landry Gatestone or Kalin March, why then those pronouncements swiftly spread throughout the buildin and beyond. Only the three surgeons, Dr. Davis Esplin, Dr. Diana Whitney, and Dr. Quincy Rowe, had escaped entirely the contagion of such news and gossip, nor were they even slightly interested in such proliferatin declamations. And in fact it was their stalwart deportment that goaded the rest of the hospital staff to honor their professional and Hippocratic duties and so attend well and closely the needs of the injured.

The police arrived at the hospital pretty quick. And they were needed. Or at least someone with authority was. Landry weren't done kickin up a commotion and while she hardly posed a threat to the orderlies surroundin her, her stallion was another matter.

Right soon as Kalin was taken from her, Landry had no one other than her dear Jojo, and she flew back to him like the breathless heave for air, orderin whoever was at hand, in that garbled way to be expected of someone with holes the size of golf balls in both cheeks, to bring warm water, to bring towels, to bring a squeegee, to bring blankets, which more than a few folks tried to deliver, and not all of them even employed by the hospital either, includin one patient with a busted wrist; that would be Carly Bunningham.

Landry first sought to soothe the great horse right there in the ER admittance area, with water from the fountain, sips delivered care of her small palms, before eventually transitionin to a silver bowl shaped like a kidney thanks to one of the nurses, Jenny Frampton. Out in the parkin lot, Landry relieved Jojo of his saddle, bit, and reins; then, after securin a lead rope to the halter-bridle, she'd rolled up one of the by-then-delivered towels and after givin it a good soak in lukewarm water, also recently provided, proceeded to gently sponge the neck and back of that extraordinary creature. Landry didn't stop either, offerin long comfortin passes across Jojo's still-heavin chest, under his belly, around his shakin legs, extra tenderly there and still only above the knees, as down closer to where both hoof and earth alike still trembled, too much pain waited.

Anyone fool enuf to approach that pair, especially unbidden by Landry, got warned off quick enuf by a flyin kick. No orderly there was so dull in the head to ignore the immense power astir there in them mortalizin hooves. Mostly they did their best to help little Landry as she continued to stroke and massage great Jojo back into some state of calmness. One someone nearby swore to fetch oats at once, but he failed so completely that he deserves no mention here given the deserved lashin he also escaped. There's been enuf blood. And Jojo's legs were still spattered with all their blood as well as his own.

Landry's momma, though, did not fail either Landry or Jojo. Allison too in the months ahead helped oversee Jojo's return to health, as he survived an episode of what was on one of those early nights diagnosed as lactic acidosis only to weeks out recover from what was never confirmed as laminitis. Farrier Terrence Olsen chalked up Jojo's podal misfortunes to runnin too long and too hard, but he also swore that Jojo would live to run again. And Terrence Olsen was right, though it did take a long time in a clean stall constantly refreshed with deep shavins plus plenty of love as well as carrots, if there's a difference between them last two, especially when it was Kalin's momma deliverin the carrots.

Allison was with Sondra when the phone rang. News of the children's arrival had already spread like lightnin, but with the police alerted first, Chief of Police Beckham had done the right thing and called Sondra at once. Suffice it to say the mothers didn't waste no time. They came tearin into that hospital parkin lot, Allison at the wheel of Sondra's dark blue Bronco, that last turn heatin tire rubber enuf to spread it like molasses on burnt toast.

What they beheld at once were several officers surroundin Landry and Jojo, though like the orderlies had already learned, they was keepin clear of that big stallion's back side, which weren't so easy given both Landry's and Jojo's near-numinous alertness, spinnin around at every impudent incursion, hooves snappin out fast and hard as you'd expect from the mountain breaker Jojo had become. Not that Officers Poulter, Mildenhall, or Unga had anywhere near as much fight as them two, their encirclement finally at a standstill, them mostly yellin at the various hospital staff, also positioned about the perimeter, to do what they was already doin: standin back.

Sondra Gatestone knew just what to do. She saw it at once in her daughter's actions, in Landry's devotions really, and while Allison had the head start runnin from the truck, Sondra lagged behind to grab from the flatbed a near-empty bag of COB, that combination of corn, oats, and rolled barley that she always kept on hand for their horses, along with two mealy carrots from a few days back.

That sight, not just of her momma, at long last, but the sight of her momma knowin what mattered most to her heart, no matter her own appearance, her wounded flesh, her blood-drenched body, why that filled Landry with a spirit that not even the long years yet left to her could ever diminish. Even Jojo sensed it, risin out of his own exhausted ire to behold a familiar and dear face racin toward them.

There's a real miracle for you, that Landry and Jojo were by this point even standin. A kind nurse, Cherry LaFranco, had at least gotten a blanket over Landry's tiny shoulders. Not that that was enuf. The night's awful cold had hardly ceased its relentless savagery, Landry's form already so dwindled and desiccated by five nights of even worse conditions, with dwindlin food hardly compensatin for caloric loss, and that weren't beginnin to factor in her wounds and exertions required for that extraordinary ride. Only her absolute devotion to Jojo kept her upright, likewise for him too, Jojo's devotion to Landry.

Your friend said Orwin Porch is alive, Officer Mildenhall had barked at Landry before either mother had raced up. *Is that true?*

Landry had nodded, not just because she knew it to be true but because she also knew that the only one who could've made that fact plain had to have been Kalin hisself.

In the Katanogos bowl? Officer Poulter had followed up with, tuggin some on his blond moustache.

Kirk's Cirque, Officer Naomi Unga had corrected Poulter.

Landry knew what they meant and had shook her head both times.

The corrie then? Officer Unga had tried to clarify. Like the other two officers, she too was still under the impression that whatever had transpired up there must have taken place west of the Katanogos summit.

But once again Landry shook her head. Jojo did too, a big swing back and forth, in his case to once again warn everyone to stand back.

The back side, Landry had finally volunteered.

The back side? All three had pretty much repeated, in understandable confusion too. And disbelief.

On the other side of Katanogos, Landry had then made clear.

You mean on the east side? Officer Mildenhall had asked.

Down off the summit ridge, there's a big meadow, Landry said then, with plenty claimin ever since that her response was because of the Church and the teachings of charity and Christian forgiveness. And, sure, while some of that may be true, there was also somethin else in Landry's tone that ticked toward a darker and more menacin reason.

You mean Pillars Meadow? Officer Unga had asked. She alone out of the officers had trekked there once before.

Landry shrugged. *He's there. They're all there.*

Officer Poulter figured Landry was disoriented and of unsound mind. To her credit, Officer Unga did call in the doubtful claim, which was passed on through the Orvop Police Department and soon enuf got over to the sheriff's department. By that point Sondra's sprint had reached its conclusion, her face unable to quiet its expressions of horror and distress before so much blood, her poor baby girl!, even as her heart grew more and more assured by the sight of her youngest still standin firm, and before such authorities too!, standin tall beside the magnificent Jojo. Landry's torn visage in turn ignited at the sight of who, without objection from Jojo, had at last reached her, enfolded her in arms that told her everythin she needed to know: she was no longer on her own and it would be okay and she could at last cease these efforts to keep fightin and it would be okay. It would be okay.

Momma! Landry said with the softest sigh, a far better last word, uttered forth too like a breeze sounds just before it gives up, or is it gives in?, producin even, and this despite the tatters of her cheeks, a smile so beamin as to outglow even the loftiest of saints before she, very much like Kalin had done, collapsed.

There's a magical moment that followed right after this. Sondra, of course, had raced inside the hospital alongside the gurney bearin the only child left to her. Allison March, though, while she kept pace with Sondra, too quick found herself barred from all access to her boy, and given how the admittance area was clotted now with law enforcement and hospital staff as well as a risin number of oglers, she quick retreated outside again to catch her breath and in some privacy attend to her own scaldin tears of rage.

Not thinkin much on it, she beelined then to the stallion like she was called to him, even if Jojo at the moment was once again ratchetin hisself up toward ear-pinned fury. The orderly that had managed to grab hold of the lead promptly dropped it when that fierce beast had turned his way, with all around then figurin the horse would bolt.

But Jojo did not bolt. The great horse seemed to take no more than a brief sideways glance at the approachin Allison March and near at once ceased his angry cloppin on the blacktop. Kalin's mother came right up to him, at once strokin him with gentle whispers, the same whispers with which she urged the same orderly who had dropped the lead, Juval Harmon, to seek out in the hospital cafeteria or any nearby eatery some apples. Juval Harmon did not let Jojo or Allison down, returnin with not only apples but fresh carrots too.

Allison March stayed beside Jojo, offerin up what remained of the corn-oat-barley mix from Sondra's bag and soon small pieces of the fruit and vegetables. There weren't much left, and the more Jojo ate, the hungrier he got. Without havin to ask, Juval Harmon slipped off again, this time managin to secure a box of oats. Upon returnin, however, he had to pause. And he weren't the only one there in that parkin lot stunned into wonderment by the sight of Allison March, now sittin on the ground, finally done with racin fer the hills, with that now-blanketed big horse, so recently so terrifyin, lowerin his head to where Allison could rest her forehead against his, her palms set upon his wide gray and speckled cheeks, caressin them. Both their eyes were closed. A mist of their slow breaths wreathin their quiet. Juval Harmon would later remark that *it weren't somethin easily believed.* Landry, if she'd been there, sure as heck wouldn't've believed it, but also knowin so well Allison's only child, Landry might not have been that surprised either.

You can bet both Chief of Police Beckham and Undersheriff Jewell were a mite bit skeptical when they heard that Orwin Porch was all the ways up on Pillars Meadow. However, a terrible chill began to run through them, with that chill runnin through more than just them too, when not a single Porch boy could be located to deny the claim. Egan Porch's neighbors volunteered up how they'd seen him with Hatch and Kelly, loadin up a trailer with snowmobiles.

By that time, the various planes commissioned to provide surveillance were grounded as well as hangared. However, one brave pilot, Scott Edwards of Lehi, took off by hisself and revisited the dark mountains, and though he later credited his success to the clear weather and the big moon above, he had skills aplenty to find his way beyond the great heaves of flight-endin rock, where he not only spied the grounded helicopter parked on a patch of blue snow but also flew low enuf, turnin sharp enuf, to permit a glimpse of somethin terribly askew down there, or as Scott Edwards would describe it over the radio: *like burnt-up matchsticks tossed on a white tablecloth.*

While what waited below would remain obscured for a little longer, a quick inquiry over at the Orvop airport, and this thanks to maintenance worker Hal Kopeck, who fortuitously was workin a double shift, confirmed that Kevin Moffet had indeed flown off with Old Porch just before noon and with a *fair number of them Porch boys.* That's what finally got a medic helicopter dispatched.

It was pilot Colby Foster and the accompanyin EMT, Lorenzo Swapp, who were the first to describe the awful scene awaitin there. The transcript of their discovery would give plenty that night, and on many subsequent nights, more than enuf shivers. But just as Kalin March had said and Landry Gatestone had confirmed, Orwin Porch was found, and despite his wound and the many hours that had already slipped by in the bone-shatterin cold up there, him bein near stiff as Pockholz wood and plenty blue too, Old Porch still had a pulse.

At about the same the time that pilot Colby Foster and EMT Lorenzo Swapp were securin Old Porch in the helicopter, Landry Gatestone had gone into surgery.

The miracle of her injuries was how much could've happened but hadn't. Not a single tooth was nicked or jarred out of alignment. No part of her tongue either had been kissed by the lethal projectile. Try pokin your own cheeks with an index finger on either side and then open your jaw just wide enuf so that any imagined projectile might get from one finger to the other with the only consequences bein to the cheeks, and you'll get an idea of just how much good fortune was shinin down on Landry Gatestone. But that's how it went, and as was already made clear, 'twas bemusement, a big guffaw, that saved her from the worst.

The suturin went well. Dr. Esplin took extra time to make sure the scars would heal narrow and smooth as possible, though Landry was still marked by what she once called *these artificial dimples* for the rest of her life.

But despite the success of the operation, Landry didn't recover near as easy as everyone expected. The journey had taken its toll, and despite the cold that a few figured should've limited infection, her little body was soon under siege. For three days she was pitched in and out of delirious fevers, cursin and wailin over the pain, sobbin over her brother, who she'd had to lose twice, which neither of the mothers, loyal at her bedside, could make sense of. What both did know, though, was that Landry needed to eat. An IV just weren't enuf. Her ribs were showin. Even them bones that make up shoulders and hips were showin too much. In the mind of those stout-hearted women, and nurses as well, the gauze on her cheeks weren't nothin compared to those indecent exposures.

Old Porch, though, was havin a harder time. The .45 hadn't passed through him like some ghost blade through the gray veils of speech. The bullet had all but pulped his spleen, shatterin ribs too along the way before lodgin in the back of his left scapula. The surgery proved long, intricate, and plagued with the second-guessin of various approaches, especially where that left scapula was concerned, which did finally give up the warped slug. But Doctors Whitney and Rowe proved worthy of the respect their colleagues and the community at large so often granted them. Many hours later, Old Porch surfaced from the ordeal lookin much improved. And that weren't even the half of it. The followin mornin, Old Porch was clear in his thoughts as a sky on the coldest night. Two weeks later, he'd quit the hospital.

Where others let pain and infirmity compromise their minds, for Old Porch they did the opposite: they honed his faculties like glowin steel pounded into hardness, hissed in oil, ground into unforgivin sharpness. Whether on the phone in his hospital bed or soon enuf at home in a wheelchair, whether talkin to whichever reporter cared to visit, and plenty did care to visit, and now and then Old Porch even lurched partially to his feet to meet, say, a state senator who had come knockin on his door, Old Porch had a story to share with whomever would listen, and when news reached him that Landry Gatestone had survived, even if she was still recoverin back in the hospital, *that poor treacherous little girl,* why that got him to tellin his story as fast and as often as he could.

F er sure, there's a heckuva good argument to be made, and plenty have made it, that one of the best titles for all this is *Old Porch.* Old Porch was somethin else. There just ain't no gettin around that fact. He was a creature of such schemin persistence, delightin in the taste of malice and astonishin in his ability to aggrandize hisself at every turn, even when there weren't a turn. He had money, folks knew that much, but there was more to Old Porch than just what kind of truck he could buy.

Consider again his home, the Porch house, surfeit with dust-covered Frederic Remingtons or boxed sets of silver or only partially unwrapped crates of chinaware. Think of the various latest-thing appliances, some used but once, some not even unpacked. Think of all them buck heads taxidermied at no small cost, shot dead, of course, by Old Porch, but few makin it up on a hook, their angled rest against whatever wall, bein at best a shelter for boluses of dust exiled from a floor no broom or mop had been at for years.

Havin a thing just didn't stir Old Porch unless it seemed to reaffirm his purchase on the world entire. He'd grown increasinly wise to the lie stuff likes to tell: how for a moment your existence seems briefly upheld, in your own upheld grip of the thing, with a kind of shimmerin permanence that calms the heart. Old Porch had learned to insulate hisself from such bunk, just crated plastic-wrapped trinkets to beguile the foolish, materialize blindness, which is maybe why Old Porch found more satisfaction in the abstract possession of property, which, as we've also come to know, he invested in heavily, from the patchwork of homes, rental units, and grazin land to apartment complexes, a travel plaza or two, and other businesses extendin beyond his own home and the Porch Meats base of operations to pretty much all over of Utah, not to mention Idaho, Colorado, and Wyoming. The history of his ambitions is rich, like his attempt to unlawfully mine granite and quartzite from Isatch Canyon back in the late '60s, or, in the years before Kalin March arrived, surrenderin the greater part of his energies and distractions to securin the realty for Four Summits, what he anticipated would become his life's crownin achievement, a mortmain for the Porch name from here on out. Old Porch never got over the idea of plain and simple ownin the mountains, and then like them mountains, or so the faulty logic of appositional association dictated, he too would stick around for near forever. Call it mountain time. And whether chrysocracy or gerontocracy, you can bet Porch's rule would extend beyond specie and age, made whole and eternal by the one thing Old Porch prized above all else, prized above even property: force. He'd be a chirocracy of one with a ledger of scars. And even that wouldn't be the end of it: from ownin a mountain, it weren't but a small skip of the eye to ownin the sky.

Not that Old Porch could admit as much to anyone, let alone to hisself; these were but intense feelins born out of the pursuit of impossible prospects.

And don't think fer a second either that Old Porch ever fancied hisself a politician inside the D.C. beltway. To him a senator, even a president, weren't but another thing he would eventually hang on a wall or more likely leave in a corner or if need be even lead by the nose to some slaughter chute. Enuf lives, unsold, undevoured, had gone to smoke under his supervision; a few more wouldn't make no difference, their position in life irrelevant, their influence on his life inconsequential. No office, rank, title, gold ring, silver spoon, government ID, student ID, or bank account was exempt before the claims of ash.

In some ways then, praise be to Old Porch's unwaverin refusal before Death, even if what hunted him now, what Old Porch didn't know but Kalin had on good authority was comin his way, was somethin far worse than just Death. Old Porch would do whatever he needed to do so he could be Old Porch. And therein lies another peculiar contradiction particular to him, in how the soft argillaceous narratives he ceaselessly formed and re-formed to benefit hisself helped perform the bedrock personality he was known for until he died.

Old Porch still stands terrible before us as that impossibly constructed identity that wishes to present hisself upon those wide, sun-beat, salt-crusted Utah flats, before those snow-rich, towerin Utah mountains, as someone who is brave, resourceful, determined, hospitable, and above all else good, in the way that Good is so denoted by the scriptures published far and wide to ratify this sentiment of worthiness and blessèdness that aura the Church and its community at large.

Puttin aside short hair, pruned language, and decaffeinated dances, and in the absence of distilled spirits, those beautiful undistilled cheers lofted up past the rafters at a local basketball game, plenty of kind folk like Gabe Bangerter, Tray Holmes, and Callista Toone, dead but never buried, have shown how the Church's most basic mission remains hitched to the humble plod of progress, daily practiced and espoused by its beleaguered but worthy citizenry, those members who declare that more important than place is example. For here is the Church entire: put in the work, church attendance, deeds of deceny, and Heaven awaits replete with the return of lost loved ones, an ever-lastin family reunion, where pain and sufferin are redeemed in the arms of the Lord.

And so the Good shall know the Good Path, and by the Good Path shall the Good be known. Which is where the trickiness starts. Especially if that path ain't all Good and more than just the Good walk there.

With a slow chuckle and amiable nod, folks like Cannon Cornaby, Scott Potter, and Ladawn Crosset, buried near Rome, have noted that when it comes to Utahns and the Chuch, such openhearted, well-intentioned folks can demonstrate more than a fair amount of gullibility, as if out of such faith and divine beguilement the resultant trust is easily preyed upon by those sellin snake oil and at a good price too. Though Ned Trimble and Reen Nakamura, buried up in Heber, are less compassionate and speak in more severe whispers of the rustin bucket in the name of the water held within, with Brinn Black, buried in Sandy, bringin up Sondra Gatestone's failure of confidence after stoppin at Egan's house. The big problem lies with havin to set store by the bucket in order to carry the Good, though the Good has no presence in what carries it. This definition of Goodness contorts until it ain't even a fiction that at least calls itself out as such, and fer sure misleadin and befuddlin, especially when the contrivance is rustin through; somethin dingier, ordinary even, then comin into view, with all its leaks and eventual emptiness, leavin no choice but to either keep tryin to carry what can't ever be carried this way or, as Veronica Lasseter said in her life's final lap: *Get brave and throw away that bucket.*

Or as Perry Metz, buried in Ogden, put it more obliquely near the end of his life, in reference to the history emblazoned in stained glass in the Milkinson Center: *Trouble comes fer you when you blind yourself to the contradiction beneath the wing.*

Maybe there's a reason the Church near leaps to accept as some kind of pleasant default its own characterization as little more than odd underwear and archaic marriage policies last practiced over a hundred years ago. Ain't it better to be lionized as hard-workin and earnest and at the same time castigated for outdated or modest peculiarities than face a scrutiny over a collaboration so long hidden, if still honored? What near came to too much light decades after The Pillars Meadow Massacre, when a United States senator, servin in a manner befittin of the Church's vision of itself, upon the back of a white horse too, that weren't, decried with distant dissatisfaction the bleachin of the flag's representative hues.

For whether by a path or in a bucket or somethin else, Good ceases to be Good when it denies the violence walkin hand in hand like a ghost. Or so at least a few have warned.

It's easy to say Old Porch weren't of the Church just as it is easy to argue that without him there'd be no Church. As often as he failed to appear in chapel on Sunday among his neighbors, to take sacrament and bow his head, *In the name of Jesus Christ, Amen*, he throughout his life remained a stalwart defender of the Church. He almost never cursed. Why he'd build with his bare hands a place in the Inferno for his boys if he ever heard one of them curse. And when he drank, well, he didn't think about that. And when he preyed upon the credulity of his neighbors, why that was just good business and them bein suckers. And when, year after year, Old Porch failed to offer up to the Church his tithe, he would hang his head and promise that next year would be different. Ever in his heart, Old Porch held true that once Four Summits was done, he'd build Orvop a new temple.

Even Old Porch's ancestral records testify to Church allegiance, all the way back to the late nineteenth century. But like many there in Utah Valley, includin those who also could trace their lineage back to that famous declaration *This is the place*, Old Porch was also of that half that the Church could not rightly claim as solely the product of its influence: he was a pioneer.

Same as was true for the Gatestones and many other locals, writ large upon Old Porch's genes was the endurin desire to disentangle oneself from authority, from the rule of law, except if that authority and law was Nature. What mattered was the will to endure, to dare the unknown, to be the spirit of ruggedness. Old Porch lived by bruised, calloused, and bloody hands. His was a spirit that could not know itself content by a home hearth; his was a spirit that devised only restlessness upon whatever clover-covered hill of whatever settlement he found hisself; his was a spirit ever driven from well-paved roads to distant ridges of existence promisin a better view, even if that way looked ready to strike life from the face of the world.

Hard and dangerous appealed to Old Porch. And what better animus for the Church to align itself with? And so, not surprisinly, the Church would and did profit from the oft-brutal energies of those foot soldiers, the Pioneers, survivalists, hardscrabbled, hard-hammered, not easily undone, whether Porch, Gatestone, Hickman, or plenty of others, who the Church whether by manifest instinct or time-veiled plan thought to yoke and instruct in the service of its own blindin and perseverin purpose: its own manifest glory.

Charlie Burton, Ikue Hayakawa, Duwayne Small, along with plenty more, some buried up around Salt Lake, some not, would demand over the years: *How do we describe the entitlements that followed our exodus from Illinois? The word-inspired trek west encounterin those who were considered inconvenient at best, brushed aside justifiably, or worse, murdered, because they loved in different languages? Whose darkness in the peculiar idiom of our texts saw them not as chosen but marked? How else do we square the killins so persistently erased in that process of settlement? The Battle of Fort Utah? And that's just fer starters. No temple wall, visitor center diorama, or Church brochure lays claim to those many earth-dismantled bones in Utah Valley put there in the name of the pioneers' right to their designs, whether homestead, pasture, or city grid. Show me the atonement.* But as Blake Kotter, never buried, would say: *For there to be atonement, there must be recognition, and after recognition, there must be reckonin with the daemon that such eminent ideals of charity and affection have partnered up with.*

Not that what all's been related here about them October days in 1982 can answer such questions, what with Tom havin raised even more questions, especially when he was caped in fire upon the Katanogos summit ridge, possessed by the inevitability of penalty from which none stand apart, the great price none are absolved from payin. Rather these were observations about how, like the inhabitants who continue to make their home in the valleys, mountains, and plains of Utah, Orwin Porch was as much of the spirit of the Church as he was of them spirits set loose, even in antediluvian times, to conquer what weren't theirs. And yet despite bein so neatly balanced, rather than encounterin some deadlock or moderate average, this divide somehow instead retains the ongoin permission to continue the rank march ahead. Which is why *Old Porch* also ain't such a bad title.

A s is obvious then, Old Porch lived on as both parts, Pioneer and Church: rugged, fearless, a terrifyin solo artist in strife, a welcome team player in collective perfidy, warm and favored in his slickeriness, cold in the execution of his ambitions, a butcher and a killer but also a father, a father of many, and a partner too to those not so unlike hisself as well as to many of the so-called Good Men he helped ascend to their lacquered mahogany chairs with arms gilt in gold leaf and backs etched with words like *Truth* and *Charity*. Like both Church and Pioneer, Old Porch never ceased in his quest to ascend from the land he knew to the land he would rule. And he never ceased to amaze others with how on one hand he could carry out so much ugly brutishness and on the other hand weep so much for the boys he'd lost.

And Old Porch sure did weep, plenty, before whomever sought to find him, even at the same time as he was marshalin the necessary financial entities and finalizin the state-sanctioned sale of the parcels and territories that included Coyote Gulch and many of the eastern routes down the back side of Katanogos, plus all of Pillars Meadow, plus another four thousand acres farther east, with some extras coverin the remainin three compass points; wranglin state officials about the approved sale of inholdins; back-and-forthin with them USFS folks and cranky BLM officers, with the banks again, and of course with Brother Mallory Guvin Hone, or Manic Guff, whose lands continued to represent the largest part of the acquisition; and followin that with calls to each of the silent investors, includin Havril Enos, goadin him and the rest with outraged sobs, until they all shared the notion that they was transfigurin Old Porch's personal tragedy into a blessin upon Orvop, a blessin upon the state of Utah, *a blessin upon the United States herself!*

And truth be told, Old Porch's stratagems darn near worked. By the time Landry surfaced, weeks later, to a clarity befittin her sharp take-no-guff mind, Old Porch's terrible albeit antigodlin narrative had lurched to life and weren't takin no prisoners. Fer sure nothin a little teenage girl could hope to change, and you can forget slay, especially with that ugly beast already growlin and clawin its way into national headlines. Of course Landry weren't no more just a teenage girl or even the little sister she'd been a week ago. Fearsome instruction had bequeathed an unanticipated resolve within her small form. And you can bet little Landry didn't flinch none either. She didn't even blink.

Not that Old Porch ever saw it comin. The echo of his every pronouncement resounded in his own ear so clearly as to keep his tears flowin, what despite his gnashin teeth couldn't help but keep that grin of his growin. A grin, mind you, that had somewhat changed.

As it turned out, many of Old Porch's teeth had for a long time, due to gross neglect and nocturnal grindin, been infected. Many fell out on their own followin his rescue, but others had to be yanked. It was surmised that their removal and the treatment of them rottin gums with gallons of antibiotics, what had been plaguin him a long time, maybe for years, only helped further assist his formidable immune system to counter the deprivations brought on by the gunshot wound and brutal exposure. *The sharp ones, though, I still got. I can tear up meat just fine,* Old Porch would say, holdin up at the same time the very thumb, once nailless and so infected, now healed over if still scarred and wrinkled like a pale tormented raisin. *I just can't chew. Not until I get my new ones.* His front teeth survived, and Old Porch had no problem leavin their brown brokenness unchanged. Besides, their appearance now helped further his most important claim: he was the injured party, the one badly abused. Old Porch believed it too. *Don't forget Job*, he'd also tell hisself. *Think of the family he lost but also of the new family he eventually got.* Old Porch was well aware that Utah Valley was full of young girls eager to start a big family, especially with a man who'd lost everythin but still had money. And anyway, no matter by what angle he pondered the state of his bein, even if through them gaps left behind by rotten teeth, he viewed hisself as a picture of progress worthy of inevitable sainthood.

Take too, fer example, Mr. Bucket #5. Old Porch knew he hadn't always been the best dog owner. And if that recognition alone weren't proof of his inherent Goodness, then it was all a lottery of who was Good and who weren't, and then what did it matter? It's true Old Porch had kicked Mr. Bucket #1 to death, but that was decades ago, and they was both different creatures then. Mr. Bucket hadn't even been Number One. He hadn't even been Mr. Bucket. He didn't even have a name, at least not until he was dead. The very drunk Old Porch had looked over the broken body and laughed and then right there named him Bucket, Mr. Bucket, *because, see, even though I was the one kickin him, he's the one that kicked the bucket! Bucket he is!* Whatever sense was or wasn't there, Old Porch hadn't stopped laughin about that one, even when he was sober, even when weeks passed, even when he'd got hisself Mr. Bucket #2, whom he'd also kicked but not to death. Mr. Bucket #3 he'd kicked only when he was a pup. Mr. Bucket #4 he'd kicked only a few times, maybe only twice, and Mr. Bucket #5, why he swore he'd never laid a boot or a hand on him, well mostly never. And sure, he'd kept him kenneled up an extra day if he was displeasin, but what dog owner don't do that? Now if that weren't near proof right there of the redemptive path Old Porch kept walkin, what was? Right?

The point of all this, and the case that Old Porch was doggedly set on makin, over and over again, was obvious: he was the victim. Plain and simple. He and his beautiful boys had sought only to recover his beloved horses in order to place them in the preserve he had always planned to include in Four Summits, which would now include pastures bearin the horses' names as well as the names of his boys and of course those others lost: Law Enforcement Ranger Bren Kelson and pilot Kevin Moffet. Now of course Old Porch never had no such plans, and folks were right who guessed he'd done got the idea from Kalin March hisself, so set on releasin Old Porch's ponies on what was now in essence Old Porch's land. Not that any reporter ever got wise to that part of the story. Not that any reporter even asked Old Porch directly for the names of the horses. But this spontaneous creation of Old Porch's, this equine field of dreams, found great reception in various papers and on local radio shows, where the phones lit up with calls of sympathy. Holly Feltzman, though, sure weren't buyin it, nor did she hesitate to voice her doubts publicly: *It just hits all the beats, don't it? Like a room that's a little too bright and just a little too cozy.*

You can also bet Old Porch made sure everyone understood that if he or any of his boys had spotted the criminals first, why they'd have called it in at once. *Done it by the book.* And who could doubt him? After all, Hatch Porch had been with them, and in Utah Valley he was a revered, near-semimythic figure of law enforcement and military authority and an Orvop High superstar to boot. Weren't he the one leadin the effort to rescue the horses? And fer his troubles, weren't he shot in the back? Gunned down in an ambush none of them had seen comin? Perpetrated by the modern day equivalent of Bonnie Parker and Clyde Barrow. Old Porch stayed crystal clear about that. This weren't just about Kalin March. Landry Gatestone was equally guilty. Sure, there was a lot of confusion at first. Hadn't there been a good spate of time when folks were certain she was Kalin's victim? *But, see, that weren't the case,* Old Porch assured everyone he could. *Them two was in league the whole time.*

And that's how Old Porch kept framin the events at Pillars Meadow: as *an ambush*. And reporters ran with it, givin ink to Old Porch's version and so further cementin how the local conversation went. *Massacre* came next, part of the same process, prodded further into use by Old Porch hisself. And detectives were writin it down too, Old Porch's amanuenses for his ongoin stultiloquy, detail by detail; their studious diligence and attention magickin in Old Porch's head that everythin he was so carefully layin out was not only to be believed but the absolute truth as well, nothin left out, not a bit outta place, what is written is Word, but what is repeated is World.

But how still had these horse-thievin teenagers, this Bonnie and Clyde, ended up on the back side of Katanogos? That's what everyone wanted to know, police included. Old Porch explained he never would've thought they could get that far east. Like everyone else, he'd figured Kirk's Cirque was the terminus of the whole tragedy. Hatch, though, had been up there in the cirque when Law Enforcement Ranger Bren Kelson was murdered and had likely got an inklin then as to what them cold-blooded killers was up to. Other than that, Old Porch couldn't speak to why his eldest had chosen on that Sunday mornin to set off gettin around the back side of Agoneeya. Two more of his sons, Egan and Kelly Porch, plus an employee at Porch Meats, had obviously seen the sense in Hatch's plan and signed on without hesitation. Of course, takin snowmobiles there was in breach of plenty of local laws, but the price they paid was far in excess of whatever fines they'd've owed. Old Porch figured that the zeal demonstrated by law enforcement to catch the murderers *no doubt added to their own zeal to find my horses,* the very same beasts that had cost Russel Porch, their youngest brother, his life.

Why no doubt? Detective Peters had asked.

Whadya mean why no doubt?

Why would the pursuit of Kalin March up Isatch Canyon have further fueled your sons' desires to locate your horses? I just don't follow.

That was the first time a detective's question had stuttered Old Porch's faith in his own narrative, though just an itsy bit, and nothin Old Porch couldn't handle, patchin up that false causal by sayin that any spirit to rectify the terrible wrongs inflicted upon the Porch family, *no matter where it was comin from,* had served to just *further charge their own spirits.* Though Old Porch also made sure Detective Peters understood, by his own sudden groan of pain from the wound in his side, with a slurp of applesauce due to the lesions where his back teeth had once been, that the spirit to do somethin, *to do anythin, so long as it were the right thing,* was always in his boys. *It's how they was raised.* Which Detective Peters grunted at with approval, dutifully writin down those words too, and with a nod that helped resettle Old Porch back into believin that whatever he was sayin like so was so.

Old Porch went on then to relate how it was Hatch, in charge of this rescue, Old Porch made sure to use that word as much as possible, *rescue,* who'd first spotted the two errant horses headin down a high ridge that would eventually wind around to become the top of Coyote Gulch. With binoculars and the help of his brothers as well as the Porch hand, they'd then confirmed that these was the same mare and geldin *we was determined to rescue.*

After that, Hatch and the rest sought out a place where they could radio the news back to Old Porch. By that point Old Porch had been up in a helicopter piloted by Kevin Moffet. He'd brought along the rest of his boys, because, A, if they did find the horses, *we'd need two riders to get them back,* and, B, they all needed some fresh air and new perspectives after the murder of their youngest brother.

No detective interrupted him then, and Old Porch was wise to treat that silence cautiously. Old Porch knew he'd better get ahead of what they was surely thinkin: why hadn't he alerted officials right then that Hatch Porch had spotted the horses? *Now I should've called the police and given them news of the horses. If my boys had spotted that murderin Kalin kid and his accomplice, Landry Gatestone, I'd've surely done just that. And, yes, in lookin back, it was a terrible mistake not to call Orvop's finest right then and there.* And once again, and this despite such furious scribblin and monitorin of their tape machines, the detectives' silence still waried Old Porch, and he further added how, despite Hatch's and Egan's reassurances, he just weren't convinced that they'd actually located his horses on the back side of Katanogos. *That still didn't make no sense. Part of me figured we'd just stumbled upon some other horses.*

When they'd landed then on Pillars Meadow, they was a good ways south of Coyote Gulch, the base of which was marked by a grove of birches and aspens. By the time Hatch, Egan, Kelly, and the hand had met up with them, they was already makin plans to split up and explore the various chutes and gullies. They all agreed that Kevin Moffet should take off and see what he could from above. While they was decidin who would go where, Francis, *who was so pained by Russel's death to be rendered near catatonic,* suddenly cried out that the horses were right up ahead. *Like it was nothin, like they'd just emerged from the trees and was now grazin smack-dab in the middle of that snowy field.*

Old Porch had paused for effect then. *We all just sauntered up that way, jovial and relaxed, and maybe even for the first time content that somethin we'd set our hearts on doin was nearly done and done right too.* Old Porch recalled makin idle chat with their pilot, Kevin Moffet, and his eldest, Hatch, while the rest of his boys broke up into various arrangements with various conversations goin on about this and that, ball games, huntin, girls and such. *My boy Hatch and me, we was rememberin how on one deer hunt we'd taken along a radio so we could listen to Conference. Even if we didn't down a buck, we had that for ourselves. Hatch didn't make it up this year for the hunt, but he was swearin to me that come next October, he weren't gonna get stuck in Texas. He put his arm around my shoulder. It felt awful nice. You all have kids?*

What neither he nor Hatch nor any of the rest knew, as Old Porch made clear, was how, upon seein the helicopter landin down the ways, the killers had released the horses and then *squirreled themselves into a depression in the field where they was lyin in wait. Or if there weren't no depression, why then they must've covered themselves in mud or whatever dead grass was around. I can't say fer sure. However they was situated, we didn't see them.* Old Porch just walked on up to the horses and got shot. Kevin Moffet tried to run but he got shot too. And even then his boys had no idea what was goin on. Not that their *stunnedness stopped the shootin none.* By then all the Porches was in the line of fire, and they paid the price. Best as Old Porch could figure, and at that point he was on the ground in a fit of pain, some of his boys did manage to shoot back, *bless their souls,* but they was still got. Others ran but they got got too. And that was the most of it. At least of what Old Porch could remember. The affliction of his wound was on him, and he was swift after swallowed up by dim perceptions and a dimmer understandin of ensuant events, in the mud and snow like he was, a barely breathin creature abandoned to the cares of gosh-awful hurt, left for dead.

Somewhere in there, the Kalin kid shot my Hatch. In the back too.

He shot him with the Colt? Detective Peters asked.

Old Porch took hisself a moment then, breathin long, lettin the pain come in long too. He seen right there how the detective was layin out a trap, and Old Porch stuck his tongue in the holes in the back of his jaw just like he then licked the teeth that was still there up front, still sharp. Of course it also shuddered him some to think how Detective Peters, like the rest of them, had no clue about what had really happened up there. And in that light, the question was understandable. Still, whether Detective Peters was huntin or just clueless, Old Porch knew he'd better keep a close eye on him.

In the end, Old Porch managed a long shake of his head. *Landry Gatestone was the one wieldin my family's Colt.*

Was she the one then who shot you? Detective Peters asked.

Old Porch nodded. *She stole the gun off Russel.*

Can you think of a reason why she'd've done that? Detective Peters asked.

Why she'd shoot me?! That best not be a serious question, Old Porch scolded the detective. *She knew I knew Russel's blood was on her hands. Plus she's a Gatestone.*

Excuse me?

Son, you best pay attention here. Porches and Gatestones have a long history of animosities. We Porches like to keep to ourselves, but them Gatestones don't pass up a chance if they can get us. Stealin our horses would be just one example.

Was she the one who cuffed you?

I don't know.

Why would she do that?

Sickos. The both of them.

And how would you say she looked when she shot you? Detective Peters asked then, his eyes fixed on his pad, still scribblin away.

Landry Gatestone?

It does take a certain look to shoot a man, especially if shootin to kill, Detective Peters added with a shrug.

Old Porch agreed. There was no doubtin that. *She was cold-eyed.*

Okay sure, but— Detective Peters looked up. *But how would you know that?*

She shot me didn't she?

Old Porch saw her then too, Landry Gatestone lookin down on him from that big horse, from under the shadow of a wide-brimmed hat. Black-eyed she was, tellin him they was in Hell, and he'd believed her too.

Detective Peters muttered then a big *Huh.*

And maybe it was that *Huh* that finally did rattle Old Porch some, the way a drunk in a pleasant haze, brought on by a long bottle and a deep glass, can suddenly in the soft thickness of his blur catch how the story he's tellin to so much laughter and appreciation is suddenly gettin no such response, how by shared glances or the stiffenin of smiles, the drunk's good mood is betrayed and he sees too clearly that his welcome has run out and the bottle is gone and his glass stands empty and the door yawns for his exit.

What were the horses' names by the way? Detective Peters asked then.

Dapple and Bay, Old Porch answered without missin a beat.

That so?

Dapple and Bay. I named them myself.

By all accounts, whether them accounts be rumor, gossip, half-informed conversations, or even some of the printed articles, whether researched pieces or thumb-suckers, at this point the truth was known, the chronology established, the case made, the jury selected, the verdict reached, with those two young belligerents, March and Gatestone, lodged at the heart of these events, just a breath away from a sentencin that would see them sent to the Point of the Mountain, where they'd be propped up against a wall just like Gary Gilmore was when he was executed in 1977. But rumor, gossip, the best-intentioned dialogues, and even the most thoroughly researched and vetted articles ain't always privy to the broader and slower grind of assemblin meanin out of solid facts, which, like a very low frequency, might go unheard by nitwits but nonetheless still endures and what's more travels a long, long ways.

It's a lot of work makin somethin up, Undersheriff Jewell would later remark. *That weren't Orwin Porch's kinda work.*

Whether folks would ever agree that Orwin Porch was representative of both State and Church, which is but one assessment, and to be clear many folks do not agree with that assessment, most folks will argue that, Old Porch aside, the Church has among its many, many members many, many good folks. Of course, it's also fair to ask if they're any better than the many, many good folks in a wide variety of devotions, not to mention organizations, which include the likes of Rotary Clubs, the Red Cross, the AMA, the ABA, the American Beekeepin Federation, AA, the PTA, the NAACP, the Peace Corps, Planned Parenthood, Panthera, United Way, the NRDC, to name just a scatterin of hopefuls? And, okay, that is another conversation altogether. But what's worth reemphasizin here is how in Orvop there were still lots of good folks around. Take even Undersheriff Jewell. Sure, he's married to Old Porch's sister, Kip-Ann. But, see, Kip-Ann can't stand her brother none, especially given his relentless taunts concernin her lack of children. *Barren Ann* is how Old Porch often referred to his estranged sister. Undersheriff Jewell might be fooled some by Old Porch, but he weren't so much the fool to ignore his wife. And he sure knew to look out for his own butt and get to crossin all his *t*'s and dottin all his *i*'s. He also knew Chief of Police Beckham was gonna make darned sure that his best people were on this.

Take Detective Peters. He was an especially good man who did give a hoot about integrity and callin things out like he saw them. He was pretty practiced too in seein how small and nonapparent details join a greater assemblage that can eventually divulge a disfigurin truth, disfigurin in how it might deform and even annihilate prevailin narratives, no matter how obvious and compellin those were at first.

Not that Old Porch noticed. It's unclear if Old Porch could even detect such Goodness except if it appeared to him as Gullibility and thus offered him a Good Mark for some new scheme. And in those days and weeks that followed The Massacre at Pillars Meadow, Old Porch was so busy payin attention to his own self speakin that he completely lost track of just how good and devoted Detective Peters was when it came to doin his job. Old Porch hardly noticed either when the FBI joined the investigation. He sure did notice, though, when his U.S. senator stopped takin his calls.

The senator didn't care one bit for any of this business. The Porch tragedy was one thing, but the involvement now of a young girl, a dark-skin girl too, struck a nerve with the shrewd and mightily intelligent Shane Hays. He sensed somethin was off. Fer one thing, she seemed too young and from too good a family to go so wild and astray; and fer another thing she was too small to wield so well a weapon like a loaded Colt Peacemaker. Senator Hays knew guns, and he knew that Colt Peacemaker. Owned one in fact. And no weak-wristed child was gonna get done on Pillars Meadow what was done. Ten shot, nine shot dead, six thanks to that gun. The math weren't addin. To the senator's discredit, he did come to his conclusion because Landry Gatestone was a child and a girl and a brown girl at that; to his credit, he whiffed early on a runty rat in the hutch. And so when Governor Matheson, who was a close friend of Chief of Police Beckham, called in his request, the senator was only too happy to help get the FBI on board. It weren't so big an ask either given the local need and the national attention the case was gettin, what with all the dead. That Hatch Porch was a Texas Ranger with an adorin commander like Chief Castor Emerson also helped. Emerson was callin in every favor he could. He didn't give a hoot if the killin had happened in Utah; one of his men had been gunned down, and in the back. *Justice will be served.*

The two FBI agents who came out couldn't have been more impartial. Linda Bruner was from Detroit, Michigan, and raised as a Lutheran. Herman Farro was from Providence, Rhode Island, and, maybe because of his Algerian heritage, or not, would never know what to make of Utah. Despite how movies and whatnot like to emphasize the conflict between various agencies, Detective Peters got on splendidly with Agents Bruner and Farro. He welcomed their participation. Anythin to get it done right. And that's exactly what they did. And they became lifelong friends too.

After Old Porch, the next thing on their agenda was to interview Landry Gatestone, but that weren't so easy given her fevers and some scary days of weakness and the kind of stillness that threatens to outlast a pulse. Also, her momma was smart enuf to retain legal counsel, and you're right if you guessed that would be Holly Feltzman, who sat beside Landry Gatestone when she finally recovered enuf to get snappy about seein Jojo and havin more Jell-O too. She ate a lot of Jell-O those weeks in the hospital.

It's hard to say if a lawyer had been necessary. For the most part, Holly Feltzman didn't say a word while Landry laid out the story, plain and simple, for Detective Peters and Agents Bruner and Farro. She told how on that night in Isatch Canyon, Russel rode up on Kalin with the Colt revolver out, and Landry sure weren't gonna stand for that sort of misbehavin. *I knocked him off his horse, knocked the wind out of him too. Then I took his gun. He was okay. The three of us just sat around the fire, and it was pretty nice. Kalin shared his food, and in the end we was all friends.* After they was done eatin, she explained how they got to settlin their differences, and that's when Russel agreed that buyin the horses off him was more than fair and would suit his old man too. *Russel knew if he came back empty-handed, he'd've likely got a beatin.* But this way he might even win some approval. *He was plenty pleased.* Landry then added how Kalin didn't have no money, *not one cent*, but she'd had a twenty-dollar bill for Mr. Chidester, for Marchin Band extras. She even wrote out their agreement on it. The only thing that Russel weren't so pleased about was her keepin the gun. Kalin hadn't liked her keepin the gun either. *But the way I seen it, I'd be goshdarned if I was gonna hand it back over to that erratic boy, what with him havin already pointed it at Kalin who'd only been cookin up some beans and rice!* Landry did swear to return it to Russel the next day, a promise she'd meant to keep. *Wednesday night was the last time we seen Russel.*

The next morning, *that would be Thursday mornin, while I was gettin out of Isatch Canyon, headin home,* Landry had come across Egan Porch with Kelly Porch and someone she didn't know. Egan seen at once the Colt in her belt. He told her Russel was dead, but Landry weren't ever gonna trust a word that came out of Egan's mouth fer reasons she weren't gonna speak on then. *Let's just say I weren't certain Egan didn't mean to harm me then, and if that was so, I figured he'd get help from these others.*

Can you give us a more specific reason why you would feel that way? Agent Bruner had asked.

Holly Feltzman was at the ready then to respond, but she didn't need to say nothin.

I felt it under my skin, and so I raced back to Kalin, who I trusted a bit already and came to trust more than anyone ever, except maybe my momma or my deceased brother Tom, bless his sorry soul.

From then on, the Porches pursued and even fired on them for reasons she and Kalin could only speculate about. They never returned fire. Landry said that a bunch of times. *We only had the one gun. I mean, I had the gun. Kalin wouldn't go near it. It had just the six bullets, five that were loaded, the sixth loose in its bag.*

They'd fer sure had nothin to do with Cavalry. Landry told them how Egan had first tried to ride up the scree and likely fell. They'd heard two shots. Landry had seen the first used to put down Cavalry, though couldn't say nothin about the second. *That was pretty awful.*

As for the killin of the ranger up in the cirque, she knew even less about that. The Colt Peacemaker was in a saddlebag. *Kalin was unarmed and trapped on the headwall because one of them Porch boys kept firin at him with a big rifle that had one heckuva roar.*

Landry had always figured it was Hatch who was the shooter until they got to the other side and she'd seen Egan pointin a rifle. Detective Peters stopped her there because he wanted to hear more about the horses and how they'd gotten out of the cirque by way of the Upecksay Headwall. He weren't alone in wonderin about that part. Agents Bruner and Farro got mighty attentive then too. For her part, even weak as she was, Landry was more than happy to spend a little time recountin the feat, though she made clear it weren't her that done it but Kalin. She'd been scared to death the whole way up.

Holly Feltzman knew full well the reason she was there, as Landry's lawyer, and she was gettin paid for it too, paid plenty, but her jaw still slackened with Landry's retellin. That went for Agents Bruner and Farro too. Sondra Gatestone, who was often on the edge of tears, was just plain gobsmacked. Detective Peters was as equally amazed by the story as he was by this fiery little girl who so sharply and fearlessly continued to regale them with her version of things. Landry even assured everyone in that hospital room that it was fine to not believe a single word. She wouldn't have believed any of it either if it weren't for the fact that she'd done it herself, up the awful face of that mountain with not just Kalin but three horses and a mule too!

Which was about when an awful headache quieted her up some. It was hard enuf havin to relive the whole thing, but the effort needed to just shape the necessary words, what was required of her tongue and lips, never failed to make the pain in her cheeks spike. Landry often had to stop to spit out the contents of her mouth lest she make the mistake of swallowin all the blood and saliva buildin up there, which in turn might upset her stomach or, worse, make her gag. That plastic cup of pink fluid on her little hospital table weren't the prettiest sight. Not that Landry was put off by it. What was hers was hers. To heck with you if you couldn't reconcile that. Truth ain't just colored glass a-glowin or even dawn light glintin off fresh snow.

Not that what she spat out or the headaches that came and went stopped her nor diminished any the bespellment upon everyone in that small room, Landry havin already laid out the wallopin rain, the traverse in the dark, their refuge in the mine, and the palace of ice that greeted them Friday mornin along with the subsequent perils such freezin posed for them. And of course, everyone there already knew about the big rockslide. Landry had assured them too how just survivin that was somethin she'd never get over. She'd sure been lucky. She knew that. Then she'd teared up somethin awful just describin how she'd thought fer sure she'd *lost them*, her tears growin even more copious as she related how Navidad and Kalin had still managed to escape, *ridin so beautifully,* findin the quiet steps in that roarin chaos in order to make their arrival on the other side seem so simple.

And still none of that compared to ridin straight up that headwall hundreds of feet high, *thousands of feet high!*, Kalin the whole time keepin the horses safe, *keepin me safe*, until he finally found hisself trapped behind that last protective bit of rock, *and why?, because them Porch boys, like the cowards they are,* had set up in the safety of distance to take shots at him until it was too dark for anyone to see, the portents of the storm then *gettin them scurryin back home, runnin for their lives.* But even with gunfire gone, Kalin, for all his blessed equine skills, *and they surpassed blessedness, they surpassed wonderment,* didn't stand a chance. *He could've crawled up the dark path if he'd left Navidad behind, but he'd never do that. He loved them horses.*

Navidad? Agent Bruner asked.

That was the name of the horse? Detective Peters asked.

That's right. Navidad and Mouse.

And then suddenly *it weren't just wind and water flyin sideways mean as knives.* Suddenly *it was even worse: snow was fallin.* And if that didn't right there spell the doom of both Kalin and Navidad, Landry didn't know what did. Except Landry had been wrong. *The snow was what saved him.* It had piled up fast in the cirque, with white layin claim to the meadow, and then for a moment the storm ceased its upbraidin of the mountain and let a big moon shine through, and Kalin could see everythin clear like Navidad could see everythin clear, and they didn't waste a second. They rode forth on that narrowest of ledges corrupted with holes and gouges, a place to fear; what Landry had had to inch along with her stomach sinkin lower than the headwall was high. Doubt fer sure had accompanied her near the whole way, *though fortunately I had more than doubt beside me,* which is why she'd made it, astounded, blinkered, elated, dumbfounded. And she'd only had to walk the thing. *Kalin had to do it on horseback.* They should've had no chance. But that didn't stop them. Kalin and Navidad had faith in their journey, down to every sharp or dull clop upon rock, down to every inhale and exhale, calmly balanced *where no horse should ever have to go, no boy neither.* And sure, maybe they was *aided some by the urgins* and exhortations *of a* wingless, some might say penitent *ghost up ahead,* the likes of whom accompanies those with the courage to do more than they are capable of because they have faced up to the fact that they ain't yet done enuf deeds of merit to match the worth of their good fortune, good fortune for just havin risen up from the muck to behold the vistas of this universe and know on top of that the nuzzles of a horse that loves them.

And, okay, maybe back then Landry didn't say it like so, but she did make clear what a miracle it was to see Kalin alive again, free of the summit ridge, and with the moon gone again too, and snow billowin down even harder, which by then fer all its whiteness was near dark as night as well. Aside from any mention of Tom, what Landry had also made darned sure not to say aloud was how fer a moment there she seemed to behold in that hospital room wings, immense ones, off the back of that magnificent black horse, wings blacker than the blackest shadow a dreamer can dream up, a black no night can ever know, risin up slow and then fallin slow but with all the force of that storm that night, with the force of every storm, with the force of the sky too, and

Kalin lookin just as dark, with that hat tilt down, hidin his face, like he was nothin now, if still poised, if still ready, he and Navidad's collective blackness so complete that it was a wonder they didn't overwhelm the night itself and right then and there fly from the world forever. No, Landry made sure not to let none of that slip.

But some things Landry did let slip, even if no one in that room thought much of when, fer example, she'd whispered, and verbatim too, *fortunately I had more than doubt beside me* or more explicitly *aided some too by the urgins of a ghost up ahead.* What earned not even a cough or a shared glance among her interrogators. No one could hear the absence she kept describin at the heart of a tale that was obviously absurd if also so spellbindin that often pens would stop scribblin, the listeners lost to the pictures Landry had brightened in their heads.

Landry did make clear that none of the rest would've happened if the Porches had just left them alone. Thanks to Kalin's plannin, they'd *managed to set up in a campsite beneath the summit ridge.* They had shelter, fire, and eventually even food. Without the Porches, they'd've just slogged their way down the back side of the mountain come mornin, then crossed Pillars Meadow, and released the horses. After that, scrawnier and muddier fer sure, they'd've made it back down to Orvop to take the cussin they deserved and after that have a warm bath and more food and a ton of sleep and be on their way back to school. They probably would've hung out some with Russel Porch too.

That cussin's still comin your way, her momma said then, strong and proud, though she still couldn't help the tears that kept gushin up anyway, so glad her little girl was alive after so much risk and misery. And terror.

Landry wanted more Jell-O then, accepted a cup of ice, then fussed some with the IV needle still in her arm. Doctor Hafen, who'd been with the Gatestones well before Evan was born, came in to make some adjustments before leavin with promises of Jell-O, and different flavors too. Detective Peters asked Landry if she needed a longer break. Right quick she replied *Heck no* and got back to it.

Landry described then how they'd broke camp, saddled up, and faced a side of Katanogos that was far more merciful compared to where they'd just been. And sure, at first it was slow goin; the snow was heavy and deep, but there were also plenty of places swept clean by winds durin the night. *Not that them rocky places didn't also require extra care.*

Eventually they'd reached a place that requirin but a quick scramble up revealed *a small valley that you can get to by way of the back side of Agoneeya* and what eventually leads to Pillars Meadow. Landry admitted that she'd forgotten about the binoculars not bein meshed no more. Agent Farro was curious about the mesh, and Landry was happy to explain how Kalin had devised the subterfuge in order to keep from gettin spotted. *Actually it was somethin his daddy had taught him.*

Landry admitted to bein amused at spottin the Porches so quickly. *But then, stupid me, Egan Porch put a bullet through my mouth. And me, I was just standin there watchin him do it!* Landry was sure too that if she hadn't got shot, she'd have convinced Kalin to take some alternate route in order to avoid that concentration of miscreants. *Kalin took Coyote Gulch because of me.*

Landry couldn't rightly remember what happened next. Gettin hit was beyond recollection. Not even her fall traipsed much across her memory. Though some sense of turmoil still lingered. *Tumblin, turnin, feelin light, and feelin that lightness replaced by heaviness.* If it weren't for the pain, she might've laid there a lot longer. *Pain was kinda my friend then.* Though she'd had no clue where she was at when at last she cleared the snow from her eyes.

Landry Gatestone took her time then describin how she came to understand how she was lodged at the base of *them amazin trees just growin on the side of them cliffs.* She made sure Detective Peters and Agents Bruner and Farro knew exactly how to find the spot where she'd got stuck. She knew it was a miracle she weren't killt by the rifle shot or in the sluice of snow that spun her off the top of them cliffs. It was another miracle that she could climb outta there. Landry laughed then, and even though it hurt, she laughed again. It felt good. It made her feel whole or least like someone who can imagine again the possibility of wholeness. *You know,* Landry said, sittin up straight-backed and amazed, *I just realized me and Kalin was both saved by a tree set in a place a tree had no business bein.* In Kalin's case, she was of course referrin to the dead ash in the middle of the Ninth Scree.

Landry did hide then how hurt she'd felt to find Kalin had left with the horses. Not even the mule had stuck around. Of course, from her hospital bed she could see plain as day how Kalin, with that shot to her head, would've figured her dead, and after bein thrown off the cliffs, dead again, and then dead a third time buried under the snow and debris that followed.

Plenty of hoofprints made followin them easy.

Kalin was ridin Navidad? Agent Bruner tested her.

Leadin Mouse.

Did this mule you keep mentionin have a name? Agent Farro followed up.

Landry didn't say nothin.

Where was the Colt Peacemaker? Detective Peters asked then.

In one of my saddlebags.

On Jojo?

That's right.

I still don't understand why it wasn't with Kalin? Agent Farro asked, and in a way that felt like he was bargin in on a picnic he weren't invited to. *You said he was fond of guns.*

I said no such thing! Ain't you been listenin? Kalin wouldn't go near it. He hated that I'd kept it. The whole time I was with him, he refused to touch it. Pretty much refused to look at it.

From here Landry's recountin sped up. *The only thing I could do I did: I started walkin downhill.* Eventually she found Jojo, who appeared to be walkin uphill in an effort to find her. They sure was happy to be reunited. Soon after they was out on Pillars Meadow. *Jojo had no interest in the place, but I meant to find Kalin and the horses. And then I seen the dead. Only Old Porch was still alive, but he thought he was dead because he was so sure I was dead!* Detective Peters and the two agents took special note of this, especially of what Landry said next: *Old Porch told me Kalin weren't around because he'd gone back to Hell.*

He said that? Detective Peters had to make sure.

I ain't makin none of this up, Landry snapped.

What do you make of what he said? Agent Bruner asked gently.

Objection, Holly Feltzman spoke up. *Speculation.*

I got no idea, Landry answered anyway. *He looked crazed.*

Are you sure about all this you're sayin? Agent Farro asked.

Objection, Holly Feltzman again.

Forget where the snake's at and you get bit, Landry responded, plenty of warnin in her voice. *I have a very good memory, Agent Herman Farro from Providence, Rhode Island.*

Detective Peters and Agent Bruner shared a light laugh there, and Agent Farro joined in as well.

I'll tell you this: I never thought a Porch, especially Old Porch hisself, could look up at me and know fear, Landry admitted.

Neither the agents nor the detective gave any indication how these last revelations had shaped their thoughts. Holly Feltzman cleared her throat then on behalf of her client. Sondra Gatestone took her daughter's hand. Landry only added that when she'd at last come upon Kalin, it took some doin and a lot of help from Jojo to get him up in the saddle. Landry admitted to not thinkin about there bein a helicopter up there let alone a radio in a helicopter. She never caught sight of it nor the snowmobiles. She repeated the troubles she'd had gettin Kalin up on Jojo and the constant fear she had from then on that they'd fall at any moment.

Upon reflection, the ride back didn't seem to take up any time in her head, but she still knew how in the middle of it, and she was sure of this, it had already seemed to have taken a forever so vast that not only did she, Jojo, and Kalin not matter, time didn't matter neither.

It was kinda weird.

The rest they knew.

Detective Peters did circle back to Navidad and Mouse. He wanted to know where they'd gone, and he asked Landry in a way that suggested he didn't have the case in mind. He was just genuinely curious. Landry didn't treat the question as any big deal. She just reported fairly that there weren't no sign of them that she could see. She just figured they'd wandered off. But it was when she'd said *wandered off*, and said it real flippant like, that all of what she'd been sayin finally caught up with her. Them dear horses! Dear, dear beautiful Navidad and beautiful ornery Mouse, with whom she'd endured such dangerous times, fostered such close ties with; where near every minute up there and even now down here had concerned their well-bein, their progress, the outcome of their lives.

Landry felt the tears come up as she heard her flippant voice now catch, and then her voice was gone, and all them tears were on her cheeks, for the sight of them, so bright in her memory, but gone from her too, leavin her with just the memory of their absence, what was just as bright too. Where were they now? How were they doin? Was it worth it? Which couldn't help but drag her back to the departure Landry couldn't speak on, not here, fer sure not in front of these men and women, certainly not in front of her momma, at least not yet.

See, unlike Navidad and Mouse, Landry never could see Tom on that journey, and yet somethin like his presence, the way he'd looked, how he'd smile, even where he'd stand, had managed still to take up residency in the air while she was up there. She could still almost see him there on the headwall when her balance had faltered and how that next step wouldn't have happened had it not been for her brother's outstretched hand. She saw him so clearly now, strollin beside Ash, whistlin, as she was strollin beside Jojo, singin, with Kalin beside Navidad, just listenin, and Mouse listenin too. That had been a pretty sweet moment, made all the more painful by the fact that Landry had never got to say goodbye to Tom.

In some ways that haunted her the most. She could relinquish the horses; Navidad and Mouse had gone on to find the life they would live. Tom, though, he was hard to let go of. She figured Kalin had had his goodbye. She hadn't. In fact Landry would go on up to Tom's Crossin near every fall to say goodbye to him, maybe hopin to catch his whistle on the wind. She often wondered about why, out of so many places, that place had been the one. She wondered about what finally happened when Tom had passed from Kalin's mind. Kalin, fer sure, and eventually her, and maybe the horses too, had borne the burden of his mysteries for but a handful of days. That too stayed with Landry for a long time: how we are all charged with the burden of shepherdin along to some far-off gate mysteries that will never divulge their hearts if in the end still awaken ours. Landry would eventually find her peace or at least a truce in the understandin that none are spared the accompaniment of ghosts. They walk beside us with allways the possibility of their own transformation right ahead. Some find that transformation. Others don't. Some are consorts of the blessèd kind. Others are not.

Over the years that awaited her, Landry would often speculate about what spectres sidled beside her and what they were to her if she couldn't see or hear them. She'd think then of the old and odd stories she carried with her. Some were rancid and weird, like how in a history class at Orvop High it was declared that homosexuality was what caused the downfall of Greek and Roman civilizations and, again in that same class, how it was a tragedy when a white man was killt by a savage defendin his family but how it was a victory when that savage and his family were all of them killt, this last story still pacin the sidewalks of near every intersection in Orvop. And there were plenty of others where that came from, but somehow the more she remembered them and spoke about them, the more she felt them let go of her. Maybe that was how reminiscin worked: you remember to forget. Funny, though, how whenever Landry was with a horse, she needed neither to forget nor remember. And if there were dead near, why they was welcome. Those were the times, when what was gone was welcome, when Landry felt most herself. Not that I ever stopped missin Tom.

Anyways, back to that moment in the hospital: it was the stabbin pain in her cheeks that had balanced out some the stabbin sadness in her heart. Of course, both pains were so different, there weren't really any balance to be had. It just checked Landry's tears is all.

Of course the FBI agents still had more questions, about Pillars Meadow, about whether or not she'd seen the Colt Peacemaker. She told them she had noticed its absence when she'd been huntin through her saddlebags for food. She'd also seen it in the mud when she was lookin for Kalin, but she hadn't had a mind to pick it up.

Why not? asked Agent Bruner.

It weren't lost on me what it had done.

The agents then asked her how she figured it had all gone down, which Holly Feltzman at once objected to, again on the grounds that it was speculation, but Landry Gatestone still said she had no idea. And then the tears came back. And this time they took a long time to stop, because this time all she could think of was Kalin.

Now over the course of these many interviews, with Landry not once refusin to revisit any of these events and her story never deviatin or much realignin, and with Detective Peters and Agents Bruner and Farro never forgettin what Old Porch was still sayin, that this here scrawny girl was the one who had wielded that Colt like some terrifyin warrior, flawlessly firin all six rounds and, as forensics would eventually reveal, killin five, an investigation of the scene of the gunfight was also underway. It weren't no perfect scene neither. After all, by her own admission, Landry had rode all over it. And that pilot, Colby Foster, and the EMT, Lorenzo Swapp, they'd trod right on through it in order to rescue Old Porch. Fortunately the freeze on Pillars Meadow set good what was still left undisturbed. Police investigators reached the area before dawn, with FBI Agents Bruner and Farro arrivin just before dusk. As you can likely already guess, this weren't some grand disquisition on the glories of GSR, meanin gunshot residue, or vagrant tangles of DNA pointin the finger at the culprit or culprits. What forensics would accomplish, they accomplished pretty quick, namely figurin out which gun killt who.

Shelly Porch shot his .38-caliber Ruger Service-Six five times and only managed to hit Woolsey Porch, who would bleed out from his injuries. Kelly Porch gutshot his brother Francis with his Remington 700 BDL. That done in Francis. It was determined that these were cross fire accidents. It was also determined that the trajectory of every shot originatin from the Colt Peacemaker was a killin shot, except one. Shelly Porch was killt by the Colt, as was Kelly Porch, as was Sean Porch. Billings Gale too. It was determined that Billings Gale, who was wieldin a .44 Magnum, Smith & Wesson Model 29-2, was the one who shot Kalin March. Egan Porch was also shot dead, and at a much closer range than the rest. Because of his position in relation to everyone else, and in accordance with Old Porch's own tellin of the facts, it was determined that Egan Porch was likely the first to die. As for Orwin Porch, he was not killt, but a bullet from the Colt still blew apart his spleen. That accounted for all six rounds. Presumedly the firearm was discarded after that.

Of great interest was how Hatch Porch had died. And Kevin Moffet too. They were not killt by the Colt but by a 9mm Smith & Wesson Model 59 with an aluminum frame, which was found frozen in the mud right where Orwin Porch had lain, the imprint of his wounded body clear as a fingerprint the followin mornin. Of course, there weren't no way to prove that, while proximal to the weapon, Old Porch was the one who'd wielded it. For one thing, the weapon was so marred and tumulted by weather that not one fingerprint upon any of its surfaces had survived as anythin better than a teasin smudge. Plus Orwin Porch firin the thing didn't occur to no one because it didn't make no sense. What kind of father shoots his own son in the back? Inconceivable! Old Porch's version then remained the only acceptable one: Landry Gatestone was firin the Colt, which left Kalin March firin the 9mm, the weapon that had not only killt Hatch Porch and Kevin Moffet but also Law Enforcement Ranger Bren Kelson.

In fact GSR might've proved a thing or two, but no residues were ever collected nor were powder burns ever looked for. Determinin that Kevin Moffet was shot dead well before the rest of the slaughterin commenced might've showed somethin too, but Assistant Medical Examiner Annabelle Kasey, MD, was not handlin the bodies, and the coroners who did carry out the examinations of those frozen and mis-handled corpses never produced a court-worthy assessment of who fell first and who fell last.

But Detective Peters and FBI Agents Bruner and Farro all agreed that that 9mm still had a story to tell. The fact that every identifyin marker had been filed off fer sure intensified their interest. It struck them as peculiar too that this weapon in particular had only shot people from behind: Bren Kelson through the back of the head, Kevin Moffet also through the back of the head, and Hatch Porch in the back.

Throughout, the investigators had kept tryin to imagine Landry Gatestone at the very center of such hellfire, and they just couldn't do it. She just didn't fit the bill. And it weren't either that she was a little girl or that her skin was darker than most in Utah Valley; Detective Peters and Agent Farro both had some color to them, as folks favorin Old Porch's side of things liked to point out. No, it was mainly about spendin time with her; neither Detective Peters nor Agents Bruner and Farro believed Landry Gatestone was lyin. She'd done no shootin. Plus there were her injuries. What projectile had pierced her cheeks remained inconclusive, thanks to surgery and whatnot, but such a wound would surely have affected her aim in the middle of a gunfight, ambush or not.

Not that they didn't keep tryin to give Old Porch's version a fair shake, but it weren't no use; more and more disturbances kept arisin. They found horse manure up in Coyote Gulch as well as near the aban-doned campsite just below summit ridge. Some climbers, all roped up, even investigated the ledges on the headwall. They found horse manure there too. One thing, though, that no one found was a vantage point on the headwall from which someone could've fired down and hit Law Enforcement Ranger Bren Kelson. None of the angles matched up. The entry wound and exit wound described a trajectory through Kelson's head that was unavailable anywhere on the face of those mighty cliffs. It was also determined by then that the shot was taken at a range much closer than even someone positioned at the base of the headwall. Imaginin someone standin right behind and a little higher than Law Enforcement Ranger Bren Kelson produced a more tenable scenario. Detective Peters sure could visualize that the clearest, and no doubt it helped that he ended up standin on the very same rock Egan Porch was standin on when he killt Kelson.

Egan Porch was dead, of course, but investigators still started takin a closer look at his body and at Billings Gale's body too, as they were both with Kelson when he was killt, as confirmed by Park Ranger Emily Brickey.

A fter what happened up at Pillars Meadow started comin out in the news, Park Ranger Emily Brickey didn't wait for no knock on her door. She at once sought out Detective Peters and Agents Bruner and Farro. And she brought with her documentation too. She already knew in her heart that, though it was only a scatterin of days since she'd been up on Katanogos, she'd already waited too long.

This happened before I heard shots over the radio, shots I likewise heard ringin out across the cirque, with Egan Porch then yellin that they'd shot Kelson in the head. In her deposition, Park Ranger Emily Brickey recalls hearin over Kelly Porch's radio, which was beside Hatch Porch and weren't but a few feet away, a softer conversation between Billings Gale and Egan Porch. *The one named Billings, he said that they'd somehow made it over, that they was clear of this place, and then I heard Egan Porch say that now they had another day on them and that they'd either better figure out a way up or head back. I was so struck by this conversation that I wrote it down.* And that weren't all that was inscribed on those pages.

It's true that Park Ranger Emily Brickey's recollections didn't exactly blow the axles off Old Porch's story, but they sure did set them wheels to wobblin. Agent Bruner and Detective Peters both began fidgetin this idea that it was either Billings Gale or Egan Porch who'd actually killt Kelson with the aluminum-frame 9mm. Old Porch hadn't been anywhere near Kirk's Cirque, but it was also pretty curious that somehow the same weapon had turned up on the other side of Kata-nogos and just a few feet from where Old Porch was lyin on Pillars

Meadow. It sure did make the mind wonder. Had whoever killt Kelson given the weapon to Old Porch later? But why? And why continue to use it up on Pillars Meadow, on the pilot Kevin Moffet, on Hatch? Though why then hadn't it been found with someone other than Old Porch? Say on Egan Porch or Billings Gale? Of course, Landry Gatestone, and we're speakin now of Landry Gatestone the Gunslinger, in the interest of protectin herself and whatever story was to emerge about her accomplice Kalin March, was fit enuf to see that weapon lost near anywhere she wanted. But if framin Old Porch was the point, and yes, sure, she could've tossed the gun beside him, she weren't sayin anythin of the kind to lead them in that direction. Landry hadn't even noted the presence of two guns in any of her recountins. It was flummoxin fer sure.

Also flummoxin was how so many of those involved in the investigation, and there got to be quite a few, continued to just overlook the whole trajectory mismatch like it weren't but an *uhm* in the middle of a sentence that didn't change the story none, or the sentence for that matter. For all them officers, it was clear: whether Landry Gatestone or Kalin March, one of them had shot Kelson from above with that 9mm and then carried the gun to Pillars Meadow, where, accordin to Old Porch, Kalin then shot Kevin Moffet and Hatch Porch.

The thing was, FBI Agents Bruner and Farro weren't willin to overlook them trajectory discrepancies, and you can bet your boots Detective Peters wasn't willin to overlook them either. All three knew this wasn't some *uhm* in a story. It weren't no minor miscalculation either. Along with the forensic reports and the many details cataloged from the headwall exploration, the data concernin the path of the 9mm bullet fired from the Smith & Wesson Model 59 that killt Law Enforcement Ranger Bren Kelson was deemed not just admissible evidence but significant evidence. Though evidence to what conclusion? That was still the question.

Park Ranger Emily Brickey's deposition also went well beyond what she'd overheard on Kelly Porch's radio. She held nothin back. She even admitted to how she'd gotten into it with Allison March after callin her son trash. She included too how Old Porch had jabbed the map so hard, his thumbnail had split in half. And she didn't stop there either. She described how Old Porch had gotten so incensed when Undersheriff Jewell called the operation a rescue that he'd tore off some of that thumbnail and stained the map with blood. She told how Old Porch then objected to her even speakin. He sure hadn't liked it none when she'd made it clear that ATVs were forbidden in the park; Undersheriff Jewel had ordered her to open the gate anyways.

What Detective Peters and Agents Bruner and Farro drew from her remarks, and from similar testimony, fer example from Undersheriff Jewell hisself, was how Old Porch had continuously demonstrated a desire for blood. And he weren't the only one. Park Ranger Emily Brickey told how Kelly Porch had sworn to her that he was gonna kill a beaver they'd spotted in Altar Lake, and how, not long after she'd warned him that she'd cite him if he did, Kelly Porch had yelled *BANG!* so loud in her ear, it had made her jump. Of course, he'd passed it off like he was just joshin, but she couldn't shake the seriousness of his intent. Somethin about Egan had troubled her too, but it weren't but intuition, and she knew that didn't count for anythin in an investigation. Hatch Porch, though, and maybe this was because he was police, had seemed pretty coolheaded throughout, though it still bothered her how, even before Kelson was shot, he'd taken out that .50-caliber rifle. *He said he was just usin the scope to get a better eye on things, but everywhere he looked, the end of that barrel went too, and his finger sure weren't far from the trigger.* It had also bothered her how later, when they was rushin Kelson out of the cirque, she'd heard a rifle shot. *It was far off but it still sounded like a cannon.* Of course she couldn't say fer sure who fired it, but what other rifle up there could utter forth a report like that?

Though the three investigators didn't reveal much to Park Ranger Emily Brickey, they did discuss among themselves, and at length too, how that rifle shot pretty much timed out with when Landry Gatestone had said Kalin March and Navidad were gettin pinned down on the Upecksay Headwall before snow started fallin.

That was another thing this trio kept comin back to: horses on the headwall.

And let's not forget there was a mule too, Agent Bruner would remind her friends as she reached for another slice of pizza one night; in fact the same night she shared how what led her to joinin the FBI was that her aunt used to rob banks. Just an odd fact.

Back in Landry's hospital room, the claim of horses on the high cliffs of Katanogos had seemed a ridiculous if enthrallin piece of fictive freestylin; no matter that it was also so specific and at times so dull as to not merit the kind of storytellin that is all about effect. Landry seemed to care little for what effect her retellin had on any of them. Rather, she looked beholden to a creation larger than what any tellin could ever handle.

As a general rule, Detective Peters never discussed his cases with his wife, Elizabeth, who was seven months pregnant too, but this time he couldn't help hisself. He and his wife would sit on the sofa, starin at the TV that was off, as he revisited beat by beat how the young girl and boy had supposedly taken three horses and a mule up a mountain wall. He told her about the pitons they'd found. He'd confirmed the numerous and ample-sized ledges. He told her about the rocky havens along the way.

Then they really did do it? Elizabeth asked. *They must really know horses. Did they ride them or lead them?*

The girl said the boy rode. She said she was so scared at times, she couldn't even move. I couldn't help but believe her, but then I went up there myself and looked first hand at what they'd supposedly done, and I didn't believe a word of it.

But you said there was horse manure?

Detective Peters nodded, continuin to stare at that black box of a TV but like it was on and ten times the size too and with the brightest colors. *Our team also found a blast hole that pretty much fits the bill for a fifty cal.*

Well, what are you frettin about? his wife asked, rubbin her belly with his hand. *Sounds like she weren't lyin.*

I walked up a little ways, her husband continued, *maybe a couple of hundred feet up, and my gosh, that was enuf. And I was doin it in the day with the sun out and the rock dry. They did it in the rain, in a snowstorm, at night.*

Detective Peters kept shakin his head. And he weren't the only one. Long after Agent Bruner had left Utah, she continued to have nightmares, *like of those mountain goats you see perched on nothin, except in my dreams they aren't goats; they're horses, and they're saddled, and children are on them! It's both mesmerizin and terrifyin!* Agent Farro never dreamt about horses, but he often used Landry's history as an example of somethin that, even after you've carefully rationalized and evidentially confirmed it, you recognize some part of yourself is still in denial. *I'd spent a lot of time lookin up at that wall and I'll tell you . . . I don't know what to tell you.*

Accordin to Park Ranger Emily Brickey, even Law Enforcement Ranger Bren Kelson doubted hisself. *I still remember what he said. I wrote it down that night, but I didn't need to,* Brickey told them. *I'll be goshdarned, Emily, I see horses up there. I don't believe it, but there they are. That's what he said. I think I answered him with somethin like Horses?!*

Detective Peters had spent a little time workin out where Kelson would have had to stand in order to catch a glimpse of Landry's and Kalin's horses. *If he'd been just a little closer to the base of the headwall,* Detective Peters would point out later, *he wouldn't have spotted them. Who knows what would've happened then. Maybe he'd still be alive today, with Brooke, havin a family. The What-ifs can drive you crazy.*

And the headwall up to the Katanogos summit ridge, though the most dramatic part, was still just a part of a journey that continues to stutter even the most imaginative. *It's really important to emphasize the quality of horsemanship goin on here,* Detective Peters liked to say. *Everyone in Orvop and pretty much Utah Valley knows Isatch Canyon terminates beyond Bridge Seven at Yell Rock Falls. There's no way outta there without rock climbin equipment. But those two kids made gettin outta there look like child's play. And on horseback too. At that level, you can understand the bond these kids had to have had with their animals, their absolute devotion to them. Of course, others will argue that takin horses into such a rocky place was a cruelty, and you'll get no argument from me. That bein said, I also have no doubt they had no intention to be cruel. Those horses were slated to die. The kids sought only to give them a second chance, and in that respect, from what we can gather, they succeeded.*

Back in Michigan, Agent Bruner would often reflect on this aspect of overcomin what everyone else assumes is the limit. *Kalin March was a dead-end kid who kept ridin into dead ends that couldn't put an end to him. Isatch Canyon. Kirk's Cirque. Of course, he left enuf dead in his wake.*

Detective Peters agreed with Agent Bruner. *A whole pile of bodies. These days folks like to imagine Pillars Meadow as this snowy field with blossoms of red here and there, bright as roses. And there was snow, and where the blood met the snow, it was bright red. Mostly, though, it was mud, mucked up, clawed at, and come night harder than granite with a layer of frost that hung on well past dawn.*

One curious aspect that preceded the matter of the horses on the cliffs: aside from those involved, and that includes Lindsey Holt, no one interviewed ever recollected Navidad and Mouse. None of the investigators ever found any records of origin. Some Orvop students who'd frequently walked past the paddocks on Willow and Oak recalled there bein horses, maybe a black one, maybe one that was piebald, maybe just a brown one. Others were certain there were horses but never paid much mind as to what they looked like. And a few were surprised to learn that Agents Bruner and Farro just assumed they should have names. *It was almost like they was never really there to begin with,* Agent Farro would sometimes muse. *But freein them changed that,* Agent Bruner would add. It was like their liberation first and foremost granted them bein. And they were right. Now no one will ever forget Navidad and Mouse.

Clop-Clop-clip-Clop.

The more the investigation checked out Landry's testimony, the more details they found to corroborate her version of things. *A tellin sturdy as oak,* admitted Detective Peters, who, along with Agents

Bruner and Farro, eventually went so far as to harness and rope up in order to rappel down and indagate the very spot where Landry claimed to have been saved by trees growin on the side of a cliff.

The agents had to search several possibilities along that ridgeline, but they didn't give up, and in the end Detective Peters was rewarded with the sight of what was later proved to be Landry's blood. Not that they needed it. They also found shreds of her clothin preserved in a squirrel's drey. Along with the help of several deputies from the sheriff's department and park rangers, they also located the round that had passed through Landry's mouth; it was lodged in the trunk of a paperbark birch. The bullet was easily matched to Egan Porch's rifle.

Another curious discovery was made in Bewilder Crick, that little thread of water that still wanders away from Altar Lake up in Kirk's Cirque: a badly wounded beaver. The round that had done her down, what Nixie Smith, the vet who saved the beaver's life, found still lodged in her poor pregnant body, traced back to that mysterious 9mm Smith & Wesson Model 59 with an aluminum frame. Now it's true, it was easy enuf to construct a series of events, in line with Old Porch's narrative, that had Kalin March all along armed with this weapon, which, upon approachin Altar Lake, he drew forth and just for spite used to shoot the animal. It troubled the investigators, however, that Landry Gatestone had made so little mention of the beaver when so much of what she'd said matched near exact their findins in the field. There was also no plausible reason for Landry to conceal the shootin of the beaver. The kids were hungry, near starvin even. They wouldn't be faulted for huntin an animal for food. It sure would've beat the jerky Kalin got sick on. And, oh yes, there was still ample evidence of that. Despite the rain, the subsequent snow and freeze had helped preserve remnants of vomit and even some of Kalin's rear effluences.

Though hardly evidence, Landry also often recalled the great beauty that had surrounded them, that had so continuously intruded upon their mission and various plights. *Out of nowhere,* Landry had told the detective and agents, *the magnificence of where we was at would just hit you, and you'd forget what you was doin or where you were goin. You'd forget even yourself. Nothin else mattered except . . . I don't know how to put it.* Her frequent praise and affection for the terrain they'd traversed kept vexin the investigators: accordin to Orwin Porch, this here was the same girl who'd not only shot him but his five boys too.

Maybe it's not so surprisin that the more folks talked with Landry, the less convinced they grew about Old Porch's claims. And that got them lookin at everythin from a different angle.

First off, there was no doubt now that Egan Porch's rifle had shot Landry Gatestone; it was also a categorical fact that she'd wound up stuck between them trees and the cliff wall. Her blood was all over the bark and branches. Secondly, there's the severity of her wounds to again consider. Tryin to imagine her hoofin it down Coyote Gulch in time for a shoot-out, which, accordin to forensic experts, coroners, but most importantly Old Porch hisself, took place around noon, gets real tricky. An examination of her footprints alone, takin into account how the snow was thawin and refreezin, indicates she came down long after the fight was over.

To be fair, no investigator ever really put much stock in Landry Gatestone's capacity for violence let alone this notion of her triumphin in an armed contest against ten men. Talkin to her doctors or just lookin at them cheeks in the raw made her success in such a mêlée seem juberous at best. And anyway, pretty much everyone deemed such speculations irrelevant in light of Orwin Porch's response when Detective Peters asked him about Landry Gatestone's appearance. *She was cold-eyed.* That was how he'd described her. *Cold-eyed.* Now ain't that an odd thing to emphasize, especially since Landry's face would've been drenched in blood with likely still more blood oozin out of the holes? Those perforations alone would've been hard to look at. But Old Porch mentioned no such sight, leavin Detective Peters certain of one thing: Old Porch was lyin. But why? He hadn't lied about seein her. And she hadn't lied about seein him. Why hadn't he mentioned her face? *Because he didn't want to let us know that she'd been shot,* Agent Farro speculated. *Because he wanted to convince us that she was a killer,* Agent Bruner added. Detective Peters thought Old Porch was lyin about the names of them horses too. *Dapple and Bay?! He didn't even get their colors right!*

Nonetheless, everyone agreed that a good defense attorney would argue that Orwin Porch's trauma had reasonably affected his memory, especially where the chronology of events was concerned if not the events themselves. After all, he'd just watched all his boys die. And there was no counterin that terrible fact: except for an estranged daughter still livin with her mother in Texas, Old Porch had lost his whole family. Old Porch could be forgiven a few confusions. What jury wouldn't accord him that?

FBI Agent Herman Farro was the one who came up with the Vengeance Narrative. In fairness, both Detective Peters and Agent Bruner had been thinkin along those lines too, but neither had managed to articulate how that singular motive might've set into motion so much of what they were tryin to puzzle out. *Somethin about the Vengeance Narrative still didn't sit right with me,* Detective Peters would say later, *but I couldn't argue with Herman either. It just made the most sense. And for a while Linda and I went with it.* Agent Bruner also had her doubts, but she too shared Detective Peters's sentiments: *At the time it just made the most sense.*

Under the organizin principle of revenge, most folks could understand why the Porches were lyin about half the things they were doin. Their youngest brother had showed up on Egan's doorstep with his throat cut, his saddle and horse splattered with blood, the one who done it on his lips. Russel Porch's last word in fact was just a name: *Kalin.* Or so most of Orvop and Utah Valley folk had come to believe. And so, yes, sure, for appearances' sake, the Porches were gonna lie about just wantin to find their horses when in fact they was lookin for some good ole Old Testament retribution. An eye for an eye. A life for a life. Blood.

And if Landry Gatestone was somehow mixed up in it, even if she was just a bystander or a curiosity seeker, that was on her. They'd take her down too. This angry spirit, Agent Bruner argued, would for the Porches justify plenty, whether it was disobeyin city and county ordinances by drivin dirt bikes, ATVs, and snowmobiles into the park or firin shots on the one who killt their brother. Even shootin a little girl. *Why to them, shootin a beaver for no other reason than to kill makes sense.*

Yet even if you did take the Porch family's repercussive fury as true, and many did, for Detective Peters enuf dissonances still remained in that narrative to give him an almost caffeinated charge. He alternately sensed that there still might exist yet another arrangement of these events or, even more unsettlin, another event not yet accounted for whose dark gravity was continuin to shape everythin else they'd thus far encountered. Detective Peters couldn't stop interrogatin this sensation either, tryin to dislodge the truth from a feelin, like a tongue that keeps jabbin at a tooth that's all but danglin from a thread of gum tissue.

One thing Detective Peters and Agents Bruner and Farro continued to suspect was that before the shoot-out, Orwin Porch believed Landry Gatestone had already been killt. *Likely Egan Porch had told his dad the second they met up on Pillars Meadow,* Agent Bruner would say. *After the shoot-out, when Mr. Porch discovered she was still alive, he would've figured she'd soon enuf point the finger at him and Egan. My guess is that he decided right there in his hospital room to cast Landry Gatestone in the worst light possible, even if that meant makin Landry Gatestone responsible for most of the killins. Obviously, he'd have seen how shot up her face was, but maybe he figured folks would think that occurred in the ensuin gunfire after she'd shot him. Maybe Mr. Porch thought that her wound would strengthen his case that she was the one wieldin the Colt.*

Saddlin Landry Gatestone with as much of the blame as Kalin March certainly fit the Vengeance Narrative. But what to do about the killin of Law Enforcement Ranger Bren Kelson?

By this point Detective Peters had interviewed a number of Orvop High students to get a better sense of those involved in the events up on Pillars Meadow. One interview had really stuck out: Staci Lithy, sister to Kenny Lithy. She'd been on the gymnastics team, where she'd managed to keep clear of Coach Pill except while she was on the parallel bars. She was an exceptional gymnast as well as an exceptional student, especially in the sciences. She never did recall seein Kalin March, but she knew the Porch boys well enuf to keep clear of them, *all of them.* She also knew Landry Gatestone. They weren't close at Orvop High, but in grade school they'd been best friends and had both hid in the Lithy basement when Egan, Sean, and Shelly had come over to help Kenny kill rats that was hidin under the many moldy heaps of loose boards and whatnot in the backyard. *The best I can figure it, the boys were just fed up with schoolin and the Church and they liked the killin. They were at it for hours. Egan's pitchfork had the most rats on it. He left it leanin by my bedroom door.*

The story sure indicated a love of violence practiced by the Porch boys, especially Egan, but the killin of Law Enforcement Ranger Bren Kelson went way beyond that, beyond the Vengeance Narrative too. Here was outright murder, senseless murder, especially given that for all intents and purposes Kelson was on the side of the Porches, aligned with the task of trackin down them kids.

Agent Bruner by then had begun to wonder aloud if maybe the Porches were troubled by the presence of Law Enforcement Ranger Bren Kelson because that meant Landry and Kalin would at best be arrested. Agent Farro added how *maybe Egan Porch and this Billings Gale came to an agreement that Kelson was only gonna get in the way of the violence they felt entitled to.*

But they'd only seen the horses on the headwall. Why kill Kelson at that moment? Detective Peters asked.

Because with Kelson gone, Hatch Porch could start firin that fifty cal. They could all start firin, Agent Farro suggested.

Don't forget Park Ranger Brickey was still up there with them.

Maybe they were gonna kill her too, Agent Farro said with a shrug.

Exactly! Detective Peters said, clappin his hands together. *But they didn't!*

Because not all the Porches were of the same mind, Agent Farro said slowly then. *Hatch Porch was still an officer of the law. He only fired the M82 once.*

Which he admitted first thing to Undersheriff Jewell, Detective Peters added.

To pin down Kalin March, Agent Bruner confirmed.

But, Agent Farro continued, *if Kelson was killt by Landry or Kalin, then shouldn't both Park Ranger Brickey and Hatch Porch been on board?*

That's supposin a lot, Agent Bruner grunted, less convinced.

Kelson's death, though, would further convince everyone down below that they were on the right trail, that Kalin March and Landry Gatestone were the ones who'd killt Russel Porch, Detective Peters said, his eyes bright, even at the late hour.

But we still have that gun, Agent Bruner said, already startin to doubt the direction of her thoughts. *Because of Kelson and the beaver, we know the 9mm Smith and Wesson Model 59 was up there in the cirque, but we also know it ended up at Pillars Meadow.*

Egan Porch or Kelly Porch or Billings Gale, one of them could've brought it down the mountain, Agent Farro responded, lettin hisself go along with wherever this was headin.

Then all they had left to do, Detective Peters said, *was make sure the gun that killt Kelson—*

And the pilot, Agent Bruner added, sittin up.

And Hatch Porch, Agent Farro threw in, also more alert than usual.

—wound up, Detective Peters said, continuin everyone's thoughts, *on Kalin March.*

Preferably in his hand, Agent Farro added.

But instead it ended up within reach of Orwin Porch, Agent Bruner concluded with a sigh.

It all seemed so close to somethin that made sense, somethin possible, at times even probable, until all at once sense itself seemed impossible. But then again, gettin horses over the Katanogos summit ridge had seemed impossible too.

Agent Bruner got up and poured herself and Agent Farro another round of tequila and Detective Peters another cup of Fanta. That particular night ended with her lamentin how they couldn't talk to none of the Porch boys. What she'd give to have a conversation with one of their ghosts. What she needed to do was figure out how to better talk to their corpses, but those weren't givin up nothin more than the name of the gun that killt them.

It was in the dark that precedes by hours any dawn that Detective Peters abruptly woke up and told his sleepy wife that he had to drive to Colorado, all the way to Greeley if need be. He at once packed a small bag and even got as far as tossin it into the trunk of his Mustang, long since repaired, his days in his wife's eggplant-colored Honda Civic over. But while preparin oatmeal and raisins, he got to thinkin he should at least call the gal one more time. Not that he hadn't tried a dozen times already. Agents Bruner and Farro too. They'd even contacted Greeley police for a little assistance but to no avail. She just weren't around no more.

So Detective Peters was understandably surprised when Lathrop Philoment picked up after the first ring. He recognized her voice at once. He'd spoken to her before, when he'd called to tell her that Trent Riddle was dead. Detective Peters apologized for the early call and introduced hisself again. He had a sense she might hang up on him, but she didn't. She apologized for not callin him back. She'd gone to Boulder to stay with friends. She still hadn't processed the accident and apologized if she started cryin.

I don't think I can talk about it no more, she even said. But they ended up talkin for a good hour. Mostly Detective Peters just listened to her anguish. She still felt guilty that her first reaction when Trent Riddle hadn't shown up that Thursday mornin was that he'd just ditched her and hadn't even had the decency to call. *I was so mad at him! I'd missed work for him!* Of course, when she'd reminded herself that it was a good seven-hour drive from Orvop to Greeley, she'd figured he might very well have just pulled over for a moment of sleep. She'd kept assurin herself that she'd be holdin his hand before noon. But then Trent's brother had called. And not long after that they found the wreck. Now she felt guilty because she was the reason he'd been drivin so late.

It wasn't your fault he was drivin so fast or that he was under the influence of alcohol, Detective Peters assured her.

I guess.

Plenty of folks drive at night and manage through just fine.

That's true.

Just an hour ago I was plannin to drive your way.

You need to look at his body or the wreck or somethin?

Trent Riddle's body was already back in Orvop. The wreck had been cleared away too. *I needed to find you.*

Me?

Did Trent ever talk about the man he worked for? Orwin Porch?

Who?

He might've called him Old Porch.

Trent didn't talk much about work except that he was sick of it.

Did he mention a poker game?

Trent played poker?

You said he called you Wednesday night to tell you he was comin your way?

He sure did but he didn't mention poker. That really surprises me. If you're in the Church, I don't think cards are allowed.

When you did speak with him that night, could you tell he was drinkin?

That's another thing that surprised me. He swore he didn't drink.

Do you?

Sure. I'm not with any church.

May I ask you a personal question, Miss Philoment?

That depends.

What did you expect would happen when Trent made it to Greeley?

We'd only met once, and that was on a flight comin into Salt Lake City. We sat next to each other. I had the window. We kissed when we landed. After that, we just, you know, called and sent postcards. Just to see him again would've made me happy.

Was he plannin to stay with you?

I didn't care, Detective Peters. What's this all about anyway? I've already told you everythin I know.

And that was true, she had. Detective Peter even admitted so. What he didn't tell her was that he needed to revisit these stories if only to apply some stress to what she earlier might have felt was fine and settled. Stories have lives of their own. Give them time and they change.

Do you recall what time he called you that Wednesday night?

Around midnight.

Did he sound drunk?

You already asked me that. Not one bit.

And he didn't tell you he'd won big at a poker game?

He said he'd got some extra money and we was gonna have fun.

How'd that strike you?

Like fun? The sharpness in her voice weren't lost on him.

No slurrin of any words?

I never once heard Trent Riddle slur a word.

After Detective Peters hung up, he sat down and ate his oatmeal. He weren't goin to Greeley anymore. Lathrop Philoment had told him all she could. He tried then to focus more clearly on Trent Riddle, but what kept comin up was Orwin Porch, standin where they slaughter cattle. Detective Peters weren't gonna forget the sight: Orwin Porch by hisself, his apron spattered with blood and bits. He'd tossed a hammer away, which had also unsettled Detective Peters. The baseball bat hadn't worried him much, but he'd noticed that somethin he couldn't quite make out was attached to one end. Maybe a horseshoe? What Detective Peters had sensed then he discovered was only more intense now: threat. But the feelin had passed at once when he'd told Orwin Porch that Trent Riddle was dead. The man's smile had vanished with that news, but what was hauntin Detective Peters now, while he was sittin at his kitchen table starin at an empty breakfast bowl, was how the smile hadn't vanished at once. It had lingered. And for a moment there Detective Peters thought it had even gotten bigger.

Lathrop Philoment's conviction that Trent Riddle weren't slurrin was a flat-out contradiction of both Orwin Porch's and Gale Billings's claim that the man had been blind drunk. That had to mean somethin, but what? And also so what? Detective Peters washed and racked his breakfast bowl.

If only to do what he'd done with Lathrop Philoment, apply some stress to settled stories, Detective Peters next called up Trent Riddle's folks. The first time he'd spoken with them, a conference call that had included Agent Farro, they were beyond heartbroken yet keen to be of as much help as possible even if what they could offer wasn't much help. Trent's father hadn't wanted to get on the line though he eventually did. This time they both picked up, and before Detective Peters could even get out one question, they were both expressin great delight to be hearin from him and at once invited him over. It turned out they lived less than nine blocks away. They needed his advice.

I just don't know what to do with it, Mrs. Jolene Riddle said in her livin room not ten minutes later. She kept presentin Detective Peters with a smile freshly glossed with fuchsia lipstick that continued to collapse into an expression so gaunt, Detective Peters kept thinkin how insufferable losin his unborn baby would be let alone losin a child who was already in his twenties. He thought then of Orwin Porch, who'd lost every single one of his boys. *It didn't feel right to spend,* Trent Riddle's mom went on. *But it feels wrong too to keep it. Do you think we ought to just give it to the Church? Maybe we'll do it on his birthday? That seems a more hopeful day to celebrate than the day he di—* Her voice caught, but she would not let that stop her. She was a determined woman, her grayin hair up in a tightly wound bun, her blouse and sweater both buttoned to the top; only her brown eyes seemed fragile and adrift. *I want people to remember his beginnin, not his end.*

Detective Peters could only nod.

What do you think? she asked him. A nod wasn't good enuf for her. She held his gaze and her smile held too.

Would you mind if I looked at the money? Detective Peters asked. He knew better than to hope, but his chest was suddenly thuddin, all of him sweatin too, and it weren't even so warm in that small livin room with, of all things, a print of Altar Lake hangin on one wall.

Despite his excitement, though, when Mrs. Jolene Riddle reappeared from the kitchen with the ziplock bag, he asked her to hold on to it until Agents Bruner and Farro arrived. Fortunately they didn't take long.

Wearin latex gloves, Agent Bruner carefully emptied the money on a clean towel she'd brought along with an evidence collection kit. Then, usin tweezers, she slowly and very methodically plucked free from the pile one bill at a time. Trent Riddle's mother was understandably puzzled. Detective Peters and Agent Farro tried to keep her entertained even if their attention continued to return to that low lacquered coffee table before which Agent Bruner kneeled. She didn't kneel for long. Not a few minutes into her inspection, Agent Bruner let loose a low whistle. There it was: one twenty-dollar bill with writin on the back side, right across the White House, in what they would confirm that day was Landry Gatestone's cursive and soon after prove was Russel Porch's signature. One bill of sale:

I accept this $20 as full payment for these two horses — Navidad & Mouse. Now owned completely by Landry Gatestone. October 27, 1982

Russel Porch

A nd then not too long after that, the very tall George Bray, accompanied by his two terriers, MacArthur and Patton, strolled into the Orvop Police Station. He wore faded jeans loose as empty laundry bags with a winter coat over a khaki vest over a plaid shirt. His hat had U.S.S. Intrepid embroidered on it. He was also smokin a Virginia Slim and refused to put it out. He smiled and told the riled-up sergeant that he had some things to say about the Russel Porch investigation and someone *of real importance* could find him outside. Maybe because one young officer there thought meetin him would be about as close as he'd get to meetin John Wayne, the resemblance was uncanny, he hurried out to hear what the old man had to say.

When Detective Peters and Agent Bruner sat down with him,

George Bray explained how he never paid the news much mind. *I gave that up some years ago. Best decision of my life.* He even sounded like John Wayne. When he finally did get wind of some kids cuttin Russel Porch's throat up in Isatch Canyon, why that lit his fuse.

You see, I seen Russel Porch returnin from the canyon later that night. George Bray was out havin hisself a cigarette *when along comes thee finest thing I seen in years.* It was young Russel Porch atop the tallest liver chestnut stallion in the area. *That would be Egan Porch's Cavalry. No mistakin that horse. And there was Russel Porch, beamin brighter than a big moon. I called him over. You bet I did. We didn't know one another much, but he smiled extra just the same, glad as most folks are when they have occasion to share some pleasant words with a neighbor. I asked him why he was out at night and in such a storm. He didn't seem at all bothered by the rain, and he was more than happy to tell me about his daddy's missin horses and how he'd been sure he was gonna find hisself in a confrontation that would leave him and the ones responsible for the theivin fairly bloodied. And in truth, he told me, it had in fact started out with some tus-slin, but then it had taken a strange turn. Those were his words: a strange turn. The horses were slated for slaughter and, accordin to his daddy, him bein Orwin Porch, they weren't worth but five bucks apiece. Russel, though, had managed a sale for twice that, which was surely gonna please his daddy. Now anyone who's lived in Orvop as long as I have knows about Orwin Porch. He's a nasty man. You can bet that boy was plenty glad to be headin home with news that would keep him clear of that nastiness. And I was glad for him. But then Russel continued to tell me about his adventure, and this time he lowered his voice some even though there weren't nobody else around. And my wife, well, Dorothy not only had the TV volume all the way up but she'd put Dolly Parton on the stereo too, and on top of that she was fast asleep on the couch! I gave Russel the nod so he understood that what he was about to confide weren't for anybody else, meanin especially not for his old man. That's when he told me how he'd ended up sittin around the fire with the two kids he'd just sold the horses to: Landry Gatestone and Kalin March. I know the Gatestone name. I still remember when the eldest Gatestone, Evan, was killt in a car accident. About five years ago. 1977 I think. Barely seventeen. A good kid. The community felt his loss. And Kalin March, I'd never heard of him. But anyways, Russel told me they'd all ate beans and rice, and they was the best beans and rice he'd ever had. He seemed astonished. Here he'd gone out without a penny in his pocket to catch a horse thief, and now he was comin back with twenty bucks in his pocket and two new friends. He was just beamin. He couldn't wait to see them again in school. That's what he told me. Suffice it to say his throat looked just fine. And then he patted that beautiful horse on the neck and tilted his hat at me and rode off into the rain. You know what I thought? Why there goes a real cowboy!*

Boy, did that change everythin, and that still weren't the most of it. Agent Farro had put in some good work, and after servin a warrant to search Porch Meats, the plant in back, as well as the main house, officers discovered somethin in the house trash bin: a plastic bag coated on the inside with dried blood.

Analysis soon enuf determined that the blood was Law Enforcement Ranger Bren Kelson's. And shortly thereafter it was confirmed that Billings Gale's prints were all over the bag.

That right there was the moment when the Vengeance Narrative was struck from the whiteboard.

Detective Peters and Agents Bruner and Farro turned their focus to Russel Porch and more specifically to the poker game at Egan Porch's house that Wednesday night on October 27. Witnesses corroborated that Francis Porch and Woolsey Porch, as well as the older brothers, Sean Porch and Shelly Porch, had all been seen after the poker game, whether they was stoppin by a 7-Eleven or callin friends. Further testimony confirmin their shock the followin mornin upon learnin about Russel Porch's death suggested that these four were in the dark about what had befallen their youngest brother. That left just Orwin Porch, Egan Porch, Kelly Porch, and Billings Gale with the dead Russel Porch. And Trent Riddle. Egan Porch and Billings Gale were also together when Cavalry was shot. A forensic team was dispatched to examine the body of the dead horse, which was still up on Aster Scree, where it would remain until wild animals, time, and curious kids scattered the bones. Egan Porch and Billings were also together when Law Enforcement Ranger Bren Kelson was murdered.

Stickin for a moment longer with the narrative line that Kalin March and Landry Gatestone were still guilty of murderin Russel Porch, if one or both were also blamed for the murder of an officer of the law, their guilt would be pretty much assured. That right there provided an alternate motive as to why Billings Gale and presumably Egan Porch would murder Law Enforcement Ranger Bren Kelson: to further assure that the kids would take the fall.

There was another tragic aspect to all this that began to materialize: it was entirely possible that like his brothers Francis, Woolsey, Sean, and Shelly, Hatch Porch too was enchained by a false narrative and put in pursuit of two kids who'd done nothin more than abscond with two horses slated for renderin. Many police officers who'd helped work the case and knew Hatch Porch by reputation if not personally would feel their hearts go blue.

Soon enuf the forensic team dispatched to examine dead Cavalry discovered not only a slug from Egan's Smith & Wesson .357 Magnum responsible for the headshot but also a 9mm slug deep in the carcass. That round was shown to have orginated from the Smith & Wesson Model 59 that had killt Law Enforcement Ranger Bren Kelson as well as the pilot Kevin Moffet. Furthermore, without prior knowledge concernin the emergin details of the case, the team felt that there was corporeal evidence to suggest that it was the .357 that had killt Cavalry and that the 9mm had come after. Those results weren't conclusive, but they weren't easily dismissed either.

What was conclusive was the casin finally found near where Law Enforcement Ranger Bren Kelson was murdered. This would be the third one that Egan never did locate. It had wandered some with the rain and snow, buried beneath pebbles and eventually more mud, where it was all set to hide forever, except it didn't hide forever, revealin itself to keen and persistent eyes: the discharge from the very same aluminum-framed Smith & Wesson Model 59.

Aided by others employed by the FBI, Agents Bruner and Farro are credited with discoverin still more about that criminally prepared 9mm Smith & Wesson Model 59. Fer starters, the identifyin markers weren't just simply scratched off. They'd been expertly removed. No amount of testin would reveal its history.

The trouble for the Porches came when it was discovered that this weren't the only weapon similarly disidentified. Quite separate from the ongoin investigation, a local man by the name of Jarold Lobland was arrested in November for the illegal possession of over one pound of marijuana as well as the possession of eight 9mm Smith & Wesson Model 59s with aluminum frames, all stripped of identifyin markers in the exact same way as the murder weapon. The wife of one of the arrestin officers, when she heard the story, quipped that old Will Rogers saw: *I never took a human life, I only sold the fellow the gun to take it with.*

When the consequences began to take hold of this not-so-brave purveyor of such armaments, mainly all those years behind bars, much like a wolf's teeth startin to exert pressure on the skin on the way to bone, why Jarold Lobland told the police everythin he could about those who was plannin to buy from him and those he'd already sold to. Of the previous buyers, one man in particular proved of great interest. In the presence of Jarold Lobland and his brother, Mane, said person of interest had purchased one ounce of marijuana and one Model 59. That buyer was none other than Egan Porch.

A nd then Assistant Medical Examiner Annabelle Kasey called.
Her news, however, weren't the best: the evidence she'd filed
for Russel Porch's case was missin. She could shed no light on why
that was so. She recalled clearly handin the evidence to Chester Walheimer, an intern from the U of U. Chester had hand-delivered the
evidence to the property room, where Officer-in-Charge Pat Stubbs
signed for the delivery. Neither Officer Brennan Hurley nor William
Mecham, who'd been called in to help reorganize some shelves, were
mentioned. Nor was the curious case of Russel H. Crop, not then nor
the followin year, with Crop's evidence box, unbeknownst to all, now
containin two evidence pouches central to Russel Porch's autopsy.

Nonetheless, while the artifacts themselves were lost, Assistant
Medical Examiner Kasey's report was not, nor was her eidetic memory of the contents of those pouches. Chester Walheimer also recalled
with great clarity the moment when Kasey demonstrated for him that
the shards were crystal.

Assistant Medical Examiner Annabelle Kasey also recalled the
wedge cuts, which a little research revealed were a Lismore pattern,
likely on a Waterford tumbler.

With Egan Porch named as the purchaser of the murder weapon,
a warrant was not hard to secure. Detective Peters and Agents Bruner
and Farro, along with a small team of qualified experts, were soon
combin through the personal effects of one Egan Porch in his residence
near Isatch Canyon. It didn't take long to locate a set of Waterford
tumblers with a Lismore pattern. It was an extraordinary moment and
even occasioned a spine-shudderin frisson that can accompany the
discovery of evidence controvertin long-held preconceived notions.

Russel Porch's throat weren't cut up in Isatch Canyon, nor had
he died outside on the sidewalk. He'd died in here. Or at least that's
how it seemed for a few minutes. Agent Bruner soon pointed out
how Assistant Medical Examiner Annabelle Kasey was free to offer up
her testimony in court, but without the actual crystal shards, an able
defense attorney would be able to stir up enuf doubt to negate her
claims if not render them entirely inadmissable.

Agent Bruner aired similar misgivins. He was standin right beside
the big table where most of the Porch family had played that last game
of poker. Agent Farro then wondered aloud where they'd all sat. Detective Peters correctly placed Old Porch at the head, closest to the foyer.
They got the rest wrong but it didn't matter. They collectively started
to imagine and even act out how Russel might've arrived, aglow with
his news, handin his daddy that twenty-dollar bill. But what happened
then? How did a good moment boil up into a bad one? A thrown glass?

The outcome of some unreported rage or maybe even jubilation? No one thought Egan Porch had just stabbed the boy with a broken glass. Maybe the glass was already broken and the boy had fallen on it? A slip? Perhaps after a hard shove?

The three of them sensed somethin like that was possible even if none of it really hung together. Then in an inspired moment Agent Farro laid it out plain and simple and real obvious: Russel Porch had come in, given the twenty dollars to his daddy, who'd promptly tossed the bill into the big pot and then promptly lost it all; Old Porch had then thrown his glass and, maybe just because Russel Porch was closest, given the boy a shove. The pivot to Old Porch was interestin, though Agent Bruner still had to point out that there weren't a single bit of corroboratin evidence.

Detective Peters, though, still ran with the scenario. He imagined where Russel might've fallen and bled out. He got that near right too. Next he surmised how the blood would need cleanin up. Maybe there was a rug that had to be tossed. Maybe into the Porch incinerator. Billings Gale had sure made the mistake of not tossin that plastic bag into the incinerator. Folks make mistakes all the time. The floors would've then been mopped and bleached, with whatever sponges and rags used also disposed of; after which the floor would be covered up by, say, this here large Sarouk rug under their feet.

When the three pulled it back, they discovered only floorly cleanliness. But was it too clean? Detective Peters got down on his knees to look for splinters of glass. He found nothin.

From there he surmised that Orwin Porch, Egan Porch, Kelly Porch, and Billings Gale would've carried Russel's body outside into the rain. Agent Bruner brought up the blood seen on Cavalry. It was a grisly suggestion, but it squared best with what they was surmisin: Russel's family would've hauled his body up on the horse and let what blood was left in him drip some more on the animal before lettin him fall to the sidewalk. After that, one of them would've carried him closer to the front door, where the police found him. Detective Peters pointed out how there'd been blood-soaked towels around the corpse. *Likely the same ones used to soak up the blood inside,* he said.

They might've even wrung some out on the horse too, Agent Bruner added. But why?

Prison for manslaughter was one obvious answer. Agents Bruner and Farro had been hard at work and knew already a great deal about the pendin Four Summits deal. Those there were big stakes, and a death like this might could've sent such a deal off the rails. So there was a motive. Old Porch and his boys stood to make plenty if Four Summits went through. *Even if the project was never completed*, Agent Farro explained, *Orwin Porch was guaranteed a well-salaried position for years to come.*

From the point of view of the prosecution then, the conclusion was obvious: whether he or one of the others had shoved Russel, Old Porch had tried to hide what had happened by blamin someone else in order to protect the pendin deal to buy and develop part of the Kata-nogos massif.

You know, it sure is spooky how Landry and Kalin wound up headin right to where Orwin Porch was buyin land, Agent Farro then pointed out.

Why spooky? Detective Peters asked.

Or funny, Agent Bruner added.

Funny? Agent Farro didn't understand.

Ironic then? Agent Bruner replied. *You steal a man's horses, take them on some crazy trek, only to give them back to him at the end.*

Like a prank, Detective Peters said, and Agent Bruner nodded.

Except by Wednesday night Landry Gatestone owned them horses, and come Sunday . . . Agent Farro just shook his head. *You see what I'm sayin, right? By the end it was Orwin Porch tryin to steal the horses from Kalin. He was the horse thief.*

Of course any competent defense team would demonstrate real quick that however logical the prosecution's version of events might seem to a jury, there wasn't a single witness from that night nor one shard of crystal. Plus Waterford glasses with a Lismore pattern could be found in plenty of households in Orvop and throughout Utah Valley. Ask Mrs. Hallie Plummer. She had the same set.

Once again Agent Bruner did a pretty good job presentin the case they didn't have. But it was also at that moment that they collectively cast their eyes downward, only to realize an instant later, also collectively, that these suppositions more fragile than gossamer might not even matter. They raced outside the house. They didn't even say a word to one another. It took a moment to find the crawl space, but they were soon enuf scramblin under the house, partin old cobwebs, until they were lyin directly under Egan Porch's dinin room, not far from the foyer, starin up together at the joists. These three weren't disappointed either: bloodstains galore, like dried molasses droolin down between the floorboards.

Prosecutors proved without a doubt that the blood was Russel Porch's and the volume present on the underside of the floorin could not be obviated by some counterclaim of a minor injury, like a cut to a finger or a foot occurin at some other time. In fact even the amount beneath Egan Porch's house suggested a fatal injury. There was no quibblin with the DNA either: the sample was flawless. Russel Porch had died in his brother's dinin room, and Orwin Porch had done everythin he could to not only hide his involvement but shift the blame to two minors who at the time were entirely ignorant of the death of someone who, there was now reason to believe, was their friend.

Now whatever else has been mislaid throughout all this, or misrepresented or even mistaken, especially in regards to the details and mechanics of municipal proceedins and civic customs, understand that those portrayals have never been the purpose here. What's of substance is how numerous officers of the law put in a great deal of honest work attemptin to disentangle the bloody mess left behind. And when it came time for the trials, prosecutors did their very best to see that justice was served. And they felt certain too that their case would prevail. Or as one prosecutor phrased it: *Now we get to watch Orwin Porch squirm and crap hisself tryin to come up with words.*

Prosecutors spent a good deal of time decidin what to try Orwin Porch for. At one point they considered goin after him for the murder of Kevin Moffet. The fact, though, that the pilot was found still in possession of the cash Old Porch had paid him, those rolls still bound up in them red rubber bands, troubled them enuf to steer clear. Who pays someone, kills them, and then leaves them with all that money? Sure, there was a case to be made, but it posed challenges. There was also still the possibility that Egan or one of the others had done the actual killin.

In the end, Orwin Porch was tried twice. The first for the death of Russel Porch. The second for the murder of Hatch Porch. In retrospect, he should've been prosecuted for accessory after the fact to murder. However, the potential for low fines and a short prison sentence exasperated the Utah County Attorney's Office. Both trials resulted in a hung jury.

These outcomes were likely helped by those proverbial good citizens who in the first trial just couldn't believe that a father would behave so terribly when handlin the accidental death of his youngest boy. That went for the second trial where there were the same number of these proverbial good citizens who could not accept that a father would shoot his eldest in the back. Prosecutors even allowed that the shot was accidental. It didn't help that a postmortem evaluation of Hatch Porch's corpse had shown, incorrectly, that he'd taken the longest to die up there. At a memorial service held for him in Texas, Chief Castor Emerson called Hatch *brave throughout.*

Stake President Havril Enos took the stand as a character witness in both trials. He described his friend, Orwin Porch, as a pillar of the community. Enos was affable, believable, and often funny. He also weren't afraid to condemn the prosecution's pleniloquence, matched only by its slovenly ineptitude. He suggested that their many documents and transcripts be overwrit with countless obeli: *that simple division sign to indicate a passage of questionable integrity.* He drew attention to a multitude of errors plaguin the depositions and various other transcripts, harpin on silly solecisms like the writin of *trail* instead of *trial* or *house* instead of *horse* or *tropes* instead of *ropes* or even *his troy* instead of *history* or the repeated transcribin of *writin* instead of *ridin,* not to mention misspellin *mountain lions* numerous times.

Havin lived here my whole life, Havril Enos had declared happily, *this is my first time hearin about mountain loins!* The jury responded with sizable laughter.

Despite objections, all of which were sustained, Havril Enos never ceased to portray Kalin March as a pestilent outsider, a peccant hooligan, a violence-peddlin gentile. The *Desert News* concocted an elegiac piece on Orwin Porch replete with the lored legacy of his ancestors whether pioneers or Church officials. For reasons the prosecution never understood, witnesses who could've testified to Orwin Porch's bilious drunkenness, his penchant for violent misbehaviors, misogyny, coded racism, and there was more, refused to take the stand. Fear was likely one answer, as was the fact that many who'd not beheld the dark nature of Orwin Porch were still involved in lucrative dealins with the man.

Evidence rangin from call logs from phone booths near the Orvop airport to testimony from residents who *thought they saw* the Porches head out onto the Agoneeya side of Isatch Canyon the day of the rockfall were either deemed inadmissible or had no impact.

Old Porch was never jailed, always out on bail, ever present in Orvop as well as throughout the valley. Famous.

Furthermore, Orwin Porch didn't shy from takin the stand in both his trials, his performance likely improved by the Hawthorne effect, what with all that attention, them jurists, the spectators, an esteemed judge!, well, Old Porch just had to exceed hisself. The prosecution couldn't do nothin with him. He hid his superbious attitudes and at the same time refuted every insinuation that he was anythin but a model citizen. He had no idea what Russel's blood was doin *under Egan's house.* He had no comment on *them fantasy crystals.* Every chance he got, he maintained that his boy's throat was slashed up in Isatch

Canyon by *the Kalin March kid and that Landry Gatestone, who also ain't from around here, you know.* As far as he was concerned, his Russel was a hero. Despite his little boy's mortal wound, he'd still rode that big Cavalry all the way back to die in his daddy's arms, though not before namin his killer: *Kalin March.* Old Porch said it as many times as he could along with the fact that George Bray's testimony didn't mean bunk. *He's a faggot who smokes lady cigarettes.* He also claimed DNA didn't exist.

DNA evidence, though, also produced another startlin revelation: Billings Gale was none other than Orwin Porch's son. Furthermore, the tiny scroll found on his person, filled with odd longins and desires and general brokenheartedness cast him, at least in the eyes of the defense, as an appealin romantic. These curious divulgences likely helped Old Porch in the end because, regardless of those accusations leveled against him, one fact that no one could contest was that every single one of his boys, includin the one no one knew about, was now dead.

Old Porch never wavered once when proclaimin his innocence. All the way through, he stood by his guns, even as he cried and wailed.

Clop-Clop-clip-Clop.

And he walked free.

What Orwin Porch, though, had always feared from a manslaughter trial did indeed come to pass: not one of his investors stood by him. Even Havril Enos withdrew his financial commitment, and given how Enos had stood up for him, on the stand and under oath, Old Porch had to apologize to him for the lost opportunity. The banks fled swift enuf. Not a state senator returned his calls. You can bet the same was true of U.S. Senator Hays, who would later further distance hisself from the Porches, at one point claimin that where Senate Bill 1245 was concerned, Orwin Porch's calendar was always off: *Perhaps his own feverish wish for how things should turn out created in his head a false impression about how Congress runs. We was still a good ways off from anythin signed into law, and even if that had happened, and that was a big if, there was nothin guaranteein that Mr. Porch would acquire the land in question for his Four Summits development project.* By the end of the second trial, Four Summits was officially dead even if some of the vast acreage where Kalin had released the two ponies was still removed from BLM oversight. State-owned inholdins found in and around the Uinta-Isatch-Cache National Forest also went up for sale. Brother Mallory Guvin Hone, along with the rest of the Hone family, remained willin to sell their substantial holdins if it was to the right buyer. Additionally, others with stranded inholdins who never would've dealt with Old Porch, havin a nose for the likes of him, agreed to surrender their parcels in the name of what they saw as the greater Good.

Ultimately the land was purchased by none other than Sondra Gatestone in a partnership with the very same Movie Star who owned Cassidy Ski Resort. This announcement alone generated a vast number of donations from across the country. Called Phains Haven, the forty-thousand-plus acres on the east side of the Katanogos massif was not only preserved through a conservation easement and protective covenant but designated a refuge for both wild and retired horses. You can bet your boots that plenty of local horses made their way there, some of the Gatestone steeds, fer sure some of those abandoned by Porch, includin Barracuda, Gads, and Gump. Eventually even Agnes Bonnie Hopper set her Ariel loose there, and while it still weren't Bozeman, Ariel lived a long, good life. By makin a portion of her donations in the name of Allison March, Sondra Gatestone was able to grant Allison March one of the board seats overseein the sanctuary and its endowment.

Not that Allison March ever had much to do with the corporate workins of the endowment and only met a few times the dozen or so lawyers and financial analysts helpin to guide allocations and investments toward a sustainable future. Instead Allison March, along with Sondra, handled the day-to-day details, every quarter meetin with the Movie Star in his Tree Room for brunch, the whole of those conversations usually focused on what backhoes they might swap out for tractors or what vet they should call or in general what not to fuss with. It was nice.

Allison March accepted a modest salary and worked for Phains Haven for the rest of her life. Sondra Gatestone, who required no salary, also worked for Phains Haven for the rest of her life. The two women remained thick as thieves. *You can make new friends any old time,* Allison March would often quip, *but you can't make new old friends.* Sondra said the same to Tucker Wyatt whenever he'd come around, which weren't as often as he'd've liked, bein called to the earth before he could ever summon up the courage for a proposal. He weren't the only one to note how both women knew every horse by color, markings, and name. They knew them forty-thousand-plus acres about as well too. Volunteers were welcome, though them were kept coralled more than the horses.

The general rule at Phains Haven was to, whenever possible, just let the horses be. Of course any horse in trouble was immediately attended to, with those who favored human companionship always welcome. Allison and Sondra even devised a commissary of sorts: a wall with numerous apertures through which horses could stick their heads for nibbles of oats and such, set close to tables where customers could enjoy their own snacks and a mug of somethin warm. It was called The Horse in the Wall. Numerous marriage proposals occurred there, as well as a few weddins and receptions.

Phains Haven was a good place. The easiest route there was by way of Heber City. You could also come up by way of Wallsburg dependin on the time of year and the tread on your tires.

Durin the summer and early fall, there were groups who hiked in by way of Isatch Canyon. They didn't climb Yell Rock Falls but took the high traverses to Cahoon's Staircase, which was finally reopened, though it took a few years, and from there to the high dells that led around to the back side of Katanogos and Pillars Meadow. Less challengin hikes could be found by goin around the back side of Agoneeya. Each year a dozen or so would come that way on horseback. Over the decades only a very few came by way of Kirk's Cirque and the summit ridge. They were experienced rock climbers, and not a one said they'd do it again. Even with the ledges, the headwall was crummy rock, not fun, not worth the risk. No one ever made it over with a horse.

Sadly, though, there are three stories of folks tryin. They all took place within two years of The Pillars Meadow Massacre.

Woody Mower, from Payson, arrived in Kirk's Cirque around noon on his quarter horse, also named Woody. Not an hour later his friends observed the pair fallin free of the wall. Park rangers were in the midst of plannin how to best commence the demolition of every starter ledge when two more gave it their carefree best. They died as well. All boys. All on fine horses. There was a fourth boy too that don't really count. Fritz Linneman came up by way of Coyote Gulch and then executed what officials determined was a suicide gallop off the summit ridge. The good news is that the horse didn't die. Indio, a powerful chestnut geldin, had the good sense and fortitude to stop short. Fritz Linneman, however, continued his journey, and his body was eventually discovered by a troop of Boy Scouts enjoyin a lunch above Altar Lake. Indio ended up at Phains Haven where he lived out his very long life.

Though movin closer would've made their commute easier, neither Sondra Gatestone nor Allison March were ever tempted by Heber City, nor had any dreams of rusticatin in some nearby cabin, and so continued to live in Orvop, Sondra in the big Gatestone family house, Allison in a house she eventually bought just above Locust Lane at the end of Cedar Avenue. Both women didn't mind the hour drive, and when it seemed too long a drive at the end of the day, they didn't mind sleepin in a tent kept on the premises; in later years, they could choose from a number of small cabins used to host retreats and seminars devoted to the discussion of how best to keep a place wild.

Sondra Gatestone didn't leave the Church, but she didn't go as often. Watchin Stake President Havril Enos repeatedly defend Old Porch hadn't helped. Him continuin to call Kalin March both a venomous viper and a coward didn't help either. When he got to talkin to congregants about the black sheep that don't return to the fold, and how that was good riddance, Enos referrin to Landry there, why that was the last straw. Sondra Gatestone just got plain fed up with them whose actions didn't match their preachin. The Church's endurin alliance too, a false alliance she agreed, that increasinly demonstrated its opposition to the declared values of the Church further eroded her trust. Sondra Gatestone knew full well that the defense of endurin loyalty don't mean squat if that loyalty comes with bigotry and hate. That was a rough awakenin for her. She began to wonder more often than not if its roots had always been rotten with bigotry and hate. It saddened her greatly because she knew many decent folks still committed to the Church's scriptures.

Sondra's husband, Dallin, had always been fond of sayin what was a kind of motto for the Gatestone family: *The best no is a better yes.* And Sondra found that yes in Phains Haven. She said nothin against the Church, she'd just come at last to The Church that mattered. Why go to what men devised with arsenic-soaked timber when the Lord provides the pillars of mountains, the vault of celestial lights, and pews decked with leaf-scatterin aspens and birches, pines, vines and mountain petals, and all of it choired with birdsong and the murmur of glacial streams? Who else but the Fallen must declare before such inimitable Majesty: *I will build another*? If you recall the Nightmare Stone Allison March gave Sondra Gatestone the night Sondra nearly took her own life, Sondra finally chose to bury that in Phains Haven so no nightmares would trouble the horses or those who lingered there. It had kept her safe. Why shouldn't it keep those she loved safe too?

Despite her continued curiosity, Church, any church, never really had served a significant role in Allison March's life. By comparison Phains Haven never shackled her with a lexicon of hallowed terms and histories. Instead the place offered her a way to just be, to stay put. She was finally done with runnin, even if unkind whispers still accosted her now and then. Fer example, fer a spit of time folks got all hot-crotched wantin to know why her number had been found in Kelly Porch's pocket. Allison paid no mind to such town-whisperin malignments. She just kept an eye on the horses, and seein them run and play was enuf to ease her heart. It probably didn't hurt either that they more than often ran to her, greetin her soft open palms with their nibblin inquiries, often answered with a piece of apple or carrot or, even if empty, the caresses of her attentive fingers. She had a way.

It sure is clear where Kalin's gifts came from, Sondra had remarked early on.

If only he could've kept them, Allison had answered.

The Angels did quite literally catch Kalin as he tumbled off Jojo in the middle of the ER waitin area: Hector Angel and Angel Rodriguez. It was to them that Kalin managed to cough out that Old Porch was still alive. From there his husk of a body was raced to an OR, where he did die but not long enuf to stay dead. Not even his surgeon, Dr. Wyman Weitzman, who worked on him for many long hours, could say fer sure how he'd managed to make it through *with any pulse at all.* Blood loss; a heart flimsy as an empty gunny sack in a howler; a lung that was even worse off, split, swollen and expellin rot; plus the rest of the damage that comes from a piece of lead routin the inside of your chest, includin the fractures of bones, well, all of that together should've kept that flat line flat. And with dehydration, hypothermia, and exhaustion, it's a wonder Kalin March hadn't died hours earlier.

Defibrillations, adrenaline, and at one point Dr. Weitzman's hand squeezin Kalin's heart helped return the mountains to that horizontal line. Kalin didn't wake up after the operation, nor the followin day, nor the followin week. He had to be intubated for near two weeks. Though even after they'd rid him of that awful tubin, he still didn't open his eyes.

At that point he was under arrest. When they moved him out of the ICU, an officer handcuffed his frail wrist to the bed's sidebar just in case. Kalin March didn't object. He didn't even stir.

You can bet Landry Gatestone, at that point still in the hospital, still in her hospital gown, had spirited words for them officers present in Kalin's room. How dare they chain decency down when Old Porch was free to go? In fact, one time an officer on duty had agreed with her and removed the handcuffs. Kalin still didn't stir. The handcuffs were back on by the end of the day, the next officer makin it clear that no matter his condition, Kalin March was still charged with the murders of Russel Porch and Law Enforcement Ranger Bren Kelson. It was sometime around then, as Landry was tryin to again reenter Kalin's room, that the officer shooin her away made clear that she too was under suspicion for murderin a handful of Porches. Landry laughed in his face. And he jumped.

The day Landry was officially discharged from the hospital, she went home to shower and then, right after purchasin a new diary, returned to the hospital. Except for the sleep she got at night when they forced her to go home, Landry spent every day right outside of Kalin's room. More than any of their nights together on the Mountain, she feared those nights away from him the most. She dreaded every mornin. The image of an empty bed made her heart shout in her ear.

You can bet Sondra Gatestone was always at her daughter's side. And you can bet too that Allison March, also disallowed from sittin at her son's bedside, was right there with them outside Kalin's room. They crowded the hallway and soon befriended the various officers who took turns standin guard. They all looked after each other. They made food runs. They played card games; Landry preferred word games. They shared books, sometimes readin them aloud. Tellin jokes was a must, anythin laugh-worthy to counter the mean-spirited falsities Old Porch kept pourin into everyone's ears while he was still free in the world.

At some point, the officers started to let Landry and the mothers sit next to Kalin. The doctors and nurses had started whisperin how there was a good chance Kalin March would never wake. The officers came in less and less until they was just droppin in to confirm with doctors that there'd been no change. Also about that time, and this did come way late for reasons they couldn't quite make sense of, both Landry and her mother realized that they was in the very same room Tom had died in, and why then they both near died themselves, right there on the spot, with terrible shivers runnin up and down their spines as well as tears runnin off their chins. Allison wanted to get Kalin moved to another room, but Landry stopped her. She didn't explain why except to say that Kalin would've liked knowin he was in Tom's room. *They had one of them friendships not even Death could get in the way of.*

And then one day, instead of the officers checkin in, Detective Peters and Agents Bruner and Farro came by and uncuffed Kalin. No case was gonna be brought against Kalin March for the murder of Law Enforcement Ranger Bren Kelson nor for the death of Russel Porch.

Does that mean if he wakes up, he's free to go? Landry asked right quick.

Detective Peter, who'd always been a straight shooter, told her that they'd still want a statement. He also warned Landry and the mothers that the Utah County Attorney's Office had yet to decide what to do about *the other shootins up on Pillars Meadow.*

Landry was at home the mornin Kalin opened his eyes. Though it weren't like a hundred watts had just flicked on. He returned to the world groggy and raspin for water that still did nothin to chase away his hoarseness. Where he was confused him plenty. Then he asked for Tom before sighin hisself back into slumber. Landry hustled over as fast as she could, but even if she'd been just down the hall lambastin a vendin machine for behavin worse than a rigged slot machine, she wouldn't have made it to his bedside. An Orvop police officer had already cleared the room and stood guardin the door no matter her protestations, which admittedly did get a little salty.

Sondra Gatestone tried her best to draw her daughter away, likely back to that vendin machine that owed them more quarters than all the quarter horses in a girl's dream. When she'd set her hands on Landry's shoulders, it was the first time the only child left to her had flat-out growled. Landry was also spinnin around so fast that Sondra at first didn't know what was even happenin, findin herself backin off too, like she was shoved away by the flash of some impossible brightness in her daughter's eyes, the sharp shine on them gritted teeth, and again the sound of rumblin stones takin down a Mountain.

It was Allison March who stepped toward this figure of fury incarnate, squattin real low so Landry was near lookin down on her.

You understand how bad I want to be in there too? Allison March whispered, and so soft too that Landry had to lean in some.

Landry nodded.

Right now they need to hear from him what happened up there. They think that if you or me get to him first, he might change his story. And we sure don't want to be the reason they think what he's sayin ain't true.

I ain't gonna tell him to lie! Landry erupted. *I just want to see him!*

I do too!

Besides, Old Porch done exhausted that fib barrel for all of us.

Allison chuckled at that. *Then let's let my boy tell his side of things. The quicker he's done, the quicker we'll be with him.*

By the time Detective Peters and Agents Bruner and Farro arrived, Holly Feltzman was sittin all cozy like next to Kalin. Suffice it to say, the interview weren't wrapped up neat after just one visit, but once the investigators were satisfied that they'd heard enuf, there weren't no surprises. No doubt it helped that Kalin laid it out plain and simple. Pretty much how he'd later tell it at both Old Porch's trials.

He started with how before Tom Gatestone died of cancer, they'd got to ridin Navidad and Mouse around the foothills of Orvop and eventually into Isatch Canyon. They knew the horses was owned by Orwin Porch. At first that was part of the fun, until they got to really lovin the horses. On the day Tom died, he made Kalin swear that if Navidad and Mouse were ever moved to Paddock B, which meant Old Porch planned to slaughter them, Kalin would take them to Tom's Crossin. And that's just what he did. It was rainin that Wednesday night, and he didn't get so far up Isatch Canyon. Never thinkin he'd been spotted, let alone followed, Kalin made camp just above Bridge Two. He was in the middle of fixin some eats when Russel Porch showed up. He was pointin a Colt .45, but Kalin weren't worried much that Russel would shoot him.

Why's that? Agent Bruner asked.

Dunno. I could just tell he weren't aimin to kill no one. And even if he was, he'd have missed.

Kalin then told how Landry had appeared out of nowhere and knocked Russel off his horse. She took the gun then, which, with a couple of exceptions, stayed in a saddlebag the rest of the time. Landry then arranged with Russel to buy the two horses for twenty dollars, and after that they had some rice and beans together. It was nice. Kalin could see Russel was a good kid who was just tryin to act like someone he weren't. Kalin figured they would likely become friends after that. Maybe go ridin together. The three of them sure loved horses.

When Russel left on Cavalry, he was plenty distraught that Landry weren't givin back the Colt. He was real afraid of what his daddy would do if he found out it was missin. Landry promised that she'd return it as soon as she got back. They all parted on good terms.

Kalin then related how Landry couldn't make it up that first scree on the north side of Isatch Canyon which suited Kalin just fine because he knew the way he was goin was dangerous. However, on her way back, as Landry would tell him later, she ran into Egan Porch, Kelly Porch, *and one whose name I never learned. They told her that Russel Porch was dead. They wanted the Colt too. They'd spied it in her belt. Landry said she'd give it to Old Porch directly. I can't say what was actually said, but I know when she came runnin back, she was plenty afraid of these men and what they had in mind. That's when I decided to help Landry ride up the scree. That's on me. From then on we had no choice but to go on together.*

Kalin told them then how the storm and rain kept gettin worse, finally forcin them to turn around and eventually take shelter in an abandoned mine. *We got through the night like we was come upon by the endless dead.*

How do you mean? Detective Peters had asked.

Bad dreams. Bad dreams.

Mornin was almost worse, *greetin us with a canyon covered in ice.* They had to wait awhile until it thawed mostly. When they got back on the traverses, most of the screes, *thank goodness,* were stable. It was on the last one, however, where all earthly stability abandoned them. A rockfall for the history books followed. They was lucky to make it across alive, especially since Kalin was bein shot at too, *rifle fire from across the canyon.*

After that, they managed to make it up to the cirque where Kalin got to eatin some bad jerky that left him real sick. Kalin never mentioned Tom, but he did tell them about the wildlife they kept seein: the white owl, the old elk, the good beaver that greeted them at Altar Lake. When the upchuckin and the rest quit, Kalin took hisself to the lake to wash. He told them then about the headwall, the maze of ledges that led to the top, which he'd sleuthed out in previous visits. He described how more rifle fire had trapped him near the top. After the sun went down, it started to snow, but in the end it was thanks to that snow and a big old moon that Kalin and Navidad were able to survive the last leg.

Their campsite was right over and below the summit ridge, which he'd scouted out and supplied over the precedin months. Landry had done one heckuva job with the ropes and tarp while he was still trapped on the headwall. *I guess she just kept believin I'd come through it okay. She looked after Mouse, Jojo, and that mule that had followed us. She didn't know about the food I'd hid up there. Maybe that was a good thing. It was a ways from the campsite, and bad things could've come from tryin to get at it at that hour and in those conditions.*

Kalin made clear that it was thanks to Landry that he survived. She'd made the fire against a fallen tree by the rock wall and built it right so the smoke slipped easily enuf away. The fire had stayed bright too and cozied them enuf so that they eventually got some rest. It was a pretty terrifyin storm too, slammin the summit hard, but they were secure, and soon enuf the snow was helpin to insulate their shelter. The horses, as if sensin their need, lay down around them to offer more heat and comfort. *That was the happiest night of my life.*

Happy? Agent Farro interrupted. *How so?*

We'd gotten the horses over the headwall. I just felt so free.

Did somethin else happen? Agent Farro pressed.

How do you mean?

Between you and Landry?

Kalin sure got a little surly then. And disgusted. *If you gotta ask that, then you got no clue what I'm sayin here. Go up there. You might learn a thing about yourself and forget some of yourself too.*

In fact a year later Agent Herman Farro did just that. He went in the summer with no chance of snow, and he camped right where Kalin and Landry had spent the night. A little wind was whippin up. He tried but once to set up his tent before skedaddlin right outta there as fast as he could. It haunted him for the rest of his life, and when his end finally did come, not havin lasted even one night up there was his only regret.

Kalin then described how on the followin mornin they finally got to eat somethin. *That was fer sure the happiest mornin of my life. Are you gonna ask me about that too?* Agent Farro didn't respond. Kalin itemized how the little they ate still amounted to a feast. After that, they made their way down to a bluff of rock, which Landry clambered up on. From there she spotted Egan Porch thanks to the sun's flare on the lenses of his binoculars. A moment later she was shot through the head, and in fallin from the rock on which she'd stood, she started a small snowfall, which sucked her over the edge of the cliffs.

To follow her that way was suicide. Kalin resolved to take Coyote Gulch and, after releasin the horses at the Crossin, go find her body.

At the bottom of Coyote Gulch, though, as he was at last comin through a grove of trees there, he spied the Porches. By Kalin's count there were ten. Kalin had decided here to retrieve the gun from Landry's saddlebag. He tried to explain some how he'd secured the Colt behind his left hand, knowin he could flip it free and shoot it if he had to. That meant comin out with his hands raised. Though he didn't like this part, he'd decided not to wear a stitch of clothin except for his hat and his boots. He figured there was a good chance they'd just gun him down from the crick bed, but his nekedness might disarm them. The trick worked. They headed out to meet him and make fun of him.

Why not go another way? Detective Peters asked.

Kalin shrugged. *They was set on findin me, and I didn't have it in me to survive elsewhere for much longer. Besides, right beyond where them Porches was at was where I was takin the horses.*

This bein the place Tom described? Agent Bruner asked.

That's right.

Wouldn't somewhere else have been just as good? Detective Peters followed up.

I don't know. Tom never mentioned no other place.

Kalin then walked them through a few times who'd shot first, that would be Old Porch, who he'd shot first, that would be Old Porch, and who he'd shot last, that would be Shelly Porch. Detective Peters and the FBI agents named for him then Billings Gale, who was the only one to hit him. Kalin shot him fifth. Egan had been second. Porches shot each other, which had lowered the number of shots he'd need to meet their number. *I guess I got lucky. It all happened so fast.*

Kalin told them then how Hatch Porch said he was under arrest, and Kalin was fine with that so long as he could release the horses where he'd promised to release them. Hatch Porch did not object. Kalin had then managed to limp to them two gateposts, where he set Navidad and Mouse free. Promise made, promise kept.

That Old Porch shot his son in the back weren't so surprisin given what Kalin had already seen, startin with Old Porch shootin some man Kalin had never seen before in the back of the head. *He took three shots to do it, and that told me he weren't so accurate, but it also told me he was a killer.* The way Kalin figured it, Hatch weren't like Old Porch; he weren't a killer, so he never understood who he was up against. Hatch's killin enraged Kalin. He couldn't even explain the feelin of angry betrayal that ran through him.

I was so mad.

Despite considerable pain, he'd marched back.

Old Porch kept firin at him too until he'd discharged every round. It didn't make no difference.

Why didn't you kill him? Agent Farro asked.

Holly Feltzman immediately objected and Kalin mostly heeded her counsel.

I cuffed him.

Agent Bruner later wondered if the fact that Orwin Porch's gun was empty by the time Kalin reached him had saved his life. Agent Farro reminded everyone that by that point Kalin was injured, unarmed, and still wearin nothin but his hat and boots. Detective Peters weren't convinced that that mattered. *I think if he'd meant to kill him, Orwin Porch would be dead now.*

Kalin then described how he'd tried to treat his wound; how he'd tried to ride Jojo. When Landry appeared later on Jojo, he was sure he was dead and this here was her ghost.

The rest was a vague blur of movement and agony encroached upon by an iciness that far exceeded anythin he'd felt upon the summit of Katanogos. But for the fire in Landry and Jojo, he'd have succumbed to it.

That Kalin March was never hisself put on trial may very well have been the worst thing. At least a trial would have processed his actions before the eyes of the state and the public and in the end produced a verdict reviewable by any yappy mouth. And to be sure, the Utah County Attorney's Office did give the Kalin March case a great deal of thought.

On one hand, nine bodies was dragged down from Pillars Meadow, and of those nine, as Kalin March had hisself admitted, five were the result of his gunplay. On the other hand, the growin evidence against

Orwin Porch and the definitive conclusion that neither Kalin March nor Landry Gatestone were involved in the death of Russel Porch or Bren Kelson made the defense's case of self-defense ultimately too strong to test.

No question plenty of Orvop folks weren't pleased to see Kalin March walk scot-free, seein as how he'd pretty much single-handedly put an end to the whole Porch family, with Old Porch still regarded by many as one of the pillars of the community. Worse still, instead of movin on, Kalin March had chosen to settle in. There were some brief uproars when he returned to Orvop High to finish out his junior year and then even came back again for his senior year. To their credit, Principal Furst and every teacher approached by an appalled parent had to make clear that it was illegal to deny the boy an education, especially since he weren't found guilty of anythin. He hadn't even been charged with the alleged theft of them two horses.

Maybe you'd've figured that at least the kids at Orvop High would've turned Kalin into a pariah. But it weren't like that. Sure, there was apprehension and timidity at first. Pretty quick, though, he became one of them, average in his studies, good for a bad joke, and as more time passed, what with him havin nothin to do with horses no more, and he didn't join the FFA, nor participatin in anythin havin to do with guns, like joinin the NRA, the harder it got to believe that this ordinary kid could've had anythin to do with what happened up on Katanogos.

A few times, though, a bigger kid did go out of his way to prove hisself against Kalin March's reputation. Let's just say it didn't go well for that brash senior with some rooster in his step. Not that Kalin did much more than stand there and wait. That was more than enuf. Some will say his shadow had gotten much longer, and a few will even claim it had become unnaturally dark. The challengers high-stepped it outta there. Darren Blicker near soiled hisself. But as Kalin's momma warned him with abidin love in her voice: *You only win for a day.* Her son still had plenty of days left ahead of him.

While Kalin's borin plainness grew more steadfast in the class-rooms, outside of Orvop High, his infamy only grew, especially where he went unobserved, like in the churches. Stake President Havril Enos continued to use The Massacre at Pillars Meadow as an example of great moral turpitude and the delinquency of justice. The more he fashioned and attempted to empanoply his narrative, the less his language incorporated themes of forgiveness, tolerance, and humility. Stake President Havril Enos took it upon hisself to tell everyone in Orvop, in Utah, in these United States, in the world if he could, that we was in a terrible crisis. And both at and away from the pulpit, with or without his gold-leafed book, he used inflammatory rhetoric to increase his popularity among congregants and his position in the Church. He was wily as well; except in private conversations, he never outright named Kalin March. His talks remained stripped of such specificity, though there were few crowdin the pews who didn't at once understand the who in his subsermonizin, and it darkened their eyes toward the Marches, the Gatestones too, them bein another fallen pillar of their community.

Stake President Havril Enos only got more toplofty as he grew more brazen with his fabrications, which he needed in order to justify the animosity he continued to direct at Kalin March and Landry Gatestone, who he more often than not characterized as *a Liminite whose very presence degraded the Church itself.* He had to either incite ire in folks or risk losin their attention, which at some point had become the only thing that mattered, what whispered in his ear the promise of power.

And, of course, the more fiery Enos got, the more folks began to wonder aloud what would happen when their stake president ran into Kalin March at some fillin station or on some street corner? But that never happened. Likely if it had, Enos would've run the other way. His wife, Myrna, had already run the other way. From Enos.

It was the Church that finally decided the time had come to temper the stake president. Whatever its faults and inconsistencies, the Church remains devoted to its Community. Except maybe for the president of the Church, responsible for direct communiqués and guidances, which are vetted or tempered, or at the very, very least offered counsel by way of the Quorum, the Church maintains a distaste for too authoritative a stance by any of its bishopry and such. After all, the Church, second only to Christ, is the authority, and any other authorial decree, unless expressly ordained, ordered, and overseen by its esteemed body, will earn a swift and sharp rebuke, no matter if the offense is an inappropriate story, general congregant clishmaclaver, or the high-minded doctrinal espousals delivered in error from the podium.

The Church proved Havril Enos's own Zoilus. And while it did not excommunicate him, the Church did install President Enos in the Church's Samoan Mission to better recalibrate his sense of self and others. And yes, you can bet Sondra Gatestone, Allison March, and Landry had a good laugh over that.

Kalin didn't care a whit for that sorta stuff. At first, he was mainly haunted by a possible trial. Every day seemed to harbor a secret that would too soon bloom with a poisonous call from Holly Feltzman: *The county attorney is gonna press charges.* But when that call never came, the memories started to resurface, at first too vivid to be declared ghosts and then, after so many visitations, with so many battlin versions, too effaced to be declared ghosts. What Kalin would have given for a visit from a real ghost. For her part, when Holly Feltz-man's time came to pass on into those mists that will one day veil the stars, she made clear she wanted nothin to do with ghosts. *Bury me like the queen,* she'd joked, and in their hearts Kalin and Landry did. *I want a month of mournin. At least.*

The *What-ifs* hounded Kalin the most. What if he'd gone another way? What if he'd released the horses farther north? Would it have made any difference? What if he'd just ignored the ghost and got-ten hisself a trailer and driven to different pastures? No answers ever came, but Kalin never stopped askin the questions.

What he seemed most unaffected by, if not outright unaware of, was the anxiety his very presence now and then provoked at some community gatherin, what he at most perceived as a faint buzzin, the way a great lion might ignore the bees beardin his chin as he pondered somethin far graver. And maybe the gravest moment since the events on Katanogos came just three years after Orwin Porch was declared free for good, about three years after Kalin hisself was rid of the med-ical care and physical rehabilitation his injuries had required. Kalin was at a pharmacy, doin his darndest to pick out the right feminine pad. Unbeknownst to him, Orwin Porch was just outside and about to head inside too. The few that was in the pharmacy didn't think to warn Kalin. They just hung back in glee, watchin, waitin. And then the strangest thing of all happened: just as Old Porch was reachin for the door, Orvop police and FBI agents swarmed in and arrested him for the murder of one Cameron Eakins back in 1973.

See, all the attention Orwin Porch had received durin his two tri-als had put his face on more than a few TV screens and newspaper pages, in some magazines too. Folks in Bexar County saw him and remembered him. Forensic tests unavailable back then were now avail-able. The third time around in a courtroom weren't no spectacle nor no hung jury neither. For the murder of Cameron Eakins, Mr. Orwin Porch was sentenced to life in prison without parole.

His one remainin child, Ginny Ward, who as a youngster had fled with her mother to Austin and, exceptin for some lingerin tolerances, fer sure some affection for Hatch Porch, continued to shun the spear side of that family, well, she showed up at Old Porch's sentencin to see that Justice was served. Old Porch never spotted her there and likely wouldn't have cared much if he had. In fact he'd so forgotten her that when Death did at last come for him, he had no idea that what remained of the shambles of his Porch Empire would go to her. Not that Ginny Ward had any interest in wealth she considered bloody and *acquired through Sin*. With the help of her mother, she arranged for the sale of all the properties along with every item upon said properties. That included them Frederic Remington sculptures, which it turned out were not originals but poor counterfeits worth not even their weight in bronze and they weren't even bronze. That at least made sense to Ginny; in the end even the best con artists get conned, and Old Porch weren't even the best, he weren't even close. And that weren't the only time Old Porch was had. In a somewhat bizarre twist, it was discovered that none other than Trent Riddle had embezzled from Porch Meats over thirty thousand dollars, which his parents eventually discovered thanks to alerts sent along by a bank in search of their boy, who was by then deceased. The Riddle people, bein honest Church folk, returned the money to Ginny Ward, who sent it right along to Phains Haven.

In fact Ginny Ward donated every last penny of her father's estate: 90 percent to Phains Haven, 10 percent to the Church.

And that weren't the end of such twists and turns either. There was a last revelation that Ginny Ward greeted with a good deal of hilarity: fed up with lyin and tired of grievin her boys, even though that grief would set her to soil not six months after Pillars Meadow, Ginny's mother eventually confessed to her daughter about havin had an affair while she was still married, with no regrets either, because it was what eventually granted her the fortitude she'd need to quit Old Porch. Not long after, DNA confirmed that Orwin Porch was not Ginny Ward's biological father. After that, Ginny regarded herself as merely a one-time inquiline creature who was only briefly enclosed by all that Porch misery, with Ginny often statin and with an irrepressible grin which as the years went by nearly matched Tom's: *From then on everywhere I went, even if I was crossin through the darkest room, I walked in sunshine.*

And that's pretty much the whole of it with only a few more notes of strangeness to include. The Colt Peacemaker, that Porch tradition as well as the corporeal instrument that signed the end of nearly all the Porches, vanished. Most assumed it was stolen by someone at the Porch trials. Plenty keep an eye out for its reemergence at some gun fair. There's little likelihood of that ever happenin.

Another bit of strangeness surfaced when, durin the presentation of evidence that would help convict Orwin Porch down in Texas, a bit of horse hair found on the body of the murdered Mr. Cameron Eakins and elsewhere at the crime scene was shown to match that item of clothin Old Porch was so fond of wearin, what had been in his possession for near three decades: his horsehair vest. Soon after none other than Assistant Medical Examiner Annabelle Kasey recalled another death in which she'd entered into evidence three strands of unidentified horse hair. What made them so interestin was that the hairs did not match the horse allegedly responsible for the death nor other horses in that stable. At the time it had been hard to object to the conclusion that the fatality was caused by a hard kick. The deceased's parietal and occipital bones bore the mark of a direct hit. However, followin the publicity surroundin the Porch trials, with Landry Gatestone's presence often remarked upon, it didn't escape Assistant Medical Examiner Annabelle Kasey that the one felled by a horse kick was none other than Dallin Gatestone. Kasey couldn't resist revisitin the evidence for that case. It took some work, but Kasey and the Orvop police eventually located those three mysterious horse hairs taken from the Gatestone stables. Tests revealed that they in fact did match the horse hair from Old Porch's vest. Not that those findins led to much else, even if eventually Kasey did share her findins with the Gatestone family. Who's to say it proved anythin: both Dallin Gatestone and Orwin Porch had crossed paths too often to make the presence of some errant hairs sufficient enuf evidence to justify foul play.

Nonetheless, the coincidence or connection stirred in Landry a need to revisit an assumption about her brother Tom's ghostly presence in Kalin's life, not to mention the real purpose of the adventure itself. On late nights, she would wonder the dark with the darkest questions: had in fact both boys, as well as herself, been conscripted into use by them immense universal wheels slowly turnin toward some levelin that is Justice, with Tom on behalf of his father sendin Kalin on a course bound to intersect Porch and his kin?

Kalin thought that was all nonsense. *Rubbish* was the word he used. *What did Old Porch do?* he'd exclaim. *Throw a horseshoe at your dad?! That might ding him but it wouldn't even give him the mark they found on his head!* Landry didn't disagree, but even so, Kalin March never was gonna understand the enmity that had lived for so long between the Porches and the Gatestones. Fer him the simplest truth would never waver: it all happened the way it happened because of his and Tom's, and in the end Landry's, abidin love for them two abused ponies.

Clop-Clop-clip-Clop.

Plenty have said it: Kalin March was a man of his word. Mostly. The promises he made throughout his life, he kept. Mostly. Like a noddin Zeus but without none of them Zeusly powers. Mostly. You can bet both bootheels that the followin year, when Landry sidled up to his locker and asked him to the girl's choice dance, he nodded. She'd meant to ask real loud so the whole school would hear who was askin, but by that point the opinion of anyone who might've heard made no difference to her. Also, her usually big and authoritative voice had on its own volition gotten real small and fragile; it was a thing of wonder that it had managed to even appear at all. But it did. And Kalin March picked her up in his mom's Dodge Dart, stood right on her front porch, with flowers too, pretty much like he said he would, and crutches and all they danced that night to *Up Where We Belong*, and, you know what?, their classmates thought they made a fine pair.

From then on they was always together, though you'd be hard pressed to prove they'd been apart since that night they ate beans and rice with Russel Porch. Landry was the class valedictorian when she graduated. Kalin was happy just to graduate. They married eventually. Not in the temple. You can bet Lindsey Holt was invited. Sondra made sure he got as many chocolate chip pancakes as he wanted. And Kalin got hisself a whole one of them orange cakes which he still insisted Landry have a bite of first, his momma too; Sondra said she'd whack him with a hot spoon if he didn't get eatin fast. And Kalin obeyed.

Folks liked to say it was Landry who tied the knot, and Kalin thought that was a fine assessment. They held off startin a family right out the gate, and like most of their decisions even that one incurred the cost of public derision, not that either paid much attention to the subsequent rounds of vulgarities that accused Kalin of shootin blanks. Despite such claims, Kalin and Landry ultimately had three precocious kids.

Some decried eucatastrophe. Others with no patience for such fifty-dollar words just said Kalin March should've gone to college like Landry had done. A good few insisted that he should've thought better of hisself, sought better for his family, and done somethin with paper that makes paper money. But there were plenty more who thought he should've just rode easy and most of all just rode. Folks never could understand Kalin. He could never ride easy. He would never ride again. Though he was never far from the horses he loved either.

Together he and Landry worked at Phains Haven. Those early years were somethin too. It weren't so much a place but an idea that ran roughshod over everyone's plans and expectations. But slowly the corrals got built for the horses that needed time and healin, and then the shelters, a barn or two, and with years passin even some cabins of sorts, with the main lodge slowly findin its way to a foundation, eventually gainin a tall chimney with a wide fireplace around which more than a few stories were told, some made-up, many true. The dogs liked those nights, especially when a snowstorm was comin up outside.

Ginny Ward had shown great gratitude when Allison March had offered to take Mr. Bucket #5, who right quick lost the *Mr.*, the *Number Five*, and *Bucket* too. Buck at once discovered that nights were no longer spent in a kennel but at the end of Allison's bed and come mornin by her side. The dog developed a lifelong love for her and he lived a long life too. Buck might not have been no Argos or Dulić Ibrahim's horse, but his later years brimmed with beautiful accompaniment. Fer example, next to Allison, Buck's best friend turned out to be Mungo. Them two were a pair, and while Sondra and Allison made sure they knew their job was to look after the horses, that didn't keep them from racin after a coyote or on one afternoon gettin after a skunk and a porcupine and then another skunk. That was a day! Stink all over with prickles in their noses and also what looked like moose dung in their hair. *Like they thought rollin in that was gonna make things better?* Allison had exclaimed. *Thought weren't any part of their process,* Sondra had dryly responded. The ladies ended up tweezin out the prickles and just shavin off their coats. *This weren't never no shaggy-dog lot anyway,* Sondra said, sweepin up the hair, while an aproned Allison, kneelin before the huge tub, finished spongin away the suds on both Mungo and Buck. The dogs looked lean and mean, creatures of terrible survival, savagin the plains of War, Guardians at the Gates of Heck itself, and maybe in some other life they'd been just that, though not now, not in this life, not to anyone at Phains Haven. Their lives were all the seasons stretched out alongside one another while Sondra and Allison in the summer dished out peach cobbler and ice cream to volunteers and come fall served hot apple cider as everyone kicked back to listen to ghost stories.

There are years that ask questions and years that answer. By Zora Neale Hurston. That was somethin Allison liked to repeat. She felt lucky to have lived enuf to live some answers, though as far as anyone could tell the answers weren't any more significant than Allison now and then wearin a blue dress. Sure, it was denim but still a dress, which Kalin and Landry thought was pretty funny, especially since Sondra would now and then wear jeans. *You always said they'd get on,* Kalin would say. *But I didn't believe it one bit.* Landry's eyebrow sure arched at that: *And now?* Kalin's eyes twinkled: *I still don't believe it.* And that kept her smilin. He was good at that. That was another one of his promises kept. Mostly.

In late 1999 they received an invitation to attend the Time Gallery exhibit down in Houston, which was to take place on February 29, 2000. They understood that they'd find on display images the community at large had concocted depictin the events that had taken place that October week in 1982. Their mild interest matured soon after into forgetfulness. News of the subsequent fire and the destruction of the various art pieces weren't somethin to take pleasure in, but for those two it didn't really register. See, they weren't even in contact with anyone who'd attended and so could never understand what was lost. *Besides, what I seen myself, I don't need to see done wrong by someone else,* Landry had said one afternoon while out walkin the northern reaches of Phains Haven in search of a speckled pony that had bolted that mornin when a truck deliverin hay bales had drove over a mason jar; popped louder than a cherry bomb. *I also can't see why Kalin and me would even be welcomed.*

Landry, though, did authorize the publication of her father's book, *Xanthos,* which Bucephalus Press proclaimed a *daedal monograph that achieved the monolithic.* It weren't monolithic, and as Sondra Gatestone snipped: *It still don't got nothin to do with my towels.* Its completion, however, did require an intense review of all papers havin to do with that talkin horse, durin which Sondra and Landry uncovered a final chapter. The editor hailed it as the perfect conclusion.

The question Landry's, Tom's, and Evan's father posed weren't so much about what permitted Achilles's horse, Xanthos, to speak but what caused that truth-tellin and prophetic voice to cease. Hera, Zeus's wife and mother to both War and Strife as well as the Graces, and Blacksmiths too, and to some Romans, even Liberty, was the one who granted Xanthos the freedom to speak. However, it was those who hunt and destroy all who break their word that silenced him. But why? Why would the Furies or Erinyes care what a horse had to say?

As Dallin Gatestone saw it, the Furies, those unforgettin and unforgivin spirits, are primarily creatures raised out of the ruin of Human Vengeance; and it is within that torturous maze constructed out of the seeminly endless repercussions of human ire where animal reflection has no place. Paper-clipped to the manuscript's last chapter had been a postcard of the nineteenth-century *Automedon with the Horses of Achilles* by the artist Henri Regnault, who soon after paintin that masterful canvas would die in the Battle of Buzenval, the siege of Paris, age twenty-seven. Depicted are two horses, Xanthos and Balios, aghast before the deeds of men, upon their mouths the foam of their great exertions and distress. Speechless. As Dallin Gatestone wrote on the back: *The Iliad cannot contain what the horses have to say. It has neither the ear for their speech nor for their hearts.*

In his quiet conclusion, Dallin Gatestone ponders whether the end of Vengeance might at last permit animals to speak their minds. He asks whether it is this spirit of Revenge that mutes the voice of horses? Great as he might seem among other men, Achilles has no life that measures even a breath against the endless lives of Xanthos and Balios, and yet the warrior still scolds them. No wonder Hera grants Xanthos his right to a reprimand. It is important to note too, Dallin Gatestone points out, that the mother of the gods does not speak through the horse; she only removes whatever impediments bridle his speech. What else might the horse have said if the Furies had not forbade another utterance? Would that immortal horse have at least answered Achilles's question: *Xanthos, why do you prophesy my end?* Dallin Gatestone admits he can't imagine a satisfactory answer. *Perhaps Xanthos seeks only to remind Achilles that he will die and they will not?*

Dallin Gatestone finished his little book wonderin about where those two horses might be now, over three thousand years old, easy, if not twenty thousand times that, and still not even an hour upon that grand clock of eternity. Where do they roam? Under what disguise? Under whose watch? Do Wrath and the Violent Designs of Humanity continue to mute their hearts? Or does the Mother of Youth now and then still grant them discourse? And if not, then to whom do they register the stories of their lives? After all, they rode upon the plains of Troy. Unless, of course, immortality does not come with immortal memory? What if they do not even know themselves as forever, forever oblivious to the strides they've made and the company they've kept? What then of such personal eternities would remain?

Suffice it to say the book was not a success and killt any notion of publishin more pieces by Dallin Gatestone, such as a florilegium of idle observations, a chrestomathy, an exoteric science fiction piece about Church pioneers designed as a feuilleton, or even a paroemiography, which Dallin Gatestone had worked on throughout his life; he loved proverbs. The modest printin of *Xanthos* produced five hundred copies and didn't sell even a fifth of that, not even a tenth, maybe a dozen, with the unsold pulped just a few years later. Three copies, though, were bought and very much treasured by none other than Mrs. Annserdodder, Ms. Melson, and Mr. Rudder. This trio relished such an unexpected reveal: who knew that the very patriarch of Tom and Landry Gatestone, central to the events that these three educators so often attempted to map out upon the familiar topography of antiquity, shared such a learnèd love of the Homeric epics, especially *The Iliad*?! Even so, the miniated monograph quickly became no more than a memento, as not one of them gave much thought to horses or even animals, unless they was huntin them, talkin about Mr. Rudder here, or eatin them, with all of them enjoyin venison. Mrs. Annserdodder had but once in her lifetime taken a sunset walk on horseback with her two daughters and hadn't cared for it a bit. The Dallin Gatestone publication, though, did revitalize their conversations about the epics in general, with *The Odyssey* now and then comin up, if not so much for the longings there for home but the stories that must accompany any return from war. Mostly, though, they talked about *The Iliad* and Pillars Meadow, even if, as Mr. Rudder kept insistin, there weren't no Troy up there and only a couple of horses.

Throughout her life, what galled Ms. Melson most, who out of the three knew *The Iliad* the best, was how so little had changed. Unlike *The Odyssey*, as Ms. Melson had idly defended once, *The Iliad* remained largely void of monsters and magical transformations or even a Hades proper where the dead, however insubstantial, could plead their case for the glories of a dull life, as Achilles did in *The Odyssey*. Mr. Rudder had pointed out then how dead Patroclus, in Book Twenty-Three of *The Iliad*, appeared before Achilles. *In a dream*, Ms. Melson countered, *seekin his own burial in order to proceed to his own dream of Hades*. Mr. Rudder still argued that *The Iliad weren't that devoid of magic*, pointin out how the gods often performed transformations of spirit on the plains of Troy, sometimes whiskin men away to rescue them from death, or in the case of Zeus's Trojan son, Sarpedon, to preserve his dead body. Mrs. Annserdodder nodded along with Mr. Rudder, recallin how Achilles even battles a river god and survives only because Hephaestus turns the water to steam. Ms. Melson accepted their objections as easily as she waved them away.

My point is how little The Iliad depends upon the assurances of an after-life. Whatever great powers may surround us or fleetinly inhabit us, they mostly remain out of reach. I speak of the Gods that maraud upon the plains of Ilion. The liberties of their deathlessness accompany us but also remain beyond us. Our mortal aggressions, however, still persist, still brutish and repellent. Thousands of years have gone by, and likely we still have in store thousands of years more where the only notable differences in our wars will be our technology and our names: the girl will still be raped; the boy's chest will still be pierced above the nipple.

Perhaps the three teachers loved *The Iliad* because of how relevant it remained to the modern apocalypse of killin machines; how it still captured the savagery, sorrow, and heroics of human conflict. And likely because these three had continued to contemplate Pillars Meadow, they couldn't help but return to the question of alignments. Though easiest was to compare Kalin to Achilles, Mr. Rudder felt somethin askew there, and Mrs. Annserdodder agreed with him: *I'm done with templates or organizin patterns,* she said, and in general declared that she would continue to resist what she called *the lazy habit of findin correlation where there weren't none,* preferrin to focus on *Kalin's kairos* or in general *observe the correlation of themes, which were aplenty and justifiable.* If Achilles had roamed up there in the Katanogos massif, it was in spirit only and likely only in brief moments here and there, a brainteaser where the tease is beside the point, *with about as much purpose as a dusty puzzle that you ain't never gonna finish because it's got too many missin pieces, and anyways you'll probably just sweep the thing back into its box, if not a trash can, before you get close to done.*

Ms. Meredith Melson would laugh. She adored Alice and Caracy but especially Alice. This was on a fall stroll not far from the mouth of Isatch Canyon. The day was cold and crisp and clear with a lastin bristle of frost upon the mountains. Winter would be here soon. Ms. Melson was agreein with Mrs. Annserdodder about how tryin to force events into a configuration delineated by some precursor, and furthermore thinkin that any failure to fit proves in turn how such juxtapositions, what Ms. Melson called *the parataxis of these individuated treatments of conflict,* requirin greater and greater nuancin, ultimately renders any similarities and most importantly any lessons null and void. *Though still, with all that bein said,* Ms. Melson chuckled, *what if we've got it backwards? Maybe the Porches weren't ever the Trojans? Maybe it was the other way around?*

How do you mean? Caracy Rudder demanded at once, rubbin his hands against the droppin temperatures. *That Kalin weren't the spirit of Achilles? That the Porches were the Achaeans?*

Mrs. Annserdodder laughed too. *Are you implyin that Shelly Porch and Sean Porch were the Greater and Lesser Ajax?*

Hatch Porch as Achilles? Ms. Melson calmly put out there. *And Egan? Probably Odysseus. A cunnin violent, opportunist. Battle always in his heart.*

Mr. Rudder scoffed.

Ms. Melson continued undeterred. *Think of Old Porch as Agamemnon. But I'm not gonna fight you over the particulars because you'll surely prove this comparison inutile. Rather more broadly I'd just like to reemphasize how it was the Greeks that were the invaders, aggressors, and pillagers afflictin a city known to be devoted to its horses.*

But the Greeks won! Mr. Rudder declared.

Not this time.

The Greeks didn't necessarily win in Homer's version either, Mrs. Annserdodder had to point out. *So many died there as well as upon their return. Agamemnon for one, murdered in his own home.*

Odysseus and Menelaus did just fine, Mr. Rudder retorted.

The Greeks paid a terrible toll! Mrs. Annserdodder responded, even raisin her voice a bit, which was unusual.

Let's not forget Mycenae, Tiryns, and Pylos, Ms. Melson said, in favor of Mrs. Annserdodder's point.

Then, Meredith, are you sayin that Landry is Andromache? Mrs. Annserdodder asked.

Ms. Melson nodded.

And Kalin March is Hector?! Mr. Rudder couldn't contain hisself and near shouted the dubious claim, though there was also a bit of joy in his voice now and an unveiled brightness in his eye.

Hector come again, Ms. Melson said real soft, though maybe not soft enuf, as the mountains before them, even with the sun declinin behind them in the west, seemed to match a darkness already born of night.

And the walls of Troy? Mrs. Annserdodder asked near as soft.

Ms. Melson nodded past Isatch Canyon, past the soft heights of Agoneeya and Kaieneewa, toward the topless towers of Katanogos wisped in cloud.

But no gods? Mr. Rudder's voice was quietin some too.

No gods, Ms. Melson answered. *Just Tom. And of course the horses.*

N ow how these three and others came to know about the ghost of Tom Gatestone deserves a little attention. As can be assumed, the first shape of the events makin up that week in October started with witnesses and rumors, further constituted by new reports, more witnesses, and then subsequent judicial proceedins. As can be imagined, there was also a great deal of speculation along with theories and summations that were just plain wrong. Over the years, it was Landry Gatestone who attempted to set the record straight. After all, she'd lived to tell the tale. She'd seen all of it too, except Pillars Meadow. Also she was married to Kalin, and though he weren't exactly the gabby type, he not only further corroborated the sequence of events he gave to Detective Peters but added more details as well, though never in one long rush. Just a little here and there, you know, as time did what time does: slip by.

Most importantly, Kalin fleshed out those conversations with Tom, about whom he often thought. Of course, Landry then, in her own jabberin with friends, and, boy, did she still love to jabber, even with scars on both cheeks, slowly let that ghostly aspect of their journey come to light. Fer certain, she'd sworn those friends to secrecy, but them was very good friends, and they weren't about to betray a good story by keepin it buried.

And as Tom's presence made its way into the weave of things, invention followed, along with fantasy, mischief too, and just pure fancy; because how so many folks came to know so intimately this journey must necessarily include the profound imagination of the few alongside the equally profound imagination of the many. To exclude such energies would be folly.

Even Kalin hisself, by then well into his gray days, would once or twice go so far as to admit that he'd made the whole thing up about Tom: *It all seems like a dream these days anyways.* A dream that seemed both inscribed as well as circumscribed by what wasn't. Then again, what dream isn't writ by absence? Kalin's heart never would forget. *Maybe I just needed to cook up a friend to see me through it,* he told Landry once. When she asked if the horses weren't companionship enuf?, Kalin assured her that they were more than enuf. And when she asked about herself, because Landry wouldn't be Landry if she didn't ask that, wasn't her companionship enuf, he assured her that she was more than enuf. Then why, she demanded, had there been a need for Tom? Kalin just shrugged: *Sometimes only a ghost will do.*

Clop-Clop-clip-Clop.

In regards to this long-discussed matter of prosopopoeia or just psychogenic invention, Broze Bearden, who'd long given up coachin sports but not his love of sports and who, late in years, would die labeled a drug dealer, addict, and a thief, had given some thought to what his sister, Radwan Crossman, once asked him: *Even if Kalin did invent Tom, what then of the hallucinations in Awides and Tom's bindin and potentially damnin deal with Pia Isan?* Broze eventually found an answer he liked: Kalin had invented Tom for company, but he'd also invented Pia Isan to put that company in peril. *You see, it was all about motivation,* Broze Bearden told his sister and her husband, Clarence Crossman, both of whom would die before Broze did, in a boatin accident. *Because what he was about to do was hard and lonely and darned scary, Kalin created Tom. He created Pia Isan, though, because she put Tom at risk and so further motivated Kalin to succeed in order to keep Tom around. And maybe Landry didn't count because he couldn't fully confide in her the terror of the headwall they was gonna have to face. Of course, there's also no gettin loose of the fact that Tom does come to know Pia Isan better along the way, carin for her maybe, but fer sure understandin that they was all in it together, includin them followin her, and so on. That there's a heart reminder. Ain't no better motivator than that.*

Some have observed how even the various accounts and comments about these events are in some ways ghosts, hauntin us with their pointless possibilities and perspectives. As Abigail Fathwell once chimed in: *The ghost isn't in the machine. The ghost is the machine!* Which really ain't so gross a mistellin, if the machine in mind is how a story is told, because stories too are ghosts, shamblin beside us with their take on things, their tales, over and over, until we can eventually shake free of their influence, another retellin, their memory. *Or not,* Nigel Thorne objected, recallin the father he'd lost and maybe, yeah, wantin to get rid of that grief but also wantin more the company of his father. *He was a great dad.* Jordan Heaton, on the other hand, too often remembered Phillip Hammond's jump from the trestle onto the shallow rocks that crippled him. *I didn't even see Phil jump, but I can't forget him jumpin either. I wish I could forget that.* Or Reed Beacham, who still experienced shivers rememberin an abandoned house down in Payson where Devil Worshippers supposedly gathered. And for a while Reed and his friends really had believed that the empty cans and spent candles evidenced some kind of demonic ritual. *But they was just kids smokin pot and drinkin beer. Just dumb kids like us. But unlike them, we wanted so bad to feel brave and righteous that we swore we'd come back and in the name of God kill them. We didn't, of course. We was too scared. And like I said, they was just partyin. But we was the ones with shotguns. That one don't leave me alone but I'd like it to.* Or Eva Thorn, who some say still walks beside Milly Lesson, because she turned her back on Milly for gettin an abortion when she was seventeen. Milly lost the Church, her friends, and that included Sue Ellen Burgess, and yet still went on to get an advanced degree and marry a fine heart with whom she raised four children, none of which happened for Eva Thorn. Or what about Karen Morrell and her family, who bought a house in the middle of a rattlesnake corridor? Nothin they put up, traps, electric fencin, could keep them dangerous fangs from turnin up in their basement or pantry. The Morrells finally had to abandon the place. Who knows if that one's true, but it's an old story of the fear that keeps plenty of folks movin along, maybe us too. And then of course there are the stories of love: lost, missed, botched, you name it, those can haunt one for a long time.

Either way, stories come at us from the past even as they get us ready for what's ahead. Ms. Melson put it this way: *Elaborate fictions, which by comparison are relatively easy to engage, prepare the mind for elaborate realities which are not easy to engage.* Though here's how that was remembered, and it's pretty much stayed this way too: *Elaborate fictions prepare us for elaborate realities.* And if nothin else, reality is elaborate.

One story that's persisted, one the Church ain't too pleased about, is that part about Tom up on the summit ridge that early Sunday mornin on October 31, 1982. There the Church is called out for false alliances. Such criticism weren't exactly welcomed, especially since the originator was either a young boy, Kalin March, tellin about the ghost of Tom Gatestone, or a young girl, Landry Gatestone, tellin about

Kalin tellin about the ghost of Tom, and not just any ghost but one who was momentarily endowed with Divine Authority and possessed by Divine Revelation. In some ways, that such a Voice would speak through Landry Gatestone, who at the time was a Church member, made it momentarily possible. But seein as how she never ceased to claim that she'd heard it from someone who weren't of the Church, even if he never bore the Church no ill will, that bein Kalin, nullified that possibility. Though that Kalin March had heard it from Tom Gatestone, albeit his ghost, who was from birth to death a Church member, made it once again seem potentially legitimate. You see the dilemma, right? The whole thing was a mess, and on that point the Church agreed. To be fair, the Church for a long time had sought to separate itself from the gears of politics, even if it still too often found itself involved with lobbyin for policies in accordance with its values, with some of those crusades extendin to as far away as California and D.C. At some point Tom was credited with sayin: *The church that seeks out the enforcement of its beliefs is a faithless settlement* which as you now know had nothin to do with him. Surprisin or not, the Church never mentioned Tom in sheets of fire talkin about horses.

The Portsmouth, New Hampshire, exhibit in 2031, which had in effect resurrected the Houston Time Gallery exhibit back in 2000, seemed mostly possible because of Landry's eventual but detailed divulgences concernin the ghost of her brother. That at least explained how Tom had regained his place in all those drawings, paintings, and songs, even if it hardly explains how the supposedly incinerated works had somehow reemerged digitally inact. The descriptions, commentaries, and debates were never detailed enuf to reconstruct the precision demonstrated in the reproduced artwork.

Still, later on, folks began sayin it weren't ever one story but a compaction of many that were locally known to those who grew up in Utah Valley. Like the one about two horses who got loose of their corral and escaped into Isatch Canyon, where they was never heard from again. Or the one about two runaways who also headed up Isatch Canyon and likewise disappeared. Or the one about a horse and rider once spied in Kirk's Cirque. Or another one about two riders with two horses. Plenty of ghostly tales surrounded the Awides Mine. Who's to say what other stories there were about Pillars Meadow. Or the murderous Porches. Some even got to sayin the whole thing was an example of a new genre: Untrue Crime. Others got headier, claimin it weren't but *liminal strategies attemptin to reincorporate ourselves within animality's spectral dominion.* Whatever that means. And that was still just the start. Many more stories with a certain familiarity have surfaced that easily could claim a place in the mosaic of this story.

And, sure, there's no denyin that some stories are made that way, many into one, even some of the most sacred ones.

Late in his life, Kalin admitted to Landry how Tom, right before he'd vanished beyond them gateposts, had shared with him how he weren't convinced he even existed, at least not in any way that he could understand: *You know, Kalin, I'm not sure there are ghosts or even the dead. There's just these poor myths that've been blindin us from ourselves for ages: who we are, where we are, what's right there in front of us.*

That moment caused Kalin great pain. Landry didn't share much of that with anyone. When Tom went over into that second oblivion, or whatever you want to call it, Tom's Crossin works just fine too, it weren't just like Tom had dissolved into thin air but rather he dissolved throughout their journey. *Like I couldn't see no more his grin at the entrance to Isatch Canyon. He weren't no more up ahead on Ash. He weren't no more outside the Awides Mine. He weren't no more on the screes. He weren't no more on the headwall. He weren't even on the summit. And he fer sure weren't with me at Pillars Meadow. He was just gone throughout. That's what haunts me the most now. That I was really there without him, that the world is ghostless. How awful is that? Or am I just gettin old?*

And Kalin March was gettin older. He'd been thinkin a lot about Pia Isan and her little chipmunk. He hadn't seen her go but in some ways that had been a blessin. Maybe she'd stayed the woman she was, dimples, scars, and all. Maybe she'd even found a name that suited the emergence of her beautiful smile. Maybe Emah? Or Ema? Or Ema Patompittseh? Or even Tokwai Ema Patompittseh? And maybe that Olk Elk had become the man he was too. Or maybe it went the other way and she had become an elk? With their little elks there too. Or what if the old elk had become somethin female and she had become somehow a man who might set a hand upon Old Elk and offer them comfort? Male or female, elk or somethin else, did any such combinations even matter? So long as they mingled the air in joy, *which they did*, Kalin assured Landry, *if gone too like a breath.*

While how to frame Tom's presence will likely remain impossible to resolve, once his spectral part in all this became more widely known, however incomplete and erroneous, it weren't the ghost that gained prominence but the Crossin itself.

Tom's Crossin.

Long before Tom's ghost began to reintegrate hisself into the history of Kalin's and Landry's journey, the matter of the destination was
already the organizin principle that had resulted in such a perilous
trek culminatin in lineage-endin bloodshed. When revisitin the gateposts that would continue to stand for many decades, Landry would
often walk back and forth between them, runnin sometimes, jumpin
through them at other times, and all to no effect; the same applyin to
whatever equine companion she was on. *Was this really the place?* she'd
demand. Which got her a nod from Kalin. *But why? Why here?* Landry
would survey again Pillars Meadow, Coyote Gulch, and the territories
east, where Navidad and Mouse had disappeared, all of which by then
was Phains Haven.

It's a place, I suppose, Kalin had answered. *A good place. Good as any.*

But as most suspected, and why the phrase itself persisted, there
had to be more at play than mere happenstance grantin significance to
that location, even if what that significance was continued to remain
so elusive. There had to be more. Folks was certain.

Fer example, what should be made of Dallin Gatestone's maps? As
Sondra discovered some years later, that very location was marked with
a red-ink *X* beside which, in green ink, was scribbled: *For the horses. Wild
them here.* Had Tom discovered this? The maps made clear the land in
question was still owned by others includin the State, the Federal Government, as well as the Porches. It's easy to conceive of Tom's puckish
personality devisin an epic journey that would in the end redeliver
Orwin Porch's horses back into his hands, especially given that Tom's
Crossin, them gateless gateposts, was situated right at the edge of the
inholdin the Porches had owned for generations.

Then there was the matter of how, durin the removal of the
corpses, additional bones were discovered, promptin an excavation
that revealed even more, all believed to be near a hundred years old,
likely from the Timpanogos or Katanogos tribes, and while there were
men among the dead, probably warriors, there were women too, and
too many children. Analysis revealed ailments rangin from malnutri-
tion to smallpox.

Kalin would hear it all out and wouldn't disagree either that it
was important, though he continued to insist that the only thing that
mattered about Tom's Crossin was how that was where *Navidad and
Mouse went free.*

The phrase certainly could not have existed without those horses.
And there were other examples like that. Hobson's choice, which we
know now as *Take it or leave it* or *It's this or nothin at all*, originated with a
sixteenth-century livery stable owner named Thomas Hobson who'd
offer either the stall with the slow horse or the stall with no horse. Few

note that Hobson's choice weren't comin from a nasty place; rather he was protectin the popular horses that were overworked and needed rest. Though, unlike a Hobson's choice, Tom's Crossin weren't so much about choosin between two options but rather described the consequences of an important choice once it's made. The thinkin bein that as soon as Kalin took them two horses from Paddock B, the conflict at Pillars Meadow became a certainty.

It's surmised that the phrase's earliest usage centered on datin and at Orvop High no less. *Go out with him and you're off to Tom's Crossin,* which got distilled down to *He's a Tom's Crossin* or even *She's a Tom's Crossin.* Soon enuf, though, this teenage usage got ditched for the more generic: *That's a Tom's Crossin,* meanin whatever you was decidin to do was gonna result in one heckuva journey endin with one heckuva conflict.

There are those, however, who continue to argue that the expression has more to do with an experience that was possible only because someone told you the way to go, the emphasis in this case bein on Tom tellin Kalin how to reach them gateposts. Fer example: *Sir, I'll tell you the way, but this here's a Tom's Crossin.* The implication bein that the route would be dangerous and fraught with opposition.

These usages endured for a good while and can still be heard from time to time, but one that's lasted the longest relies more on the notion of that which ain't really there to begin with but becomes somethin by goin there. Put another way: Tom's Crossin is that ideal that through hardship, strife, and too often great antagonism becomes a reality. *You're on your way to Tom's Crossin.*

There is also a psychological usage that emerged after Tom's ghost was well established in the recountin of these events. For example: *I owe it to my deceased wife. I'm on a Tom's Crossin.* In this regard a Tom's Crossin describes a promise made in life to a loved one who's passed but whose ghost still accompanies you until that promise is kept. As Dr. Yvette Ruffel put it: *Would that my mind let fall its dead ideas, as the tree does its withered leaves. André Gide wrote that. And I think that starts to get at it. Would that our minds shed as easily the dead and especially our debts to the dead. Gone like raked piles on the front lawn, soon bagged, soon hauled away. Of course, debts to the dead are more often like evergreens even if they do goad us to do remarkable things, foolish things, dangerous things. I don't doubt the amount of challenges and crises that can come out of that kind of companionship. If my husband were alive now, he'd have wonderful things to say about such notions.* And as Kim Kapp would add on the subject, *Tom's Crossin is not like Virgil leadin Dante to some Earthly Paradise atop some mountain. Tom's accompaniment is less auspicious, though admittedly some kind of victory is part of the formula.*

And finally there is a darker usage that addresses not just the release from the past that the livin accomplish but the past's own release from itself. Not that Cavil Cox cared for this approach: *We need the dead. Because of them, the sufferin endured in yesteryears has a chance to find a solution in the present. Maybe that's the dead's true curse: they have to stick around.* Of course, there are those folks, like Dayton Banner, who are more magnanimous when it comes to them we've lost: *What about the dead? The dead need their Tom's Crossin too. They need to move on, and sometimes they might even need our help.* Patroclus upon his pyre.

I've changed my mind. I realize that, sure, as far as titles go, *Landry's Ride* makes way more sense than, say, *Pillars Meadow, Kalin March, Old Porch,* or even *The Fourth Rider,* not to mention whatever else nonsense the dull-witted still come up with, but though my ride was pretty fantastic, with me and Jojo haulin that vengeful angel back home, it still weren't the most of it. Hard as this is for me to say, because gobs of tears will come up, it really was all along about Tom: his dyin and how in life we can begin to see all we might've done but didn't do and then desire suddenly and desperately in our last moments to make amends for what our heart kept too close, to still do somethin with the livin opportunities we took for granted and likely wasted on foolishness. Leadin Navidad and Mouse to the open weren't ever foolish. You'll never hear me say otherwise. Tom, from beyond the grave, got to see that much through, and on Ash as well, and in the company of his dear friend Kalin March, and however indirectly with me too, his sister, whom he loved beyond death like I will always love him beyond death. Which is to say *Tom's Crossin* is as fine a title as any.

Though that does raise the question: why not *Navidad's and Mouse's Crossin?* That's a pretty darn good question too, but I don't have the answer.

When Kalin's daddy died, we left our children with Sondra and went down to Texas, just the two of us. At first Kalin swore he weren't goin, but he eventually heeded my advice, which really bordered more on insistence. As he later confided: *It was way easier freein Navidad and Mouse from Paddock B that night than it was gettin on this plane.* And it weren't so long a flight either.

After the service, some in attendance got to sharin stories about Connor Mayhew. One in particular was worth the whole trip. Orwin Porch had ended up in Ellis Unit, a maximum security prison in Walker County. It turns out Kalin's daddy had been moved there too, and he went out of his way to find Old Porch. He sat down right beside him and wouldn't leave until he'd heard the whole story. And when Old Porch was finally finished, Kalin's daddy leaned back as if to remeasure in his mind all that he had just heard against what all he knew first-hand. And then he started laughin, howled until tears ran from the sides of his eyes. *I guess I should be glad,* he finally managed to say, *that he ain't never came lookin for me.* In the end, it was a cold that got Kalin's daddy, just took away his breath.

Old Porch didn't outlive him by much, and he went out near the same way too, except instead of a cold, somethin just weakened in his blood, and he paled out, with them scars on his hands lookin more like veins of bright gypsum. It's still hard, though, to think of his death without seein Russel comin out of them woods on Cavalry, rage in his eyes, Pia Isan's rusty ax-head in his hands, with them angry dogs beside him. Tom had only said but a few words on it, lookin horrified, but for Kalin, as the years got on, it only got more terrifyin and vivid too. *Like I can see it myself: that lone boy, lonelier than all around, ridin out slow but real deliberate.* And then I get to seein it too, Russel weighin what he carried against what he would do with such a burden when the father who'd betrayed him emerged from beyond the veil of his life, because however many years might interpose themselves, let me tell you, far as I know, the dead don't forget.

Who doesn't wonder whether or not it was possible for some-one like Old Porch to make peace with the ghost of this youngest son stalkin his every breath? If that don't trouble your sleep. And it makes you wonder too: of those who find themselves immaculate in their mind's mirror, how many abide the brightness of their allotted years unaware that a vengeful ghost strides beside them, savagely countin the fast-departin hours? How would any of us greet such a vision? With surprise? Regret? Confusion? Likely just horror. We fear vio-lence for the death it may presage, but what of violence after death's already suffered? Ain't that right there at least one definition of Hell?

Not that Kalin went in for any of this. His heart stayed with the horses even if it was the horses that kept breakin his heart. And that's likely puttin it too lightly. Maybe it's more direct to say that a good part of Kalin March just flat-out died up there on Pillars Meadow. Him and me, along with our mothers, devoted pretty much the rest of our lives to Phains Haven and the horses. For me it was a labor not once separate from joy. For Kalin it was his penance, an awful purgatory he refused to quit. As he'd tell me often: *I can think of plenty else I could be doin that would be worse. I'm here with those I love.* The trouble was that no horses loved him back. Not a one.

For those fortunate enuf to have seen Kalin ride, his gift near supernatural if not outright divine, it was plenty disturbin in those long gray later years to see the way horses avoided him, shyin from his presence, with some audacious enuf to dare a snip, plenty pinnin their ears, but the most of them just outright fearin him. Kalin would still muck their stalls, haul hay out to the far fields, refill the water tubs, maybe sneak a scratch between the ears, not that a one ever welcomed such a scratch or the sight of him comin near. If he tried to give one a brushin, their skin would crawl, their hooves would stomp. Sure, some could stand it, at least with a snort and switch of a tail, but Kalin hisself couldn't stand causin a horse any discomfort and eventually ceased with such solicitous attempts to befriend any of them, leavin those joys to me and our numerous volunteers.

Not that Kalin didn't want to make amends. He just didn't have no clue how to do so. After all, how often have any of us found ourselves battlin some impossible storm, and at night too, with but a candle in hand, still tryin to find a way to credibly discount the ills for which we know ourselves responsible? No wonder so many fall to them pretensions espousin the Good way, a one true path, or any other such guarantee of redemption. Let me tell you, Redemption is a hard road to take, to proceed always in such doubt, tryin to keep lit that frail flickerin flame. Of course maybe it ain't the worst road either.

As has already been said, Kalin always considered hisself a man of his word, and plenty who knew him or didn't know him would confirm that statement. But though it was mostly true, it weren't exactly true. For weren't it in the Awides Mine that, in exchange for the warnin not to mess with Godder Ford, Kalin swore to Brad P. Hone to deliver a message to his wife and children, a message, to be fair, that Tom had kept silent on and Kalin had plumb forgot, if he'd ever really heard it to begin with. There was also somethin Tom had promised the boy Robert Gaff that likewise lay beyond Memory's Palace. I can sure see that now. Nonetheless, they was promises made in a place where promises have endlessly grave consequences.

In fact it was historians who decades later solved these mysteries, thanks to a meticulous tracin of the Porch family's interactions with folks gone missin, fueled now by the understandin that both Orwin Porch and Egan Porch were, plain and simple, nasty killers. Very explicit movie clips eventually emerged, their origin questionable, the contents henceforth considered creations, if nonetheless vividly examinin murders by both men: Old Porch layin down Cameron Eakins with a chop knife; Egan Porch tossin into a dumpster that poor boy, Robert Gaff, who didn't die then, though he did lose consciousness only to awaken as he was bein buried in a landfill, unobserved by any there. If he only could've muttered but one sound. Alas, he was unable to expel in time the refuse that clogged his mouth. Anyways, the historians got it right, and it's best left to them to tell those stories. They also discovered more than just Eakins had been killt by Old Porch's murderous hands.

There's no discountin the possibility that Kalin hisself, beyond the fields of life, will be held accountable for his deeds and non-deeds. And if that ain't the greatest dread for us all: that there's somethin we must still do, and by golly would do too, if we could only remember it. Personally, though, I don't think that's the case. Ghosts got a lot to offer, but they can talk loads of crap too. One of the things that's hard to get at, what I think really got under the skin of any horse Kalin came across, was how it weren't simply the awfulness of Pillars Meadow that haunted him.

In Kalin's later years, he became obsessed with self-control. He was so measured that it got so as he was effectively achievin nothin. Like he weren't just pumpin the brakes to slow; the brakes always had to go to the floor, emergency brake too. He confessed once how he'd come to feel that who he was was but a small, broke part of hisself, *like a hawk that can't fly because she's staked to the ground, or a horse that can't run because she's locked in a stall, or a tiger that can't be a tiger no more because he's trapped by concrete walls with just an old barrel to hunt.* And maybe that last comparison suits the truth best, one that he never could resolve or let go of: the only time he ever felt the very limit of hisself was out there on Pillars Meadow, facin off against those nine. He was fluid, he was powerful, he was unerrin, as if inhabited and just as soon abandoned by a God whose authority had been ordained by Destiny.

Now that particular reflection was but just one moment of late-night thought in the long life of Kalin March, when he was much older and worn down and recollections of these sorts often just got the best of him. He'd rock hisself by the firelight, arms crossed tight like it was too cold to bear, though our livin room was always plenty warm, plus I was on that couch too with my arms around him. Fortunately that misery would pass as he finally found his way to a kind of prayer, what did uncross his arms and deliver him to sleep, and me there next to him tendin the coals. *Of course, with Navidad,* he'd whispered, and on that night it seemed nearly a song, *out there on the rocks when the ground was givin way and clouds of dust was upon us and there was nowhere for us to go but down, we were beyond what any animal or person can matter. And on Katanogos too, when we were right up beneath the summit, takin that last turn, we was beyond what even a mountain can matter.*

From that Halloween in 1982 on, Kalin March was mauled by guilt, which as he got older only got worse. Add to that an extra load of disappointment, frailty, maybe surprise over how bereft a life can be in the aftermath of somethin that seemed for a moment suffused with the movements of timeless beings, coagulate before the attentions of the Gods, the God of All, which anyways too soon afterward dimmed into disbelief, all regard for that mighty young man gone, so that none of this pageant of doins was of real concern anymore, especially with Kalin cast into exile from all of it, from those in the community, from hisself, lost and loathed by near everyone but especially by the horses he loved so much, though never loathed by me. I weren't afraid to be his country, his city, his insurmountable defenses.

Folks tended to agree with Tom's early assessment that Kalin March was bequeathed but two gifts with neither of them suited for this world. But I would say he had three gifts, and to me the third was the most important: he was a loyal husband, a lovin father, and my greatest friend. Now I know that sounds like an additional three things, but if you know what I'm talkin about, you know they're the same. And see, Love beats drawin a gun any day.

I'll tell you this: never a year went by that Kalin March didn't stand before Tom's grave. Sometimes he'd say somethin or bring somethin to set on his headstone, like a can of tobacco. The older he got, the more tragic Tom's departure seemed. My brother was just so dang young when he went to ground. Most of the time Kalin would just stand there awhile. *Just listenin*, he'd say. Sometimes he swore he could hear a whistle and then swore just as fast that he was a liar. *What I'd give to hear that whistle one more time.* I might prod him now and then to tell again what it had been like to hear me sing and Tom whistle on that long-ago Sunday mornin. *In truth, Landry, I can't right remember none of it, not a bit of the tune, not a word, but I do remember the feelin: it was just so darned beautiful, and I felt grateful that I could hear you and sad that the world couldn't.*

Kalin also visited every year the graves of all them Porches. There he'd kneel. Even before the headstone of that old spit of poison, Orwin Porch, who got his plot when he was at last lugged home in a wooden box and interred beside his boys in the Orvop City Cemetery. Kalin mourned most of all Russel and Hatch. Kalin made sure all their graves were kept neat and free of graffiti. Some fine Orvop citizens regarded these visits as pure posturin or even perverse, but as Kalin might've pointed out, if even one of them gabbers had had the courage to say as much to his face, he was the only one who ever visited.

Kalin did get a curious visit one day from, of all people, Rico Gale. That's right, the half brother of Billings Gale.

We had the same mother but I never knew him, he told Kalin. *Still, he was family, and you killt him.*

You come for revenge then? Kalin asked.

Nah. Just to sit with you awhile.

We can manage that.

Kalin ended up givin him a tour of Phains Haven. Rico Gale had become somethin of a watercolorist and later sent along some paintins of Kalin from that day. He never did come into any of the cash Billings had hid in his wall, a substantial sum accompanied by broken pieces of rotten red rubber bands, all of it gone when his buildin was torn down. Probably for the best. You know what they say about bad money.

Some years later, Rico Gale did come into his own and designated Phains Haven as one of his annual charitable contributions. It was needed. While in their day both the Porches and Gatestones were considered monied, as the years went by and new wealth was upon the land, well, Phains Haven was often teeterin on the edge of financial ruin. At one point the Gatestone family house was sold to pay for risin costs. Donations continued to keep it afloat, but new sets of politicians alignin with new tides of capital kept circlin ways to put the land to private use and of course get rid of the horses.

One visit that had held little meanin for Landry and Kalin, mostly because they weren't around most of that day but also because neither of them had any notion of who Cal Carneros was, occurred so close to Rico Gale's visit that it can't help but provoke an unfulfilled wish that Cal and Rico might've intersected again and, for a little while at least, on the back of Katanogos or even upon the soils of Pillars Meadow itself, conversed about the Time Gallery show and the reality they could now glimpse some of together. A few friendly Phains Haven volunteers gave their afternoon to Cal, showin him the various stables, barns, large paddocks, larger fields, finally offerin to guide him up to Pillars Meadow. Cal weren't interested in ridin horses. They drove him up instead.

Along the way he saw for hisself a stallion snakin a small herd, with another stallion in pursuit through the simmerin dust of the day. All at once Cal Carneros beheld how this immense, beautiful World will always defeat Art's sublime approximations. He was released from any need for Majesty. He told the volunteers they could turn around. He'd got what he came for.

On gettin back, Cal encountered Kalin March, who'd also just returned. It was dusk. Kalin passed Cal with a quiet hello nod, which he offered to every visitor. Cal didn't say more than *Hello* back, but what scared him at once was how little an impression the man left on him, almost like he weren't there at all. If one of his guides had not said *Good evenin, Mr. March. The mare's with foal now,* Cal might not have even noticed him. For certain nothin exceptional haloed him. At best he would've seemed a battered and very retired athlete, if there were such a sport that could accommodate so slight a man. And yet as he'd neared a stable for animals still recoverin from injury, where in fact six horses were cranin their heads over the stall doors in anticipation of feed time, with Kalin's arrival all six retreated from sight, with one or two proceedin to kick at the walls.

Not long after the trials, Kalin March started goin to Alcoholics Anonymous. He didn't even drink nor ever took up anythin narcotic. In those meetins, he told his lie: whenever he talked about *the feelin to get back to it,* which everyone assumed was drinkin, Kalin was really talkin about guns. He never stopped goin to meetins either. He came to appreciate the gift that boredom is to trauma, how repetition finally pries loose the past's hold on the present. He never objected much to the notion of a higher power often brought up in meetings but he also never put much stock in sacred texts, especially when it came to the United States Constitution, and when he got north of sixty he joined a group set on repealin the Second Amendment. One thing he never could make up his mind about was whether unanchored thoughts tended to float toward Good. He tended to believe unanchored thoughts weren't a good thing, at least for him, and if he weren't always pullin on the oars, he'd drift straight for the worst.

Twice more his palm knew that cursèd steel. Once egregiously, the last time less so. It was partly my fault too. I'd asked some of the workers and summer volunteers to drill holes in the bottoms of about a dozen tin pails so I could use them as planters for some flower arrangements I had in mind to brighten up the main lodge as well as some of the nearby cabins. They decided to achieve this by gettin out their pistols. A few of them thought pretty highly of their shootin.

Not far off, Kalin was handlin a colt just brought in with an abscess under his front left hoof. Kalin had already had to duck an angry kick. When it happened again, why that was just the last straw. Earlier that day, Kalin had also slipped in some mud and banged his head on a fence rail. It weren't so bad, but the fall had left a welt above his eye. When that colt's hoof flew past his ear for the second time, Kalin couldn't help the red anger that suddenly out-redded the blood in his veins. When one of the summer volunteers, a kid who'd come all the way from Maine and knew nothin about Kalin, saw him go stompin by, he asked if he'd like to fire off a few rounds, makin it clear that if he ruined one of the buckets, he'd have to pay for it. Much to everyone's surprise, Kalin accepted the offer.

It didn't take but a moment, but all there, except for that kid from Maine, suffered a chill at the sight of it. Kalin fired eight times. It was like watchin water move. Nothin out of place. The Maine kid, though, upon inspectin them buckets, started to laugh. *Well, you didn't hit one, but I bet you feel better, right?* Kalin had forced a smile and marched off. After that he didn't talk much to anyone for a good month, and for another month he spent most of his time livin up on the high ridges. I finally had to go up there and get him. Rumor is I threatened him with a wooden spoon, and that that had been enuf to retreat him back to the penance of livin. Truth is I just gave him a kiss and held him.

Of course, that Maine kid, and this weren't his fault, just didn't understand a thing about what had just happened. He had his view of things, and the others there confirmed that that view of things weren't wrong: none of them buckets had any extra holes. Which is how it would have rested if one of the volunteers, and she was smart and had an inklin, hadn't decided to examine a birch about fifty yards off. They all went over to where she was standin, the Maine kid too, which is when he finally understood, and, boy, did that discovery rob him of his smile, and he had a nice smile too. Because right smack-dab in the middle of that narrow trunk was a tight cluster of holes. And at least this much can be said of those kids: they knew better than to start diggin up bullets for souvenirs. Some say that birch still stands with a heart of metal, a reminder of who once walked those hills. Later on the story changed so that Kalin was shootin out the shape of a heart in the bark, but those who were there, especially that kid from Maine, knew it weren't no heart. More like a metal fist. An angry fist.

After that, the horses shied from Kalin even more. A lesser man might've grown to hate those equine sensitivities, but my husband bore his burden like some stoic, in silence, without an expression of disgust or despair, and though the horses continued to despise his presence, he never stopped watchin over them, from the wild ones that lived out in the open to those closer in the monitored pastures to those periodically stabled near the Phains Haven center. Not that the horses cared. They knew him as a predator, to be feared or fought, and maybe they weren't wrong. Kalin, though, remained their guardian throughout his life and never asked of them anythin in return.

I've always liked that bit by Alice Walker: *The animals of the world exist for their own reasons. They were not made for humans any more than black people were made for whites or women for men.* In the early years of our courtship, and after we'd married too, Kalin and I often went out on foot in search of Navidad and Mouse, but we never did see them again. No one did. And that didn't exactly spare us from too many worst-case scenarios: come that first spring, Mouse chowin down on skunk cabbage or locoweed so he could go chargin challengers that weren't there until he finally fell over, or Navidad dyin even faster on fitweed or foxglove. Poisons, disease, and injury, and them was just a start. There weren't a prayer of well-bein that weren't matched by predation. The local accusations of *cruel refoulement* weren't easily dismissed. It didn't take much imagination to find hardships on hardships in that future we'd delivered them to. But it was also hard to imagine Mouse or Navidad dead. Now and then I'd joke with Kalin that, since Mouse was a geldin, maybe Jojo had somehow managed to sire foals with Navidad and that one day we'd come across fillies and colts blue as they was black. But we never did see any of those either.

Back then I would've taken a glimpse of even that mule. She'd never done more than come along and then move on. I always loved that I never knew more. I told the kids about Effy, and I always loved hearin what stories they'd make up. What a child's mind can find.

When Jojo died, it was my turn to find speech lost. I didn't freeze up no more, that was a condition I'd rid myself of back on Katanogos, but the whole winter I hardly said a word, and I might've took to the hills too if Kalin hadn't kept close. Even then he could make me smile. He always was my rainbow in the rain.

Hope did finally enter his heart, for his children, for me, and so then fear had to follow. He didn't escape the effects of age neither, wrinkles risin up on his face like scars hidden by the energies of youth. He died just shy of eighty under a white elm or weepin American elm, take your pick, either way exceedinly rare up in the Utah hills. But that tree sure fit right in at Phains Haven. Kalin's back was against the trunk, his legs stretched out, the canopy above thick enuf to hold off the snow. It was the last snowfall of the year and durin a time too when there weren't much snow. Our breathless daughter was who beheld him there first in that halo of white, which was magical enuf but not near the extent of the magic that was at hand on that afternoon.

Okay, quibble if you will with that word. Maybe it weren't magic. Maybe it was just magical thinkin, but our little girl will to this day swear a Kalin Oath to what she saw. She's a wonder, that little girl, bright with confidence and fer sure her own person. Beautiful as beautiful can be, and you bet she knows Aunt Lissie's words: *Beauty ain't beautiful if it ain't unique.* She was wearin my hat that day too. You remember the one: wool felt, sage, with a front pinch. Not that it means anythin to me. A hat's a hat no matter the color. But she loved it. And I loved seein her in it. She reminded me of my braver self. Once upon a time. A long, long time ago.

Her brother, who was laggin behind, also swore hisself a Kalin Oath that day: how he'd heard the most wondrous whistle threadin the wind. It gladdened him about as much as the absence of origin had shivered him. But it weren't nothin compared to the shivers my baby girl experienced as she ran to her daddy. He was still a good ways off, but the closer she got, the clearer it became that her daddy weren't alone. A great black horse lay beside him, forehooves curled under, with her great head restin in his lap.

M e, I died four years later. The goin weren't swift nor painless either. As long ago as October 1982 is for you, or me now, that week with Kalin and the horses on the backs of mountains set to buck us from our tomorrows helped steel me fer my final days. I'd lived quite a sum of years, but the memory of them handful of long-ago days, those hours of great boldness, why I know them still as a forever.

Funny how when we're young we think our time will go on and on, and even if we frame ourselves in later years as gray and grizzled, why we still believe we'll be made of the same stuff. Of course, when age comes, we see how that ain't so, and if there are regrets, it's that we didn't hurl ourselves more into the dark while we still thought our heart a lamp. Make no mistake, I got no regrets. Except maybe that I let Egan Porch shoot me. Keep your lenses meshed. My heart is still my lamp. It lights my way, and maybe it'll light yours some of the way too.

I'll say this: when my dyin was over, I sure as heck was grateful not to find any of my children waitin for me. I even pitied Orwin Porch if that was his fate; it's plenty awful to imagine not only Russel but all his boys steppin forth from whatever shadows were fashioned for his passin . . . That there is a horror show I wouldn't visit on anyone.

It's an unfortunate quality of life that too often when you care the least about somethin, it does happen, and when you care the most, it don't. I did expect to find my Kalin, but he weren't here. I sure would've taken Tom with his big red ears and bigger smile, but except for a shallow ache in this rustlin wind that only a fool could dream was a whistle, he weren't around either. *Clop-Clop-clip-Clop.* Who did come to meet me then? Oh, I think you know. *Clop-Clop-clip-Clop.* With a snort and shake of his long mane, that big beautiful blue horse shrugged off the dark and trotted to my side. I didn't know how much I'd missed his touch until my dear Jojo was knockin me off my boots with that big, waggin head of his.

As we rode on from there, and along the way findin ourselves fer a spell in your good company, and thank you for your company, I began to understand for myself the clarity of that understandin that Kalin had so poorly tried to convey to me about what Tom had tried to convey to him. Neither ornature nor idyll can describe the vividness I now inhabit. So incorporeal in its shape and without prejudice that not even dust is dulled from existence. And yet it does not overwhelm either. Maybe because there is no time demandin preference. I behold effortlessly all I've shared with you and to my shame find it not even a worthy abridgment; so small a part of a whole that it seems not even the tiniest fleck of snow landin upon the back of big Katanogos that long-ago Saturday night when Kalin and I and the horses huddled together in the jaws of Death and still knew ourselves alive.

I recall now for some reason how me and Tom once got into our momma's bakin drawer, and though we only meant to make somethin sweet, and for her too, we had somehow loosed cake flour and confectioner's sugar over the entire kitchen. How mad was she! *What in the world have you done?!* she'd cried, and Tom had laughed, and I knew then he was somehow charmed because despite our chaos he'd made our momma laugh. But I still think of her words: *What in the world have you done? That ain't so bad a question: What in the World have we done?* I also remember often what Kalin's momma never stopped sayin, how nobody's free until they set somethin else free that ain't you. I wonder about both those things: What did I do while I was of the World? Who did I help set free that weren't me? It ain't more complicated than that. Sometimes the shortest path takes the longest time to find. Of course, when Death's there to warn your every step, findin your way ain't always so easy, though as Kalin once told me when his hair had gone white: *When you've ridden with the dead, well, dyin ain't got nothin on you.*

And ain't that what you've been doin for some time now? And you managed it okay, right? Even when the switchbacks got steep, or worse, forlorn, until we was there, with no higher left to us, and then over the back of it too, like for a moment we had wings but didn't need to fly because we weren't ever gonna fall. And now look at us, on this wide, wild field and, fer a little while longer, still together.

As I'm sure you can also tell now, me and Jojo are little left, Jojo no more now than his trusty *Clop-Clop-clip-Clop* and me no more than this twang, maybe more Arkansan than Utahn, either way of my own fashionin and even worse overwrappin the voices of others. I ain't no ventriloquist. I ain't no Scheherazade neither. Whether by basilect or the highfalutin, I am just I not even I. But I do still remain determined. Deliberate too. Like when I said *Calvary* instead of *Cavalry*, why that weren't no flub. *Son of a gun, made-up mind,* and *hectorin rain,* them weren't said just because. Or how that last *thunder* was with Jojo at the hospital. Someone along the way needs to jot down *straight on til mournin, with a u,* if this ever gets to bein jotted down. And all them names? Like startin with Lucy? We all go forth in the name of somethin else. There are so many names. I got lists now that go on forever. I got answers too that go on forever. But ask me who got Tom's smolderin brand and I can't tell you. Ask me how Navidad and Mouse got from Paddock A into Paddock B; I can't tell you that either. There's where memory cannot follow. And ask me what's ahead for you; I can only say that, yes, your moment will come, and the only question is whether or not you'll be ready.

As for the ghost who travels beside me, I wish I could ease their burden. Burdens here, though, are singular. None are spared. Mine grants me no end of grief and awful speculation. As gladdened as I am by Jojo, by you, I remain troubled by this thing bequeathed to me beyond the edge of life.

Have you already guessed?

Clop-Clop-clip-Clop.

That someone will come for it, I've no doubt. Know, though, that I've resolved that even if it's my Kalin, or Tom, or my momma, or Kalin's momma, or even my dear little babies, whether they're friend or foe, stranger or beggar, or even the Good Lord On High, I shall refuse the demand.

For, yes, again in my belt, I carry that very same Colt Peacemaker, fully loaded too, all six chambers, six chambers I cannot empty, and I've tried many, many times.

But I shall not unhand it.

Ever.

Enuf is enuf.

Clop~Clop~clip~

From the Transcriber

As many will note, Orvop is just a jiggle of letters from Provo, just as Rome is from Orem, just as Isatch is near enough to Wasatch, these latter names hailing from Utah proper, where Mark Z. Danielewski grew up. Unlike Mount Timpanogos, the Katanogos massif is not there. It is but a dream lifted up amidst very real mountains that will stand there tomorrow and the tomorrow after that, no matter what they're called or what's said about them. There's no Pillars Meadow either. Tom's Crossing, though, is real. Ask anyone who's been there. They'll tell you a story.